Toc H Cymru

Patient Library Service
I hope you enjoyed this book
Thank you for its return

Toc H registered Charity No. 211042

DEAN R KOONTZ

DEAN R KOONTZ

LIGHTNING

MIDNIGHT

THE BAD PLACE

CHANCELLOR
PRESS

Lightning first published in Great Britain in 1988
by Headline Book Publishing Plc.

Midnight first published in Great Britain in 1989
by Headline Book Publishing Plc.

The Bad Place first published in Great Britain in 1990
by Headline Book Publishing Plc.

The collected volume first published in Great Britain in 1992
by Chancellor Press
an imprint of
Reed Consumer Books Limited
Michelin House, 81 Fulham Road, London SW3 6RB
and Auckland, Melbourne, Singapore and Toronto

Published by arrangement with Headline Book Publishing Plc.

ISBN 1 85152 214 X

A CIP catalogue record for this book is available at the British Library

Printed in Great Britain by The Bath Press

CONTENTS

LIGHTNING

To Greg and Joan Benford. Sometimes I think that you're the most interesting people we know. Then I always take two aspirin and lie down. But the thought persists.

The wailing of the newborn infant
is mingled with the dirge for the dead.

LUCRETIUS

I'm not afraid to die.
I just don't want to be there when it happens.

WOODY ALLEN

Roller coaster:
1) a small gravity railroad . . . with steep inclines
that produce sudden, speedy plunges
for thrill-seeking passengers.

THE RANDOM HOUSE DICTIONARY

PART ONE

LAURA

*Being deeply loved by someone
gives you strength;
while loving someone deeply
gives you courage.*

LAO TZU

One

A Candle in the Wind

• 1 •

A storm struck on the night Laura Shane was born, and there was a strangeness about the weather that people would remember for years.

Wednesday, January 12, 1955, was frigid, gray, and somber. At twilight thick, fluffy snowflakes spiraled out of the low sky, and the people of Denver huddled in expectation of a Rocky Mountain blizzard. By ten o'clock that night, a bitterly cold gale blew in from the west, howling out of the mountain passes and shrieking down those rugged, wooded slopes. The snowflakes grew smaller, until they were as fine as sand, and they sounded as abrasive as sand, too, when the wind blew them across the windows of Dr. Paul Markwell's book-lined study.

Markwell slumped in the chair behind his desk, drinking Scotch to keep warm. The persistent chill that troubled him was not caused by a winter draft but by an internal frigidity of the mind and heart.

In the four years since his only child, Lenny, had died of polio, Markwell's drinking had gotten steadily worse. Now, though on call for emergencies at County Medical, he picked up the bottle and poured more Chivas Regal.

In the enlightened year of 1955, children were being inoculated with Dr. Jonas Salk's vaccine, and the day was near when no child would be paralyzed or die from poliomyelitis. But Lenny had been afflicted in 1951, a year before Salk tested the vaccine. The boy's respiratory muscles had been paralyzed, too, and the case had been complicated by bronchopneumonia. Lenny never had a chance.

From the mountains to the west, a low rumble echoed across the winter night, but at first Markwell thought nothing of it. He was so involved with his own enduring, bile-black grief that sometimes he was only subliminally aware of events that transpired around him.

A photograph of Lenny stood on his desk. Even after four years he was tortured by his son's smiling face. He should have put the photo away but instead left it in view because unceasing self-flagellation was his method of attempting to atone for his guilt.

None of Paul Markwell's colleagues was aware of his drinking problem. He never appeared to be drunk. The errors he made in the treatment of some patients had resulted in complications that might have arisen naturally and were not attributed to malpractice. But *he* knew that he had blundered, and self-loathing only induced him to drink more.

The rumbling came again. This time he recognized the thunder, but he still did not wonder about it.

The phone rang. The Scotch had left him numb and slow to react, so he did not pick up the receiver until the third ring. 'Hello?'

'Dr. Markwell? Henry Yamatta.' Yamatta, an intern at County Medical, sounded nervous. 'One of your patients, Janet Shane, was just brought in by her husband. She's in labor. Fact is, they were delayed by the storm, so she was well along when they got here.'

Markwell drank Scotch while he listened. Then, pleased to hear that his voice was not slurred, he asked, 'She still in first stage?'

'Yes, but her labor pains are intense and unusually protracted for this point in the process. There's blood-tinged vaginal mucus—'

'That's to be expected.'

Impatiently Yamatta said, 'No, no. This isn't ordinary show.'

Show, or blood-tainted vaginal mucus, was a reliable sign that labor was impending. However Yamatta had said Mrs. Shane was already well into labor. Markwell had blundered by suggesting that the intern was reporting ordinary show.

Yamatta said, 'Not enough blood for hemorrhage, but something's wrong. Uterine inertia, obstruction of the pelvis, systemic disease—'

'I'd have noticed any physiological irregularity that would've made pregnancy dangerous,' Markwell said sharply. But he knew that he might *not* have noticed . . . if he had been drunk. 'Dr. Carlson's on duty tonight. If something goes wrong before I get there, he—'

'We've just had four accident victims brought in, two in bad shape. Carlson's hands are full. We need you, Dr. Markwell.'

'I'm on my way. Twenty minutes.'

Markwell hung up, finished his Scotch, and took a peppermint lozenge from his pocket. Since becoming a heavy drinker, he always carried mints. As he unwrapped the lozenge and popped it into his mouth, he left the study and went along the hall to the foyer closet.

He was drunk, and he was going to deliver a baby, and maybe he was going to botch it, which would mean the end of his career, the destruction of his reputation, but he did not care. In fact he anticipated that catastrophe with a perverse longing.

He was pulling on his overcoat when a peal of thunder rocked the night. The house reverberated with it.

He frowned and looked at the window beside the front door. Fine, dry snow swirled against the glass, briefly hung suspended as the wind held its breath, then swirled again. On a couple of other occasions over the years, he had heard thunder in a snowstorm, though always at the beginning, always soft and far away, nothing as menacing as this.

Lightning flashed, then again. Falling snow flickered queerly in the inconstant light, and the window was briefly transformed into a mirror in which Markwell saw his own haunted face. The subsequent crash of thunder was the loudest yet.

He opened the door and peered curiously at the turbulent night. The hard-driving wind hurled snow under the porch roof, drifting it against the front wall of the house. A fresh, two-or three-inch white mantle covered the lawn, and the windward boughs of the pine trees were flocked as well.

Lightning flared bright enough to sting Markwell's eyes. The thunderclap was so tremendous that it seemed to come not only from the sky but from the ground, too, as if heaven and earth were splitting open, announcing Armageddon. Two extended, overlapping, brilliant bolts seared the darkness. On all sides eerie silhouettes leaped, writhed, throbbed. The shadows of porch railings, balusters, trees, barren shrubs, and streetlamps were so weirdly distorted by every flash that Markwell's familiar world acquired the characteristics of a Surrealistic painting: the unearthly light illuminated common objects in such a way as to give them mutant forms, altering them hauntingly.

Disoriented by the blazing sky, thunder, wind, and billowing white curtains of the storm, Markwell abruptly *felt* drunk for the first time that night. He wondered how much of the bizarre electrical phenomenon was real and how much was alcohol-induced hallucination. He edged cautiously across the slippery porch to the head of the steps that led to the snow-covered front walk, and he leaned against a porch post, craning his head out to look up at the light-shattered heavens.

A chain of thunderbolts made the front lawn and street appear to jump repeatedly as if that scene were a length of motion picture film stuttering in a jammed projector. All color was burned out of the night, leaving only the dazzling white of the lightning, the starless sky, the sparkling white of snow, and ink-black shuddering shadows.

As he stared in awe and fear at the freakish celestial display, another jagged crack opened in the heavens. The earth-seeking tip of the hot bolt touched an iron streetlamp only sixty feet away, and Markwell cried out in fear. At the moment of contact the night became incandescent, and the glass panes in the lamp exploded. The clap of thunder vibrated in Markwell's teeth; the porch floor rattled. The cold air instantly reeked of ozone and hot iron.

Silence, stillness, and darkness returned.

Markwell had swallowed the peppermint.

Astonished neighbors appeared on their porches along the street. Or perhaps they were present throughout the tumult, and perhaps he saw them only when the comparative calm of an ordinary blizzard was restored. A few trudged through the snow to have a closer look at the stricken streetlamp, the iron crown of which appeared half melted. They called to one another and to Markwell, but he did not respond.

He had not been sobered by the terrifying exhibition. Afraid that neighbors would detect his drunkenness, he turned away from the porch steps and went into the house.

Besides, he had no time to chat about the weather. He had a pregnant woman to treat, a baby to deliver.

Striving to regain control of himself, he took a wool scarf from the foyer closet, wound it around his neck, and crossed the ends over his chest. His hands were trembling, and his fingers were slightly stiff, but he managed to button his overcoat. Fighting dizziness, he pulled on a pair of galoshes.

He was gripped by the conviction that the incongruous lightning had some special meaning for him. A sign, an omen. Nonsense. Just the whiskey confusing him. Yet the feeling remained as he went into the garage, put up the door, and backed the car into the driveway, the chain-wrapped winter tires crunching and clinking softly in the snow.

As he shifted the car into park, intending to get out and close the garage, someone rapped hard on the window beside him. Startled, Markwell turned his head and saw a man bending down and peering at him through the glass.

The stranger was approximately thirty-five. His features were bold, well-formed. Even through the partly fogged window he was a striking man. He was wearing a navy peacoat with the collar turned up. In the arctic air his nostrils smoked, and when he spoke, the words were dressed in pale puffs of breath. 'Dr. Markwell?'

Markwell rolled down the window. 'Yes?'

'Dr. Paul Markwell?'

'Yes, yes. Didn't I just say so? But I've no office hours here tonight, and I'm on my way to see a patient at the hospital.'

The stranger had unusually blue eyes that conjured in Markwell the image of a clear winter sky reflected in the millimeter-thin ice of a just-freezing pond. They were arresting, quite beautiful, but he knew at once that they were also the eyes of a dangerous man.

Before Markwell could throw the car into gear and reverse toward the street where help might be found, the man in the peacoat thrust a pistol through the open window. 'Don't do anything stupid.'

When the muzzle pressed into the tender flesh under his chin, the physician realized with some surprise that he did not want to die. He had long nursed the idea that he was ready to embrace death. Yet now, instead of welcoming the realization of his will to live, he was guilt-stricken. To embrace life seemed a betrayal of the son with whom he could be joined only in death.

'Kill the headlights, Doctor. Good. Now switch off the engine.'

Markwell withdrew the key from the ignition. 'Who are you?'

'That's not important.'

'It is to me. What do you want? What're you going to do to me?'

'Cooperate, and you won't be hurt. But try to get away, and I'll blow your damn head off, then empty the gun into your dead body just for the hell of it.' His voice was soft, inaptly pleasant, but full of conviction. 'Give me the keys.'

Markwell passed them through the open window.

'Now come out of there.'

Slowly sobering, Markwell got out of the car. The vicious wind bit his face. He had to squint to keep the fine snow out of his eyes.

'Before you close the door, roll up the window.' The stranger crowded him, allowing no avenue of escape. 'Okay, very good. Now, Doctor, walk with me to the garage.'

'This is crazy. What—'

'*Move.*'

The stranger stayed at Markwell's side, holding him by the left arm. If someone was watching from a neighboring house or from the street, the gloom and falling snow would conceal the gun.

In the garage, at the stranger's direction, Markwell pulled the big door shut. The cold, unoiled hinges squealed.

'If you want money—'

'Shut up and get in the house.'

'Listen, a patient of mine is in labor at the county—'

'If you don't shut up, I'll use the butt of this pistol to smash every tooth in your head, and you won't be *able* to talk.'

Markwell believed him. Six feet tall, about a hundred and eighty pounds, the man was Markwell's size but was intimidating. His blond hair was frosted with melting snow, and as the droplets trickled down his brow and temples, he appeared to be as devoid of humanity as an ice statue at a winter carnival. Markwell had no doubt that in a physical confrontation the stranger in the peacoat would win handily against most adversaries, especially against one middle-aged, out-of-shape, drunken physician.

Bob Shane felt claustrophobic in the cramped maternity-ward lounge provided for expectant fathers. The room had a low acoustic-tile ceiling, drab green walls, and a single window rimed with frost. The air was too warm. The six chairs and two end tables were too much furniture for the narrow space. He had an urge to push through the double swinging doors into the corridor, race to the other end of the hospital, cross the main public lounge, and break out into the cold night, where there was no stink of antiseptics or illness.

He remained in the maternity lounge, however, to be near to Janet if she needed him. Something was wrong. Labor was supposed to be painful but not as agonizing as the brutal, extended contractions that Janet had endured for so long. The physicians would not admit that serious complications had arisen, but their concern was apparent.

Bob understood the source of his claustrophobia. He was not actually afraid that the walls were closing in. What was closing in was death, perhaps that of his wife or of his unborn child – or both.

The swinging doors opened inward, and Dr. Yamatta entered.

As he rose from his chair, Bob bumped the end table, scattering half a dozen magazines across the floor. 'How is she, Doc?'

'No worse.' Yamatta was a short, slender man with a kind face and large, sad eyes. 'Dr. Markwell will be here shortly.'

'You're not delaying her treatment until he arrives, are you?'

'No, no, of course not. She's getting good care. I just thought you'd be relieved to know that your own doctor is on his way.'

'Oh. Well, yeah . . . thank you. Listen, can I see her, Doc?'

'Not yet,' Yamatta said.

'When?'

'When she's . . . in less distress.'

'What kind of answer's that? When will she *be* in less distress? When the hell will she come out of this?' He instantly regretted the outburst. 'I . . . I'm sorry, Doc. It's just . . . I'm afraid.'

'I know. I know.'

An inside door connected Markwell's garage to the house. They crossed the kitchen and followed the first-floor hallway, switching on lights as they went. Clumps of melting snow fell off their boots.

The gunman looked into the dining room, living room, study, medical office, and the patients' waiting room, then said, 'Upstairs.'

In the master bedroom the stranger snapped on one of the lamps. He moved a straight-backed, needlepoint chair away from the vanity and stood it in the middle of the room.

'Doctor, please take off your gloves, coat, and scarf.'

Markwell obeyed, dropping the garments to the floor, and at the gunman's direction he sat in the chair.

The stranger put the pistol on the dresser and produced a coiled length of sturdy rope from one pocket. He reached beneath his coat and withdrew a short, wide-bladed knife that was evidently kept in a sheath attached to his belt. He cut the rope into pieces with which, no doubt, to bind Markwell to the chair.

The doctor stared at the pistol on the dresser, calculating his chances of reaching the weapon before the gunman could get it. Then he met the stranger's winter-blue eyes and realized that his scheming was as transparent to his adversary as a child's simple cunning was apparent to an adult.

The blond man smiled as if to say, Go ahead, go for it.

Paul Markwell wanted to live. He remained docile and compliant, as the intruder tied him, hand and foot, to the needlepoint chair.

Making the knots tight but not painfully so, the stranger seemed oddly concerned about his captive. 'I don't want to have to gag you. You're drunk, and with a rag jammed in your mouth, you might vomit, choke to death. So to some extent I'm going to trust you. But if you cry out for help at any time, I'll kill you on the spot. Understand?'

'Yes.'

When the gunman spoke more than a few words, he revealed a vague accent, so mild that Markwell could not place it. He clipped the ends of some words, and occasionally his pronunciation had a guttural note that was barely perceptible.

The stranger sat on the edge of the bed and put one hand on the telephone. 'What's the number of the county hospital?'

Markwell blinked. 'Why?'

'Damn it, I asked you the number. If you won't give it to me, I'd rather beat it out of you than look it up in the directory.'

Chastened, Markwell gave him the number.

'Who's on duty there tonight?'

'Dr. Carlson. Herb Carlson.'

'Is he a good man?'

'What do you mean?'

'Is he a better doctor than you – or is he a lush too?'

'I'm not a lush. I have—'

'You're an irresponsible, self-pitying, alcoholic wreck, and you know it. Answer my question, Doctor. Is Carlson reliable?'

Markwell's sudden nausea resulted only partly from overindulgence in Scotch; the other cause was revulsion at the truth of what the intruder had said. 'Yeah, Herb Carlson's good. A very good doctor.'

'Who's the supervising nurse tonight?'

Markwell had to ponder that for a moment. 'Ella Hanlow, I think. I'm not sure. If it isn't Ella, it's Virginia Keene.'

The stranger called the county hospital and said he was speaking on behalf of Dr. Paul Markwell. He asked for Ella Hanlow.

A blast of wind slammed into the house, rattling a loose window, whistling in the eaves, and Markwell was reminded of the storm. As he watched the fast-falling snow at the window, he felt another gust of disorientation blow through him. The night was so eventful – the lightning, the inexplicable intruder – that suddenly it did not seem real. He pulled at the ropes that bound him to the chair, certain that they were fragments of a whiskey dream and would dissolve like gossamer, but they held him fast, and the effort made him dizzy again.

At the phone the stranger said, 'Nurse Hanlow? Dr. Markwell won't be able to come to the hospital tonight. One of his patients there, Janet Shane, is having a difficult labor. Hmmmm? Yes, of course. He wants Dr. Carlson to handle the delivery. No, no, I'm afraid he can't possibly make it. No, not the weather. He's drunk. That's right. He'd be a danger to the patient. No . . . he's so drunk, there's no point putting him on the line. Sorry. He's been drinking a lot lately, trying to cover it, but tonight he's worse than usual. Hmmmm? I'm a neighbor. Okay. Thank you, Nurse Hanlow. Good-bye.'

Markwell was angry but also surprisingly relieved to have his secret revealed. 'You bastard, you've ruined me.'

'No, Doctor. You've ruined yourself. Self-hatred is destroying your career. And it drove your wife away from you. The marriage was already troubled, sure, but it might've been saved if Lenny had lived, and it might even have been saved after he died if you hadn't withdrawn into yourself so completely.'

Markwell was astonished. 'How the hell do you know what it was like with me and Anna? And how do you know about Lenny? I've never met you before. How can you know anything about me?'

Ignoring the questions, the stranger piled two pillows against the padded headboard of the bed. He swung his wet, dirty, booted feet onto the covers and stretched out. 'No matter how you feel about it, losing your son wasn't your fault. You're just a physician, not a miracle worker. But losing Anna *was* your fault. And what you've become – an extreme danger to your patients – that's your fault too.'

Markwell started to object, then sighed and let his head drop forward until his chin was on his chest.

'You know what your trouble is, Doctor?'

'I suppose you'll tell me.'

'Your trouble is you never had to struggle for anything, never knew adversity. Your father was well-to-do, so you got everything you wanted, went to the finest schools. And though you were successful in your practice, you never needed the money – you had your inheritance. So when Lenny got polio, you didn't know how to deal with adversity because you'd never had any practice. You hadn't been *inoculated*, so you had no resistance, and you got a bad case of despair.'

Lifting his head, blinking until his vision cleared, Markwell said, 'I can't figure this.'

'Through all this suffering, you've learned something, Markwell, and if you'll sober up long enough to think straight, you might get back on track. You've still got a slim chance to redeem yourself.'

'Maybe I don't want to redeem myself.'

'I'm afraid that could be true. I think you're scared to die, but I don't know if you have the guts to go on living.'

The doctor's breath was sour with stale peppermint and whiskey. His mouth was dry, and his tongue swollen. He longed for a drink.

He halfheartedly tested the ropes that bound his hands to the chair. Finally, disgusted by the self-pitying whine in his own voice but unable to regain his dignity, he said, 'What do you want from me?'

'I want to prevent you from going to the hospital tonight. I want to be damn sure you don't deliver Janet Shane's baby. You've become a butcher, a potential killer, and you have to be stopped this time.'

Markwell licked his dry lips. 'I still don't know who you are.'

'And you never will, Doctor. You never will.'

Bob Shane had never been so scared. He repressed his tears, for he had the superstitious feeling that revealing his fear so openly would tempt the fates and insure Janet's and the baby's deaths.

He leaned forward in the waiting-room chair, bowed his head, and prayed silently: Lord, Janet could've done better than me. She's so pretty, and I'm as homely as a rag rug. I'm just a grocer, and my corner store isn't ever going to turn big profits, but she loves me. Lord, she's good, honest, humble . . . she doesn't deserve to die. Maybe You want to take her 'cause she's already good enough for heaven. But *I'm* not good enough yet, and I need her to help me be a better man.

One of the lounge doors opened.

Bob looked up.

Doctors Carlson and Yamatta entered in their hospital greens.

The sight of them frightened Bob, and he rose slowly from his chair.

Yamatta's eyes were sadder than ever.

Dr. Carlson was a tall, portly man who managed to look dignified even in his baggy hospital uniform. 'Mr. Shane . . . I'm sorry. I'm so sorry, but your wife died in childbirth.'

Bob stood rock-still, as if the dreadful news had transformed his flesh to stone. He heard only part of what Carlson said:

'. . . major uterine obstruction . . . one of those women not really designed to have children. She should never have gotten pregnant. I'm sorry . . . so sorry . . . everything we could . . . massive hemorrhaging . . . but the baby . . .'

The word 'baby' broke Bob's paralysis. He took a halting step toward Carlson. 'What did you say about the baby?'

'It's a girl,' Carlson said. 'A healthy little girl.'

Bob had thought everything was lost. Now he stared at Carlson, cautiously hopeful that a part of Janet had not died and that he was not, after all, entirely alone in the world. 'Really? A girl?'

'Yes,' Carlson said. 'She's an exceptionally beautiful baby. Born with a full head of dark brown hair.'

Looking at Yamatta, Bob said, 'My baby lived.'

'Yes,' Yamatta said. His poignant smile flickered briefly. 'And you've got Dr. Carlson to thank. I'm afraid Mrs. Shane never had a chance. In less experienced hands the baby might've been lost too.'

Bob turned to Carlson, still afraid to believe. 'The . . . the baby lived, and that's something to be thankful for, anyway, isn't it?'

The physicians stood in awkward silence. Then Yamatta put one hand on Bob Shane's shoulder, perhaps sensing that the contact would comfort him.

Though Bob was five inches taller and forty pounds heavier than the diminutive doctor, he leaned against Yamatta. Overcome with grief he wept, and Yamatta held him.

―――

The stranger stayed with Markwell for another hour, though he spoke no more and would respond to none of Markwell's questions. He lay on the bed, staring at the ceiling, so intent on his thoughts that he seldom moved.

As the doctor sobered, a throbbing headache began to torment him. As usual his hangover was an excuse for even greater self-pity than that which had driven him to drink.

Eventually the intruder looked at his wristwatch. 'Eleven-thirty. I'll be going now.' He got off the bed, came to the chair, and again drew the knife from beneath his coat.

Markwell tensed.

'I'm going to saw part way through your ropes, Doctor. If you struggle with them for half an hour or so, you'll be able to free yourself. Which gives me time enough to get out of here.'

As the man stooped behind the chair and set to work, Markwell expected to feel the blade slip between his ribs.

But in less than a minute the stranger put the knife away and went to the bedroom door. 'You do have a chance to redeem yourself, Doctor. I think you're too weak to do it, but I hope I'm wrong.'

Then he walked out.

For ten minutes, as Markwell struggled to free himself, he heard occasional noises downstairs. Evidently the intruder was searching for valuables. Although he had seemed mysterious, perhaps he was nothing but a burglar with a singularly odd modus operandi.

Markwell finally broke loose at twenty-five past midnight. His wrists were severely abraded, bleeding.

Though he had not heard a sound from the first floor in half an hour, he took his pistol from the nightstand drawer and descended the stairs with caution. He went to his office in the professional wing, where he expected to find drugs missing from his medical supplies; neither of the two tall, white cabinets had been touched.

He hurried into his study, convinced that the flimsy wall safe had been opened. The safe was unbreached.

Baffled, turning to leave, he saw empty whiskey, gin, tequila, and vodka bottles piled in the bar sink. The intruder had paused only to locate the liquor supply and pour it down the drain.

A note was taped to the bar mirror. The intruder had printed his message in neat block letters:

IF YOU DON'T STOP DRINKING, IF YOU DON'T LEARN TO ACCEPT LENNY'S DEATH, YOU WILL PUT A GUN IN YOUR MOUTH AND BLOW YOUR BRAINS OUT WITHIN ONE YEAR. THIS IS NOT A PREDICTION. THIS IS A FACT.

Clutching the note and the gun, Markwell looked around the empty room, as if the stranger was still there, unseen, a ghost that could choose at will between visibility and invisibility. 'Who are you?' he demanded. 'Who the *hell* are you?'

Only the wind at the window answered him, and its mournful moan had no meaning that he could discern.

At eleven o'clock the next morning, after an early meeting with the funeral director regarding Janet's body, Bob Shane returned to the county hospital to see his newborn daughter. After he donned a cotton gown, a cap, and a surgical mask, and after thoroughly scrubbing his hands under a nurse's direction, he was permitted into the nursery, where he gently lifted Laura from her cradle.

Nine other newborns shared the room. All of them were cute in one way or another, but Bob did not believe he was unduly prejudiced in his judgement that Laura Jean was the cutest of the crop. Although the popular image of an angel required blue eyes and blond hair, and though Laura had brown eyes and hair, she was nevertheless angelic in appearance. During the ten minutes that he held her, she did not cry; she blinked, squinted, rolled her eyes, yawned. She looked pensive, too, as if perhaps she knew that she was motherless and that she and her father had only each other in a cold, difficult world.

A viewing window, through which relatives could see the newborns, filled one wall. Five people were gathered at the glass. Four were smiling, pointing, and making funny faces to entertain the babies.

The fifth was a blond man wearing a navy peacoat and standing with his hands in his pockets. He did not smile or point or make faces. He was staring at Laura.

After a few minutes during which the stranger's gaze did not shift from the child, Bob became concerned. The guy was good looking and clean-cut but there was a hardness in his face, too, and some quality that could not be put into words but that made Bob think this was a man who had seen and done terrible things.

He began to remember sensational tabloid stories of kidnappers, babies being sold on the black market. He told himself that he was paranoid, imagining a danger where none existed because, having lost Janet, he was now worried about losing his daughter as well. But the longer the blond man studied Laura, the more uneasy Bob became.

As if sensing that uneasiness, the man looked up. They stared at each other. The stranger's blue eyes were unusually bright, intense. Bob's fear deepened. He held his daughter closer, as if the stranger might smash through the nursery window to seize her. He considered calling one of the crèche nurses and suggesting that she speak to the man, make inquiries about him.

Then the stranger smiled. His was a broad, warm, genuine smile that transformed his face. In an instant he no longer looked sinister but friendly. He winked at Bob and mouthed one word through the thick glass: 'Beautiful.'

Bob relaxed, smiled, realized his smile could not be seen behind his mask, and nodded a thank you.

The stranger looked once more at Laura, winked at Bob again, and walked away from the window.

Later, after Bob Shane had gone home for the day, a tall man in dark clothing approached the crèche window. His name was Kokoschka. He studied the infants; then his field of vision shifted, and he became aware of his colorless reflection in the polished glass. He had a broad, flat face with sharp-edged features, lips so thin and hard that they seemed to be made of horn. A two-inch dueling scar marked his left cheek. His dark eyes had no depth, as if they were painted ceramic spheres, much like the cold eyes of a shark cruising in shadowy ocean trenches. He was amused to realize how starkly his face contrasted to the innocent visages of the cradled babies beyond the window; he smiled, a rare expression for him, which imparted no warmth to his face but actually made him appear more threatening.

He looked beyond his reflection again. He had no trouble finding Laura Shane among the swaddled infants, for the surname of each child was printed on a card and affixed to the back of his or her cradle.

Why is there such interest in you, Laura? he wondered. Why is your life so important? Why all this energy expended to see that you are brought safely into the world? Should I kill you now and put an end to the traitor's scheme?

He'd be able to murder her without compunction. He had killed children before, though none quite so young as this. No crime was too terrible if it furthered the cause to which he had devoted his life.

The babe was sleeping. Now and then her mouth worked, and her tiny face briefly wrinkled, as perhaps she dreamed of the womb with regret and longing.

At last he decided not to kill her. Not yet.

'I can always eliminate you later, little one,' he murmured. 'When I understand what part you play in the traitor's plans, *then* I can kill you.'

Kokoschka walked away from the window. He knew he would not see the girl again for more than eight years.

• **2** •

In southern California rain falls rarely in the spring, summer, and autumn. The true rainy season usually begins in December and ends in March. But on Saturday the second of April, 1963, the sky was overcast, and humidity was high. Holding open the front door of his small, neighborhood grocery in Santa Ana, Bob Shane decided that the prospects were good for one last big downpour of the season.

The ficus trees in the yard of the house across the street and the date palm on the corner were motionless in the dead air and seemed to droop as if with the weight of the oncoming storm.

By the cash register, the radio was turned low. The Beach Boys were singing their new hit 'Surfin' U.S.A.'. Considering the weather, their tune was as appropriate as 'White Christmas' sung in July.

Bob looked at his watch: three-fifteen.

There'll be rain by three-thirty, he thought, and a lot of it.

Business had been good during the morning, but the afternoon had been slow. At the moment no shoppers were in the store.

The family-owned grocery faced new, deadly competition from convenience-store chains like 7-Eleven. He was planning to shift to a deli-style operation, offering more fresh foods, but was delaying as long as possible because a deli required considerably more work.

If the oncoming storm was bad he would have few customers the rest of the day. He might close early and take Laura to a movie.

Turning from the door, he said, 'Better get the boat, doll.'

Laura was kneeling at the head of the first aisle, across from the cash register, absorbed in her work. Bob had carried four cartons of canned soup from the stockroom, then Laura had taken over. She was only eight years old, but she was a reliable kid, and she liked to help out around the store. After stamping the correct price on each of the cans, she stacked them on the shelves, remembering to cycle the merchandise, putting the new soup behind the old.

She looked up reluctantly. 'Boat? What boat?'

'Upstairs in the apartment. The boat in the closet. From the look of the sky, we're going to need it to get around later today.'

'Silly,' she said. 'We don't have a boat in the closet.'

He walked behind the checkout counter. 'Nice little blue boat.'

'Yeah? In a closet? Which closet?'

He began to clip packages of Slim Jims to the metal display rack beside the snack pack crackers. 'The library closet, of course.'

'We don't have a library.'

'We don't? Oh. Well, now that you mention it, the boat isn't in the library. It's in the closet in the toad's room.'

She giggled. 'What toad?'

'Why, you mean to tell me that you don't know about the toad?'

Grinning, she shook her head.

'As of today we are renting a room to a fine, upstanding toad from England. A gentleman toad who's here on the queen's business.'

Lightning flared and thunder rumbled through the April sky. On the radio, static crackled through the The Cascades' 'Rhythm of the Rain.'

Laura paid no attention to the storm. She was not frightened of things that scared most kids. She was so self-confident and self-contained that sometimes she seemed to be an old lady masquerading as a child. 'Why would the queen let a toad handle her business?'

'Toads are excellent businessmen,' he said, opening one of the Slim Jims and taking a bite. Since Janet's death, since moving to California to start over, he had put on fifty pounds. He had never been a handsome man. Now at thirty-eight he was pleasantly round, with little chance of turning a woman's head. He was not a great success, either; no one got rich operating a corner grocery. But he didn't care. He had Laura, and he was a good father, and she loved him with all her heart, as he loved her, so what the rest of the world might think of him was of no consequence. 'Yes, toads are excellent businessmen indeed. And this toad's family has served the crown for hundreds of years. In fact he's been knighted. Sir Thomas Toad.'

Lightning crackled brighter than before. The thunder was louder as well.

Having finished stocking the soup shelves, Laura rose from her knees and wiped her hands on the white apron that she was wearing over T-shirt and jeans. She was lovely; with her thick, brown hair and large, brown eyes, she bore more than a passing resemblance to her mother. 'And how much rent is Sir Thomas Toad paying?'

'Six pence a week.'

'Is he in the room next to mine?'

'Yes, the room with the boat in the closet.'

She giggled again. 'Well, he better not snore.'

'He said the same of you.'

A battered, rusted Buick pulled up in front of the store, and as the driver's door opened, a third thunderbolt blasted a hole in the darkening sky. The day was filled with molten light that appeared to flow liquidly along the street outside, sprayed lavalike over the parked Buick and the passing cars. The accompanying thunder shook the building from roof to foundation, as though the stormy heavens were reflected in the land below, precipitating an earthquake.

'Wow!' Laura said, moving fearlessly toward the windows.

Though no rain had fallen yet, wind suddenly swept in from the west, harrying leaves and litter before it.

The man who got out of the decrepit, blue Buick was looking at the sky in astonishment.

Bolt after bolt of lightning pierced the clouds, seared the air, cast their blazing images in windows and automobile chrome, and with each flash came thunder that struck the day with god-size fists.

The lightning spooked Bob. When he called to Laura – 'Honey, get away from the windows' – she rushed behind the counter and let him put an arm around her, probably more for his comfort than hers.

The man from the Buick hurried into the store. Looking out at the fulminous sky, he said, 'You see that, man? Whew!'

The thunder faded; silence returned.

Rain fell. Fat droplets at first struck the windows without much force then came in blinding torrents that blurred the world beyond the small shop.

The customer turned and smiled. 'Some show, huh?'

Bob started to respond but fell silent when he took a closer look at the man, sensing trouble as a deer might sense a stalking wolf. The guy was wearing scuffed engineer boots, dirty jeans, and a stained windbreaker half zipped over a soiled white T-shirt. His windblown hair was oily, and his face was shaded with beard stubble. He had bloodshot, fevered eyes. A junkie. Approaching the counter, he drew a revolver from his windbreaker, and the gun was no surprise.

'Gimme what's in the register, asshole.'

'Sure.'

'Make it quick.'

'Just take it easy.'

The junkie licked his pale, cracked lips. 'Don't hold out on me, asshole.'

'Okay, okay, sure. You got it,' Bob said, trying to push Laura behind him with one hand.

'Leave the girl so I can see her! I want to *see* her. Now, right now, get her the fuck out from behind you!'

'Okay, just cool off.'

The guy was strung out as taut as a dead man's grin, and his entire body vibrated visibly. 'Right where I can see her. And don't you reach for nothin' but the cash register, don't you go reachin' for no gun, or I'll blow your fuckin' head off.'

'I don't have a gun,' Bob assured him. He glanced at the rain-washed windows, hoping that no other customers would arrive while the holdup was in progress. The junkie seemed so unstable that he might shoot anyone who walked through the door.

Laura tried to ease behind her father, but the junkie said, 'Hey, don't move!'

Bob said, 'She's only eight—'

'She's a bitch, they're all fuckin' bitches no matter how big or little.' His shrill voice cracked repeatedly. He sounded even more frightened than Bob was, which scared Bob more than anything else.

Though he was focused intently on the junkie and the revolver, Bob was also crazily aware that the radio was playing Skeeter Davis singing 'The End of the World,' which struck him as uncomfortably prophetic. With the excusable superstition of a man being held at gunpoint, he wished fervently that the song would conclude before it magically precipitated the end of his and Laura's world.

'Here's the money, here's all of it, take it.'

Scooping the cash off the counter and stuffing it into a pocket of his dirty windbreaker, the man said, 'You got a storeroom in back?'

'Why?'

With one arm the junkie angrily swept the Slim Jims, Life Savers, crackers, and chewing gum off the counter onto the floor. He thrust the gun at Bob. 'You got a storeroom, asshole, I know you do. We're gonna go back there in the storeroom.'

Bob's mouth was suddenly dry. 'Listen, take the money and go. You got what you want. Just go. Please.'

Grinning, more confident now that he had the money, emboldened by Bob's fear but still visibly trembling, the gunman said, 'Don't worry, I ain't gonna kill no one. I'm a lover not a killer. All I want's a piece of that little bitch, and then I'm out of here.'

Bob cursed himself for not having a gun. Laura was clinging to him, trusting in him, but he could do nothing to save her. On the way to the storeroom, he'd lunge at the junkie, try to grab the revolver. He was overweight, out of shape. Unable to move fast enough, he would be shot in the gut and left to die on the floor, while the filthy bastard took Laura into the back room and raped her.

'Move,' the junkie said impatiently. '*Now!*'

A gun fired, Laura screamed, and Bob pulled her tight against him, sheltering her, but it was the junkie who had been shot. The bullet struck his left temple, blowing out part of his skull, and he went down hard atop the Slim Jims and crackers and chewing gum that he had knocked off the counter, dead so instantaneously that he did not even reflexively pull the trigger of his own revolver.

Stunned, Bob looked to his right and saw a tall, blond man with a pistol. Evidently he had entered the building through the rear service door and had crept silently through the storage room. Upon entering the grocery he had shot the junkie without warning. As he stared at the dead body, he looked cool, dispassionate, as if he were an experienced executioner.

'Thank God,' Bob said, 'police.'

'I'm not the police.' The man wore gray slacks, a white shirt, and a dark gray jacket under which a shoulder holster was visible.

Bob was confused, wondering if their rescuer was *another* thief about to take over where the junkie had been violently interrupted.

The stranger looked up from the corpse. His eyes were pure blue, intense, and direct.

Bob was sure that he had seen the guy before, but he could not remember where or when.

The stranger looked at Laura. 'You all right, sweetheart?'

'Yes,' she said, but she clung to her father.

The pungent odor of urine rose from the dead man, for he had lost control of his bladder at the moment of death.

The stranger crossed the room, stepping around the corpse, and engaged the dead-bolt lock on the front door. He pulled down the shade. He looked worriedly at the big display windows over which flowed a continuous film of rain, distorting the stormy afternoon beyond. 'No way to cover those, I guess. We'll just have to hope nobody comes along and looks in.'

'What're you going to do to us?' Bob asked.

'Me? Nothing. I'm not like that creep. I don't want anything from you. I just locked the door so we could work out the story you're going to have to tell the police. We have to get it straight before anyone walks in here and sees the body.'

'Why do I need a story?'

Stooping beside the corpse, the stranger took a set of car keys and the wad of money from the pockets of the blood-stained windbreaker. Rising again, he said, 'Okay, what you have to tell them is that there were *two* gunmen. This one wanted Laura, but the other was sickened by the idea of raping a little girl, and he just wanted to get out. So they argued, it got nasty, the other one shot this bastard and skipped with the money. Can you make that sound right?'

Bob was reluctant to believe that he and Laura had been spared. With one arm he held his daughter tightly against him. 'I . . . I don't understand. You weren't really with him. You're not in trouble for killing him – after all, he was going to kill us. So why don't we just tell them the truth?'

Stepping to the end of the checkout counter, returning the money to Bob, the man said, 'And what is the truth?'

'Well . . . you happened along and saw the robbery in progress—'

'I didn't just *happen* along, Bob. I've been watching over you and Laura.' Slipping his pistol into his shoulder holster, the man looked down at Laura. She stared at him wide-eyed. He smiled and whispered, 'Guardian angel.'

Not believing in guardian angels, Bob said, 'Watching over us? From where, how long, why?'

In a voice colored by urgency and by a vague, unplaceable accent that Bob heard for the first time, the stranger said, 'Can't tell you that.' He glanced at the rain-washed windows. 'And I can't afford to be questioned by police. So you've got to get this story straight.'

Bob said, 'Where do I know you from?'

'You don't know me.'

'But I'm sure I've seen you before.'

'You haven't. You don't need to know. Now for God's sake, hide that money and leave the register empty; it'll seem odd if the second man left without what he came for. I'll take his Buick, abandon it in a few blocks, so you can give the cops a description of it. Give them a description of me, too. It won't matter.'

Thunder rumbled outside, but it was low and distant, not like the explosions with which the storm had begun.

The humid air thickened as the slower-spreading, coppery scent of blood mixed with the stench of urine.

Queasy, leaning on the counter but still holding Laura at his side, Bob said, 'Why can't I just tell them how you interrupted the robbery, shot the guy, and didn't want publicity, so you left?'

Impatient, the stranger raised his voice. 'An armed man just happens to stroll by while the robbery's in progress and decides to be a hero? The cops won't believe a cockeyed story like that.'

'That's what happened—'

'But they won't buy it! Listen, they'll start thinking maybe *you* shot the junkie. Since you don't own a gun, at least not according to public record, they'll wonder if maybe it was an illegal weapon and if you disposed of it after you shot this guy, then cooked up a crazy story about some Lone Ranger type walking in and saving your ass.'

'I'm a respectable businessman with a good reputation.'

In the stranger's eyes a peculiar sadness arose, a haunted look. 'Bob, you're a nice man . . . but you're a little naive sometimes.'

'What're you—'

The stranger held up a hand to silence him. 'In a crunch a man's reputation never counts for as much as it ought to. Most people are good-hearted and willing to give a man the benefit of the doubt, but the poisonous few are eager to see others brought down, ruined.' His voice had fallen to a whisper, and although he continued to look at Bob, he seemed to be seeing other places, other people. 'Envy, Bob. Envy eats them alive. If you had money, they'd envy you that. But since you don't, they envy you for having such a good, bright, loving daughter. They envy you for just being a happy man. They envy you for *not* envying them. One of the greatest sorrows of human existence is that some people aren't happy merely to be alive but find their happiness only in the misery of others.'

The charge of naiveté was one that Bob could not refute, and he knew the stranger spoke the truth. He shivered.

After a moment of silence, the man's haunted expression gave way to a look of urgency again. 'And when the cops decide you're lying about the Lone Ranger who saved you, then they'll begin to wonder if maybe the junkie wasn't here to rob you at all, if maybe you knew him, had a falling out with him over something, even *planned* his murder and tried to make it look like a robbery. That's how cops think, Bob. Even if they can't pin this on you, they'll try so hard that they'll make a mess of your life. Do you want to put Laura through that?'

'No.'

'Then do it my way.'

Bob nodded. 'I will. Your way. But who the hell are you?'

'That doesn't matter. We don't have time for it anyway.' He stepped behind the counter and stooped in front of Laura, face to face with her. 'Did you understand what I told your father? If the police ask you what happened—'

'You were with that man,' she said, pointing in the general direction of the corpse.

'That's right.'

'You were his friend,' she said, 'but then you started arguing about me, though I'm not sure why, 'cause I didn't do anything—'

'It doesn't matter why, honey,' the stranger said.

Laura nodded. 'And the next thing you shot him and ran out with all our money and drove away, and I was very scared.'

The man looked up at Bob. 'Eight years old, huh?'

'She's a smart girl.'

'But it'd still be best if the cops didn't question her much.'

'I won't let them.'

'If they do,' Laura said, 'I'll just cry and cry till they stop.'

The stranger smiled. He stared at Laura so lovingly that he made Bob uneasy. His manner was not that of the pervert who had wanted to take her into the storeroom; his expression was tender, affectionate. He touched her cheek. Astonishingly, tears shimmered in his eyes. He blinked, stood. 'Bob, put that money away. Remember, *I* left with it.'

Bob realized the wad of cash was still in his hand. He jammed it into his pants pocket, and his loose apron concealed the bulge.

The stranger unlocked the door and put up the shade. 'Take care of her, Bob. She's special.' Then he dashed into the rain, letting the door stand open behind him, and got into the Buick. The tires squealed as he pulled out of the parking lot.

The radio was on, but Bob heard it for the first time since 'The End of the World' had been playing, before the junkie had been shot. Now Shelley Fabares was singing 'Johnny Angel.'

Suddenly he heard the rain again, not just as a dull background hiss and patter but really *heard* it, beating furiously on the windows and on the roof of the apartment above. In spite of the wind rushing through the open door, the stink of blood and urine was abruptly far worse than it had been a moment ago, and just as precipitously, as if coming out of a trance of terror and regaining his full senses, he realized how close his precious Laura had come to dying. He scooped her into his arms, lifted her off the floor, and held her, repeating her name, smoothing her hair. He buried his face against her neck and smelled the sweet freshness of her skin, felt the pulse of the artery in her throat, and thanked God that she was alive.

'I love you, Laura.'

'I love you, too, Daddy. I love you because of Sir Tommy Toad and a million other reasons. But we've got to call the police now.'

'Yes, of course,' he said, reluctantly putting her down.

His eyes were full of tears. He was so unnerved that he could not recall where the telephone was.

Laura had already taken the handset off the hook. She held it out to him. 'Or I can call them, Daddy. The number's right here on the phone. Do you want me to call them?'

'No. I'll do it, baby.' Blinking back tears, he took the phone from her and sat on the old wooden stool behind the cash register.

She put one hand on his arm, as if she knew he needed her touch.

Janet had been emotionally strong. But Laura's strength and self-possession were unusual for her age, and Bob Shane was not sure where they came from. Maybe being motherless made her self-reliant.

'Daddy?' Laura said, tapping the phone with one finger. 'The police, remember?'

'Oh, yeah,' he said. Trying not to gag on the odor of death that permeated the store, he dialed the police emergency number.

———

Kokoschka sat in a car across the street from Bob Shane's small grocery, thoughtfully fingering the scar on his cheek.

The rain had stopped. The police had gone. Neon shop signs and lampposts lit at nightfall, but the macadam streets glistened darkly in spite of that illumination, as if the pavement absorbed the light instead of reflecting it.

Kokoschka had arrived in the neighborhood simultaneously with Stefan, the blond and blue-eyed traitor. He had heard the shooting, had seen Stefan flee in the dead man's car, had joined the crowd of onlookers when the police arrived, and had learned most of the details of what had happened in the store.

He had, of course, seen through Bob Shane's preposterous story about Stefan having been merely a second thief. Stefan was not their assailant but their self-appointed guardian, and he had no doubt lied to cover his true identity.

Laura had been saved again.

But why?

Kokoschka tried to imagine what part the girl could possibly play in the traitor's plans, but he was stumped. He knew nothing would be gained by interrogating the girl, for she was too young to have been told anything useful. The reason for her rescue would be as much a mystery to her as it was to Kokoschka.

He was sure that her father knew nothing, either. The girl was obviously the one who interested Stefan, not the father, so Bob Shane would not have been made privy to Stefan's origins or intentions.

Finally Kokoschka drove several blocks to a restaurant, had dinner, then returned to the grocery well after nightfall. He parked on the side street, in the shadows under the expansive fronds of a date palm. The store was dark, but lights shone at the windows of the second-floor apartment.

From a deep pocket of his raincoat, he withdrew a revolver. It was a snub-nosed Colt Agent .38, compact but powerful. Kokoschka admired well-designed and well-made weapons, and he especially liked the feel of this gun in his hand: this was Death himself imprisoned in steel.

Kokoschka could cut the Shanes' phone wires, quietly force entry, kill the girl and her father, and slip away before police responded to the shots. He had a talent and affinity for that kind of work.

But if he killed them without knowing *why* he was killing them, without understanding what role they played in Stefan's schemes, he might later discover that eliminating them was a mistake. He had to know Stefan's purpose before acting.

Reluctantly he put the revolver in his pocket.

In the windless night, rain fell straight down on the city, as if every droplet was enormously heavy. It drummed noisily on the roof and windshield of the small, black car.

At one o'clock in the morning on that Tuesday in late March, the rainswept streets, flooded at some intersections, were generally deserted but for military vehicles. Stefan chose an indirect route to the institute to avoid known inspection stations, but he was afraid of encountering an impromptu checkpoint. His papers were in order, and his security clearance exempted him from the new curfew. Nevertheless he preferred not to come under the scrutiny of military police. He could not afford to have the car searched, for the suitcase on the back seat contained copper wire, detonators, and plastic explosives not legally in his possession.

Because his breath fogged the windshield, because rain obscured the eerily dark city, because the car's wipers were worn, and because the hooded headlights illuminated a limited field of vision, he almost missed the narrow, cobblestone street that led behind the institute. He braked, turned the wheel sharply. The sedan took the corner with a shudder and a squeal of tires, sliding slightly on the slick cobbles.

He parked in darkness near the rear entrance, got out of the car, and took the suitcase from the back seat. The institute was a drab, four-story brick building with heavily barred windows. An air of menace hung about the place, though it did not look as if it harbored secrets that would radically change the world. The metal door had concealed hinges and was painted black. He pushed the button, heard the buzzer ring inside, and waited nervously for a response.

He was wearing rubber boots and a trenchcoat with the collar turned up, but he had neither a hat nor an umbrella. The cold rain pasted his hair to his skull and drizzled down the nape of his neck.

Shivering, he looked at a slit window that was set in the wall beside the door. It was six inches wide, a foot high, with glass that was mirrored from outside, transparent from inside.

He patiently listened to the rain beating on the car, splashing in puddles, and gurgling in a nearby downspout. With a cold sizzle it struck the leaves of plane trees at the curb.

A light came on above the door. It was in a cone-shaped shade, the yellow glow tightly contained and directed straight down on him.

Stefan smiled at the mirrored observation window, at the guard he could not see.

The light went out, the lock bolts clattered open, and the door swung inward. He knew the guard: Viktor something, a stout, fiftyish man with close-cropped gray hair and steel-rimmed spectacles, who was more pleasant-tempered than he looked and was in fact a mother hen who worried about the health of friends and acquaintances.

'Sir, what are you doing out at this hour, in this downpour?'

'Couldn't sleep.'

'Dreadful weather. Come in, in! You'll catch cold for sure.'

'Kept worrying about work I'd left undone, so I thought I might as well come in and *do* it.'

'You'll work yourself into an early grave, sir. Truly you will.'

As Stefan stepped into the antechamber and watched the guard close the door, he searched his memory for a scrap of knowledge about Viktor's personal life. 'From the look of you, I guess your wife still makes those incredible noodle dishes you've told me about.'

Turning from the door, Viktor laughed softly, patted his belly. 'I swear, she's employed by the devil to lead me into sin, primarily gluttony. What's that, sir, a suitcase? Are you moving in?'

Wiping rain from his face with one hand, Stefan said, 'Research data. Took it home weeks ago, been working on it evenings.'

'Have you no private life at all?'

'I get twenty minutes for myself every second Thursday.'

Viktor clucked his tongue disapprovingly. He stepped to the desk that occupied a third of the floor space in the small room, picked up the phone, and called the other night guard, who was stationed in a similar antechamber at the front entrance to the institute. When anyone was let in after hours, the admitting guard always alerted his colleague at the other end of the building, in part to avoid false alarms and perhaps the accidental shooting of an innocent visitor.

Dripping rain on the worn carpet runner, fishing a set of keys from his trenchcoat pocket, Stefan went to the inner door. Like the outer portal, it was made of steel with concealed hinges. However, it could be unlocked only with two keys turned in tandem – one belonging to an authorized employee, the other carried by the guard on duty. The work being conducted at the institute was so extraordinary and secret that even the night watchmen could not be trusted to have access to the labs and file rooms.

Viktor put down the phone. 'How long are you staying, sir?'

'A couple of hours. Is anyone else working tonight?'

'No. You're the only martyr. And no one truly appreciates martyrs, sir. You'll work yourself to death, I swear, and for what? Who'll care?'

'Eliot wrote: "Saints and martyrs rule from the tomb." '

'Eliot? He a poet or something?'

'T. S. Eliot, a poet, yes.'

' "Saints and martyrs rule from the tomb"? I don't know about this fellow. Doesn't sound like an *approved* poet. Sounds subversive.' Viktor laughed warmly, apparently amused by the ridiculous notion that his hard-working friend could be a traitor.

Together they opened the inner door.

Stefan lugged the suitcase of explosives into the institute's ground-floor hallway, where he switched on the lights.

'If you're going to make a habit of working in the middle of the night,' Viktor said, 'I'll bring you one of my wife's cakes to give you energy.'

'Thank you, Viktor, but I hope not to make a habit of this.'

The guard closed the metal door. The lock bolt clanked shut automatically.

Alone in the hallway Stefan thought, not for the first time, that he was fortunate in his appearance: blond, strong-featured, blue-eyed. His looks partly explained why he could brazenly carry explosives into the institute without expecting to be searched. Nothing about him was dark, sly, or suspect; he was the ideal, angelic when he smiled, and his devotion to country would never be questioned by men like Viktor, men whose blind obedience to the state and whose beery, sentimental patriotism prevented them from thinking clearly about a lot of things. A lot of things.

He rode the elevator to the third floor and went directly to his office where he turned on a brass, gooseneck lamp. After removing his rubber boots and trenchcoat, he selected a manila folder from the file cabinet and arranged its contents across the desk to create a convincing impression that work was underway. In the unlikely event that another staff member decided to put in an appearance in the heart of the night, as much as possible must be done to allay suspicion.

Carrying the suitcase and a flashlight that he had taken from an inner pocket of his trenchcoat, he climbed the stairs past the fourth floor and ascended all the way to the attic. The flashlight revealed huge timbers from which a few misdriven nails bristled here and there. Though the attic had a rough wood floor, it was not used for storage and was empty of all but a film of gray dust and spider-webs. The space under the highly pitched slate roof was sufficient to allow him to stand erect along the center of the building, though he would have to drop to his hands and knees when he worked closer to the eaves.

With the roof only inches away, the steady roar of the rain was as thunderous as the flight of an endless fleet of bombers crossing low overhead. That image came to mind perhaps because he believed that exactly such ruination would be the inevitable fate of his city.

He opened the suitcase. Working with the speed and confidence of a demolitions expert, he placed the bricks of plastic explosives and shaped each charge to direct the power of the explosion downward and inward. The blast must not merely blow the roof off but pulverize the middle floors and bring the heavy roof slates and timbers crashing down through the debris to cause further destruction. He secreted the plastique among the rafters and in the corners of the long room, even pried up a couple of floorboards and left explosives under them.

Outside, the storm briefly abated. But soon more ominous peals of thunder rolled across the night, and the rain returned, falling harder than before. The long-delayed wind arrived, too, keening along the gutters and moaning under the eaves; its strange, hollow voice seemed simultaneously to threaten and mourn the city.

Chilled by the unheated attic air, he conducted his delicate work with increasingly tremulous hands. Though shivering, he broke out in a sweat.

He inserted a detonator in every charge and strung wire from all the charges to the northwest corner of the attic. He braided them to a single copper line and dropped it down a ventilation chase that went all the way to the basement.

The charges and wire were as well concealed as possible and would not be spotted by someone who merely opened the attic door for a quick look. But on closer inspection or if the space was needed for storage, the wires and molded plastique surely would be noticed.

He needed twenty-four hours during which no one would go into the attic. That wasn't much to ask, considering that he was the only one who had visited the institute's garret in months.

Tomorrow night he would return with a second suitcase and plant charges in the basement. Crushing the building between simultaneous explosions above and below was the only way to be certain of reducing it – and its contents – to splinters, gravel, and twisted scraps. After the blast and accompanying fire, no files must remain to rekindle the dangerous research now conducted there.

The great quantity of explosives, although carefully placed and shaped, would damage structures on all sides of the institute, and he was afraid that other people, some of them no doubt innocent, would be killed in the blast. Those deaths could not be avoided. He dared not use less plastique, for if every file and every duplicate of every file throughout the institute were not utterly destroyed, the project might be quickly relaunched. And this was a project that must be brought to an end swiftly, for the hope of all mankind hinged on its destruction. If innocent people perished, he would just have to live with the guilt.

In two hours, at a few minutes past three o'clock, he finished his work in the attic.

He returned to his office on the third floor and sat for a while behind his desk. He did not want to leave until his sweat-soaked hair had dried and he had stopped trembling, for Viktor might notice.

He closed his eyes. In his mind he summoned Laura's face. He could always calm himself with thoughts of her. The mere fact of her existence brought him peace and greater courage.

• 4 •

Bob Shane's friends did not want Laura to attend her father's funeral. They believed that a twelve-year-old girl ought to be spared such a grim ordeal. She insisted, however, and when she wanted anything as badly as she wanted to say one last goodbye to her father, no one could thwart her.

That Thursday, July 24, 1967, was the worst day of her life, even more distressing than the preceding Tuesday when her father had died. Some of the anesthetizing shock had worn off, and Laura no longer felt numb; her emotions were closer to the surface and less easily controlled. She was beginning to realize fully how much she had lost.

She chose a dark blue dress because she did not own a black one. She wore black shoes and dark blue socks, and she worried about the socks because they made her feel childish, frivolous. Having never worn nylons, however, she didn't think it a good idea to don them for the first time at the funeral. She expected her father to look down from heaven during the service, and she intended to be just the way he remembered her. If he saw her in nylons, a changeling striving awkwardly to be grown up, he might be embarrassed for her.

At the funeral home she sat in the front row between Cora Lance, who owned a beauty shop half a block from Shane's Grocery, and Anita Passadopolis, who had done charity work with Bob at St. Andrew's Presbyterian Church. Both were in their late fifties, grand-motherly types who touched Laura reassuringly and watched her with concern.

They did not need to worry about her. She would not cry, become hysterical, or tear out her hair. She understood death. Everyone had to die. People died, dogs died, cats died, birds died, flowers died. Even the ancient redwood trees died sooner or later, though they lived twenty or thirty times longer than a person, which didn't seem right. On the other hand, living a thousand years as a tree would be a lot duller than living just forty-two years as a happy human being. Her father had been forty-two when his heart failed – bang, a sudden attack – which was too young. But that was the way of the world, and crying about it was pointless. Laura prided herself on her sensibleness.

Besides, death was not the end of a person. Death was actually only the beginning. Another and better life followed. She knew that must be true because her father had told her so, and her father never lied. Her father was the most truthful man, and kind, and sweet.

As the minister approached the lectern to the left of the casket, Cora Lance leaned close to Laura. 'Are you okay, dear?'

'Yes. I'm fine,' she said, but she did not look at Cora. She dared not meet anyone's eyes, so she studied inanimate things with great interest.

This was the first funeral home she had ever entered, and she did not like it. The burgundy carpet was ridiculously thick. The drapes and upholstered chairs were burgundy, too, with only minimal gold trim, and the lamps had burgundy shades, so all the rooms appeared to have been decorated by an obsessed interior designer with a burgundy fetish.

Fetish was a new word for her. She used it too much, just as she always overused a new word, but in this case it was appropriate.

Last month, when she'd first heard the lovely word 'sequestered,' meaning 'secluded or isolated,' she had used it at every opportunity, until her father had begun to tease her with silly variations: 'Hey, how's my little sequestrian this morning?' he would say, or 'Potato chips are a high turnover item, so we'll shift them into the first aisle, closer to the register, 'cause the corner they're in now is sort of sequesteriacious.' He enjoyed making her giggle, as with his tales of Sir Tommy Toad, a British amphibian he had invented when she was eight years old and whose comic biography he embellished nearly every day. In some ways her father had been more of a child than she was, and she had loved him for that.

Her lower lip trembled. She bit it. Hard. If she cried, she'd be doubting what her father had always told her about the next life, the better life. By crying she would be pronouncing him dead, dead for once and all, forever, *finito*.

She longed to be sequestered in her room above the grocery, in bed, the covers pulled over her head. That idea was so appealing, she figured she could easily develop a fetish for sequestering herself.

From the funeral home they went to the cemetery.

The graveyard had no headstones. The plots were marked by bronze plaques on marble bases set flush with the ground. The rolling green lawns, shaded by huge Indian laurels and smaller magnolias, might have been mistaken for a park, a place to play games and run and laugh – if not for the open grave over which Bob Shane's casket was suspended.

Last night she'd awakened twice to the sound of distant thunder, and though half asleep she had thought she'd seen lightning flickering at the windows, but if unseasonal storms had passed through during the darkness, there was no sign of them now. The day was blue, cloudless.

Laura stood between Cora and Anita, who touched her and murmured reassurances, but she was not comforted by anything they did or said. The bleak chill in her deepened with each word of the minister's final prayer, until she felt as if she were standing unclothed in an arctic winter instead of in the shade of a tree on a hot, windless July morning.

The funeral director activated the motorized sling on which the casket was suspended. Bob Shane's body was lowered into the earth.

Unable to watch the slow descent of the casket, having difficulty drawing breath, Laura turned away, slipped out from under the caring hands of her two honorary grandmothers, and took a few steps across the cemetery. She was as cold as marble; she needed to escape the shade. She stopped as soon as she reached sunlight, which felt warm on her skin but which failed to relieve her chills.

She stared down the long, gentle hill for perhaps a minute before she saw the man standing at the far end of the cemetery in shadows at the edge of a large grove of laurels. He was wearing light tan slacks and a white shirt that appeared faintly luminous in that gloom, as if he were a ghost who had forsaken his usual night haunts for daylight. He was watching her and the other mourners around Bob Shane's grave near the top of the slope. At that distance Laura could not see his face clearly, but she could discern that he was tall and strong and blond – and disturbingly familiar.

The observer intrigued her, though she did not know why. As if spellbound, she descended the hill, stepping between and across the graves. The nearer she drew to the blond, the more familiar he looked. At first he did not react to her approach, but she knew he was studying her intently; she could feel the weight of his gaze.

Cora and Anita called to her, but she ignored them. Seized by an inexplicable excitement, she walked faster, now only a hundred feet from the stranger.

The man retreated into the false twilight among the trees.

Afraid that he would slip away before she had gotten a good look at him – yet not certain why seeing him more clearly was so important – Laura ran. The soles of her new black shoes were slippery, and several times she nearly fell. At the place where he had been standing, the grass was tramped flat, so he was no ghost.

Laura saw a flicker of movement among the trees, the spectral white of his shirt. She hurried after him. Only sparse, pale grass grew under the laurels, beyond the reach of the sun. However, surface roots and treacherous shadows sprouted everywhere. She stumbled, grabbed the trunk of a tree to avoid a bad fall, regained her balance, looked up – and discovered that the man had vanished.

The grove was comprised of perhaps a hundred trees. The branches were densely interlaced, allowing sunlight through only in thin golden threads, as if the fabric of the sky had begun unraveling into the woods. She hurried forward, squinting at the darkness. Half a dozen times she thought she saw him, but it was always phantom movement, a trick of light or of her own mind. When a breeze sprang up, she was certain she heard his furtive footsteps in the masking rustle of the leaves, but when she pursued the crisp sound, its source eluded her.

After a couple of minutes she came out of the trees to a road that served another section of the sprawling cemetery. Cars were parked along the verge, sparkling in the brightness, and a hundred yards away was a group of mourners at another graveside service.

Laura stood at the edge of the lane, breathing hard, wondering where the man in the white shirt had gone and why she had been compelled to chase him.

The blazing sun, the cessation of the short-lived breeze, and the return of perfect silence to the cemetery made her uneasy. The sun seemed to pass through her as if she were transparent, and she was strangely light, almost weightless, and mildly dizzy too: She felt as if she were in a dream, floating an inch above an unreal landscape.

I'm going to pass out, she thought.

She put one hand against the front fender of a parked car and gritted her teeth, struggling to hold on to consciousness.

Though she was only twelve she did not often think or act like a child, and she never *felt* like a child – not until that moment in the cemetery when suddenly she felt very young, weak, and helpless.

A tan Ford came slowly along the road, slowing even further as it drew near her. Behind the wheel was the man in the white shirt.

The moment she saw him, she knew why he'd seemed familiar. Four years ago. The robbery. Her guardian angel. Although she had been just eight years old at the time, she would never forget his face.

He brought the Ford almost to a halt and drifted by her slowly, scrutinizing her as he passed. They were just a few feet apart.

Through the open window of his car, every detail of his handsome face was as clear as on that terrible day when she had first seen him in the store. His eyes were as brilliantly blue and riveting as she had remembered. When their gazes locked, she shuddered.

He said nothing, did not smile, but studied her intently, as if trying to fix every detail of her appearance in his mind. He stared at her the way a man might stare at a tall glass of cool water after crossing a desert. His silence and unwavering gaze frightened Laura but also filled her with an inexplicable sense of security.

The car was rolling past her. She shouted, 'Wait!'

She pushed away from the car against which she had been leaning, dashed toward the tan Ford. The stranger accelerated and sped out of the graveyard, leaving her alone in the sun until a moment later she heard a man speak behind her, 'Laura?'

When she turned she could not see him at first. He called her name again, softly, and she spotted him fifteen feet away at the edge of the trees, standing in the purple shadows under an Indian laurel. He wore black slacks, a black shirt, and seemed out of place in this summer day.

Curious, perplexed, wondering if somehow this man was connected with her guardian angel, Laura started forward. She closed to within two steps of the new stranger before she realized that the disharmony between him and the bright, warm summer day was not solely a result of his black clothing; wintry darkness was an integral part of the man himself; a coldness seemed to come from within him, as if he had been born to dwell in polar regions or in the high caves of ice-bound mountains.

She stopped less than five feet from him.

He said no more but stared at her intently, with a look that seemed as much puzzlement as anything.

She saw a scar on his left cheek.

'Why you?' the wintry man asked, and he took a step forward, reaching for her.

Laura stumbled backward, suddenly too scared to cry out.

From the middle of the copse of trees, Cora Lance called, 'Laura? Are you all right, Laura?'

The stranger reacted to the nearness of Cora's voice, turned, and moved away through the laurels, his black-clad body disappearing quickly in the shadows, as if he had not been a real man at all but a bit of darkness briefly come to life.

Five days after the funeral, on Tuesday the twenty-ninth of July, Laura was back in her own room above the grocery store for the first time in a week. She was packing and saying goodbye to the place that had been home to her for as long as she could recall.

Pausing to rest, she sat on the edge of the rumpled bed, trying to remember how secure and happy she had been in that room only days ago. A hundred paperback books, mostly dog and horse stories, were shelved in one corner. Fifty miniature dogs and cats – glass, brass, porcelain, pewter – filled the shelves above the headboard of her bed.

She had no pets, for the health code prohibited animals in an apartment above a grocery. Some day she hoped to have a dog, perhaps even a horse. But more importantly she might be a veterinarian when she grew up, a healer of sick and injured animals.

Her father had said she could be anything: a vet, a lawyer, a movie star, anything. 'You can be a moose herder if you want, or a ballerina on a pogo stick. Nothing can stop you.'

Laura smiled, remembering how her father had imitated a ballerina on a pogo stick. But she also remembered he was gone, and a dreadful emptiness opened in her.

She cleaned out the closet, carefully folded her clothes, and filled two large suitcases. She had a steamer trunk as well, into which she packed her favorite books, a few games, a teddy bear.

Cora and Tom Lance were taking an inventory of the contents of the rest of the small apartment and of the grocery store downstairs. Laura was going to stay with them, though she was not yet clear as to whether the arrangement was permanent or temporary.

Made nervous and fretful by thoughts of her uncertain future, Laura returned to her packing. She pulled open the drawer in the nearest of the two nightstands and froze at the sight of the elfin boots, tiny umbrella, and four-inch-long neck scarf that her father had acquired as proof that Sir Tommy Toad indeed rented quarters from them.

He had persuaded one of his friends, a skilled leatherworker, to make the boots, which were wide and shaped to accommodate webbed feet. He had obtained the umbrella from a shop that sold miniatures, and he had made the green-plaid scarf himself, laboriously fashioning fringe for the ends of it. On her ninth birthday, when she came home from school, the boots and umbrella were standing against the wall just inside the apartment door, and the scrap of scarf was hung carefully on the coatrack. 'Sssshh,' her father whispered dramatically. 'Sir Tommy has just returned from an arduous trip to Ecuador on the queen's business – she owns a diamond farm there, you know – and he's exhausted. I'm sure he'll sleep for *days*. However, he told me to wish you a very happy birthday, and he left a gift in the yard out back.' The gift had been a new Schwinn bicycle.

Now, staring at the three items in the nightstand drawer, Laura realized that her father had not died alone. With him had gone Sir Tommy Toad, the many other characters he had created, and the silly but wonderful fantasies with which he'd entertained her. The webbed-foot boots, the tiny umbrella, and the little scarf looked so sweet and pathetic; she could almost believe that Sir Tommy, in fact, had been real and that he was now gone to a better world of his own. A low, miserable groan escaped her. She fell onto the bed and buried her face in the pillows, muffling her agonized sobs, and for the first time since her father's death she finally let her grief overwhelm her.

She did not want to live without him, yet she must not only live but prosper because every day of her life would be a testament to him. Even as young as she was, she understood that by living well and being a good person, she would make it possible for her father to go on living in some small way through her.

But facing the future with optimism and finding happiness was going to be hard. She now knew that life was frighteningly subject to tragedy and change, blue and warm one moment, cold and stormy the next, so you never knew when a bolt of lightning might strike someone you cared about. Nothing lasts forever. Life is a candle in the wind. That was a hard lesson for a girl her age, and it made her feel old, very old, ancient.

When the flood of warm tears abated, she did not take long to collect herself, for she did not want the Lances to discover that she had been crying. If the world was hard and cruel and unpredictable, then it did not seem wise to show the slightest weakness.

She carefully wrapped the webbed-foot boots, umbrella, and little scarf in tissue paper. She tucked them away in the steamer trunk.

When she had disposed of the contents of both nightstands, she went to her desk to clean that out as well, and on the felt blotter she found a folded sheet of tablet paper with a message for her in clear, elegant, almost machine-neat handwriting.

Dear Laura,

Some things are meant to be, and no one can prevent them. Not even your special guardian. Be content with the knowledge that your father loved you with all his heart in a way that few people are ever lucky enough to be loved. Though you think now that you will never be happy again, you are wrong. In time happiness will come to you. This is not an empty promise. This is a fact.

The note was unsigned, but she knew who must have written it: the man who had been at the cemetery, who had studied her from the passing car, who years ago saved her and her father from being shot. No one else could call himself her special guardian. A tremor swept through her not because she was afraid but because the strangeness and the mystery of her guardian filled her with curiosity and wonder.

She hurried to the bedroom window and pushed aside the sheer curtain that hung between the drapes, certain that she would see him standing in the street, watching the store, but he was not there.

The man in dark clothing was not there, either, but she had not expected to see him. She had half convinced herself that the other stranger was unrelated to her guardian, that he had been in the cemetery for some other reason. He had known her name . . . but perhaps he had heard Cora calling her earlier, from the top of the graveyard hill. She was able to put him out of her mind because she did not *want* him to be part of her life, not as she so desperately wanted to have a special guardian.

She read the message again.

Although she did not understand who the blond man was or why he had taken an interest in her, Laura was reassured by the note he had left. Understanding wasn't always necessary, as long as you *believed*.

• 5 •

The following night, after he had planted explosives in the attic of the institute, Stefan returned with the same suitcase, claiming he had insomnia again. Anticipating the post-midnight visit, Viktor had brought half of one of his wife's cakes as a gift.

Stefan nibbled at the cake while he shaped and placed the plastic explosives. The enormous basement was divided into two rooms, and unlike the attic it was used daily by employees. He would have to conceal the charges and wires with considerable care.

The first chamber contained research files and a pair of long, oak worktables. The file cabinets were six feet tall and stood in banks along two of the walls. He was able to place the explosives atop the cabinets, tucking them toward the back, against the walls, where not even the tallest man on the staff could see them.

He strung the wires behind the cabinets, though he was forced to drill a small hole in the partition between halves of the cellar in order to continue the detonation line into the next chamber. He managed to put the hole in an inconspicuous place, and the wires were visible only for a couple of inches on either side of the partition.

The second room was used for storage of office and lab supplies and to cage the score of animals – several hamsters, a few white rats, two dogs, one energetic monkey in a big cage with three bars to swing on – that had participated in (and survived) the institute's early experiments. Though the animals were of no more use, they were kept in order to learn if over the long term they developed unforeseen medical problems that could be related to their singular adventures.

Stefan molded powerful charges of plastique into hollow spaces toward the back of the stacked supplies and brought all of the wires to the screened ventilation chase down which he had dropped the attic wires the previous night, and as he worked, he felt the animals watching with unusual intensity, as if they knew they had less than twenty-four hours to live. His cheeks flushed with guilt, which strangely he had failed to feel when contemplating the deaths of the men who worked in the institute, perhaps because the animals were innocent and the men were not.

By four o'clock in the morning, Stefan had finished both the job in the basement and the work he had to do in his office on the third floor. Before leaving the institute, he went to the main lab on the ground floor and for a minute stared at the gate.

The gate.

The scores of dials and gauges and graphs in the gate's support machinery all glowed softly orange, yellow, or green, for the power to it was never turned off. The thing was cylindrical, twelve feet long and eight feet in diameter, barely visible in the dim light; its stainless-steel outer skin gleamed with faint reflections of the spots of light in the machinery that lined three of the room's walls.

He had used the gate scores of times, but he was still in awe of it – not so much because it was an astonishing scientific breakthrough but because its potential for evil was unlimited. It was not a gate to hell, but in the hands of the wrong men, it might as well have been just that. And it was indeed in the hands of the wrong men.

After thanking Viktor for the cake and claiming to have eaten all that he had been given – though in fact he fed the larger part of it to the animals – Stefan drove back to his apartment.

For the second night in a row, a storm raged. Rain slashed out of the northwest. Water foamed out of downspouts into nearby drains, drizzled off roofs, puddled in the streets, and overflowed gutters, and because the city was almost entirely dark, the pools and streams looked more like oil than water. Only a few military personnel were out, and they all wore dark slickers that made them look as if they were creatures from an old Gothic novel by Bram Stoker.

Stefan took a direct route home, making no effort to skirt the known police inspection stations. His papers were in order; his exemption from curfew was current; and he was no longer transporting illegally obtained explosives.

In his apartment he set the alarm on the large bedside clock and fell almost immediately to sleep. He desperately needed his rest because, in the afternoon to come, there would be two arduous journeys and much killing. If he was not fully alert, he might find himself on the wrong end of a bullet.

His dreams were of Laura, which he interpreted as a good omen.

Two

The Enduring Flame

• 1 •

Laura Shane was swept from her twelfth through her seventeenth years as if she were a tumbleweed blown across the California deserts, coming to rest briefly here and there in becalmed moments, torn loose and sent rolling again as soon as the wind gusted.

She had no relatives, and she could not stay with her father's best friends, the Lances. Tom was sixty-two, and Cora was fifty-seven, and though married thirty-five years, they had no children. The prospect of raising a young girl daunted them.

Laura understood and bore no grudge against them. On the day in August when she left the Lance house in the company of a woman from the Orange County Child Welfare Agency, Laura kissed both Cora and Tom and assured them that she would be fine. Riding away in the social worker's car, she waved gaily, hoping they felt absolved.

Absolved. That word was a recent acquisition. Absolved: freed from the consequences of one's actions; to set free or release from some duty, obligation, or responsibility. She wished that she could grant herself absolution from the obligation to make her way in the world without the guidance of a loving father, absolution from the responsibility to live and carry on his memory.

From the Lances' house she was conveyed to a child shelter – the McIlroy Home – an old, rambling, twenty-seven-room Victorian mansion built by a produce magnate in the days of Orange County's agricultural glory. Later it had been converted to a dormitory where children in public custody were housed temporarily between foster homes.

That institution was unlike any she had read about in fiction. For one thing, it lacked kindly nuns in flowing black habits.

And there was Willy Sheener.

Laura first noticed him shortly after arriving at the home, while a social worker, Mrs. Bowmaine, was showing her to the room she would share with – she had been told – the Ackerson twins and a girl named Tammy. Sheener was sweeping a tile-floored hallway with a pushbroom.

He was strong, wiry, pale, freckled, about thirty, with hair the color of a new copper penny and green eyes. He smiled and whistled softly while he worked. 'How're you this morning, Mrs. Bowmaine?'

'Right as rain, Willy.' She clearly liked Sheener. 'This is Laura Shane, a new girl. Laura, this is Mr. Sheener.'

Sheener stared at Laura with a creepy intensity. When he managed to speak, the words were thick, 'Uhhh . . . welcome to McIlroy.'

Following the social worker, Laura glanced back at Sheener. With no one but

Laura to see, he lowered one hand to his crotch and lazily massaged himself.

Laura did not look at him again.

Later, as she was unpacking her meager belongings, trying to make her quarter of the third-floor bedroom more like home, she turned and saw Sheener in the doorway. She was alone, for the other kids were at play in the backyard or the game room. His smile was different from the one with which he'd favored Mrs. Bowmaine: predatory, cold. Light from one of the two small windows fell across the doorway and met his eyes at such an angle as to make them appear silver instead of green, like the cataract-filmed eyes of a dead man.

Laura tried to speak but could not. She edged backward until she came up against the wall beside her bed.

He stood with his arms at his sides, motionless, hands fisted.

The McIlroy Home was not air conditioned. The bedroom windows were open, but the place was tropically hot. Yet Laura had not been sweating until she turned and saw Sheener. Now her T-shirt was damp.

Outside, children at play shouted and laughed. They were nearby, but they sounded far away.

The hard, rhythmic rasp of Sheener's breathing seemed to grow louder, gradually drowning out the voices of the children.

For a long time neither of them moved or spoke. Then abruptly he turned and walked away.

Weak-kneed, sweat-soaked, Laura moved to her bed and sat on the edge of it. The mushy mattress sagged, and the springs creaked.

As her thudding heartbeat decelerated, she surveyed the gray-walled room and despaired of her circumstances. In the four corners were narrow, iron-framed beds with tattered chenille spreads and lumpy pillows. Each bed had a battered, Formica-topped nightstand, and on each was a metal reading lamp. The scarred dresser had eight drawers, two of which were hers. There were two closets, and she was allotted half of one. The ancient curtains were faded, stained; they hung limp and greasy from rust-spotted rods. The entire house was moldering and haunted; the air had a vaguely unpleasant odor; and Willy Sheener roamed the rooms and halls as if he were a malevolent spirit waiting for the full moon and the blood games attendant thereon.

———

That night after dinner the Ackerson twins closed the door to the room and encouraged Laura to join them on the threadbare maroon carpet where they could sit in a circle and share secrets.

Their other roomie – a strange, quiet, frail blonde named Tammy – had no interest in joining them. Propped up by pillows, she sat in bed and read a book, nibbling her nails continuously, mouselike.

Laura liked Thelma and Ruth Ackerson immediately. Having just turned twelve, they were only months younger than Laura and were wise for their age. They had been orphaned when they were nine and had lived at the shelter for almost three years. Finding adoptive parents for children their age was difficult, especially for twins who were determined not to be split up.

Not pretty girls, they were astonishingly identical in their plainness: lusterless brown hair, myopic brown eyes, broad faces, blunt chins, wide mouths. Although lacking in good looks, they were abundantly intelligent, energetic, and good-natured.

Ruth was wearing blue pajamas with dark green piping on the cuffs and collar, blue slippers; her hair was tied in a ponytail. Thelma wore raspberry-red pajamas and furry yellow slippers, each with two buttons painted to represent eyes, and her hair was unfettered.

With darkfall the insufferable heat of the day had passed. They were less than ten miles from the Pacific, so the night breezes made comfortable sleep possible. Now, with the windows open, currents of mild air stirred the aged curtains and circulated through the room.

'Summer's a bore here,' Ruth told Laura as they sat in a circle on the floor. 'We're not allowed off the property, and it's just not big enough. And in the summer all the do-gooders are busy with their own vacations, their own trips to the beach, so they forget about us.'

'Christmas is great, though,' Thelma said.

'All of November and December are great,' Ruth said.

'Yeah,' Thelma said. 'Holidays are fine because the do-gooders start feeling guilty about having so much when we poor, drab, homeless waifs have to wear newspaper coats, cardboard shoes, and eat last year's gruel. So they send us baskets of goodies, take us on shopping sprees and to the movies, though never the *good* movies.'

'Oh, I like some of them,' Ruth said.

'The kind of movies where no one ever, ever gets blown up. And *never* any feelies. They'll never take us to a movie in which some guy puts his hand on a girl's boob. Family films. Dull, dull, dull.'

'You'll have to forgive my sister,' Ruth told Laura. 'She thinks she's on the trembling edge of puberty—'

'I *am* on the trembling edge of puberty! I feel my sap rising!' Thelma said, thrusting one thin arm into the air above her head.

Ruth said, 'The lack of parental guidance has taken a toll on her, I'm afraid. She hasn't adapted well to being an orphan.'

'You'll have to forgive *my* sister,' Thelma said. 'She's decided to skip puberty and go directly from childhood to senility.'

Laura said, 'What about Willy Sheener?'

The Ackerson twins glanced knowingly at each other and spoke with such synchronization that not a fraction of a second was lost between their statements: 'Oh, a disturbed man,' Ruth said, and Thelma said, 'He's scum,' and Ruth said, 'He needs therapy,' and Thelma said, 'No, what he needs is a hit over the head with a baseball bat maybe a dozen times, maybe two dozen, then locked away for the rest of his life.'

Laura told them about encountering Sheener in her doorway.

'He didn't say anything?' Ruth asked. 'That's creepy. Usually he says "You're a very pretty little girl" or—'

'—he offers you candy.' Thelma grimaced. 'Can you *imagine?* Candy? How trite! It's as if he learned to be a scumbag by reading those booklets the police hand out to warn kids about perverts.'

'No candy,' Laura said, shivering as she remembered Sheener's sun-silvered eyes and heavy, rhythmic breathing.

Thelma leaned forward, lowering her voice to a stage whisper. 'Sounds like the White Eel was tongue-tied, too hot even to *think* of his usual lines. Maybe he has a special lech for you, Laura.'

'White Eel?'

'That's Sheener,' Ruth said. 'Or just the Eel for short.'

'Pale and slick as he is,' Thelma said, 'the name fits. I'll bet the Eel has a special lech for you. I mean, kid, you *are* a knockout.'

'Not me,' Laura said.

'Are you kidding?' Ruth said. 'That dark hair, those big eyes.'

Laura blushed and started to protest, and Thelma said, 'Listen, Shane, the Dazzling Ackerson Duo – Ruth and moi – cannot abide false modesty any more than we can tolerate bragging. We're straight-from-the-shoulder types. We know what *our* strengths are, and we're proud of them. God knows, neither of us will win the Miss America contest, but we're intelligent, very intelligent, and we're not reluctant to admit to brains. And *you* are gorgeous, so stop being coy.'

'My sister is sometimes too blunt and too colorful in the way she expresses herself,' Ruth said apologetically.

'And *my* sister,' Thelma told Laura, 'is trying out for the part of Melanie in *Gone With the Wind*.' She put on a thick Southern accent and spoke with exaggerated sympathy: 'Oh, Scarlett doesn't mean any harm. Scarlett's a lovely girl, really she is. Rhett is so lovely at heart, too, and even the Yankees are lovely, even those who sacked Tara, burned our crops, and made boots out of the skin of our babies.'

Laura began to giggle halfway through Thelma's performance.

'So drop the modest maiden act, Shane! You're gorgeous.'

'Okay, okay. I know I'm . . . pretty.'

'Kiddo, when the White Eel saw you, a fuse blew in his brain.'

'Yes,' Ruth agreed, 'you stunned him. That's why he couldn't even think to reach in his pocket for the candy he always carries.'

'Candy!' Thelma said. 'Little bags of M&Ms, Tootsie Rolls!'

'Laura, be real careful,' Ruth warned. 'He's a sick man—'

'He's a geek!' Thelma said. 'A sewer rat!'

From the far corner of the room, Tammy said softly, 'He's not as bad as you say.'

The blond girl was so quiet, so thin and colorless, so adept at fading into the background that Laura had forgotten her. Now she saw that Tammy had put her book aside and was sitting up in bed; she had drawn her bony knees against her chest and wrapped her arms around her legs. She was ten, two years younger than her roommates, small for her age. In a white nightgown and socks Tammy looked more like an apparition than like a real person.

'He wouldn't hurt anyone,' Tammy said hesitantly, tremulously, as though stating her opinion about Sheener – about anything, anyone – was like walking on a tightrope without a net.

'He *would* hurt someone if he could get away with it,' Ruth said.

'He's just . . .' Tammy bit her lip. 'He's . . . lonely.'

'No, honey,' Thelma said, 'he's not lonely. He's so much in love with himself that he'll never be lonely.'

Tammy looked away from them. She got up, slipped her feet into floppy slippers, and mumbled, 'Almost bedtime.' She took her toiletry kit from her nightstand and shuffled out of the room, closing the door behind her, heading for one of the baths at the end of the hall.

'She takes the candy,' Ruth explained.

An icy wave of revulsion washed through Laura. 'Oh, no.'

'Yes,' Thelma said. 'Not because she wants the candy. She's . . . messed up. She needs the kind of approval she gets from the Eel.'

'But why?' Laura asked.

Ruth and Thelma exchanged another of their looks, through which they seemed to debate an issue and reach a decision in a second or two, without words. Sighing, Ruth said, 'Well, see, Tammy needs that kind of approval because . . . her father taught her to need it.'

Laura was jolted. 'Her own *father?*'

'Not all the kids at McIlroy are orphans,' Thelma said. 'Some are here because their parents committed crimes and went to jail. And others were abused by their folks physically or . . . sexually.'

The freshening air coming through the open windows was probably only a degree or two colder than when they had sat down in a circle on the floor, but it seemed to Laura like a chilly late-autumn wind that had mysteriously leaped the months and infiltrated the August night.

Laura said, 'But Tammy doesn't really *like* it?'

'No, I don't think she does,' Ruth said. 'But she's—'

'—compelled,' Thelma said, 'can't help herself. Twisted.'

They were all silent, thinking the unthinkable, and finally Laura said, 'Strange and . . . so sad. Can't we stop it? Can't we tell Mrs. Bowmaine or one of the other social workers about Sheener?'

'It wouldn't do any good,' Thelma said. 'The Eel would deny it, and *Tammy* would deny it, too, and we don't have any proof.'

'But if she's not the only kid he's abused, one of the others—'

Ruth shook her head. 'Most have gone to foster homes, adoptive parents, or back to their own families. Those two or three still here . . . well, they're either like Tammy, or they're just scared to death of the Eel, too scared ever to rat on him.'

'Besides,' Thelma said, 'the adults don't want to know, don't want to deal with it. Bad publicity for the home. And it makes them look stupid to have this going on under their noses. Besides, who can believe children?' Thelma imitated Mrs. Bowmaine, catching the note of phoniness so perfectly that Laura recognized it at once: 'Oh, my dear, they're horrible, lying little creatures. Noisy, rambunctious, bothersome little beasts, capable of destroying Mr. Sheener's fine reputation for the fun of it. If only they could be drugged, hung on wall hooks, and fed intravenously, how much more efficient the system would be, my dear – and really so much better for them, too.'

'Then the Eel would be cleared,' Ruth said, 'and he'd come back to work, and he'd find ways to make us pay for speaking against him. It happened that way before with another perv who used to work here, a guy we called Ferret Fogel. Poor Denny Jenkins . . .'

'Denny ratted on Ferret Fogel; he told Bowmaine the Ferret molested him and two other boys. Fogel was suspended. But the two other boys wouldn't support Denny's story. They were afraid of the Ferret . . . but they also had this sick need for his approval. When Bowmaine and her staff interrogated Denny—'

'They hammered at him,' Ruth said angrily, 'with trick questions, trying to trip him up. He got confused, contradicted himself, so they said he was making it all up.'

'And Fogel came back to work,' Thelma said.

'He bided his time,' Ruth said, 'and then he found ways to make Denny miserable. He tormented the boy relentlessly until one day . . . Denny just started screaming and couldn't stop. The doctor had to give him a shot, and then they took him away. Emotionally disturbed, they said.' She was on the brink of tears. 'We never saw him again.'

Thelma put one hand on her sister's shoulder. To Laura, she said, 'Ruth was fond of Denny. He was a nice boy. Small, shy, sweet . . . he never had a chance. That's why you've got to be tough with the White Eel. You can't let him see that you're afraid of him. If he tries anything, scream. And kick him in the crotch.'

Tammy returned from the bathroom. She did not look at them but stepped out of her slippers and got under the covers.

Although Laura was repulsed by the thought of Tammy submitting to Sheener, she regarded the frail blonde with less disgust than sympathy. No sight could be more pitiful than that small, lonely defeated girl lying on her narrow, sagging bed.

That night Laura dreamed of Sheener. He had his own human head, but his body was that of a white eel, and wherever Laura ran, Sheener slithered after her, wriggling under closed doors and other obstacles.

• 2 •

Sickened by what he'd just seen, Stefan returned from the institute's main lab to his third-floor office. He sat at his desk with his head in his hands, shaking with horror and anger and fear.

That red-haired bastard, Willy Sheener, was going to rape Laura repeatedly, beat her half to death, and leave her so traumatized that she would never recover. That was not just a possibility; it would come to pass if Stefan did not move to prevent it. He had *seen* the aftermath: Laura's bruised face, broken mouth. Her eyes had been the worst of it, so flat looking and half-dead, the eyes of a child who no longer had the capacity for joy or hope.

Cold rain tapped on the office windows, and that hollow sound seemed to reverberate within him, as if the terrible things he had seen had left him burnt out, an empty shell.

He had saved Laura from the junkie in her father's grocery, but here was another pedophile already. One of the things he had learned from the experiments in the institute was that reshaping fate was not always easy. Destiny struggled to reassert the pattern that was meant to be. Perhaps being molested and psychologically destroyed was such an immutable part of Laura's fate that Stefan could not prevent it from happening sooner or later. Perhaps he could not save her from Willy Sheener, or perhaps if he thwarted Sheener, *another* rapist would enter the girl's life. But he had to try.

Those half-dead, joyless eyes . . .

Seventy-six children resided at the McIlroy Home, all twelve or younger; upon turning thirteen, they were transferred to Caswell Hall in Anaheim. Since the oak-paneled dining hall would hold only forty, meals were served in two shifts. Laura was on the second shift, as were the Ackerson twins.

Standing in the cafeteria line between Thelma and Ruth on her first morning at the shelter, Laura saw that Willy Sheener was one of the four attendants serving from behind the counter. He monitored the milk supply and dispensed sweet rolls with a pair of tongs.

As Laura moved along the line, the Eel spent more time looking at her than at the kids he was serving.

'Don't let him intimidate you,' Thelma whispered.

Laura tried to meet Sheener's gaze – and his challenge – boldly. But she was the one who always broke the staring match.

When she reached his station, he said, 'Good mornng, Laura,' and put a sweet roll on her tray, a particular pastry he had saved for her. It was twice as large as the others, with more cherries and icing.

On Thursday, Laura's third full day at the shelter, she endured a how-are-we-adjusting meeting with Mrs. Bowmaine in the social worker's first-floor office. Etta Bowmaine was stout, with an unflattering wardrobe of flower-print dresses. She spoke in cliches and platitudes with that gushy insincerity that Thelma had imitated perfectly, and she asked a lot of questions to which she actually did not want honest answers. Laura lied about how happy she was at McIlroy, and the lies pleased Mrs. Bowmaine enormously.

Returning to her room on the third floor, Laura encountered the Eel on the north stairs. She turned at the second landing, and he was on the next flight, wiping the oak handrail with a rag. An unopened bottle of furniture polish stood on the step below him.

She froze, and her heart began to pound double time, for she knew he had been lying in wait for her. He'd have known about her summons to Mrs. Bowmaine's office and would have counted on her using the nearest stairs to return to her room.

They were alone. At any time another child or staff member might come along, but for the moment they were alone.

Her first impulse was to retreat and use the south stairs, but she remembered what Thelma had said about standing up to the Eel and about how his type preyed only on weaklings. She told herself that the best thing to do was walk past him without saying a word, but her feet seemed to have been nailed to the step; she could not move.

Looking down at her from half a flight up, the Eel smiled. It was a horrible smile: His skin was white, and his lips were colorless, but his crooked teeth were as yellow and mottled with brownish spots as the skin of a ripe banana. Under his unruly copper-red hair, his face resembled a clown's countenance – not the kind of clown you'd see in a circus but the kind you might run into on Halloween night, the kind that might carry a chainsaw instead of a seltzer bottle.

'You're a very pretty little girl, Laura.'

She tried to tell him to go to hell. She couldn't speak.

'I'd like to be your friend,' he said.

Somehow she found the strength to start up the steps toward him.

He smiled even more broadly, perhaps because he thought she was responding to his offer of friendship. He reached into a pocket of his khaki pants and withdrew a couple of Tootsie Rolls.

Laura recalled Thelma's comical assessment of the Eel's stupidly unimaginative gambits, and suddenly he did not look as scary to her as he had before. Offering Tootsie Rolls, leering at her, Sheener was a ridiculous figure, a caricature of evil, and she would have laughed at him if she had not known what he had done to Tammy and other girls. Though she could not quite laugh, the Eel's ludicrous appearance and manner gave her the courage to move swiftly around him.

When he realized she was not going to take the candy or respond to his offer of friendship, he put a hand on her shoulder to stop her.

She angrily took hold of his hand and threw it off. 'Don't you ever touch me, you geek.'

She hurried up the stairs, struggling against a desire to run. If she ran he would know that her fear of him had not been entirely banished. He must see absolutely no weakness in her, for weakness would encourage him to continue harassing her.

By the time she was only two steps from the next landing, she allowed herself to hope that she had won, that her toughness had impressed him. Then she heard the unmistakable sound of a zipper. Behind her, in a loud whisper he said, 'Hey, Laura, look at this. Look at what I have for you.' There was a demented, hateful tone in his voice. 'Look, look at what's in my hand now, Laura.'

She did not glance back.

She reached the landing and started up the next flight, thinking: There's no reason to run; you don't *dare* run, don't run, don't run.

From one flight below, the Eel said, 'Look at the big Tootsie Roll I have in my hand now, Laura. It's lots bigger than those others.'

On the third floor Laura hurried directly to the bathroom where she vigorously scrubbed her hands. She felt filthy after taking hold of Sheener's hand in order to remove it from her shoulder.

Later, when she and the Ackerson twins convened their nightly powwow on the floor of their room, Thelma howled with laughter when she heard about the Eel wanting Laura to look at his 'big Tootsie Roll.' She said, 'He's priceless, isn't he? Where do you think he gets these lines of his? Does Doubleday publish the *Perverts' Book of Classic Come-ons* or something?'

'The point is,' Ruth said worriedly, 'he wasn't turned off when Laura stood up to him. I don't think he's going to give up on her as quickly as he gives up on other girls who resist him.'

That night Laura had difficulty sleeping. She thought about her special guardian, and she wondered if he would appear as miraculously as before and if he would deal with Willy Sheener. Somehow she didn't think she could count on him this time.

During the following ten days, as August waned, the Eel shadowed Laura as reliably as the moon shadowed the earth. When she and the Ackerson twins went to the game room to play cards or Monopoly, Sheener arrived within ten minutes and set to work ostensibly washing windows or polishing furniture or repairing a drapery rod, though in fact his attention was primarily focused on Laura. If the girls sought refuge in a corner of the playground behind the mansion, either to talk or play a game of their own devising, Sheener entered the yard shortly thereafter, having suddenly found shrubbery that had to be pruned or fertilized. And although the third floor was for girls only, it was open to male staff members for the purpose of maintenance between ten in the morning and four in the afternoon on weekdays, so Laura could not escape to her room during those hours with any degree of safety.

Worse than the Eel's diligence was the frightening rate at which his dark passion for her grew, a sick need revealed by the steadily increasing intensity of his gaze and the sour sweat that burst from him when he was in the same room with her for more than a few minutes.

Laura, Ruth, and Thelma tried to convince themselves that the threat from the Eel lessened with every day he did not act, that his hesitation revealed his awareness of Laura as unsuitable prey. At heart they knew they were hoping to slay the dragon with a wish, but they were unable to face the full extent of the danger till a Saturday afternoon late in August, when they returned to their room and found Tammy destroying Laura's book collection in a fit of twisted jealousy.

The library of fifty paperbacks – her favorite books, which she had brought with her from the apartment above the grocery – were kept under Laura's bed. Tammy had brought them out into the middle of the room and in a hateful frenzy had ripped apart two-thirds of them.

Laura was too shocked to act, but Ruth and Thelma pulled the girl away from the books and restrained her.

Because those were her favorite books, because her father bought them for her and they were therefore a link to him, but most of all because she owned so little, Laura was pained by the destruction. Her possessions were so meager, of no value, but she suddenly realized that they formed ramparts against the worst cruelties of life.

Tammy lost interest in the books now that the true object of her rage stood before her. 'I hate you, I hate you!' Her pale, drawn face was alive for the first time since Laura had known her, flushed and contorted with emotion. The bruiselike circles around her eyes hadn't vanished, but they no longer made her appear weak or broken; instead she looked wild, savage. 'I hate you, Laura, I hate you!'

'Tammy, honey,' Thelma said, struggling to hold on to the girl, 'Laura's never done anything to you.'

Breathing hard but no longer thrashing to break free of Ruth and Thelma, Tammy shrieked at Laura: 'You're all he talks about, he isn't interested in me any more, just you, he can't stop talking about you, I hate you, why did you have to come here, I hate you!'

No one had to ask her to whom she was referring. The Eel.

'He doesn't want me any more, nobody wants me now, he only wants me so I can help him get to you. Laura, Laura, Laura. He wants me to trick you into a place where he can get you alone, where it'll be safe for him, but I won't do it, I won't! 'Cause then what would I have once he's got you? Nothing.' Her face was a furious red. Worse than her rage was the awful desperation that lay behind it.

Laura ran out of the room, down the long hall into the lavatory. Sick with disgust and fear, she fell to her knees on the cracked yellow tiles before one of the toilets and threw up. Once her stomach was purged she went to one of the sinks, rinsed her mouth repeatedly, then splashed cold water on her face. When she raised her head and looked in the mirror, the tears came at last.

It was not her own loneliness or fear that brought her to tears. She was crying for Tammy. The world was an unthinkably mean place if it would allow a ten-year-old girl's life to be devalued to such an extent that the only words of approval she ever heard from an adult were those spoken by the demented man who abused her, that the only possession in which she could take pride was the under-developed sexual aspect of her own thin, prepubescent body.

Laura realized that Tammy's situation was infinitely worse than her own. Even stripped of her books, Laura had good memories of a loving, kind, gentle father, which Tammy did not. If what few things she owned were taken from her, Laura would still be whole of mind, but Tammy was psychologically damaged, perhaps beyond repair.

• 4 •

Sheener lived in a bungalow on a quiet street in Santa Ana. It was one of those neighborhoods built after World War II: small, neat houses with interesting architectural details. In this autumn of 1967, the various types of ficus trees had reached maturity, spreading their limbs protectively over the homes; Sheener's place was further cloaked by overgrown shrubbery – azaleas, eugenias, and red-flowering hibiscus.

Near midnight, using a plastic loid, Stefan popped the lock on the back door and let himself into the house. As he inspected the bungalow, he boldly turned on the lights and did not bother to draw the drapes at the windows.

The kitchen was immaculate. The blue Formica counters glistened. The chrome handles on the appliances, the faucet in the sink, and the metal frames of the kitchen chairs all gleamed, unmarred by a single fingerprint.

He opened the refrigerator, not sure what he expected to find there. Perhaps an indication of Willy Sheener's abnormal psychology; a former victim of his molestations, murdered and frozen to preserve the memories of twisted passion? Nothing that dramatic. However, the man's fetish for neatness was obvious: All the food was stored in matching Tupperware containers.

Otherwise, the only thing odd about the contents of both the refrigerator and cupboards was the preponderance of sweets: ice cream, cookies, cakes, candies, pies, doughnuts, even animal crackers. There were a great many novelty foods, too, like Spaghetti-Os and cans of vegetable soup in which the noodles were shaped like popular cartoon characters. Sheener's larder looked as if it had been stocked by a child with a checkbook but no adult supervision.

Stefan moved deeper into the house.

The confrontation over the shredded books was sufficient to drain what little spirit Tammy possessed. She said no more about Sheener and seemed no longer to harbor any animosity toward Laura. Retreating further into herself day by day, she averted her eyes from everyone, hung her head lower; her voice grew softer.

Laura wasn't sure which was less tolerable – the constant threat posed by the White Eel or watching Tammy's already wispy personality fading further as she slid toward a state hardly more active than catatonia. But on Thursday, August 31, those two burdens were lifted unexpectedly from Laura's shoulders when she learned that she would be transferred to a foster home in Costa Mesa the following day, Friday.

However, she regretted leaving the Ackersons. Though she'd known them only a few weeks, friendships forged in extremity solidified faster and felt more enduring than those made in more ordinary times.

That night, as the three of them sat on the floor of their room, Thelma said, 'Shane, if you wind up with a good family, a happy home, just settle down snug and *enjoy*. If you're in a good place, forget us, make new friends, get on with your life. *But* the legendary Ackerson sisters – Ruth and moi – have been through the foster-family mill, three bad ones, so let me assure you that if you wind up in a *rotten* place, you don't have to stay there.'

Ruth said, 'Just weep a lot and let everyone know how unhappy you are. If you can't weep, pretend to.'

'Sulk,' Thelma advised. 'Be clumsy. Accidentally break a dish each time you've got to wash them. Make a nuisance of yourself.'

Laura was surprised. 'You did all that to get back into McIlroy?'

'That and more,' Ruth said.

'But didn't you feel terrible – breaking their things?

'It was harder for Ruth than me,' Thelma said. 'I've got the devil in me, while Ruth is the reincarnation of an obscure, treacly, fourteenth-century nun whose name we've not yet ascertained.'

———

Within one day Laura knew she did not want to remain in the care of the Teagel family, but she tried to make it work because at first she thought their company was preferable to returning to McIlroy.

Real life was just a misty backdrop to Flora Teagel, for whom only crossword puzzles were of interest. She spent days and evenings at the table in her yellow kitchen, wrapped in a cardigan regardless of the weather, working through books of crossword puzzles one after another with a dedication both astonishing and idiotic.

She usually spoke to Laura only to give her lists of chores and to seek help with knotty crossword clues. As Laura stood at the sink, washing dishes, Flora might say, 'What's a seven-letter word for cat?'

Laura's answer was always the same: 'I don't know.'

' "I don't know, I don't know, I don't know," ' Mrs. Teagel mocked. 'You don't seem to know anything, girl. Aren't you paying attention in school? Don't you care about language, about words?'

Laura, of course, was *fascinated* with words. To her, words were things of beauty, each like a magical powder or potion that could be combined with other words to create powerful spells. But to Flora Teagel, words were game chips needed to fill blank puzzle squares, annoyingly elusive clusters of letters that frustrated her.

Flora's husband, Mike, was a squat, baby-faced truck driver. He spent evenings in an armchair, poring over the *National Enquirer* and its clones, absorbing useless facts from dubious stories about alien contact and devil-worshipping movie stars. His taste for what he called 'exotic news' would have been harmless if he'd been as self-absorbed as his wife, but he often popped in on Laura when she was doing chores or in those rare moments when she was given time for homework, and he insisted on reading aloud the more bizarre articles.

She thought these stories were stupid, illogical, pointless, but she could not tell him so. She had learned that he would not be offended if she said his newspapers were rubbish. Instead he'd regard her pityingly; then with maddening patience, with an infuriating know-it-all manner found only in the overeducated and totally ignorant, he would proceed to explain how the world worked. At length. Repeatedly. 'Laura, you've got a lot to learn. The big shots who run things in Washington, *they* know about the aliens and the secrets of Atlantis . . .'

As different as Flora was from Mike, they shared one belief: that the purpose of sheltering a foster child was to obtain a free servant. Laura was expected to clean, do laundry, iron clothes, and cook.

Their own daughter – Hazel, an only child – was two years older than Laura and thoroughly spoiled. Hazel never cooked, washed dishes, did laundry, or cleaned house. Though she was just fourteen, she had perfectly manicured, painted fingernails and toenails. If you had deducted from her age the number of hours she had spent primping in front of a mirror, she would have been only five years old.

'On laundry day,' she explained on Laura's first day in the Teagel house, 'you must press *my* clothes first. And always be sure that you hang them in my closet arranged according to color.'

I've read this book and seen this movie, Laura thought. Gad, I've got the lead in *Cinderella!*

'I'm going to be a major movie star or a model,' Hazel said. 'So my face, hands, and body are my future. I've got to protect them.'

When Mrs. Ince – the wire-thin, whippet-faced child-welfare worker assigned to the case – paid a scheduled visit to the Teagel house on Saturday morning, September 16, Laura intended to demand to be returned to McIlroy Home. The threat posed by Willy Sheener had come to seem less of a problem than everyday life with the Teagels.

Mrs. Ince arrived on schedule to find Flora washing the first dishes she had washed in two weeks. Laura was sitting at the kitchen table, apparently working a crossword puzzle that in fact had been shoved into her hands only when the doorbell had rung.

In that portion of the visit devoted to a private interview with Laura in her bedroom, Mrs. Ince refused to believe what she was told about Laura's load of housework. 'But dear, Mr. and Mrs. Teagel are exemplary foster parents. You don't look to me as if you've been worked to the bone. You've even gained a few pounds.'

'I didn't accuse them of starving me,' Laura said. 'But I never have time for schoolwork. I go to bed every night exhausted—'

'Besides,' Mrs. Ince interrupted, 'foster parents are expected not merely to house children but to *raise* them, which means teaching manners and deportment, instilling good values and good work habits.'

Mrs. Ince was hopeless.

Laura resorted to the Ackersons' plan for shedding an unwanted foster family. She began to clean haphazardly. When she was done with the dishes, they were spotted and streaked. She ironed wrinkles *into* Hazel's clothes.

Because the destruction of most of her book collection had taught her a profound respect for property, Laura could not break dishes or anything else that belonged to the Teagels, but for that part of the Ackerson Plan she substituted scorn and disrespect. Working a puzzle, Flora asked for a six-letter word meaning 'a species of ox,' and Laura said, 'Teagel.' When Mike began to recount a flying-saucer story he had read in the *Enquirer*, she interrupted to spin a tale about mutated mole men living secretly in the local supermarket. To Hazel, Laura suggested that her big break in show business might best be achieved by applying to serve as Ernest Borgnine's stand-in: 'You're a dead-ringer for him, Hazel. They've *got* to hire you!'

Her scorn led swiftly to a spanking. With his big, calloused hands Mike had no need of a paddle. He thumped her across the bottom, but she bit her lip and refused to give him the satisfaction of her tears. Watching from the kitchen doorway, Flora said, 'Mike, that's enough. Don't mark her.' He quit reluctantly only when his wife entered the room and stayed his hand.

That night Laura had difficulty sleeping. For the first time she had employed her love of words, the power of language, to achieve a desired effect, and the Teagels' reactions were proof that she could use words well. Even more exciting was the half-formed thought, still too new to be fully understood, that she might possess the ability not only to defend herself with words but to earn her way in the world with them, perhaps even as an author of the kind of books she so much enjoyed. With her father she'd talked of being a doctor, ballerina, veterinarian, but that had been just talk. None of those dreams had filled her with as much excitement as the prospect of being a writer.

The next morning, when she went down to the kitchen and found the three Teagels at breakfast, she said, 'Hey, Mike, I've just discovered there's an intelligent squid from Mars living in the toilet tank.'

'What *is* this?' Mike demanded.

Laura smiled and said, 'Exotic news.'

Two days later Laura was returned to McIlroy Home.

• 6 •

Willy Sheener's living room and den were furnished as if an ordinary man lived there. Stefan was not sure what he had expected. Evidence of dementia, perhaps, but not this neat, orderly home.

One of the bedrooms was empty, and the other was decidedly odd. The only bed was a narrow mattress on the floor. The pillowcases and sheets were for a child's room, emblazoned with the colorful, antic figures of cartoon rabbits.

The nightstand and dresser were scaled to a child's dimensions, pale blue, with stenciled animals on the sides and drawers: giraffes, rabbits, squirrels. Sheener owned a collection of Little Golden Books, as well, and other children's picture books, stuffed animals, and toys suitable for a six- or seven-year-old.

At first Stefan thought that the room was designed for the seduction of neighborhood children, that Sheener was unstable enough to seek out prey even on his home ground, where the risk was greatest. But there was no other bed in the house, and the closet and dresser drawers were filled with a man's clothing. On the walls were a dozen framed photos of the same red-headed boy, some as an infant, some when he was seven or eight, and the face was identifiably that of a younger Sheener. Gradually Stefan realized the decor was for Willy Sheener's benefit alone. The creep slept here. At bedtime Sheener evidently retreated into a fantasy of childhood, no doubt finding a desperately needed peace in his eerie, nightly regression.

Standing in the middle of that strange room, Stefan felt both saddened and repelled. It seemed that Sheener molested children not solely or even primarily for the sexual thrill of it but to absorb their youth, to become young again like them; through perversion he seemed to be trying to descend not into moral squalor so much as into a lost innocence. He was equally pathetic and despicable, inadequate to the challenges of adult life but nonetheless dangerous for his inadequacies.

Stefan shivered.

• 7 •

Her bed in the Ackerson twins' room was now occupied by another kid. Laura was assigned to a small, two-bed room at the north end of the third floor near the stairs. Her bunkmate was nine-year-old Eloise Fischer, who had pig-tails, freckles, and a demeanor too serious for a child. 'I'm going to be an accountant when I grow up,' she told Laura. 'I like numbers a lot. You can add up a column of numbers and get the same answer every time. There're no surprises with numbers; they're not at all like people.' Eloise's parents had been convicted of drug dealing and sent to prison, and she was in McIlroy while the court decided which relative would be given custody of her.

As soon as Laura had unpacked, she hurried to the Ackersons' room. Bursting in on them, she cried, 'I is free, I is free!'

Tammy and the new girl looked at her blankly, but Ruth and Thelma ran to her and hugged her, and it was like coming home to real family.

'Your foster family didn't like you?' Ruth asked.

Thelma said, 'Ah ha! You used the Ackerson Plan.'

'No, I killed them all while they slept.'

'That'll work,' Thelma agreed.

The new girl, Rebecca Bogner, was about eleven. She and the Ackersons obviously were not sympatico. Listening to Laura and the twins, Rebecca kept saying 'you're weird' and 'too weird' and 'jeez, what weirdos,' with such an air of superiority and disdain that she poisoned the atmosphere as effectively as a nuclear detonation.

Laura and the twins went outside to a corner of the playground where they could share five weeks of news without Rebecca's snotty commentary. It was early October, and the days were still warm, though at a quarter till five the air was cooling. They wore jackets and sat on the lower branches of the jungle gym, which was abandoned now that the younger children were washing up for the early dinner.

They had not been in the yard five minutes before Willy Sheener arrived with an electric shrub trimmer. He set to work on a eugenia hedge about thirty feet from them, but his attention was on Laura.

At dinner the Eel was at his serving station on the cafeteria line, passing out cartons of milk and pieces of cherry pie. He had saved the largest slice for Laura.

On Monday she entered a new school where the other kids already had had four weeks to make friends. Ruth and Thelma were in a couple of her classes, which made it easier to adjust, but she was reminded that the primary condition of an orphan's life was instability.

Tuesday afternoon, when Laura returned from school, Mrs. Bowmaine stopped her in the hall. 'Laura, may I see you in my office?'

Mrs. Bowmaine was wearing a purple floral-pattern dress that clashed with the rose and peach floral patterns of her office drapes and wallpaper. Laura sat in a rose-patterned chair. Mrs. Bowmaine stood at her desk, intending to deal with Laura quickly and move on to other tasks. Mrs. Bowmaine was a bustler, a busy-busy type.

'Eloise Fischer left our charge today,' Mrs. Bowmaine said.

'Who got custody?' Laura asked. 'She liked her grandmother.'

'It was her grandmother,' Mrs. Bowmaine confirmed.

Good for Eloise. Laura hoped the pigtailed, freckled, future accountant would find something to trust besides cold numbers.

'Now you've no roommate,' Mrs. Bowmaine said briskly, 'and we've no vacant bed elsewhere, so you can't just move in with—'

'May I make a suggestion?'

Mrs. Bowmaine frowned with impatience and consulted her watch.

Laura said quickly, 'Ruth and Thelma are my best friends, and their roomies are Tammy Hinsen and Rebecca Bogner. But I don't think Tammy and Rebecca get along well with Ruth and Thelma, so—'

'We want you children to learn how to live with people different from you. Bunking with girls you already like won't build character. Anyway, the point is, I can't make new arrangements until tomorrow; I'm busy today. So I want to know if I can trust you to spend the night alone in your current room.'

'Trust me?' Laura asked in confusion.

'Tell me the truth, young lady. Can I trust you alone tonight?'

Laura could not figure what trouble the social worker anticipated from a child left alone for one night. Perhaps she expected Laura to barricade herself in the room so effectively that police would have to blast the door, disable her with tear gas, and drag her out in chains.

Laura was as insulted as she was confused. 'Sure, I'll be okay. I'm not a baby. I'll be fine.'

'Well . . . all right. You'll sleep by yourself tonight, but we'll make other arrangements tomorrow.'

After leaving Mrs. Bowmaine's colorful office for the drab hallways, climbing the stairs to the third floor, Laura suddenly thought: *the White Eel!* Sheener would know she was going to be alone tonight. He knew everything that went on at McIlroy, and he had keys, so he could return in the night. Her room was next to the north stairs, so he could slip out of the stairwell into her room, overpower her in seconds. He'd club her or drug her, stuff her in a burlap sack, take her away, lock her in a cellar, and no one would know what had happened to her.

She turned at the second-floor landing, descended the stairs two at a time, and rushed back toward Mrs. Bowmaine's office, but when she turned the corner into the front hall, she nearly collided with the Eel. He had a mop and a wringer-equipped bucket on wheels, which was filled with water reeking of pine-scented cleanser.

He grinned at her. Maybe it was only her imagination, but she was certain that he already knew she would be alone that night.

She should have stepped by him, gone to Mrs. Bowmaine, and begged a change in the night's sleeping arrangements. She could not make accusations about Sheener, or she would wind up like Denny Jenkins – disbelieved by the staff, tormented relentlessly by her nemesis – but she could have found an acceptable excuse for her change of mind.

She also considered rushing at him, shoving him into his bucket, knocking him on his butt, and telling him that she was tougher than him, that he had better not mess with her. But he was different from the Teagels. Mike, Flora, and Hazel were small-minded, obnoxious, ignorant, but comparatively sane. The Eel was insane, and there was no way of knowing how he would react to being knocked flat.

As she hesitated, his crooked, yellow grin widened.

A flush touched his pale cheeks, and Laura realized it might be a flush of desire, which made her nauseous.

She walked away, dared not run until she had climbed the stairs and was out of his sight. Then she sprinted for the Ackersons' room.

'You'll sleep here tonight,' Ruth said.

'Of course,' Thelma said, 'you'll have to stay in your room until they finish the bed check, then sneak down here.'

From her corner where she was sitting in bed doing math homework, Rebecca Bogner said, 'We've only got four beds.'

'I'll sleep on the floor,' Laura said.

'This is against the rules,' Rebecca said.

Thelma made a fist and glowered at her.

'Okay, all right,' Rebecca agreed. 'I never said *I* didn't want her to stay. I just pointed out that it's against the rules.'

Laura expected Tammy to object, but the girl lay on her back in bed, atop the covers, staring at the ceiling, apparently lost in her own thoughts and uninterested in their plans.

In the oak-paneled dining room, over an inedible dinner of pork chops, gluey mashed potatoes, and leathery green beans – and under the watchful eyes of the Eel – Thelma said, 'As for why Bowmaine wanted to know if she could trust you alone . . . she's afraid you'll try suicide.'

Laura was incredulous.

'Kids have done it here,' Ruth said sadly. 'Which is why they stuff at least two of us into even very small rooms. Being alone too much . . . that's one of the things that seems to trigger the impulse.'

Thelma said, 'They won't let Ruth and me share one of the small rooms because, since we're identical twins, they think we're really like *one* person. They think they'd no sooner close the door on us than we'd hang ourselves.'

'That's ridiculous,' Laura said.

'Of course it's ridiculous,' Thelma agreed. 'Hanging isn't flamboyant enough. The amazing Ackerson sisters – Ruth and moi – have a flair for the dramatic. We'd commit hara-kiri with stolen kitchen knives, or if we could get hold of a chainsaw . . .'

Throughout the room conversations were conducted in moderate voices, for adult monitors patrolled the dining hall. The third-floor Resident Advisor, Miss Keist, passed behind the table where Laura sat with the Ackersons, and Thelma whispered, 'Gestapo.'

When Miss Keist had passed, Ruth said, 'Mrs. Bowmaine means well, but she just isn't good at what she does. If she took time to learn what kind of person you are, Laura, she'd never worry about you committing suicide. You're a survivor.'

As she pushed her inedible food around her plate, Thelma said, 'Tammy Hinsen was once caught in the bathroom with a packet of razor blades, trying to get up the nerve to slash her wrists.'

Laura was suddenly impressed by the mix of humor and tragedy, absurdity and bleak realism, that formed the peculiar pattern of their lives at McIlroy. One moment they were bantering amusingly with one another; a moment later they were discussing the suicidal tendencies of girls they knew. She realized that such an insight was beyond her years, and as soon as she returned to her room, she would write it down in the notebook of observations she had recently begun to keep.

Ruth had managed to choke down the food on her plate. She said, 'A month after the razor-blade incident, they held a surprise search of our rooms, looking for dangerous objects. They found Tammy had a can of lighter fluid and matches. She'd intended to go into the showers, cover herself with lighter fluid, and set herself on fire.'

'Oh, God.' Laura thought of the thin, blond girl with the ashen complexion and the sooty rings around her eyes, and it seemed that her plan to immolate herself was only a desire to speed up the slow fire that for a long time had been consuming her from within.

'They sent her away two months for intense therapy,' Ruth said.

'When she came back,' Thelma said, 'the adults talked about how much better she was, but she seemed the same to Ruth and me.'

Ten minutes after Miss Keist's nightly room check, Laura left her bed. The deserted, third-floor hall was lit only by three safety lamps. Dressed in pajamas, carrying a pillow and blanket, she hurried barefoot to the Ackersons' room.

Only Ruth's bedside lamp was aglow. She whispered, 'Laura, you sleep on my bed. I've made a place for myself on the floor.'

'Well, unmake it and get back in your bed,' Laura said.

She folded her blanket several times to make a pad on the floor, near the foot of Ruth's bed, and she lay on it with her pillow.

From her own bed Rebecca Bogner said, 'We're all going to get in trouble over this.'

'What're you afraid they'll do to us?' Thelma asked. 'Stake us in the backyard, smear us with honey, and leave us for the ants?'

Tammy was sleeping or pretending to sleep.

Ruth turned out her light, and they settled down in darkness.

The door flew open, and the overhead light snapped on. Dressed in a red robe, scowling fiercely, Miss Keist entered the room. 'So! Laura, what're you doing here?'

Rebecca Bogner groaned. 'I *told* you we'd get in trouble.'

'Come back to your room right this minute, young lady.'

The swiftness with which Miss Keist appeared was suspicious, and Laura looked at Tammy Hinsen. The blonde was no longer feigning sleep. She was leaning on one elbow, smiling thinly. Evidently she had decided to assist the Eel in his quest for Laura, perhaps with the hope of regaining her status as his favorite.

Miss Keist escorted Laura to her room. Laura got into bed, and Miss Keist stared at her for a moment. 'It's warm. I'll open the window.' Returning to the bed, she studied Laura thoughtfully. 'Is there anything you want to tell me? Is anything wrong?'

Laura considered telling her about the Eel. But what if Miss Keist waited to catch the Eel as he crept into her room, and what if he didn't show? Laura would never be able to accuse the Eel again because she'd have a *history* of accusing him; no one would take her seriously. Then even if Sheener raped her, he'd get away with it.

'No, nothing's wrong,' she said.

Miss Keist said, 'Thelma's too sure of herself for a girl her age, full of false sophistication. If you're foolish enough to break the rules again just to have an all-night gabfest, develop some friends worth taking the risk for.'

'Yes, ma'am,' Laura said just to get rid of her, sorry that she had even considered responding to the woman's moment of concern.

After Miss Keist left, Laura did not get out of bed and flee. She lay in darkness, certain there would be another bed check in half an hour. Surely the Eel would not slither around until midnight, and it was only ten, so between Miss Keist's next visit and the Eel's arrival, she'd have plenty of time to get to a safe place.

Far, far away in the night, thunder grumbled. She sat up in bed. Her guardian! She threw back the covers and ran to the window. She saw no lightning. The distant rumble faded. Perhaps it had not been thunder after all. She waited ten minutes or more, but nothing else happened. Disappointed, she returned to bed.

Shortly after ten-thirty the doorknob creaked. Laura closed her eyes, let her mouth fall open, and feigned sleep.

Someone stepped quietly across the room, stood beside the bed.

Laura breathed slowly, evenly, deeply, but her heart was racing.

It was Sheener. She *knew* it was him. Oh, God, she had forgotten he was insane, that he was unpredictable, and now he was here earlier than she'd expected, and he was preparing the hypodermic. He'd jam her into a burlap sack and carry her away as if he was a brain-damaged Santa Claus come to steal children rather than leave gifts.

The clock ticked. The cool breeze rustled the curtains.

At last the person beside the bed retreated. The door closed.

It had been Miss Keist, after all.

Trembling violently, Laura got out of bed and pulled on her robe. She folded the blanket over her arm and left the room without slippers because she would make less noise if she was barefoot.

She could not return to the Ackersons' room. Instead she went to the north stairs, cautiously opened the door, and stepped onto the dimly lit landing. She listened for the sound of the Eel's footsteps below. She descended warily, expecting to encounter Sheener, but she reached the ground floor safely.

Shivering as the cool tile floor imparted its chill to her bare feet, she took refuge in the game room. She didn't turn on the lights but relied on the ghostly glow of the streetlamps that penetrated the windows and silvered the edges of the furniture. She eased past chairs and game tables, bedding down on her folded blanket behind the sofa.

She dozed fitfully, waking repeatedly from nightmares. The old mansion was filled with stealthy sounds in the night: the creaking of floorboards overhead, the hollow popping of ancient plumbing.

• 8 •

Stefan turned out all the lights and waited in the bedroom that was furnished for a child. At three-thirty in the morning, he heard Sheener returning. Stefan moved silently behind the bedroom door. A few minutes later Willy Sheener entered, switched on the light, and started toward the mattress. He made a queer sound as he crossed the room, partly a sigh and partly the whimper of an animal escaping from a hostile world into its burrow.

Stefan closed the door, and Sheener spun around at the sound of movement, shocked that his nest had been invaded. 'Who . . . who are you? What the hell are you doing here?'

From a Chevy parked in the shadows across the street, Kokoschka watched Stefan depart Willy Sheener's house. He waited ten minutes, got out of the car, walked around to the back of the bungalow, found the door ajar, and cautiously went inside.

He located Sheener in a child's bedroom, battered and bloody and still. The air reeked of urine, for the man had lost control of his bladder.

Someday, Kokoschka thought with grim determination and a thrill of sadism, I'm going to hurt Stefan even worse than this. Him and that damned girl. As soon as I understand what part she plays in his plans and why he's jumping across decades to reshape her life, I'll put both of them through the kind of pain that no one knows this side of hell.

He left Sheener's house. In the backyard he stared up at the star-spattered sky for a moment, then returned to the institute.

• 9 •

Shortly after dawn, before the first of the shelter's residents had arisen but when Laura felt the danger from Sheener had passed, she left her bed in the game room and returned to the third floor. Everything in her room was as she had left it. There was no sign that she'd had an intruder during the night.

Exhausted, bleary-eyed, she wondered if she had given the Eel too much credit for boldness and daring. She felt somewhat foolish.

She made her bed – a housekeeping chore every McIlroy child was expected to perform – and when she lifted her pillow she was paralyzed by the sight of what lay under it. A single Tootsie Roll.

That day the White Eel did not come to work. He had been awake all night preparing to abduct Laura and no doubt needed his sleep.

'How does a man like that sleep at all?' Ruth wondered as they gathered in a corner of McIlroy's playground after school. 'I mean, doesn't his conscience keep him awake?'

'Ruthie,' Thelma said, 'he doesn't have a conscience.'

'Everyone does, even the worst of us. That's how God made us.'

'Shane,' Thelma said, 'prepare to assist me in an exorcism. Our Ruth is once again possessed by the moronic spirit of Gidget.'

In an uncharacteristic stroke of compassion, Mrs. Bowmaine moved Tammy and Rebecca to another room and allowed Laura to bunk with Ruth and Thelma. For the time being the fourth bed was vacant.

'It'll be Paul McCartney's bed,' Thelma said, as she and Ruth helped Laura settle in. 'Anytime the Beatles are in town, Paul can come use it. And *I'll* use Paul!'

'Sometimes,' Ruth said, 'you're embarrassing.'

'Hey, I'm only expressing healthy sexual desire.'

'Thelma, you're only twelve!' Ruth said exasperatedly.

'Thirteen's next. Going to have my first period any day now. We'll wake up one morning, and there'll be so much blood this place will look like there's been a massacre.'

'*Thelma!*'

Sheener did not come to work on Thursday, either. His days off that week were Friday and Saturday, so by Saturday evening, Laura and the twins speculated excitedly that the Eel would never show up again, that he had been run down by a truck or had contracted beriberi.

But at Sunday morning breakfast, Sheener was at the buffet. He had two black eyes, a bandaged right ear, a swollen upper lip, a six-inch scrape along his left jaw, and he was missing two front teeth.

'Maybe he *was* hit by a truck,' Ruth whispered as they moved forward in the cafeteria line.

Other kids were commenting on Sheener's injuries, and some were giggling. But they either feared and despised him or scorned him, so none cared to speak to him directly about his condition.

Laura, Ruth, and Thelma fell silent as they reached the buffet. The closer they drew to him, the more battered he appeared. His black eyes were not new but a few days old, yet the flesh was still horribly discolored and puffy; initially both eyes must have been nearly swollen shut. His split lip looked raw. Where his face was not bruised or abraded, his usually milk-pale skin was gray. Under his mop of frizzy, copper-red hair, he was a ludicrous figure – a circus clown who had taken a pratfall down a set of stairs without knowing how to land properly and avoid injury.

He did not look up at any of the kids as he served them but kept his eyes on the milk and breakfast pastries. He seemed to tense when Laura came before him, but he did not raise his eyes.

At their table Laura and the twins arranged their chairs so they could watch the Eel, a turn of events they would not have contemplated an hour ago. But he was now less fearful than intriguing. Instead of avoiding him, they spent the day following him on his chores, trying to be casual about it, as if they just happened to wind up in the same places he did, watching him surreptitiously. Gradually it became clear that he was aware of Laura but was avoiding even glancing at her. He looked at other kids, paused in the game room to speak softly to Tammy Hinsen on one occasion, but seemed as loath to meet Laura's eyes as he would have been to stick his fingers in an electric socket.

By late morning Ruth said, 'Laura, he's afraid of you.'

'Damned if he isn't,' Thelma said. 'Was it *you* who beat him up, Shane? Have you been hiding the fact that you're a karate expert?'

'It *is* strange, isn't it? Why's he afraid of me?'

But she knew. Her special guardian. Though she had thought she would have to deal with Sheener herself, her guardian had come through again, warning Sheener to stay away from her.

She was not sure why she was reluctant to share the story of her mysterious protector with the Ackersons. They were her best friends. She trusted them. Yet intuitively she felt that the secret of her guardian was meant to remain a secret, that what little she knew of him was sacred knowledge, and that she had no right to prattle on about him to other people, reducing sacred knowledge to mere gossip.

During the following two weeks the Eel's bruises faded, and the bandage came off his ear to reveal angry red stitches where that flap of flesh nearly had been torn off. He continued to keep his distance from Laura. When he served her in the dining hall, he no longer saved the best dessert for her, and he continued to refuse to meet her eyes.

Occasionally, however, she caught him glaring at her from across a room. Each time he quickly turned away, but in his fiery green eyes she now saw something worse than his previous twisted hunger: rage. Obviously he blamed her for the beating he had suffered.

On Friday, October 27, she learned from Mrs. Bowmaine that she was going to be transferred to another foster home the following day. A couple in Newport Beach, Mr. and Mrs. Dockweiler, were new to the foster-child program and eager to have her.

'I'm sure this will be a more compatible arrangement,' Mrs. Bowmaine said, standing at her desk in a blazing yellow floral-print dress that made her look like a sun-porch sofa. 'The trouble you caused at the Teagels' better not be repeated with the Dockweilers.'

That night in their room, Laura and the twins tried to put on brave faces and discuss the approaching separation in the equanimous spirit with which they had faced her departure for the Teagels'. But they were closer now than a month ago, so close that Ruth and Thelma had begun to speak of Laura as if she were their sister. Thelma even once had said, 'The amazing Ackerson sisters – Ruth, Laura, and moi,' and Laura had felt more wanted, more loved, more *alive* than at any time in the three months since her father died.

'I love you guys,' Laura said.

Ruth said, 'Oh, Laura,' and burst into tears.

Thelma scowled. 'You'll be back in no time. These Dockweilers will be horrid people. They'll make you sleep in the garage.'

'I hope so,' Laura said.

'They'll beat you with rubber hoses—'

'That would be good.'

———

This time the lightning that struck her life was *good* lightning, or at least that was how it seemed at first.

The Dockweilers lived in a huge house in an expensive section of Newport Beach. Laura had her own bedroom with an ocean view. It was decorated in earth tones, mostly beige.

Showing her the room for the first time, Carl Dockweiler said, 'We didn't know what your favorite colors were, so we left it like this, but we can repaint the whole thing, however you want it.' He was fortyish, big as a bear, barrel-chested, with a broad, rubbery face that reminded her of John Wayne if John Wayne had been a bit amusing looking. 'Maybe a girl your age wants a pink room.'

'Oh, no, I like it just the way it is!' Laura said. Still in a state of shock over the sudden opulence into which she had been plunged, she moved to the window and looked out at the splendid view of Newport Harbor, where yachts bobbed on sun-spangled water.

Nina Dockweiler joined Laura and put one hand on her shoulder. She was lovely, with smoky coloring, dark hair, and violet eyes, a china doll of a woman. 'Laura, the child-welfare file said you loved books, but we didn't know what kind of books, so we're going straight to the bookstore and buy whatever you'd like.'

At Waldenbooks Laura chose five paperbacks, and the Dockweilers urged her to buy more, but she felt guilty about spending their money. Carl and Nina scouted the shelves, plucking off volumes and reading cover copy to her, adding them to her pile if she showed the slightest interest. At one point he was crawling on his hands and knees in the young-adult section, scanning titles on the bottom shelf – 'Hey, here's one about a dog. You like animal stories? Here's a spy story!' – and he was such a comical sight that Laura giggled. By the time they left the store, they'd bought one hundred books, *bagsful* of books.

Their first dinner together was at a pizza parlor, where Nina exhibited a surprising talent for magic by plucking a pepperoni ring from behind Laura's ear, then making it vanish.

'That's amazing,' Laura said. 'Where'd you learn that?'

'I owned an interior design firm, but I had to give it up eight years ago. Health reasons. Too stressful. I wasn't used to sitting at home like a lump, so I did all the things I'd dreamed of when I was a businesswoman with no spare time. Like learning magic.'

'Health reasons?' Laura said.

Security was a treacherous rug that people kept pulling out from under her, and now someone was getting ready to jerk the rug again.

Her fear must have been evident, for Carl Dockweiler said, 'Don't worry. Nina was born with a bum heart, a structural defect, but she'll live as long as you or me if she avoids stress.'

'Can't they operate?' Laura asked, putting down the slice of pizza she had just picked up, her appetite having suddenly fled.

'Cardiovascular surgery's advancing rapidly,' Nina said. 'In a couple years maybe. But, honey, it's nothing to worry about. I'll take care of myself, especially now I've got a daughter to spoil!'

'More than anything,' Carl said, 'we wanted kids, but couldn't have them. By the time we decided to adopt, we discovered Nina's heart condition, so then the adoption agencies wouldn't approve us.'

'But we qualify as foster parents,' Nina said, 'so if you like living with us, you can stay forever, just as if you were adopted.'

That night in her big bedroom with its view of the sea – now an almost scary, vast expanse of darkness – Laura told herself that she must not like the Dockweilers too much, that Nina's heart condition foreclosed any possibility of real security.

The following day, Sunday, they took her shopping for clothes and would have spent fortunes if she had not finally begged them to stop. With their Mercedes crammed full of her new clothes, they went to a Peter Sellers comedy, and after the movie they had dinner at a hamburger restaurant where the milkshakes were humongous.

Pouring catsup on her french fries, Laura said, 'You guys are lucky that child-welfare sent me to you instead of some other kid.'

Carl raised his eyebrows. 'Oh?'

'Well, you're nice, *too* nice – and a lot more vulnerable than you realize. Any kid would see how vulnerable you really are, and a lot would take advantage of you. Mercilessly. But you can relax with me. I'll never take advantage of you or make you sorry you took me in.'

They stared at her in amazement.

At last Carl looked at Nina. 'They've tricked us. She's not twelve. They've palmed off a dwarf on us.'

That night in bed, as she waited for sleep, Laura repeated her litany of self-protection: 'Don't like them too much, don't like them too much . . .' But already she liked them enormously.

———————————

The Dockweilers sent her to a private academy where the teachers were more demanding than those in the public schools she had attended, but she relished the challenge and performed well. Slowly she made new friends. She missed Thelma and Ruth, but she took some comfort from knowing they would be pleased that she had found happiness.

She even began to think that she could have faith in the future and could dare to *be* happy. After all, she had a special guardian, didn't she? Perhaps even a guardian angel. Surely any girl blessed with a guardian angel was destined for love, happiness, and security.

But would a guardian angel actually shoot a man in the head? Beat another man to a bloody pulp? Never mind. She had a handsome guardian, angel or not, and foster parents who loved her, and she could not refuse happiness when it showered on her by the bucketful.

On Tuesday, December 5, Nina had her monthly appointment with her cardiologist, so no one was at home when Laura returned from school that afternoon. She let herself in with her key and put her textbooks on the Louis XIV table in the foyer near the foot of the stairs.

The enormous living room was decorated in shades of cream, peach, and pale green, which made it cozy in spite of its size. As she paused at the windows to enjoy the view, she thought of how much better it would be if Ruth and Thelma could enjoy it with her – and suddenly it seemed the most natural thing that they should be there.

Why not? Carl and Nina loved kids. They had enough love for a houseful of kids, for a thousand kids.

'Shane,' she said aloud, 'you're a genius.'

She went to the kitchen and prepared a snack to take to her room. She poured a glass of milk, heated a chocolate croissant in the oven, and got an apple from the refrigerator, as she mulled over the ways in which she might broach the subject of the twins with the Dockweilers. The plan was such a natural that by the time she carried her snack to the swinging door that separated kitchen and dining room and pushed it open with her shoulder, she had been unable to think of a single approach that would fail.

The Eel was waiting in the dining room, and he grabbed her and slammed her up against the wall so hard that he knocked the wind out of her. The apple and chocolate croissant flew off the plate, the plate flew out of her hand, he knocked the glass of milk out of her other hand, and it struck the dining-room table, shattering noisily. He pulled her away from the wall but slammed her into it again, pain flashed down her back, her vision clouded, she knew she dared not black out, so she held on to consciousness, held on tenaciously though she was racked with pain, breathless, and half concussed.

Where was her guardian? Where?

Sheener shoved his face close to hers, and terror seemed to sharpen her senses, for she was acutely aware of every detail of his rage-wrenched countenance: the still red suture marks where his torn ear had been reattached to his head, the blackheads in the creases around his nose, the acne scars in his mealy skin. His green eyes were too strange to be human, as alien and fierce as those of a cat.

Her guardian would pull the Eel off her at any second now, pull him off her and kill him. Any second now.

'I got you,' he said, his voice shrill, manic, 'now you're mine, honey, and you're gonna tell me who that son of a bitch was, the one who beat on me, I'll blow his head off.'

He was holding her by her upper arms, his fingers digging into her flesh. He lifted her off the floor, raised her to his eye level, and pinned her against the wall. Her feet dangled in the air.

'Who is the bastard?' He was so strong for his size. He lifted her away from the wall, slammed her against it again, keeping her at eye level. 'Tell me, honey, or I'll tear *your* ear off.'

Any second now. Any second.

Pain still throbbed through her back, but she was able to draw breath, although what she drew in was *his* breath, sour and nauseating.

'Answer me, honey.'

She could die waiting for a guardian angel to intervene.

She kicked him in the crotch. It was a perfect shot. His legs were planted wide, and he was so unaccustomed to girls who fought back that he never saw it coming. His eyes widened – they actually looked like human eyes for an instant – and he made a low, strangled sound. His hands dropped away from her. Laura collapsed to the floor, and Sheener staggered backward, lost his balance, fell against the dining-room table, folded to his side on the Chinese carpet.

Nearly immobilized by pain, shock, and fear, Laura could not get to her feet. Rag legs. Limp. So crawl. She could crawl. Away from him. Frantically. Toward the dining-room archway. Hoping to be able to stand by the time she reached the living room. He grabbed her left ankle. She tried to kick loose. No good. Rag legs. Sheener held on. Cold fingers. Corpse-cold. He made a thin, shrieking sound. Weird. She put her hand in a milk-soaked patch of carpet. Saw the broken glass. The top of the tumbler had shattered. The heavy base was intact, crowned with sharp spears. Drops of milk clinging to it. Still winded, half paralyzed by pain, the Eel seized her other ankle. Hitched-twitched-dragged himself toward her. He was still shrieking. Like a bird. Going to throw himself on top of her. Pin her. She seized the broken glass. Cut her thumb. Didn't feel a thing. He let go of her ankles to grab at her thighs. She flipped-writhed onto her back. As if *she* were an eel. Thrust the jagged end of the broken tumbler at him, not intending to stab him, hoping only to ward him off. But he was heaving himself onto her, falling onto her, and the three glass points speared into his throat. He tried to pull away. Twisted the tumbler. The points broke off in his flesh. Choking, gagging, he nailed her to the floor with his body. Blood streamed from his nose. She squirmed. He clawed at her. His knee bore down hard on her hip. His mouth was at her throat. He bit her. Just nipped her skin. He'd get a bigger bite next time if she let him. She thrashed. Breath whistled and rattled in his ruined throat. She slithered free. He grabbed. She kicked. Her legs worked better now. The kick landed solidly. She crawled toward the living room. Gripped the frame of the dining-room archway. Pulled herself to her feet. Glanced back. The Eel was on his feet as well, a dining-room chair raised like a club. He swung it. She dodged. The chair hit the frame of the archway with a thunderous sound. She staggered into the living room, heading for the foyer, the door, escape. He threw the chair. It struck her shoulder. She went down. Rolled. Looked up. He towered over her, seized her left arm. Her strength faded. Darkness pulsed at the edges of her vision. He gripped her other arm. She was finished. Would have been finished, anyway, if the glass in his throat had not finally worked through one more artery. Blood suddenly *gushed* from his nose. He collapsed atop her, a great and terrible weight, dead.

She could not move, could barely breathe, and had to struggle to hold fast to consciousness. Above the eerie sound of her own strangled sobs, she heard a door open. Footsteps.

'Laura? I'm home.' It was Nina's voice, light and cheery at first, then shrill with horror: 'Laura? Oh, my God, *Laura!*'

Laura strove to push the dead man off her, but she was able to squirm only half free of the corpse, just far enough to see Nina standing in the foyer archway.

For a moment the woman was paralyzed by shock. She stared at her cream and peach and seafoam-green living room, the tasteful decor now liberally accented with crimson smears. Then her violet eyes returned to Laura, and she snapped out of her trance. 'Laura, oh, dear God, Laura.' She took three steps forward, halted abruptly, and bent over, hugging herself as if she had been hit in the stomach. She made an odd sound: 'Uh, uh, uh, uh, uh.' She tried to straighten up. Her face was contorted. She could not seem to stand erect, and finally she crumpled to the floor and made no sound at all.

It could not happen like this. This wasn't fair, damn it.

New strength, born of panic and of love for Nina, filled Laura. She wriggled free of Sheener and crawled quickly to her foster mother.

Nina was limp. Her beautiful eyes were open, sightless.

Laura put her bloody hand to Nina's neck, feeling for a pulse. She thought she found one. Weak, irregular, but a pulse.

She pulled a cushion off a chair and put it under Nina's head, then ran into the kitchen where the numbers of the police and fire departments were on the wall phone. Shakily, she reported Nina's heart attack and gave the fire department their address.

When she hung up, she knew everything was going to be all right because she had already lost one parent to a heart attack, her father, and it would be just too absurd to lose Nina the same way. Life had absurd moments, yes, but life *itself* wasn't absurd. Life was strange, difficult, miraculous, precious, tenuous, mysterious, but not flat-out absurd. So Nina would live because Nina dying made no sense.

Still scared and worried but feeling better, Laura hurried back to the living room and knelt beside her foster mother, held her.

Newport Beach had first-rate emergency services. The ambulance arrived no more than three or four minutes after Laura had called for it. The two paramedics were efficient and well equipped. Within just a few minutes, however, they pronounced Nina dead, and no doubt she had been dead from the moment she collapsed.

One week after Laura returned to McIlroy and eight days before Christmas, Mrs. Bowmaine reassigned Tammy Hinsen to the fourth bed in the Ackersons' room. In an unusual private session with Laura, Ruth, and Thelma, the social worker explained the reasoning behind that reassignment: 'I know you say Tammy isn't happy with you girls, but she seems to get along better there than anywhere else. We've had her in several rooms, but the other children can't tolerate her. I don't know what it is about the child that makes her an outcast, but her other roommates usually end up using her as a punching bag.'

Back in their room, before Tammy arrived, Thelma settled into a basic yoga position on the floor, legs folded in a pretzel form, heels against hips. She had become interested in yoga when the Beatles endorsed Eastern meditation, and she had said that when she finally met Paul McCartney (which was her indisputable destiny), 'it would be nice if we have something in common, which we will if I can talk with some authority about this yoga crap.'

Now, instead of meditating she said, 'What would that cow have done if I'd said, "Mrs. Bowmaine, the kids don't like Tammy because she let herself be diddled by the Eel, and she helped him target other vulnerable girls, so as far as they're concerned, she's the enemy." What would Bovine Bowmaine have done when I laid *that* on her?'

'She'd have called you a lying scuz,' Laura said, flopping down on her sway-backed bed.

'No doubt. Then she'd have eaten me for lunch. Do you believe the size of that woman? She gets bigger by the week. Anyone that big is dangerous, a ravenous omnivore capable of eating the nearest child, bones and all, as casually as she'd consume a pint of fudge ripple.'

At the window, looking down at the playground behind the mansion, Ruth said, 'It's not fair the way the other kids treat Tammy.'

'Life isn't fair,' Laura said.

'Life isn't a weenie roast, either,' Thelma said. 'Jeez, Shane, don't wax philosophical if you're going to be trite. You know we hate triteness here only slightly less than we hate turning on the radio and hearing Bobbie Gentry singing *Ode to Billy Joe*.'

When Tammy moved in an hour later, Laura was tense. She had killed Sheener, after all, and Tammy had been dependent on him. She expected Tammy to be bitter and angry, but in fact the girl greeted her only with a sincere, shy, and piercingly sad smile.

After Tammy had been with them two days, it became clear that she viewed the loss of the Eel's twisted affections with perverse regret but also with relief. The fiery temper she had revealed when she tore apart Laura's books was quenched. She was once again that drab, bony, washed-out girl who, on Laura's first day at McIlroy, had seemed more of an apparition than a real person, in danger of dissolving into smoky ectoplasm and, with the first good draft, dissipating entirely.

———

After the deaths of the Eel and Nina Dockweiler, Laura attended half-hour sessions with Dr. Boone, a psychotherapist, when he visited McIlroy every Tuesday and Saturday. Boone was unable to understand that Laura could absorb the shock of Willy Sheener's attack and Nina's tragic death without psychological damage. He was puzzled by her articulate discussions of her feelings and the adult vocabulary with which she expressed her adjustment to events in Newport Beach. Having been motherless, having lost her father, having endured many crises and much terror – but most of all, having benefited from her father's wondrous love – she was as resilient as a sponge, absorbing what life presented. However, though she could speak of Sheener with dispassion and of Nina with as much affection as sadness, the psychiatrist viewed her adjustment as merely apparent and not real.

'So you dream about Willy Sheener?' he asked as he sat beside her on the sofa in the small office reserved for him at McIlroy.

'I've only dreamed of him twice. Nightmares, of course. But all kids have nightmares.'

'You dream about Nina, too. Are those nightmares?'

'Oh, no! Those are lovely dreams.'

He looked surprised. 'When you think of Nina, you feel sad?'

'Yes. But also . . . I remember the fun of shopping with her, trying on dresses and sweaters. I remember her smile and her laugh.'

'And guilt? Do you feel guilty about what happened to Nina?'

'No. Maybe Nina wouldn't have died if I hadn't moved in with them and drawn Sheener after me, but I can't feel guilty about that. I tried hard to be a good foster daughter to them, and they were happy with me. What happened was that life dropped a big custard pie on us, and that's not my fault; you can never see the custard pies coming. It's not good slapstick if you see the pie coming.'

'Custard pie?' he asked, perplexed. 'You see life as slapstick comedy? Like the Three Stooges?'

'Partly.'

'Life is just a joke then?'

'No. Life is serious *and* a joke at the same time.'

'But how can that be?'

'If you don't know,' she said, 'maybe I should be the one asking the questions here.'

She filled many pages of her current notebook with observations about Dr. Will Boone. Of her unknown guardian, however, she wrote nothing. She tried not to think of him, either. He had failed her. Laura had come to depend on him; his heroic efforts on her behalf had made her feel *special*, and feeling special had helped her cope since her father's death. Now she felt foolish for ever looking beyond herself for survival. She still had the note he had left on her desk after her father's funeral, but she no longer reread it. And day by day her guardian's previous efforts on her behalf seemed more like fantasies akin to those of Santa Claus, which must be outgrown.

On Christmas afternoon they returned to their room with the gifts they received from charities and do-gooders. They wound up in a sing-along of holiday songs, and both Laura and the twins were amazed when Tammy joined in. She sang in a low, tentative voice.

Over the next couple of weeks she nearly ceased biting her nails altogether. She was only slightly more outgoing than usual, but she seemed calmer, more content with herself than she had ever been.

'When there's no perv around to bother her,' Thelma said, 'maybe she gradually starts to feel clean again.'

Friday, January 12, 1968, was Laura's thirteenth birthday, but she did not celebrate it. She could find no joy in the occasion.

On Monday, she was transferred from McIlroy to Caswell Hall, a shelter for older children in Anaheim, five miles away.

Ruth and Thelma helped her carry her belongings downstairs to the front foyer. Laura had never imagined that she would so intensely regret leaving McIlroy.

'We'll be coming in May,' Thelma assured her. 'We turn thirteen on May second, and then we're out of here. We'll be together again.'

When the social worker from Caswell arrived, Laura was reluctant to go. But she went.

Caswell Hall was an old high school that had been converted to dormitories, recreational lounges, and offices for social workers. As a result the atmosphere was more institutional than at McIlroy.

Caswell was also more dangerous than McIlroy because the kids were older and because many were borderline juvenile delinquents. Marijuana and pills were available, and fights among the boys – and even among the girls – were not infrequent. Cliques formed, as they had at McIlroy, but at Caswell some of the cliques were perilously close in structure and function to street gangs. Thievery was common.

Within a few weeks Laura realized that there were two types of survivors in life: those, like her, who found the requisite strength in having once been loved with great intensity; and those who, having not been loved, learned to thrive on hatred, suspicion, and the meager rewards of revenge. They were at once scornful of the need for human feeling and envious of the capacity for it.

She lived with great caution at Caswell but never allowed fear to diminish her. The thugs were frightening but also pathetic and, in their posturing and rituals of violence, even funny. She found no one like the Ackersons with whom to share the black humor, so she filled her notebooks with it. In those neatly written monologues, she turned inward while she waited for the Ackersons to be thirteen; that was an intensely rich time of self-discovery and increasing understanding of the slapstick, tragic world into which she had been born.

On Saturday, March 30, she was in her room at Caswell, reading, when she heard one of her roomies – a whiny girl named Fran Wickert – talking to another girl in the hall, discussing a fire in which kids had been killed. Laura was eavesdropping with only half an ear until she heard the word 'McIlroy.'

A chill pierced her, freezing her heart, numbing her hands. She dropped the book and raced into the hallway, startling the girls. 'When? When was this fire?'

'Yesterday,' Fran said.

'How many were k-killed?'

'Not many, two kids I think, maybe only one, but I heard if you was there you could smell burnin' meat. Isn't that the grossest thing—'

Advancing on Fran, Laura said, 'What were their names?'

'Hey, let me go.'

'Tell me their names!'

'I don't know any names. Christ, what's the matter with you?'

Laura did not remember letting go of Fran, and she did not recall leaving the grounds of the shelter, but suddenly she found herself on Katella Avenue, blocks from Caswell Hall. Katella was a commercial street in that area, and in some places there was no sidewalk, so she ran on the shoulder of the road, heading east, with traffic whizzing by on her right side. Caswell was five miles from McIlroy, and she was not sure she knew the entire route, but trusting to instinct she ran until she was exhausted, then walked until she could run again.

The rational course would have been to go straight to one of the Caswell counselors and ask for the names of those kids killed in the fire at McIlroy. But Laura had the peculiar idea that the Ackerson twins' fate rested entirely upon her willingness to make the difficult trip to McIlroy to inquire about them, that if she asked about them by phone she would be told they were dead, that if instead she endured the physical punishment of the five-mile run, she'd find the Ackersons were safe. That was superstition, but she succumbed to it anyway.

Twilight descended. The late-March sky was filled with muddy-red and purple light, and the edges of the scattered clouds appeared to be aflame by the time Laura came within sight of the McIlroy Home. With relief she saw that the front of the old mansion was unmarked by fire.

Although she was soaked with sweat and shaking with exhaustion, though she had a throbbing headache, she did not slow when she saw the unscorched mansion but maintained her pace for the final block. She passed six kids in the ground-floor hallways and three more on the stairs, and two of them spoke to her by name. But she did not stop to ask them about the blaze. She had to *see*.

On the last flight of stairs she caught the scent of a fire's aftermath: the acrid, tarry stench of burnt things; the lingering, sour smell of smoke. When she went through the door at the top of the stairwell, she saw that the windows were open at each end of the third-floor hall and that electric fans had been set up in the middle of the corridor to blow the tainted air in both directions.

The Ackersons' room had a new, unpainted door frame and door, but the surrounding wall was scorched and smeared with black soot. A hand-printed sign warned of danger. Like all the doors in McIlroy, this one had no lock, so she ignored the sign and flung open the door and stepped across the threshold and saw what she had been so afraid of seeing: destruction.

The hall lights behind her and the purple glow of twilight at the windows did not adequately illuminate the room, but she saw that the remains of the furniture had been cleaned out; the place was empty but for the reeking ghost of the fire. The floor was blackened by soot and charred, though it looked structurally sound. The walls were smoke-damaged. The closet doors had been reduced to ashes but for a few burnt chunks of wood clinging to the hinges, which had partially melted. Both windows had blown out or been broken by those fleeing the flames; now those gaps were temporarily covered by sections of clear-plastic dropcloths stapled to the walls. Fortunately for the other kids at McIlroy, the fire had burned upward rather than outward, eating through the ceiling. She looked overhead into the mansion's attic where massive, blackened beams were dimly visible in the gloom. Apparently the flames had been stopped before they'd broken through the roof, for she could not see the sky.

She was breathing laboriously, noisily, not only because of the exhausting trip from Caswell but because a vise of panic was squeezing her chest painfully, making it difficut to inhale. And every breath of the bitterly scented air brought the nauseating taste of carbon.

From that moment in her room at Caswell when she had heard of the fire at McIlroy, she had known the cause, though she had not wanted to admit to the knowledge. Tammy Hinsen once had been caught with a can of lighter fluid and matches with which she planned to set herself afire. On hearing of that intended self-immolation, Laura had known that Tammy had been serious about it because immolation seemed such a *right* form of suicide for her, an externalization of the inner fire that had been consuming her for years.

Please, God, she was alone in the room when she did it, please.

Gagging on the stink and taste of destruction, Laura turned away from the fire-blasted room and stepped into the third-floor corridor.

'Laura?'

She looked up and saw Rebecca Bogner. Laura's breath came and went in wrenching inhalations, shuddering exhalations, but somehow she croaked their names: 'Ruth . . . Thelma?'

Rebecca's bleak expression denied the possibility that the twins had escaped unharmed, but Laura repeated the precious names, and in her ragged voice she heard a pathetic, beseeching note.

'Down there,' Rebecca said, pointing toward the north end of the hall. 'The next to the last room on the left.'

With a sudden rush of hope, Laura ran to the indicated room. Three beds were empty, but in the fourth, revealed by the light of a reading lamp, was a girl lying on her side, facing the wall.

'Ruth? Thelma?'

The girl on the bed slowly rose – one of the Ackersons, unharmed. She wore a drab, badly wrinkled, gray dress; her hair was in disarray; her face was puffy, her eyes moist with tears. She took a step toward Laura but stopped as if the effort of walking was too great.

Laura rushed to her, hugged her.

With her head on Laura's shoulder, face against Laura's neck, she spoke at last in a tortured voice. 'Oh, I wish it'd been me, Shane. If it had to be one of us, why couldn't it have been me?'

Until the girl spoke, Laura had assumed that she was Ruth.

Refusing to accept that horror, Laura said, 'Where's Ruthie?'

'Gone. Ruthie's gone. I thought you knew, my Ruthie's dead.'

Laura felt as if something deep within her had torn. Her grief was so power-ful that it precluded tears; she was stunned, numb.

For the longest time they just held each other. Twilight faded toward night. They moved to the bed and sat on the edge.

A couple of kids appeared at the door. They evidently shared the room with Thelma, but Laura waved them away.

Looking at the floor, Thelma said, 'I woke up to this shrieking, such a horrible shrieking . . . and all this *light* so bright it hurt my eyes. And then I realized the room was on fire. *Tammy* was on fire. Blazing like a torch. Thrashing in her bed, blazing and shrieking . . .'

Laura put an arm around her and waited.

'. . . the fire leaped off Tammy – *whoosh* up the wall, her bed was on fire, and fire was spreading across the floor, the rug was burning . . .'

Laura remembered how Tammy had sung with them on Christmas and had thereafter been calmer day by day, as if gradually finding inner peace. Now it was obvious that the peace she'd found had been based on the determination to end her torment.

'Tammy's bed was nearest the door, the door was on fire, so I broke the window over my bed. I called to Ruth, she . . . s-she said she was coming, there was smoke, I couldn't see, then Heather Dorning, who was bunking in your old bed, she came to the window, so I helped her get out, and the smoke was sucked out of the window, so the room cleared a little, which was when I saw Ruth was trying to throw her own blanket over Tammy to s-smother the flames, but that blanket had caught f-fire, too, and I saw Ruth . . . Ruth . . . Ruth on fire . . .'

Outside, the last purple light melted into darkness.

The shadows in the corners of the room deepened.

The lingering burnt odor seemed to grow stronger.

'. . . and I would've gone to her, I would've gone, but just then the f-fire *exploded*, it was everywhere in the room, and the smoke was black and so thick, and I couldn't see Ruth any more or anything . . . then I heard sirens, loud and close, sirens, so I tried to tell myself they'd get there in time to help Ruth, which was a l-l-lie, a lie I told myself and wanted to believe, and . . . I left her there, Shane. Oh, God, I went out the window and left Ruthie on f-f-fire, burning . . .'

'You couldn't do anything else,' Laura assured her.

'I left Ruthie burning.'

'There was nothing you could do.'

'I left Ruthie.'

'There was no point in you dying too.'

'I left Ruthie burning.'

———

In May, after her thirteenth birthday, Thelma was transferred to Caswell and assigned to a room with Laura. The social workers agreed to that arrangement because Thelma was suffering from depression and was not responding to therapy. Maybe she would find the succor she needed in her friendship with Laura.

For months Laura despaired of reversing Thelma's decline. At night Thelma was plagued by dreams, and by day she stewed in self-recrimination. Eventually, time healed her, though her wounds never entirely closed. Her sense of humor gradually returned, and her wit became as sharp as ever, but there was a new melancholy in her.

They shared a room at Caswell Hall for five years, until they left the custody of the state and embarked on lives under no one's control but their own. They shared many laughs during those years. Life was good again but never the same as it had been before the fire.

• 11 •

In the main lab of the institute, the dominant object was the gate through which one could step into other ages. It was a huge, barrel-shaped device, twelve feet long and eight feet in diameter, of highly polished steel on the outside, lined with polished copper on the inside. It rested on copper blocks that held it eighteen inches off the floor. Thick electrical cables trailed from it, and within the barrel strange currents made the air shimmer as if it were water.

Kokoschka returned through time to the gate, materializing inside that enormous cylinder. He had made several trips that day, shadowing Stefan in far times and places, and at last he had learned why the traitor was obsessed with reshaping the life of Laura Shane. He hurried to the mouth of the gate and stepped down onto the lab floor, where two scientists and three of his own men were waiting for him.

'The girl has nothing to do with the bastard's plot against the government, nothing to do with his attempts to destroy the time-travel project,' Kokoschka said. 'She's an entirely separate matter, just a personal crusade of his.'

'So now we know everything he's done and why,' said one of the scientists, 'and you can eliminate him.'

'Yes,' Kokoschka said, crossing the room to the main programming board. 'Now that we've uncovered all the traitor's secrets, we can kill him.'

As he sat down at the programming board, intending to reset the gate to deliver him to yet another time, where he could surprise the traitor, Kokoschka decided to kill Laura, too. It would be an easy job, something he could handle by himself, for he would have the element of surprise on his side; he preferred to work alone, anyway, whenever possible; he disliked sharing the pleasure. Laura Shane was no danger to the government or to its plans to reshape the future of the world, but he would kill her first and in front of Stefan, merely to break the traitor's heart before putting a bullet in it. Besides, Kokoschka liked to kill.

Three

A Light in the Dark

• 1 •

On Laura Shane's twenty-second birthday, January 12, 1977, she received a toad in the mail. The box in which it came bore no return address, and no note was enclosed. She opened it at the desk by the window in the living room of her apartment, and the clear sunlight of the unusually warm winter day glimmered pleasingly on the charming little figurine. The toad was ceramic, two inches tall, standing on a ceramic lily pad, wearing a top hat and holding a cane.

Two weeks earlier the campus literary magazine had published 'Amphibian Epics,' a short story of hers about a girl whose father spun fanciful tales of an imaginary toad, Sir Tommy of England. Only she knew that the piece was as much fact as fiction, though someone apparently intuited at least something of the true importance that the story had for her, because the grinning toad in the top hat was packed with extraordinary care. It was carefully wrapped in a swatch of soft cotton cloth tied with red ribbon, then further wrapped in tissue paper, nestled in a plain white box in a bed of cotton balls, and that box was packed in a nest of shredded newspaper inside a still larger box. No one would go to such trouble to protect a five-dollar, novelty figurine unless the packing was meant to signify the sender's perception of the depth of her emotional involvement with the events of 'Amphibian Epics.'

To afford the rent, she shared her off-campus apartment in Irvine with two juniors at the university, Meg Falcone and Julie Ishimina, and at first she thought perhaps one of them had sent the toad. They seemed unlikely candidates, for Laura was not close to either of them. They were busy with studies and interests of their own; and they had lived with her only since the previous September. They claimed to have no knowledge of the toad, and their denials seemed sincere.

She wondered if Dr. Matlin, the faculty adviser to the literary magazine at UCI, might have sent the figurine. Since her sophomore year, when she had taken Matlin's course in creative writing, he had encouraged her to pursue her talent and polish her craftsmanship. He had been particularly fond of 'Amphibian Epics,' so maybe he had sent the toad to say 'well done.' But why no return address, no card? Why the secrecy? No, that was out of character for Harry Matlin.

She had a few casual friends at the university, but she was not truly close to anyone because she had little time to make and sustain deep friendships. Between her studies, her job, and her writing, she used up all the hours of the day not devoted to sleeping or eating. She could think of no one who would have gone out of his way to buy the toad, package it, and mail it anonymously.

A mystery.

The following day her first class was at eight o'clock and her last at two. She returned to her nine-year-old Chevy in the campus parking lot at a quarter till four, unlocked the door, got behind the wheel – and was startled to see another toad on the dash-board.

It was two inches high and four inches long. This one was also ceramic, emerald green, reclining with one arm bent and its head propped on its hand. It was smiling dreamily.

She was sure she had left the car locked, and in fact it had been locked when she returned from class. The enigmatic giver of toads had evidently gone to considerable trouble to open the Chevy without a key – a loid of some kind or a coathanger worked through the top of the window to the lock button – and leave the toad in a dramatic fashion.

Later she put the reclining toad on her nightstand where the top-hat-and-cane fellow already stood. She spent the evening in bed, reading. From time to time her attention drifted away from the page to the ceramic figures.

The next morning when she left the apartment, she found a small box on her doorstep. Inside was another meticulously wrapped toad. It was cast in pewter, sitting upon a log, holding a banjo.

The mystery deepened.

———

In the summer she put in a full shift as a waitress at Hamburger Hamlet in Costa Mesa, but during the school year her course load was so heavy that she could work only three evenings a week. The Hamlet was an upscale hamburger restaurant providing good food for reasonable prices in a moderately plush ambience – crossbeam ceiling, lots of wood paneling, hugely comfortable armchairs – so the customers were usually happier than those in other places where she had waited tables.

Even if the atmosphere had been seedy and the customers surly, she would have kept the job; she needed the money. On her eighteenth birthday, four years ago, she learned that her father had established a trust fund, consisting of the assets liquidated upon his death, and that the trust could not be touched by the state to pay for her care at McIlroy Home and Caswell Hall. At that time the funds had become hers to spend, and she had applied them toward living and college expenses. Her father hadn't been rich; there was only twelve thousand dollars even after six years of accrued interest, not nearly enough for four years of rent, food, clothing, and tuition, so she depended upon her income as a waitress to make up the difference.

On Sunday evening, January 16, she was halfway through her shift at the Hamlet when the host escorted an older couple, about sixty, to one of the booths in Laura's station. They asked for two Michelobs while they studied the menu. A few minutes later, when she returned from the bar with the beers and two frosted mugs on a tray, she saw a ceramic toad on their table. She nearly dropped the tray in surprise. She looked at the man, at the woman, and they were grinning at her, but they weren't *saying* anything, so she said, '*You've* been giving me toads? But I don't even know you – do I?'

The man said, 'Oh, you've gotten more of these, have you?'

'This is the fourth. You didn't bring this for me, did you? But it wasn't here a few minutes ago. Who put it on the table?'

He winked at his wife, and she said to Laura, 'You've got a secret admirer, dear.'

'Who?'

'Young fella was sitting at that table over there,' the man said, pointing across the room to a station served by a waitress named Amy Heppleman. The table was now empty; the busboy had just finished clearing away the dirty dishes. 'Soon as you left to get our beers, he comes over and asks if he can leave this here for you.'

It was a Christmas toad in a Santa suit, without a beard, a sack of toys over its shoulder.

The woman said, 'You don't really know who he is?'

'No. What'd he look like?'

'Tall,' the man said. 'Quite tall and husky. Brown hair.'

'Brown eyes too,' his wife said. 'Soft-spoken.'

Holding the toad, staring at it, Laura said, 'There's something about this . . . something that makes me uneasy.'

'Uneasy?' the woman said. 'But it's just a young man who's smitten with you, dear.'

'Is it?' she wondered.

Laura found Amy Heppleman at the salad preparation counter and sought a better description of the toad-giver.

'He had a mushroom omelet, whole-wheat toast, and a Coke,' Amy said, using a pair of stainless-steel tongs to fill two bowls with salad greens. 'Didn't you see him sitting there?'

'I didn't notice him, no.'

'Biggish guy. Jeans. A blue-checkered shirt. His hair was cut too short, but he was kinda cute if you like the moose type. Didn't talk much. Seemed kinda shy.'

'Did he pay with a credit card?'

'No. Cash.'

'Damn,' Laura said.

She took the Santa toad home and put it with the other figurines.

The following morning, Monday, as she left the apartment, she found yet another plain white box on the doorstep. She opened it reluctantly. It contained a clear glass toad.

When Laura returned from the UCI campus that same afternoon, Julie Ishimina was sitting at the dinette table, reading the daily paper and drinking a cup of coffee. 'You got another one,' she said, pointing to a box on the kitchen counter. 'Came in the mail.'

Laura tore open the elaborately wrapped package. The sixth toad was actually a pair of toads – salt and pepper shakers.

She put the shakers with the other figurines on her nightstand, and for a long while she sat on the edge of her bed, frowning at that growing collection.

At five o'clock that afternoon she called Thelma Ackerson in Los Angeles and told her about the toads.

Lacking a trust fund of any size, Thelma had not even considered college, but as she said, that was no tragedy because she was not interested in academics. Upon completing high school, she had gone straight from Caswell Hall to Los Angeles, intent upon breaking into show business as a stand-up comic.

Nearly every night, from about six o'clock until two in the morning, she hung around the comedy clubs – the Improv, the Comedy Store, and all their imitators – angling for a six-minute, unpaid shot on the stage, making contacts (or hoping to make them), competing with a horde of young comics for the coveted exposure.

She worked days to pay the rent, moving from job to job, some of them decidedly peculiar. Among other things she had worn a chicken suit and sung songs and waited tables in a weird 'theme' pizza parlor, and she'd been a picket-line stand-in for a few Writers Guild West members who were required by their union to participate in a strike action but who preferred to pay someone a hundred bucks a day to carry a placard for them and sign their names on the duty roster.

Though they lived just ninety minutes apart, Laura and Thelma got together only two or three times a year, usually just for a long lunch or dinner, because they led busy lives. But regardless of the time between visits, they were instantly comfortable with each other and quick to share their most intimate thoughts and experiences. 'The McIlroy-Caswell bond,' Thelma once said, 'is stronger than being blood brothers, stronger than the Mafia convenant, stronger than the bond between Fred Flintstone and Barney Rubble, and those two are *close*.'

Now, after she listened to Laura's story, Thelma said, 'So what's your problem, Shane? Sounds to me like some big, shy hunk of a guy has a crush on you. Lots of women would swoon over this.'

'Is that what it is, though? An innocent crush?'

'What else?'

'I don't know. But it . . . makes me uneasy.'

'Uneasy? These toads are all cute little things, aren't they? None of them is a snarling toad? None of them is holding a bloody little butcher knife? Or a little ceramic chainsaw?'

'No.'

'He hasn't sent you any *beheaded* toads, has he?'

'No, but—'

'Shane, the last few years have been calm, though of course you've had a pretty eventful life. It's understandable that you'd expect this guy to be Charles Manson's brother. But it's almost a sure bet he's just what he appears to be – a guy who admires you from afar, is maybe a little shy, and has a streak of romance in him about eighteen inches wide. How's your sex life?'

'I don't have any,' Laura said.

'Why not? You're not a virgin. There was that guy last year—'

'Well, you know that didn't work out.'

'Nobody since?'

'No. What do you think – I'm promiscuous?'

'Sheesh! Kiddo, two lovers in twenty-two years would not make you promiscuous even by the pope's definition. Unbend a little. Relax. Stop being a worrier. Flow with this, see where it goes. He might just turn out to be prince charming.'

'Well . . . maybe I will. I guess you're right.'

'But, Shane?'

'Yeah?'

'Just for luck, from now on you better carry a .357 Magnum.'
'Very funny.'
'Funny is my business.'

During the following three days Laura received two more toads, and by Saturday morning, the twenty-second, she was equally confused, angry, and afraid. Surely no secret admirer would string the game out so long. Each new toad seemed to be mocking rather than honoring her. There was a quality of obsession in the giver's relentlessness.

She spent much of Friday night in a chair by the big living-room window, sitting in the dark. Through the half-open drapes, she had a view of the apartment building's covered veranda and the area in front of her own door. If he came during the night, she intended to confront him in the act. By three-thirty in the morning he had not arrived, and she dozed off. When she woke in the morning, no package was on the doorstep.

After she showered and ate a quick breakfast, she went down the outside stairs and around to the back of the building where she kept her car in the covered stall assigned to her. She intended to go to the library to do some research work, and it looked like a good day for being indoors. The winter sky was gray and low, and the air had a prestorm heaviness that filled her with foreboding – a feeling that intensified when she found another box on the dashboard of her locked Chevy. She wanted to scream in frustration.

Instead she sat behind the wheel and opened the package. The other figurines had been inexpensive, no more than ten or fifteen dollars each, some probably as cheap as three bucks, but the newest was an exquisite miniature porcelain that surely cost at least fifty dollars. However she was less interested in the toad than in the box in which it had come. It was not plain, as before, but imprinted with the name of a gift shop – Collectibles – in the South Coast Plaza shopping mall.

Laura drove directly to the mall, arrived fifteen minutes before Collectibles opened, waited on a bench in the promenade, and was first through the shop's door when it was unlocked. The store's owner and manager was a petite, gray-haired woman named Eugenia Farvor. 'Yes, we handle this line,' she said after listening to Laura's succinct explanation and examining the porcelain toad, 'and in fact I sold it myself just yesterday to the young man.'

'Do you know his name?'
'I'm sorry, no.'
'What did he look like?'
'I remember him well because of his size. Very tall. Six five, I'd say. And very broad in the shoulders. He was quite well dressed. A gray pinstripe suit, blue and gray striped tie. I admired the suit, in fact, and he said it wasn't easy finding clothes to fit him.'
'Did he pay cash?'
'Mmmmm . . . no, I believe he used a credit card.'
'Would you still have the charge slip?'
'Oh, yes, we usually run a day or two behind in organizing them and transferring them to the master ticket for deposit.' Mrs. Farvor led Laura past glass

display cases filled with porcelains, Lalique and Waterford crystal, Wedgwood plates, Hummel figurines, and other expensive items, to the cramped office at the back of the store. Then she suddenly had second thoughts about sharing her customer's identity. 'If his intentions are innocent, if he's just an admirer of yours – and I must say there seemed no harm in him; he seemed quite nice – then I'll be spoiling everything for him. He'll want to be revealing himself to you according to his own plan.'

Laura tried hard to charm the woman and win her sympathy. She could not recall ever having spoken more eloquently or with such feeling; usually she was not as good at vocalizing her feelings as she was at putting them down in print. Genuine tears sprang to her assistance, surprising her even more than they did Eugenia Farvor.

From the Mastercard charge slip, she obtained his name – Daniel Packard – and his telephone number. She went directly from the gift shop to a public telephone in the mall and looked him up. There were two Daniel Packards in the book, but the one with that number lived on Newport Avenue in Tustin.

When she returned to the mall parking lot, a cold drizzle was falling. She turned up her coat collar, but she had neither a hat nor an umbrella. By the time she got to her car, her hair was wet, and she was chilled. She shivered all the way from Costa Mesa to North Tustin.

She figured there was a good chance he would be at home. If he was a student, he would not be in class on Saturday. If he worked an ordinary nine-to-five job, he would probably not be at the office, either. And the weather ruled out many of the usual weekend pastimes for outdoor-oriented southern Californians.

His address was an apartment complex of two-story, Spanish-style buildings, eight of them, in a garden setting. For a few minutes she hurried from building to building on winding walkways under dripping palms and coral trees, looking for his apartment. By the time she found it – a first-floor, end unit in the building farthest from the street – her hair was soaked. Her chill had deepened. Discomfort dulled her fear and sharpened her anger, so she rang his bell without hesitation.

He evidently did not peek through the fisheye security lens, for when he opened the door and saw her, he looked stunned. He was maybe five years older than she, and he was a big man indeed, fully six feet five, two hundred and forty pounds, all muscle. He was wearing jeans and a pale-blue T-shirt smeared with grease and spotted with another oily substance; his well-developed arms were formidable. His face was shadowed by beard stubble and smudged with more grease, and his hands were black.

Carefully staying back from the door, beyond his reach, Laura simply said, 'Why?'

'Because . . .' He shifted from one foot to the other, almost too big for the doorway in which he stood. 'Because . . .'

'I'm waiting.'

He wiped one grease-covered hand through his close-cropped hair and seemed oblivious of the resultant mess. His eyes shifted away from her; he looked out at the rain-lashed courtyard as he spoke. 'How . . . how'd you find out it was me?'

'That's not important. What's important is that I don't know you, I've never seen you before, and yet I've got a toad menagerie that you've sent me, you come around in the middle of the night to leave them on my doorstep, you break into my car to leave them on the dashboard, and it's been going on for *weeks*, so don't you think it's time I knew what this is all about?'

Still not looking at her, he flushed and said, 'Well, sure, but I didn't . . . wasn't ready . . . didn't think the time was right.'

'The time was right a week ago!'

'Ummmm.'

'So tell me. *Why?*'

Looking down at his greasy hands, he said quietly, 'Well, see . . .'

'Yes?'

'I love you.'

She stared at him, incredulous. He finally looked at her. She said, 'You *love* me? But you don't even *know* me. How can you love a person you've never met?'

He looked away from her, rubbed his filthy hand through his hair again, and shrugged. 'I don't know, but there it is, and I . . . uh . . . well, ummmm, I have this feeling, see, this feeling that I've got to spend the rest of my life with you.'

With cold rainwater trickling from her wet hair down the nape of her neck and along the curve of her spine, with her day at the library shot – how could she concentrate on research after this insane scene? – and with more than a little disappointment that her secret admirer had turned out to be this dirty, sweaty, inarticulate lummox, Laura said, 'Listen, Mr. Packard, I don't want you sending me any more toads.'

'Well, see, I really want to send them.'

'But I don't want to receive them. And tomorrow I'll mail back the ones you've sent me. No, today. I'll mail them back today.'

He met her eyes again, blinked in surprise, and said, 'I thought you liked toads.'

With growing anger, she said, 'I *do* like toads. I love toads. I think toads are the cutest things in creation. Right now I even wish I *were* a toad, but I don't want *your* toads. Understand?'

'Ummmm.'

'Don't harass me, Packard. Maybe some women surrender to your weird mix of heavy-handed romance and sweaty macho charm, but I'm not one of them, and I can protect myself, don't think I can't. I'm a lot tougher than I look, and I've dealt with worse than you.'

She turned away from him, walked out from under the veranda into the rain, returned to her car, and drove back to Irvine. She shook all the way home, not only because she was wet and chilled but because she was in the grip of anger. The nerve of him!

At her apartment she undressed, bundled up in a quilted robe, and brewed a pot of coffee with which to ward off the chills.

She had just taken her first sip of coffee when the phone rang. She answered it in the kitchen. It was Packard.

Speaking so rapidly that he ran his sentences together in long gushes, he said, 'Please don't hang up on me, you're right, I'm stupid about these things, an idiot, but give me just one minute to explain myself, I was fixing the dishwasher when you came, that's why I was such a mess, greasy and sweaty, had to pull it from under the counter myself, the landlord would have fixed it, but going through management takes a week, and I'm good with my hands, I can fix anything, it was a rainy day, nothing else to do, so why not fix it myself, I never figured you to show up. My name's Daniel Packard, but you know that already, I'm twenty-eight, I was in the army until '73, graduated from the University of California at Irvine with a degree in business just three years ago, work as a stockbroker now, but I take a couple night courses at the university, which is how I came across your story about the toad in the campus literary magazine, it was terrific, I loved it, a great story, really, so I went to the library and searched through back issues to find everything else you'd written, and I read it all, and a *lot* of it was good, damned good, not all of it, but a lot. I fell in love with you somewhere along the way, with the person I knew from her writing, because the writing was so beautiful and so real. One evening I was sitting there in the library reading one of your stories – they won't let anyone check out back issues of the literary magazine, they have them in binders, and you have to read them in the library – and this librarian was passing behind my chair, and she leaned over and asked if I liked the story, I said I did, and she said, "Well, the author's right over there, if you want to tell her it's good," and there you were just three tables away with a stack of books, doing research, scowling, making notes, and you were gorgeous. See, I knew you would be beautiful *inside* because your stories are beautiful, the sentiment in them is beautiful, but it never occurred to me that you'd be beautiful *outside*, too, and there was no way I could approach you because I've always been tongue-tied and stumble-footed around beautiful women, maybe because my mother was beautiful but cold and forbidding, so now maybe I think all beautiful women will reject me the way my mother did – a little half-baked analysis there – but it sure would've been a lot easier for me if you'd been ugly or at least plain looking. Because of your story I thought I'd use the toads, that whole secret admirer bit with the gifts, as a way to soften you up, and I planned to reveal myself after the third or fourth toad, I really did, but I kept delaying because I didn't want to be rejected, I guess, and I knew it was getting crazy, toad after toad after toad, but I just couldn't stop it and forget you, yet I wasn't able to face you, either, and that's it. I never meant you any harm, I sure didn't mean to upset you, can you forgive me, I hope you can.'

He stopped at last, exhausted.

She said, 'Well.'

He said, 'So will you go out with me?'

Surprised by her own response, she said, 'Yes.'

'Dinner and a movie?'

'All right.'

'Tonight? Pick you up at six?'

'Okay.'

After she hung up she stood for a while, staring at the phone. Finally she said aloud, 'Shane, are you nuts?' Then she said, 'But he told me my writing was "so beautiful and so real." '

She went into her bedroom and looked at the collection of toads on the nightstand. She said, 'He's inarticulate and silent one time, a babbler the next. He could be a psycho killer, Shane.' Then she said, 'Yeah, he could be, but he's also a great literary critic.'

Because he had suggested dinner and a movie, Laura dressed in a gray skirt, white blouse, and maroon sweater, but he showed up in a dark blue suit, white shirt with French cuffs, blue silk tie with tie chain, silk display handkerchief, and highly polished black wingtips, as if he were going to the season opener at the opera. He carried an umbrella and escorted her from her apartment to his car with one hand under her right arm, with such solemn concern that he seemed convinced that she would dissolve if touched by one drop of rain or shatter into a million pieces if she slipped and fell.

Considering the difference in their dress and the considerable difference in their size – at five-five, she was one foot shorter than he was; at a hundred fifteen pounds, she was less than half his weight – she felt almost as if she were going on a date with her father or an older brother. She was not a petite woman, but on his arm and under his umbrella she felt positively tiny.

He was uncommunicative again in the car, but he blamed it on the need to drive with special care in such rotten weather. They went to a small Italian restaurant in Costa Mesa, a place in which Laura had eaten a few good meals in the past. They sat down at their table and were given menus, but even before the waitress could ask if they would like a drink, Daniel said, 'This is no good, this is all wrong, let's find another place.'

Surprised, she said, 'But why? This is fine. Their food's very good here.'

'No, really, this is all wrong. No atmosphere, no style, I don't want you to think, ummmm,' and now he was babbling as he'd done on the phone, blushing, 'ummmm, well, anyway, this is not good, not right for our first date, I want this to be special,' and he got up, 'ummm, I think I know just the place, I'm sorry, Miss' – this to the startled young waitress – 'I hope we haven't inconvenienced you,' and he was pulling back Laura's chair, helping her up, 'I know just the place, you'll like it, I've never eaten there but I've heard it's really good, excellent.' Other customers were staring, so Laura stopped protesting. 'It's close, too, just a couple of blocks from here.'

They returned to his car, drove two blocks, and parked in front of an unpretentious-looking restaurant in a strip shopping centre.

By now Laura knew him well enough to realize that his sense of courtliness required her to wait for him to come around and open her car door, but when he opened it she saw he was standing in a ten-inch-deep puddle. 'Oh, your shoes!' she said.

'They'll dry out. Here, you hold the umbrella over yourself, and I'll lift you across the puddle.'

Nonplussed, she allowed herself to be plucked from the car and carried over the puddle as if she weighed no more than a feather pillow. He put her down on higher pavement and, without the umbrella, he sloshed back to the car to close the door.

The French restaurant had less atmosphere than the Italian place. They were shown to a corner table too near the kitchen, and Daniel's saturated shoes squished and squeaked all the way across the room.

'You'll catch pneumonia,' she worried when they were seated and had ordered two Dry Sacks on the rocks.

'Not me. I've got a good immune system. Never get sick. One time in Nam, during an action, I was cut off from my unit, spent a week on my own in the jungle, rained every minute, I was *shriveled* by the time I found my way back to friendly territory, but I never even got the sniffles.'

As they sipped their drinks and studied the menu and ordered, he was more relaxed than Laura had yet seen him, and he actually proved to be a coherent, pleasant, even amusing conversationalist. But when the appetizers were served – salmon in dill sauce for her, scallops in pastry for him – it swiftly became clear that the food was terrible, even though the prices were twice those at the Italian place that they had left, and course by course, as his embarrassment grew, his ability to sustain his end of the conversation declined drastically. Laura proclaimed everything delicious and choked down every bite, but it was no use; he was not fooled.

The kitchen staff and the waiter were also slow. By the time Daniel had paid the check and escorted her back to the car – lifting her across the puddle again as if she were a little girl – they were half an hour late for the movie they had intended to see.

'That's all right,' she said, 'we can go in late and stay to see the first half hour of the next showing.'

'No, no,' he said. 'That's a terrible way to see a movie. It'll ruin it for you. I wanted this night to be perfect.'

'Relax,' she said. 'I'm having fun.'

He looked at her with disbelief, and she smiled, and he smiled, too, but his smile was sick.

'If you don't want to go to the movie now,' she said, 'that's all right, too. Wherever you want to go, I'm game.'

He nodded, started the car, and drove out to the street. They had done a few miles before she realized that he was taking her home.

All the way from his car to her door, he apologized for what a lousy evening it had been, and she repeatedly assured him that she was not in the least disappointed with a moment of it. At her apartment, the instant she inserted her key in the door, he turned and fled down the stairs from the second-floor veranda, neither asking for a goodnight kiss nor giving her a chance to invite him in.

She stepped to the head of the stairs and watched him descend, and he was halfway down when a gust of wind turned his umbrella inside out. He fought with it the rest of the way, twice almost losing his balance. When he reached the walk below, he finally got the umbrella corrected – and the wind immediately turned it inside out again. In frustration he threw it into some nearby shrubbery, then looked up at Laura. He was soaked from head to toe by then, and in the pale light from a lamppost she could see that his suit hung on him shapelessly. He was a *huge* man, strong as two bulls, but he had been done in by little things – puddles, a gust of wind – and there was something quite funny about that. She knew she should not laugh, *dared* not laugh, but a laugh burst from her anyway.

'You're too damned beautiful, Laura Shane!' he shouted from the walk below. 'God help me, you're just too beautiful.' Then he hurried away through the night.

Feeling bad about laughing but unable to stop, she went into the apartment and changed into pajamas. It was only twenty till nine.

He was either a hopeless basket case or the sweetest man she had known since her father died.

At nine-thirty the phone rang. He said, 'Will you ever go out with me again?'

'I thought you'd never call.'

'You will?'

'Sure.'

'Dinner and a movie?' he asked.

'Sounds good.'

'We won't go back to that horrible French place. I'm sorry about that, I really am.'

'I don't care where we go,' she said, 'but once we sit down in the restaurant, promise me we'll *stay* there.'

'I'm a bonehead about some things. And like I said . . . I never have been able to cope around beautiful women.'

'Your mother.'

'That's right. Rejected me. Rejected my father. Never felt *any* warmth from that woman. Walked out on us when I was eleven.'

'Must've hurt.'

'You're more beautiful than she was, and you scare me to death.'

'How flattering.'

'Well, sorry, but I meant it to be. The thing is, beautiful as you are, you're not *half* as beautiful as your writing, and that scares me even more. Because what could a genius like you ever see in a guy like me – except maybe comic relief?'

'Just one question, Daniel.'

'Danny.'

'Just one question, Danny. What the hell kind of stockbroker are you? Any good at all?'

'I'm first-rate,' he said with such genuine pride that she knew he was telling the truth. 'My clients swear by me, and I've got a nice little portfolio of my own that's out-performed the market three years running. As a stock analyst, broker, and investment adviser, I never give the wind a chance to turn my umbrella inside out.'

• 2 •

The afternoon following the placement of the explosives in the basement of the institute, Stefan took what he expected to be his next to last trip on the Lightning Road. It was an illicit jaunt to January 10, 1988, not on the official schedule and conducted without the knowledge of his colleagues.

Light snow was falling in the San Bernardino Mountains when he arrived, but he was dressed for the weather in rubber boots, leather gloves, and navy peacoat. He took cover under a dense copse of pines, intending to wait until the fierce lightning stopped flaring.

He checked his wristwatch in the flickering celestial light and was startled to see how late he had arrived. He had less than forty minutes to reach Laura before she was killed. If he screwed up and arrived too late, there would be no second chance.

Even while the last white flashes seared the overcast sky, while hard crashes of thunder still echoed back to him from distant peaks and ridges, he hurried away from the trees and down a sloping field where the snow was knee-deep from previous winter storms. There was a crust on the snow, through which he kept breaking with each step, and progress was as difficult as if he had been wading through deep water. He fell twice, and snow got down the tops of his boots, and the savage wind tore at him as if it possessed consciousness and the desire to destroy him. By the time he reached the end of the field and climbed over a snowbank onto the two-lane state highway that led to Arrowhead in one direction and Big Bear in the other, his pants and coat were crusted with frozen snow, his feet freezing, and he had lost more than five minutes.

The recently plowed highway was clean except for the wispy snow snakes that slithered across the pavement on shifting currents of air. But already the tempo of the storm had increased. The flakes were much smaller than when he had arrived and were falling twice as fast as they had been minutes ago. Soon the road would be treacherous.

He noticed a sign by the side of the pavement – LAKE ARROWHEAD 1 MILE – and was shocked to discover how much farther he was from Laura than he had expected to be.

Squinting into the wind, looking north, he saw a warm glimmer of electric lighting in the dreary, iron-gray afternoon: a single-story building and parked cars about three hundred yards away, on the right. He headed immediately in that direction, keeping his head tucked down to protect his face from the icy teeth of the wind.

He had to find a car. Laura had less than half an hour to live, and she was ten miles away.

• **3** •

Five months after that first date, on Saturday, July 16, 1977, six weeks after graduating from UCI, Laura married Danny Packard in a civil ceremony before a judge in his chambers. The only guests in attendance, both of whom served as witnesses, were Danny's father, Sam Packard, and Thelma Ackerson.

Sam was a handsome, silver-haired man of about five ten, dwarfed by his son. Throughout the brief ceremony, he wept, and Danny kept turning around and saying, 'You all right, Dad?' Sam nodded and blew his nose and told them to go on with it, but a moment later he was crying again, and Danny was asking him if he was all right, and Sam blew his nose as if imitating the mating calls of geese. The judge said, 'Son, your father's tears are tears of joy, so if we could get on with this – I have three more ceremonies to perform.'

Even if the groom's father had not been an emotional wreck, and even if the groom had not been a giant with the heart of a fawn, their wedding party would have been memorable because of Thelma. Her hair was cut in a strange, shaggy style, with a pompom-like spray in front that was tinted purple. In the middle of summer – and at a wedding, yet – she was wearing red high heels, tight black slacks, and tattered black blouse – carefully, purposefully tattered – gathered at the waist with a length of ordinary steel chain used as a belt. She was wearing exaggerated purple eye makeup, blood-red lipstick, and one earring that looked like a fishhook.

After the ceremony, as Danny was having a private word with his father,

Thelma huddled with Laura in a corner of the courthouse lobby and explained her appearance. 'It's called the punk look, the latest thing in Britain. No one's wearing it over here yet. In fact hardly anyone's wearing it in Britain, either, but in a few years everyone will dress like this. It's great for my act. I look freaky, so people want to laugh as soon as I step on the stage. It's also good for *me*. I mean, face it, Shane, I'm not exactly blossoming with age. Hell, if homely was a disease and had an organized charity, I'd be their poster child. But the two great things about punk style is you get to hide behind flamboyant makeup and hair, so no one can tell just how homely you are – and you're supposed to look weird, anyway. Jesus, Shane, Danny's a big guy. You've told me so much about him on the phone, but you never once said he was so huge. Put him in a Godzilla suit, turn him loose in New York, film the results, and you could make one of those movies without having to build expensive miniature sets. So you love him, huh?'

'I *adore* him,' Laura said. 'He's as gentle as he is big, maybe because of all the violence he saw and was a part of in Vietnam, or maybe because he's always been gentle at heart. He's sweet, Thelma, and he's thoughtful, and he thinks I'm one of the best writers he's ever read.'

'And when he first started giving you toads, you thought he was a psychopath.'

'A minor misjudgment.'

Two uniformed police officers passed through the courthouse lobby, flanking a bearded young man in handcuffs, taking him to one of the courtrooms. The prisoner gave Thelma a looking over as he passed and said, 'Hey, mama, let's get it on!'

'Ah, the Ackerson charm,' Thelma said to Laura. 'You get a guy who's a combination of a Greek god, a teddy bear, and Bennett Cerf, and I get crude propositions from the dregs of society. But come to think of it, I never even used to get that, so maybe my time is coming yet.'

'You underrate yourself, Thelma. You always have. Some very special guy's going to see what a treasure you are—'

'Charles Manson when he's paroled.'

'No. Someday you're going to be every bit as happy as I am. I know it. Destiny, Thelma.'

'Good heavens, Shane, you've become a raging optimist! What about the lightning? All those deep conversations we had on the floor of our room at Caswell – you remember? We decided that life is just an absurdist comedy, and every once in a while it's suddenly interrupted with thunderbolts of tragedy to give the story balance, to make the slapstick seem funnier by comparison.'

'Maybe it's struck for the last time in my life,' Laura said.

Thelma stared hard at her. 'Wow. I know you, Shane, and I know you realize what emotional risk you're putting yourself at by even just *wanting* to be this happy. I hope you're right, kid, and I bet you are. I bet there'll be no more lightning for you.'

'Thank you, Thelma.'

'And I think your Danny is a sweetheart, a jewel. But I'll tell you something that ought to mean a lot more than my opinion: Ruthie would have loved him too; Ruthie would have thought he was perfect.'

They held each other tightly, and for a moment they were young girls again,

defiant yet vulnerable, filled with both the cockeyed confidence and the terror
of blind fate that had shaped their shared adolescence.

———

Sunday, July 24, when they returned from a week-long honeymoon in Santa
Barbara, they went grocery shopping, then cooked dinner together – tossed
salad, sourdough bread, microwave meatballs, and spaghetti – at the apartment
in Tustin. She'd given up her own place and moved in with him a few days
before the wedding. According to the plan that they had worked out, they
would stay at the apartment for two years, maybe three. (They had talked about
their future so often and in such detail that they now capitalized those two
words in their minds – The Plan – as if they were referring to some cosmic
owner's manual that had come with their marriage and that could be relied
upon for an accurate picture of their destiny as husband and wife.) So after two
years, maybe three, they would be able to afford the down payment on the right
house without dipping into the tidy stock portfolio that Danny was building,
and only then would they move.

They dined at the small table in the alcove off the kitchen, where they had a
view of the king palms in the courtyard in the golden late-afternoon sun, and
they discussed the key part of The Plan, which was for Danny to support them
while Laura stayed home to write her first novel. 'When you're wildly rich and
famous,' he said, twirling spaghetti on his fork, 'then I'll leave the brokerage
and spend my time managing our money.'

'What if I'm never rich and famous?'

'You will be.'

'What if I can't even get published?'

'Then I'll divorce you.'

She threw a crust of bread at him. 'Beast.'

'Shrew.'

'You want another meatball?'

'Not if you're going to throw it.'

'My rage has passed. I make good meatballs, don't I?'

'Excellent,' he agreed.

'That's worth celebrating, don't you think – that you have a wife who makes
good meatballs?'

'Definitely worth celebrating.'

'So let's make love.'

Danny said, 'In the middle of dinner?'

'No, in bed.' She pushed back her chair and got up. 'Come on. Dinner can
always be reheated.'

During that first year they made love frequently, and in their intimacies
Laura found more than sexual release, something far more than she had
expected. Being with Danny, holding him within her, she felt so close to him
that at times it almost seemed as if they were one person – one body and one
mind, one spirit, one dream. She loved him wholeheartedly, yes, but that
feeling of oneness was more than love, or at least different from love. By their
first Christmas together, she understood that what she felt was a sense of
belonging not experienced in a long time, a sense of family; for this was her

husband and she was his wife, and one day from their union would come children – after two or three years, according to The Plan – and within the shelter of the family was a peace not to be found elsewhere.

She would have thought that working and living in continuous happiness, harmony, and security day after day would lead to mental lethargy, that her writing would suffer from too much happiness, that she needed a balanced life with down days and miseries to keep the sharp edge on her work. But the idea that an artist needed to suffer to do her best work was a conceit of the young and inexperienced. The happier she grew, the better she wrote.

Six weeks before their first wedding anniversary, Laura finished a novel, *Jericho Nights,* and sent a copy to a New York literary agent, Spencer Keene, who had responded favorably to a query letter a month earlier. Two weeks later Keene called to say he would represent the book, expected a quick sale, and thought she had a splendid future as a novelist. With a swiftness that startled even the agent, he sold it to the first house to which it was submitted, Viking, for a modest but perfectly respectable advance of fifteen thousand dollars, and the deal was concluded on Friday, July 14, 1978, two days before Laura and Danny's anniversary.

• 4 •

The place he had seen from farther up the road was a restaurant and tavern in the shadows of enormous Ponderosa pines. The trees stood over two hundred feet tall, bedecked with clusters of six-inch cones, with beautifully fissured bark, some boughs bent low under the weight of snow from previous storms. The single-story building was made of logs; it was so sheltered by trees on three sides that its slate roof was covered with more pine needles than snow. The windows were either steamed over or frosted, and the light from within was pleasingly diffused by that translucent film on the glass.

In the parking lot in front of the building were two Jeep wagons, two pickup trucks, and a Thunderbird. Relieved that no one would be able to see him through the tavern windows, Stefan went directly to one of the Jeeps, tried the door, found it unlocked, and got in behind the steering wheel, closing the door after him.

He drew the Walther PPK/S .380 from the shoulder holster he was wearing inside his peacoat. He put it on the seat at his side.

His feet were painfully cold, and he wanted to pause and empty the snow out of his boots. But he had arrived late, and his original schedule was shot, so he dared not waste a minute. Besides, if his feet hurt, they weren't frozen; he wasn't in danger of frostbite yet.

The keys were not in the ignition. He slid the seat back, bent down, groped under the dashboard, located the ignition wires, and had the engine running in a minute.

Stefan sat up just as the owner of the Jeep, breath reeking of beer, pulled open the door. 'Hey, what the hell you doing, pal?'

The rest of the snowswept parking lot was still deserted. They were alone.

Laura would be dead in twenty-five minutes.

The Jeep's owner reached for him, and he allowed himself to be dragged from behind the steering wheel, plucking his pistol off the seat as he went, and in fact he threw himself into the other man's grasp, using the momentum to send his adversary staggering backward on the slippery parking lot. They fell. As they hit the ground, he was on top, and he jammed the muzzle under the guy's chin.

'Jesus, mister! Don't kill me.'

'We're getting up now. Easy, damn you, no sudden moves.'

When they were on their feet Stefan moved behind the guy, quickly reversed his grip on the Walther, used it as a club, struck once, hard enough to knock the man unconscious without doing permanent damage. The owner of the Jeep went down again, stayed down, limp.

Stefan glanced at the tavern. No one else had come out.

He could hear no traffic approaching on the road, but then again the howling wind might mask the sound of an engine.

As the snow began to fall harder, he put the pistol in the deep pocket of his peacoat and dragged the unconscious man to the nearest other vehicle, the Thunderbird. It was unlocked, and he heaved the guy into the rear seat, closed the door, and hurried back to the Jeep.

The engine had died. He hot-wired it again.

As he put the Jeep in gear and swung it around toward the road, the wind shrieked at the window beside him. The falling snow grew denser, blizzard-thick, and clouds of yesterday's snow were whipped up from the ground and spun in sparkling columns. The giant, shadow-swaddled pines swayed and shuddered under winter's assault.

Laura had little more than twenty minutes to live.

• 5 •

They celebrated the publishing contract for *Jericho Nights* and the otherworldly harmony of their first year of marriage by spending their anniversary at a favorite place – Disneyland. The sky was blue, cloudless; the air was dry and hot. Virtually oblivious of the summer crowds, they rode the Pirates of the Caribbean, had their pictures taken with Mickey Mouse, got dizzy spinning in the Mad Hatter's teacups, had their portraits drawn by a caricaturist, ate hot dogs and ice cream and chocolate-covered frozen bananas on sticks, and danced that evening to a Dixieland band in New Orleans Square.

The park became even more magical after nightfall, and they rode the Mark Twain paddlewheel steamboat around Tom Sawyer's Island for the third time, standing at the railing on the top level, near the bow, with their arms around each other. Danny said, 'You know why we like this place so much? 'Cause it's of the world yet untainted *by* the world. And that's our marriage.'

Later, over strawberry sundaes at the Carnation Pavilion, at a table beneath trees strung with white Christmas lights, Laura said, 'Fifteen thousand bucks for a year's work . . . not exactly a fortune.'

'It isn't slave wages either.' He pushed his sundae aside, leaned forward, slid her sundae aside, too, and took her hands across the table. 'The money will come eventually because you're brilliant, but money isn't what I care about. What I care about is that you've got something special to share. No. That's not exactly what I mean. You don't just *have* something special, you *are* something special. In some way I understand but can't explain, I know that what you *are*, when shared, will bring as much hope and joy to people in far places as it brings to me here at your side.'

Blinking away sudden tears, she said, 'I love you.'

Jericho Nights was published ten months later, in May of 1979. Danny insisted she use her maiden name because he knew that through all the bad years in McIlroy Home and Caswell Hall, she had endured in part because she wanted to grow up and make something of herself as a testament to her father and perhaps, as well, to the mother she had never known. The book sold few copies, was not chosen by any book clubs, and was licensed by Viking to a paperback publisher for a small advance.

'Doesn't matter,' Danny told her. 'It'll come in time. It'll all come in time. Because of what you *are*.'

By then she was deep into her second novel, *Shadrach*. Working ten hours a day, six days a week, she finished it that July.

On a Friday she sent one copy to Spencer Keene in New York and gave the original script to Danny. He was the first to read it. He left work early and began reading at one o'clock Friday afternoon in his living-room armchair, then shifted to the bedroom, slept only four hours, and by ten o'clock Saturday morning he was back in the armchair and two-thirds of the way through the script. He would not talk about it, not a word. 'Not until I'm done. It wouldn't be fair to you to start analyzing and reacting until I've finished, until I've grasped your entire pattern, and it wouldn't be fair to me, either, because in discussing it you're sure to give away some plot turn or other.'

She kept peeking at him to see if he was frowning, smiling, or responding to the story in any way, and even when he was reacting she worried that it was the *wrong* reaction to whatever scene he might be reading. By ten-thirty Saturday, she couldn't bear to stay around the apartment any longer, so she drove to South Coast Plaza, browsed in bookstores, ate an early lunch though she was not hungry, drove to the Westminster Mall, window-shopped, ate a cone of frozen yogurt, drove to the Orange Mall, looked in a few shops, bought a square of fudge and ate half of it. 'Shane,' she told herself, 'go home, or you'll be a double for Orson Welles by dinnertime.'

As she parked in the carport at the apartment complex, she saw that Danny's car was gone. When she let herself into the apartment, she called his name but got no answer.

The script of *Shadrach* was piled on the dinette table.

She looked for a note. There was none.

'Oh, God,' she said.

The book was bad. It stank. It reeked. It was mule puke. Poor Danny had gone out somewhere to have a beer and find the courage to tell her that she should study plumbing while she was still young enough to get launched on a new career.

She was going to throw up. She hurried to the bathroom, but the nausea passed. She washed her face with cold water.

The book was mule puke.

Okay, she would just have to live with that. She'd thought *Shadrach* was pretty good, better than *Jericho Nights* by a mile, but evidently she had been wrong. So she would write another book.

She went to the kitchen and opened a Coors. She had taken only two swallows when Danny came home with a gift-wrapped box about the right size to hold a basketball. He put it on the dinette table beside the manuscript, looked at her solemnly. 'It's for you.'

Ignoring the box, she said, 'Tell me.'

'Open your gift first.'

'Oh, God, is it *that* bad? Is it so bad you have to soften the blow with a gift? Tell me. I can take it. Wait! Let me sit down.' She pulled out a chair from the table and dropped into it. 'Hit me with your best, big guy. I'm a survivor.'

'You've got too strong a sense of drama, Laura.'

'What're you saying? The book's melodramatic?'

'Not the book. You. Right now, anyway. Will you for God's sake stop being the shattered young artiste and open your gift?'

'All right, all right, if I've got to open the gift before you'll talk, then I'll open the bloody gift.'

She put the box in her lap – it was heavy – and tore at the ribbon while Danny pulled up a chair and sat in front of her, watching.

The box was from an expensive shop, but she was not prepared for the contents: a large, gorgeous Lalique bowl; it was clear except for two handles that were partly clear green and partly frosted crystal; each handle was formed by two leaping toads, four toads altogether.

She looked up, wide-eyed. 'Danny, I've never seen anything like this. It's the most beautiful piece ever.'

'Like it, then?'

'Good God, how much was it?'

'Three thousand.'

'Danny, we can't afford this!'

'Oh, yes, we can.'

'No, we can't, really we can't. Just because I wrote a lousy book and you want to make me feel better—'

'You didn't write a lousy book. You wrote a toad-worthy book. A *four*-toad book on a scale of one to four, four being the best. We can afford that bowl precisely because you wrote *Shadrach*. This book is beautiful, Laura, infinitely better than the last one, and it's beautiful because it's you. This book is what you *are*, and it shines.'

In her excitement and in her eagerness to hug him, she nearly dropped the three-thousand-dollar bowl.

• 6 •

A skin of new snow covered the highway now. The Jeep wagon had four-wheel drive and was equipped with tire chains, so Stefan was able to make reasonably good time in spite of the road conditions.

But not good enough.

He estimated that the tavern, where he had stolen the Jeep, was about eleven miles from the Packard house, which was just off state route 330 a few miles south of Big Bear. The mountain roads were narrow, twisty, full of dramatic rises and falls, and blowing snow ensured poor visibility, so his average speed was about forty miles an hour. He could not risk driving faster or more recklessly, for he would be of no use at all to Laura, Danny, and Chris if he lost control of the Jeep and plunged over an embankment to his death. At his current speed, however, he would arrive at their place at least ten minutes after they had left.

His intention had been to delay them at their house until the danger had passed. That plan was no longer viable.

The January sky seemed to have sunk so low under the weight of the storm that it was no higher than the tops of the serried ranks of massive evergreens that flanked both sides of the roadway. Wind shook the trees and hammered the Jeep. Snow stuck to the windshield wipers and became ice, so he turned up the defroster and hunched over the wheel, squinting through the inadequately cleaned glass.

When he next glanced at his watch, he saw that he had less than fifteen minutes. Laura, Danny, and Chris would be getting into their Chevy Blazer. They might even be pulling out of their driveway already.

He would have to intercept them on the highway, scant seconds ahead of Death.

He tried to squeeze slightly more speed out of the Jeep without shooting wide of a turn and into an abyss.

• 7 •

Five weeks after the day that Danny bought her the Lalique bowl, on August 15, 1979, a few minutes after noon, Laura was in the kitchen, heating a can of chicken soup for lunch, when she got a call from Spencer Keene, her literary agent in New York. Viking loved *Shadrach* and were offering a hundred thousand.

'*Dollars?*' she asked.

'Of course, dollars,' Spencer said. 'What do you think, Russian rubles? What would that buy you – a hat maybe?'

'Oh, God.' She had to lean against the kitchen counter because suddenly her legs were weak.

Spencer said, 'Laura, honey, only you can know what's best for you, but unless they're willing to let the hundred grand stand for a floor bid in an auction, I want you to consider turning this down.'

'Turn down a hundred thousand dollars?' she asked in disbelief.

'I want to send this out to maybe six or eight houses, set an auction date, see what happens. I think I *know* what will happen, Laura, I think they'll all love this book as much as I do. On the other hand . . . maybe not. It's a hard decision, and you've got to go away and think about it before you answer me.'

The moment Spencer said goodbye and hung up, Laura dialed Danny at work and told him about the offer.

He said, 'If they won't make it a floor bid, turn it down.'

'But, Danny, can we afford to? I mean, my car is eleven years old and falling apart. Yours is almost four years old—'

'Listen, what did I tell you about this book? Didn't I tell you that it was *you*, a reflection of what you are?'

'You're sweet, but—'

'Turn it down. Listen, Laura. You're thinking that scorning a hundred K is like spitting in the faces of all the gods of good fortune; it's like inviting that lightning you've spoken about. But you *earned* this payoff, and fate isn't going to cheat you out of it.'

She called Spencer Keene and told him her decision.

Excited, nervous, already missing the hundred thousand dollars, she returned to the den and sat at her typewriter and stared at the unfinished short story for a while until she became aware of the odor of chicken soup and remembered she had left it on the stove. She hurried into the kitchen and found that all but half an inch of soup had boiled away; burnt noodles were stuck to the bottom of the pot.

At two-ten, which was five-ten New York time, Spencer called again to say that Viking had agreed to let the hundred thousand stand as a floor bid. 'Now, that's the very least you make from *Shadrach* – a hundred grand. I think I'll set September twenty-sixth as the auction date. It's going to be a big one, Laura. I feel it.'

She spent the remainder of the afternoon trying to be elated but unable to shake off her anxiety. *Shadrach* was already a big success, no matter what happened in the auction. She had no reason for her anxiety, but it held her in a tight grip.

Danny came home from work that day with a bottle of champagne, a bouquet of roses, and a box of Godiva chocolates. They sat on the sofa, nibbling chocolates, sipping champagne, and talking about the future, which seemed entirely bright; yet her anxiety lingered.

Finally she said, 'I don't want chocolates or champagne or roses or a hundred thousand dollars. I want you. Take me to bed.'

They made love for a long time. The late summer sun ebbed from the windows and the tide of night rolled in before they parted with a sweet, aching reluctance. Lying at her side in the darkness, Danny tenderly kissed her breasts, her throat, her eyes, and finally her lips. She realized that her anxiety had at last faded. It was not sexual release that expelled her fear. Intimacy, total surrender of self, and the sense of shared hopes and dreams and destinies had been the true medicines; the great, good feeling of *family* that she had with him was a talisman that effectively warded off cold fate.

———————

On Wednesday, September 26, Danny took the day off from work to be at Laura's side as the news came in from New York.

At seven-thirty in the morning, ten-thirty New York time, Spencer Keene called to report that Random House had made the first offer above the auction floor. 'One hundred and twenty-five thousand, and we're on our way.'

Two hours later Spencer called again. 'Everyone's off to lunch, so there'll be a lull. Right now, we're up to three hundred and fifty thousand and six houses are still in the bidding.'

'Three hundred and fifty thousand?' Laura repeated.

At the kitchen sink where he was rinsing the breakfast dishes, Danny dropped a plate.

When she hung up and looked at Danny, he grinned and said, 'Am I mistaken, or is this the book you were afraid might be mule puke?'

Four and a half hours later, as they were sitting at the dinette table pretending to be concentrating on a game of five-hundred rummy, their inattention betrayed by their mutual inability to keep score with any degree of mathematical accuracy whatsoever, Spencer Keene called again. Danny followed her into the kitchen to listen to her side of the conversation.

Spencer said, 'You sitting down, honey?'

'I'm ready, Spencer. I don't need a chair. Tell me.'

'It's over. Simon and Schuster. One million, two hundred and twenty-five thousand dollars.'

Weak with shock, shaky, she spoke with Spencer for another ten minutes, and when she hung up, she wasn't sure of a thing that had been said after he had told her the price. Danny was staring at her expectantly, and she realized that he didn't know what had happened. She told him the name of the buyer and the figure.

For a moment they stared at each other in silence.

Then she said, 'I think maybe now we can afford to have a baby.'

• 8 •

Stefan topped a hill and peered ahead at the half-mile stretch of snowswept road on which it would happen. On his left, beyond the southbound lane, the tree-covered mountainside sloped steeply down to the highway. On his right the northbound lane was edged by a soft shoulder only about four feet wide, beyond which the mountainside fell away again into a deep gorge. No guardrails protected travelers from that deadly drop-off.

At the bottom of the slope, the road turned left, out of sight. Between that turn below and the crest of the hill, which he had just topped, the two-lane blacktop was deserted.

According to his watch, Laura would be dead in a minute. Two minutes at most.

He suddenly realized that he should never have tried to drive toward the Packards, not after he had arrived so late. Instead he should have given up the idea of stopping the Packards and should have tried instead to identify and stop the Robertsons' vehicle farther back on the road to Arrowhead. That would have worked just as well.

Too late now.

Stefan had no time to go back, nor could he risk driving farther north toward the Packards. He did not know the exact moment of their deaths, not to the second, but that catastrophe was now approaching swiftly. If he tried to go even another half mile and stop them before they arrived at this fateful incline, he might reach the bottom of the slope and, in taking the turn, pass them going the other way, at which point he would not be able to swing around and catch up with them and stop them before the Robertsons' truck hit them head-on.

He braked gently and angled across the ascending southbound lane, stopping the Jeep on a wide portion of that shoulder of the road about halfway down the slope, so close to the embankment that he could not get out of the driver's door. His heart was thudding almost painfully as he shifted the Jeep into park, put on the emergency brake, cut the engine, slid across the seat, and got out the passenger-side door.

The blowing snow and icy air stung his face, and all along the mountainside the wind shrieked and howled like many voices, perhaps the voices of the three sisters of Greek myth, the Fates, mocking him for his desperate attempt to prevent what they had ordained.

• 9 •

After receiving editorial suggestions, Laura undertook an easy revision of *Shadrach*, delivering the final version of the script in mid-December, 1979, and Simon and Schuster scheduled the book for publication in September, 1980.

It was such a busy year for Laura and Danny that she was only peripherally aware of the Iranian hostage crisis and presidential campaign, and even more vaguely cognizant of the countless fires, plane crashes, toxic spills, mass murders, floods, earthquakes, and other tragedies that constituted the news. That was the year the rabbit died. That was the year she and Danny bought their first house – a four-bedroom, two-and-a-half-bath, Spanish model in Orange Park Acres – and moved out of the apartment in Tustin. She started her third novel, *The Golden Edge*, and one day when Danny asked her how it was going, she said, 'Mule puke,' and he said, 'That's great!' The first of September, upon receipt of a substantial check for the film rights to *Shadrach*, which had sold to MGM, Danny quit his job at the brokerage house and became her full-time financial manager. On Sunday, September 21, three weeks after it arrived in the stores, *Shadrach* appeared on the *New York Times* bestseller list at number twelve. On October 5, 1980, when Laura gave birth to Christopher Robert Packard, *Shadrach* was in a third printing, sitting comfortably at number eight on the *Times*, and received what Spencer Keene called a 'thunderously good' review on page five of that same book section.

The boy entered the world at 2:23 P.M. in a greater rush of blood than that which usually carried babies out of their prenatal darkness. Pain-racked and hemorrhaging, Laura required three pints during the afternoon and evening. She spent a better night than expected, however, and by morning she was sore, weary, but well out of danger.

The following day during visiting hours, Thelma Ackerson came to see the baby and the new mother. Still dressed punkish and ahead of her time – hair long on the left side of her head, with a white streak like the bride of Frankenstein, and short on the right side, with no streak – she breezed into Laura's private room, went straight to Danny, threw her arms around him, hugged him hard, and said, 'God, you're big. You're a mutant. Admit it, Packard, your mother might have been human, but your father was a grizzly bear.' She came to the bed where Laura was propped up against three pillows, kissed her on the forehead and then on the cheek. 'I went to the nursery before I came here, had a peek at Christopher Robert through the glass, and he's adorable. But I think you're going to need all the millions you can make from your books, kiddo, because that boy is going to take after his father, and your food bill's going to run thirty thousand a month. Until you get him housebroken, he'll be eating your furniture.'

Laura said, 'I'm glad you came, Thelma.'

'Would I miss it? Maybe if I was playing a Mafia-owned club in Bayonne,

New Jersey, and had to cancel out part of a date to fly back, maybe *then* I'd miss it because if you break a contract with those guys they cut off your thumbs and make you use them as suppositories. But I was west of the Mississippi when I got the news last night, and only nuclear war or a date with Paul McCartney could keep me away.'

Almost two years ago Thelma had finally gotten time on the stage at the Improv, and she'd been a hit. She landed an agent and began to get paid bookings in sleazy, third-rate – and eventually second-rate – clubs across the country. Laura and Danny had driven into Los Angeles twice to see her perform, and she had been hilarious; she wrote her own material and delivered it with the comic timing she had possessed since childhood but had honed in the intervening years. Her act had one unusual aspect that would either make her a national phenomenon or ensure her obscurity: Woven through the jokes was a strong thread of melancholy, a sense of the tragedy of life that existed simultaneously with the wonder and humor of it. In fact it was similar to the tone of Laura's novels, but what appealed to book readers was less likely to appeal to audiences who had paid for belly laughs.

Now Thelma leaned across the bed railing, peered closely at Laura and said, 'Hey, you look pale. And those rings around your eyes . . .'

'Thelma, dear, I hate to shatter your illusions, but a baby isn't really brought by the stork. The mother has to expel it from her own womb, and it's a tight fit.'

Thelma stared hard at her, then directed an equally hard stare at Danny, who had come around the other side of the bed to hold Laura's hand. 'What's wrong here?'

Laura sighed and, wincing with discomfort, shifted her position slightly. To Danny, she said, 'See? I told you she's a bloodhound.'

'It wasn't an easy pregnancy, was it?' Thelma demanded.

'The pregnancy was easy enough,' Laura said. 'It was the delivery that was the problem.'

'You didn't . . . almost die or anything, Shane?'

'No, no, no,' Laura said, and Danny's hand tightened on hers. 'Nothing that dramatic. We knew from the start there were going to be some difficulties along the way, but we found the best doctor, and he kept a close watch. It's just . . . I won't be able to have any more. Christopher will be our last.'

Thelma looked at Danny, at Laura, and said quietly, 'I'm sorry.'

'It's all right,' Laura said, forcing a smile. 'We have little Chris, and he's beautiful.'

They endured an awkward silence, and then Danny said, 'I haven't had lunch yet, and I'm starved. I'm going to slip down to the coffee shop for a half hour or so.'

When Danny left, Thelma said, 'He's not really hungry, is he? He just knew we wanted a girl-to-girl talk.'

Laura smiled. 'He's a lovely man.'

Thelma put down the railing on one side of the bed and said, 'If I hop up here and sit beside you, I won't shake up your insides, will I? You won't suddenly bleed all over me, will you, Shane?'

'I'll try not to.'

Thelma eased up onto the high hospital bed. She took one of Laura's hands in both of hers. 'Listen, I read *Shadrach*, and it's damned good. It's what all writers try to do and seldom achieve.'

'You're sweet.'

'I'm a tough, cynical, hard-nosed broad. Listen, I'm serious about the book. It's brilliant. And I saw Bovine Bowmaine in there, and Tammy. And Boone, the child-welfare psychologist. Different names but I saw them. You've captured them perfectly, Shane. God, there were times you brought it all back, times when chills ran up and down my back so bad I had to put down the book and go for a walk in the sun. And there were times when I laughed like a loon.'

Laura ached in every muscle, in every joint. She did not have the strength to lean away from the pillows and put her arms around her friend. She just said, 'I love you, Thelma.'

'The Eel wasn't there, of course.'

'I'm saving him for another book.'

'And me, damn it. I'm not in the book, though I'm the most colorful character you've ever known!'

'I'm saving you for a book all your own,' Laura said.

'You mean it, don't you?'

'Yes. Not the one I'm working on now but the one after it.'

'Listen, Shane, you better make me *gorgeous*, or I'll sue your ass off. You hear me?'

'I hear you.'

Thelma chewed her lip, then said, 'Will you—'

'Yes. I'm going to put Ruthie in it too.'

They were silent a while, just holding hands.

Unshed tears clouded Laura's vision, but she saw that Thelma was blinking back tears too. 'Don't. It'll streak all that elaborate punk eye makeup.'

Thelma raised one of her feet. 'Are these boots freaky or what? Black leather, pointy toes, stud-ringed heels. Makes me look like a damned dominatrix, doesn't it?'

'When you walked in, the first thing I wondered was how many men you've whipped lately.'

Thelma sighed and sniffed hard to clear her nose. 'Shane, listen and listen good. This talent of yours is maybe more precious than you think. You're able to capture people's lives on the page, and when the people are gone, the page is still there, the life is still *there*. You can put feelings on the page, and anyone, anywhere, can pick up that book and *feel* those same feelings, you can touch the heart, you can remind us what it means to be human in a world that's increasingly bent on forgetting. That's talent and a reason to live that's more than most people ever have. So . . . well, I know how much you want to have a family . . . three or four kids, you've said . . . so I know how bad you must be hurting right now. But you've got Danny and Christopher and this amazing talent, and that's so very much to have.'

Laura's voice was unsteady. 'Sometimes . . . I'm just so afraid.'

'Afraid of what, baby?'

'I wanted a big family because . . . then it's less likely they'll all be taken away from me.'

'Nobody's going to be taken away from you.'

'With just Danny and little Chris . . . just two of them . . . something might happen.'

'Nothing will happen.'

'Then I'd be alone.'

'Nothing will happen,' Thelma repeated.

'Something always seems to happen. That's life.'

Thelma slid farther onto the bed, stretched out beside Laura, and put her head against Laura's shoulder. 'When you said it was a hard birth . . . and the way you look, so pale . . . I was scared. I have friends in LA, sure, but all of them are show-biz types. You're the only *real* person I'm close to, even though we don't see each other that much, and the idea that you might have nearly . . .'

'But I didn't.'

'Might've, though.' Thelma laughed sourly. 'Hell, Shane, once an orphan, always an orphan, huh?'

Laura held her and stroked her hair.

Shortly after Chris's first birthday, Laura delivered *The Golden Edge*. It was published ten months later, and by the boy's second birthday, the book was number one on the *Times* bestseller list, which was a first for her.

Danny managed Laura's book income with such diligence, caution, and brilliance that within a few years, in spite of the savage bite of income taxes, they would be not just rich – they were already rich by most standards – but seriously rich. She didn't know what she thought about that. She had never expected to be rich. When she considered her enviable circumstances, she thought perhaps she should be thrilled or, given the want of much of the world, appalled, but she felt nothing much one way or the other about the money. The security that money provided was welcome; it inspired confidence. But they had no plans to move out of their quite pleasant four-bedroom house, though they could have afforded an estate. The money was *there*, and that was the end of it; she gave it little thought. Life was not money; life was Danny and Chris and, to a lesser extent, her books.

With a toddler in the house, she no longer had the ability or desire to work sixty hours a week at her word processor. Chris was talking, walking, and he exhibited none of the moodiness or mindless rebellion that the child-rearing books described as normal behavior for the year between two and three. Mostly he was a pleasure to be with, a bright and inquisitive boy. She spent as much time with him as she could without risk of spoiling him.

The Amazing Appleby Twins, her fourth novel, was not published until October, 1984, two years after the *The Golden Edge*, but there was none of the drop-off in audience that is sometimes the case when a writer does not publish a book each year. The advance sales were her biggest yet.

On October first, she was sitting with Danny and Chris on the sofa in the family room, watching old Road Runner cartoons on the VCR – 'Vooom, vooom!' Christopher said each time Road Runner took off in a flash of speed – eating popcorn, when Thelma called from Chicago, in tears. Laura took the call on the kitchen phone, but on the TV in the adjoining room the beleaguered coyote was trying to blow up his nemesis and was blowing himself up instead, so Laura said, 'Danny, I better take this in the den.'

In the four years since Chris was born, Thelma's career had gone straight up. She had been booked in a couple of Vegas casino lounges. ('Hey, Shane, I must be pretty good because the cocktail waitresses are nearly naked, all boobs and butts, and sometimes the guys in the audience actually look at me instead of them. On the other hand maybe I only appeal to fags.') In the past year she had moved into the main showroom at the MGM Grand as an opening act for Dean Martin, and she had made four appearances on the *Tonight* show with Johnny Carson. There was talk of a movie or even a television series to be built around her, and she seemed poised for stardom as a comedienne. Now she was in Chicago, opening soon as the headliner at a major club.

Perhaps the long chain of positive developments in their lives was what panicked Laura when she heard Thelma crying. For some time she had been waiting for the sky to fall with a horrid suddenness that would have caught Chicken Little unaware. She dropped into the chair behind the desk in the den, snatched up the phone. 'Thelma? What is it, what's wrong?'

'I just read . . . the new book.'

Laura could not figure what in *The Amazing Appleby Twins* could have affected Thelma so profoundly, and then she suddenly wondered if something in the characterization of Carrie and Sandra Appleby had offended. Though none of the major events in the story mirrored those in the lives of Ruthie and Thelma, the Applebys were, of course, based on the Ackersons. But both characters had been drawn with great love and good humor; surely there was nothing about them that would offend Thelma, and in panic Laura tried to say as much.

'No, no, Shane, you hopeless fool,' Thelma said between bouts of tears. 'I'm not offended. The reason I can't stop crying is because you did the most wonderful thing. Carrie Appleby is Ruthie as sure as I ever knew her, but in your book you let Ruthie live a long time. You let Ruthie live, Shane, and that's a whole hell of a lot better job than God did in real life.'

They talked for an hour, mostly about Ruthie, reminiscing, not with a lot of tears, now, but mostly with affection. Danny and Chris appeared in the open doorway of the den a couple of times, looking abandoned, and Laura blew them kisses, but she stayed on the telephone with Thelma because it was one of those rare times when remembering the dead was more important than tending to the needs of the living.

Two weeks before Christmas, 1985, when Chris was five and then some, the southern California rainy season started with a downpour that made palm fronds rattle like bones, battered the last remaining blossoms off the impatiens, and flooded streets. Chris could not play outside. His father was off inspecting a potential real estate investment, and the boy was in no mood to entertain himself. He kept finding excuses to bother Laura in her office, and by eleven o'clock she gave up trying to work on the current book. She sent him to the kitchen to get the baking sheets out of the cupboard, promising to let him help her make chocolate-chip cookies.

Before joining him, she got Sir Tommy Toad's webbed-foot boots, tiny umbrella, and miniature scarf from the dresser drawer in the bedroom, where she had been keeping them for just such a day as this. On her way to the kitchen she arranged those items near the front door.

Later, as she was slipping a tray of cookies into the oven, she sent him to the front door to see if the United Parcel deliveryman had left a package that she professed to be expecting, and Chris came back flushed with excitement. 'Mommy, come look, come see.'

In the foyer he showed her the three miniature items, and she said, 'I suppose they belong to Sir Tommy. Oh, did I forget to tell you about the lodger we've taken in? A fine, upstanding toad from England here on the queen's business.'

She had been eight when her father had invented Sir Tommy, and she had accepted the fabulous toad as a fun fantasy, but Chris was only five and took it more seriously. 'Where's he going to sleep – the spare bedroom? Then what do we do when Grandpa comes to visit?'

'We've rented Sir Tommy a room in the attic,' Laura said, 'and we must not disturb him or tell anyone about him except Daddy because Sir Tommy is here on *secret* business for Her Majesty.'

He looked at her wide-eyed, and she wanted to laugh but dared not. He had brown hair and eyes, like she and Danny, but his features were delicate, more his mother's than his father's. In spite of his smallness there was something about him that made her think he would eventually shoot up to be tall and solidly constructed like Danny. He leaned close and whispered: 'Is Sir Tommy a *spy?*'

Throughout the afternoon, as they baked cookies, cleaned up, and played a few games of Old Maid, Chris was full of questions about Sir Tommy. Laura discovered that tale-telling for children was in some ways more demanding than writing novels for adults.

When Danny came home at four-thirty, he shouted a greeting on his way along the hall from the connecting door to the garage.

Chris jumped up from the breakfast-nook table, where he and Laura were playing cards, and urgently shushed his father. 'Sssshhh, Daddy, Sir Tommy might be sleeping now, he had a long trip, he's the Queen of England, and he's spying in our attic!'

Danny frowned. 'I go away from home for just a few hours, and while I'm gone we've invaded by scaly, transvestite, British spies?'

That night in bed, after Laura made love with a special passion that surprised even her, Danny said, 'What's gotten into you today? All evening you were so . . . buoyant, so up.'

Snuggling against him under the covers, enjoying the feel of his nude body against hers, she said, 'Oh, I don't know, it's just that I'm *alive*, and Chris is alive, you're alive, we're all together. And it's this Tommy Toad thing.'

'It tickles you?'

'Tickles me, yes. But it's more than that. It's . . . well, somehow it makes me feel that life goes on, that it always goes on, the cycle is renewed – does this sound crazy? – and that life is going to go on for us, too, for all of us, for a long time.'

'Well, yeah, I think you're right,' he said. 'Unless you're that energetic *every* time you make love from now on, in which case you'll kill me in about three months.'

In October, 1986, when Chris turned six, Laura's fifth novel, *Endless River*, was published to critical acclaim and bigger sales than any of her previous titles. Her editor had predicted the greater success: 'It's got all the humor, all the tension, all the tragedy, that whole weird mix of a Laura Shane novel, but it's somehow not as *dark* as the others, and that makes it especially appealing.'

For two years, Laura and Danny had been taking Chris up to the San Bernardino Mountains at least one weekend a month, to Lake Arrowhead and Big Bear, both during the summer and winter, to make sure he learned that the whole world was not like the pleasant but thoroughly urbanized and sub-urbanized realms of Orange County. With the continued flowering of her career and the success of Danny's investment strategies, and considering her recent willingness not only to entertain optimism but to *live* it, they decided it was time to indulge themselves, so they bought a second home in the mountains.

It was an eleven-room stone and redwood place on thirty acres just off state route 330, a few miles south of Big Bear. It was, in fact, a more expensive house than the one they lived in during the week in Orange Park Acres. The property was mostly covered with western juniper, Ponderosa pine, and sugar pine, and their nearest neighbor was far beyond sight. During their first weekend at the retreat, as they were making a snowman, three deer appeared at the edge of the looming forest, twenty yards away, and watched curiously.

Chris was thrilled at the sight of the deer, and by the time he had been tucked in bed that night, he was sure that they were Santa Claus's deer. *This* was where the jolly fat man went after Christmas, he insisted, and not, as legend had it, to the North Pole.

Wind and Stars appeared in October of '87, and it was a still bigger hit than any of her previous books. The movie of *Endless River* was released that Thanksgiving, enjoying the biggest opening-week box office of any film that year.

On Friday, January 8, 1988, buoyed by the knowledge that *Wind and Stars* would hold the number one spot on the *Times* list that Sunday for the fifth week in a row, they drove up to Big Bear in the afternoon, as soon as Chris came home from school. The following Tuesday was Laura's thirty-third birthday, and they intended to have an early celebration, just the three of them, high in the mountains, with the snow like icing on a cake and the wind to sing for her.

Accustomed to them, the deer ventured within twenty feet of their house on Saturday morning. But Chris was seven now, and in school he heard the rumor that Santa Claus was not real, and he was no longer so sure that these were more than ordinary deer.

The weekend was perfect, perhaps the best they had spent in the mountains, but they had to cut it short. They had intended to leave at six o'clock Monday morning, returning to Orange County in time to deliver Chris to school. How-ever a major storm moved into the area ahead of schedule late Sunday after-noon, and though they were little more than ninety minutes from the balmy temperatures nearer the coast, the weather report called for two feet of new snow by morning. Not wanting to risk being snowbound and causing Chris to miss a day of school – a possibility even with their four-wheel-drive Blazer – they closed up the big stone and redwood house and headed south on state route 330 at a few minutes past four o'clock.

Southern California was one of the few places in the world where you could drive from a winterscape to subtropical heat in less than two hours, and Laura always enjoyed – and marveled at – the journey. The three of them were dressed for snow – wool socks, boots, thermal underwear, heavy slacks, warm sweaters, ski jackets – but in an hour and a quarter they would be in milder climes where no one was bundled up, and in two hours they would be in shirtsleeve weather.

Laura drove while Danny, sitting in front, and Chris, sitting behind him, played a word-association game that they had devised on previous trips to amuse themselves. Rapidly falling snow found even those sections of the highway that were largely protected by trees on both sides, and in unsheltered areas the hard-driven flakes sheeted and whirled by the millions in the capricious currents of the high-mountain winds, sometimes half obscuring the way ahead. She drove with caution, not caring if the two-hour drive home required three hours or four; since they had left early, they had plenty of time to spare, all the time in the world.

When she came out of the big curve a few miles south of their house and entered the half-mile incline, she saw a red Jeep station wagon parked on the right shoulder and a man in a navy peacoat in the middle of the road. He was coming down the hill, waving both arms to halt them.

Leaning forward and squinting between the thumping windshield wipers, Danny said, 'Looks like he broke down, needs help.'

'Packard's Patrol to the rescue!' Chris said from the back seat.

As Laura slowed, the guy on the road began frantically gesturing for them to pull to the right shoulder.

Danny said uneasily, 'Something odd about him. . . .'

Yes, odd indeed. He was her special guardian. The sight of him after all these years shocked and frightened Laura.

• 10 •

He had just gotten out of the stolen Jeep when the Blazer turned the bend at the bottom of the hill. As he rushed toward it, he saw Laura slow the Blazer to a crawl a third of the way up the slope, but she was still in the middle of the roadway, so he signaled her more frantically to get off onto the shoulder, as close to the embankment as possible. At first she continued to creep forward, as if unsure whether he was only a motorist in trouble or dangerous, but when they drew close enough to each other for her to see his face and perhaps recognize him, she immediately obeyed.

As she accelerated past him and whipped the Blazer onto the wider portion of the shoulder, only twenty feet downhill from Stefan's Jeep, he reversed direction and ran to her, yanked open her door. 'I don't know if being off the road's good enough. Get out, up the embankment, quickly, *now!*'

Danny said, 'Hey, wait just—'

'Do what he says!' Laura shouted. 'Chris, come on, get out!'

Stefan gripped Laura's hand and helped her out of the driver's seat. As Danny and Chris also scrambled from the Blazer, Stefan heard a laboring engine above the skirling wind. He looked up the long hill and saw that a big pickup truck had topped the crest and was starting down toward them. Pulling Laura after him, he ran around the front of the Blazer.

Her guardian said, 'Up the embankment, come on,' and began to climb the hard-packed, ice-crusted snow that had been shoved there by plows and that sloped steeply toward the nearby trees.

Laura looked up the highway and saw the truck, a quarter-mile from them and only a hundred feet below the crest, beginning a long, sickening slide on the treacherous pavement until it was coming sideways down the road. If they had not stopped, if her guardian had not delayed them, they would have been just below the crest when the truck went out of control; already they would have been hit.

Beside her, with Chris riding him piggyback and holding on tight, Danny obviously had seen the danger. The truck might come all the way down the hill without the driver in control, might slam into the Jeep and Blazer. Lugging Chris, he scrambled up the snow-packed embankment, yelling for Laura to *move*.

She climbed, grabbing for handholds, kicking footholds as she went. The snow was not only ice-mantled but ice-marbled and rotten in places, breaking away in chunks, and a couple of times she nearly fell backward to the shoulder of the highway below. By the time she joined her guardian, Danny, and Chris fifteen feet above the highway, on a narrow but snow-free shelf of rock near the trees, it seemed as if she had been climbing for minutes. But in fact her sense of time must have been distorted by fear, for when she looked up the highway she saw that the truck was still sliding toward them, that it was two hundred feet away, had made one complete revolution, and was turning sideways again.

On it came through the streaming snow, as if in slow motion, fate in the form of a few tons of steel. A snowmobile stood in the big pickup's cargo bed, and it was apparently not secured by chains or in any way restrained; the driver foolishly had relied on inertia to keep it in place. But now the snowmobile was slamming from side to side against the walls of the cargo hold and forward into the back wall of the cab, and through the quarter-mile slide its violent shifts contributed to the destabilization of the vehicle under it, until it seemed as if the truck, leaning radically, would roll instead of spin through another complete turn.

Laura saw the driver fighting the wheel, and she saw a woman beside him, screaming, and she thought: Oh, my god, those poor people!

As if sensing her thoughts, her guardian shouted above the wind, 'They're drunk, both of them, and no snow chains.'

If you know that much about them, she thought, you must know who they are, so why didn't you stop them, why didn't you save them too?

With a terrible crash the front end of the truck rammed into the side of the Jeep, and unrestrained by a seat belt, the woman was thrown halfway through the windshield, where she hung partly in and partly out of the cab—

Laura yelled, 'Chris!' But she saw that Danny had already taken the boy off his back and was holding him close, turning his head away from the ongoing accident.

—the collision didn't stop the truck; it had too much momentum, and the pavement was too slippery for chainless tread to grip. But the brutal impact did reverse the direction of the truck's slide: it abruptly whipped around to its driver's right, heading backward down the hill, and the snowmobile exploded through the tailgate, *flew* free, crashing onto the hood of the parked Blazer, smashing the windshield. An instant later the rear of the pickup slammed into the front of the Blazer with enough force to shove that vehicle ten feet backward in spite of its firmly engaged emergency brakes—

Though viewing the destruction from the safety of the embankment, Laura gripped Danny's arm, horrified by the thought that they surely would have been injured and perhaps killed if they had taken refuge either in front of or behind the Blazer.

—now the pickup bounced off the Blazer; the bloodied woman fell back into the cab; and, sliding more slowly but still out of control, the battered truck turned three hundred and sixty degrees in an eerily graceful ballet of death, angling down the slope and across the snowy pavement and over the far shoulder, over the unguarded brink, out into emptiness, down, out of sight, gone.

Though no horror remained to be seen, Laura covered her face with her hands, perhaps trying to block out the mental image of the pickup carrying its occupants down the rocky, nearly treeless wall of that gorge, tumbling hundreds upon hundreds of feet. The driver and his companion would be dead before they hit bottom. Even above the raging wind, she heard the truck strike an outcropping of rock, then another. But in seconds the noise of its violent descent faded, and the only sound was the mad shrieking of the storm.

Stunned, they slid and groped their way down the embankment to the shoulder of the road between the Jeep and the Blazer, where bits of glass and metal littered the snowy surface. Steam rose from under the Blazer as hot radiator fluid drizzled onto the frozen ground, and the ruined vehicle creaked under the weight of the snowmobile embedded in its hood.

Chris was crying. Laura reached for him. He came into her arms, and she lifted him, held him, while he sobbed against her neck.

Dazed, Danny turned to their savior. 'Who . . . who in the name of God are you?'

Laura stared at her guardian, finding it difficult to cope with the fact that he really was there. She had not seen him in over twenty years, since she was twelve, that day in the cemetery when she had spotted him watching her father's interment from the grove of Indian laurels. She had not seen him close up for almost twenty-*five* years, since the day he had killed the junkie in her father's grocery. When he failed to save her from the Eel, when he left her to handle *that* one on her own, a loss of faith set in, and doubt was encouraged when he did nothing to save Nina Dockweiler, either – or Ruthie. With the passage of so much time, he had become a dream figure, more myth than reality, and in the last couple of years she had not thought about him at all, had abandoned belief in him just as Chris was currently abandoning belief in Santa Claus. She still had the note that he'd left on her desk, after her father's funeral. But she had long ago convinced herself that it had not in fact been written by a magical guardian but perhaps by Cora or Tom Lance, her father's friends. Now he had saved her again, miraculously, and Danny wanted to know who in the name of God he was, and that was what Laura wanted to know as well.

The strangest part of it was that he looked the same as when he had shot the junkie. *Exactly the same.* She had recognized him at once, even after the passage of so much time, because he had not aged. He still appeared to be in his middle to late thirties. Impossibly, the years had left no mark on him, no hint of gray in his blond hair, no wrinkles in his face. Though he had been her father's age that bloody day in the grocery store, he now was of her own generation or nearly so.

Before the man could answer Danny's question or find a way to avoid an answer, a car topped the hill and started down toward them. It was a late-model Pontiac equipped with tire chains that sang on the pavement. The driver apparently saw the damage to the Jeep and the Blazer and noted the pickup's still fresh skid marks that had not yet been obliterated by wind and snow; he slowed – with reduced speed the song of the chains quickly changed to a clatter – and pulled across the pavement into the southbound lane. Instead of going all the way to the shoulder and out of traffic, however, the car continued north in the wrong lane, stopping only fifteen feet from them, near the back of the Jeep. When he threw open the door and got out of the Pontiac, the driver – a tall man in dark clothing – was holding an object that, too late, Laura identified as a submachine gun.

Her guardian said, 'Kokoschka!'

Even as his name was spoken, Kokoschka opened fire.

Though he was more than fifteen years from Vietnam, Danny reacted with the instincts of a soldier. As bullets ricocheted off the red Jeep in front of them and off the Blazer behind them, Danny grabbed Laura, pushing her and Chris to the ground between the two vehicles.

As Laura dropped below the line of fire, she saw Danny struck in the back. He was hit at least once, maybe twice, and she jerked as if the slugs had hit her. He fell against the front of the Blazer, dropped to his knees.

Laura cried out and, holding Chris with one arm, reached for her husband.

He was still alive, and in fact he swung toward her on his knees. His face was as white as the snow falling around them, and she had the bizarre and terrible feeling that she was looking into the countenance of a ghost rather than that of a living man. 'Get under the Jeep,' Danny said, pushing her hand away. His voice was thick and wet, as if something had broken in his throat. 'Quick!'

One of the bullets had passed completely through him. Bright blood oozed down the front of his blue, quilted ski jacket.

When she hesitated, he moved to her on hands and knees, pushed her toward the Jeep just a few feet away.

Another loud burst of submachine-gun fire crackled through the wintry air.

The gunman would no doubt move cautiously forward toward the front of the Jeep and slaughter them as they cowered there. Yet they had nowhere to run: If they went up the embankment toward the trees, he would cut them down long before they reached the safety of the forest; if they crossed the road, he would blow them away before they reached the other side, and at the other side there was nothing but the steep-walled gorge, anyway; running uphill, they would be heading toward him; running downhill, they would be putting their backs to him, making even easier targets of themselves.

The submachine gun rattled. Windows burst. Bullets punctured sheet metal with a hard *pock-twang*.

Crawling to the front of the Jeep, dragging Chris with her, Laura saw her guardian slipping into the narrow space between that vehicle and the snow-packed embankment. He was crouched below the fender, out of sight of the man he had called Kokoschka. In his fear he no longer seemed magical, no guardian angel but merely a man; and in fact he was no longer a savior, either, but an agent of Death, for his presence here had attracted the killer.

At Danny's urging she frantically squirmed under the Jeep. Chris squirmed, too, not crying now, being brave for his father; but then he had not seen his father shot, for his face had been pressed to Laura's breast, buried in her ski jacket. It seemed useless to get under the Jeep because Kokoschka would find them anyway. He could not be so dim-witted as to fail to look under the Jeep when they could be found nowhere else, so at most they were just buying a little time, an extra minute of life at most.

When she was completely under the Jeep, pulling Chris against her to give him what little additional protection her body could provide, she heard Danny speak to her from the front of the vehicle. 'I love you.' Anguish pierced her as she realized that those three short words also meant goodbye.

Stefan slipped between the Jeep and the dirty, mounded snow along the embankment. There was little space, not enough for him to have gotten out of the driver's door on that side when he had parked there, but barely enough to squeeze along toward the rear bumper where Kokoschka might not expect him to show up, where he might get off one good shot before Kokoschka swung around and sprayed him with the submachine gun.

Kokoschka. He had never been so surprised in his life as when Kokoschka had gotten out of that Pontiac. It meant they were aware of his traitorous activities at the institute. And they were also aware that he had interposed himself between Laura and her true destiny. Kokoschka had taken the Lightning Road with the intention of eliminating the traitor and evidently Laura as well.

Now, keeping his head down, Stefan urgently forced his way between the Jeep and the embankment. The submachine gun chattered and windows blew out above him. At his back the snowbank was ice-crusted in many places, jabbing painfully into him; when he endured the pain and pressed hard with his body, the ice cracked, and the snow beneath it compacted just enough to give him passage. Wind streamed through the narrow space he occupied, shrieking between sheet metal and snow, so it seemed that he was not alone there but was in the company of some invisible creature that hooted and gibbered in his face.

He had seen Laura and Chris wriggling under the Jeep, but he knew that cover would provide only an additional minute of safety, perhaps even less. When Kokoschka got to the front of the Jeep and didn't find them there, he would look under the vehicle, get down at road level, and open fire, chopping them to pieces in their confinement.

And what of Danny? He was such a big man, barrel-chested, surely too big to slide swiftly under the Jeep. And already he'd been shot; he must be stiff with pain. Besides, Danny wasn't the kind of man who hid from trouble, not even trouble like this.

At last Stefan reached the rear bumper. Cautiously he looked out and saw the

Pontiac parked eight feet away in the southbound lane with its driver's door standing open, engine running. No Kokoschka. So with his Walther PPK/S.380 in hand he eased away from the snowbank, moved behind the Jeep. He crouched against the tailgate and peered around the other rear bumper.

Kokoschka was in the middle of the roadway, moving toward the front of the Jeep where he believed everyone had taken cover. His weapon was an Uzi with an extended magazine, chosen for the mission because it would not be anachronistic. As Kokoschka reached the gap between the Jeep and the Blazer, he opened fire again, sweeping the submachine gun from left to right. Bullets screamed off metal, blew out tires, and thudded into the embankment.

Stefan fired at Kokoschka, missed.

Suddenly, with berserk courage, Danny Packard launched himself at Kokoschka, coming out from his hiding place tight up against the Jeep's grille, so low that he must have been lying flat, low enough to have been under the spray of bullets the submachine gun had just laid down. He was wounded from the initial burst of fire but still quick and powerful, and for a moment it seemed that he might even reach the gunman and disable him. Kokoschka was sweeping the Uzi from left to right, already moving away from his target when he saw Danny coming at him, so he had to reverse himself, bring the muzzle around. If he had been a few feet closer to the Jeep instead of in the middle of the highway, he would not have nailed Danny in time.

'Danny, no!' Stefan shouted, squeezing off three shots at Kokoschka even as Packard was going for him.

But Kokoschka had kept a cautious distance, and he brought the spitting muzzle around, straight at Danny, when they were still three or four feet apart. Danny was kicked backward by the impact of several slugs.

Stefan took no consolation from the fact that even as Danny was hit, Kokoschka was hit, too, taking two rounds from the Walther, one in his left thigh and one in his left shoulder. He was knocked down. He dropped the submachine gun as he fell; it spun along the pavement.

Under the Jeep, Laura was screaming.

Stefan rose from the cover of the rear bumper and ran toward Kokoschka, who was on the ground only thirty feet downslope, near the Blazer now. He slipped on the snowy pavements, struggled to keep his balance.

Badly wounded, no doubt in shock, Kokoschka nevertheless saw him coming. He rolled toward the Uzi carbine, which had come to rest by the rear tire of the Blazer.

Stefan fired three times as he ran, but he did not have the steadiness required for a good aim, and Kokoschka was rolling away from him, so he missed the son of a bitch. Then Stefan slipped again and fell to one knee in the middle of the road, landing so hard that pain shot up his thigh and into his hip.

Rolling, Kokoschka reached the submachine gun.

Realizing he'd never get to the man in time, Stefan dropped onto both knees and raised the Walther, holding it with both hands. He was twenty feet from Kokoschka, not far. But even a good marksman could miss at twenty feet if the circumstances were bad enough, and these were bad: a state of panic, a weird firing angle, gale-force wind to deflect the shot.

Downslope, lying on the ground, Kokoschka opened fire the instant he got his hands on the Uzi, even before he brought the weapon around, loosing the first twenty rounds under the Blazer, blowing out the front tires.

As Kokoschka swung the gun toward him, Stefan squeezed off his last three rounds with deliberation. In spite of the wind and the angle, he had to make them count, for if he missed he would have no time to reload.

The first round from the Walther missed.

Kokoschka continued to bring the submachine gun around, and the arc of fire reached the front of the Jeep. Laura was under the Jeep with Chris, and Kokoschka was shooting from ground level, so surely a couple of rounds had passed under the vehicle.

Stefan fired again. The slug hit Kokoschka in the upper body, and the submachine gun stopped firing. Stefan's next and last shot took Kokoschka in the head. It was over.

From beneath the Jeep, Laura saw Danny's incredibly brave charge, saw him go down again, flat on his back, unmoving, and she knew that he was dead, no possibility of a reprieve this time. A flash of grief like the terrible light from an explosion swept through her, and she glimpsed a future without Danny, a vision so starkly illuminated and of such dreadful power that she almost blacked out.

Then she thought of Chris, still alive and sheltering against her. She blocked out the grief, knowing she would return to it later – if she survived. The important thing right now was keeping Chris alive and, if possible, protecting him from the sight of his father's bullet-riddled corpse.

Danny's body blocked part of her view, but she saw Kokoschka hit by gunfire. She saw her guardian approaching the downed gunman, and for a moment it seemed the worst was over. Then her guardian slipped and fell to one knee, and Kokoschka rolled toward the submachine gun that he had dropped. More gunfire. A lot of it in a few seconds. She heard a couple of rounds passing under the Jeep, frighteningly close, lead cutting through the air with a deadly whisper, that was louder than any other sound in the world.

The silence after the gunfire was at first perfect. Initially she could not hear the wind or her son's low sobbing. Gradually those sounds impinged upon her.

She saw her guardian was alive, and part of her was relieved, but part of her was irrationally angry that he had survived because he had drawn this Kokoschka with him, and Kokoschka had killed Danny. On the other hand Danny – and she and Chris – would surely have been killed in the collision with the truck, anyway, if her guardian had not come along. Who the hell was he? Where did he come from? Why was he so interested in her? She was frightened, angry, shocked, sick in her soul, and badly confused.

Clearly in pain, her guardian rose from his knees and hobbled to Kokoschka. Laura twisted farther around to look directly down the hill, just past Danny's unmoving head. She could not quite see what her guardian was doing, though he appeared to be tearing open Kokoschka's clothes.

After a while he hobbled back up the hill, carrying something he had taken off the corpse.

When he reached the Jeep, he crouched and looked under at her. 'Come out. It's over.' His face was pale, and in the past few minutes he seemed to have aged at least a couple of his twenty-five lost years. He cleared his throat. In a voice filled with what seemed like genuine, deeply felt remorse, he said, 'I'm sorry, Laura. I'm so very sorry.'

She squirmed on her belly toward the rear of the Jeep, bumping her head on the undercarriage. She pulled Chris and encouraged him to come with her, for if they wriggled out nearer the front, the boy might see his father. Her guardian pulled them into the open. Laura sat back against the rear bumper and clutched Chris to her.

Tremulously, the boy said, 'I want Daddy.'

I want him too, Laura thought. Oh, baby, I want him, too, I want him so bad, all I want in the world is your daddy.

The storm was a full-fledged blizzard now, pumping snow out of the sky under tremendous pressure. The afternoon was dying; light was fading, and all around the grim, gray day was succumbing to the queer, phosphorescent darkness of a snowy night.

In this weather few people would be traveling, but he was sure that someone would come along soon. No more than ten minutes had passed since he had stopped Laura in the Blazer, but even on this rural road in a storm, the gap in traffic would not last much longer. He needed to have a talk with her and leave before he got entangled in the aftermath of this bloody encounter.

Hunkering down in front of her and the weeping boy, behind the Jeep, Stefan said, 'Laura, I've got to get out of here, but I'll be back soon, in just a couple of days—'

'Who are you?' she demanded angrily.

'There's no time for that now.'

'I want to know, damn you. I have a right to know.'

'Yes, you do, and I'll tell you in a few days. But right now we have to get your story straight, the way we did that day in the grocery store. Remember?'

'To hell with you.'

Unfazed, he said, 'It's for your own good, Laura. You can't tell the authorities the exact truth because it won't seem real, will it? They'll think you're making it all up. Especially when you see me leave . . . well, if you tell them how I went, they'll either be sure that you're somehow an accomplice to murder or a mad-woman.'

She glared at him and said nothing. He did not blame her for being angry. Perhaps she even wanted him dead, but he understood that too. The only emotions she stirred in him, however, were love and pity and a profound respect.

He said, 'You'll tell them that when you and Danny turned the curve at the bottom of the hill and started up, there were *three* cars in the roadway: the Jeep parked here along the embankment, the Pontiac in the wrong lane just where it is now, and another car was stopped in the north-bound lane. There were . . . four men, two of them with guns, and they seemed to have forced the Jeep off the road. You just came along at the wrong time, that's all. They pointed a submachine gun at you, made you pull off the road, made you and Danny and Chris get out of the car. At one point you heard talk about cocaine . . . somehow it involved drugs, you don't know how, but they were arguing over drugs, and they seemed to have chased down the man in the Jeep—'

'Drug dealers out here in the middle of nowhere?' she said scornfully.

'There could be processing labs out here – a cabin in the woods, processing PCP maybe. Listen, if the story makes at least *some* sense, they'll want to buy it. The *real* story makes no sense at all, so you can't rely on it. So you tell them the Robertsons came over the crest of the hill in their pickup – of course you don't know their name – and the road was blocked by all these cars, and when he braked the pickup it started to slide—'

'You've got an accent,' she said angrily. 'A slight one but I can hear it. Where are you from?'

'I'll tell you all of that in a few days,' he said impatiently, looking up and down the snow-blasted road. 'I really will, but now you've got to promise me you'll work with this false story, embellish it as best you can, and not tell them the truth.'

'I don't have any choice, do I?'

'No,' he said, relieved that she realized her position.

She clung to her son and said nothing.

Stefan had begun to feel the pain in his half-frozen feet again. The heat of action had dissipated, leaving him racked by shivers. He handed her the belt that he had taken off Kokoschka. 'Put this inside your ski jacket. Don't let anyone see it. When you get home, put it away somewhere.'

'What is it?'

'Later. I'll try to return in a few hours. Only a few hours. Right now just promise me you'll hide it. Don't get curious, don't put it on, and for God's sake don't push the yellow button on it.'

'Why not?'

'Because you don't want to go where it'll take you.'

She blinked at him in confusion. 'Take me?'

'I'll explain but not now.'

'Why can't you take it with you, whatever it is?'

'Two belts, one body – it's an anomaly, it'll cause a disruption of some kind in the energy field, and God only knows where I might wind up or in what condition.'

'I don't understand. What're you talking about?'

'Later. But, Laura, if for some reason I'm unable to come back, you better take precautions.'

'What kind of precautions?'

'Arm yourself. Be prepared. There's no *reason* they should come after you if they get me, but they might. Just to teach me a lesson, to humble me. They thrive on vengeance. And if they come for you . . . there'll be a squad of them, well armed.'

'Who the hell *are* they?'

Without answering, he got to his feet, wincing at the pain in his right knee. He backed away, taking one last, long look at her. Then he turned, leaving her on the ground, in the cold and snow, against the back of the battered and bullet-pocked Jeep, with her terrified child and her dead husband.

Slowly he walked out into the middle of the highway where more light seemed to come from the shifting snow on the pavement than from the sky overhead. She called to him, but he ignored her.

He holstered his empty gun beneath his coat. He reached inside his shirt, felt for and located the yellow button on his own travel belt, and hesitated.

They had sent Kokoschka to stop him. Now they would be waiting anxiously at the institute to learn the outcome. He would be arrested on arrival. He probably never again would have an opportunity to take the Lightning Road to return to her as he had promised.

The temptation to stay was great.

If he stayed, however, they would only send someone else to kill him, and he would spend the rest of his life running from one assassin after another – while watching the world around him change in ways that would be too horrible to endure. On the other hand, if he went back, there was a slim chance that he might still be able to destroy the institute. Dr. Penlovski and the others obviously knew everything about his meddling in the natural flow of events in this one woman's life, but perhaps they did not know that he had planted explosives in the attic and basement of the institute. In that case, if they gave him an opportunity to get into his office for just a moment, he could throw the hidden switch and blow the place – and all its files – to hell where it belonged. More likely than not, they had found the explosive charges and removed them. But as long as there was any possibility whatsoever that he could bring an end forever to the project and close the Lightning Road, he was morally obliged to return to the institute, even if it meant that he would never see Laura again.

As the day died, the storm seemed to come more fiercely alive. On the mountainside above the highway, the wind rumbled and keened through the enormous pines, and the boughs made an ominous rustling sound, as if some many-legged, giant creature were scuttling down the slope. The snowflakes had become fine and dry, almost like bits of ice, and they seemed to be abrading the world, smoothing it the way that sandpaper smoothed wood, until eventually there would be no peaks and valleys, nothing but a featureless, highly polished plain as far as anyone could see.

With his hand still inside his coat and shirt, Stefan pressed the yellow button three times in quick succession, triggering the beacon. With regret and fear he returned to his own time.

Holding Chris, whose sobbing had subsided, Laura sat on the ground at the back of the Jeep and watched her guardian walk into the slanting snow, past the rear of Kokoschka's Pontiac.

He stopped in the middle of the highway, stood for a long moment with his back to her, and then an incredible thing happened. First the air became heavy; she was aware of a strange pressure, something she had never felt before, as if the atmosphere of the earth were being condensed in some cosmic cataclysm, and abruptly she found it hard to draw breath. The air acquired a curious odor, too, exotic but familiar, and after a few seconds she realized it smelled like hot electrical wires and scorched insulation, much like what she had smelled in her own kitchen when a toaster plug had shorted out a few weeks ago; that stink was overlaid with the crisp but not unpleasant scent of ozone, which was the same odor that filled the air during any violent thunderstorm. The pressure grew greater, until she almost felt pinned to the ground, and the air shimmered and rippled as if it were water. With a sound like an enormous cork popping out of a bottle, her guardian vanished from the purple-gray, winter twilight, and simultaneously with that *pop* came a great *whoosh* of wind, as if massive quantities of air were rushing in to fill some void. Indeed for an instant she felt trapped in a vacuum, unable to breathe. Then the crushing pressure was gone, the air smelled only of snow and pine, and everything was normal again.

Except, of course, after what she had seen, nothing could ever be normal for her again.

The night grew very dark. Without Danny it was the blackest night of her life. Only one light remained to illuminate her struggle toward some distant hope of happiness: Chris. He was the last light in her darkness.

Later, at the top of the hill, a car appeared. Headlights bored through the gloom and the heavily falling snow.

She struggled to her feet and took Chris into the middle of the roadway. She waved for help.

As the descending car slowed, she suddenly wondered if when it stopped another man with another submachine gun would get out and open fire. She would never again feel safe.

Four

The Inner Fire

• 1 •

On Saturday, August 13, 1988, seven months after Danny was shot down, Thelma Ackerson came to the mountain house to stay for four days.

Laura was in the backyard, conducting target practice with her Smith & Wesson .38 Chief's Special. She had just reloaded, snapped the cylinder in place, and was about to put on her Hearing Guard headset when she heard a car approaching on the long gravel driveway from the state route. She picked up a pair of binoculars from the ground at her feet and took a closer look at the vehicle to be sure it was not an unwanted visitor. When she saw Thelma behind the wheel, she put the glasses down and continued firing at the target – an outline of a man's head and torso – that was lashed to a hay-bale backstop.

Sitting on the grass nearby, Chris plucked six more cartridges from the box and prepared to hand them to her when she had fired the last round currently in the cylinder.

The day was hot, clear, and dry. Wildflowers by the hundred blazed along the edge of the yard where the mown area gave way to wild grass and weeds near the forest line. Squirrels had been at play on the grass a while ago, and birds had been singing, but the shooting had temporarily frightened them away.

Laura might have been expected to associate her husband's death with the high retreat and to sell it. Instead she had sold the house in Orange County four months ago and moved with Chris to the San Bernardinos.

She believed that what had happened to them the previous January on route 330 could have happened anywhere. The place was not to blame; the fault lay in her destiny, in the mysterious forces at work in her strangely troubled life. Intuitively she knew that if her guardian had not stepped in to save her on that stretch of snowy highway, he would have entered her life elsewhere, at another moment of crisis. At *that* place Kokoschka would have shown up with a submachine gun, and the same set of violent, tragic events would have transpired.

Their other home had held more memories of Danny than did the stone and redwood place south of Big Bear. She was better able to deal with her grief in the mountains than in Orange Park Acres.

Besides, oddly enough, the mountains felt much safer to her. In the highly populated suburbs of Orange County, where the streets and freeways teemed with more than two million people, an enemy would not be perceived among the crowd until he chose to act. In the mountains, however, strangers were highly visible, especially since the house sat almost in the center of their thirty-acre property.

And she had not forgotten her guardian's warning: *Arm yourself. Be prepared. If they come for you . . . there'll be a squad of them.*

When Laura fired the last round in the .38 and pulled off the ear guards,

Chris handed her six more cartridges. He removed his muffs, too, and ran to the target to check her accuracy.

The backstop consisted of hay bales piled seven feet high and four deep; it was fourteen feet wide. Behind it were acres of pine woods, her private land, so the need for an elaborate backstop was questionable, but she did not want to shoot anyone. At least not accidentally.

Chris lashed up a new target and returned to Laura with the old one. 'Four hits out of six, Mom. Two deaders, two good wounds, but looks like you're pulling off to the left a little.'

'Let's see if I can correct that.'

'You're just getting tired, that's all,' Chris said.

The grass around her was littered with over a hundred and fifty empty brass shell casings. Her wrists, arms, shoulders, and neck were beginning to ache from the cumulative recoil, but she wanted to get in another full cylinder before quitting for the day.

Back near the house, Thelma's car door slammed.

Chris put on his ear guards again and picked up the binoculars to watch the target while his mother fired.

Sorrow plucked at Laura as she paused to look at the boy, not merely because he was fatherless but because it seemed so unfair that a child two months short of his eighth birthday should already know how dangerous life was and should have to live in constant expectation of violence. She did her best to make sure there was as much fun in his life as possible: They still played with the Tommy Toad fantasy, though Chris no longer believed that Tommy was real; through a large personal library of children's classics, Laura also was showing him the pleasure and escape to be found in books; she even did her best to make target practice a game and thereby divert the focus from the deadly necessity of being able to protect themselves. Yet for the time being their lives were dominated by loss and danger, by a fear of the unknown. That reality could not be hidden from the boy, and it could not fail to have a profound and lasting effect on him.

Chris lowered the binoculars and looked at her to see why she was not shooting. She smiled at him. He smiled at her. He had such a sweet smile it almost broke her heart.

She turned to the target, raised the .38, gripped it with both hands, and squeezed off the first shot of the new series.

By the time Laura fired four rounds, Thelma stepped up beside her. She stood with her fingers in her ears, wincing.

Laura squeezed off the last two shots and removed her ear guards, and Chris retrieved the target. The roar of gunfire was still echoing through the mountains when she turned to Thelma and hugged her.

'What's all this gun stuff?' Thelma asked. 'Are you going to write new movies for Clint Eastwood? No, hey, better yet, write the female equal of Clint's role – *Dirty Harriet*. And I'm just the broad to play it – tough, cold, with a sneer that would make Bogart cringe.'

'I'll keep you in mind for the part,' Laura said, 'but what I'd really like to see is Clint play it in drag.'

'Hey, you've still got a sense of humor, Shane.'

'Did you think I wouldn't?'

Thelma frowned. 'I didn't know what to think when I saw you blasting away, looking mean as a snake with fang decay.'

'Self-defense,' Laura said. 'Every good girl should learn some.'

'You were plinking away like a pro.' Thelma noted the glitter of brass shell casings in the grass. 'How often do you do this?'

'Three times a week, a couple of hours each time.'

Chris returned with the target. 'Hi, Aunt Thelma. Mom, you got four deaders out of six that time, one good wound, and a miss.'

'Deaders?' Thelma said.

'Still pulling to the left, do you think?' Laura asked the boy.

He showed her the target. 'Not so much as last time.'

Thelma said, 'Hey, Christopher Robin, is that all I get – just a lousy "Hi, Aunt Thelma"?'

Chris put the target with the pile of others that he had taken down before it, went to Thelma, and gave her a big hug and a kiss. Noticing that she was no longer done up in punk style, he said, 'Gee, what happened to you, Aunt Thelma? You look normal.'

'I look normal? What is that – a compliment or an insult? Just you remember, kid, even if your old Aunt Thelma looks normal, she is no such a thing. She is a comic genius, a dazzling wit, a legend in her own scrapbook. Anyway, I decided punk was passé.'

They enlisted Thelma to help them collect empty shell casings.

'Mom's a terrific shot,' Chris said proudly.

'She better be terrific with all this practice. There's enough brass here to make balls for an entire army of Amazon warriors.'

To his mother, Chris said, 'What's that mean?'

'Ask me again in ten years,' Laura said.

When they went into the house, Laura locked the kitchen door. Two deadbolts. She closed the Levelor blinds over the windows so no one could see them.

Thelma watched these rituals with interest but said nothing.

Chris put *Raiders of the Lost Ark* on the VCR in the family room and settled in front of the television with a bag of cheese popcorn and a Coke. In the adjacent kitchen Laura and Thelma sat at the table and drank coffee while Laura disassembled and cleaned the .38 Chief's Special.

The kitchen was big but cozy with lots of dark oak, used brick on two walls, a copper range hood, copper pots hung on hooks, and a dark blue, ceramic-tile floor. It was the kind of kitchen in which TV sitcom families worked out their nonsensical crises and attained transcendental enlightenment (with heart) in thirty minutes each week, minus commercials. Even to Laura it seemed like an odd place to be cleaning a weapon designed primarily to kill other human beings.

'Are you really afraid?' Thelma asked.

'Bet on it.'

'But Danny was killed because you were unlucky enough to wander into the middle of a drug deal of some kind. Those people are long gone, right?'

'Maybe not.'

'Well, if they were afraid that you might be able to identify them, they'd have come to get you long before this.'

'I'm taking no chances.'

'You got to ease up, kid. You can't live the rest of your life expecting someone to jump at you from the bushes. All right, you can keep a gun around the house. That's probably wise. But aren't you ever going to go out into the world again? You can't tote a gun with you everywhere you go.'

'Yes, I can. I've got a permit.'

'A permit to carry that cannon?'

'I take it in my purse wherever we go.'

'Jesus, how'd you get a permit to carry?'

'My husband was killed under strange circumstances by persons unknown. Those killers tried to shoot my son and me – and they are still at large. On top of all that, I'm a rich and relatively famous woman. It'd be a little odd if I *couldn't* get a permit to carry.'

Thelma was silent for a minute, sipping her coffee, watching Laura clean the revolver. Finally she said, 'This is kind of spooky, Shane, seeing you so serious about this, so tense. I mean, it's seven months since . . . Danny died. But you're as skittish as if someone had shot at you yesterday. You can't maintain this level of tension or readiness or whatever you want to call it. That way lies madness. Paranoia. You've got to face the fact that you can't really be on guard the rest of your life, every minute.'

'I can, though, if I have to.'

'Oh, yeah? What about right now? Your gun's disassembled. What if some barbarian thug with tattoos on his tongue started kicking down the kitchen door?'

The kitchen chairs were on rubber casters, so when Laura suddenly shoved way from the table, she rolled swiftly to the counter beside the refrigerator. She pulled open a drawer and brought out another .38 Chief's Special.

Thelma said, 'What – am I sitting in the middle of an arsenal?'

Laura put the second revolver back in the drawer. 'Come on. I'll give you a tour.'

Thelma followed her to the pantry. Hung on the back of the pantry door was an Uzi semiautomatic carbine.

'That's a machine gun. Is it legal to have one?'

'With federal approval, you can buy them at gunshops, though you can only get a semiautomatic; it's illegal to have them modified for full automatic fire.'

Thelma studied her, then sighed. 'Has this one been modified?'

'Yes. It's fully automatic. But I bought it that way from an illegal dealer, not a gunshop.'

'This is too spooky, Shane. Really.'

She led Thelma into the dining room and showed her the revolver that was clipped to the bottom of the sideboard. In the living room a fourth revolver was clipped under an end table next to one of the sofas. A second modified Uzi was hung on the back of the foyer door at the front of the house. Revolvers were also hidden in the desk drawer in the den, in her office upstairs, in the master bathroom, and in the nightstand in her bedroom. Finally, she kept a third Uzi in the master bedroom.

Staring at the Uzi that Laura pulled from under the bed, Thelma said,

'Spookier and spookier. If I didn't know you better, Shane, I'd think you'd gone mad, a raving paranoid gun nut. But knowing you, if you're really *this* scared, you've got to have some reason. But what about Chris around all these guns?'

'He knows not to touch them, and I know he can be trusted. Most Swiss families have members in the militia – nearly every male citizen there is prepared to defend his country, did you know that? – with guns in almost every house, but they have the lowest rate of accidental shootings in the world. Because guns are a way of life. Children are taught to respect them from an early age. Chris'll be okay.'

As Laura put the Uzi under the bed again, Thelma said, 'How on earth do you find an illegal gun dealer?'

'I'm rich, remember?'

'And money can buy anything? Okay, maybe that's true. But, come on, how does a gal like you find an arms dealer? They don't advertise on Laundromat bulletin boards, I presume.'

'I've researched the backgrounds to several complicated novels, Thelma. I've learned how to find anyone or anything I need.'

Thelma was silent as they returned to the kitchen. From the family room came the heroic music that accompanies Indiana Jones on all of his exploits. While Laura sat at the table and continued cleaning the revolver, Thelma poured fresh coffee for both of them.

'Straight talk now, kiddo. If there's really some threat out there that justifies all this armament, then it's bigger than you can handle yourself. Why not bodyguards?'

'I don't trust anyone. Anyone but you and Chris, that is. And Danny's father, except he's in Florida.'

'But you can't go on like this, alone, afraid. . . .'

Working a spiral brush into the barrel of the revolver, Laura said, 'I'm afraid, yeah, but I feel good about being prepared. All my life I've stood by while people I love have been taken from me. I've done nothing about it but endure. Well, to hell with that. From now on, I fight. If anyone wants to take Chris from me, they're going to have to go *through* me to get him, they'll have to fight a war.'

'Laura, I know what you're going through. But listen, let me play psychoanalyst here and tell you that you're reacting less to any real threat than you are *over*reacting to a sense of helplessness in the face of fate. You can't thwart Providence, kid. You can't play poker with God and expect to win because you've got a .38 in your purse. I mean, you lost Danny to violence, yeah, and maybe you could say that Nina Dockweiler would have lived if someone had put a bullet in the Eel when he first deserved it, but those are the only cases where lives of people you loved might've been saved with guns. Your mother died in childbirth. Your father died of a heart attack. We lost Ruthie to fire. Learning to defend yourself with guns is fine, but you've got to keep perspective, you've got to have a sense of humor about our vulnerability as a species, or you'll wind up in an institution with people who talk to tree stumps and eat their belly-button lint. God forbid, but what if Chris got cancer? You're all prepared to blow away anyone who touches him, but you can't kill cancer with a revolver, and I'm afraid you're so crazy determined to protect him that you'll fall to pieces if something like that happens, something you can't deal with, that no one can deal with. I worry about you, kid.'

Laura nodded and felt a rush of warmth for her friend. 'I know you do, Thelma. And you can put your mind at ease. For thirty-three years I just endured; now I'm fighting back as best I can. If cancer were to strike me or Chris, I'd hire all the best specialists, seek the finest possible treatment. But if all failed, if for example Chris died of cancer, then I'd accept defeat. Fighting doesn't preclude enduring. I can fight, and if fighting fails, I can still endure.'

For a long time Thelma stared at her across the table. At last she nodded. 'That's what I hoped to hear. Okay. End of discussion. On to other things. When do you plan to buy a tank, Shane?'

'They're delivering it Monday.'

'Howitzers, grenades, bazookas?'

'Tuesday. What about the Eddie Murphy movie?'

'We closed the deal two days ago,' Thelma said.

'Really. My Thelma is going to star in a movie with Eddie Murphy?'

'Your Thelma is going to *appear* in a movie with Eddie Murphy. I don't think I qualify as a star yet.'

'You had fourth lead in that picture with Steve Martin, third lead in the picture with Chevy Chase. And this is second lead, right? And how many times have you hosted the *Tonight* show? Eight times, isn't it? Face it, you're a star.'

'Low magnitude, maybe. Isn't it weird, Shane? Two of us come from nothing, McIlroy Home, and we make it to the top. Strange?'

'Not so strange,' Laura said. 'Adversity breeds toughness, and the tough succeed. And survive.'

· **2** ·

Stefan left the snow-filled night in the San Bernardino Mountains and an instant later was inside the gate at the other end of Lightning Road. The gate resembled a large barrel, not unlike one of those that were popular in carnival funhouses, except that its inner surface was of highly polished copper rather than wood, and it did not turn under his feet. The barrel was eight feet in diameter and twelve feet long, and in a few steps he walked out of it, into the main, ground-floor lab of the institute, where he was certain that he'd be met by armed men.

The lab was deserted.

Astonished, he stood for a moment in his snow-flecked peacoat and looked around in disbelief. Three walls of the thirty-by-forty-foot room were lined floor to ceiling with machinery that hummed and clicked unattended. Most of the overhead lamps were off, so the room was softly, eerily lit. The machinery supported the gate, and it featured scores of dials and gauges that glowed pale green or orange, for the gate – which was a breach in time, a tunnel to anywhen – was never shut down; once closed, it could be reopened only with great difficulty and a tremendous expenditure of energy, but once open it could be maintained with comparatively little effort. These days, because the primary research work was no longer focused on developing the gate itself, the main lab was attended by institute personnel only for routine maintenance of the machinery and, of course, when a jaunt was in progress. If different circumstance had pertained, Stefan would never have been able to make the scores of secret, unauthorized trips that he had taken to monitor – and sometimes correct – the events of Laura's life.

But though it was not unusual to find the lab deserted most times of the day, it was singularly strange now, for they had sent Kokoschka to stop him, and surely they would be waiting anxiously to learn how Kokoschka had fared in those wintry California mountains. They had to have entertained the possibility that Kokoschka would fail, that the wrong man would return from 1988, and that the gate would have to be guarded until the situation was resolved. Where were the secret police in their black trenchcoats with padded shoulders? Where were the guns with which he had expected to be greeted?

He looked at the large clock on the wall and saw that it was six minutes past eleven o'clock, local time. That was as it should have been. He'd begun the jaunt at five minutes till eleven that morning, and every jaunt ended exactly eleven minutes after it began. No one knew why, but no matter how long a time traveler spent at the other end of his journey, only eleven minutes passed at home base. He had been in the San Bernardinos for nearly an hour and a half, but only eleven minutes had transpired in his own life, in his own time. If he had stayed with Laura for months before pressing the yellow button on his belt, activating the beacon, he would still have returned to the institute only – and precisely – eleven minutes after he had left it.

But where were the authorities, the guns, his angry colleagues expressing their outrage? After discovering his meddling in the events of Laura's life, after sending Kokoschka to get him and Laura, why would they walk away from the gate when they had to wait only *eleven minutes* to learn the outcome of the confrontation?

Stefan took off his boots, peacoat, and shoulder holster, and tucked them out of sight in a corner behind some equipment. He had left his white lab coat in the same place when he had departed on the jaunt, and now he slipped into it again.

Baffled, still worried in spite of the lack of a hostile greeting committee, he stepped out of the lab into the ground-floor corridor and went looking for trouble.

• 3 •

At two-thirty Sunday morning Laura was at her word processor in the office adjacent to the master bedroom, dressed in pajamas and a robe, sipping apple juice, and working on a new book. The only light in the room came from the electronic-green letters on the computer screen and from a small desk lamp tightly focused on a printout of yesterday's pages. A revolver lay on the desk beside the script.

The door to the dark hallway was open. She never closed any but the bathroom door these days because sooner or later a closed door might prevent her from hearing the stealthy progress of an intruder in another part of the house. The house had a sophisticated alarm system, but she kept interior doors open just in case.

She heard Thelma coming down the hallway, and she turned just as her friend looked through the door. 'Sorry if I've made any noise that's kept you awake.'

'Nah. We nightclub types work late. But I sleep till noon. What about you? You usually up at this hour?'

'I don't sleep well any more. Four or five hours a night is good for me. Instead of lying in bed, fidgeting, I get up and write.'

Thelma pulled up a chair, sat, and propped her feet on Laura's desk. Her taste in sleepwear was even more flamboyant than it had been in her youth: baggy silk pajamas in a red, green, blue, and yellow abstract pattern of squares and circles.

'I'm glad to see you're still wearing bunny slippers,' Laura said. 'It shows a certain constancy of personality.'

'That's me. Rock-solid. Can't buy bunny slippers in my size any more, so I have to buy a pair of furry adult slippers *and* a pair of kids' slippers, snip the eyes and ears off the little ones and sew them on the big ones. What're you writing?'

'A bile-black book.'

'Sounds like just the thing for a fun weekend at the beach.'

Laura sighed and relaxed in her spring-backed armchair. 'It's a novel about death, about the injustice of death. It's a fool's project because I'm trying to explain the unexplainable. I'm trying to explain death to my ideal reader because then maybe I can finally understand it myself. It's a book about why we have to struggle and go on in spite of that knowledge of our mortality, why we have to fight and endure. It's a black, bleak, grim, moody, depressing, bitter, deeply disturbing book.'

'Is there a big market for that?'

Laura laughed. 'Probably no market at all. But once an idea for a novel seizes a writer . . . well, it's like an inner fire that at first warms you and makes you feel good but then begins to eat you alive, burn you up from within. You can't just walk away from the fire; it keeps burning. The only way to put it out is to write the damned book. Anyway, when I get stuck on this one, I turn to a nice little children's book I'm writing all about Sir Tommy Toad.'

'You're nuts, Shane.'

'Who's wearing the bunny slippers?'

They talked about this and that, with the easy camaraderie they had shared for twenty years. Perhaps it was Laura's loneliness, more acute than in the days immediately following Danny's murder, or maybe it was a fear of the unknown, but for whatever reason she began to speak of her special guardian. In all the world only Thelma might believe the tale. In fact Thelma was spellbound, soon lowering her feet from the desk and sitting forward on her chair, never expressing disbelief, as the story unrolled from the day the junkie was shot until the guardian vanished on the mountain highway.

When Laura had quenched *that* inner fire, Thelma said, 'Why didn't you tell me about this . . . this guardian years ago? Back in McIlroy?'

'I don't know. It seemed like something . . . magical. Something I should keep to myself because if I shared it I'd break the spell and never see him again. Then after he left me to deal with the Eel on my own, after he had done nothing to save Ruthie, I guess I just stopped believing in him. I never told Danny about him because by the time I met Danny my guardian was no more real to me than Santa Claus. Then suddenly . . . there he was again on the highway.'

'That night on the mountain, he said he'd be back to explain everything in a few days . . .?'

'But I haven't seen him since. I've been waiting seven months, and I figure that when someone suddenly materializes it might be my guardian or, just as likely, another Kokoschka with a submachine gun.'

The story had electrified Thelma, and she fidgeted on her chair as if a current were crackling through her. Finally she got up and paced. 'What about Kokoschka? The cops find out anything about him?'

'Nothing. He was carrying no identification whatsoever. The Pontiac he was driving was stolen, just like the red Jeep. They ran his fingerprints through every file they've got, came up empty-handed. And they can't interrogate a corpse. They don't know who he was or where he came from or why he wanted to kill us.'

'You've had a long time to think about all this. So any ideas? Who is this guardian? Where did he come from?'

'I don't know.' She had one idea in particular that she focused on, but it sounded mad, and she had no evidence to support the theory. She withheld it from Thelma not because it was crazy, however, but because it would sound so egomaniacal. 'I just don't know.'

'Where's this belt he left with you?'

'In the safe,' Laura said, nodding toward the corner where a floor-set box was hidden under the carpet.

Together they pulled the wall-to-wall carpet off its tack strip in that corner, revealing the face of the safe, which was a cylinder twelve inches in diameter and sixteen inches deep. Only one item reposed within, and Laura withdrew it.

They moved back to the desk to look at the mysterious article in better light. Laura adjusted the flexible neck of the lamp.

The belt was four inches wide and was made of a stretchy, black fabric, perhaps nylon, through which were woven copper wires that formed intricate and peculiar patterns. Because of its width, the belt required two small buckles rather than one; those were also made of copper. In addition, sewn on the belt just to the left of the buckles, was a thin box the size of an old-fashioned cigarette case – about four inches by three inches, only three-quarters of an inch thick – and this, too, was made of copper. Even on close examination no way to open the rectangular copper box could be discerned; its only feature was a yellow button toward the lower left corner, less than an inch in diameter.

Thelma fingered the odd material. 'Tell me again what he said would happen if you pushed the yellow button.'

'He just told me for God's sake not to push it, and when I asked why not, he said, "You won't want to go where it'll take you." '

They stood side by side in the glow of the desk lamp, staring at the belt that Thelma held. It was after four in the morning, and the house was as silent as any dead, airless crater on the moon.

Finally Thelma said, 'You ever been tempted to push the button?'

'No, never,' Laura said without hesitation. 'When he mentioned the place to which it would take me . . . there was a terrible look in his eyes. And I know he returned there himself only with reluctance. I don't know where he comes from, Thelma, but if I didn't misunderstand what I saw in his eyes, the place is just one step this side of hell.'

Sunday afternoon they dressed in shorts and T-shirts, spread a couple of blankets on the rear lawn, and made a long, lazy picnic of potato salad, cold cuts, cheese, fresh fruit, potato chips, and plump cinnamon rolls with lots of crunchy pecan topping. They played games with Chris, and he enjoyed the day enormously, partly because Thelma was able to shift her comic engine into a lower gear, producing one-liners designed for eight-year-olds.

When Chris saw squirrels frolicking farther back in the yard, near the woods, he wanted to feed them. Laura gave him a pecan roll and said, 'Tear it into little pieces and toss the pieces to them. They won't let you get too near. And you stay close to me, you hear?'

'Sure, Mom.'

'Don't you go all the way to the woods. Only about halfway.'

He ran thirty feet from the blanket, only a little more than halfway to the trees, then dropped to his knees. He tore pieces from the cinnamon roll and threw them to the squirrels, making those quick and cautious creatures edge a bit closer for each successive scrap.

'He's a good kid,' Thelma said.

'The best.' Laura moved the Uzi to her side.

'He's only ten or twelve yards away,' Thelma said.

'But he's closer to the woods than to me.' Laura studied the shadows under the serried pines.

Plucking a few potato chips from the bag, Thelma said, 'Never been on a picnic with someone who brought a submachine gun. I sort of like it. Don't have to worry about bears.'

'It's hell on ants, too.'

Thelma stretched out on her side on the blanket, her head propped up on one bent arm, but Laura continued to sit with her legs crossed Indian-fashion. Orange butterflies, as bright as condensed sunshine, darted through the warm August air.

'The kid seems to be coping,' Thelma said.

'More or less,' Laura agreed. 'There was a very bad time. He cried a lot, wasn't emotionally stable. But that passed. They're flexible at his age, quick to adapt, to accept. But as good as he seems . . . I'm afraid there's a darkness in him now that wasn't there before and that isn't going to go away.'

'No,' Thelma said, 'it won't go away. It's like a shadow on the heart. But he'll live, and he'll find happiness, and there'll be times when he's not aware of the shadow at all.'

While Thelma watched Chris luring the squirrels, Laura studied her friend's profile. 'You still miss Ruth, don't you?'

'Every day for twenty years. Don't you still miss your dad?'

'Sure,' Laura said. 'But when I think of him, I don't believe what I feel is like what you feel. Because we *expect* our parents to die before us, and even when they die prematurely, we can accept it because we've always known it was going to happen sooner or later. But it's different when the one who dies is a wife, husband, child . . . or sister. We don't expect them to die on us, not early in life. So it's harder to cope. Especially, I suppose, if she's a twin sister.'

'When I get a piece of good news – career news, I mean – the first thing I always think of is how happy Ruthie would have been for me. What about you, Shane? You coping?'

'I cry at night.'

'That's healthy now. Not so healthy a year from now.'

'I lie awake at night and listen to my heartbeat, and it's a lonely sound. Thank God for Chris. He gives me purpose. And you. I've got you and Chris, and we're sort of family, don't you think?'

'Not just sort of. We *are* family. You and me – sisters.'

Laura smiled, reached out, and rumpled Thelma's tousled hair.

'But,' Thelma said, 'being sisters doesn't mean you get to borrow my clothes.'

• 4 •

In the corridors and through the open doors of the institute's offices and labs, Stefan saw his colleagues at work, and none of them had any special interest in him. He took the elevator to the third floor where just outside his office he encountered Dr. Wladyslaw Januskaya, who was Dr. Vladimir Penlovski's long-time protégé and second in charge of the time-travel research which originally had been called Project Scythe but which for several months now had been known by the apt code name Lightning Road.

Januskaya was forty, ten years younger than his mentor, but he looked older than the vital, energetic Penlovski. Short, overweight, balding, with a blotchy complexion, with two bright gold teeth in the front of his mouth, wearing thick glasses that made his eyes look like painted eggs, Januskaya should have been a comic figure. But his unholy faith in the state and his zeal in working for the totalitarian cause were sufficient to counteract his comic potential; indeed he was one of the more disturbing men involved with Lightning Road.

'Stefan, dear Stefan,' Januskaya said, 'I've been meaning to tell you how grateful we are for your timely suggestion, last October, that the power supply to the gate should be provided by a secure generator. Your foresight has saved the project. If we were still drawing from the municipal power lines . . . why, the gate would have collapsed half a dozen times by now, and we'd be woefully behind schedule.'

Having returned to the institute in expectation of arrest, Stefan was confused to find his treachery undiscovered and startled to hear himself being praised by this evil worm. He had suggested switching the gate to a secure generator not because he wanted to see their vile project achieve success but because he had not wanted his own jaunts into Laura's life to be interrupted by the failure of the public power supply.

'I would not have thought last October that by this time we would have come to such a situation as this, with ordinary public services no longer to be trusted,' Januskaya said, shaking his head sadly, 'the social order so thoroughly disturbed. What must the people endure to see the socialist state of their dreams triumph, eh?'

'These are dark times,' Stefan said, meaning very different things than Januskaya meant.

'But we will triumph,' Januskaya said forcefully. His magnified eyes filled with the madness that Stefan knew too well. 'Through the Lightning Road, we will triumph.'

He patted Stefan on the shoulder and continued down the hall.

After Stefan watched the scientist walk nearly to the elevators, he said, 'Oh, Dr. Januskaya?'

The fat white worm turned and looked at him. 'Yes?'

'Have you seen Kokoschka today?'

'Today? No, not yet today.'

'He's here, isn't he?'

'Oh, I'd imagine so. He's here pretty much as long as there's anyone working, you know. He's a diligent man. If we had more like Kokoschka we'd have no doubt of ultimate triumph. Do you need to talk to him? If I see him, should I send him to you?'

'No, no,' Stefan said. 'It's nothing urgent. I wouldn't want to interrupt him in other work. I'm sure I'll see him sooner or later.'

Januskaya continued to the elevators, and Stefan went into his office, closing the door behind him.

He crouched beside the filing cabinet that he had repositioned slightly to cover one-third of the grille in the corner ventilation chase. In the narrow space behind it, a bundle of copper wires was barely visible, coming out of the bottom slot in the grille. The wires were connected to a simple dial-type timer that was in turn plugged into a wall outlet farther behind the cabinet. Nothing had been disconnected. He could reach behind the cabinet, set the timer, and in one to five minutes, depending on how big a twist he gave the dial, the institute would be destroyed.

What the hell is going on? he wondered.

He sat for a while at his desk, staring at the square of sky that he could see from one of his two windows: scattered, dirty gray clouds moving sluggishly across an azure backdrop.

Finally he left his office, went to the north stairs, and climbed quickly past the fourth floor to the attic. The door opened with only a brief squeak. He flipped the light switch and entered the long, half-finished room, stepping as softly as possible on the board floor. He checked three of the charges of plastique that he had hidden in the rafters two nights ago. The explosives had not been disturbed.

He had no need to examine the charges in the basement. He left the attic and returned to his office.

Obviously no one knew about either his intention of destroying the institute or his attempts to turn Laura's life away from a series of ordained tragedies. No one except Kokoschka. Damn it, Kokoschka *had* to know because he had shown up on the mountain road with an Uzi.

So why hadn't Kokoschka told anyone else?

Kokoschka was an officer of the state's secret police, a true fanatic, obedient and eager servant of the government, and personally responsible for the security of Lightning Road. On discovering a traitor at the institute, Kokoschka would not have hesitated to call in squads of agents to encircle the building, guard the gate, and interrogate everyone.

Surely he would not have allowed Stefan to go to Laura's aid on that mountain highway, then follow with the intent of killing them all. For one thing, he would want to detain Stefan and interrogate him to determine if Stefan had conspirators in the institute.

Kokoschka had learned of Stefan's meddling in the ordained flow of events in one woman's life. And he had either discovered or had not discovered the explosives in the institute – probably not, or he would have at least unwired them. Then for reasons of his own he had not reacted as a policeman but as an individual. This morning he had followed Stefan through the gate, to that wintry afternoon in January of '88, with intentions that Stefan did not now understand at all.

It made no sense. Yet that was what had to have happened.

What had Kokoschka been up to?

He would probably never know.

Now Kokoschka was dead on a highway in 1988, and soon someone at the institute would realize that he was missing.

This afternoon at two o'clock, Stefan was scheduled to take an approved jaunt under the direction of Penlovski and Januskaya. He had intended to blow the institute – in two senses – at one o'clock, an hour before the scheduled event. Now, at 11:43, he decided that he would have to move faster than he originally intended, before Kokoschka's disappearance caused alarm.

He went to one of the tall files, opened the bottom drawer, which was empty, and disconnected it from its slides, lifting it all the way out of the cabinet. Wired to the back of the drawer was a pistol, a Colt Commander 9mm Parabellum with a nine-round magazine, acquired on one of his illicit jaunts and brought back secretly to the institute. From behind another drawer he removed two high-tech silencers and four additional, fully loaded magazines. At his desk, working quickly lest someone enter without knocking, he screwed one of the silencers onto the pistol, flicked off the safety, and distributed the other silencer and magazines in the pockets of his lab coat.

When he left the institute by way of the gate for the last time, he could not trust to the explosives to kill Penlovski, Januskaya, and certain other scientists. The blast would bring down the building and no doubt destroy all machinery and paper files, but what if just one of the key researchers survived? The necessary knowledge to rebuild the gate was in Penlovski's and Januskaya's minds, so Stefan planned to kill them and one other man, Volkaw, before he set the timer on the explosives and entered the gate to return to Laura.

With the silencer attached, the Commander was too long to fit all the way in the pocket of his lab coat, so he turned the pocket inside out and tore the bottom of it. With his finger on the trigger, he shoved the gun into his now bottomless pocket and held it there as he opened his office door and went into the hallway.

His heart pounded furiously. This was the most dangerous part of his plan, the killing, because there were so many opportunities for something to go wrong before he finished with the gun and returned to his office to set the timer on the explosives.

Laura was a long way off, and he might never see her again.

· 5 ·

On Monday afternoon Laura and Chris dressed in gray sweat suits. After Thelma helped them unroll the thick gym mats on the patio at the back of the house, Laura and Chris sat side by side and did deep-breathing exercises.

'When does Bruce Lee arrive?' Thelma asked.

'At two,' Laura said.

'He's not Bruce Lee, Aunt Thelma,' Chris said exasperatedly. 'You keep calling him Bruce Lee, but Bruce Lee is dead.'

Mr. Takahami arrived promptly at two o'clock. He was wearing a dark blue sweat suit, on the back of which was the logo for his martial arts school: QUIET STRENGTH. When introduced to Thelma, he said, 'You're a very funny lady. I love your record album.'

Glowing from the praise, Thelma said, 'And I can honestly tell you that I sincerely wish Japan had won the war.'

Henry laughed. 'I think we did.'

Sitting on a sun lounger, sipping iced tea, Thelma watched while Henry instructed Laura and Chris in self-defense.

He was forty years old, with a well-developed upper body and wiry legs. He was a master of judo and karate, as well as an expert kick boxer, and he taught a form of self-defense based on various martial arts, a system which he had devised himself. Twice a week he drove out from Riverside and spent three hours with Laura and Chris.

The kicking, punching, poking, grunting, twisting, throwing, off-the-hip rolling combat was conducted gently enough not to cause injury but with enough force to teach. Chris's lessons were less strenuous and less elaborate than Laura's, and Henry gave the boy plenty of breaks to pause and recoup. But by the end of the session, Laura was, as always, dripping sweat and exhausted.

When Henry left, Laura sent Chris upstairs to shower while she and Thelma rolled up the mats.

'He's cute,' Thelma said.

'Henry? I guess he is.'

'Maybe I'll take up judo or karate.'

'Have your audiences been *that* dissatisfied lately?'

'That one was below the belt, Shane.'

'Anything's fair when the enemy's formidable and merciless.'

———————

The following afternoon, as Thelma was putting her suitcase in the trunk of her Camaro for the return trip to Beverly Hills, she said, 'Hey, Shane, you remember that first foster family you were sent to from McIlroy?'

'The Teagels,' Laura said. 'Flora, Hazel, and Mike.'

Thelma leaned against the sun-warmed side of the car next to Laura. 'You remember what you told us about Mike's fascination with newspapers like the *National Enquirer?*'

'I remember the Teagels as if I lived with them yesterday.'

'Well,' Thelma said, 'I've been thinking a lot about what's happened to you – this guardian, the way he never ages, the way he disappeared into thin air – and I thought of the Teagels, and it all seems sort of ironic to me. All those nights at McIlroy, we laughed at nutty old Mike Teagel . . . and now what you find yourself in the middle of is a prime bit of exotic news.'

Laura laughed softly. 'Maybe I'd better reconsider all those tales of aliens living secretly in Cleveland, huh?'

'I guess what I'm trying to say is . . . life is full of wonders and surprises. Some of them are nasty surprises, yeah, and some days are as dark as the inside of the average politician's head. But just the same, there are moments that make me realize we're all here for some reason, enigmatic as it might be. It's not meaningless. If it was meaningless, there'd be no mystery. It'd be as dull and clear and lacking in mystery as the mechanism of a Mr. Coffee machine.'

Laura nodded.

'God, listen to me! I'm torturing the English language to come up with a half-baked philosophical statement that ultimately means nothing more than "keep your chin up, kid." '

'You're not half-baked.'

'Mystery,' Thelma said. 'Wonder. You're in the middle of it, Shane, and that's what life's all about. If it's dark right now . . . well, this too shall pass.'

They stood by the car, hugging, not needing to say more, until Chris ran out from the house with a crayon drawing he had done for Thelma and that he wanted her to take back to LA with her. It was a crude but charming scene of Tommy Toad standing outside a movie theater, gazing up at a marquee on which Thelma's name was huge.

He had tears in his eyes. 'But do you really have to go, Aunt Thelma? Can't you stay one more day?'

Thelma hugged him, then carefully rolled up the drawing as if in possession of a priceless masterwork. 'I'd love to stay, Christopher Robin, but I can't. My adoring fans are crying for me to make this movie. Besides, I've got a big mortgage.'

'What's a mortgage?'

'The greatest motivator in the world,' Thelma said, giving him a last kiss. She got into the car, started the engine, put down the side window, and winked at Laura. 'Exotic news, Shane.'

'Mystery.'

'Wonder.'

Laura gave her the four-finger greeting from *Star Trek*.

Thelma laughed. 'You'll make it, Shane. In spite of the guns and all I've learned since I came here on Friday, I'm less worried about you now than I was then.'

Chris stood at Laura's side, and they watched Thelma's car until it went down the long driveway and disappeared onto the state route.

• 6 •

Dr. Vladimir Penlovski's large office suite was on the fourth floor of the institute. When Stefan entered the reception lounge, it was deserted, but he heard voices coming from the next room. He went to the inner door, which was ajar, pushed it all the way open, and saw Penlovski giving dictation to Anna Kaspar, his secretary.

Penlovski looked up, mildly surprised to see Stefan. He must have perceived the tension in Stefan's face, for he frowned and said, 'Is something wrong?'

'Something's been wrong for a long time,' Stefan said, 'but it'll all be fine now, I think.' Then, as Penlovski's frown deepened, Stefan pulled the silencer-equipped Colt Commander from the pocket of his lab coat and shot the scientist twice in the chest.

Anna Kaspar sprang up from her chair, dropping her pencil and dictation pad, a scream caught in her throat.

He did not like killing women – he did not like killing anyone – but there was no choice now, so he shot her three times, knocking her backward onto the desk, before the scream could tear free of her.

Dead, she slid off the desk and crumpled to the floor. The shots had been no louder than the hissing of an angry cat, and the sound of the body dropping had been insufficient to draw attention.

Penlovski was slumped in his chair, eyes and mouth open, staring sightlessly. One of the shots must have pierced his heart, for there was only a small spot of blood on his shirt; his circulation had been cut off in an instant.

Stefan backed out of the room, closed the door. He crossed the reception lounge and, stepping into the hall, shut the outer door too.

His heart was racing. With those two murders he had cut himself off forever from his own time, his own people. From here on, the only life for him was in Laura's time. Now there was no turning back.

With his hands – and the gun – jammed in his lab-coat pockets, he went down the hall toward Januskaya's office. As he neared the door, two of his other colleagues came out of it. They said hello as they passed him, and he stopped to see if they were heading for Penlovski's office. If they were he'd have to kill them too.

He was relieved when they stopped at the elevators. The more corpses he left strewn around, the more likely someone would be to stumble across one of them and sound an alarm that would prevent him from setting the timer on the explosives and escaping by way of the Lightning Road.

He went into Januskaya's office, which also had a reception area. At the desk, the secretary – provided, as Anna Kaspar had been, by the secret police – looked up and smiled.

'Is Dr. Januskaya here?' Stefan asked.

'No. He's down in the documents room with Dr. Volkaw.'

Volkaw was the third man whose overview of the project was great enough to require that he be eliminated. It seemed a good omen that he and Wladyslaw Januskaya were conveniently in the same place.

In the documents room, they stored and studied the many books, newspapers, magazines, and other materials that had been brought back by time travelers from scheduled jaunts. These days the men who had conceived of Lightning Road were engaged in an urgent analysis of the key points at which alterations in the natural flow of events could provide the changes in the course of history that they desired.

On the way down in the elevator, Stefan replaced the pistol's silencer with the unused spare. The first would muffle another dozen shots before its sound baffles were seriously damaged. But he did not want to overuse it. The second silencer was additional insurance. He also quickly exchanged the half-empty magazine for a full one.

The first-floor corridor was a busy place, with people coming and going from one lab and research room to another. He kept his hands in his pockets and went directly to the documents room.

When Stefan entered, Januskaya and Volkaw were standing at an oak table, bent over a copy of a magazine, arguing heatedly but in low voices. They glanced up, then immediately continued their discussion, assuming that he was there for research purposes of his own.

Stefan put two bullets in Volkaw's back.

Januskaya reacted with confusion and shock as Volkaw flew forward into the table, driven by the impact of the nearly silent gunfire.

Stefan shot Januskaya in the face, then turned and left the room, closing the door behind him. Not trusting himself to speak to one of his colleagues with any degree of self-control or coherence, he tried to appear to be lost in thought, hoping that would dissuade them from approaching him. He went to the elevators as quickly as possible without running, went to his third-floor office, reached behind the file cabinet, and twisted the dial on the timer as far as it would go, giving himself just five minutes to get to the gate and away before the institute was reduced to burning rubble.

• 7 •

By the time the school year began, Laura had won approval for Chris to receive his education at home, from a state-accredited tutor. Her name was Ida Palomar, and she reminded Laura of Marjorie Main, the late actress in the Ma and Pa Kettle movies. Ida was a big woman, a bit gruff, but with a generous heart, and she was a good teacher.

By the Thanksgiving school break, instead of feeling as if they were imprisoned, both she and Chris had accommodated to the relative isolation in which they lived. In fact they had actually come to enjoy the special closeness that developed between them as a result of having so few other people in their lives.

On Thanksgiving Day Thelma called from Beverly Hills to wish them a happy holiday. Laura took the call in the kitchen, which was full of the aroma of roasting turkey. Chris was in the family room, reading Shel Silverstein.

'Besides wishing you a happy holiday,' Thelma said, 'I'm calling to invite you down here to spend Christmas week with me and Jason.'

'Jason?' Laura said.

'Jason Gaines, the director,' Thelma said. 'He's the guy who's directing this film I'm making. I've moved in with him.'

'Does he know it yet?'

'Listen, Shane, *I* make the wisecracks.'

'Sorry.'

'He says he loves me. Is that crazy or what? I mean, Jeez, here's this decent-looking guy, only five years older than me, with no visible mutations, who's a *hugely* successful film director, worth many millions, who could just about have any stacked little starlet he wanted, and the only one he wants is me. Now obviously he's brain-damaged, but you wouldn't know it to talk to him, he could pass for normal. He says what he loves about me is I've got a *brain*—'

'Does he know how diseased it is?'

'There you go again, Shane. He says he loves my brain and sense of humor, and he's even excited by my body – or if he isn't excited then he's the first guy in history who could *fake* an erection.'

'You've got a perfectly lovely body.'

'Well, I'm beginning to consider the possibility that it's not as bad as I always thought. That is, if you consider *boniness* to be the sine qua non of feminine beauty. But even if I am able to look at my body in a mirror now, it's still got *this* face perched atop it.'

'You've got a perfectly lovely face – especially now that it's not surrounded by green and purple hair.'

'It's not *your* face, Shane. Which means I'm mad for inviting you here for Christmas week. Jason will see you, and the next thing I'll be sitting in a Glad trash bag at the curb. But what about it? Will you come? We're shooting the film in and around LA, and we'll finish principal photography December tenth. Then Jason's got a lot of work to do, what with the editing, the whole schmear, but Christmas week we're just *stopping*. We'd like you to be here. Say you will.'

'I'd sure like to meet the man smart enough to fall for you, Thelma, but I don't know. I feel . . . safe here.'

'What do you think – we're dangerous?'

'You know what I mean.'

'You can bring an Uzi.'

'What will Jason think of that?'

'I'll tell him you're a radical leftist, save-the-sperm-whale, get-toxic-preserva-tives-out-of-Spam, parakeet liberationist and that you keep an Uzi with you at all times in case the revolution comes without warning. He'll buy it. This is Holly-wood, kid. Most of the actors he works with are politically crazier than that.'

Through the family-room archway, Laura could see Chris curled up in the armchair with his book.

She sighed. 'Maybe it is time we got out in the world once in a while. And it's going to be a difficult Christmas if it's just Chris and me, this being the first without Danny. But I feel uneasy . . .'

'It's been over ten months, Laura,' Thelma said gently.

'But I'm not going to let down my guard.'

'You don't have to. I'm serious about the Uzi. Bring your whole arsenal if that'll make you feel better. Just come.'

'Well . . . all right.'

'Fantastic! I can't wait for you to meet Jason.'

'Do I detect that the love this brain-damaged Hollywood maven feels for you is reciprocated?'

'I'm crazy about him,' Thelma admitted.

'I'm happy for you, Thelma. In fact I'm standing here now with a grin that won't stop, and nothing's made me feel so good in months.'

Everything she said was true. But after she hung up, she missed Danny more than ever.

• 8 •

As soon as he set the timer behind the filing cabinet, Stefan left his third-floor office and went to the main lab on the ground floor. It was 12:14, and because the scheduled jaunt was not until two o'clock, the main lab was deserted. The windows were sealed, and most of the overhead lights were still off, as they had been little more than an hour ago, when he had returned from the San Bernardinos. The multitude of dials, gauges, and lighted graphs of the support machinery glowed green and orange. More in shadow than in the light, the gate awaited him.

Four minutes till detonation.

He went directly to the primary programming board and carefully adjusted the dials and switches and levers, setting the gate for the desired destination: southern California, near Big Bear, at eight o'clock on the night of January 10, 1988, just a few hours after Danny Packard had been killed. He had done the necessary calculations days ago and had them on a sheet of paper to which he referred, so he was able to program the machinery in only a minute.

If he could have traveled to the afternoon of the tenth, prior to the accident and the shoot-out with Kokoschka, he would have done so in the hope of saving Danny. However, they had learned that a time traveler could not revisit a place if he scheduled his second arrival shortly *before* his previous jaunt; there was a natural mechanism that prevented a traveler from being in a place where he might encounter himself on a previous jaunt. He could return to Big Bear *after* he had left Laura that January night, for having already departed from the highway, he was no longer at risk of encountering himself there. But if he set the gate for an arrival time that would make it possible for him to meet himself, he would simply bounce back to the institute without going anywhere. That was one of many mysterious aspects of time travel which they had learned, around which they worked, but which they did not understand.

When he finished programming the gate, he glanced at the latitude and longitude indicator to confirm that he would arrive in the general area of Big Bear. Then he looked at the clock that noted his arrival time, and he was startled to see that it showed 8:00 P.M., January 10, 1989, instead of 1988. The gate was now set to deliver him to Big Bear not hours after Danny's death but a full year later.

He was sure that his calculations were correct; he'd had plenty of time to make them and recheck them over the past couple of weeks. Evidently, nervous as he was, he had made a mistake when entering the numbers. He would have to reprogram the gate.

Less than three minutes until detonation.

He blinked sweat out of his eyes and studied the numbers on the paper, the end product of his extensive calculations. As he reached for a control knob to cancel out the current program and re-enter the first of the figures again, a shout of alarm went up in the ground-floor corridor. The cries sounded as if they were coming from the north end of the building, in the general area of the document room.

Someone had found the bodies of Januskaya and Volkaw.

He heard more shouting. People running.

Glancing nervously at the closed door to the hall, he decided he had no time to reprogram. He would have to settle for returning to Laura one year after he had last left her.

With the silencer-fitted Colt Commander in his right hand, he rose from the programming console and headed toward the gate – that eight-foot-high, twelve-foot-long, polished steel, open-ended barrel resting a foot off the floor on copper-plated blocks. He did not even want to risk taking time to recover his peacoat from the corner where he had left it an hour ago.

The commotion in the corridor was louder.

When he was only a couple of steps from the entrance to the gate, the lab door was thrown open behind him with such force that it hit the wall with a crash.

'Stop right there!'

Stefan recognized the voice, but he did not want to believe what he heard. He brought up the pistol as he swung around to confront his challenger: The man who had raced into the lab was Kokoschka.

Impossible. Kokoschka was dead. Kokoschka had followed him to Big Bear on the night of January 10, 1988, and he had killed Kokoschka on that snow-swept highway.

Stunned, Stefan squeezed off two shots, both wide.

Kokoschka returned his fire. One slug took Stefan in the chest, high on the left side, knocking him backward against the edge of the gate. He stayed on his feet and got off three shots at Kokoschka, forcing the bastard to dive for cover and roll behind a lab bench.

They were less than two minutes from detonation.

Stefan felt no pain because he was in shock. But his left arm was useless; it hung limply at his side. And an insistent, oily blackness seeped in at the edges of his vision.

Only a few overhead lights had been left on, but suddenly even they flickered and went out, leaving the room vaguely illuminated by the wan glow of the many glass-covered dials and gauges. For an instant Stefan thought the dying light was a further surrender of his consciousness, a subjective development, but then he realized the public power supply had failed again, evidently due to the work of saboteurs, for there had been no sirens to warn of an air attack.

Kokoschka fired twice from darkness, the muzzle flash marking his position, and Stefan loosed the last three rounds in his pistol, though there was no hope of hitting Kokoschka through the marble lab bench.

Thankful that the gate was powered by a secure generator and still functional, Stefan threw away the pistol and with his good hand gripped the rim of the barrel-shaped portal. He pulled himself inside and crawled frantically toward the three-quarter point, where he would cross the energy field and depart this place for Big Bear, 1989.

As he hitched on two knees and one good arm through the gloomy interior of the barrel, he abruptly realized that the timer on the detonator in his office was connected to the public power supply. The countdown to destruction had been interrupted when the lights had gone out.

With dismay he understood why Kokoschka was not dead in Big Bear in 1988. *Kokoschka had not made that trip yet.* Kokoschka had only now learned of Stefan's perfidy, when he had discovered the bodies of Januskaya and Volkaw. Before the public power supply was restored, Kokoschka would search Stefan's office, find the detonator, and disarm the explosives. The institute would not be destroyed.

Stefan hesitated, wondering if he should go back.

Behind him he heard other voices in the lab, other security men arriving to reinforce Kokoschka.

He crawled forward.

And what of Kokoschka? The security chief evidently would travel to January 10, 1988, trying to kill Stefan on state route 330. But he would only manage to kill Danny before being killed himself. Stefan was pretty sure that

Kokoschka's death was an immutable destiny, but he would need to think more about the paradoxes of time travel, to see if there was any way Kokoschka could escape being gunned down in 1988, a death that Stefan had already witnessed.

The complications of time travel were confusing even when one pondered them with a clear head. In his condition, wounded and struggling to remain conscious, he only grew dizzier thinking about such things. Later. He would worry about it later.

Behind him in the dark laboratory, someone began firing into the entrance of the gate, hoping to hit him before he reached the point of departure.

He crawled the last couple of feet. Toward Laura. Toward a new life in a distant time. But he had hoped to close forever the bridge between the era he was leaving and that to which he was now pledging himself. Instead the gate would remain open. And they could come across time to get him . . . and Laura.

• 9 •

Laura and Chris spent Christmas with Thelma at Jason Gaines's house in Beverly Hills. It was a twenty-two-room, Tudor-style mansion on six, walled acres, a phenomenally large property in an area where the cost per acre had long ago escalated far beyond reason. During construction in the '40s – it had been built by a producer of screwball comedies and war movies – no compromises had been made in quality, and the rooms were marked by beautiful detail work that could not have been duplicated these days at ten times the original cost: There were intricately coffered ceilings, some made of oak, some of copper; crown moldings were elaborately carved; the leaded windows were of stained or beveled glass, and they were set so deep in the castle-thick walls that one could comfortably sit on the wide sills; interior lintels were decorated with hand-carved panels – vines and roses, cherubs and banners, leaping deer, birds with ribbons trailing from their bills; exterior lintels were of carved granite, and in two were set mortared clusters of colorful della Robbia-style ceramic fruits. The six-acre property around the house was a meticulously maintained private park where winding stone pathways led through a tropical landscape of palms, benjaminas, ficus nidida, azaleas laden with brilliant red blossoms, impatiens, ferns, birds of paradise, and seasonal flowers of so many species that Laura could identify only half of them.

When Laura and Chris arrived early on Saturday afternoon, the day before Christmas, Thelma took them on a long tour of the house and grounds, after which they drank hot cocoa and ate miniature pastries prepared by the cook and served by the maid in the airy sun porch that looked out upon the swimming pool.

'Is this a crazy life, Shane? Can you believe that the same girl who spent almost ten years in holes like McIlroy and Caswell could end up living *here* without first having to be reincarnated as a princess?'

The house was so imposing that it encouraged anyone who owned it to feel Important with a capital I, and anyone in possession of it would be hard-pressed to avoid smugness and pomposity. But when Jason Gaines came home at four o'clock, he proved to be as unpretentious as anyone Laura knew, amazingly so for a man who had spent seventeen years in the movie business. He was thirty-eight, five years older than Thelma, and he looked like a younger Robert Vaughn, which was a lot better than 'decent-looking,' as Thelma had referred to him. He was home less than half an hour before he and Chris were huddled in one of his three hobby rooms, playing with an electric train set that covered a fifteen-by-twenty-foot platform, complete with detailed villages, rolling countryside, windmills, waterfalls, tunnels, and bridges.

That night, with Chris asleep in the room adjoining Laura's, Thelma visited her. In their pajamas they sat cross-legged on her bed, as if they were girls again, though they ate roasted pistachios and drank Christmas champagne instead of cookies and milk.

'The weirdest thing of all, Shane, is that in spite of where I came from, I feel as if I belong here. I don't feel out of place.'

She did not look out of place, either. Though she was still recognizably Thelma Ackerson, she had changed in the past few months. Her hair was better cut and styled; she had a tan for the first time in her life; and she carried herself more like a woman and less like a comic trying to win laughter – meaning approval – with each funny gesture and posture. She was wearing less flamboyant – and sexier – pajamas than usual: clingy, unpatterned, peach-colored silk. She was, however, still sporting bunny slippers.

'Bunny slippers,' she said, 'remind me of who I am. You can't get a swelled head if you wear bunny slippers. You can't lose your sense of perspective and start acting like a star or a rich lady if you keep on wearing bunny slippers. Besides, bunny slippers give me confidence because they're so jaunty; they make a statement; they say, "Nothing the world does to me can ever get me so far down that I can't be silly and frivolous." If I died and found myself in hell, I could endure the place if I had bunny slippers.'

Christmas Day was like a wonderful dream. Jason proved to be a sentimentalist with the undiminished wonder of a child. He insisted they gather at the Christmas tree in pajamas and robes, that they open their gifts with as much popping of ribbons and noisy tearing of paper and as much general drama as possible, that they sing carols, that while opening gifts they abandon the idea of a healthy breakfast and instead eat cookies, candy, nuts, fruitcake, and caramel popcorn. He proved that he had not just been trying to be a good host when he had spent the previous evening with Chris at the trains, for all Christmas Day he engaged the boy in one form of play or another, both inside and outside the house, and it was clear that he had a love of and natural rapport with kids. By dinnertime Laura realized Chris had laughed more in one day than in the entire past eleven months.

When she tucked the boy into bed that night, he said, 'What a great day, huh, Mom?'

'One of the all-time greats,' she agreed.

'All I wish,' he said as he dropped toward sleep, 'is that Daddy could've been here to play with us.'

'I wish the same thing, honey.'

'But in a way he was here, 'cause I thought of him a lot. Will I always remember him, Mom, the way he was, even after dozens and dozens of years, will I remember him?'

'I'll help you remember, baby.'

'Because sometimes already there are little things I don't quite remember about him. I have to think hard to remember them. But I don't want to forget 'cause he was my daddy.'

When he was asleep, Laura went through the connecting door to her own bed. She was immensely relieved when a few minutes later Thelma came by for another girl-to-girl, because without Thelma, she would have had a few very bad hours there.

'If I had babies, Shane,' Thelma said, climbing into Laura's bed, 'do you think there's any chance at all that they'd be allowed to live in society, or would they be banished to some ugly-kid equivalent of a leper colony?'

'Don't be silly.'

'Of course, I could afford *massive* plastic surgery for them. I mean, even if it turns out that their species is questionable, I could afford to have them made passably human.'

'Sometimes your put-downs of yourself make me angry.'

'Sorry. Chalk it up to not having a supportive mom and dad. I've got both the confidence and doubt of an orphan.' She was quiet for a moment, then laughed and said, 'Hey, you know what? Jason wants to marry me. I thought at first he was possessed by a demon and unable to control his tongue, but he assures me we've no need of an exorcist, though he's evidently suffered a minor stroke. So what do you think?'

'What do *I* think? What's that matter? But for what it's worth, he's a terrific guy. You are going to grab him, aren't you?'

'I worry that he's too good for me.'

'No one's too good for you. Marry him.'

'I worry that it won't work out, and then I'll be devastated.'

'And if you don't give it a try,' Laura said, 'you'll be worse than devastated – you'll be alone.'

• 10 •

Stefan felt the familiar, unpleasant tingle that accompanied time travel, a peculiar vibration that passed inward from his skin, through his flesh, into the marrow of his bones, then swiftly back out again from bones to flesh to skin. With a *pop-whoooosh* he left the gate, and in the same instant he was stumbling down a steep, snow-covered slope in the California mountains on the night of January 10, 1989.

He tripped, fell on his wounded side, rolled to the bottom of the slope, where he came to rest against a rotted log. Pain flashed through him for the first time since he had been shot. He cried out and flopped onto his back, biting his tongue to keep from passing out, blinking up at the tumultuous night.

Another thunderbolt ripped the sky, and light seemed to pulse from the jagged wound. By the spectral glow of the snow-covered earth and by the fierce but fitful flashes of lightning, Stefan saw that he was in a clearing in a forest. Leafless, black trees thrust bare limbs toward the fulminous sky, as if they were fanatical cultists praising a violent god. Evergreens, boughs drooping under surplices of snow, stood like the solemn priests of a more decorous religion.

Arriving in a time other than his own, a traveler disrupted the forces of nature in some way that required the dissipation of tremendous energy. Regardless of the weather at the point of arrival, the imbalance was corrected by a sky-shattering display of lightning, which was why the ethereal highway on which time travelers journeyed was called the Lightning Road. For reasons no one had been able to ascertain, a return to the institute, to the traveler's own era, was marked by no celestial pyrotechnics.

The lightning subsided, as it always did, from bolts worthy of the Apocalypse to distant flickerings. In a minute the night was dark and calm again.

As the thunderbolts had faded, his pain had increased. It almost seemed as if the lightning that had cracked the vaults of heaven was now captured within his chest, left shoulder, and left arm, too great a power for mortal flesh to contain or endure.

He got onto his knees and rose shakily to his feet, worried that he had little chance of getting out of the woods alive. But for the phosphorescent glow of the snow-mantled clearing the cloudy night was cellar-black, forbidding. Though undisturbed by wind, the winter air was icy, and he was wearing only a thin lab coat over shirt and pants.

Worse, he might be miles from a highway or any landmark by which he could reckon his position. If the gate was considered as a gun, its accuracy was remarkable for the temporal distance covered to the target, but it was far from perfect in its aim. A traveler usually arrived within ten or fifteen minutes of the *time* he intended, but not always with the desired geographic precision. Sometimes he touched down within a hundred yards of his physical destination, but on other occasions he was as far as ten or fifteen miles off, as on the day that he had traveled to January 10, 1988, to save Laura, Danny, and Chris from the Robertsons' sliding pickup truck.

On all previous trips, he had carried both a map of the target area and a compass, lest he find himself in just such a place of isolation as he had arrived at now. But this time, having left his peacoat in the corner of the lab, he had neither compass nor map, and the occluded sky deprived him of the hope of finding his way out of the forest with the help of the stars.

He stood in snow almost to his knees, wearing street shoes, no boots, and he felt as if he must start moving immediately or freeze to the ground. He looked around the clearing, hoping for inspiration, for a twinge of intuition, but at last he chose a direction at random and headed to his left, searching for a deer trail or other natural course that would provide him a passage through the forest.

His entire left side from neck to waist throbbed with pain. He hoped that the bullet, in passing through him, had torn no arteries and that the rate of blood loss was slow enough to allow him at least to reach Laura and see her face, the face he loved, one last time before he died.

The one-year anniversary of Danny's death fell on a Tuesday, and although Chris did not mention the significance of the date, he was aware of it. The boy was unusually quiet. He spent most of that somber day playing silently with his Masters of the Universe action figures in the family room, which was the kind of play ordinarily characterized by vocal imitations of laser weapons, clashing swords, and spaceship engines. Later he sprawled on his bed in his room, reading comic books. He resisted Laura's every effort to draw him out of his self-imposed isolation, which was probably for the best; any attempt she made to be cheerful would have been transparent, and he would have been further depressed by the perception that she was also struggling mightily to turn her thoughts away from their grievous loss.

Thelma, who had called only days before to report the good news that she had decided to marry Jason Gaines, called again at seven-fifteen that evening, just to chat, as if she were unaware of the importance of the date. Laura took the call in her office, where she was still struggling with the bile-black book that had occupied her for the past year.

'Hey, Shane, guess what? I met Paul McCartney! He was in LA to negotiate a recording contract, and we were at the same party Friday night. When I first saw him, he was stuffing an hors d'oeuvre in his mouth, he said hello, he had crumbs on his lip, and he was *gorgeous*. He said he'd seen my movies, thought I was very good, and we talked – you believe this? – we must've chatted twenty minutes, and gradually the strangest thing happened.'

'You discovered that you'd undressed him while you were talking.'

'Well, he still looks very good, you know, still that cherub face we swooned over twenty years ago but marked now by experience, *très* sophisticated and with an extremely appealing touch of sadness about his eyes, and he was enormously amusing and charming. At first maybe I did want to tear his clothes off, yeah, and live out the fantasy at last. But then the longer we talked, the less he seemed like a god, the more he seemed like a person, and in *minutes*, Shane, the myth evaporated, and he was just this very nice, attractive, middle-aged man. Now what do you make of that?'

'What am I supposed to make of it?'

'I don't know,' Thelma said. 'I'm a little disturbed. Shouldn't a living legend continue to awe you longer than twenty minutes after you meet him? I mean, I've met lots of stars by now, and none of them have remained godlike, but this was *McCartney*.'

'Well, if you want my opinion, his swift loss of mythological stature says nothing negative about him, but it says plenty positive about you. You've achieved a new maturity, Ackerson.'

'Does this mean I've got to give up watching old Three Stooges movies every Saturday morning?'

'The Stooges are permitted, but food fights are definitely a thing of the past for you.'

By the time Thelma hung up at ten minutes till eight, Laura was feeling slightly better, so she switched from the bile-black book to the tale about Sir Tommy Toad. She had written only two sentences of the children's story when the night beyond the windows was lit by a bolt of lightning bright enough to spark dire thoughts of nuclear holocaust. The subsequent thunderclap shook the house from roof to foundation, as if a wrecker's ball had slammed into one of the walls. She came to her feet with a start, so surprised that she did not even hit the 'save' key on the computer. A second bolt seared the night, making the windows as luminous as television screens, and the thunder that followed was louder than the first explosion.

'Mom!'

She turned and saw Chris standing in the doorway. 'It's okay,' she said. He ran to her. She sat in the spring-backed armchair and pulled him onto her lap. 'It's all right. Don't be afraid, honey.'

'But it's not raining,' he said. 'Why's it booming like that if it's not raining?'

Outside, an incredible series of lightning bolts and overlapping thunderclaps continued for nearly a minute, then subsided. The power of the event had been so great, Laura was able to imagine that in the morning they would find the broken sky lying about in huge chunks like fragments of a giant eggshell.

Before he walked five minutes from the clearing in which he had arrived, Stefan was forced to pause and lean against the thick trunk of a pine whose branches began just above his head. The pain of his wound wrung streams of sweat from him, yet he was shivering in the bitter January cold, too dizzy to stand up, yet terrified of sitting down and falling into an endless sleep. With the drooping boughs of that mammoth pine overhead and all around, he felt as if he had taken refuge under Death's black robe, from which he might not emerge.

Before putting Chris to bed for the night, she made sundaes for them with coconut-almond ice cream and Hershey's syrup. They ate at the kitchen table, and the boy's depression seemed to have lifted. Perhaps by marking the end of that sad anniversary with such drama, the bizarre weather phenomenon had startled him out of thoughts of death and into the contemplation of wonders. He was filled with talk of the lightning that had crackled down a kite string and into Dr. Frankenstein's laboratory in the old James Whale film, which he'd seen for the first time a week ago, and of the lightning that had frightened Donald Duck in a Disney cartoon, and of the stormy night in *101 Dalmatians* during which Cruella DeVille had posed such a dire threat to the title-role puppies.

By the time she tucked him in and kissed him goodnight, he was approaching sleep with a smile – a half smile, at least – rather than with the frown that had weighed upon his face all day. She sat in a chair by the side of his bed until he was fast asleep, though he was no longer afraid and did not require her presence. She stayed simply because she needed to look at him for a while.

She returned to her office at nine-fifteen, but before going to the word processor, she stopped at a window and stared out at the snow-swathed front lawn, at the black ribbon of the graveled driveway leading to the distant state route, and up at the starless, night sky. Something about the lightning deeply disturbed her: not that it had been so strange, not that it had been potentially destructive, but that the unprecedented and almost supernatural power of it had been somehow . . . familiar. She seemed to recall having witnessed a similar stormy display on another occasion, but she could not remember when. It was an uncanny feeling, akin to déjà vu, and it would not fade.

She went into the master bedroom and checked the security-control panel in her closet to be sure the perimeter alarm covering all the windows and doors was engaged. From beneath the bed, she withdrew the Uzi, which had an extended magazine holding four hundred exotic, light-weight, alloy-jacketed rounds. She took the gun back to her office and put it on the floor by her chair.

She was about to sit down when lightning split the night again, frightening her, and it was followed at once by a crack of thunder she felt in her bones. Another bolt and another and another blazed in the windows like a series of leering, ghostly faces formed of ectoplasmic light.

As the heavens quaked with scintillant shudders, Laura hurried to Chris's room to calm him. To her surprise, though the lightning and thunder were shockingly more violent than they had been previously, the boy was not awakened, perhaps because the din seemed a part of some dream he was having about Dalmatian puppies on a stormy night of adventure.

Again, no rain fell.

The lightning and thunder quickly subsided, but her anxiety remained high.

He saw strange ebony shapes in the darkness, things that slipped between the trees and watched him with eyes blacker than their bodies, but though they startled and frightened him, he knew that they were not real, only phantoms spawned by his increasingly disoriented mind. He plodded onward in spite of outer cold, inner heat, prickling pine needles, sharp bramble thorns, icy ground that sometimes tilted out from beneath his feet and sometimes spun like a phonograph turntable. The pain in his chest and shoulder and arm was so intense that he was assailed by delirium images of rats gnawing at his flesh from within his body, though he could not figure how they had gotten *in* there.

After wandering for at least an hour – it seemed like many hours, even days, but it could not have been days because the sun had not risen – he came to the perimeter of the forest and, at the far end of a sloping half acre of snow-mantled lawn, he saw the house. Lights were vaguely visible at the edges of the blind-covered windows.

He stood, disbelieving, at first convinced that the house was no more real than the Stygian figures that had accompanied him through the woods. Then he began moving toward the mirage – in case it wasn't a fever dream, after all.

When he had taken only a few steps, a flash of lightning whipped the night, scarred the sky. The whip cracked repeatedly, and each time a stronger arm seemed to power it.

Stefan's shadow leaped and writhed on the snow around him, though he was temporarily paralyzed by fear. Sometimes he had two shadows because lightning silhouetted him simultaneously from two directions. Already well-trained hunters had followed him on the Lightning Road, determined to stop him before he had a chance to warn Laura.

He looked back at the trees out of which he had come. Under the stroboscopic sky, the evergreens seemed to jump toward him, then back, then toward him again. He saw no hunters there.

As the lightning faded, he staggered toward the house again. He fell twice, struggled up, kept moving, though he was afraid that if he fell again he would not be able to get to his feet or shout loud enough to be heard.

Staring at the computer screen, trying to think about Sir Tommy Toad and thinking instead of the lightning, Laura suddenly recalled when she previously had seen such a preternaturally stormy sky: the very day on which her father had first told her about Sir Tommy, the day that the junkie had come into the grocery, the day that she had seen her guardian for the first time, that summer of her eighth year.

She sat up straight in her chair.

Her heart began to hammer hard, fast.

Lightning of that unnatural power meant trouble of a specific nature, trouble for *her*. She could recall no lightning on the day that Danny died or when her guardian appeared in the cemetery during her father's burial service. But with an absolute certainty that she could not explain, she knew that the phenomenon she had witnessed tonight held a terrible meaning for her; it was an omen and not a good one.

She grabbed the Uzi and made a circuit of the upstairs, checking all the windows, looking in on Chris, making sure everything was as it should be. Then she hurried downstairs to inspect those rooms.

As she stepped into the kitchen, something thumped against the back door. With a gasp of surprise and fear, she whirled in that direction, swung the Uzi around, and nearly opened fire.

But it was not the determined sound of someone breaking in. It was an unthreatening thump, barely louder than a knock, repeated twice. She thought she heard a voice, too, weakly calling her name.

Silence.

She edged to the door and listened for perhaps half a minute.

Nothing.

The door was a high-security model with a steel core sandwiched between two-inch slabs of oak, so she was not worried about being shot by a gunman on the other side. Yet she hesitated to move directly to it and peer through the fisheye lens because she feared seeing an eye pressed to the other side, trying to peer in at *her*. When at last she had the courage for it, the peephole gave her a wide-angled view of the patio, and she saw a man sprawled on the concrete, his arms flung out at his sides, as if he had fallen backward after knocking on the door.

Trap, she thought. Trap, trick.

She switched on the outdoor spotlights and crept to the Levelor-covered window above the built-in writing desk. Cautiously she lifted one of the slats. The man on the concrete patio was her guardian. His shoes and trousers were caked with snow. He wore what appeared to be a white lab coat, the front darkly stained with blood.

As far as she could see, no one was crouched on the patio or on the lawn beyond, but she had to consider the possibility that someone had dumped his body there as a lure to bring her out of the house. Opening the door at night, under these circumstances, was foolhardy.

Nevertheless she could not leave him out there. Not her guardian. Not if he was hurt and dying.

She pressed the alarm bypass button next to the door, disengaged the dead-bolt locks, and reluctantly stepped into the wintry night with the Uzi at the ready. No one shot at her. On the dimly snow-illumined lawn, all the way back to the forest, nothing moved.

She went to her guardian, knelt at his side, and felt for his pulse. He was alive. She peeled back one of his eyelids. He was unconscious. The wound high in the left side of his chest looked bad, though it did not appear to be bleeding at the moment.

Her training with Henry Takahami and her regular exercise program had dramatically increased her strength, but she was not strong enough to lift the wounded man with one arm. She propped the Uzi by the back door and found she could not lift him even with both arms. It seemed dangerous to move a man who was so badly hurt, but more dangerous to leave him in the frigid night, especially when someone was apparently in pursuit of him. She managed to half lift and half drag him into the kitchen, where she stretched him out on the floor. With relief she retrieved the Uzi, relocked the door, and engaged the alarm again.

He was frighteningly pale and cold to the touch, so the immediate necessity was to strip off his shoes and socks, which were crusted with snow. By the time she dealt with his left foot and was unlacing his right shoe, he was mumbling in a strange language, the words too slurred for her to identify the tongue, and in English he muttered about explosives and gates and 'phantoms in the trees.'

Though she knew that he was delirious and very likely could not understand her any more than she could understand him, she spoke to him reassuringly: 'Easy now, just relax, you'll be all right; as soon as I get your foot out of this block of ice, I'll call a doctor.'

The mention of a doctor brought him briefly out of his confusion. He gripped her arm weakly, fixed her with an intense, fearful gaze. 'No doctor. Get out . . . got to get out. . . .'

'You're in no condition to go anywhere,' she told him. 'Except by ambulance to a hospital.'

'Got to get out. Quick. They'll be coming . . . soon coming. . . .'

She glanced at the Uzi. 'Who will be coming?'

'Assassins,' he said urgently. 'Kill me for revenge. Kill you, kill Chris. Coming. Now.'

At that moment there was no delirium in his eyes or voice. His pale, sweat-slick face was no longer slack but taut with terror.

All her training with guns and in the martial arts no longer seemed like hysterical precautions. 'Okay,' she said, 'we'll get out as soon as I've had a look at that wound, see if it needs to be dressed.'

'No! Now. Out now.'

'But—'

'Now,' he insisted. In his eyes was such a haunted look, she could almost believe that the assassins of whom he spoke were not ordinary men but creatures of some supernatural origin, demons with the ruthlessness and relentlessness of the soulless.

'Okay,' she said. 'We'll get out now.'

His hand fell away from her arm. His eyes shifted out of focus, and he began to mumble thickly, senselessly.

As she hurried across the kitchen, intending to go upstairs and wake Chris, she heard her guardian speak dreamily yet anxiously of a 'great, black, rolling machine of death,' which meant nothing to her but frightened her nonetheless.

PART TWO

PURSUIT

The long habit of living indisposeth us for dying.

SIR THOMAS BROWNE

Five

An Army of Shadows

• 1 •

Laura switched on a lamp and shook Chris awake. 'Get dressed, honey. Quickly.'

'What's happening?' he asked sleepily, rubbing his eyes with his small fists.

'Some bad men are coming, and we've got to get out of here before they arrive. Now hurry.'

Chris had spent a year not only mourning his father but preparing for the moment when the deceptively placid events of daily life would be disrupted by another unexpected explosion of the chaos that lay at the heart of human existence, the chaos that from time to time erupted like an active volcano, as it had done the night his father had been murdered. Chris had watched his mother become a first-rate shot with a handgun, had seen her collect an arsenal, had taken self-defense classes with her, and through it all he had retained the point of view and attitudes of a child, had seemed pretty much like any other child, if understandably melancholy since the death of his father. But now in a moment of crisis he did not react like an eight-year-old; he did not whine or ask unnecessary questions; he was not quarrelsome or stubborn or slow to obey. He threw back the covers, got out of bed at once, and hurried to the closet.

'Meet me in the kitchen,' Laura said.

'Okay, Mom.'

She was proud of his responsible reaction and relieved that he would not delay them, but she was also saddened that at eight years of age he understood enough about the brevity and harshness of life to respond to a crisis with the swiftness and equanimity of an adult.

She was wearing jeans and a blue-plaid, flannel shirt. When she went to her bedroom, she only had to slip into a wool sweater, pull off her Rockport walking shoes, and put on a pair of rubberized hiking boots with lace-up tops.

She had gotten rid of Danny's clothes, so she had no coat for the wounded man in the kitchen. She had plenty of blankets, however, and she grabbed two of those from the linen closet in the hall.

As an afterthought, she went to her office, opened the safe, and removed the strange black belt with copper fittings that her guardian had given her a year ago. She jammed it in her satchel-like purse.

Downstairs she stopped at the front foyer closet for a blue ski jacket and the Uzi carbine that hung on the back of the door. As she moved she was alert for unusual noises – voices in the night beyond the house or the sound of a car engine – but all remained silent.

In the kitchen she put the submachine gun on the table with the other one, then knelt beside her guardian, who was unconscious again. She unbuttoned his snow-wet lab coat, then his shirt, and looked at the gunshot wound in his chest. It was high in his left shoulder, well above the heart, which was good, but he had lost a lot of blood; his clothes were soaked with it.

'Mom?' Chris was in the doorway, dressed for a winter night.

'Take one of those Uzis from the table, get the one from the back of the pantry door, and put them both in the Jeep.'

'It's him,' Chris said, wide-eyed with surprise.

'Yes, it is. He showed up like this, hurt bad. Besides the Uzis, get two of the revolvers – the one in the drawer over there and the one in the dining room. And be careful not to accidentally—'

'Don't worry, Mom,' he said, setting off on the errands.

As gently as possible she rolled her guardian onto his right side – he groaned but did not awaken – to see if there was an exit wound in his back. Yes. The bullet had gone through him, exiting under the scapula. His back was soaked with blood, too, but neither the entry nor exit point was bleeding heavily any longer; if there was serious bleeding, it was internal, and she could not detect or treat it.

Under his clothing he wore one of the belts. She unbuckled it. The belt wouldn't fit in the center compartment of her purse, so she had to stuff it into a zippered side compartment after dumping out the items she usually kept in there.

She rebuttoned his shirt and debated whether she should take off his damp lab coat. She decided it would be too difficult to wrestle the sleeves down his arms. Rolling him gently from side to side, she worked a gray wool blanket under and around him.

While Laura bundled up the wounded man, Chris made a couple of trips to the Jeep with the guns, using the inner door that connected the laundry room to the garage. Then he came in with a two-foot-wide, four-foot-long, flat dolly – essentially a wooden platform on casters – that had accidentally been left behind by some furniture delivery men almost a year and a half ago. Riding it like a skateboard toward the pantry, he said, 'We gotta take the ammo box, but it's too heavy for me to carry. I'll put it on this.'

Pleased by his initiative and cleverness, she said, 'We have twelve rounds in the two revolvers and twelve *hundred* rounds in the three Uzis, so I don't think we'll need more than that, no matter what happens. Bring the board here. Quick now. I've been trying to figure how we can get him to the Jeep without shaking him up too bad. That looks like the ticket.'

They were moving fast, as if they had drilled for just this particular emergency, yet Laura felt that they were taking too much time. Her hands were shaking, and her belly fluttered continuously. She expected someone to hammer on the door at any moment.

Chris held the dolly still while Laura heaved the wounded man onto it. When she got the board under his head, shoulders, back, and buttocks, she was able to lift his legs and push him as if he were a wheelbarrow. Chris scooted along at a crouch by the front wheels, one hand on the unconscious man's right shoulder to keep him from sliding off and to prevent the board from rolling out from beneath him. They had a little trouble easing across the door sill at the end of the laundry room, but they got him into the three-car garage.

The Mercedes was on the left, the Jeep wagon on the right, with the middle slot empty. They wheeled her guardian to the Jeep.

Chris had opened the tailgate. He had also unrolled a small gym mat in there for a mattress.

'You're a great kid,' she told him.

Together they managed to transfer the wounded man from the dolly into the cargo bed by way of the open tailgate.

'Bring the other blanket and his shoes from the kitchen,' she told Chris.

By the time the boy returned with those items, Laura had gotten her guardian stretched out flat on his back on the gym mat. They covered his bare feet with the second blanket and put his soggy shoes beside him.

As Laura shut the tailgate, she said, 'Chris, get in the front seat and buckle up.'

She hurried back into the house. Her purse, which contained all of her credit cards, was on the table; she slipped the straps over her shoulder. She picked up the third Uzi and headed back toward the laundry room, but before she had taken three steps, something hit the rear door with tremendous force.

She whirled, bringing up the gun.

Something slammed into the door again, but the steel core and Schlage deadbolts could not be defeated easily.

Then the nightmare began in earnest.

A submachine gun chattered, and Laura threw herself against the side of the refrigerator, sheltering there. They were trying to blow open the back door, but the heavy steel core held against that assault too. The door shook, however, and bullets pierced the wall on both sides of the reinforced frame, tearing holes in the drywall.

Family-room and kitchen windows exploded as a second submachine gun opened fire. The metal Levelors danced on their mountings. Metal slats twanged as slugs passed between them, and some slats bent, but most of the shattered window glass was contained behind the blinds, where it rained on sills and from there to the floor. Cabinet doors splintered and cracked as bullets pierced them, and chips of brick flew off one wall, and bullets ricocheted off the copper range hood, leaving it dented, creased. Hanging from ceiling hooks, the copper pots and pans took a lot of hits, producing a variety of *clinks* and *ponks*. One overhead light blew out. The Levelor at the window above the writing desk was torn off its mountings at last, and half a dozen slugs plowed into the refrigerator door just inches from her.

Her heart was racing, and a flood of adrenaline had made her senses almost painfully sharp. She wanted to run for the Jeep in the garage and try to get out before they realized she was in the process of leaving, but a primal warrior instinct told her to stay put. She pressed flat against the side of the refrigerator, out of the direct line of fire, hoping that she would not be hit by a ricochet.

Who the hell *are* you people? she wondered angrily.

The firing stopped, and her instinct proved true: The barrage was followed by the gunmen themselves. They stormed the house. The first one clambered through the imploded window above the kitchen desk. She stepped away from the refrigerator and opened fire, blowing him back out onto the patio. A second man, dressed in black like the first, entered by the shattered sliding door in the family room – she saw him through the archway a second before he saw her – and she swung the Uzi in that direction, spraying bullets, destroying the Mr. Coffee machine, tearing the hell out of the kitchen wall beside the archway, then cutting him down as he brought his weapon around toward her. She had practiced with the Uzi but not recently, and she was surprised at how controllable it was. She was also surprised at how sickened she was by the need to kill them, though they were trying to slaughter her and her child; like a wave of oily sludge, nausea washed through her, but she choked down the gorge that rose in her throat. A third man started into the family room, and she was ready to kill him, too, and a hundred like him, no matter how sick the killing made her, but he threw himself backward, out of the line of fire, when he saw his companion blown away.

Now the Jeep.

She didn't know how many killers were outside, maybe only the three, two dead and one still living, maybe four or ten or a hundred, but regardless of how many there were, they would not have expected to be met with such a bold response and certainly not with so much firepower, no way, not from a woman and a small boy, and they had known that her guardian was wounded and unarmed. So right now they were stunned, and they'd be taking cover, assessing the situation, planning their next move. This might be her first and last chance to get away in the Jeep wagon. She sprinted through the laundry room into the garage.

She saw that Chris had started the Jeep's engine when he'd heard the gunfire; bluish exhaust fumes billowed from the tailpipes. As she ran to the Jeep, the garage door started up; Chris had evidently used the Genie remote-control unit the moment he saw her.

By the time she got behind the wheel, the garage door was a third open. She shifted into gear. 'Get down!'

As Chris instantly obeyed, sliding down in his seat below window level, Laura let up on the brakes. She rammed the accelerator against the floorboards, peeled rubber on the concrete, and roared out into the night, clearing the still rising garage door by only an inch or two, ripping off the radio antenna.

The Jeep's big tires, though not swaddled in chains, had heavy winter tread. They dug into the frozen slush and gravel that formed the surface of the driveway, finding traction with no trouble, spewing shrapnel of stone and ice.

From off to her left came a dark figure, a man in black, running across the front lawn, kicking up snow, forty or fifty feet away, and he was such a featureless shape that he might have been just a shadow, except that over the screaming of the engine she heard the rattle of automatic gunfire. Slugs slammed into the side of the Jeep, and the window behind her blew in, but the window beside her remained intact, and then she was speeding away, heading out of range, a few seconds from safety now, with wind shrieking at the broken window. She prayed none of the tires would be hit, and she heard more rounds striking sheet metal, or maybe it was gravel and ice churned up by the Jeep.

When she reached the state route at the end of the drive-way, she was certain that she was out of range. As she braked hard for the left turn, she glanced into the rearview mirror and saw, far back, a pair of headlights at the open garage. The killers had arrived at her house without a vehicle – God only knew how they had traveled, perhaps with the use of those strange belts – and they were using her Mercedes to pursue her.

She had intended to turn left on the state route, head down past Running Springs, past the turnoff to Lake Arrowhead, on to the superhighway and into the city of San Bernardino, where there were people and safety in numbers, where men dressed in black and toting automatic weapons would not stalk her so boldly, and where she could get medical treatment for her guardian. But when she saw the headlights behind her, she responded to an innate proclivity for survival, turning right instead, heading east-northeast toward Big Bear Lake.

If she had gone left they would have come to that fateful half mile of inclined highway on which Danny had been murdered a year ago; and Laura felt intuitively – almost superstitiously – that the most dangerous place in the world for them at the moment was that sloping length of two-lane blacktop. She and Chris had been meant to die twice on that hill: first, when the Robertsons' pickup slid out of control; second, when Kokoschka opened fire on them. Sometimes she perceived that there were both benign and ominous patterns in life and that, once thwarted, fate strove to reassert those predestined designs. Though she had no intellectually sound reason for believing that they would die if they headed down toward Running Springs, she knew in her heart that death in fact awaited them there.

As they pulled onto the state route and headed for Big Bear, tall evergreens rising darkly on both sides, Chris sat up and looked back.

'They're coming,' Laura told him, 'but we'll outrun them.'

'Are they the ones that got Daddy?'

'Yes, I think so. But we didn't know about them then, and we weren't prepared.'

The Mercedes was on the state route now, out of sight most of the time because the roadway rose and fell and twisted, putting hills and turns between the two vehicles. The car seemed to be about two hundred yards behind, but it was probably closing because it had a bigger engine and a lot more power than the Jeep.

'Who are they?' Chris asked.

'I'm not sure, honey. And I don't know why they want to hurt us, either. But I know *what* they are. They're thugs, they're scum, I learned all about their type a long time ago at Caswell Hall, and I know the only thing you can do with people like them is stand up to them, fight back, because they only respect toughness.'

'You were terrific back there, Mom.'

'You were darned good yourself, kiddo. That was very smart of you to start the Jeep when you heard the gunfire, and to have the garage door on the way up by the time I got behind the wheel. That probably saved us.'

Behind them the Mercedes had closed the distance to about one hundred yards. It was a road-hugger, a 420 SEL, which handled as well as anything on the highway, much better than the Jeep.

'They're coming fast, Mom.'

'I know.'

'Real fast.'

Approaching the eastern point of the lake, Laura pulled up behind a rattle-trap Dodge pickup with one broken taillight and a rusted bumper that appeared to be held together by stickers with supposedly funny sayings – I BRAKE FOR BLONDES, MAFIA STAFF CAR. It chugged along at thirty miles an hour, below the speed limit. If Laura hesitated, the Mercedes would close the gap; when they were near enough the killers might use their guns again. They were in a no-passing zone, but she could see enough clear road ahead to risk the maneuver;

she swung around the pickup, tramped the accelerator hard, got in front of the truck, and returned to the right lane. Immediately ahead was a Buick doing about forty, and she passed that, too, just before the road got too twisty to allow the Mercedes to get around the old truck.

'They're hung up back there!' Chris said.

Laura put the Jeep up to fifty-five, which was too fast for some of the turns, though she held it on the road and began to think they were going to escape. But the highway split at the lake, and neither the Buick nor the old Ford pickup followed her along the south shore toward Big Bear City; they both turned toward Fawnskin and the north shore, leaving the road empty between her and the Mercedes, which at once began to close the distance between them.

Houses were everywhere now, both on the high ground to the right and on the lower ground down toward the lake on her left. Some of them were dark, probably vacation homes used only on winter weekends and in the summers, but the lights of other places were visible among the trees.

She knew she could follow any of those lanes and driveways to a hundred different houses where she and Chris would have been taken in. People would open their doors without hesitation. This was not the city; in the small-town atmosphere of the mountains, people were not instantly suspicious of unannounced night visitors.

The Mercedes closed to within a hundred yards, and the driver flicked the headlights from low beam to high beam again and again, as if gleefully saying, *Hey, here we come, Laura, we're gonna get you, we're the bogeymen, the real thing, and nobody can run from us forever, here we come, here we come.*

If she tried to take refuge in one of the nearby houses, the killers probably would follow, murdering not only her and Chris but the people who sheltered them. The bastards might be reluctant to chase her to ground in the heart of San Bernardino or Riverside or even Redlands, where they were likely to encounter police response, but they would not be intimidated by a mere handful of bystanders because no matter how many people they slaughtered, they could no doubt elude capture by pushing the yellow buttons on their belts and vanishing as her guardian had vanished one year ago. She had no idea where they would be vanishing *to*, but she suspected that it was a place where the police could never touch them. She would not risk innocent lives, so she passed house after house without slowing.

The Mercedes was about fifty yards back, closing fast.

'Mom—'

'I see them, honey.'

She was headed toward Big Bear City, but unfortunately the place was inaptly named. It was not only less than a city but not even much of a village, hardly a hamlet. There were not enough streets for her to hope to lose their pursuers, and the police presence was inadequate to deal with a couple of fanatics armed with submachine guns.

Light traffic passed them going the other way, and she got behind another car in their lane, a gray Volvo, around which she whipped on an almost blind stretch of road, but she had no choice because the Mercedes was within forty yards. The killers passed the Volvo with equal recklessness.

'How's our passenger?' she asked.

Without unfastening his safety harness, Chris turned to look into the back of the Jeep wagon. 'He looks okay, I guess. He's getting bounced around a lot.'

'I can't help that.'

'Who is he, Mom?'

'I don't know much about him,' she said. 'But when we get out of this fix, I'm going to tell you what I do know. I haven't told you before because . . . I guess because I didn't know what was going on, and I was afraid it might be dangerous somehow for you to know anything about him at all. But it can't get more dangerous than this, huh? So I'll tell you later.'

Assuming there was going to *be* a later.

When she was two-thirds of the way along the south shore of the lake, pushing the Jeep as fast as she dared, with the Mercedes just thirty-five yards behind, she saw the ridge-road turnoff ahead. It led up through the mountains past Clark's Summit, a ten-mile county road that cut off the thirty- or thirty-five-mile eastern loop of state route 38, rejoining that two-lane highway south near Barton Flats. As she recalled, the ridge road was paved for a couple of miles at each end but was only a graded dirt lane for six or seven miles in the middle. Unlike the Jeep, the Mercedes did not have four-wheel drive; it had winter tires, but they were not currently equipped with chains. The men driving the Mercedes were unlikely to know that the ridge road's pavement would give way to a rutted dirt surface patched with ice and in some places drifted over with snow.

'Hold on!' she told Chris.

She didn't use the brakes until the last moment, taking the right turn onto the ridge road so fast that the Jeep slid sideways with a tortured squeal of tires. It shuddered, too, as if it were an old horse that had been forced to make a frightening jump.

The Mercedes cornered better, though the driver had not known what she was going to do. As they headed into higher elevations and greater wilderness, the car closed the gap to about thirty yards.

Twenty-five. Twenty.

Thorny branches of lightning abruptly grew across the sky to the south. It was not as near to them as the lightning at the house but near enough to turn night to day around them. Even above the sound of the engine she could hear the roar of thunder.

Gaping at the stormy display, Chris said, 'Mommy, what's going on? What's happening?'

'I don't know,' she said, and she had to shout to be heard above the cacophony of the racing engine and clashing heavens.

She did not hear the gunfire itself but heard bullets smacking into the Jeep, and a slug punched a hole through the tailgate window and thudded into the back of the seat in which she and Chris were riding; she felt as well as heard its solid impact. She began to turn the wheel back and forth, weaving from one side of the road to the other, making as difficult a target as possible, which made her dizzy in the flickering light. Either the gunman stopped firing or missed them with every shot, because she did not hear any more incoming rounds. However, the weaving slowed her, and the Mercedes closed even faster.

She had to use the side mirrors instead of the rearview. Though most of the tailgate window was intact, the safety glass was webbed with thousands of tiny cracks that left it translucent and useless.

Fifteen yards, ten.

In the southern sky the lightning and thunder passed, as before.

She topped a rise, and the pavement ended halfway down the hill ahead of them. She stopped weaving, accelerated. When the Jeep left the blacktop, it shimmied for a moment, as if surprised by the change in road surface, but then streaked forward on the snow-spotted, ice-crusted, frozen dirt. They jolted across a series of ruts, through a short hollow where trees arched over them, and up the next hill.

In the side mirrors she saw the Mercedes cross the hollow on the dirt lane and start up the slope behind her. But as she reached the crest, the car began to founder in her wake. It slid sideways, its headlights swinging away from her. The driver overcorrected instead of turning the wheel into the slide, as he should have done. The car's tires began to spin uselessly. It slid not only off to the side but backward twenty yards, until the right rear wheel jolted into the drainage ditch that flanked the road; the headlight beams were canted up and angled across the dirt track.

'They're stuck!' Chris said.

'They'll need half an hour to get out of that mess.' Laura continued over the crest, down the next slope of the dark ridge road.

Although she should have been exultant over their escape, or at least relieved, her fear was undiminished. She had a hunch that they were not yet safe, and she had learned to trust her hunches more than twenty years ago, when she had suspected the White Eel was going to come for her the night that she would have been alone in the end room by the stairs at McIlroy, the night when in fact he had left a Tootsie Roll under her pillow. After all, hunches were just messages from the subconscious, which was thinking furiously all the time and processing information she had not consciously noted.

Something was wrong. But what?

They made less than twenty miles an hour on that narrow, winding, potholed, rutted, frozen dirt track. For a while the road followed the rocky spine of a ridge where there were no trees, then traced the course of a declivity in the ridge wall, all the way to the floor of the parallel ravine, where trees were so thick on both sides that the headlights bouncing back from their trunks seemed to reveal phalanxes of pines as solid as board walls.

In the back of the wagon, her guardian murmured wordlessly in his fevered sleep. She was worried about him, and she wished that she could go faster, but she dared not.

For the first two miles after they lost their pursuers, Chris was silent. Finally he said, 'At the house . . . did you kill any of them?'

She hesitated. 'Yes. Two.'

'Good.'

Disturbed by the grim pleasure in the single word that he spoke, Laura said, 'No, Chris, it isn't good to kill. It made me sick.'

'But they deserved to be killed,' he said.

'Yes, they did. But that doesn't mean it's pleasant to kill them. It's not. There's no satisfaction in it. Just . . . disgust at the necessity of it. And sadness.'

'I wish I could've killed one of them,' he said with tight, cold anger that was disturbing in a boy his age.

She glanced at him. With his face carved by shadows and the pale yellow light from the dashboard, he looked older than he was, and she had a glimpse of the man he would become.

When the ravine floor became too rocky to provide passage, the road rose again, following a shelf on the ridge wall.

She kept her eyes on the rude track. 'Honey, we'll have to talk about this later at more length. Right now I just want you to listen carefully and try to understand something. There are a lot of bad philosophies in the world. You know what a philosophy is?'

'Sorta. No . . . not really.'

'Then let's just say people believe in a lot of things that are bad for them to believe. But there are two things that different kinds of people believe that are the worst, most dangerous, *wrongest* of all. Some people believe the best way to solve a problem is with violence; they beat up or kill anyone who disagrees with them.'

'Like these guys who're after us.'

'Yes. Evidently that's the kind of people they are. That's a real bad way of thinking because violence leads to more violence. Besides, if you settle differences with a gun, there's no justice, no moment of peace, no hope. You follow me?'

'I guess so. But what's the other worst kind of bad thinking?'

'Pacifism,' she said. 'That's just the opposite of the first kind of bad thinking. Pacifists believe you should never lift a hand against another human being, no matter what he has done or what you know he's going to do. If a pacifist was standing beside his brother, and if he saw a man coming to kill his brother, he'd urge his brother to run, but he wouldn't pick up a gun and stop the killer.'

'He'd let the guy go after his brother?' Chris asked, astonished.

'Yes. If worse came to worst, he'd let his brother be murdered rather than violate his own principles and become a killer himself.'

'That's whacko.'

They rounded the point of the ridge, and the road descended into another valley. The branches of overhanging pines were so low they scraped the roof; clumps of snow fell onto the hood and windshield.

Laura turned on the wipers and hunched over the steering wheel, using the change in terrain as an excuse not to talk until she had time to think how to make her point most clearly. They had endured a lot of violence in the past hour; much more violence no doubt lay ahead of them, and she was concerned that Chris develop a proper attitude toward it. She did not want him to get the idea that guns and muscle were acceptable substitutes for reason. On the other hand she did not want him to be traumatized by violence and learn to fear it at the cost of personal dignity and ultimate survival.

At last she said, 'Some pacifists are cowards in disguise, but some really believe it's right to permit the murder of an innocent person rather than kill to stop it. They're wrong because by not fighting evil, they've become part of it. They're as bad as the guy who pulls the trigger. Maybe this is above your head right now, and maybe you'll have to do a lot of thinking before you understand, but it's important you realize there's a way to live that's in the middle, between killers and pacifists. You try to avoid violence. You never start it. But if someone else starts it, you defend yourself, friends, family, anyone who's in trouble. When I had to shoot those men at the house, it made me sick. I'm no hero. I'm not proud of having shot them, but I'm not ashamed of it, either. I don't want you to be proud of me for it, or think that killing them was satisfying, that revenge in any way makes me feel better about your dad's murder. It doesn't.'

He was silent.

She said, 'Did I dump too much on you?'

'No. I just gotta think about it a while,' he said. 'Right now, I'm thinking bad, I guess. 'Cause I want them all dead, all of them who had anything to do with . . . what happened to Dad. But I'll work on it, Mom. I'll try to be a better person.'

She smiled. 'I know you will, Chris.'

———————

During her conversation with Chris and for the few minutes of mutual silence that followed it, Laura continued to be plagued by the feeling that they were not yet out of imminent danger. They had gone about seven miles on the ridge road, with perhaps another mile of dirt track and two miles of pavement ahead before they connected with state route 38. The farther she drove, the more certain she became that she was overlooking something and that more trouble was drawing near.

She suddenly stopped on the spine of another ridge, just before the road dipped down again – and for the last time – toward lower land. She switched off the engine and the lights.

'What's wrong? Chris asked.

'Nothing. I just need to think, have a look at our passenger.'

She got out and went around to the back of the Jeep. She opened the tailgate, where a bullet had punched through the window. Chunks of safety glass broke out and fell on the ground at her feet. She climbed into the cargo bed and, lying next to her guardian, checked the wounded man's pulse. It was still weak, perhaps even slightly weaker than before, but it was regular. She put a hand to his head and found he was no longer cold; he seemed to be afire within. At her request Chris gave her the flashlight from the glove compartment. She pulled back the blankets to see if the man was bleeding worse than when they had loaded him into the Jeep. His wound looked bad, but there was not much fresh blood in spite of the bouncing that he had endured. She replaced the blankets, returned the flashlight to Chris, got out of the Jeep, and closed the tailgate.

She broke all of the remaining glass out of the tailgate window and out of the smaller rear window on the driver's side. With the glass missing completely, the damage was less conspicuous and less likely to draw the attention of a cop or anyone else.

For a while she stood in the cold air beside the wagon, staring out at the lightless wilderness, trying to force a connection between instinct and reason: Why was she so sure that she was heading for trouble and that the night's violence was not yet at an end?

The clouds were shredding in a high-altitude wind that harried them eastward, a wind that had not yet reached the ground, where the air was almost peculiarly still. Moonlight found its way through those ragged holes and eerily illuminated the snow-cloaked landscape of rising and falling hills, evergreens leeched of their color by the night, and clustered rock formations.

Laura looked south where in a few miles the ridge road led to state route 38, and everything in that direction seemed serene. She looked east, west, then back to the north from which they had come, and on all sides the San Bernardino Mountains were without a sign of human habitation, without a single light, and seemed to exist in primeval purity and peace.

She asked herself the same questions and gave the same answers that had been part of an interior dialogue for the past year. Where did the men with the belts come from? Another planet, another galaxy? No. They were as human as she was. So maybe they came from Russia. Maybe the belts acted like matter transmitters, devices akin to the teleportation chamber in that old movie, *The Fly*. That might explain her guardian's accent – if he'd teleported from Russia – but it didn't explain why he had not aged in a quarter of a century; besides, she did not seriously believe that the Soviet Union or anyone else had been perfecting matter transmitters since she was eight years old. Which left time travel.

She had been considering that possibility for some months, though she'd not even felt confident enough about her analysis to mention it to Thelma. But if her guardian had been entering her life at crucial points by time travel, he could have made all of his journeys in the space of a single month or week in his own era while many years had passed for her, so he would have appeared not to have aged. Until she could question him and learn the truth, the time-travel theory was the only one on which she could operate: Her guardian had traveled to her from some future world; and evidently it was an unpleasant future, because when speaking of the belt he had said, 'You don't want to go where it'll take you,' and there had been a bleak, haunted look in his eyes. She had no idea why a time traveler would come back from the future to protect her, of all people, from armed junkies and runaway pickup trucks, and she had no time to ponder the possibilities.

The night was quiet, dark, and cold.

They were heading straight into trouble.

She *knew* it, but she didn't know what it was or where it would come from.

When she got back into the Jeep, Chris said, 'What's wrong now?'

'You're crazy about *Star Trek, Star Wars, Batteries Not Included*, all that stuff, so maybe what I've got here is the kind of background expert I seek out when I'm writing a novel. You're my resident expert in the weird.'

The engine was switched off, and the interior of the Jeep was brightened only by the cloud-cloaked moonlight. But she was able to see Chris's face reasonably well because, during the few minutes she had been outside, her eyes had adapted to the night. He blinked at her and looked puzzled. 'What're you talking about?'

'Chris, like I said earlier, I'm going to tell you all about the man lying back there, about the other strange appearances he's made in my life, but we don't have time for that now. So don't snow me under with lots of questions, okay? But just suppose my guardian – that's how I think of him, because he's pro-tected me from terrible things when he could – suppose he was a time traveler from the future. Suppose he doesn't come in a big clumsy time machine. Suppose the whole machine is in a belt that he wears around his waist, under his clothes, and he just materializes out of thin air when he arrives here from the future. Are you with me so far?'

Chris was staring wide-eyed. 'Is that what he is?'

'He might be, yes.'

The boy freed himself from his safety harness, scrambled onto his knees on the seat, and looked back at the man lying in the compartment behind them. 'Holy shit.'

'Given the unusual circumstances,' she said, 'I'll overlook the foul language.'

He glanced at her sheepishly. 'Sorry. But a *time* traveler!'

If she had been angry with him, the anger would not have held, for she now saw in him a sudden rush of that boyish excitement and a capacity for wonder that he had not exhibited in a year, not even at Christmas when he had enjoyed himself immensely with Jason Gaines. The prospect of an encounter with a time traveler instantly filled him with a sense of adventure and joy. That was the splendid thing about life: Though it was cruel, it was also mysterious, filled with wonder and surprise; sometimes the surprises were so amazing that they qualified as miraculous, and by witnessing those miracles, a despondent person could discover a reason to live, a cynic could obtain unexpected relief from ennui, and a profoundly wounded boy could find the will to heal himself and medicine for melancholy.

She said, 'Okay, suppose that when he wants to leave our time and return to his own, he presses a button on the special belt he wears.'

'Can I see the belt?'

'Later. Remember, you promised not to ask a lot of questions just now.'

'Okay.' He looked again at the guardian, then turned and sat down, focusing his attention on his mother. 'When he presses the button – what happens?'

'He just vanishes.'

'Wow! And when he arrives from the future, does he just appear out of thin air?'

'I don't know. I've never seen him arrive. Though I think for some reason there's lightning and thunder—'

'The lightning tonight!'

'Yes, but there's not always lightning. All right. Suppose that he came back in time to help us, to protect us from certain dangers—'

'Like the runaway pickup.'

'We don't know why he wants to protect us, can't know why until he tells us. Anyway, suppose other people from the future *don't* want us to be protected. We can't understand their motivations, either. But one of them was Kokoschka, the man who shot your father—'

'And the guys who showed up tonight at the house,' Chris said, 'they're from the future, too.'

'I think so. They were planning to kill my guardian, you, and me. But we killed some of them instead and left two of them stranded in the Mercedes. So . . . what are they going to do next, kiddo? You're the resident expert on the weird. Do you have any ideas?'

'Let me think.'

Moonlight gleamed dully on the dirty hood of the Jeep.

The interior of the station wagon was growing cold; their breath issued in frosty plumes, and the windows were beginning to fog over. Laura switched on the engine, heater, defroster, but not the lights.

Chris said, 'Well, see, their mission failed, so they won't hang around. They'll go back to the future where they came from.'

'Those guys in our car?'

'Yeah. They probably already pushed the buttons on the belts of the guys you killed, sent the bodies back to the future, so there're no dead men at the house, no proof time travelers were ever there. Except maybe some blood. So when the last two or three guys got stuck in the ditch, they probably gave up and went home.'

'So they aren't back there any more? They wouldn't walk back to Big Bear maybe, steal a car, and try to find us?'

'Nope. That would be too hard. I mean, they have an easier way to find us than to just drive around looking for us like regular bad guys would have to do.'

'What way?'

The boy screwed up his face and squinted through the windshield at the snow and moonglow and darkness ahead. 'See, Mom, as soon as they lost us, they'd push the buttons on their belts, go home to the future, and then make a *new* trip back to our time to set another trap for us. They knew we took this road. So what they probably did was make another trip back to our time, but earlier tonight, and they set a trap at the other end of this road, and now they're waiting there for us. Yeah, that's where they are! I'll just bet that's where they are.'

'But why couldn't they come back even earlier tonight, earlier than they came the first time, back to the house, and attack us before my guardian ever showed up to warn us?'

'Paradox,' the boy said. 'You know what that means?'

The word seemed too complex for a boy his age, but she said, 'Yes, I know what a paradox is. Anything that's self-contradictory but possibly true.'

'See, Mom, the neat thing is that time travel is full of all kinds of possible paradoxes. Things that couldn't be true, shouldn't be true – but then might be.' Now he was talking in that excited voice with which he described scenes in his favorite fantastic films and comic books, but with more intensity than she had ever heard before, probably because this was not a story but reality even more amazing than fiction. 'Like suppose you went back in time and married your own grandfather. See, then you'd be your own grandmother. If time travel was possible, maybe you could do that – but then how could you have ever been born if your *real* grandmother had never married your grandfather in the first place? Paradox! Or what if you went back in time and met up with your mom when she was a kid and accidentally killed her? Would you just cease to exist – *pop!* – like you'd never been born? But if you ceased to exist – then how could you have gone back in time in the first place? Paradox! Paradox!'

Staring at him in the moon-painted darkness of the Jeep, Laura felt as though she was looking at a different boy from the one she had always known. Of course, she had been aware of his great fascination with space-age tales, which seemed to preoccupy most kids these days, regardless of age. But until now she hadn't gotten a deep look inside the mind shaped by those influences. Evidently the American children of the late twentieth century not only lived interior

fantasy lives richer than those of children at any other time in history, but they
seemed to have gotten from their fantasies something not provided by the elves
and fairies and ghosts with which earlier generations of kids had entertained
themselves: The ability to think about abstract concepts like space and time in a
manner far beyond their intellectual and emotional age. She had the peculiar
feeling that she was speaking to a little boy and a rocket scientist coexisting in
one body.

Disconcerted, she said, 'So . . . when these men failed to kill us on their first
trip tonight, why wouldn't they make a second trip *earlier* than the first, to kill
us before my guardian warned us that they were coming?'

'See, your guardian already showed up in the time stream to warn us. So if
they came back *before* he warned us – then how could he have warned us in the
first place, and how could we be here where we are now, alive? Paradox!'

He laughed and clapped his hands like a gnome chortling over some particularly amusing side-effect of a magical spell.

In contrast to his good humor, Laura was getting a headache from trying to
sort out the complexities of this thing.

Chris said, 'Some people believe time travel isn't even possible 'cause of all
the paradoxes. But some believe it's possible so long as the trip you make into
the past doesn't create a paradox. Now if *that's* true, see, then the killers
couldn't come back on a second, earlier trip 'cause two of them had already been
killed on the *first* trip. They couldn't do it because they were already dead, and
it was a paradox. But the guys you didn't kill and maybe some *new* time travelers
could make another trip to cut us off at the end of this road.' He leaned forward
to peer through the streaked windshield again. 'That's what all that lightning
was off to the south when we were weaving to keep them from shooting us –
more guys from the future were arriving. Yeah, I'll bet they're waiting for us
down there somewhere, down there in the dark.'

Rubbing her temples with her fingertips, Laura said, 'But if we turn around
and go back, if we don't drive into the trap ahead, then they'll realize we've
outthought them. And so they'll make a *third* trip back in time and return to the
Mercedes and shoot us when we try to drive back that way. They'll get us no
matter which way we go.'

He shook his head vigorously. 'No. Because by the time they realize we're on
to them, maybe half an hour from now, we'll already have turned around and
driven back past the Mercedes.' The boy was bouncing up and down in his seat
with excitement now. 'So if they try to make a *third* trip in time to go back to the
beginning of this road and trap us there, they can't do it, because we'll already
have driven back that way and out, we'll already be safe. Paradox! See, they got
to play by the rules, Mom. They're not magical. They got to play by the rules,
and they can be beat!'

In thirty-three years she had never had a headache that had gone from a mild
throb to a pounding skull-splitter as quickly as this one. The more she tried to
puzzle out the difficulties of avoiding a pack of time-traveling hitmen, the
deeper rooted the pain became.

Finally she said, 'I give up. I guess I should've been watching *Star Trek* and
reading Robert Heinlein all these years instead of being a serious adult, because
I'm just not able to cope with this. So I'll tell you what: I'm going to rely on *you*
to outsmart them. You'll have to try to keep one step ahead of them. They want

us dead. So how can they try to kill us without creating one of these paradoxes? Where will they show up next . . . and next? Right now, we're going back the way we came, past the Mercedes, and if you're right, no one will be waiting there for us. So where will they show up after that? Will we see them again tonight? Think about those things, and when you have any ideas, let me know what they are.'

'I will, Mom.' He slumped down in his seat, grinning broadly for a moment, then chewing on his lip as he settled deeper into the game.

Except it was not a game, of course. Their lives were really at stake. They had to elude killers with nearly superhuman abilities, and they were pinning their hopes of survival on nothing more than the richness of an eight-year-old boy's imagination.

Laura started the Jeep, put it in reverse, and backed up a couple of hundred yards until she found a place in the road wide enough to turn around. Then they headed back the way they had come, toward the Mercedes in the ditch, toward Big Bear.

She was beyond terror. Their situation contained such a large element of the unknown – and unknowable – that terror could not be sustained. Terror was not like happiness or depression; it was an *acute* condition that by its very nature had to be of a short term. Terror wilted fast. Or it escalated until you passed out or until you died of it, frightened to death; you screamed until a blood vessel burst in your brain. She wasn't screaming, and in spite of her headache she didn't think any vessels were going to burst. She settled into a low-key, chronic fear, hardly more than anxiety.

What a day this had been. What a year. What a life.

Exotic news.

• 2 •

They passed the stranded Mercedes and drove all the way to the north end of the ridge road without encountering men with submachine guns. At the inter-section with the lakeside highway, Laura stopped and looked at Chris. 'Well?'

'As long as we're driving around,' he said, 'and as long as we go to a place where we've never been and don't usually go, we're pretty safe. They can't find us if they don't have any idea where we might be. Just like your regular-type scumbags.'

Scumbags? she thought. What is this – H. G. Wells meets *Hill Street Blues*?

He said, 'See, now that we've given them the slip, these guys are going to go back to the future and look over the records they've got about you, Mom, your history, and they're going to see where you show up next – like when you want to go live in the house again. Or if you hid out for a year and wrote another book and then went on a tour for it, they'd show up at a store where you're signing books because, see, there'd be a *record* of that in the future; they'd know you could be found in that store at a certain time on a certain day.'

She frowned. 'You mean the only way to avoid them for the rest of my life is to change my name, go on the run forever, and leave no trace of myself on any public records, just vanish from recorded history from here on out?'

'Yeah, I think maybe that's what you'll have to do,' he said excitedly.

He was smart enough to have figured out how to defeat a pack of time-traveling hitmen but not adult enough to perceive how hard it would be for them to forsake everything they owned and start with only the cash in their pockets. In a way he was like an idiot savant, tremendously insightful and gifted in one narrow area, but naive and severely limited in all other ways. In matters of time-travel theory, he was a thousand years old, but otherwise he was going on nine.

She said, 'I can never write another book because I'd have to have contact with editors, agents, even if by phone. So there'd be phone records that could be traced. And I can't collect royalties because no matter how many blinds I use, no matter how many different bank accounts I shift the money through, sooner or later I have to collect the funds personally, which would leave a public record. So then they'd have that record in the future, and they'd travel back to the bank to wipe me out when I showed up. How am I supposed to get my hands on the money we *already* have? How can I cash a check anywhere without leaving a record that they would have in the future?' She blinked at him. 'Good God, Chris, we're in a box!'

Now it was the boy's turn to be baffled. He looked at her with little understanding of where money came from, how it was put aside for future use, or how difficult it was to obtain. 'Well, for a couple of days, we can just drive around, sleep in motels—'

'We can only sleep in motels if I pay cash. A credit card record might be all they need to find us. Then they'd come back in time to the night I used the credit card, and they'd kill us at the motel.'

'Yeah, so we use cash. Hey, we can eat at McDonald's all the time! That doesn't take much money, and it's *good*.'

They drove down from the mountains, out of the snow, into San Bernardino, a city of about 300,000, without encountering assassins. She needed to get their guardian to a doctor, not only because she owed him a debt of life, but also because without him she might never learn the truth of what was happening and might never find a way out of the box they were in.

She could not take him to a hospital because hospitals kept records, which might give her enemies from the future a way of finding her. She would have to obtain medical care secretly, from someone who would not have to be told her name or anything about the patient.

Shortly before midnight she stopped at a telephone booth near a Shell service station. The phone was at the corner of the property, away from the station itself, which was ideal because she could not risk an attendant noticing the Jeep's broken windows or the unconscious man.

In spite of the hour-long nap the boy had gotten earlier and in spite of the excitement, Chris had dozed off. In the compartment behind the front seat, their guardian was sleeping, too, but his sleep was neither restful nor natural. He was not mumbling much any more, but for minutes at a stretch he drew breath with a dismaying wheeze and rattle.

She left the Jeep in park, the engine running, and went into the telephone booth to look through the directory. She tore out the Yellow Pages' listings for physicians.

After obtaining a street map of San Bernardino from the attendant in the service station, she began searching for a doctor who did not operate out of a clinic or medical office building but from an office attached to his home, which was how most doctors in small towns and cities had worked in years gone by, though these days few continued to keep home and office together. She was acutely aware that the longer she took to find help, the smaller the chance that their guardian would survive.

At a quarter past one, in a quiet residential neighborhood of older homes, she pulled in front of a two-story, white, Victorian house built in another era, in a lost California, before everything had been constructed of stucco. It stood on a corner lot, with a two-car garage, shaded by alders that were leafless in the middle of winter, a touch that made it seem like a place transported entirely, landscaping and all, from the East. According to the pages she had torn from the telephone directory, this was the address for Dr. Carter Brenkshaw, and beside the driveway a small sign suspended between two wrought-iron posts confirmed the directory's accuracy.

She drove to the end of the block and parked at the curb. She got out of the Jeep, scooped a handful of damp earth from a flowerbed in front of a nearby house, and smeared the dirt over the front and back license plates as best she could.

By the time she wiped her hand in the grass and got back in the Jeep, Chris had awakened but was groggy and confused after being asleep for more than two hours. She patted his face and pushed his hair back from his forehead and rapidly talked him awake. The cold night air, flowing through the broken windows, helped too.

'Okay,' she said when she was sure he was awake, 'listen closely, partner. I've found a doctor. Can you act sick?'

'Sure.' He made a face as if he was going to puke, then gagged and moaned.

'Don't overplay it.' She explained what they were going to do.

'Good plan, Mom.'

'No, it's nuts. But it's the only plan I've got.'

She swung the Jeep around and drove back to Brenkshaw's, where she parked in the driveway in front of the closed garage, which was set back from the house. Chris slid out by the driver's door, and she picked him up and held him against her left side, his head against her shoulder. He held on to her, so she only needed her left arm to keep him in place, though he was quite heavy; her baby was not a baby any more. In her free hand she gripped the revolver.

As she carried Chris along the walk, past the stark alders, with no light except a purplish glow from one of the widely spaced mercury-vapor streetlamps out at the curb, she hoped no one was at a window in any of the nearby houses. On the other hand it probably wasn't unusual for someone to visit a doctor's house in the middle of the night, needing treatment.

She went up the front steps, across the porch, and rang the bell three times, quick, as a frantic mother might do. She waited only a few seconds before ringing it three more times.

In a couple of minutes, after she had rung the bell again and was beginning to think that no one was home, the porch lights came on. She saw a man studying her through the three-pane, fan-shaped window in the top third of the door.

'Please,' she said urgently, holding the revolver at her side where it could not be seen, 'my boy, poison, he's swallowed poison!'

The man opened the door inward, and there was an outward-opening glass storm door, as well, so Laura stepped out of its way.

He was about sixty-five, white-haired, with a face that was Irish except for a strong Roman nose and dark brown eyes. He was dressed in a brown robe, white pajamas, and slippers. Peering at her over the rims of tortoiseshell glasses, he said, 'What's wrong?'

'I live two blocks down, you're so close, and my boy – poison.' At the height of her hysteria, she let go of Chris, and he got out of her way as she shoved the muzzle of the .38 against the man's belly. 'I'll blow your guts out if you call for help.'

She had no intention of shooting him, but she apparently sounded convincing, for he nodded and said nothing.

'Are you Dr. Brenkshaw?' He nodded again, and she said, 'Who else is in the house, Doctor?'

'No one. I'm alone here.'

'Your wife?'

'I'm a widower.'

'Children?'

'All grown and gone.'

'Don't lie to me.'

'I've made a lifetime habit of not lying,' he said. 'It's gotten me in trouble a few times, but telling the truth generally makes life simpler. Look, it's chilly, and this robe's thin. You can intimidate me as well if you come inside.'

She stepped across the threshold, keeping the gun in his belly and pushing him backward with it. Chris followed her. 'Honey,' she whispered, 'go check out the house. Quietly. Start upstairs, and don't miss a room. If there's anyone here, tell them the doctor has an emergency patient and needs their help.'

Chris headed for the stairs, and Laura kept Carter Brenkshaw in the foyer at gunpoint. Nearby a grandfather clock was ticking softly.

'You know,' he said, 'I've been a lifelong reader of thrillers.'

She frowned. 'What do you mean?'

'Well, I've often read a scene in which a gorgeous villainess held the hero against his will. As often as not, when he finally turned the tables on her, she surrendered to the inevitability of masculine triumph, and they made wild, passionate love. So when it happens to me, why do I have to be too old to enjoy the prospect of the second half of this showdown?'

Laura held back a smile because she could not continue to pretend to be dangerous once she allowed herself to smile. 'Shut up.'

'Surely you can do better than that.'

'Just shut up, all right? Shut up.'

He did not go pale or begin to tremble. He smiled.

Chris returned from upstairs. 'Nobody, Mom.'

Brenkshaw said, 'I wonder how many dangerous thugs have pint-size accomplices who call them Mom?'

'Don't misjudge me, Doctor. I'm desperate.'

Chris disappeared into the downstairs rooms, turning on lights as he went.

To Brenkshaw, Laura said, 'I've got a wounded man in the car—'

'Of course, a gunshot.'

'—I want you to treat him and keep your mouth shut about it, 'cause if you don't, we'll come back some night and blow you away.'

'This,' he said almost merrily, 'is perfectly delicious.'

As Chris returned, he switched off the lights he had switched on moments ago. 'Nobody, Mom.'

'You have a stretcher?' Laura asked the physician.

Brenkshaw stared at her. 'You really do have a wounded man?'

'What the hell else would I be doing here?'

'How peculiar. Well, all right, how badly is he bleeding?'

'A lot earlier, not so much now. But he's unconscious.'

'If he's not bleeding badly now, we can roll him in. I've got a collapsible wheelchair in my office. Can I get an overcoat,' he said, pointing to the foyer closet, 'or do tough molls like you get a thrill out of making old men shiver in their peejays?'

'Get your coat, Doctor, but damn it, don't underestimate me.'

'Yeah,' Chris said. 'She shot two guys already tonight.' He imitated the sound of an Uzi. 'She just cut 'em down, and they never had a chance to lay a hand on her.'

The boy sounded so sincere that Brenkshaw looked at Laura with new concern. 'There's nothing but coats in the closet. Umbrellas. A pair of galoshes. I don't keep a gun in there.'

'Just be careful, Doctor. No fast moves.'

'No fast moves – yes, I knew you'd say that.' Though he still seemed to find the situation to some degree amusing, he was not quite as lighthearted about it as he had been.

When he had pulled on his overcoat, they went with him through a door to the left of the foyer. Without snapping on a light, relying on the glow from the foyer and on his familiarity with the place, Dr. Brenkshaw led them through a patients' waiting room that contained straight-backed chairs and a couple of end tables. Another door led into his office – a desk, three chairs, medical books – where he did turn on a light, and a door from the office led farther back in the house to his examination room.

Laura had expected to see an examination table and equipment that had been in use and well maintained for thirty-odd years, a homely den of medicine straight out of a Norman Rockwell painting, but everything looked new. There was even an EKG machine, and at the far end of the room was a door with a sign that warned X-RAY: KEEP CLOSED IN USE.

'You have X-ray equipment here?' she asked.

'Sure. It's not as expensive as it once was. Every clinic has X-ray equipment these days.'

'Every clinic, yes, but this is just a one-man—'

'I may look like Barry Fitzgerald playing at being a doctor in an old movie, and I may prefer the old-fashioned convenience of an office in my home, but I don't give patients outdated care just to be quaint. I dare say, I'm a more serious physician than you are a desperado.'

'Don't bet on that,' she said harshly, though she was getting tired of pretending to be cold-blooded.

'Don't worry,' he said. 'I'll play along. Seems like it'll be more fun if I do.' To

Chris, he said, 'When we came through my office, did you notice a big, red-ceramic jar on the desk? It's full of orange-slice candies and Tootsie Pops if you want some.'

'Wow, thanks!' Chris said. 'Uh . . . can I have a piece, Mom?'

'A piece or two,' she said, 'but don't make yourself sick.'

Brenkshaw said, 'When it comes to giving sweet treats to young patients, I'm old-fashioned, I guess. No sugar-free gum here. What the hell fun is that stuff? Tastes like plastic. If their teeth rot out after they visit me, that's their dentist's problem.'

While he talked, he got a folding wheelchair from the corner, unfolded it, and rolled it to the middle of the room.

Laura said, 'Honey, you stay here while we go out to the Jeep.'

'Okay,' Chris said from the next room, where he was peering into the red-ceramic jar, selecting his treat.

'Your Jeep in the driveway?' Brenkshaw asked. 'Then let's go out the back. Less conspicuous, I think.'

Pointing the revolver at the physician but feeling foolish, Laura followed him out of a side door in the examination room, which opened onto a ramp, so there was no need to descend stairs.

'Handicapped entrance,' Brenkshaw said quietly over his shoulder as he pushed the wheelchair along a walk toward the back of the house. His bedroom slippers made a crisp sound on the concrete.

The physician had a large property, so the neighboring house did not loom over them. Instead of being planted with alders as was the front lawn, the side yard was graced with ficus and pines, which were green all year. In spite of the screening branches and the darkness, however, Laura could see the blank windows of the neighboring place, so she supposed that she could be seen, as well, if anyone looked.

The world had the hushed quality that it possessed only between midnight and dawn. Even if she had not known it was going on two in the morning, she would have been able to guess the time within half an hour. Though faint city noises echoed in the distance, there was a cemeterial stillness that would have made her feel like a woman on a secret mission even if she had only been taking out the garbage.

The walk led around the house, crossing another walk that extended to the back of the property. They went past the rear porch, through an areaway between house and garage, into the driveway.

Brenkshaw halted at the back of the Jeep and chuckled. 'Mud on the license plates,' he whispered. 'Convincing touch.'

After she put the tailgate down, he got into the back of the Jeep to have a look at the wounded man.

She looked out toward the street. All was silent. Still.

But if a San Bernardino Police cruiser happened to drive by now on a routine patrol, the officer would surely stop to see what was up at kindly old Doc Brenkshaw's place. . . .

Brenkshaw was already crawling out of the Jeep. 'By God, you *do* have a wounded man in there.'

'Why the hell do you keep being surprised? Would I pull this kind of stunt for laughs?'

'Let's get him inside. Quickly,' Brenkshaw said.

He could not handle her guardian by himself. In order to help him, Laura had to stick the .38 in the waistband of her jeans.

Brenkshaw made no attempt to run or to knock her down and get the weapon away from her. Instead, as soon as he had the wounded man in the wheelchair, he rolled him out of the drive, through the areaway, and around the house to the handicapped entrance at the far side.

She grabbed one of the Uzis from the front seat and followed Brenkshaw. She didn't think she'd have any use for the automatic carbine, but she felt better with it in her hands.

Fifteen minutes later, Brenkshaw turned from the developed X-rays that hung on a lightboard in a corner of his examination room. 'The bullet didn't fragment, made a clean exit. Didn't nick any bones, so we don't have chips to worry about.'

'Terrific,' Chris said from a corner chair, happily sucking on a Tootsie Pop. In spite of the warm air in the house, Chris was still wearing his jacket, as was Laura, because she wanted them to be ready to get out on short notice.

'Is he in a coma or what?' Laura asked the doctor.

'Yes, he's comatose. Not from any fever associated with a bad infection of the wound. Too early for that. And now that he's gotten treatment, there probably won't be an infection. It's traumatic coma from being shot, the loss of blood, the shock and all. He shouldn't have been moved, you know.'

'I had no choice. Will he come out of it?'

'Probably. In this case a coma is the body's way of shutting down to conserve energy, facilitate healing. He's not lost as much blood as it appears; he's got a good pulse, so this probably won't last long. When you see his shirt and lab coat soaked like that, you think he's bled quarts, but he hasn't. Not that it was a spoonful, either. He's had a bad time of it. But no major blood vessels were torn, or he'd be in worse shape. Still, he should be in a hospital.'

'We've already been through that,' Laura said impatiently. 'We can't go to a hospital.'

'What bank did you rob?' the physician asked teasingly, but with noticeably less twinkle in his eyes than there had been when he had made his other little jokes.

While he waited for the pictures to develop, he had cleaned the wound, flooded it with iodine, dusted it with antibiotic powder, and prepared a bandage. Now he got a needle, another implement she could not identify, and heavy thread from a cabinet and put them on a stainless-steel tray that he had hung on the side of the examination table. The wounded man lay there, unconscious, propped on his right side with the help of several foam pillows.

'What're you doing?' Laura asked.

'Those holes are fairly large, especially the exit wound. If you insist on endangering his life by keeping him out of a hospital, then the least I can do is throw a few stitches in him.'

'Well, all right, but be quick about it.'

'You expect G-men to break down the door any minute?'

'Worse than that,' she said. 'Far worse than that.'

Since they had arrived at Brenkshaw's, she had been expecting a sudden, night-shattering display of lightning, thunder like the giant hooves of apocalyptic horsemen, and the arrival of more well-armed time travelers. Fifteen minutes ago, as the doctor had been X-raying her guardian's chest, she'd thought she heard thunder so distant that it was barely audible. She hurried to the nearest window to search the sky for far-off lightning, but she saw none through the breaks in the trees, perhaps because the sky over San Bernardino already had a ruddy glow from city lights or perhaps because she had not heard thunder in the first place. She had finally decided that she might have heard a jet passing overhead and, in her panic, had misinterpreted it as a more distant sound.

Brenkshaw stitched up his patient, snipped the thread – 'sutures will dissolve' – and bound the bandages in place with wide adhesive tape that he repeatedly wound around the guardian's chest and back.

The air had a pungent, medicinal smell that made Laura slightly ill, but it did not bother Chris. He sat in the corner, happily working on another Tootsie Pop.

While waiting for the X-rays, Brenkshaw also had administered an injection of penicillin. Now he went to the tall, white, metal cabinets along the far wall and poured capsules from a large jar into a pill bottle, then from another large jar into a second small bottle. 'I keep some basic drugs here, sell them to poorer patients at cost so they don't have to go broke at the pharmacy.'

'What're these?' Laura asked when he returned to the examination table, where she stood, and gave her the two small plastic bottles.

'More penicillin in this one. Three a day, with meals – if he can take meals. I *think* he'll come around soon. If he doesn't he'll begin to dehydrate, and he'll need intravenous fluid. Can't give him liquid by mouth when he's in a coma – he'd choke. This other is a painkiller. Only when needed, and no more than two a day.'

'Give me more of these. In fact give me your whole supply.' She pointed to two quart jars that contained hundreds of both capsules.

'He won't need that much of either one. He—'

'No, I'm sure he won't,' she said, 'but I don't know what the hell other problems we're going to have. We may need both penicillin and painkillers for me – or my boy.'

Brenkshaw stared at her for a long moment. 'What in the name of God have you gotten into? It's like something in one of your books.'

'Just give me—' Laura stopped, stunned by what he had said. 'Like something in one of my books? *In one of my books!* Oh, my God, you know who I am.'

'Of course. I've known almost from the moment I saw you on the porch. I read thrillers, as I said, and although your books aren't strictly in that genre, they're very suspenseful, so I read them, too, and your photograph's on the back of the jacket. Believe me, Ms. Shane, no man would forget your face once he'd seen it, even if he'd seen it only in pictures and even if he was an old crock like me.'

'But why didn't you say—'

'At first I thought it was a joke. After all, the melodramatic way you appeared on my doorstep in the dead of night, the gun, the corny, hard-boiled dialogue

. . . it all seemed like a gag. Believe me, I have certain friends who might think of such an elaborate hoax and, if they knew you, might be able to persuade you to join in the fun.'

Pointing to her guardian, she said, 'But when you saw him—'

'Then I knew it was no joke,' the physician said.

Hurrying to his mother's side, Chris pulled the Tootsie Pop from his mouth. 'Mom, if he tells on us . . .'

Laura had drawn the .38 from her waistband. She began to raise it, then lowered her hand as she realized the gun no longer had any power to intimidate Brenkshaw; in fact it had never frightened him. For one thing she now realized he was not the kind of man who could be intimidated, and for another thing she could not convincingly portray a lawless, dangerous woman when he knew who she really was.

On the examination table her guardian groaned and tried to shift in his unnatural sleep, but Brenkshaw put a hand upon his chest and stilled him.

'Listen, Doctor, if you tell anyone what happened here tonight, if you can't keep my visit a secret for the rest of your life, it'll be the death of me and my boy.'

'Of course the law requires a physician to report any gunshot wounds he treats.'

'But this is a special case,' Laura said urgently. 'I'm not on the run from the law, Doctor.'

'Who are you running from?'

'In a sense . . . from the same men who killed my husband, Chris's father.'

He looked surprised and pained. 'Your husband was killed?'

'You must've read about it in the papers,' she said bitterly. 'It made a sensational story there for a while, the kind of thing the press loves.'

'I'm afraid I don't read newspapers or watch television news,' Brenkshaw said. 'It's all fires, accidents, and crazed terrorists. They don't report real news, just blood and tragedy and politics. I'm sorry about your husband. And if these people who killed him, whoever they are, want to kill you now, you should go straight to the police.'

Laura liked this man and thought they shared more views and sympathies than not. He seemed reasonable, kind. Yet she had little hope of persuading Brenkshaw to keep his mouth shut. 'The police can't protect me, Doctor. No one can protect me except *me* – and maybe that man whose wounds you just sewed up. These people who're after us . . . they're relentless, implacable, and they're beyond the law.'

He shook his head. 'No one is beyond the law.'

'*They* are, Doctor. It'd take me an hour to explain to you why they are, and then you probably wouldn't believe me. But I beg of you, unless you want our deaths on your conscience, keep your mouth shut about our being here. Not just for a few days but forever.'

'Well . . .'

Studying him, she knew it was no use. She remembered what he had told her in the foyer earlier, when she had warned him not to lie about the presence of other people in the house: He did not lie, he said, because always telling the truth made life simpler; telling the truth was a lifelong habit. Hardly forty-five minutes later, she knew him well enough to believe that he was indeed an unusually truthful man. Even now, as she begged him to keep their visit secret, he was not able to tell the lie that would placate her and get her out of his office. He stared at her guiltily and could not tease the falsehood from his tongue. He would do his duty when she left; he would file a police report. The cops would look for her at her house near Big Bear, where they would discover the blood if not the bodies of the time travelers, and where they would find hundreds of expended bullets, shattered windows, slug-pocked walls. By tomorrow or the next day the story would be splashed across the newspapers. . . .

The airliner that had flown overhead more than half an hour ago might not have been a passing jet, after all. It might well have been what she had first thought it was – very distant thunder, fifteen or twenty miles away.

More thunder on a night without rain.

'Doctor, help me get him dressed,' she said, indicating her guardian on the table beside them. 'Do at least that much for me, since you're going to betray me later.'

He winced visibly at the word *betray*.

Earlier she'd sent Chris upstairs to get one each of Brenkshaw's shirts, sweaters, jackets, slacks, a pair of his socks, and shoes. The physician was not as muscular and trim as her guardian, but they were approximately the same size.

At the moment the wounded man was wearing only his blood-stained pants, but Laura knew there would not be time to put all the clothes on him. 'Just help me get him into the jacket. Doctor. I'll take the rest and dress him later. The jacket will be enough to protect him from the cold.'

Reluctantly lifting the unconscious man into a sitting position on the examination table, the doctor said, 'He shouldn't be moved.'

Ignoring Brenkshaw, struggling to pull the wounded man's right arm through the sleeve of the warmly lined corduroy jacket, Laura said, 'Chris, go to the waiting room at the front of the house. It's dark in there. Don't turn on the lights. Go to the windows and give the street a good looking over, and for God's sake don't let yourself be seen.'

'You think they're here?' the boy asked fearfully.

'If not now, they will be soon,' she said, working her guardian's left arm through the other jacket sleeve.

'What're you talking about?' Brenkshaw asked, as Chris dashed into the adjoining office and on into the dark waiting room.

Laura didn't answer. 'Come on, let's get him in the wheelchair.'

Together, they lifted the wounded man off the examination table, into the chair, and buckled a restraining strap around his waist.

As Laura was gathering up the other clothes and the two quart-sized jars of drugs, making a bundle, padding the clothes around the jars and tying it all together in the shirt, Chris raced back from the waiting room. 'Mom, they're just pulling up outside, it must be them, two cars full of men across the street, six or eight of 'em, anyway. What're we going to do?'

'Damn,' she said, 'we can't get to the Jeep now. And we can't go out the side door because they might see us from the front.'

Brenkshaw headed toward his office. 'I'll call the police—'

'No!' She put the bundle of clothes and drugs on the wheelchair between her guardian's legs, put her purse there, too, and snatched up the Uzi and .38 Chief's Special. 'There's no time, damn you. They'll be in here in a couple of minutes, and they'll kill us. You've got to help me get the wheelchair out the back, down the rear porch steps.'

Apparently her terror was at last conveyed to the physician, for he did not hesitate or continue to work at cross purposes to her. He grabbed the chair and wheeled it swiftly through a door that connected the examination room to the downstairs hall. Laura and Chris followed him along the gloomy corridor, then across a kitchen lit only by the illuminated digital clocks on the oven and microwave oven. The chair thumped over the sill between the kitchen and the back porch, badly jarring the wounded man, but he had been through worse.

Slinging the Uzi over her shoulder and jamming the revolver into her waistband, Laura hurried around Brenkshaw to the bottom of the porch steps. She took hold of the wheelchair from the front, helping him trundle it to the concrete walk below.

She glanced at the areaway between the house and garage, half expecting to see an armed man coming through there already, and she whispered to Brenkshaw, 'You'll have to go with us. They'll kill you if you stay here, I'm sure they will.'

Again he offered no argument but followed Chris, as the boy led the way down the walk that struck across the rear lawn to the gate in the redwood fence at the back of the long property. Having unslung the Uzi from her shoulder, Laura came last, ready to turn and open fire if she heard a noise from the house behind them.

As Chris reached the gate, it opened in front of him, and a man dressed in black stepped through from the alley, darker than the night around them except for his moon-pale face and white hands, every bit as surprised by them as they were by him. He'd come along the street beside the house and into the alley to cover the place from the back. In his left hand, gleaming darkly, was a submachine gun, not at the ready, but he started to bring it up – Laura could not blow him away, not without cutting her son down as well – but Chris reacted as Henry Takahami had spent months teaching him to react. The boy spun and kicked the assassin's right arm, knocking the gun out of his grasp – it hit the lawn with a thump and soft clatter – then kicked again at his adversary's crotch, and with a grunt of pain, the man in black fell backward against the gatepost.

By then Laura had stepped around the wheelchair and interposed herself between Chris and the killer. She reversed the Uzi, raised it overhead, and brought the stock of it down on the assassin's skull, struck him again with all her might, and he dropped to the lawn, away from the walk, without having had a chance to cry out.

Events were moving fast now, too fast, they were on a downhill ride, and already Chris was going through the gate, so Laura followed, and they surprised a second man in black, eyes like holes in his white face, a vampiric figure, but this one was beyond the reach of a karate kick, so she had to open fire before he could use his own weapon. She shot over Chris's head, a tightly placed burst that pounded into the assassin's chest, throat, and neck, virtually decapitating him as it catapulted him backward onto the alley pavement.

Brenkshaw had come through the gate behind them, pushing the wheelchair into the alley, and Laura felt bad about having gotten him into this, but there was no going back now. The back street was narrow, flanked by the fenced yards of houses on both sides, with a few garages and clusters of garbage cans behind each property, poorly revealed by the lamps on the intersecting streets at each end of the block, with no light of its own.

To Brenkshaw, Laura said, 'Wheel him across the alley and down a couple of doors. Find a gate that's open and get him into somebody else's yard, out of sight. Chris, you go with them.'

'What about you?'

'I'll follow you in a second.'

'Mom—'

'Go, Chris!' she said, for the physician had already rolled the wheelchair fifty feet, angling across the alleyway.

As the boy reluctantly followed the doctor, Laura returned to the open redwood gate at the rear of Brenkshaw's property. She was just in time to see two dark figures scuttle out of the areaway between the house and garage, thirty yards from her, barely visible, noticeable only because they were moving. They ran crouched, one of them heading toward the porch and the other toward the lawn because they didn't yet know exactly where the trouble was, where the gunfire had come from.

She stepped through the gate, onto the walk, and opened up on them before they saw her, spraying the back of the house with bullets. Though she was not on top of her targets, she was in range – ninety feet was not far – and they dove for cover. She could not tell if she hit them, and she didn't continue to fire because even with a magazine of four hundred rounds expended in short bursts, the Uzi could empty quickly; and now it was the only automatic weapon she still possessed. She backed out of the gate and ran after Brenkshaw and Chris.

They were just going through a wrought-iron gate at the back of a property on the other side of the alley, two doors down. When she got there and stepped into the yard, she found that old eugenias were planted along the iron fence to the left and right of the gate; they had grown into a dense hedge, so no one would spot her easily from the alley unless they were directly in front of the gate itself.

The physician had pushed the wheelchair all the way to the back of the house. It was Tudor, not Victorian like Brenkshaw's, but also built at least forty or fifty years ago. The doctor was starting around the side of the place, into the driveway, heading toward the next major street.

Lights winked on in houses all over the neighborhood. She was sure that faces were pressed to windows, including those where lights had not appeared, but she didn't think anyone would see much.

She caught up with Brenkshaw and Chris at the front of the house and halted them in shadows near some overgrown shrubbery. 'Doc, I'd like you to wait here with your patient,' she whispered.

He was shaking, and she hoped to God he didn't have a heart attack, but he was still game. 'I'll be here.'

She took Chris out to the next street, where at least a score of cars were parked at the near and far curbs along that block. In the rain of bluish light from the streetlamps, the boy looked bad but not as awful as she had feared, not as frightened as the physician; he was growing accustomed to terror. She said, 'Okay, let's start trying car doors. You take this side, I'll take the far side. If the door is open, check the ignition, under the driver's seat, and behind the sun visor for keys.'

'Gotcha.'

Having once done research for a book in which a character had been a car thief, she had learned among other things that on average one out of seventeen drivers left his keys in his car overnight. She hoped the figure might be even more in their favor in a place like San Bernardino; after all, in New York and Chicago and LA and other big cities, nobody but masochists left their keys in their cars, so for the average to work out to one in seventeen, there had to be more trusting people among other Americans.

She attempted to keep an eye on Chris as she tried the doors of the cars along the far side of the street, but she soon lost track of him. Out of the first eight vehicles, four were unlocked, but no keys were in any of them.

In the distance rose the wail of sirens.

That would probably drive off the men in black. Anyway, they were most likely still searching along the alleyway behind Brenkshaw's house, moving cautiously, expecting to be fired upon again.

Laura moved boldly, with no caution whatsoever, not concerned about being seen by residents in the flanking houses. The street was lined with mature but squat, stunted date palms that provided a lot of cover. Anyway, if anyone had been aroused at this dead hour of the night, they were probably at second-floor windows, not trying to look down at their own street through the palms but over toward the next street, toward Brenkshaw's place, where all the shooting had been.

The ninth vehicle was an Oldsmobile Cutlass, and there were keys under the seat. Just as she started the engine and pulled her door shut, Chris opened the door on the passenger's side and showed her a set of keys that he had found.

'Brand new Toyota,' he said.

'This'll do,' she said.

The sirens were closer.

Chris pitched the Toyota's keys away, hopped into the car, and rode with her to the driveway of the house on the other side of the street, farther up toward the corner, where the doctor was waiting in the shadows along the driveway of a house in which no lights had yet come on. Maybe they were in luck; maybe no one was home at that place. They lifted her guardian out of the wheelchair and laid him on the rear seat of the Cutlass.

The sirens were very close now, and in fact a police cruiser shot past at the far end of that block, on the side street, red beacons flashing, heading toward Brenkshaw's block.

'You'll be okay, Doctor?' she asked, turning to him as she closed the back door of the Cutlass.

He had dropped into the wheelchair. 'No apoplexy, if that's what you're afraid of. What the *hell* is going on with you, girl?'

'No time, Doc. I have to split.'

'Listen,' he said, 'maybe I won't tell them anything.'

'Yes, you will,' she said. 'You may think you won't, but you'll tell them everything. If you weren't going to tell them, then there wouldn't have been a police report or a newspaper story, and without that record in the future, those gunmen couldn't have found me.'

'What're you jibbering about?'

She leaned down and kissed his cheek. 'No time to explain, Doc. Thanks for your help. And, sorry, but I'd better take that wheelchair too.'

He folded it and put it in the trunk for her.

The night was full of sirens now.

She got behind the wheel, slammed her door. 'Buckle up, Chris.'

'Buckled,' he said.

She turned left at the end of the driveway and drove to the far corner of the block, away from Brenkshaw's end of the neighborhood, to the intersecting street on which a cruiser had flashed by only a moment ago. She figured that if police were converging in answer to reports of automatic-weapons fire, they would be coming from different areas of the city, from different patrols, so maybe no other car would approach by that same route. The avenue was nearly deserted, and the only other vehicles she saw were not fitted with rooftop emergency beacons. She turned right, heading steadily farther away from the Brenkshaw place, across San Bernardino, wondering where she would find sanctuary.

• **3** •

Laura reached Riverside at 3:15 in the morning, stole a Buick from a quiet residential street, shifted her guardian to it with the wheelchair, and abandoned the Cutlass. Chris slept through the entire operation and had to be carried from one car to the other.

Half an hour later, in another neighborhood, exhausted and in need of sleep, she used a screwdriver from a tool pouch in the Buick's trunk to steal a set of license plates from a Nissan. She put the Nissan's plates on the Buick and put the Buick's plates in the trunk because they would eventually turn up on a police hot sheet.

A couple of days might pass before the Nissan's owner noticed his plates were missing, and even when he reported them stolen, the police would not treat that news with the same attention they gave to stolen cars. Plates were usually taken by kids playing a stupid prank, or vandals, and their recovery was not a high priority for overworked police laboring under heavy caseloads of major crimes. That was one more useful fact she had learned while researching the book in which a car thief had played a secondary role.

She also paused long enough to dress her guardian in wool socks, shoes, and a pullover sweater to keep him from catching a chill. At one point he opened his eyes, blinked at her, and said her name, and she thought he was coming around, but then he slipped away again, muttering in a language that she could not identify because she could not hear any of the words clearly.

She drove from Riverside to Yorba Linda in Orange County, where she parked in a corner of a Ralph's Supermarket lot, behind a Goodwill collection station, at 4:50 in the morning. She killed the engine and lights, unbuckled her safety harness. Chris was still buckled up, leaning against the door, sound asleep. Lying on the back seat, her guardian was still unconscious, though his breathing was not quite as wheezy as it had been before they had visited Carter Brenkshaw. Laura did not think she would be able to doze off; she hoped just to collect her wits and rest her eyes, but in a minute or two she was asleep.

After killing at least three men, after being shot at repeatedly, after stealing two cars, after surviving a chase that had harried her through three counties, she might have expected to dream of death, of blasted bodies and blood, with the cold chatter of automatic-weapons fire as background music to the nightmare. She might have expected to dream of losing Chris, for he was one of the two remaining lights in her personal darkness, he and Thelma, and she dreaded the thought of going on without him. But instead she dreamed of Danny, and they were lovely dreams, not nightmares. Danny was alive again, and they were reliving the sale of *Shadrach* for more than one million dollars, but Chris was there, too, and he was eight years old, though in fact Chris had not been born at that time, and they were celebrating their good fortune by spending the day at Disneyland, where the three of them had their picture taken with Mickey Mouse, and in the Carnation Pavilion Danny told her he'd love her forever, while Chris pretended that he could speak in an all-snort pig language that he had learned from Carl Dockweiler, who was sitting at the next table with Nina and with Laura's father, and at another table the amazing Ackerson twins were eating strawberry sundaes. . . .

She woke more than three hours later at 8:26, feeling rested as much because of that familial communion, provided by her subconscious, as because of the sleep itself. Sunlight from a cloudless sky sparkled on the car's chrome and fell in a bright, brassy shaft through the rear window. Chris was still dozing. In the back seat the wounded man had not regained consciousness.

She risked a quick walk to a telephone booth beside the market, which was within sight of the car. With change she had in her purse, she called Ida Palomar, Chris's tutor in Lake Arrowhead, to tell her they would be away from home for the rest of the week. She did not want poor Ida to walk unsuspecting into the bullet-riddled, blood-spattered house near Big Bear, where police forensic teams were no doubt hard at work. She did not tell Ida where she was calling from; nevertheless, she did not intend to remain in Yorba Linda much longer.

After she returned to the car, she sat yawning, stretching, and massaging the back of her neck, as she watched early shoppers entering and leaving the supermarket a couple of hundred feet away. She was hungry. With sleep-matted eyes and sour breath, Chris woke less than ten minutes later, and she gave him money to go into the market and buy a package of sweet rolls and two pints of orange juice, not the most nutritional breakfast but energy-giving.

'What about him?' Chris asked, indicating her guardian.

She remembered Dr. Brenkshaw's warning about the patient's risk of dehydration. But she also knew that she could not force-feed him liquids when he was comatose; he would choke to death. 'Well . . . bring a third orange juice. Maybe I can coax him awake.' As Chris got out of the car, she said, 'Might as well get us something for lunch, something that won't spoil – say a loaf of bread and a jar of peanut butter. And get a can of spray deodorant and a bottle of shampoo.'

He grinned. 'Why won't you let me eat this way at home?'

'Because if you don't get good nutrition, you're going to wind up with a brain even more twisted than the one you've got now, kiddo.'

'Even on the lam from hired killers, I'm surprised you didn't pack a microwave, fresh vegetables, and a bottle of vitamins.'

'Are you saying I'm a good mother but a fuss-budget? Compliment noted and point taken. Now go.'

He started to close his door.

She said, 'And, Chris . . .'

'I know,' the boy said. 'Be careful.'

While Chris was gone, she started the engine and switched on the radio to listen to the nine o'clock news. She heard a story about herself: the scene at her house near Big Bear, the shoot-out in San Bernardino. Like most news stories it was inaccurate, disjointed, and made little sense. But it confirmed that the police were looking for her throughout southern California. According to the reporter, the authorities expected to locate her soon, largely because her face was already widely known.

She had been shocked last night when Carter Brenkshaw recognized her as Laura Shane, famous writer. She did not think of herself as a celebrity; she was only a storyteller, a weaver of tales, who worked with a loom of language, making a special fabric from words. She had done only one book tour for an early novel, had loathed that dreary trek, and had not repeated the experience. She was not a regular guest on television talkshows. She had never endorsed a product in a TV commercial, had never gone public in support of a politician, and had in general attempted to avoid being part of the media circus. She observed the tradition of having a dust jacket photograph on her books because it seemed harmless, and by the age of thirty-three she could admit without severe embarrassment that she was an unusually striking woman, but she never imagined, as the police put it, that her face was widely known.

Now she was dismayed not only because her loss of anonymity made her easier quarry for the police but because she knew that becoming a celebrity in modern America was tantamount to a loss of one's self-critical faculties and a severe decline of artistic power. A few managed to be both public figures and worthwhile writers, but most seemed to be corrupted by the media attention. Laura dreaded that trap almost as much as she dreaded being picked up by the police.

Suddenly, with some surprise, she realized that if she could worry about becoming a celebrity and losing her artistic center, she must still believe in a safe future in which she would write more books. At times during the night, she had vowed to fight to the death, to struggle to a bloody end to protect her son, but throughout she had felt that their situation was virtually hopeless, their enemy too powerful and unreachable to be destroyed. Now something had changed her, had brought her around to a dim, guarded optimism.

Maybe it had been the dream.

Chris returned with a large package of pecan-cinnamon rolls, three one-pint containers of orange juice, and the other items. They ate the rolls and drank the juice, and nothing had ever tasted better.

When she finished her own breakfast, Laura got in the back seat and tried to wake her guardian. He could not be roused.

She gave the third carton of orange juice to Chris and said, 'Keep it for him. He'll probably wake up soon.'

'If he can't drink, he can't take his penicillin,' Chris said.

'He doesn't need to take any for a few hours yet. Dr. Brenkshaw gave him a pretty potent shot last night; it's still working.'

But Laura was worried. If he did not regain consciousness, they might never learn the true nature of the dangerous maze in which they were now lost – and might never find a way out of it.

'What next?' Chris asked.

'We'll find a service station, use the rest rooms, then stop at a gunshop and buy ammunition for the Uzi and the revolver. After that . . . we start looking for a motel, just the right kind of motel, a place where we can hide out.'

When they settled in somewhere, they would be at least fifty miles from Dr. Brenkshaw's place, where their enemies had last found them. But did distance matter to men who measured their journeys strictly in days and years rather than miles?

Parts of Santa Ana, neighborhoods on the south side of Anaheim, and adjoining areas offered the greatest number of motels of the type she was seeking. She did not want a modern, gleaming Red Lion Inn or Howard Johnson's Motor Lodge with color television sets, deep-pile carpet, and a heated swimming pool, because reputable establishments required valid ID and a major credit card, and she dared not risk leaving a paper trail that would bring either the police or the assassins down on her. Instead she was seeking a motel that was no longer clean enough or in good enough repair to attract tourists, a seedy place where they were happy to get the business, eager to take cash, and reluctant to ask questions that would drive away guests.

She knew she would have a hard time finding a room, and she was not surprised to discover that the first twelve places she tried were unable or unwilling to accommodate her. The only people who could be seen going from or coming to those dead-end motels were young Mexican women with babies in their arms or young children in tow, and young or middle-aged Mexican men in sneakers, chinos, flannel shirts, and lightweight denim or corduroy jackets, some wearing straw cowboy hats and some baseball caps, and all of them with an air of watchfulness and suspicion. Most decrepit motels had become boarding houses for illegal immigrants, hundreds of thousands of whom had taken up not-so-secret residence in Orange County alone. Whole families lived in a single room, five or six or seven of them crowded into that cramped space, sharing one ancient bed and two chairs and a bathroom with minimally functional plumbing, for which they paid a hundred and fifty dollars or more every week, with no linen or maid service or amenities of any kind, but with cockroaches by the thousands. Yet they were willing to endure those conditions and let themselves be outrageously exploited as underpaid workers rather than return to their homeland and live under the rule of the 'revolutionary people's government' that for decades had given them no brotherhood but that of despair.

At the thirteenth motel, The Bluebird of Happiness, the owner-manager still hoped to serve the lower end of the tourist trade, and he had not yet succumbed to the temptation to squeeze a rich living from the blood of poor immigrants. A few of the twenty-four units were obviously rented to illegals, but the management still provided fresh linen daily, maid service, television sets, and two spare pillows in every closet. However the fact that the desk clerk took cash, did not press her for ID, and avoided meeting her eyes was sad proof that in another year The Bluebird of Happiness would be one more monument to political stupidity and human avarice in a world as crowded with such monuments as any old city cemetery was crowded with tombstones.

The motel had three wings in a U-shape, with parking in the middle, and their unit was in the right rear corner of the back wing. A big fan palm flourished near the door to their room, not visibly touched by smog or limited by its small patch of ground midst so much concrete and blacktop, bristling with new growth even in winter, as if nature had chosen it as a subtle omen of her intention to seize every corner of the earth again when humankind passed on.

Laura and Chris unfolded the wheelchair and got the wounded man into it, making no effort to conceal what they were doing, as if they were simply caring for a disabled person. Fully dressed, with his wounds concealed, her guardian could pass for a paraplegic – except for the way his head lolled against his shoulder.

Their room was small though passably clean. The carpet was worn but recently shampooed, and a pair of dustballs in one corner were far from the size of tumbleweeds. The maroon-plaid spread on the queen-size bed was tattered at the edges, and its pattern was not quite busy enough to conceal two patches, but the sheets were crisp and smelled faintly of detergent. They moved her guardian from the wheelchair to the bed and put two pillows under his head.

The seventeen-inch television set was firmly bolted to a table with a scarred, laminated top, and the back legs of the table were in turn bolted to the floor. Chris sat in one of the two mismatched chairs, switched on the set, and turned the cracked dial in search of either a cartoon show or reruns of an old sitcom. He settled for *Get Smart* but complained that it was 'too stupid to be funny,' and Laura wondered how many boys his age would have thought so.

She sat in the other chair. 'Why don't you get a shower?'

'Then just get back in these same clothes?' he asked doubtfully.

'I know it sounds like purest folly, but try it. I guarantee you'll feel cleaner even without fresh clothes.'

'But all that trouble to shower, then get into *wrinkled* clothes?'

'When did you become such a fashion plate that you're offended by a few wrinkles?'

He grinned, got up from his chair, and pranced to the bathroom as he thought a hopeless fop might prance. 'The king and queen would be shocked to see me such a mess.'

'We'll make them put on blindfolds when they visit,' she said.

He returned from the bathroom in a minute. 'There's a dead bug in the toilet bowl. I think it's a cockroach, but I'm not really sure.'

'Does the species matter? Will we be notifying next of kin?'

Chris laughed. God, she loved to hear him laugh. He said, 'What should I do – flush him?'

'Unless you want to fish him out, put him in a matchbox, and bury him in the flowerbed outside.'

He laughed again. 'Nope. Burial at sea.' In the bathroom, he hummed 'Taps,' then flushed the john.

While the boy was showering, *Get Smart* ended and a movie came on, *The Harlem Globetrotters on Gilligan's Island*. Laura was not actually watching the set; she left it on for background, but there were limits to what even a woman on the lam could endure, so she quickly switched to channel eleven and *Hour Magazine*.

She stared at her guardian for a while, but his unnatural slumber depressed her. From her chair she reached to the drapes a few times, parting them far enough to scan the motel's parking lot, but no one on earth could know where she was; she was in no imminent danger. So she stared at the TV screen, uninterested in what it offered, until she was half hypnotized by it. The *Hour Magazine* host was interviewing a young actor who droned on about himself, not always making much sense, and after a while she was vaguely aware that he kept saying something about water, but now she was beginning to doze off, and his insistent talk of water was both mesmeric and annoying.

'Mom?'

She blinked, sat up, and saw Chris in the bathroom doorway. He'd just gotten out of the shower. His hair was damp, and he was dressed only in his briefs. The sight of his thin, boyish body – all ribs and elbows and knees – pulled at her heart, for he looked so innocent and vulnerable. He was so small and fragile that she wondered how she could ever protect him, and renewed fear rose in her.

'Mom, he's talking,' Chris said, pointing to the man on the bed. 'Didn't you hear him? He's talking.'

'Water,' her guardian said thickly. 'Water.'

She went quickly to the bed and bent over him. He was no longer comatose. He was trying to sit up, but he had no strength. His blue eyes were open, and although they were bloodshot, they focused on her, alert and observant.

'Thirsty,' he said.

She said, 'Chris—'

He was already there with a glass of water from the bathroom.

She sat on the bed beside her guardian, lifted his head, took the water from Chris, and helped the wounded man drink. She allowed him only small sips; she didn't want him to choke. His lips were fever-chapped, and his tongue was coated with a white film, as if he had eaten ashes. He drank more than a third of a glass of water, then indicated that he'd had enough.

After she lowered his head to the pillow, she put a hand to his forehead. 'Not so hot as he was.'

He rolled his head from side to side, trying to look at the room. In spite of the water, his voice was dry, burnt out. 'Where are we?'

'Safe,' she said.

'Nowhere . . . is safe.'

'We may have figured out more of this crazy situation than you realize,' she told him.

'Yeah,' Chris said, sitting on the bed beside his mother. 'We know you're a time traveler!'

The man looked at the boy, managed a weak smile, winced in pain.

'I've got drugs,' Laura said. 'A painkiller.'

'No,' he said. 'Not now. Later maybe. More water?'

Laura lifted him once more, and this time he drank most of what remained in the glass. She remembered the penicillin and put a capsule between his teeth. He washed it down with the last two swallows.

'When do you come from?' Chris asked, intensely interested, oblivious of the

droplets of bathwater that tracked out of his damp hair and down his face.
'When?'

'Honey,' Laura said, 'he's very weak, and I don't think we should bother him with too many questions just yet.'

'He can tell us that much, anyway, Mom.' To the wounded man, Chris said, 'When do you come from?'

He stared at Chris, then at Laura, and the haunted look was in his eyes again.
'When do you come from ? Huh? The year 2100? 3000?'

In his paper-dry voice, her guardian said, 'Nineteen forty-four.'

The little bit of activity had clearly tired him already, for his eyelids looked heavy, and his voice was fainter than it had been, so Laura was certain that he had lapsed into delirium again.

'When?' Chris repeated, baffled by the answer he had been given.

'Nineteen forty-four.'

'That's impossible,' Chris said.

'Berlin,' her guardian said.

'He's delirious,' Laura told Chris.

His voice was slurred now as weariness dragged him down, but what he said was unmistakable: 'Berlin.'

'Berlin?' Chris said. 'You mean – Berlin, Germany?'

Sleep claimed the wounded man, not the unnatural sleep of a coma but restful sleep that was immediately marked by soft snoring, though in the moment before he slipped away, he said, '*Nazi* Germany.'

• 4 •

One Life to Live was on the television, but neither she nor Chris was paying any attention to the soap opera. They had drawn the two chairs closer to the bed, where they could watch the sleeping man. Chris was dressed, and his hair was mostly dry, though it remained damp at the nape of his neck. Laura felt grimy and longed for a shower, but she was not going to leave her guardian in case he woke again and was able to talk. She and the boy spoke in whispers:

'Chris, it just occurred to me, if these people were from the future, why wouldn't they have been carrying laser guns or something futuristic when they came for us?'

'They wouldn't want everyone to *know* they were from the future,' Chris said. 'They'd bring weapons and wear clothes that wouldn't be out of place here. But, Mom, he said he was from—'

'I know what he said. But it doesn't make sense, does it? If they had time travel in 1944, we'd know about it by now, wouldn't we?'

At one-thirty her guardian woke and seemed briefly confused as to his whereabouts. He asked for more water, and Laura helped him drink. He said he was feeling a little better, though very weak and still surprisingly sleepy. He asked to be propped up higher. Chris got the two spare pillows from the closet and helped his mother raise the wounded man.

'What is your name?' Laura asked.

'Stefan. Stefan Krieger.'

She repeated the name softly, and it was all right, not melodic but solid, a masculine-sounding name. It was just not the name of a guardian angel, and she was mildly amused to realize that after so many years, including two decades during which she had professed to have no belief in him, she still expected his name to be musical and unearthly.

'And you really come from—'

'Nineteen forty-four,' he repeated. Just the effort required to move to a sitting position had wrung fine beads of perspiration from his brow – or perhaps the sweat resulted in part from thoughts of the time and place where his long journey had begun. 'Berlin, Germany. There was a brilliant Polish scientist, Vladimir Penlovski, considered a madman by some, and very likely mad in fact – very mad, I think – but also a genius. He was in Warsaw, working on certain theories about the nature of time for more than twenty-five years before Germany and Russia collaborated to invade Poland in 1939 . . .'

Penlovski, according to Stefan Krieger, was a Nazi sympathizer and welcomed Hitler's forces. Perhaps he knew that from Hitler he would receive the kind of financial backing for his researches that he could not get from sources more rational. Under the personal patronage of Hitler himself, Penlovski and his closest assistant, Wladyslaw Januskaya, went to Berlin to establish an institute for temporal research, which was so secret that it was given no name. It was simply called the institute. There, in association with German scientists no less committed and no less farsighted than he, financed by a seemingly inexhaustible river of funds from the Third Reich, Penlovski had found a way to pierce the artery of time and move at will through that bloodstream of days and months and years.

'*Blitzstrasse*,' Stefan said.

'*Blitz* – that part of it means lightning,' Chris said. 'Like *Blitzkrieg* – lightning war – in all those old movies.'

'Lightning Road in this case,' Stefan said. 'The road through time. The road to the future.'

It literally could have been called *Zukunftstrasse*, or Future Road, Stefan explained, for Vladimir Penlovski had been unable to discover a way to send men backward in time from the gate he had invented. They could travel only forward, into their future, and return automatically to their own era.

'There seems to be some cosmic mechanism that prohibits time travelers from meddling with their own pasts in order to change their present-day circumstances. You see, if they *could* travel back in time to their own past, there would develop certain—'

'Paradoxes!' Chris said excitedly.

Stefan looked surprised to hear the boy speak that word.

Smiling, Laura said, 'As I told you, we've had rather a long discussion about your possible origins, and time travel turned out to be the most logical. And in Chris here, you're looking at my resident expert on the weird.'

'Paradox,' Stefan agreed. 'It's the same word in English and German. If a time traveler could go back in time to his own past and affect some event in history, that change would have tremendous ramifications. It would alter the future from which he had come. Therefore he wouldn't be able to return to the same world he'd left—'

'Paradox!' Chris said gleefully.

'Paradox,' Stefan agreed. 'Apparently nature abhors a paradox and generally

will not permit a time traveler to create one. And thank God for that. Because
. . . suppose, for example, Hitler sent an assassin back in time to kill Franklin
Roosevelt and Winston Churchill long before they rose to high office, which
would have resulted in the election of different men in the U.S. and England,
men who might have been less brilliant and more easily dealt with, leading to
Hitler's triumph by '44 or sooner.'

He was speaking now with a passion that his physical condition would not
allow him to sustain, and Laura could see it taking a toll of him word by word.
The perspiration had almost dried on his brow; but now, although he was not
even gesturing, a new thin film of sweat silvered his pale forehead again. The
circles of fatigue around his eyes appeared to grow darker. But she could not
stop him and order him to rest, because she wanted and needed to hear everything he had to say – and because he would not have allowed her to stop him.

'Suppose *der Führer* could send back assassins to kill Dwight Eisenhower,
George Patton, Field Marshal Montgomery, kill them in their *cradles*, when
they were babies, eliminating them and others, all the best military minds the
Allies possessed. Then most of the world would have been his by '44, in which
case time travelers would have been going back in time to kill those men *who had
already long been dead and posed no threat*. Paradox, you see. And thank God that
nature permits no such paradox, no such tampering with the time traveler's
own past, for otherwise Adolf Hitler would have turned the entire world into a
concentration camp, a crematorium.'

They were silent a while, as the possibility of such hell on earth struck each of
them. Even Chris responded to the picture of an altered world that Stefan
painted, for he was a child of the eighties, in which the villains of film and
television melodramas were usually either voracious aliens from a distant star or
Nazis. The swastika, the silver death's-head symbol, and the black uniforms of
the SS, and that strange fanatic with the small mustache were to Chris especially terrifying because they were part of the media-created mythology on
which he had been raised. Laura knew that real people and events, once
subsumed by mythology, were somehow *more* real to a child than the very bread
he ate.

Stefan said, 'So from the institute we could go only forward in time, but that
had its uses too. We could leap forward a few decades to discover if Germany
had held on in the dark days of the war and had somehow turned the tide. But of
course we found that Germany had not done any such thing, that the Third
Reich had been defeated. Yet with all the knowledge of the future to draw from,
could not that tide be turned, after all? Surely there were things Hitler could do
to save the Reich even as late as '44. And there were things that might be
brought back from the future with which the war might be won—'

'Such as,' Chris said, 'atomic bombs!'

'Or the knowledge of how they were built,' Stefan said. 'The Reich already
had a nuclear research program, you know, and if they'd had a breakthrough
early enough, had split the atom . . .'

'They'd have won the war,' Chris said.

Stefan asked for water and drank half a glass this time. He wanted to hold the
glass in his good hand, but he was shaking too much; water slopped on the
bedclothes, and Laura had to help him.

When he spoke again, Stefan's voice wavered at times. 'Because the time traveler exists *outside* of time during his journey, he is not only able to move in time but geographically, as well. Picture him hanging above the earth, unmoving, as the globe turns below him. That's not what he does, of course, but it's easier to see that image than to imagine him hovering in another dimension. Now, as he hangs above the world, it turns below him, and if his journey to the future is gauged properly, he can travel to a precise time at which he will find himself in Berlin, the same city he left years before. But if he chooses to travel a few hours more or less, the world will have turned that much more beneath him, and he will arrive at a different place on its surface. The calculations to achieve a precise arrival are monumentally difficult in my era, 1944—'

'But they'd be easy these days,' Chris said, 'with computers.'

Shifting in discomfort against the pillows that propped him up, putting his trembling right hand against his wounded left shoulder as if to quell the pain by his own touch, he said, 'Teams of German physicists, accompanied by Gestapo, were sent secretly to various cities in Europe and the United States in the year 1985, to accumulate vital information on the making of nuclear weapons. The material they were after was not classified or difficult to find. With what they already knew from their own researches, they could obtain the rest from textbooks and scientific publications readily available at any major university library in '85. Four days before I departed the institute for the last time, those teams returned from '85 to March, 1944, with material that would give the Third Reich a nuclear arsenal before the autumn of that year. They were to spend a few weeks studying the material at the institute before deciding how and where to introduce that knowledge into the German nuclear program without revealing how it had been obtained. I knew then that I had to destroy the institute and everything it contained, key personnel as well as files, to prevent a future shaped by Adolf Hitler.'

As Laura and Chris listened, rapt, Stefan Krieger told them how he had planted explosives in the institute, how on the last of his days in '44 he had shot Penlovski, Januskaya, and Volkaw, and had programmed the time gate to bring him to Laura in present-day America.

But something had gone wrong at the last minute, as Stefan was leaving. The public power supply failed. The RAF had bombed Berlin for the first time in January that year, and U.S. bombers had made the first daylight runs on March 6, so the power supply had been interrupted often, not merely due to bomb damage but also because of the work of saboteurs. It was to guard against such interruptions that the gate itself was powered by a secure generator. Stefan heard no bombers that day when, wounded by Kokoschka, he had crawled into the gate, so apparently the power failed because of saboteurs.

'And the timer on the explosives stopped. The gate was not destroyed. It's still open back there, and they can come after us. And . . . they can still win the war.'

Laura was getting another headache. She put her fingertips to her temples. 'But wait. Hitler can't have succeeded in building atomic weapons and winning World War Two, because we don't live in a world where that happened. You don't have to worry. Somehow, in spite of all the knowledge they took back through the gate, they obviously failed to develop a nuclear arsenal.'

'No,' he said. 'They've failed so far, but we can't assume they will continue to fail. To those men at the institute in Berlin in 1944, their past is immutable, as I have said. They cannot travel backward in time and change their own past. But they can change their future and ours, because a time traveler's future is mutable; he can take steps to alter it.'

'But *his* future is *my* past,' Laura said. 'And if the past can't be changed, how can he change mine?'

'Yeah,' Chris said. 'Paradox.'

Laura said, 'Listen, I haven't spent the last thirty-four years in a world ruled by Adolf Hitler and his heirs; therefore, in spite of the gate, Hitler failed.'

Stefan's expression was dismal. 'If time travel were invented now, in 1989, that past of which you speak – World War Two and every event since – would be unalterable. You could not change it, for nature's rule against backward time-travel and time-travel paradoxes would apply to you. But time travel has not been discovered here – or rediscovered. The time travelers at the institute in Berlin in '44 are free to change *their* future, apparently, and though they will simultaneously be changing your past, nothing in the laws of nature will stop them. And there you have the greatest paradox of all – the only one that for some reason nature seems to allow.'

'You're saying they could still build nuclear weapons back then with the information they got in '85,' Laura said, 'and win the war?'

'Yes. Unless the institute is destroyed first.'

'And what then? Suddenly, all around us, we find things changed, find ourselves living under Nazism?'

'Yes. And you won't even know what's happened, because you will be a different person than you are now. Your entire past will never have occurred. You will have lived a *different* past altogether, and you will remember nothing else, none of what has happened to you in *this* life because this life will never have existed. You will think the world has always been as it is, that there was never a world in which Hitler lost.'

What he was proposing terrified and appalled her because it made life seem even more fragile than she had always thought it was. The world under her feet suddenly seemed no more real than the world of a dream; it was apt to dissolve without warning and send her tumbling into a great, dark void.

With growing horror she said, 'If they change the world in which I grew up, I might never have met Danny, never married.'

'I might never have been born,' Chris said.

She reached to Chris and put a hand on his arm, not only to reassure him but to reassure herself of his current solidity. 'I might not have been born myself. Everything I've seen, the good and bad of the world that's been since 1944 . . . it'll all wash away like an elaborate sandcastle, and a new reality will exist in its place.'

'A new and worse reality,' Stefan said, clearly exhausted by the effort he had made to explain what was at stake.

'In that new world, I might never have written my novels.'

'Or if you wrote novels,' Stefan said, 'they would be different from those you've done in this life, grotesque works produced by an artist laboring under the rule of an oppressive government, in the iron fist of Nazi censorship.'

'If those guys build the atom bomb in 1944,' Chris said, 'then we'll all just crumble into dust and blow away.'

'Not literally. But like dust, yes,' Stefan Krieger agreed. 'Gone, with no trace that we've ever been.'

'We've gotta stop them,' Chris said.

'If we can,' Stefan agreed. 'But first we've got to stay alive in *this* reality, and that might not be easy.'

Stefan needed to relieve himself, and Laura helped him into the motel bathroom, handling him as if she were a nurse accustomed to matter-of-fact dealings with the plumbing of sick men. By the time she returned him to the bed, she was worried about him again; though he was muscular, he felt limp, clammy, and he was frighteningly weak.

She told him briefly about the shoot-out at Brenkshaw's, through which he had remained comatose. 'If these assassins are coming from the past instead of the future, how do they know where to find us? How did they know in 1944 that we'd be at Dr. Brenkshaw's when we were, forty-five years later?'

'To find you,' Stefan said, 'they made two trips. First, they went farther into the future, a couple of days farther, to this coming weekend perhaps, to see if you had shown up anywhere by then. If you hadn't – and apparently you had not – then they started checking the public record. Back issues of newspapers, for one thing. They looked for the stories about the shooting at your house last night, and in those stories they read that you'd taken a wounded man to Brenkshaw's place in San Bernardino. So they simply returned to '44 and made a second trip – this time to Dr. Brenkshaw's in the early hours of this morning, January 11.'

'They can hopscotch around us,' Chris told Laura. 'They can pop ahead in time to see where we show up, then they pick and choose the easiest place along the time stream to ambush us. It's sorta like . . . if we were cowboys and the Indians were all psychic.'

'Who was Kokoschka?' Chris wanted to know. 'Who was the man who killed my dad?'

'Head of institute security,' Stefan said. 'He claimed to be a distant relation of Oskar Kokoschka, the noted Austrian expressionist painter, but I doubt if it was true because in *our* Kokoschka there was no hint of an artist's sensitivity. *Standartenführer* – which means Colonel – Heinrich Kokoschka was an efficient killer for the Gestapo.'

'Gestapo,' Chris said, awestruck. 'Secret police?'

'State police,' Stefan said. 'Widely known to exist but allowed to operate in secrecy. When he showed up on that mountain road in 1988, I was as surprised as you. There'd been no lightning. He must have arrived far away from us, fifteen or twenty miles, in some other valley of the San Bernardinos, and the lightning had been beyond our notice.' The lightning associated with time travel was in fact a very localized phenomenon, Stefan explained. 'After Kokoschka showed up there, on my trail, I thought I would return to the institute and find all of my colleagues outraged at my treason, but when I got there, no one took special notice of me. I was confused. Then after I killed

Penlovski and the others, when I was in the main lab preparing for my final jaunt into the future, Heinrich Kokoschka burst in and shot me. He wasn't dead! Not dead on that highway in 1988. Then I realized that Kokoschka had obviously only just learned of my treason when he'd found the men I'd shot. He would travel to 1988 and try to kill me – and all of you – at a later time. Which meant that the gate would have to remain open to allow him to do so, and that I was destined to fail to destroy it. At least at that time.'

'God, this headache,' Laura said.

Chris seemed to have no trouble whatsoever following the tangled threads of time travel. He said, 'So after you traveled to our house last night, Kokoschka traveled to 1988 and killed my dad. Jeez! In a way, Mr. Krieger, you killed Kokoschka forty-three years *after* he shot you in that lab . . . yet you had shot him *before* he shot you. This is wild stuff. Mom, isn't this wild? Isn't this great?'

'It's something,' she agreed. 'And how did Kokoschka know to find you on that mountain road?'

'After he discovered I'd shot Penlovski, and after I escaped through the gate, Kokoschka must have found the explosives in the attic and basement. Then he must have dug into the automatic records the machinery keeps of all the times the gate is used. That was a bit of data tracking that was *my* responsibility, so no one previously had noticed all my jaunts into your life, Laura. Anyway, Kokoschka must have done some time traveling of his own, must have taken a lot of trips to see where I'd been going, secretly watching me watch you, watching me alter your destiny for the better. He must have been watching the day I came to the cemetery when your father was buried, and he must have been watching when I beat Sheener, but I never saw him. So from all the trips I made into your life, from all the times I just observed you and the times I acted to save you, he picked a place at which to kill us. He wanted to kill me because I was a traitor, and he wanted to kill you and your family because . . . well because he realized you were so important to me.'

Why? she thought. Why am I so important to you, Stefan Krieger? Why have you intruded in my destiny, trying to give me a better life?

She would have asked those questions then, but he had more to say about Kokoschka. His strength seemed to be fading fast, and he was having some difficulty holding on to the thread of his reasoning. She did not want to interrupt and confuse him.

He said, 'From the clocks and graphs on the gate's programming board, Kokoschka could have discovered my final destination: last night, your house. But, you see, I actually had intended to return to the night that Danny died, as I promised you I would, and instead I returned one year later only because I made some mistake when entering my calculations in the machine. After I left through the gate, wounded, Heinrich Kokoschka would have found those calculations. He would have realized my mistake, and would have known where to find me not only last night but on the night that Danny died. In a way, by coming to save you from that runaway truck last year, I brought Danny's killer with me. I feel responsible for that, even though Danny would have died in the accident, anyway. At least you and Chris are alive. For now.'

'Why wouldn't Kokoschka have followed you to 1989, to our house last night? He knew you were already wounded, easy prey.'

'But he also knew that I would expect him to follow me, and he was afraid I was armed and would be prepared for him. So he went to 1988, where I was not expecting him, where he had the advantage of surprise. Also, Kokoschka probably figured if he followed me to 1988 and killed me there, I would not therefore have ever returned to the institute from that mountain highway and would not have had a chance to kill Penlovski. He no doubt thought he could pull a trick with time and *undo* those murders, thereby saving the head of the project. But of course he could not do so, because then he would be altering his *own* past, an impossibility. Penlovski and the others were already dead by then and would stay dead. If Kokoschka had better understood the laws of time travel, he would have known that I would kill him in 1988 when he followed me there, because by the time he made that jaunt to avenge Penlovski, I had already returned to the institute from that night, safe!'

Chris said, 'Are you all right, Mom?'

'Do they make Excedrin in one-pound tablets?' she asked.

'I know it's a lot to absorb,' Stefan said. 'But that's who Heinrich Kokoschka is. Or who he was. He removed the explosives I'd planted. Because of him – and that inconvenient power failure that stopped the timer on the detonator – the institute still stands, the gate is still open, and Gestapo agents are trying to track us here in our own time – and kill us.'

'Why?' Laura asked.

'For revenge,' Chris said.

'They're crossing forty-five years of time to kill us just for revenge?' Laura said. 'Surely there's more than that.'

'There is,' Stefan said. 'They want to kill us because they believe we are the only people in existence who can find a way to close the gate before they win the war and alter their future. And in that assumption, they're correct.'

'How?' she asked, astounded. 'How can we destroy the institute forty-five years ago?'

'I'm not sure yet,' he said. 'But I'll think about it.'

She began to ask more questions, but Stefan shook his head. He pleaded exhaustion and soon drifted off to sleep again.

Chris made a late lunch of peanut butter sandwiches with the fixings he had bought at the supermarket. Laura had no appetite.

She could see that Stefan was going to sleep for a few hours, so she showered. She felt better afterward, even in wrinkled clothes.

Throughout the afternoon the television fare was relentlessly idiotic: Soap operas, game shows, more soap operas, reruns of *Fantasy Island*, *The Bold and the Beautiful*, and Phil Donahue dashing back and forth through the studio audience, exhorting them to raise their consciousness about – and find compassion for – the singular plight of transvestite dentists.

She replenished the Uzi's magazine with the ammunition she had bought at a gunshop that morning.

Outside, as the day waned, clots of dark clouds formed and grew until no blue sky could be seen. The fan palm beside the stolen Buick seemed to pull its fronds closer together in expectation of a storm.

She sat in one of the chairs, propped her feet up on the edge of the bed, closed her eyes, and dozed for a while. She woke from a bad dream in which she had discovered she was made of sand and was swiftly dissolving in a rainstorm. Chris was sleeping in the other chair, and Stefan was still snoring softly on the bed.

Rain was falling, drumming hollowly on the motel roof, pattering in the puddles on the parking lot outside, a sound like bubbling-hot grease, though the day was cool. It was a typical southern California storm, tropically heavy and steady but lacking thunder and lightning. Occasionally such pyrotechnics accompanied rain in this part of the world, but less often than elsewhere. Now Laura had special reason to be thankful for that climatological fact, because if there had been thunder and lightning, she would not have known whether it was natural or signaled the arrival of Gestapo agents from another era.

Chris woke at five-fifteen, and Stefan Krieger came around five minutes later. Both said they were hungry, and in addition to his appetite, Stefan showed other signs of recovery. His eyes had been bloodshot and watery; now they were clear. He was able to raise himself up in bed with his good arm. His left hand, which had been numb and virtually useless, was full of feeling now, and he was able to flex it, wriggle his fingers, and make a weak fist.

Instead of dinner she wanted answers to her questions, but she'd led a life that had taught her patience – among other things. When they had checked into the motel shortly after eleven that morning, Laura had noticed a Chinese restaurant across the street. Now, though reluctant to leave Stefan and Chris, she went out into the rain to get some take-out food.

She carried the .38 under her jacket and left the Uzi on the bed with Stefan. Though the carbine was too big and powerful for Chris to handle, Stefan might be able to brace himself against the headboard and trigger a burst even with just his right hand, though the shock of recoil would shatter through his wound.

When she returned, dripping rain, they put the waxed-cardboard containers of food on the bed – except for the two orders of egg-flower soup, which were for Stefan, and which she put on the night-stand near him. Upon walking into the aromatic restaurant, she had found her own appetite, and naturally she had ordered far too much food: lemon chicken, beef with orange flavor, brown-pepper shrimp, moo goo gai pan, moo shu pork, and two containers of rice.

As she and Chris sampled all of the dishes with plastic forks and washed the food down with Cokes that she had gotten from the motel's soda machine, Stefan drank his soup. He had thought he could not hold down more solid food, but with the soup disposed of, he cautiously began to try the moo goo gai pan and the lemon chicken.

At Laura's request he told them about himself while they ate. He had been born in 1909 in the German town of Gittelde in the Harz Mountains, which made him thirty-five years old. ('Well,' Chris said, 'on the other hand, if you count the forty-five years you skipped when you traveled in time from '44 to '89, you're actually eighty years old!' He laughed, pleased with himself. 'Boy, you sure look *good* for an eighty-year-old geezer!') After moving the family to Munich following the First World War, Stefan's father, Franz Krieger, had been an early supporter of Hitler in 1919, a member of the German Workers' Party from the very week that Hitler began his political career in that organization. He even worked with Hitler and Anton Drexler to write the platform with which that group, essentially a debating society, was eventually transformed into a true political party, later to become the National Socialists.

'I was one of the first members of the Hitler Youth in 1926, when I was seventeen,' he said. 'Less than a year later I joined the *Sturmabteilung* or the SA, the brown shirts, the enforcement arm of the party, virtually a private army. By 1928, however, I was a member of the *Schutzstaffel*—'

'The SS!' Chris said, speaking in the same tone of horror mixed with strange attraction that he would have used if he had been talking of vampires or werewolves. 'You were a member of the SS? You wore the black uniform and the silver death's-head, carried the dagger?'

'I'm not proud of it,' Stefan Krieger said. 'Oh, at the time I was proud, of course. I was a fool. My father's fool. In the early days the SS was a small group, the essence of elitism, and our purpose was to protect *der Führer* with our own lives if that was necessary. We were all eighteen to twenty-two, young and ignorant and hot-headed. In my own defense I'll say that I was not particularly hot-headed, not as committed as those around me. I was doing what my father wanted, but of ignorance I'll admit to having more than my fair share.'

Windblown rain rattled against the window and gurgled noisily in a downspout beyond the outside wall against which the bed stood.

Since awakening from his nap, Stefan had looked healthier, and he had perked up even more with the hot soup. But now, as he recalled a youth spent in a cauldron of hatred and death, he paled again, and his eyes seemed to sink deeper into the darkness under his brow. 'I never left the SS because it was such a desired position and there was no way to leave without arousing suspicion that I'd lost my faith in our revered leader. But year by year, month by month, then day by day I became sickened by what I saw, by the madness and murder and terror.'

Neither the brown-pepper shrimp nor the lemon chicken tasted too good any longer, and Laura's mouth was so dry that the rice stuck to the roof of it. She pushed the food aside, sipped her Coke. 'But if you never left the SS . . . when did you go to college, when did you get involved in scientific research?'

'Oh,' he said, 'I wasn't at the institute as a researcher. I've no university education. Except . . . for two years I received intensive instruction in English, trying to learn to speak with an acceptable American accent. I was part of a project that dropped hundreds of deep-cover agents into Britain and the United States. But I never could quite cast off the accent, so I was never sent overseas; besides, because my father was an early supporter of Hitler, they felt I was trustworthy, so they found other uses for me. I was on special assignment to *der Führer*'s staff, where I was given sensitive jobs, usually as a liaison between squabbling factions of the government. It was an excellent position from which to obtain information useful to the British, which I did from 1938 on.'

'You were a spy?' Chris asked excitedly.

'Of a sort. I had to do what little I could to bring down the Reich, to make up for ever having been a willing part of it. I had to atone – though atoning seemed impossible. And then, in the autumn of 1943, when Penlovski began to have some success with his time gate, sending animals off to God-knew-where and bringing them back, I was assigned to the institute as an observer, as *der Führer*'s personal representative. Also as a guinea pig, as the first human to be sent forward in time. You see, when they were ready to send a man into the future, they did not want to risk Penlovski or Januskaya or Helmut Volkaw or

Mitter or Shenck or one of the other scientists whose loss would damage the project. No one knew if a man would come back as reliably as the animals did – or if he would come back sane and whole.'

Chris nodded solemnly. 'It's possible time travel might've been painful or mentally unbalancing or something, yeah. Who could know?'

Who could know indeed? Laura thought.

Stefan said, 'They also wanted whomever they sent to be reliable and capable of keeping his mission a secret. I was the ideal choice.'

'An SS officer, a spy, and the first chrononaut,' Chris said. 'Wow, what a fascinating life.'

'May God give you a life far less eventful,' Stefan Krieger said. Then he looked at Laura more directly than previously. His eyes were a beautiful, pure blue, yet they revealed a tortured soul. 'Laura . . . what do you think of your guardian now? Not an angel but an aide to Hitler, an SS thug.'

'No thug,' she said. 'Your father, your time, and your society may have tried to make a thug of you, but there was an inner core they couldn't bend. Not a thug, Stefan Krieger. Never. Not you.'

'No angel, though,' he said. 'Far from an angel, Laura. Upon my death, when the stains on my soul are read by He who sits in judgment, I'll be given my own small space in hell.'

The rain drumming on the roof seemed like time flowing away, many millions of precious minutes, hours and days and years pouring through gutters and downspouts, draining away, wasted.

After she had gathered up the unfinished food and thrown it in a dumpster behind the motel office, after she'd gotten three more Cokes from the machines, one for each of them, she at last asked her guardian the question she had wanted to ask him from the moment he had come out of his coma: 'Why? Why did you focus on me, on my life, and why did you want to help me along, to save my butt now and then? For God's sake, how does my fate tie up with Nazis, time travelers, the fate of the world?'

On his third trip into the future, he explained, he had traveled to California in 1984. California because his previous two trips – two weeks in 1954, two weeks in 1964 – had shown him that California was perhaps the coming cultural and current scientific center of the most advanced nation on earth. Nineteen eighty-four because it was a neat forty years from his own time. He was not the only man going through the gate by then; four others began making jaunts as soon as it was proved safe. On that third trip Stefan had still been scouting the future, learning in detail what had happened to the world during and after the war. He was also learning what scientific developments of the intervening forty years would most likely be taken back to Berlin in '44 to win the war for Hitler, not because he intended to help in that design but because he hoped to sabotage it. His researches involved reading newspapers, watching television, and just circulating in American society, getting a feel for the late twentieth century.

Leaning back on his pillows now, recalling that third journey in a voice utterly different from the gloom with which he had described his grim life up to 1944, he said, 'You can't imagine what it was like for me to walk the streets of

Los Angeles for the first time. If I had traveled one thousand years into the future instead of forty, it couldn't have seemed more wondrous. The cars! Cars everywhere – and so many of them German, which seemed to indicate a certain forgiveness for the war, acceptance of the new Germany, and I was moved by that.'

'We have a Mercedes,' Chris said. 'It's neat, but I like the Jeep better.'

'The cars,' Stefan said, 'the styles, the amazing advancements everywhere: digital watches, home computers, videotape recorders for watching movies in your own living room! Even after five days of my visit had passed, I was in a state of pleasant shock, and looked forward each morning to new wonders. On the sixth day, as I passed a bookstore in Westwood, I saw a line of people waiting to have copies of a novel signed by the author. I went inside to browse and to see what kind of book was so popular, to help me a bit in understanding American society. And there you were, Laura, at a table piled with copies of your third novel and your first major success, *Ledges*.'

Laura leaned forward, as if puzzlement were a force drawing her to the edge of her chair. '*Ledges?* But I've never written a book with that title.'

Again, Chris understood. 'That was a book you wrote in the life you would've lived if Mr. Krieger hadn't meddled in it.'

'You were twenty-nine years old when I saw you for the first time at that book-signing party in Westwood,' Stefan said. 'You were in a wheelchair because your legs were twisted, useless. Your left arm was partly paralyzed, as well.'

'Crippled?' Chris said. 'Mom was crippled?'

Laura was literally on the edge of her chair now, for though what her guardian said seemed too fantastic to be believed, she sensed that it was true. On a deep level even more primitive than instinct, she perceived a *rightness* to the image of herself in a wheelchair, her legs useless and wasted; perhaps what she apprehended was the faint echo of destiny thwarted.

'You'd been that way since birth,' Stefan said.

'Why?'

'I only learned that much later, after conducting much research into your life. The doctor who had delivered you in Denver, Colorado, in 1955 – Markwell was his name – had been an alcoholic. Yours was a difficult birth anyway—'

'My mother died delivering me.'

'Yes, in *that* reality she died too. But in that reality Markwell botched the delivery, and you received a spinal injury that crippled you for life.'

A shudder passed through her. As if to prove to herself that she had indeed escaped the life that fate had originally planned for her, she got up and walked to the window, using her legs, her undamaged and blessedly useful legs.

To Chris, Stefan said, 'That day I saw her in the wheelchair, your mother was so beautiful. Oh, so very beautiful. Her face, of course, was the same as it is now. But it wasn't the face alone that made her beautiful. There was such an aura of *courage* about her, and she was in such good humor in spite of her handicaps. Each person who came to her with *Ledges* was sent away not only with a signature but with a laugh. In spite of being condemned to a life in a wheelchair, your mother was so amusing, lighthearted. I watched from a distance and was charmed and profoundly moved, as I'd never been before.'

'She's great,' Chris said. 'Nothing scares my mom.'

'Everything scares your mom,' Laura said. 'This whole crazy conversation is scaring your mom half to death.'

'You never run from anything or hide,' Chris said, turning to look at her. He blushed; a boy his age was supposed to be cool, at a stage where he was beginning to wonder if he was not infinitely wiser than his mother. In an ordinary relationship, such expressions of admiration for one's mother seldom were expressed so directly short of the child's fortieth birthday or the mother's death, whichever came first. 'Maybe you're afraid, but you never *act* afraid.'

She had learned young that those who showed fear were seen as easy targets.

'I bought a copy of *Ledges* that day,' Stefan said, 'and took it back to the hotel where I was staying. I read it overnight, and it was so beautiful that in places I wept . . . and so amusing that in other places I laughed out loud. The next day I got your other two books, *Silverlock* and *Fields of Night*, which were as fine, as moving, as the book that made you famous, *Ledges*.'

It was strange to listen to favorable reviews of books that in this life she had never written. But she was less concerned about learning the storylines of those novels than hearing the answer to a chilling question that had just occurred to her: 'In this life I was meant to live, in this other 1984 . . . was I married?'

'No.'

'But I'd met Danny and—'

'No. You had never met Danny. You had never married.'

'I'd never been born!' Chris said.

Stefan said, 'All of those things happened because I went back to Denver, Colorado, in 1955, and prevented Dr. Markwell from delivering you. The doctor who took Markwell's place couldn't save your mother, but he brought you into the world whole and sound. And everything in your life changed from that point on. It was your past that I was changing, yes, but it was *my* future, therefore flexible. And thank God for that peculiarity of time travel, for otherwise I wouldn't have been able to save you from a life as a paraplegic.'

The wind gusted, and another barrage of rain rattled against the window at which Laura stood.

She was plagued again by the feeling that the room in which she stood, the earth on which it was built, and the universe in which it turned were as insubstantial as smoke, subject to sudden change.

'I monitored your life thereafter,' Stefan said. 'Between mid-January of '44 and mid-March, I made over thirty secret jaunts to see how you were getting along. On the fourth of those trips, when I went to 1964, I discovered you had been dead for one year, you and your father, killed by that junkie who had held up the grocery store. So I journeyed to 1963 and killed him before he could kill you.'

'Junkie?' Chris said, baffled.

'I'll tell you about it later, honey.'

Stefan said, 'And until the night that Kokoschka showed up on that mountain road, I was pretty successful, I think, at making your life easier and better. Yet my interference did not deprive you of your art or result in books that were any less beautiful than the ones that you'd written in that other life. Different books but not lesser ones, books in the same voice, in fact, that you write in now.'

Feeling weak-kneed, Laura returned to her chair. 'But *why*? Why did you go to such great lengths to improve my life?'

Stefan Krieger looked at Chris, then at her, then closed his eyes when he finally spoke. 'After seeing you in that wheelchair, signing copies of *Ledges*, and after reading your books, I fell in love with you . . . deeply in love with you.'

Chris squirmed in his chair, obviously embarrassed to hear such feelings expressed when the object of affection was his own mother.

'Your mind was even more beautiful than your face,' Stefan said softly. His eyes were still closed. 'I fell in love with your great courage, perhaps because real courage was something I'd seen none of in my own world of strutting, uniformed fanatics. They committed atrocities in the name of the people and called that courage. They were willing to die for a twisted totalitarian ideal, and they called *that* courage when it was really stupidity, insanity. And I fell in love with your dignity, for I had none of my own, no self-respect like that I saw shining in you. I fell in love with your compassion, which was so rich a part of your books, for in my world I had seen little compassion. I fell in love, Laura, and realized that I could do for you what all men would do for those they loved if they had the power of gods: I did my best to spare you the worst that fate had planned for you.'

He opened his eyes at last.

They were a beautiful blue. And tortured.

She was immeasurably grateful to him. She did not love him in return, for she hardly knew him. But in stating the depth of his love, a passion that had caused him to transform her destiny and that had driven him to sail across vast tides of time to be with her, he had to some degree restored the magical aura in which she had once viewed him. Again he seemed larger than life, a demigod if not a god, elevated from mere mortal status by the degree of his selfless commitment to her.

That night Chris shared the creaky-springed bed with Stefan Krieger. Laura tried to sleep in one chair with her feet propped on the other.

Rain fell in ceaseless, lulling rhythms that soon put Chris to sleep. Laura could hear him snoring softly.

After she sat for perhaps an hour in darkness, she said quietly, 'Are you asleep?'

'No,' Stefan said at once.

'Danny,' she said. 'My Danny . . .'

'Yes?'

'Why didn't you . . .'

'Make a second trip to that night in 1988 and kill Kokoschka before he could kill Danny?'

'Yes. Why didn't you?'

'Because . . . you see, Kokoschka was from the world of 1944, so his killing of Danny and his own death were a part of *my* past, which I could not undo. If I'd attempted to travel again to that night in '88, to an earlier point in the evening, to stop Kokoschka *before* he killed Danny – I would have bounced immediately back through the gate, back to the institute, without going anywhere; nature's law against paradox would have prevented me from going in the first place.'

Laura was silent.

Stefan said, 'Do you understand?'

'Yes.'

'Do you accept it?'

'I'll never accept his death.'

'But . . . do you believe me?'

'I think I do, yes.'

'Laura, I know how much you loved Danny Packard. If I could have saved him, even at the cost of my own life, I would have done so. I would not have hesitated.'

'I believe you,' she said. 'Because without you . . . I'd never have had Danny at all.'

<hr>

'The Eel,' she said.

'Destiny struggles to reassert the pattern that was meant to be,' Stefan said in the darkness. 'When you were eight years old, I shot that junkie, prevented him from raping and killing you, but inevitably fate brought you to another pedophile who had the potential to be a murderer. Willy Sheener. The Eel. But fate also determined that you would be a writer and a successful one, that you would bring the same message to the world in your books regardless of what I did to change your life. That's a *good* pattern. There's something frightening yet reassuring in the way some power tries to reestablish destiny's broken designs . . . almost as if there's meaning in the universe, something that in spite of its insistence on our suffering, we might even call God.'

For a while they listened to the rain and wind sweep clean the world outside.

She said, 'But why didn't you take care of the Eel for me?'

'I waited for him one night in his apartment—'

'You gave him a bad beating. Yes, I knew that was you.'

'Beat him and warned him to stay away from you. I told him I'd kill him the next time.'

'But the beating only made him more determined to have me. Why didn't you kill him right off?'

'I should have. But . . . I don't know. Perhaps I'd seen so much killing and participated in enough of it that . . . I just hoped for once that killing wouldn't be necessary.'

She thought of his world of war, concentration camps, genocide, and she could understand why he might have hoped to avoid murder even though Sheener had hardly deserved to live.

'But when Sheener came after me at the Dockweilers' house, why weren't you there to stop him?'

'The next time I monitored your life was when you were thirteen, after you'd already killed Sheener yourself and survived, so I decided not to go back and deal with him for you.'

'I survived,' she said. 'But Nina Dockweiler didn't. Maybe if she hadn't come home and seen the blood, the body . . .'

'Maybe,' he said. 'And maybe not. Destiny struggles to restore the ordained pattern as best it can. Maybe she'd have died anyway. Besides, I couldn't protect you from every trauma, Laura. I would have needed ten thousand trips through time to have done that. And perhaps that degree of tampering wouldn't have been good for you. Without any adversity in your life, perhaps you wouldn't have become the woman with whom I fell in love.'

Silence settled between them.

She listened to the wind, the rain.

She listened to her heartbeat.

At last she said, 'I don't love you.'

'I understand.'

'Seems like I should – a little.'

'You don't even really know me yet.'

'Maybe I can never love you.'

'I know.'

'In spite of all you've done for me.'

'I know. But if we live through this . . . well, there's always time.'

'Yes,' she said, 'I suppose there's always time.'

Six

Night's Companion

• 1 •

On Saturday, March 18, 1944, in the main, ground-floor lab of the institute, SS *Obersturmführer* Erich Klietmann and his squad of three highly trained men were prepared to jump into the future and eliminate Krieger, the woman, and the boy. They were dressed to pass as young California executives in 1989: pinstripe suits by Yves St. Laurent, white shirts, dark ties, black Bally loafers, black socks, and Ray-Ban sunglasses if the weather required them; they had been told that in the future this was called the 'power look,' and though Klietmann didn't know what that meant exactly, he liked the sound of it. Their clothes had been purchased in the future by institute researchers on previous jaunts; nothing about them, down to their underwear, was anachronistic.

Each of the four was carrying a Mark Cross attaché case, as well, a smart-looking model made of calfskin with gold-plated fixtures. The cases had also been brought back from the future, as had the modified Uzi carbine and spare magazines that were packed in each attaché.

A team of institute researchers had been on a mission to the U.S. in the year and month when John Hinckley had attempted to assassinate Ronald Reagan. While watching the film of the attack on television, they had been immensely impressed by the compact automatic weapons that the Secret Service agents had been carrying in attaché cases. The agents had been able to withdraw those submachine guns and bring them into firing position in but a second or two. Now the Uzi was not only the automatic carbine of choice in many of the police agencies and armies of 1989, but was the preferred weapon of the time-traveling *Schutzstaffel* commandos.

Klietmann had practiced with the Uzi. He regarded the weapon with as much affection as he had ever lavished upon a human being. The only thing about it that bothered him was the fact that it was an Israeli-designed and -manufactured gun, the product of a bunch of Jews. On the other hand, within a few days the new directors of the institute were likely to approve the integration of the Uzi into the world of 1944, and German soldiers equipped with it would be better able to drive back the subhuman hordes who would depose *der Führer*.

He looked at the clock on the gate's programming board and saw that seven minutes had passed since the research team had left for California on February 15, 1989. They were there to search public records – mostly back issues of newspapers – to discover if Krieger, the woman, and the boy had been found by police and detained for questioning in the month following the shoot-outs at Big Bear and San Bernardino. Then they would return to '44 and tell Klietmann the day, time, and place where Krieger and the woman could be found. Because every time traveler returned from a jaunt exactly eleven minutes after departing, regardless of how long he spent in the future, Klietmann and his squad had only four more minutes to wait.

Thursday, January 12, 1989, was Laura's thirty-fourth birthday, and they spent it in the same room at The Bluebird of Happiness Motel. Stefan needed another day of rest to regain his strength and let the penicillin do its work. He also needed the time to think; he had to devise a plan for destroying the institute, and that problem was sufficiently knotty to require hours of intense concentration.

The rain had stopped, but the sky still looked bruised, swollen. The forecast was for another storm to follow the first by midnight.

They watched the local five o'clock television news and saw a story about her and Chris and the wounded mystery man they had taken to Dr. Brenkshaw. Police were still looking for her, and the best guess anyone could make about the situation was that the drug dealers who had killed her husband were after her and her son, either because they were afraid she would eventually identify them in a police lineup or because she was somehow involved in drug traffic herself.

'My mom a drug dealer?' Chris said, offended by that insinuation. 'What a bunch of bozos!'

Although no bodies had been found at Big Bear or San Bernardino, there had been a sensational development that guaranteed the media's continued interest. Reporters had learned that considerable blood had been found at both scenes – and that a man's severed head had been discovered in the alleyway behind the Brenkshaw house, between two garbage cans.

Laura remembered stepping through the redwood gate behind Carter Brenkshaw's property, seeing the second surprised gunman, and opening fire on him with the Uzi. The burst had taken him in the throat and head, and at the time she had thought that the concentrated automatic fire might well have decapitated him.

'The surviving SS men pushed the call-home button on the dead man's belt,' Stefan said, 'and sent his body back.'

'But why not his head?' Laura said, sickened by the subject but too curious not to ask the question.

'It must've rolled away from the body, between the garbage cans,' Stefan said, 'and they couldn't find it in the few seconds they had to look. If they'd located it, they could have laid it on the corpse and folded his arms around it. Anything a time traveler wears or carries is taken with him on a jaunt. But with the sirens approaching and the darkness in the alley . . . they didn't have time to find the head.'

Chris, who might have been expected to revel in these bizarre complications, slumped in his chair, legs curled up under him, and was silent. Perhaps the hideous image of a severed head had made Death's presence more real for him than had all the gunfire directed at him.

Laura made a special point of hugging him and subtly reassuring him that they were going to come out of this together and unscathed. The hugs, however, were as much for her as for him, and the pep talks she gave him must have seemed at least somewhat false, for she had not yet convinced herself that in fact they would triumph.

For lunch and dinner she got take-out from the Chinese restaurant just across the street. The previous night none of the restaurant's employees had recognized her as either the famous author or the fugitive, so she felt reasonably safe there. It seemed foolish to go elsewhere and risk being spotted.

At the end of dinner, while Laura was cleaning up the cardboard containers, Chris produced two chocolate cupcakes with a yellow candle on each. He had bought the packet of Hostess pastries and a box of birthday candles at the Ralph's supermarket yesterday morning and had hidden them until now. With great ceremony he carried the cupcakes from the bathroom, where he had secretly inserted and lit the candles, and golden reflections of the two flames shimmered brightly in his eyes. He grinned when he saw that he had surprised and delighted her. In fact she had to strive to hold back tears. She was moved that even in the thrall of fear, in the midst of danger, he'd still had the presence of mind to think of her birthday, and the desire to please her; it seemed, to her, to be the essence of what mothers and children were all about.

The three of them ate wedges of the cupcakes. In addition five fortune cookies had come with the take-out food.

From his pillowed perch upon the bed, Stefan opened his cookie. 'If only this were true: "You'll live in times of peace and plenty." '

'It might turn out to be true,' Laura said. She cracked her cookie and withdrew the slip of paper. 'Oh, well, I think I've had enough of this, thank you: "Adventure will be your companion." '

When Chris opened his cookie, there was no slip of paper inside, no fortune.

A flicker of fear passed through Laura, as if the empty cookie actually meant that he had no future. Superstitious nonsense. But she could not suppress her sudden anxiety.

'Here,' she said, quickly handing him both of the remaining cookies. 'Getting none in that one just means you get *two* fortunes.'

Chris opened the first, read it to himself, laughed, then read it to them: ' "You will achieve fame and fortune." '

'When you're stinking rich, will you support me in my old age?' Laura asked.

'Sure, Mom. Well . . . as long as you'll still cook for me, and especially your vegetable soup.'

'Going to make your old mom *earn* her way, huh?'

Smiling at the interplay between Laura and Chris, Stefan Krieger said, 'He's a tough customer, isn't he?'

'He'll probably have me scrubbing his floors when I'm eighty,' Laura said.

Chris opened the second cookie. ' "You'll have a good life of little pleasures – books, music, art." '

Neither Chris nor Stefan seemed to notice that the two fortunes made opposed predictions, effectively canceling each other, which in a way confirmed the ominous meaning of the empty cookie.

Hey, you're losing your mind, Shane, you really are, she thought. They're just fortune cookies. They don't *really* predict anything.

Hours later, after the lights were out and Chris was asleep, Stefan spoke to Laura from the darkness. 'I've devised a plan.'

'A way to destroy the institute?'

'Yes. But it's very complicated, and there are many things we'll need. I don't know for sure ... but I suspect some of these items can't be purchased by private citizens.'

'I can get anything you need,' she said confidently. 'I have the contacts. Anything.'

'We'll have to have quite a lot of money.'

'That's thorny. I've only got forty bucks left, and I can't go to the bank and withdraw funds because that would leave a record—'

'Yes. That would draw them straight to us. Is there someone you can trust and who trusts you, someone who would give you a lot of their own money and tell no one they'd seen you?'

'You know all about me,' Laura said, 'so you know about Thelma Ackerson. But, God, I don't want to drag her into this. If anything happened to Thelma—'

'It can be arranged without risk to her,' he insisted.

Outside, the promised rain arrived in a sudden downpour.

Laura said, 'No.'

'But she's our only hope.'

'No.'

'Where else can you raise the money?'

'We'll find another way that doesn't require a lot of financing.'

'Whether we come up with another plan or not, we'll need money. Your forty dollars won't last another day. And I have nothing.'

'I won't risk Thelma,' she said adamantly.

'As I said, we can do it without risk, without—'

'No.'

'Then we're defeated,' he said dismally.

She listened to the rain, which in her mind became the heavy roar of World War II bombers – and then the sound of a chanting, maddened crowd.

At last she said, 'But even if we could arrange it without any risk to Thelma, what if the SS has a tail on her? They must know she's my best friend – my only real friend. So why wouldn't they have sent one of their teams forward in time to just keep a watch on Thelma with the hope she'd lead them to me?'

'Because that's an unnecessarily tedious way to find us,' he said. 'They can just send research teams into the future, to February of this year and then March and April, month after month, to check the newspapers until they find out where we first showed up. Each of those jaunts only takes eleven minutes in *their* time, remember, so it's quick; and that method is almost certain to work sooner or later because it's doubtful we could stay in hiding the rest of our lives.'

'Well . . .'

He waited a long time. Then he said, 'You're like sisters, you two. And if you can't turn for help to a sister at a time like this, who can you turn to, Laura?'

'If we can get Thelma's help without putting her at risk . . . I guess we have to try.'

'First thing in the morning,' he said.

That was a night of rain, and rain also filled her dreams, and in those dreams were explosive thunderclaps and lightning, as well. She woke in terror, but the rainy night in Santa Ana was unmarred by those bright, noisy omens of death. It was a comparatively peaceful storm, without thunder, lightning, and wind, though she knew that it would not always be so.

· 3 ·

The machinery clicked and hummed.

Erich Klietmann looked at the clock. In just three minutes the research team would return to the institute.

Two scientists, heirs of Penlovski and Januskaya and Volkaw, stood at the programming board, studying the myriad dials and gauges.

All the light in the room was unnatural, for the windows were not merely blacked out to avoid providing beacons for night-flying enemy bombers, but were bricked in for security reasons. The air was stuffy.

Standing in one corner of the main lab, near the gate, Lieutenant Klietmann anticipated his trip to 1989 with excitement, not because that future was filled with wonders but because the mission gave him an opportunity to serve *der Führer* in a way that few men ever could. If he succeeded in killing Krieger, the woman, and the boy, he would have earned a personal meeting with Hitler, a chance to see the great man face to face, to know the touch of his hand and through that touch to feel the power, the tremendous power of the German state and people and history and destiny. The lieutenant would have risked death ten times, a thousand times, for the chance to be brought to the personal attention of *der Führer*, to make Hitler aware of him, not aware of him as just another SS officer, but aware of him as an individual, as Erich Klietmann, the man who saved the Reich from the dire fate that it had almost been forced to endure.

Klietmann was not the Aryan ideal, and he was acutely aware of his physical shortcomings. His maternal grandfather had been Polish, a disgusting slavic mongrel, which made Klietmann only three-quarters German. Furthermore, though his other three grandparents and both of his parents had been blond, blue-eyed, with Nordic features, Erich had hazel eyes, dark hair, and the heavier, more sensuous features of his barbarian grandfather. He loathed the way he looked, and he tried to compensate for his physical shortcomings by being the most vigilant Nazi, most courageous soldier, and most ardent supporter of Hitler in the entire *Schutzstaffel*, which was tough because he had so much competition for that honor. Sometimes he had despaired of ever being singled out for glory. But he never gave up, and now here he was, on the brink of heroism that would earn him Valhalla.

He wanted to kill Stefan Krieger personally, not only because that would win *der Führer*'s favor but because Krieger *was* the Aryan ideal, blond and blue-eyed, every feature truly Nordic, and from fine breeding stock. With every advantage, the hateful Krieger had chosen to betray his *Führer*, and that enraged Klietmann, who had to labor toward greatness under the burden of mongrel genes.

Now, with little more than two minutes left before the research team would return through the gate from 1989, Klietmann looked at his three subordinates, all dressed as young executives of another age, and he felt both a fierce and a sentimental pride in them so strong it almost brought tears to his eyes.

They had all come from humble beginnings. *Unterscharführer* Felix Hubatsch, Klietmann's sergeant and second in command of the unit, was the son of an alcoholic lathe operator and a slattern mother, both of whom he despised. *Rottenführer* Rudolph von Manstein was the son of a poor farmer whose lifetime of failure shamed him, and *Rottenführer* Martin Bracher was an orphan. In spite of coming from four different corners of Germany, the two corporals, the sergeant, and Lieutenant Klietmann shared one thing that made them as close as brothers: They understood that a man's truest, deepest, and dearest relationship was not to his family but to the state, to the fatherland, and to their leader in whom the fatherland was embodied; the state was the only family that mattered; this single bit of wisdom elevated them and made them worthy fathers of the super-race to come.

Klietmann discreetly dabbed at the corners of his eyes with his thumb, blotting the nascent tears that he was not able to suppress.

In one minute the research team would return.

The machinery clicked and hummed.

• 4 •

At three o'clock, Friday afternoon, January 13, a white pickup entered the rainswept motel lot, came straight to the rear wing, and parked next to the Buick that bore a Nissan's license plates. The truck was about five or six years old. The passenger-side door was dented, and that rocker panel was spotted with rust. The owner was evidently refinishing the pickup in a patchwork fashion, because some spots had been sanded and primed but not yet repainted.

Laura watched the truck from behind the barely parted drapes at the motel-room window. She held the Uzi in one hand at her side.

The truck's headlights blinked off, and its windshield wipers stopped, and a moment later a woman with frizzy blond hair got out and walked to the door of Laura's unit. She rapped three times.

Chris was standing behind the door, looking at his mother.

Laura nodded.

Chris opened the door and said, 'Hi, Aunt Thelma. Jeez, that's an ugly wig.'

Stepping inside, hugging Chris fiercely, Thelma said, 'Well, thanks a lot. And what would you say if I told you that was a monumentally ugly nose you were born with, but you're stuck with it, while I'm not stuck with the wig? Huh? what would you say then?'

Chris giggled. 'Nothing. 'Cause I know I've got a cute nose.'

'Cute nose? God, kid, you've got an actor's ego.' She let go of him, glanced at Stefan Krieger, who was sitting in one of the chairs near the TV set, then turned to Laura. 'Shane, did you see the heap I pulled up in? Am I clever? As I was getting in my Mercedes, I said to myself, Thelma – I call myself Thelma – I said, Thelma, isn't it going to draw a hell of a lot of attention at that sleazy motel when you pull up in a sixty-five-thousand-dollar car? So I tried to borrow the butler's car, but you know what *he* drives? A Jaguar. Is Beverly Hills the Twilight Zone, or what? So I had to borrow the gardener's truck. But here I am, and what do you think of this disguise?'

She was wearing a kinky blond wig glittering with droplets of rain, horn-rimmed glasses, and a pair of false dentures that gave her an overbite.

'You look better this way,' Laura said, grinning.

Thelma popped out the fake teeth. 'Listen, once I turned up a set of wheels that wouldn't draw attention, I realized that *I'd* draw some attention myself,

being a major star and everything. And since the media's already dug up the fact
that you and I are friends and have tried to ask me some pointed questions about
you, the famous machine-gun-packing authoress, I decided to come incognito.'
She dropped her purse and the stage teeth on the bed. 'This getup was for a new
character I created in my nightclub act, tried it about eight times at Bally's in
Vegas. It was a primo flop, that character. The audience *spat* at me, Shane, they
brought in the casino's security guard and tried to have me arrested, they
questioned my right to share the same planet with them – oh, they were rude,
Shane, they were—'

Suddenly she halted in the middle of her patter and burst into tears. She
rushed to Laura, threw her arms around her. 'Oh, Jesus, Laura, I was scared, I
was so scared. When I heard the news about San Bernardino, machine guns,
and then the way they found your house at Big Bear, I thought you . . . or
maybe Chris . . . I was so worried . . .'

Holding Thelma as tightly as Thelma was holding her, Laura said, 'I'll tell
you all about it, but the main thing is we're all right, and we think maybe we
have a way to get out of the hole we're in.'

'Why didn't you call me, you silly bitch?'

'I did call you.'

'Only this morning! Two *days* after you're splashed all over the newspapers.
I nearly went crazy.'

'I'm sorry. I should've called sooner. I just didn't want to get you involved if I
could avoid it.'

Reluctantly Thelma let go of her. 'I'm inevitably, deeply, and hopelessly
involved, you idiot, because *you're* involved.' She pulled a Kleenex from a
pocket of her suede jacket and blotted her eyes.

'You have another one of those?' Laura asked.

Thelma gave her a Kleenex, and they both blew their noses.

'We were on the lam, Aunt Thelma,' Chris said. 'It's hard to stay in touch
with people when you're on the lam.'

Taking a deep, shuddery breath, Thelma said, 'So, Shane, where are you
keeping your collection of severed heads? In the bathroom? I heard you left one
behind in San Bernardino. Sloppy. Is this a new hobby of yours, or have you
always had an appreciation for the beauty of the human head unencumbered by
all the messy extremities?'

'I want you to meet someone,' Laura said. 'Thelma Ackerson, this is Stefan
Krieger.'

'Pleased to meet you,' Thelma said.

'You'll excuse me if I don't get up,' Stefan said. 'I'm still recuperating.'

'If you can excuse this wig, I can excuse anything.' To Laura, Thelma said,
'Is he who I think he is?'

'Yes.'

'Your guardian?'

'Yes.'

Thelma went to Stefan and kissed him wetly on both cheeks. 'I've no idea
where you come from or who the hell you are, Stefan Krieger, but I love you for
all the times you've helped my Laura.' She stepped back and sat on the foot of
the bed beside Chris. 'Shane, this man you have here is gorgeous. Look at him,
he's a hunk. I'll bet *you* shot him just so he couldn't get away. He looks just like

a guardian angel ought to look.' Stefan was embarrassed, but Thelma would not be stopped. 'You're a real dish, Krieger. I want to hear all about you. But first, here's the money you asked for, Shane.' She opened her voluminous purse and withdrew a thick wad of hundred-dollar bills.

Examining the money, Laura said, 'Thelma, I asked you for four thousand. There's at least twice that here.'

'Ten or twelve thousand, I think.' Thelma winked at Chris and said, 'When my friends are on the lam, I *insist* they go first class.'

———

Thelma listened to the story, never expressing disbelief. Stefan was surprised by her open-mindedness, but she said, 'Hey, once you've lived at McIlroy Home and Caswell Hall, the universe holds no more surprises. Time travelers from 1944? Pah! At McIlroy I could've shown you a woman as big as a sofa, who wore clothes made of bad upholstery fabric, and who was paid a handsome civil-service wage to treat orphaned children like vermin. Now *there* is an amazement.' She was clearly affected by Stefan's origins, chilled and amazed by the trap they were in, but even under these circumstances she was Thelma Ackerson, always looking for the laugh in everything.

At six o'clock she put in the stage teeth again and went up the street to get take-out from a Mexican restaurant. 'When you're on the run from the law, you need beans in your belly, tough-guy food.' She came back with rain-dampened bags of tacos, containers of enchiladas, two orders of nachos, burritos, and chimichangas. They spread the food out on the bottom half of the bed, and Thelma and Chris sat on the top half. Laura and Stefan sat in chairs at the foot of the bed.

'Thelma,' Laura said, 'there's enough food here for ten.'

'Well, I figured that would feed us and the cockroaches. If we didn't have food for the cockroaches, they might get mean, might go outside and overturn my gardener's pickup. You *do* have cockroaches here, don't you? I mean, after all, a swell place like this without cockroaches would be like the Beverly Hills Hotel without tree rats.'

As they ate, Stefan outlined the plan he had devised for closing the gate and destroying the institute. Thelma interrupted with wisecracks, but when he was finished, she was solemn. 'This is damned dangerous, Stefan. Brave enough to be foolish, maybe.'

'There's no other way.'

'I can see that,' she said. 'So what can I do to help?'

Pausing with a wad of corn chips halfway to his mouth, Chris said, 'We need you to buy the computer, Aunt Thelma.'

Laura said, 'An IBM PC, their best model, the same one I have at home, so I'll know how to use all the software. We don't have time to learn the operating procedures of a new machine. I've written it all down for you. I could go buy it myself, I guess, with the money you gave me, but I'm afraid of showing my face too many places.'

'And we'll need a place to stay,' Stefan said.

'We can't stay here,' Chris said, enjoying being a part of the discussion, 'not if we're going to be doing stuff with a computer. The maid would see it no matter how hard we tried to hide it, and she'd talk about it because that would be weird, people holing up in a place like this with a computer.'

Stefan said, 'Laura tells me that you and your husband have a second house in Palm Springs.'

'We have a house in Palm Springs, a condo in Monterey, another condo in Vegas, and it wouldn't surprise me if we owned – or at least had time shares in – our very own Hawaiian volcano. My husband is too rich. So take your pick. My houses are your houses. Just don't use the towels to polish the hubcaps on your car, and if you must chew tobacco and spit on the floors, try to keep it in the corners.'

'I thought the house in Palm Springs would be ideal,' Laura said. 'You've told me it's fairly secluded.'

'It's on a large property with lots of trees, and there're other show-biz people on that block, all of 'em busy, so they don't tend to drop over for a cup of coffee. No one'll disturb you there.'

'All right,' Laura said, 'there's just a few other things. We need changes of clothes, comfortable shoes, some basic necessities. I've made a list, sizes and everything. And, of course, when this is all over, I'll pay you back the cash you gave me and whatever you spend on the computer and these other things.'

'Damn right you will, Shane. And forty percent interest. Per week. Compounded hourly. Plus your child. Your child will be mine.'

Chris laughed. 'My Aunt Rumpelstiltskin.'

'You won't make smart remarks when you're *my* child, Christopher Robin. Or at least you'll call me Mother Rumpelstiltskin, Sir.'

'Mother Rumpelstiltskin, Sir!' Chris said, and saluted her.

At eight-thirty Thelma prepared to leave with the shopping list that Laura had composed and the information about the computer. 'I'll be back tomorrow afternoon, as soon as I can,' she said, giving Laura and then Chris one last hug. 'You'll really be safe here, Shane?'

'I think we will. If they'd discovered we were staying here, they would've shown up sooner.'

Stefan said, 'Remember, Thelma, they're time travelers; once they discover where we've been hiding, they could just jaunt forward to the moment when we first arrived here. In fact they could've been waiting for us when we pulled into the motel on Wednesday. The fact that we've stayed here so long unmolested is almost proof there'll never be public knowledge that this was our hideout.'

'My head spins,' Thelma said. 'And I thought reading a major studio's contract was complicated!'

She went out into the night and rain, still wearing the wig and the horn-rimmed glasses but carrying her stage teeth in her pocket, and she drove away in her gardener's truck.

Laura, Chris, and Stefan watched her from the big window, and Stefan said, 'She's a special person.'

'Very,' Laura said. 'I hope to God I haven't endangered her.'

'Don't worry, Mom,' Chris said. 'Aunt Thelma's a tough broad. She always says so.'

That night at nine o'clock, shortly after Thelma left, Laura drove to Fat Jack's place in Anaheim. The rain was not as heavy as it had been but fell in a steady drizzle. The macadamized pavement glistered silver-black, and gutters still overflowed with water that looked like oil in the queer light of the sodium-vapor streetlamps. Fog had crept in, too, not on little cat feet but slithering like a snake on its belly.

She had been loath to leave Stefan at the motel. But it was not wise for him to spend much time in the chilly, rainy January night in his debilitated condition. Besides, he could do nothing to help her.

Though Stefan remained behind, Chris accompanied Laura, for she would not be separated from him for the time it would take to cut a deal for the weapons. The boy had gone with her when she had first visited Fat Jack a year ago, when she'd bought the illegally modified Uzis, so the fat man would not be surprised to see him. Displeased, yes, since Fat Jack was no lover of children, but not surprised.

As she drove, Laura looked frequently in the rearview mirror, in the side mirrors, and took the measure of the other drivers around her with a diligence that gave new meaning to the term defensive driving. She could not afford to be broadsided by a dunderhead who was driving too fast for the road conditions. Police would put in an appearance at the scene of the crash, would routinely check out her license plates, and before they even arrested her, men carrying submachine guns would materialize and kill her and Chris.

She had left her own Uzi with Stefan, although he had protested. However, she was unable to abandon him with no means of self-defense. She still carried the .38 Chief's Special. And fifty spare rounds were distributed in the zippered pockets of her ski jacket.

Near Disneyland, when the neon-drenched phantasmagoria of Fat Jack's Pizza Party Palace appeared in the fog like the starship in *Close Encounters of the Third Kind* descending from clouds of its own making, Laura was relieved. She pulled into the crowded parking lot and switched off the engine. The windshield wipers stopped thumping, and rain washed down the glass in rippling sheets. Orange, red, blue, yellow, green, white, purple, and pink reflections of neon glimmered in that flowing film of water, so Laura felt curiously as if she were inside one of those old-fashioned, gaudy jukeboxes from the 1950s.

Chris said, 'Fat Jack's put up more neon since we were here.'

'I think you're right,' Laura said.

They got out of the car and looked up at the blinking, flashing, rippling, winking, grotesquely flamboyant façade of Fat Jack's Pizza Party Palace. Neon was not reserved solely for the name of the place. It was also used to outline the building, the roofline, every window, and the front doors. In addition there were a pair of giant neon sunglasses on one end of the roof, and a huge neon rocket-ship poised for takeoff on the other end, with neon vapors perpetually curling and sparkling beneath its exhaust jets. The ten-foot-diameter neon pizza was an old feature, but the grinning neon clown's face was new.

The quantity of neon was so great that every falling raindrop was brightly tinted, as if it was part of a rainbow that had broken apart at nightfall. Every puddle shimmered with rainbow fragments.

The effect was disorienting, but it prepared the visitor for the inside of Fat Jack's, which seemed to be a glimpse of the chaos out of which the universe had

formed trillions of years ago. The waiters and waitresses were dressed as
clowns, ghosts, pirates, spacemen, witches, gypsies, and vampires, and a
singing trio in bear costumes moved from table to table, delighting young
children with pizza-smeared faces. In alcoves off the main room, older kids were
at banks of videogames, so the *beep-zing-zap-bong* of that electronic play served
as background music to singing bears and shouting children.

'Asylum,' Chris said.

They were met inside the front door by the host, Dominick, who was Fat
Jack's minority partner. Dominick was tall, cadaverous, with mournful eyes,
and he seemed out of place midst the forced hilarity.

Raising her voice to be heard over the din, Laura asked for Fat Jack and said,
'I called earlier, I'm an old friend of his mother's,' which was what you were to
say to indicate you wanted guns not pizza.

Dominick had learned to project his voice clearly through the cacophony
without shouting. 'You've been here before, I believe.'

'Good memory,' she said. 'A year ago.'

'Please follow me,' Dominick said in a funereal voice.

They did not have to go through the cyclonic commotion of the dining room,
which was good because that meant Laura was less likely to be seen and recognized by one of the customers. A door off the other side of the host's foyer opened
onto a corridor that led past the kitchen and the storeroom to Fat Jack's private
office. Dominick knocked on the door, ushered them inside, and said to Fat Jack,
'Old friends of your mother,' then left Laura and Chris with the big man.

Fat Jack took his nickname seriously and tried to live up to it. He was five feet
ten and weighed about three hundred and fifty pounds. Wearing immense gray
sweatpants and sweatshirt that fit him almost as tightly as Spandex, he looked
like the fat man in that magnetized photograph that dieters could buy to put on
refrigerators to scare them off food; in fact he looked like the refrigerator.

He sat in a baronial swivel chair behind a desk sized for him, and he did not
get up. 'Listen to the little beasts.' He spoke to Laura, ignored Chris. 'I put my
office at the back of the building, had it specially soundproofed, and I can still
hear them out there, shrieking, squealing; it's as if I'm just down the hall from
hell.'

'They're only children having fun,' Laura said, standing with Chris in front
of the desk.

'And Mrs. O'Leary was just an old lady with a clumsy cow, but she burned
down Chicago,' Fat Jack said sourly. He was eating a Mars bar. In the distance
children's voices, insulated by soundproofing, rose in a dull roar, and as if talking
to that unseen multitude, the fat man said, 'Ah, choke on it, you little trolls.'

'It's a nuthouse out there,' Chris said.

'Who asked you?'

'Nobody, sir.'

Jack had a grainy complexion with gray eyes nearly buried in a puff-adder
face. He focused on Laura and said, 'You see my new neon?'

'The clown is new, isn't it?'

'Yeah. Isn't it a beauty? I designed it, had it made, and then had it erected in
the dead of night, so the next morning it was too late for anybody to get a
restraining order to stop me. The damn city council just about croaked, all of
them at once.'

Fat Jack had been embroiled in a decade-long legal battle with the Anaheim Zoning Commission and the city council. The authorities disapproved of his garish neon displays, especially now that the area around Disneyland was slated for urban renewal. Fat Jack had spent tens if not hundreds of thousands of dollars fighting them in the courts, paying fines, being sued, countersuing, and he had even spent time in jail for contempt of court. He was a former libertarian who now claimed to be an anarchist, and he would not tolerate infringement of his rights – real and imagined – as a free-thinking individual.

He dealt in illegal weapons for the same reason he erected neon signs that violated city codes: as a statement against authority, to champion individual rights. He could talk for hours about the evils of government, any kind of government, in any degree whatsoever, and on Laura's last visit with Chris, in order to get the modified Uzis she wanted, she had listened to a lengthy explanation of why the government did not even have the right to pass laws forbidding murder.

Laura had no great love of big government, whether of the left or right, but she had little sympathy with Fat Jack, either. He did not acknowledge the legitimacy of any authority whatsoever, not that of proven institutions, not even that of family.

Now, after she gave Fat Jack her new shopping list, after he quoted a price and counted her money, he led her and Chris through the hidden door in the back of his office closet, down a narrow stairwell – he seemed in danger of becoming wedged tight – to the basement where he kept his illegal stock. Though his restaurant was a madhouse, his arsenal was stored with fetishistic neatness: Cartons upon cartons of handguns and automatic weapons were stacked on metal shelves, arranged according to caliber and also according to price; he kept at least a thousand guns in the basement of the Pizza Party Palace.

He was able to provide her with two modified Uzis – 'An immensely popular gun since the attempt to kill Reagan,' he said – and another .38 Chief's Special. Stefan had hoped to obtain a Colt Commander 9mm Parabellum with a nine-round magazine and the barrel machined for a silencer. 'Don't have it,' Fat Jack said, 'but I can let you have a Colt Commander Mark IV in .38 Super, which has a nine-round magazine, and I've got two of those machined for silencers. Got the silencers, too, plenty of 'em.' She already knew that he wasn't able to provide her with ammunition, but as he finished his Mars bar, he explained anyway: 'Don't stock ammunition or explosives. Look, I don't believe in authority, but I'm not totally irresponsible. I got a restaurant full of shrieking, snot-faced kids upstairs, and I can't risk blowing them to bits, even if that'd bring more peace to the world. Besides, I'd destroy all my pretty neon too.'

'All right,' Laura said, putting one arm around Chris to keep him at her side, 'what about the gas on my list?'

'You sure you don't mean tear gas?'

'No. Vexxon. That's the stuff I want.' Stefan had given her the name of the gas. He said it was one of the chemical weapons that was on the list of items the institute hoped to bring back to 1944 and introduce into the German military arsenal. Now perhaps it could be used *against* the Nazis. 'We need something that will kill fast.'

Fat Jack leaned his backside against the metal worktable in the middle of the room, where he had laid out the Uzis, revolvers, pistol, and silencers. The table creaked ominously. 'Well, what we're talking about here is army ordnance, tightly controlled stuff.'

'You can't get it?'

'Oh, sure, I can get you some Vexxon,' Fat Jack said. He moved away from the table, which creaked in relief as his weight was lifted from it, and went to a set of metal shelves where he withdrew a couple of Hershey bars from between boxes of guns, a secret stash. He did not offer one to Chris, but put the second bar in the side pocket of his sweatpants and began to eat the other. 'I don't have that sort of crap here; just as dangerous as explosives. But I can have it for you late tomorrow, if that's not inconvenient.'

'That'll be fine.'

'It'll cost you.'

'I know.'

Fat Jack grinned. Bits of chocolate were stuck between his teeth. 'Don't get much call for this kind of thing, not from someone like yourself, a small buyer. Tickles me to try to figure what you'd be up to with it. Not that I expect you to tell me. But usually it's big buyers from South America or the Middle East who want these neuroactive and respirative gases. Iraq and Iran used plenty the last few years.'

'Neuroactive, respirative? What's the difference?'

'Respirative – they have to breathe it in; it kills them seconds after it hits the lungs and spreads through the bloodstream. When you release it, you've got to be wearing a gas mask. Your neuroactive, on the other hand, kills even quicker, just on touching the skin, and with certain types of it – like Vexxon – you won't need a gas mask or protective clothing, 'cause you can take a couple of pills before you use it, and they're like an advance antidote.'

'Yes, I was supposed to ask for the pills, too,' Laura said.

'Vexxon. Easiest-to-use gas on the market. You're a real smart shopper,' Fat Jack said.

Already he had finished the candy bar, and he appeared to have grown noticeably since Laura and Chris had entered his office half an hour ago. She realized that Fat Jack's commitment to political anarchy was reflected not only in the atmosphere of his pizza parlor but in the condition of his body, for his flesh swelled unrestrained by social or medical considerations. He seemed to revel in his size, as well, frequently patting his gut or grabbing the rolls of fat on his sides and kneading them almost affectionately, and he walked with belligerent arrogance, pushing the world away from him with his belly. She had a vision of Fat Jack growing ever more huge, soaring past four hundred pounds, past five hundred, even as the wildly pyramiding neon structures on the roof grew ever more elaborate, until one day the roof collapsed and Fat Jack exploded simultaneously.

'I'll have the gas by five o'clock tomorrow,' he said as he put the Uzis, .38 Chief's Special, Colt Commander, and silencers in a box labeled BIRTHDAY PARTY FAVORS, which had probably contained paper hats or noisemakers for the restaurant. He slipped the lid on the box and indicated that Laura was to carry it upstairs; among other things, Fat Jack did not believe in chivalry.

Back in Fat Jack's office, when Chris opened the door to the hall for his mother, Laura was pleased by the squealing of the children in the pizza parlor.

That sound was the first normal, sane thing she had heard in more than half an hour.

'Listen to the little cretins,' Fat Jack said. 'They're not children; they're shaved baboons trying to pass for children.' He slammed his soundproofed office door behind Chris and Laura.

In the car on the way back to the motel, Chris said, 'When this is all over . . . what're you going to do about Fat Jack?'

'Turn his butt in to the cops,' Laura said. 'Anonymously.'

'Good. He's a nut.'

'He's worse than a nut, honey. He's a fanatic.'

'What's a fanatic exactly?'

She thought for a moment, then said, 'A fanatic is a nut who has something to believe in.'

• 5 •

Lieutenant Erich Klietmann, SS, watched the second hand on the programming board clock, and when it neared the twelve, he turned and looked at the gate. Inside that twelve-foot-long, gloom-filled tube, something shimmered, a fuzzy gray-black patch that resolved into the silhouette of a man – then three more men, one behind the other. The research team came out of the gate, into the room, and were met by the three scientists who had been monitoring the programming board.

They had returned from February, 1989, and were smiling, which made Klietmann's heart pound because they would not be smiling if they had not located Stefan Krieger, the woman, and the boy. The first two assassination squads that had been sent into the future – the one that had attacked the house near Big Bear and the one in San Bernardino – had been composed of Gestapo officers. Their failures had led *der Führer* to insist the third team be *Schutzstaffel*, and now Erich judged the researchers' smiles to mean that his squad was going to have a chance to prove the SS was filled with better men than the Gestapo.

The failures of the two previous squads were not the only black marks on the Gestapo's record in this affair. Heinrich Kokoschka, the head of the institute's security, had been a Gestapo officer, as well, and he had apparently turned traitor. Available evidence seemed to support the theory that two days ago, on March 16, he had defected to the future with five other members of the institute's staff.

On the evening of March 16, Kokoschka had jaunted alone to the San Bernardino Mountains with the claimed intention of killing Stefan Krieger there in the future before Krieger returned to 1944 and killed Penlovski, thereby undoing the deaths of the project's best men. But Kokoschka never came back. Some argued that Kokoschka had been killed up there in 1988, that Krieger had won the confrontation – but that did not explain what had happened to the five other men in the institute that evening: the two Gestapo agents waiting for Kokoschka's return and the three scientists monitoring the gate's programming board. All vanished, and five homing belts were missing; so the evidence pointed to a group of traitors within the institute who had become convinced that Hitler would lose the war even with the advantage of exotic weapons brought back from the future, and who had defected to another age rather than stay in a doomed Berlin.

But Berlin was not doomed. Klietmann would not entertain that possibility. Berlin was the new Rome; the Third Reich would last a thousand years. Now that the SS was being given the chance to find and kill Krieger, *der Führer*'s dream would be protected and fulfilled. Once they had eliminated Krieger, who was the main threat to the gate and whose execution was the most urgent task before them, they would then focus on finding Kokoschka and the other traitors. Wherever those swine had gone, in whatever distant year and place they had taken refuge, Klietmann and his SS brethren would exterminate them with extreme prejudice and great pleasure.

Now Dr. Theodore Juttner – director of the institute since the murders of Penlovski, Januskaya, and Volkaw, and the disappearances on March 16 – turned to Erich and said, 'We've perhaps found Krieger, *Obersturmführer* Klietmann. Get your men ready to go.'

'We're ready, Doctor,' Erich said. Ready for the future, he thought, ready for Krieger, ready for glory.

• 6 •

At three-forty on Saturday afternoon, January 14, little more than one day after her first visit, Thelma returned to The Bluebird of Happiness Motel in her gardener's battered white pickup. She had two changes of clothes for each of them, suitcases in which to pack all the stuff, and a couple of thousand rounds of ammunition for the revolvers and the Uzis. She also had the IBM PC in the truck, plus a printer, a variety of software, a box of diskettes, and everything else they would need to make the system work for them.

With the wound in his shoulder only four days old, Stefan was recuperating surprisingly fast, although he was not ready to do any lifting, heavy or otherwise. He stayed in the motel room with Chris and packed the suitcases while Laura and Thelma moved the computer boxes to the trunk and back seat of the Buick.

The storm had passed during the night. Shredded gray clouds hung beardlike from the sky. The day had warmed to sixty-five degrees, and the air smelled clean.

Closing the Buick's trunk on the last of the boxes, Laura said, 'You went shopping in that wig and those glasses, those *teeth*?'

'Nah,' Thelma said, removing the stage teeth and putting them in a jacket pocket because they made her lisp when she talked. 'Up close a salesclerk might've recognized me, and being disguised would arouse more attention than if I shopped as myself. But after I'd bought everything, I drove the truck to the deserted end of another shopping center's parking lot and made myself look like a cross between Harpo Marx and Bucky Beaver before heading here, just in case someone in another car looked over at me in traffic. You know, Shane, I sorta like this kind of intrigue. Maybe I'm the reincarnation of Mata Hari, 'cause when I think about seducing men to learn their secrets and then selling the secrets to a foreign government, I get delicious chills.'

'It's the part about seducing men that gives you chills,' Laura said, 'not the secret-selling part. You're no spy, just a lech.'

Thelma gave her the keys to the house in Palm Springs. 'There's no full-time staff there. We just call a housekeeping service to spruce the place up a couple of days before we go. I didn't call them this time, of course, so you're liable to find some dust, but no real filth, and none of the severed heads *you* tend to leave behind.'

'You're a love.'

'There's a gardener. Not full-time like the one at our house in Beverly Hills. This guy just comes around once a week, Tuesdays, to mow the lawn, trim the hedges, and trample some flowers so he can charge us to replace them. I'd advise staying away from the windows and keeping a low profile on Tuesday, until he comes and goes.'

'We'll hide under the bed.'

'You'll notice a lot of whips and chains under the bed, but don't get the idea Jason and I are kinky. The whips and chains belonged to his mother, and we keep them strictly for sentimental reasons.'

They brought the packed suitcases out of the motel room and put those in the back seat with the other packages that would not fit in the Buick's trunk. After a round of hugs, Thelma said, 'Shane, I'm between nightclub appearances for the next three weeks, so if you need me for anything more, you can get hold of me at the house in Beverly Hills, night or day. I'll stay by the phone.' Reluctantly she left.

Laura was relieved when the truck disappeared in traffic; Thelma was safe, out of it. She dropped the room keys at the motel office, then drove away in the Buick with Chris in the other seat and Stefan in the back seat with the luggage. She regretted leaving The Bluebird of Happiness because they had been safe there for four days, and there was no guarantee they'd be safe anywhere else in the world.

They stopped at a gunshop first. Because it was best to keep Laura out of sight as much as possible, Stefan went in to buy a box of ammunition for the pistol. They had not put that item on the shopping list they had given Thelma, for at that time they had not known whether they would get the 9mm Parabellum that Stefan wanted. And in fact they had gotten the .38 Colt Commander Mark IV instead.

After the gunshop they drove to Fat Jack's Pizza Party Palace to pick up two canisters of deadly nerve gas. Stefan and Chris waited in the car, under neon signs that were already burning at twilight, though they would not be in their full glory until nightfall.

The canisters were on Jack's desk. They were the size of small household fire extinguishers with a stainless-steel finish instead of fire-red, with a skull-and-crossbones label that said VEXXON/AEROSOL/WARNING – DEADLY NERVE TOXIN/UNAUTHORIZED POSSESSION IS A FELONY UNDER U.S. LAW, followed by a lot of fine print.

With a finger as plump as an overstuffed sausage, Jack pointed to a half-dollar-size dial on the top of each cylinder. 'These here are timers, calibrated in minutes, one to sixty. If you set the timer and push the button in the center of it, you can release the gas remote, sort of like setting off a time bomb. But if you want to release it manually, then you hold the bottom of the canister in one hand, take this pistol-grip handle in your other hand, and just squeeze this loop the way you would a trigger. This crap, released under pressure, will disperse through a five-thousand-square-foot building in a minute and a half, faster if the heating or air conditioning is running. Exposed to light and air, it breaks down fast into nontoxic components, but it remains deadly for forty to sixty minutes. Just three milligrams on the skin kills in thirty seconds.'

'The antidote?' Laura asked.

Fat Jack smiled and tapped the sealed, four-inch-square, blue-plastic bags that were fixed to the handles of the cylinders. 'Ten capsules in each bag. Two will protect one person. Instructions are in the bag, but I was told you have to take the pills at least one hour before dispersing the gas. Then they'll protect you for three to five hours.'

He took her money and put the Vexxon cylinders in a cardboard box labeled MOZZARELLA CHEESE – KEEP REFRIGERATED. As he put the lid on the box, he laughed and shook his head.

'What's wrong?' Laura asked.

'It just tickles me,' Fat Jack said. 'A looker like you, clearly well educated, with a little boy . . . if someone like *you* is involved in shit like this, society must be really coming apart at the seams a lot faster than I ever hoped. Maybe I will live to see the day when the establishment falls, when anarchy rules, when the only laws are those that individuals make between themselves and seal with a handshake.'

As an afterthought, he lifted the lid on the box, plucked a few green slips of paper from a desk drawer, and dropped them on top of the cylinders of Vexxon.

'What're those?' Laura asked.

'You're a good customer,' Fat Jack said, 'so I'm throwing in a few coupons for free pizza.'

Thelma and Jason's house in Palm Springs was indeed secluded. It was a curious but attractive cross between Spanish and Southwest adobe-style architecture on a one-acre property surrounded by a nine-foot-tall, peach-colored stucco wall that was interrupted only by the entrance and exit from the circular driveway. The grounds were heavily planted with olive trees, palms, and ficus, so neighbors were screened out on three sides, with only the front of the house revealed.

Though they arrived at eight o'clock that Saturday night, after driving into the desert from Fat Jack's place in Anaheim, the house and grounds were visible in detail because they were illuminated by cunningly designed, photocell-controlled landscape lighting that provided both security and aesthetic value. Palm and fern shadows made dramatic patterns on stucco walls.

Thelma had given them the remote garage door opener, so they drove the Buick into the three-car garage and entered the house through the connecting door to the laundry room – after deactivating the alarm system with the code Thelma had also given them.

It was far smaller than the Gaines's mansion in Beverly Hills, but still sizable, with ten rooms and four baths. The unique stamp of Steve Chase, the interior designer of choice in Palm Springs, was on every room: dramatic spaces dramatically lit; simple colors – warm apricot, dusty salmon – accented with turquoise here and there; suede walls, cedar ceilings; here, copper tables with a rich patina; there, granite tables contrasting interestingly with comfortably upholstered furniture in a variety of textured fabrics; elegant yet livable.

In the kitchen Laura found most of the pantry bare except for one shelf of canned goods. As they were all too tired to go grocery shopping, they made a dinner of what was at hand. Even if Laura had broken into the house without a key and had not known who owned the place, she would have realized it belonged to Thelma and Jason as soon as she looked in the pantry, for she could not imagine that any other pair of millionaires would still be so childlike at heart as to stock their larder with Chef Boyardee canned ravioli and spaghetti. Chris was delighted. For dessert they finished off two boxes of chocolate-covered Klondike ice-cream nuggets that they found in the otherwise empty freezer.

Laura and Chris shared the king-size bed in the master bedroom, and Stefan bunked across the hall in a guest room. Though she had re-engaged the perimeter alarm system that monitored every door and window, though a loaded Uzi was on the floor beside her, though a loaded .38 was on the nightstand, and though no one in the world but Thelma could know where they were, Laura slept only fitfully. Each time she woke, she sat straight up in bed, listening for noises in the night – stealthy footsteps, whispering voices.

Toward morning, when she could not get back to sleep, she stared at the shadowy ceiling for a long time, thinking about something that Stefan had said a couple of days ago when explaining some of the fine points of time travel and the changes that travelers could effect in their futures: *Destiny struggles to reassert the pattern that was meant to be.* When Stefan had saved her from the junkie in the grocery store in 1963, fate eventually had brought her to another pedophile, Willy Sheener, in 1967. She had been destined to be an orphan, so when she found a new home with the Dockweilers, fate had conspired to shock Nina Dockweiler with a fatal heart attack, sending Laura back to the orphanage again.

Destiny struggles to reassert the pattern that was meant to be.

What next?

In the pattern that was meant to be, Chris had never been born. Therefore would fate arrange his death soon, to bring events back as close as possible to those which had been ordained and with which Stefan Krieger had meddled? She had been destined to spend her life in a wheelchair before Stefan held Dr. Paul Markwell at gunpoint and prevented him from delivering her. So perhaps now fate would put her in the way of Gestapo gunfire that would sever her spine and render her paraplegic in accordance with the original plan.

How long did the forces of destiny strive to reassert the pattern after a change had been made in it? Chris had been alive for more than eight years. Was that long enough for destiny to decide that his existence was acceptable? She had lived thirty-four years out of a wheelchair. Was destiny still troubling itself with that unnatural squiggle in the ordained design?

Destiny struggles to reassert the pattern that was meant to be.

As dawn's light glowed softly at the edges of the drapes, Laura tossed and turned, growing angry but not sure at whom or what her anger could be directed. What *was* destiny? What was the power that shaped the patterns and attempted to enforce them? God? Should she be raging at God – or begging

Him to let her son live and to spare her from the life of a cripple? Or was the power behind destiny merely a natural mechanism, a force no different in origin from gravity or magnetism?

Because there was no logical target at which her emotions could be vented, Laura felt her anger slowly metamorphosing to fear. They seemed to be safe at the Gaines's Palm Springs house. After passing one uneventful night in the place, they almost could be assured that their presence would never be public knowledge, for otherwise killers from the past no doubt already would have appeared. Yet Laura was afraid.

Something bad was going to happen. Something very bad.

Trouble was coming, but she did not know from what direction.

Lightning. Soon.

Too bad the old saw wasn't true: In fact lightning did strike twice in the same place, three times, a hundred, and she was the reliable rod that drew it.

• 7 •

Dr. Juttner entered the last of the numbers in the programming board that controlled the gate. To Erich Klietmann, he said, 'You and your men will be traveling to the vicinity of Palm Springs, California, in January, 1989.'

'Palm Springs?' Klietmann was surprised.

'Yes. Of course, we had expected you'd have to go somewhere in the Los Angeles or Orange County area, where you would have found your young-executive dress more appropriate than in a resort town, but you'll still pass without notice. For one thing, it's winter there, and even in the desert dark suits will be appropriate for the season.' Juttner handed Klietmann a sheet of paper on which he had written directions. 'Here's where you'll find the woman and the boy.'

Folding the paper and putting it in an inside coat pocket, the lieutenant said, 'What about Krieger?'

'The researchers didn't find mention of him,' Juttner said, 'but he must be with the woman and the boy. If you don't see him, then do your best to take the woman and boy captive. If you have to torture them to learn Krieger's whereabouts, so be it. And if worse comes to worst and they won't give you Krieger – kill them. That might draw him into the open somewhere down the time line.'

'We'll find him, Doctor.'

Klietmann, Hubatsch, von Manstein, and Bracher were all wearing their homing belts beneath their Yves St. Laurent suits. Carrying their Mark Cross attaché cases, they walked to the gate, stepped up into that giant barrel, and moved toward the two-thirds point where they would pass in a wink from 1944 to 1989.

The lieutenant was afraid but also exhilarated. He was the iron fist of Hitler, from which Krieger could not hide even forty-five years in the future.

On their first full day in the Palm Springs house, Sunday the fifteenth of January, they set up the computer, and Laura instructed Stefan in its use. IBM's operating program and the software for the tasks they needed to perform were extremely user-friendly, and though by nightfall Stefan was far from expert at operating the computer, he was able to understand how it functioned, how it thought. He would not be doing most of the work with the machine, anyway; that would be left to Laura, who was already experienced with the system. His job would be to explain to her the calculations that would have to be done, so she would be able to apply the computer to the solution of the many problems ahead of them.

Stefan's intention was to go back to 1944, using the gate-homing belt he had taken off Kokoschka. The belts were not time machines. The gate itself was the machine, the vehicle of transport, and it remained always in 1944. The belts were in tune with the temporal vibrations of the gate, and they simply brought the traveler home when he pushed the button to activate that link.

'How?' Laura asked when he explained the use of the belt. 'How does it take you back?'

'I don't know. Would you know *how* a microchip functions inside a computer? No. But that doesn't prevent you from using the computer any more than my ignorance prevents me from using the gate.'

Having returned to the institute in 1944, having seized control of the main lab, Stefan would make two crucial jaunts, each only days into the future from March of '44, to arrange the destruction of the institute. Those two trips had to be meticulously planned, so he would arrive at each destination in *exactly* the geographical location and *precisely* at the time that he desired. Such refined calculations were impossible to make in 1944, not only because computer assistance was unavailable but because in those days marginally – but vitally – less was known then about the angle and rate of rotation of the earth and about other planetary factors that affected a jaunt, which was why time travelers from the institute frequently arrived off schedule by minutes and out of place by miles. With the ultimate numbers provided by the IBM, he could program the gate to deliver him within one yard and within a split second of his desired point of arrival.

They used all of the books that Thelma had bought. These were not merely science and mathematics texts, but histories of the Second World War, in which they could pinpoint the whereabouts of certain major figures on certain dates.

In addition to performing complex calculations for the jaunts, they had to allow time for Stefan to heal. When he returned to 1944, he would be re-entering the wolf's lair, and even equipped with nerve gas and a first-rate firearm, he would have to be quick and agile to avoid being killed. 'Two weeks,' he said. 'I think I'll have enough flexibility in the shoulder and arm to go back in two more weeks.'

It did not matter if he took two weeks or ten, for when he used Kokoschka's homing belt, he would return to the institute only eleven minutes after Kokoschka had left it. His date of departure from current time would not affect his date of return in 1944.

The only worry was that the Gestapo would find them first and send a hit squad to 1989 to eliminate them before Stefan could return to his era to implement his plan. Though it was their only worry – it was worry enough.

With considerable caution, more than half expecting a sudden flash of lightning and a roll of thunder, they took a break and went grocery shopping Sunday afternoon. Laura, still the object of media attention, remained in the car while Chris and Stefan went into the market. No lightning struck, and they returned to the house with a trunkful of groceries.

Unpacking the market bags in the kitchen, Laura discovered that a third of the sacks contained nothing but snack food: three different kinds of ice-cream bars, plus one quart each of chocolate, rocky road, butter almond, and almond fudge; family-size bags of M&Ms, Kit Kats, Reese's Cups, and Almond Joys; potato chips, pretzels, tortilla chips, cheese popcorn, peanuts; four kinds of cookies; one chocolate cake, one cherry pie, one box of doughnuts, four packages of Ding Dongs.

Stefan was helping her put things away, and she said, 'You must have the world's biggest sweet tooth.'

'See, this is another thing I find so amazing and wonderful about this future of yours,' he said. 'Just imagine – there's no longer any nutritional difference between a chocolate cake and a steak. Just as many vitamins and minerals in these potato chips as in a green salad. You can eat nothing but desserts and remain as healthy as a man who eats balanced meals. Incredible! How was this advance achieved?'

Laura turned in time to see Chris slinking out of the kitchen. 'Whoa, you little con artist.'

Looking sheepish, he said, 'Doesn't Mr. Krieger get some funny ideas about our culture.'

'I know where he got this one,' she said. 'What a sneaky thing to have done.'

Chris sighed and tried to sound mournful. 'Yeah. But I figure . . . if we're being hunted down by Gestapo agents, we ought to be able to eat as many Ding Dongs as we want, at least, 'cause every meal could be our last.' He looked at her sideways to see if she was buying his condemned-man routine.

In fact what the boy said contained enough truth to make his trickery understandable if not excusable, and she could not find the will to punish him.

That night after dinner, Laura changed the dressing on Stefan's wound. The impact of the slug had left an enormous bruise on his chest with the bullet hole at its approximate center, a smaller bruise around the exit point. The suture threads and the inside of the old bandage were crusted with fluid that had seeped from him and dried. After she carefully bathed the wounds, cleaning the material away as much as possible without disturbing the scab, she gently palpated the flesh, producing a trace of clear seepage, but there was no sign of pus formation that would indicate a serious infection. Of course, he might have an abscess within the wound, draining internally, but that was not likely because he had no fever.

'Keep taking the penicillin,' she said, 'and I think you'll be fine. Doc Brenkshaw did a good job.'

While Laura and Stefan spent long hours at the computer Monday and Tuesday, Chris watched television, looked through the bookshelves for something to read, puzzled over a hardcover collection of old Barbarella cartoons—

'Mom, what does orgasm mean?'

'What're you reading? Give me that.'

—and generally entertained himself without a fuss. He came to the den once in a while and stood for a minute or two at a time, watching them use the computer. After about a dozen visits he said, 'In *Back to the Future* they just had this time-traveling car, and they pushed a few buttons on the dashboard, and they were *off – Pow*! – like that. How come nothing in real life's ever as easy as it is in the movies?'

On Tuesday, January 17, they kept a low profile while the gardener mowed the lawn and trimmed some shrubbery. In four days he was the only person they had seen; no door-to-door salesmen had called, not even a Jehovah's Witness pushing *Watchtower* magazine.

'We're safe here,' Stefan said. 'Obviously, our presence in the house never becomes public knowledge. If it did, the Gestapo would have visited us already.'

Nevertheless Laura kept the perimeter alarm system switched on nearly twenty-four hours a day. And at night she dreamed of destiny reasserting itself, of Chris erased from existence, of waking up to find herself in a wheelchair.

• 9 •

They were supposed to arrive at eight o'clock to give them plenty of time to reach the location at which the researchers had pinpointed the woman and the boy, if not Krieger. But when Lieutenant Klietmann blinked and found himself forty-five years beyond his own era, he knew at once that they were a couple of hours late. The sun was too high above the horizon. The temperature was about seventy-five, too warm for an early, winter morning in the desert.

Like a white crack in a blue-glazed bowl, lightning splintered down the sky. Other cracks opened, and sparks flashed above as if struck from the hooves of a bull loose in some celestial china shop.

As the thunder faded, Klietmann turned to see if von Manstein, Hubatsch, and Bracher had made the journey safely. They were with him, all carrying attaché cases, with sunglasses stuck in the breast pockets of their expensive suits.

The problem was that thirty feet beyond the sergeant and the two corporals, a pair of elderly, white-haired women in pastel stretch pants and pastel blouses were standing at a white car near the rear door to a church, staring in astonishment at Klietmann and his squad. They were holding what appeared to be casseroles.

Klietmann glanced around and saw that he and his men had arrived in the parking lot behind the church. There were two other cars in addition to the one that seemed to belong to the women, but there were no other onlookers. The lot was encircled by a wall, so the only way out was past the women and along the side of the church.

Deciding that boldness was the best course, Klietmann walked straight toward the women, as if there was nothing whatsoever unusual about his having materialized out of thin air, and his men followed him. Mesmerized, the women watched them approach.

'Good morning, ladies.' Like Krieger, Klietmann had learned to speak English with an American accent in hopes of serving as a deep-cover agent, but he'd been unable to lose his accent entirely, no matter how hard he studied and practiced. Though his own watch was set to local time, he knew he could no longer trust it, so he said, 'Could you please be so kind as to tell me what time it is?'

They stared at him.

'The time?' he repeated.

The woman in yellow pastel twisted her wrist without letting go of the casserole, looked at her watch, and said, 'Uh, it's ten-forty.'

They were two hours and forty minutes late. They couldn't waste time searching for a car to hot-wire, especially not when a perfectly good one was available, with keys, right in front of them. Klietmann was prepared to kill both women for the car. He could not leave their bodies in the parking lot; an alarm would go up when they were found, and shortly thereafter the police would be looking for their car – a nasty complication. He'd have to stuff the bodies in the trunk and take them with him.

The woman in blue pastels said, 'Why've you come to us, are you angels?'

Klietmann wondered if she was senile. Angels in pinstripe suits? Then he realized that they were in the vicinity of a church and had appeared miraculously, so it might be logical for a religious woman to assume they were angels, regardless of their clothing. Maybe it would not be necessary to waste time killing them, after all. He said, 'Yes, ma'am, we are angels, and God needs your car.'

The woman in yellow said, 'My Toyota here?'

'Yes, ma'am.' The driver's door was standing open, and Klietmann put his attaché on the front seat. 'We're on an urgent mission for God, you saw us step through the pearly gate from Heaven right before your eyes, and we must have transportation.'

Von Manstein and Bracher had gone around to the other side of the Toyota, opened those doors, and gotten inside.

The woman in blue said, 'Shirley, you've been *chosen* to give your car.'

'God will return it to you,' Klietmann said, 'when our work here is done.' Remembering the gasoline shortages of his own war-torn era and not sure how plentiful fuel was in 1989, he added: 'Of course, no matter how much gas is in the tank now, it'll be full when we return it and perpetually full thereafter. The loaves and fishes thing.'

'But there's potato salad in there for the church brunch,' the woman in yellow said.

Felix Hubatsch had already opened the rear door on the driver's side and had found the potato salad. Now he took it out of the car and put it on the macadam at the woman's feet.

Klietmann got in, closed the door, heard Hubatsch slam the door behind him, found the keys in the ignition, started the car, and drove out of the church lot. When he looked in the rearview mirror just before turning into the street, the old women were still back there, holding their casseroles, staring after him.

Day by day they refined their calculations, and Stefan exercised his left arm and shoulder as much as he dared, trying to prevent it from growing stiff as it healed, hoping to maintain as much muscle tone as possible. On Saturday afternoon, January 21, as their first week in Palm Springs drew to a close, they completed the calculations and arrived at the precise time and space coordinates that Stefan would require for the jaunts he would make once he returned to 1944.

'Now I just need a bit more time to heal,' he said, as he stood up from the computer and testingly moved his left arm in circles.

She said, 'It's been eleven days since you were shot. Do you still have pain?'

'Some. A deeper, duller pain. And not all the time. But the strength isn't back. I think I'd better wait a few days yet. If it feels all right by next Wednesday, the twenty-fifth, I'll return to the institute then. Sooner, if I improve faster, but certainly no later than next Wednesday.'

That night, Laura woke from a nightmare in which she was confined yet again to a wheelchair and in which destiny, in the form of a faceless man in a black robe, was busily erasing Chris from reality, as if the boy was only a crayon drawing on a pane of glass. She was soaked in sweat, and for a while she sat up in bed, listening for noises in the house but hearing nothing other than her son's steady, low breathing on the bed beside her.

Later, unable to get back to sleep, she lay thinking about Stefan Krieger. He was an interesting man, extremely self-contained and at times hard to figure.

Since Wednesday of the previous week, when he explained that he had become her guardian because he had fallen in love with her and wanted to improve the life she had been meant to live, he'd said nothing more of love. He had not restated his feelings for her, had not subjected her to meaningful looks, had not played the part of a pining suitor. He made his case and was willing to give her time to think about him and get to know him before she decided what she thought of him. She suspected he would wait years, if necessary, and without complaint. He had the patience born of extreme adversity, which was something she understood.

He was quiet, pensive a lot of the time, occasionally downright melancholy, which she supposed was a result of the horrors he had seen in his long-ago Germany. Perhaps that core of sadness had its roots in things he had done himself and had come to regret, things for which he felt he could never atone. After all, he had said that a place in hell was reserved for him. He had revealed no more about his past than what he had told her and Chris in the motel room more than ten days ago. She sensed, however, that he was willing to tell her all the details, those that were a discredit to him as well as those that reflected well on him; he would not conceal anything from her; he was merely waiting for her to decide what she thought of him and whether, in any case, she wanted to know more.

In spite of the sorrow in him, deep as marrow and dark as blood, he had a quiet sense of humor. He was good with Chris and could make the boy laugh, which Laura counted in his favor. His smile was warm and gentle.

She still did not love him, and she did not think that she ever would. She wondered how she could be so sure of that. In fact she lay in the dark bedroom for a couple of hours, wondering, until at last she began to suspect that the reason she could not love him was because he was not Danny. Her Danny had been a unique man, and with him she had known a love as close to perfection as the world allowed. Now, in seeking her affections, Stefan Krieger would be forever in competition with a ghost.

She recognized the pathos in their situation, and she was glumly aware of the loneliness that her attitude assured. In her heart she wanted to be loved and to love in return, but in her relationship with Stefan, she saw only his passion unrequited, her hope unfulfilled.

Beside her, Chris murmured in his sleep, then sighed.

I love you, honey, she thought. I love you so much.

Her son, the only child she could ever have, was the center of her existence now and for the foreseeable future, her primary reason for going on. If anything happened to Chris, Laura knew she would no longer be able to find relief in the dark humor of life; this world in which tragedy and comedy were married in all things would become, for her, exclusively a place of tragedy, too black and bleak to be endured.

• 11 •

Three blocks from the church Erich Klietmann pulled the white Toyota to the curb and parked on a side street off Palm Canyon Drive in Palm Springs' main shopping district. Scores of people strolled along the sidewalks, window-shopping. Some of the younger women were wearing shorts and brief tops that Klietmann found not only scandalous but embarrassing, casually displaying their bodies in a way unknown in his own age. Under the iron rule of *der Führer's* National Socialist Workers' Party, such shameless behavior wouldn't be permitted; Hitler's triumph would result in a different world, where morality would be strictly enforced, where these bare-limbed, brassiereless women would parade themselves only at the risk of imprisonment and re-education, where decadent creatures wouldn't be tolerated. As he watched their buttocks clench and flex beneath their tight shorts, as he watched unrestrained breasts swaying under the thin fabric of T-shirts, what most disturbed Klietmann was that he desperately wanted to lay with every one of these women even if they were representatives of the deviant strains of humanity that Hitler would abolish.

Beside Klietmann, Corporal Rudy von Manstein had unfolded the map of Palm Springs provided by the team of researchers that had located the woman and the boy. He said, 'Where do we make the hit?'

From an inside pocket of his suit jacket, Klietmann withdrew the folded paper that Dr. Juttner had given him in the lab. He opened it and read aloud: 'On state route 111, approximately six miles north of the Palm Springs city limits, the woman will be arrested by an officer of the California Highway Patrol at eleven-twenty, Wednesday morning, January 25. She will be driving a black Buick Riviera. The boy will be with her and will be taken into protective custody. Apparently Krieger is there, but we're not sure; apparently he escapes from the police officer, but we don't know how.'

Von Manstein had already traced a route on the map that would take them out of Palm Springs and onto highway 111.

'We've got thirty-one minutes,' Klietmann said, glancing at the dashboard clock.

'We'll make it easily,' von Manstein said. 'Fifteen minutes at the most.'

'If we get there early,' Klietmann said, 'we can kill Krieger before he slips away from the highway-patrol officer. In any event we have to get there before the woman and boy are taken into custody because it'll be far more difficult to get at them once they're in jail.' He turned around to look at Bracher and Hubatsch in the back seat. 'Understood?'

They both nodded, but then Sergeant Hubatsch patted the breast pocket of his suit and said, 'Sir, what about these sunglasses?'

'What about them?' Klietmann asked impatiently.

'Should we put them on now? Will that help us blend with the local citizenry? I've been studying the people on the street, and though a lot of them are wearing dark glasses, many of them aren't.'

Klietmann looked at the pedestrians, trying not to be distracted by scantily clad women, and he saw that Hubatsch was correct. More to the point, he realized that not even one of the men in sight was dressed in the power look preferred by young executives. Maybe all young executives were in their offices at this hour. Whatever the reason for the lack of dark suits and black Bally loafers, Klietmann felt conspicuous even though he and his men were in a car. Because many pedestrians were wearing sunglasses, he decided that wearing his own would give him one thing in common with some of the locals.

When the lieutenant put on his Ray-Bans, so did von Manstein, Bracher, and Hubatsch.

'All right, let's go,' Klietmann said.

But before he could pop the emergency brake and put the car in gear, someone knocked on the driver's window beside him. It was a Palm Springs police officer.

• 12 •

Laura sensed that, one way or the other, their ordeal was soon coming to an end. They would succeed in destroying the institute or die trying, and she had almost reached the point at which an end to fear was desirable regardless of how it was achieved.

Wednesday morning, January 25, Stefan still suffered deep-muscle soreness in his shoulder but no sharp pain. No numbness remained in his hand or arm, which meant the bullet had not damaged any nerves. Because he cautiously had exercised every day, he had more than half of his usual strength in his left arm and shoulder, just enough to make him confident that he would be able to implement his plan. But Laura could see that he was afraid of the trip ahead of him.

He put on Kokoschka's gate-homing belt, which Laura had taken from her safe the night that Stefan had arrived wounded on her doorstep. His fear remained apparent, but the moment that he put on the belt, his anxiety was overlaid with a steely determination.

In the kitchen at ten o'clock, each of them, including Chris, took two of the capsules that would render them impervious to the effects of the nerve gas, Vexxon. They washed down the preventive with glasses of Hi-C orange drink.

The three Uzis, one of the .38 revolvers, the silencer-equipped Colt

Commander Mark IV, and a small nylon backpack full of books had been loaded into the car.

The two pressurized, stainless-steel bottles of Vexxon were still in the Buick's trunk. After studying the informational pamphlets in the blue plastic bags attached to the containers, Stefan had decided he would need only one cylinder for the job. Vexxon was a designer gas tailored primarily for use indoors – to kill the enemy in barracks, shelters, and bunkers deep under-ground – rather than against troops in the field. In the open air the stuff dispersed too fast – and broke down too quickly in sunlight – to be effective beyond a radius of two hundred yards from point of release. However, when opened full-cock, a single cylinder could contaminate a fifty-thousand-square-foot structure in a few minutes, which was good enough for his purposes.

At 10:35 they got in the car and left the Gaines's house, heading for the desert off route 111, north of Palm Springs. Laura made sure Chris's safety harness was buckled, and the boy said, 'See, if you had a car that was a time machine, we'd drive back to 1944 in comfort.'

Days ago they had taken a night drive to the open desert to find a spot suitable for Stefan's departure. They needed to know the exact geographical location in advance in order to do the calculations that would make it possible for him to return conveniently to them after his work in 1944 was done.

Stefan intended to open the valve on the Vexxon cylinder *before* he pushed the button on the gate-homing belt, so the nerve gas would be dispersing even as he returned through the gate to the institute, killing everyone who was in the lab at the 1944 end of the Lightning Road. Therefore he would be releasing a quantity of the toxin at his point of departure, too, and it seemed prudent to do so only in an isolated place. The street in front of the Gaines's house was less than two hundred yards away, within Vexxon's effective range, and they did not want to kill innocent bystanders.

Besides, though the gas was supposed to remain poisonous only for forty to sixty minutes, Laura was concerned that the deactivated residue, although not lethal, might have unknown, long-range toxic effects. She did not intend to leave any such substance in Thelma and Jason's house.

The day was clear, blue, serene.

When they had driven only a couple of blocks and were descending into a hollow where the road was flanked by huge date plams, Laura thought she saw a strange pulse of light in the fragment of sky that was captured by her rearview mirror. What would lightning be like in a bright, cloudless sky? Not as dramatic as on a stormclouded day, for it would be competing with the brightness of the sun. What it might look like in fact was the very thing she thought she had seen – a strange, brief *pulse* of brightness.

Though she braked, the Buick was into the bottom of the hollow, and she could no longer see the sky in the rearview mirror, just the hill behind them. She thought she heard a rumble, too, like distant thunder, but she could not be sure because of the roar of the car's air conditioner. She pulled quickly to the side of the road, fumbling with the ventilation controls.

'What's wrong?' Chris asked as she put the car in park, threw open her door, and got out.

Stefan opened the rear door and got out too. 'Laura?'

She was looking at the limited expanse of sky that she could see from the bottom of the hollow, using her flattened hand as a visor over her eyes. 'You hear that, Stefan?'

In the warm, desert-dry day, a faraway rumble slowly died.

He said, 'Could be jet noise.'

'No. The last time I thought it might be a jet, it was *them*.'

The sky pulsed again, one last time. She did not actually see the lightning itself, not the jagged bolt scored on the heavens, but just the reflection of it in the upper atmosphere, a faint wave of light flushing across the blue vault above.

'They're here,' she said.

'Yes,' he agreed.

'Somewhere on our way out to route 111, someone's going to stop us, maybe a traffic cop, or maybe we'll be in an accident, so there'll be a public record, and then *they'll* show up. Stefan, we've got to turn around, go back to the house.'

'It's no use,' he said.

Chris had gotten out of the other side of the car. 'He's right, Mom. It doesn't matter what we do. Those time travelers came here 'cause they've already peeked into the future and know where they're gonna find us maybe half an hour from now, maybe ten minutes from now. It doesn't matter if we go back to the house or go on ahead; they've already seen us someplace – maybe even back at the house. See, no matter how much we change our plans, we'll cross their path.'

Destiny.

'Shit!' she said and kicked the side of the car, which didn't do any good, didn't even make her feel better. 'I *hate* this. How can you hope to win against goddamn time travelers? It's like playing blackjack when the dealer is God.'

No more lightning flared.

She said, 'Come to think of it, all of life is a blackjack game with God as the dealer, isn't it? So this is no worse. Get in the car, Chris. Let's go on with it.'

As she drove through the western neighborhoods of the resort city, Laura's nerves were as taut as garroting wire. She was alert for trouble on all sides, though she knew it would come when and where she least expected it.

Without incident they connected with the northern end of Palm Canyon Drive, then state route 111. Ahead lay twelve miles of mostly barren desert before 111 intersected Interstate 10.

• 13 •

Hoping to avoid catastrophe, Lieutenant Klietmann lowered the driver's window and smiled up at the Palm Springs policeman who had rapped on the glass to get his attention and who was now bending down, squinting in at him. 'What is it, officer?'

'Didn't you see the red curb when you parked here?'

'Red curb?' Klietmann said, smiling, wondering what the hell the cop was talking about.

'Now, sir,' the officer said in a curiously playful tone, 'are you telling me you didn't see the red curb?'

'Yes, sir, of course I saw it.'

'I didn't think *you'd* fib,' the cop said as if he knew Klietmann and trusted his reputation for honesty, which baffled the lieutenant. 'So if you saw the red curb, sir, why'd you park here?'

'Oh, I see,' Klietmann said, 'parking is restricted to curbs that aren't red. Yes, of course.'

The patrolman blinked at the lieutenant. He shifted his attention to von Manstein in the passenger's seat, then to Bracher and Hubatsch in the rear, smiled and nodded at them.

Klietmann did not have to look at his men to know they were on edge. The air in the car was heavy with tension.

When he shifted his gaze to Klietmann, the police officer smiled tentatively and said, 'Am I right – you fellas are four preachers?'

'Preachers?' Klietmann said, disconcerted by the question.

'I've got a bit of a deductive mind,' the cop said, his tentative smile still holding. 'I'm no Sherlock Holmes. But the bumper stickers on your car say "I Love Jesus" and "Christ Has Risen." And there's a Baptist convention in town, and you're all dressed in dark suits.'

That was why he had thought he could trust Klietmann not to fib: He believed they were Baptist ministers.

'That's right,' Klietmann said at once. 'We're with the Baptist convention, officer. Sorry about the illegal parking. We don't have red curbs where I come from. Now if—'

'Where *do* you hail from?' the cop asked, not with suspicion but in an attempt to be friendly.

Klietmann knew a lot about the United States but not enough to carry on a conversation of this sort when he did not control its direction to any degree whatsoever. He believed that Baptists were from the southern part of the country; he wasn't sure if there were any of them in the north or west or east, so he tried to think of a southern state. He said, 'I'm from Georgia,' before he realized how unlikely that claim seemed when spoken in his German accent.

The smile on the cop's face faltered. Looking past Klietmann to von Manstein, he said, 'And where you from, sir?'

Following his lieutenant's lead, but speaking with an even stronger accent, von Manstein said, 'Georgia.'

From the back seat, before they could be asked, Hubatsch and Bracher said, 'Georgia, we're from Georgia,' as if that word was magic and would cast a spell over the patrolman.

The cop's smile had vanished altogether. He frowned at Erich Klietmann and said, 'Sir, would you mind stepping out of the car for a moment?'

'Certainly, officer,' Klietmann said, as he opened his door, noticing how the cop backed up a couple of steps and rested his right hand on the butt of his holstered revolver. 'But we're late for a prayer meeting—'

In the back seat Hubatsch snapped open his attaché case and snatched the Uzi from it as quickly as a presidential bodyguard might have done. He did not roll down the window but put the muzzle against the glass and opened fire on the cop, giving him no time to draw his revolver. The car window blew out as bullets pounded through it. Struck by at least twenty rounds at close range, the cop pitched backward into traffic. Brakes squealed as a car made a hard stop to avoid the body, and across the street display windows shattered as bullets hit a men's clothing shop.

With the cool detachment and quick thinking that made Klietmann proud to
be in the *Schutzstaffel*, Martin Bracher got out of the Toyota on his side and
loosed a wide arc of fire from the Uzi to add to the chaos and give them a better
chance of escaping. Windows imploded in the exclusive shops not only on the
side street at the end of which they were parked but all the way across the
intersection on the east flank of Palm Canyon Drive as well. People screamed,
dropped to the pavement, scuttled for the cover of doorways. Klietmann saw
passing cars hit by bullets out on Palm Canyon, and maybe a few drivers were
hit or maybe they only panicked, but the vehicles swung wildly from lane to
lane; a tan Mercedes side-swiped a delivery truck, and a sleek, red sportscar
jumped the curb, crossed the sidewalk, grazed the bole of a palm tree, and
plowed into the front of a gift shop.

Klietmann got behind the wheel again and released the emergency brake. He
heard Bracher and Hubatsch leap into the car, so he threw the white Toyota in
gear and shot forward onto Palm Canyon, hanging a hard left, heading north.
He discovered at once that he was on a one-way street, going in the wrong
direction. Cursing, he dodged oncoming cars. The Toyota rocked wildly on bad
springs, and the glove compartment popped open, emptying its contents in von
Manstein's lap. Klietmann turned right at the next intersection. A block later
he ran a red light, narrowly avoiding pedestrians in the crosswalk, and turned
left onto another avenue that allowed northbound traffic.

'We only have twenty-one minutes,' von Manstein said, pointing at the
dashboard clock.

'Tell me where to go,' Klietmann said. 'I'm lost.'

'No, you're not,' von Manstein said, brushing the contents of the glove
compartment – spare keys, paper napkins, a pair of white gloves, individual
packets of catsup and mustard, documents of various kinds – off the map that
he was still holding open in his lap. 'You're not lost. This will connect with
Palm Canyon where it becomes a two-way street. From there we head straight
north onto route 111.'

• 14 •

Approximately six miles north of Palm Springs, where the barren land looked
particularly empty, Laura pulled to the shoulder of the highway. She slowly
proceeded a few hundred yards until she found the place where the embankment declined almost to the level of the surrounding desert and sloped sufficiently to allow her to drive out onto the flat plain. Aside from a little
bunchgrass that bristled in dry clumps and a few gnarly mesquite bushes, the
only vegetation was tumbleweed – some green and rooted, some dry and rolling free. The fixed weeds scraped softly against the Buick, and the loose ones
flew away on the wind that the car created.

The hard ground had a shale base over which an alkaline sand was drifted and
whorled in places. As she had done when they found the place a few nights ago,
Laura stayed away from the sand, kept to the bare gray-pink shale. She did not
stop until she was three hundred yards from the highway, putting that well-
traveled road beyond the radius of Vexxon's open-air effectiveness. She parked
not far from an arroyo, a twenty-foot-wide and thirty-foot-deep natural drainage

channel formed by flash floods during hundreds of the desert's brief rainy seasons; previously, at night, proceeding with caution but guided only by head-lights, they'd been fortunate not to drive into that enormous ditch.

Though the lightning had not been followed by any sign of armed men, urgency informed the moment; Laura, Chris, and Stefan moved as if they could hear a clock ticking toward an impending detonation. While Laura removed one of the thirty-pound Vexxon cylinders from the trunk of the Buick, Stefan put his arms through the straps on the small, green nylon backpack that was full of books, pulled the chest strap in place, and pressed the Velcro fasteners together. Chris carried one of the Uzis twenty feet from the car to the center of a circle of utterly barren shale where not even a tuft of bunchgrass grew, which looked like a good staging area for Stefan's debarkation from 1989. Laura joined the boy there, and Stefan followed, holding the silencer-fitted Colt Commander in his right hand.

North of Palm Springs on state route 111, Klietmann was pushing the Toyota as hard as it would go, which was not hard enough. The car had forty thousand miles on the odometer, and no doubt the old woman who owned it never drove faster than fifty, so it wasn't responding well to the demands Klietmann made on it. When he tried to go faster than sixty, the Toyota began to shimmy and sputter, forcing him to ease up.

Nevertheless, just two miles north of the Palm Springs city limits, they fell in behind a California Highway Patrol cruiser, and Klietmann knew they must have caught up with the officer who was going to encounter and arrest Laura Shane and her son. The cop was doing just under fifty-five in a fifty-five-mile-per-hour zone.

'Kill him,' Klietmann said over his shoulder to Corporal Martin Bracher, who was in the right rear seat.

Klietmann glanced in the rearview mirror, saw no traffic behind; there was oncoming traffic, but it was in the southbound lanes. He swung into the northbound passing lane and began to move around the patrol car at sixty.

In the back Bracher rolled down his window. The other rear window was already open because Hubatsch had shot it out when he had killed the Palm Springs cop, so wind roared noisily through the back of the Toyota and reached into the front seat to flutter the map that was still in von Manstein's lap.

The CHP officer glanced over in surprise, for motorists probably seldom dared pass a policeman who was already driving within a couple of miles of the speed limit. When Klietmann pressed the Toyota past sixty, it shimmied and coughed, still accelerating but grudgingly. The policeman took note of this indication of Klietmann's determined breaking of the law, and he tapped his siren lightly, making it whoop and die, which apparently meant that Klietmann was to fall back and pull to the shoulder of the road.

Instead the lieutenant nursed the protesting Toyota up to sixty-four miles an hour, where it seemed in danger of shaking itself apart, and that was just fast enough to pull slightly ahead of the startled CHP officer, bringing Bracher's rear window in line with the patrol car's front window. The corporal opened fire with his Uzi.

The police cruiser's windows imploded, and the officer was dead in an instant. He had to be dead, for he had not seen the attack coming and surely had taken several rounds in the head and upper body. The patrol car swung toward the Toyota and brushed it before Klietmann could get out of the way, then veered toward the shoulder of the road.

Klietmann braked, falling back from the out-of-control cruiser.

The four-lane highway was elevated about ten feet above the desert floor, and the patrol car shot past the unguarded brink of the shoulder. It was airborne for a few seconds, then came down so hard that some of its tires no doubt blew out on impact. Two doors popped open, including that on the driver's side.

As Klietmann moved into the right lane and drove slowly by the wreckage, von Manstein said, 'I can see him in there, slumped over the wheel. He's no more trouble to us.'

Oncoming drivers had witnessed the patrol car's spectacular flight. They pulled to the verge on their side of route 111. When Klietmann glanced in his rearview mirror, he saw people getting out of those vehicles, good Samaritans hurrying across the highway to the CHP officer's rescue. If some of them realized why the cruiser had crashed, they had decided not to pursue Klietmann and bring him to justice. Which was wise.

He accelerated again, glanced at the odometer, and said, 'Three miles from here, that cop would've arrested the woman and boy. So be on the lookout for a black Buick. Three miles.'

Standing in the bright desert sun on the patch of barren shale near the Buick, Laura watched Stefan slip the strap of the Uzi over his right shoulder. The carbine hung freely and did not interfere with the backpack full of books.

'But now I wonder if I should take it,' he said. 'If the nerve gas works as well as it ought to, I probably won't even need the pistol, let alone a submachine gun.'

'Take it,' Laura said grimly.

He nodded. 'You're right. Who knows.'

'Too bad you don't have a couple of grenades too,' Chris said. 'Grenades would be good.'

'Let's hope it doesn't get *that* nasty back there,' Stefan said.

He switched off the pistol's safeties and held it ready in his right hand. Gripping the canister of Vexxon by its heavy-duty, fire-extinguisher-type handle, he picked it up with his left hand and tested its weight to see how his injured shoulder would react.

'Hurts a little,' he said. 'Pulls at the wound. But it's not bad, and I'll be able to control it.'

They had cut the wire on the canister's trigger, which allowed the manual venting of the Vexxon. He curled his finger through the release loop.

When he finished his work in 1944, he would make a final jaunt to their time again, 1989, and the plan was for him to arrive only five minutes after he departed. Now he said, 'I'll see you very soon. You'll hardly know I'm gone.'

Suddenly Laura was afraid that he would never return. She put a hand to his face and kissed him on the cheek. 'Good luck, Stefan.'

It was not a kiss that a lover might have given, nor was there even a promise of

passion; it was just the affectionate kiss of a friend, the kiss of a woman who
owed eternal gratitude but who did not owe her heart. She saw an awareness of
that in his eyes. At the core, in spite of flashes of humor, he was a melancholy
man, and she wished that she could make him happy. She regretted that she
could not at least pretend to feel more for him; yet she knew he would see
through any such pretense.

'I want you to come back,' she said. 'I really do. Very much.'

'That's enough.' He looked at Chris and said, 'Take care of your mother
while I'm gone.'

'I'll try,' Chris said. 'But she's pretty good at taking care of herself.'

Laura pulled her son to her side.

Stefan lifted the thirty-pound Vexxon cylinder higher, squeezed the release
loop.

As the gas vented under high pressure with a sound like a dozen snakes
hissing at once, Laura was seized by a brief panic, certain that the capsules they
had taken would not protect them from the nerve toxin, that they would drop to
the ground, twitching in the grip of muscle spasms and convulsions, where they
would die in thirty seconds. Vexxon was colorless but not odorless or tasteless;
even in the open air, where it dispersed quickly, she detected a sweet odor of
apricots and a tart, nauseating taste that seemed half lemon juice and half
spoiled milk. But in spite of what she could smell and taste, she felt no adverse
effects.

Holding the pistol across his body, Stefan reached beneath his shirt with a
free finger of his gun hand and pressed the button on the homing belt three
times.

Von Manstein was the first to spot the black car standing in that expanse of
white sand and pale rock, a few hundred yards east of the highway. He called it
to their attention.

Of course, Lieutenant Klietmann could not see the make of the car from so
far away, but he was sure it was the one for which they were searching. Three
people stood together near the car; they were hardly more than stick figures at
that distance, and they appeared to shimmer like mirages in the desert sun, but
Klietmann could see that two of them were adults, the other a child.

Abruptly one of the adults vanished. It was not a trick of desert air and light.
The figure did not shimmer into view again a moment later. It was gone, and
Klietmann knew that it had been Stefan Krieger.

'He went back!' Bracher said, astonished.

'Why would he go back,' von Manstein said, 'when everyone at the institute
wants his ass?'

'Worse,' Hubatsch said from behind the lieutenant. 'He came to 1989 days
before we did. So that belt of his will have taken him back to the same point, to the
day that Kokoschka shot him – to just eleven minutes after Kokoschka shot him.
Yet we know for a fact he never returned that day. What the hell's going on here?'

Klietmann was worried, too, but he didn't have time to figure out what was
going on. His job was to kill the woman and her son if not Krieger. He said,
'Get ready,' and he slowed the Toyota to look for a way down the embankment.

Hubatsch and Bracher had already withdrawn the Uzis from their attaché cases in Palm Springs. Now von Manstein armed himself with his weapon.

The land rose to meet the highway. Klietmann swung the Toyota off the pavement, down the sloped embankment, and onto the desert floor, heading toward the woman and the boy.

When Stefan activated the homing belt, the air became heavy, and Laura felt a great, invisible weight pressing on her. She grimaced at the stench of hot electrical wiring and burnt insulation, overlaid by the scent of ozone, underlaid by the apricot smell of the Vexxon. The air pressure grew, the blend of odors intensified, and Stefan left her world with a sudden, loud *pop*. For an instant there seemed to be no air to breathe, but the brief vacuum was followed by a blustery inrush of hot wind tainted by the faintly alkaline smell of the desert.

Standing close at her side and holding fast to her, Chris said, 'Wow! Wasn't that something, Mom, wasn't that great?'

She did not answer because she noticed a white car driving off state route 111, onto the desert floor. It turned toward them and leaped forward as its driver accelerated.

'Chris, get in front of the Buick. Stay down!'

He saw the oncoming vehicle and obeyed her without question.

She ran to the open door of the Buick and snatched one of the submachine guns off the seat. She stepped to the rear, standing by the open trunk, and faced the oncoming car.

It was less than two hundred yards away, closing fast. Sunlight starred and flashed off the chrome, coruscated across the windshield.

She considered the possibility that the occupants were not German agents from 1944 but innocent people. However that was so unlikely, she could not allow the possibility to inhibit her.

Destiny struggles to reassert the pattern that was meant to be.

No. Damn it, no.

When the white car was within one hundred yards, she squeezed off two solid bursts from the Uzi and saw bullets punch at least two holes in the windshield. The rest of the tempered glass instantly crazed.

The car – she could see now that it was a Toyota – spun out, turning a full three hundred and sixty degrees, then ninety degrees more, throwing up clouds of dust, tearing through a couple of still green tumbleweeds. It came to rest about sixty yards away, the front end pointed north, the passenger's side toward her.

Doors flew open on the far side, and Laura knew the occupants were scrambling out of the car where she could not see them, staying low. She opened fire again, not with the hope of hitting them through the Toyota but with the intention of puncturing the fuel tank; then perhaps a lucky spark, struck by a bullet passing through sheet metal, might ignite the gasoline and catch some or all of those men in the sudden flames as they huddled against the far flank of the vehicle. But she emptied the Uzi's extended magazine without igniting a fire, even though she had almost certainly riddled the fuel tank.

She threw down the gun, pulled open the back door of the Buick, and snatched up the other, fully loaded Uzi. She got the .38 Chief's Special from the front seat, too, never taking her eyes off the white Toyota for more than a second or two. She wished that Stefan had left the third submachine gun, after all.

From the other car, sixty yards away, one of the gunmen opened fire with an automatic weapon, and now there was no doubt who they were. As Laura crouched against the side of the Buick, bullets thudded into the open trunk lid, blew out the rear window, tore into the rear fenders, ricocheted off the bumper, bounced off surrounding shale with sharp *cracks*, and kicked up puffs of powdery, white sand.

She heard a couple of rounds cutting the air close to her head – deadly, high-pitched, whispery whines – and she began to edge backward toward the front of the Buick, staying close to it, trying to make as small a target of herself as possible. In a moment she joined Chris where he huddled against the Buick's grille.

The gunman at the Toyota ceased firing.

'Mom?' Chris said fearfully.

'It's all right,' she said, trying hard to believe what she told him. 'Stefan will be back in less than five minutes, honey. He's got another Uzi, and that'll even the odds a lot. We'll be okay. We only have to hold them off for a few minutes. Just a few minutes.'

• 15 •

Kokoschka's belt returned Stefan to the institute in a blink, and he entered the gate with the nozzle on the Vexxon cylinder wide open. He was squeezing the handle and trigger so hard that his hand ached, and the pain already was beginning to travel up his arm into his wounded shoulder.

From within the gloom of the barrel, he could see only a small portion of the lab. He glimpsed two men in dark suits, who were peering in the far end of the gate. They very much resembled Gestapo agents – all of the bastards looked as if they'd been cloned from the same small group of degenerates and fanatics – and he was relieved to know that they could not see him as clearly as he could see them; for a moment at least they would think he was Kokoschka.

He moved forward, the noisily hissing canister of Vexxon held before him in his left hand, the pistol in his right hand, and before the men in the lab realized something was wrong, the nerve gas hit them. They dropped to the floor, below the elevated gate, and by the time Stefan stepped down into the laboratory, they were writhing in agony. They had vomited explosively. Blood was running from their nostrils. One of them was on his side, kicking his legs and clawing at his throat; the other was curled fetally on his side and, with fingers hooked like claws, was ripping horribly at his eyes. Near the gate-programming board three men in lab coats – Stefan knew them: Hoepner, Eicke, Schmauser – had collapsed. They tore at themselves as if mad or rabid. All five dying men were trying to scream, but their throats had swollen shut in an instant; they were able to make only faint, pathetic, chilling sounds like the mewling of small, tortured animals. Stefan stood among them, physically unaffected but appalled, horrified, and in thirty to forty seconds they were dead.

A cruel justice was served in the use of Vexxon against these men, for it had been Nazi-sponsored researchers who had synthesized the first nerve gas in 1936, an organo-phosphorous ester called tabun. Virtually all subsequent nerve gases – which killed by interfering with the transmission of electrical nerve impulses – had been related to that original chemical compound. Including Vexxon. These men in 1944 had been killed by a futuristic weapon, yet it was a substance that had its origins in their own twisted, death-centered society.

Nevertheless Stefan took no satisfaction from these five deaths. He had seen so much killing in his life that even the extermination of the guilty to protect the innocent, even murder in the service of justice, repulsed him. But he could do what he had to do.

He put the pistol on a lab bench. He shrugged the Uzi off his shoulder and put that aside as well.

From a pocket of his jeans, he withdrew a few inches of wire, which he used to lock open the trigger on the Vexxon. He stepped into the ground-floor corridor and put the canister in the center of that hallway. In a few minutes the gas would spread through the building by way of stairwells, elevator shafts, and ventilation ducts.

He was surprised to see that only the night lights illuminated the hallway and that the other labs on the ground floor appeared to be deserted. Leaving the gas to disperse, he returned to the gate-programming board in the main lab to learn the date and time to which Heinrich Kokoschka's homing device had brought him. It was eleven minutes past nine o'clock on the night of March 16.

This was a piece of singularly good luck. Stefan had expected to return to the institute at an hour when most of its staff – some of whom began work as early as six in the morning and some of whom stayed as late as eight o'clock – would be in residence. That would have meant as many as a hundred bodies scattered throughout the four-floor building; and when they were discovered, it would be known that only Stefan Krieger, using Kokoschka's belt and penetrating the institute from the future by way of the gate, could have been responsible. They would realize that he had not come back merely to kill as many of the staff as were on the premises, but that he had been up to something else, and they would launch a major investigation to discover the nature of his scheme and undo what damage he had done. But now . . . if the building was mostly empty, he might be able to dispose of the few bodies in a fashion that would cover his presence and direct all suspicion to these dead men.

After five minutes the Vexxon cylinder was empty. The gas had spread throughout the structure, with the exception of the two guard foyers at the front and back entrances, which did not share even ventilation ducts with the rest of the building. Stefan went from floor to floor, room to room, looking for more victims. The only bodies he found were those of the animals in the basement, the first time-travelers, and the sight of their pathetic corpses disturbed him as much or more than the five gassed men.

Stefan returned to the main lab, took five of the special belts from a white cabinet, and buckled the devices on the dead men, over their clothes. He quickly reprogrammed the gate to send the bodies roughly six billion years into the future. He had read somewhere that the sun would have gone nova or would have died in six billion years, and he wanted to dispose of the five men in a place where no one would exist to notice them or to use their belts to home in on the gate.

Dealing with the dead in that silent, deserted building was an eerie business. Repeatedly he froze, certain that he'd heard stealthy movement. A couple of times he even paused in his labors to go in search of the imagined sound but found nothing. Once he looked at one of the dead men behind him, half convinced that the lifeless thing had started to rise, that the soft scrape he'd heard had been its cool hand clawing for a grip on the machinery, as it tried to drag itself erect. That was when he realized how deeply disturbed he had been by bearing witness to so many deaths over so many years.

One by one he dragged the reeking corpses into the gate, shoved them along to the point of transmission, and heaved them across that energy field. Tumbling through the invisible doorway in time, they vanished. At an unimaginably distant point they would reappear – either on an earth long cold and dead, where not even one plant or insect lived, or in the airless and empty space where the planet had existed before being consumed by the exploding sun.

He was exceedingly careful not to venture across the transmission point. If he was suddenly transported to the vacuum of deep space, six billion years hence, he would be dead before he had a chance to press the button on his homing belt and return to the lab.

By the time he disposed of the five cadavers and cleaned up all traces of their messy deaths, he was weary. Fortunately the nerve gas left no apparent residue; there was no need to wipe down every surface in the institute. His wounded shoulder throbbed as badly as in the days immediately after he had been shot.

But at least he had cleverly covered his trail. In the morning it might appear as if Kokoschka, Hoepner, Eicke, Schmauser, and the two Gestapo agents had decided that the Third Reich was doomed and had defected to a future in which peace and plenty could be found.

He remembered the animals in the basement. If he left them in their cages, tests would be run to discover what had killed them, and perhaps the results would cast doubt on the theory that Kokoschka and the others had defected through the gate. Then once again the primary suspect would be Stefan Krieger. Better the animals should disappear. That would be a mystery, but it would not point directly toward the truth, as would the condition of their carcasses.

The hot, pounding pain in his shoulder became hotter, as he used clean lab coats for burial shrouds, bundling groups of animals together, tying them up with cord. Without belts he sent them six billion years into the future. He retrieved the empty nerve-gas canister from the hall and sent that to the far end of time as well.

At last he was ready to make the two crucial jaunts that he hoped would lead to the utter destruction of the institute and the certain defeat of Nazi Germany. Moving to the gate-programming board again, he took a folded sheet of paper from the hip pocket of his jeans; it contained the results of days of calculations that he and Laura had done on the IBM PC in the house in Palm Springs.

If he had been able to return from 1989 with enough explosives to reduce the institute to smoldering rubble, he would have done the job himself, right here, right now. However, in addition to the heavy canister of Vexxon, the rucksack filled with six books, the pistol, and the Uzi, he would have been unable to carry more than forty or fifty pounds of plastique, which was insufficient to the task.

The explosives he had planted in the attic and basement had been removed by Kokoschka a couple of days ago, of course, in local time. He might have come back from 1989 with a couple of cans of gasoline, might have attempted to burn the place to the ground; but many research documents were locked in fireproof file cabinets to which even he did not have access, and only a devastating explosion would split them open and expose their contents to flames.

He could no longer destroy the institute alone.

But he knew who could help him.

Referring to the numbers arrived at with the aid of the IBM PC, he reprogrammed the gate to take him three and a half days into the future from that night of March 16. Geographically, he would be arriving on British soil in the heart of the extensive underground shelters beneath the government offices overlooking St. James's Park by Storey's Gate, where bombproof offices and quarters for the prime minister and other officials had been constructed during the Blitz, and where the War Room was still located. Specifically, Stefan hoped to arrive in a particular conference room at 7.30 A.M., a jaunt of such precision that only the knowledge and computers available in 1989 could allow the complex calculations to determine the necessary time and space coordinates.

Carrying no weapons, taking with him only the rucksack full of books, he entered the gate, crossed the point of transmission, and materialized in the corner of a low-ceilinged conference room in the center of which stood a large table encircled by twelve chairs. Ten of the chairs were empty. Only two men were present. The first was a male secretary in a British army uniform, a pen in one hand and a pad of paper in the other. The second man, engaged in the dictation of an urgent message, was Winston Churchill.

· 16 ·

As he crouched against the Toyota, Klietmann decided they could not have been more inappropriately dressed for their mission if they had been made up as circus clowns. The surrounding desert was mostly white and beige, pale pink and peach, with little vegetation and only a few rock formations significant enough to provide cover. In their black suits, as they tried to circle and get behind the woman, they would be as visible as bugs on a wedding cake.

Hubatsch, who had been standing near the front of the Toyota, directing short barrages of automatic fire at the Buick, dropped down. 'She's gone to the front of the car with the boy, out of sight.'

'Local authorities will show up soon,' Bracher said, looking west toward state route 111, then southwest in the general direction of the patrol car they had blown off the road four miles back.

'Remove your coats,' Klietmann said, stripping out of his own. 'White shirts will blend with the landscape better. Bracher, you stay here, prevent the bitch from doubling back this way. Von Manstein and Hubatsch, try to circle around on the right side. Stay well apart and don't move from one point of cover until you've picked out the next. I'll go north and east, around on the left.'

'Do we kill her without trying to find out what Krieger is up to?' Bracher asked.

'Yes,' Klietmann said at once. 'She's too heavily armed to be taken alive.

Anyway, I'd bet my honor that Krieger will be coming back to them, returning here through the gate in a few minutes, and we'll be better able to deal with him when he arrives if we've already taken out the woman. Now go. *Go.*'

Hubatsch, followed a few seconds later by von Manstein, left the cover of the Toyota, staying low, moving fast, and heading south-southeast.

Lieutenant Klietmann went north from the Toyota, holding his submachine gun in one hand, running in a crouch, making for the meager cover of a sprawling mesquite bush upon which a few tumbleweeds had gotten hung up.

Laura rose slightly and peered around the front fender of the Buick just in time to see two men in white shirts and black trousers sprint away from the Toyota, heading east toward her but also angling to the south, obviously intending to circle behind her. She stood and squeezed off a short burst at the first man, who made for the cover of a tooth-like formation of rock, behind which he safely vanished.

At the sound of gunfire, the second man sprawled flat in a shallow depression that did not entirely conceal him, but the angle of fire and the distance made him a hard target. She did not intend to waste any more rounds.

Besides, even as she saw where the second man had gone to ground, a third gunman opened fire on her from behind the Toyota. Bullets cracked off the Buick, missing her by inches, and she was forced to drop down again.

Stefan would be back in just three or four minutes. Not long. Not long at all. But an eternity.

Chris was sitting with his back against the front bumper of the Buick, his knees drawn up against his chest, hugging himself, and shaking visibly.

'Hang on, kiddo,' she said.

He looked at her but said nothing. Through all the terrors they had endured in the past couple of weeks, she had not seen him look so dispirited. His face was pale and slack. He realized that this game of hide and seek had never been a game at all for anyone but him, that nothing *was* in fact as easy as in the movies, and this frightening perception brought to his gaze a bleak detachment that scared Laura.

'Hang on,' she repeated, then scrambled past him to the other front fender, on the driver's side, where she crouched to study the desert to the north of them.

She was worried that other men were circling her on that flank. She could not let them do that because then the Buick would be of no use as a barricade, and there would be no place to run except into the open desert, where they would kill her and Chris within fifty yards. The Buick was the only good cover around. She had to keep the Buick between her and them.

She could see no one out there on her north flank. The land was more uneven in that direction, with a few low spines of rock, a few drifts of white sand, and no doubt many man-size depressions in the desert floor that were not visible from her position, places where a stalker might even now be taking cover. But the only things that moved were three dry tumble-weeds; they rolled slowly, errat-ically, in the mild, inconstant breeze.

She slipped past Chris and returned to the other fender in time to see that the two men to the south were already on the move again. They were thirty yards south of her but only twenty yards in front of the Buick, closing with frightening speed. Though the leader was staying low and weaving as he ran, the follower was bolder; perhaps he thought Laura's attention would be focused on the front man.

She fooled him, stood up, leaned out from the Buick as far as she had to, using it for cover as best she could, and squeezed off a two-second burst. The gunman at the Toyota opened fire on her, giving his buddies cover, but she hit the second running man hard enough to lift him off his feet and pitch him through a bristling manzanita.

Though not dead, he was clearly out of action, for his screams were so shrill and agonized, there could be no doubt he was mortally wounded.

As she dropped down below the line of fire again, she found that she was grinning fiercely. She was intensely pleased by the pain and horror that the wounded man's screams conveyed. Her savage reaction, the primitive power of her thirst for blood and revenge, startled her, but she held fast to it because she sensed that she would be a better and more clever fighter while in the spell of that primal rage.

One down. Perhaps only two more to go.

And soon Stefan would be here. No matter how long his work required in 1944, Stefan would program the gate to bring him back here shortly after he had left. He would rejoin her – and enter the fight – in only two or three minutes.

• 17 •

The prime minister happened to be looking directly at Stefan when he materialized, but the man in uniform – a sergeant – became aware of him because of the discharge of electrical energy that accompanied his arrival. Thousands of bright snakes of blue-white light wriggled away from Stefan, as if his very flesh had generated them. Perhaps deep crashes of thunder and bolts of lightning shattered the sky in the world above these underground rooms, but some of the displaced energy of time travel was expended here, as well, in a sizzling display that brought the uniformed man straight to his feet in surprise and fear. The hissing serpents of electricity streaked across the floor, up the walls, coalesced briefly on the ceiling, then dissipated, leaving everyone unharmed; the only damage was to a large wall map of Europe, which had been seared in several places but not set aflame.

'Guards!' the sergeant shouted. He was unarmed but evidently quite sure that his cry would be heard and answered swiftly, for he repeated it only once and made no move toward the door. 'Guards!'

'Mr. Churchill, please,' Stefan said, ignoring the sergeant, 'I'm not here to do you any harm.'

The door flew open and two British soldiers entered the room, one holding a revolver, the other an automatic carbine.

Speaking hastily, afraid he was about to be shot, Stefan said, 'The future of the world depends on your hearing me out, sir, please.'

Throughout the excitement, the prime minister had remained seated in the armchair at the end of the table. Stefan believed that he had seen a brief flash of surprise and perhaps even a glimmer of fear on the great man's face, but he would not have bet on it. Now the prime minister looked as bemused and implacable as in every photograph that Stefan had ever seen of him. He raised one hand to the guards: 'Hold a moment.' When the sergeant began to protest, the prime minister said, 'If he had meant to kill me, certainly he would have done so already, on arrival.' To Stefan he said, 'And that was *some* entrance, sir. As dramatic as any that young Olivier has ever made.'

Stefan could not help but smile. He stepped out of the corner, but when he moved toward the table, he saw the guards stiffen, so he stopped and spoke from a distance. 'Sir, by the very manner that I've arrived here, you know I'm no ordinary messenger and that what I have to tell you must be . . . unusual. It's also highly sensitive, and you may not wish to have my information conveyed to any ears but yours.'

'If you expect us to leave you alone with the PM,' the sergeant said, 'you're . . . you're mad!'

'He may be mad,' the prime minister said, 'but he's got flair. You must admit that much, Sergeant. If the guards search him and find no weapons, I'll give the gentleman a bit of my time, as he asks.'

'But, sir, you don't know who he is. You don't know *what* he is. The way he exploded into—'

Churchill cut him off. 'I know how he arrived, Sergeant. And please remember that only you and I *do* know. I will expect you to remain as tight-lipped about what you've seen here as you would about any other bit of war information that might be considered classified.'

Chastened, the sergeant stood to one side and glowered at Stefan while the guards conducted a body search.

They found no weapons, only the books in the rucksack and a few papers in Stefan's pockets. They returned the papers and stacked the books in the middle of the long table, and Stefan was amused to see that they had not noticed the nature of the volumes they'd handled.

Reluctantly, carrying his pencil and dictation pad, the sergeant accompanied the guards out of the room, as the prime minister had instructed. When the door closed, Churchill motioned Stefan to the chair that the sergeant had vacated. They sat in silence a moment, regarding each other with interest. Then the prime minister pointed to a steaming pot that stood on a serving tray. 'Tea?'

———

Twenty minutes later, when Stefan had told only half of the condensed version of his story, the prime minister called for the sergeant in the corridor. 'We'll be here a while yet, Sergeant. I will have to delay the War Cabinet meeting by an hour, I'm afraid. Please see that everyone is informed – and with my apologies.'

Twenty-five minutes after *that*, Stefan finished.

The prime minister asked a few more questions – surprisingly few but well-thought and to the heart of the matter. Finally he sighed and said, 'It's terribly early for a cigar, I suppose, but I'm in the mood to have one. Will you join me?'

'No, thank you, sir.'

As he prepared the cigar for smoking, Churchill said, 'Aside from your spectacular entrance – which really proves nothing but the existence of a revolutionary means of travel, which might or might not be *time* travel – what evidence do you have to convince a reasonable man that the particulars of your story are true?'

Stefan had expected such a test and was prepared for it. 'Sir, because I have been to the future and read portions of your account of the war, I knew you would be in this room at this hour on this day. Furthermore I knew what you would be doing here in the hour before your meeting with the War Cabinet.'

Drawing on his cigar, the prime minister raised his eyebrows.

'You were dictating a message to General Alexander in Italy, expressing your concerns about the conduct of the battle for the town of Cassino, which has been dragging on at a terrible cost of life.'

Churchill remained inscrutable. He must have been surprised by Stefan's knowledge, but he would not provide encouragement even with a nod or a narrowing of his eyes.

Stefan needed no encouragement because he knew that what he said was correct. 'From the account of the war that you will eventually write, I memorized the opening of that message to General Alexander – which you had not even finished dictating to the sergeant when I arrived a short while ago: "I wish you would explain to me why this passage by Cassino Monastery Hill, etcetera, all on a front of two or three miles, is the only place which you must keep butting at." '

The prime minister drew on his cigar again, blew out smoke, and studied Stefan intensely. Their chairs were only a few feet apart, and being the object of Churchill's thoughtful scrutiny was more unnerving than Stefan would have expected.

At last the prime minister said, 'And you got that information from something I will write in the future?'

Stefan rose from his chair, retrieved the six thick books that the guards had taken from his rucksack – Houghton Mifflin Company's trade-paperback reprints published at $9.95 each – and spread them out on the end of the table in front of Winston Churchill. 'This, sir, is your six-volume history of the Second World War, which will stand as the definitive account of that conflict and be hailed as both a great work of history and literature.' He was going to add that those books were largely responsible for Churchill's being awarded the Nobel Prize for literature in 1953, but decided not to make that revelation. Life would be less interesting if robbed of such grand surprises.

The prime minister examined the covers of all six books, front and back, and permitted himself a smile when he read the three-line excerpt from the review that had appeared in the *Times Literary Supplement*. He opened one volume and swiftly riffled the pages, not pausing to read anything.

'They aren't elaborate forgeries,' Stefan assured him. 'If you will read any page at random, you'll recognize your own unique and unmistakable voice. You will—'

'I've no need to read them. I believe you, Stefan Krieger.' He pushed the books away and leaned back in his chair. 'And I believe I understand why you've come to me. You want me to arrange an aerial bombardment of Berlin, targeted tightly to the district in which this institute of yours is located.'

'Yes, Prime Minister, that's exactly right. It must be done before the scientists working at the institute have finished studying the material on nuclear weapons that's been brought back from the future, before they agree upon a means of introducing that information into the German scientific community at large – which they may do any day now. You must act before they come back from the future with something else that might turn the tide against the Allies. I'll give you the precise location of the institute. American and RAF bombers have been making both daylight and night runs on Berlin since the first of the year, after all—'

'There has been considerable uproar in Parliament about bombing cities, even enemy cities,' Churchill noted.

'Yes, but it's not as if Berlin can't be hit. Because of the narrowly defined target, of course, this mission will have to take place in daylight. But if you strike that district, if you utterly pulverize that block—'

'Several blocks on all sides of it would have to be reduced to rubble,' the prime minister said. 'We can't strike with sufficient accuracy to surgically remove the buildings on one block alone.'

'Yes, I understand. But you *must* order it, sir. More tons of explosives must be dropped on that district – and within the next few days – than will be dropped on any other scrap of land in the entire European theater at any time in the entire war. Nothing must be left of the institute but *dust*.'

The prime minister was silent for a minute or so, watching the thin, bluish plume of his cigar smoke, thinking. Finally: 'I'll need to consult with my advisers, of course, but I believe the earliest we could prepare and launch the bombardment would be two days hence, on the twenty-second, but perhaps as late as the twenty-third.'

'I think that'll be soon enough,' Stefan said with great relief. 'But no later. For God's sake, sir, no later.'

• 18 •

As the woman crouched by the driver's-side fender of the Buick and surveyed the desert to the north of her position, Klietmann was watching her from behind a tangle of mesquite and tumbleweed. She did not see him. When she moved to the other fender and turned her back to Klietmann, he got up at once and ran in a crouch toward the next bit of cover, a wind-scalloped knob of rock narrower than he was.

The lieutenant silently cursed the Bally loafers he was wearing, because the soles were too slippery for this kind of action. It now seemed foolish to have come on a mission of assassination dressed like young executives – or Baptist ministers. At least the Ray-Bans were useful. The bright sun glared off every stone and slope of drifted sand; without the sunglasses, he would not have been able to see the ground ahead of him as clearly as he could now, and he certainly would have put a foot wrong and fallen more than once.

He was about to dive for cover again when he heard the woman open fire in the other direction. With this proof that she was distracted, he kept going. Then he heard screaming so shrill and ululant that it hardly sounded like the screaming of a man; it was more like the cry of a wild animal gutted by another creature's claws but still alive.

Shaken, he took cover in a long, narrow basin of rock that was below the woman's line of sight. He crawled on his belly to the end of that trough and lay there, breathing hard. When he raised his head to bring his eyes up to the level of the surrounding ground, he saw that he was fifteen yards directly north of the Buick's rear door. If he could move just a few more yards east, he would be behind the woman, in the perfect position to cut her down.

The screaming faded.

Figuring that the other man to the south of her would lie low for a while because he would be spooked by the death of his partner, Laura shifted again to the other front fender. As she passed Chris, she said, 'Two minutes, baby. Two minutes at most.'

Crouching against the corner of the car, she surveyed their north flank. The desert out there still seemed untenanted. The breeze had died, and not even the tumbleweed moved.

If there were only three of them, they surely would not leave one man at the Toyota while the other two tried to circle her from the *same* direction. If there were only three, then the two on her south side would have split, one of them going north. Which meant there had to be a fourth man, perhaps even a fifth, out there in the shale and sand and desert scrub to the northwest of the Buick.

But where?

• 19 •

As Stefan expressed his gratitude to the prime minister and got up to leave, Churchill pointed to the books on the table and said, 'I wouldn't want you to forget those. If you left them behind – what a temptation to plagiarize myself!'

'It's a mark of your character,' Stefan said, 'that you haven't importuned me to leave them with you for that very purpose.'

'Nonsense.' Churchill put his cigar in an ashtray and rose from his chair. 'If I possessed those books now, all written, I'd not be content to have them published just as they are. Undoubtedly I would find things needing improvement, and I'd spend the years immediately after the war tinkering endlessly with them – only to find, upon completion and publication, that I had destroyed the very elements of them that in your future have made them classics.'

Stefan laughed.

'I'm quite serious,' Churchill said. 'You've told me that my history will be the definitive one. That's enough foreknowledge to suit me. I'll write them as I wrote them, so to speak, and not risk second-guessing myself.'

'Perhaps that's wise,' Stefan agreed.

As Stefan packed the six books in the rucksack, Churchill stood with his hands behind his back, rocking slightly on his feet. 'There are so many things I'd like to ask you about the future that I'm helping to shape. Things that are of more interest to me than whether I will write successful books or not.'

'I really must be going, sir, but –'

'I know, yes,' the prime minister said. 'I won't detain you. But tell me at least one thing. Curiosity's killing me. Let's see . . . well, for instance, what of the Soviets after the war?'

Stefan hesitated, closed the rucksack, and said, 'Prime Minister, I'm sorry to tell you that the Soviets will become far more powerful than Britain, rivaled only by the United States.'

Churchill looked surprised for the first time. 'That abominable system of theirs will actually produce economic success, abundance?'

'No, no. Their system will produce economic ruin – but tremendous military power. The Soviets will relentlessly militarize their entire society and eliminate all dissidents. Some say their concentration camps rival those of the Reich.'

The expression on the prime minister's face remained inscrutable, but he could not conceal the troubled look in his eyes. 'Yet they are allies of ours now.'

'Yes, sir. And without them perhaps the war against the Reich wouldn't have been won.'

'Oh, it would be won,' Churchill said confidently, 'Just not as quickly.' He sighed. 'They say politics makes strange bedfellows, but the alliances necessitated by war make stranger ones yet.'

Stefan was ready to depart.

They shook hands.

'Your institute shall be reduced to pebbles, splinters, dust, and ashes,' the prime minister said. 'You've my word on that.'

'That's all the assurance I need,' Stefan said.

He reached beneath his shirt and pushed three times on the button that activated the homing belt's link with the gate.

In what seemed like the same instant, he was in the institute in Berlin. He stepped out of the barrel-like gate and returned to the programming board. Exactly eleven minutes had elapsed on the clock since he had departed for those bombproof rooms below London.

His shoulder still ached, but the pain had not increased. The relentless throbbing, however, was gradually taking a toll on him, and he sat in the programmer's chair for a while, resting.

Then, using more numbers provided by the IBM computer in 1989, he programmed the gate for his next-to-last jaunt. This time he would go five days into the future, arriving at eleven o'clock at night, March 21, in other bombproof, underground quarters – not in London but in his own city of Berlin.

When the gate was ready, he entered it, taking no weapons. This time he did not take the six volumes of Churchill's history, either.

When he crossed the point of transmission inside the gate, the familiar unpleasant tingle passed inward from his skin, through his flesh, into his marrow, then instantly back out again from marrow to flesh to skin.

The windowless, subterranean room in which Stefan arrived was lit by a single lamp on the corner desk and briefly by the crackling light he brought with him. In that weird glow Hitler was clearly revealed.

• 20 •

One minute.

Laura huddled with Chris against the Buick. Without shifting her position she looked first toward the south where she knew one man was hiding, then to the north where she suspected that other enemies lay concealed.

A preternatural calm had befallen the desert. Windless, the day had no more breath than a corpse. The sun had shed so much of itself upon the arid plain that the land seemed as full of light as the sky; at the far edges of the world, the bright heavens blended into the bright earth with so little demarcation that the horizon effectively disappeared. Though the temperature was only in the high seventies, everything – every bush and rock and weed and sweep of sand – appeared to have been welded by the heat to the object beside it.

One minute.

Surely only a minute or less remained until Stefan would return from 1944, and somehow he would be of great help to them, not only because he had an Uzi but because he was her guardian. Her *guardian*. Although she understood his origins now and was aware that he was not supernatural, in some ways he remained for her a figure larger than life, capable of working wonders.

No movement to the south.

No movement to the north.

'They're coming,' Chris said.

'We'll be okay, honey,' she softly. However, her heart not only raced with fear but ached with a sense of loss, as if she knew on some primitive level that her son – the only child she could ever have, the child who had never been meant to live – was already dead, not because of her failure to protect him so much as because destiny would not be thwarted. No. Damn it, no. She would beat fate this time. She would hold on to her boy. She would not lose him as she had lost so many people she had loved over the years. He was hers. He did not belong to destiny. He did not belong to fate. He was hers. He was *hers*. 'We'll be okay, honey.'

Only half a minute now.

Suddenly she saw movement to the south.

• 21 •

In the private study of Hitler's Berlin bunker, the displaced energy of time travel hissed and squirmed away from Stefan in snakes of blazing light, tracing hundreds of serpentine paths across the floor and up the concrete walls, as it had done in the subterranean conference room in London. That bright and noisy phenomenon did not draw guards from other chambers, however, for at that moment Berlin was enduring another bombing by Allied planes; the bunker shook with the impact of blockbusters in the city far above, and even at that depth the thunder of the attack masked the particular sounds of Stefan's arrival.

Hitler turned in his swivel chair to face Stefan. He showed no more surprise than Churchill, though of course he knew about the work of the institute, as Churchill had not, and he understood at once how Stefan had materialized within these private quarters. Furthermore he knew Stefan both as the son of a loyal and early supporter and as an SS officer who had worked long for the cause.

Though Stefan had not expected to see surprise on Hitler's face, he had hoped to see those vulturine features twist with fear. After all, if *der Führer* had read Gestapo reports on recent events at the institute – which he had certainly done – he knew that Stefan stood accused of having killed Penlovski, Januskaya, and Volkaw six days ago, on March 15, fleeing thereafter into the future. He probably thought that Stefan had made this trip illicitly just six days ago, shortly before killing those scientists, and was going to kill him as well. Yet if he was frightened, he controlled his fear; remaining seated, he calmly opened a desk drawer and withdrew a Luger.

Even as the last of the electricity discharged, Stefan threw his arm forth in the Nazi salute, and said with all the false passion he could muster, 'Heil Hitler!' To prove quickly that his intentions were not hostile, he dropped to one knee, as if genuflecting before the altar of a church, and bowed his head, making of himself an easy and unresisting target. '*Mein Führer*, I come to you to clear my name and to alert you to the existence of traitors in the institute and in the Gestapo contingent responsible for the institute's security.'

For a long moment the dictator did not speak.

From far above, the shockwaves of the night bombardment passed through the earth, through twenty-foot-thick steel and concrete walls, and filled the bunker with a continuous, low, ominous sound. Each time that a blockbuster hit nearby, the three paintings – removed from the Louvre following the conquest of France – rattled against the walls, and on *der Führer*'s desk a hollow, vibrant sound rose from a tall copper pot filled with pencils.

'Get up, Stefan,' Hitler said. 'Sit there.' He indicated a maroon leather armchair, one of only five pieces of furniture in the cramped, windowless study. He put the Luger on his desk – but within easy reach. 'Not just for your honor but for your father's honor and that of the SS, as well, I hope you're as innocent as you claim.'

Stefan spoke forcefully because he knew Hitler greatly admired forcefulness. But at all times he also spoke with feigned reverence, as if he truly believed he was in the presence of the man in whom the very spirit of the German people, past and present and future, was embodied. Even more than forcefulness, Hitler was pleased by the awe in which certain of his subordinates held him. It was a thin line to tread, but this was not Stefan's first encounter with the man; he'd had some practice ingratiating himself with this megalomaniac, this viper cloaked in a human disguise.

'*Mein Führer*, it was not I who killed Vladimir Penlovski, Januskaya, and Volkaw. It was Kokoschka. He was a traitor to the Reich, and I caught him in the documents room at the institute just after he had shot Januskaya and Volkaw. He shot me there, as well.' Stefan put his right hand against the upper left side of his chest. 'I can show you the wound if you wish. Shot, I fled from him to the main lab. I was stunned, not sure how many in the institute were involved in his subversion. I didn't know to whom I could safely turn, so there was only one way to save myself – I fled through the gate to the future before Kokoschka could catch me and finish me off.'

'Colonel Kokoschka's report tells a quite different story. He said that he shot you *as* you fled through the gate, after *you* had killed Penlovski and the others.'

'If that were so, *Mein Führer*, would I have returned here to attempt to clear my name? If I were a traitor with more faith in the future than I have in you, would I not have stayed in that future, where I was safe, rather than return to you?'

'But were you safe there, Stefan?' Hitler said, and smiled slyly. 'As I understand, two Gestapo squads and later an SS squad were sent after you in that distant time.'

Stefan was jolted by the mention of an SS squad because he knew it must have been the group that arrived in Palm Springs less than an hour before he left, the group that had occasioned the lightning in the clear desert sky. He was suddenly more worried for Laura and Chris than he had been, because his respect for the dedication and murderous abilities of the SS was far greater than that with which he regarded the Gestapo.

He also realized Hitler had not been told that the Gestapo squads had been outgunned by a woman; he thought Stefan had gone up against them himself, not realizing that Stefan had been comatose throughout those encounters. That played into the lies that Stefan intended to tell, so he said, 'My *Führer*, I dealt with those men when they came after me, yes, and did so in good conscience because I knew they were all traitors to you, intent on killing me so that I would not be able to return to you and warn you of the nest of subversives who were – and still are – at work within the institute. Kokoschka has since vanished – am I correct? And so have five other men at the institute, as I understand. They had no faith in the future of the Reich, and fearing that their roles in the murders of March fifteenth would soon be revealed, they fled to the future, to hide in another era.'

Stefan paused to let what he had said sink in.

As the explosions far overhead subsided and a lull developed in the bombardment, Hitler studied him intently. This man's scrutiny was every bit as direct as that of Winston Churchill, but there was none of the clean, straightforward, man-to-man assessment in it that had marked the prime minister's attitude. Instead Hitler appraised Stefan from the perspective of a self-appointed god viewing one of his own creations for indications of a dangerous mutation. And this was a malign god who had no love for his creatures; he loved only the fact of their obedience.

At last *der Führer* said, 'If there are traitors at the institute, what is their goal?'

'To mislead you,' Stefan said. 'They are presenting you with false information about the future in hopes of encouraging you to make serious military blunders. They've told you that in the last year and a half of the war, virtually all of your military decisions will prove to be mistakes, but that's not true. As the future stands now, you will lose the war by only the thinnest of margins. With but a few changes in your strategies, you can *win*.'

Hitler's face hardened, and his eyes narrowed, not because he was suspicious of Stefan but because suddenly he was suspicious of all those at the institute who had told him he would make fatal military misjudgments in the days ahead. Stefan was encouraging him to believe again in his infallibility, and the madman was only too eager to trust once more in his genius.

'With a few *small* changes in my strategies?' Hitler asked. 'And what might those changes be?'

Stefan quickly summarized six alterations in military strategy that he claimed would be decisive in certain key battles to come; in fact those changes would make no difference to the outcome, and the battles of which he spoke were not to be the major engagements of the remainder of the war.

But *der Führer* wanted to believe that he had been very nearly a winner rather than a certain loser, and now he seized upon Stefan's advice as the truth, for it suggested bold strategies only slightly different from those the dictator would have endorsed himself. He rose from his chair and paced the small room in excitement. 'From the first reports presented to me by the institute, I've felt there was a *wrongness* in the future they portrayed. I sensed that I could not have managed this war as brilliantly as I have – then suddenly be plagued by such a long string of misjudgments. Oh, yes, we are in a dark period now, but this will not last. When the Allies launch their long-awaited invasion of Europe, they will fail; we will drive them back into the sea.' He spoke almost in a whisper, though with the mesmerizing passion so familiar from his many public speeches. 'In that failed assault they will have expended most of their reserves; they will have to retreat on a broad front, and they will not be able to regain their strength and mount a new offensive for many months. During that time we will strengthen our hold on Europe, defeat the Russian barbarians, and be stronger than we have ever been!' He stopped pacing, blinked as if rising from a self-induced trance, and said, 'Yes, what of the invasion of Europe? D-Day as I'm told it came to be called. Reports from the institute tell me that the Allies will land at Normandy.'

'Lies,' Stefan said. Now they had come to the issue that was the entire purpose behind Stefan's trip to this bunker on this night in March. Hitler had learned from the institute that the Beaches of Normandy would be the site of the invasion. In the future that fate had ordained for him, *der Führer* would misjudge the Allies and would prepare for a landing elsewhere, leaving Normandy inadequately defended. He must be encouraged to stick with the strategy that he would have followed had the institute never existed. He must lose the war as fate intended, and it was up to Stefan to undermine the influence of the institute and thereby assure the success of the Normandy invasion.

• 22 •

Klietmann had managed to ease a few more yards east, past the Buick, out-flanking the woman. He lay prone behind a low spine of white rock veined with pale blue quartz, waiting for Hubatsch to make a move on the south of her. When the woman was thus distracted, Klietmann would spring from conceal-ment and close on her, firing the Uzi as he ran. He would cut her to pieces before she even had a chance to turn and see the face of her executioner.

Come on, Sergeant, don't huddle out there like a cowardly Jew, Klietmann thought savagely. Show yourself. Draw her fire.

An instant later Hubatsch broke from cover, and the woman saw him run-ning. As she focused on Hubatsch, Klietmann leaped up from behind the quartz-veined rock.

Leaning forward in the leather armchair in the bunker, Stefan said, 'Lies, all lies, my *Führer*. This attempt to misdirect you toward Normandy is the key part of the plot by the subversives at the institute. They want to force you to make the sort of major mistake that you're not really destined to make. They want you to focus on Normandy, when the real invasion will come at—'

'Calais!' Hitler said.

'Yes.'

'I have believed it will be in the area of Calais, farther north than Normandy. They will cross the Channel where it's narrowest.'

'You're correct, my *Führer*,' Stefan said. 'Troops *will* be put ashore at Normandy on June seventh—'

Actually it would be June 6, but the weather would be so bad on the sixth that the German High Command would not believe the Allies capable of conducting the operation in such rough seas.

'—but that will be a minor force, a diversion, to pull your elite Panzer divisions to the Normandy coast while the real front subsequently opens near Calais.'

This information played to all of the dictator's prejudices and to his belief in his own infallibility. He returned to his chair and thumped his desk with one fist. '*This* has the feel of reality, Stefan. But . . . I have seen documents, selected pages from histories of the war that were brought back from the future—'

'Forgeries,' Stefan said, counting on the man's paranoia to make the lie seem plausible. 'Rather than show you the real documents from the future, they created forgeries to mislead you.'

With luck, Churchill's promised bombardment of the institute would take place tomorrow, eradicating the gate, everyone who knew how to re-create the gate, and every scrap of material that had been brought back from the future. Then *der Führer* would never have the opportunity to conduct a thorough investigation to test Stefan's truthfulness.

Hitler sat in silence for perhaps a minute, staring at the Luger on his desk, thinking intently.

Overhead the bombing began to escalate once more, rattling the paintings on the walls and the pencils in the copper pot.

Stefan waited anxiously to discover if he would be believed.

'How have you come to me?' Hitler asked. 'How could you use the gate now? I mean, it has been so closely guarded since the defection of Kokoschka and the other five.'

'I didn't come to you by way of the gate,' Stefan said. 'I came to you straight from the future, using only the time-travel belt.'

This was the boldest lie of all, for the belt was not a time machine, only a homing device that could do nothing but bring the wearer back to the institute. He was counting on the ignorance of politicians to save him: They knew a little bit about everything that was done under their rule, but there were no matters that they understood in depth. Hitler knew of the gate and of the nature of time travel, of course, but perhaps only in a general sense; he might lack knowledge of most of the details, such as how the belts actually functioned.

If Hitler realized that Stefan had come from the institute after returning there with Kokoschka's device, he would know that Kokoschka and the other five had been dispatched by Stefan and had not been defectors, after all, at which point the entire elaborate tale of conspiracy would collapse. And Stefan would be a dead man.

Frowning, the dictator said, 'You used the belt without the gate? Is that possible?'

Dry-mouthed with fear but speaking with conviction, Stefan said, 'Oh, yes, my *Führer*, it is quite simple to . . . adjust the belt and use it not merely to home in on the beacon of the gate but to skip through time as one wishes. And we are fortunate that such is the case, for otherwise, if I'd had to return to the gate to get here, I would have been stopped by the Jews who control it.'

'Jews?' Hitler said, startled.

'Yes, sir. The conspiracy within the institute is organized, I believe, by staff members who have Jewish blood but have concealed their heritage.'

The madman's face hardened further in a look of sudden anger. 'Jews. Always the same problem. Everywhere, the same problem. Now in the institute as well.'

Upon hearing that statement, Stefan knew that he had pushed the course of history back toward the proper path.

Destiny struggles to reassert the pattern that was meant to be.

• 24 •

Laura said, 'Chris, I think you better hide under the car.'

Even as she spoke, the gunman to the southwest of her rose from concealment and sprinted along the edge of the arroyo, angling toward her and toward the meager cover offered by another low dune.

She leaped to her feet, confident that the Buick would shelter her from the man at the Toyota, and opened fire. The first dozen rounds kicked up sand and chips of shale at the running man's heels, but then the bullets caught up with him, tearing into his legs. He went down, screaming, and was hit on the ground as well. He rolled twice and fell over the edge of the arroyo to the floor thirty feet below.

Even as the gunman slipped over the brink, Laura heard automatic fire, not from the Toyota but behind her. Before she could turn to meet the threat, she took several bullets in the back and was thrown forward, facedown on the hard shale.

• 25 •

'Jews,' Hitler said again, angrily. Then: 'What of this nuclear weapon that they say may win the war for us?'

'Another lie, my *Führer*. Though many attempts to develop such a weapon were made in the future, there were never any successes. This is a fantasy the conspirators have created to further misdirect the resources and energies of the Reich.'

A rumbling came through the walls, as if they were not underground but suspended high in the heavens, in a thunderstorm.

The heavy frames of the paintings thumped against the concrete.

The pencils jiggled in the copper pot.

Hitler met Stefan's eyes and studied him for a long time. Then: 'I suppose that if you were not loyal to me, you'd simply have come armed and would have killed me the instant you arrived.'

He had considered doing just that, for only in killing Adolf Hitler might he expunge some of the stain on his own soul. But that would have been a selfish act, for by killing Hitler he would have radically changed the course of history and would have put the future as he knew it at extreme risk. He could not forget that his future was also Laura's past; if he meddled sufficiently to change the series of events that fate ordained, perhaps he would change the world for the worse in general and for Laura in particular. What if he killed Hitler here and, upon returning to 1989, found a world so drastically altered that for some reason Laura had never even been born?

He wanted to kill this snake in human skin, but he could not take the responsibility for the world that might follow. Common sense said that only a better world could result, but he knew that common sense and fate were mutually exclusive concepts.

'Yes,' he said, 'had I been a traitor, my *Führer*, I could've done just that. And I worry that the *real* traitors at the institute may sooner or later think of just such a method of assassination.'

Hitler paled. 'Tomorrow, I shut the institute down. The gate will be closed until I know the staff is purged of traitors.'

Churchill's bombers may beat you to the punch, Stefan thought.

'We will win, Stefan, and we'll do so by retaining faith in our great destiny, not by playing fortune teller. We will win because it is our fate to win.'

'It's our destiny,' Stefan agreed. 'We're on the side of truth.'

Finally the madman smiled. Overcome by a sentimentality that was strange because of the extremely sudden change of mood, Hitler spoke of Stefan's father, Franz, and the early days in Munich: the secret meetings in Anton Drexler's apartment, the public meetings at the beer halls – the *Hofbräuhaus* and *Eberlbräu*.

Stefan listened for a while, pretending to be enthralled, but when Hitler expressed his continued and unshakable faith in the son of Franz Krieger, Stefan seized the opportunity to leave. 'And I, my *Führer*, have undying faith in you and will be, forever, your loyal disciple.' He stood, saluted the dictator, put one hand under his shirt to the button on the belt, and said, 'Now I must return to the future, for I've more work to do in your behalf.'

'Go?' Hitler said, rising from the desk chair. 'But I thought you'd stay now in your own time? Why go there now that you've cleared your name with me?'

'I think I may know where the traitor Kokoschka has gone, in what corner of the future he's taken refuge. I've got to find him, bring him back, for perhaps only Kokoschka knows the names of the traitors at the institute and can be made to reveal them.'

He saluted quickly, pushed the button on the belt, and left the bunker before Hitler could respond.

He returned to the institute on the night of March 16, the night that Kokoschka had set out for the San Bernardinos in pursuit of him, never to return. To the best of his ability, he had arranged for the destruction of the institute and had almost ensured Hitler's distrust of any information that came from it. He would have been exhilarated if he had not been so worried about the SS squad that apparently was stalking Laura in 1989.

At the programming board, he entered the computer-derived numbers for the last jaunt that he would ever make: to the desert outside of Palm Springs, where Laura and Chris waited for him on the morning of January 25, 1989.

• 26 •

Even as she fell to the ground, Laura knew that her spinal column had been severed or shattered by one of the bullets, for she felt no pain whatsoever – nor any sensation of any kind in any part of her body below the neck.

Destiny struggles to reassert the pattern that was meant to be.

The gunfire ceased.

She could move only her head, and only enough to turn and see Chris on his feet in front of the Buick, as paralyzed by terror as she was by the bullet that had cracked her spine. Beyond the boy, hurrying toward them from the north, only fifteen yards away, was a man in sunglasses, a white shirt, and black slacks, carrying a submachine gun.

'Chris,' she said thickly, 'run! *Run!*'

His face twisted with an expression of purest grief, as if he knew he was leaving her to die. Then he ran as fast as his small legs would carry him, east into the desert, and he was smart enough to weave back and forth as he ran, making as difficult a target of himself as possible.

Laura saw the killer raise the submachine gun.

In the main lab, Stefan opened the hinged panel that covered the automatic jaunt-recorder.

A spool of two-inch-wide paper indicated that tonight's uses of the gate had included a jaunt to January 10, 1988, which was the trip Heinrich Kokoschka had made to the San Bernardinos, when he had killed Danny Packard. The tape additionally recorded eight trips to the year A.D. 6,000,000,000 – the five men and three bundles of lab animals. Also noted were Stefan's own jaunts: to March 20, 1944, with the latitudes and longitudes of the bombproof underground facility near St. James's Park in London; to March 21, 1944, with the precise latitudes and longitudes of Hitler's bunker; and the destination of the jaunt that he had just programmed but not yet made – Palm Springs, January 25, 1989. He tore the tape, pocketed the evidence, and respooled the blank paper. He'd already set the programming-board clocks to clear themselves and reset to zero when he passed through the gate. They would know someone had tampered with the records, but they would think it had been Kokoschka and the other defectors covering their trail.

He closed the panel and strapped on the backpack that was filled with Churchill's books. He slipped the strap of the Uzi over his shoulder and picked up the silencer-fitted pistol from the lab bench.

He quickly scanned the room to see if he had left anything behind that might betray his presence here tonight. The IBM printouts were folded away in the pockets of his jeans again. The Vexxon cylinder had long ago been sent into a future where the sun was dead or dying. As far as he could see, he had overlooked nothing.

He stepped into the gate and approached the point of transmission with more hope than he had dared entertain in many years. He had been able to assure the destruction of the institute and the defeat of Nazi Germany through a series of Machiavellian manipulations of time and people, so surely he and Laura would be able to deal with that single squad of SS gunmen who were somewhere in Palm Springs in 1989.

Lying paralyzed upon the desert shale, Laura screamed, 'No!' The word came out as a whisper, for she didn't have the strength or lung power to make more of it.

The submachine gun opened fire on Chris, and for a moment she was sure that the boy was going to weave his way out of range, which was a last desperate fantasy, of course, because he was only a small boy, such a very small boy, with short legs, and he was well within range when the bullets found him, stitching a pattern across the center of his frail back, pitching him into the sand where he lay motionless in spreading blood.

All the unfelt pain of her ruined body would have been as a pinprick compared to the anguish that wrenched her at the sight of her little boy's lifeless body. Through all the tragedies of her life, she had known no pain to equal this. It was as if all the losses she had experienced – the mother she had never known, her sweet father, Nina Dockweiler, gentle Ruthie, and Danny, for whom she would gladly have sacrificed herself – were manifested again in this new brutality that fate insisted she endure, so she felt not only the shattering grief at Chris's death but felt anew the terrible agony of all the deaths that had come before it. She lay paralyzed and unfeeling but in torment, spiritually lacerated, at last emotionally broken on the hateful wheel of fate, no longer able to be brave, no longer able to hope or care. Her boy was dead. She had failed to save him, and with him all prospects of joy had died. She felt horribly alone in a cold and hostile universe, and all she hoped for now was death, emptiness, infinite nothingness, and at last an end to all loss and grief.

She saw the gunman approaching her.

She said, 'Kill me, please kill me, finish me,' but her voice was so faint that he probably did not hear her.

What had been the point of living? What had been the point of enduring all the tragedies that she had endured? Why had she suffered and gone on with life if it was all to end like this? What cruel consciousness lay behind the workings of the universe that it could even conceive of forcing her to struggle through a troubled life that turned out, in the end, to have no apparent meaning or purpose?

Christopher Robin was dead.

She felt hot tears spilling down her face, but that was all she could feel physically – that and the hardness of the shale against the right side of her face.

In a few steps the gunman reached her, stood over her, and kicked her in the side. She knew he kicked her, for she was looking back along her own immobile body and saw his foot land in her ribs, but she felt nothing whatsoever.

'Kill me,' she murmured.

She was suddenly terrified that destiny would try too faithfully to reassert the pattern that was meant to be, in which case she might be permitted to live but only in the wheelchair that Stefan had saved her from when he had meddled with the ordained circumstances of her birth. Chris was the child who had never been a part of destiny's plans, and now he had been scrubbed from existence. But she might not be erased, for it had been *her* destiny to live as a cripple. Now she had a vision of her future: alive, paraplegic or quadriplegic, confined to a wheelchair, but trapped in something else far worse – trapped in a life of tragedy, of bitter memories, of endless sorrow, of unendurable longing for her son, her husband, her father, and all the others she had lost.

'Oh, God, please, please kill me.'

Standing over her, the gunman smiled and said, 'Well, I must be God's messenger.' He laughed unpleasantly. 'Anyway, I'm answering your prayer.'

Lightning flashed and thunder crashed across the desert.

Thanks to the calculations performed on the computer, Stefan returned to the precise spot in the desert from which he had departed for 1944, exactly five minutes after he had left. The first thing he saw in the too-bright desert light was Laura's bloody body and the SS gunman standing over it. Then beyond them, he saw Chris.

The gunman reacted to the thunder and lightning. He began to turn in search of Stefan.

Stefan pushed the button on his homing belt three times. The air pressure instantly increased; the odor of hot electric wires and ozone filled the day.

The SS thug saw him, brought up the submachine gun, and opened fire, wide of him at first, then bringing the muzzle around to bear straight on him.

Before the bullets hit, Stefan popped out of 1989 and back to the institute on the night of March 16, 1944.

'Shit!' Klietmann said when Krieger slipped into the time stream and away, unhurt.

Bracher was running over from the Toyota, shouting, 'That was him! That was him!'

'I know it was him,' Klietmann said when Bracher arrived. 'Who else would it be – Christ on His second coming?'

'What's he up to?' Bracher said. 'What's he doing back there, where's he been, what's this all about?'

'I don't know,' Klietmann said irritably. He looked down at the badly wounded woman and said to her, 'All I know is that he saw you and your boy's dead body, and he didn't even make an attempt to kill me for what I'd done to you. He cut and ran to save his own skin. What do you think of your hero now?'

She only continued to beg for death.

Stepping back from the woman, Klietmann said, 'Bracher, get out of the way.'

Bracher moved, and Klietmann squeezed off a burst of perhaps ten or twenty rounds, all of which pierced the woman, killing her instantly.

'We could have questioned her,' Corporal Bracher said. 'About Krieger, about what he was doing here—'

'She was paralyzed,' Klietmann said impatiently. 'She could feel nothing. I kicked her in the side, must've broken half her ribs, and she didn't even cry out. You can't torture information from a woman who can feel no pain.'

March 16, 1944. The institute.

His heart hammering like a blacksmith's sledge, Stefan jumped down from the gate and ran to the programming board. He pulled the list of computer-derived numbers from his pocket and spread it out on the small programmer's desk that filled a niche in the machinery.

He sat in the chair, picked up a pencil, pulled a tablet from the drawer. His hands shook so badly that he dropped the pencil twice.

He already had the numbers that would put him in that desert five minutes after he had first left it. He could work backward from those figures and find a new set that would put him in the same place four minutes and fifty-five seconds earlier, only five seconds after he had originally left Laura and Chris.

If he was gone only five seconds, the SS assassins would not yet have killed her and the boy by the time Stefan returned. He would be able to add his fire-power to the fight, and perhaps that would be enough to change the outcome.

He had learned the necessary mathematics when first assigned to the institute in the autumn of 1943. He could do the calculations. The work was not impossible because he didn't have to begin from scratch; he had only to refine the computer's numbers, work backward a few minutes.

But he stared at the paper and could not *think* because Laura was dead and Chris was dead.

Without them he had nothing.

You can get them back, he told himself. Damn it, shape up. You can stop it before it happens.

He bent himself to the task, working for nearly an hour. He knew that no one was likely to come to the institute so late at night and discover him, but he repeatedly imagined that he heard footsteps in the ground-floor hall, the *click-click-click* of SS boots. Twice he looked toward the gate, half convinced he had heard the five dead men returning from A.D. 6,000,000,000, somehow revitalized and in search of him.

When he had the numbers and doubled-checked them, he entered them in the board. Carrying the submachine gun in one hand and the pistol in the other, he climbed into the gate and passed through the point of transmission—

—and returned to the institute.

He stood for a moment in the gate, surprised, confused. Then he stepped through the energy field again—

—and returned to the institute.

The explanation hit him with such force that he bent forward as if he actually had been punched in the stomach. He could *not* go back earlier now, for he had already showed up at that place five minutes after leaving it; if he went back now he would be creating a situation in which he would surely be there to see himself arrive the first time. Paradox! The mechanism of the cosmos would not permit a time traveler to encounter himself anywhere along the time stream; when such a jaunt was attempted, it invariably failed. Nature despised a paradox.

In memory he could hear Chris in the sleazy motel room where they had first discussed time travel: 'Paradox! Isn't this wild stuff, Mom? Isn't this wild? Isn't this great?' And the charming, excited, boyish laughter.

But there had to be a way.

He returned to the programming board, dropped the guns on the work desk, and sat down.

Sweat was pouring off his brow. He blotted his face on his shirt-sleeves.

Think.

He stared at the Uzi and wondered if he could send *that* back to her at least. Probably not. He had been carrying the machine gun and the pistol when he had returned to her the first time, so if he sent either of the guns back four minutes and fifty seconds earlier, they would exist twice in the same place when he showed up just four minutes and fifty seconds later. Paradox.

But maybe he could send her something else, something that came from this room, something he had not been carrying with him and that would not, therefore, create a paradox.

He pushed the guns aside, picked up a pencil, and wrote a brief message on a sheet of tablet paper: THE SS WILL KILL YOU AND CHRIS IF YOU STAY AT THE CAR. GET AWAY. HIDE. He paused, thinking. Where could they hide on that flat desert plain? He wrote: MAYBE IN THE ARROYO. He tore the sheet of paper from the tablet. Then as an after-thought he hastily added: THE SECOND CANISTER OF VEXXON. IT'S A WEAPON TOO.

He searched the drawers of the lab bench for a glass beaker with a narrow top, but there were no such vessels in that lab, where all of the research had been related to electromagnetism rather than to chemistry. He went down the hall, searching through other labs, until he found what he needed.

Back in the main lab, carrying the beaker with the note inside it, he entered the gate and approached the point of transmission. He threw the object through the energy field as if he were a man stranded on an island, throwing a bottled message into the sea.

It did not bounce back to him.

———

—but the brief vacuum was followed by a blustery inrush of hot wind tainted by the faintly alkaline smell of the desert.

Standing close at her side, holding fast to her, delighted by Stefan's magical departure, Chris said, 'Wow! Wasn't that something, Mom, wasn't that great?'

She did not answer because she noticed a white car driving off state route 111, onto the desert floor.

Lightning flared, thunder shook the day, startling her, and a glass bottle appeared in midair, fell at her feet, shattering on the shale, and she saw that there had been a paper inside.

Chris snatched the paper from among the shards of glass. With his usual aplomb in these matters, he said, 'It must be from Stefan!'

She took it from him, read the words, aware that the white car had turned toward them. She did not understand how and why this message had been sent, but she believed it implicitly. Even as she finished reading, with the lightning and thunder still flickering and rumbling through the sky, she heard the engine of the white car roar.

She looked up and saw the vehicle leap toward them as its driver accelerated. They were almost three hundred yards away, but were closing as fast as the rough desert terrain permitted.

'Chris, get both Uzis from the car and meet me at the edge of the arroyo. Hurry!'

As the boy sprinted to the open door of the nearby Buick, Laura raced to the open trunk. She grabbed the canister of Vexxon, lifted it out, and caught up with Chris before he had reached the brink of the deep, naturally carved water channel, which was a raging river during a flash flood but dry now.

The white car was less than a hundred and fifty yards away.

'Come on,' she said, leading him eastward along the brink, 'we've got to find a way down into the arroyo.'

The walls of the channel sloped slightly to the bottom thirty feet below, but only slightly. They were carved by erosion, filled with miniature vertical channels leading down to the main channel, some as narrow as a few inches, some as wide as three and four feet; during a rainstorm, water poured off the surface of the desert, down those gulleys to the floor of the arroyo, where it was carried away in great, surging torrents. In some of the downsloping drains the soil had washed away to reveal rocks here and there that would impede a swift descent, while others were partially blocked by hardy mesquite bushes that had taken root in the very wall of the arroyo.

Little more than a hundred yards away, the car strayed off the shale into sand that pulled at the tires and slowed it down.

When Laura had gone only twenty yards along the edge of the arroyo, she discovered a wide channel leading straight down to the floor of that dry river, unobstructed by rocks or mesquite. What lay before her was essentially a four-foot-wide, thirty-foot-long, water-smoothed, dirt slide.

She dropped the canister of Vexxon into that natural run, and it slipped down halfway before halting.

She took one of the Uzis from Chris, turned to the approaching car, which was now about seventy-five yards away, and opened fire. She saw bullets punch at least two holes in the windshield. The rest of the tempered glass instantly crazed.

The car – she could see now that it was a Toyota – spun out, turning a full three hundred and sixty degrees, then ninety degrees more, throwing up clouds of dust, tearing through a couple of still green tumbleweeds. It came to rest about forty yards from the Buick, sixty yards from her and Chris, the front end pointed north. Doors flew open on the far side. Laura knew the occupants were scrambling out of the car where she would not see them, staying low.

She took the other Uzi from Chris and said, 'Into the slide, kiddo. When you reach the canister of gas, push it ahead of you all the way to the bottom.'

He went down the wall of the arroyo, pulled most of the way by the force of gravity but having to scoot along a couple of times when friction stopped him. It was exactly the kind of daredevil stunt that would have raised a mother's ire under other circumstances, but now she cheered him on.

She pumped at least a hundred rounds into the Toyota, hoping to pierce the fuel tank and set off the gasoline with a bullet-made spark, roasting the bastards as they huddled against the far side. But she emptied the magazine without the desired result.

When she stopped shooting, they took a crack at her. She did not stay long enough to give them a target. With the second Uzi held before her in both hands, she sat on the edge of the arroyo and shoved off into the slide that Chris had already used. In seconds she was at the bottom.

Dry tumbleweeds had blown down to the floor of the gulch from the desert above. Gnarled driftwood, some time-grayed lumber washed from the distant ruins of an old desert shack, and a few stones littered the powder-soft soil that formed the bed of the arroyo. None of those things offered a place to hide or protection from the gunfire that would soon be directed down at them.

'Mom?' Chris said, meaning: What now?

The arroyo would have scores of tributaries spread out across the desert, and many of those tributaries would have tributaries of their own. The drainage network was like a maze. They could not hide in it forever, but perhaps by putting a few branches of the system between themselves and their pursuers, they would gain time to plan an ambush.

She said, 'Run, baby. Follow the main arroyo, take the first right-hand branch you come to, and wait there for me.'

'What're you going to do?'

'I'll wait for them to look over the edge up there,' she said, pointing to the top of the palisades, 'then pick them off if I can. Now go, go.'

He ran.

Leaving the canister of Vexxon in plain sight, Laura returned to the wall of the arroyo down which they'd slid. She went to a different vertical channel, however, one that was carved deeper into the wall, had less of a slope, and was half-blocked at its midpoint by a mesquite bush. She stood in the bottom of that deep hollow, confident that the bush overhead blocked their view of her from the desert above.

To the east, Chris vanished around a turn into a tributary of the main channel.

A moment later she heard voices. She waited, waited, giving them time to feel confident that both she and Chris were gone. Then she stepped out from the erosion channel in the arroyo wall, turned, and swept the top of the cliff with bullets.

Four men were there, peering down, and she killed the first two, but the third and fourth leaped backward, out of sight before the arc of fire reached them. One of the bodies lay at the top of the arroyo wall, one arm and leg over the brink. The other fell all the way to the floor of the channel, losing his sunglasses on the way.

March 16, 1944. The institute.

When the bottle with the message did not bounce back to him, Stefan was reasonably confident that it had reached Laura before she had been killed, only seconds after he had first departed for 1944.

Now he returned to the programmer's desk and set to work on the calculations that would return him to the desert a few minutes *after* his previous arrival there. He could make that trip because he would be arriving subsequent to his previous hasty departure, and there would be no possibility of encountering himself, no paradox.

Again the calculations were not terribly difficult because he needed only to work forward from the numbers that the IBM PC had provided him. Though he knew that the time he spent here was not passing in equal measure in the desert of 1989, he was eager to rejoin Laura nevertheless. Even if she had taken the advice of the message in the bottle, even if the future he had seen had been changed and she was still alive, she would have to deal with those SS gunmen, and she would need help.

In forty minutes he had the numbers that he required, and he reprogrammed the gate.

Again he opened the panel on the jaunt recorder and tore the evidence off that spool of paper.

Carrying the Uzi and the pistol, gritting his teeth as the dull throbbing in his half-healed shoulder grew worse, he entered the gate.

Lugging both the Vexxon canister and the Uzi, Laura joined Chris in the narrower tributary off the main channel, about sixty feet from the point at which they had descended into the system. Crouching at the corner formed by the two earth walls, she looked back into the primary arroyo from which she had come.

On the desert above, one of the surviving assassins shoved the dangling corpse off the brink, into the deep gulch, apparently to see if she was still immediately below them and if she would be tricked into opening fire. When there was no fire, the two survivors became bolder. One lay at the brink with a submachine gun, covering the other man while he slid down. Then the first gunman covered the second's descent.

When the second man joined the first, Laura stepped boldly around the corner and squeezed off a two-second burst. Both of her pursuers were so startled by her aggressiveness that they did not return fire but threw themselves toward the deep, vertical erosion channels in the arroyo wall, seeking shelter there as she had sheltered while waiting for the opportunity to shoot them off the top of the cliff. Only one of them made it to cover. She blew the other one away.

She stepped back around the corner, picked up the cylinder of nerve gas, and said to Chris, 'Come on. Let's hustle.'

As they ran along the tributary, seeking yet another branch in the maze, lightning and thunder split the blue sky above.

'Mr. Krieger!' Chris said.

He returned to the desert seven minutes after he had originally departed for his meetings with Churchill and Hitler in 1944, just *two* minutes after his initial return when he had seen Laura and Chris dead at the hands of SS gunmen. There were no bodies this time, just the Buick – and the bullet-riddled Toyota in a different position.

Daring to hope that his scheme had worked, Stefan hurried to the arroyo and ran along the brink, searching for someone, anyone, friend or foe. Before long he saw the three dead men on the floor of the channel, thirty feet below.

There would be a fourth. No SS squad would have been composed of only three men. Somewhere in the network of zigzagging arroyos that crossed the desert like a chain of jagged lightning bolts, Laura was still on the run from the last man.

In the arroyo wall Stefan found a vertical channel that appeared to have been used already; he stripped off his book-filled rucksack, slid to the bottom. On the way down, his back scraped against the earth, and hot pain flared in the partly healed exit wound. At the end of the slope, when he stood up, a wave of dizziness washed through him, and bile rose in his throat.

Somewhere in the maze to the east, automatic weapons chattered.

She halted just inside the mouth of a new tributary and signaled Chris to be quiet.

Breathing through her open mouth, she waited for the last killer to turn the corner into the channel that she had just left. Even in the soft soil his running footsteps were audible.

She leaned out to gun him down. But he was extremely cautious now; he entered low and at a dead run. When her gunfire alerted him to her position, he crossed the channel and hid against the same wall off which her new tributary opened, so she could get a clear shot at him only if she stepped out into the arroyo where he waited.

In fact she tried that, risking his fire, but when she squeezed off a two-second burst, it ended in less than a second. The Uzi spat out its last ten or twelve rounds, then failed her.

Klietmann heard her Uzi go empty. He looked out from the crevice in the arroyo wall where he was sheltering and saw her throw the gun down. She disappeared into the mouth of the tributary where she had been laying in wait for him.

He considered what he had seen in the Buick, up on the desert: a .38 revolver lying on the driver's seat. He assumed that she had not had time to grab it or, in her haste to get that curious canister from the trunk, had forgotten about the handgun.

She'd had two Uzis, both discarded now. Could she have had two handguns – and left only one in the car?

He thought not. Two automatic carbines made sense because they were useful at a distance and in a variety of circumstances. But unless she was an expert marksman, a handgun would be of little use except at close range, where six shots was about all she would need before she either dealt with her assailant or died at his hands. A second revolver would be superfluous.

Which meant that for self-defense she had – what? That canister? It had looked like nothing more than a chemical fire extinguisher.

He went after her.

The new tributary was narrower than the one before it, just as that one had been narrower than the main channel. It was twenty-five feet deep and only ten feet wide at the mouth, growing shallower and half that narrow as it cut a crooked path through the desert floor. In a hundred yards, it funneled to an end.

At the terminus, she looked for a way out. On two sides the cliffs were too steep, soft, and crumbly to be easily climbed, but the wall behind her sloped at a scalable angle and was studded with mesquite that offered handholds. She knew, however, that they would be only halfway up the slope when their pursuer found them; suspended on that high ground, they would make easy targets.

This was where she would have to make her last stand.

Cornered at the bottom of this big, natural ditch, she looked up at the rectangular patch of blue sky and thought they might have been at the bottom of an enormous grave in a cemetery where only giants were buried.

Destiny struggles to reassert the pattern that was meant to be.

She pushed Chris behind her, into the point of the dead-end arroyo. Ahead of her, she could see forty feet back the way they had come, along the five-foot-wide channel, to the point where it angled to the left. He would appear at that turn within a minute or two.

She dropped to her knees with the canister of Vexxon, intending to strip the safety wire off the manual trigger. But the wire was not merely looped and braided through the trigger; it was repeatedly wound and then sealed with solder. It could not be unwound; it had to be cut, and she had nothing with which to cut it.

Maybe a stone. A sharp-edged stone might wear through the wire if scraped across it often enough.

'Get me a stone,' she said urgently to the boy behind her. 'One with a rough, sharp edge.'

As he searched the soft, flood-carried soil that had washed down from the desert floor, looking for a suitable scrap of slate, she examined the automatic timer on the canister, which provided a second means of releasing the gas. It was a simple device: a rotating dial was calibrated in minutes; if you wanted to set the timer for twenty minutes, you twisted the dial until the 20 was lined up with the red mark on the dial frame; when you pushed the button in the center, the countdown began.

The problem was that the dial could be set for no fewer than five minutes. The gunman would reach them sooner than that.

Nevertheless she twisted the dial to 5 and pushed the button that started it ticking.

'Here, Mom,' Chris said, presenting her with a blade of slate that just might do the job.

Though the timer was ticking, she set to work, frantically sawing at the strong, twined wire that prevented manual release. Every few seconds she looked up to see if the assassin had found them, but the narrow arroyo ahead of them remained deserted.

———

Stefan followed the footprints in the soft soil that formed the bed of the arroyo. He had no idea how far behind them he might be. They had only a few minutes' head start, but they were probably moving faster than he was because the pain in his shoulder, exhaustion, and dizziness slowed him.

He had unscrewed the silencer from the pistol, thrown it away, and tucked the handgun under his belt. He carried the Uzi in both hands at the ready.

———

Klietmann had thrown away his Ray-Bans because the floor of the arroyo network was shadow-swaddled in many places, especially as they moved into narrower tributaries, where the walls closed in and left less of an opening above for sunlight to enter.

His Bally loafers filled with sand and provided no surer footing here than on the slate of the desert above. Finally he paused, kicked off the shoes, stripped off the socks, and proceeded barefoot, which was a great improvement.

He was not tracking the woman and the boy as swiftly as he would have liked, partly because of the shoes that he had discarded, but mainly because he kept a watch on his backside every step of the way. He had heard and seen the recent display of thunder and lightning; he knew Krieger must have returned. Most likely, as Klietmann stalked the woman and boy, Krieger was stalking him. He did not intend to be meat for *that* tiger.

———

On the timer two minutes had ticked off.

Laura had sawed almost as long at the wire, initially with the blade of slate that Chris had found, then with a second that he turned up when the first piece crumbled in her fingers. The government could not make a postage stamp that could be trusted to stay on an envelope, could not build a battle tank that was capable of crossing a river on every attempt, could not protect the environment or eliminate poverty, but it sure as hell knew how to procure indestructible wire; this stuff must be some wonder material which they had developed for the space shuttle and for which they'd eventually found more mundane uses; it was the wire God would use to guy the tilting pillars that held up the world.

Her fingers were raw, the second chip of slate was slick with her blood, and only half the strands of wire were cut when the barefoot man in black slacks and a white shirt rounded the bend in the narrow arroyo, forty feet away.

———

Klietmann edged forward warily, wondering why the hell she was struggling so frantically with the fire extinguisher. Did she really think a blast of chemical fog would disorient him and protect her from submachine-gun fire!

Or was the extinguisher not what it appeared to be? Since arriving in Palm Springs less than two hours ago, he had encountered several things that were not what they appeared to be. A red curb, for instance, did not mean EMER-GENCY PARKING, as he had thought, but NO PARKING AT ANY TIME. Who could know? And who could know for sure about this canister with which she was struggling?

She looked up at him, then went right back to work on the handle of the extinguisher.

Klietmann edged along the narrow arroyo, which was now not even wide enough for two men to walk abreast. He would not have gone any closer to her except that he could not see the boy. If she had tucked the boy in some crevice along the way, he would have to force her to reveal the child's whereabouts, for his orders were to kill them all – Krieger and the woman and the boy. He did not think the boy could be a danger to the Reich, but he was not one to question orders.

Stefan found a discarded pair of shoes and a tangled pair of black socks caked with sand. Earlier he had found a pair of sunglasses.

He had never before pursued a man who had undressed during a chase, and at first there seemed to be something funny about it. But then he thought of the world portrayed in the novels of Laura Shane, a world in which comedy and terror were intermingled, a world in which tragedy frequently struck in the middle of a laugh, and suddenly the discarded shoes and socks scared him *because* they were funny; he had the crazy idea that if he laughed, that would be the catalyst of Laura's and Chris's deaths.

And if they died this time, he would not be able to save them by going back in time and sending them another message sooner than the one he had sent in the bottle, for the remaining window for such a feat was only five seconds. Even with an IBM PC, he could not split a hair that fine.

In the silt, the prints of the barefoot man led away to the mouth of a tributary. Although the pain in Stefan's half-healed shoulder had wrung sweat from him and left him dizzy, he followed that trail as Robinson Crusoe had followed Friday but with more dread.

With growing despair Laura watched the Nazi assassin approach through the shadows along the earthen corridor. His Uzi was trained on her, but for some reason he did not immediately blow her away. She used that inexplicable period of grace to saw relentlessly at the safety wires on the trigger of the Vexxon canister.

Even in those circumstances she held on to hope, largely because of a line from one of her own novels that had come back to her just a moment ago: *In tragedy and despair, when an endless night seems to have fallen, hope can be found in the realization that the companion of night is not another night, that the companion of night is day, that darkness always gives way to light, and that death rules only half of creation, life the other half.*

Only twenty feet away now, the killer said, 'Where is the boy? The boy. Where is the boy?'

She felt Chris against her back, curled in the shadows between her and the wall of the cul-de-sac. She wondered if her body would protect him from the bullets and that if, after killing her, this man would leave without realizing that Chris lived in the dark niche at her back.

The timer on the cylinder clicked. Nerve gas erupted from the nozzle with the rich odor of apricots and the disgusting taste of lemon juice mixed with sour milk.

Klietmann could see nothing escaping the canister, but he could hear it: Like a hissing score of serpents.

An instant later he felt as if someone had shoved a hand through his mid-section, had seized his stomach in a viselike grip, and had torn that organ loose of him. He doubled over, vomiting explosively on the ground and on his bare feet. With a painful flash that seared the *backs* of his eyes, something seemed to burst in his sinuses, and blood gushed from his nose. As he fell to the floor of the arroyo, he reflexively triggered the Uzi; aware that he was dying and losing all control of himself in the process, he tried as a last effort of will to fall on his side, facing the woman, so the final burst from the submachine gun would take her with him.

Soon after Stefan entered the narrowest of all the tributaries, where the walls seemed to tilt in above him instead of sloping away toward the sky, as they had in the other channels, he heard a long rattle of submachine-gun fire, very near, and he hurried forward. He stumbled a lot and bounced off the earthen walls, but he followed the crooked corridor into the cul-de-sac, where he saw the SS officer dead of Vexxon poisoning.

Beyond that corpse, Laura sat splay-legged, with the canister of nerve gas between her thighs, her bloodied hands hooked around it. Her head hung down, her chin on her breast; she looked as limp and lifeless as a doll made of rags.

'Laura, no,' he said in a voice that he hardly recognized as his own. 'No, no.'

She raised her head and blinked at him, shuddered, and finally smiled weakly. Alive.

'Chris,' he said, stepping over the dead man. 'Where's Chris?'

She pushed the still hissing canister of nerve gas away from her and moved to one side.

Chris looked out from the dark niche behind her and said, 'Mr. Krieger, are you all right? You look like shit. Sorry, Mom, but he really does.'

For the first time in more than twenty years – or for the first time in more than *sixty-five* years if you wanted to count those over which he had jumped when he had come to live with Laura in her time – Stefan Krieger wept. He was surprised by his own tears, for he thought that his life under the Third Reich had left him incapable of weeping for anyone or anything ever again. More surprising still – these first tears in decades were tears of joy.

Seven

Ever After

• 1 •

More than an hour later, when the police moved north from the site of the machine-gun attack on the CHP patrolman along route 111, when they found the bullet-riddled Toyota and saw blood on the sand and shale near the brink of the arroyo, when they saw the discarded Uzi, and when they saw Laura and Chris struggling out of the channel near the Buick with the Nissan plates, they expected to find the immediate area littered with bodies, and they were not disappointed. The first three were at the bottom of the nearby gulch, and the fourth was in a distant tributary to which the exhausted woman directed them.

In the days that followed she appeared to cooperate fully with the local, state, and federal authorities – yet none of them was satisfied that she was telling the whole truth. The drug dealers who had killed her husband a year ago had finally sent hired killers after her, she said, for they had evidently been afraid that she would identify them. They had attacked with such force at her house near Big Bear and had been so relentless that she'd had to run, and she'd not gone to the police because she did not believe that the authorities could protect her and her son adequately. She had been on the move for fifteen days, ever since that submachine-gun assault on the night of January 10, the first anniversary of her husband's murder; in spite of every precaution she had taken, hitmen found her in Palm Springs, pursued her on route 111, forced her off the highway into the desert, and chased her on foot into the arroyos where she finally got the best of them.

That story – one woman wiping out four experienced hitmen, plus at least the one additional whose head had been found in the alley behind Brenkshaw's house – would have been unbelievable if she had not proved to be a superb marksman, the beneficiary of considerable martial-arts training, and the owner of an illegal arsenal the envy of some third-world countries. During interrogation to determine how she had obtained illegally modified Uzis and a nerve gas kept under lock and key by the army, she had said, 'I write novels. It's part of my job to do a lot of research. I've learned how to find out anything I want to know, how to obtain anything I need.' Then she gave them Fat Jack, and the raid on his Pizza Party Palace turned up everything she had said it would.

'I don't hold it against her,' Fat Jack told the press at his arraignment. 'She owes me nothing. None of us owes anybody nothing that we don't *want* to owe them. I'm an anarchist, I love broads like her. Besides, I won't go to prison. I'm too fat, I'd die, it'd be cruel and unusual punishment.'

She would not tell them the name of the man she had brought to Carter Brenkshaw's house in the early morning hours of January 11, the man whose bullet wounds the physician had treated. She would only say that he was a good friend who had been staying with her at the house near Big Bear when the hitmen had struck. He was, she insisted, an innocent bystander whose life would be wrecked if she involved him in this sordid affair, and she implied that he was a married man with whom she had been having an affair. He was recovering from the bullet wound quite well, and he had suffered enough.

The authorities pressed her hard on the issue of this nameless lover, but she would not budge, and they were limited in the pressures that they could apply to her, especially since she could afford the finest legal counsel in the country. They never believed the claim that the mystery man was her lover. Little investigation was required to learn that her husband, only one year deceased, had been unusually close to her and that she had not recovered from the loss of him sufficiently to convince anyone that she was able to conduct an affair in the shadow of Danny Packard's memory.

No, she could not explain why none of the dead hitmen carried identification or why they were all dressed identically, or why they had been without their own car and had been forced to steal one from two women at a church, or why they had panicked in downtown Palm Springs and killed a policeman there. The abdominal flesh on two of the bodies had borne the marks of what appeared to be tightly fitted trusses of some kind, yet neither had been wearing such a device, and she knew nothing of that, either. Who knew, she asked, what reasons men like that had for their antisocial actions? That was a mystery that the finest criminologists and sociologists could not adequately explain. And if all those experts could not begin to shed light on the deepest and truest reasons for such sociopathic behaviour, how could she be expected to provide an answer to the more mundane but also more bizarre mystery of the disappearing trusses? Confronted by the woman whose Toyota had been stolen and who claimed that the hitmen had been angels, Laura Shane listened with evident interest, even fascination, but subsequently inquired of the police if they were going to subject her to the cuckoo fantasies of every nut who took an interest in her case.

She was granite.

She was iron.

She was steel.

She could not be broken. The authorities hammered at her as relentlessly and with as much force as the god Thor had wielded his hammer Mjollnir but with no effect. After several days they were angry with her. After several weeks they were furious. After three months they loathed her and wanted to punish her for not shivering in awe of their power. In six months they were weary. In ten months they were bored. In a year they forced themselves to forget her.

In the meantime, of course, they had seen her son, Chris, as the weak link. They had not pounded at him as they had at her, choosing instead to use false affection, guile, trickery, and deceit to lure the boy into making the revelations that his mother refused to make. But when they questioned him about the missing, wounded man, he told them all about Indiana Jones and Luke Skywalker and Han Solo instead. When they tried to pry from him a few details about the events in the arroyos, he told them all about Sir Tommy Toad, servant of the queen, who rented quarters in his house. When they sought to elicit at least a hint of where his mother and he had hidden out – and what they had done – in the fourteen days between January 10 and 25, the boy said, 'I slept through it all, I was in a coma, I think I had malaria or maybe even Mars fever, see, and now I got amnesia like Wily Coyote got that one time when the Road Runner tricked him into dropping a boulder on his own head.' Eventually, frustrated with their inability to get the point, he said, 'This is *family* stuff, see. Don't you know about family stuff? I can only talk with my mom about this stuff, and it's nobody else's business. If you start talking family stuff with strangers, pretty soon where do you go when you want to go home?'

To complicate matters for the authorities, Laura Shane publicly apologized to everyone whose property she had appropriated or damaged during the course of her attempts to escape from the hired killers who had been sent after her. To the family whose Buick she had stolen, she gave a new Cadillac. To the man whose Nissan plates she had taken, she gave a new *Nissan*. In every case she made restitution to excess and won friends at every hand.

Her old books went back to press repeatedly, and some of them reappeared on paperback bestseller lists now, years after their original successes. Major film studios bid competitively for the few movie rights to her books that had remained unsold. Rumors, perhaps encouraged by her own agent but very likely true, circulated to the effect that publishers were standing six deep for a chance to pay her a record advance for her next novel.

• 2 •

During that year Stefan Krieger missed Laura and Chris terribly, but life at the Gaines's mansion in Beverly Hills was not a hardship. The accommodations were superb; the food was delicious; Jason enjoyed teaching him how film could be manipulated in his home editing studio; and Thelma was unfailingly amusing.

'Listen, Krieger,' she said one summer day by the pool. 'Maybe you would rather be with them, maybe you're getting tired of hiding here, but consider the alternative. You could be stuck back there in your own age, when there weren't plastic garbage bags, Pop Tarts, Day-Glo underwear, Thelma Ackerson movies, or reruns of *Gilligan's Island*. Count your blessings, that you should find yourself in this enlightened era.'

'It's just that . . .' He stared for a while at the spangles of sunlight on the chlorine-scented water. 'Well, I'm afraid that during this year of separation, I'm losing any slim chance I might have had to win her.'

'You can't win her, anyway, *Herr* Krieger. She's not a set of cereal containers raffled off at a Tupperware party. A woman like Laura can't be won. She decides when she wants to *give* herself, and that's that.'

'You're not very encouraging.'

'Being encouraging is not my job—'

'I know—'

'—my job—'

'—yes, yes—'

'—is comedy. Although with my devastating looks, I'd probably be just as successful as a traveling slut – at least in really remote logging camps.'

At Christmas Laura and Chris came to stay at the Gaines's house, and her gift to Stefan was a new identity. Although rather closely monitored by various authorities for the better part of the year, she had managed through surrogates to obtain a driver's license, social security card, credit cards, and a passport in the name of Steven Krieger.

She presented them to him on Christmas morning, wrapped in a box from Neiman-Marcus. 'All the documents are valid. In *Endless River*, two of my characters are on the run, in need of new identities—'

'Yes,' Stefan said, 'I read it. Three times.'

'The same book three times?' Jason said. They were all sitting around the Christmas tree, eating junk food and drinking cocoa, and Jason was in his cheeriest mood of the year. 'Laura, beware this man. He sounds like an obsessive-compulsive to me.'

'Well, of course,' Thelma said, 'to you Hollywood types, anyone who reads *any* book, even once, is viewed either as an intellectual giant or a psychopath. Now, Laura, how *did* you come up with all these convincing-looking, phony papers?'

'They're not phony,' Chris said. 'They're *real*.'

'That's right,' Laura said. 'The driver's license and everything else is supported by government files. In researching *Endless River*, I had to find out how you go about obtaining a new identity of high quality, and I found this interesting man in San Francisco who runs a veritable document industry from the basement beneath a topless nightclub—'

'It doesn't have a roof?' Chris asked.

Laura ruffled the boy's hair and said, 'Anyway, Stefan, if you look deeper into that box, you'll find a couple of bank books as well. I've opened accounts for you under your new identity at Security Pacific Bank and Great Western Savings.'

He was startled. 'I can't take money from you. I can't—'

'You save me from a wheelchair, repeatedly save my life, and I can't give you money if I feel like it? Thelma, what's wrong with him?'

'He's a man,' Thelma said.

'I guess that explains it.'

'Hairy, Neanderthalic,' Thelma said, 'perpetually half-crazed from excessive levels of testosterone, plagued by racial memories of the lost glory of mammoth-hunting expeditions – they're all alike.'

'Men,' Laura said.

'Men,' Thelma said.

To his surprise and almost against his will, Stefan Krieger felt some of the darkness fading from within him, and light began to find a pane through which to shine into his heart.

———

In late February of the next year, thirteen months after the events in the desert outside Palm Springs, Laura suggested that he come to stay with her and Chris at the house near Big Bear. He went the next day, driving there in the sleek new Russian sports car that he had bought with some of the money she had given him.

For the next seven months he slept in the guest room. Every night. He needed nothing more. Just being with them, day after day, being accepted by them, being included, was all the love he could handle for a while.

In mid-September, twenty months after he had appeared on her doorstep with a bullet hole in his chest, she asked him into her bed. Three nights later he found the courage to go.

• 3 •

The year that Chris was twelve, Jason and Thelma bought a getaway house in Monterey, overlooking the most beautiful coastline in the world, and they insisted that Laura, Stefan, and Chris visit them for the month of August, when they were both between film projects. The mornings on the Monterey peninsula were cool and foggy, the days warm and clear, the nights downright chilly in spite of the season, and that daily pattern of weather was invigorating.

On the second Friday of the month, Stefan and Chris went for a beach walk with Jason. On the rocks not far from shore, sea lions were sunning themselves and barking noisily. Tourists were parked bumper to bumper along the road that served the beach; they ventured onto the sand to take photographs of the sun-worshipping 'seals,' as they called them.

'Year by year,' Jason said, 'there're more foreign tourists. It's a regular invasion. And you notice – they're mostly either Japanese, Germans, or Russians. Less than half a century ago, we fought the greatest war in history against all three of them, and now they're all more prosperous than we are. Japanese electronics and cars, Russian cars and computers, German cars and quality machinery of all kinds . . . Honest to God, Stefan, I think Americans frequently treat old enemies better than they do old friends.'

Stefan paused to watch the sea lions that had drawn the interest of the tourists, and he thought of the mistake that he had made in his meeting with Winston Churchill.

But tell me at least one thing. Curiosity's killing me. Let's see . . . well, for instance, what of the Soviets after the war?

The old fox had spoken so casually, as if the question was one that had occurred to him by chance, as if he might as likely have asked whether the cut of men's suits would change in the future, when in fact his query had been calculated and the answer of intense interest to him. Operating on what Stefan had told him, Churchill had rallied the Western Allies to continue fighting in Europe after the Germans were defeated. Using the Soviets' land grab of Eastern Europe as an excuse to turn against them, the other Allies had fought the Russians, driving them back into their motherland and ultimately defeating them entirely; in fact, throughout the war with Germany, the Soviets had been propped up with weapons and supplies from the United States, and when that support was withdrawn they collapsed in a matter of months. After all, they had been exhausted after the war with their old ally, Hitler. Now the modern world was far different from what destiny had intended, and all because Stefan had answered Churchill's one question.

Unlike Jason or Thelma or Laura or Chris, Stefan was a man out of time, a man for whom this era was not his destined home; the years since the Great

Wars were his future, while those same years were in these people's past; therefore he recalled both the future that had once been and the future that had now come to pass in place of the old. They, however, could remember no different world but this one in which no great world powers were hostile toward one another, in which no huge nuclear arsenals awaited launch, in which democracy flourished even in Russia, in which there were plenty and peace.

Destiny struggles to reassert the pattern that was meant to be. But sometimes, happily, it fails.

Laura and Thelma remained in rocking chairs on the porch, watching their menfolk walk down to the sea and then north along the beach, out of sight.

'Are you happy with him, Shane?'

'He's a melancholy man.'

'But lovely.'

'He'll never be Danny.'

'But Danny is gone.'

Laura nodded. They rocked.

'He says I redeemed him,' Laura said.

'Like grocery coupons, you mean?'

Finally Laura said, 'I love him.'

'I know,' Thelma said.

'I never thought I would . . . again. I mean, love a man that way.'

'What way is that, Shane? Are you talking about some kinky new position? You're heading toward middle age, Shane; you'll be forty before too many moons, so isn't it time you reformed your libidinous ways?'

'You're incorrigible.'

'I try to be.'

'How about you, Thelma? Are you happy?'

Thelma patted her large belly. She was seven months pregnant. 'Very happy, Shane. Did I tell you – maybe twins?'

'You told me.'

'Twins,' Thelma said, as if the prospect awed her. 'Think how pleased Ruthie would be for me.'

Twins.

Destiny struggles to reassert the pattern that was meant to be, Laura thought. And sometimes, happily, it succeeds.

They sat for a while in companionable silence, breathing the healthful sea air, listening to the wind sough softly in the Monterey pines and cypress.

After a while Thelma said, 'Remember that day I came to your house in the mountains, and you were taking target practice in the backyard?'

'I remember.'

'Blasting away at those human silhouettes. Snarling, daring the world to tackle you, guns hidden everywhere. That day you told me you'd spent your life enduring what fate threw at you, but you were not just going to endure any more – you were going to fight to protect your own. You were very angry that day, Shane, and very bitter.'

'Yes.'

'Now, I know you're still an endurer. And I know you're still a fighter. The world is still full of death and tragedy. In spite of all that, somehow you just aren't bitter any more.'

'No.'

'Share the secret?'

'I've learned the third great lesson, that's all. As a kid I learned to endure. After Danny was killed, I learned to fight. Now I'm still an endurer and a fighter – but I've also learned to accept. Fate *is*.'

'Sounds very Eastern-mystic-transcendental-bull-shit, Shane. Jeez. "Fate *is*." Next you'll be telling me to chant a mantra and contemplate my navel.'

'Stuffed with twins, as you are,' Laura said, 'you can't even see your navel.'

'Oh, yes, I can – with just the right arrangement of mirrors.'

Laura laughed. 'I love you, Thelma.'

'I love you, Sis.'

They rocked and rocked.

Down on the shore, the tide was coming in.

MIDNIGHT

To Ed and Pat Thomas
of the Book Carnival,
who are such nice people
that sometimes I suspect
they're not really human
but aliens from
another, better world.

PART ONE

ALONG THE NIGHT COAST

*Where eerie figures caper
to some midnight music
that only they can hear.*

THE BOOK OF COUNTED SORROWS

Janice Capshaw liked to run at night.

Nearly every evening between ten and eleven o'clock, Janice put on her gray sweats with the reflective blue stripes across the back and chest, tucked her hair under a headband, laced up her New Balance shoes, and ran six miles. She was thirty-five but could have passed for twenty-five, and she attributed her glow of youth to her twenty-year-long commitment to running.

Sunday night, September 21, she left her house at ten o'clock and ran four blocks north to Ocean Avenue, the main street through Moonlight Cove, where she turned left and headed downhill toward the public beach. The shops were closed and dark. Aside from the faded-brass glow of the sodium-vapor street-lamps, the only lights were in some apartments above the stores, at Knight's Bridge Tavern, and at Our Lady of Mercy Catholic Church, which was open twenty-four hours a day. No cars were on the street, and not another person was in sight. Moonlight Cove always had been a quiet little town, shunning the tourist trade that other coastal communities so avidly pursued. Janice liked the slow, measured pace of life there, though sometimes lately the town seemed not merely sleepy but dead.

As she ran down the sloping main street, through pools of amber light, through layered night shadows cast by wind-sculpted cypresses and pines, she saw no movement other than her own – and the sluggish, serpentine advance of the thin fog through the windless air. The only sounds were the soft *slap-slap* of her rubber-soled running shoes on the sidewalk and her labored breathing. From all available evidence, she might have been the last person on earth, engaged upon a solitary post-Armageddon marathon.

She disliked getting up at dawn to run before work, and in the summer it was more pleasant to put in her six miles when the heat of the day had passed, though neither an abhorrence of early hours nor the heat was the real reason for her nocturnal preference; she ran on the same schedule in the winter. She exercised at that hour simply because she liked the night.

Even as a child, she had preferred night to day, had enjoyed sitting out in the yard after sunset, under the star-speckled sky, listening to frogs and crickets. Darkness soothed. It softened the sharp edges of the world, toned down the too-harsh colors. With the coming of twilight, the sky seemed to recede; the universe expanded. The night was *bigger* than the day, and in its realm, life seemed to have more possibilities.

Now she reached the Ocean Avenue loop at the foot of the hill, sprinted across the parking area and onto the beach. Above the thin fog, the sky held only scattered clouds, and the full moon's silver-yellow radiance penetrated the mist, providing sufficient illumination for her to see where she was going. Some nights the fog was too thick and the sky too overcast to permit running on the shore. But now the white foam of the incoming breakers surged out of the black sea in ghostly phosphorescent ranks, and the wide crescent of sand gleamed palely between the lapping tide and the coastal hills, and the mist itself was softly aglow with reflections of the autumn moonlight.

As she ran across the beach to the firmer, damp sand at the water's edge and turned south, intending to run a mile out to the point of the cove, Janice felt wonderfully alive.

Richard – her late husband, who had succumbed to cancer three years ago – had said that her circadian rhythms were so post-midnight focused that she was more than just a night person. 'You'd probably love being a vampire, living between sunset and dawn,' he'd said, and she'd said, 'I vant to suck your blood.' God, she had loved him. Initially she worried that the life of a Lutheran minister's wife would be boring, but it never was, not for a moment. Three years after his death, she still missed him every day – and even more at night. He had been—

Suddenly, as she was passing a pair of forty-foot, twisted cypresses that had grown in the middle of the beach, halfway between the hills and the waterline, Janice was sure that she was not alone in the night and fog. She saw no movement, and she was unaware of any sound other than her own footsteps, raspy breathing, and thudding heartbeat; only instinct told her that she had company.

She was not alarmed at first, for she thought another runner was sharing the beach. A few local fitness fanatics occasionally ran at night, not by choice, as was the case with her, but of necessity. Two or three times a month she encountered them along her route.

But when she stopped and turned and looked back the way she had come, she saw only a deserted expanse of moonlit sand, a curved ribbon of luminously foaming surf, and the dim but familiar shapes of rock formations and scattered trees that thrust up here and there along the strand. The only sound was the low rumble of the breakers.

Figuring that her instinct was unreliable and that she was alone, she headed south again, along the beach, quickly finding her rhythm. She went only fifty yards, however, before she saw movement from the corner of her eye, thirty feet to her left: a swift shape, cloaked by night and mist, darting from behind a sandbound cypress to a weather-polished rock formation, where it slipped out of sight again.

Janice halted and, squinting toward the rocks, wondered what she had glimpsed. It had seemed larger than a dog, perhaps as big as a man, but having seen it only peripherally, she had absorbed no details. The formation – twenty feet long, as low as four feet in some places and as high as ten feet in others – had been shaped by wind and rain until it resembled a mound of half-melted wax, more than large enough to conceal whatever she had seen.

'Someone there?' she asked.

She expected no answer and got none.

She was uneasy but not afraid. If she had seen something more than a trick of fog and moonlight, it surely had been an animal – and not a dog because a dog would have come straight to her and would not have been so secretive. As there were no natural predators along the coast worthy of her fear, she was curious rather than frightened.

Standing still, sheathed in a film of sweat, she began to feel the chill in the air.

To maintain high body heat, she ran in place, watching the rocks, expecting to see an animal break from that cover and sprint either north or south along the beach.

Some people in the area kept horses, and the Fosters even ran a breeding and boarding facility near the sea about two and a half miles from there, beyond the northern flank of the cove. Perhaps one of their charges had gotten loose. The thing she'd seen from the corner of her eye had not been as big as a horse, though it might have been a pony. On the other hand, wouldn't she have heard a pony's thudding hoofbeats even in the soft sand? Of course, if it was one of the Fosters' horses – or someone else's – she ought to attempt to recover it or at least let them know where it could be found.

At last, when nothing moved, she ran to the rocks and circled them. Against the base of the formation and within the clefts in the stone were a few velvet-smooth shadows, but for the most part all was revealed in the milky, shimmering, lunar glow, and no animal was concealed there.

She never gave serious thought to the possibility that she had seen someone other than another runner or an animal, that she was in real danger. Aside from an occasional act of vandalism or burglary – which was always the work of one of a handful of disaffected teenagers – and traffic accidents, local police had little to occupy them. Crimes against person – rape, assault, murder – were rare in a town as small and tightly knit as Moonlight Cove; it was almost as if, in this pocket of the coast, they were living in a different and more benign age from that in which the rest of California dwelt.

Rounding the formation and returning to the firmer sand near the roiling surf, Janice decided that she had been snookered by moonlight and mist, two adept deceivers. The movement had been imaginary; she was alone on the shore.

She noted that the fog was rapidly thickening, but she continued along the crescent beach toward the cove's southern point. She was certain that she would get there and be able to return to the foot of Ocean Avenue before visibility declined too drastically.

A breeze sprang up from the sea and churned the incoming fog, which seemed to solidify from a gauzy vapor into a white sludge, as if it were milk being transformed into butter. By the time Janice reached the southern end of the dwindling strand, the breeze was stiffening and the surf was more agitated as well, casting up sheets of spray as each wave hit the piled rocks of the man-made breakwater that had been added to the natural point of the cove.

Someone stood on that twenty-foot high wall of boulders, looking down at her. Janice glanced up just as a cloak of mist shifted and moonlight silhouetted him.

Now fear seized her.

Though the stranger was directly in front of her, she could not see his face in the gloom. He seemed tall, well over six feet, though that could have been a trick of perspective.

Other than his outline, only his eyes were visible, and they were what ignited her fear. They were a softly radiant amber like the eyes of an animal revealed in headlight beams.

For a moment, peering directly up at him, she was transfixed by his gaze. Backlit by the moon, looming above her, standing tall and motionless upon ramparts of rock, with sea spray exploding to the right of him, he might have been a carved stone idol with luminous jewel eyes, erected by some demon-worshiping cult in a dark age long passed. Janice wanted to turn and run, but she could not move, was rooted to the sand, in the grip of that paralytic terror she had previously felt only in nightmares.

She wondered if she was awake. Perhaps her late-night run was indeed part of a nightmare, and perhaps she was actually asleep in bed, safe beneath warm blankets.

Then the man made a queer low growl, partly a snarl of anger but also a hiss, partly a hot and urgent cry of need but also cold, cold.

And he moved.

He dropped to all fours and began to descend the high breakwater, not as an ordinary man would climb down those jumbled rocks but with catlike swiftness and grace. In seconds he would be upon her.

Janice broke her paralysis, turned back on her own tracks, and ran toward the entrance to the public beach – a full mile away. Houses with lighted windows stood atop the steep-walled bluff that overlooked the cove, and some of them had steps leading down to the beach, but she was not confident of finding those stairs in the darkness. She did not waste any energy on a scream, for she doubted anyone would hear her. Besides, if screaming slowed her down, even only slightly, she might be overtaken and silenced before anyone from town could respond to her cries.

Her twenty-year commitment to running had never been more important than it was now; the issue was no longer good health but, she sensed, her very survival. She tucked her arms close to her sides, lowered her head, and sprinted, going for speed rather than endurance, because she felt that she only needed to get to the lower block of Ocean Avenue to be safe. She did not believe the man – or whatever the hell he was – would continue to pursue her into that lamplit and populated street.

High-altitude, striated clouds rushed across a portion of the lunar face. The moonlight dimmed, brightened, dimmed, and brightened in an irregular rhythm, pulsing through the rapidly clotting fog in such a way as to create a host of phantoms that repeatedly startled her and appeared to be keeping pace with her on all sides. The eerie, palpitant light contributed to the dreamlike quality of the chase, and she was half convinced that she was really in bed, fast asleep, but she did not halt or look over her shoulder because, dream or not, the man with the amber eyes was still behind her.

She had covered half the strand between the point of the cove and Ocean Avenue, her confidence growing with each step, when she realized that two of the phantoms in the fog were not phantoms after all. One was about twenty feet to her right and ran erect like a man; the other was on her left, less than fifteen feet away, splashing through the edge of the foam-laced sea, loping on all fours, the size of a man but certainly not a man, for no man could be so fleet and graceful in the posture of a dog. She had only a general impression of their shape and size, and she could not see their faces or any details of them other than their oddly luminous eyes.

Somehow she knew that neither of these pursuers was the man she had seen on the breakwater. He was behind her, either running erect or loping on all fours. She was nearly encircled.

Janice made no attempt to imagine who or what they might be. Analysis of this weird experience would have to wait for later; now she simply accepted the existence of the impossible, for as the widow of a preacher and a deeply spiritual woman, she had the flexibility to bend with the unknown and unearthly when confronted by it.

Powered by the fear that had formerly paralyzed her, she picked up her pace. But so did her pursuers.

She heard a peculiar whimpering and only slowly realized that she was listening to her own tortured voice.

Evidently excited by her terror, the phantom forms around her began to keen. Their voices rose and fell, fluctuating between a shrill, protracted bleat and a guttural gnarl. Worst of all, punctuating those ululant cries were bursts of words, too, spoken raspily, urgently: 'Get the bitch, get the bitch, get the bitch . . .'

What in God's name *were* they? Not men, surely, yet they could stand like men and speak like men, so what else could they *be* but men?

Janice felt her heart swelling in her breast, pounding hard.

'Get the bitch . . .'

The mysterious figures flanking her began to draw closer, and she tried to put on more speed to pull ahead of them, but they could not be shaken. They continued to narrow the gap. She could see them peripherally but did not dare look at them directly because she was afraid that the sight of them would be so shocking that she would be paralyzed again and, frozen by horror, would be brought down.

She was brought down anyway. Something leaped upon her from behind. She fell, a great weight pinning her, and all three creatures swarmed over her, touching her, plucking and tugging at her clothes.

Clouds slipped across most of the moon this time, and shadows fell in as if they were swatches of a black cloth sky.

Janice's face was pressed hard into the damp sand, but her head was turned to one side, so her mouth was free, and she screamed at last, though it was not much of a scream because she was breathless. She thrashed, kicked, flailed with her hands, desperately trying to strike them, but hitting mostly air and sand.

She could see nothing now, for the moon was completely lost.

She heard fabric tearing. The man astride her tore off her Nike jacket, ripped it to pieces, gouging her flesh in the process. She felt the hot touch of a hand, which seemed rough but human.

His weight briefly lifted from her, and she wriggled forward, trying to get away, but they pounced and crushed her into the sand. This time she was at the surf line, her face in the water.

Alternately keening, panting like dogs, hissing and snarling, her attackers loosed frantic bursts of words as they grabbed at her:

'. . . get her, get her, get, get, get . . .'

'. . . want, want, want it, want it . . .'

'. . . now, now, quick, now, quick, quick, quick . . .'

They were pulling at her sweat pants, trying to strip her, but she wasn't sure if they wanted to rape or devour her; perhaps neither; what they wanted was, in fact, beyond her comprehension. She just knew they were overcome by some tremendously powerful urge, for the chilly air was as thick with their *need* as with fog and darkness.

One of them pushed her face deeper into the wet sand, and the water was all around her now, only inches deep but enough to drown her, and they wouldn't let her breathe. She knew she was going to die, she was pinned now and helpless, going to die, and all because she liked to run at night.

• 2 •

On Monday, October 13, twenty-two days after the death of Janice Capshaw, Sam Booker drove his rental car from the San Francisco International Airport to Moonlight Cove. During the trip, he played a grim yet darkly amusing game with himself, making a mental list of reasons to go on living. Although he was on the road for more than an hour and a half, he could think of only four things: Guinness Stout, really good Mexican food, Goldie Hawn, and fear of death.

That thick, dark, Irish brew never failed to please him and to provide a brief surcease from the sorrows of the world. Restaurants consistently serving first-rate Mexican food were more difficult to locate than Guinness; its solace was therefore more elusive. Sam had long been in love with Goldie Hawn – or the screen image she projected – because she was beautiful *and* cute, earthy and intelligent, and seemed to find life so much damn fun. His chances of meeting Goldie Hawn were about a million times worse than finding a great Mexican restaurant in a northern California coastal town like Moonlight Cove, so he was glad that she was not the *only* reason he had for living.

As he drew nearer his destination, tall pines and cypresses crowded Highway 1, forming a gray-green tunnel, casting long shadows in the late-afternoon light. The day was cloudless yet strangely forbidding; the sky was pale blue, bleak in spite of its crystalline clarity, unlike the tropical blue to which he was accustomed in Los Angeles. Though the temperature was in the fifties, hard sunshine, like glare bouncing off a field of ice, seemed to freeze the colors of the landscape and dull them with a haze of imitation frost.

Fear of death. That was the best reason on his list. Though he was just forty-two years old – five feet eleven, a hundred and seventy pounds, and currently healthy – Sam Booker had skated along the edge of death six times, had peered into the waters below, and had not found the plunge inviting.

A road sign appeared on the right side of the highway: OCEAN AVENUE, MOONLIGHT COVE, 2 MILES.

Sam was not afraid of the pain of dying, for that would pass in a flicker. Neither was he afraid of leaving his life unfinished; for several years he had harbored no goals or hopes or dreams, so there was nothing to finish, no purpose or meaning. But he *was* afraid of what lay beyond life.

Five years ago, more dead than alive on an operating-room table, he had undergone a near-death experience. While surgeons worked frantically to save him, he had risen out of his body and, from the ceiling, looked down on his carcass and the medical team surrounding it. Then suddenly he'd found himself rushing through a tunnel, toward dazzling light, toward the Other Side: the entire near-death cliché that was a staple of sensationalistic supermarket tabloids. At the penultimate moment, the skillful physicians had pulled him back into the land of the living, but not before he had been afforded a glimpse of what lay beyond the mouth of that tunnel. What he'd seen had scared the crap out of him. Life, though often cruel, was preferable to confronting what he now suspected lay beyond it.

He reached the Ocean Avenue exit. At the bottom of the ramp, as Ocean Avenue turned west, under Pacific Coast Highway, another sign read: MOONLIGHT COVE ½ MILE.

A few houses were tucked in the purple gloom among the trees on both sides of the two-lane blacktop; their windows glowed with soft yellow light even an hour before nightfall. Some were of that half-timbered, deep-eaved, Bavarian architecture that a few builders, in the 1940s and '50s, had mistakenly believed was in harmony with the northern California coast. Others were Monterey-style bungalows with white clapboard or shingle-covered walls, cedar-shingled roofs, and rich – if fairy tale rococo – architectural details. Since Moonlight Cove had enjoyed much of its growth in the past ten years, a large number of houses were sleek, modern, many-windowed structures that looked like ships tossed up on some unimaginably high tide, stranded now on these hillsides above the sea.

When Sam followed Ocean Avenue into the six-block-long commercial district, a peculiar sense of *wrongness* immediately overcame him. Shops, restaurants, taverns, a market, two churches, the town library, a movie theater, and other unremarkable establishments lined the main drag, which sloped down toward the ocean, but to Sam's eyes there was an indefinable though powerful strangeness about the community that gave him a chill.

He could not identify the reasons for his instant negative reaction to the place, though perhaps it was related to the somber interplay of light and shadow. At this dying end of the autumn day, in the cheerless sunlight, the gray stone Catholic church looked like an alien edifice of steel, erected for no human purpose. A white stucco liquor store gleamed as if built from time-bleached bones. Many shop windows were cataracted with ice-white reflections of the sun as it sought the horizon, as if painted to conceal the activities of those who worked beyond them. The shadows cast by the buildings, by the pines and cypresses, were stark, spiky, razor-edged.

Sam braked at a stoplight at the third intersection, halfway through the commercial district. With no traffic behind him, he paused to study the people on the sidewalks. Not many were in sight, eight or ten, and they also struck him as wrong, though his reasons for thinking ill of them were less definable than those that formed his impression of the town itself. They walked briskly, purposefully, heads up, with a peculiar air of urgency that seemed unsuited to a lazy, seaside community of only three thousand souls.

He sighed and continued down Ocean Avenue, telling himself that his imagination was running wild. Moonlight Cove and the people in it probably would not have seemed the least unusual if he had just been passing by on a long trip and turned off the coast highway only to have dinner at a local restaurant. Instead, he had arrived with the knowledge that something was rotten there, so of course he saw ominous signs in a perfectly innocent scene.

At least that was what he told himself. But he knew better.

He had come to Moonlight Cove because people had died there, because the official explanations for their deaths were suspicious, and he had a hunch that the truth, once uncovered, would be unusually disturbing. Over the years he had learned to trust his hunches; that trust had kept him alive.

He parked the rented Ford in front of a gift shop.

To the west, at the far end of a slate-gray sea, the anemic sun sank through a sky that was slowly turning muddy red. Serpentine tendrils of fog began to rise off the choppy water.

• 3 •

In the pantry off the kitchen, sitting on the floor with her back against a shelf of canned goods, Chrissie Foster looked at her watch. In the harsh light of the single bare bulb in the ceiling socket, she saw that she had been locked in that small, windowless chamber for nearly nine hours. She had received the wrist-watch on her eleventh birthday, more than four months ago, and she had been thrilled by it because it was not a kid's watch with cartoon characters on the face; it was delicate, ladylike, gold-plated, with roman numerals instead of digits, a real Timex like her mother wore. Studying it, Chrissie was overcome by sadness. The watch represented a time of happiness and family togetherness that was lost forever.

Besides feeling sad, lonely, and a little restless from hours of captivity, she was scared. Of course, she was not as scared as she had been that morning, when her father had carried her through the house and thrown her into the pantry. Then, kicking and screaming, she had been *terrified* because of what she had seen. Because of what her parents had become. But that white-hot terror could not be sustained; gradually it subsided to a low-grade fever of fear that made her feel flushed and chilled at the same time, queasy, headachy, almost as if she were in the early stages of flu.

She wondered what they were going to do to her when they finally let her out of the pantry. Well, no, she didn't worry about what they were going to do, for she was pretty sure she already knew the answer to that one: They were going to change her into one of them. What she wondered about, actually, was how the change would be effected – and what, exactly, she would become. She knew that her mother and father were no longer ordinary people, that they were something else, but she had no words to describe what they had become.

Her fear was sharpened by the fact that she lacked the words to explain to herself what was happening in her own home, for she had always been in love with words and had faith in their power. She liked to read just about anything: Poetry, short stories, novels, the daily newspaper, magazines, the backs of cereal boxes if nothing else was at hand. She was in sixth grade at school, but her teacher, Mrs. Tokawa, said she read at a tenth-grade level. When she was not reading, she was often writing stories of her own. Within the past year she had decided she was going to grow up to write novels like those of Mr. Paul Zindel or the sublimely silly Mr. Daniel Pinkwater or, best of all, like those of Ms. Andre Norton.

But now words failed; her life was going to be far different from what she had imagined. She was frightened as much by the loss of the comfortable, bookish future she had foreseen as she was by the changes that had taken place in her parents. Eight months shy of her twelfth birthday, Chrissie had become acutely aware of life's uncertainty, grim knowledge for which she was ill prepared.

Not that she had already given up. She intended to fight. She was not going to let them change her without resistance. Soon after she had been thrown into the pantry, once her tears had dried, she had looked over the contents of the shelves, searching for a weapon. The pantry contained mostly canned, bottled, and packaged food, but there were also laundry and first-aid and handyman supplies. She had found the perfect thing: a small aerosol-spray can of WD-40, an oil-based lubricant. It was a third the size of an ordinary spray can, easily concealed. If she could surprise them, spray it in their eyes and temporarily blind them, she could make a break for freedom.

As though reading a newspaper headline, she said, 'Ingenious Young Girl Saves Self with Ordinary Household Lubricant.'

She held the WD-40 in both hands, taking comfort from it.

Now and then a vivid and unsettling memory recurred: her father's face as it had looked when he had thrown her into the pantry – red and swollen with anger, his eyes darkly ringed, nostrils flared, lips drawn back from his teeth in a feral snarl, every feature contorted with rage. 'I'll be back for you,' he had said, spraying spittle as he spoke. 'I'll be back.'

He slammed the door and braced it shut with a straight-backed kitchen chair that he wedged under the knob. Later, when the house fell silent and her parents seemed to have gone away, Chrissie had tried the door, pushing on it with all her might, but the tilted chair was an immovable barricade.

I'll be back for you. I'll be back.

His twisted face and bloodshot eyes had made her think of Mr. Robert Louis Stevenson's description of the murderous Hyde in the story of Dr. Jekyll, which she had read a few months ago. There was madness in her father; he was not the same man that he once had been.

More unsettling was the memory of what she had seen in the upstairs hall when she had returned home after missing the school bus and had surprised her parents. No. They were not really her parents any more. They were . . . something else.

She shuddered.

She clutched the can of WD-40.

Suddenly, for the first time in hours, she heard noise in the kitchen. The back door of the house opened. Footsteps. At least two, maybe three or four people.

'She's in there,' her father said.

Chrissie's heart stuttered, then found a new and faster beat.

'This isn't going to be quick,' said another man. Chrissie did not recognize his deep, slightly raspy voice. 'You see, it's more complicated with a child. Shaddack's not sure we're even ready for the children yet. It's risky.'

'She's got to be converted, Tucker.' That was Chrissie's mother, Sharon, though she did not sound like herself. It was her voice, all right, but without its usual softness, without the natural, musical quality that had made it such a perfect voice for reading fairy tales.

'Of course, yes, she's got to be done,' said the stranger, whose name was evidently Tucker. 'I know that. Shaddack knows it too. He sent me here, didn't he? I'm just saying it might take more time than usual. We need a place where we can restrain her and watch over her during the conversion.'

'Right here. Her bedroom upstairs.'

Conversion?

Trembling, Chrissie got to her feet and stood facing the door.

With a scrape and clatter, the tilted chair was removed from under the knob. She held the spray can in her right hand, down at her side and half behind her, with her forefinger on top of the nozzle.

The door opened, and her father looked in at her.

Alex Foster. Chrissie tried to think of him as Alex Foster, not as her father, just Alex Foster, but it was difficult to deny that in some ways he was still her dad. Besides, 'Alex Foster' was no more accurate than 'father' because he was someone altogether new.

His face was no longer warped with rage. He appeared more like himself: thick blond hair; a broad, pleasant face with bold features; a smattering of freckles across his cheeks and nose. Nevertheless, she could see a terrible difference in his eyes. He seemed to be filled with a strange urgency, an edgy tension. Hungry. Yes, that was it: Daddy seemed hungry . . . consumed by hunger, frantic with hunger, *starving* . . . but for something other than food. She did not understand his hunger but she sensed it, a fierce *need* that engendered a constant tension in his muscles, a need of such tremendous power, so hot, that waves of it seemed to rise from him like steam from boiling water.

He said, 'Come out of there, Christine.'

Chrissie let her shoulders sag, blinked as if repressing tears, exaggerated the shivers that swept through her, and tried to look small, frightened, defeated. Reluctantly she edged forward.

'Come on, come on,' he said impatiently, motioning her out of the pantry.

Chrissie stepped through the doorway and saw her mother, who was beside and slightly behind Alex. Sharon was pretty – auburn hair, green eyes – but there was no softness or motherliness about her any more. She was hard looking and changed and full of the same barely contained nervous energy that filled her husband.

By the kitchen table stood a stranger in jeans and plaid hunting jacket. He was evidently the Tucker to whom her mother had spoken: tall, lean, all sharp edges and angles. His close-cropped black hair bristled. His dark eyes were set under a deep, bony brow; his sharply ridged nose was like a stone wedge driven into the center of his face; his mouth was a thin slash, and his jaws were as prominent as those of a predator that preyed on small animals and snapped them in half with one bite. He was holding a physician's black leather bag.

Her father reached for Chrissie as she came out of the pantry, and she whipped up the can of WD-40, spraying him in the eyes from a distance of less than two feet. Even as her father howled in pain and surprise, Chrissie turned and sprayed her mother, too, straight in the face. Half-blinded, they fumbled for her, but she slipped away from them and dashed across the kitchen.

Tucker was startled but managed to grab her by the arm.

She spun toward him and kicked him in the crotch.

He did not let go of her, but the strength went out of his big hands. She tore herself away from him and sprinted into the downstairs hallway.

From the east, twilight drifted down on Moonlight Cove, as if it were a mist not of water but of smoky purple light. When Sam Booker got out of his car, the air was chilly; he was glad that he was wearing a wool sweater under his corduroy sportcoat. As a photocell activated all the streetlamps simultaneously, he strolled along Ocean Avenue, looking in shop windows, getting a feel for the town.

He knew that Moonlight Cove was prosperous, that unemployment was virtually nonexistent – thanks to New Wave Microtechnology, which had headquartered there ten years ago – yet he saw signs of a faltering economy. Taylor's Fine Gifts and Saenger's Jewelry had vacated their shops; through their dusty, plate-glass windows, he saw bare shelves and empty display cases and deep, still shadows. New Attitudes, a trendy clothing store, was having a going-out-of-business sale, and judging by the dearth of shoppers, their merchandise was moving sluggishly even at fifty to seventy percent off the original prices.

By the time he had walked two blocks west, to the beach end of town, crossed the street, and returned three blocks along the other side of Ocean Avenue to Knight's Bridge Tavern, twilight was swiftly waning. A nacreous fog was moving in from the sea, and the air itself seemed iridescent, shimmering delicately; a plum-colored haze lay over everything, except where the streetlamps cast showers of mist-softened yellow light, and above it all was a heavy darkness coming down.

A single moving car was in sight, three blocks away, and at the moment Sam was the only pedestrian. The solitude combined with the queer light of the dying day to give him the feeling that this was a ghost town, inhabited only by the dead. As the gradually thickening fog seeped up the hill from the Pacific, it contributed to the illusion that *all* of the surrounding shops were vacant, that they offered no wares other than spider webs, silence, and dust.

You're a dour bastard, he told himself. Too grim by half.

Experience had made a pessimist of him. The traumatic course of his life to date precluded grinning optimism.

Tendrils of fog slipped around his legs. At the far edge of the darkening sea, the pallid sun was half extinguished. Sam shivered and went into the tavern to get a drink.

Of the three other customers, none was in a noticeably upbeat mood. In one of the black vinyl booths off to the left, a middle-aged man and woman were leaning toward each other, speaking in low voices. A gray-faced guy at the bar was hunched over his glass of draft beer, holding it in both hands, scowling as if he had just seen a bug swimming in the brew.

In keeping with its name, Knight's Bridge reeked ersatz British atmosphere. A different coat of arms, each no doubt copied from some official heraldic reference book, had been carved from wood and hand-painted and inset in the back of every barstool. A suit of armor stood in one corner. Fox-hunting scenes hung on the walls.

Sam slid onto a stool eight down from the gray-faced man. The bartender hurried to him, wiping a clean cotton rag over the already immaculate, highly polished oak counter.

'Yes, sir, what'll it be?' He was a round man from every aspect: a small round potbelly; meaty forearms with a thick thatching of black hair; a chubby face; a mouth too small to be in harmony with his other features; a puggish nose that ended in a round little ball; eyes round enough to give him a perpetual look of surprise.

'You have Guinness?' Sam asked.

'It's a fundamental of a *real* pub, I'd say. If we didn't have Guinness . . . why, we might as well convert to a tea shop.' His was a mellifluous voice; every word he spoke sounded as smooth and round as he looked. He seemed unusually eager to please. 'Would you like it cold or just slightly chilled? I keep it both ways.'

'Very slightly chilled.'

'Good man!' When he returned with a Guinness and a glass, the bartender said, 'Name's Burt Peckham. I own the joint.'

Carefully pouring the stout down the side of the glass to ensure the smallest possible head, Sam said, 'Sam Booker. Nice place, Burt.'

'Thanks. Maybe you could spread the word. I try to keep it cozy and well stocked, and we used to have quite a crowd, but lately it seems like most of the town either joined a temperance movement or started brewing their own in their basements, one or the other.'

'Well, it's a Monday night.'

'These last couple months, it's not been unusual to be half empty even on a Saturday night, which never used to happen.' Burt Peckham's round face dimpled with worry. He slowly polished the bar while he talked. 'What it is – I think maybe this health kick Californians have been on for so long has finally just gone too far. They're all staying home, doing aerobics in front of the VCR, eating wheat germ and egg whites or whatever the hell it is they eat, drinking nothing but bottled water and fruit juice and titmouse milk. Listen, a tipple or two a day is *good* for you.'

Sam drank some of the Guinness, sighed with satisfaction, and said, 'This sure tastes as if it ought to be good for you.'

'It is. Helps your circulation. Keeps your bowels in shape. Ministers ought to be touting its virtues each Sunday, not preaching against it. *All* things in moderation – and that includes a couple of brews a day.' Perhaps realizing that he was polishing the bar a bit obsessively, he hung the rag on a hook and stood with his arms folded across his chest. 'You just passing through, Sam?'

'Actually,' Sam lied, 'I'm taking a long trip up the coast from L.A. to the Oregon line, loafing along, looking for a quiet place to semi-retire.'

'Retire? You kidding?'

'*Semi*-retire.'

'But you're only, what, forty, forty-one?'

'Forty-two.'

'What are you – a bank robber?'

'Stockbroker. Made some good investments over the years. Now I think I can drop out of the rat race and get by well enough just managing my own portfolio. I want to settle down where it's quiet, no smog, no crime. I've had it with L.A.'

'People really make money in stocks?' Peckham asked. 'I thought it was about as good an investment as a craps table in Reno. Wasn't everybody wiped out when the market blew up a couple of years ago?'

'It's a mug's game for the little guy, but you can do all right if you're a broker and if you don't get swept up in the euphoria of a bull market. No market goes up forever or down forever; you just have to guess right about when to start swimming against the current.'

'Retiring at forty-two,' Peckham said wonderingly. 'And when I got into the bar business, I thought I was set for life. Told my wife – in good times, people drink to celebrate, in bad times they drink to forget, so there's no better business than a tavern. Now look.' He indicated the nearly empty room with a sweeping gesture of his right hand. 'I'd have done better selling condoms in a monastery.'

'Get me another Guinness?' Sam asked.

'Hey, maybe this place will turn around yet!'

When Peckham returned with the second bottle of stout, Sam said, 'Moonlight Cove might be what I've been looking for. I guess I'll stay a few days, get the feel of it. Can you recommend a motel?'

'There's only one left. Never been much of a tourist town. No one here really wanted that, I guess. Up until this summer, we had four motels. Now three are out of business. I don't know . . . even as pretty as it is, maybe this burg is dying. As far as I can see, we aren't losing population but . . . dammit, we're losing *something*.' He snatched up the bar rag again and began to polish the oak. 'Anyway, try Cove Lodge on Cypress Lane. That's the last cross street on Ocean Avenue; it runs along the bluff, so you'll probably have a room with an ocean view. Clean, quiet place.'

• 5 •

At the end of the downstairs hall, Chrissie Foster threw open the front door. She raced across the wide porch and down the steps, stumbled, regained her balance, turned right, and fled across the yard, past a blue Honda that evidently belonged to Tucker, heading for the stables. The hard slap of her tennis shoes seemed to boom like cannon fire through the swiftly fading twilight. She wished that she could run silently – and faster. Even if her parents and Tucker couldn't reach the front porch until she was swallowed by shadows, they would still be able to hear where she was going.

Most of the sky was a burnt-out black, though a deep red glow marked the western horizon, as if all the light of the October day had been boiled down to that intense crimson essence, which had settled at the bottom of the celestial cauldron. Wispy fog crept in from the nearby sea, and Chrissie hoped it would swiftly thicken, dense as pudding, because she was going to need more cover.

She reached the first of the two long stables and rolled aside the big door. The familiar and not unpleasant aroma – straw, hay, feed grain, horseflesh, liniment, saddle leather, and dry manure – wafted over her.

She snapped the night-light switch, and three low-wattage bulbs winked on, bright enough to dimly illuminate the building without disturbing the occupants. Ten generously proportioned stalls flanked each side of the dirt-floored main aisle, and curious horses peered out at her from above several of the half-size doors. A few belonged to Chrissie's parents, but most were being boarded for people who lived in and around Moonlight Cove. The horses snuffled and snorted, and one whinnied softly, as Chrissie ran past them to the last box on the left, where a dapple-gray mare named Godiva was in residence.

Access to the stalls also could be had from outside the building, although in this cool season the exterior Dutch-style doors were kept bolted both top and bottom to prevent heat escaping from the barn. Godiva was a gentle mare and particularly amicable with Chrissie, but she was skittish about being approached in the dark; she might rear or bolt if surprised by the opening of her exterior stall door at this hour. Because Chrissie could not afford to lose even a few seconds in calming her mount, she had to reach the mare from inside the stable.

Godiva was ready for her. The mare shook her head, tossing the thick and lustrous white mane for which she had been named, and blew air through her nostrils in greeting.

Glancing back toward the stable entrance, expecting to see Tucker and her parents storm in at any moment, Chrissie unlatched the half-door. Godiva came out into the aisle between the rows of stalls.

'Be a lady, Godiva. Oh, please be sweet for me.'

She could not take time to saddle the mare or slip a bit between her teeth. With a hand against Godiva's flank, she guided her mount past the tack room and feed shed that occupied the last quarter of the barn, startling a mouse that scurried across her path into a shadowy corner. She rolled open the door at that end, and cool air swept in.

Without a stirrup to give her a leg up, Chrissie was too small to mount Godiva.

A blacksmith's shoeing stool stood in the corner by the tack room. Keeping a hand against Godiva to gentle her, Chrissie hooked the stool with one foot and pulled it to the horse's side.

Behind her, from the other end of the barn, Tucker shouted, 'Here she is! The stable!' He ran toward her.

The stool did not give her much height and was no substitute for a stirrup.

She could hear Tucker's pounding footsteps, close, closer, but she didn't look at him.

He cried, 'I got her!'

Chrissie grabbed Govida's magnificent white mane, threw herself against the big horse and up, up, swinging her leg high, scrabbling desperately against the mare's side, pulling hard on the mane. It must have hurt Govida, but the old girl was stoic. She didn't rear or whinny in pain, as if some equine instinct told her that this little girl's life depended on equanimity. Then Chrissie was on Godiva's back, tilting precariously but aboard, holding tight with her knees, one hand full of mane, and she slapped the horse's side.

'Go!'

Tucker reached her as she shouted that single word, grabbed at her leg, snared her jeans. His deep-set eyes were wild with anger; his nostrils flared, and his thin lips pulled back from his teeth. She kicked him under the chin, and he lost his grip on her.

Simultaneously Godiva leaped forward, through the open door, into the night.

'She's got a horse!' Tucker shouted. 'She's on a horse!'

The dapple-gray sprinted straight toward the meadowed slope that led to the sea a couple of hundred yards away, where the last muddy-red light of the sunset painted faint, speckled patterns on the black water. But Chrissie didn't want to go down to the shore because she was not sure how high the tide was. At some places along the coast, the beach was not broad even at low tide; if the tide were high now, deep water would meet rocks and bluffs at some points, making passage impossible. She could not risk riding into a dead end with her parents and Tucker in pursuit.

Even without the benefit of a saddle and at a full gallop, Chrissie managed to pull herself into a better position astride the mare, and as soon as she was no longer leaning to one side like a stunt rider, she buried both hands in the thick white mane, gripped fistsful of that coarse hair, and tried to use it as a substitute for reins. She urged Godiva to turn left, away from the sea, away from the house as well, back along the stables, and out toward the half-mile driveway that led to the county road, where they were more likely to find help.

Instead of rebelling at this crude method of guidance, patient Godiva responded immediately, turning to the left as prettily as if she had a bit in her teeth and had felt the tug of a rein. The thunder of her hooves echoed off the barn walls as they raced past that structure.

'You're a great old girl!' Chrissie shouted to the horse. 'I love you, girl.'

They passed safely wide of the east end of the stable, where she had first entered to get the mare, and she spotted Tucker coming out of the door. He was clearly surprised to see her heading that way instead of down to the ocean. He sprinted toward her, and he was startlingly quick, but he was no match for Godiva.

They came to the driveway, and Chrissie kept Godiva on the soft verge, parallel to that hard-surfaced lane. She leaned forward, as tight against the horse as she could get, terrified of falling off, and every hard thud of hooves jarred through her bones. Her head was turned to the side, so she saw the house off to the left, the windows full of light but not welcoming. It was no longer her home; it was hell between four walls, so the light at the windows seemed, to her, to be demonic fires in the rooms of Hades.

Suddenly she saw something racing across the front lawn toward the driveway, toward her. It was low and fast, the size of a man but running on all fours – or nearly so – loping, about twenty yards away and closing. She saw another equally bizarre figure, almost the size of the first, running behind it. Though both creatures were backlit by the house lights, Chrissie could discern little more than their shapes, yet she knew what they were. No, correct that: She knew *who* they probably were, but she still didn't know *what* they were, though she had seen them in the upstairs hall this morning; she knew what they had been – people like her – but not what they were now.

'Go, Godiva, go!'

Even without the flap of reins to signal the need for greater speed, the mare increased the length of her stride, as if she shared a psychic link with Chrissie.

Then they were past the house, tearing flat-out across a grassy field, paralleling the macadam driveway, whizzing toward the country road less than half a mile to the east. The nimble-footed mare worked her great haunch muscles, and her powerful stride was so lullingly rhythmic and exhilarating that Chrissie soon was hardly aware of the rocking-jolting aspect of the ride; it seemed as if they were skimming across the earth, nearly flying.

She looked over her shoulder and did not see the two loping figures, although they were no doubt still pursuing her through the multilayered shadows. With the muddy-red candescence along the western horizon fading to deep purple, with the lights of the house rapidly dwindling, and with a crescent moon beginning to thrust one silver-bright point above the line of hills in the east, visibility was poor.

Though she could not see those pursuers who were on foot, she had no difficulty spotting the headlights of Tucker's blue Honda. In front of the house, a couple of hundred yards behind her now, Tucker swung the car around in the driveway and joined the chase.

Chrissie was fairly confident that Godiva could outrun any man or beast other than a better horse, but she knew that the mare was no match for a car. Tucker would catch them in seconds. The man's face was clear in her memory: the bony brow, sharp-ridged nose, deeply set eyes like a pair of hard, black marbles. He'd had about him that aura of unnatural vitality that Chrissie sometimes had seen in her parents – abundant nervous energy coupled with a queer look of hunger. She knew he would do anything to stop her, that he might even attempt to ram Godiva with the Honda.

He could not, of course, use the car to follow Godiva overland. Reluctantly Chrissie employed her knees and the mane in her right hand to turn the mare away from the driveway and the county road, where they were most likely to reach help quickly. Godiva responded without hesitation, and they headed toward the woods that lay at the far side of the meadow, five hundred yards to the south.

Chrissie could see the forest only as a black, bristly mass vaguely silhouetted against the marginally less dark sky. The details of the terrain she must cross appeared to her more in memory than in reality. She prayed that the horse's night vision was keener than hers.

'That's my girl, go, go, you good old girl, go!' she shouted encouragingly to the mare.

They made their own wind in the crisp, still air. Chrissie was aware of Godiva's hot breath streaming past her in crystallized plumes, and her own breath smoked from her open mouth. Her heart pounded in time with the frantic thumping of hooves, and she felt almost as if she and Godiva were not rider and horse but one being, sharing the same heart and blood and breath.

Though fleeing for her life, she was as pleasantly thrilled as she was terrified, and that realization startled her. Facing death – or in this case something perhaps worse than death – was peculiarly exciting, darkly attractive in a way and to an extent that she could never have imagined. She was almost as frightened of the unexpected thrill as of the people who were chasing her.

She clung tightly to the dapple-gray, sometimes bouncing on the horse's bare back, lifting dangerously high, but holding fast, flexing and contracting her own muscles in sympathy with those of the horse. With every ground-pummelling stride, Chrissie grew more confident that they would escape. The mare had heart and endurance. When they had traversed three quarters of the field, with the woods looming, Chrissie decided to turn east again when they reached the trees, not straight toward the county road but in that general direction, and—

Godiva fell.

The mare had put a foot in some depression – a ground squirrel's burrow, the entrance to a rabbit's warren, perhaps a natural drainage ditch – stumbled, and lost her balance. She tried to recover, failed, and fell, bleating in terror.

Chrissie was afraid that her mount would crash down on her, that she would be crushed, or at least break a leg. But there were no stirrups to ensnare her feet, no saddle horn to snag her clothes, and because she instinctively let go of the dapple-gray's mane, she was thrown free at once, straight over the horse's head and high into the air. Though the ground was soft and further cushioned by a thick growth of wild grass, she met it with numbing impact, driving the air from her lungs and banging her teeth together so hard that her tongue would have been bitten off if it had been between them. But she was three yards away from the horse and safe in that regard.

Godiva was the first to rise, scrambling up an instant after crashing down. Eyes wide with fright, she cantered past Chrissie, favoring her right foreleg, which evidently was only sprained; if it had been broken, the horse would not have gotten up.

Chrissie called to the mare, afraid the horse would wander off. But her breath was coming in ragged gasps, and the name issued from her in a whisper: '*Godiva!*'

The horse kept going west, back toward the sea and the stables.

By the time Chrissie got up on her hands and knees, she realized that a lame horse was of no use to her, so she made no further effort to recall the mare. She was gasping for breath and mildly dizzy, but she knew she had to get moving because she was no doubt still being stalked. She could see the Honda, headlights on, parked along the lane more than three hundred yards to the north. With all the bloody glow of sunset having seeped out of the horizon, the meadow was black. She could not determine if low, swift-moving figures were out there, though she knew they must be approaching and that she would surely fall into their hands within a minute or two.

She got to her feet, turned south toward the woods, staggered ten or fifteen yards until her legs recovered from the shock of her fall, and finally broke into a run.

• 6 •

Over the years Sam Booker had discovered that the length of the California coast was graced by charming inns that featured master-quality stonework, weathered wood, cove ceilings, beveled-glass, and lushly planted courtyards with used-brick walkways. In spite of the comfortable images its name evoked and the singularly scenic setting that it enjoyed, Cove Lodge was not one of those California jewels. It was just an ordinary stucco, two-story, forty-room, rectangular box, with a drab coffee shop at one end, no swimming pool. Amenities were limited to ice and soda machines on both floors. The sign above the motel office was neither garish nor in the artistic mode of some modern neon, just small and simple – and cheap.

The evening desk clerk gave him a second-floor room with an ocean view, though location didn't matter to Sam. Judging by the dearth of cars in the lot, however, rooms with a view were not in short supply. Each level of the motel had twenty units in banks of ten, serviced by an interior hall carpeted in short-nap orange nylon that seared his eyes. Rooms on the east overlooked Cypress Lane; those on the west faced the Pacific. His quarters were at the northwest corner; a queen-size bed with a sagging mattress and worn blue-green spread, cigarette-scarred nightstands, a television bolted to a stand, table, two straight-back chairs, cigarette-scarred bureau, phone, bathroom, and one big window framing the night-blanketed sea.

When disheartened salesmen, down on their luck and teetering on the edge of economic ruin, committed suicide on the road, they did the deed in rooms like this.

He unpacked his two suitcases, putting his clothes in the closet and bureau drawers. Then he sat on the edge of the bed and stared at the telephone on the nightstand.

He should call Scott, his son, who was back home in Los Angeles, but he couldn't do it from this phone. Later, if the local police became interested in him, they would visit Cove Lodge, examine his long-distance charges, investigate the numbers he had dialed, and try to piece together his real identity from the identities of those with whom he had spoken. To maintain his cover, he must use his room phone only to call his contact number at the Bureau office in L.A., a secure line that would be answered with 'Birchfield Securities, may I help you?' Furthermore, in phone-company records that line *was* registered to Birchfield, the nonexistent firm with which Sam was supposedly a stock-broker; it could not be traced ultimately to the FBI. He had nothing to report yet, so he did not lift the receiver. When he went out to dinner, he could call Scott from a pay phone.

He did not want to talk to the boy. It would be purely a duty call. Sam dreaded it. Conversation with his son had ceased to be pleasurable at least three years ago, when Scott had been thirteen and, at that time, already motherless for a year. Sam wondered if the boy would have gone wrong quite so rapidly or so completely if Karen had lived. That avenue of thought led him, of course, to the contemplation of his own role in Scott's decline: Would the boy have turned bad regardless of the quality of the parental guidance that he received; was his fall inevitable, the weakness in him or in his stars? Or was Scott's descent a direct result of his father's failure to find a way to steer him to a better, brighter path?

If he kept brooding about it, he was going to pull a Willy Loman right there in Cove Lodge, even though he was not a salesman.

Guinness stout.

Good Mexican food.

Goldie Hawn.

Fear of death.

As a list of reasons for living, it was damned short and too pathetic to contemplate, but perhaps it was just long enough.

After he used the bathroom, he washed his hands and face in cold water. He still felt tired, not the least refreshed.

He took off his corduroy jacket and put on a thin, supple leather shoulder holster that he retrieved from a suitcase. He'd also packed a Smith & Wesson .38 Chief's Special, which he now loaded. He tucked it into the holster before slipping into his jacket again. His coats were tailored to conceal the weapon; it made no bulge, and the holster fit so far back against his side that the gun could not be seen easily even if he left the jacket unbuttoned.

For undercover assignments, Sam's body and face were as well tailored as his jackets. He was five eleven, neither tall nor short. He weighed one hundred and seventy pounds, mostly bone and muscle, little fat, yet he was not a thick-necked weightlifter type in such superb condition that he would draw attention. His face was nothing special: neither ugly nor handsome, neither too broad nor too narrow, marked by neither unusually sharp nor blunt features, unblemished and unscarred. His sandy-brown hair was barbered in a timelessly moderate length and style that would be unremarkable in an age of brushcuts or in an era of shoulder-length locks.

Of all the aspects of his appearance, only his eyes were truly arresting. They were gray-blue with darker blue striations. Women had often told him that his were the most beautiful eyes they had ever seen. At one time he had cared what women said of him.

He shrugged, making sure the holster was hanging properly.

He did not expect to need the gun that evening. He had not begun to nose around and draw attention to himself; and since he had not yet pushed anyone, no one was ready to push back.

Nevertheless, from now on he would carry the revolver. He could not leave it in the motel room or lock it in his rental car; if someone conducted a determined search, the gun would be found, and his cover would be blown. No middle-aged stockbroker, searching for a coastal haven in which to take early retirement, would go armed with a snub-nosed .38 of that make and model. It was a cop's piece.

Pocketing his room key, he went out to dinner.

• 7 •

After she checked in, Tessa Jane Lockland stood for a long time at the big window in her room at the Cove Lodge, with no lights on. She stared out at the vast, dark Pacific and down at the beach from which her sister, Janice, supposedly had ventured forth on a grimly determined mission of self-destruction.

The official story was that Janice had gone to the shore alone at night, in a state of acute depression. She had taken a massive overdose of Valium, swallowing the capsules with several swigs from a can of Diet Coke. Then she had stripped off her clothes and had swum out toward far Japan. Losing consciousness because of the drugs, she soon slipped into the cold embrace of the sea, and drowned.

'Bullshit,' Tessa said softly, as if speaking to her own vague reflection in the cool glass.

Janice Lockland Capshaw had been a hopeful person, unfailingly optimistic – a trait so common in members of the Lockland clan as to be genetic. Not once in her life had Janice sat in a corner feeling sorry for herself; if she had tried it, within seconds she would have begun laughing at the foolishness of self-pity and would have gotten up and gone to a movie, or for a psychologically therapeutic run. Even when Richard died, Janice had not allowed grief to metastasize into depression, though she loved him greatly.

So what would have sent her into such a steep emotional spiral? Contemplating the story the police wanted her to believe, Tessa was driven to sarcasm.

Maybe Janice had gone out to a restaurant, been served a bad dinner, and been so crushed by the experience that suicide had been her only possible response. Yeah. Or maybe her television went on the blink, and she missed her favorite soap opera, which plunged her into irreversible despair. Sure. Those scenarios were about as plausible as the nonsense that the Moonlight Cove police and coroner had put in their reports.

Suicide.

'Bullshit,' Tessa repeated.

From the window of her motel room, she could see only a narrow band of the beach below, where it met the churning surf. The sand was dimly revealed in the wintry light of a newly risen quarter moon, a pale ribbon curving southwest and northwest around the cove.

Tessa was overcome by the desire to stand on the beach from which her sister had supposedly set out on that midnight swim to the graveyard, the same beach to which the tide had returned her bloated, ravaged corpse days later. She turned from the window and switched on a bedside lamp. She removed a brown leather jacket from a hanger in the closet, pulled it on, slung her purse over her shoulder, and left the room, locking the door behind her. She was certain – irrationally so – that merely by going to the beach and standing where Janice supposedly had stood, she would uncover a clue to the true story, through an amazing insight or flicker of intuition.

• 8 •

As the hammered-silver moon rose above the dark eastern hills, Chrissie raced along the tree line, looking for a way into the woods before her strange pursuers found her. She quickly arrived at Pyramid Rock, thus named because the formation, twice as tall as she was, had three sides and came to a weather-rounded point; when younger, she had fantasized that it had been constructed ages ago by a geographically displaced tribe of inch-high Egyptians. Having played in this meadow and forest for years, she was as familiar with the terrain as with the rooms of her own house, certainly more at home there than her parents or Tucker would be, which gave her an advantage. She slipped past Pyramid Rock, into the gloom beneath the trees, onto a narrow deer trail that led south.

She heard no one behind her and did not waste time squinting back into the darkness. But she suspected that, as predators, her parents and Tucker would be silent stalkers, revealing themselves only when they pounced.

The coastal woodlands were comprised mostly of a wide variety of pines, although a few sweet gums flourished, too, their leaves a scarlet blaze of autumn color in daylight but now as black as bits of funeral shrouds. Chrissie followed the winding trail as the land began to slope into a canyon. In more than half the forest, the trees grew far enough apart to allow the cold glow of the partial moon to penetrate to the underbrush and lay an icy crust of light upon the trail. The incoming fog was still too thin to filter out much of that wan radiance, but at other places the interlacing branches blocked the lunar light.

Even where moonlight revealed the way, Chrissie dared not run, for she would surely be tripped by the surface roots of the trees, which spread across the deer-beaten path. Here and there low-hanging branches presented another danger to a runner, but she hurried along.

As if reading from a book of her own adventures, a book like one of those she so much enjoyed, she thought, *Young Chrissie was as surefooted as she was resourceful and quick-thinking, no more intimidated by the darkness than by the thought of her monstrous pursuers. What a girl she was!*

Soon she would reach the bottom of the slope, where she could turn west toward the sea or east toward the county route, which bridged the canyon. Few people lived in that area, more than two miles from the outskirts of Moonlight Cove; fewer still lived by the sea, since portions of the coastline were protected by state law and were closed to construction. Though she had little chance of finding help toward the Pacific, her prospects to the east were not noticeably better, because the county road was lightly traveled and few houses were built along it; besides, Tucker might be patrolling that route in his Honda, expecting her to head that way and flag down the first passing car she saw.

Frantically wondering where to go, she descended the last hundred feet. The trees flanking the trail gave way to low impenetrable tangles of bristly scrub oaks called chaparral. A few immense ferns, ideally suited to the frequent coastal fogs, overgrew the path, and Chrissie shivered as she pushed through them, for she felt as if scores of small hands were grabbing at her.

A broad but shallow stream cut a course through the bottom of the canyon, and she paused by its bank to catch her breath. Most of the streambed was dry. At this time of year, only a couple of inches of water moved lazily through the center of the channel, glimmering darkly in the moonlight.

The night was windless.

Soundless.

Hugging herself, she realized how cold it was. In jeans and a blue-plaid flannel shirt, she was adequately dressed for a crisp October day, but not for the cold, damp air of an autumn night.

She was chilled, breathless, scared, and unsure of what her next move ought to be, but most of all she was angry with herself for those weaknesses of mind and body. Ms. Andre Norton's wonderful adventure stories were filled with dauntless young heroines who could endure far longer chases – and far greater cold and other hardships – than this, and always with wits intact, able to make quick decisions and, usually, right ones.

Spurred by comparing herself to a Norton girl, Chrissie stepped off the bank of the stream. She crossed ten feet of loamy soil eroded from the hills by last season's heavy rains and tried to jump across the shallow, purling band of water. She splashed down a few inches short of the other side, soaking her tennis shoes. Nevertheless she went on through more loam, which clumped to her wet shoes, ascended the far bank, and headed neither east nor west but south, up the other canyon wall toward the next arm of the forest.

Though she was entering new territory now, at the extremity of the section of the woods that had been her playground for years, she was not afraid of getting lost. She could tell east from west by the movement of the thin, incoming fog and by the position of the moon, and from those signs she could stay on a reliably southward course. She believed that within a mile she would come to a score of houses and to the sprawling grounds of New Wave Microtechnology, which lay between Foster Stables and the town of Moonlight Cove. There she would be able to find help.

Then, of course, her *real* problems would begin. She would have to convince someone that her parents were no longer her parents, that they had changed or been possessed or been somehow taken over by some spirit or . . . force. And that they wanted to turn her into one of them.

Yeah, she thought, good luck.

She was bright, articulate, responsible, but she was also just an eleven-year-old kid. She would have a hard time making anyone believe her. She had no illusions about that. They would listen and nod their heads and smile, and then they would call her parents, and her parents would sound more plausible than she did . . .

But I've got to try, she told herself, as she began to ascend the sloped southern wall of the canyon. If I don't try to convince someone, what else can I do? Just surrender? No chance.

Behind her, a couple of hundred yards away, from high on the far canyon wall down which she had recently descended, something shrieked. It was not an entirely human cry – not that of any animal, either. The first shrill call was answered by a second, a third, and each shriek was clearly that of a different creature, for each was in a noticeably variant voice.

Chrissie halted on the steep trail, one hand against the deeply fissured bark of a pine, under a canopy of sweet-scented boughs. She looked back and listened as her pursuers simultaneously began to wail, an ululant cry reminiscent of the baying of a pack of coyotes . . . but stranger, more frightening. The sound was so cold, it penetrated her flesh and pierced like a needle to her marrow.

Their baying was probably a sign of their confidence: They were certain they would catch her, so they no longer needed to be quiet.

'What *are* you?' she whispered.

She suspected they could see as well as cats in the dark.

Could they smell her, as if they were dogs?

Her heart began to slam almost painfully within her breast.

Feeling vulnerable and alone, she turned from the puling hunters and scrambled up the trail toward the southern rim of the canyon.

· 9 ·

At the foot of Ocean Avenue, Tessa Lockland walked through the empty parking lot and onto the public beach. The night breeze off the Pacific was just cranking up, faint but chilly enough that she was glad to be wearing slacks, a wool sweater, and her leather jacket.

She crossed the soft sand, toward the seaside shadows that lay beyond the radius of the glow from the last streetlamp, past a tall cypress growing on the beach and so radically shaped by ocean winds that it reminded her of an Erté sculpture, all curved lines and molten form. On the damp sand at the surf's edge, with the tide lapping at the strand inches from her shoes, Tessa stared westward. The partial moon was insufficient to light the vast, rolling main; all she could see were the nearest three lines of low, foam-crested breakers surging toward her from out of the gloom.

She tried to picture her sister standing on this deserted beach, washing down thirty or forty Valium capsules with a Diet Coke, then stripping naked and plunging into the cold sea. No. Not Janice.

With growing conviction that the authorities in Moonlight Cove were incompetent fools or liars, Tessa walked slowly south along the curving shoreline. In the pearly luminescence of the immature moon, she studied the sand, the widely separated cypresses farther back on the beach, and the time-worn formations of rock. She was not looking for physical clues that might tell her what had happened to Janice; those had been erased by wind and tide during the past three weeks. Instead, she was hoping that the very landscape itself and the elements of night – darkness, cool wind, and arabesques of pale but slowly thickening fog – would inspire her to develop a theory about what had *really* happened to Janice and an approach she might use to prove that theory.

She was a filmmaker specializing in industrials and documentaries of various kinds. When in doubt about the meaning and purpose of a project, she often found that immersion in a particular geographical locale could inspire narrative and thematic approaches to making a film about it. In the developmental stages of a new travel film, for instance, she often spent a couple of days casually strolling around a city like Singapore or Hong Kong or Rio, just absorbing details, which was more productive than thousands of hours of background reading and brain-storming, though of course the reading and brainstorming had to be a part of it too.

She had walked less than two hundred feet south along the beach, when she heard a shrill, haunting cry that halted her. The sound was distant, rising and falling, rising and falling, then fading.

Chilled more by that strange call than by the brisk October air, she wondered what she had heard. Although it had been partly a canine howl, she was certain it was not the voice of a dog. Though it was also marked by a feline whine and wail, she was equally certain it had not issued from a cat; no domestic cat could produce such volume, and to the best of her knowledge, no cougars roamed the coastal hills, certainly not in or near a town the size of Moonlight Cove.

Just as she was about to move on, the same uncanny cry cut the night again, and she was fairly sure it was coming from atop the bluff that overlooked the beach, farther south, where the lights of sea-facing houses were fewer than along the middle of the cove. This time the howl ended on a protracted and more guttural note, which might have been produced by a large dog, though she still felt it had to have come from some other creature. Someone living along the bluff must be keeping an exotic pet in a cage: a wolf, perhaps, or some big mountain cat not indigenous to the northern coast.

That explanation did not satisfy her, either, for there was some peculiarly familiar quality to the cry that she could not place, a quality not related to a wolf or mountain cat. She waited for another shriek, but it did not come.

Around her the darkness had deepened. The fog was clotting, and a lumpish cloud slid across half of the two-pointed moon.

She decided she could better absorb the details of the scene in the morning, and she turned back toward the mist-shrouded streetlamps at the bottom of Ocean Avenue. She didn't realize she was walking so fast – almost running – until she had left the shore, crossed the beach parking lot, and climbed half the first steep block of Ocean Avenue, at which point she became aware of her pace only because she suddenly heard her own labored breathing.

Thomas Shaddack drifted in a perfect blackness that was neither warm nor cool, where he seemed weightless, where he had ceased to feel any sensation against his skin, where he seemed limbless and without musculature or bones, where he seemed to have no physical substance whatsoever. A tenuous thread of thought linked him to his corporeal self, and in the dimmest reaches of his mind, he was still aware that he was a man – an Ichabod Crane of a man, six feet two, one hundred and sixty-five pounds, lean and bony, with a too narrow face, a high brow, and brown eyes so light they were almost yellow.

He was also vaguely aware that he was nude and afloat in a state-of-the-art sensory-deprivation chamber, which looked somewhat like an old-fashioned iron lung but was four times larger. The single low wattage bulb was not lit, and no light penetrated the shell of the tank. The pool in which Shaddack floated was a few feet deep, a ten-percent solution of magnesium sulfate in water for maximum buoyancy. Monitored by a computer – as was every element of that environment – the water cycled between ninety-three degrees Fahrenheit, the temperature at which a floating body was least affected by gravity, and ninety-eight degrees, at which the heat differential between human body temperature and surrounding fluid was marginal.

He suffered from no claustrophobia. A minute or two after he stepped into the tank and closed the hatch behind him, his sense of confinement entirely faded.

Deprived of sensory input – no sight, no sound, little or no taste, no olfactory stimulation, no sense of touch or weight or place or time – Shaddack let his mind break free of the dreary restraints of the flesh, soaring to previously unattainable heights of insight and exploring ideas of a complexity otherwise beyond his reach.

Even without the assistance of sensory deprivation, he was a genius. *Time* magazine had said he was, so it must be true. He had built New Wave Microtechnology from a struggling firm with initial capital of twenty thousand dollars to a three-hundred-million-a-year operation that conceived, researched, and developed cutting-edge micro-technology.

At the moment, however, Shaddack was making no effort to focus his mind on current research problems. He was using the tank strictly for recreational purposes, for the inducement of a specific vision that never failed to enthrall and excite him.

His vision.

Except for that thin thread of thought that tethered him to reality, he believed himself to be within a great, laboring machine, so immense that its dimensions could be ascertained no more easily than could those of the universe itself. It was the landscape of a dream but infinitely more textured and intense than a dream. Like an airborne mote within the eerily lit bowels of that colossal imaginary mechanism, he drifted past massive walls and interconnected columns of whirling driveshafts, rattling drive chains, myriad thrusting piston rods joined by sliding blocks to connecting rods that were in turn joined by crank wrists to well-greased cranks that turned flywheels of all dimensions. Servomotors hummed, compressors huffed, distributors sparked as electrical current flashed through millions of tangled wires to far reaches of the construct.

For Shaddack, the most exciting thing about this visionary world was the manner in which steel drive shafts and alloy pistons and hard rubber gaskets and aluminum cowlings were joined with organic parts to form a revolutionary entity possessed of two types of life: efficient mechanical animation and the throb of organic tissue. For pumps, the designer had employed glistening human hearts that pulsated tirelessly in that ancient lub-dub rhythm, joined by thick arteries to rubber tubing that snaked into the walls; some of them pumped blood to parts of the system that required organic lubrication, while others pumped high-viscosity oil. Incorporated into other sections of the infinite machine were tens of thousands of lung sacs functioning as bellows and filters; tendons and tumorlike excrescences of flesh were employed to join lengths of pipe and rubber hoses with more flexibility and surety of seal than could have been attained with ordinary nonorganic couplings.

Here was the best of organic and machine systems wedded in one perfect structure. As Thomas Shaddack imagined his way through the endless avenues of this dream place, he was enraptured even though he did not understand – or care – what ultimate function any of it had, what product or service it labored to bring forth. He was excited by the entity because it was clearly efficient at whatever it was doing, because its organic and inorganic parts were brilliantly integrated.

All of his life, for as many of his forty-one years as he could recall, Shaddack had struggled against the limitations of the human condition, striving with all his will and heart to rise above the destiny of his species. He wanted to be more than merely a man. He wanted to have the power of a god and to shape not only his own future but that of all mankind. In his private sensory-deprivation chamber, transported by this vision of a cybernetic organism, he was closer to that longed-for metamorphosis than he could be in the real world, and that was what invigorated him.

For him the vision was not simply intellectually stimulating and emotionally moving, but powerfully erotic too. As he floated through that imaginary semi-organic machine, watching it throb and pulsate, he surrendered to an orgasm that he felt not merely in his genitals but in every fiber; indeed he was unaware of his fierce erection, unaware of the forceful ejaculations around which his entire body contracted, for he perceived the pleasure to be diffused throughout him rather than focused in his penis. Milky threads of semen spread through the dark pool of magnesium-sulfate solution.

A few minutes later the sensory-deprivation chamber's automatic timer activated the interior light and sounded a soft alarm. Shaddack was called back from his dream to the real world of Moonlight Cove.

• 11 •

Chrissie Foster's eyes adjusted to the darkness, and she was able to find her way swiftly through even unfamiliar territory.

When she reached the rim of the canyon, she passed between a pair of Monterey cypresses and onto another mule-deer trail leading south through the forest. Protected from the wind by the surrounding trees, those enormous cypresses were lush and full, neither badly twisted nor marked by antlerlike branches as they were along the windswept shore. For a moment she considered climbing high into those leafy reaches, with the hope that her pursuers would pass beneath, unaware of her. But she dared not take that chance; if they smelled her or divined her presence by some other means, they would ascend, and she would be unable to retreat.

She hurried on and quickly reached a break in the trees. Beyond lay a meadow that sloped from east to west, as did most of the land thereabouts. The breeze picked up and was strong enough to ruffle her blond hair continuously. The fog was not as thin as it had been when she'd left Foster Stables on horseback, but the moonlight was still unfiltered enough to frost the knee-high, dry grass that rippled when the wind blew.

As she ran across the field toward the next stand of woods, she saw a large truck, strung with lights as if it were a Christmas tree, heading south on the interstate, nearly a mile east of her, along the crest of the second tier of coastal hills. She ruled out seeking help from anyone on the distant freeway, for they were all strangers headed to faraway places, therefore even less likely than locals to believe her. Besides, she read newspapers and watched TV, so she had heard all about the serial killers that roamed the interstates, and she had no trouble imagining tabloid headlines summing up her fate: YOUNG GIRL KILLED AND EATEN BY ROVING CANNIBALS IN DODGE VAN; SERVED WITH A SIDE OF BROCCOLI AND PARSLEY FOR GARNISH; BONES USED FOR SOUP.

The county road lay half a mile closer, along the tops of the first hills, but no traffic moved on it. In any case she already had rejected the idea of seeking help there, for fear of encountering Tucker in his Honda.

Of course she believed that she had heard three distinct voices among the eerie pulings of those who stalked her, which had to mean that Tucker had abandoned his car and was with her parents now. Maybe she could safely head toward the county highway, after all.

She thought about that as she sprinted across the meadow. But before she had made up her mind to change course, those dreadful cries rose behind her again, still in the woods but closer than before. Two or three voices yowled simultaneously, as if a pack of baying hounds was at her heels, though stranger and more savage than ordinary dogs.

Abruptly Chrissie stepped into thin air and found herself falling into what, for an instant, seemed to be a terrible chasm. But it was only an eight-foot-wide, six-foot-deep drainage channel that cleaved the meadow, and she rolled to the bottom of it unharmed.

The angry shrieking of her pursuers grew louder, nearer, and now their voices had a more frenetic quality . . . a note of need, of hunger.

She scrambled to her feet and started to clamber up the six-foot wall of the channel, when she realized that to her left, upslope, the ditch terminated in a large culvert that bored away into the earth. She froze halfway up the arroyo and considered this new option.

The pale concrete pipe offered the lambent moonlight just enough of a reflective surface to be visible. When she saw it, she knew immediately that it was the main drainage line that carried rainwater off the interstate and county road far above and east of her. Judging by the shrill cries of the hunters, her lead was dwindling. She was increasingly afraid that she would not make the trees at the far side of the meadow before being brought down. Perhaps the culvert was a dead end and would provide her with a haven no more secure than the cypress that she had considered climbing, but she decided to risk it.

She slid to the floor of the arroyo again and scurried to the conduit. The pipe was four feet in diameter. By stooping slightly she was able to walk into it. She went only a few steps, however, before she was halted by a stench so foul that she gagged.

Something was dead and rotting in that lightless passage. She could not see what it was. But maybe she was better off not seeing; the carcass might look worse than it smelled. A wild animal, sick and dying, must have crawled into the pipe for shelter, where it perished from its disease.

She backed hastily out of the drain, drawing deep breaths of the fresh night air.

From the north came intermingled, ululant wails that literally put the hair up on the back of her neck.

They were closing fast, almost on top of her.

She had no choice but to hide deep in the culvert and hope they could not catch her scent. She suddenly realized that the decaying animal might be to her benefit, for if those stalking her *were* able to smell her as though they were hounds, the stench of decomposition might mask her own odor.

Entering the pitch-black culvert again, she followed the convex floor, which sloped gradually upward beneath the meadow. Within ten yards she put her foot in something soft and slippery. The horrid odor of decay burst upon her with even greater strength, and she knew she had stepped in the dead thing.

'Oh, yuck.'

She gagged and felt her gorge rise, but she gritted her teeth and *refused* to throw up. When she was past the putrid mass, she paused to scrape her shoes on the concrete floor of the pipe.

Then she hurried farther into the drain. Scurrying with her knees bent, shoulders hunched, and head tucked down, she realized she must have looked like a troll scuttling into its secret burrow.

Fifty or sixty feet past the unidentified dead thing, Chrissie stopped, crouched, and turned to look back toward the mouth of the culvert. Through that circular aperture she had a view of the ditch in moonlight, and she could see more than she had expected because, by contrast with the darkness of the drain, the night beyond seemed brighter than when she had been out there.

All was silent.

A gentle breeze flowed down the pipe from drainage grilles in the highways above and to the east, pushing the odor of the decomposing animal away from her, so she could not detect even a trace of it. The air was tainted only by a mild dankness, a whiff of mildew.

Silence gripped the night.

She held her breath for a moment and listened intently.

Nothing.

Still crouching, she shifted her weight from foot to foot.

Silence.

She wondered if she should head deeper into the culvert. Then she wondered whether snakes were in the pipe. Wouldn't that be a perfect place for snakes to nest when the oncoming night's cool air drove them to shelter?

Silence.

Where were her parents? Tucker? A minute ago they had been close behind her, within striking distance.

Silence.

Rattlesnakes were common in the coastal hills, though not active at this time of year. If a nest of rattlers—

She was so unnerved by the continuing, unnatural silence that she had the urge to scream, just to break that eerie spell.

A shrill cry shattered the quietude outside. It echoed through the concrete tunnel, past Chrissie, and bounced from wall to wall along the passage behind her, as if the hunters were approaching her not only from outside but from the depths of the earth behind her.

Shadowy figures leaped into the arroyo beyond the culvert.

· 12 ·

Sam found a Mexican restaurant on Serra Street, two blocks from his motel. One sniff of the air inside the place was enough to assure him the food would be good. That melange was the odiferous equivalent of a José Feliciano album: chilli powder, bubbling hot *chorizo*, the sweet fragrance of tortillas made with *masa harina*, cilantro, bell peppers, the astringent tang of jalapeño chiles, onions . . .

The Perez Family Restaurant was as unpretentious as its name, a single rectangular room with blue vinyl booths along the side walls, tables in the middle, kitchen at the rear. Unlike Burt Peckham at Knight's Bridge Tavern, the Perez Family had as much business as they could handle. Except for a two-chair table at the back, to which Sam was led by the teenage hostess, the restaurant was filled to capacity.

The waiters and waitresses were dressed casually in jeans and sweaters, the only nod to a uniform being white half-aprons tied around their waists. Sam didn't even ask for Guinness, which he had never found in a Mexican restaurant, but they had Corona, which would be fine if the food was good.

The food was *very* good. Not truly, unequivocally great, but better than he had a right to expect in a northern coastal town of just three thousand people. The corn chips were homemade, the salsa thick and chunky, the albondigas soup rich and sufficiently peppery to break him out in a light sweat. By the time he received an order of crab enchiladas in tomatillo sauce, he was half convinced that he *should* move to Moonlight Cove as soon as possible, even if it meant robbing a bank to finance early retirement.

When he got over his surprise at the food's quality, he began to pay as much attention to his fellow diners as to the contents of his plate. Gradually he noted several odd things about them.

The room was unusually quiet, considering that it was occupied by eighty or ninety people. High-quality Mexican restaurants – with fine food, good beer, and potent margaritas – were festive places. At Perez's, however, diners were talking animatedly at only about a third of the tables. The other two-thirds of the customers ate in silence.

After he tilted his glass and poured from the fresh bottle of Corona that had just been served to him, Sam studied some of the silent eaters. Three middle-age men sat in a booth on the right side of the room, scarfing up tacos and enchiladas and chimichangas, staring at their food or at the air in front of them, occasionally looking at each other but exchanging not a word. On the other side of the room, in another booth, two teenage couples industriously devoured a double platter of mixed appetizers, never punctuating the meal with the chatter and laughter one expected of kids their age. Their concentration was so intense that the longer Sam watched them, the odder they seemed.

Throughout the room, people of all ages, in groups of all kinds, were fixated on their food. Hearty eaters, they had appetizers, soup, salads, and side dishes as well as entrees; on finishing, some ordered 'a couple more tacos' or 'another burrito', before also asking for ice cream or flan. Their jaw muscles bulged as they chewed, and as soon as they swallowed, they quickly shoveled more into their mouths. A few ate with their mouths open. Some swallowed with such force that Sam could actually hear them. They were red-faced and perspiring, no doubt from jalapeño-spiced sauces, but not one offered a comment like, 'Boy, this is hot,' or 'Pretty good grub,' or even the most elementary conversational gambit to his companions.

To the third of the customers who were happily jabbering away at one another and progressing through their meals at an ordinary pace, the almost fevered eating of the majority apparently went unnoticed. Bad table manners were not rare, of course; at least a quarter of the diners in any town would give Miss Manners a stroke if she dared to eat with them. Nevertheless, the gluttony of many of the customers in the Perez Restaurant seemed astonishing to Sam. He supposed that the polite diners were inured to the behavior of the other patrons because they had witnessed it so many times before.

Could the cool sea air of the northern coast be *that* appetite-enhancing? Did some peculiar ethnic background or fractured social history in Moonlight Cove mitigate against the universal development of commonly accepted Western table manners?

What he saw in the Perez Family Restaurant seemed a puzzle for which any sociologist, desperately seeking a doctoral thesis subject, would be eager to find a solution. After a while, however, Sam had to turn his attention away from the more ravenous patrons because their behavior was killing his own appetite.

Later, when he was figuring the tip and putting money on the table to cover his bill, he surveyed the crowd again, and this time realized that none of the heavy eaters was drinking beer, margaritas, or anything alcoholic. They had ice water or Cokes, and some were drinking milk, glass after glass, but every last man and woman of these gourmands seemed to be a teetotaler. He might not have noticed their temperance if he had not been a cop – and a good one – trained not only to observe but to think about what he observed.

He remembered the scarcity of drinkers at Knight's Bridge Tavern.

What ethnic culture or religious group inculcated a disdain for alcohol while encouraging mannerlessness and gluttony?

He could think of none.

By the time Sam finished his beer and got up to leave, he was telling himself that he'd overreacted to a few crude people, that this queer fixation on food was limited to a handful of patrons and not as widespread as it seemed. After all, from his table in the back, he had not been able to see the entire room and every last one of the customers. But on his way out, he passed a table where three attractive and well-dressed young women were eating hungrily, none of them speaking, their eyes glazed; two of them had flecks of food on their chins, of which they seemed oblivious, and the third had so many corn-chip crumbs sprinkled across the front of her royal-blue sweater that she appeared to be breading herself with the intention of going into the kitchen, climbing into an oven, and *becoming* food.

He was glad to get out in the clean night air.

Sweating both from the chilli-spiced dishes and the heat in the restaurant, he had wanted to take his jacket off, but he had not been able to do so because of the gun he was packing in a shoulder holster. Now he relished the chilling fog that was being harried eastward by a gentle but steady breeze.

• 13 •

Chrissie saw them enter the drainage channel, and for a moment she thought they were all going to clamber up the far side of it and off across the meadow in the direction she had been heading. Then one of them turned toward the mouth of the culvert. The figure approached the drain on all fours, in a few stealthy and sinuous strides. Though Chrissie could see nothing more of it than a shadowy shape, she had trouble believing that this thing was either one of her parents or the man called Tucker. But who else could it be?

Entering the concrete tunnel, the predator peered forward into the gloom. Its eyes shone softly amber-green, not as bright here as in moonlight, dimmer than glow-in-the-dark paint, but vaguely radiant.

Chrissie wondered how well it could see in absolute darkness. Surely its gaze could not penetrate eighty or a hundred feet of lightless pipe to the place where she crouched. Vision of that caliber would be supernatural.

It stared straight at her.

Then again, who was to say that what she was dealing with here was not supernatural? Perhaps her parents had become . . . werewolves.

She was soaked in sour sweat. She hoped the stench of the dead animal would screen her body odor.

Rising from all fours into a crouch, blocking most of the silvery moonlight at the drain entrance, the stalker slowly came forward.

Its heavy breathing was amplified by the curved concrete walls of the culvert. Chrissie breathed shallowly through her open mouth lest she reveal her presence.

Suddenly, only ten feet into the tunnel, the stalker spoke in a raspy, whispery voice and with such urgency that the words were almost run together in a single long string of syllables: *'Chrissie, you there, you, you? Come me, Chrissie, come me, come, want you, want, want, need, my Chrissie, my Chrissie.'*

That bizarre, frantic voice gave rise in Chrissie's mind to a terrifying image of a creature that was part lizard, part wolf, part human, part something unidentifiable. Yet she suspected that its actual appearance was even worse than anything she could imagine.

'Help you, want help you, help, now, come me, come, come. You there, there, you there?'

The worst thing about the voice was that, in spite of its cold hoarse note and whispery tone, in spite of its alienness, it was familiar. Chrissie recognised it as her mother's. Changed, yes, but her mother's voice just the same.

Chrissie's stomach was cramped with fear, but she was filled with another pain, too, that for a moment she could not identify. Then she realized that she ached with loss; she missed her mother, wanted her mother back, her *real* mother. If she'd had one of those ornate silver crucifixes like they always used in the fright films, she probably would have revealed herself, advanced on this hateful thing, and demanded that it surrender possession of her mother. A crucifix probably would not work because nothing in real life was as easy as in the movies; besides, whatever had happened to her parents was far stranger than vampires and werewolves and demons jumped up from hell. But if she'd had a crucifix, she would have tried it anyway.

'*Death, death, smell death, stink, death . . .*'

The mother-thing quickly advanced into the tunnel until it came to the place where Chrissie had stepped in a slippery, putrefying mass. The brightness of the shining eyes was directly related to the nearness of moonlight, for now they dimmed. Then the creature lowered its gaze to the dead animal on the culvert floor.

From beyond the mouth of the drain came the sound of something descending into the ditch. Footfalls and the clatter of stones were followed by another voice, equally as fearsome as that of the stalker now hunched over the dead animal. Calling into the pipe, it said, '*She there, there, she? What found, what, what?*'

'*. . . raccoon . . .*'

'*What, what it, what?*'

'*Dead raccoon, rotten, maggots, maggots,*' the first one said.

Chrissie was stricken by the macabre fear that she had left a tennis-shoe imprint in the rotting muck of the dead raccoon.

'*Chrissie?*' the second asked as it ventured into the culvert.

Tucker's voice. Evidently her father was searching for her across the meadow or in the next section of the forest.

Both stalkers were fidgeting constantly. Chrissie could hear them scraping – claws? – against the concrete floor of the pipe. Both sounded panicky, too. No, not panicky, really, because no fear was audible in their voices. Frantic. Frenzied. It was as if an engine in each of them was racing faster, faster, almost out of control.

'*Chrissie there, she there, she?*' Tucker asked.

The mother-thing raised its gaze from the dead raccoon and peered straight at Chrissie through the lightless tunnel.

You can't see me, Chrissie thought-prayed. I'm invisible.

The radiance of the stalker's eyes had faded to twin spots of tarnished silver. Chrissie held her breath.

Tucker said, '*Got to eat, eat, want eat.*'

The creature that had been her mother said, '*Find girl, girl, find her first, then eat, then.*'

They sounded as if they were wild animals magically gifted with crude speech.

'*Now, now, burning it up, eat now, now, burning,*' Tucker said urgently, insistently.

Chrissie was shaking so badly that she was half afraid they would hear the shudders that rattled her.

Tucker said, *'Burning it up, little animals in meadow, hear them, smell them, track, eat, eat, now.'*

Chrissie held her breath.

'Nothing here,' the mother-thing said. *'Only maggots, stink, go, eat, then find her, eat, eat, then find her, go.'*

Both stalkers retreated from the culvert and vanished.

Chrissie dared to breathe.

After waiting a minute to be sure they were really gone, she turned and troll-walked deeper into the upsloping culvert, blindly feeling the walls as she went, hunting a side passage. She must have gone two hundred yards before she found what she wanted: a tributary drain, half the size of the main line. She slid into it, feetfirst and on her back, then squirmed onto her belly and faced out toward the bigger tunnel. That was where she would spend the night. If they returned to the culvert to see if they could detect her scent in the cleaner air beyond the decomposing raccoon, she would be out of the downdraught that swept the main line, and they might not smell her.

She was heartened because their failure to probe deeper into the culvert was proof that they were not possessed of supernatural powers, neither all-seeing nor all-knowing. They were abnormally strong and quick, strange and terrifying, but they could make mistakes too. She began to think that when daylight came she had a fifty-fifty chance of getting out of the woods and finding help before she was caught.

• 14 •

In the lights outside of the Perez Family Restaurant, Sam Booker checked his watch. Only 7:10.

He went for a walk along Ocean Avenue, building up the courage to call Scott in Los Angeles. The prospect of that conversation with his son soon preoccupied him and drove all thoughts of the mannerless, gluttonous diners out of his mind.

At 7:30, he stopped at a telephone booth near a Shell service station at the corner of Juniper Lane and Ocean Avenue. He used his credit card to make a long-distance call to his house in Sherman Oaks.

At sixteen Scott thought he was mature enough to be home alone when his father was away on an assignment. Sam did not entirely agree and preferred that the boy stay with his Aunt Edna. But Scott won his way by making life pure hell for Edna, so Sam was reluctant to put her through that ordeal.

He had repeatedly drilled the boy in safety procedures – keep all doors and windows locked; know where the fire extinguishers are; know how to get out of the house from any room in an earthquake or other emergency – and had taught him how to use a handgun. In Sam's judgement Scott was still too immature to be home alone for days at a time; but at least the boy was well prepared for every contingency.

The number rang nine times. Sam was about to hang up, guiltily relieved that he'd failed to get through, when Scott finally answered.

'Hello.'

'It's me, Scott. Dad.'

'Yeah?'

Heavy-metal rock was playing at high volume in the background. He was probably in his room, his stereo cranked up so loud that the windows shook.

Sam said, 'Could you turn the music down?'

'I can hear you,' Scott mumbled.

'Maybe so, but I'm having trouble hearing you.'

'I don't have anything to say, anyway.'

'Please turn it down,' Sam said, with emphasis on the 'please.'

Scott dropped the receiver, which clattered on his nightstand. The sharp sound hurt Sam's ear. The boy lowered the volume on the stereo but only slightly. He picked up the phone and said, 'Yeah?'

'How're you doing?'

'Okay.'

'Everything all right there?'

'Why shouldn't it be?'

'I just asked.'

Sullenly: 'If you called to see if I'm having a party, don't worry. I'm not.'

Sam counted to three, giving himself time to keep his voice under control. Thickening fog swirled past the glass-walled phone booth. 'How was school today?'

'You think I didn't go?'

'I know you went.'

'You don't trust me.'

'I trust you,' Sam lied.

'You think I didn't go.'

'Did you?'

'Yeah.'

'So how was it?'

'Ridiculous. The same old shit.'

'Scott, please, you know I've asked you not to use that kind of language when you're talking to me,' Sam said, realizing that he was being forced into a confrontation against his will.

'So sorry. Same old *poop*,' Scott said in such a way that he might have been referring either to the day at school or to Sam.

'It's pretty country up here,' Sam said.

The boy did not reply.

'Wooded hillsides slope right down to the ocean.'

'So?'

Following the advice of the family counsellor whom he and Scott had been seeing both together and separately, Sam clenched his teeth, counted to three again, and tried another approach. 'Did you have dinner yet?'

'Yeah.'

'Do your homework?'

'Don't have any.'

Sam hesitated, then decided to let it pass. The counsellor, Dr. Adamski, would have been proud of such tolerance and cool self-control.

Beyond the phone booth, the Shell station's lights acquired multiple halos, and the town faded into the slowly congealing mist.

At last Sam said, 'What're you doing this evening?'

'I *was* listening to music.'

Sometimes it seemed to Sam that the music was part of what had turned the boy sour. That pounding, frenetic, unmelodic heavy-metal rock was a collection of monotonous chords and even more monotonous atonal riffs, so soulless and mind-numbing that it might have been the music produced by a civilization of intelligent machines long after man had passed from the face of the earth. After a while Scott had lost interest in most heavy-metal bands and switched allegiance to U2, but their simplistic social consciousness was no match for nihilism. Soon he grew interested in heavy-metal again, but the second time around he focused on black metal, those bands espousing – or using the dramatic trappings of – satanism; he became increasingly self-involved, antisocial, and somber. On more than one occasion, Sam had considered confiscating the kid's record collection, smashing it to bits, and disposing of it, but that seemed an absurd overreaction. After all, Sam himself had been sixteen when the Beatles and Rolling Stones were coming on the scene, and his father had railed against *that* music and predicted it would lead Sam and his entire generation into perdition. He'd turned out all right in spite of John, Paul, George, Ringo, and the Stones. He was the product of an unparalleled age of tolerance, and he did not want his mind to close up as tight as his father's mind had been.

'Well, I guess I better go,' Sam said.

The boy was silent.

'If any unexpected problems come up, you call your Aunt Edna.'

'There's nothing *she* could do for me that I couldn't do myself.'

'She loves you, Scott.'

'Yeah, sure.'

'She's your mother's sister; she'd like to love you as if you were her own. All you have to do is give her the chance.' After more silence, Sam took a deep breath and said, 'I love you, too, Scott.'

'Yeah? What's that supposed to do – turn me all gooey inside?'

'No.'

''Cause it doesn't.'

'I was just stating a fact.'

Apparently quoting from one of his favorite songs, the boy said:

> 'Nothing lasts forever;
> even love's a lie,
> a tool for manipulation;
> there's no God beyond the sky.'

Click.

Sam stood for a moment, listening to the dial tone. 'Perfect.' He returned the receiver to its cradle.

His frustration was exceeded only by his fury. He wanted to kick the shit out of something, anything, and pretend that he was savaging whomever or whatever had stolen his son from him.

He also had an empty, achy feeling in the pit of his stomach, because he *did* love Scott. The boy's alienation was devastating.

He knew he could not go back to the motel yet. He was not ready to sleep, and the prospect of spending a couple of hours in front of the idiot box, watching mindless sitcoms and dramas, was intolerable.

When he opened the phone-booth door, tendrils of fog slipped inside and seemed to pull him out into the night. For an hour he walked the streets of Moonlight Cove, deep into the residential neighborhoods, where there were no streetlamps and where trees and houses seemed to float within the mist, as if they were not rooted to the earth but tenuously tethered and in danger of breaking loose.

Four blocks north of Ocean Avenue, on Iceberry Way, as Sam walked briskly, letting the exertion and the chilly night air leech the anger from him, he heard hurried footsteps. Someone running. Three people, maybe four. It was an unmistakable sound, though curiously stealthy, not the straightforward slap-slap-slap of joggers' approach.

He turned and looked back along the gloom-enfolded street.

The footsteps ceased.

Because the partial moon had been engulfed by clouds, the scene was brightened mostly by light fanning from the windows of Bavarian-, Monterey-, English-, and Spanish-style houses nestled among pines and junipers on both sides of the street. The neighborhood was long-established, with great character, but the lack of big-windowed modern homes contributed to the murkiness. Two properties in that block had hooded, downcast Malibu landscape lighting, and a few had carriage lamps at the ends of front walks, but the fog damped those pockets of illumination. As far as Sam could see, he was alone on Iceberry Way.

He began to walk again but went less than half a block before he heard the hurried footfalls. He swung around, but as before saw no one. This time the sound faded, as though the runner had moved off a paved surface onto soft earth, then between two of the houses.

Perhaps they were on another street. Cold air and fog could play tricks with sound.

He was cautious and intrigued, however, and he quietly stepped off the cracked and root-canted sidewalk, onto someone's front lawn, into the smooth blackness beneath an immense cypress. He studied the neighborhood, and within half a minute he saw furtive movement on the north side of the street. Four shadowy figures appeared at the corner of a house, running low, in a crouch. When they crossed a lawn that was patchily illuminated by a pair of hurricane lamps on iron poles, their freakishly distorted shadows leaped wildly over the front of a white stucco house. They went to ground again in dense shrubbery before he could ascertain their size or anything else about them.

Kids, Sam thought, and they're up to no good.

He didn't know why he was so sure they were kids, perhaps because neither their quickness nor behavior was that of adults. They were either engaged on some prank against a disliked neighbor – or they were after Sam. Instinct told him that he was being stalked.

Were juvenile delinquents a problem in a community as small and closely knit as Moonlight Cove?

Every town had a few bad kids. But in the semirural atmosphere of a place like this, juvenile crime rarely included gang activities like assault and battery, armed robbery, mugging, or thrill killing. In the country, kids got into trouble with fast cars, booze, girls, and a little unsophisticated theft, but they did not prowl the streets in packs the way their counterparts did in the inner cities.

Nevertheless, Sam was suspicious of the quartet that crouched, invisible, among shadow-draped ferns and azaleas, across the street and three houses west of him. After all, something was wrong in Moonlight Cove, and conceivably the trouble was related to juvenile delinquents. The police were concealing the truth about several deaths in the past couple of months, and perhaps they were protecting someone; as unlikely as it seemed, maybe they were covering for a few kids from prominent families, kids who had taken the privileges of class too far and had gone beyond permissible, civilized behavior.

Sam was not afraid of them. He knew how to handle himself, and he was carrying a .38. Actually he would have enjoyed teaching the brats a lesson. But a confrontation with a group of teenage hoods would mean a subsequent scene with the local police, and he preferred not to bring himself to the attention of the authorities, for fear of jeopardizing his investigation.

He thought it peculiar that they would consider assaulting him in a residential neighborhood like this. One shout of alarm from him would bring people to their front porches to see what was happening. Of course, because he wanted to avoid calling even that much notice to himself, he would not cry out.

The old adage about discretion being the better part of valor was in no circumstance more applicable than in his. He moved back from the cypress under which he had taken shelter, away from the street and toward the lightless house behind him. Confident that those kids were not sure where he had gone, he planned to slip out of the neighborhood and lose them altogether.

He reached the house, hurried alongside it, and entered a rear yard, where a looming swing set was so distorted by shadows and mist that it looked like a giant spider stilting toward him through the gloom. At the end of the yard he vaulted a rail fence, beyond which was a narrow alley that serviced the block's detached garages. He intended to go south, back toward Ocean Avenue and the heart of town, but a shiver of prescience shook him toward another route. Stepping straight across the narrow backstreet, past a row of metal garbage cans, he vaulted another low fence, landing on the back lawn of another house that faced out on the street parallel to Iceberry Way.

No sooner had he left the alley than he heard soft, running footsteps on that hard surface. The juvies – if that's what they were – sounded as swift but not quite as stealthy as they had been.

They were coming in Sam's direction from the end of the block. He had the odd feeling that with some sixth sense they would be able to determine which yard he had gone into and that they would be on him before he could reach the next street. Instinct told him to stop running and go to ground. He was in good shape, yes, but he was forty-two, and they were no doubt seventeen or younger, and any middle-aged man who believed he could outrun kids was a fool.

Instead of sprinting across that new yard, he moved swiftly to a side door on the nearby clapboard garage, hoping it would be unlocked. It was. He stepped into total darkness and pulled the door shut, just as he heard the four pursuers halt in the alleyway in front of the big roll-up door at the other end of the building. They had stopped there not because they knew where he was but probably because they were trying to decide which way he might have gone.

In tomblike blackness Sam fumbled for a lock button or dead-bolt latch to secure the door by which he had entered. He found nothing.

He heard the four kids murmuring to one another, but he could not make out what they were saying. Their voices sounded strange: whispery and urgent.

Sam remained at the smaller door. He gripped the knob with both hands to keep it from turning, in case the kids searched around the garage and gave it a try.

They fell silent.

He listened intently.

Nothing.

The cold air smelled of grease and dust. He could see nothing, but he assumed a car or two occupied that space.

Although he was not afraid, he was beginning to feel foolish. How had he gotten himself into this predicament? He was a grown man, an FBI agent trained in a variety of self-defense techniques, carrying a revolver with which he possessed considerable expertise, yet he was hiding in a garage from four kids. He had gotten there because he had acted instinctively, and he usually trusted instinct implicitly, but this was—

He heard furtive movement along the outer wall of the garage. He tensed. Scraping footsteps. Approaching the small door at which he stood. As far as Sam could tell, he was hearing only one of the kids.

Leaning back, holding the knob in both hands, Sam pulled the door tight against the jamb.

The footsteps stopped in front of him.

He held his breath.

A second ticked by, two seconds, three.

Try the damn lock and move on, Sam thought irritably.

He was feeling more foolish by the second and was on the verge of confronting the kid. He could pop out of the garage as if he were a jack-in-the-box, probably scare the hell out of the punk, and send him screaming into the night.

Then he heard a voice on the other side of the door, inches from him, and although he did not know what in God's name he was hearing, he knew at once that he had been wise to trust to instinct, wise to go to ground and hide. The voice was thin, raspy, utterly chilling, and the urgent cadences of the speech were those of a frenzied psychotic or a junkie long overdue for a fix:

'Burning, need, need . . .'

He seemed to be talking to himself and was perhaps unconscious of speaking, as a man in a fever might babble deliriously.

A hard object scraped down the outside of the wooden door. Sam tried to imagine what it was.

'Feed the fire, fire, feed it, feed,' the kid said in a thin, frantic voice that was partly a whisper and partly a whine and partly a low and menacing growl. It was not much like the voice of any teenager Sam had ever heard – or any adult, for that matter.

In spite of the cold air, his brow was covered with sweat.

The unknown object scraped down the door again.

Was the kid armed? Was it a gun barrel being drawn along the wood? The blade of a knife? Just a stick?

'. . . burning, burning . . .'

A claw?

That was a crazy idea. Yet he could not shake it. In his mind was the clear image of a sharp and hornlike claw – a talon – gouging splinters from the door as it carved a line in the wood.

Sam held tightly to the knob. Sweat trickled down his temples.

At last the kid tried the door. The knob twisted in Sam's grip, but he would not let it move much.

'. . . *oh, God, it burns, hurts, oh God . . .*'

Sam was finally afraid. The kid sounded so damned weird. Like a PCP junkie flying out past the orbit of Mars somewhere, only worse than that, far stranger and more dangerous than any angel-dust freak. Sam was scared because he didn't know what the hell he was up against.

The kid tried to pull the door open.

Sam held it tight against the jamb.

Quick, frenetic words: '. . . *feed the fire, feed the fire . . .*'

I wonder if he can smell me in here? Sam thought, and under the circumstances that bizarre idea seemed no crazier than the image of the kid with claws.

Sam's heart was hammering. Stinging perspiration seeped into the corners of his eyes. The muscles in his neck, shoulders, and arms ached fiercely; he was straining much harder than necessary to keep the door shut.

After a moment, apparently deciding that his quarry was not in the garage after all, the kid gave up. He ran along the side of the building, back toward the alley. As he hurried away, a barely audible keening issued from him; it was a sound of pain, need . . . and animal excitement. He was struggling to contain that low cry, but it escaped him anyway.

Sam heard cat-soft footsteps approaching from several directions. The other three would-be muggers rejoined the kid in the alley, and their whispery voices were filled with the same frenzy that had marked his, though they were too far away now for Sam to hear what they were saying. Abruptly, they fell silent and, a moment later, as if they were members of a wolfpack responding instinctively to the scent of game or danger, they ran as one along the alleyway, heading north. Soon their sly footsteps faded, and again the night was grave-still.

For several minutes after the pack left, Sam stood in the dark garage, holding fast to the doorknob.

· **15** ·

The dead boy was sprawled in an open drainage ditch along the county road on the southeast side of Moonlight Cove. His frost-white face was spotted with blood. In the glare of the two tripod-mounted police lamps flanking the ditch, his wide eyes stared unblinkingly at a shore immeasurably more distant than the nearby Pacific.

Standing by one of the hooded lamps, Loman Watkins looked down at the small corpse, forcing himself to bear witness to the death of Eddie Valdoski because Eddie, only six years old, was his godson. Loman had gone to high school with Eddie's father, George, and in a strictly platonic sense he had been in love with Eddie's mother, Nella, for almost twenty years. Eddie had been a great kid, bright and inquisitive and well behaved. Had been. But now . . . Hideously bruised, savagely bitten, scratched and torn, neck broken, the boy was little more than a pile of decomposing trash, his promising potential destroyed, his flame snuffed, deprived of life – and life of him.

Of the innumerable terrible things Loman had encountered in twenty-one years of police work, this was perhaps the worst. And because of his personal relationship with the victim, he should have been deeply shaken if not devastated. Yet he was barely affected by the sight of the small, battered body. Sadness, regret, anger, and a flurry of other emotions touched him, but only lightly and briefly, the way unseen fish might brush past a swimmer in a dark sea. Of grief, which should have pierced him like nails, he felt nothing.

Barry Sholnick, one of the new officers on the recently expanded Moonlight Cove police force, straddled the ditch, one foot on each bank, and took a photograph of Eddie Valdoski. For an instant the boy's glazed eyes were silvery with a reflection of the flash.

Loman's growing inability to *feel* was, strangely, the one thing that evoked strong feelings: It scared the shit out of him. Lately he was increasingly frightened by his emotional detachment, an unwanted but apparently irreversible hardening of the heart that would soon leave him with auricles of marble and ventricles of common stone.

He was one of the New People now, different in many ways from the man he had once been. He still looked the same – five ten, squarely built, with a broad and remarkably innocent face for a man in his line of work – but he wasn't only what he appeared to be. Perhaps a greater control of emotions, a more stable and analytical outlook, was an unanticipated benefit of the Change. But was that really beneficial? Not to feel? Not to grieve?

Though the night was chilly, sour sweat broke out on his face, the back of his neck, and under his arms.

Dr. Ian Fitzgerald, the coroner, was busy elsewhere, but Victor Callan, owner of Callan's Funeral Home and the assistant coroner, was helping another officer, Jules Timmerman, scour the ground between the ditch and the nearby woods. They were looking for clues that the killer might have left behind.

Actually they were just putting on a show for the benefit of the score of area residents who had gathered on the far side of the road. Even if clues were found, no one would be arrested for the crime. No trial would ever take place. If they found Eddie's killer, they would cover for him and deal with him in their own way, in order to conceal the existence of the New People from those who had not yet undergone the Change. Because without doubt the killer was what Thomas Shaddack called a 'regressive', one of the New People gone bad. Very bad.

Loman turned away from the dead boy. He walked back along the county road, toward the Valdoski house, which was a few hundred yards north and veiled in mist.

He ignored the onlookers, although one of them called to him: 'Chief? What the hell's going on, Chief?'

This was a semirural area barely within the town limits. The houses were widely separated, and their scattered lights did little to hold back the night. Before he was halfway to the Valdoski place, though he was within hailing distance of the men at the crime scene, he felt isolated. Trees, tortured by ages of sea wind on nights far less calm than this one, bent toward the two-lane road, their scraggly branches overhanging the gravel shoulder on which he walked.

He kept imagining movement in the dark boughs above him, and in the blackness and fog between the twisted trunks of the trees.

He put his hand on the butt of the revolver that was holstered at his side.

Loman Watkins had been the chief of police in Moonlight Cove for nine years, and in the past month more blood had been spilled in his jurisdiction than in the entire preceding eight years and eleven months. He was convinced that worse was coming. He had a hunch that the regressives were more numerous and more of a problem than Shaddack realized – or was willing to admit.

He feared the regressives almost as much as he feared his own new, cool, dispassionate perspective.

Unlike happiness and grief and joy and sorrow, stark fear was a survival mechanism, so perhaps he would not lose touch with it as thoroughly as he was losing touch with other emotions. That thought made him as uneasy as did the phantom movement in the trees.

Is fear, he wondered, the only emotion that will thrive in this brave new world we're making?

• 16 •

After a greasy cheeseburger, soggy fries, and an icy bottle of Dos Equis in the deserted coffee shop at Cove Lodge, Tessa Lockland returned to her room, propped herself up in bed with pillows, and called her mother in San Diego. Marion answered the phone on the first ring, and Tessa said, 'Hi, Mom.'

'Where are you, Teejay?' As a kid, Tessa could never decide whether she wanted to be called by her first name or her middle, Jane, so her mother always called her by her initials, as if that were a name in itself.

'Cove Lodge,' Tessa said.

'Is it nice?'

'It's the best I could find. This isn't a town that worries about having first-rate tourist facilities. If it didn't have such a spectacular view, Cove Lodge is one of those places that would be able to survive only by showing closed-circuit porn movies on the TV and renting rooms by the hour.'

'Is it clean?'

'Reasonably.'

'If it wasn't clean, I'd insist you move out right now.'

'Mom, when I'm on location, shooting a film, I don't always have luxury accommodations, you know. When I did that documentary on Miskito Indians in Central America, I went on hunts with them and slept in the mud.'

'Teejay, dear, you must never tell people that you slept in the mud. Pigs sleep in the mud. You must say you roughed it or camped out, but never that you slept in the mud. Even unpleasant experiences can be worthwhile if one keeps one's sense of dignity and style.'

'Yes, Mom, I know. My point was that Cove Lodge isn't great, but it's better than sleeping in the mud.'

'Camping out.'

'Better than camping out,' Tessa said.

Both were silent a moment. Then Marion said, 'Dammit, I should be there with you.'

'Mom, you've got a broken leg.'

'I should have gone to Moonlight Cove as soon as I heard they'd found poor Janice. If I'd been there, they wouldn't have cremated the body. By God, they wouldn't! I'd have stopped that, and I'd have arranged another autopsy by *trustworthy* authorities, and now there'd be no need for you to get involved. I'm so angry with myself.'

Tessa slumped back in the pillows and sighed. 'Mom, don't do this to yourself. You broke your leg three days before Janice's body was even found. You can't travel easily now, and you couldn't travel easily then, either. It's not your fault.'

'There was a time when a broken leg couldn't have stopped me.'

'You're not twenty any more, Mom.'

'Yes, I know, I'm old,' Marion said miserably. 'Sometimes I think about how old I am, and it's scary.'

'You're only sixty-four, you look not a day past fifty, and you broke your leg skydiving, for God's sake, so you're not going to get any pity from me.'

'Comfort and pity is what an elderly parent expects from a good daughter.'

'If you caught me calling you elderly or treating you with pity, you'd kick my ass halfway to China.'

'The chance to kick a daughter's ass now and then is one of the pleasures of a mother's later life, Teejay. Damn, where did that tree come from, anyway? I've been skydiving for thirty years, and I've never landed in a tree before, and I swear it wasn't there when I looked down on the final approach to pick my drop spot.'

Though a certain amount of the Lockland family's unshakable optimism and spirited approach to life came from Tessa's late father, Bernard, a large measure of it – with a full measure of indomitability as well – flowed from Marion's gene pool.

Tessa said, 'Tonight, just after I got here, I went down to the beach where they found her.'

'This must be awful for you, Teejay.'

'I can handle it.'

When Janice died, Tessa had been traveling in rural regions of Afghanistan, researching the effects of genocidal war on the Afghan people and culture, intending to script a documentary on that subject. Her mother had been unable to get word of Janice's death to Tessa until two weeks after the body washed up on the shore of Moonlight Cove. Five days ago, on October 8, she had flown out of Afghanistan with a sense of having failed her sister somehow. Her load of guilt was at least as heavy as her mother's, but what she said was true: She *could* handle it.

'You were right, Mom. The official version stinks.'

'What've you learned?'

'Nothing yet. But I stood right there on the sand, where she was supposed to have taken the Valium, where she set out on her last swim, where they found her two days later, and I knew their whole story was garbage. I feel it in my guts, Mom. And one way or another, I'm going to find out what really happened.'

'You've got to be careful, dear.'

'I will.'

'If Janice was . . . murdered . . .'

'I'll be okay.'

'And if, as we suspect, the police up there can't be trusted . . .'

'Mom, I'm five feet four, blond, blue-eyed, perky, and about as dangerous-looking as a Disney chipmunk. All my life I've had to work against my looks to be taken seriously. Women all want to mother me or be my big sister, and men either want to be my father or get me in the sack, but darned few can see immediately through the exterior and realize I've got a brain that is, I strongly believe, bigger than that of a gnat; usually they have to know me a while. So I'll just use my appearance instead of struggling against it. No one here will see me as a threat.'

'You'll stay in touch?'

'Of course.'

'If you feel you're in danger, just leave, get out.'

'I'll be all right.'

'Promise you won't stay if it's dangerous,' Marion persisted.

'I promise. But you have to promise *me* that you won't jump out of any more airplanes for a while.'

'I'm too old for that, dear. I'm elderly now. Ancient. I'm going to have to pursue interests suitable for my age. I've always wanted to learn to water-ski, for instance, and that documentary you did on dirt-bike racing made those little motorcycles look like so much fun.'

'I love you to pieces, Mom.'

'I love you, Teejay. More than life itself.'

'I'll make them pay for Janice.'

'If there's anyone who deserves to pay. Just remember, Teejay, that our Janice is gone, but you're still here, and your *first* allegiance should never be to the dead.'

• 17 •

George Valdoski sat at the formica-topped kitchen table. Though his work-scarred hands were clasped tightly around a glass of whiskey, he could not prevent them from trembling; the surface of the amber bourbon shivered constantly.

When Loman Watkins entered and closed the door behind him, George didn't even look up. Eddie had been his only child.

George was tall, solid in the chest and shoulders. Thanks to deeply and closely set eyes, a thin-lipped mouth, and sharp features, he had a hard, mean look in spite of his general handsomeness. His forbidding appearance was deceptive, however, for he was a sensitive man, soft-spoken and kind.

'How you doin'?' Loman asked.

George bit his lower lip and nodded as if to say that he would get through this nightmare, but he did not meet Loman's eyes.

'I'll look in on Nella,' Loman said.

This time George didn't even nod.

As Loman crossed the too-bright kitchen, his hard-soled shoes squeaked on the linoleum floor. He paused at the doorway to the small dining room and looked back at his friend. 'We'll find the bastard, George. I swear we will.'

At last George looked up from the whiskey. Tears shimmered in his eyes, but he would not let them flow. He was a proud, hardheaded Pole, determined to be strong. He said, 'Eddie was playin' in the backyard toward dusk, just right out there in the backyard, where you could see him if you looked out any window, right in his *own* yard. When Nella called him for supper just after dark, when he didn't come or answer, we thought he'd gone to one of the neighbor's to play with some other kids, without asking like he should've.' He had related all of this before, more than once, but he seemed to need to go over it again and again, as if repetition would wear down the ugly reality and thereby change it as surely as ten thousand playings of a tape cassette would eventually scrape away the music and leave a hiss of white noise. 'We started lookin' for him, couldn't find him, wasn't scared at first; in fact we were a little angry with him; but then we got worried and then scared, and I was just about to call you for help when we found him there in the ditch, sweet Jesus, all torn up in the ditch.' He took a deep breath and another, and the pent-up tears glistened brightly in his eyes. 'What kind of monster would do that to a child, take him away somewhere and do that, and *then* be cruel enough to bring him back here and drop him where we'd find him? Had to've been that way, 'cause we'd have heard . . . heard the screaming if the bastard had done all that to Eddie right here somewheres. *Had* to've taken him away, done all that, then brought him back so we'd find him. What kind of man, Loman? For God's sake, what kind of man?'

'Psychotic,' Loman said, as he had said before, and that much was true. The regressives were psychotic. Shaddack had coined a term for their condition: metamorphic-related psychosis. 'Probably on drugs,' he added, and he was lying now. Drugs – at least the conventional illegal pharmacopoeia – had nothing to do with Eddie's death. Loman was still surprised at how easy it was for him to lie to a close friend, something that he had once been unable to do. The immorality of lying was a concept more suited to the Old People and their turbulently emotional world. Old-fashioned concepts of what was immoral might ultimately have no meaning to the New People, for if they changed as Shaddack believed they would, efficiency and expediency and maximum performance would be the only moral absolutes. 'The country's rotten with drug freaks these days. Burnt-out brains. No morals, no goals but cheap thrills. They're our inheritance from the recent age of Do Your Own Thing. This guy was a drug-disoriented freak, George, and I swear we'll get him.'

George looked down at his whiskey again. He drank some.

Then to himself more than to Loman, he said, 'Eddie was playin' in the backyard toward dusk, just right out there in the backyard, where you could see him if you looked out any window . . .' His voice trailed away.

Reluctantly Loman went upstairs to the master bedroom to see how Nella was coping.

She was lying on the bed, propped up a bit with pillows, and Dr. Jim Worthy was sitting in a chair that he had moved to her side. He was the youngest of Moonlight Cove's three doctors, thirty-eight, an earnest man with a neatly trimmed mustache, wire-rimmed glasses, and a proclivity for bow ties.

The physician's bag was on the floor at his feet. A stethoscope hung around his neck. He was filling an unusually large syringe from a six-ounce bottle of golden fluid.

Worthy turned to look at Loman, and their eyes met, and they did not need to say anything.

Either having heard Loman's soft footsteps or having sensed him by some subtler means, Nella Valdoski opened her eyes, which were red and swollen from crying. She was still a lovely woman with flaxen hair and features that seemed too delicate to be the work of nature, more like the finely honed art of a master sculptor. Her mouth softened and trembled when she spoke his name: 'Oh, Loman.'

He went around the bed, to the side opposite Dr. Worthy, and took hold of the hand that Nella held out to him. It was clammy, cold, and trembling.

'I'm giving her a tranquilizer,' Worthy said. 'She needs to relax, even sleep if she can.'

'I don't want to sleep,' Nella said. 'I *can't* sleep. Not after . . . not after this . . . not ever again after this.'

'Easy,' Loman said, gently rubbing her hand. He sat on the edge of the bed. 'Just let Dr. Worthy take care of you. This is for the best, Nella.'

For half his life, Loman had loved this woman, his best friend's wife, though he had never acted upon his feelings. He had always told himself that it was a strictly platonic attraction. Looking at her now, however, he knew passion had been a part of it.

The disturbing thing was . . . well, though he *knew* what he had felt for her all these years, though he remembered it, he could not feel it any longer. His love, his passion, his pleasant yet melancholy longing had faded as had most of his other emotional responses; he was still aware of his previous feelings for her, but they were like another aspect of him that had split off and drifted away like a ghost departing a corpse.

Worthy set the filled syringe on the nightstand. He unbuttoned and pushed up the loose sleeve on Nella's blouse, then tied a length of rubber tubing around her arm, tight enough to make a vein more evident.

As the physician swabbed Nella's arm with an alcohol-soaked cottonball, she said, 'Loman, what are we going to do?'

'Everything will be fine,' he said, stroking her hand.

'No. How can you say that? Eddie's dead. He was so sweet, so small and sweet, and now he's gone. Nothing will be fine again.'

'Very soon you'll feel better,' Loman assured her. 'Before you know it the hurt will be gone. It won't matter as much as it does now. I promise it won't.'

She blinked and stared at him as if he were talking nonsense, but then she did not know what was about to happen to her.

Worthy slipped the needle into her arm.

She twitched.

The golden fluid flowed out of the syringe, into her bloodstream.

She closed her eyes and began to cry softly again, not at the pain of the needle but at the loss of her son.

Maybe it *is* better not to care so much, not to love so much, Loman thought.

The syringe was empty.

Worthy withdrew the needle from her vein.

Again Loman met the doctor's gaze.

Nella shuddered.

The Change would require two more injections, and someone would have to stay with Nella for the next four or five hours, not only to administer the drugs but to make sure that she did not hurt herself during the conversion. Becoming a New Person was not a painless process.

Nella shuddered again.

Worthy tilted his head, and the lamplight struck his wire-rimmed glasses at a new angle, transforming the lenses into mirrors that for a moment hid his eyes, giving him an uncharacteristically menacing appearance.

Shudders, more violent and protracted this time, swept through Nella.

From the doorway George Valdoski said, 'What's going on here?'

Loman had been so focused on Nella that he had not heard George coming. He got up at once and let go of Nella's hand. 'The doctor thought she needed—'

'What's that horse needle for?' George said, referring to the huge syringe. The needle itself was no larger than an ordinary hypodermic.

'Tranquilizer,' Dr. Worthy said. 'She needs to—'

'Tranquilizer?' George interrupted. 'Looks like you gave her enough to knock down a bull.'

Loman said, 'Now, George, the doctor knows what he's—'

On the bed Nella fell under the thrall of the injection. Her body suddenly stiffened, her hands curled into tight fists, her teeth clenched, and her jaw muscles bulged. In her throat and temples, the arteries swelled and throbbed visibly as her heartbeat drastically accelerated. Her eyes glazed over, and she passed into the peculiar twilight that was the Change, neither conscious nor unconscious.

'What's wrong with her?' George demanded.

Between clenched teeth, lips peeled back in a grimace of pain, Nella let out a strange, low groan. She arched her back until only her shoulders and heels were in contact with the bed. She appeared to be full of violent energy, as if she were a boiler straining with excess steam pressure, and for a moment she seemed about to explode. Then she collapsed back onto the mattress, shuddered more violently than ever, and broke out in a copious sweat.

George looked at Worthy, at Loman. He clearly realized that something was very wrong, though he could not begin to understand the nature of that wrongness.

'Stop.' Loman drew his revolver as George stepped backward toward the second-floor hall. 'Come all the way in here, George, and lie down on the bed beside Nella.'

In the doorway George Valdoski froze, staring in disbelief and dismay at the revolver.

'If you try to leave,' Loman said, 'I'll have to shoot you, and I don't really want to do that.'

'You wouldn't,' George said, counting on decades of friendship to protect him.

'Yes, I would,' Loman said coldly. 'I'd kill you if I had to, and we'd cover it with a story you wouldn't like. We'd say that we caught you in a contradiction, that we found some evidence that *you* were the one who killed Eddie, killed your own boy, some twisted sex thing, and that when we confronted you with proof, you grabbed my revolver out of my holster. There was a struggle. You were shot. Case closed.'

Coming from someone who was supposed to be a close and treasured friend, Loman's threat was so monstrous that at first George was speechless. Then, as he stepped back into the room, he said, 'You'd let everyone think . . . think I did those terrible things to Eddie? Why? What're you doing, Loman? What the hell are you doing? Who . . . who are you protecting?'

'Lie down on the bed,' Loman said.

Dr. Worthy was preparing another syringe for George.

On the bed Nella was shivering ceaselessly, twitching, writhing. Sweat trickled down her face; her hair was damp and tangled. Her eyes were open, but she seemed unaware that others were in the room. Maybe she was not even conscious of her whereabouts. She was seeing a place beyond this room or looking within herself; Loman didn't know which and could remember nothing of his own conversion except that the pain had been excruciating.

Reluctantly approaching the bed, George Valdoski said, 'What's happening, Loman? Christ, what is this? What's wrong?'

'Everything'll be fine,' Loman assured him. 'It's for the best, George. It's really for the best.'

'*What's* for the best? What in God's name—'

'Lie down, George. Everything'll be fine.'

'What's happening to Nella?'

'Lie down, George. It's for the best,' Loman said.

'It's for the best,' Dr. Worthy agreed as he finished filling the syringe from a new bottle of the golden fluid.

'It's really for the best,' Loman said. 'Trust me.' With the revolver he waved George toward the bed and smiled reassuringly.

• 18 •

Harry Talbot's house was Bauhaus-inspired redwood, with a wealth of big windows. It was three blocks south of the heart of Moonlight Cove, on the east side of Conquistador Avenue, a street named for the fact that Spanish conquerors had bivouacked in that area centuries earlier, when accompanying the Catholic clergy along the California coast to establish missions. On rare occasions Harry dreamed of being one of those ancient soldiers, marching northward into unexplored territory, and it was always a nice dream because, in that adventure fantasy, he was never wheelchair-bound.

Most of Moonlight Cove was built on wooded hillsides facing the sea, and Harry's lot sloped down to Conquistador, providing a perfect perch for a man whose main activity in life was spying on his fellow townsmen. From his third-floor bedroom at the northeast corner of the house, he could see at least portions of all the streets between Conquistador and the cove – Juniper Lane, Serra Street, Roshmore Way, and Cypress Lane – as well as the intersecting streets which ran east-west. To the north, he could glimpse pieces of Ocean Avenue and even beyond. Of course the breadth and depth of his field of vision would have been drastically limited if his house hadn't been one story higher than most of those around it and if he hadn't been equipped with a 60mm f/8 refractor telescope and a good pair of binoculars.

At 9:30 Monday night, October 13, Harry was in his custom-made stool, between the enormous west and north windows, bent to the eyepiece of the telescope. The high stool had arms and a backrest like a chair, four wide-spread sturdy legs for maximum balance, and a weighted base to prevent it from tipping over easily when he was levering himself into it from the wheelchair. It also had a harness, something like that in an automobile, allowing him to lean forward to the telescope without slipping off the stool and falling to the floor.

Because he had no use whatsoever of his left leg and left arm, because his right leg was too weak to support him, because he could rely only on his right arm – which, thank God, the Viet Cong had spared – even transferring from the battery-powered wheelchair to a custom-made stool was a torturous undertaking. But the effort was worthwhile because every year Harry Talbot lived more through his binoculars and telescope than he had the year before. Perched on his special stool, he sometimes almost forgot his handicaps, for in his own way he was participating in life.

His favorite movie was *Rear Window* with Jimmy Stewart. He had watched it probably a hundred times.

At the moment the telescope was focused on the back of Callan's Funeral Home, the only mortuary in Moonlight Cove, on the east side of Juniper Lane, which ran parallel to Conquistador but was one block closer to the sea. He was able to see the place by focusing between two houses on the opposite side of his own street, past the thick trunk of a Big Cone pine, and across the service alley that ran between Juniper and Conquistador. The funeral home backed up to that alley, and Harry had a view that included a corner of the garage in which the hearse was parked, the rear entrance to the house itself, and the entrance to the new wing in which the corpses were embalmed and prepared for viewing, or cremated.

During the past two months he had seen some strange things at Callan's. Tonight, however, no unusual activity enlivened Harry's patient watch over the place.

'Moose?'

The dog rose from his resting place in the corner and padded across the unlighted bedroom to Harry's side. He was a full-grown black Labrador, virtually invisible in the darkness. He nuzzled Harry's leg: the right one, in which Harry still had some feeling.

Reaching down, Harry petted Moose. 'Get me a beer, old fella.'

Moose was a service dog raised and trained by Canine Companions for Independence, and he was always happy to be needed. He hurried to the small refrigerator in the corner, which was designed for under-the-counter use in restaurants and could be opened with a foot pedal.

'None there,' Harry said. 'I forgot to bring a six-pack up from the kitchen this afternoon.'

The dog had already discovered that the bedroom fridge contained no Coors. He padded into the hallway, his claws clicking softly on the polished wood floor. No room had carpets, for the wheelchair rolled more efficiently on hard surfaces. In the hall the dog leaped and hit the elevator button with one paw, and immediately the purr and whine of the lift machinery filled the house.

Harry returned his attention to the telescope and to the rear of Callan's Funeral Home. Fog drifted through the town in waves, some thick and blinding, some wispy. But lights brightened the rear of the mortuary, giving him a clear view; through the telescope, he seemed to be standing between the twin brick pilasters flanking the driveway that served the back of the property.

If the night had been fogless, he would have been able to count the rivets in the metal door of the embalmery-crematorium.

Behind him the elevator doors rolled open. He heard Moose enter the lift. Then it started down to the first floor.

Bored with Callan's, Harry slowly swiveled the scope to the left, moving the field of vision southward to the large vacant lot adjacent to the funeral home. Adjusting the focus, he looked across that empty property and across the street to the Gosdale house on the west side of Juniper, drawing in on the dining-room window.

With his good hand, he unscrewed the eyepiece and put it on a high metal table beside his stool, quickly and deftly replacing it with one of several other eyepieces, thus allowing a clearer focus on the Gosdales. Because the fog was at that moment in a thinning phase, he could see into the Gosdale dining room almost as well as if he had been crouched on their porch with his face to the window. Herman and Louise Gosdale were playing pinochle with their neighbors, Dan and Vera Kaiser, as they did every Monday night and on some Fridays.

The elevator reached the ground floor; the motor stopped whining, and silence returned to the house. Moose was now two floors below, hurrying along the hallway to the kitchen.

On an unusually clear night, when Dan Kaiser was sitting with his back to the window and at the correct angle, Harry occasionally could see the man's pinochle hand. A few times he had been tempted to call Herman Gosdale and describe his adversary's cards to him, with some advice on how to play out the trick.

But he dared not let people know he spent much of his day in his bedroom – darkened at night to avoid being silhouetted at the window – vicariously participating in their lives. They would not understand. Those whole of limb were uneasy about a handicapped person from the start, for they found it too easy to believe that the crippling twist of legs and arms extended to the mind. They would think he was nosy; worse, they might mark him as a peeping Tom, a degenerate voyeur.

That was not the case. Harry Talbot had set down strict rules governing his use of the telescope and binoculars, and he faithfully abided by them. For one thing, he would never try to get a glimpse of a woman undressed.

Arnella Scarlatti lived across the street from him and three doors north, and he once discovered, by accident, that she spent some evenings in her bedroom, listening to music or reading in the nude. She turned on only a small bedside lamp, and gauzy sheers hung between the drapes, and she always stayed away from the windows, so she saw no need to draw the drapes on every occasion. In fact she could not be seen by anyone less prepared to see her than Harry was. Arnella was lovely. Even through the sheers and in the dim lamplight, her exquisite body had been revealed to Harry in detail. Astonished by her nakedness, riveted by surprise and by the sensuous concavities and convexities of her full-breasted, long-legged body, he had stared for perhaps a minute. Then, as hot with embarrassment as with desire, he had turned the scope from her. Though Harry had not been with a woman in more than twenty years, he never invaded Arnella's bedroom again. On many mornings he looked at an angle into the side window of her tidy first-floor kitchen and watched her at breakfast, studying her perfect face as she had her juice and muffin or toast and eggs. She was beautiful beyond his abilities of description, and from what he knew of her life, she seemed to be a nice person, as well. In a way he supposed he was in love with her, as a boy could love a teacher who was forever beyond his reach, but he never used unrequited love as an excuse to caress her unclothed body with his gaze.

Likewise, if he caught one of his neighbors in another kind of embarrassing situation, he looked away. He watched them fight with one another, yes, and he watched them laugh together, eat, play cards, cheat on their diets, wash dishes, and perform the countless other acts of daily life, but not because he wanted to get any dirt on them or find reason to feel superior to them. He got no cheap thrill from his observations of them. What he wanted was to be a part of their lives, to reach out to them – even if one-sidedly – and make of them an extended family; he wanted to have reason to *care* about them and, through that caring, to experience a fuller emotional life.

The elevator motor hummed again. Moose evidently had gone into the kitchen, opened one of the four doors of the under-the-counter refrigerator, and fetched a cold can of Coors. Now he was returning with the brew.

Harry Talbot was a gregarious man, and on coming home from the war with only one useful limb, he was advised to move into a group home for the disabled, where he might have a social life in a caring atmosphere. The counselors warned him that he would not be accepted if he tried to live in the world of the whole and healthy; they said he would encounter unconscious yet hurtful cruelty from most people he met, especially the cruelty of thoughtless exclusion, and would finally fall into the grip of a deep and terrible loneliness. But Harry was as stubbornly independent as he was gregarious, and the prospect of living in a group home, with only the companionship of disabled people and caretakers, seemed worse than no companionship at all. Now he lived alone, but for Moose, with few visitors other than his once-a-week housekeeper, Mrs. Hunsbok (from whom he hid the telescope and binoculars in a bedroom closet). Much of what the counselors warned him about was proved true daily; however, they had not imagined Harry's ability to find solace and a sufficient sense of family through surreptitious but benign observation of his neighbors.

The elevator reached the third floor. The door slid open, and Moose padded into the bedroom, straight to Harry's high stool.

The telescope was on a wheeled platform, and Harry pushed it aside. He reached down and patted the dog's head. He took the cold can from the Labrador's mouth. Moose had held it by the bottom for maximum cleanliness. Harry put the can between his limp legs, plucked a penlight off the table on the other side of his stool, and directed the beam on the can to be sure it was Coors and not Diet Coke.

Those were the two beverages that the dog had been taught to fetch, and for the most part the good pooch recognized the difference between the words 'beer' and 'Coke', and was able to keep the command in mind all the way to the kitchen. On rare occasions he forgot along the way and returned with the wrong drink. Rarer still, he brought odd items that had nothing to do with the command he'd been given: a slipper; a newspaper; twice, an unopened bag of dog biscuits; once, a hardboiled egg, carried so gently that the shell was not cracked between his teeth; strangest of all, a toilet-bowl brush from the housekeeper's supplies. When he brought the wrong item, Moose always proved successful on the second try.

Long ago Harry had decided that the pooch often was not mistaken but only having fun with him. His close association with Moose had convinced him that dogs were gifted with a sense of humor.

This time, neither mistaken nor joking, Moose had brought what he'd been asked to bring. Harry grew thirstier at the sight of the can of Coors.

Switching off the penlight, he said, 'Good boy. Good, good, *gooood* dog.'

Moose whined happily. He sat at attention in the darkness at the foot of the stool, waiting to be sent on another errand.

'Go, Moose. Lie down. That's a good dog.'

Disappointed, the Lab moseyed into the corner and curled up on the floor, while his master popped the tab on the beer and took a long swallow.

Harry set the Coors aside and pulled the telescope in front of him. He returned to his scrutiny of the night, the neighborhood, and his extended family.

The Gosdales and Kaisers were still playing cards.

Nothing but eddying fog moved at Callan's Funeral Home.

One block south on Conquistador, at the moment illuminated by the walkway lamps at the Sternbach house, Ray Chang, the owner of the town's only television and electronics store, was coming this way. He was walking his dog, Jack, a golden retriever. They moved at a leisurely pace, as Jack sniffed each tree along the sidewalk, searching for just the right one on which to relieve himself.

The tranquillity and familiarity of those scenes pleased Harry, but the mood was shattered abruptly when he shifted his attention through his north window to the Simpson place. Ella and Denver Simpson lived in a cream-colored, tile-roofed Spanish house on the other side of Conquistador and two blocks north, just beyond the old Catholic cemetery and one block this side of Ocean Avenue. Because nothing in the graveyard – except part of one tree – obstructed Harry's view of the Simpsons' property, he was able to get an angled but tight focus on all the windows on two sides of the house. He drew in on the lighted kitchen. Just as the image in the eyepiece resolved from a blur to a sharp-lined picture, he saw Ella Simpson struggling with her husband, who was pressing her against the refrigerator; she was twisting in his grasp, clawing at his face, screaming.

A shiver sputtered the length of Harry's shrapnel-damaged spine.

He knew at once that what was happening at the Simpsons' house was connected with other disturbing things he had seen lately. Denver was Moonlight Cove's postmaster, and Ella operated a successful beauty parlor. They were in their mid-thirties, one of the few local black couples, and as far as Harry knew, they were happily married. Their physical conflict was so out of character that it had to be related to the recent inexplicable and ominous events that Harry had witnessed.

Ella wrenched free of Denver. She took only one twisting step away from him before he swung a fist at her. The blow caught her on the side of the neck. She went down. Hard.

In the corner of Harry's bedroom, Moose detected the new tension in his master. The dog raised his head and chuffed once, twice.

Bent forward on his stool, riveted to the eyepiece, Harry saw two men step forward from a part of the Simpson kitchen that was out of line with the window. Though they were not in uniform, he recognized them as Moonlight Cove police officers: Paul Hawthorne and Reese Dorn. Their presence confirmed Harry's intuitive sense that this incident was part of the bizarre pattern of violence and conspiracy of which he had become increasingly aware during the past several weeks. Not for the first time, he wished to God he could figure out what was going on in his once serene little town. Hawthorne and Dorn plucked Ella off the floor and held her firmly between them. She appeared to be only half conscious, dazed by the punch her husband had thrown.

Denver was speaking to Hawthorne, Dorn, or his wife. Impossible to tell which. His face was contorted with rage of such intensity that Harry was chilled by it.

A third man stepped into sight, moving straight to the windows to close the Levolor blinds. A thicker vein of fog flowed eastward from the sea, clouding the view, but Harry recognized this man too: Dr. Ian Fitzgerald, the oldest of Moonlight Cove's three physicians. He had maintained a family practice in town for almost thirty years and had long been known affectionately as Doc Fitz. He was Harry's own doctor, an unfailingly warm and concerned man, but at the moment he looked colder than an iceberg. As the slats of the Levolor blind came together, Harry stared into Doc Fitz's face and saw a hardness of features and a fierceness in the eyes that weren't characteristic of the man; thanks to the telescope, Harry seemed to be only a foot from the old physician, and what he saw was a familiar face but, simultaneously, that of a total stranger.

Unable to peer into the kitchen any longer, he pulled back for a wider view of the house. He was pressing too hard against the eyepiece; dull pain radiated outward from the socket, across his face. He cursed the curdling fog but tried to relax.

Moose whined inquisitively.

After a minute, a light came on in the room at the southeast corner of the second floor of the Simpson house. Harry immediately zoomed in on a window. The master bedroom. In spite of the occluding fog, he saw Hawthorne and Dorn bring Ella in from the upstairs hall. They threw her onto the quilted blue spread on the queen-size bed.

Denver and Doc Fitz entered the room behind them. The doctor put his black leather bag on a nightstand. Denver drew the drapes at the front window that looked out on Conquistador Avenue, then came to the graveyard-side window on which Harry was focused. For a moment Denver stared out into the night, and Harry had the eerie feeling that the man saw him, though they were two blocks away, as if Denver had the vision of Superman, a built-in biological telescope of his own. The same sensation had gripped Harry on other occasions, when he was 'eye-to-eye' with people this way, long before odd things had begun to happen in Moonlight Cove, so he knew that Denver was not actually aware of him. He was spooked nonetheless. Then the postmaster pulled those curtains shut, as well, though not as tightly as he should have done, leaving a two-inch gap between the panels.

Trembling now, damp with cold perspiration, Harry worked with a series of eyepieces, adjusting the power on the scope and trying to sharpen the focus, until he had pulled in so close to the window that the lens was filled by the narrow slot between the drapes. He seemed to be not merely *at* the window but beyond it, standing in that master bedroom, behind the drapes.

The denser scarves of fog slipped eastward, and a thinner veil floated in from the sea, further improving Harry's view. Hawthorne and Dorn were holding Ella Simpson on the bed. She was thrashing, but they had her by the legs and arms, and she was no match for them.

Denver held his wife's face by the chin and stuffed a wadded handkerchief or piece of white clothing into her mouth, gagging her.

Harry had a brief glimpse of the woman's face as she struggled with her assailants. Her eyes were wide with terror.

'Oh, shit.'

Moose got up and came to him.

In the Simpsons' house, Ella's valiant struggle had caused her skirt to ride up. Her pale yellow panties were exposed. Buttons had popped open on her green blouse. In spite of that, the scene conveyed no feeling that rape was imminent, not even a hint of sexual tension. Whatever they were doing to her was perhaps even more menacing and cruel – and certainly stranger – than rape.

Doc Fitz stepped to the foot of the bed, blocking Harry's view of Ella and her oppressors. The physician held a bottle of amber fluid, from which he was filling a hypodermic syringe.

They were giving Ella an injection.

But of what?

And why?

• 19 •

After talking with her mother in San Diego, Tessa Lockland sat on her motel bed and watched a nature documentary on PBS. Aloud, she critiqued the camerawork, the composition of shots, lighting, editing techniques, scripted narration, and other aspects of the production, until she abruptly realized she sounded foolish talking to herself. Then she mocked herself by imitating various television movie critics, commenting on the documentary in each of their styles, which turned out to be fun because most TV critics were pompous in one way or another, with the exception of Roger Ebert. Nevertheless, although having fun, Tessa *was* talking to herself, which was too eccentric even for a nonconformist who had reached the age of thirty-three without ever having to take a nine-to-five job. Visiting the scene of her sister's 'suicide' had made her edgy. She was seeking comic relief from that grim pilgrimage. But at certain times, in certain places, even the irrepressible Lockland buoyancy was inappropriate.

She clicked off the television and retrieved the empty plastic ice bucket from the bureau. Leaving the door to her room ajar, taking only some coins, she headed toward the south end of the second floor to the ice-maker and soda-vending machine.

Tessa had always prided herself on avoiding the nine-to-five grind. Absurdly proud, actually, considering that she often put in twelve and fourteen hours a day instead of eight, and was a tougher boss than any she could have worked for in a routine job. Her income was nothing to preen about, either. She had enjoyed a few flush years, when she could not have stopped making money if she'd tried, but they were far outnumbered by the years in which she had earned little more than a subsistence living. Averaging her income for the twelve years since she had finished film school, she'd recently calculated that her annual earnings were around twenty-one thousand, though that figure would be drastically readjusted downward if she did not have another boom year soon.

Though she was not rich, though freelance documentary filmmaking offered no security to speak of, she *felt* like a success, and not just because her work generally had been well received by the critics and not only because she was blessed with the Lockland disposition toward optimism. She felt successful because she had always been resistant to authority and had found, in her work, a way to be the master of her own destiny.

At the end of the long corridor, she pushed through a heavy fire door and stepped onto a landing, where the ice-maker and soda cooler stood to the left of the head of the stairs. Well stocked with cola, root beer, orange crush, and 7-Up, the tall vending machine was humming softly, but the ice-maker was broken and empty. She would have to fill up her bucket at the machine on the ground floor. She descended the stairs, her footsteps echoing off the concrete-block walls. The sound was so hollow and cold that she might have been in a vast pyramid or some other structure, alone but for the companionship of unseen spirits.

At the foot of the stairs, she found no soda or ice machines, but a sign on the wall indicated that the ground-floor refreshment center was at the north end of the motel. By the time she got her ice and Coke, she would have walked off enough calories to deserve a regular, sugar-packed cola instead of a diet drink.

As she reached for the handle of the fire door that led to the ground-floor corridor, she thought she heard the upper door open at the head of the stairs. If so, it was the first indication she'd had, since checking in, that she was not the only guest in the motel. The place had an abandoned air.

She went through the fire door and found that the lower corridor was carpeted in the same hideous orange nylon as was the upper hall. The decorator had a clown's taste for bright colors. It made her squint.

She would have preferred to be a more successful filmmaker, if only because she could have afforded lodgings that did not assault the senses. Of course, this was the only motel in Moonlight Cove, so even wealth could not have saved her from that eye-blistering orange glare. By the time she walked to the end of the hall, pushed through another fire door, and stepped into the bottom of the north stairwell, the sight of gray concrete-block walls and concrete steps was positively restful and appealing.

There, the ice-maker was working. She slid open the top of the chest and dipped the plastic bucket into the deep bin, filling it with half-moon pieces of ice. She set the full bucket atop the machine. As she closed the chest, she heard the door at the head of the stairs open with a faint but protracted squeak of hinges.

She stepped to the soda vendor to get her Coke, expecting someone to descend from the second floor. Only as she dropped a third quarter into the slot did she realize something was *sneaky* about the way the overhead door opened: the long, slow squeak . . . as if someone knew the hinges were unoiled, and was trying to minimize the noise.

With one finger poised over the Diet Coke selection button, Tessa hesitated, listening.

Nothing.

Cool concrete silence.

She felt exactly as she had felt on the beach earlier in the evening, when she had heard that strange and distant cry. Now, as then, her flesh prickled.

She had the crazy notion that someone was on the landing above, holding the fire door open now that he had come through it. He was waiting for her to push the button, so the squeak of the upper door's hinges would be covered by the clatter-thump of the can rolling into the dispensing trough.

Many modern women, conscious of the need to be tough in a tough world, would have been embarrassed by such apprehension and would have shrugged off the intuitive chill. But Tessa knew herself well. She was not given to hysteria or paranoia, so she did not wonder for a moment if Janice's death had left her overly sensitive, did not doubt her mental image of a hostile presence at the upper landing, out of sight around the turn.

Three doors led from the bottom of that concrete shaft. The first was in the south wall, through which she had come and through which she could return to the ground-floor corridor. The second was in the west wall, which opened to the back of the motel, where a narrow walk or service passage evidently lay between the building and the edge of the sea-facing bluff, and the third was in the east wall, through which she probably could reach the parking lot in front of the motel. Instead of pushing the vendor button to get her Coke, leaving her full ice bucket as well, she stepped quickly and quietly to the south door and pulled it open.

She glimpsed movement at the distant end of the ground-floor hall. Someone ducked back through that other fire door into the south stairwell. She didn't see much of him, only his shadowy form, for he had not been on the orange carpet in the corridor itself but at the far threshold, and therefore able to slip out of sight in a second. The door eased shut in his wake.

At least two men – she presumed they were men, not women – were stalking her.

Overhead, in her own stairwell, the unoiled hinges of that door produced a barely audible, protracted rasp and squeal. The other man evidently had tired of waiting for her to make a covering noise.

She could not go into the hallway. They'd trap her between them.

Though she could scream in the hope of calling forth other guests and frightening these men away, she hesitated because she was afraid the motel might be as deserted as it seemed. Her scream might elicit no help, while letting the stalkers know that she was aware of them and that they no longer had to be cautious.

Someone was stealthily descending the stairs above her.

Tessa turned away from the corridor, stepped to the east door, and ran out into the foggy night, along the side of the building, into the parking lot beyond which lay Cypress Lane. Gasping, she sprinted past the front of Cove Lodge to the motel office, which was adjacent to the now closed coffee shop.

The office was open, the doorstep was bathed in a mist-diffused glow of pink and yellow neon, and the man behind the counter was the same one who had registered her hours ago. He was tall and slightly plump, in his fifties, clean-shaven and neatly barbered if a little rumpled looking in brown corduroy slacks and a green and red flannel shirt. He put down a magazine, lowered the volume of the country music on the radio, got up from his spring-backed desk chair, and stood at the counter, frowning at her while she told him, a bit too breathlessly, what had happened.

'Well, this isn't the big city, ma'am,' he said when she had finished. 'It's a peaceful place, Moonlight Cove. You don't have to worry about that sort of thing here.'

'But it happened,' she insisted, nervously glancing out at the neon-painted mist that drifted through the darkness beyond the office door and window.

'Oh, I'm sure you saw and heard someone, but you put the wrong spin on it. We *do* have a couple other guests. That's who you saw and heard, and they were probably just getting a Coke or some ice, like you.' He had a warm, grandfatherly demeanor when he smiled. 'This place can seem a little spooky when there aren't many guests.'

'Listen, mister . . .'

'Quinn. Gordon Quinn.'

'Listen, Mr. Quinn, it wasn't that way at all.' She felt like a skittish and foolish female, though she knew she was no such thing. 'I didn't mistake innocent guests for muggers and rapists. I'm not an hysterical woman. These guys were up to no damn good.'

'Well . . . all right. I think you're wrong, but let's have a look.' Quinn came through the gate in the counter, to her side of the office.

'Are you just going like that?' she asked.

'Like what?'

'Unarmed?'

He smiled again. As before, she felt foolish.

'Ma'am,' he said, 'in twenty-five years of motel management, I haven't yet met a guest I couldn't handle.'

Though Quinn's smug, patronizing tone angered Tessa, she did not argue with him but followed him out of the office and through the eddying fog to the far end of the building. He was big, and she was petite, so she felt somewhat like a little kid being escorted back to her room by a father determined to show her that no monster was hiding either under the bed or in the closet.

He opened the metal door through which she had fled the north service stairs, and they went inside. No one waited there.

The soda-vending machine purred, and a faint clinking arose from the ice-maker's laboring mechanism. Her plastic bucket still stood atop the chest, filled with half-moon chips.

Quinn crossed the small space to the door that led to the ground-floor hall, pulled it open. 'Nobody there,' he said, nodding toward the silent corridor. He opened the door in the west wall, as well, and looked outside, left and right. He motioned her to the threshold and insisted that she look too.

She saw a narrow, railing-flanked serviceway that paralleled the back of the lodge, between the building and the edge of the bluff, illuminated by a yellowish night light at each end. Deserted.

'You said you'd already put your money in the vendor but hadn't got your soda?' Quinn asked, as he let the door swing shut.

'That's right.'

'What did you want?'

'Well . . . Diet Coke.'

At the vending machine, he pushed the correct button, and a can rolled into the trough. He handed it to her, pointed at the plastic container that she had brought from her room, and said, 'Don't forget your ice.'

Carrying the ice bucket and Coke, a hot blush on her cheeks and cold anger in her heart, Tessa followed him up the north stairs. No one lurked there. The unoiled hinges of the upper door squeaked as they went into the second-floor hallway, which was also deserted.

The door to her room was ajar, which was how she had left it. She was hesitant to enter.

'Let's check it out,' Quinn said.

The small room, closet, and adjoining bath were untenanted.

'Feel better?' he asked.

'I wasn't imagining things.'

'I'm sure you weren't,' he said, still patronizing her.

As Quinn returned to the hallway, Tessa said, 'They were there, and they were real, but I guess they're gone now. Probably ran away when they realized I was aware of them and that I went for help.'

'Well, all's well then,' he said. 'You're safe. If they're gone, that's almost as good as if they'd never existed in the first place.'

Tessa required all of her restraint to avoid saying more than 'Thank you,' then she closed the door. On the knob was a lock button, which she depressed. Above the knob was a dead-bolt lock, which she engaged. A brass security chain was also provided; she used it.

She went to the window and examined it to satisfy herself that it couldn't be opened easily by a would-be assailant. Half of it slid to the left when she applied pressure to a latch and pulled, but it could not be opened from outside unless someone broke it and reached through to disengage the lock. Besides, as she was on the second floor, an intruder would need a ladder.

For a while she sat in bed, listening to distant noises in the motel. Now every sound seemed strange and menacing. She wondered what, if any, connection her unsettling experience had with Janice's death more than three weeks ago.

• 20 •

After a couple of hours in the storm drain under the sloping meadow, Chrissie Foster was troubled by claustrophobia. She had been locked in the kitchen pantry a great deal longer than she had been in the drain, and the pantry had been smaller, yet the grave-black concrete culvert was by far the worse of the two. Maybe she began to feel caged and smothered because of the cumulative effect of spending all day and most of the evening in cramped places.

From the superhighway far above, where the drainage system began, the heavy roar of trucks echoed down through the tunnels, giving rise in her mind to images of growling dragons. She put her hands over her ears to block out the noise. Sometimes the trucks were widely spaced, but on occasion they came in trains of six or eight or a dozen, and the continuous rumble became oppressive, maddening.

Or maybe her desire to get out of the culvert had something to do with the fact that she was underground. Lying in the dark, listening to the trucks, searching the intervening silences for the return of her parents and Tucker, Chrissie began to feel she was in a concrete coffin, a victim of premature burial.

Reading aloud from the imaginary book of her own adventures, she said, 'Little did young Chrissie know that the culvert was about to collapse and fill with earth, squishing her as if she were a bug and trapping her forever.'

She knew she should stay where she was. They might still be prowling the meadow and woods in search of her. She was safer in the culvert than out of it.

But she was cursed with a vivid imagination. Although she was no doubt the only occupant of the lightless passageway in which she sprawled, she envisioned unwanted company in countless grisly forms: slithering snakes; spiders by the hundreds; cockroaches; rats; colonies of blood-drinking bats. Eventually she began to wonder if over the years a child might have crawled into the tunnels to play and, getting lost in the branching culverts, might have died there, undiscovered. His soul, of course, would have remained restless and earthbound, for his death had been unjustly premature and there had been no proper burial service to free his spirit. Now perhaps that ghost, sensing her presence, was animating those hideous skeletal remains, dragging the decomposed and age-dried corpse toward her, scraping off pieces of leathery and half-petrified flesh as it came. Chrissie was eleven years old and level-headed for her age, and she repeatedly told herself that there were no such things as ghosts, but then she thought of her parents and Tucker, who seemed to be some kind of *werewolves*, for God's sake, and when the big trucks passed on the interstate, she was afraid to cover her ears with her hands for fear that the dead child was using the cover of that noise to creep closer, closer.

She had to get out.

• 21 •

When he left the dark garage where he had taken refuge from the pack of drugged-out delinquents (which is what he had to believe they were; he knew no other way to explain them), Sam Booker went straight to Ocean Avenue and stopped in Knight's Bridge Tavern just long enough to buy a six-pack of Guinness Stout to go.

Later, in his room at Cove Lodge, he sat at the small table and drank beer while he pored over the facts of the case. On September 5, three National Farmworkers Union organizers – Julio Bustamante, his sister Maria Bustamante, and Maria's fiancé, Ramon Sanchez – were driving south from the wine country, where they had been conducting discussions with vineyard owners about the upcoming harvest. They were in a four-year-old, tan Chevy van. They stopped for dinner in Moonlight Cove. They'd eaten at the Perez Family Restaurant and had drunk too many margaritas (according to witnesses among the waiters and customers at Perez's that night), and on their way back to the interstate, they'd taken a dangerous curve too fast; their van had rolled and caught fire. None of the three had survived.

That story might have held up and the FBI might never have been drawn into the case, but for a few inconsistencies. For one thing, according to the

Moonlight Cove police department's official report, Julio Bustamante had been driving. But Julio had never driven a car in his life; furthermore, he was unlikely to do so after dark, for he suffered from a form of night blindness. Furthermore, according to witnesses quoted in the police report, Julio and Maria and Ramon were *all* intoxicated, but no one who knew Julio or Ramon had ever seen them drunk before; Maria was a lifelong teetotaler.

The Sanchez and Bustamante families, of San Francisco, also were made suspicious by the behavior of the Moonlight Cove authorities. None of them was told of the three deaths until September 10, five days after the accident. Police chief Loman Watkins had explained that Julio's, Maria's, and Ramon's paper ID had been destroyed in the intense fire and that their bodies had been too completely burned to allow swift identification by fingerprints. What of the van's license plates? Curiously, Loman had not found any on the vehicle or torn loose and lying in the vicinity of the crash. Therefore, with three badly mangled and burned bodies to deal with and no way to locate next of kin on a timely basis, he had authorized the coroner, Dr. Ian Fitzgerald, to fill out death certificates and thereafter dispose of the bodies by cremation. 'We don't have the facilities of a big-city morgue, you understand,' Watkins had explained. 'We just can't keep cadavers long term, and we had no way of knowing how much time we'd need to identify these people. We thought they might be itinerants or even illegals, in which case we might never be able to ID them.'

Neat, Sam thought grimly, as he leaned back in his chair and took a long swallow of Guinness.

Three people had died violent deaths, been certified victims of an accident, and cremated before their relatives were notified, before any other authorities could step in to verify, through the application of modern forensic medicine, whether the death certificates and police report in fact contained the whole story.

The Bustamantes and Sanchezes were suspicious of foul play, but the National Farmworkers Union was convinced of it. On September 12, the union's president sought the intervention of the Federal Bureau of Investigation on the grounds that anti-union forces were responsible for the deaths of Bustamante, Bustamante, and Sanchez. Generally, the crime of murder fell into the FBI's jurisdiction only if the suspected killers had crossed state borders either to commit the act, or during its commission, or to escape retribution subsequent to the act; or as in this case, if federal authorities had reason to believe that murder had been committed as a consequence of the willful violation of the victims' civil rights.

On September 26, after the absurd if standard delays associated with government bureaucracy and the federal judiciary, a team of six FBI agents – including three men from the Scientific Investigation Division – moved into picturesque Moonlight Cove for ten days. They interviewed police officers, examined police and coroner files, took statements from witnesses who were at the Perez Family Restaurant on the night of September 5, sifted through the wreckage of the Chevy van at the junkyard, and sought whatever meager clues might remain at the accident site itself. Because Moonlight Cove had no agricultural industry, they could find no one interested in the farm-union issue let alone angered by it, which left them short of people motivated to kill union organizers.

Throughout their investigation, they received the full and cordial cooperation of the local police and coroner. Loman Watkins and his men went so far as
to volunteer to submit to lie-detector tests, which subsequently were administered, and all of them passed without a hint of deception. The coroner also took
the tests and proved to be a man of unfailing honesty.

Nevertheless, something about it reeked.

The local officials were almost too eager to cooperate. And all six of the FBI
agents came to feel that they were objects of scorn and derision when their backs
were turned – though they never saw any of the police so much as raise an
eyebrow or smirk or share a knowing look with another local. Call it Bureau
Instinct, which Sam knew was at least as reliable as that of any creature in the
wild.

Then the *other* deaths had to be considered.

While investigating the Sanchez-Bustamante case, the agents had reviewed
police and coroner records for the past couple of years to ascertain the usual
routine with which sudden deaths – accidental and otherwise – were handled
in Moonlight Cove, in order to determine if local authorities had dealt with this
recent case differently from previous ones, which would be an indication of
police complicity in a coverup. What they discovered was puzzling and
disturbing – but not like anything they had *expected* to find. Except for one spectacular car crash involving a teenage boy in an extensively souped-up Dodge,
Moonlight Cove had been a singularly safe place to live. During that time, its
residents were untroubled by violent death – until August 28, eight days before
the deaths of Sanchez and the Bustamantes, when an unusual series of mortal-
ities began to show up on the public records.

In the pre-dawn hours of August 28, the four members of the Mayser family
were the first victims: Melinda, John, and their two children, Carrie and Billy.
They had perished in a house fire, which the authorities later attributed to Billy
playing with matches. The four bodies were so badly burned that identification
could be made only from dental records.

Having finished his first bottle of Guinness, Sam reached for a second but
hesitated. He had work to do yet tonight. Sometimes, when he was in a particularly dour mood and started drinking stout, he had trouble stopping short of
unconsciousness.

Holding the empty bottle for comfort, Sam wondered why a boy, having
started a fire, would not cry out for help and wake his parents when he saw the
blaze was beyond control. Why would the boy not run before being overcome
with smoke? And just what kind of fire, except one fueled by gasoline or another
volatile fluid (of which there was no indication in official reports), would spread
so fast that none of the family could escape and would reduce the house –
and the bodies therein – to heaps of ashes before firemen could arrive and
quench it?

Neat again. The bodies were so consumed by flames that autopsies would be
of little use in determining if the blaze had been started not by Billy but by
someone who wanted to conceal the true causes of death. At the suggestion of
the funeral director – who was the owner of Callan's Funeral Home and also
the assistant coroner, therefore a suspect in any official coverup – the Maysers'
next of kin, Melinda Mayser's mother, authorized cremation of the remains.
Potential evidence not destroyed by the original fire was thus obliterated.

'How tidy,' Sam said aloud, putting his feet up on the other straight-back chair. 'How splendidly clean and tidy.'

Body count: four.

Then the Bustamantes and Sanchez on September 5. Another fire. Followed by more speedy cremations.

Body count: seven.

On September 7, while trace vapors of the Bustamante and Sanchez remains might still have lingered in the air above Moonlight Cove, a twenty-year resident of the town, Jim Armes, put to sea in his thirty-foot boat, the *Mary Leandra*, for an early-morning sail – and was never seen again. Though he was an experienced seaman, though the day was clear and the ocean calm, he'd apparently gone down in an outbound tide, for no identifiable wreckage had washed up on local beaches.

Body count: eight.

On September 9, while fish presumably were nibbling on Armes's drowned body, Paula Parkins was torn apart by five Dobermans. She was a twenty-nine-year-old woman living alone, raising and training guard dogs, on a two-acre property near the edge of town. Evidently one of her Dobermans turned against her, and the others flew into a frenzy at the scent of her blood. Paula's savaged remains, unfit for viewing, had been sent in a sealed casket to her family in Denver. The dogs were shot, tested for rabies, and cremated.

Body count: nine.

Six days after entering the Bustamante-Sanchez case, on October 2, the FBI had exhumed Paula Parkins's body from a grave in Denver. An autopsy revealed that the woman indeed had been bitten and clawed to death by multiple animal assailants.

Sam remembered the most interesting part of that autopsy report word for word: . . . *however, bite marks, lacerations, tears in the body cavity, and specific damage to breasts and sex organs are not entirely consistent with canine attack. The teeth pattern and size of bite do not fit the dental profile of the average Doberman or other animals known to be aggressive and capable of successfully attacking an adult.* And later in the same report, when referring to the specific nature of Parkins's assailants: *Species unknown.*

How had Paula Parkins really died?

What terror and agony had she known?

Who was trying to blame it on the Dobermans?

And in fact what evidence might the Dobermans' bodies have provided about the nature of their own deaths and, therefore, the truthfulness of the police story?

Sam thought of the strange, distant cry he had heard tonight – like that of a coyote but not a coyote, like that of a cat but not a cat. And he thought also of the eerie, frantic voices of the kids who had pursued him. Somehow it all fit. Bureau Instinct.

Species unknown.

Unsettled, Sam tried to soothe his nerves with Guinness. The bottle was still empty. He clinked it thoughtfully against his teeth.

Six days after Parkins's death and long before the exhumation of her body in Denver, two more people met untimely ends in Moonlight Cove. Steve Heinz and Laura Dalcoe, unmarried but living together, were found dead in their house on Iceberry Way. Heinz left a typed, incoherent, unsigned suicide note, then killed Laura with a shotgun while she slept, and took his own life. Dr. Ian Fitzgerald's report was murder-suicide, case closed. At the coroner's suggestion, the Dalcoe and Heinz families authorized cremation of the grisly remains.

Body count: eleven.

'There's an ungodly amount of cremation going on in this town,' Sam said aloud, and turned the empty beer bottle around in his hands.

Most people still preferred to have themselves and their loved ones embalmed and buried in a casket, regardless of the condition of the body. In most towns cremations accounted for perhaps one in four or one in five dispositions of cadavers.

Finally, while investigating the Bustamante-Sanchez case, the FBI team from San Francisco found that Janice Capshaw was listed as a Valium suicide. Her sea-ravaged body had washed up on the beach two days after she disappeared, three days before the agents arrived to launch their investigation into the death of the union organizers.

Julio Bustamante, Maria Bustamante, Ramon Sanchez, the four Maysers, Jim Armes, Paula Parkins, Steven Heinz, Laura Dalcoe, Janice Capshaw: a body count of twelve in less than a month – exactly twelve times the number of violent deaths that had occurred in Moonlight Cove during the previous *twenty-three months*. Out of a population of just three thousand, twelve violent deaths in little more than three weeks was one hell of a mortality rate.

Queried about his reaction to this astonishing chain of deadly events, Chief Loman Watkins had said, 'It's horrible, yes. And it's sort of frightening. Things were so calm for so long that I guess, statistically, we were just overdue.'

But in a town that size, even spread over two years, twelve such violent deaths went off the top of the statisticians' charts.

The six-man Bureau team was unable to find one shred of evidence of any local authorities' complicity in those cases. And although a polygraph was not an entirely dependable determiner of truth, the technology was not so unreliable that Loman Watkins, his officers, the coroner, and the coroner's assistant could all pass the examination without a single indication of deception if in fact they were guilty.

Yet . . .

Twelve deaths. Four cremated in a house fire. Three cremated in a demolished Chevy van. Three suicides, two by shotgun and one by Valium, all subsequently cremated at Callan's Funeral Home. One lost at sea – no body at all. And the only victim available for autopsy appeared not to have been killed by dogs, as the coroner's report claimed, though she had been bitten and clawed by something, dammit.

It was enough to keep the Bureau's file open. By the ninth of October, four days after the San Francisco team departed Moonlight Cove, a decision was made to send in an undercover operative to have a look at certain aspects of the case that might be more fruitfully explored by a man who was not being watched.

One day after that decision, on October 10, a letter arrived in the San Francisco office that clinched the Bureau's determination to maintain involvement. Sam had that note committed to memory as well:

Gentlemen:

I have information pertinent to a recent series of deaths in the town of Moonlight Cove. I have reason to believe local authorities are involved in a conspiracy to conceal murder.

I would prefer you contact me in person, as I do not trust the privacy of our telephones here. I must insist on absolute discretion because I am a disabled Vietnam veteran with severe physical limitations, and I am naturally concerned about my ability to protect myself.

It was signed, Harold G. Talbot.

United States Army records confirmed that Talbot was indeed a disabled Vietnam vet. He had been repeatedly cited for bravery in combat. Tomorrow, Sam would discreetly visit him.

Meanwhile, considering the work he had to do tonight, he wondered if he could risk a second bottle of stout on top of what he'd drunk at dinner. The six-pack was on the table in front of him. He stared at it for a long time. Guinness, good Mexican food, Goldie Hawn, and fear of death. The Mexican food was in his belly, but the taste of it was forgotten. Goldie Hawn was living on a ranch somewhere with Kurt Russell, whom she had the bad sense to prefer to one ordinary-looking, scared, and hope-deserted federal agent. He thought of twelve dead men and women, of bodies roasting in a crematorium until they were reduced to bone splinters and ashes, and he thought of shotgun murder and shotgun suicide and fish-gnawed corpses and a badly bitten woman, and all those thoughts led him to morbid philosophizing about the way of all flesh. He thought of his wife, lost to cancer, and he thought of Scott and their long-distance telephone conversation, too, and that was when he finally opened a second beer.

• 22 •

Chased by imaginary spiders, snakes, beetles, rats, bats, and by the *possibly* imaginary reanimated body of a dead child, and by the real if dragonlike roar of distant trucks, Chrissie crawled out of the tributary drain in which she had taken refuge, troll-walked down the main culvert, stepped again in the slippery remains of the decomposing raccoon, and plunged out into the silt-floored drainage channel. The air was clean and sweet. In spite of the six-foot-high walls of the ditch, fog-filtered moonlight, and fog-hidden stars, Chrissie's claustrophobia abated. She drew deep lungfuls of the cool, moist air but tried to breathe with as little noise as possible.

She listened to the night, and before long she was rewarded by those alien cries, echoing faintly across the meadow from the woods to the south. As before, she was sure that she heard three distinct voices. If her mother, father, and Tucker were off to the south looking for her in the forest that eventually led to the edge of New Wave Microtech's property, she might be able to head back the way she had come, through the northern woods, into the meadow where Godiva had thrown her, then east toward the county road and into Moonlight Cove by that route, leaving them searching fruitlessly in the wrong place.

For sure, she could not stay where she was.

And she could not head south, straight toward *them*.

She clambered out of the ditch and ran north across the meadow, retracing the route she had taken earlier in the evening, and as she went she counted her miseries. She was hungry because she'd had no dinner, and she was tired. The muscles in her shoulders and back were cramped from the time she had spent in the tight, cold concrete tributary drain. Her legs ached.

So what's your problem? she asked herself as she reached the trees at the edge of the meadow. Would you rather have been dragged down by Tucker and 'converted' into one of them?

· 23 ·

Loman Watkins left the Valdoski house, where Dr. Worthy was overseeing the conversion of Ella and George. Farther down the county road, his officers and the coroner were loading the dead boy into the hearse. The crowd of onlookers was entranced by the scene.

Loman got into his cruiser and switched on the engine. The compact video display lit at once, a soft green. The computer link was mounted on the console between the front seats. It began to flash, indicating that HQ had a message for him – one that they chose not to broadcast on the more easily intercepted police-band radio.

Though he had been working with microwave-linked mobile computers for a few years, he was still sometimes surprised upon first getting into a cruiser and seeing the VDT light up. In major cities like Los Angeles, for the better part of the past decade, most patrol cars had been equipped with computer links to central police data banks, but such electronic wonders were still rare in smaller cities and unheard of in jurisdictions as comparatively minuscule as Moonlight Cove. His department boasted state-of-the-art technology not because the town's treasury was overflowing but because New Wave – a leader in mobile microwave-linked data systems, among other things – had equipped his office and cars with their in-development hardware and software, updating the system constantly, using the Moonlight Cove police force as something of a proving ground for every advancement that they hoped ultimately to integrate into their line of products.

That was one of the many ways Thomas Shaddack had insinuated himself into the power structure of the community even before he had reached for *total* power through the Moonhawk Project. At the time Loman had been thick-headed enough to think New Wave's largesse was a blessing. Now he knew better.

From his mobile VDT, Loman could access the central computer in the department's headquarters on Jacobi Street, one block south of Ocean Avenue, to obtain any information in the data banks or to 'speak' with the on-duty dispatcher who could communicate with him almost as easily by computer as by police-band radio. Furthermore, he could sit comfortably in his car and, through HQ computer, reach out to the Department of Motor Vehicles computer in Sacramento to get a make on a license plate, or the Department of Prisons data banks in the same city to call up information on a particular felon, or any other computer tied in to the nationwide law-enforcement electronic network.

He adjusted his holster because he was sitting on his revolver.

Using the keyboard under the display terminal, he entered his ID number, accessing the system.

The days when *all* fact-gathering required police legwork had begun to pass in the mid '80s. Now only TV cops like Hunter were forced to rush hither and yon to turn up the smallest details because that was more dramatic than a depiction of the high-tech reality. In time, Watkins thought, the gumshoe might be in danger of becoming the gumbutt, with his ass parked for hours in front of either a mobile VDT or one on a desk at HQ.

The computer accepted his number.

The VDT stopped flashing.

Of course, if all the people of the world were New People, and if the problem of the regressives were solved, ultimately there would be no more crime and no need of policemen. Some criminals were spawned by social injustice, but all men would be equal in the new world that was coming, as equal as one machine to another, with the same goals and desires, with no competitive or conflicting needs. Most criminals were genetic defectives, their sociopathic behavior virtually encoded in their chromosomes; however, except for the regressive element among them, the New People would be in perfect genetic repair. That was Shaddack's vision, anyway.

Sometimes Loman Watkins wondered where free will fit into the plan. Maybe it didn't. Sometimes he didn't seem to care if it fit in or not. At other times his inability to care ... well, it scared the hell out of him.

Lines of words began to appear left to right on the screen, one line at a time, in soft green letters on the dark background:

FOR: LOMAN WATKINS
SOURCE: SHADDACK
JACK TUCKER HAS NOT REPORTED IN FROM THE FOSTER PLACE. NO ONE ANSWERS PHONE THERE. URGENT THAT SITUATION BE CLARIFIED. AWAIT YOUR REPORT.

Shaddack had direct entry to the police-department computer from his own computer in his house out on the north point of the cove. He could leave messages for Watkins or any of the other men, and no one could call them up except the intended recipient.

The screen went blank.

Loman Watkins popped the hand brake, put the patrol car in gear, and set out for Foster Stables, though the place was actually outside the city limits and beyond his bailiwick. He no longer cared about such things as jurisdictional boundaries and legal procedures. He was still a cop only because it was the role he had to play until all of the town had undergone the Change. None of the old rules applied to him any more because he was a New Man. Such disregard for the law would have appalled him only a few months ago, but now his arrogance and his disdain for the rules of the Old People's society did not move him in the least.

Most of the time nothing moved him any more. Day by day, hour by hour, he was less emotional.

Except for fear, which his new elevated state of consciousness still allowed:

fear because it was a survival mechanism, useful in a way that love and joy and hope and affection were not. He was afraid right now, in fact. Afraid of the regressives. Afraid that the Moonhawk Project would somehow be revealed to the outside world and crushed – and him with it. Afraid of his only master, Shaddack. Sometimes, in fleeting bleak moments, he was afraid of himself, too, and of the new world coming.

• 24 •

Moose dozed in a corner of the unlighted bedroom. He chuffed in his sleep, perhaps chasing bushy-tailed rabbits in a dream – although, being the good service dog that he was, even in his dreams he probably ran errands for his master.

Belted in his stool at the window, Harry leaned to the eyepiece of the telescope and studied the back of Callan's Funeral Home over on Juniper Lane, where the hearse had just pulled into the service drive. He watched Victor Callan and the mortician's assistant, Ned Ryedock, as they used a wheeled gurney to transfer a body from the black Cadillac hearse into the embalming and cremation wing. Zippered inside a half-collapsed, black plastic body bag, the corpse was so small that it must have been that of a child. Then they closed the door behind them, and Harry could see no more.

Sometimes they left the blinds raised at the two high, narrow windows, and from his elevated position Harry was able to peer down into that room, to the tilted and guttered table on which the dead were embalmed and prepared for viewing. On those occasions he could see much more than he wanted to see. Tonight, however, the blinds were lowered all the way to the windowsills.

He gradually shifted his field of vision southward along the fog-swaddled alley that served Callan's and ran between Conquistador and Juniper. He was not looking for anything in particular, just slowly scanning, when he saw a pair of grotesque figures. They were swift and dark, sprinting along the alley and into the large vacant lot adjacent to the funeral home, running neither on all fours nor erect, though closer to the former than the latter.

Boogeymen.

Harry's heart began to race.

He'd seen their like before, three times in the past four weeks, though the first time he had not believed what he had seen. They had been so shadowy and strange, so briefly glimpsed, that they seemed like phantoms of the imagination; therefore he named them Boogeymen.

They were quicker than cats. They slipped through his field of vision and vanished into the dark, vacant lot before he could overcome his surprise and follow them.

Now he searched that property end to end, back to front, seeking them in the three- to four-foot grass. Bushes offered concealment too. Wild holly and a couple of clumps of chaparral snagged and held the fog as if it were cotton.

He found them. Two hunched forms. Man-size. Only slightly less black than the night. Featureless. They crouched together in the dry grass in the middle of the lot, just to the north of the immense fir that spread its branches (all high ones) like a canopy over half the property.

Trembling, Harry pulled in even tighter on that section of the lot and adjusted the focus. The Boogeymen's outlines sharpened. Their bodies grew paler in contrast to the night around them. He still could not see any details of them because of the darkness and eddying mist.

Although it was quite expensive and tricky to obtain, he wished that through his military contacts he had acquired a Tele-Tron, which was a new version of the Star Tron night-vision device that had been used by most armed services for years. A Star Tron took available light – moonlight, starlight, meager electric light if any, the vague natural radiance of certain minerals in soil and rocks – and amplified it eighty-five thousand times. With that single-lens gadget, an impenetrable nightscape was transformed into a dim twilight or even late-afternoon grayness. The Tele-Tron employed the same technology as the Star Tron, but it was designed to be fitted to a telescope. Ordinarily, available light was sufficient to Harry's purposes, and most of the time he was looking through windows into well-lighted rooms; but to study the quick and furtive Boogeymen, he needed some high-tech assistance.

The shadowy figures looked west toward Juniper Lane, then north toward Callan's, then south toward the house that, with the funeral home, flanked that open piece of land. Their heads turned with a quick, fluid movement that made Harry think of cats, although they were definitely not feline.

One of them glanced back to the east. Because the telescope put Harry right in the lot with the Boogeymen, he saw the thing's eyes – soft gold, palely radiant. He had never seen their eyes before. He shivered, but not just because they were so uncanny. Something was familiar about those eyes, something that reached deeper than Harry's conscious or subconscious mind to stir dim recognition, activating primitive racial memories carried in his genes.

He was suddenly cold to the marrow and overcome by fear more intense than anything he had known since Nam.

Dozing, Moose was atuned nonetheless to his master's mood. The Labrador got up, shook himself as if to cast off sleep, and came to the stool. He made a low, mewling, inquisitive sound.

Through the telescope Harry glimpsed the nightmare face of one of the Boogeymen. He had no more than the briefest flash of it, at most two seconds, and the malformed visage was limned only by an ethereal spray of moonlight, so he saw little; in fact the inadequate lunar glow did less to reveal the thing than to deepen the mystery of it.

But he was gripped by it, stunned, frozen.

Moose issued an interrogatory '*Woof?*'

For an instant, unable to look up from the eyepiece if his life had depended on it, Harry stared at an apelike countenance, though it was leaner and uglier and more fierce and infinitely stranger than the face of an ape. He was reminded, as well, of wolves, and in the gloom the thing even seemed to have something of a reptilian aspect. He thought he saw the enameled gleam of wickedly sharp teeth, gaping jaws. But the light was poor, and he could not be certain how much of what he saw was a trick of shadow or a distortion of fog. Part of this hideous vision had to be attributed to his fevered imagination. A man with a pair of useless legs and one dead arm *had* to have a vivid imagination if he was to make the most of life.

As suddenly as the Boogeyman looked toward him, it looked away. At the same time both creatures moved with an animal fluidity and quickness that startled Harry. They were nearly the size of big jungle cats and as fast. He turned the scope to follow them, and they virtually flew through the darkness, south across the vacant lot, disappearing over a split-rail fence into the backyard of the Claymore house, up and gone with such alacrity that he could not hold them in his field of view.

He continued to search for them, as far as the junior-senior high school on Roshmore, but he found only night and fog and the familiar buildings of his neighborhood. The Boogeymen had vanished as abruptly as they always did in a small boy's bedroom the moment the lights were turned on.

At last he lifted his head from the eyepiece and slumped back in his stool.

Moose immediately stood up with his forepaws on the arm of the stool, begging to be petted, as if he had seen what his master had seen and needed to be reassured that malign spirits did not actually run loose in the world.

With his good right hand, which at first trembled violently, Harry stroked the Labrador's head. In a while the petting calmed him almost as much as it calmed the dog.

If the FBI eventually responded to the letter he had sent over a week ago, he did not know if he would tell them about the Boogeymen. He would tell them everything else he had seen, and a lot of it might be useful to them. But this . . . On the one hand, he was sure that the beasts he had glimpsed so fleetingly on three occasions – four now – were somehow related to all the other curious events of recent weeks. They were a different magnitude of strangeness, however, and in speaking of them he might appear addled, even crazed, causing the Bureau agents to discount everything else he said.

Am I addled? he wondered as he petted Moose. Am I crazed?

After twenty years of confinement to a wheelchair, housebound, living vicariously through his telescope and binoculars, perhaps he had become so desperate to be more involved with the world and so starved for excitement that he had evolved an elaborate fantasy of conspiracy and the uncanny, putting himself at the center of it as The One Man Who Knew, convinced that his delusions were real. But that was highly unlikely. The war had left his body pathetically damaged and weak, but his mind was as strong and clear as it had ever been, perhaps even tempered and made stronger by adversity. *That*, not madness, was his curse.

'Boogeymen,' he said to Moose.

The dog chuffed.

'What next? Will I look up at the moon some night and see the silhouette of a witch on a broomstick?'

• 25 •

Chrissie came out of the woods by Pyramid Rock, which once had inspired her fantasies of inch-high Egyptians. She looked west toward the house and Foster Stables, where lights now wore rainbow-hued halos in the fog. For a moment she entertained the idea of going back for Godiva or another horse. Maybe she could even slip into the house and grab a jacket. But she decided that she would be less conspicuous and safer on foot. Besides, she was not as dumb as movie heroines who repeatedly returned to the Bad House, knowing the Bad Thing was likely to find them there. She turned east-northeast and headed up through the meadow toward the county road.

Exhibiting her usual cleverness (she thought, as if reading a line from an adventure novel), *Chrissie wisely turned away from the cursed house and set off into the night, wondering if she would ever again see that place of her youth or find solace in the arms of her now alienated family.*

Tall, autumn-dry grass lashed at her legs, as she angled out toward the middle of the field. Instead of staying near the tree line, she wanted to be in the open in case something leaped at her from the forest. She didn't think she could outrun them once they spotted her, not even if she had a minute's head start, but at least she intended to give herself a chance to try.

The night chill had deepened during the time she'd taken refuge in the culvert. Her flannel shirt seemed hardly more warming than a short-sleeved summer blouse. If she were an adventurer-heroine of the breed that Ms. Andre Norton created, she would know how to weave a coat out of available grass and other plants, with a high insulation factor. Or she would know how to trap, painlessly kill, and skin fur-bearing animals, how to tan their hides and stitch them together, clothing herself in garments as astonishingly stylish as they were practical.

She simply had to stop thinking about the heroines of those books. Her comparative ineptitude depressed her.

She already had enough to be depressed about. She'd been driven from her home. She was alone, hungry, cold, confused, afraid – and stalked by weird and dangerous creatures. But more to the point . . . though her mother and father always had been a bit distant, not given to easy displays of affection, Chrissie had loved them, and now they were gone, perhaps gone forever, changed in some way she did not understand, alive but soulless and, therefore, as good as dead.

When she was less than a hundred feet from the two-lane county route, paralleling the long driveway at about the same distance, she heard a car engine. She saw headlights on the road, coming from the south. Then she saw the car itself, for the fog was thinner in that direction than toward the sea, and visibility was reasonably good. Even at that distance she identified it as a police cruiser; though no siren wailed, blue and red lights were revolving on its roof. The patrol car slowed and turned in the driveway by the sign for Foster Stables.

Chrissie almost shouted, almost ran toward the car, because she always had been taught that policemen were her friends. She actually raised one hand and waved, but then realized that in a world where she could not trust her own parents, she certainly could not expect all policemen to have her best interests in mind.

Spooked by the thought that the cops might have been 'converted' the way Tucker had intended to convert her, the way her parents had been converted, she dropped down, crouching in the tall grass. The headlights had not come anywhere near her when the car had turned into the driveway. The darkness on the meadow and the fog no doubt made her invisible to the occupants of the cruiser, and she was not exactly so tremendously tall that she stood out on the flat land. But she did not want to take any chances.

She watched the car dwindle down the long driveway. It paused briefly beside Tucker's car, which was abandoned halfway along the lane, then drove on. The thicker fog in the west swallowed it.

She rose from the grass and hurried eastward again, toward the county route. She intended to follow that road south, all the way into Moonlight Cove. If she remained watchful and alert, she could scramble off the pavement into a ditch or behind a patch of weeds each time she heard approaching traffic.

She would not reveal herself to anyone she did not know. Once she reached town, she could go to Our Lady of Mercy and seek help from Father Castelli. (He said he was a modern priest and preferred to be called Father Jim, but Chrissie had never been able to address him so casually.) Chrissie had been an indefatigable worker at the church's summer festival and had expressed a desire to be an altar girl next year, much to Father Castelli's delight. She was sure he liked her and would believe her story, no matter how wild it was. If he didn't believe her . . . well, then she would try Mrs. Tokawa, her sixth-grade teacher.

She reached the county road, paused, and looked back toward the distant house, which was only a collection of glowing points in the fog. Shivering, she turned south toward Moonlight Cove.

• 26 •

The front door of the Foster house stood open to the night.

Loman Watkins went through the place from bottom to top and down again. The only odd things he found were an overturned chair in the kitchen and Jack Tucker's abandoned black bag filled with syringes and doses of the drug with which the Change was effected – and a spray-can of WD-40 on the floor of the downstairs hall.

Closing the front door behind him, he went out onto the porch, stood at the steps that led down to the front yard, and listened to the ethereally still night. A sluggish breeze had risen and fallen fitfully during the evening, but now it had abated entirely. The air was uncannily still. The fog seemed to dampen all sounds, leaving a world as silent as if it had been one vast graveyard.

Looking toward the stables, Loman called out: 'Tucker! Foster! Is anyone here?'

An echo of his voice rolled back to him. It was a cold and lonely sound.

No one answered him.

'Tucker? Foster?'

Lights were on at one of the long stables, and a door was open at the nearest end. He supposed he should go have a look.

Loman was halfway to that building when an ululant cry, like the wavering note of a distant horn, came from far to the south, faint but unmistakable. It was shrill yet guttural, filled with anger, longing, excitement, and need. The shriek of a regressive in mid-hunt.

He stopped and listened, hoping that he had misheard.

The sound came again. This time he could discern at least two voices, perhaps three. They were a long way off, more than a mile, so their eerie keening could not be in reply to Loman's shouts.

Their cries chilled him.

And filled him with a strange yearning.

No.

He made such tight fists of his hands that his fingernails dug into his palms, and he fought back the darkness that threatened to well up within him. He tried to concentrate on police work, the problem at hand.

If those cries came from Alex Foster, Sharon Foster, and Jack Tucker – as was most likely the case – where was the girl, Christine?

Maybe she escaped as they were preparing her for conversion. The overturned kitchen chair, Tucker's abandoned black bag, and the open front door seemed to support that unsettling explanation. In pursuit of the girl, caught up in the excitement of the chase, the Fosters and Tucker might have surrendered to a latent urge to regress. Perhaps not so latent. They might have regressed on other occasions, so this time they had slipped quickly and eagerly into that altered state. And now they were stalking her in the wildlands to the south – or had long ago run her down, torn her to pieces, and were still regressed because they got a dark thrill from being in that debased condition.

The night was cool, but suddenly Loman was sweating.

He wanted . . . needed . . .

No!

Earlier in the day, Shaddack had told Loman that the Foster girl had missed her school bus and, returning home from the bus stop at the county road, had walked in on her parents as they were experimenting with their new abilities. So the girl had to be conducted through the Change slightly sooner than planned, the first child to be elevated. But maybe 'experimenting' was a lie that the Fosters had used to cover their asses. Maybe they had been in deep regression when the girl had come upon them, which they could not reveal to Shaddack without marking themselves as degenerates among the New People.

The Change was meant to elevate mankind; it was forced evolution.

Willfull regression, however, was a sick perversion of the power bestowed by the Change. Those who regressed were outcasts. And those regressives who killed for the primal thrill of blood sport were the worst of all: psychotics who had chosen devolution over evolution.

The distant cries came again.

A shiver crackled the length of Loman's spine. It was a pleasant shiver. He was seized by a powerful longing to shed his clothes, drop closer to the ground, and race nude and unrestrained through the night in long, graceful strides, across the broad meadow and into the woods, where all was wild and beautiful, where prey waited to be found and run down and broken and torn . . .

No.

Control.

Self-control.

The faraway cries pierced him.

He must exhibit self-control.

His heart pounded.

The cries. The sweet, eager, wild cries . . .

Loman began to tremble, then to shake violently, as in his mind's eye he saw himself freed from the rigid posture of *Homo erectus*, freed from the constraints of civilized form and behavior. If the primal man within him could be set loose at long last and allowed to live in a natural state—

No. Unthinkable.

His legs became weak, and he fell to the ground, though not onto all fours, no, because that posture would encourage him to surrender to these unspeakable urges; instead he curled into the fetal position, on his side, knees drawn up to his chest, and struggled against the swelling desire to regress. His flesh grew as hot as if he had been lying for hours in midday summer sun, but he realized that the heat was coming not from any external source but from deep within him; the fire arose not merely from vital organs or the marrow of his bones, but from the material within the walls of his cells, from the billions of nuclei that harbored the genetic material that made him what he was. Alone in the dark and fog in front of the Foster house, seduced by the echoey cry of the regressives, he longed to exercise the control of his physical being that the Change had granted him. But he knew if once he succumbed to that temptation, he would never be Loman Watkins again; he would be a degenerate masquerading as Loman Watkins, Mr. Hyde in a body from which he had banished Dr. Jekyll forever.

With his head tucked down, he was looking at his hands, which were curled against his chest, and in the dim light from the windows of the Foster house, he thought he saw several of his fingers begin to change. Pain flashed through his right hand. He *felt* the bones crunching and re-forming, knuckles swelling, digits lengthening, the pads of his fingers growing broader, sinews and tendons thickening, nails hardening and sharpening into talonlike points.

He screamed in stark terror and denial, and he *willed* himself to hold fast to his born identity, to what remained of his humanity. He resisted the lavalike movement of his living tissue. Through clenched teeth he repeated his name – 'Loman Watkins, Loman Watkins, Loman Watkins' – as if that were a spell that would prevent this evil transformation.

Time passed. Perhaps a minute. Perhaps ten. An hour. He didn't know. His struggle to retain his identity had conveyed him into a state of consciousness beyond time.

Slowly, he returned to awareness. With relief he found himself still on the ground in front of the house, unchanged. He was drenched in sweat. But the white-hot fire in his flesh had subsided. His hands were as they'd always been, with no freakish elongation of the fingers.

For a while he listened to the night. He heard no more of the distant cries, and he was grateful for that silence.

Fear, the only emotion that had not daily lost vividness and power since he had become one of the New People, was now as sharp as knives within him, causing him to cry out. For some time he had been afraid that he was one of those with the potential to become a regressive, and now that dark speculation was proven true. But if he surrendered to the yearning, he would have lost both the old world he'd known before he'd been converted *and* the brave new world Shaddack was making; he would belong in neither.

Worse: He was beginning to suspect that he was not unique, that in fact *all* of the New People had within them the seeds of devolution. Night by night, the regressives seemed to be increasing in number.

Shakily, he got to his feet.

The film of sweat was like a crust of ice on his skin now that his inner fires had been banked.

Moving dazedly toward his patrol car, Loman Watkins wondered if Shaddack's research – and the technological application of it – was so fundamentally flawed that there was no benefit whatsoever in the Change. Maybe it was an unalloyed curse. If the regressives were not a statistically insignificant percentage of the New People, if instead they were *all* doomed to drift toward regression sooner or later . . .

He thought of Thomas Shaddack out there in the big house on the north point of the cove, overlooking the town where beasts of his creation roamed the shadows, and a terrible bleakness overcame him. Because reading for pleasure had been his favorite pastime since he was a boy, he thought of H.G. Wells's Dr. Moreau, and he wondered if that was who Shaddack had become. Moreau reincarnate. Shaddack might be a Moreau for the age of microtechnology, obsessed with an insane vision of transcendence through the forced melding of man and machine. Certainly he suffered from delusions of grandeur, and had the hubris to believe that he could lift mankind to a higher state, just as the original Moreau had believed he could make men from savage animals and beat God at His game. If Shaddack was not *the* genius of his century, if he was an overreacher like Moreau, then they were all damned.

Loman got in the car and pulled the door shut. He started the engine and turned on the heater to warm his sweat-chilled body.

The computer screen lit, awaiting use.

For the sake of protecting the Moonhawk Project – which, flawed or not, represented the only future open to him – he had to assume the girl, Christine, had escaped, and that the Fosters and Tucker hadn't caught her. He must arrange for men to stand watch surreptitiously along the county road and on the streets entering the north end of Moonlight Cove. If the girl came into town seeking help, they could intercept her. More likely than not, she would unknowingly approach one of the New People with her tale of possessed parents, and that would be the end of her. Even if she got to people not yet converted, they weren't likely to believe her wild story. But he could take no chances.

He had to talk to Shaddack about a number of things, and attend to several pieces of police business.

He also had to get something to eat.

He was inhumanly hungry.

• 27 •

Something was wrong, something was wrong, something, something.

Mike Peyser had slipped through the dark woods to his house on the southeast edge of town, down through the wild hills and trees, stealthy and alert, slinking and quick, naked and quick, returning from a hunt, blood in his mouth, still excited but tired after two hours of playing games with his prey, cautiously bypassing the homes of his neighbors, some of whom were his kind and some of whom were not. The houses in that area were widely separated, so he found it relatively easy to creep from shadow to shadow, tree to tree, through tall grass, low to the ground, cloaked in the night, swift and sleek, silent and swift, naked and silent, powerful and swift, straight to the porch of the single-story house where he lived alone, through the unlocked door, into the kitchen, still tasting the blood in his mouth, blood, the lovely blood, exhilarated by the hunt though also glad to be home, but then—

Something was wrong.

Wrong, wrong, God, he was burning up, full of fire, hot, burning up, in need of food, nourishment, fuel, fuel, and that was normal, that was to be expected – the demands on his metabolism were tremendous when he was in his altered state – but the fire was not wrong, not the inner fire, not the frantic and consuming need for nourishment. What was wrong was that he could not, he could not, he could not—

He could not change back.

Thrilled by the exquisitely fluid movement of his body, by the way his muscles flexed and stretched, flexed and stretched, he came into the darkened house, seeing well enough without lights, not as well as a cat might but better than a man, because he was more than just a man now, and he roamed for a couple of minutes through the rooms, silent and swift, almost hoping he would find an intruder, someone to savage, someone to savage, savage, someone to savage, bite and tear, but the house was deserted. In his bedroom, he settled to the floor, curled on his side, and called his body back to the form that had been his birthright, to the familiar form of Mike Peyser, to the shape of a man who walked erect and looked like a man, and within himself he felt a surge toward normalcy, a *shift* in the tissues, but not *enough* of a shift, and then a sliding away, away, like an outgoing tide pulling back from a beach, away, away from normalcy, so he tried again, but this time there was no shift at all, not even a partial return to what he had been. He was stuck, trapped, locked in, locked, locked in a form that earlier had seemed the essence of freedom and inexpressibly desirable, but now it was not a desirable form at all because he could not forsake it at will, was trapped in it, trapped, and he panicked.

He sprang up and hurried out of the room. Although he could see fairly well in the darkness, he brushed a floor lamp, and it fell with a crash, the brittle sound of shattering glass, but he kept going into the short hall, the living room. A rag rug spun out from under him. He felt that he was in a prison; his body, his own transformed body, had become his prison, prison, metamorphosed bones serving as the bars of a cell, bars holding him captive from within; he was restrained by his own reconfigured flesh. He circled the room, scrambled this way and that, circled, circled, frenzied, frantic. The curtains fluttered in the wind of his passage. He weaved among the furniture. An end table toppled over in his wake. He could run but not escape. He carried his prison with him. No escape. No escape. Never. That realization made his heart thump more wildly. Terrified, frustrated, he knocked over a magazine rack, spilling its contents, swept a heavy glass ashtray and two pieces of decorative pottery off the cocktail table, tore at the sofa cushions until he had shredded both the fabric and the foam padding within, whereupon a terrible pressure filled his skull, pain, such pain, and he wanted to scream but he was afraid to scream, afraid that he would not be able to stop.

Food.

Fuel.

Feed the fire, feed the fire.

He suddenly realized that his inability to return to his natural form might be related to a severe shortage of energy reserves needed to fuel the tremendous acceleration of his metabolism associated with a transformation. To do what he was demanding, his body must produce enormous quantities of enzymes, hormones, and complex biologically active chemicals; in mere minutes the body must undergo a forced degeneration and rebuilding of tissues equal in energy requirements to years of ordinary growth, and for that it needed fuel, material to convert, proteins and minerals, carbohydrates in quantity.

Hungry, starving, starving, Peyser hurried into the lightless kitchen, clutched the handle on the refrigerator door, pulled himself up, tore the door open, hissed as the light stung his eyes, saw two-thirds of a three-pound canned ham, solid ham, good ham, sealed in Saran Wrap on a blue plate, so he seized it, ripped away the plastic, threw the plate aside, where it smashed against a cabinet door, and he dropped back to the floor, bit into the hunk of meat, bit and bit into it, bit deep, ripped, chewed feverishly, bit deep.

He loved to strip out of his clothes and seek another form as soon after nightfall as possible, sprinting into the woods behind his house, up into the hills, where he chased down rabbits and raccoons, foxes and ground squirrels, tore them apart in his hands, with his teeth, fed the fire, the deep inner burning, and he loved it, loved it, not merely because he felt such freedom in that incarnation but because it gave him an overwhelming sense of power, godlike power, more intensely erotic than sex, more satisfying than anything he had experienced before, power, savage power, raw power, the power of a man who had tamed nature, transcended his genetic limits, the power of the wind and the storm, freed of all human limitations, set loose, liberated. He had fed tonight, sweeping through the woods with the confidence of an inescapable predator, as irresistible as the darkness itself, but whatever he had consumed must have been insufficient to empower his return to the form of Michael Peyser, software designer, bachelor, Porsche-owner, ardent collector of movies on video disk, marathon runner, Perrier-drinker.

So now he ate the ham, all two pounds of it, and he snatched other items out of the refrigerator and ate them as well, stuffing them into his mouth with both tine-fingered hands: a bowlful of cold leftover rigatoni and one meatball; half of an apple pie that he'd bought yesterday at the bakery in town; a stick of butter, an entire quarter of a pound, greasy and cloying but good food, good fuel, just the thing to feed the fire; four raw eggs; and more, more. This was a fire that, when fed, did not burn brighter but cooled, subsided, for it was not a real fire at all but a physical symptom of the desperate need for fuel to keep the metabolic processes running smoothly. Now the fire began to lose some of its heat, shrinking from a roaring blaze to sputtering flames to little more than the glow of hot coals.

Sated, Mike Peyser collapsed to the floor in front of the open refrigerator, in a litter of broken dishes and food and Saran Wrap and eggshells and Tupperware containers. He curled up again and willed himself toward that form in which the world would recognize him, and once more he felt a *shift* taking place in his marrow and bones, in his blood and organs, in sinews and cartilage and muscles and skin, as tides of hormones and enzymes and other biological chemicals were produced by his body and washed through it, but as before the change was arrested with transformation woefully incomplete, and his body eased toward its more savage stage, inevitably regressing though he strained with all his will, all his will, strained and struggled to seek the higher form.

The refrigerator door had swung shut. The kitchen was in the grasp of shadows again, and Mike Peyser felt as if that darkness was not merely all around him but also within him.

At last he screamed. As he had feared, once he began to scream, he could not stop.

• 28 •

Shortly before midnight Sam Booker left Cove Lodge. He wore a brown leather jacket, blue sweater, jeans, and blue running shoes – an outfit that allowed him to blend effectively with the night but that didn't look suspicious, though perhaps slightly too youthful for a man of his relentlessly melancholy demeanor. Ordinary as it looked, the jacket had several unusually deep and capacious inner pockets, in which he was carrying a few basic burglary and auto-theft tools. He descended the south stairs, went out the rear door at the bottom, and stood for a moment on the walkway behind the lodge.

Thick fog poured up the face of the bluff and through the open railing, driven by a sudden sea breeze that finally had disturbed the night's calm. In a few hours the breeze would harry the fog inland and leave the coast in relative clarity. By then Sam would have finished the task ahead of him and, no longer needing the cover that the mist provided, would be at last asleep – or more likely fighting insomnia – in his motel-room bed.

He was uneasy. He had not forgotten the pack of kids from whom he'd run on Iceberry Way, earlier in the evening. Because their true nature remained a mystery, he continued to think of them as punks, but he knew they were more than just juvenile delinquents. Strangely, he had the feeling that he *did* know what they were, but the knowledge stirred in him far below even a subconscious plane, in realms of primitive consciousness.

He rounded the south end of the building, walked past the back of the coffee shop, which was now closed, and ten minutes later, by a roundabout route, he arrived at the Moonlight Cove Municipal Building on Jacobi Street. It was exactly as the Bureau's San Francisco agents had described it: a two-story structure – weathered brick on the lower floor, white siding on the upper – with a slate roof, forest-green storm shutters flanking the windows, and large iron carriage lamps at the main entrance. The municipal building and the property on which it stood occupied half a block on the north side of the street, but its anti-institutional architecture was in harmony with the otherwise residential neighborhood. Exterior and interior ground-floor lights were on even at that hour because in addition to the city-government offices and water authority, the municipal building housed the police department, which of course never closed.

From across the street, pretending to be out for a late-night constitutional, Sam studied the place as he passed it. He saw no unusual activity. The sidewalk in front of the main entrance was deserted. Through the glass doors he saw a brightly-lit foyer.

At the next corner he went north and into the alley in the middle of the block. That unlighted serviceway was bracketed by trees and shrubbery and fences that marked the rear property lines of the houses on Jacobi Street and Pacific

Drive, by some garages and outbuildings, by groups of garbage cans, and by the large unfenced parking area behind the municipal building.

Sam stepped into a niche in an eight-foot-tall evergreen hedge at the corner of the yard that adjoined the public property. Though the alley was very dark, two sodium-vapor lamps cast a jaundice glow over the city lot, revealing twelve vehicles: four late-model Fords of the stripped-down, puke-green variety that was produced for federal, state, and local government purchase; a pickup and van both bearing the seal of the city and the legend WATER AUTHORITY; a hulking street-sweeping machine; a large truck with wooden sides and tailgate; and four police cars, all Chevy sedans.

The quartet of black-and-whites were what interested Sam because they were equipped with VDTs linking them to the police department's central computer. Moonlight Cove owned eight patrol cars, a large number for a sleepy coastal town, five more than other communities of similar size could afford and surely in excess of need.

But everything about this police department was bigger and better than necessary, which was one of the things that had triggered silent alarms in the minds of the Bureau agents who'd come to investigate the deaths of Sanchez and the Bustamantes. Moonlight Cove had twelve full-time and three part-time officers plus four full-time office support personnel. A lot of manpower. Furthermore, they were all receiving salaries competitive with law-enforcement pay scales in major West Coast cities, therefore excessive for a town as small as this. They had the finest uniforms, the finest office furniture, a small armory of handguns and riot guns and tear gas, and – most astonishing of all – they were computerized to an extent that would have been the envy of the boys manning the end-of-the-world bunkers at the Strategic Air Command in Colorado.

From his bristly nook in the fragrant evergreen hedge, Sam studied the lot for a couple of minutes to be sure no one was sitting in any of the vehicles or standing in deep shadows along the back of the building. Levolor blinds were closed at the lighted windows on the ground floor, so no one inside had a view of the parking area.

He took a pair of soft, supple goatskin gloves from a jacket pocket and pulled them on.

He was ready to move when he heard something in the alley behind him. A scraping noise. Back the way he'd come.

Pressing deeper into the hedge, he turned his head to search for the source of the sound. A pale, crumpled cardboard box, twice the size of a shoebox, slid along the blacktop, propelled by the breeze that was increasingly rustling the leaves of the shrubs and trees. The carton met a garbage can, wedged against it, and fell silent.

Streaming across the alley, flowing eastward on the breeze, the fog now looked like smoke, as if the whole town were afire. Squinting back through that churning vapor, he satisfied himself that he was alone, then turned and sprinted to the nearest of the four patrol cars in the unfenced lot.

It was locked.

From an inner jacket pocket, he withdrew a Police Automobile-Lock Release Gun, which could instantly open any lock without damaging the mechanism. He cracked the car, slipped in behind the steering wheel, and closed the door as quickly and quietly as possible.

Enough light from the sodium-vapor lamps penetrated the car for him to see what he was doing, though he was experienced enough to work virtually in the dark. He put the lock gun away and took an ignition-socket wrench from another pocket. In seconds he popped the ignition-switch cylinder from the steering column, exposing the wires.

He hated this part. To click on the video-display mounted on the car's console, he had to start the engine; the computer was more powerful than a lap-top model and communicated with its base data center by energy-intensive microwave transmissions, drawing too much power to run off the battery. The fog would cover the exhaust fumes but not the sound of the engine. The black-and-white was parked eighty feet from the building, so no one inside was likely to hear it. But if someone stepped out of the back door for some fresh air or to take one of the off-duty cruisers out on a call, the idling engine would not escape notice. Then Sam would be in a confrontation that – given the frequency of violent death in this town – he might not survive.

Sighing softly, lightly depressing the accelerator with his right foot, he separated the ignition wires with one gloved hand and twisted the bare contact points together. The engine turned over immediately, without any harsh grinding.

The computer screen blinked on.

The police department's elaborate computerization was provided by New Wave Microtechnology because they were supposedly using Moonlight Cove as a sort of testing ground for their own systems and softwares. The source of the excess funds so evident in every other aspect of the department was not easy to pin down, but the suspicion was that it came from New Wave or from New Wave's majority stockholder and chief executive officer, Thomas Shaddack. Any citizen was free to support his local police or other arms of government in excess of his taxes, of course, but if that was what Shaddack was doing, why wasn't it a matter of public record? No innocent man gives large sums of money to a civic cause with *complete* self-effacement. If Shaddack was being secretive about supporting the local authorities with private funds, then the possibility of bought cops and in-the-pocket officials could not be discounted. And if the Moonlight Cove police were virtually soldiers in Thomas Shaddack's private army, it followed that the suspicious number of violent deaths in recent weeks could be related to that unholy alliance.

Now the VDT in the car displayed the New Wave logo in the bottom right-hand corner, just as the IBM logo would have been featured if this had been one of their machines.

During the San Francisco office's investigation of the Sanchez-Bustamante case, one of the Bureau's better agents, Morrie Stein, had been in a patrol car with one of Watkins' officers, Reese Dorn, when Dorn accessed the central computer for information in departmental files. By then Morrie had suspected that the computer was even more sophisticated than Watkins or his men had revealed, serving them in some way that exceeded the legal limits of police authority and that they were not willing to discuss, so he had memorized the code number with which Reese had tapped into the system. When he had flown to the Los Angeles office to brief Sam, Morrie had said, 'I think every cop in that twisted little town has his own computer-access number, but Dorn's ought to work as well as any. Sam, you've got to get into their computer and let it throw some menus at you, see what it offers, play around with it when Watkins and his men aren't looking over your shoulder. Yeah, I sound paranoid, but there's too much high-tech for their size and needs, unless they're up to something dirty. At first it seems like any town, even more pleasant than most, rather pretty . . . but, dammit, after a while you get the feeling the whole burg is wired, that you're watched everywhere you go, that Big Brother is looking over your shoulder every damn minute. Honest to God, after a few days you're gut-sure you're in a miniature police state, where the control is so subtle you can hardly see it but still complete, iron-fisted. Those cops are bent, Sam; they're deep into something – maybe drug traffic, who knows – and the computer is part of it.'

Reese Dorn's number was 262699, and Sam tapped it out on the VDT keyboard. The New Wave logo disappeared. The screen was blank for a second. Then a menu appeared.

> CHOOSE ONE
> A. DISPATCHER
> B. CENTRAL FILES
> C. BULLETIN BOARD
> D. OUTSYSTEM MODEM

To Sam, the first item on the menu indicated that a cruising office could communicate with the dispatcher at headquarters not only by means of the police-band radio with which the car was equipped but also through the computer link. But why would he want to go to all the trouble of typing in questions to the dispatcher and reading the transmitted replies off the VDT when the information could be gotten so much easier and quicker on the radio? Unless . . . there were some things that these cops did not want to talk about on radio frequencies that could be monitored by anyone with a police-band receiver.

He did not open the link to the dispatcher because then he would have to begin a dialogue, posing as Reese Dorn, and that would be like shouting, *Hey, I'm out here in one of your cruisers, poking my nose in just where you don't want it, so why don't you come and chop it off.*

Instead, he tapped B and entered it. Another menu appeared.

> CHOOSE ONE:
> A. STATUS – CURRENT ARRESTEES
> B. STATUS – CURRENT COURT CASES
> C. STATUS – PENDING COURT CASES
> D. PAST ARREST RECORDS – COUNTY
> E. PAST ARREST RECORDS – CITY
> F. CONVICTED CRIMINALS LIVING IN COUNTY
> G. CONVICTED CRIMINALS LIVING IN CITY

Just to satisfy himself that the offerings on the menu were what they appeared to be and not code for other information, he punched in selection F, to obtain data on convicted criminals living in the county. Another menu appeared, offering him ten choices: MURDER, MANSLAUGHTER, RAPE, SEX OFFENSES, ASSAULT AND BATTERY, ARMED ROBBERY, BURGLARY, BREAKING AND ENTERING, OTHER THEFT, MISCELLANEOUS LESSER OFFENSES.

He called forth the file on murder and discovered three convicted killers – all guilty of murder in either the first or second degree – were now living as free men in the county after having served anywhere from twelve to forty years for their crimes before being released on parole. Their names, addresses, and telephone numbers appeared on the screen with the names of their victims, economically summarized details of their crimes, and the dates of their imprisonment; none lived in the city limits of Moonlight Cove.

Sam looked up from the screen and scanned the parking lot. It remained deserted. The omnipresent mist was filled with thicker veins of fog that rippled bannerlike as they flowed past the car, and he felt almost as if he were under the sea in a bathyscaphe, peering out at long ribbons of kelp fluttering in marine currents.

He returned to the main menu and asked for item C, BULLETIN BOARD. That proved to be a collection of messages that Watkins and his officers had left for one another regarding matters that seemed sometimes related to policework and sometimes private. Most were in such cryptic shorthand that Sam didn't feel he could puzzle them out or that they would be worth the effort to decipher.

He tried item D on the main menu, OUTSYSTEM MODEM, and was shown a list of computers nationwide with which he could link through the telephone modem in the nearby municipal building. The department's possible connections were astonishing: LOS ANGELES PD (for police department), SAN FRANCISCO PD, SAN DIEGO PD, DENVER PD, HOUSTON PD, DALLAS PD, PHOENIX PD, CHICAGO PD, MIAMI PD, NEW YORK CITY PD, and a score of other major cities; CALIFORNIA DEPARTMENT OF MOTOR VEHICLES, DEPARTMENT OF PRISONS, HIGHWAY PATROL, and many other state agencies with less obvious connections to police work; U.S. ARMY PERSONNEL FILES, NAVY PERSONNEL FILES, AIR FORCE; FBI CRIMINAL RECORDS; FBI LLEAS (Local Law-Enforcement Assistance System, a relatively new Bureau program); even INTERPOL's New York office, through which the international organization could access its central files in Europe.

What in the hell would a small police force in rural California need with all those sources of information?

And there was more: data to which even fully computerized police agencies in cities like Los Angeles would not have easy access. By law, some of it was stuff that police could not obtain without a court order, such as the files at TRW, the nation's premier credit-reporting firm. The Moonlight Cove Police Department's ability to access TRW's data base at will had to be a secret kept from TRW itself, for the company would not have cooperated in a wholesale disgorgement of its files without a subpoena. The system also offered entrance to CIA data bases in Virginia, which were supposedly secured against access from any computer beyond the Agency's walls, and to certain FBI files which were likewise believed to be inviolate.

Shaken, Sam retreated from the OUTSYSTEM MODEM options and returned to the main menu.

He stared out at the parking lot, thinking.

When briefing Sam a few days ago, Morrie Stein had suggested that Moonlight Cove's police might somehow be trafficking in drugs, and that New Wave's generosity with computer systems might indicate complicity on the part of certain unidentified officers of that firm. But the Bureau was also interested in the possibility that New Wave was illegally selling sensitive high technology to the Soviets and that it had bought the Moonlight Cove police because, through these law-enforcement contacts, the company would be alerted at the earliest possible moment to a nascent federal probe into its activities. They had no explanation of how either of those crimes accounted for all the recent deaths, but they had to start with *some* theory.

Now Sam was ready to discount both the idea that New Wave was selling to the Soviets and that some executives of the firm were in the drug trade. The far-reaching web of data bases that the police had made available to themselves through their modem – one hundred and twelve were listed on that menu! – was greatly in excess of anything they would require for either drug trafficking or sniffing out federal suspicions of possible Soviet connections at New Wave.

They had created an informational network more suitable to the operational necessities of an entire state government – or, even more accurately, a small nation. A small, *hostile* nation. This data web was designed to provide its owner with enormous power. It was as if this picturesque little town suffered under the governing hand of a megalomaniac whose central delusion was that he could create a tiny kingdom from which he would eventually conquer vast territory.

Today, Moonlight Cove; tomorrow, the world.

'What the fuck are they doing?' Sam wondered aloud.

• 29 •

Safely locked in her room at Cove Lodge – dressed for bed in pale yellow panties and a white T-shirt emblazoned with Kermit the Frog's smiling face – Tessa drank Diet Coke and tried to watch a repeat of the *Tonight* show, but she couldn't get interested in the conversations that Johnny Carson conducted with a witless actress, a witless singer, and a witless comedian. Diet thought to accompany Diet Coke.

The more time that passed after her unsettling experiences in the motel's halls and stairwells, the more she wondered if indeed she had imagined being stalked. She was distraught about Janice's death, after all, preoccupied by the thought that it was murder rather than suicide. And she was still dyspeptic from the cheeseburger she'd eaten for dinner, which had been so greasy that it might have been deep-fried, bun and all, in impure yak lard. As Scrooge had first believed of Marley's ghost, so Tessa now began to view the phantoms that had frightened her earlier: Perhaps they'd been nothing more than an undigested bit of beef, a blot of mustard, a crumb of cheese, a fragment of an underdone potato.

As Carson's current guest talked about a weekend he'd spent at an arts festival in Havana with Fidel Castro – 'a great guy, a funny guy, a compassionate guy' – Tessa got up from the bed and went to the bathroom to wash her face and brush her teeth. As she was squeezing Crest onto the brush, she heard someone try the door to her room.

The small bath was off the smaller foyer. When she stepped to the threshold, she was within a couple of feet of the door to the hall, close enough to see the knob twisting back and forth as someone tested the lock. They weren't even being subtle about it. The knob clicked and rattled, and the door clattered against the frame.

She dropped her toothbrush and hurried to the telephone that stood on the nightstand.

No dial tone.

She jiggled the cutoff buttons, pressed O for operator, but nothing worked. The motel switchboard was shut down. The phone was dead.

• 30 •

Several times Chrissie had to scurry off the road, taking cover in the brush along the verge, until an approaching car or truck went past. One of them was a Moonlight Cove police car, heading toward town, and she was pretty sure it was the one that had come out to the house. She hunkered down in tall grass and milkweed stalks, and remained there until the black-and-white's taillights dwindled to tiny red dots and finally vanished around a turn.

A few houses were built along the first mile and a half of that two-lane blacktop. Chrissie knew some of the people who lived in them: the Thomases, the Stones, the Elswicks. She was tempted to go to one of those places, knock on the door, and ask for help. But she couldn't be sure that those people were still the nice folks they had once been. They might have changed, too, like her parents. Either something supernatural or from outer space was taking possession of people in and around Moonlight Cove, and she had seen enough scary movies and read enough scary books to know that when *those* kind of forces were at work, you could no longer trust anyone.

She was betting nearly everything on Father Castelli at Our Lady of Mercy because he was a holy man, and no demons from hell would be able to get a grip on him. Of course, if the problem was aliens from another world, Father Castelli would not be protected just because he was a man of God.

In that case, if the priest had been taken over, and if Chrissie managed to get away from him after she discovered he was one of the enemy, she'd go straight to Mrs. Irene Tokawa, her teacher. Mrs. Tokawa was the smartest person Chrissie knew. If aliens were taking over Moonlight Cove, Mrs. Tokawa would have realized something was wrong before it was too late. She would have taken steps to protect herself, and she would be one of the last that the monsters would get their hooks into. Hooks or tentacles or claws or pincers or whatever.

So Chrissie hid from passing traffic, sneaked past the houses scattered along the county road, and proceeded haltingly but steadily toward town. The horned moon, sometimes revealed above the fog, had traversed most of the sky; it would soon be gone. A stiff breeze had swept in from the west, marked by periodic gusts strong enough to whip her hair straight up in the air as if it were a blond flame leaping from her head. Although the temperature had fallen to only about fifty degrees, the night felt much colder during those turbulent moments when the breeze temporarily became a blustering wind. The positive side was that the more miserable the cold and wind made her, the less aware she was of that other discomfort – hunger.

'Waif Found Wandering Hungry and Dazed After Encounter with Space

Aliens,' she said, reading that imagined headline from an issue of *The National Enquirer* that existed only in her mind.

She was approaching the intersection of the county route and Holliwell Road, feeling good about the progress she was making, when she nearly walked into the arms of those she was trying to avoid.

To the east of the county route, Holliwell was a dirt road leading up into the hills, under the interstate, and all the way to the old, abandoned Icarus Colony – a dilapidated twelve-room house, barn, and collapsing out-buildings – where a group of artists had tried to establish an ideal communal society back in the 1950s. Since then it had been a horse-breeding facility (failed), the site of a weekly flea market and auction (failed), a natural-food restaurant (failed), and had long ago settled into ruin. Kids knew all about it because it was a spooky place and thus the site of many tests of courage. To the west, Holliwell Road was paved and led along the edge of the town limits, past some of the newer homes in the area, past New Wave Microtech, and even-tually out to the north point of the cove, where Thomas Shaddack, the com-puter genius, lived in a huge, weird-looking house. Chrissie didn't intend to go either east or west on Holliwell; it was just a milestone on her trek, and when she crossed it she would be at the northeast corner of the Moonlight Cove city limits.

She was within a hundred feet of Holliwell when she heard the low but swiftly swelling sound of a racing engine. She stepped away from the road, over a narrow ditch at the verge, waded through weeds, and took cover against the thick trunk of an ancient pine. Even as she hunkered down by the tree, she got a fix on the direction from which the vehicle was approaching – west – and then she saw its headlights spearing into the intersection just south of her. A truck pulled into view on Holliwell, ignoring the stop sign, and braked in the middle of the intersection. Fog whirled and plumed around it.

Chrissie could see that heavy-duty, black, extended-bed pickup fairly well because, as the junction of Holliwell and the county road was the site of frequent accidents, a single streetlight had been installed on the northeast corner for better visibility and as a warning to drivers. The truck bore the distinctive New Wave insignia on the door, which she could recognize even at a distance because she had seen it maybe a thousand times before: a white and blue circle the size of a dinner plate, the bottom half of which was a cresting blue wave. The truck had a large bed, and at the moment its cargo was men; six or eight were sitting in the back.

The instant that the pickup halted in the intersection, two men vaulted over the tailgate. One of them went to the wooded point at the northwest corner of the intersection and slipped into the trees, no more than a hundred feet south of the pine from which Chrissie was watching him. The other crossed to the southeast corner of the junction and took up a position in weeds and chaparral.

The pickup turned south on the county road and sped away.

Chrissie suspected that the remaining men in the truck would be let off at other points along the eastern perimeter of Moonlight Cove, where they would take up watch positions. Furthermore, the truck had been big enough to carry at least twenty men, and no doubt others had been dropped off as it had come eastward along Holliwell from the New Wave building in the west. They were surrounding Moonlight Cove with sentries. She was quite sure they were looking for her. She had seen something she had not been meant to see – her parents in the act of a hideous transformation, shucking off their human disguise – and now she had to be found and 'converted' – as Tucker had put it – before she had a chance to warn the world.

The sound of the black truck receded.

Silence settled in like a damp blanket.

Fog swirled and churned and eddied in countless currents, but the overriding tidal forces in the air pushed it relentlessly toward the dark and serried hills.

Then the breeze abruptly ratcheted up until it became a real wind again, whispering in the tall weeds, soughing through the evergreens. It produced a soft and strangely forlorn thrumming from a nearby road sign.

Though Chrissie knew where the two men had gone to ground, she could not see them. They were well hidden.

• 31 •

Fog flew past the patrol car and eastward through the night, driven by a breeze that was swiftly becoming a full wind, and ideas flew through Sam's mind with the same fluidity. His thoughts were so disturbing that he would have preferred to have sat in mindless stupefaction.

From considerable prior computer experience, he knew that part of a system's capabilities could be hidden if the program designer simply deleted some choices from the task menus that appeared on the screen. He stared at the primary menu on the car's display – A. DISPATCHER; B. CENTRAL FILES; C. BULLETIN BOARD; D. OUTSYSTEM MODEM – and he pressed E. though no E task was offered.

Words appeared on the terminal: HELLO, OFFICER DORN.

There *was* an E. He'd entered either a secret data base requiring ritual responses for access or an interactive information system that would respond to questions he typed on the keyboard. If the former was the case, if passwords or phrases were required, and if he typed the wrong response, he was in trouble; the computer would shut him out and sound an alarm in police headquarters to warn them that an impersonator was using Dorn's number.

Proceeding with caution, he typed: HELLO.

MAY I BE OF ASSISTANCE?

Sam decided to proceed as if this was just what it seemed to be – a straightforward, question-and-answer program. He tapped the keyboard: MENU.

The screen blanked for a moment, then the same words reappeared: MAY I BE OF ASSISTANCE?

He tried again: PRIMARY MENU.

MAY I BE OF ASSISTANCE?

MAIN MENU.

MAY I BE OF ASSISTANCE?

Using a system accessed by question and response, with which one was unfamiliar, meant finding the proper commands more or less by trial and error. Sam tried again: FIRST MENU.

At last he was rewarded.

CHOOSE ONE
A. NEW WAVE PERSONNEL
B. PROJECT MOONHAWK
C. SHADDACK

He had found a secret connection between New Wave, its founder Thomas Shaddack, and the Moonlight Cove police. But he didn't know yet what the connection was or what it meant.

He suspected that choice C might link him to Shaddack's personal computer terminal, allowing him to have a dialogue with Shaddack that would be more private than a conversation conducted on police-band radio. If that was the case, then Shaddack and the local cops were indeed involved in a conspiracy so criminal that it required a very high degree of security. He did not punch C because, if he called up Shaddack's computer and got Mr. Big himself on the other end, there was no way he could successfully pretend to be Reese Dorn.

Choice A probably would provide him with a roster of New Wave's executives and department heads, and maybe with codes that would allow him to link up with their personal terminals as well. He didn't want to talk with any of them either.

Besides, he felt that he was on borrowed time. He surveyed the parking lot again and peered especially hard at the deeper pools of shadow beyond the reach of the sodium-vapor lamps. He'd been in the patrol car for fifteen minutes, and no one had come or gone from the municipal-building lot in that time. He doubted his luck would hold much longer, and he wanted to learn as much as possible in whatever minutes remained before he was interrupted.

PROJECT MOONHAWK was the most mysterious and interesting of the three choices, so he pushed B, and another menu appeared.

CHOOSE ONE:
A. CONVERTED
B. PENDING CONVERSION
C. SCHEDULE OF CONVERSION – LOCAL
D. SCHEDULE OF CONVERSION – SECOND STAGE

He punched choice A, and a column of names and addresses appeared on the screen. They were people in Moonlight Cove, and at the head of the column was the notation 1967 NOW CONVERTED.

Converted? From what? To what? Was there something religious about this conspiracy? Some strange cult? Or maybe 'converted' was used in some euphemistic sense or as a code.

The word gave him the creeps.

Sam discovered that he could either scroll through the list or access it in alphabetized chunks. He looked up the names of residents whom he either knew or had met. Loman Watkins was on the converted list. So was Reese Dorn. Burt Peckham, the owner of Knight's Bridge Tavern, was not among the converted, but the entire Perez family, surely the same that operated the restaurant, was on that roster.

He checked Harold Talbot, the disabled vet with whom he intended to make contact in the morning. Talbot was not on the converted list.

Puzzled as to the meaning of it all, Sam closed out that file, returned to the main menu, and punched B. PENDING CONVERSION. This brought another list of names and addresses to the VDT, and the column was headed by the words 1104 PENDING CONVERSION. On this roster he found Burt Peckham and Harold Talbot.

He tried C. SCHEDULE OF CONVERSION – LOCAL, and a submenu of three headings appeared:

A. MONDAY, OCTOBER 13, 6:00 P.M.
    THROUGH
    TUESDAY, OCTOBER 14, 6:00 A.M.

B. TUESDAY, OCTOBER 14, 6:00 A.M.
    THROUGH
    TUESDAY, OCTOBER 14, 6:00 P.M.

C. TUESDAY, OCTOBER 14, 6:00 P.M.
    THROUGH
    MIDNIGHT

It was now 12:39 a.m., Tuesday, about halfway between the times noted in Choice A, so he punched that one first. It was another list of names headed by the notation 380 CONVERSIONS SCHEDULED.

The fine hairs were bristling on the back of Sam's neck, and he didn't know why except that the word 'conversions' unsettled him. It made him think of that old movie with Kevin McCarthy, *Invasion of the Body Snatchers*.

He also thought of the pack that had pursued him earlier in the night. Had they been . . . converted?

When he looked up Burt Peckham, he found the tavern owner on the schedule for conversion before 6:00 a.m. However, Harry Talbot was not listed.

The car shook.

Sam snapped his head up and reached for the revolver holstered under his jacket.

Wind. It was only wind. A series of hard gusts shredded holes in the fog and lightly rocked the car. After a moment the wind died to a strong breeze again, and the torn fabric of fog mended itself, but Sam's heart was still thudding painfully.

• 32 •

As Tessa put down the useless telephone, the doorknob stopped rattling. She stood by the bed for a while, listening, then ventured warily into the foyer to press her ear against the door.

She heard voices but not immediately beyond that portal. They were farther down the hallway, peculiar voices that spoke in urgent, raspy whispers. She could not make out anything they said.

She was sure they were the same ones who had stalked her, unseen, when she had gone for ice and a Diet Coke. Now they were back. And somehow they had knocked out the phones, so she couldn't call for help. It was crazy, but it was happening.

Such persistence on their part indicated to Tessa that they were not ordinary rapists or muggers, that they had focused on her because she was Janice's sister, because she was there to look into Janice's death. However, she wondered how they had become aware of her arrival in town and why they had chosen to move against her so precipitously, without even waiting to see if she was just going to settle Janice's affairs and leave. Only she and her mother knew that she intended to attempt a murder investigation of her own.

Gooseflesh prickled her bare legs, and she felt vulnerable in just T-shirt and panties. She went quickly to the closet, pulled on jeans and a sweater.

She wasn't alone in the motel. There were other guests. Mr. Quinn had said so. Maybe not many, perhaps only another two or three. But if worse came to worst, she could scream, and the other guests would hear her, and her would-be assailants would have to flee.

She picked up her Rockports, in which she had stuffed the white athletic socks she'd been wearing, and returned to the door.

Low, hoarse voices hissed and muttered at the far end of the hall – then a bone-jarring crash slammed through the lodge, making her cry out and twitch in surprise. Another crash followed at once. She heard a door give way at another room.

A woman screamed, and a man shouted, but the *other* voices were what brought a chill of horror to Tessa. There were several of them, three or even four, and they were eerie and shockingly savage. The public corridor beyond her door was filled with harsh wolflike growls, murderous snarls, shrill and excited squeals, an icy keening that was the essence of blood hunger, and other less describable sounds, but worst of all was that those same inhuman voices, clearly belonging to beasts not men, nevertheless also spat out a few recognizable words: '. . . *need, need . . . get her, get . . . get, get . . . blood, bitch, blood . . .*'

Leaning against the door, holding on to it for support, Tessa tried to tell herself that the words she heard were from the man and woman whose room had been broken into, but she knew that was not true, because she also heard both a man and woman screaming. Their screams were horrible, almost unbearable, full of terror and agony, as if they were being beaten to death or worse, much worse, being torn apart, ripped limb from limb and gutted.

A couple of years ago Tessa had been in Northern Ireland, making a documentary about the pointlessness of the endless violence there, and she'd been unfortunate enough to be at a cemetery, at the funeral of one of the endless series of 'martyrs' – Catholic or Protestant, it didn't matter any more, both sides had a surfeit of them – when the crowd of mourners had metamorphosed into a pack of savages. They had streamed from the churchyard into nearby streets, looking for those of a different faith, and soon they'd come across two British plainclothes army officers patrolling the area in a unmarked car. By its sheer size, the mob blocked the car's advance, encircled it, smashed in the windows, and dragged the would-be peacekeepers out onto the pavement. Tessa's two technical assistants had fled, but she had waded into the mêlée with her shoulder-mounted videotape camera, and through the lens she had seemed to be looking beyond the reality of this world into hell itself. Eyes wild, faces distorted with hatred and rage, grief forgotten and bloodlust embraced, the mourners had tirelessly kicked the fallen Britons, then pulled them to their feet only to pummel and stab them, slammed them repeatedly against the car until their spines broke and their skulls cracked, then dropped them and stomped them and tore at them and stabbed them again, though by that time they were both dead. Howling and shrieking, cursing, chanting slogans that degenerated into meaningless chains of sounds, mindless rhythms, like a flock of carrion-eating birds, they plucked at the shattered bodies, though they weren't like earthly birds, neither buzzards nor vultures, but like demons that had flown up from the pit, tearing at the dead men not only with the intention of consuming their flesh but with the hot desire to rip out and steal their souls. Two of those frenzied men had noticed Tessa, had seized her camera and smashed it, and had thrown her to the ground. For one terrible moment she was sure that they would dismember her in their frenzy. Two of them leaned down, grabbing at her clothes. Their faces were so wrenched with hatred that they no longer looked human, but like gargoyles that had come to life and had climbed down from the roofs of cathedrals. They had surrendered all that was human in themselves and let loose the gene-encoded ghosts of the primitives from whom they were descended. 'For God's sake, no!' she had cried. 'For God's sake, please!' Perhaps it was the mention of God or just the sound of a human voice that had *not* devolved into the hoarse gnarl of a beast, but for some reason they let go and hesitated. She seized that reprieve to scramble away from them, through the churning, blood-crazed mob to safety.

What she heard now, at the other end of the motel corridor, was just like that. Or worse.

· **33** ·

Beginning to sweat even though the patrol car's heater was not on, still spooked by every sudden gust of wind, Sam called up submenu item B, which showed the conversions scheduled from 6:00 this coming morning until 6:00 p.m. that evening. Those names were preceded by the heading 450 CONVERSIONS SCHEDULED. Harry Talbot's name was not on that list either.

Choice C, six o'clock Tuesday evening through midnight the same day, indicated that 274 conversions were scheduled. Harry Talbot's name and address were on that third and final list.

Sam mentally added the numbers mentioned in each of the three conversion periods – 380, 450, and 274 – and realized they totaled 1104, which was the same number that headed the list of PENDING CONVERSIONS. Add that number to 1967, the total listed as already converted, and the grand total, 3071, was probably the population of Moonlight Cove. By the next time the clock struck midnight, a little less than twenty-three hours from now, the entire town would be converted – whatever the hell *that* meant.

He keyed out of the submenu and was about to switch off the car's engine and get out of there when the word ALERT appeared on the VDT and began to flash. Fear thrilled through him because he was sure they had discovered an intruder poking around in their system; he must have tripped some subtle alarm in the program.

Instead of opening the door and making a run for it, however, he watched the screen for a few more seconds, held by curiosity.

TELEPHONE SWEEP INDICATES FBI
AGENT IN MOONLIGHT COVE.
POINT OF CALL:
PAY PHONE, SHELL STATION,
OCEAN AVENUE.

The alert *was* related to him, though not because they knew he was currently sitting in one of their patrol cars and probing the New Wave/Moonhawk conspiracy. Evidently the bastards were tied into the phone company's data banks and periodically swept those records to see who had made calls from what numbers to what numbers – even from all of the town's pay telephones, which in ordinary circumstances could have been counted on to provide secure communications for a field agent. They were paranoid and security conscious and electronically connected to an extent and degree that proved increasingly astounding with each revelation.

TIME OF CALL:
7:31 P.M., MONDAY,
OCTOBER 13.

At least they didn't keep a minute-by-minute or even hour-by-hour link with the telephone company. Their computer obviously swept those records on a programmed schedule, perhaps every four or six or eight hours. Otherwise they would have been on the lookout for him shortly after he had made the call to Scott earlier in the evening.

After the legend CALL PLACED TO, his home phone number appeared, then his name and his address in Sherman Oaks. Followed by:

CALL PLACED BY:
SAMUEL H. BOOKER.

MEANS OF PAYMENT:
TELEPHONE CREDIT CARD.

TYPE OF CARD:
EMPLOYER-BILLED.

BILLING ADDRESS:
FEDERAL BUREAU OF INVESTIGATION,
WASHINGTON, D.C.

They would start checking motels in the entire county, but as he was staying in Moonlight Cove's only lodgings, the search would be a short one. He wondered if he had time to sprint back to Cove Lodge, get his car, and drive to the next town, Aberdeen Wells, where he could call the Bureau office in San Francisco from an unmonitored phone. He had learned enough to know that something damned strange was going on in this town, enough to justify an imposition of federal authority and a far-reaching investigation.

But the very next words that appeared on the VDT convinced him that if he went back to Cove Lodge to get his car, he would be caught before he could get out of town. And if they got their hands on him, he might be just one more nasty accidental-death statistic.

They knew his home address, so Scott might be in danger too – not right now, not down there in Los Angeles, but maybe by tomorrow.

DIALOGUE INVOKED
WATKINS: SHOLNICK, ARE YOU LINKED IN?
SHOLNICK: HERE.
WATKINS: TRY COVE LODGE.
SHOLNICK: ON MY WAY.

Already an officer, Sholnick, was on his way to see if Sam was a registered guest at Cove Lodge. And the cover story that Sam had established with the desk clerk – that he was a successful stockbroker from Los Angeles, contemplating early retirement in one coastal town or another – was blown.

WATKINS: PETERSON?
PETERSON: HERE.

They probably didn't have to type in their names. Each man's link would identify him to the main computer, and his name would be automatically printed in front of the brief input that he typed. Clean, swift, easy to use.

WATKINS: BACK UP SHOLNICK.
PETERSON: DONE.
WATKINS: DON'T KILL HIM UNTIL WE CAN QUESTION.

All over Moonlight Cove, cops in patrol cars were talking to one another by computer, off the public airwaves, where they could not be easily overheard. Even though Sam was eavesdropping on them without their knowledge, he felt that he was up against a formidable enemy nearly as omniscient as God.

WATKINS: DANBERRY?
DANBERRY: HERE. HQ.
WATKINS: BLOCK OCEAN AVENUE TO INTERSTATE.
DANBERRY: DONE.
SHADDACK: WHAT ABOUT THE FOSTER GIRL?

Sam was startled to see Shaddack's name appear on the screen. The alert apparently had flashed on his computer at home, perhaps also sounding an audible alarm and waking him.

WATKINS: STILL LOOSE.
SHADDACK: CAN'T RISK BOOKER STUMBLING ACROSS HER.
WATKINS: TOWN'S RINGED WITH SENTRIES. THEY'LL CATCH HER COMING IN.
SHADDACK: SHE'S SEEN TOO MUCH.

Sam had read about Thomas Shaddack in magazines, newspapers. The guy was a celebrity of sorts, the computer genius of the age, and somewhat geeky looking besides.

Fascinated by this revealing dialogue, which incriminated the famous man and his bought police force, Sam had not immediately picked up on the meaning of the exchanges between Chief Watkins and Danberry: *Danberry . . . Here, HQ . . . Block Ocean Avenue to interstate . . . Done.* He realized that Officer Danberry was at headquarters, HQ, which was the municipal building, and that any moment he was going to come out the back door and rush to one of the four patrol cars in the parking lot.

'Oh, shit.' Sam grabbed the ignition wires, tearing them apart. The engine coughed and died, and the video display went dark.

A fraction of a second later, Danberry threw open the rear door of the municipal building and ran into the parking lot.

• 34 •

When the screaming stopped, Tessa broke out of a trance of terror and went straight to the phone again. The line was still dead.

Where was Quinn? The motel office was closed at this hour, but didn't the manager have an adjacent apartment? He would respond to the ruckus. Or was he one of the savage pack in the corridor?

They had broken down one door. They could break down hers too.

She grabbed one of the straight-backed chairs from the table by the window, hurried to the door with it, tilted it back, and wedged it under the knob.

She no longer thought they were after her just because she was Janice's sister and bent on uncovering the truth. That explanation didn't account for their attack on the other guests, who had nothing to do with Janice. It was nuts. She didn't understand what was happening, but she clearly understood the implications of what she had heard: a psychotic killer – no, several psychotics, judging by the noise they had made, some bizarre cult like the Manson family maybe, or worse – were loose in the motel. They had already killed two people, and they would kill her, too, evidently for the sheer pleasure of it. She felt as if she were in a bad dream.

She expected the walls to bulge and flow in that amorphous fashion of nightmare places, but they remained solid, fixed, and the colors of things were too sharp and clear for this to be a dreamscape.

Frantically she pulled on her socks and shoes, unnerved by being barefoot, as earlier her near nakedness had made her feel vulnerable – as if death could be foiled by an adequate wardrobe.

She heard those voices again. Not at the end of the hallway any more. Near her own door. Approaching. She wished the door featured one of those one-way, fisheye lenses that allowed a wide-angled view, but there was none.

At the sill was a half-inch crack, however, so Tessa dropped to the floor, pressed one side of her face against the carpet, and squinted out at the corridor. From that limited perspective, she saw something move past her room so quickly that her eyes could not quite track it, though she caught a glimpse of its feet, which was enough to alter dramatically her perception of what was happening. This was not an incidence of human savagery akin to the bloodbath she had witnessed – and to which she nearly had succumbed – in Northern Ireland. This was, instead, an encounter with the unknown, a breach of reality, a sudden sideslip out of the normal world into the uncanny. They were leathery, hairy, dark-skinned feet, broad and flat and surprisingly long, with toes so extrusile and multiple jointed that they almost seemed to have the function of fingers.

Something hit the door. Hard.

Tessa scrambled to her feet and out of the foyer.

Crazed voices filled the hall: that same weird mix of harsh animal sounds punctuated by bursts of breathlessly spoken but for the most part disconnected words.

She went around the bed to the window, disengaged the pressure latch, and slid the movable pane aside.

Again the door shook. The boom was so loud that Tessa felt as if she were inside a drum. It would not collapse as easily as the other guests' door, thanks to the chair, but it would not hold for more than a few additional blows.

She sat on the sill, swung her legs out, looked down. The fog-dampened walk glistened in the dim yellow glow of the serviceway lamps about twelve feet below the window. An easy jump.

They hit the door again, harder. Wood splintered.

Tessa pushed off the windowsill. She landed on the wet walkway and, because of her rubber-soled shoes, skidded but did not fall.

Overhead, in the room she had left, wood splintered more noisily than before, and tortured metal screeched as the lock on the door began to disintegrate.

She was near the north end of the building. She thought she saw something moving in the darkness in that direction. It might have been nothing more than a clotting of fog churning eastward on the wind, but she didn't want to take a chance, so she ran south, with the vast black sea beyond the railing at her right side. By the time she reached the end of the building, a crash echoed through the night – the sound of the door to her room going down – which was followed by the howling of the pack as it entered that place in search of her.

• 35 •

Sam could not have slipped out of the patrol car without drawing Danberry's attention. Four cruisers awaited the cop's use, so there was a seventy-five-percent chance that Sam would be undetected if he stayed in the car. He slid down in the driver's seat as far as he could and leaned to his right, across the computer keyboard on the console.

Danberry went to the next car in line.

With his head on the console, his neck twisted so he could look up through the window on the passenger's side, Sam watched as Danberry unlocked the door of that other cruiser. He prayed that the cop would keep his back turned, because the interior of the car in which Sam slouched was revealed by the sulfurous glow of the parking-lot lights. If Danberry even glanced his way, Sam would be seen.

The cop got into the other black-and-white and slammed the door, and Sam sighed with relief. The engine turned over. Danberry pulled out of the municipal lot. When he hit the alley he gunned the engine, and his tires spun and squealed for a moment before they bit in, and then he was gone.

Though Sam wanted to hot-wire the car and switch on the computer again to find out whether Watkins and Shaddack were still conversing, he knew he dared not stay any longer. As the manhunt escalated, the police department's offices in the municipal building were sure to become busy.

Because he didn't want them to know that he had been probing in their computer or that he had eavesdropped on their VDT conversation – the greater they assumed his ignorance to be, the less effective they would be in their search for him – Sam used his tools to replace the ignition core in the steering column. He got out, pushed the lock button down, and closed the door.

He didn't want to leave the area by the alleyway because a patrol car might turn in from one end or the other, capturing him in its headlights. Instead he dashed straight across that narrow backstreet from the parking lot and opened a gate in a simple wrought-iron fence. He entered the rear yard of a slightly decrepit Victorian-style house whose owners had let the shrubbery run so wild that it looked as if a macabre cartoon family from the pen of Gahan Wilson might live in the place. He walked quietly past the side of the house, across the front lawn, to Pacific Drive, one block south of Ocean Avenue.

The night calm was not split by sirens. He heard no shouts, no running footsteps, no cries of alarm. But he knew he had awakened a many-headed beast and that this singularly dangerous Hydra was looking for him all over town.

• 36 •

Mike Peyser didn't know what to do, didn't know, he was scared, confused and scared, so he could not think clearly, though he *needed* to think sharp and clear like a man, except the wild part of him kept intruding; his mind worked quickly, and it was sharp, but he could not hold to a single train of thought for more than a couple of minutes. Quick thinking, rapid-fire thinking, was not good enough to solve a problem like this; he had to think quick *and* deep. But his attention span was not what it should have been.

When he finally was able to stop screaming and get up from the kitchen floor, he hurried into the dark dining room, through the unlit living room, down the short hall to the bedroom, then into the master bathroom, going on all fours part of the way, rising onto his hind feet as he crossed the bedroom threshold, unable to rise all the way up and stand entirely straight, but flexible enough to get more than halfway erect. In the bathroom, which was lit only by the vague and somewhat scintillant moonglow that penetrated the small window above the shower stall, he gripped the edges of the sink and stared into the mirrored front of the medicine cabinet, where he could see only a shadowy reflection of himself, without detail.

He wanted to believe that in fact he had returned to his natural form, that his feeling of being trapped in the altered state was pure hallucination, yes, yes, he wanted to believe that, badly needed to believe, believe, even though he could not stand fully erect, even though he could feel the difference in his impossibly long-fingered hands and in the queer set of his head on his shoulders and in the way his back joined his hips. He needed to believe.

Turn on the light, he told himself.

He could not do it.

Turn on the light.

He was afraid.

He had to turn on the light and look at himself.

But he gripped the sink and could not move.

Turn on the light.

Instead he leaned toward the tenebrous mirror, peering intently at the indistinct reflection, seeing little more than the pale amber radiance of strange eyes.

Turn on the light.

He let out a thin mewl of anguish and terror.

Shaddack, he thought suddenly. Shaddack, he must tell Shaddack, Tom Shaddack would know what to do, Shaddack was his best hope, maybe his only hope, Shaddack.

He let go of the sink, dropped to the floor, hurried out of the bathroom, into the bedroom, toward the telephone on the nightstand. As he went, in a voice alternately shrill and guttural, piercing and whispery, he repeated the name as if it were a word with magic power: '*Shaddack, Shaddack, Shaddack, Shaddack . . .*'

• 37 •

Tessa Lockland took refuge in a twenty-four-hour coin-operated laundry four blocks east of Cove Lodge and half a block off Ocean Avenue. She wanted to be someplace bright, and the banks of overhead fluorescents allowed no shadows. Alone in the laundry, she sat in a badly scarred, yellow plastic chair, staring at rows of clothes-dryer portals, as if understanding would be visited upon her from some cosmic source communicating in those circles of glass.

As a documentarist, she had to have a keen eye for the patterns in life that would give coherence to a film narratively and visually, so she had no trouble seeing patterns of darkness, death, and unknown forces in this deeply troubled town. The fantastic creatures in the motel surely had been the source of the cries she'd heard on the beach earlier that night, and her sister had no doubt been killed by those same beings, whatever the hell they were. Which sort of explained why the authorities had been so insistent that Marion okay the cremation of Janice's body – not because the remains were corroded by seawater and half-devoured by fish, but because cremation would cover wounds that would raise unanswerable questions in an unbiased autopsy. She also saw reflections of the corruption of local authorities in the physical appearance of Ocean Avenue, where too many storefronts were empty and too many businesses were suffering, which was inexplicable for a town in which unemployment was virtually nil. She had noted an air of solemnity about the people she had seen on the streets, as well as a briskness and purposefulness that seemed odd in a laidback northern coastal town where the hurly-burly of modern life hardly intruded.

However, her awareness of the patterns included no explanation of *why* the police would want to conceal the true nature of Janice's killing. Or why the town seemed in an economic depression in spite of its prosperity. Or what in the name of God those nightmare things in the motel had been. Patterns were clues to underlying truths, but her ability to recognize them did not mean she could find the answers and reveal the truths at which the patterns hinted.

She sat, shivering, in the fluorescent glare and breathed trace fumes of detergents, bleaches, fabric softeners, and the lingering staleness of the cigarette butts in the two free-standing sand-filled ashtrays, while she tried to figure what to do next. She had not lost her determination to probe into Janice's death. But she no longer had the audacity to think she could play detective all by herself. She was going to need help and would probably have to obtain it from county or state authorities.

The first thing she had to do was get out of Moonlight Cove in one piece.

Her car was at Cove Lodge, but she did not want to go back there for it. Those . . . creatures might still be in the motel or watching it from the dense shrubs and trees and omnipresent shadows that were an integral part of the town. Like Carmel, California, elsewhere along the coast, Moonlight Cove was a town virtually built in a seaside forest. Tessa loved Carmel for its splendid integration of the works of man and nature, where geography and architecture often appeared to be the product of the same sculptor's hand. Right now, however, Moonlight Cove did not draw style and grace from its verdant lushness and artful night shadows, as did Carmel; rather, this town seemed to be dressed in the thinnest veneer of civilization, beneath which something savage – even primal – watched and waited. Every grove of trees and every dark street was not the home of beauty but of the uncanny and of death. She would have found Moonlight Cove far more attractive if every street and alley and lawn and park had been lit with the same plenitude of fluorescent bulbs as the Laundromat in which she had taken refuge.

Maybe the police had shown up at Cove Lodge by now in response to the screams and commotion. But she would not feel any safer returning there just because cops were around. Cops were part of the problem. They would want to question her about the murders of the other guests. They would find out that Janice had been her sister, and though she might not tell them she was in town to poke into the circumstances of Janice's death, they would suspect as much. If they *had* participated in a conspiracy to conceal the true nature of Janice's death, they probably wouldn't hesitate to deal with Tessa in a firm and final way.

She had to abandon the car.

But damned if she was going to walk out of town at night. She might be able to hitch a ride on the interstate – perhaps even from an honest trucker instead of a mobile psychopath – but between Moonlight Cove and the freeway, she would have to walk through a dark and semirural landscape, where surely she would be at even greater risk of encountering more of those mysterious beasts that had broken down her motel-room door.

Of course, they had come after her in a relatively public and well-lighted place. She had no real reason to assume that she was safer in this coin-operated laundry than in the middle of the woods. When the membrane of civilization ruptured and the primordial terror burst through, you weren't safe anywhere, not even on the steps of a church, as she had learned in Northern Ireland and elsewhere.

Nevertheless, she would cling to the light and shun the darkness. She had stepped through an invisible wall between the reality she had always known and a different, more hostile world. As long as she remained in that Twilight Zone, it seemed wise to assume that shadows offered even less comfort and security than did bright places.

Which left her with no plan of action. Except to sit in the Laundromat and wait for morning. In daylight she might risk a long walk to the freeway.

The blank glass of the dryer windows returned her stare.

An autumn moth thumped softly against the frosted plastic panels that were suspended under the fluorescent bulbs.

• 38 •

Unable to walk boldly into Moonlight Cove as she had planned, Chrissie retreated from Holliwell Road, heading back the way she had come. She stayed in the woods, moving slowly and cautiously from tree to tree, trying to avoid making a sound that might carry to the nearer of the sentries who had been posted at the intersection.

In a couple of hundred yards, when she was beyond those men's sight and hearing, she moved more aggressively. Eventually she came to one of the houses that lay along the county route. The single-story ranch home was set behind a large front lawn and sheltered by several pines and firs, barely visible now that the moon was waning. No lights were on inside or out, and all was silent.

She needed time to think, and she wanted to get out of the cold, dampish night. Hoping there were no dogs at the house, she hurried to the garage, staying off the gravel driveway to keep from making a lot of noise. As she expected, in addition to the large front door through which the cars entered and exited, there was a smaller side entrance. It was unlocked. She stepped into the garage and closed the door behind her.

'Chrissie Foster, secret agent, penetrated the enemy facility by the bold and clever use of a side door,' she said softly.

The secondhand radiance of the sinking moon penetrated the panes in the door and two high, narrow windows on the west wall, but it was insufficient to reveal anything. She could see only a few darkly gleaming curves of chrome and windshield glass, just enough to suggest the presence of two cars.

She edged toward the first of those vehicles with the caution of a blind girl, hands out in front of her, afraid of knocking something over. The car was unlocked. She slipped inside behind the wheel, leaving the door open for the welcome glow of the interior lamp. She supposed a trace of that light might be visible at the garage windows if anyone in the house woke up and looked out, but she had to risk it.

She searched the glove compartment, the map-storage panels on the doors, and under the seats, hoping to find food, because most people kept candy bars or bags of nuts or crackers or *something* to snack on in their cars. Though she had eaten midafternoon, while locked in the pantry, she'd had nothing for ten hours. Her stomach growled. She wasn't expecting to find a hot fudge sundae or the fixings for a jelly sandwich, but she certainly hoped to do better than a single stick of chewing gum and one green Lifesaver that, retrieved from beneath the seat, was furry with dirt, lint, and carpet fuzz.

As if reading tabloid headlines, she said, 'STARVATION IN THE LAND OF PLENTY, A MODERN TRAGEDY, YOUNG GIRL FOUND DEAD IN GARAGE, "I ONLY WANTED A FEW PEANUTS" WRITTEN IN HER OWN BLOOD.'

In the other car she found two Hershey bars with almonds.

'Thank you, God. Your friend, Chrissie.'

She hogged down the first bar but savored the second one in small bites, letting it melt on her tongue.

While she ate, she thought about ways to get into Moonlight Cove. By the time she finished the chocolate—

CHOCOHOLIC YOUNG GIRL FOUND DEAD IN GARAGE FROM TERMINAL CASE OF GIANT ZITS.

—she had devised a plan.

Her usual bedtime had passed hours ago, and she was exhausted from all the physical activity with which the night had been filled, so she just wanted to stay there in the car, her belly full of milk chocolate and almonds, and sleep for a couple of hours before putting her plan into effect. She yawned and slumped down in the seat. She ached all over, and her eyes were as heavy as if some overanxious mortician had weighted them with coins.

That image of herself as a corpse was so unsettling that she immediately got out of the car and closed the door. If she dozed off in the car, she most likely wouldn't wake until someone found her in the morning. Maybe the people who kept their cars in this garage were converted, like her own parents, in which case she'd be doomed.

Outside, shivering as the wind nipped at her, she headed back to the county road and turned north. She passed two more dark and silent houses, another stretch of woods, and came to a fourth house, another single-story ranch-style place with shake-shingle roof and redwood siding.

She knew the people who lived there, Mr. and Mrs. Eulane. Mrs. Eulane managed the cafeteria at school. Mr. Eulane was a gardener with many accounts in Moonlight Cove. Early every morning, Mr. Eulane drove into town in his white truck, the back of which was loaded with lawnmowers and hedge clippers and rakes and shovels and bags of mulch and fertilizer and everything else a gardener might need; only a few students had arrived by the time he dropped Mrs. Eulane off at school, then went about his own work. Chrissie figured she could find a place to hide in the back of the truck – which had board sides – among Mr. Eulane's gardening supplies and equipment.

The truck was in the Eulanes' garage, which was unlocked, just as the other one had been. But this was the country, after all, where people still trusted one another – which was good except that it gave invading aliens an extra edge.

The only window was small and in the wall that could not be seen from the house, so Chrissie risked turning on the overhead light when she stepped inside. She quietly scaled the side of the truck and made her way in among the gardening equipment, which was stored in the rear two-thirds of the cargo bed, nearest the tailgate. Toward the front, against the back wall of the truck cab, flanked by fifty-pound bags of fertilizer, snail bait, and potting soil, was a three-foot-high stack of folded burlap tarps in which Mr. Eulane bundled grass clippings that had to be hauled to the dump. She could use some tarps as a mattress, others as blankets, and bed down until morning, remaining hidden in the burlap and between the piles of fifty-pound bags all the way to Moonlight Cove.

She climbed out of the truck, switched off the garage lights, then returned in the dark and carefully climbed aboard once more. She made a nest for herself in the tarps. The burlap was a little scratchy. After years of use it was permeated with the scent of new-mown grass, which was nice at first but quickly palled. At least a few layers of tarps trapped her body heat, and in minutes she was warm for the first time all night.

And as the night deepened (she thought), *young Chrissie, masking her telltale human odors in the scent of grass that saturated the burlap, cleverly concealed herself from the pursuing aliens – or maybe werewolves – whose sense of smell was almost as good as that of hounds.*

• 39 •

Sam took temporary refuge on the unlit playground of Thomas Jefferson Elementary School on Palomino Street on the south side of town. He sat on one of the swings, holding the suspension chains with both hands, actually swinging a bit, while he considered his options.

He could not leave Moonlight Cove by car. His rental was back at the motel, where he'd be apprehended if he showed his face. He could steal a car, but he remembered the exchange on the computer when Loman Watkins had ordered Danberry to establish a blockade on Ocean Avenue, between town and the interstate. They'd have sealed off every exit.

He could go overland, sneaking from street to street, to the edge of the town limits, then through the woods and fields to the freeway. But Watkins had also said something about having ringed the entire community with sentries, to intercept the 'Foster girl'. Although Sam was confident of his instincts and survival abilities, he had not had experience in taking evasive action over open territory since his service in the war more than twenty years ago. If men were stationed around the town, waiting to intercept the girl, Sam was likely to walk straight into one or more of them.

Though he was willing to risk getting caught, he must not fall into their hands until he had placed a call to the Bureau to report and to ask for emergency backup. If he became a statistic in this accidental-death capital of the world, the Bureau would send new men in his place, and ultimately the truth would come out – but perhaps too late.

As he swung gently back and forth through the rapidly thinning fog, pushed mostly by the wind, he thought about those schedules he had seen on the VDT. Everyone in town would be 'converted' in the next twenty-three hours. Although he had no idea what the hell people were being converted *to*, he didn't like the sound it. And he sensed that once those schedules had been met, once everyone in town was converted, getting to the truth in Moonlight Cove would be no easier than cracking open an infinite series of laser-welded, titanium boxes nested in Chinese-puzzle fashion.

Okay, so the first thing he had to do was get to a phone and call the Bureau. The phones in Moonlight Cove were compromised, but he did not care if the call was noted in a computer sweep or even recorded word for word. He just needed thirty seconds or a minute on the line with the office, and massive reinforcements would be on the way. Then he'd have to keep moving around, dodging cops for a couple of hours, until other agents arrived.

He couldn't just walk up to a house and ask to use their phone because he didn't know whom he could trust. Morrie Stein had said that after being in town a day or two, you were overcome with the paranoid feeling that eyes were on you wherever you went and that Big Brother was always just at arm's reach away. Sam had attained that stage of paranoia in only a few hours and was rapidly moving beyond it to a state of constant tension and suspicion unlike anything he'd known since those jungle battlegrounds two decades ago.

A pay phone. But not the one at the Shell station that he had used earlier. A wanted man was foolish to return to a place he was known to have frequented before.

From his walks around town, he remembered one or maybe two other pay phones. He got up from the swing, slipped his hands in his jacket pockets, hunched his shoulders against the chilling wind, and started across the school-yard toward the street beyond.

He wondered about the Foster girl to whom Shaddack and Watkins referred on the computer link. Who was she? What had she seen? He suspected she was a key to understanding this conspiracy. Whatever she had witnessed might explain what they meant by 'conversion'.

• 40 •

The walls appeared to be bleeding. Red ooze, as if seeping from the sheetrock, tracked down the pale yellow paint in many rivulets.

Standing in that second-floor room at Cove Lodge, Loman Watkins was repelled by the carnage . . . but also strangely excited.

The male guest's body was sprawled near the disarranged bed, hideously bitten and torn. In worse condition, the dead woman lay outside the room, in the second-floor hall, a scarlet heap on the orange carpet.

The air reeked of blood, bile, feces, urine – a mélange of odors with which Loman was becoming increasingly familiar, as the victims of the regressives turned up more frequently week by week and day by day. This time, however, as never before, an alluring sweetness lay under the acrid surface of the stench. He drew deep breaths, unsure why that terrible redolence should have any appeal whatsoever. But he was unable to deny – or resist – its attraction any more than a hound could resist the fox's scent. Though he could not withstand the tempting fragrance, he was frightened by his response to it, and the blood in his veins seemed to grow colder as his pleasure in the biological stink grew more intense.

Barry Sholnick, the officer Loman had dispatched to Cove Lodge via com-puter link to apprehend Samuel Booker, and who had found this death and destruction instead of the Bureau agent, now stood in the corner by the win-dow, staring intently at the dead man. He had been at the motel longer than anyone, almost half an hour, long enough to have begun to regard the victims with the detachment that police had to cultivate, as if dead and ravaged bodies were no more remarkable a part of the scene than the furniture. Yet Sholnick could not shift his gaze from the eviscerated corpse, the gore-spattered wreckage, and the blood-streaked walls. He was clearly electrified by that horrendous detritus and the violence of which it was a remembrance.

We hate what the regressives have become and what they do, Loman thought, but in some sick way we're also envious of them, of their ultimate freedom.

Something within him – and, he suspected, in all of the New People – cried out to join the regressives. As at the Foster place, Loman felt the urge to employ his newfound bodily control not to elevate himself, as Shaddack had intended, but to devolve into a wild state. He yearned to descend to a level of consciousness in which thoughts of the purpose and meaning of life would not trouble him, in which intellectual challenge would be nonexistent, in which he would be a creature whose existence was defined almost entirely by *sensation*, in which every decision was made solely on the basis of what would give him pleasure, a condition untroubled by complex thought. Oh, God, to be freed from the burdens of civilization and higher intelligence!

Sholnick made a low sound in the back of his throat.

Loman looked up from the dead man.

In Sholnick's brown eyes a wild light burned.

Am I as pale as he? Loman wondered. As sunken-eyed and strange?

For a moment Sholnick met the chief's gaze, then looked away as if he had been caught in a shameful act.

Loman's heart was pounding.

Sholnick went to the window. He stared out at the lightless sea. His hands were fisted at his sides.

Loman was trembling.

The smell, darkly sweet. The smell of the hunt, the kill.

He turned away from the corpse and walked out of the room, into the hallway, where the sight of the dead woman – half naked, gouged, lacerated – was no relief. Bob Trott, one of several recent additions to the force when it expanded to twelve men last week, stood over the battered body. He was a big man, four inches taller and thirty pounds heavier than Loman, with a face of hard planes and chiseled edges. He looked down at the cadaver with a faint, unholy smile.

Flushed, his vision beginning to blur, his eyes smarting in the harsh fluorescent glare, Loman spoke sharply: 'Trott, come with me.' He set off along the hall to the other room that had been broken into. With evident reluctance, Trott finally followed him.

By the time Loman reached the shattered door of that unit, Paul Amberlay, another of his officers, appeared at the head of the north stairs, returning from the motel office where Loman had sent him to check the register. 'The couple in room twenty-four were named Jenks, Sarah and Charles,' Amberlay reported. He was twenty-five, lean and sinewy, intelligent. Perhaps because the young officer's face was slightly pointed, with deep-set eyes, he had always reminded Loman of a fox. 'They're from Portland.'

'And in thirty-six here?'

'Tessa Lockland from San Diego.'

Loman blinked. 'Lockland?'

Amberlay spelled it.

'When did she check in?'

'Just tonight.'

'The minister's widow, Janice Capshaw,' Loman said. 'Her maiden name was Lockland. I had to deal with her mother by phone, and she was in San Diego. Persistent old broad. A million questions. Had some trouble getting her to consent to cremation. She said her other daughter was out of the country, somewhere really remote, couldn't be reached quickly, but would come around within a month to empty the house and settle Mrs. Capshaw's affairs. So this is her, I guess.'

Loman led them into Tessa Lockland's room, two doors down from unit forty, in which Booker was registered. Wind huffed at the open window. The place was littered with broken furniture, torn bedding, and the glass from a shattered TV set, but unmarked by blood. Earlier they had checked the room for a body and found none; the open window indicated that the occupant fled before the regressives had managed to smash through the door.

'So Booker's out there,' Loman said, 'and we've got to assume he saw the regressives or heard the killing. He knows something's wrong here. He doesn't understand it, but he knows enough . . . too much.'

'You can bet he's busting his ass to get a call out to the damn Bureau,' Trott said.

Loman agreed. 'And now we've also got this Lockland bitch, and she's got to be thinking her sister never committed suicide, that she was killed by the same things that killed the couple from Portland—'

'Most logical thing for her to do,' Amberlay said, 'is come straight to us – to the police. She'll walk right into our arms.'

'Maybe,' Loman said, unconvinced. He began to pick through the rubble. 'Help me find her purse. With them bashing down the door, she'd have gone out the window without pausing to grab her purse.'

Trott found it wedged between the bed and one of the nightstands.

Loman emptied the contents onto the mattress. He snatched up the wallet, flipped through the plastic windows full of credit cards and photographs, until he found her driver's license. According to the license data, she was five-four, one hundred and four pounds, blond, blue-eyed. Loman held up the ID so Trott and Amberlay could see the photograph.

'She's a looker,' Amberlay said.

'I'd like to get a bite of that,' Trott said.

His officer's choice of words gave Loman a chill. He couldn't help wondering whether Trott meant 'bite' as a euphemism for sex or whether he was expressing a very real subconscious desire to savage the woman as the regressive had torn apart the couple from Portland.

'We know what she looks like,' Loman said. 'That helps.'

Trott's hard, sharp features were inadequate for the expression of gentler emotions like affection and delight, but they perfectly conveyed the animal hunger and urge to violence that seethed deep within him. 'You want us to bring her in?'

'Yes. She doesn't know anything, really, but on the other hand she knows too much. She knows the couple down the hall were killed, and she probably saw a regressive.'

'Maybe the regressives followed her through the window and got her,' Amberlay suggested. 'We might find her body somewhere outside, on the grounds of the lodge.'

'Could be,' Loman said. 'But if not, we have to find her and bring her in. You called Callan?'

'Yeah,' Amberlay said.

'We've got to get this place cleaned up,' Loman said. 'We've got to keep a lid on until midnight, until everyone in town's been put through the Change. Then, when Moonlight Cove's secure, we can concentrate on finding the regressives and eliminating them.'

Trott and Amberlay met Loman's eyes, then looked at each other. In the glances they exchanged, Loman saw the dark knowledge that they all were potential regressives, that they, too, felt the call toward that unburdened, primitive state. It was an awareness of which none of them dared speak, for to give it voice was to admit that Moonhawk was a deeply flawed project and that they might all be damned.

• 41 •

Mike Peyser heard the dial tone and fumbled with the buttons, which were too small and closely set for his long, tinelike fingers. Abruptly he realized that he could not call Shaddack, *dared* not call Shaddack, though they had known each other for more than twenty years, since their days together at Stanford, could not call Shaddack even though it was Shaddack who had made him what he was, because Shaddack would consider him an outlaw now, a regressive, and Shaddack would have him restrained in a laboratory and either treat him with all the tenderness that a vivisectionist bestowed upon a white rat or destroy him because of the threat he posed to the ongoing conversion of Moonlight Cove. Peyser shrieked in frustration. He tore the telephone out of the wall and threw it across the bedroom, where it hit the dresser mirror, shattering the glass.

His sudden perception of Shaddack as a powerful enemy rather than a friend and mentor was the last entirely clear and rational thought that Peyser had for a while. His fear was a trapdoor that opened under him, casting him down into the darkness of the primeval mind that he had unleashed for the pleasure of a night hunt. He moved back and forth through the house, sometimes in a frenzy, sometimes in a sullen slouch, not sure why he was alternately excited, depressed, or smoldering with savage needs, driven more by feelings than intellect.

He relieved himself in a corner of the living room, sniffed his own urine, then went into the kitchen in search of more food. Now and then his mind cleared, and he tried to call his body back to its more civilized form, but when his tissues would not respond to his will, he cycled down into the darkness of animal thought again. Several times he was clear-headed enough to appreciate the irony of having been reduced to savagery by a process – the Change – meant to elevate him to superhuman status, but that line of thought was too bleak to be endured, and a new descent into the savage mind was almost welcome.

Repeatedly, both when in the grip of a primitive consciousness and when the clouds lifted from his mind, he thought of the boy, Eddie Valdoski, the boy, the tender boy, and he thrilled to the memory of blood, sweet blood, fresh blood steaming in the cold night air.

• 42 •

Physically and mentally exhausted, Chrissie nevertheless was not able to sleep. In the burlap tarps in the back of Mr. Eulane's truck, she hung from the thin line of wakefulness, wanting nothing more than to let go and fall into unconsciousness.

She felt incomplete, as though something had been left undone – and suddenly she was crying. Burying her face in the fragrant and slightly scratchy burlap, she bawled as she'd not done in years, with the abandon of a baby. She wept for her mother and father, perhaps lost forever, not taken cleanly by death but by something foul, dirty, inhuman, satanic. She wept for the adolescence that would have been hers – horses and seaside pastures and books read on the beach – but that had been shattered beyond repair. She wept, as well, over some loss she felt but could not quite identify, though she suspected it was innocence or maybe faith in the triumph of good over evil.

None of the fictional heroines she admired would have indulged in uncontrolled weeping, and Chrissie was embarrassed by her torrent of tears. But to weep was as human as to err, and perhaps she needed to cry, in part, to prove to herself that no monstrous seed had been planted in her of the sort that had germinated and spread tendrils through her parents. Crying, she was still Chrissie. Crying was proof that no one had stolen her soul.

She slept.

• 43 •

Sam had seen another pay phone at a Union 76 service station one block north of Ocean. The station was out of business. The windows were filmed with gray dust, and a hastily lettered FOR SALE sign hung in one of them, as if the owner actually didn't care whether the place was sold or not and had made the sign only because it was expected of him. Crisp, dead leaves and dry pine needles from surrounding trees had blown against the gasoline pumps and lay in snowlike drifts.

The phone booth was against the south wall of the building and visible from the street. Sam stepped through the open door but did not pull it shut, for fear of completing a circuit that would turn on the overhead bulb and draw him to the attention of any cops who happened by.

The line was dead. He deposited a coin, hoping that would activate the dial tone. The line was still dead.

He jiggled the hook from which the handset hung. His coin was returned.

He tried again but to no avail.

He believed that pay phones in or adjacent to a service station or privately owned store were sometimes joint operations, the income shared between the telephone company and the businessman who allowed the phone to be installed. Perhaps they had turned off the phone when the Union 76 had closed up.

However, he suspected the police had used their access to the telephone-company's computer to disable all coin-operated phones in Moonlight Cove. The moment they had learned an undercover federal agent was in town, they could have taken extreme measures to prevent him from contacting the world outside.

Of course he might be overestimating their capabilities. He had to try another phone before giving up hope of contacting the Bureau.

On his walk after dinner, he had passed a coin laundry half a block north of Ocean Avenue and two blocks west of this Union 76. He was pretty sure that when glancing through the plate-glass window, he had seen a telephone on the rear wall, at the end of a row of industrial-size dryers with stainless-steel fronts.

He left the Union 76. As much as possible staying away from the streetlamps – which illuminated side streets only in the first block north and south of Ocean – using alleyways where he could, he slipped through the silent town, toward where he remembered having seen the laundry. He wished the wind would die and leave some of the rapidly dissipating fog.

At an intersection one block north of Ocean and half a block from the laundry, he almost walked into plain sight of a cop driving south toward the center of town. The patrolman was half a block from the intersection, coming slowly, surveying both sides of the street. Fortunately he was looking the other way when Sam hurried into the unavoidable fall of lamplight at the corner.

Sam scrambled backward and pressed into a deep entranceway on the side of a three-story brick building that housed some of the town's professionals: A plaque in the recess, to the left of the door, listed a dentist, two lawyers, a doctor, and a chiropractor. If the patrol turned left at the corner and came past him, he'd probably be spotted. But if it either went straight on toward Ocean or turned right and headed west, he would not be seen.

Leaning against the locked door and as far back in the shadows as he could go, waiting for the infuriatingly slow car to reach the intersection, Sam had a moment for reflection and realized that even for one-thirty in the morning, Moonlight Cove was peculiarly quiet and the streets unusually deserted. Small towns had night owls as surely as did cities; there should have been a pedestrian or two, a car now and then, *some* signs of life other than police patrols.

The black-and-white turned right at the corner, heading west and away from him.

Although the danger had passed, Sam remained in the unlit entranceway, mentally retracing his journey from Cove Lodge to the municipal building, from there to the Union 76, and finally to his current position. He could not recall passing a house where music was playing, where a television blared, or where the laughter of late revelers indicated a party in progress. He had seen no young couples sharing a last kiss in parked cars. The few restaurants and taverns were apparently closed, and the movie theater was out of business, and except for his movements and those of the police, Moonlight Cove might have been a ghost town. Its living rooms, bedrooms, and kitchens might have been peopled only by moldering corpses – or by robots that posed as people during the day and were turned off at night to save energy when it was not as essential to maintain the illusion of life.

Increasingly worried by the word 'conversion' and its mysterious meaning in the context of this thing they called the Moonhawk Project, he left the entranceway, turned the corner, and ran along the brightly lit street to the laundry. He saw the phone as he was pushing open the glass door.

He hurried halfway through the long room – dryers on the right, a double row of washers back-to-back in the middle, some chairs at the end of the washers, more chairs along the left wall with the candy and detergent machines and the laundry-folding counter – before he realized the place was not deserted. A petite blonde in faded jeans and a blue pullover sweater sat on one of the yellow plastic chairs. None of the washers or dryers was running, and the woman did not seem to have a basket of clothes with her.

He was so startled by her – a live person, a live *civilian*, in this sepulchral night – that he stopped and blinked.

She was perched on the edge of the chair, visibly tense. Her eyes were wide. Her hands were clenched in her lap. She seemed to be holding her breath.

Realizing that he had frightened her, Sam said, 'Sorry.'

She stared at him as if she were a rabbit facing down a fox.

Aware that he must look wild-eyed, even frantic, he added, 'I'm not dangerous.'

'They all say that.'

'They do?'

'But I *am*.'

Confused, he said, 'You are what?'

'Dangerous.'

'Really?'

She stood up. 'I'm a black belt.'

For the first time in days, a genuine smile pulled at Sam's face. 'Can you kill with your hands?'

She stared at him for a moment, pale and shaking. When she spoke, her defensive anger was excessive. 'Hey, don't laugh at me, asshole, or I'll bust you up so bad that when you walk, you'll clink like a bag of broken glass.'

At last, astonished by her vehemence, Sam began to assimilate the observations he'd made on entering. No washers or dryers in operation. No clothes basket. No box of detergent or bottle of fabric softener.

'What's wrong?' he asked, suddenly suspicious.

'Nothing, if you keep your distance.'

He wondered if she knew somehow that the local cops were eager to get hold of him. But that seemed nuts. How could she know? 'What're you doing here if you don't have clothes to wash?'

'What's it your business? You own this dump?' she demanded.

'No. And don't tell me you own it, either.'

She glared at him.

He studied her, gradually absorbing how attractive she was. She had eyes as piercingly blue as a June sky and skin as clear as summer air, and she seemed radically out of place along this dark, October coast, let alone in a grungy Laundromat at one-thirty in the morning. When her beauty finally, fully registered with him, so did other things about her, including the intensity of her fear, which was revealed in her eyes and in the lines around them and in the set of her mouth. It was fear far out of proportion to any threat he could pose. If he had been a six-foot-six, three-hundred-pound, tattooed biker with a revolver in one hand and a ten-inch knife in the other, and if he had burst into the laundry chanting paeans to Satan, the utterly bloodless paleness of her face and the hard edge of terror in her eyes would have been understandable. But he was only Sam Booker, whose greatest attribute as an agent was his guy-next-door ordinariness and an aura of harmlessness.

Unsettled by *her* unsettledness, he said, 'The phone.'

'What?'

He pointed at the pay phone.

'Yes,' she said, as if confirming it was indeed a phone.

'Just came in to make a call.'

'Oh.'

Keeping one eye on her, he went to the phone, fed it his quarter, but got no dial tone. He retrieved his coin, tried again. No luck.

'Damn!' he said.

The blonde had edged toward the door. She halted, as though she thought he might rush at her and drag her down if she attempted to leave the Laundromat.

The Cove engendered in Sam a powerful paranoia. Increasingly over the past few hours he had come to think of everyone in town as a potential enemy. And suddenly he perceived that this woman's peculiar behavior resulted from a state of mind precisely like his. 'Yes, of course, you're not *from* here, are you, from Moonlight Cove?'

'So?'

'Neither am I.'

'So?'

'And you've seen something.'

She stared at him.

He said, 'Something's happened, you've seen something, and you're scared, and I'll bet you've got damned good reason to be.'

She looked as if she'd sprint for the door.

'Wait,' he said quickly. 'I'm with the FBI.' His voice cracked slightly. 'I really am.'

• 44 •

Because he was a night person who had always preferred to sleep during the day, Thomas Shaddack was in his teak-paneled study, dressed in a gray sweat suit, working on an aspect of Moonhawk at a computer terminal, when Evan, his night servant, rang through to tell him that Loman Watkins was at the front door.

'Send him to the tower,' Shaddack said. 'I'll join him shortly.'

He seldom wore anything but sweat suits these days. He had more than twenty in the closet – ten black, ten gray, and a couple navy blue. They were more comfortable than other clothes, and by limiting his choices, he saved time that otherwise would be wasted coordinating each day's wardrobe, a task at which he was not skilled. Fashion was of no interest to him. Besides, he was gawky – big feet, lanky legs, knobby knees, long arms, bony shoulders – and too thin to look good even in finely tailored suits. Clothes either hung strangely on him or emphasized his thinness to such a degree that he appeared to be Death personified, an unfortunate image reinforced by his flour-white skin, nearly black hair, sharp features, and yellowish eyes.

He even wore sweat suits to New Wave board meetings. If you were a genius in your field, people expected you to be eccentric. And if your personal fortune was in the hundreds of millions, they accepted all eccentricities without comment.

His ultramodern, reinforced-concrete house at cliff's edge near the north point of the cove was another expression of his calculated nonconformity. The three stories were like three layers of a cake, though each layer was of a different size than the others – the largest on top, the smallest in the middle – and they were not concentric but misaligned, creating a profile that in daylight lent the house the appearance of an enormous piece of avant-garde sculpture. At night, its myriad windows aglow, it looked less like sculpture than like the star-traveling mothership of an invading alien force.

The tower was eccentricity piled on eccentricity, rising off-center from the third level, soaring an additional forty feet into the air. It was not round but oval, not anything like a tower in which a princess might pine for a crusade-bound prince or in which a king might have his enemies imprisoned and tortured, but reminiscent of the conning tower of a submarine. The large, glass-walled room at the top could be reached by elevator or by stairs that spiraled around the inside of the tower wall, circling the metal core in which the elevator was housed.

Shaddack kept Watkins waiting for ten minutes, just for the hell of it, then chose to take the lift to meet him. The interior of the cab was panelled with burnished brass, so although the mechanism was slow, he seemed to be ascending inside a rifle cartridge.

He had added the tower to the architect's designs almost as an afterthought, but it had become his favorite part of the huge house. That high place offered endless vistas of calm (or wind-chopped), sun-spangled (or night-shrouded) sea to the west. To the east and south, he looked out and *down* on the whole town of Moonlight Cove; his sense of superiority was comfortably reinforced by that lofty perspective on the only other visible works of man. From that room, only four months ago, he had seen the moonhawk for the third time in his life, a sight that few men were privileged to see even once – which he took to be a sign that he was destined to become the most influential man ever to walk the earth.

The elevator stopped. The doors opened.

When Shaddack entered the dimly lit room that encircled the elevator, Loman Watkins rose quickly from an armchair and respectfully said, 'Good evening, sir.'

'Please be seated, chief,' he said graciously, even affably, but with a subtle note in his voice that reinforced their mutual understanding that it was Shaddack, not Watkins, who decided how formal or casual the meeting would be.

Shaddack was the only child of James Randolph Shaddack, a former circuit-court judge in Phoenix, now deceased. The family had not been wealthy, though solidly upper middle-class, and that position on the economic ladder, combined with the prestige of a judgeship, gave James considerable stature in his community. And power. Throughout his childhood and adolescence, Tom had been fascinated by how his father, a political activist as well as a judge, had used that power not only to acquire material benefits but to control others. The control – the exercise of power for power's sake – was what had most appealed to James, and that was what had deeply excited his son, too, from an early age.

Now Tom Shaddack held power over Loman Watkins and Moonlight Cove by reason of his wealth, because he was the primary employer in town, because he gripped the reins of the political system, and because of the Moonhawk Project, named after the thrice-received vision. But his ability to manipulate them was more extensive than anything old James had enjoyed as a judge and canny politico. He possessed the power of life and death over them – literally. If an hour from now he decided they all must die, they would be dead before midnight. Furthermore he could condemn them to the grave with no more chance of being punished than a god risked when raining fire on his creations.

The only lights in the tower room were concealed in a recess under the immense windows, which extended from the ceiling to within ten inches of the floor. The hidden lamps ringed the chamber, subtly illuminating the plush carpet but casting no glare on the huge panes. Nevertheless, if the night had been clear, Shaddack would have flicked the switch next to the elevator button, plunging the room into near darkness, so his ghostly reflection and those of the starkly modern furnishings would not fall on the glass between him and his view of the world over which he held dominion. He left the lights on, however, because some milky fog still churned past glass walls, and little could be seen now that the horned moon had found the horizon.

Barefoot, Shaddack crossed the charcoal-gray carpet. He settled into a second armchair, facing Loman Watkins across a low, white-marble cocktail table.

The policeman was forty-four, less than two years older than Shaddack, but he was Shaddack's complete physical opposite: five-ten, a hundred and eighty pounds, large-boned, broad in the shoulders and chest, thick-necked. His face was broad, too, as open and guileless as Shaddack's was closed and cunning. His blue eyes met Shaddack's yellow-brown gaze, held it only for a moment, then lowered to stare at his strong hands, which were clasped so rigidly in his lap that the sharp knuckles seemed in danger of piercing the taut skin. His darkly tanned scalp showed through brush-cut brown hair.

Watkins's obvious subservience pleased Shaddack, but he was even more gratified by the chief's fear, which was evident in the tremors that the man was struggling – with some success – to repress and in the haunted expression that deepened the colour of his eyes. Because of the Moonhawk Project, because of what had been done to him, Loman Watkins was in many ways superior to most men, but he was also now and forever in Shaddack's thrall as surely as a laboratory mouse, clamped down and attached to electrodes, was at the mercy of the scientist who conducted experiments on him. In a manner of speaking, Shaddack was Watkins's maker, and he possessed, in Watkins's eyes, the position and power of a god.

Leaning back in his chair, folding his pale, long-fingered hands on his chest, Shaddack felt his manhood swelling, hardening. He was not aroused by Loman Watkins, because he had no tendency whatsoever toward homosexuality; he was aroused not by anything in Watkins's physical appearance but by the awareness of the tremendous authority he wielded over the man. Power aroused Shaddack more fully and easily than sexual stimuli. Even as an adolescent, when he saw pictures of naked women in erotic magazines, he was turned on not by the sight of bared breasts, not by the curve of a female bottom or the elegant line of long legs, but by the thought of *dominating* such women, totally controlling them, holding their very lives in his hands. If a woman looked at him with undisguised fear, he found her infinitely more appealing than if she regarded him with desire. And since he reacted more strongly to terror than to lust, his arousal was not dependent upon the sex or age or physical attractiveness of the person who trembled in his presence.

Enjoying the policeman's submissiveness, Shaddack said, 'You've got Booker?'

'No, sir.'

'Why not?'

'He wasn't at Cove Lodge when Sholnick got there.'

'He's got to be found.'

'We'll find him.'

'And converted. Not just to prevent him from telling anyone what he's seen . . . but to give us one of our own *inside* the Bureau. That'd be a coup. His being here could turn out to be an incredible plus for the project.'

'Well, whether Booker's a plus or not, there's worse than him. Regressives attacked some of the guests at the lodge. Quinn himself was either carried off, killed, and left where we haven't found him yet . . . or he was one of the regressives himself and is off now . . . doing whatever they do after a kill, maybe baying at the goddamn moon.'

With growing dismay and agitation, Shaddack listened to the report.

Perched on the edge of his chair, Watkins finished, blinked, and said, 'These regressives scare the hell out of me.'

'They're disturbing.' Shaddack agreed.

On the night of September fourth, they had cornered a regressive, Jordan Coombs, in the movie theater on Main Street. Coombs had been a maintenance man at New Wave. That night, however, he had been more ape than man, although actually neither, but something so strange and savage that no single word could describe him. The term 'regressive' was only adequate, Shaddack had discovered, if you never came face to face with one of the beasts. Because once you'd seen one close up, 'regressive' insufficiently conveyed the horror of the thing, and in fact all words failed. Their attempt to take Coombs alive had failed, too, for he had proved too aggressive and powerful to be subdued; to save themselves, they'd had to blow his head off.

Now Watkins said, 'They're more than disturbing. Much more than just that. They're . . . psychotic.'

'I know they're psychotic,' Shaddack said impatiently. 'I've named their condition myself; metamorphic-related psychosis.'

'They *enjoy* killing.'

Thomas Shaddack frowned. He had not foreseen the problem of the regressives, and he refused to believe that they constituted more than a minor anomaly in the otherwise beneficial conversion of the people of Moonlight Cove. 'Yes, all right, they enjoy killing, and in their regressed state they're designed for it, but we've only a few of them to identify and eliminate. Statistically, they're an insignificant percentage of those we've put through the Change.'

'Maybe not so insignificant,' Watkins said hesitantly, unable to meet Shaddack's eyes, a reluctant bearer of bad tidings. 'Judging by all the bloody wreckage lately, I'd guess that among those nineteen hundred converted as of this morning, there were fifty or sixty of these regressives out there.'

'Ridiculous!'

To admit regressives existed in large numbers, Shaddack would have to consider the possibility that his research was flawed, that he had rushed his discoveries out of the laboratory and into the field with too little consideration of the potential for disaster, and that his enthusiastic application of the Moonhawk Project's revolutionary discoveries to the people of Moonlight Cove was a tragic mistake. He could admit nothing of the sort.

He had yearned all his life for the nth degree of power that was now nearly within his reach, and he was psychologically incapable of retreating from the course he had set. Since puberty he had denied himself certain pleasures because, had he acted upon those needs, he would have been hunted down by the law and made to pay a heavy price. All those years of denial had created a tremendous internal pressure that he desperately needed to relieve. He had sublimated his antisocial desires in his work, focused his energies into socially acceptable endeavors – which had, ironically, resulted in discoveries that would make him immune to authority and therefore free to indulge his long-suppressed urges without fear of censure or punishment.

Besides, not just psychologically but also in practical terms, he had gone too far to turn back. He had brought something revolutionary into the world. Because of him, nineteen hundred New People walked the earth, as different from other men and women as CroMagnons had been different from their more primitive Neanderthal ancestors. He did not have the ability to undo what he had done any more than other scientists and technicians could *un*invent the wheel or atomic bomb.

Watkins shook his head. 'I'm sorry . . . but I don't think it's ridiculous at all. Fifty or sixty regressives. Or more. Maybe a lot more.'

'You'll need proof to convince me of that. You'll have to name them for me. Are you any closer to identifying even *one* of them – other than Quinn?'

'Alex and Sharon Foster, I think. And maybe even your own man, Tucker.'

'Impossible.'

Watkins described what he had found at the Foster place – and the cries he had heard in the distant woods.

Reluctantly Shaddack considered the possibility that Tucker was one of those degenerates. He was disturbed by the likelihood that his control among his inner circle was not as absolute as he had thought. If he could not be sure of those men closest to him, how could he be certain of his ability to control the masses? 'Maybe the Fosters are regressives, though I doubt it's true of Tucker. But even if Tucker's one of them, that means you've found four. Not fifty or sixty. Just *four*. Who're all these others you imagine are out there?'

Loman Watkins stared at the fog, which pressed in ever-changing patterns against the glass walls of the tower room. 'Sir, I'm afraid it isn't easy. I mean . . . think about it. If the state or federal authorities learned what you've done, if they could *understand* what you've done and really believe it, and if then they wanted to prevent us from bringing the Change to everyone beyond Moonlight Cove, they'd have one hell of a time stopping us, wouldn't they? After all, those of us who've been converted . . . we walk undetected among ordinary people. We seem like them, no different, unchanged.'

'So?'

'Well . . . that's the same problem *we* have with the regressives. They're New People like us, but the thing that makes them different from us, the rottenness in them, is impossible to see; they're as indistinguishable from us as we are from the unchanged population of Old People.'

Shaddack's iron erection had softened. Impatient with Watkins's negativism, he rose from his armchair and moved to the nearest of the big windows. Standing with his hands fisted in the pockets of his sweat-suit jacket, he stared at the vague reflection of his own long, lupine face, which was ghostlike in its transparency. He met his own gaze, as well, then quickly looked through the reflection of his eye sockets and past the glass into the darkness beyond, where vagrant sea breezes worked the loom of night to bring forth a fragile fabric of fog. He kept his back to Watkins, for he did not want the man to see that he was concerned, and he avoided the glass-caught image of his own eyes because he did not want to admit to himself that his concern might be marbled with veins of fear.

• 45 •

He insisted on moving to the chairs, so they could not be seen as easily from the street. Tessa was leery about sitting beside him. He said that he was operating undercover and therefore carried no Bureau ID, but he showed her everything else in his wallet: driver's license, credit cards, library card, video rental card, photos of his son and his late wife, a coupon for a free chocolate-chip cookie at any Mrs. Fields store, a picture of Goldie Hawn torn from a magazine. Would a homicidal maniac carry a cookie coupon? In a while, as he took her back through her story of the massacre at Cove Lodge and picked relentlessly at the details, making sure that she told him everything and that he understood all of it, she began to trust him. If he was only pretending to be an agent, his pretense would not have been so elaborate or sustained.

'You didn't actually *see* anybody murdered?'

'They were killed,' she insisted. 'You wouldn't have any doubt if you'd heard their screams. I've stood in a mob of human monsters in Northern Ireland and seen them beat men to death. I was filming an industrial in a steel mill once, when there was a spill of molten metal that splattered all over workers' bodies, their faces. I've been with Miskito Indians in the Central American jungles when they were hit with antipersonnel bombs – millions of little bits of sharp steel, bodies pierced by a thousand needles – and I've heard *their* screams. I know what death sounds like. And this was the worst I've ever heard.'

He stared at her for a long time. Then he said, 'You look deceptively . . .'

'Cute?'

'Yes.'

'Therefore innocent? Therefore naive?'

'Yes.'

'My curse.'

'And an advantage sometimes?'

'Sometimes,' she acknowledged. 'Listen, you know something, so tell me: What's going on in this town?'

'Something's happening to the people here.'

'What?'

'I don't know. They're not interested in movies, for one thing. The theater closed. And they're not interested in luxury goods, fine gifts, that sort of thing, because those stores have all closed too. They no longer get a kick from champagne . . .' He smiled thinly. 'The barrooms are all going out of business. The only thing they seem to be interested in is food. And killing.'

• 46 •

Still standing at a tower-room window, Tom Shaddack said, 'All right, Loman, here's what we'll do. Everyone at New Wave has been converted, so I'll assign a hundred of them to you, to augment the police force. You can use them to help in your investigation in any way you see fit – starting now. With that many at your command, you'll catch one of the regressives in the act, surely . . . and you'll be more likely to find this man Booker too.'

The New People did not require sleep. The additional deputies could be brought into the field immediately.

Shaddack said, 'They can patrol the streets on foot and in their cars – quietly, without drawing attention. And with that assistance, you'll grab at least one of the regressives, maybe all of them. If we can catch one in a devolved state, if I've a chance to *examine* one of them, I might be able to develop a test – physical or psychological – with which we can screen the New People for degenerates.'

'I don't feel adequate to deal with this.'

'It's a police matter.'

'No, it isn't, really.'

'It's no different than if you were tracking down an ordinary killer,' Shaddack said irritably 'You'll apply the same techniques.'

'But . . .'

'What is it?'

'Regressives could be among the men you assign me.'

'There won't be any.'

'But . . . how can you be sure?'

'I told you there won't be,' Shaddack said sharply, still facing the window, the fog, the night.

They were both silent a moment.

Then Shaddack said, 'You've got to put everything into finding these damned deviants. Everything, you hear me? I want at least one of them to examine by the time we've taken all of Moonlight Cove through the Change.'

'I thought . . .'

'Yes?'

'Well, I thought . . .'

'Come on, come on. You thought what?'

'Well . . . just that maybe you'd suspend the conversions until we understand what's happening here.'

'Hell, no.' Shaddack turned from the window and glared at the police chief, who flinched satisfactorily. 'These regressives are a minor problem, very minor.

What the shit do you know about it? You're not the one who designed a new race, a new world. *I* am. The dream was mine, the vision mine. I had the brains and nerve to make the dream real. And I *know* this is an anomaly indicative of nothing. So the Change will take place according to schedule.'

Watkins looked down at his white-knuckled hands.

As he spoke, Shaddack paced barefoot along the curved glass wall, then back again. 'We now have more than enough doses to deal with the remaining townspeople. In fact, we've initiated a new round of conversions this evening. Hundreds will be brought into the fold by dawn, the rest by midnight. Until everyone in town is with us, there's a chance we'll be found out, a risk of someone carrying a warning to the outside world. Now that we've overcome the problems with the production of the biochips, we've got to take Moonlight Cove quickly, so we can proceed with the confidence that comes from having a secure home base. Understand?'

Watkins nodded.

'*Understand?*' Shaddack repeated.

'Yes. Yes, sir.'

Shaddack returned to his chair and sat down. 'Now what's this other thing you called me about earlier, this Valdoski business?'

'Eddie Valdoski, six years old,' Watkins said, looking at his hands, which he was now virtually wringing, as if trying to squeeze something from them in the way he might have squeezed water from a rag. 'He was found dead a few minutes past eight. In a ditch along the county road. He'd been . . . tortured . . . bitten, gutted.'

'You think one of the regressives did it?'

'Definitely.'

'Who found the body?'

'Eddie's folks. His dad. The boy had been playing in the backyard, and then he . . . disappeared near sunset. They started searching, couldn't find him, got scared, called us, continued to search while we were on our way . . . and found the body just before my men got there.'

'Evidently the Valdoskis aren't converted?'

'They weren't. But they are now.'

Shaddack sighed. 'There won't be any trouble about the boy if they've been brought into the fold.'

The police chief raised his head and found the courage to look directly at Shaddack again. 'But the boy's still dead.' His voice was rough.

Shaddack said, 'That's a tragedy, of course. This regressive element among the New People could not have been foreseen. But no great advancement in human history has been without its victims.'

'He was a fine boy,' the policeman said.

'You knew him?'

Watkins blinked. 'I went to high school with his father, George Valdoski. I was Eddie's godfather.'

Considering his words carefully, Shaddack said, 'It's a terrible thing. And we'll find the regressive who did it. We'll find all of them and eliminate them. Meanwhile, we can take some comfort in the fact that Eddie died in a great cause.'

Watkins regarded Shaddack with unconcealed astonishment. 'Great cause? What did Eddie know of a great cause? He was six years old.'

'Nevertheless,' Shaddack said, hardening his voice, 'Eddie was caught up in an unexpected side-effect of the conversion of Moonlight Cove, which makes him part of this wonderful, historical event.' He knew that Watkins had been a patriot, absurdly proud of his flag and country, and he supposed that some of that sentiment still reposed in the man, even subsequent to conversion, so he said: 'Listen to me, Loman. During the Revolutionary War, when the colonists were fighting for independence, some innocent bystanders died, women and children, not just combatants, and those people did not die in vain. They were martyrs every bit as much as the soldiers who perished in the field. It's the same in any revolution. The important thing is that justice prevail and that those who die can be said to have given their lives for a noble purpose.'

Watkins looked away from him.

Rising from his armchair again, Shaddack rounded the low cocktail table to stand beside the policeman. Looking down at Watkins's bowed head, he put one hand on the man's shoulder.

Watkins cringed from the touch.

Shaddack did not move his hand, and he spoke with the fervor of an evangelist. He was a cool evangelist, however, whose message did not involve the hot passion of religious conviction but the icy power of logic, reason. 'You're one of the New People now, and that does not just mean that you're stronger and quicker than ordinary men, and it doesn't just mean you're virtually invulnerable to disease and have a greater power to mend your injuries than anything any faith healer ever dreamed of. It *also* means you're clearer of mind, more rational than the Old People, so if you consider Eddie's death carefully and in the context of the miracle we're working here, you'll see that the price he paid was not too great. Don't deal with this situation emotionally, Loman; that's definitely not the way of New People. We're making a world that'll be more efficient, more ordered, and infinitely more stable precisely because men and women will have the power to control their emotions, to view every problem and event with the analytical coolness of a computer. Look at Eddie Voldoski's death as but another datum in the great flow of data that is the birth of the New People. You've got the power in you now to transcend human emotional limitations, and when you *do* transcend them, you'll know true peace and happiness for the first time in your life.'

After a while Loman Watkins raised his head. He turned to look up at Shaddack. 'Will this really lead to peace?'

'Yes.'

'When there's no one left unconverted, will there be brotherhood at last?'

'Yes.'

'Tranquility?'

'Eternal.'

• 47 •

The Talbot house on Conquistador was a three-story redwood with lots of big windows. The property was sloped, and steep stone steps led up from the sidewalk to a shallow porch. No streetlamps lit that block, and there were no walkway or landscape lights at Talbot's for which Sam was grateful.

Tessa Lockland stood close to him on the porch as he pressed the buzzer, just as she had stayed close all the way from the laundry. Above the noisy rustle of the wind in the trees, he could hear the doorbell ring inside.

Looking back toward Conquistador, Tessa said, 'Sometimes it seems more like a morgue than a town, peopled by the dead, but then . . .'

'Then?'

'. . . in spite of the silence and the stillness, you can feel the energy of the place, tremendous pent-up energy, as if there's a huge hidden machine just beneath the streets, beneath the ground . . . and as if the houses are filled with machinery, too, all of it powered up and straining at cogs and gears, just waiting for someone to engage a clutch and set it all in motion.'

That was *exactly* Moonlight Cove, but Sam had not been able to put the feeling of the place into words. He rang the bell again and said, 'I thought filmmakers were required to be borderline illiterates.'

'Most Hollywood filmmakers are, but I'm an outcast documentarian, so I'm permitted to think – as long as I don't do too much of it.'

'Who's there?' said a tinny voice, startling Sam. It came from an intercom speaker that he'd not noticed. 'Who's there, please?'

Sam leaned close to the intercom. 'Mr Talbot? Harold Talbot ?'

'Yes. Who're you?'

'Sam Booker,' he said quietly, so his voice would not carry past the perimeter of Talbot's porch. 'Sorry to wake you, but I've come in response to your letter of October eighth.'

Talbot was silent. Then the intercom clicked, and he said, 'I'm on the third floor. I'll need time to get down there. Meanwhile I'll send Moose. Please give him your ID so he can bring it to me.'

'I have no Bureau ID,' Sam whispered. 'I'm undercover here.'

'Driver's license?' Talbot asked.

'Yes.'

'That's enough.' He clicked off.

'Moose?' Tessa asked.

'Damned if I know,' Sam said.

They waited almost a minute, feeling vulnerable on the exposed porch, and they were both startled again when a dog pushed out through a pet door they had not seen, brushing between their legs. For an instant Sam didn't realize what it was, and he stumbled backward in surprise, nearly losing his balance.

Stooping to pet the dog, Tessa whispered, 'Moose?'

A flicker of light had come through the small swinging door with the dog; but that was gone now that the door was closed. The dog was black and hardly visible in the night.

Squatting beside it, letting it lick his hand, Sam said, 'I'm supposed to give my ID to you?'

The dog wuffed softly, as if answering in the affirmative.

'You'll eat it,' Sam said.

Tessa said, 'He won't.'

'How do you know?'

'He's a good dog.'

'I don't trust him.'

'I guess that's your job.'

'Huh?'

'Not to trust anyone.'

'And my nature.'

'Trust him,' she insisted.

He offered his wallet. The dog plucked it from Sam's hand, held it in his teeth, and went back into the house through the pet door.

They stood on the dark porch for another few minutes, while Sam tried to stifle his yawns. It was after two in the morning, and he was considering adding a fifth item to his list of reasons for living: good Mexican food, Guinness Stout, Goldie Hawn, fear of death, and *sleep*. Blissful sleep. Then he heard the clack and rattle of locks being laboriously disengaged, and the door finally opened inward on a dimly lighted hallway.

Harry Talbot waited in his motorized wheelchair, dressed in blue pajamas and a green robe. His head was tilted slightly to the left in a permanently quizzical angle that was part of his Vietnam legacy. He was a handsome man, though his face was prematurely aged, too deeply lined for that of a forty-year-old. His thick hair was half white, and his eyes were ancient. Sam could see that Talbot had once been a strapping young man, though he was now soft from years of paralysis. One hand lay in his lap, the palm up, fingers half curled, useless. He was a living monument to what might have been, to hopes destroyed, to dreams incinerated, a grim remembrance of war pressed between the pages of time.

As Tessa and Sam entered and closed the door behind them, Harry Talbot extended his good hand and said, 'God, am I glad to see you!' His smile transformed him astonishingly. It was the bright, broad, warm, and genuine smile of a man who believed he was perched in the lap of the gods, with too many blessings to count.

Moose returned Sam's wallet, uneaten.

· 48 ·

After leaving Shaddack's house on the north point, but before returning to headquarters to coordinate the assignments of the hundred men who were being sent to him from New Wave, Loman Watkins stopped at his home on Iceberry Way, on the north side of town. It was a modest, two-story, three-bedroom, Monterey-style house, white with pale-blue trim, nestled among conifers.

He stood for a moment in the driveway beside his patrol car, studying the place. He had loved it as if it were a castle, but he could not find that love in himself now. He remembered much happiness related to the house, to his family, but he could not *feel* the memory of that happiness. A lot of laughter had graced life in that dwelling, but now the laughter had faded until recollection of it was too faint even to induce a smile in remembrance. Besides, these days, his smiles were all counterfeit, with no humor behind them.

The odd thing was that laughter and joy had been a part of his life as late as this past August. It had all seeped away only within the past couple of months, after the Change. Yet it seemed an ancient memory.

Funny.

Actually, not so funny at all.

When he went inside he found the first floor dark and silent. A vague, stale odor lingered in the deserted rooms.

He climbed the stairs. In the unlit, second-floor hallway he saw a soft glow along the bottom of the closed door to Denny's bedroom. He went in and found the boy sitting at his desk, in front of the computer. The PC had an oversize screen, and currently that was the only light in the room.

Denny did not look up from the terminal.

The boy was eighteen years old, no longer a child; therefore, he had been converted with his mother, shortly after Loman himself had been put through the Change. He was two inches taller than his dad and better looking. He'd always done well in school, and on IQ tests he'd scored so high it spooked Loman a bit to think his kid was *that* smart. He had always been proud of Denny. Now, at his son's side, staring down at him, Loman tried to resurrect that pride but could not find it. Denny had not fallen from favor; he had done nothing to earn his father's disapproval. But pride, like so many other emotions, seemed an encumbrance to the higher consciousness of the New People and interfered with their more efficient thought patterns.

Even before the Change, Denny had been a computer fanatic, one of those kids who called themselves hackers, to whom computers were not only tools, not only fun and games, but a way of life. After the conversion, his intelligence and high-tech expertise were put to use by New Wave. He was provided with a more powerful home terminal and a modem link to the supercomputer at New Wave headquarters – a behemoth that, according to Denny's description, incorporated four thousand miles of wiring and thirty-three thousand high-speed processing units – which, for reasons Loman didn't understand, they called Sun, though perhaps that was its name because all research at New Wave made heavy use of the machine and therefore revolved around it.

As Loman stood beside his son, voluminous data flickered across the terminal screen. Words, numbers, graphs, and charts appeared and disappeared at such speed that only one of the New People, with somewhat heightened senses and powerfully heightened concentration, could extract meaning from them.

In fact Loman could not read them because he had not undergone the training that Denny had received from New Wave. Besides, he'd had neither the time nor the need to learn to fully focus his new powers of concentration.

But Denny absorbed the rushing waves of data, staring blankly at the screen, no frown lines in his brow, his face completely relaxed. Since being converted, the boy was as much a solid-state electronic entity as he was flesh and blood, and that new part of him related to the computer with an intimacy that exceeded any man-machine relationship any of the Old People had ever known.

Loman knew that his son was learning about the Moonhawk Project. Ultimately he would join the task group at New Wave that was endlessly refining the software and hardware related to the project, working to make each generation of New People superior to – and more efficient than – the one before it.

An endless river of data washed across the screen.

Denny stared unblinkingly for so long that tears would have formed in his eyes if he had been one of the Old People.

The light of the ever-moving data danced on the walls and sent a continuous blur of shadows chasing around the room.

Loman put one hand on the boy's shoulder.

Denny did not look up or in any way respond. His lips began to move, as if he were talking, but he made no sound. He was speaking to himself, oblivious of his father.

In a garrulous, evangelistic moment, Thomas Shaddack had spoken of one day developing a link that would connect a computer directly to a surgically implanted socket in the base of the human spine, thereby merging real and artificial intelligence. Loman had not understood why such a thing was either wise or desirable, and Shaddack had said, 'The New People are a bridge between man and machine, Loman. But one day our species will entirely cross that bridge, become *one* with the machines, because only then will mankind be *completely* efficient, *completely* in control.'

'Denny,' Loman said softly.

The boy did not respond.

At last Loman left the room.

Across the hall and at the end of it was the master bedroom. Grace was lying on the bed, in the dark.

Of course, since the Change, she could never be entirely blinded by a mere insufficiency of light, for her eyesight had improved. Even in this lightless room, she could see – as Loman could – the shapes of the furniture and some textures, though few details. For them, the night world was no longer black but darkish gray.

He sat on the edge of the mattress. 'Hello.'

She said nothing.

He put one hand on her head and stroked her long auburn hair. He touched her face and found her cheeks wet with tears, a detail that even his improved eyes could not discern.

Crying. She was crying, and that jolted him because he had never seen one of the New People cry.

His heartbeat accelerated, and a brief but wonderful thrill of hope throbbed through him. Perhaps the deadening of emotions was a transient condition.

'What is it?' he asked. 'What're you crying about?'

'I'm afraid.'

The pulse of hope swiftly faded. Fear had brought her to tears, fear and the desolation associated with it, and he already knew those feelings were a part of this brave new world, those and no other.

'Afraid of what?'

'I can't sleep,' Grace said.

'But you don't need to sleep.'

'Don't I?'

'None of us needs to sleep any more.'

Prior to the Change, men and women had needed to sleep because the human body, being strictly a biological mechanism, was terribly inefficient. Downtime was required to rest and repair the damage of the day, to deal with the toxic substances absorbed from the external world and the toxics created internally. But in the New People, every bodily process and function was superbly regulated. Nature's work had been highly refined. Every organ, every system, every cell operated at a far higher efficiency, producing less waste, casting off waste faster than before, cleansing and rejuvenating itself every hour of the day. Grace knew that as well as he did.

'I long for sleep,' she said.

'All you're feeling is the pull of habit.'

'Too many hours in the day now.'

'We'll fill up the time. The new world will be a busy one.'

'What're we going to do in this new world when it comes?'

'Shaddack will tell us.'

'Meanwhile . . .'

'Patience,' he said.

'I'm afraid.'

'Patience.'

'I yearn for sleep, hunger for it.'

'We don't need to sleep,' he said, exhibiting the patience that he had encouraged in her.

'We don't need sleep,' she said cryptically, 'but we *need* to sleep.'

They were both silent a while.

Then she took his hand in hers, and moved it to her breasts. She was nude.

He tried to pull away from her, for he was afraid of what might happen, of what had happened before, since the Change, when they had made love. No. Not love. They didn't make love any more. They had sex. There was no feeling beyond physical sensation, no tenderness or affection. They thrust hard and fast at each other, pushed and pulled, flexed and writhed against each other, striving to maximize the excitation of nerve endings. Neither of them cared for or about the other, only about himself, his own satisfaction. Now that their emotional life was no longer rich, they tried to compensate for that loss with pleasures of the senses, primarily food and sex. However, without the emotional factor, every experience was . . . hollow, and they tried to fill that emptiness by overindulgence: A simple meal became a feast; a feast became an unrestrained indulgence in gluttony. And sex degenerated into a frenzied, bestial coupling.

Grace pulled him onto the bed.

He did not want to go. He could not refuse. Literally *could not* refuse.

Breathing hard, shuddering with excitement, she tore at his clothes and mounted him. She was making strange wordless sounds.

Loman's excitement matched hers and swelled, and he thrust at her, into her, into, losing all sense of time and place, existing only to stoke the fire in his loins, stoke it relentlessly until it was an unbearable heat, heat, friction and heat, wet and hot, heat, stoking the heat to a flashpoint at which his entire body would be consumed in the flames. He shifted positions, pinning her down, hammering himself into her, into her, into, into, pulling her against him so roughly that he must be bruising her, but he didn't care. She reached back and clawed at him, her fingernails digging into his arm, drawing blood, and he tore at her, too, because the blood was exciting, the smell of the blood, the sweet smell, so exciting, blood, and it didn't matter that they wounded each other, for these were superficial wounds and would heal within seconds, because they were New People; their bodies were efficient; blood flowed briefly, and then the wounds closed, and they clawed again, again. What he really wanted – what they *both* wanted – was to let go, indulge the wild spirit within, cast off all the inhibitions of civilization, including the inhibition of higher human form, go wild, go savage, regress, surrender, because then sex would have an even greater thrill, a purer thrill; surrender, and the emptiness would be filled; they would be fulfilled, and when the sex was done they could hunt together, hunt and kill, swift and silent, sleek and swift, bite and tear, bite deep and hard, hunt and kill, sperm and then blood, sweet fragrant blood. . . .

====

For a while Loman was disoriented.

When a sense of time and place returned to him, he first glanced at the door, realizing that it was ajar. Denny could have seen them if he'd come down the hall – surely *had* heard them – but Loman couldn't make himself care whether they had been seen or heard. Shame and modesty were two more casualties of the Change.

As he became fully oriented to the world around him, fear slipped into his heart, and he quickly touched himself – his face, arms, chest, legs – to be sure that he was in no way less than he ought to be. In the midst of sex, the wildness in him grew, and sometimes he thought that approaching orgasm he *did* change, regress, if only slightly. But upon regaining awareness, he never found evidence of backsliding.

He was, however, sticky with blood.

He switched on the bedside lamp.

'Turn it off,' Grace said at once.

But he was not satisfied with even his enhanced night vision. He wanted to look at her closely to determine if she was in any way . . . different.

She had not regressed. Or, if she *had* regressed, she had already returned to the higher form. Her body was smeared with blood, and a few welts showed on her flesh, where he had gouged her and where she had not finished healing.

He turned the light off and sat on the edge of the bed.

Because the recuperative powers of their bodies had been vastly improved by the Change, superficial cuts and scrapes healed in only minutes; you could actually watch your flesh knit its wounds. They were impervious to disease now, their immune systems too aggressive for the most infectious virus or bacterium to survive long enough to replicate. Shaddack believed that their life spans would prove to be of great duration, as well, perhaps hundreds of years.

They could be killed, of course, but only by a wound that tore and stopped the heart or shattered the brain or destroyed their lungs and prevented a flow of oxygen to the blood. If a vein or artery was severed, the blood supply was drastically reduced to that vessel for the few minutes required to heal it. If a vital organ other than the heart or lungs or brain was damaged, the body could limp along for hours while accelerated repairs were under way. They were not yet as fully reliable as machines, for machines could not die; with the right spare parts, a machine could be rebuilt even from rubble and could work again; but they were closer to that degree of corporeal endurance than anyone outside Moonlight Cove would have believed.

To live for hundreds of years . . .

Sometimes Loman brooded about that.

To live for hundreds of years, knowing only fear and physical sensation . . .

He rose from the bed, went into the adjacent bathroom, and took a quick shower to sluice off the blood.

He could not meet his eyes in the bathroom mirror.

In the bedroom again, without turning on a light, he pulled on a fresh uniform that he took from his closet.

Grace was still lying on the bed.

She said, 'I wish I could sleep.'

He sensed that she was still crying silently.

When he left the room, he closed the door behind him.

• 49 •

They gathered in the kitchen, which Tessa liked because some of her happiest memories of childhood and adolescence involved family conferences and impromptu chats in the kitchen of their house in San Diego. The kitchen was the heart of a home and in a way the heart of a family. Somehow the worst problems became insignificant when you discussed them in a warm kitchen redolent of coffee and hot cocoa, nibbling on home-baked cake or pastry. In a kitchen she felt *secure*.

Harry Talbot's kitchen was large, for it had been remodeled to suit a man in a wheelchair, with lots of clearance around the central cooking island, which was built low – as were the counters along the walls – to be accessible from a sitting position. Otherwise it was a kitchen like many others: cabinets painted a pleasant creamy shade; pale yellow ceramic tile; a quietly purring refrigerator. The Levolor blinds at the windows were electrically operated by a button on one of the counters, and Harry put them down.

After trying the phone and discovering that the line was dead, that not just the pay phones but the town's entire phone system had been interdicted, Sam and Tessa sat at a round table in one corner, at Harry's insistence, while he made a pot of good Colombian in a Mr. Coffee machine. 'You look cold,' he said. 'This'll do you good.'

Chilled and tired, in need of the caffeine, Tessa did not decline the offer. Indeed, she was fascinated that Harry, with such severe disabilities, could function well enough to play the gracious host to unexpected visitors.

With his one good hand and some tricky moves, he got a package of apple-cinnamon muffins from the bread box, part of a chocolate cake from the refrigerator, plates and forks, and paper napkins. When Sam and Tessa offered to help, he gently declined their assistance with a smile.

She sensed that he was not trying to prove anything either to them or to himself. He was simply enjoying having company, even at this hour and under these bizarre circumstances. Perhaps it was a rare pleasure.

'No cream,' he said. 'Just a carton of milk.'

'That's fine,' Sam said.

'And no elegant porcelain cream pitcher, I'm afraid,' said Harry, putting the milk carton on the table.

Tessa began to consider shooting a documentary about Harry, about the courage required to remain independent in his circumstances: She was drawn by the siren call of her art in spite of what had transpired in the past few hours. Long ago, however, she had learned that an artist's creativity could not be turned off; the eye of a filmmaker could not be capped as easily as the lens of her camera. In the midst of grief over her sister's death, ideas for projects had continued to come to her, narrative concepts, interesting shots, angles. Even in the terror of war, running with Afghan rebels as Soviet planes strafed the ground at their heels, she'd been excited by what she was getting on film and by what she would be able to make of it when she got into an editing room – and her three-man crew had reacted much the same. So she no longer felt awkward or guilty about being an artist on the make, even in times of tragedy; for her, that was just natural, a part of being creative and *alive*.

Customized to his needs, Harry's wheelchair included a hydraulic lift that raised the seat a few inches, bringing him nearly to normal chair height, so he could sit at an ordinary table or writing desk. He took a place beside Tessa and across from Sam.

Moose was lying in the corner, watching, occasionally raising his head as if interested in their conversation – though more likely drawn by the smell of chocolate cake. The Labrador did not come sniffing and pawing around, whining for handouts, and Tessa was impressed by his discipline.

As they passed the coffee pot and carved up the cake and muffins, Harry said, 'You've told me what brings you here, Sam – not just my letter but all these so-called accidents.' He looked at Tessa, and because she was on his right side, the permanent cock of his head to the left made it seem as if he were leaning back from her, regarding her with suspicion or at least skepticism, though his true attitude was belied by his warm smile. 'But just where do you fit in, Miss Lockland?'

'Call me Tessa, please. Well . . . my sister was Janice Capshaw—'

'Richard Capshaw's wife, the Lutheran minister's wife?' he said, surprised. 'That's right.'

'Why, they used to come to visit me. I wasn't a member of their congregation, but that's how they were. We became friends. And after he died, she still stopped by now and then. Your sister was a dear and wonderful person, Tessa.' He put down his coffee cup and reached out to her with his good hand. 'She was my friend.'

Tessa held his hand. It was leathery and calloused from use, and very strong, as if all the frustrated power of his paralyzed body found expression through that single extremity.

'I watched them take her into the crematorium at Callen's Funeral Home,' Harry said. 'Through my telescope. I'm a watcher. That's what I do with my life, for the most part. I watch.' He blushed slightly. He held Tessa's hand a bit tighter. 'It's not just snooping. In fact it isn't snooping at all. It's . . . participating. Oh, I like to read, too, and I've got a lot of books, and I do a heavy load of thinking, for sure, but it's watching, mainly, that gets me through. We'll go upstairs later. I'll show you the telescope, the whole setup. I think maybe you'll understand. I hope you will. Anyway, I saw them take Janice into Callan's that night . . . though I didn't know who it was until two days later, when the story of her death was in the county paper. I couldn't believe she died the way they said she did. Still don't believe it.'

'Neither do I,' Tessa said. 'And that's why I'm here.'

Reluctantly, with a final squeeze, Harry let go of Tessa's hand. 'So many bodies lately, most of them hauled into Callan's at night, and more than a few times with cops hanging around, overseeing things – it's strange as hell for a quiet little town like this.'

From across the table, Sam said, 'Twelve accidental deaths or suicides in less than two months.'

'Twelve?' Harry said.

'Didn't you realize it was that many?' Sam asked.

'Oh, it's more than that.'

Sam blinked.

Harry said, 'Twenty, by my count.'

• **50** •

After Watkins left, Shaddack returned to the computer terminal in his study, reopened his link to Sun, the supercomputer at New Wave, and set to work again on a problematic aspect of the current project. Though it was two-thirty in the morning, he would put in a few more hours, for the earliest he went to bed was dawn.

He had been at the terminal a few minutes when his most private phone line rang.

Until Booker was apprehended, the telephone company computer was allowing service only among those who had been converted, *from* one of their numbers *to* one of their numbers. Other lines were cut off, and calls to the outside world were interrupted before being completed.

Incoming calls to Moonlight Cove were answered by a recording that pleaded equipment failure, promised a return to full service within twenty-four hours, and expressed regret at the inconvenience.

Therefore, Shaddack knew the caller must be among the converted and, because it was his most private line, must also be one of his closest associates at New Wave. A LED readout on the base of the phone displayed the number from which the call was being placed, which he recognized as that of Mike Peyser. He picked up the receiver and said, 'Shaddack here.'

The caller breathed heavily, raggedly into the phone but said nothing.

Frowning, Shaddack said, 'Hello?'

Just the breathing.

Shaddack said, 'Mike, is that you?'

The voice that finally responded to him was hoarse, guttural, but with a shrill edge, whispery yet forceful, Peyser's voice yet not his, strange: '. . . *something wrong, wrong, something wrong, can't change, can't . . . wrong . . . wrong . . .*'

Shaddack was reluctant to admit that he recognized Mike Peyser's voice in those queer inflections and eerie cadences. He said, 'Who is this?'

'. . . *need, need . . . need, want, I need . . .*'

'Who is this?' Shaddack demanded angrily, but in his mind was another question: *What* is this?

The caller issued a sound that was a groan of pain, a mewl of deepest anguish, a thin cry of frustration, and a snarl, all twisted into one rolling bleat. The receiver dropped from his hand with a hard clatter.

Shaddack put his own phone down, turned back to the VDT, tapped into the police data system, and sent an urgent message to Loman Watkins.

<h2 style="text-align:center">• 51 •</h2>

Sitting on the stool in the dark third-floor bedroom, bent to the eyepiece, Sam Booker studied the rear of Callan's Funeral Home. All but scattered scrims of fog had blown away on the wind, which still blustered at the windows and shook the trees all along the hillsides on which most of Moonlight Cove was built. The serviceway lamps were extinguished now, and the rear of Callan's lay in darkness but for the thin light radiating from the blind-covered windows of the crematorium wing. No doubt they were busily feeding the flames with the bodies of the couple who had been murdered at Cove Lodge.

Tessa sat on the edge of the bed behind Sam, petting Moose, who was lying with his head in her lap.

Harry was in his wheelchair nearby. He used a penlight to study a spiral-bound notebook in which he had kept a record of the unusual activities at the mortuary.

'First one – at least the first unusual one I noticed – was on the night of August twenty-eighth,' Harry said. 'Twenty minutes to midnight. They brought four bodies at once, using the hearse and the city ambulance. Police accompanied them. The corpses were in body bags, so I couldn't see anything about them, but the cops and the ambulance attendants and the people at Callan's were visibly . . . well . . . upset. I saw it in their faces. Fear. They kept looking around at the neighboring houses and the alleyway, as if they were afraid someone was going to see what they were up to, which seemed peculiar because they were only doing their jobs. Right? Anyway, later, in the county paper, I read about the Mayser family dying in a fire, and I knew that was who'd been brought to Callan's that night. I suppose they didn't die in a fire any more than your sister killed herself.'

'Probably not,' Tessa said.

Still watching the back of the funeral home, Sam said, 'I have the Maysers on my list. They were turned up in the investigation of the Sanchez-Bustamante case.'

Harry cleared his throat and said, 'Seven days later, September third, two bodies were brought to Callan's shortly after midnight. And this was even weirder because they didn't come in a hearse or an ambulance. Two police cars pulled in at the back of Callan's and they unloaded a body from the rear seat of each of them, wrapped in blood-streaked sheets.'

'September third?' Sam said. 'There's no one on my list for that date. Sanchez and the Bustamantes were on the fifth. No death certificates were issued on the third. They kept those two off the official records.'

'Nothing in the county paper about anyone dying then, either,' Harry said.

Tessa said, 'So who were those two people?'

'Maybe they were out-of-towners who were unlucky enough to stop in Moonlight Cove and stumble into something dangerous,' Sam said. 'People whose deaths could be completely covered up, so no one would know *where* they'd died. As far as anyone knows, they just vanished on the road somewhere.'

'Sanchez and the Bustamantes were on the night of the fifth,' Harry said, 'and then Jim Armes on the night of the seventh.'

'Armes disappeared at sea,' Sam said, looking up from the telescope and frowning at the man in the wheelchair.

'They brought the body to Callan's at eleven o'clock at night,' Harry said, consulting his notebook for details. 'The blinds weren't drawn at the crematorium windows, so I could see straight in there, almost as good as if I'd been right there in that room. I saw the body . . . the mess it was in. And the face. Couple of days later, when the paper ran a story about Armes's disappearance, I recognized him as the guy they'd fed to the furnace.'

The large bedroom was dressed in cloaks of shadow except for the narrow beam of the penlight, which was half shielded by Harry's hand and confined to the open notebook. Those white pages seemed to glow with light of their own, as if they were the leaves of a magic or holy – or unholy – book.

Harry Talbot's careworn countenance was more dimly illumined by the backsplash from those pages, and the peculiar light emphasized the lines in his face, making him appear older than he was. Each line, Sam knew, had its provenance in tragic experience and pain. Profound sympathy stirred in him. Not pity. He could never pity anyone as determined as Talbot. But Sam appreciated the sorrow and loneliness of Harry's restricted life. Watching the wheelchair-bound man, Sam grew angry with the neighbors. Why hadn't they done more to bring Harry into their lives? Why hadn't they invited him to dinner more often, drawn him into their holiday celebrations? Why had they left him so much on his own that his primary means of participating in the life of his community was through a telescope and binoculars? Sam was cut by a pang of despair at people's reluctance to reach out to one another, at the way they isolated themselves and one another. With a jolt, he thought of his inability to communicate with his own son, which only left him feeling bleaker still.

To Harry, he said, 'What do you mean when you say Armes's body was a mess?'

'Cut. Slashed.'

'He didn't drown?'

'Didn't look it.'

'Slashed . . . Exactly what do you mean?' Tessa asked.

Sam knew that she was thinking about the people whose screams she had heard at the motel – and about her own sister.

Harry hesitated, then said: 'Well, I saw him on the table in the crematorium, just before they slipped him into the furnace. He'd been . . . disemboweled. Nearly decapitated. Horribly . . . *torn*. He looked as bad as if he'd been standing on an antipersonnel mine when it went off and been riddled by shrapnel.'

They sat in mutual silence considering that description.

Only Moose seemed unperturbed. He made a soft, contented sound as Tessa gently scratched behind his ears.

Sam thought it might not be so bad to be one of the lower beasts, a creature mostly of feelings, untroubled by a complex intellect. Or at the other extreme

. . . a genuinely intelligent computer, all intellect and no feelings whatsoever. The great dual burden of emotion and high intelligence was singular to human-kind, and it was what made life so hard; you were always thinking about what you were feeling instead of just going with the moment, or you were always trying to feel what you thought you *should* feel in a given situation. Thoughts and judgment were inevitably colored by emotions – some of them on a sub-conscious level, so you didn't even entirely understand *why* you made certain decisions, acted in certain ways. Emotions clouded your thinking; but thinking too hard about your feelings took the edge off them. Trying to feel deeply and think perfectly clearly at the same time was like simultaneously juggling six Indian clubs while riding a unicycle backward along a high wire.

'After the story in the paper about Armes disappearing,' Harry said, 'I kept waiting for a correction, but none was printed, and that's when I began to realize that the odd goings-on at Callan's weren't *just* odd but probably crimi-nal, as well – and that the cops were part if it.'

'Paula Parkins was torn apart too,' Sam said.

Harry nodded. 'Supposedly by her Dobermans.'

'Dobermans?' Tessa asked.

At the laundry Sam had told her that her sister was one of many curious suicides and accidental deaths, but he had not gone into any detail about the others. Now he quickly told her about Parkins.

'Not her own dogs,' Tessa agreed. 'She was savaged by whatever killed Armes. And the people tonight at Cove Lodge.'

This was the first that Harry Talbot had heard about the murders at Cove Lodge. Sam had to explain about that and about how he and Tessa had met at the laundry.

A strange expression settled on Harry's prematurely aged face. To Tessa, he said, 'Uh . . . you didn't see these things at the motel? Not even a glimpse?'

'Only the foot of one of them, through the crack under the door.' Harry started to speak, stopped, and sat in thoughtful silence. He knows something, Sam thought. More than we do.

For some reason Harry was not ready to share what he knew, for he returned his scrutiny to the notebook on his lap and said, 'Two days after Paula Parkins died, there was one body taken to Callan's, around nine-thirty at night.'

'That would be September eleventh?' Sam asked.

'Yes.'

'There's no record of a death certificate issued that day.'

'Nothing about it in the paper, either.'

'Go on.'

Harry said, 'September fifteenth –'

'Steve Heinz, Laura Dalcoe. He supposedly killed her, then took his own life,' Sam said. 'Lovers' quarrel, we're to believe.'

'Another quick cremation,' Harry noted. 'And three nights later, on the eighteenth, two more bodies delivered to Callan's shortly after one in the morning, just as I was about to go to bed.'

'No public record of those, either,' Sam said.

'Two more out-of-towners who drove off the interstate for a visit or just dinner?' Tessa wondered. 'Or maybe someone from another part of the county, passing on the county road along the edge of town?'

'Could even have been locals,' Harry said. 'I mean, there're always a few people around who haven't lived here a long time, newcomers who rent instead of own their houses, don't have many ties to the community, so if you wanted to cover their murders, you could maybe concoct an acceptable story about them moving away suddenly, for a new job, whatever, and their neighbors might buy it.'

If their neighbors weren't already 'converted' and participating in the coverup, Sam thought.

'Then September twenty-third,' Harry said. 'That would have been your sister's body, Tessa.'

'Yes.'

'By then I knew I had to tell someone what I'd seen. Someone in authority. But who? I didn't trust anyone local because I'd watched the cops bring in some of those bodies that were never reported in the newspaper. County Sheriff? He'd believe Watkins before he'd believe me, wouldn't he? Hell, everyone thinks a cripple is a little strange anyway – strange in the head, I mean – they equate physical disabilities with mental disabilities at least a little, at least subconsciously. So they'd be predisposed not to believe me. And admittedly it *is* a wild story, all these bodies, secret cremations . . .' He paused. His face clouded. 'The fact that I'm a decorated veteran wouldn't have made me any more believable. That was a long time ago, ancient history – for them. In fact . . . no doubt they'd hold the war against me in a way. Post-Vietnam stress syndrome, they'd call it. Poor old Harry finally went crackers – don't you see? – from the war.'

Thus far Harry had been speaking matter-of-factly, without much emotion. But the words he had just spoken were like a piece of glass held against the surface of a rippled pool, revealing realms below – in his case, realms of pain, loneliness, and alienation.

Now emotion not only entered his voice but, a few times, made it crack: 'And I've got to say, part of the reason I didn't try to tell anyone what I'd seen was because . . . I was afraid. I didn't know what the hell was going on. I couldn't be sure how big the stakes were. I didn't know if they'd silence me, feed *me* to the furnace at Callan's one night. You'd think that having lost so much I'd be reckless now, unconcerned about losing more, about dying, but that's not the way it is, not at all. Life's probably more precious to me than to men who're whole and healthy. This broken body slowed me down so much that I've spent the last twenty years out of the whirl of activity in which most of you exist, and I've had time to really *see* the world, the beauty and intricacy of it. In the end my disabilities have led me to appreciate and love life more. So I was afraid they'd come for me, kill me, and I hesitated to tell anyone what I'd seen. God help me, if I'd spoken out, if I'd gotten in touch with the Bureau sooner, maybe some people might have been saved. Maybe . . . your sister would've been saved.'

'Don't even think of that,' Tessa said at once. 'If you'd done anything differently, no doubt you'd be ashes now, scraped out of the bottom of Callan's furnace and thrown in the sea. My sister's fate was sealed. You couldn't unseal it.'

Harry nodded, then switched off the penlight, plunging the room into deeper darkness, though he had not yet finished going through the information in his notebook. Sam suspected that Tessa's unhesitating generosity of spirit had brought tears to Harry's eyes and that he did not want them to see.

'On the twenty-fifth,' he continued, not needing to consult the notebook for details, 'one body was brought to Callan's at ten-fifteen at night. Weird, too, because it didn't come in either an ambulance or hearse or police car. It was brought by Loman Watkins—'

'Chief of police,' Sam said for Tessa's benefit.

'—but he was in his private car, out of uniform,' Harry said. 'They took the body out of his trunk. It was wrapped in a blanket. The blinds weren't shut at their windows that night, either, and I was able to get in tight with the scope. I didn't recognize the body, but I did recognize the condition of it – the same as Armes.'

'Torn?' Sam asked.

'Yes. Then the Bureau *did* come to town on the Sanchez-Bustamante thing, and when I read about it in the newspaper, I was so relieved, because I thought it was all going to come out in the open at last, that we'd have revelations, explanations. But then there were two more bodies disposed of at Callan's on the night of October fourth—'

'Our team was in town then,' Sam said, 'in the middle of their investigation. They didn't realize any death certificates were filed during that time. You're saying this happened under their noses?'

'Yeah. I don't have to look in the notebook; I remember it clearly. The bodies were brought around in Reese Dorn's camper truck. He's a local cop, but he was out of uniform that night. They hauled the stiffs into Callan's and the blind at one window was open, so I saw them shove both bodies into the crematorium together, as if they were in a real sweat to dispose of them. And there was more activity at Callan's late on the night of the seventh, but the fog was so thick, I can't swear that it was more bodies being taken in. And finally . . . earlier tonight. A child's body. A small child.'

'Plus the two who were killed at Cove Lodge,' Tessa said. 'That makes twenty-two victims, not the twelve that brought Sam here. This town's become a slaughterhouse.'

'Could be even more than we think,' Harry said.

'How so?'

'Well, after all, I don't watch the place every evening, all evening long. And I go to bed by one-thirty, no later than two. Who's to say there weren't visits I missed, that more bodies weren't brought in during the dead hours of the night?'

Brooding about that, Sam looked through the eyepiece again. The rear of Callan's remained dark and still. He slowly moved the scope to the right, shifting the field of vision northward through the neighborhood.

Tessa said, 'But *why* were they killed?'

No one had an answer.

'And by what?' she added.

Sam studied a cemetery farther north on Conquistador, then sighed and looked up and told them about his experience earlier in the night, on Iceberry Way. 'I thought they were kids, delinquents, but now what I think is that they were the same things that killed the people at Cove Lodge, the same as the one whose foot you saw through the crack under the door.'

He could almost feel Tessa frowning with frustration in the darkness when she said, 'But what *are* they?'

Harry Talbot hesitated. Then: 'Boogeymen.'

Not daring to use sirens, dousing headlights on the last quarter mile of the approach, Loman came down on Mike Peyser's place at three-ten in the morning, with two cars, five deputies, and shotguns. Loman hoped they did not have to use the guns for more than intimidation. In their only previous encounter with a regressive – Jordan Coombs on the fourth of September – they had not been prepared for its ferocity and had been forced to blow its head off to save their own lives. Shaddack had been left with only a carcass to examine. He'd been furious at the lost chance to delve into the psychology – and the functioning physiology – of one of these metamorphic psychopaths. A tranquilizer gun would be of little use, unfortunately, because regressives were New People gone bad, and all New People, regressive or not, had radically altered metabolisms that not only allowed for magically fast healing but also for the rapid absorption, breakdown, and rejection of toxic substances like poison or tranquilizers. The only way to sedate a regressive would be to get him to agree to be put on a continuous IV drip, which wasn't very damn likely.

Mike Peyser's house was a one-story bungalow with front and rear porches on the west and east sides respectively, nicely maintained, on an acre and a half, sheltered by a few huge sweet gums that had not yet lost their leaves. No lights shone at the windows.

Loman sent one man to watch the north side, another the south, to prevent Peyser from escaping through a window. He stationed a third man at the foot of the front porch to cover that door. With the other two men – Sholnick and Penniworth – he circled to the rear of the place and quietly climbed the steps to the back porch.

Now that the fog had been blown away, visibility was good. But the huffing and skirling wind was a white noise that blocked out other sounds they might need to hear while stalking Peyser.

Penniworth stood against the wall of the house to the left of the door, and Sholnick stood to the right. Both carried semiautomatic 20-gauge shotguns.

Loman tried the door. It was unlocked. He pushed it open and stepped back.

His deputies entered the dark kitchen, one after the other, their shotguns lowered and ready to fire, though they were aware that the objective was to take Peyser alive if at all possible. But they were not going to sacrifice themselves just to bring the living beast to Shaddack. A moment later one of them found a light switch.

Carrying a 12-gauge of his own, Loman went into the house after them. Empty bowls, broken dishes, and dirty Tupperware containers were scattered on the floor, as were a few rigatoni red with tomato sauce, half of a meatball, eggshells, a chunk of pie crust, and other bits of food. One of the four wooden chairs from the breakfast set was lying on its side; another had been hammered to pieces against a counter top, cracking some of the ceramic tiles.

Straight ahead, an archway led into a dining room. Some of the spill-through light from the kitchen vaguely illuminated the table and chairs in there.

To the left, beside the refrigerator, was a door. Barry Sholnick opened it defensively. Shelves of canned goods flanked a landing. Stairs led down to the basement.

'We'll check that later,' Loman said softly. 'After we've gone through the house.'

Sholnick soundlessly snatched a chair from the breakfast set and braced the door shut so nothing could come up from the cellar and creep in behind them after they went into other rooms.

They stood for a moment, listening.

Gusting wind slammed against the house. A window rattled. From the attic above came the creaking of rafters, and from higher still the muffled clatter of a loose cedar shingle on the roof.

His deputies looked at Loman for guidance. Penniworth was only twenty-five, could pass for eighteen, and had a face so fresh and guileless that he looked more like a door-to-door peddler of religious tracts than a cop. Sholnick was ten years older and had a harder edge to him.

Loman motioned them toward the dining room.

They entered, turning the lights on as they went. The dining room was deserted, so they moved cautiously into the living room.

Penniworth clicked a wall switch that turned on a chrome and brass lamp, which was one of the few items not broken or torn apart. The cushions on the sofa and chairs had been slashed; wads of foam padding, like clumps of a poisonous fungus, lay everywhere. Books had been pulled from shelves and ripped to pieces. A ceramic lamp, a couple of vases, and the glass top of a coffee table were shattered. The doors had been torn off the cabinet-style television set, and the screen had been smashed. Blind rage and savage strength had been at work here.

The room smelled strongly of urine . . . and of something else less pungent and less familiar. It was, perhaps, the scent of the creature responsible for the wreckage. Part of that subtler stink was the sour odor of perspiration, but something stranger was in it, too, something that simultaneously turned Loman's stomach and tightened it with fear.

To the left, a hallway led back to the bedrooms and baths. Loman kept it covered with his shotgun.

The deputies went into the foyer, which was connected to the living room by a wide archway. A closet was on the right, just inside the front door. Sholnick stood in front of it, his 20-gauge lowered. From the side Penniworth jerked open the door. The closet contained only coats.

The easy part of the search was behind them. Ahead lay the narrow hall with three doors off it, one half open and two ajar, dark rooms beyond. There was less space in which to maneuver, more places from which an assailant might attack.

Night wind soughed in the eaves. It fluted across a rain gutter, producing a low, mournful note.

Loman had never been the kind of leader who sent his men ahead into danger while he stayed back in a position of safety. Although he had shed pride and self-respect and a sense of duty along with most other Old People attitudes and emotions, duty was still a habit with him – in fact, less conscious than a habit, more like a reflex – and he operated as he would have done before the Change. He entered the hall first, where two doors waited on the left and one on the right. He moved swiftly to the end, to the second door on the left, which was half open; he kicked it inward, and in the light from the hall he saw a small, deserted bathroom before the door bounced off the wall and swung shut again.

Penniworth took the first room on the left. He went in and found the light switch by the time Loman reached that threshold. It was a study with a desk, worktable, two chairs, cabinets, tall bookshelves crammed full of volumes with brightly colored spines, two computers. Loman moved in and covered the closet, where Penniworth warily rolled aside first one and then the other of two mirrored doors.

Nothing.

Barry Sholnick remained in the hallway, his 20-gauge leveled at the room they hadn't investigated. When Loman and Penniworth rejoined him, Sholnick shoved that door all the way open with the barrel of his shotgun. As it swung wide, he jerked back, certain that something would fly at him from the darkness, though nothing did. He hesitated, then stepped into the doorway, fumbled with one hand for the light switch, found it, said, 'Oh, my God,' and stepped quickly back into the hall.

Looking past his deputy into a large bedroom, Loman saw a hellish thing crouched on the floor and huddled against the far wall. It was a regressive, no doubt Peyser, but it did not look as much like the regressed Jordan Coombs as Loman expected. There were similarities, yes, but not many.

Easing by Sholnick, Loman crossed the threshold. 'Peyser?'

The thing at the other end of the room blinked at him, moved its twisted mouth. In a voice that was whispery yet guttural, savage yet tortured as only the voice of an at least halfway intelligent creature could be, it said, '. . . *Peyser, Peyser, Peyser, me, Peyser, me, me . . .*'

The odor of urine was here, too, but that other scent was now the dominant one – sharp, musky.

Loman moved farther into the room. Penniworth followed. Sholnick stayed at the doorway. Loman stopped twelve feet from Peyser and Penniworth moved off to one side, his 20-gauge held ready.

When they'd cornered Jordan Coombs in the shuttered movie theater back on September fourth, he had been in an altered state somewhat resembling a gorilla with a squat and powerful body. Mike Peyser, however, had a far leaner appearance, and as he crouched against the bedroom wall, his body looked more lupine than apelike. His hips were set at an angle to his spine, preventing him from standing or sitting completely erect, and his legs seemed too short in the thighs, too long in the calves. He was covered in thick hair but not so thick that it could be called a pelt.

'. . . *Peyser, me, me, me . . .*'

Coombs's face had been partly human though mostly that of a higher primate, with a bony brow, flattened nose, and thrusting jaw to accommodate large, wickedly sharp teeth like those of a baboon. Mike Peyser's hideously transformed countenance had, instead, a hint of the wolf in it, or dog; his mouth and nose were drawn forward into a deformed snout. His massive brow *was* like that of an ape, though exaggerated, and in his bloodshot eyes, set in shadowy sockets deep beneath that bony ridge, was a look of anguish and terror that was entirely human.

Raising one hand and pointing at Loman, Peyser said, '. . . *help me, me, help, something wrong, wrong, wrong, help . . .*'

Loman stared at that mutated hand with both fear and amazement, remembering how his own hand had begun to change when he had felt the call of regression at the Fosters' place earlier in the night. Elongated fingers. Large, rough knuckles. Fierce claws instead of fingernails. Human hands in shape and degree of dexterity, they were otherwise utterly alien.

Shit, Loman thought, those hands, those *hands*. I've seen them in the movies, or at least on the TV, when we rented the cassette of *The Howling*. Rob Botin. That was the name of the special-effects artist who created the werewolf. He remembered it because Denny had been a nut about special effects before the Change. More than anything else these looked like the goddamn hands of the werewolf in *The Howling!*

Which was too crazy to contemplate. Life imitating fantasy. The fantastic made flesh. As the twentieth century rushed into its last decade, scientific and technological progress had reached some divide, where mankind's dreams of a better life often could be fulfilled but also where nightmares could be made real. Peyser was a bad, bad dream that had crawled out of the subconscious and become flesh, and now there was no escaping him by waking up; he would not disappear as did the monsters that haunted sleep.

'How can I help you?' Loman asked warily.

'Shoot him,' Penniworth said.

Loman responded sharply: 'No!'

Peyser raised both of his tine-fingered hands and looked at them for a moment, as if seeing them for the first time. A groan issued from him, then a thin and miserable wail. '. . . *change, can't change, can't, tried, want, need, want, want, can't, tried, can't . . .*'

From the doorway Sholnick said, 'My God, he's stuck like that, he's trapped. I thought the regressives could change back at will.'

'They can,' Loman said.

'*He* can't,' Sholnick said.

'That's what he said,' Penniworth agreed, his voice quick and nervous. 'He said he can't change.'

Loman said, 'Maybe, maybe not. But the other regressives can change, because if they couldn't, then we'd have found all of them by now. They retreat from their altered state and then walk among us.'

Peyser seemed oblivious of them. He was staring at his hands, mewling in the back of his throat as if what he saw terrified him.

Then the hands began to change.

'You see,' Loman said.

Loman had never witnessed such a transformation; he was gripped by curiosity, wonder, and terror. The claws receded. The flesh was suddenly as malleable as soft wax: It bulged, blistered, pulsed not with the rhythmic flow of blood in arteries but strangely, obscenely; it assumed new form, as if an invisible sculptor were at work on it. Loman heard bones crunching, splintering, as they were broken down and remade; the flesh melted and resolidified with a sickening, wet sound. The hands became nearly human. Then the wrists and forearms began to lose some of their rawboned lupine quality. In Peyser's face were indications that the human spirit was struggling to banish the savage that was now in control; the features of a predator began to give way to a gentler and more civilized mien. It was as if the monstrous Peyser was only a beast's reflection in a pool of water out of which the real and human Peyser was now rising.

Though he was no scientist, no genius of microtechnology, only a policeman with a high-school education, Loman knew that this profound and rapid transformation could not be attributed solely to the New People's drastically improved metabolic processes and ability to heal themselves. No matter what great tides of hormones, enzymes, and other biological chemicals Peyser's body could now produce at will, there was no way that bone and flesh could be re-formed so dramatically in such a brief period of time. Over days or weeks, yes, but not in *seconds*. Surely it was physically impossible. Yet it was happening. Which meant that another force was at work in Mike Peyser, something more than biological processes, something mysterious and frightening.

Suddenly the transformation halted. Loman could see that Peyser was straining toward full humanity, clenching his half-human yet still wolflike jaws together and grinding his teeth, a look of desperation and iron determination in his strange eyes, but to no avail. For a moment he trembled on the edge of human form. It seemed that if he could just push the transformation one step farther, just one more small step, then he would cross a watershed after which the rest of the metamorphosis would take place almost automatically, without the strenuous exertion of will, as easily as a stream flowing downhill. But he could not reach that divide.

Penniworth made a low, strangled sound, as if he were sharing Peyser's anguish.

Loman glanced at his deputy. Penniworth's face glistened with a thin film of perspiration.

Loman realized he was perspiring too; he felt a bead trickle down his left temple. The bungalow was warm – an oil furnace kept clicking on and off – but not warm enough to wring moisture from them. This was a cold sweat of fear, but more than that. He also felt a tightness in his chest, a thickening in his throat that made it hard to swallow, and he was breathing fast, as if he'd sprinted up a hundred steps—

Letting out a thin, agonized cry, Peyser began to regress again. With the brittle splintering noise of bones being remade, with the oily-wet sound of flesh being rent and re-knit, the savage creature reasserted itself, and in moments Peyser was as he had been when they had first seen him: a hellish beast.

Hellish, yes, and a beast, but enviably powerful and with an odd, terrible beauty of its own. The forward carriage of the large head was awkward by comparison to the set of the human head, and the thing lacked the sinuous inward curve of the human spine, yet it had a dark grace of its own.

They stood in silence for a moment.

Peyser huddled on the floor, head bowed.

From the doorway, Sholnick finally said, 'My God, he *is* trapped.'

Although Mike Peyser's problem could have been related to some glitch in the technology on which conversion from Old to New Person was based, Loman suspected that Peyser still possessed the power to reshape himself, that he could become a man if he wanted to badly enough, but that he lacked the desire to be fully human again. He had become a regressive because he found that altered state appealing, so maybe he found it so much more exciting and satisfying than the human condition that now he did not truly *want* to return to a higher state.

Peyser raised his head and looked at Loman, then at Penniworth, then at Sholnick, and finally at Loman again. His horror at his condition was no longer apparent. The anguish and terror were gone from his eyes. With his twisted muzzle he seemed to smile at them, and a new wildness – both disturbing and appealing – appeared in his eyes. He raised his hands before his face again and flexed the long fingers, clicked the claws together, studying himself with what might have been wonder.

'. . . *hunt, hunt, chase, hunt, kill, blood, blood, need, need . . .*'

'How the hell can we take him alive if he doesn't want to be taken?' Penniworth's voice was peculiar, thick and slightly slurred.

Peyser dropped one hand to his genitals and scratched lightly, absent-mindedly. He looked at Loman again, then at the night pressing against the windows.

'I feel . . .' Sholnick left the sentence unfinished.

Penniworth was no more articulate: 'If we . . . well, we could . . .'

The pressure in Loman's chest had grown greater. His throat was tighter, too, and he was still sweating.

Peyser let out a soft, ululant cry as eerie as any sound Loman had ever heard, an expression of longing, yet also an animal challenge to the night, a statement of his power and his confidence in his own strength and cunning. The wail should have been harsh and unpleasant in the confines of that bedroom, but instead it stirred in Loman the same unspeakable yearning that had gripped him outside of the Fosters' house when he had heard the trio of regressives calling to one another faraway in the darkness.

Clenching his teeth so hard that his jaws ached, Loman strove to resist that unholy urge.

Peyser loosed another cry, then said, '*Run, hunt, free, free, need, free, need, come with me, come, come, need, need . . .*'

Loman realized that he was relaxing his grip on the 12-gauge. The barrel was tilting down. The muzzle was pointing at the floor instead of at Peyser.

'. . . *run, free, free, need . . .*'

From behind Loman came an unnerving, orgasmic cry of release.

He glanced back at the bedroom doorway in time to see Sholnick drop his shotgun. Subtle transformations had occurred in the deputy's hands and face. He pulled off his quilted, black uniform jacket, cast it aside, and tore open his shirt. His cheekbones and jaws dissolved and flowed forward, and his brow retreated as he sought an altered state.

• 53 •

When Harry Talbot finished telling them about the Boogeymen, Sam leaned forward on the high stool to the telescope eyepiece. He swung the instrument to the left, until he focused on the vacant lot beside Callan's, where the creatures had most recently put in an appearance.

He was not sure what he was looking for. He didn't believe that the Boogeymen would have returned to that same place at precisely this time to give him a convenient look at them. And there were no clues in the shadows and trampled grass and shrubs, where they had crouched only a few hours ago, to tell him what they might have been or on what mission they had been embarked. Maybe he was just trying to anchor the fantastic image of ape-dog-reptilian Boogeymen in the real world, tie them in his mind to that vacant lot, and thereby make them more concrete, so he could deal with them.

In any event Harry had another story besides that one. As they sat in the darkened room, as if listening to ghost stories around a burnt-out campfire, he told them how he'd seen Denver Simpson, Doc Fitz, Reese Dorn, and Paul Hawthorne overpower Ella Simpson, take her upstairs to the bedroom, and prepare to inject her with an enormous syringeful of some golden fluid.

Operating the telescope at Harry's direction, Sam was able to find and draw in tight on the Simpsons' house, on the other side of Conquistador and just north of the Catholic cemetery. All was dark and motionless.

From the bed where she still had the dog's head in her lap, Tessa said, 'All of it's got to be connected somehow: these "accidental" deaths, whatever those men were doing to Ella Simpson, and these . . . Boogeymen.'

'Yes, it's tied together,' Sam agreed. 'And the knot is New Wave Microtechnology.'

He told them what he had uncovered while working with the VDT in the patrol car behind the municipal building.

'Moonhawk?' Tessa wondered. 'Conversions? What on earth are they converting people into?'

'I don't know.'

'Surely not into . . . these Boogeymen?'

'No, I don't see the purpose of *that*, and besides, from what I turned up, I gather almost two thousand people in town have been . . . given this treatment, put through this change, whatever the hell it is. If there were that many of Harry's Boogeymen running loose, they'd be everywhere; the town would be crawling with them, like a zoo in the Twilight Zone.'

'Two thousand,' Harry said. 'That's two-thirds of the town.'

'And the rest by midnight,' Sam said, 'just under twenty-one hours from now.'

'Me, too, I guess?' Harry asked.

'Yeah. I looked you up on their lists. You're scheduled for conversion in the final stage, between six o'clock this coming evening and midnight. So we've got about fourteen and a half hours before they come looking for you.'

'This is nuts,' Tessa said.

'Yeah,' Sam agreed. 'Totally nuts.'

'It can't be happening,' Harry said. 'But if it isn't happening, then why's the hair standing up on the back of my neck?'

• 54 •

'Sholnick!'

Throwing aside his uniform shirt, kicking off his shoes, frantic to strip out of all his clothes and complete his regression, Barry Sholnick ignored Loman.

'Barry, stop, for God's sake, don't let this happen,' Penniworth said urgently. He was pale and shaking. He glanced from Sholnick to Peyser and back again, and Loman suspected that Penniworth felt the same degenerate urge to which Sholnick had surrendered himself.

'. . . *run free, hunt, blood, blood, need . . .*'

Peyser's insidious chant was like a spike through Loman's head, and he wanted it to stop. No, truthfully, it wasn't like a spike splitting his skull, because it wasn't at all painful and was, in fact, thrilling and strangely melodic, reaching deep into him, piercing him not like a shaft of steel but like music. *That* was why he wanted it to stop: because it appealed to him, enticed him; it made him want to shed his responsibilities and concerns, retreat from the too-complex life of the intellect to an existence based strictly on feelings, on physical pleasures, a world whose boundaries were defined by sex and food and the thrill of the hunt, a world where disputes were settled and needs were met strictly by the application of muscle, where he'd never have to think again or worry or care.

'. . . *need, need, need, need, need, kill . . .*'

Sholnick's body bent forward as his spine re-formed. His back lost the concave curvature distinctive of the human form. His skin appeared to be giving way to scales—

'. . . *come, quick, quick, the hunt, blood, blood . . .*'

—and as Sholnick's face was reshaped, his mouth split impossibly wide, opening nearly to each ear, like the mouth of some ever-grinning reptile.

The pressure in Loman's chest was growing greater by the second. He was hot, sweltering, but the heat came from within him, as if his metabolism was racing at a thousand times ordinary speed, readying him for transformation. 'No.' Sweat streamed from him. 'No!' He felt as if the room were a cauldron in which he would be reduced to his essence; he could almost feel his flesh beginning to melt.

Penniworth was saying, 'I want, I want, I want, want,' but he was vigorously shaking his head, trying to deny what he wanted. He was crying and trembling and sheet-white.

Peyser rose from his crouch and stepped away from the wall. He moved sinuously, swiftly, and although he could not stand entirely erect in his altered state, he was taller than Loman, simultaneously a frightening and seductive figure.

Sholnick shrieked.

Peyser bared his fierce teeth and hissed at Loman as if to say, *Either join us or die.*

With a cry composed partly of despair and partly of joy, Neil Penniworth dropped his 20-gauge and put his hands to his face. As if that contact had exerted an alchemical reaction, both his hands and face began to change.

Heat *exploded* in Loman, and he shouted wordlessly, but without the joy that Penniworth had expressed and without Sholnick's orgasmic cry. While he still had control of himself, he raised the shotgun and squeezed off a round point-blank at Peyser.

The blast took the regressive in the chest, blowing him backwards against the bedroom wall in a tremendous spray of blood. Peyser went down, squealing, gasping for breath, wriggling on the floor like a half-stomped bug, but he was not dead. Maybe his heart and lungs had not sustained sufficient damage. If oxygen was still being conveyed to his blood and if blood was still being pumped throughout his body, he was already repairing the damage; his invulnerability was in some ways even greater than the supernatural imperviousness of a werewolf, for he could not be easily killed even with a *silver* bullet; in a moment he would be up, strong as ever.

Wave after wave of heat, each markedly hotter than the one before it, washed through Loman. He felt pressure from within, not only in his chest but in every part of his body now. He had only seconds left in which his mind would be clear enough for him to act and his will strong enough to resist. He scuttled to Peyser, shoved the muzzle of the shotgun against the writhing regressive's chest, and pumped another round into him.

The heart *had* to have been pulverized by that round. The body leaped off the floor as the load tore through it. Peyser's monstrous face contorted, then froze with his eyes open and sightless, his lips peeled back from his inhumanly large, sharp, hooked teeth.

Someone screamed behind Loman.

Turning, he saw the Sholnick-thing coming for him. He fired a third round, then a fourth, hitting Sholnick in the chest and stomach.

The deputy went down hard, and began to crawl toward the hall, away from Loman.

Neil Penniworth was curled in the fetal position on the floor by the foot of the bed. He was chanting but not about blood and needs and being free; he was chanting his mother's name, over and over, as if it were a verbal talisman to protect him from the evil that wanted to claim him.

Loman's heart was pounding so hard that the sound of it seemed to have an external source, as if someone were thumping timpani in another room of the house. He was half-convinced that he could feel his entire body throbbing with his pulse, and that with each throb he was changing in some subtle yet hideous way.

Stepping in behind Sholnick, standing over him, Loman rammed the muzzle of the shotgun against the regressive's back, about where he thought the heart would be, and pulled the trigger. Sholnick let out a shrill scream when he felt the muzzle touch him, but he was too weak to roll over and grab the gun away from Loman. The scream was cut off forever by the blast.

The room steamed with blood. That complex scent was so sweet and compelling that it took the place of Peyser's seductive chanting, inducing Loman to regress.

He leaned against the dresser and squeezed his eyes shut, trying to establish a firmer grip on himself. He clung to the shotgun with both hands, clasping it tightly, not for its defensive value – it held no more rounds – but because it was an expertly crafted weapon, which was to say that it was a *tool*, an artifact of civilization, a reminder that he was a man, at the pinnacle of evolution, and that he must not succumb to the temptation to cast away all his tools and knowledge in exchange for the more primal pleasures and satisfactions of a beast.

But the blood smell was strong and so alluring . . .

Desperately trying to impress himself with all that would be lost in this surrender, he thought of Grace, his wife, and remembered how much he once had loved her. But he was beyond love now, as were all of the New People. Thoughts of Grace could not save him. Indeed, images of their recent, bestial rutting flashed through his mind, and she was not Grace to him any more; she was simply *female*, and the recollection of their savage coupling excited him and drew him closer to the vortex of regression.

The intense desire to degenerate made him feel as though he were in a whirlpool, being sucked down, down, and he thought that this was how the nascent werewolf was supposed to feel when he looked up into the night sky and

saw, ascending at the horizon, a full moon. The conflict raged within him:
... blood ...
... freedom ...
—*no. Mind, knowledge*—
... hunt ...
... Kill ...
—*no. Explore, learn*—
... eat ...
... run ...
... hunt ...
... fuck ...
... kill ...
—*no, no! Music, art, language*—
His turmoil grew.

He was trying to resist the siren call of savagery with reason, but that did not seem to be working, so he thought of Denny, his son. He must hold fast to his humanity if only for Denny's sake. He tried to summon the love he had once known for his boy, tried to let that love rebuild in him until he could shout of it, but there was only a whisper of remembered emotion deep in the darkness of his mind. His ability to love had receded from him in much the way that matter had receded from the center of existence following the Big Bang that created the universe; his love for Denny was now so faraway and long ago that it was like a star at the outer edge of the universe, its light only dimly perceived, with little power to illuminate and no power to warm. Yet even that glimmer of feeling was something around which to build an image of himself as human, human, first and always a man, not some thing that ran on all fours or with its knuckles dragging the ground, but a man, a man.

His stentorian breathing slowed a little. His heartbeat fell from an impossibly rapid *dubdubdubdubdubdubdub* to perhaps a hundred or a hundred and twenty beats a minute, still fast, as if he were running, but better. His head cleared, too, though not entirely, because the scent of blood was an inescapable perfume.

He pushed away from the dresser and staggered to Penniworth.

The deputy was still curled in the tightest fetal position that a grown man could achieve. Traces of the beast were in his hands and face, but he was considerably more human than not. The chanting of his mother's name seemed to be working nearly as well as the thread-thin lifeline of love had worked for Loman.

Letting go of his shotgun with one cramped hand, Loman reached down to Penniworth and took him by the arm. 'Come on, let's get out of here, boy, let's get away from this smell.'

Penniworth understood and got laboriously to his feet. He leaned against Loman and allowed himself to be led out of the room, away from the two dead regressives, along the hallway into the living room.

Here, the stink of urine completely smothered what trace of the blood scent might have ridden the currents of air outward from the bedroom. That was better. It was not a foul odor at all, as it had seemed previously, but acidic and cleansing.

Loman settled Penniworth in an armchair, the only upholstered item in the room that had not been torn to pieces.

'You going to be okay?'

Penniworth looked up at him, hesitated, then nodded. All signs of the beast had vanished from his hands and countenance, though his flesh was strangely lumpy, still in transition. His face appeared to be swollen with a disabling case of the hives, large round lumps from forehead to chin and ear to ear, and there were long, diagonal welts, too, that burned an angry red against his pale skin. However, even as Loman watched, those phenomena faded, and Neil Penniworth laid full claim to his humanity. To his *physical* humanity, at least.

'You sure?' Loman asked.

'Yes.'

'Stay right there.'

'Yes.'

Loman went into the foyer and opened the front door. The deputy standing guard outside was so tense because of all the shooting and screaming in the house that he almost fired on his chief before he realized who it was.

'What the hell?' the deputy said.

'Get on the computer link to Shaddack,' Loman said. 'He has to come out here now. Right now. I have to see him *now.*'

• 55 •

Sam drew the heavy blue drapes, and Harry turned on one bedside lamp. Soft as it was, too dim to chase away more than half the shadows, the light nevertheless stung Tessa's eyes, which were already tired and bloodshot.

For the first time she actually saw the room. It was sparely furnished: the stool; the tall table beside the stool; the telescope; a long modern-oriental, black lacquered dresser; a pair of matching nightstands; a small refrigerator in one corner; and an adjustable hospital-type bed, queen-size, without a spread but with plenty of pillows and brightly colored sheets patterned with splashes and streaks and spots of red, orange, purple, green, yellow, blue, and black, like a giant canvas painted by a demented and color-blind abstract artist.

Harry saw her and Sam's reaction to the sheets and said, 'Now, *that's* a story, but first you've got to know the background. My housekeeper, Mrs. Hunsbok, comes in once a week, and she does most of my shopping for me. But I send Moose on errands every day, if only to pick up a newspaper. He wears this set of . . . well, sort of saddlebags strapped around him, one hanging on each side. I put a note and some money in the bags, and he goes to the local convenience store – it's the only place he'll go when he's wearing the bags, unless I'm with him. The clerk at the little grocery, Jimmy Ramis, knows me real well. Jimmy reads the note, puts a quart of milk or some candy bars or whatever I want in the saddlebags, puts the change in there, too, and Moose brings it all back to me. He's a good, reliable service dog, the best. They train them real well at Canine Companions for Independence. Moose never chases after a cat with my newspaper and fresh milk in his backpack.'

The dog raised his head off Tessa's lap, panted and grinned, as if acknowledging the praise.

'One day he came home with a few items I'd sent him for, and he also had a set of these sheets and pillow cases. I call up Jimmy Ramis, see, and ask him what's the idea, and Jimmy says he doesn't know what I'm talking about, says he never saw any such sheets. Now, Jimmy's dad owns the convenience store, and he also owns Surplus Outlet, out on the country road. He gets all kinds of discontinued merchandise and stuff that didn't sell as well as the manufacturers expected, picks it up at ten cents on the dollar sometimes, and I figure these sheets were something he was having trouble unloading even at Surplus Outlet. Jimmy no doubt saw them, thought they were pretty silly, and decided to have some fun with me. But on the phone Jimmy says, "Harry, if I knew anything about the sheets, I'd tell you, but I don't." And I says, "You trying to make me believe Moose went and bought them all on his own, with his own money?" And Jimmy says, "Well, no, I'd guess he shoplifted them somewhere," and I says, "And just how did he manage to stuff them in his own backpack so neat?" and Jimmy says, "I don't know, Harry, but that there is one hell of a clever dog – though it sounds like he doesn't have good taste." '

Tessa saw how Harry relished the story, and she also saw why he was so pleased by it. For one thing the dog was child and brother and friend, all rolled into one, and Harry was proud that people thought of Moose as clever. More important, Jimmy's little joke made Harry a part of his community, not just a homebound invalid but a participant in the life of his town. His lonely days were marked by too few such incidents.

'And you *are* a clever dog,' Tessa told Moose.

Harry said, 'Anyway, I decided to have Mrs. Hunsbok put them on the bed next time she came, as a joke, but then I sort of liked them.'

After drawing the drapes at the second window, Sam returned to the stool, sat down, swiveled to face Harry, and said, 'They're the loudest sheets I've ever seen. Don't they keep you awake at night?'

Harry smiled. 'Nothing can keep me awake. I sleep like a baby. What keeps people awake is worry about the future, about what might happen to them. But the worst has *already* happened to me. Or they lie awake thinking about the past, about what might have been, but I don't do that because I just don't dare.' His smile faded as he spoke, 'So now what? What do we do next?'

Gently removing Moose's head from her lap, standing, and brushing a few dog hairs from her jeans, Tessa said, 'Well, the phones aren't working, so Sam can't call the Bureau, and if we walk out of town we risk an encounter with Watkins's patrols or these Boogeymen. Unless you know a ham radio enthusiast who'd let us use his set to get a message relayed, then so as far as I can see, we've got to drive out.'

'Roadblocks, remember,' Harry said.

She said, 'Well, I figure we'll have to drive out in a truck, something big and mean, ram straight through the damn roadblock, make it to the highway, then out of their jurisdiction. Even if we do get chased down by county cops, that's fine, because Sam can get them to call the Bureau, verify his assignment, then they'll be on our side.'

'Who's the federal agent here, anyway?' Sam asked.

Tessa felt herself blush. 'Sorry. See, a documentary filmmaker is almost always her own producer, sometimes producer and director and writer too. That means if the art part of it is going to work, the business part of it has to work first, so I'm used to doing a lot of planning, logistics. Didn't mean to step on your toes.'

'Step on them any time.'

Sam smiled, and she liked him when he smiled. She realized she was even attracted to him a little. He was neither handsome nor ugly, and not what most people meant by 'plain,' either. He was rather . . . nondescript but pleasant-looking. She sensed a darkness in him, something deeper than his current worries about events in Moonlight Cove – maybe sadness at some loss, maybe long-repressed anger related to some injustice he had suffered, maybe a general pessimism arising from too much contact in his work with the worst elements of society. But when he smiled he was transformed.

'You really going to smash out in a truck?' Harry asked.

'Maybe as a last resort,' Sam said. 'But we'd have to find a rig big enough and then steal it, and that's an operation in itself. Besides, they might have riot guns at the roadblock, loaded with magnum rounds, maybe automatic weapons. I wouldn't want to run that kind of flak even in a Mack truck. You can ride into hell in a tank, but the devil will get his hands on you anyway, so it's best not to go there in the first place.'

'So where *do* we go?' Tessa asked.

'To sleep,' Sam said. 'There's a way out of this, a way to get through to the Bureau. I can sort of see it out of the corner of my eye, but when I try to look directly at it, it goes away, and that's because I'm tired. I need a couple of hours in the sack to get fresh and think straight.'

Tessa was exhausted, too, though after what had happened at Cove Lodge, she was somewhat surprised that she not only could sleep but wanted to. As she'd stood in her motel room, listening to the screams of the dying and the savage shrieks of the killers, she wouldn't have thought she'd ever sleep again.

• 56 •

Shaddack arrived at Peyser's at five minutes till four in the morning. He drove his charcoal-gray van with heavily tinted windows, rather than his Mercedes, because a computer terminal was mounted on the console of the van, between the seats, where the manufacturer had originally intended to provide a built-in cooler. As eventful as the night had been thus far, it seemed a good idea to stay within reach of the data link that, like a spider, spun a silken web enmeshing all of Moonlight Cove. He parked on the wide shoulder of the two-lane rural blacktop, directly in front of the house.

As Shaddack walked across the yard to the front porch, distant rumbling rolled along the Pacific horizon. The hard wind that had harried the fog eastward had also brought a storm in from the west. During the past couple of hours, churning clouds had clothed the heavens, shrouding the naked stars that had burned briefly between the passing of the mist and the coming of the thunderheads. Now the night was very dark and deep. He shivered inside his cashmere topcoat, under which he still wore a sweat suit.

A couple of deputies were sitting in black-and-whites in the driveway. They watched him, pale faces beyond dusty car windows, and he liked to think they regarded him with fear and reverence, for he was in a sense their maker.

Loman Watkins was waiting for him in the front room. The place had been wrecked. Neil Penniworth sat on the only undamaged piece of furniture; he looked badly shaken and could not meet Shaddack's gaze. Watkins was pacing. A few spatters of blood marked his uniform, but he looked unhurt; if he'd sustained injuries, they had been minor and had already healed. More likely, the blood belonged to someone else.

'What happened here?' Shaddack asked.

Ignoring the question, Watkins spoke to his officer: 'Go out to the car, Neil. Stay close to the other men.'

'Yes, sir,' Penniworth said. He was huddled in his chair, bent forward, looking down at his shoes.

'You'll be okay, Neil.'

'I think so.'

'It wasn't a question. It was a statement: You'll be okay. You have enough strength to resist. You've proven that already.'

Penniworth nodded, got up, and headed for the door.

Shaddack said, 'What's this all about?'

Turning toward the hallway at the other end of the room, Watkins said, 'Come with me.' His voice was as cold and hard as ice, informed by fear and anger, but noticeably devoid of the grudging respect with which he had spoken to Shaddack ever since he had been converted in August.

Displeased by that change in Watkins, uneasy, Shaddack frowned and followed him down the hall.

The cop stopped at a closed door, turned to Shaddack. 'You told me that what you've done to us is improve our biological efficiency by injecting us with these . . . these biochips.'

'A misnomer, really. They're not chips at all, but incredibly small microspheres.'

In spite of the regressives and a few other problems that had developed with the Moonhawk Project, Shaddack's pride of achievement was undiminished. Glitches could be fixed. Bugs could be worked out of the system. He was still *the* genius of his age; he not only felt this to be true, but knew it as well as he knew in which direction to look for the rising sun each morning.

Genius . . .

The ordinary silicon microchip that made possible the computer revolution had been the size of a fingernail, and had contained one million circuits etched onto it by photo lithography. The smallest circuits on the chip had been one-hundredth as wide as a human hair. Breakthroughs in X-ray lithography, using giant particle accelerators called synchrotrons, eventually made possible the imprinting of one *billion* circuits on a chip, with features as small as one-thousandth the width of a human hair. Shrinking dimensions was the primary way to gain computer speed, improving both function and capabilities.

The microspheres developed by New Wave were one four-thousandth the size of a microchip. Each was imprinted with a quarter-million circuits. This had been achieved by the application of a radically new form of X-ray lithography that made it possible to etch circuits on amazingly small surfaces *and* without having to hold those surfaces perfectly still.

Conversion of Old People into New People began with the injection of hundreds of thousands of those microspheres, in solution, into the bloodstream. They were biologically interactive in function, but the material itself was biologically inert, so the immune system wasn't triggered. There were different kinds of microspheres. Some were heart-tropic, meaning they moved through the veins to the heart and took up residence there, attaching themselves to the walls of the blood vessels that serviced the cardiac muscle. Some spheres were liver-tropic, lung-tropic, kidney-tropic, bowel-tropic, brain-tropic, and so on. They settled in clusters at those sites and were designed in such a way that, when touching, their circuits linked.

Those clusters, spread throughout the body, eventually provided about fifty billion usable circuits that had the potential for data processing, considerably more than in the largest supercomputers of the 1980s. In a sense, by injection, a super-supercomputer had been put inside the human body.

Moonlight Cove and the surrounding area were constantly bathed in micro-wave transmissions from dishes on top of the main building at New Wave. A fraction of those transmissions involved the police computer system, and another fraction could be drawn upon to power-up the microspheres inside each of the New People.

A small number of spheres were of a different material and served as transducers and power distributors. When one of the Old People received his third injection of microspheres, the power spheres at once drew on those microwave transmissions, converting them into electrical current and distributing it throughout the network. The amount of current needed to operate the system was exceedingly small.

Other specialized spheres in each cluster were memory units. Some of those carried the program that would operate the system; that program was loaded the moment power entered the network.

To Watkins, Shaddack said, 'Long ago I became convinced that the basic problem with the human animal is its extremely emotional nature. I've freed you from that burden. In so doing, I've made you not only mentally healthier but physically healthier as well.'

'How? I know so little of how the Change is effected.'

'You're a cybernetic organism now – that is, part man and part machine – but you don't *need* to understand it, Loman. You use a telephone, yet you've no idea of how to build a phone system from scratch. You don't know how a computer works, yet you can use one. And you don't have to know how the computer *in* you works in order to use it, either.'

Watkins's eyes were clouded with fear. 'Do I use it . . . or does it use me?'

'Of course, it doesn't use you.'

'Of course . . .'

Shaddack wondered what had happened here tonight to have put Watkins in such a state of extreme anxiety. He was more curious than ever to see what was in the bedroom at the threshold of which they had halted. But he was acutely aware that Watkins was in a dangerously excited state and that it was necessary, if frustrating, to take the time to calm his fears.

'Loman, the clustered microspheres within you don't constitute a *mind*. The system's not in any way truly intelligent. It's a servant, your servant. It frees you from toxic emotions.'

Strong emotions – hatred, love, envy, jealousy, the whole long list of human sensibilities – regularly destabilized the biological functions of the body. Medi-cal researchers had proved that different emotions stimulated the production of different brain chemicals, and that those chemicals in turn induced the various organs and tissues of the body to either increase or reduce or alter their function in a less than productive fashion. Shaddack was convinced that a man whose body was ruled by his emotions could not be a totally healthy man and *never* entirely clear-thinking.

The microsphere computer within each of the New People monitored every organ in the body. When it detected the production of various amino-acid compounds and other chemical substances that were produced in response to strong emotion, it used electrical stimuli to override the brain and other organs, shutting off the flow, thus eliminating the physical consequences of an emotion if not the emotion itself. At the same time the microsphere computer stimulated the copious production of other compounds known to repress those same emotions, thereby treating not only the cause but the effect.

'I've released you from all emotions but fear,' Shaddack said, 'which is necessary for self-preservation. Now that the chemistry of your body is no longer undergoing wild swings, you'll think more clearly.'

'So far as I've noticed, I've not suddenly become a genius.'

'Well, you might not notice a greater mental acuity yet, but in time you will.'

'When?'

'When your body is fully purged of the residue of a lifetime of emotional pollution. Meanwhile, your interior computer' – he lightly tapped Watkins's chest – 'is also programmed to use complex electrical stimuli to induce the body to create wholly new amino-acid compounds that keep your blood vessels scoured and free of plaque and clots, kill cancerous cells the moment they appear, and perform a double score of other chores, keeping you far healthier than ordinary men, no doubt dramatically lengthening your life-span.'

Shaddack had expected the healing process to be accelerated in New People, but he had been surprised at the almost miraculous speed with which their wounds closed. He still could not entirely understand how new tissue could be formed so quickly, and his current work on Moonhawk was focused on discovering an explanation for that effect. The healing was not accomplished without a price, for the metabolism was fantastically accelerated; stored body fat was burned prodigiously in order to close a wound in seconds or minutes, leaving the healed man pounds lighter, sweat-drenched, and fiercely hungry.

Watkins frowned and wiped one shaky hand across his sweaty face. 'I can maybe see that healing would be speeded up, but what gives us the ability to so completely reshape ourselves, to regress to another form? Surely not even buckets of these biological chemicals could tear down our bodies and rebuild them in just a minute or two. How can that be?'

For a moment Shaddack met the other man's gaze, then looked away, coughed, and said, 'Listen, I can explain all of this to you later. Right now I want to see Peyser. I hope you were able to restrain him without doing much damage.'

As Shaddack reached toward the door to push it open, Watkins seized his wrist, staying his hand. Shaddack was shocked. He did not allow himself to be touched.

'Take your hand off me.'

'How can the body be so suddenly reshaped?'

'I told you, we'll discuss it later.'

'Now.' Watkins's determination was so strong that it carved deep lines in his face. 'Now. I'm so scared I can't think straight. I can't function at this level of fear, Shaddack. Look at me. I'm shaking. I feel like I'm going to blow apart. A million pieces. You don't know what happened here tonight, or you'd feel the same way. I've got to know: How can our bodies change so suddenly?'

Shaddack hesitated. 'I'm working on that.'

Surprised, Watkins let go of his wrist and said, 'You . . . you mean you don't know?'

'It's an unexpected effect. I'm beginning to understand it' – which was a lie – 'but I've got a lot more work to do.' First he had to understand the New People's phenomenal healing powers, which were no doubt an aspect of the same process that allowed them to completely metamorphose into subhuman forms.

'You subjected us to this without knowing what all it might do to us?'

'I knew it would be a benefit, a great gift,' Shaddack said impatiently. 'No scientist can ever predict all the side effects. He has to proceed with the confidence that whatever side effects arise will not outweigh the benefits.'

'But they *do* outweigh the benefits,' Watkins said, as close to anger as a New Man could get. 'My God, how could you have done this to us?'

'I did this *for* you.'

Watkins stared at him, then pushed open the bedroom door and said, 'Have a look.'

Shaddack stepped into the room, where the carpet was damp – and some of the walls festooned – with blood. He grimaced at the stink. He found all biological odors unusually repellent, perhaps because they were a reminder that human beings were far less efficient and clean than machines. After stopping at the first corpse – which lay facedown near the door – and studying it, he looked across the room at the second body. 'Two of them? Two regressives, and you killed *both?* Two chances to study the psychology of these degenerates, and you threw away both opportunities?'

Watkins was unbowed by the criticism. 'It was a life-or-death situation here. It couldn't have been handled differently.'

He seemed angry to a degree inconsistent with the personality of a New Man, though perhaps the emotion sustaining his icy demeanor was less rage than fear. Fear was acceptable.

'Peyser was regressed when we got here,' Watkins continued. 'We searched the house, confronted him in this room.'

As Watkins described that confrontation in detail, Shaddack was gripped by an apprehension that he tried not to reveal and to which he did not even want to admit. When he spoke he let only anger touch his voice, not fear: 'You're telling me that your men, both Sholnick and Penniworth, are regressives, that even *you* are a regressive?'

'Sholnick was a regressive, yes. In my book Penniworth isn't – not yet anyway – because he successfully resisted the urge. Just as I resisted it.' Watkins boldly maintained eye contact, not once glancing away, which further disturbed Shaddack. 'What I'm telling you is the same thing I told you in so many words a few hours ago at your place: Each of us, every damned one of us, is potentially a regressive. It's not a rare sickness among the New People. It's in all of us. You've not created new and better men any more than Hitler's policies of genetic breeding could've created a master race. You're not God; you're Dr. Moreau.'

'You will not speak to me like this,' Shaddack said, wondering who this

Moreau was. The name was vaguely familiar, but he could not place it. 'When you talk to me, I'd suggest you remember who I am.'

Watkins lowered his voice, perhaps realizing anew that Shaddack could extinguish the New People almost as easily as snuffing out a candle. But he continued to speak forcefully and with too little respect. 'You still haven't responded to the worst of this news.'

'And what's that?'

'Didn't you hear me? I said that Peyser was *stuck*. He couldn't remake himself.'

'I doubt very much that he was trapped in an altered state. New Men have complete control of their bodies, more control than I ever anticipated. If he could not return to human form, that was strictly a psychological block. He didn't really want to return.'

For a moment Watkins stared at him, then shook his head and said, 'You aren't really that dense, are you? *It's the same thing.* Hell, it doesn't matter whether something went wrong with the microsphere network inside him or whether it was strictly psychological. Either way, the effect was the same, the result was the same: He was stuck, trapped, locked into that degenerate form.'

'You will not speak to me like this,' Shaddack repeated firmly, as if repetition of the command would work the same way it did when training a dog.

For all their physiological superiority and potential for mental superiority, New People were still dismayingly *people*, and to the degree they were people, they were that much less effective machines. With a computer, you only had to program a command once. The computer retained it and acted upon it always. Shaddack wondered if he would ever be able to perfect the New People to the point at which future generations functioned as smoothly and reliably as the average IBM PC.

Damp with sweat, pale, his eyes strange and haunted, Watkins was an intimidating figure. When the cop took two steps to reduce the gap between them, Shaddack was afraid and wanted to retreat, but he held his ground and continued to meet Watkins's eyes the way he would have defiantly met those of a dangerous German shepherd if he had been cornered by one.

'Look at Sholnick,' Watkins said, indicating the corpse at their feet. He used the toe of his shoe to turn the dead man over.

Even riddled with shotgun pellets and soaked in blood, Sholnick's bizarre mutation was unmistakable. His sightlessly staring eyes were perhaps the most frightful thing about him: yellow with black irises, not the round irises of the human eye but elongated ovals as in the eyes of a snake.

Outside, thunder rolled across the night, a louder peal than the one Shaddack had heard when he'd been crossing Peyser's front lawn.

Watkins said, 'The way you explained it to me – these degenerates undergo willful devolution.'

'That's right.'

'You said the whole history of human evolution is carried in our genes, that we still have in us traces of what the species once was, and that the regressives somehow tap that genetic material and devolve into creatures somewhere farther back on the evolutionary ladder.'

'What's your point?'

'That explanation made some sort of crazy sense when we trapped Coombs in the theater and got a good look at him back in September. He was more ape than man, something in between.'

'It doesn't make crazy sense; it makes perfect sense.'

'But, Jesus, look at Sholnick. *Look* at him! When I gunned him down, he'd halfway transformed himself into some goddamned creature that's part man, part . . . hell, I don't know, part lizard or snake. You telling me that we evolved from reptiles, we're carrying lizard genes from ten million years ago?'

Shaddack thrust both hands in his coat pockets lest they betray his apprehension with a nervous gesture or tremble. 'The first life on earth was in the sea, then something crawled onto the land – a fish with rudimentary legs – and the fish evolved into the early reptiles, and along the way mammals split off. If we don't contain actual fragments of the genetic material of those very early reptiles – and I believe we do – then at least we have racial memory of that stage of evolution encoded in us in some other way we don't really understand.'

'You're jiving me, Shaddack.'

'And you're *irritating* me.'

'I don't a give damn. Come here, come with me, take a closer look at Peyser. He was a friend of yours from way back, wasn't he? Take a good, long look at what he was when he died.'

Peyser was flat on his back, naked, right leg straight in front of him, left leg bent under him at an angle, one arm flung out at his side, the other across his chest, which had been shattered by a couple of shotgun blasts. The body and the face – with its inhuman muzzle and teeth, yet vaguely recognizable as Mike Peyser – were those of a shockingly horrific freak, a dog-man, a werewolf, something that belonged in either a carnival sideshow or an old horror movie. The skin was coarse. The patchy coat of hair was wiry. The hands looked powerful, the claws sharp.

Because his fascination exceeded his disgust and fear, Shaddack pulled up his topcoat to keep the hem of it from brushing the bloody corpse, and stooped beside Peyser's body for a closer look.

Watkins hunkered down on the other side of the cadaver.

While another avalanche of thunder rumbled down the night sky, the dead man stared at the bedroom ceiling with eyes that were too human for the rest of his twisted countenance.

'You going to tell me that somewhere along the way we evolved from dogs, wolves?' Watkins asked.

Shaddack did not reply.

Watkins pressed the issue. 'You going to tell me that we've got dog genes in us that we can tap when we want to transform ourselves? Am I supposed to believe God took a rib from some prehistoric Lassie and made man from it before he took man's rib to make a woman?'

Curiously Shaddack touched one of Mike Peyser's hands, which was designed for killing as surely as was a soldier's bayonet. It felt like flesh, just cooler than that of a living man.

'This can't be explained biologically,' Watkins said, glaring at Shaddack across the corpse. 'This wolf form isn't something Peyser could dredge up from racial memory stored in his genes. So how could he change like this? It's not just your biochips at work here. It's something else . . . something stranger.'

Shaddack nodded. 'Yes.' An explanation had occurred to him, and he was excited by it. 'Something a great deal stranger . . . but perhaps I understand it.'

'So tell me. *I'd* like to understand it. Damned if I wouldn't. I'd like to understand it real well. Before it happens to me.'

'There's a theory that form is a function of consciousness.'

'Huh?'

'It holds that we are what we think we are. I'm not talking pop psychology here, that you can be what you want to be if you'll only like yourself, nothing of that sort. I mean *physically*, we may have the potential to be whatever we think we are, to override the morphic stasis dictated by our genetic heritage.'

'Gobbledegook,' Watkins said impatiently.

Shaddack stood. He put his hands in his pockets again. 'Let me put it this way: The theory says that consciousness is the greatest power in the universe, that it can bend the physical world to its desire.'

'Mind over matter.'

'Right.'

'Like some talkshow psychic bending a spoon or stopping a watch,' Watkins said.

'Those people are usually fakes, I suspect. But, yes, maybe that power is really in us. We just don't know how to tap it because for millions of years we've allowed the physical world to dominate us. By habit, by stasis, and by preference for order over chaos, we remain at the mercy of the physical world. But what we're talking about here,' he said, pointing to Sholnick and Peyser, 'is a lot more complex and exciting than bending a spoon with the mind. Peyser felt the urge to regress, for reasons I don't understand, perhaps for the sheer thrill of it—'

'For the thrill.' Watkins's voice lowered, became quiet, almost hushed, and was filled with such intense fear and mental anguish that it deepened Shaddack's chill. 'Animal power is thrilling. Animal need. You feel animal hunger, animal lust, bloodthirst – and you're drawn toward that because it seems so . . . so simple and powerful, so natural. It's freedom.'

'Freedom?'

'Freedom from responsibility, from worry, from the pressure of the civilized world, from having to *think* too much. The temptation to regress is tremendously powerful because you feel life will be so much easier and exciting then,' Watkins said, evidently speaking about what he had felt when drawn toward an altered state. 'When you become a beast, life is all sensation, just pain and pleasure, with no need to intellectualize anything. That's part of it, anyway.'

Shaddack was silent, unsettled by the passion with which Watkins – not ordinarily an expressive man – had spoken of the urge to regress.

Another detonation rocked the sky, more powerful than any before it. The first hard crack of thunder reverberated in the bedroom windows.

Mind racing, Shaddack said, 'Anyway, the important thing is that when Peyser felt this urge to become a beast, a hunter, he didn't regress along the human genetic line. Evidently, in his opinion, a wolf is the greatest of all hunters, the most desirable form for a predatory beast, so he *willed* himself to become wolflike.'

'Just like that,' Watkins said skeptically.

'Yes, just like that. Mind over matter. The metamorphosis is mostly a *mental* process. Oh, certainly, there are physical changes. But we might not be talking

complete alteration of matter . . . only of biological structures. The basic
nucleotides remain the same, but the sequence in which they're read changes
drastically. Structural genes are transformed into operator genes by a force of
will . . .'

Shaddack's voice trailed off as his excitement rose to match his fear and left
him breathless. He'd done far more than he'd hoped to do with the Moonhawk
Project. That stunning accomplishment was the source of both his sudden joy
and escalating fear: joy, because he had given men the ability to control their
physical form and, eventually, perhaps all matter, simply by the exercise of will;
fear, because he was not sure that the New People could learn to control and
properly use their power . . . or that he could continue to control them.

'The gift I've given to you – computer-assisted physiology and release from
emotion – unleashes the mind's power over matter. It allows consciousness to
dictate form.'

Watkins shook his head, clearly appalled by what Shaddack was suggesting.
'Maybe Peyser willed himself to become what he did. Maybe Sholnick willed it
too. But I'll be damned if I did. When I was overcome by the desire to change, I
fought it like an ex-addict sweating out a craving for heroin. I didn't want it. It
came over me . . . the way the force of the full moon comes over a werewolf.'

'No,' Shaddack said. 'Subconsciously, you *did* want to change, Loman, and
you no doubt partially wanted it even on a conscious level. You *must* have
wanted it to some extent because you spoke so forcefully about how attractive
regression was. You resisted using your power of mind over body only because
you found metamorphosis marginally more frightening than appealing. If you
lose some of your fear of it . . . or if an altered state becomes just a little more
appealing . . . well, then your psychological balance will shift, and you'll
remake yourself. But it won't be some outside force at work. It'll be your own
mind.'

'Then why couldn't Peyser come back?'

'As I said, and as *you* suggested, he didn't want to.'

'He was trapped.'

'Only by his own desire.'

Watkins looked down at the grotesque corpse of the regressive. 'What have
you done to us, Shaddack?'

'Haven't you grasped what I've said?'

'What have you done to us?'

'This is a great gift!'

'To have no emotions but fear?'

'That's what frees your mind and gives you the power to control your very
form,' Shaddack said excitedly. 'What I don't understand is why the regressives
have all chosen a subhuman condition. Surely you have the power within you to
undergo evolution rather than devolution, to lift yourself up from mere humanity to something higher, cleaner, purer. Perhaps you even have the power to
become a being of pure consciousness, intellect without *any* physical form.
Why have all these New People chosen to regress instead?'

Watkins raised his head, and his eyes had a half-dead look, as if they had
absorbed death from the very sight of the corpse. 'What good is it to have the
power of a god if you can't also experience the simple pleasures of a
man?'

'But you can do and experience anything you want,' Shaddack said exasperatedly.

'Not love.'

'What?'

'Not love or hate or joy or any emotion but fear.'

'But you don't *need* them. Not having them has freed you.'

'You're not thickheaded,' Watkins said, 'so I guess you don't understand because you're psychologically . . . twisted, warped.'

'You must not speak to me like—'

'I'm trying to tell you why they all choose a subhuman form over a super-human form. It's because, for a thinking creature of high intellect, there can be no pleasure separate from emotion. If you deny men emotions you deny them pleasure, so they seek an altered state in which complex emotions and pleasure *aren't* linked – the life of an unthinking beast.'

'Nonsense. You are—'

Watkins interrupted him again, sharply. 'Listen to me, for God's sake! If I remember, even Moreau listened to his creatures.'

His face was flushed now instead of pale. His eyes no longer looked half dead; a certain wildness had returned to them. He was only a step or two from Shaddack and seemed to loom over him, though he was the shorter of the two. He looked scared, badly scared – and dangerous.

He said, 'Consider sex – a basic human pleasure. For sex to be *fully* satis-fying, it has to be accompanied by love or at least some affection. To a psycho-logically damaged man, sex can still be good if it's linked to hate or pride of domination; even negative emotions can make the act pleasurable for a twisted man. But done with *no emotion at all*, it's pointless, stupid, just the breeding impulse of an animal, just the rhythmic function of a machine.'

A flash of lightning burned the night and blazed briefly on the bedroom windows, followed by a crash of thunder that seemed to shake the house. That celestial flicker was, for an instant, brighter than the soft glow of the single bedroom lamp.

In that queer light Shaddack thought he saw something happen to Loman Watkins's face . . . a *shift* in the relationship of the features. But when the lightning passed, Watkins looked quite like himself, so it must have been Shaddack's imagination.

Continuing to speak with great force, with the passion of stark fear, Watkins said, 'It's not just sex, either. The same goes for other physical pleasures. Eating, for example. Yeah, I still taste a piece of chocolate when I eat it. But the taste gives me only a tiny fraction of the satisfaction that it did before I was converted. Haven't you noticed?'

Shaddack did not reply, and he hoped that nothing in his demeanor would reveal that he had not undergone conversion himself. He was, of course, wait-ing until the process had been more highly refined through additional genera-tions of the New People. But he suspected Watkins would not react well to the discovery that their maker had not chosen to submit himself to the blessing that he had bestowed on them.

Watkins said, 'And do you know why there's less satisfaction? Before conver-sion, when we ate chocolate, the taste had thousands of associations for us. When we ate it, we subconsciously remembered the first time we ate it and all the times in between, and subconsciously we remembered how often that taste was associated with holidays and celebrations of all kinds, and because of all that the taste made us *feel good*. But now when I eat chocolate, it's just a taste, a good taste, but it doesn't make me feel good any more. I know it should; I remember that such a thing as "feeling good" was a part of it once, but not now. The taste of chocolate doesn't generate emotional echoes any more. It's an empty sensation, its richness has been stolen from me. The richness of everything but fear has been stolen from me, and everything is gray now – strange, gray, drab – as if I'm half dead.'

The left side of Watkins's head bulged. His cheekbone enlarged. That ear began to change shape and draw toward a point.

Stunned, Shaddack backed away from him.

Watkins followed, raising his voice, speaking with a slight slur but with no less force, not with real anger but with fear and an unsettling touch of savagery: 'Why the hell would any of us want to evolve to some higher form with even fewer pleasures of the body and the heart? Intellectual pleasures aren't enough, Shaddack. Life is more than that. A life that's *only* intellectual isn't tolerable.'

As Watkins's brow gradually sloped backward, slowly melting away like a wall of snow in the sun, heavier accretions of bone began to build up around his eyes.

Shaddack backed into the dresser.

Still approaching, Watkins said, 'Jesus! Don't you see yet? Even a man confined to a hospital bed, paralyzed from the neck down, has more in his life than intellectual interests; no one's stolen his emotions from him; no one's reduced him to fear and pure intellect. We need pleasure, Shaddack, pleasure, pleasure. Life without it is terrifying. Pleasure makes life worth living.'

'Stop.'

'You've made it impossible for us to experience the pleasurable release of emotion, so we can't fully experience pleasures of the flesh, either, because we're creatures of a high order and need the emotional aspect to truly enjoy physical pleasure. It's both or neither in human beings.'

Watkins's hands, fisted at his sides, were becoming larger, with swollen knuckles and tobacco-brown, pointed nails.

'You're transforming,' Shaddack said.

Ignoring him, speaking more thickly as the shape of his mouth began to change subtly, Watkins said, 'So we revert to a savage, altered state. We retreat from our intellect. In the cloak of the beast, our *only* pleasure is the pleasure of the flesh, the flesh, flesh . . . but at least we're no longer aware of what we've lost, so the pleasure remains intense, so intense, deep and sweet, sweet, so sweet. You've made . . . made our lives intolerable, gray and dead, dead, all dead, dead . . . so we have to devolve in mind and in body . . . to find a worthwhile existence. We . . . we have to flee . . . from the horrible restrictions of this narrowed life . . . this very narrowed life you've given us. Men aren't machines. Men . . . men . . . men are not *machines!*'

'You're regressing. For God's sake, Loman!'

Watkins halted and seemed disoriented. Then he shook his head, as if to cast off his confusion as he might a veil. He raised his hands, looked at them, and cried out in terror. He glanced past Shaddack, at the dresser mirror, and his cry grew louder, shriller.

Abruptly Shaddack was acutely aware of the stench of blood, to which he had somewhat accustomed himself. Watkins must be even more affected by it, though not repulsed, no, not in the least repulsed, but excited.

Lightning flashed and thunder shook the night again, and rain suddenly came down in torrents, beating on the windows and drumming on the roof.

Watkins looked from the mirror to Shaddack, raised a hand as if to strike him, then turned and staggered out of the room, into the hall, away from the ripe stink of blood. Out there he dropped to his knees, then onto his side. He curled into a ball, shaking violently, gagging, whimpering, snarling, and intermittently chanting, 'No, no, no, no.'

• 57 •

When he pulled back from the brink and felt in control of himself once more, Loman sat up and leaned against the wall. He was wet with perspiration again, and shaky with hunger. The partial transformation and the energy expended to keep it from going all the way had left him drained. He was relieved but also felt unfulfilled, as if some great prize had been within his reach but then had been snatched away just as he had touched it.

A hollow, somewhat susurrant sound surrounded him. At first he thought it was an internal noise, all in his head, perhaps the soft boom and sizzle of brain cells flaring and dying from the strain of thwarting the regressive urge. Then he realized it was rain hammering the roof of the bungalow.

When he opened his eyes, his vision was blurred. It cleared, and he was staring at Shaddack, who stood on the other side of the hall, just beyond the open bedroom door. Gaunt, long-faced, pale enough to pass for an albino, with those yellowish eyes, in his dark topcoat, the man looked like a visitation, perhaps Death himself.

If this *had* been Death, Loman might well have stood up and warmly embraced him.

Instead, while he waited for the strength to get up, he said, 'No more conversions. You've got to stop the conversions.'

Shaddack said nothing.

'You're not going to stop, are you?'

Shaddack merely stared at him.

'You're mad,' Loman said. 'You're stark, raving mad, yet I've no choice but to do what you want . . . or kill myself.'

'Never talk to me like that again. Never. Remember who I am.'

'I remember who you are.' Loman said. He struggled to his feet at last, dizzy, weak. 'You did this to me without my consent. And if the time comes when I can no longer resist the urge to regress, when I sink down into savagery, when I'm no longer scared shitless of you, I'll somehow hold on to enough of my mind to remember *where* you are, too, and I'll come for you.'

'You threaten me?' Shaddack said, clearly amazed.

'No,' Loman said. 'Threat isn't the right word.'

'It better not be. Because if anything happens to me, Sun is programmed to broadcast a command that'll be received by the clusters of microspheres inside you and—'

'—will instantly kill us all,' Loman finished. 'Yeah, I know. You've told me. If you go, we all go with you, just like people down there at Jonestown years ago, drinking their poisoned Kool-Aid and biting the big one right along with Reverend Jim. You're our Reverend Jim Jones, a Jim Jones for the high-tech age, Jim Jones with a silicon heart and tightly packed semiconductors between the ears. No, I'm not threatening you, Reverend Jim, because "threat" is too dramatic a word for it. A man making a threat has to be feeling something powerful, has to be hot with anger. I'm a New Person. I'm only afraid. That's all I can be. Afraid. So it's not a threat. No such a thing. It's a *promise.*'

Shaddack stepped through the bedroom doorway, into the hall. A draft of cold air seemed to come with him. Maybe it was Loman's imagination, but the hall seemed chillier with Shaddack in it.

They stared at each other for a long moment.

At last Shaddack said, 'You'll continue to do what I say.'

'I don't have a choice,' Loman noted. 'That's the way you made me – without a choice. I'm right there in the palm of your hand, Lord, but it isn't love that keeps me there – it's fear.'

'Better,' Shaddack said.

He turned his back on Loman and walked down the hall, into the living room, out of the house, and into the night, the rain.

PART TWO

DAYBREAK IN HADES

I could not stop something I knew was wrong and terrible. I had an awful sense of powerlessness.

ANDREI SAKHAROV

Power dements even more than it corrupts, lowering the guard of foresight and raising the haste of action.

WILL AND ARIEL DURANT

Before dawn, having slept less than an hour, Tessa Lockland was awakened by a coldness in her right hand and then the quick, hot licking of a tongue. Her arm was draped over the edge of the mattress, hand trailing just above the carpet, and something down there was taking a taste of her.

She sat straight up in bed, unable to breathe.

She had been dreaming of the carnage at Cove Lodge, of half-seen beasts, shambling and swift, with menacing teeth and claws like curved and well-honed blades. Now she thought that the nightmare had become real, that Harry's house had been invaded by those creatures, and that the questing tongue was but the prelude to a sudden, savage bite.

But it was only Moose. She could see him vaguely in the dim glow that came through the doorway from the night light in the second-floor hall, and at last she was able to draw breath. He put his forepaws on the mattress, too well trained to climb all the way onto the bed. Whining softly, he seemed only to want affection.

She was sure that she had closed the door before retiring. But she had seen enough examples of Moose's cleverness to suppose that he was able to open a door if he was determined. In fact she suddenly realized that the interior doors of the Talbot house were fitted with hardware that made the task easier for Moose: not knobs but lever-action handles that would release the latch when depressed either by a hand or paw.

'Lonely?' she asked, gently rubbing the Labrador behind the ears.

The dog whined again and submitted to her petting.

Fat drops of rain rattled against the window. It was falling with such force that she could hear it slashing through the trees outside. Wind pressed insistently against the house.

'Well, as lonely as you are, fella, I'm a thousand times that sleepy, so you're going to have to scoot.'

When she stopped petting him, he understood. Reluctantly he dropped to the floor, padded to the door, looked back at her for a moment, then went into the hall, glanced both ways, and turned left.

The light from the hall was minimal, but it bothered her. She got up and closed the door, and by the time she returned to bed in the dark, she knew she would not be able to go back to sleep right away.

For one thing, she was wearing all her clothes – jeans and T-shirt and sweater – having taken off only her shoes, and she was not entirely comfortable. But she hadn't the nerve to undress, for that would make her feel so vulnerable that she wouldn't sleep at all. After what had happened at Cove Lodge, Tessa wanted to be prepared to move fast.

Furthermore, she was in the only spare bedroom – there was another but unfurnished – and the mattress and quilted spread had a musty odor from years of disuse. It had once been Harry's father's room, as the house had once been Harry's father's house, but the elder Talbot had died seventeen years ago, three years after Harry had been brought home from the war. Tessa had insisted she could do without sheets and just sleep on top of the spread or, if cold, slip under the spread and sleep on the bare mattress. After shooing Moose out and closing the door, she felt chilled, and when she got under the spread, the musty odor seemed to carry a new scent of mildew, faint but unpleasant.

Above the background patter and hiss of the rain, she heard the hum of the elevator ascending. Moose probably had called it. Was he usually so peripatetic at night?

Though she was grindingly weary, she was now too awake to shut her mind off easily. Her thoughts were deeply troubling.

Not the massacre at Cove Lodge. Not the grisly stories of dead bodies being shoveled like so much refuse into crematoriums. Not the Parkins woman being torn to pieces by some species unknown. Not the monstrous night stalkers. All of those macabre images no doubt helped determine the channel into which her thoughts flowed, but for the most part they were only a somber background for more personal ruminations about her life and its direction.

Having recently brushed against death, she was more aware than usual of her mortality. Life was finite. In the business and the busyness of daily life, that truth was often forgotten.

Now she was unable to escape thinking about it, and she wondered if she was playing too loose with life, wasting too many years. Her work was satisfying. She was a happy woman; it was damned hard for a Lockland to be unhappy, predisposed as they were to good humor. But in all honesty she had to admit she was not getting what she truly wanted. If she remained on her current course, she'd never get it.

What she wanted was a family, a place to belong. That came, of course, from her childhood and adolescence in San Diego, where she had idolized her big sister, Janice, and had basked in the love of her mother and father. The tremendous amount of happiness and security she'd known in her youth was what allowed her to deal with the misery, despair, and terror that she sometimes encountered when working on one of her more ambitious documentaries. The first two decades of her life had been so full of joy, they balanced anything that followed.

The elevator had arrived on the second floor, and now, with a soft thump and a renewed hum, it descended. She was intrigued that Moose, so accustomed to using the elevator for and with his master, used it himself at night, though the stairs would have been quicker. Dogs, too, could be creatures of habit.

They'd had dogs at home when she was a kid, first a great golden retriever named Barney, then an Irish Setter named Mickey Finn. . . .

Janice had married and moved away from home sixteen years ago, when Tessa was eighteen, and thereafter entropy, the blind force of dissolution, had pulled apart that cozy life in San Diego. Tessa's dad died three years later, and soon after his funeral Tessa hit the road to make her industrials and documentaries and travel films, and although she had remained in touch with her mother and sister on a regular basis, that golden time had passed.

Janice was gone now. And Marion wouldn't live forever, not even if she actually gave up skydiving.

More than anything, Tessa wanted to recreate that home life with a husband of her own and children. She had been married, at twenty-three, to a man who wanted kids more than he wanted her, and when they had learned that she could never have children, he had left. Adoption wasn't enough for him. He wanted children that were biologically his. Fourteen months from wedding day to divorce. She had been badly hurt.

Thereafter she had thrown herself into her work with a passion she'd not shown previously. She was insightful enough to know that through her art she was trying to reach out to all the world as if it were one big extended family. By boiling down complex stories and issues to thirty, sixty, or ninety minutes of film, she was trying to pull the world in, reduce it to essences, to the size of one family.

But, lying awake in Harry Talbot's spare bedroom, Tessa knew .he was never going to be fully satisfied if she didn't radically shake up her life and more directly seek the thing she so much wanted. It was impossible to be a person of depth if you lacked a love for humankind, but that generalized love could swiftly become airy and meaningless if you didn't have a particular family close to you; for in your family you saw, day to day, those specific things in specific people that justified, by extension, a broader love of fellow men and women. She was a stickler for specificity in her art, but she lacked it in her emotional life.

Breathing dust and the faint odor of mildew, she felt as if her potential as a person had long been lying as unused as that bedroom. But not having dated for years, having sought refuge from heartbreak in hard work, how did a woman of thirty-four begin to open herself to that part of life she had so purposefully sealed off? Just then she felt more barren than at any time since first learning that she would never have children of her own. And at the moment, finding a way to remake her life seemed a more important issue than learning where the Boogeymen came from and what they were.

A brush with death could stir up peculiar thoughts.

In a while her weariness overcame her inner turmoil, and she drifted into sleep again. Just as she dropped off, she realized that Moose might have come to her room because he sensed something wrong in the house. Perhaps he had been trying to alert her. But surely he would have been more agitated and would have barked if there was danger.

Then she slept.

• 2 •

From Peyser's, Shaddack returned to his ultramodern house on the north point of the cove, but he didn't stay long. He made three ham sandwiches, wrapped them, and put them in a cooler with several cans of Coke. He put the cooler in the van along with a couple of blankets and a pillow. From the gun cabinet in his study he fetched a Smith & Wesson .357 Magnum, a Remington 12-gauge semi-automatic pistol-grip shotgun, and plenty of ammunition for both. Thus equipped, he set out in the storm to cruise Moonlight Cove and immediate outlying areas, intending to keep on the move, monitoring the situation by computer until the first phase of Moonhawk was concluded at midnight, in less than nineteen hours.

Watkins's threat unnerved him. Staying mobile, he wouldn't be easy to find if Watkins regressed and, true to his promise, came after him. By midnight, when the last conversions were performed, Shaddack would have consolidated his power. Then he could deal with the cop.

Watkins would be seized and shackled before he transformed. Then Shaddack could strap him down him in a lab and study his psychology and physiology to find an explanation for this plague of regression.

He did not accept Watkins's explanation. They weren't regressing to escape life as New People. To accept that theory, he would have to admit that the Moonhawk Project was an unmitigated disaster, that the Change was not a boon to mankind but a curse, and that all his work was not only misguided but calamitous in its effect. He could admit no such thing.

As maker and master of the New People, he had tasted godlike power. He was unwilling to relinquish it.

The rainswept, pre-dawn streets were deserted except for cars – some police cruisers, some not – in which pairs of men patrolled in the hope of spotting either Booker, Tessa Lockland, the Foster girl, or regressives on the prowl. Though they could not see through his van's heavily smoked windows, they surely knew to whom the vehicle belonged.

Shaddack recognized many of them, for they worked at New Wave and were among the contingent of one hundred that he had put on loan to the police department only a few hours ago. Beyond the rain-washed windshields, their pale faces floated like disembodied spheres in the dark interiors of their cars, so expressionless that they might have been mannequins or robots.

Others were patrolling the town on foot but were circumspect, keeping to the deeper shadows and alleyways. He saw none of them.

Shaddack also passed two conversion teams as they went quietly and briskly from one house to another. Each time a conversion was completed, the team keyed in that data on one of their car VDTs so the central system at New Wave could keep track of their progress.

When he paused at an intersection and used his own VDT to call the current roster onto the screen, he saw that only five people remained to be dealt with in the midnight-to-six-o'clock batch of conversions. They were slightly ahead of schedule.

Hard rain slanted in from the west, silvery as ice in his headlights. Trees shook as if in fear. And Shaddack kept on the move, circling through the night as if he were some strange bird of prey that preferred to hunt on storm winds.

· 3 ·

With Tucker leading, they had hunted and killed, bitten and torn, clawed and bitten, hunted and killed and eaten the prey, drunk blood, blood, warm and sweet, thick and warm, sweet and thick, blood, feeding the fire in their flesh, cooling the fire with food. Blood.

Gradually Tucker had discovered that the longer they stayed in their altered state, the less intensely the fire burned and the easier it was to *remain* in subhuman form. Something told him that he should be worried that it was increasingly easy to cling to the shape of a beast, but he could not raise much concern about it, partly because his mind no longer seemed able to focus on complex thoughts for more than a few seconds.

So they had raced over the fields and hills in the moonlight, raced and roamed, free, so free in moonlight and fog, in fog and wind, and Tucker had led them, pausing only to kill and eat, or to couple with the female, who took her own pleasure with an aggressiveness that was exciting, savage and exciting.

Then the rains came.

Cold.

Slashing.

Thunder, too, and blazing light in the sky.

Part of Tucker seemed to know what the long, jagged bolts of sky-ripping light were. But he could not quite remember, and he was frightened, dashing for the cover of trees when the light caught him in the open, huddling with the other male and the female until the sky went dark again and stayed that way for a while.

Tucker began to look for a place to take shelter from the storm. He knew that they should go back to where they had started from, to a place of light and dry rooms, but he could not remember where that had been exactly. Besides, going back would mean surrendering freedom and assuming their born identities. He did not want to do that. Neither did the other male and the female. They wanted to race and roam and kill and rut and be free, free. If they went back they could not be free, so they went ahead, crossing a hard-surface road, slinking up into higher hills, staying away from the few houses in the area.

Dawn was coming, not yet on the eastern horizon but coming, and Tucker knew they had to find a haven, a den, before daylight, a place where they could curl up around one another, down in darkness, sharing warmth, darkness and warmth, safely curled up with memories of blood and rutting, darkness and warmth and blood and rutting. They would be out of danger there, safe from a world in which they were still alien, safe also from the necessity to return to human form. When night fell again, they could venture forth to roam and kill, kill, bite and kill, and maybe the day would come when there were so many of their kind in the world that they would no longer be outnumbered and could venture forth in bright daylight as well, but not now, not yet.

They came to a dirt road, and Tucker had a dim memory of where he was, a sense that the road would quickly lead him to a place that could provide the shelter that he and his pack needed. He followed it farther into the hills, encouraging his companions with low growls of reassurance. In a couple of minutes they came to a building, a huge old house fallen to ruin, with the windows smashed in and the front door hanging open on half-broken hinges. Other gray structures loomed out of the rain: a barn in worse shape than the house, several outbuildings that had mostly collapsed.

Large, hand-painted signs were nailed to the house, between two of the second-floor windows, one sign above the other, in different styles of lettering, as though a lot of time had passed between the hanging of the first and the second. He knew they had meaning, but he couldn't read them, though he strained to recall the lost language used by the species to which he had once belonged.

The two members of his pack flanked him. They, too, stared up at the dark letters on the white background. Murky symbols in the rain and gloom. Eerily mysterious runes.

ICARUS COLONY

And under that:

THE OLD ICARUS COLONY RESTAURANT
NATURAL FOODS

On the dilapidated barn was another sign – FLEA MARKET – but that meant nothing more to Tucker than the signs on the house, and after a while he decided it didn't matter if he understood them. The important thing was that no people were nearby, no fresh scent or vibration of human beings, so the refuge that he sought might be found here, a burrow, a den, a warm and dark place, warm and dark, safe and dark.

• 4 •

With one blanket and pillow, Sam had made his bed on a long sofa in the living room, just off the front hall downstairs. He wanted to sleep on the ground floor so he might be awakened by the sound of an intruder. According to the schedule that Sam had seen on the VDT in the patrol car, Harry Talbot wouldn't be converted until the following evening. He doubted that they would accelerate their schedule simply because they knew an FBI man was in Moonlight Cove. But he was taking no unnecessary chances.

Sam often suffered from insomnia, but it did not trouble him that night. After he took off his shoes and stretched out on the sofa, he listened to the rain for a couple of minutes, trying not to think. Soon he slept.

His was not a dreamless sleep. It seldom was.

He dreamed of Karen, his lost wife, and as always in nightmares, she was spitting up blood and emaciated, in the final stages of her cancer, after the chemotherapy had failed. He knew that he must save her. He could not. He felt small, powerless, and terribly afraid.

But that nightmare did not wake him.

Eventually the dream shifted from the hospital to a dark and crumbling building. It was rather like a hotel designed by Salvador Dali: The corridors branched off randomly; some were very short and some were so long that the ends of them could not be seen; the walls and floors were at surreal angles to one another, and the doors to the rooms were of different sizes, some so small that only a mouse could have passed through, others large enough for a man, and still others on a scale suitable to a thirty-foot giant.

He was drawn to certain rooms. When he entered them he found in each a person from his past or current life.

He encountered Scott in several rooms and had unsatisfactory, disjointed conversations with him, all ending in unreasoning hostility on Scott's part. The nightmare was made worse by the variation in Scott's age: Sometimes he was a sullen sixteen-year-old and sometimes ten or just four or five. But in every incarnation he was alienated, cold, quick to anger, and seething with hatred. 'This isn't right, this isn't true, you weren't like this when you were younger,' Sam told a seven-year-old Scott, and the boy made an obscene reply.

In every room and regardless of his age, Scott was surrounded by huge posters of black-metal rockers dressed in leather and chains, displaying satanic symbols on their foreheads and in the palms of their hands. The light was flickering and strange. In a dark corner Sam saw something lurking, a creature of which Scott was aware, something the boy did not fear but which scared the hell out of Sam.

But that nightmare did not wake him, either.

In other chambers of that surreal hotel, he found dying men, the same ones every time – Arnie Taft and Carl Sorbino. They were two agents with whom he had worked and whom he had seen gunned down.

The entrance to one room was a car door – the gleaming door of a blue '54 Buick, to be exact. Inside he found an enormous, gray-walled chamber in which was the front seat, dashboard, and steering wheel, nothing else of the car, like parts of a prehistoric skeleton lying on a vast expanse of barren sand. A woman in a green dress sat behind the wheel, her head turned away from him. Of course, he knew who she was, and he wanted to leave the room at once, but he could not. In fact he was drawn to her. He sat beside her, and suddenly he was seven years old, as he had been on the day of the accident, though he spoke with his grown-up voice: 'Hello, Mom.' She turned to him, revealing that the right side of her face was caved in, the eye gone from the socket, bone punching through torn flesh. Broken teeth were exposed in her cheek, so she favored him with half of a hideous grin.

Abruptly they were in the *real* car, cast back in time. Ahead of them on the highway, coming toward them, was the drunk in the white pickup truck, weaving across the double yellow line, bearing down on them at high speed. Sam cried out – 'Mom!' – but she couldn't evade the pickup this time any more than she had been able to avoid it thirty-five years ago. It came at them as if they were a magnet and slammed into them head-on. He thought it must be like that at the center of a bomb blast: a great roar pierced by the shriek of shredding metal. Everything went black. Then, when he swam up from that gloom, he found himself pinned in the wreckage. He was face to face with his dead mother, peering into her empty eye socket. He began to scream.

That nightmare also failed to wake him.

Now he was in a hospital, as he'd been after the accident, for that had been the first of the six times he'd nearly died. He was no longer a boy, however, but a grown man, and he was on the operating table, undergoing emergency surgery because he had been shot in the chest during the same gun battle in which Carl Sorbino had died. As the surgical team labored over him, he rose out of his body and watched them at work on his carcass. He was amazed but not afraid, which was just how he had felt when it had *not* been a dream.

Next he was in a tunnel, rushing toward dazzling light, toward the Other Side. This time he knew what he would find at the other end because he had been there before, in real life instead of in a dream. He was terrified of it, didn't want to face it again, didn't want to look Beyond. But he moved faster, faster, faster through the tunnel, *bulleted* through it, his terror escalating with his speed. Having to look again at what lay on the Other Side was worse than his dream confrontations with Scott, worse than the battered and one-eyed face of his mother, infinitely worse (faster, faster), intolerable, so he began to scream (faster) and scream (faster) and scream—

That one woke him.

He sat straight up on the sofa and pinched off the cry before it left his throat.

An instant later he became aware that he was not alone in the unlit living room. He heard something move in front of him, and he moved simultaneously, snatching his .38 revolver from the holster, which he had taken off and laid beside the sofa.

It was Moose.

'Hey, boy.'

The dog chuffed softly.

Sam reached out to pat the dark head, but already the Labrador was moving away. Because the night outside was marginally less black than the interior of the house, the windows were visible as fuzzy-gray rectangles. Moose went to one at the side of the house, putting his paws on the sill and his nose to the glass.

'Need to go out?' Sam asked, though they had let him out for ten minutes just before they'd gone to bed.

The dog made no response but stood at the window with a peculiar rigidity.

'Something out there?' Sam wondered, and even as he asked the question, he knew the answer.

Quickly and gingerly he crossed the dark room. He bumped into furniture but didn't knock anything down, and joined the dog at the window.

The rain-battered night seemed at its blackest in this last hour before dawn, but Sam's eyes were adjusted to darkness. He could see the side of the neighboring house, just thirty feet away. The steeply sloping property between the two structures was not planted with grass but with a variety of shrubs and several starburst pines, all of which swayed and shuddered in the gusty wind.

He quickly spotted the two Boogeymen because their movement was in opposition to the direction of the wind and therefore in sharp contrast to the storm dance of the vegetation. They were about fifteen feet from the window, heading downslope toward Conquistador. Though Sam could discern no details of them, he could see by their hunchbacked movement and shambling yet queerly graceful gait that they were not ordinary men.

As they paused beside one of the larger pines, one of them looked toward the Talbot house, and Sam saw its softly radiant, utterly alien amber eyes. For a moment he was transfixed, frozen not by fear so much as by amazement. Then he realized that the creature seemed to be staring straight at the window, as if it could see him, and suddenly it loped straight toward him.

Sam dropped below the sill, pressing against the wall under the window, and pulled Moose down with him. The dog must have had some sense of the danger, for he didn't bark or whine or resist in any way, but lay with his belly to the floor and allowed himself to be held there, still and silent.

A fraction of a second later, over the sounds of wind and rain, Sam heard furtive movement on the other side of the wall against which he crouched. A soft scuttling sound. Scratching.

He held his .38 in his right hand, ready in case the thing was bold enough to smash through the window.

A few seconds passed in silence. A few more.

Sam kept his left hand on Moose's back. He could feel the dog shivering.

Tick-tick-tick.

After long seconds of silence, the sudden ticking startled Sam, for he had just about decided that the creature had gone away.

Tick-tick-tick-tick.

It was tapping the glass, as if testing the solidity of the pane or calling to the man it had seen standing there.

Tick-tick. Pause. *Tick-tick-tick.*

• 5 •

Tucker led his pack out of the mud and rain, onto the sagging porch of the decrepit house. The boards creaked under their weight. One loose shutter was banging in the wind; all the others had rotted and torn off long ago.

He struggled to speak of his intentions, but he found it very difficult to remember or produce the necessary words. Amidst snarls and growls and low brute mutterings, he only managed to say, '. . . *here . . . hide . . . here . . . safe . . .*'

The other male seemed to have lost his speech entirely, for he could produce no words at all.

With considerable difficulty, the female said, '. . . *safe . . . here . . . home . . .*'

Tucker studied his two companions for a moment and realized they had changed during their night adventures. Earlier, the female had possessed a feline quality – sleek, sinuous, with cat ears and sharply pointed teeth that she revealed when she hissed either in fear, anger, or sexual desire. Though something of the cat was still in her, she had become more like Tucker, wolfish, with a large head drawn forward into a muzzle more canine than feline. She had lupine haunches, as well, and feet that appeared to have resulted from the crossbreeding of man and wolf, not paws but not hands either, tipped with claws longer and more murderous than those of a real wolf. The other male, once unique in appearance, combining a few insectile features with the general form of a hyena, had now largely conformed to Tucker's appearance.

By unspoken mutual agreement, Tucker had become the leader of the pack. Upon submitting to his rule, his followers evidently had used his appearance as a model for their own. He realized that this was an important turn of events, maybe even an ominous one.

He did not know why it should spook him, and he no longer had the mental clarity to concentrate on it until understanding came to him. The more pressing concern of shelter demanded his attention.

'. . . *here . . . safe . . . here . . .*'

He led them through the broken, half-open door, into the front hall of the moldering house. The plaster was pocked and cracked, and in some places missing altogether, with lath showing through like the rib cage of a half-decomposed corpse. In the empty living room, long strips of wallpaper were peeling off, as if the place was shedding its skin in the process of a metamorphosis as dramatic as any that Tucker and his pack had undergone.

He followed scents through the house, and that was interesting, not exciting but definitely interesting. His companions followed as he investigated patches of mildew, toadstools growing in a dank corner of the dining room, colonies of vaguely luminescent fungus in a room on the other side of the hall, several deposits of rat feces, the mummified remains of a bird that had flown in through one of the glassless windows and broken a wing against a wall, and the still ripe carcass of a diseased coyote that had crawled into the kitchen to die.

During the course of that inspection, Tucker realized the house did not offer ideal shelter. The rooms were too large and drafty, especially with windows broken out. Though no human scent lingered on the air, he sensed that people still came here, not frequently but often enough to be troublesome.

In the kitchen, however, he found the entrance to the cellar, and he was excited by that subterranean retreat. He led the others down the creaking stairs into that deeper darkness, where cold drafts could not reach them, where the floor and walls were dry, and where the air had a clean, lime smell that came off the concrete-block walls.

He suspected that trespassers seldom ventured into the basement. And if they did . . . they would be walking into a lair from which they could not possibly escape.

It was a perfect, windowless den. Tucker prowled the perimeter of the room, his claws ticking and scraping on the floor. He sniffed in corners and examined the rusted furnace. He was satisfied they'd be safe. They could curl up secure in the knowledge that they would not be found and if, by some chance, they were found, they could cut off the only exit and dispense with an intruder quickly.

In such a deep, dark, secret place, they could become anything they wanted, and no one would see them.

That last thought startled Tucker. Become anything they wanted?

He was not sure where that thought originated or what it meant. He suddenly sensed that by regressing he had initiated some process that was now beyond his conscious control, that some more primitive part of his mind was permanently in charge. Panic seized him. He had shifted to an altered state many times before and had always been able to shift back again. But now . . . His fear was sharp only for a moment, because he could not concentrate on the problem, didn't even remember what he meant by 'regressing,' and was soon distracted by the female, who wanted to couple with him.

Soon the three of them were in a tangle, pawing at one another, thrusting and thrashing. Their shrill, excited cries rose through the abandoned house, like ghost voices in a haunted place.

• 6 •

Tick-tick-tick.

Sam was tempted to rise, look through the window, and confront the creature face to face, for he was eager to see what one of them looked like close up.

But as violent as these beings evidently were, a confrontation was certain to result in an attack and gunfire, which would draw the attention of the neighbors and then the police. He couldn't risk his current hiding place, for at the moment he had nowhere else to go.

He clutched his revolver and kept one hand on Moose and remained below the windowsill, listening. He heard voices, either wordless or so muffled that the words did not come clearly through the glass above his head. The second creature had joined the first at the side of the house. Their grumbling sounded like a low-key argument.

Silence followed.

Sam crouched there for a while, waiting for the voices to resume or for the amber-eyed beast to tap once more – *tick-tick* – but nothing happened. At last, as the muscles in his thighs and calves began to cramp, he took his hand off Moose and eased up to the window. He half expected the Boogeyman to be there, malformed face pressed to the glass, but it was gone.

With the dog accompanying him, he went from room to room on the ground floor, looking out all the windows on four sides of the house. He would not have been surprised to find those creatures trying to force entry somewhere.

But for the sound of rain drumming on the roof and gurgling in the downspouts, the house was silent.

He decided they were gone and that their interest in the house had been coincidental. They weren't looking for him in particular, just for prey. They very likely had glimpsed him at the window, and they didn't want to let him go if he had seen them. But if they had come to deal with him, they apparently had decided that they could no more risk the sound of breaking glass and a noisy confrontation than he could, not in the heart of town. They were secretive creatures. They might rarely cut loose with an eerie cry that would echo across Moonlight Cove, but only when in the grip of some strange passion. And thus far, for the most part, they had limited their attacks to people who had been relatively isolated.

Back in the living room he slipped the revolver into the holster again and stretched out on the sofa.

Moose sat watching him for a while, as if unable to believe that he could calmly lie down and sleep again after seeing what had been on the prowl in the rain.

'Some of my dreams are worse than what's out there tonight,' he told the dog. 'So if I spooked easily, I'd probably never want to go to sleep again.'

The dog yawned and got up and went out into the dark hall, where he boarded the elevator. The motor hummed as the lift carried the Labrador upstairs.

As he waited for sleep to steal over him again, Sam attempted to shape his dreams into a more appealing pattern by concentrating on a few images he would not mind dreaming about: good Mexican food, barely chilled Guinness stout, and Goldie Hawn. Ideally, he'd dream about being in a great Mexican restaurant with Goldie Hawn, who'd look even more radiant than usual, and they'd be eating and drinking Guinness and laughing.

Instead, when he did fall asleep, he dreamed about his father, a mean-tempered alcoholic, into whose hands he had fallen at the age of seven, after his mother had died in the car crash.

• 7 •

Nestled in the stack of grass-scented burlap tarps in the back of the gardener's truck, Chrissie woke when the automatic garage door ascended with a groan and clatter. She almost sat up in surprise, revealing herself. But remembering where she was, she pulled her head under the top half-dozen tarps, which she was using as blankets. She tried to shrink into the pile of burlap.

She heard rain striking the roof. It sliced into the gravel driveway just beyond the open door, making a sizzling noise like a thousand strips of bacon on an immense griddle. Chrissie was hungry. That sound made her hungrier.

'You got my lunch box, Sarah?'

Chrissie didn't know Mr. Eulane well enough to recognize his voice, but she supposed that was him, for Sarah Eulane, whose voice Chrissie did recognize, answered at once:

'Ed, I wish you'd just come back home after you drop me at the school. Take the day off. You shouldn't work in such foul weather.'

'Well, I can't cut grass in this downpour,' he said, 'but I can do some other chores. I'll just pull on my vinyl anorak. Keeps me dry as bone. Moses could've walked through the Red Sea in that anorak and wouldn't have needed God's miracle to help him.'

Breathing air filtered through the coarse, grass-stained cloth, Chrissie was troubled by a tickling sensation in her nose, all the way into her sinuses. She was afraid that she was going to sneeze.

STUPID YOUNG GIRL SNEEZES, REVEALING HERSELF TO RAVENOUS ALIENS; EATEN ALIVE; 'SHE WAS A TASTY LITTLE MORSEL,' SAYS ALIEN NEST QUEEN, 'BRING US MORE OF YOUR ELEVEN-YEAR-OLD BLOND FEMALES.'

Opening the passenger door of the truck, a couple of feet from Chrissie's hiding place, Sarah said, 'You'll catch your death, Ed.'

'You think I'm some delicate violet?' he asked playfully as he opened the driver's door and got into the truck.

'I think you're a withered old dandelion.'

He laughed. 'You didn't think so last night.'

'Yes, I did. But you're *my* withered old dandelion, and I don't want you to just blow away on the wind.'

One door slammed shut, then the other.

Certain that they could not see her, Chrissie pulled back the burlap, exposing her head. She pinched her nose and breathed through her mouth until the tickling in her sinuses subsided.

As Ed Eulane started the truck, let the engine idle a moment, then reversed out of the garage, Chrissie could hear them talking in the cab at her back. She couldn't make out everything they were saying, but they still seemed to be bantering with each other.

Cold rain struck her face, and she immediately pulled her head under the tarps again, leaving just a narrow opening by which a little fresh air might reach her. If she sneezed while in transit, the sound of the rain and the rumble of the truck's engine would cover it.

Thinking about the conversation she had overheard in the garage and listening to Mr. Eulane laughing now in the cab, Chrissie thought she could trust them. If they were aliens, they wouldn't be making dumb jokes and lovey talk. Maybe they would if they were putting on a show for non-aliens, trying to convince the world that they were still Ed and Sarah Eulane, but not when they were in private. When aliens were together without unconverted humans nearby, they probably talked about . . . well, planets they had sacked, the weather on Mars, the price of flying-saucer fuel, and recipes for serving human beings. Who knew? But surely they didn't talk as the Eulanes were talking.

On the other hand . . .

Maybe these aliens had only taken control of Ed and Sarah Eulane during the night, and maybe they were not yet comfortable in their human roles. Maybe they were practicing being human in private so they could pass for human in public. Sure as the devil, if Chrissie revealed herself, they'd probably sprout tentacles and lobster pincers from their chests and either eat her alive, without condiments, or freeze-dry her and mount her on a plaque and take her to their home world to hang on their den wall, or pop her brain out of her skull and plug it into their spaceship and use it as a cheap control mechanism for their in-flight coffeemaker.

In the middle of an alien invasion, you could give your trust only with reluctance and considerable deliberation. She decided to stick to her original plan.

The fifty-pound, plastic sacks of fertilizer and mulch and snail bait, piled on both sides of her burlap niche, protected her from some rain, but enough reached her to soak the upper layers of tarps. She was relatively dry and toasty warm when they set out, but soon she was saturated with grass-scented rainwater, cold to the bone.

She peeked out repeatedly to determine where they were. When she saw that they were turning off the county route onto Ocean Avenue, she peeled back the soggy burlap and crawled out of her hiding place.

The wall of the truck cab featured a window, so the Eulanes would see her if they turned and looked back. Mr. Eulane might even see her in the rearview mirror if she didn't keep very low. But she had to get to the rear of the truck and be ready to jump off when they passed Our Lady of Mercy.

On her hands and knees, she moved between – and over – the supplies and gardening equipment. When she reached the tailgate, she huddled there, head down, shivering and miserable in the rain.

They crossed Shasta Way, the first intersection at the edge of town, and headed down through the business district of Ocean Avenue. They were only about four blocks from the church.

Chrissie was surprised that no people were on the sidewalks and that no cars traveled the streets. It was early – she checked her watch, 7:03 – but not so early that everyone would still be home in bed. She supposed the weather also had something to do with the town's deserted look; no one was going to be out and about in that mess unless he absolutely had to be.

There was another possibility: Maybe the aliens had taken over such a large percentage of the people in Moonlight Cove that they no longer felt it necessary to enact the charade of daily life; with complete conquest only hours away, all their efforts were bent on seeking the last of the unpossessed. *That* was too unsettling to think about.

When they were one block from Our Lady of Mercy, Chrissie climbed onto the white-board tailgate. She swung one leg over the top, then the other leg, and clung to the outside of the gate with both hands, her feet on the rear bumper. She could see the backs of the Eulanes' heads through the rear window of the cab, and if they turned her way – or if Mr. Eulane glanced at his rearview mirror – she'd be seen.

She kept expecting to be spotted by a pedestrian who would yell, 'Hey, you, hanging on that truck, are you nuts?' But there were no pedestrians, and they reached the next intersection without incident.

The brakes squealed as Mr. Eulane slowed for the stop sign.

As the truck came to a stop, Chrissie dropped off the tailgate.

Mr. Eulane turned left on the cross street. He was heading toward Thomas Jefferson Elementary School on Palomino, a few blocks south, where Mrs. Eulane worked and where, on an ordinary Tuesday morning, Chrissie would soon be going to her sixth-grade classroom.

She sprinted across the intersection, splashed through the dirty streaming water in the gutter, and ran up the steps to the front doors of Our Lady of Mercy. A flush of triumph warmed her, for she felt that she had reached sanctuary against all odds.

With one hand on the ornate brass handle of the carved-oak door, she paused to look uphill and down. The windows of shops, offices, and apartments were as frost-blank as cataracted eyes. Smaller trees leaned with the stiff wind, and larger trees shuddered, which was the only movement other than the driving rain. The wind was inconstant, blustery; sometimes it stopped pushing the rain relentlessly eastward and gathered it into funnels, whirling them up Ocean Avenue, so if she squinted her eyes and ignored the chill in the air, she could almost believe that she was standing in a desert ghost town, watching dust devils whirl along its haunted streets.

At the corner beside the church, a police car pulled up to the stop sign. Two men were in it. Neither was looking toward her.

She already suspected that the police were not to be trusted. Pulling open the church door, she quickly slipped inside before they glanced her way.

The moment she stepped into the oak-paneled narthex and drew in a deep breath of the myrrh- and spikenard-scented air, Chrissie felt safe. She stepped through the archway to the nave, dipped her fingers in the holy water that filled the marble font on the right, crossed herself, and moved down the center aisle to the fourth pew from the rear. She genuflected, crossed herself again, and took a seat.

She was concerned about getting water all over the polished oak pew, but there was nothing she could do about that. She was dripping.

Mass was under way. Besides herself, only two of the faithful were present, which seemed to be a scandalously poor turnout. Of course, to the best of her memory, though her folks always attended Sunday Mass, they had brought her to a weekday service only once in her life, many years ago, and she could not be sure that weekday Masses ever drew more worshipers. She suspected, however, that the alien presence – or demons, whatever – in Moonlight Cove was responsible for the low attendance. No doubt space aliens were godless or, worse yet, bowed to some dark deity with a name like Yahgag or Scogblatt.

She was surprised to see that the priest celebrating Mass, with the assistance of one altarboy, was not Father Castelli. It was the young priest – the curate, they called him – whom the archdiocese had assigned to Father Castelli in August. His name was Father O'Brien. His first name was Tom, and following his rector's lead, he sometimes insisted that parishioners call him Father Tom. He was nice – though not as nice or as wise or as amusing as Father Castelli – but she could no more bring herself to call him Father Tom than she could call the older priest Father Jim. Might as well call the Pope Johnny. Her parents sometimes talked about how much the church had changed, how less formal it had become over the years, and they spoke approvingly of those changes. In her conservative heart, Chrissie wished that she had been born and raised in a time when the Mass had been in Latin, elegant and mysterious, and when the service had not included the downright silly ritual of 'giving peace' to worshipers around you. She had gone to Mass at a cathedral in San Francisco once, when they were on vacation, and the service had been a special one, in Latin, conducted according to the old liturgy, and she had *loved* it. Making ever faster airplanes, improving television from black and white to color, saving lives with better medical technology, junking those clumsy old records for compact discs – all those changes were desirable and good. But there were some things in life that shouldn't change, because it was their changelessness that you loved about them. If you lived in a world of constant, rapid change in *all* things, where did you turn for stability, for a place of peace and calm and quiet in the middle of all that buzz and clatter? That truth was so evident to Chrissie that she could not understand why grownups were not aware of it. Sometimes adults were thickheaded.

She sat through only a couple of minutes of the Mass, just long enough to say a prayer and beseech the Blessed Virgin to intercede on her behalf, and to be sure that Father Castelli was not somewhere in the nave – sitting in a pew like an ordinary worshiper, which he did sometimes – or perhaps at one of the confessionals. Then she got up, genuflected, crossed herself, and went back into the narthex, where candle-shaped electric bulbs flickered softly behind the amber-glass panes of two wall-mounted lamps. She opened the front door a crack, peeking out at the rain-washed street.

Just then a police car came down Ocean Avenue. It was not the same one she'd seen when she had gone into the church. It was newer, and only one officer was in it. He was driving slowly, scanning the streets as if looking for someone.

As the police cruiser reached the corner on which Our Lady of Mercy stood, another car passed it, coming uphill from the sea. That one wasn't a patrol car but a blue Chevy. Two men were in it, giving everything a slow looking over, peering left and right through the rain, as the policeman was doing. And though the men in the Chevy and the policeman did not wave to each other or signal in any way, Chrissie sensed that they were involved in the same pursuit. The cops had linked up with a civilian posse to search for something, someone.

Me, she thought.

They were looking for her because she knew too much. Because yesterday morning, in the upstairs hall, she had seen the aliens in her parents. Because she was the only obstacle to their conquest of the human race. And maybe because she would taste good if they cooked her up with some Martian potatoes.

Thus far, although she had learned that aliens were taking possession of some people, she had seen no evidence that they were actually eating others, yet she continued to believe that somewhere, right now, they were snacking on body parts. It just *felt* right.

When the patrol car and the blue Chevy passed, she pushed the heavy door open another few inches and stuck her head out in the rain. She looked left and right, then again, to be very sure that no one was in sight either in a car or on foot. Satisfied, she stepped outside and dashed east to the corner of the church. After looking both ways on the cross street, she turned the corner and hurried along the side of the church toward the rectory behind it.

The two-story house was all brick with carved granite lintels and a white-painted front porch with scalloped eaves, respectable-looking enough to be the perfect residence for a priest. The old plane trees along the front walk protected her from the rain, but she was already sodden. When she reached the porch and approached the front door, her tennis shoes made squelching-squeaking noises.

As she was about to put her finger on the doorbell button, she hesitated. She was concerned that she might be walking into an alien lair – an unlikely possibility but one which could not be lightly dismissed. She also realized that Father O'Brien might be saying Mass in order that Father Castelli, a hard worker by nature, could enjoy a rare sleep-in, and she was loath to disturb him if that was the case.

Young Chrissie, she thought, *undeniably courageous and clever, was nonetheless too polite for her own good. While standing on the priest's porch, debating the proper etiquette of an early-morning visit, she suddenly was snatched up by slavering, nine-eyed aliens and eaten on the spot. Fortunately she was too dead to hear the way they belched and farted after eating her, for surely her refined sensibilities would have been gravely offended.*

She rang the bell. Twice.

A moment later a shadowy and strangely lumpish figure appeared beyond the crackle-finished, diamond-shaped panes in the top half of the door. She almost turned and ran but told herself that the glass was distorting the image and that the figure beyond was not actually grotesque.

Father Castelli opened the door and blinked in surprise when he saw her. He was wearing black slacks, a black shirt, a Roman collar, and a tattered gray cardigan, so he hadn't been fast asleep, thank God. He was a shortish man, about five feet seven, and round but not really fat, with black hair going gray at the temples. Even his proud beak of a nose was not enough to dilute the effect of his otherwise soft features, which gave him a gentle and compassionate appearance.

He blinked again – this was the first time Chrissie had seen him without his glasses – and said, 'Chrissie?' He smiled, and she knew that she had done the right thing by coming to him, because his smile was warm and open and loving. 'Whatever brings you here at this hour in this weather?' He looked past her to the rest of the porch and the walkway beyond. 'Where're your parents?'

'Father,' she said, not altogether surprised to hear her voice crack, 'I have to see you.'

His smile wavered. 'Is something wrong?'

'Yes, Father. Very wrong. Terribly, awfully wrong.'

'Come in, then, come in. You're soaked!' He ushered her into the foyer and closed the door. 'Dear girl, what *is* this all about?'

'Aliens, F-f-father,' she said, as a chill made her stutter.

'Come on back to the kitchen,' he said. 'It's the warmest room in the house. I was just fixing breakfast.'

'I'll ruin the carpet,' she said, indicating the oriental runner that lay the length of the hallway, with oak flooring on both sides.

'Oh, don't worry about that. It's old thing, but it stands up well to abuse. Sort of like me! Would you like some hot cocoa? I was making breakfast, including a big pot of piping hot cocoa.'

She followed him gratefully back the dimly lighted hall, which smelled of lemon oil and pine disinfectant and vaguely of incense.

The kitchen was homey. A well-worn, yellow linoleum floor. Pale yellow walls. Dark wood cabinets with white porcelain handles. Gray and yellow Formica counter tops. There were appliances – refrigerator, oven, microwave oven, toaster, electric can opener – as in any kitchen, which surprised her, though when she thought about it, she didn't know why she would have expected it to be any different. Priests needed appliances too. They couldn't just summon up a fiery angel to toast some bread or work a miracle to brew a pot of hot cocoa.

The place smelled wonderful. Cocoa was brewing. Toast was toasting. Sausages were sizzling over a low flame on the gas stove.

Father Castelli showed her to one of the four padded vinyl chairs at the chrome and Formica breakfast set, then scurried about, taking care of her as if she were a chick and he a mother hen. He rushed upstairs, returned with two clean, fluffy bath towels, and said, 'Dry your hair and blot your damp clothes with one of them, then wrap the other one around you like a shawl. It'll help you get warm.' While she was following his instructions, he went to the bathroom off the downstairs hall and fetched two aspirins. He put those on the table in front of her and said, 'I'll get you some orange juice to take them with. Lots of vitamin C in orange juice. Aspirin and vitamin C are like a one-two punch; they'll knock a cold right out of you before it can take up residence.' When he returned with the juice, he stood for a moment looking down at her, shaking his head, and she figured she must look bedraggled and pitiful. 'Dear girl, what on *earth* have you been up to?' He seemed not to have heard what she'd said about aliens when she'd first crossed his threshold. 'No, wait. You can tell me over breakfast. Would you like some breakfast?'

'Yes, please, Father. I'm starved. The only thing I've eaten since yesterday afternoon was a couple of Hershey bars.'

'Nothing but Hershey bars?' He sighed. 'Chocolate is one of God's graces, but it's also a tool the devil uses to lead us into temptation – the temptation of gluttony.' He patted his round belly. 'I, myself, have often partaken of this particular grace, but I would *never*' – he exaggerated the word never and winked at her – 'never, not ever, heed the devil's call to overindulge! But, see here, if you've been eating only chocolate, your teeth will fall out. So . . . I've got plenty of sausages, plenty to share. I was about to cook a couple of eggs for myself too. Would you like a couple of eggs?'

'Yes, please.'

'And toast?'

'Yes.'

'We've got some wonderful cinnamon sweetrolls there on the table. And the hot chocolate, of course.'

Chrissie washed down the two aspirins with orange juice.

As he carefully cracked eggs into the hot frying pan, Father Castelli glanced at her again. 'Are you all right?'

'Yes, Father.'

'Are you sure?'

'Yes. Now. I'm all right now.'

'It'll be nice having company for breakfast,' he said.

Chrissie drank the rest of her juice.

He said, 'When Father O'Brien finishes saying Mass, he never wants to eat. Nervous stomach.' He chuckled. 'They all have bad stomachs when they're new. For the first few months they're scared to death up there on the altar. It's such a sacred duty, you see, offering the Mass, and the young priests are always afraid of flubbing up in some way that'll be . . . oh, I don't know . . . that'll be an insult to God, I guess. But God doesn't insult very easily. If He did, He'd have washed His hands of the human race a long time ago! All young priests come to that realization eventually, and then they're fine. Then they come back from saying Mass, and they're ready to run through the entire week's food budget in one breakfast.'

She knew that he was talking just to soothe her. He had noticed how distraught she was. He wanted to settle her down so they could discuss it in a calm, reasonable manner. She didn't mind. She *needed* to be soothed.

Having cracked all four eggs, he turned the sausages with a fork, then opened a drawer and took out a spatula, which he placed on the counter near the egg pan. As he got plates, knives, and forks for the table, he said, 'You look more than a little scared, Chrissie, like you'd just seen a ghost. You can calm down now. After so many years of schooling and training, if a young priest can be afraid of making a mistake at Mass, then anyone can be afraid of anything. Most fears are things we create in our own minds, and we can banish them as easily as we called them forth.'

'Maybe not this one,' she said.

'We'll see.'

He transferred eggs and sausages from frying pans to plates.

For the first time in twenty-four hours, the world seemed *right*. As Father Castelli put the food on the table and encouraged her to dig in, Chrissie sighed with relief and hunger.

• 8 •

Shaddack usually went to bed after dawn, so by seven o'clock Tuesday morning he was yawning and rubbing at his eyes as he cruised through Moonlight Cove, looking for a place to hide the van and sleep for a few hours safely beyond Loman Watkins's reach. The day was overcast, gray and dim, yet the sunlight seared his eyes.

He remembered Paula Parkins, who'd been torn apart by regressives back in September. Her 1.5-acre property was secluded, at the most rural end of town. Though the dead woman's family – in Colorado – had put it up for sale through a local real-estate agent, it had not sold. He drove out there, parked in the empty garage, cut the engine, and pulled the big door down behind him.

He ate a ham sandwich and drank a Coke. Brushing crumbs from his fingers, he curled up on the blankets in the back of the van and drifted toward sleep.

He never suffered insomnia, perhaps because he was so sure of his role in life, his destiny, and had no concern about tomorrow. He was absolutely convinced he would bend the future to his agenda.

All of his life Shaddack had seen signs of his uniqueness, omens that foretold his ultimate triumph in any pursuit he undertook.

Initially he had noticed those signs only because Don Runningdeer had pointed them out to him. Runningdeer had been an Indian – of what tribe, Shaddack had never been able to learn – who had worked for the judge, Shaddack's father, back in Phoenix, as a full-time gardener and all-around handyman. Runningdeer was lean and quick, with a weathered face, ropy muscles, and calloused hands; his eyes were bright and as black as oil, singularly powerful eyes from which you sometimes had to look away . . . and from which you sometimes could *not* look away, no matter how much you might want to. The Indian took an interest in young Tommy Shaddack, occasionally letting him help with some yard chores and household repairs, when neither the judge nor Tommy's mother was around to disapprove of their boy doing common labor or associating with 'social inferiors'. Which meant he hung out with Runningdeer almost constantly between the ages of five and twelve, the period during which the Indian had worked for the judge, because his parents were hardly ever there to see and object.

One of the earliest detailed memories he had was of Runningdeer and the sign of the self-devouring snake . . .

He had been five years old, sprawled on the rear patio of the big house in Phoenix, among a collection of Tonka Toys, but he'd been more interested in Runningdeer than in the miniature trucks and cars. The Indian was wearing jeans and boots, shirtless in the bright desert sun, trimming shrubs with a large pair of wood-handled shears. The muscles in Runningdeer's back, shoulders, and arms worked fluidly, stretching and flexing, and Tommy was fascinated by the man's physical power. The judge, Tommy's father, was thin, bony, and pale. Tommy himself, at five, was already visibly his father's son, fair and tall for his age and painfully thin. By the day he showed Tommy the self-devouring snake, Runningdeer had been working for the Shaddacks two weeks, and Tommy had been increasingly drawn to him without fully understanding why. Running-deer often had a smile for him and told funny stories about talking coyotes and rattlesnakes and other desert animals. Sometimes he called Tommy 'Little Chief,' which was the first nickname anyone had given him. His mother always called him Tommy or Tom; the judge called him Thomas. So he sprawled among his Tonka Toys, playing with them less and less, until at last he stopped playing altogether and simply watched Runningdeer, as if mesmerized.

He was not sure how long he lay entranced in the patio shade, in the hot dry air of the desert day, but after a while he was surprised to hear Runningdeer call to him.

'Little Chief, come look at this.'

He was in such a daze that at first he could not respond. His arms and legs would not work. He seemed to have been turned to stone.

'Come on, come on, Little Chief. You've *got* to see this.'

At last Tommy sprang up and ran out onto the lawn, to the hedges surrounding the swimming pool, where Runningdeer had been trimming.

'This is a rare thing,' Runningdeer said in a somber voice, and he pointed to a green snake that lay at his feet on the sun-warmed decking around the pool.

Tommy began to pull back in fear.

But the Indian seized him by the arm, held him close, and said, 'Don't be afraid. It's only a harmless garden snake. It's not going to hurt you. In fact it's been sent here as a sign to you.'

Tommy stared wide-eyed at the eighteen-inch reptile, which was curled to form an O, its own tail in its mouth, as if eating itself. The serpent was motionless, glassy eyes unblinking. Tommy thought it was dead, but the Indian assured him that it was alive.

'This is a great and powerful sign that all Indians know,' said Runningdeer. He squatted in front of the snake and pulled the boy down beside him. 'It is a sign,' he whispered, 'a supernatural sign, sent from the great spirits, and it's always meant for a young boy, so it must have been meant for you. A very powerful sign.'

Staring wonderingly at the snake, Tommy said. 'Sign? What do you mean? It's not a sign. It's a snake.'

'An omen. A presentiment. A sacred sign,' Runningdeer said.

As they hunkered before the snake, he explained such things to Tommy in an intense, whispery voice, all the while holding him by one arm. Sun glare bounced off the concrete decking. Shimmering waves of heat rose from it too. The snake lay so motionless that it might have been an incredibly detailed jeweled choker rather than a real snake – each scale a chip of emerald, twin rubies for the eyes. After a while Tommy drifted back into the queer trance that he'd been in while lying on the patio, and Runningdeer's voice slithered serpentlike into his head, deep inside his skull, curling and sliding through his brain.

Stranger still, it began to seem that the voice was not really Runningdeer's at all, but the snake's. He stared unwaveringly at the reptile and almost forgot that Runningdeer was there, for what the snake said to him was so compelling and exciting that it filled Tommy's senses, demanded his entire attention, even though he did not fully understand what he was hearing. This is a sign of destiny, the snake said, a sign of power and destiny, and you will be a man of great power, far greater than your father, a man to whom others will bow down, a man who will be obeyed, a man who will never fear the future because he will *make* the future, and you will have anything you want, anything in the world. But for now, said the snake, this is to be our secret. No one must know that I've brought this message to you, that the sign has been delivered, for if they know that you are destined to hold power over them, they will surely kill you, slit your throat in the night, tear out your heart, and bury you in a deep grave. They must not know that you are the king-to-be, a god-on-earth, or they will smash you before your strength has fully flowered. Secret. This is our secret. I am the self-devouring snake, and I will eat myself and vanish now that I've delivered this message, and no one will know I've been here. Trust the Indian but no one else.

No one. Ever.

Tommy fainted on the pool decking and was ill for two days. The doctor was baffled. The boy had no fever, no detectable swelling of lymph glands, no nausea, no soreness in the joints or muscles, no pain whatsoever. He was merely gripped by a profound malaise, so lethargic that he did not even want to bother holding a comic book; watching TV was too much effort. He had no appetite. He slept fourteen hours a day and lay in a daze most of the rest of the time. 'Perhaps mild sunstroke,' the doctor said, 'and if he doesn't snap out of it in a couple of days, we'll put him in the hospital for tests.'

During the day, when the judge was in court or meeting with his investment associates, and when Tommy's mother was at the country club or at one of her charity luncheons, Runningdeer slipped into the house now and then to sit by the boy's bed for ten minutes. He told Tommy stories, speaking in that soft and strangely rhythmic voice.

Miss Karval, their live-in housekeeper and part-time nanny, knew that neither the judge nor Mrs. Shaddack would approve of the Indian's sickbed visits or any of his other associations with Tommy. But Miss Karval was kindhearted, and she disapproved of the lack of attention that the Shaddacks gave to their offspring. And she liked the Indian. She turned her head because she saw no harm in it – if Tommy promised not to tell his folks how much time he spent with Runningdeer.

Just when they decided to admit the boy to a hospital for tests, he recovered, and the doctor's diagnosis of sunstroke was accepted. Thereafter, Tommy tagged along with Runningdeer most days from the time his father and mother left the house until one of them returned. When he started going to school, he came right home after classes; he was never interested when other kids invited him to their houses to play, for he was eager to spend a couple of hours with Runningdeer before his mother or father appeared in the late afternoon.

And week by week, month by month, year by year, the Indian made Tommy acutely aware of signs that foretold his great – though as yet unspecified – destiny. A patch of four-leaf clovers under the boy's bedroom window. A dead rat floating in the swimming pool. A score of chirruping crickets in one of the boy's bureau drawers when he came home from school one afternoon. Occasionally coins appeared where he had not left them – a penny in every shoe in his closet; a month later, a nickle in every pocket of every pair of his pants; later still, a shiny silver dollar *inside* an apple that Runningdeer was peeling for him – and the Indian regarded the coins with awe, explaining that they were some of the most powerful signs of all.

'Secret,' Runningdeer whispered portentously on the day after Tommy's ninth birthday, when the boy reported hearing soft bells ringing under his window in the middle of the night.

On arising, he had seen nothing but a candle burning on the lawn. Careful not to wake his parents, he sneaked outside to take a closer look at the candle, but it was gone.

'Always keep these signs secret, or they'll realize that you're a child of destiny, that one day you'll have tremendous power over them, and they'll kill you now, while you're still a boy, and weak.'

'Who's "they"?' Tommy asked.

'They, them, everyone,' the Indian said mysteriously.

'But who?'

'Your father, for one.'

'Not him.'

'Him especially,' Runningdeer whispered. 'He's a man of power. He enjoys having power over others, intimidating, arm-twisting to get his way. You've seen how people bow and scrape to him.'

Indeed, Tommy had noticed the respect with which everyone spoke to his father – especially his many friends in politics – and a couple of times had glimpsed the unsettling and perhaps more honest looks they gave the judge behind his back. They appeared to admire and even revere him to his face, but when he was not looking they seemed not only to fear but loathe him.

'He is satisfied only when he has all the power, and he won't let go of it easily, not for anyone, not even for his son. If he finds out that you're destined to be greater and more powerful than he is . . . no one can save you then. Not even me.'

Perhaps if their family life had been marked by more affection, Tommy would have found the Indian's warning difficult to accept. But his father seldom spoke to him in more than a perfunctory way, and even more seldom touched him – never a real hug and *never* a kiss.

Sometimes Runningdeer brought a gift of homemade candy for the boy. 'Cactus candy,' he called it. There was always just one piece for each of them, and they always ate it together, either sitting on the patio when the Indian was on his lunch break, or as Tommy followed his mentor around the two-acre property on a series of chores. Soon after eating the cactus candy, the boy was overcome by a curious mood. He felt euphoric. When he moved, he seemed to float. Colors were brighter, prettier. The most vivid thing of all was Runningdeer: His hair was impossibly black, his skin a beautiful bronze, his teeth radiantly white, his eyes as dark as the end of the universe. Every sound – even the crisp *snick-snick-snick* of hedge clippers, the roar of a plane passing overhead on its way to Phoenix airport, the insect-hum of the pool motor – became music; the world was full of music, though the most musical of all things was Runningdeer's voice. Odors also became sharper: flowers, cut grass, the oil with which the Indian lubricated his tools. Even the stink of perspiration was pleasant. Runningdeer smelled like fresh-baked bread and hay and copper pennies.

Tommy seldom remembered what Runningdeer talked about after they ate their cactus candy, but he did recall that the Indian spoke to him with a special intensity. A lot of it had to do with the sign of the moonhawk. 'If the great spirits send the sign of the moonhawk, you'll know you're to have tremendous power and be invincible. Invincible! But if you *do* see the moonhawk, it'll mean the great spirits want something from you in return, an act that will truly prove your worthiness.' That much stuck with Tommy, but he remembered little else. Usually, after an hour, he grew weary and went to his room to nap; his dreams then were particularly vivid, more real than waking like, and always involved the Indian. They were simultaneously frightening and comforting dreams.

On a rainy Saturday in November, when Tommy was ten, he sat on a stool by the workbench at one end of the four-car garage, watching as Runningdeer repaired an electric carving knife that the judge always used to slice the turkey on Thanksgiving and Christmas. The air was pleasantly cool and unusually humid for Phoenix. Runningdeer and Tommy were talking about the rain, the up-coming holiday, and things that had happened at school recently. They didn't always talk about signs and destiny, or otherwise Tommy might not have liked the Indian so much; Runningdeer was a great listener.

When the Indian finished repairing the electric knife, he plugged it in and switched it on. The blade shivered back and forth so fast that the cutting edge was a blur.

Tommy applauded.

'You see this?' Runningdeer asked, raising the knife higher and squinting at it in the glow from the fluorescent bulbs overhead.

Bright glints flew from the shuttling blade, as if it were busily slicing up the light itself.

'What?' Tommy asked.

'This knife, Little Chief. It's a machine. A frivolous machine, not a really important machine like a car or airplane or electric wheelchair. My brother is ... crippled ... and must get around in an electric wheelchair. Did you know that, Little Chief?'

'No.'

'One of my brothers is dead, the other crippled.'

'I'm sorry.'

'They are my half-brothers, really, but the only ones I have.'

'How did it happen? Why?'

Runningdeer ignored the questions. 'Even if this knife's purpose is just to carve a turkey that could be carved as well by hand, it's still efficient and clever. Most machines are much more efficient and clever than people.'

The Indian lowered the cutting instrument slightly and turned to face Tommy. He held the purring knife between them and looked past the shuttling blade into Tommy's eyes.

The boy felt himself slipping into a spell similar to that he'd experienced after eating cactus candy, though they had eaten none.

'The white man puts great faith in machines,' Runningdeer said. 'He thinks machines are ever so much more reliable and clever than people. If you want to be truly great in the white man's world, Little Chief, you must make yourself as much like a machine as you can. You must be efficient. You must be relentless like a machine. You must be determined in your goals, allowing no desires or emotions to distract you.'

He moved the purring blade slowly toward Tommy's face, until the boy's eyes crossed in an attempt to focus on the cutting edge.

'With this I could lop away your nose, slice off your lips, carve away your cheeks and ears ...'

Tommy wanted to slip off the workbench stool and run.

But he could not move.

He realized that the Indian was holding him by one wrist.

Even if he had not been held, he would have been unable to flee. He was paralyzed. Not entirely by fear, either. There was something seductive about the moment; the potential for violence was in an odd way ... exciting.

'... cut off the round ball of your chin, scalp you, lay bare the bone, and you'd bleed to death or die of one cause or another but ...'

The blade was no more than two inches from his nose.

'... *but* the machine would go on ...'

One inch.

'... the knife would still purr and slice, purr and slice ...'

Half an inch.

'... because machines don't die ...'

Tommy could feel the faint, faint breeze stirred by the continuously moving electric blade.

'... machines are efficient and reliable. If you want to do well in the white man's world, Little Chief, you must be like a machine.'

Runningdeer switched off the knife. He put it down.

He did not let go of Tommy.

Leaning close, he said, 'If you wish to be great, if you wish to please the spirits and do what they ask of you when they send you the sign of the moon-hawk, then you must be determined, relentless, cold, single-minded, uncaring of consequences, just *like a machine.*'

Thereafter, especially when they ate cactus candy together, they often talked of being as dedicated to a purpose and as reliable as a machine. As he approached puberty, Tommy's dreams were less often filled with sexual refer-ences than with images of the moonhawk and with visions of people who looked normal on the outside but who were all wires and transistors and clicking metal switches on the inside.

In the summer of his twelfth year, after seven years in the Indian's company, the boy learned what had happened to Runningdeer's half-brothers. At least he learned some of it. He surmised the rest.

He and the Indian were sitting on the patio, having lunch and watching the rainbows that appeared and faded in the mist thrown up by the lawn sprinklers. He had asked about Runningdeer's brothers a few times since that day at the workbench, more than a year and a half earlier, but the Indian had never answered him. This time, however, Runningdeer stared off toward the distant, hazy mountains and said, 'This is a secret I tell you.'

'All right.'

'As secret as all the signs you've been given.'

'Sure.'

'Some white men, just college boys, got drunk and were cruising around, maybe looking for women, certainly looking for trouble. They met my brothers by accident, in a restaurant parking lot. One of my brothers was married, and his wife was with him, and the college boys started playing tease-the-Indians, but they also really liked the look of my brother's wife. They wanted her and were drunk enough to think they could just take her. There was a fight. Five against my two brothers. They beat one to death with a tire iron. The other will never walk again. They took my brother's wife with them, used her.'

Tommy was stunned by this revelation.

At last the boy said, 'I *hate* white men.'

Runningdeer laughed.

'I really do,' Tommy said. 'What happened to those guys who did it? Are they in prison now?'

'No prison.' Runningdeer smiled at the boy. A fierce, humorless smile. 'Their fathers were powerful men. Money. Influence. So the judge let them off for "insufficient evidence." '

'My father should've been the judge. He wouldn't let them off.'

'Wouldn't he?' the Indian said.

'Never.'

'Are you so sure?'

Uneasily, Tommy said, 'Well . . . sure I'm sure.'

The Indian was silent.

'I hate white men,' Tommy repeated, this time motivated more by a desire to curry favor with the Indian than by conviction.

Runningdeer laughed again and patted Tommy's hand.

Near the end of that same summer, Runningdeer came to Tommy late on a blazing August day and, in a portentous and ominous voice, said, 'There will be a full moon tonight, Little Chief. Go into the backyard and watch it for a while. I believe that tonight the sign will finally come, the most important sign of all.'

After moonrise, which came shortly after nightfall, Tommy went out and stood on the pool apron, where Runningdeer had shown him the self-devouring snake seven years earlier. He stared up at the lunar sphere for a long time, while an elongated reflection of it shimmered on the surface of the water in the swimming pool. It was a swollen yellow moon, still low in the sky and immense.

Soon the judge came out onto the patio, calling to him, and Tommy said, 'Here.'

The judge joined him by the pool. 'What're you doing, Thomas?'

'Watching for . . .'

'For what?'

Just then Tommy saw the hawk silhouetted by the moon. For years he had been told he would see it one day, had been prepared for it and all that it would mean, and suddenly there it was, frozen for a moment in midflight against the round lunar lamp.

'There!' he said, for the moment having forgotten that he could trust no one but the Indian.

'There what?' the judge asked.

'Didn't you see it?'

'Just the moon.'

'You weren't looking or you'd have seen it.'

'Seen what?'

His father's blindness to the sign only proved to Tommy that he was, indeed, special and that the portent had been meant for his eyes only – which reminded him that he could not trust his own father. He said, 'Uh . . . a shooting star.'

'You're standing out here watching for shooting stars?'

'They're actually meteors,' Tommy said, talking too fast. 'See, tonight the earth's supposed to be passing through a meteor belt, so there'll be lots of them.'

'Since when are you interested in astronomy?'

'I'm not.' Tommy shrugged. 'Just wondered what it'd look like. Pretty boring.' He turned away from the pool and started back toward the house, and after a moment the judge accompanied him.

The next day, Wednesday, the boy told Runningdeer about the moonhawk. 'But I didn't get any messages from it. I don't know what the great spirits want me to do to prove myself.'

The Indian smiled and stared at him in silence for what began to be an uncomfortably long time. Then he said, 'Little Chief, we'll talk about that at lunch.'

Miss Karval had Wednesdays off, and Runningdeer and Tommy were at home alone. They sat side by side on patio chairs for lunch. The Indian seemed to have brought nothing but cactus candy, and Tommy had no appetite for anything else.

Long ago the boy had ceased to eat the candy for its flavor but devoured it eagerly for its effect. And over the years its impact on him had grown constantly more profound.

Soon the boy was in that much-desired dreamlike plane, where colors were bright and sounds were loud and odors were sharp and all things were comforting and appealing. He and the Indian talked for nearly an hour, and at the end of that time Tommy came to understand that the great spirits expected him to kill his father four days hence. Sunday morning. 'That's my day off,' said Runningdeer, 'so I will not be here to offer you support. But in fact that's probably the spirits' intention – that you should have to prove yourself all on your own. At least we'll have the next few days to plan it together, so that when Sunday comes you'll be prepared.'

'Yes,' the boy said dreamily. 'Yes. We'll plan it together.'

Later that afternoon, the judge came home from a business meeting that had followed his court session. Complaining of the heat, he went straight upstairs to take a shower. Tommy's mother had come home half an hour earlier. She was in an armchair in the living room, feet on a low upholstered stool, reading the latest issue of *Town & Country* and sipping at what she called a 'precocktail-hour cocktail'. She barely looked up when the judge leaned in from the hall to announce his intention of showering.

As soon as his father went upstairs, Tommy went to the kitchen and got a butcher's knife from the rack by the stove.

Runningdeer was outside, mowing the lawn.

Tommy went into the living room, walked up to his mother, and kissed her on the cheek. She was surprised by the kiss but more surprised by the knife, which he rammed into her chest three times. He carried the same knife upstairs and buried it in the judge's stomach as he stepped out of the shower.

He went to his room and took off his clothes. There was no blood on his shoes, little on his jeans, but a lot on his shirt. After he quickly washed up in his bathroom sink and sluiced all traces of blood down the drain, he dressed in fresh jeans and shirt. He carefully bundled his bloody clothes in an old towel and carried them into the attic, where he hid them in a corner behind a seaman's trunk. He could dispose of them later.

Downstairs he passed the living room without looking in at his dead mother. He went straight to the desk in the judge's study and opened the right bottom drawer. From behind a stack of files, he withdrew the judge's revolver.

In the kitchen he turned off the overhead fluorescents, so the only light was what came through the windows, which was bright enough but left some parts of the room in cool shadows. He put the butcher's knife on the counter by the refrigerator, squarely in some of those shadows. He put the revolver on one of the chairs at the table, and pulled the chair only partway out, so the gun could be reached but not easily seen.

He went out through the French doors that connected the kitchen to the patio, and yelled for Runningdeer. The Indian did not hear the boy over the roar of the lawnmower, but happened to look up and see him waving. Frowning, he shut off the mower and crossed the half-cut lawn to the patio. 'Yes, Thomas?' he said, because he knew that the judge and Mrs. Shaddack were at home.

'My mother needs your help with something,' Tommy said. 'She asked me to fetch you.'

'My help?'

'Yeah. In the living room.'

'What's she want?'

'She needs some help with . . . well, it's easier to show you than to talk about it.'

The Indian followed him through the French doors, into the large kitchen, past the refrigerator, toward the hall door.

Tommy halted abruptly, turned, and said, 'Oh, yeah, Mother says you'll need that knife, that one there behind you on the counter, by the refrigerator.'

Runningdeer turned, saw the knife lying on the shadowed tile top of the counter, and picked it up. His eyes went very wide. 'Little Chief, there's blood on this knife. There's blood—'

Tommy had already plucked the revolver off the kitchen chair. As the Indian turned toward him in surprise, Tommy held the gun in both hands and fired until he emptied the cylinder, though the recoil slammed painfully through his arms and shoulders, nearly knocking him off his feet. At least two of the rounds hit Runningdeer, and one of them tore out his throat.

The Indian went down hard. The knife clattered out of his hand and spun across the floor.

With one shoe, Tommy kicked the knife closer to the corpse, so it would definitely look as if the dying man had been wielding it.

The boy's understanding of the great spirits' message had been clearer than his mentor's. They wanted him to free himself at once from *everyone* who had more than a little power over him: the judge, his mother, and Runningdeer. Only then could he achieve his own lofty destiny of power.

He had planned the three murders with the coolness of a computer and had executed them with machinelike determination and efficiency. He felt nothing. Emotions had not interfered with his actions. Well, in truth, he was scared and a little excited – even exhilarated – but those feelings had not distracted him.

After staring for a moment at Runningdeer's body, Tommy went to the kitchen phone, dialed the police, and hysterically reported that the Indian, shouting of revenge, had killed his parents and that he, Tommy, had killed the Indian with his father's gun. But he didn't put it so succinctly. He was so hysterical, they had to pry it from him. In fact he was so shattered and disoriented by what had happened that they had to work patiently with him for three or four tedious minutes to get him to stop babbling and give them his name and address. In his mind he had practiced hysteria all afternoon, since lunch with the Indian. Now he was pleased that he sounded so convincing.

He walked out to the front of the house and sat in the driveway and wept until the police arrived. His tears were more genuine than his hysteria. He was crying with relief.

He'd seen the moonhawk twice again, later in life. He saw it when he needed to see it, when he wanted to be reassured that some course of action he wished to follow was correct.

But he never killed anyone again – because he never needed to.

His maternal grandparents took him into their home and raised him in another part of Phoenix. Because he had endured such tragedy, they more or less gave him everything that he wanted, as if to deny him anything would be unbearably cruel and, just possibly, might be the additional straw of burden that would break him at last. He was the sole heir of his father's estate, which was fattened by large life-insurance policies; therefore he was guaranteed a first-rate education and plenty of capital with which to start out in life after graduation from the university. The world lay before him, filled with opportunity. And thanks to Runningdeer, he had the additional advantage of knowing beyond a doubt that he had a great destiny and that the forces of fate and heaven wanted him to achieve tremendous power over other men.

Only a madman killed without a compelling need.

With but rare exception, murder simply was not an *efficient* method of solving problems.

Now, curled up in the back of the van in Paula Parkins's dark garage, Shaddack reminded himself that he was destiny's child, that he had seen the moonhawk three times. He put all fear of Loman Watkins and of failure out of his mind. He sighed and slipped over the edge of sleep.

He dreamed the familiar dream. The vast machine. Half metal and half flesh. Steel pistons stroking. Human hearts dependably pumping lubricants of all kinds. Blood and oil, iron and bone, plastic and tendon, wires and nerves.

• 9 •

Chrissie was amazed that priests ate so well. The table in the rectory kitchen was heavily laden with food; an immense plateful of sausages, eggs, a stack of toast, a package of sweetrolls, another of blueberry muffins, a bowl of hashbrown potatoes that had been warming in the oven, fresh fruit, and a bag of marshmallows for the hot cocoa. Father Castelli was pudgy, sure, but Chrissie had always thought of priests as abstemious in all things, denying themselves at least some of the pleasures of food and drink just as they denied themselves marriage. If Father Castelli consumed as much at every meal, he ought to weigh twice what he did. No, three times as much!

As they ate, she told him about the aliens taking over her folks. In deference to Father Castelli's predisposition toward spiritual answers, and as a means of keeping him hooked, she left the door open on demonic possession, though personally she much favored the alien-invasion explanation. She told him what she'd seen in the upstairs hall yesterday, how she'd been locked in the pantry and, later, had been pursued by her parents and Tucker in their strange new shapes.

The priest expressed astonishment and concern, and several times he demanded more details, but he did not once pause significantly in his eating. In fact he ate with such tremendous gusto that his table manners suffered. Chrissie was as surprised by his sloppiness as she was by the size of his appetite. A couple of times he had egg yolk on his chin, and when she got up the nerve to point it out to him, he made a joke about it and immediately wiped it off. But a moment later she looked up, and there was more egg yolk. He dropped a few miniature marshmallows and didn't seem to care. The front of his black shirt was speckled with toast crumbs, a couple of tiny pieces of sausage, flecks of potatoes, sweetroll crumbs, muffin crumbs . . .

Really, she was beginning to think that Father Castelli was as guilty as any man had ever been of the sin of gluttony.

But she loved him in spite of his eating habits because he never once doubted her sanity or expressed a lack of belief in her wild story. He listened with interest and utmost seriousness, and seemed genuinely concerned, even frightened, by what she told him. 'Well, Chrissie, they've made maybe a thousand movies about alien invasions, hostile creatures from other worlds, and they've written maybe ten thousand books about it, and I've always said that man's mind can't imagine anything that isn't possible in God's world. So who knows, hmmmm? Who's to say they might *not* have landed here in Moonlight Cove? I'm a film buff, and I've always liked scary movies best, but I never imagined that I'd find myself in the middle of a *real-life* scary movie.' He was sincere. He never patronized her.

Although Father Castelli continued to eat with undiminished appetite, Chrissie finished breakfast and her story at the same time. Because the kitchen was warm, she was rapidly drying out, and only the seat of her pants and her running shoes were still really wet. She felt sufficiently reinvigorated to consider what lay ahead of her now that she had reached help. 'What next? We've got to call in the Army, don't you think, Father?'

'Perhaps the Army *and* the Marines,' he said after a moment of deliberation. 'The Marines might be better at this sort of thing.'

'Do you think . . .'

'What is it, dear girl?'

'Do you think there's any chance . . . well, any chance of getting my folks back? The way they were, I mean?'

He put down a muffin that he had been raising to his mouth, and he reached across the table, between the plates and tins of food, to take her hand. His fingers were slightly greasy with butter, but she did not mind, for he was so reassuring and comforting; right now she needed a lot of reassuring and comforting.

'You'll be reunited with your parents,' Father Castelli said with great sympathy. 'I absolutely guarantee that you will.'

She bit her lower lip, trying to hold back her tears.

'I guarantee it,' he repeated.

Abruptly his face *bulged*. Not evenly like an inflating balloon. Rather, it bulged in some places and not others, rippled and pulsed, as if his skull had turned to mush and as if balls of worms were writhing and squirming just under the skin.

'I guarantee it!'

Chrissie was too terrified to scream. For a moment she could not move. She was paralyzed by fear, frozen in her chair, unable to summon even enough motor control to blink or draw a breath.

She could hear his bones loudly crackling-crunching-popping as they splintered and dissolved and reshaped themselves with impossible speed. His flesh made a disgusting, wet, oozing sound as it flowed into new forms almost with the ease of hot wax.

The priest's skull swelled upward and swept back in a bony crest, and his face was hardly human at all now but partly crustacean, partly insectile, vaguely wasplike, with something of the jackal in it, too, and with fiery hateful eyes.

At last Chrissie cried out explosively, 'No!' Her heart was pounding so hard that each beat was painful. 'No, go away, let me alone, let me go!'

His jaws lengthened, then split back nearly to his ears in a menacing grin defined by double rows of immense sharp teeth.

'No, no!'

She tried to get up.

She realized that he was still holding her left hand.

He spoke in a voice eerily reminiscent of those of her mother and Tucker when they had stalked her as far as the mouth of the culvert last night:

'. . . *need, need . . . want . . . give me . . . give me . . . need . . .*'

He didn't look like her parents had looked when transformed. Why wouldn't all the aliens look the same?

He opened his mouth wide and hissed at her, and thick yellowish saliva was strung like threads of taffy from his upper to his lower teeth. Something stirred inside his mouth, a strange-looking tongue; it thrust out at her like a jack-in-the-box popping forth on its spring, and it proved to be a mouth *within* his mouth, another set of smaller and even sharper teeth on a stalk, designed to get into tight places and bite prey that took refuge there.

Father Castelli was becoming something startlingly familiar: the creature from the movie *Alien*. Not exactly that monster in every detail but uncannily similar to it.

She was trapped in a movie, just as the priest had said, a real-life horror flick: no doubt one of his favorites. Was Father Castelli able to assume whatever shape he wanted, and was he becoming this beast only because it pleased him to do so and because it would best fulfill Chrissie's expectations of alien invaders?

This was crazy.

Beneath his clothes, the priest's body was changing too. His shirt sagged on him in some places, as if the substance of him had melted away beneath it, but in other places it strained at the seams as his body acquired new bony extrusions and inhuman excrescences. Shirt buttons popped. Fabric tore. His Roman collar came apart and fell askew on his hideously resculpted neck.

Gasping, making a curious *uh-uh-uh-uh-uh* sound in the back of her throat but unable to stop, she tried to pull free of him. She stood up, knocking her chair over, but she was still held fast. He was very strong. She could not tear loose.

His hand also had begun to change. His fingers had lengthened. They were plated with a hornlike substance – smooth, hard, and shiny black – more like pincers with digits than like human hands.

'. . . *need . . . want, want . . . need . . .*'

She plucked up her breakfast knife, swung it high over her head, and drove it down with all her might, stabbing him in the forearm, just above the wrist, where his flesh still looked more human than not. She had hoped that the blade would pin him to the table, but she didn't feel it bite all the way through him to the wood beneath.

His shriek was so shrill and piercing that it seemed to vibrate through Chrissie's bones.

His armored, demonic hand spasmed open. She yanked free of him. Fortunately she was quick, for his hand clamped shut again a fraction of a second later, pinching her fingertips but unable to hold her.

The kitchen door was on the priest's side of the table. She could not reach it without exposing her back to him.

With a cry that was half scream and half roar, he tore the knife from his arm and threw it aside. He knocked the dishes and food from the table with one sweep of his bizarrely mutated arm, which was now eight or ten inches longer than it had been. It protruded from the cuff of his black shirt in nightmarish gnarls and planes and hooks of the dark, chitinous stuff that had replaced his flesh.

Mary, Mother of God, pray for me; Mother most pure, pray for me; Mother most chaste, pray for me. *Please*, Chrissie thought.

The priest grabbed hold of the table and threw it aside, too, as if it weighed only ounces. It crashed into the refrigerator.

Now nothing separated her from him.

From *it*.

She feinted toward the kitchen door, taking a couple of steps in that direction.

The priest – not really a priest any more; a *thing* that sometimes masqueraded as a priest – swung to his right, intending to cut her off and snare her.

Immediately she turned, as she'd always intended, and ran in the opposite direction, toward the open door that led to the downstairs hall, leaping over scattered toast and links of sausage. The trick worked. Wet shoes squishing and squeaking on the linoleum, she was past him before he realized she actually was going to his left.

She suspected that he was quick as well as strong. Quicker than she, no doubt. She could hear him coming behind her.

If she could only reach the front door, get out onto the porch and into the yard, she would probably be safe. She suspected that he would not follow her beyond the house, into the street, where others might see him. Surely not everyone in Moonlight Cove had already been possessed by these aliens, and until the last real person in town was taken over, they could not strut around in a transformed state, eating young girls with impunity.

Not far. Just the front door and a few steps beyond.

She had covered two-thirds of the distance, expecting to feel a claw snag her shirt from behind, when the door opened ahead of her. The other priest, Father O'Brien, stepped across the threshold and blinked in surprise.

At once she knew that she couldn't trust him, either. He could not have lived in the same house as Father Castelli without the alien seed having been planted in him. Seed, spoor, slimy parasite, spirit – whatever was used to effect possession, Father O'Brien undoubtedly had had it rammed or injected into him.

Unable to go forward or back, unwilling to swerve through the archway on her right and into the living room because that was a dead end – in every sense of the word – she grabbed hold of the newel post, which she was just passing, and swung herself onto the stairs. She ran pell-mell for the second floor.

The front door slammed below her.

By the time she turned at the landing and started up the second flight of stairs, she heard both of them climbing behind her.

The upper hall had white plaster walls, a dark wood floor, and a wood ceiling. Rooms lay on both sides.

She sprinted to the end of the hall and into a bedroom furnished only with a simple dresser, one nightstand, a double bed with a white chenille spread, a bookcase full of paperbacks, and a crucifix on the wall. She threw the door shut after her, but didn't bother trying to lock or brace it. There was no time. They'd smash through it in seconds, anyway.

Repeating, 'MarymotherofGod, MarymotherofGod,' in a breathless and desperate whisper, she rushed across the room to the window that was framed by emerald-green drapes. Rain washed down the glass.

Her pursuers were in the upstairs hall. Their footsteps boomed through the house.

She grabbed the handles on the sash and tried to pull the window up. It would not budge. She fumbled with the latch, but it already was disengaged.

Farther back the hall toward the head of the stairs, they were throwing open doors, looking for her.

The window was either painted shut or perhaps swollen tight because of the high humidity. She stepped back from it.

The door behind her crashed inward, and something snarled.

Without glancing behind her, she tucked her head down and crossed her arms over her face and threw herself through the window, wondering if she could kill herself by jumping from the second story, figuring it depended where she landed. Grass would be good. Sidewalk would be bad. The pointed spires of a wrought-iron fence would be *real* bad.

The sound of shattering glass was still in the air when she hit a porch roof two feet below the window, which was virtually a miracle, – she was uncut too – so she kept saying *MarymotherofGod* as she did a controlled roll through hammering rain toward the edge of the shingled expanse. When she reached the brink, she clung there for a moment, her left side on the roof, right side supported by a creaking and rapidly sagging rain gutter, and she looked back at the window.

Something wolfish and grotesque was coming after her.

She dropped. She landed on a walkway, on her left side, jarring her bones, clacking her teeth together so hard that she feared they'd fall out in pieces, and scraping one hand badly on the concrete.

But she didn't lie there pitying herself. She scrambled up and, huddled around her pain, turned from the house to run into the street.

Unfortunately she wasn't in front of the rectory. She was behind it, in the rear yard. The back wall of Our Lady of Mercy bordered the lawn on her right, and a seven-foot-high brick wall encircled the rest of the property.

Because of the wall and the trees on both sides of it, she could not see either the neighboring house to the south or the one to the west, on the other side of the alley that ran behind the property. If she couldn't see the rectory's neighbors, they couldn't see her, either, even if they happened to be looking out a window.

That privacy explained why the wolf-thing dared to come onto the roof, pursuing her in broad – if rather gray and dismal – daylight.

She briefly considered going into the house, through the kitchen, down the hall, out the front door, into the street, because that was the last thing they'd expect. But then she thought: Are you *insane?*

She did not bother to scream for help. Her thudding heart seemed to have swollen until her lungs had too little room to expand, so she could barely get enough air to remain conscious, on her feet, and moving. No breath was left for a scream. Besides, even if people heard her call for help, they wouldn't necessarily be able to tell where she was; by the time they tracked her down, she would be either torn apart or possessed, because the scream would have slowed her by a fateful second or two.

Instead, limping slightly to favor a pulled muscle in her left leg but losing no time, she hurried across the expansive rear lawn. She knew she could not scale a blank seven-foot wall fast enough to save herself, especially not with one stingingly abraded hand, so she studied the trees as she ran. She needed one close to the wall; maybe she could climb into it, crawl out on a branch, and drop into the alleyway or into the neighbor's yard.

Above the slosh and patter of the rain, she heard a low growl behind her, and she dared to glance over her shoulder. Wearing only tatters of a shirt, freed entirely from shoes and trousers, the wolf-thing that had been Father O'Brien leaped from the edge of the porch roof in pursuit.

She finally saw a suitable tree – but an instant later noticed a gate in the wall at the southwest corner. She hadn't seen it sooner because it had been screened from her by some shrubbery that she had just passed.

Gasping for air, she put her head down, tucked her arms against her sides, and ran to the gate. She hit the bar latch with her hand, popping it out of the slot in which it had been cradled, and burst through into the alley. Turning left, away from Ocean Avenue toward Jacobi Street, she ran through deep puddles nearly to the end of the block before risking a glance behind her.

Nothing followed her out of the rectory gate.

Twice she had been in the hands of the aliens, and twice she had escaped. She knew she would not be so lucky if she were captured a third time.

• 10 •

Shortly before nine o'clock, after less than four hours of sleep altogether, Sam Booker woke to the quiet clink and clatter of someone at work in the kitchen. He sat up on the living-room sofa, wiped at his matted eyes, put on his shoes and shoulder holster, and went down the hall.

Tessa Lockland was humming softly as she lined up pans, bowls, and food on the wheelchair-low counter near the stove, preparing to make breakfast.

'Good morning,' she said brightly when Sam came into the kitchen.

'What's good about it?' he asked.

'Just listen to that rain,' she said. 'Rain always makes me feel clean and fresh.'

'Always depresses me.'

'And it's nice to be in a warm, dry kitchen, listening to the storm but cozy.'

He scratched at the stubble of beard on his unshaven cheeks. 'Seems a little stuffy in here to me.'

'Well, anyway, we're still alive, and *that's* good.'

'I guess so.'

'God in heaven!' She banged an empty frying pan down on the stove and scowled at him. 'Are all FBI agents like you?'

'In what way?'

'Are they all sourpusses?'

'I'm not a sourpuss.'

'You're a classic Gloomy Gus.'

'Well, life isn't a carnival.'

'It isn't?'

'Life is hard and mean.'

'Maybe. But isn't it a carnival too?'

'Are all documentary filmmakers like you?'

'In what way?'

'Pollyannas?'

'That's ridiculous. I'm no Pollyanna.'

'Oh, no?'

'No.'

'Here we are trapped in a town where reality seems to have been temporarily suspended, where people are being torn apart by species unknown, where Boogeymen roam the streets at night, where some mad computer genius seems to have turned human biology inside out, where we're all likely to be killed or "converted" before midnight tonight, and when I come in here you're grinning and sprightly and humming a Beatles tune.'

'It wasn't the Beatles.'

'Huh?'

'Rolling Stones.'

'And that makes a difference?'

She signed. 'Listen, if you're going to help eat this breakfast, you're going to help make it, so don't just stand there glowering.'

'All right, okay, what can I do?'

'First, get on the intercom there and call Harry, make sure he's awake. Tell him breakfast in ... ummmm ... forty minutes. Pancakes and eggs and shaved, fried ham.'

Sam pressed the intercom button and said, 'Hello, Harry,' and Harry answered at once, already awake. He said he'd be down in about half an hour.

'Now what?' Sam asked Tessa.

'Get the eggs and milk from the refrigerator – but for God's sake don't look in the cartons.'

'Why not?'

She grinned. 'You'll spoil the eggs and curdle the milk.'

'Very funny.'

'I thought so.'

While making pancake mix from scratch, cracking six eggs into glass dishes and preparing them so they could be quickly slipped into the frying pans when she needed them, directing Sam to set the table and help her with other small chores, chopping onions, and shaving ham, Tessa alternately hummed and sang songs by Patti La Belle and the Pointer Sisters. Sam knew whose music it was because she told him, announcing each song as if she were a disc jockey or as if she hoped to educate him and loosen him up. While she worked and sang, she danced in place, shaking her bottom, swiveling her hips, rolling her shoulders, sometimes snapping her fingers, really getting into it.

She was genuinely enjoying herself, but he knew that she was also needling him a little and getting a kick out of that too. He tried to hold fast to his gloom, and when she smiled at him, he did not return her smile, but *damn* she was cute. Her hair was tousled, and she wasn't wearing any makeup, and her clothes were wrinkled from having been slept in, but her slightly disheveled look only added to her allure.

Sometimes she paused in her soft singing and humming to ask him questions, but she continued to sing and dance in place even while he answered her. 'You figured what we're going to do yet to get out of this corner we're in?'

'I have an idea.'

'Patti La Belle, "New Attitude," ' she said, identifying the song she was singing. 'Is this idea of yours a deep, dark secret?'

'No. But I have to go over it with Harry, get some information from him, so I'll tell you both at breakfast.'

At her direction he was hunched over the low counter, cutting thin slices of cheese from a block of Cheddar when she broke into her song long enough to ask, 'Why did you say life is hard and mean?'

'Because it is.'

'But it's also full of fun—'

'No.'

'—and beauty—'

'No.'

'—and hope—'

'Bullshit.'

'It is.'

'It isn't.'

'Yes, it is.'

'It isn't.'

'Why are you so negative?'

'Because I want to be.'

'But why do you want to be?'

'Jesus, you're relentless.'

'Pointer Sisters, "Neutron Dance." ' She sang a bit, dancing in place as she put eggshells and other scraps down the garbage disposal. Then she interrupted her tune to say, 'What could've happened to you to make you feel that life's only mean and hard?'

'You don't want to know.'

'Yes, I do.'

He finished with the cheese and put down the slicer. 'You really want to know?'

'I really do.'

'My mother was killed in a traffic accident when I was just seven. I was in the car with her, nearly died, was actually trapped in the wreckage with her for more than an hour, face to face, staring into her eyeless socket, one whole side of her head bashed in. After that I had to go live with my dad, whom she'd divorced, and he was a mean-tempered son of a bitch, an alcoholic, and I can't tell you how many times he beat me or threatened to beat me or tied me to a chair in the kitchen and left me there for hours at a time, until I couldn't hold myself any more and peed in my pants, and then he'd finally come to untie me and he'd see what I'd done and he'd beat me for *that*.'

He was surprised by how it all spilled from him, as if the floodgates of his subconscious had been opened, pouring forth all the sludge that had been pent up through long years of stoic self-control.

'So as soon as I graduated from high school, I got out of that house, worked my way through junior college, living in cheap rented rooms, shared my bed with armies of cockroaches every night, then applied to the Bureau as soon as I could, because I wanted to see justice in the world, be a part of *bringing* justice to the world, maybe because there'd been so little fairness or justice in my life. But I discovered that more than half the time justice doesn't triumph. The bad guys get away with it, no matter how hard you work to bring them down, because the bad guys are often pretty damned clever, and the good guys never allow themselves to be as mean as they have to be to get the job done. But at the same time, when you're an agent, mainly what you see is the sick underbelly of society, you deal with the scum, one kind of scum or another, and day by day it makes you more cynical, more disgusted with people and sick of them.'

He was talking so fast that he was almost breathless.

She had stopped singing.

He continued with an uncharacteristic lack of emotional control, speaking so fast that his sentences sometimes ran together: 'And my wife died, Karen, she was wonderful, you'd have liked her, everybody liked her, but she got cancer and she died, painfully, horribly, with a lot of suffering, not easy like Ali McGraw in the movies, not with just a sigh and a smile and a quiet goodbye, but in agony. And then I lost my son too. Oh, he's alive, sixteen, nine when his mother died and sixteen now, physically alive and mentally alive, but he's emotionally dead, burnt out in his heart, cold inside, so damned cold inside. He likes computers and computer games and television, and he listens to black metal. You know what black metal is? It's heavymetal music with a twist of satanism, which he likes because it tells him there are no moral values, that everything is relative, that his alienation is right, that his coldness inside is *right*, it tells him that whatever feels good *is* good. You know what he said once?'

She shook her head.

'He said to me, "People aren't important. People don't count. Only *things* are important. Money is important, liquor is important, my stereo is important, anything that makes me *feel* good is important, but I'm not important." He tells me that nuclear bombs are important because they'll blow up all those nice things some day, not because they'll blow up people – after all, people are nothing, just polluting animals that spoil the world. That's what he says. That's what he tells me he believes. He says he can prove it's all true. He says that next time you see a bunch of people standing around a Porsche, admiring the car, look real hard at their faces and you'll see that they care more about that car than about each other. They're not admiring the workmanship, either, not in the sense that they're thinking about the people who *made* the car. It's as if the Porsche was organic, as if it grew or somehow made itself. They admire it for itself, not for what it represents of human engineering skills and craftsmanship. The car is more *alive* than they are. They draw energy from the car, from the sleek lines of it, from the thrill of imagining its power under their hands, so the car becomes more real and far more important than any of the people admiring it.'

'That's bullshit,' Tessa said with conviction.

'But that's what he tells me, and I know it's crap, and I try to reason with him, but he's got all the answers – or thinks he has. And sometimes I wonder . . . if I wasn't so soured on life myself, so sick of so many people, would I be able to argue with him more persuasively? If I wasn't who I am, would I be more able to save my son?'

He stopped.

He realized he was trembling.

They were both silent for a moment.

Then he said, '*That's* why I say life is hard and mean.'

'I'm sorry, Sam.'

'Not your fault.'

'Not yours either.'

He sealed the Cheddar in a piece of Saran Wrap and returned it to the refrigerator while she returned to the pancake mix she was making.

'But you had Karen,' she said. 'There's been love and beauty in your life.'

'Sure.'

'Well, then—'

'But it doesn't last.'

'Nothing lasts forever.'

'Exactly my point,' he said.

'But that doesn't mean we can't enjoy a blessing while we have it. If you're always looking ahead, wondering when this moment of joy is going to end, you can never know any real pleasure in life.'

'Exactly my point,' he repeated.

She left the wooden mixing spoon in the big metal bowl and turned to face him. 'But that's *wrong*. I mean life is filled with moments of wonder, pleasure, joy ... and if we don't seize the moment, if we don't sometimes turn off thoughts of the future and relish the moment, then we'll have no memory of joy to carry us through the bad times – and no hope.'

He stared at her, admiring her beauty and vitality. But then he began to think about how she would age, grow infirm, and die just as everything died, and he could no longer bear to look at her. Instead he turned his gaze to the rain-washed window above the sink. 'Well, I'm sorry if I've upset you, but you'll have to admit you asked for it. You insisted on knowing how I could be such a Gloomy Gus.'

'Oh, you're no Gloomy Gus,' she said. 'You go way beyond that. You're a regular Dr. Doom.'

He shrugged.

They returned to their culinary labors.

• 11 •

After escaping through the gate at the rear of the rectory yard, Chrissie stayed on the move for more than an hour while she tried to decide what to do next. She had planned to go to school and tell her story to Mrs. Tokawa if Father Castelli proved unhelpful. But now she was no longer willing to trust even Mrs. Tokawa. After her experience with the priests, she realized the aliens would probably have taken possession of all the authority figures in Moonlight Cove as a first step toward conquest. She already knew the priests were possessed. She was certain that the police had been taken over as well, so it was logical to assume that teachers also had been among the early victims.

As she moved from neighborhood to neighborhood, she alternately cursed the rain and was grateful for it. Her shoes and jeans and flannel shirt were sodden again, and she was chilled through and through. But the darkish-gray daylight and the rain kept people indoors and provided her with some cover. In addition, as the wind subsided, a thin cold fog drifted in from the sea, not a fraction as dense as it had been last night, just a beardlike mist that clung to the trees, but enough to further obscure the passage of one small girl through those unfriendly streets.

Last night's thunder and lightning were gone too. She was no longer in danger of being flash-roasted by a sudden bolt, which was at least some comfort.

YOUNG GIRL FRIED TO A CRISP BY LIGHTNING THEN EATEN BY ALIENS; SPACE CREATURES ENJOY HUMAN POTATO CHIPS; 'IF WE CAN MAKE THEM WITH RUFFLES,' SAYS ALIEN NEST QUEEN, 'THEY'LL BE PERFECT WITH ONION DIP.'

She moved as much as possible through alleyways and backyards, crossing streets only when necessary and always quickly, for out there she saw too many pairs of somber-faced, sharp-eyed men in slow-moving cars, obvious patrols. Twice she almost ran into them in alleys, too, and had to dive for cover before they spotted her. About a quarter of an hour after she fled through the rectory gate, she noticed more patrols in the area, a sudden influx of cars and men on foot. Foot patrols scared her most. Pairs of men in rain slickers were better able to conduct a search and were more difficult to escape from than men in cars. She was terrified of walking into them unexpectedly.

Actually she spent more time in hiding than on the move. Once she huddled for a while behind a cluster of garbage cans in an alley. She took refuge under a brewer's spruce, the lower branches of which nearly touched the ground, like a skirt, providing a dark and mostly dry retreat. Twice she crawled under cars and lay for a while.

She never stayed in one place for more than five or ten minutes. She was afraid that some alien-possessed busybody would see her as she crawled into her hiding place and would call the police to report her, and that she would be trapped.

By the time she reached the vacant lot on Juniper Lane, beside Callan's Funeral Home, and curled up in the deepest brush – dry grass and bristly chaparral – she was beginning to wonder if she would ever think of someone to turn to for help. For the first time since her ordeal had begun, she was losing hope.

A huge fir spread its branches across part of the lot, and her clump of brush was within its domain, so she was sheltered from the worst of the rain. More important, in the deep grass, curled on her side, she could not be seen from the street or from the windows of nearby houses.

Nevertheless, every minute or so, she cautiously raised her head far enough to look quickly around, to be sure that no one was creeping up on her. During that reconnoitering, looking east past the alleyway at the back of the lot, toward Conquistador, she saw a part of the big redwood-and-glass house on the east side of that street. The Talbot place. At once she remembered the man in the wheelchair.

He had come to Thomas Jefferson to speak to the fifth- and sixth-grade students last year, during Awareness Days, a week-long program of studies that was for the most part wasted time, though *he* had been interesting. He had talked to them about the difficulties and the amazing abilities of disabled people.

At first Chrissie had felt so sorry for him, had just pitied him half to death, because he'd looked so pathetic, sitting there in his wheelchair, his body half wasted away, able to use only one hand, his head slightly twisted and tilted permanently to one side. But then as she listened to him she realized that he had a wonderful sense of humor and did not feel sorry for himself, so it seemed more and more absurd to pity him. They had an opportunity to ask him questions, and he had been so willing to discuss the intimate details of his life, the sorrows and joys of it, that she had finally come to admire him a whole lot.

And his dog Moose had been terrific.

Now, looking at the redwood-and-glass house through the tips of the rain-shiny stalks of high grass, thinking about Harry Talbot and Moose, Chrissie wondered if *that* was a place she could go for help.

She dropped back down in the brush and thought about it for a couple of minutes.

Surely a wheelchair-bound cripple was one of the last people the aliens would bother to possess – if they wanted him at all.

She immediately was ashamed of herself for thinking such a thing. A wheelchair-bound cripple was not a second-class human being. He had just as much to offer the aliens as anyone else.

On the other hand . . . would a bunch of aliens have an enlightened view of disabled people? Wasn't that a bit much to expect? After all, they were *aliens*. Their values weren't supposed to be the same as those of human beings. If they went around planting seeds – or spoors or slimy baby slugs or whatever – in people, and if they ate people, surely they couldn't be expected to treat disabled people with the proper respect any more than they would help old ladies to cross the street.

Harry Talbot.

The more she thought about him, the more certain Chrissie became that he had thus far been spared the horrible attention of the aliens.

• 12 •

After she called him Dr. Doom, she sprayed the Jenn-Air griddle with Pam, so the pancakes wouldn't stick.

She turned on the oven and put a plate in there, to which she could transfer the cakes to keep them warm as she made them.

Then, in a tone of voice that immediately clued him to the fact that she was bent on persuading him to reconsider his bleak assessment of life, she said, 'Tell me—'

'Can't you leave it alone *yet*?'

'No.'

He sighed.

She said, 'If you're this damned glum, why not . . .'

'Kill myself?'

'Why not?'

He laughed bitterly. 'On the drive up here from San Francisco, I played a little game with myself – counted the reasons that life was worth living. I came up with just four, but I guess they're enough, because I'm still hanging around.'

'What were they?'

'One – good Mexican food.'

'I'll go along with that.'

'Two – Guinness Stout.'

'I like Heineken dark myself.'

'It's okay, but it's not a reason to live. *Guinness* is a reason to live.'

'What's number three?'

'Goldie Hawn.'

'You know Goldie Hawn?'

'Nope. Maybe I don't want to, 'cause maybe I'd be disappointed. I'm talking about her screen image, the idealized Goldie Hawn.'

'She's your dream girl, huh?'

'More than that. She . . . hell, I don't know . . . she seems untouched by life, undamaged, vital and happy and innocent and . . . fun.'

'Think you'll ever meet her?'

'You've got to be kidding.'

She said, 'You know what?'

'What?'

'If you *did* meet Goldie Hawn, if she walked up to you at a party and said something funny, something cute, and giggled in that way she has, you wouldn't even recognize her.'

'Oh, I'd recognize her, all right.'

'No, you wouldn't. You'd be so busy brooding about how unfair, unjust, hard, cruel, bleak, dismal, and stupid life is that you would not seize the moment. You wouldn't even *recognize* the moment. You'd be too shrouded in a haze of gloom to see who she was. Now, what's your fourth reason for living?'

He hesitated. 'Fear of death.'

She blinked at him. 'I don't understand. If life's so awful, why is death to be feared?'

'I underwent a near-death experience. I was in surgery, having a bullet taken out of my chest, and I almost bought the farm. Rose out of my body, drifted up to the ceiling, watched the surgeons for a while, then found myself rushing faster and faster down a dark tunnel toward this dazzling light – the whole screwy scenario.'

She was impressed and intrigued. Her clear blue eyes were wide with interest. 'And?'

'I saw what lies beyond.'

'You're serious, aren't you?'

'Damned serious.'

'You're telling me that you *know* there's an afterlife?'

'Yes.'

'A God?'

'Yes.'

Astonished, she said, 'But if you *know* there's a God and that we move on from this world, then you know life has purpose, meaning.'

'So?'

'Well, it's doubt about the purpose of life that lies at the root of most people's spells of gloom and depression. Most of us, if we'd experienced what you'd experienced . . . well, we'd never worry again. We'd have the strength to deal with any adversity, knowing there was meaning to it and a life beyond. So what's wrong with you, mister? Why didn't you lighten up after that? Are you just a bullheaded dweeb or what?'

'Dweeb?'

'Answer the question.'

The elevator kicked in and ascended from the first-floor hall.

'Harry's coming,' Sam said.

'Answer the question,' she repeated.

'Let's just say that what I saw didn't give me hope. It scared the hell out of me.'

'Well? Don't keep me hanging. What'd you see on the Other Side?'

'If I tell you, you'll think I'm crazy.'

'You've got nothing to lose. I already think you're crazy.'

He sighed and shook his head and wished that he'd never brought it up. How had she gotten him to open himself so completely?

The elevator reached the third floor and halted.

Tessa stepped away from the kitchen counter, moving closer to him, and said, 'Tell me what you saw, dammit.'

'You won't understand.'

'What am I – a moron?'

'Oh, you'd understand what I saw, but you wouldn't understand what it meant to me.'

'Do *you* understand what it meant to you?'

'Oh, yes,' he said solemnly.

'Are you going to tell me willingly, or do I have to take a meat fork from that rack and torture it out of you?'

The elevator had started down from the third floor.

He glanced toward the hall. 'I really don't want to discuss it.'

'You don't, huh?'

'No.'

'You saw God but you don't want to discuss it.'

'That's right.'

'Most guys who see God – that's the *only* thing they ever want to discuss. Most guys who see God – they form whole religions based on the one meeting with Him, and they tell *millions* of people about it.'

'But I—'

'Fact is, according to what I've read, most people who undergo a near-death experience are changed forever by it. And always for the better. If they were pessimists, they become optimists. If they were atheists, they become believers. Their values change, they learn to love life for itself, they're goddamned *radiant!* But not you. Oh, no, you become even more dour, even more grim, even more bleak.'

The elevator reached the ground floor and fell silent.

'Harry's coming,' Sam said.

'Tell me what you saw.'

'Maybe I can tell *you*,' he said, surprised to find that he was actually willing to discuss it with her at the right time, in the right place. 'Maybe you. But later.'

Moose padded into the kitchen, panting and grinning at them, and Harry rolled through the doorway a moment later.

'Good morning,' Harry said chipperly.

'Did you sleep well?' Tessa asked, favoring him with a genuine smile of affection that Sam envied.

Harry said, 'Soundly, but not as soundly as the dead – thank God.'

'Pancakes?' Tessa asked him.

'Stacks, please.'

'Eggs?'

'Dozens.'

'Toast?'

'Loaves.'

'I like a man with an appetite.'

Harry said, 'I was running all night, so I'm famished.'

'Running?'

'In my dreams. Chased by Boogeymen.'

While Harry got a package of dog food from under one of the counters and filled Moose's dish in the corner, Tessa went to the griddle, sprayed it with Pam again, told Sam that he was in charge of the eggs, and started to ladle out the first of the pancakes from the bowl of batter. After a moment she said, 'Patti La Belle, "Stir It Up," ' and began to sing and dance in place again.

'Hey,' Harry said, 'I can give you music if you want music.'

He rolled to a compact under-the-counter-mounted radio that neither Tessa nor Sam had noticed, clicked it on, and moved the tuner across the dial until he came to a station playing 'I Heard It Through the Grapevine' by Gladys Knight and the Pips.

'All *right*,' Tessa said, and she began to sway and bump and grind with such enthusiasm that Sam couldn't figure out how she poured the pancake batter onto the griddle in such neat puddles.

Harry laughed and turned his motorized wheelchair in circles, as if dancing with her.

Sam said, 'Don't you people know that the world is coming to an end around us?'

They ignored him, which he supposed was what he deserved.

• 13 •

By a roundabout route, cloaking herself in the rain and mist and whatever shadows she could find, Chrissie reached the alley to the east of Conquistador. She entered Talbot's backyard through a gate in a redwood fence and scurried from one clump of shrubbery to another, twice nearly stepping in dog poop – Moose was an amazing dog, but not without faults – until she reached the steps to the back porch.

She heard music playing inside. It was an oldie, from the days when her parents had been teenagers. And in fact it had been one of their favorites. Though Chrissie didn't remember the title, she did recall the name of the group – Junior Walker and the All-Stars.

Figuring that the music, combined with the drumming rain, would cover any sounds she made, she crept up the steps onto the redwood porch and, in a crouch, moved to the nearest window. She hunkered below the sill for a while, listening to them in there. They were talking, often laughing, sometimes singing along with the songs on the radio.

They didn't sound like aliens. They sounded pretty much like ordinary people.

Were aliens likely to enjoy the music of Stevie Wonder and the Four Tops and the Pointer Sisters? Hardly. To human ears, alien music probably sounded like knights in armor playing bagpipes while simultaneously falling down a long set of stairs amidst a pack of baying hounds. More like Twisted Sister than like the Pointer Sisters.

Eventually she rose up just far enough to peer over the sill, through a gap in the curtains. She saw Mr. Talbot in his wheelchair, Moose, and a strange man and woman. Mr. Talbot was beating time with his good hand on the arm of his wheelchair, and Moose was wagging his tail vigorously if out of synch with the music. The other man was using a spatula to scoop eggs out of a couple of frying pans and shift them onto plates, glowering at the woman now and then as he did so, maybe not approving of the way she abandoned herself to the song, but still tapping his right foot to the music. The woman was making flapjacks and transferring them to a warming platter in the oven, and as she worked she shimmied and swayed and dipped; she had good moves.

Chrissie crouched down again and thought about what she had seen. Nothing about their behavior was particularly odd if they were people, but if they were aliens they surely wouldn't be bopping to the radio while they made breakfast. Chrissie had a real hard time believing that aliens – like the thing masquerading as Father Castelli – could have either a sense of humor or rhythm. Surely, all that aliens cared about was taking possession of new hosts and finding new recipes for cooking tender children.

Nevertheless she decided to wait until she had a chance to watch them eating. From what she'd heard her mother and Tucker say in the meadow last night, and from what she had seen at breakfast with the Father Castelli creature, she believed that aliens were ravenous, each with the appetite of half a dozen men. If Harry Talbot and his guests didn't make absolute hogs of themselves when they sat down to eat, she could probably trust them.

• 14 •

Loman had stayed at Peyser's house, supervising the cleanup and overseeing the transfer of the regressives' bodies to Callan's hearse. He was afraid to let his men handle it alone, for fear that the sight of the mutated bodies or the smell of blood would induce them to seek altered states of their own. He knew that all of them – not least of all himself – were walking a taut wire over an abyss. For the same reason, he followed the hearse to the funeral home and stayed with Callan and his assistant until Peyser's and Sholnick's bodies were fed into the white-hot flames of the crematorium.

He checked on the progress of the search for Booker, the Lockland woman, and Chrissie Foster, and he made a few changes in the pattern of the patrols. He was in the office when the report came in from Castelli, and he went directly to the rectory at Our Lady of Mercy to hear firsthand how the girl could have slipped away from them. They were full of excuses, mostly lame. He suspected they had regressed in order to toy with the girl, just for the thrill of it, and while playing with her had unintentionally given her a chance to escape. Of course they would not admit to regression.

Loman increased the patrols in the immediate area, but there was no sign of the girl. She had gone to ground. Still, if she had come into town instead of heading out to the freeway, they were more likely to catch her and convert her before the day was done.

At nine o'clock he returned to his house on Iceberry Way to get breakfast. Since he'd nearly degenerated in Peyser's blood-spattered bedroom, his clothes had felt loose on him. He had lost a few pounds as his catabolic processes had consumed his own flesh to generate the tremendous energy needed to regress – and to *resist* regression.

The house was dark and silent. Denny was no doubt upstairs, in front of his computer, where he had been last night. Grace had left for work at Thomas Jefferson, where she was a teacher; she had to keep up the pretense of an ordinary life until everyone in Moonlight Cove had been converted.

At the moment no children under twelve had been put through the Change, partly because of difficulties New Wave technicians had had in determining the correct dosage for younger converts. Those problems had been solved, and tonight the kids would be brought into the fold.

In the kitchen Loman stood for a moment, listening to the rain on the windows and the ticking of the clock.

At the sink he drew a glass of water. He drank it, another, then two more. He was dehydrated after the ordeal at Peyser's.

The refrigerator was chock full of five-pound hams, roast beef, a half-eaten turkey, a plate of porkchops, chicken breasts, sausages, and packages of bologna and dried beef. The accelerated metabolisms of the New People required a diet high in protein. Besides, they had a craving for meat.

He took a loaf of pumpernickel from the breadbox and sat down with that, the roast beef, the ham, and a jar of mustard. He stayed at the table for a while, cutting or ripping thick hunks of meat, wrapping them in mustard-slathered bread, and tearing off large bites with his teeth. Food offered him less subtle pleasure than when he'd been an Old Person; now the smell and taste of it raised in him an animal excitement, a thrill of greed and gluttony. He was to some degree repelled by the way he tore at his food and swallowed before he'd finished chewing it properly, but every effort that he made to restrain himself soon gave way to even more feverish consumption. He slipped into a half-trance, hypnotized by the rhythm of chewing and swallowing. At one point he became clearheaded enough to realize he had gotten the chicken breasts from the refrigerator and was eating them with enthusiasm, though they were uncooked. He let himself slip mercifully back into the half-trance again.

Finished eating, he went upstairs to look in on Denny.

When he opened the door to the boy's room, everything at first seemed to be just as it had been the last time he'd seen it, during the previous night. The shades were lowered, the curtains drawn, the room dark except for the greenish light from the VDT. Denny sat in front of the computer, engrossed in the data that flickered across the screen.

Then Loman saw something that made his skin prickle.

He closed his eyes.

Waited.

Opened them.

It was not an illusion.

He felt sick. He wanted to step back into the hall and close the door, forget what he'd seen, go away. But he could not move and could not avert his eyes.

Denny had unplugged the computer keyboard and put it on the floor beside his chair. He'd unscrewed the front cover plate from the data-processing unit. His hands were in his lap, but they weren't exactly hands any more. His fingers were wildly elongated, tapering not to points and fingernails but to metallic-looking wires, as thick as lamp cords, that snaked into the guts of the computer, vanishing there.

Denny no longer needed the keyboard.

He had become part of the system. Through the computer and its modem link to New Wave, Denny had become one with Sun.

'Denny?'

He had assumed an altered state, but nothing like that sought by the regressives.

'Denny?'

The boy did not answer.

'Denny!'

An odd, soft clicking and electronic pulsing sounds came from the computer.

Reluctantly, Loman entered the room and walked to the desk. He looked down at his son and shuddered.

Denny's mouth hung open. Saliva drooled down his chin. He had become so enraptured by his contact with the computer that he had not bothered to get up and eat or go to the bathroom; he had urinated in his pants.

His eyes were gone. In their place were what appeared to be twin spheres of molten silver as shiny as mirrors. They reflected the data that swarmed across the screen in front of them.

The pulsing sounds, soft electronic oscillations, were not coming from the computer but from Denny.

• 15 •

The eggs were good, the pancakes were better, and the coffee was strong enough to endanger the porcelain finish of the cups but not so strong that it had to be chewed. As they ate, Sam outlined the method he had devised for getting a message out of town to the Bureau.

'Your phone's still dead, Harry. I tried it this morning. And I don't think we can risk heading out to the interstate on foot or by car, not with the patrols and roadblocks they've established; that'll have to be a last resort. After all, as far as we know, we're the only people who realize that something truly . . . twisted is happening here and that the need to stop it is urgent. Us and maybe the Foster girl, the one the cops talked about in their VDT conversation last night.'

'If she's literally a girl,' Tessa said, 'just a child, even if she's a teenager, she won't have much of a chance against them. We've got to figure they'll catch her if they haven't already.'

Sam nodded. 'And if they nail us, too, while we're trying to get out of town, there'll be no one left to do the job. So first we've got to try a low-risk course of action.'

'Is *any* option low risk?' Harry wondered as he mopped up some egg yolk with a piece of toast, eating slowly and with a touching precision necessitated by his having only one useful hand.

Pouring a little more maple syrup over his pancakes, surprised by how much he was eating, attributing his appetite to the possibility that this was his last meal, Sam said, 'See . . . this is a wired town.'

'Wired?'

'Computer-linked. New Wave gave computers to the police, so they'd be tied into the web—'

'And the schools,' Harry said, 'I remember reading about it in the paper last spring or early summer. They gave a lot of computers and software to both the elementary and the high schools. A gesture of civic involvement, they called it.'

'Seems more ominous than that now, doesn't it?' Tessa said.

'Sure as hell does.'

Tessa said, 'Seems now like maybe they wanted their computers in the schools for the same reason they wanted the cops computerized – to tie them all in tightly with New Wave, to monitor and control.'

Sam put down his fork. 'New Wave employs, what, about a third of the people in town?'

'Probably that,' Harry said. 'Moonlight Cove really grew after New Wave moved in ten years ago. In some ways it's an old-fashioned company town – life here isn't just dependent upon the main employer but pretty much socially centered around it too.'

After sipping some coffee so strong it was nearly as bracing as brandy, Sam said, 'A third of the people . . . which works out to maybe forty percent or so of the adults.'

Harry said, 'I guess so.'

'And you've got to figure everyone at New Wave is part of the conspiracy, that they were among the first to be . . . converted.'

Tessa nodded. 'I'd say that's a given.'

'And they're even more than usually interested in computers, of course, because they're working in that industry, so it's a good bet most or all of them have computers in their homes.'

Harry agreed.

'And no doubt many if not all of their home computers can be tied by modem directly to New Wave, so they can work at home in the evening or on weekends if they have to. And now, with this conversion scheme nearing a conclusion, I'll bet they're working 'round the clock; data must be flying back and forth over their lines half the night. If Harry can tell me of someone within a block of here who works for New Wave—'

'There're several,' Harry said.

'—then I could slip out in the rain, try their house, see if anyone's home. At this hour they'll probably be at work. If no one's there, then maybe I could get a call out on their phone.'

'Wait, wait,' Tessa said. 'What's all this about phones? The phones don't work.'

Sam shook his head. 'All we know is that the public phones are out of service, as is Harry's. But remember: New Wave controls the telephone-company computer, so they can probably be selective about what lines they shut down. I'll bet they haven't cut off the service of those who've already undergone this . . .

conversion. They wouldn't deny *themselves* communication. Especially not now, in a crisis, and with this scheme of theirs nearly accomplished. There's a better than fifty-percent chance that the only lines they've shut down are the ones they figured we might get to: Pay phones, phones in public places – like the motel – and the phones in the homes of people who haven't yet been converted.'

· **16** ·

Fear permeated Loman Watkins, saturated him so completely that if it had possessed substance, it could have been wrung from his flesh in quantities to rival the rivers currently pouring forth from the storm-racked sky outside. He was afraid for himself, for what he might yet become. He was afraid for his son, too, who sat at the computer in an utterly alien guise. And he was also afraid *of* his son, no use denying that, scared half to death of him and unable to touch him.

A flood of data coruscated across the screen in blurred green waves. Denny's glistening, liquid, silvery eyes – like puddles of mercury in his sockets – reflected the luminescent tides of letters, numbers, graphs, and charts. Unblinkingly.

Loman remembered what Shaddack had said at Peyser's house when he had seen that the man had regressed to a lupine form that could not have been a part of human genetic history. Regression was not merely – or even primarily – a physical process. It was an example of mind over matter, of consciousness dictating form. Because they could no longer be ordinary people, and because they simply could not tolerate life as emotionless New People, they were seeking altered states in which existence was more endurable. And the boy had sought *this* state, had willed himself to become this grotesque thing.

'Denny?'

No response.

The boy had fallen entirely silent. Not even electronic noises issued from him any longer.

The metallic cords, in which the boy's fingers ended, vibrated continuously and sometimes throbbed as if irregular pulses of thick, inhuman blood were passing through them, cycling between organic and inorganic portions of the mechanism.

Loman's heart was pounding as fast as his running footsteps would have been if he could have fled. But he was held there by the weight of his fear. He had broken out in a sweat. He struggled to keep from throwing up the enormous meal he had just eaten.

Desperately he considered what he must do, and the first thing that occurred to him was to call Shaddack and seek his help. Surely Shaddack would understand what was happening and would know how to reverse this hideous metamorphosis and restore Denny to human form.

But that was wishful thinking. The Moonhawk Project was now out of control, following dark routes down into midnight horrors that Tom Shaddack had never foreseen and could not avert.

Besides, Shaddack would not be frightened by what was happening to Denny. He would be delighted, exuberant. Shaddack would view the boy's transformation as an *elevated* altered state, as much to be desired as the degeneration of the regressives was to be avoided and scorned. Here was what Shaddack truly sought, the forced evolution of man into machine.

In memory even now, Loman could hear Shaddack talking agitatedly in Peyser's blood-spattered bedroom: '. . . *what I don't understand is why the regressives have all chosen a subhuman condition. Surely you have the power within you to undergo evolution rather than devolution, to lift yourself up from mere humanity to something higher, cleaner, purer . . .*'

Loman was certain that Denny's drooling, silver-eyed incarnation was not a higher form than ordinary human existence, neither cleaner nor purer. In its way it was as much a degeneration as Mike Peyser's regression to a lupine shape or Coombs's descent into apelike primitiveness. Like Peyser, Denny had surrendered intellectual individuality to escape awareness of the emotionless life of a New Person; instead of becoming just one of a pack of subhuman beasts, he had become one of many data-processing units in a complex supercomputer network. He had relinquished the last of what was human in him – his mind – and had become something simpler than a gloriously complex human being.

A bead of drool fell from Denny's chin, leaving a wet circle on his denim-clad thigh.

Do you know fear now? Loman wondered. You can't love. Not any more than I can. But do you fear anything now?

Surely not. Machines could not feel terror.

Though Loman's conversion had left him unable to experience any emotion but fear, and though his days and nights had become one long ordeal of anxiety of varying intensity, he had in a perverse way come to love fear, to cherish it, for it was the only feeling that kept him in touch with the unconverted man he had once been. If his fear were taken from him, too, he would be only a machine of flesh. His life would have no human dimension whatsoever.

Denny had surrendered that last precious emotion. All he had left to fill his gray days were logic, reason, endless chains of calculations, the never-ending absorption and interpolation of facts. And if Shaddack was correct about the longevity of the New People, those days would mount into centuries.

Suddenly eerie electronic noises came from the boy again. They echoed off the walls.

Those sounds were as strange as the cold, mournful songs and cries of some species dwelling in the deepest reaches of the sea.

To call Shaddack and reveal Denny to him in this condition would be to encourage the madman in his insane and unholy pursuits. Once he saw what Denny had become, Shaddack might find a way to induce or force all of the New People to transform themselves into identical, thoroughgoing cybernetic entities. That prospect boosted Loman's fear to new heights.

The boy-thing fell silent again.

Loman drew his revolver from its holster. His hand was shaking badly.

Data rushed ever more frantically across the screen and swam simultaneously across the surface of Denny's molten eyes.

Staring at the creature that had once been his son, Loman dragged memories from the trunk of his pre-Change life, desperately trying to recall something of what he'd once felt for Denny – the love of father for son, the sweet ache of pride, hope for the boy's future. He remembered fishing trips they had taken together, evenings spent in front of the TV, favorite books shared and discussed, long hours during which they'd worked happily together on science projects for school, the Christmas that Denny had gotten his first bicycle, the kid's first date when he had nervously brought the Talmadge girl home to meet his folks. . . . Loman could summon forth images of those times, quite detailed memory-pictures, but they had no power to warm him. He knew he should *feel* something if he was going to kill his only child, something more than fear, but he no longer had that capacity. To hold fast to whatever remained of the human being in him, he ought to be able to squeeze out one tear, at least one, as he squeezed off the shot from the Smith & Wesson, but he remained dry-eyed.

Without warning something erupted from Denny's forehead.

Loman cried out and stumbled backward two steps in surprise.

At first he thought the thing was a worm, for it was shiny-oily and segmented, as thick as a pencil. But as it continued to extrude, he saw that it was more metalic than organic, terminating in a fish-mouth plug three times the diameter of the 'worm' itself. Like the feeler of a singularly repulsive insect, it weaved back and forth in front of Denny's face, growing longer and longer, until it touched the computer.

He is *willing* this to happen, Loman reminded himself.

This was mind over matter, not short-circuited genetics. Mental power made concrete, not merely biology run amok. This was what the boy wanted to become, and if this was the only life he could tolerate now, the only existence he desired, then why shouldn't he be allowed to have it?

The hideous wormlike extrusion probed the exposed mechanism, where the cover plate had once been. It disappeared inside, making some linkage that helped the boy achieve a more intimate bond with Sun than could be had solely through his mutated hands and mercuric eyes.

A hollow, electronic, blood-freezing wail came from the boy's mouth, though neither his lips nor tongue moved.

Loman's fear of taking action was at last outweighed by his fear of *not* acting. He stepped forward, put the muzzle of the revolver against the boy's right temple, and fired two rounds.

• 17 •

Crouching on the back porch, leaning against the wall of the house, rising up now and then to look cautiously through the window at the three people gathered around the kitchen table, Chrissie grew slowly more confident that they could be trusted. Above the dull roar and sizzle of the rain, through the closed window, she could hear only snatches of their conversation. After a while, however, she determined that they knew something was terribly wrong in Moonlight Cove. The two strangers seemed to be hiding out in Mr. Talbot's house and were on the run as much as she was. Apparently they were working on a plan to get help from authorities outside of town.

She decided against knocking on the door. It was solid wood, with no panes in the upper half, so they would not be able to see who was knocking. She had heard enough to know they were tense, maybe not as completely frazzle-nerved as she was herself, but definitely on edge. An unexpected knock at the door would give them all massive heart attacks – or maybe they'd pick up guns and blast the door to smithereens, and her with it.

Instead she rose up in plain sight and rapped on the window.

Mr. Talbot jerked his head in surprise and pointed, but even as he was pointing, the other man and the woman flew to their feet with the suddenness of marionettes snapped upright on strings. Moose barked once, twice. The three people – and the dog – stared in surprise at Chrissie. From the expressions on their faces, she might have been not a bedraggled eleven-year-old girl but a chainsaw-wielding maniac wearing a leather hood to conceal a deformed face.

She supposed that right now, in alien-infested Moonlight Cove, even a pathetic, rain-soaked, exhausted little girl could be an object of terror to those who didn't know that she was still human. In hope of allaying their fear, she spoke through the windowpane:

'Help me. Please, help me.'

• 18 •

The machine screamed. Its skull shattered under the impact of the two slugs, and it was blown out of its seat, toppling to the floor of the bedroom and pulling the chair with it. The elongated fingers tore loose of the computer on the desk. The segmented wormlike probe snapped in two, halfway between the computer and the forehead from which it had sprung. The thing lay on the floor, twitching, spasming.

Loman had to think of it as a machine. He could not think of it as his son. That was too terrifying.

The face was misshapen, wrenched into an asymmetrical, surreal mask by the impact of the bullets as they'd torn through the cranium.

The silvery eyes had gone black. Now it appeared as if puddles of oil, not mercury, were pooled in the sockets in the thing's skull.

Between plates of shattered bone, Loman saw not merely the gray matter he had expected but what appeared to be coiled wire, glinting shards that looked almost ceramic, odd geometrical shapes. The blood that seeped from the wounds was accompanied by wisps of blue smoke.

Still, the machine screamed.

The electronic shrieks no longer came from the boy-thing but from the computer on the desk. Those sounds were so bizarre that they were as out of place in the machine half of the organism as they had been in the boy half.

Loman realized these were not entirely electronic wails. They also had a tonal quality and character that were unnervingly human.

The waves of data ceased flowing across the screen. One word was repeated hundreds of times, filling line after line on the display:

NO NO NO NO NO NO NO NO NO NO NO NO NO NO NO . . .

He suddenly knew that Denny was only half dead. The part of the boy's mind that had inhabited his body was extinguished, but another fragment of his consciousness still lived somehow within the computer, kept alive in silicon instead of brain tissue. *That* part of him was screaming in this machine-cold voice.

On the screen:

WHERE'S THE REST OF ME WHERE'S THE REST OF ME WHERE'S THE REST OF ME NO NO NO NO NO NO NO NO . . .

Loman felt as if his blood was icy sludge pumped by a heart as gelid as the meat in the freezer downstairs. He had never known a chill that penetrated as deep as this one.

He stepped away from the crumpled body, which at last stopped twitching, and turned his revolver on the computer. He emptied the gun into the machine, first blowing out the screen. Because the blinds and drapes were closed, the room was nearly dark. He blasted the circuitry to pieces. Thousand of sparks flared in the blackness, spraying out of the data-processing unit. But with a final sputter and crackle, the machine died, and the gloom closed in again.

The air stank of scorched insulation. And worse.

Loman left the room and walked to the head of the stairs. He stood there a moment, leaning against the railing. Then he descended to the front hall.

He reloaded his revolver, holstered it.

He went out into the rain.

He got in his car and started the engine.

'Shaddack,' he said aloud.

• 19 •

Tessa immediately took charge of the girl. She led her upstairs, leaving Harry and Sam and Moose in the kitchen, and got her out of her wet clothes.

'Your teeth are chattering, honey.'

'I'm lucky to have any teeth to chatter.'

'Your skin's positively blue.'

'I'm lucky to have skin,' the girl said.

'I noticed you're limping too.'

'Yeah. I twisted an ankle.'

'Sure it's just sprained?'

'Yeah. Nothing serious, besides—'

'I know,' Tessa said, 'you're lucky to *have* ankles.'

'Right. For all I know, aliens find ankles particularly tasty, the same way some people like pig's feet. Yuch.'

She sat on the edge of the bed in the guest room, a wool blanket pulled around her nakedness, and waited while Tessa got a sheet from the linen supplies and several safety pins from a sewing box that she noticed in the same closet.

Tessa said, 'Harry's clothes are much too big for you, so we'll wrap you in a sheet temporarily. While your clothes are in the dryer, you can come downstairs and tell Harry and Sam and me all about it.'

'It's been quite an adventure,' the girl said.

'Yes, you look as if you've been through a lot.'

'It'd make a great book.'

'You like books?'

'Oh, yes, I love books.'

Blushing but evidently determined to be sophisticated, she threw back the blanket and stood and allowed Tessa to drape the sheet around her. Tessa pinned it in place, fashioning a toga of sorts.

As Tessa worked, Chrissie said, 'I think I'll write a book about all of this one day. I'll call it *The Alien Scourge* or maybe *Nest Queen*, although naturally I won't title it *Nest Queen* unless it turns out there really is a nest queen somewhere. Maybe they don't reproduce like insects or even like animals. Maybe they're basically a vegetable lifeform. Who knows? If they're basically a vegetable lifeform, then I'd have to call the book something like *Space Seeds* or *Vegetables of the Void* or maybe *Murderous Martian Mushrooms*. It's sometimes good to use alliteration in titles. Alliteration. Don't you like that word? It sounds so nice. I like words. Of course, you could always go with a more poetic title, haunting, like *Alien Roots, Alien Leaves*. Hey, if they're vegetables, we may be in luck, because maybe they'll eventually be killed off by aphids or tomato worms, since they won't have developed protection against earth pests, just like a few tiny germs killed off the mighty Martians in *War of the Worlds*.'

Tessa was reluctant to disclose that their enemies were not from the stars, for she was enjoying the girl's precocious chatter. Then she noticed that Chrissie's left hand was injured. The palm had been badly abraded; the center of it looked raw.

'I did that when I fell off the porch roof at the rectory,' the girl said.

'You fell off a roof?'

'Yeah. Boy, *that* was exciting. See, the wolf-thing was coming through the window after me, and I didn't have anywhere else to go. Twisted my ankle in the same fall and then had to run across the yard to the back gate before he caught me. You know, Miss Lockland—'

'Please call me Tessa.'

Apparently Chrissie was unaccustomed to addressing adults by their Christian names. She frowned and was silent for a moment, struggling with the invitation to informality. Evidently she decided it would be rude not to use first names when asked to do so. 'Okay . . . Tessa. Well, anyway, I can't decide what the aliens are most likely to do if they catch us. Maybe eat our kidneys? Or don't they eat us at all? Maybe they just shove alien pill bugs in our ears, and the bugs crawl into our brains and take over. Either way, I figure it's worth falling off a roof to avoid them.'

Having finished pinning the toga, Tessa led Chrissie down the hall to the bathroom and looked in the medicine cabinet for something with which to treat the scraped palm. She found a bottle of iodine with a faded label, a half-empty roll of adhesive tape, and a package of gauze pads so old that the paper wrapper around each bandage square was yellow with age. The gauze itself looked fresh and white, and the iodine was undiluted by time, still strong enough to sting.

Barefoot, toga-clad, with her blond hair frizzing and curling as it dried, Chrissie sat on the lowered lid of the toilet seat and submitted stoically to the treatment of her wound. She didn't protest in any way, didn't cry out – or even hiss – in pain.

But she *did* talk: 'That's the second time I've fallen off a roof, so I guess I must have a guardian angel looking over me. About a year and a half ago, in the spring, these birds – starlings, I think they were – built a nest on the roof of one of our stables at home, and I just *had* to see what baby birds looked like in the nest, so when my folks weren't around, I got a ladder and waited for the mama bird to fly off for more food, and then I real quick climbed up there to have a peek. Let me tell you, before they get their feathers, baby birds are just about the ugliest things you'd want to see – except for aliens, of course. They're withered little wrinkled things, all beaks and eyes, and stumpy little wings like deformed arms. If human babies looked that bad when they were born, the first people back a few million years ago would've flushed their newborns down the toilet – if they'd *had* toilets – and wouldn't have *dared* have any more of them, and the whole race would've died out before it even really got started.'

Still painting the wound with iodine, trying without success to repress a grin, Tessa looked up and saw that Chrissie was squeezing her eyes tightly shut, wrinkling her nose, struggling very hard to be brave.

'Then the mama or papa bird came back,' the girl said, 'and saw me at the nest and flew at my face, shrieking. I was so startled that I slipped and fell off the roof. Didn't hurt myself at all that time – though I did land in some horse manure. Which isn't a thrill, let me tell you. I love horses, but they'd be ever so much more lovable if you could teach them to use a litterbox like a cat.'

Tessa was crazy about this kid.

• 20 •

Sam leaned forward with his elbows on the kitchen table and listened attentively to Chrissie Foster. Though Tessa had heard the Boogeymen in the middle of a kill at Cove Lodge and had glimpsed one of them under the door of her room, and though Harry had watched them at a distance in night and fog, and though Sam had spied two of them last night through a window in Harry's living room, the girl was the only one present who had seen them close up and more than once.

But it was not solely her singular experience that held Sam's attention. He also was captivated by her sprightly manner, good humor, and articulateness. She obviously had considerable inner strength, real toughness, for otherwise she would not have survived the previous night and the events of this morning. Yet she remained charmingly innocent, tough but not hard. She was one of those kids who gave you hope for the whole damn human race.

A kid like Scott used to be.

And that was why Sam was fascinated by Chrissie Foster. He saw in her the child that Scott had been. Before he . . . changed. With regret so poignant that it manifested itself as a dull ache in his chest and a tightness in his throat, he watched the girl and listened to her, not only to hear what information she had to impart but with the unrealistic expectation that by studying her he would at last understand why his own son had lost both innocence and hope.

• 21 •

Down in the darkness of the Icarus Colony cellar, Tucker and his pack did not sleep, for they did not require it. They lay curled in the deep blackness. From time to time, he and the other male coupled with the female, and they tore at one another in savage frenzy, gashing flesh that began to heal at once, drawing one another's blood simply for the pleasure of the scent – immortal freaks at play.

The darkness and the barren confines of their concrete-walled burrow contributed to Tucker's growing disorientation. By the hour he remembered less of his

existence prior to the past night's exciting hunt. He ceased to have much sense
of self. Individuality was not to be encouraged in the pack when hunting, and in
the burrow it was even a less desirable trait; harmony in that windowless, claustrophobic space required the relinquishment of self to group.

His waking dreams were filled with images of dark, wild shapes creeping
through night-clad forests and across moon-washed meadows. When occasionally a memory of human form flickered through his mind, its origins were a
mystery to him; more than that, he was frightened by it and quickly shifted his
fantasies back to running-hunting-killing-coupling scenes in which he was just
a part of the pack, one aspect of a single shadow, one extension of a larger
organism, free from the need to think, having no desire but to *be.*

At one point he became aware that he had slipped out of his wolflike form,
which had become too confining. He no longer wanted to be the leader of a
pack, for that position carried with it too much responsibility. He didn't want to
think at all. Just be. *Be.* The limitations of all rigid physical forms seemed
insufferable.

He sensed that the other male and the female were aware of his degeneration
and were following his example.

He felt his flesh flowing, bones dissolving, organs and vessels surrendering
form and function. He devolved beyond the primal ape, far beyond the four-
legged thing that laboriously had crawled out of the ancient sea millennia ago,
beyond, beyond, until he was but a mass of pulsing tissue, protoplasmic soup,
throbbing in the darkness of the Icarus Colony cellar.

• 22 •

Loman rang the doorbell at Shaddack's house on the north point, and Evan, the
manservant, answered.

'I'm sorry, Chief Watkins, but Mr. Shaddack isn't here.'

'Where's he gone?'

'I don't know.'

Evan was one of the New People. To be sure of dispatching him, Loman shot
him twice in the head and then twice in the chest while he lay on the foyer floor,
shattering both brain and heart. Or data-processor and pump. Which was
needed now – biological or mechanical terminology? How far had they progressed toward becoming machines?

Loman closed the door behind him and stepped over Evan's body. After
replenishing the expended rounds in the revolver's cylinder, he searched the
huge house room by room, floor by floor, looking for Shaddack.

Though he wished that he could be driven by a hunger for revenge, could be
consumed by anger, and could take satisfaction in bludgeoning Shaddack to
death, that depth of feeling was denied him. His son's death had not melted the
ice in his heart. He couldn't feel grief or rage.

Instead he was driven by fear. He wanted to kill Shaddack before the
madman made them into something worse then they'd already become.

By killing Shaddack – who was always linked to the supercomputer at New
Wave by a simple cardiac telemetry device – Loman would activate a program
in Sun that would broadcast a microwave death order. That transmission would

be received by all the microsphere computers wedded to the innermost tissues of the New People. Upon receiving the death order, each biologically interactive computer in each New Person would instantly still the heart of its host. Every one of the converted in Moonlight Cove would die. He too would die.

But he no longer cared. His fear of death was outweighed by his fear of living, especially if he had to live either as a regressive or as that more hideous thing that Denny had become.

In his mind he could see himself in that wretched condition – gleaming mercurial eyes, a wormlike probe bursting bloodlessly from his forehead to seek obscene conjugation with the computer. If skin actually could crawl, his own would have crept off his body.

When he could not find Shaddack at home, he set out for New Wave, where the maker of the new world was no doubt in his office busily designing neighborhoods for this hell that he called paradise.

• 23 •

Shortly after eleven o'clock, as Sam was leaving, Tessa stepped out onto the back porch with him and closed the door, leaving Harry and Chrissie in the kitchen. The trees at the rear of the property were just tall enough to prevent neighbors, even those uphill, from looking into the yard. She was sure they could not be seen in the deeper shadows of the porch.

'Listen,' she said, 'it makes no sense for you to go alone.'

'It makes perfect sense.'

The air was chilly and damp. She hugged herself.

She said, 'I could ring the front doorbell, distract anyone inside, while you went in the back.'

'I don't want to have to worry about you.'

'I can take care of myself.'

'Yeah, I believe you can,' he said.

'Well?'

'But I work alone.'

'You seem to do everything alone.'

He smiled thinly. 'Are we going to get into another argument about whether life is a tea party or hell on earth?'

'That wasn't an argument we had. It was a discussion.'

'Well, anyway, I've shifted to undercover assignments for the very reason that I can pretty much work alone. I don't want a partner any more, Tessa, because I don't want to see any more of them die.'

She knew he was referring not only to the other agents who had been killed in the line of duty with him but also to his late wife.

'Stay with the girl,' he said. 'Take care of her if anything happens. She's like you, after all.'

'What?'

'She's one of those who knows how to love life. How to really, deeply love it, no matter what happens. It's a rare and precious talent.'

'You know too,' she said.

'No. I've never known.'

'Dammit, everyone is born with a love of life. You still have it, Sam. You've just lost touch with it, but you can find it again.'

'Take care of her,' he said, turning away and descending the porch steps into the rain.

'You better come back, damn you. You promised to tell me what you saw at the other end of that tunnel, on the Other Side. You just better come back.'

Sam departed through silver rain and thin patches of gray fog.

As she watched him go, Tessa realized that even if he never told her about the Other Side, she wanted him to come back for many other reasons both complex and surprising.

• 24 •

The Coltrane house was two doors south of the Talbot place, on Conquistador. Two stories. Weathered cedar siding. A covered patio instead of a rear porch.

Moving quickly along the back of the house, where rain drizzled off the patio cover with a sound inaptly like crackling fire, Sam peered through sliding glass doors into a gloomy family room and then through French windows into an unlit kitchen. When he reached the kitchen door, he withdrew his revolver from the holster under his leather jacket and held it down at his side, against his thigh.

He could have walked around front and rung the bell, which might have seemed less suspicious to the people inside. But that would mean going out to the street, where he was more likely to be seen not only by neighbors but by the men Chrissie said were patrolling the town.

He knocked on the door, four quick raps. When no one responded, he knocked again, louder, and then a third time, louder still. If anyone was home, the knock would have been answered.

Harley and Sue Coltrane must be at New Wave, where they worked.

The door was locked. He hoped it had no dead bolt.

Though he had left his other tools at Harry's, he had brought a thin, flexible metal loid. Television dramas had popularized the notion that any credit card made a convenient and unincriminating loid, but those plastic rectangles too often got wedged in the crack or snapped before the latch bolt was slipped. He preferred time-proven tools. He worked the loid between the door and frame, below the lock, and slid it up, applying pressure when he met resistance. The lock popped. He tried the door, and there was no dead bolt; it opened with a soft creak.

He stepped inside and quietly closed the door, making sure that the lock did not engage. If he had to get out fast, he did not want to fumble with a latch.

The kitchen was illuminated only by the dismal light of the rain-darkened day that barely penetrated the windows. Evidently the vinyl flooring, wall-covering, and tile were of the palest hues, for in that dimness everything seemed to be one shade of gray or another.

He stood for almost a minute, listening intently.

A kitchen clock ticked.

Rain drummed on the patio cover.

His soaked hair was pasted to his forehead. He pushed it aside, out of his eyes.

When he moved, his wet shoes squished.

He went directly to the phone, which was mounted on the wall above a corner secretary. When he picked it up, he got no dial tone, but the line was not dead, either. It was filled with strange sounds: clicking, low beeping, soft oscillations – all of which blended into mournful and alien music, an electronic threnody.

The back of Sam's neck went cold.

Carefully, silently, he returned the handset to its cradle.

He wondered what sounds could be heard on a telephone that was being used as a link between two computers, with a modem. Was one of the Coltranes at work elsewhere in the house, tied in by a home computer to New Wave?

Somehow he sensed that what he had heard on the line was not as simply explained as that. It had been damned eerie.

A dining room lay beyond the kitchen. The two large windows were covered with gauzy sheers, which further filtered the ashen daylight. A hatch, buffet, table, and chairs were revealed as blocks of black and slate-gray shadows.

Again he stopped to listen. Again he heard nothing unusual.

The house was laid out in a classic California design, with no downstairs hall. Each room led directly to the next in an open and airy floorplan. Through an archway he entered the large living room, grateful that the house had wall-to-wall carpet, on which his wet shoes made no sound.

The living room was less shadowy than any other part of the house that he had seen thus far, yet the brightest color was a pearly gray. The west windows were sheltered by the front porch, but rain streamed over those facing north. Leaden daylight, passing through the panes, speckled the room with the watery-gray shadows of the hundreds of beads that tracked down the glass, and Sam was so edgy that he could almost feel those small ameboid phantoms crawling over him.

Between the lighting and his mood, he felt as if he were in an old black-and-white movie. One of those bleak exercises in *film noir*.

The living room was deserted, but abruptly a sound came from the last room downstairs. At the southwest corner. Beyond the foyer. The den, most likely. It was a piercing trill that made his teeth ache, followed by a forlorn cry that was neither the voice of a man nor that of a machine but something in between, a semi-metallic voice wrenched by fear and twisted with despair. That was followed by low electronic pulsing, like a massive heartbeat.

Then silence.

He had brought up his revolver, holding it straight out in front of him, ready to shoot anything that moved. But everything was as still as it was silent.

The trill, the eerie cry, and the base throbbing surely could not be associated with the Boogeymen that he'd seen last night outside of Harry's house, or with the other shape-changers Chrissie described. Until now, an encounter with one of them had been the thing he feared most. But suddenly the unknown entity in the den was more frightening.

Sam waited.

Nothing more.

He had the queer feeling that something was listening for his movements as tensely as he was listening for it.

He considered returning to Harry's to think of some other way to send a message to the Bureau, because Mexican food and Guinness Stout and Goldie Hawn movies – even *Swing Shift* – now seemed precious beyond value, not pathetic reasons to live but pleasures so exquisite that no words existed to adequately describe them.

The only thing that kept him from getting the hell out of there was Chrissie Foster. The memory of her bright eyes. Her innocent face. The enthusiasm and animation with which she had recounted her adventures. Perhaps he had failed Scott, and perhaps it was too late for the boy to be hauled back from the brink. But Chrissie was still alive in every vital sense of the word – physically, intellectually, emotionally – and she was dependent on him. No one else could save her from conversion.

Midnight was little more than twelve hours away.

He edged through the living room and quietly crossed the foyer. He stood with his back against the wall beside the half-open door to the room from which the weird sounds had come.

Something clicked in there.

He stiffened.

Low, soft clicks. Not the *tick-tick-tick* of claws like those he had heard tapping on the window last night. More like a long series of relays being tripped, scores of switches being closed, dominoes falling against one another: *click-click-click-clickety-clickety-click-click-clickety*. . .

Silence once more.

Holding the revolver in both hands, Sam stepped in front of the door and pushed it open with one foot. He crossed the threshold and assumed a shooter's stance just inside the room.

The windows were covered by interior shutters, and the only light was from two computer screens. Both were fitted with filters that resulted in black text on an amber background. Everything in the room not wrapped in shadows was touched by that golden radiance.

Two people sat before the terminals, one on the right side of the room, the other on the left, their backs to each other.

'Don't move,' Sam said sharply.

They neither moved nor spoke. They were so still that at first he thought they were dead.

The peculiar light was brighter yet curiously less revealing than the half-burnt-out daylight that vaguely illuminated the other rooms. As his eyes adjusted, Sam saw that the two people at the computers were not only unnaturally still but were not really people any more. He was drawn forward by the icy grip of horror.

Oblivious of Sam, a naked man, probably Harley Coltrane, sat in a wheeled, swivel-based chair at the computer to the right of the door, against the west wall. He was connected to the VDT by a pair of inch-thick cables that looked less metallic than organic, glistening wetly in the amber glow. They extended from within the bowels of the data-processing unit – from which the cover plate had been removed – and into the man's bare torso below his rib cage, melding bloodlessly with the flesh. They throbbed.

'Dear God,' Sam whispered.

Coltrane's lower arms were utterly fleshless, just golden bones. The meat of his upper arms ended smoothly two inches above the elbows; from those stumps, bones thrust out as cleanly as robotic extrusions from a metal casing. The skeletal hands were locked tightly around the cables, as if they were merely a pair of clamps.

When Sam stepped nearer to Coltrane and looked closer, he saw the bones were not as well differentiated as they should have been but had half melted together. Furthermore, they were veined with metal. As he watched, the cables pulsed with such vigor that they began to vibrate wildly. If not held fast by the clamping hands, they might have torn loose either from the man or the machine.

Get out.

A voice spoke within him, telling him to flee, and it was his own voice, though not that of the adult Sam Booker. It was the voice of the child he had once been and to which his fear was encouraging him to revert. Extreme terror is a time machine a thousand times more efficient than nostalgia, hurtling us backward through the years, into that forgotten and intolerable condition of helplessness in which so much of childhood is spent.

Get out, run, run, get out!

Sam resisted the urge to bolt.

He wanted to understand. What was happening? What had these people become? *Why?* What did this have to do with the Boogeymen who prowled the night? Evidently through microtechnology Thomas Shaddack had found a way to alter, radically and forever, human biology. That much was clear to Sam, but knowing just that and nothing else was like sensing that something lived within the sea without ever having seen a fish. So much more lay beneath the surface, mysterious.

Get out.

Neither the man before him nor the woman across the room seemed remotely aware of him. Apparently he was in no imminent danger.

Run, said the frightened boy within.

Rivers of data – words, numbers, charts and graphs of myriad types – flowed in a floodlike rampage across the amber screen, while Harley Coltrane stared unwaveringly at that darkly flickering display. He could not have seen it as an ordinary man would have, for he had no eyes. They'd been torn from his sockets and replaced by a cluster of other sensors: tiny beads of ruby glass, small knots of wire, waffle-surfaced chips of some ceramic material, all bristling and slightly recessed in the deep black holes in his skull.

Sam was holding the revolver in only one hand now. He kept his finger on the trigger guard rather than on the trigger itself, for he was shaking so badly that he might unintentionally let off a shot.

The man-machine's chest rose and fell. His mouth hung open, and bitterly foul breath rushed from him in rhythmic waves.

A rapid pulse was visible in his temples and in the gruesomely swollen arteries in his neck. But other pulses throbbed where none should have been: in the center of his forehead; along each jawline; at four places in his chest and belly; in his upper arms, where dark ropy vessels had thickened and risen above subcutaneous fat, sheathed now only by his skin. His circulatory system seemed to have been redesigned and augmented to assist new functions that his body was being called upon to perform. Worse yet, those pulses beat in a strange syncopation, as if at least two hearts pounded within him.

A shriek erupted from the thing's gaping mouth, and Sam twitched and cried out in surprise. This was akin to the unearthly sounds that he had heard while in the living room, that had drawn him here, but he had thought they'd come from the computer.

Grimacing as the electronic wail spiraled higher and swelled into painful decibels, Sam let his gaze rise from the man-machine's open mouth to its 'eyes'. The sensors still bristled in the sockets. The beads of ruby glass glowed with inner light, and Sam wondered if they registered him on the infrared spectrum or by some other means. Did Coltrane see him at all? Perhaps the man-machine had traded the human world for a different reality, moving from this physical plane to another level, and perhaps Sam was an irrelevancy to him, unnoticed.

The shriek began to fade, then cut off abruptly.

Without realizing what he'd done, Sam had raised his revolver and, from a distance of about eighteen inches, pointed it at Harley Coltrane's face. He was startled to discover that he also had slipped his finger off the guard and onto the trigger itself and that he was going to destroy this thing.

He hesitated. Coltrane was, after all, still a man – at least to some extent. Who was to say that he didn't desire his current state more than life as an ordinary human being? Who was to say that he was not happy like this? Sam was uneasy in the role of judge, but an even uneasier executioner. As a man who believed that life was hell on earth, he had to consider the possibility that Coltrane's condition was an improvement, an escape.

Between man and computer, the glistening, semiorganic cables *thrummed*. They rattled against the skeletal hands in which they were clamped.

Coltrane's rank breath was redolent with both the stench of rotting meat and overheated electronic components.

Sensors glinted and moved within the lidless eye sockets.

Tinted gold by the light from the screen, Coltrane's face seemed to be frozen in a perpetual scream. The vessels pulsing in his jaws and temples looked less like reflections of his own heartbeat than like parasites squirming under his skin.

With a shudder of revulsion, Sam squeezed the trigger. The blast was thunderous in that confined space.

Coltrane's head snapped back with the impact of the pointblank shot, then dropped forward, chin on his chest, smoking and bleeding.

The repulsive cables continued to swell and shrink and swell as if with the rhythmic passage of inner fluid.

Sam sensed that the man was not entirely dead. He turned the gun on the computer screen.

One of Coltrane's skeletal hands released the cable around which it had been firmly clamped. With a *click-snick-snack* of bare bones, it whipped up and seized Sam's wrist.

Sam cried out.

The room filled with electronic clicks and snaps and beeps and warblings.

The hellish hand held him fast and with such tremendous strength that the bony fingers pinched his flesh, then began to cut through it. He felt warm blood trickle down his arm, under his shirtsleeve. With a flash of panic he realized that the unhuman power of the man-machine was ultimately sufficient to crush his wrist and leave him crippled. At best his hand would swiftly go numb from lack of circulation, and the revolver would drop from his grasp.

Coltrane was struggling to raise his half-shattered head.

Sam thought of his mother in the wreckage of the car, face torn open, grinning at him, grinning, silent and unmoving but grinning . . .

Frantically he kicked at Coltrane's chair, hoping to send it rolling and spinning away. The wheels had been locked.

The bony hand squeezed tighter, and Sam screamed. His vision blurred.

Still, he saw that Coltrane's head was coming up slowly, slowly.

Jesus, I don't want to see that ruined face!

With his right foot, putting everything he had into the kick, Sam struck once, twice, three times at the cables between Coltrane and the computer. They tore loose from Coltrane, popping out of his flesh with a hideous sound, and the man slumped in his chair. Simultaneously the skeletal hand opened and fell away from Sam's wrist. With a cold rattle it struck the hard plastic mat under the chair.

Bass electronic pulses thumped like soft drumbeats and echoed off the walls, while under them a thin bleat wavered continuously through three notes.

Gasping and half in shock, Sam clamped his left hand around his bleeding wrist, as if that would still the stinging pain.

Something brushed against his legs.

He looked down and saw the semiorganic cables, like pale headless snakes, still attached to the computer and full of malevolent life. They seemed to have grown, as well, until they were twice the length they had been when linking Coltrane to the machine. One snared his left ankle, and the other curled sinuously around his right calf.

He tried to tear loose.

They held him fast.

They twined up his legs.

Instinctively he knew they were seeking bare flesh on the upper half of his body, and that upon contact they would burrow into him and make him part of the system.

He was still holding the revolver in his blood-slicked right hand. He aimed at the screen.

Data was no longer flowing across that amber field. Instead, Coltrane's face looked out from the display. His eyes had been restored, and it seemed as if he could see Sam, for he was looking directly at him and speaking to him:

'. . . need . . . need . . . want, need . . .'

Without understanding a damned thing about it, Sam knew Coltrane was still alive. He had not died – or at least not all of him had perished – with his body. He was there, in the machine somehow.

As if to confirm that insight, Coltrane influenced the glass screen of the VDT to relinquish the convex plane of its surface and adapt to the contours of his face. The glass became as flexible as gelatin, thrusting outward, as if Coltrane actually existed within the machine, physically, and was now pushing his face out of it.

This was impossible. Yet it was happening. Harley Coltrane seemed to be controlling matter with the power of his mind, a mind not even any longer linked to a human body.

Sam was mesmerized by fear, frozen, paralyzed. His finger lay immovable against the trigger.

Reality had been ripped, and through that tear a nightmare world of infinite malign possibilities seemed to be rushing into the world that Sam knew and – suddenly – loved.

One of the snakelike cables had reached his chest and found its way under his sweater to bare skin. He felt as if he'd been touched by a white-hot brand, and the pain broke his trance.

He fired three rounds into the computer, shattering the screen first, which was the second face of Coltrane's into which he'd pumped a .38 slug. Though Sam half expected it to absorb the bullet without effect, the cathode-ray tube imploded as if still made of glass. The other rounds scrambled the guts of the data-processing unit, at last finishing off the thing that Coltrane had become.

The pale, oily tentacles fell away from him. They blistered, began to bubble, and seemed to be putrefying before his eyes.

Eerie electronic beeps, crackles, and oscillations, not ear-torturingly loud but uncannily piercing, still filled the room.

When Sam looked toward the woman who had been seated at the other computer, against the east wall, he saw that the mucus-slick cables between her and the machine had lengthened, allowing her to turn in her chair to face him. Aside from those semiorganic connections and her nakedness, she was in a different but no less hideous condition from her husband. Her eyes were gone, but her sockets did not bristle with a host of sensors. Rather, twin reddish orbs, three times the size of ordinary eyes, filled enlarged sockets in a face redesigned to accommodate them; they were less eyes than eye-shaped receptors no doubt designed to see in many spectrums of light, and in fact Sam became aware of an image of himself in each red lens, reversed. Her legs, belly, breasts, arms, throat, and face were heavily patterned with swollen blood vessels that lay just beneath her skin and that seemed to stretch it to the breaking point, so she looked as if she were a design board for branch-pattern circuitry. Some of those vessels might, indeed, have carried blood, but some of them throbbed with waves of radiumlike illumination, some green and some sulfurous yellow.

A segmented, wormlike probe, the diameter of a pencil, erupted from her forehead, as if shot from a gun, and streaked toward Sam, closing the ten feet between them in a split second, striking him above the right eye before he could duck. The tip bit into his skin on contact. He heard a whirring sound, as of tiny blades spinning at maybe a thousand revolutions a minute. Blood ran down his brow and along the side of his nose. But he was squeezing off the last two rounds in his gun even as the probe came at him. Both shots found their mark. One slammed into the woman's upper body, and one took out the computer behind her in a blaze of sparks and crackling electrical bolts that jumped to the ceiling and snaked briefly across the plaster before dissipating. The probe went limp and fell away from him before it could link his brain to hers, which evidently had been its intention.

Except for gray daylight that entered through the paper-thin cracks between the slats of the shutters, the room was dark.

Crazily, Sam remembered something a computer specialist had said at a seminar for agents, when explaining how the Bureau's new system worked: *'Computers can perform more effectively when linked, allowing parallel processing of data.'*

Bleeding from the forehead and the right wrist, he stumbled backward to the door and flicked the light switch, turning on a floor lamp. He stood there – as far as he could get from the two grotesque corpses and still see them – while he began to reload the revolver with rounds he dug out of the pockets of his jacket.

The room was preternaturally silent.

Nothing moved.

Sam's heart was hammering with such force that his chest ached dully with each blow.

Twice he dropped cartridges because his hands were shaking. He didn't stoop to retrieve them. He was half convinced that the moment he wasn't in a position to fire with accuracy or to run, one of the dead creatures would prove not to be dead, after all, and like a flash would come at him, spitting sparks, and would seize him before he could rise and scramble out of its way.

Gradually he became aware of the sound of rain. After losing half of its force during the morning, it was now falling harder than at any time since the storm had first broken the previous night. No thunder shook the day, but the furious drumming of the rain itself – and the insulated walls of the house – had probably muffled the gunfire enough to prevent it being heard by neighbors. He hoped to God that was the case. Otherwise, they were coming even now to investigate, and they would prevent his escape.

Blood continued to trickle down from the wound on his forehead, and some of it got into his right eye. It stung. He wiped at his eye with his sleeve and blinked away the tears as best he could.

His wrist hurt like hell. But if he had to, he could hold the revolver with his left hand and shoot well enough in close quarters.

When the .38 was reloaded, Sam edged back into the room, to the smoking computer on the worktable along the west wall, where Harley Coltrane's mutated body was slumped in a chair, trailing its bone-metal arms. Keeping one eye on the dead man-machine, he took the phone off the modem and hung it up. Then he lifted the receiver and was relieved to hear a dial tone.

His mouth was so dry that he wasn't sure he'd be able to speak clearly when his call got through.

He punched out the number of the Bureau office in Los Angeles.

The line clicked.

A pause.

A recording came on: 'We are sorry that we are unable to complete your call at this time.'

He hung up, then tried again.

'We are sorry that we are unable to complete—'

He slammed the phone down.

Not all of the telephones in Moonlight Cove were operable. And evidently, even from those in service, calls could be placed only to certain numbers. Approved numbers. The local phone company had been reduced to an elaborate intercom to serve the converted.

As he turned away from the phone, he heard something move behind him. Stealthy and quick.

He swung around, and the woman was three feet away. She was no longer connected to the ruined computer, but one of those organic-looking cables trailed across the floor from the base of her spine and into a electrical socket.

Free-associating in his terror, Sam thought: So much for your clumsy kites, Dr. Frankenstein, so much for the need for storms and lightning; these days we just plug the monsters into the wall, give them a jolt of the juice direct, courtesy of Pacific Power & Light.

A reptilian hiss issued from her, and she reached for him. Instead of fingers, her hand had three multiple-pronged plugs similar to the couplings with which the elements of a home computer were joined, though these prongs were as sharp as nails.

Sam dodged to the side, colliding with the chair in which Harley Coltrane still slumped, and nearly fell, firing at the woman-thing as he went. He emptied the five-round .38.

The first three shots knocked her backward and down. The other two tore through vacant air and punched chunks of plaster out of the walls because he was too panicked to stop pulling the trigger when she fell out of his line of fire.

She was trying to get up.

Like a goddamn vampire, he thought.

He needed the high-tech equivalent of a wooden stake, a cross, a silver bullet.

The artery-circuits that webbed her naked body were still pulsing with light, although in places she was sparking, just as the computers themselves had done when he had pumped a couple of slugs into them.

No rounds were left in the revolver.

He searched his pockets for cartridges.

He had none.

Get out.

An electronic wail, not deafening but more nerve-splintering than a thousand sharp fingernails scraped simultaneously down a blackboard, shrilled from her.

Two segmented, wormlike probes burst from her face and flew straight at him. Both fell inches short of him – perhaps a sign of her waning energy – and returned to her like splashes of quicksilver streaming back into the mother mass.

But she *was* getting up.

Sam scrambled to the doorway, stooped, and snatched up the two cartridges he had dropped when he had reloaded the gun. He broke open the cylinder, shook out the empty brass casings, jammed in the last two rounds.

'. . . *neeeeeeeeeeeeeeeeed . . . neeeeeeeeeeeeeeeeed . . .*'

She was on her feet, coming toward him.

This time he held the Smith & Wesson in both hands, aimed carefully, and shot her in the head.

Take out the data processor, he thought with a flash of black humor. Only way to stop a determined machine. Take out its data processor, and it's nothing but a tangle of junk.

She crumpled to the floor. The red light went out of her unhuman eyes; they were black now. She was perfectly still.

Suddenly flames erupted from her bullet-cracked skull, spurting from the wound, from her eyes, nostrils, and gaping mouth.

He moved quickly to the socket to which she was still tethered, and he kicked at the semiorganic plug that she had extruded from her body, knocking it loose.

The flames still leaped from her.

He could not afford a house fire. The bodies would be found, and the neighborhood, Harry's house included, would be searched door-to-door. He looked around for something to throw over her to smother the flames, but already the blaze within her skull was subsiding. In a moment it burned itself out.

The air reeked of a dozen foul odors, some of which did not bear contemplation.

He was mildly dizzy. Nausea stole over him. He gagged, clenched his teeth, and forced back his gorge.

Though he wanted desperately to get out of there, he took time to unplug both computers. They were inoperable and damaged beyond repair, but he was irrationally afraid that, like Dr. Frankenstein's homebuilt man in movie sequel after sequel, they would somehow come to life if exposed to electricity.

He hesitated at the doorway, leaned against the jamb to take some of the weight off his weak and trembling legs, and studied the strange corpses. He had expected them to revert to their normal appearance when they were dead, the way werewolves in the movies, upon taking a silver bullet in the heart or being beaten with a silver-headed cane, always metamorphosed one last time, becoming their tortured, too-human selves, finally released from the curse. Unfortunately this was not lycanthropy. This was not a supernatural affliction, but something worse that men had brought upon themselves with no help from demons or spirits or other things that went bump in the night. The Coltranes remained as they had been, monstrous half-breeds of flesh and metal, blood and silicon – human and machine.

He could not comprehend *how* they had become what they had become, but he half remembered that a word existed for them, and in a moment he recalled it. *Cyborg*: a person whose physiological functioning was aided by or dependent on a mechanical or electronic device. People wearing pacemakers to regulate arrhythmic hearts were cyborgs, and that was a good thing. Those whose kidneys had both failed – and who received dialysis on a regular basis – were cyborgs, and that was good too. But with the Coltranes the concept had been carried to extremes. They were the nightmare side of advanced cybernetics, in whom not merely physiological but mental function had become aided by and almost certainly dependent on a machine.

Sam began to gag again. He turned quickly away from the smoke-hazed den and backtracked through the house to the kitchen door, by which he had entered.

Every step of the way, he was certain that he would hear a voice behind him, half human and half electronic – *'neeeeeeeeeeed'* – and would look back to see one of the Coltranes lumbering toward him, reanimated by a last small supply of current stored in battery cells.

• 25 •

At the main gate of New Wave Microtechnology, on the highlands along the northern perimeter of Moonlight Cove, the guard, wearing a black rain slicker with the corporate logo on the breast, squinted at the oncoming police cruiser. When he recognized Loman, he waved him through without stopping him. Loman had been well known there even before he and they had become New People.

New Wave power, prestige, and profitability were not hidden in an unassuming corporate headquarters. The place had been designed by a leading architect who favored rounded corners, gentle angles, and the interesting juxtaposition of curved walls – some concave, some convex. The two large three-story buildings – one erected four years after the other – were faced with buff-colored stone, had huge tinted windows, and blended well with the landscape.

Of the fourteen hundred people employed there, nearly a thousand lived in Moonlight Cove. The rest resided in outlying communities elsewhere in the county. All of them, of course, lived within the effective reach of the microwave broadcasting dish on the roof of the main structure.

As he followed the entrance road around the big buildings toward the parking areas behind, Loman thought: Sure as hell, Shaddack's our very own Reverend Jim Jones. Needs to be sure he can take every last one of his devoted followers with him any time he wants. A modern pharaoh. When he dies, those attending him die, too, as if he expects them to continue to attend him in the next world. Shit. Do we even believe in a next world any more?

No. Religious faith was akin to hope, and it required emotional commitment. New People did not believe in God any more than they believed in Santa Claus. The only thing they believed in was the power of the machine and the cybernetic destiny of humanity.

Maybe some of them didn't even believe in that.

Loman didn't. He no longer believed in anything at all – which scared him because he had once believed in so many things.

He entered the first parking area.

The ratio of New Wave's gross sales and profits to its number of employees was high even for the microtechnology industry, and its ability to pay for the best talent in its field was reflected in the percentage of high-ticket cars in the two enormous lots. Mercedes. BMW. Porsche. Corvette. Cadillac Seville. Jaguar. High-end-Japanese imports with every bell and whistle.

Only half the usual number of cars were in the lot. It looked as if a high percentage of the staff was at home, working by modem. How many were already like Denny?

Side by side on the rainswept macadam, those cars reminded Loman of the orderly ranks of tombstones in a cemetery. All those quiescent engines, all that cold metal, all those hundreds of wet windshields reflecting the flat gray autumn sky, suddenly seemed a presentiment of death. To Loman, that parking lot represented the future of the entire town: silence, stillness, the terrible eternal peace of the graveyard.

If the authorities outside of Moonlight Cove tumbled to what was happening there, or if it turned out that virtually every one of the New People *was* a regressive – or worse – and the Moonhawk Project was a disaster, the remedy would not be poisoned Kool-Aid this time, like Reverend Jim Jones used down there in Jonestown, but lethal commands broadcast in bursts of microwaves, received by microsphere computers inside the New People, instantly translated into the language of the governing program, and acted upon. Thousands of hearts would stop as one. The New People would fall, as one, and Moonlight Cove would in an instant become a graveyard of the unburied.

Loman drove through the first parking lot, into the second, and headed toward the row of spaces reserved for the top executives.

If I wait for Shaddack to see that Moonhawk's gone bad and to take us with him, Loman thought, he won't be doing it because he cares about cleaning up the messes he makes, not that damn albino-spider-of-a-man. He'll take us with him just for the bloody hell of it, just so he can go out with a big bang, so the world will stand in awe of his power, a man of such incredible power that he could command thousands to die simultaneously with him.

More than a few sickos would see him as a hero, idolize him. Some budding young genius might want to emulate him. That was no doubt what Shaddack had in mind. At best, if Moonhawk succeeded and all of mankind was eventually converted, Shaddack literally would be the master of his world. At worst, if it all went bad and he had to kill himself to avoid falling into the hands of the authorities, he would become a nearly mythic figure of dark inspiration, whose malign legend would encourage legions of the mad and power-mad, a Hitler for the silicon age.

Loman braked at the end of a row of cars.

He wiped at his greasy face. His hand was shaking.

He was filled with a longing to abandon this responsibility and seek the pressure-free existence of the regressive.

But he resisted.

If Loman killed Shaddack first, before Shaddack had a chance to kill himself, the legend would be tarnished. Loman would die a few seconds after Shaddack died, as would all the New People, but at least the legend would have to incorporate the fact that this high-tech Jim Jones had perished at the hands of one of the creatures he'd created. His power would be shown to be finite; he would be seen as clever but not clever enough, a flawed god, sharing both the hubris and the fate of Wells's Moreau, and his work more universally would be viewed as folly.

Loman turned right, drove to the row of executive parking spaces, and was disappointed to see that neither Shaddack's Mercedes nor his charcoal-gray van was in his reserved slot. He might still be there. He could have been driven to the office by someone else or could have parked elsewhere.

Loman swung his cruiser into Shaddack's reserved space. He cut the engine.

He was carrying his revolver in a hip holster. He had checked twice before to be sure it was fully loaded. He checked again.

Between Shaddack's house and New Wave, Loman had parked along the road to write a note, which he would leave on Shaddack's body, clearly explaining that he had killed his maker. When authorities entered Moonlight Cove from the unconverted world beyond, they would find the note and know.

He would execute Shaddack not because he was motivated by noble purpose. Such high-minded self-sacrifice required a depth of feeling he could no longer achieve. He would murder Shaddack strictly because he was terrified that Shaddack would learn about Denny, or would discover that others had become what Denny had become, and would find a way to make *all* of them enter into an unholy union with machines.

Molten silver eyes . . .

Drool spilling from the gaping mouth . . .

The segmented probe bursting from the boy's forehead and seeking the vaginal heat of the computer . . .

Those blood-freezing images, and others, played through Loman's mind on an endless loop of memory.

He'd kill Shaddack to save himself from being forced to become what Denny had become, and the destruction of Shaddack's legend would just be a beneficial side-effect.

He holstered his gun and got out of the car. He hurried through the rain to the main entrance, pushed through the etched-glass doors into the marble-floored lobby, turned right, away from the elevators, and approached the main reception desk. In corporate luxury, the place rivaled the most elaborate headquarters of high-tech companies in the more famous Silicon Valley, farther south. Detailed marble moldings, polished brass trim, fine crystal sconces, and modernistic crystal chandeliers were testament to New Wave's success.

The woman on duty was Dora Hankins. He had known her all of his life. She was a year older than he. In high school he had dated her sister a couple of times.

She looked up as he approached, said nothing.

'Shaddack?' he said.

'Not in.'

'You sure?'

'Yes.'

'When's he due?'

'His secretary will know.'

'I'll go up.'

'Fine.'

As he boarded an elevator and pushed the 3 on the control board, Loman reflected on the small talk in which he and Dora Hankins would have engaged in the days before they had been put through the Change. They would have bantered with each other, exchanged news about their families, and commented on the weather. Not now. Small talk was a pleasure of their former world. Converted, they had no use for it. In fact, though he recalled that small talk had once been a part of civilized life, Loman could no longer quite remember why he ever had found it worthwhile or what kind of pleasure it had given him.

Shaddack's office suite was on the northwest corner of the third floor. The first room off the hall was the reception lounge, plushly carpeted in beige Edward Fields originals, impressively furnished in plump Roche-Bobois leather couches and brass tables with inch-thick glass tops. The single piece of art was a painting by Jasper Johns – an original, not a print.

What happens to artists in the new world coming? Loman wondered.

But he knew the answer. There would be none. Art was emotion embodied in paint on a canvas, words on a page, music in a symphony hall. There would be no art in the new world. And if there was, it would be the art of fear. The writer's most frequently used words would all be synonyms for darkness. The musician would write dirges of one form or another. The painter's most used pigment would be black.

Vicky Lanardo, Shaddack's executive secretary, was at her desk. She said, 'He's not in.'

Behind her the door to Shaddack's enormous private office stood open. No lights were on in there. It was illuminated only by the light of the storm-torn day, which came through the blinds in ash-gray bands.

'When will he be in?' Loman asked.

'I don't know.'

'No appointments?'

'None.'

'Do you know where he is?'

'No.'

Loman walked out. For a while he prowled the half-deserted corridors, offices, labs, and tech rooms, hoping to spot Shaddack.

Before long, however, he decided that Shaddack was not lurking about the premises. Evidently the great man was staying mobile on this last day of Moonlight Cove's conversion.

Because of me, Loman thought. Because of what I said to him last night at Peyser's. He's afraid of me, and he's either staying mobile or gone to ground somewhere, making himself difficult to find.

Loman left the building, returned to his patrol car, and set out in search of his maker.

• 26 •

In the downstairs half-bath off the kitchen, naked from the waist up, Sam sat on the closed lid of the commode, and Tessa performed the same kind of nursely duties she'd performed earlier for Chrissie. But Sam's wounds were more serious than the girl's.

In a dime-size circle on his forehead, above his right eye, the skin had been flensed off, and in the center of the circle the flesh had been entirely eaten away, revealing a speck of bared bone about an eighth of an inch in diameter. Staunching the flow of blood from those tiny, severed capillaries required a few minutes of continuous pressure, followed by the application of iodine, a liberal coating of NuSkin, and a tightly taped gauze bandage. But even after all these efforts, the gauze slowly darkened with a red stain.

As Tessa worked on him, Sam told them what had happened:

'. . . so if I hadn't shot her in the head, just then . . . if I'd been a second or two slower, I think that damn thing, that probe, whatever it was, it would have bored right through my skull and sunk into my brain, and she'd have connected with me the way she was connected with that computer.'

Her toga forsaken in favor of dry jeans and blouse, Chrissie stood just inside the bathroom, white-faced but wanting to hear all.

Harry had pulled his wheelchair into the doorway.

Moose was lying at Sam's feet, rather than at Harry's. The dog seemed to realize that at the moment the visitor needed comforting more than Harry did.

Sam was colder to the touch than could be explained by his time in the chilly rain. He was trembling, and periodically the shivers that passed through him were so powerful that his teeth chattered.

The more Sam talked, the colder Tessa became, too, and in time his shivers were communicated to her.

His right wrist had been cut on both sides, when Harley Coltrane had gripped him with a powerful bony hand. No major blood vessels had been severed; neither gash required stitches, and Tessa quickly stopped the bleeding there. The bruises, which had barely begun to appear and would not fully flower for hours yet, were going to be worse than the cuts. He complained of pain in the joint, and his hand was weak, but she did not think that any bones had been broken or crushed.

'. . . as if they'd somehow been given the ability to control their physical form,' Sam said shakily, 'to make anything they wanted of themselves, mind over matter, just like Chrissie said when she told us about the priest, the one who started to become the creature from that movie . . .'

The girl nodded.

'I mean, they changed *before my eyes*, grew these probes, tried to spear me. Yet with this incredible control of their bodies, of their physical substance, all they apparently wanted to make of themselves was . . . something out of a bad dream.'

The wound on his abdomen was the least of the three. As on his forehead, the skin was stripped away in a dime-sized circle, though the probe that had struck him there seemed to have been meant to burn rather than cut its way into him. His flesh was scorched, and the wound itself was pretty much cauterized.

From his wheelchair Harry said, 'Sam, do you think they're really people who control themselves, who have *chosen* to become machinelike, or are they people who've somehow been taken over by machines, against their will?'

'I don't know,' Sam said. 'It could be either, I guess.'

'But how could they be taken over, how could this happen, how could such a change in the human body be accomplished? And how does what's happened to the Coltranes tie in with the Boogeymen?'

'Damned if I know,' Sam said. 'Somehow it's all related to New Wave. Got to be. And none of us here knows anything much about the cutting edge of that kind of technology, so we don't even have the basic knowledge required to speculate intelligently. It might as well be magic to us, supernatural. The only way we'll ever really understand what's happened is to get help from outside, quarantine Moonlight Cove, seize New Waves' labs and records, and reconstruct it the way fire marshals reconstruct the history of a fire from what they sift out of the ashes.'

'Ashes?' Tessa asked as Sam stood up and as she helped him into his shirt. 'This talk about fires and ashes – and other things you've said – make it sound as if you think whatever's going on in Moonlight Cove is building real fast toward an explosion or something.'

'It is,' he said.

At first he tried to button his shirt with one hand, but then he allowed Tessa to do it for him. She noticed that his skin was still cold and that his shivers were not subsiding with time.

He said, 'All these murders they've got to cover up, these things that stalk the night . . . there's a sense that a collapse has begun, that whatever they tried to do here isn't turning out like they expected, and that the collapse is accelerating.' He was breathing too quickly, too shallowly. He paused, took a deeper breath. 'What I saw in the Coltranes' house . . . that didn't look like anything anyone could have planned, not something you'd *want* to do to people or that they'd want for themselves. It looked like an experiment out of control, biology run amok, reality turned inside out, and I swear to God that if *those* kinds of secrets are hidden in the houses of this town, then the whole project has to be collapsing on New Wave right now, coming down fast and hard on their heads, whether they want to admit it or not. It's all blowing up now, right now, one hell of an explosion, and we're in the middle of it.'

From the moment he'd stumbled through the kitchen door, dripping rain and blood, throughout the time Tessa had cleaned and bandaged his wounds, she had noticed something that frightened her more than his paleness and shivering. He kept touching them. He had embraced Tessa in the kitchen when she gasped at the sight of the bleeding hole in his forehead; he'd held her and leaned against her and assured her that he was okay. Primarily he seemed to be reassuring himself that she and Harry and Chrissie were okay, as if he had expected to come back and find them . . . changed. He hugged Chrissie, too, as if she were his own daughter, and he said, 'It'll be all right, everything'll be all right,' when he saw how frightened she was. Harry held out a hand in concern, and Sam grasped it and was reluctant to let go. In the bathroom, while Tessa dressed his wounds, he had repeatedly touched her hands, her arms, and had once put a hand against her cheek as if wondering at the softness and warmth of her skin. He reached out to touch Chrissie, too, where she stood inside the bathroom door, patting her shoulder, holding her hand for a moment and giving it a reassuring squeeze. Until now he had not been a toucher. He had been reserved, self-contained, cool, even distant. But during the quarter of an hour he'd spent in the Coltrane house, he had been so profoundly shaken by what he had seen that his shell of self-imposed isolation had cracked wide open; he had come to want and need the human contact that, only a short while ago, he had not even ranked as desirable as good Mexican food, Guinness Stout, and Goldie Hawn films.

When she contemplated the intensity of the horror necessary to transform him so completely and abruptly, Tessa was more frightened than ever because Sam Booker's redemption seemed akin to that of a sinner who, on his deathbed, glimpsing hell, turns desperately to the god he once shunned, seeking comfort and reassurance. Was he less sure now of their chances of escaping? Perhaps he was seeking human contact because, having denied it to himself for so many years, he believed that only hours remained in which to experience the communion of his own kind before the great, deep, endless darkness settled over them.

• 27 •

Shaddack awoke from his familiar and comforting dream of human and machine parts combined in a world-spanning engine of incalculable power and mysterious purpose. He was, as always, refreshed as much by the dream as by sleep itself.

He got out of the van and stretched. Using tools he found in the garage, he forced open the connecting door to the late Paula Parkins's house. He used her bathroom, then washed his hands and face.

Upon returning to the garage, he raised the big door. He pulled the van out into the driveway, where it could better transmit and receive data by microwave.

Rain was still falling, and depressions in the lawn were filled with water. Already wisps of fog stirred in the windless air, which probably meant the banks that rolled in from the sea later in the day would be even denser than those last night.

He took another ham sandwich and a Coke from the cooler and ate while using the van's VDT to check on the progress of Moonhawk. The 6:00 a.m. to 6:00 p.m. schedule of four hundred and fifty conversions was still under way. Already, at 12:50, slightly less than seven hours into the twelve-hour program, three hundred and nine had been injected with full-spectrum microspheres. The conversion teams were well ahead of schedule.

He checked on the progress of the search for Samuel Booker and the Lockland woman. Neither had been found.

Shaddack should have been worried about their disappearance. But he was unconcerned. He had seen the moonhawk, after all, not once but three times, and he had no doubt that ultimately he would achieve all of his goals.

The Foster girl was still missing too. He didn't trouble himself about her either. She had probably encountered something deadly in the night. At times regressives could be useful.

Perhaps Booker and the Lockland woman had fallen victim to those same creatures. It would be ironic if the regressives – the only flaw in the project, and a potentially serious one – should prove to have preserved the secret of Moonhawk.

Through the VDT, he tried to reach Tucker at New Wave, then at his home, but the man was at neither place. Could Watkins be correct? Was Tucker a regressive and, like Peyser, unable to find his way back to human form? Was he out there in the woods right now, trapped in an altered state?

Clicking off the computer, Shaddack sighed. After everyone had been converted at midnight, this first phase of Moonhawk would not be finished. Not quite. They'd evidently have a few messes to mop up.

• 28 •

In the cellar of the Icarus Colony, three bodies had become one. The resultant entity was without rigid shape, boneless, featureless, a mass of pulsing tissue that lived in spite of lacking a brain and heart and blood vessels, without organs of any kind. It was primal, a thick protein soup, brainless but aware, eyeless but seeing, earless but hearing, without a gut but hungry.

The agglomerations of silicon microspheres had dissolved within it. That inner computer could no longer function in the radically altered substance of the creature, and in turn the beast had no use any more for the biological assistance that the microspheres had been designed to provide. Now it was not linked to Sun, the computer at New Wave. If the microwave transmitter there sent a death order, it would not receive the command – and would live.

It had become the master of its physiology by reducing itself to the uncomplicated essence of physical existence.

Their three minds also had become one. The consciousness now dwelling in that darkness was as lacking in complex form as the amorphous, jellid body it inhabited.

It had relinquished its memory because memories were inevitably of events and relationships that had consequences, and consequences – good or bad – implied that one was responsible for one's actions. Flight from responsibility had driven the creature to regression in the first place. Pain was another reason for shedding memory – the pain of recalling what had been lost.

Likewise, it had surrendered the capacity to consider the future, to plan, to dream.

Now it had no past of which it was aware, and the concept of a future was beyond its ken. It lived only for the moment, unthinking, unfeeling, uncaring.

It had one need. To survive.

And to survive, it needed only one thing. To feed.

• 29 •

The breakfast dishes had been cleared from the table while Sam Booker was at the Coltranes' house, battling monsters that apparently had been part human and part computer and part zombies – and maybe, for all they knew, part toaster oven. After Sam was bandaged, Chrissie gathered with him and Tessa and Harry around the kitchen table again, to listen to them discuss what action to take next.

Moose stayed at Chrissie's side, regarding her with soulful brown eyes, as if he adored her more than life itself. She couldn't resist giving him all the petting and scratching-behind-the-ears that he wanted.

'The greatest problem of our age,' Sam said, 'is how to keep technological progress accelerating, how to use it to improve the quality of life – without being overwhelmed by it. Can we employ the computer to redesign our world, to remake our lives, without one day coming to worship it?' He blinked at Tessa and said, 'It's not a silly question.'

Tessa frowned. 'I didn't say it was. Sometimes we have a blind trust in machines, a tendency to believe that whatever a computer tells us is gospel—'

'To forget the old maxim,' Harry injected, 'which says – "garbage in, garbage out." '

'Exactly,' Tessa agreed. 'Sometimes, when we get data or analysis from computers, we treat it as if the machines were all infallible. Which is dangerous because a computer application can be conceived, designed, and implemented by a madman, perhaps not as easily as by a benign genius but certainly as effectively.'

Sam said, 'Yet people have a tendency – no, even a deep desire – to *want* to depend on the machines.'

'Yeah,' Harry said, 'that's our sorry damn need to shift responsibility whenever we possibly can. A spineless desire to get out from under responsibility is in our genes, I swear it is, and the only way we get anywhere in this world is by constantly fighting our natural inclination to be utterly irresponsible. Sometimes I wonder if *that's* what we got from the devil when Eve listened to the serpent and ate the apple – this aversion to responsibility. Most evil has its roots there.'

Chrissie noticed this subject energized Harry. With his one good arm and a little help from his half-good leg, he levered himself higher in his wheelchair. Color seeped into his previously pale face. He made a fist of one hand and stared at it intently, as if holding something precious in that tight grip, as if he held the idea there and didn't want to let go of it until he had fully explored it.

He said, 'Men steal and kill and lie and cheat because they feel no responsibility for others. Politicians want power, and they want acclaim when their policies succeed, but they seldom stand up and take the responsibility for failure. The world's full of people who want to tell you how to live your life, how to make heaven right here on earth, but when their ideas turn out half-baked, when it ends in Dachau or the Gulag or the mass murders that followed our departure from Southeast Asia, they turn their heads, avert their eyes, and pretend they had no responsibility for the slaughter.'

He shuddered, and Chrissie shuddered too, though she was not entirely sure that she entirely understood everything he was saying.

'Jesus,' he continued, 'if I've thought about this once, I've thought about it a thousand times, ten thousand, maybe because of the war.'

'Vietnam, you mean?' Tessa said.

Harry nodded. He was still staring at his fist. 'In the war, to survive, you had to be responsible every minute of every day, unhesitatingly responsible for yourself, for your every action. You had to be responsible for your buddies, too, because survival wasn't something that could be achieved alone. That's maybe the one positive thing about fighting in a war – it clarifies your thinking and makes you realize that a sense of responsibility is what separates good men from the damned. I don't regret the war, not even considering what happened to me there. I learned that great lesson, learned to be responsible in all things, and I still feel responsible to the people we were fighting for, always will, and some-times when I think of how we abandoned them to the killing fields, the mass graves, I lay awake at night and cry because they depended on me, and to the extent that I was a part of the process, I'm responsible for failing them.'

They were all silent.

Chrissie felt a peculiar pressure in her chest, the same feeling she always got in school when a teacher – any teacher, any subject – began to talk about something which had been previously unknown to her and which so impressed her that it changed the way she looked at the world. It didn't happen often,but it was always both a scary and wonderful sensation. She felt it now, because of what Harry had said, but the sensation was ten times or a hundred times stronger than it had ever been when some new insight or idea had been passed to her in geography or math or science.

Tessa said, 'Harry, I think your sense of responsibility in this case is excessive.'

He finally looked up from his fist, 'No. It can never be. Your sense of responsibility to others can never be excessive.' He smiled at her. 'But I know you just well enough to suspect you're already aware of that, Tessa, whether you realize it or not.' He looked at Sam and said, 'Some of those who came out of the war saw no good at all in it. When I meet up with them, I always suspect they were the ones who never learned the lesson, and I avoid them – though I suppose that's unfair. Can't help it. But when I meet a man from the war and see he learned the lesson, then I'd trust him with my life. Hell, I'd trust him with my soul, which in this case seems to be what they want to steal. You'll get us out of this, Sam.' At last he opened his fist. 'I've no doubt of that.'

Tessa seemed surprised. To Sam she said, 'You were in Vietnam?'

Sam nodded. 'Between junior college and the Bureau.'

'But you never mentioned it. This morning, when we were making breakfast, when you told me all the reasons you saw the world so differently from the way I saw it, you mentioned your wife's death, the murder of your partners, your situation with your son, but not that.'

Sam stared at his bandaged wrist for a while and finally said, 'The war is the most personal experience of my life.'

'What an odd thing to say.'

'Not odd at all,' Harry said. 'The most intense and the most personal.'

Sam said, 'If I'd not come to terms with it, I'd probably still talk about it, probably run on about it all the time. But I *have* come to terms with it. I've understood. And now to talk about it casually with someone I've just met would . . . well, cheapen it, I guess.'

Tessa looked at Harry and said, 'But you knew he was in Vietnam?'

'Yes.'

'Just *knew* it somehow.'

'Yes.'

Sam had been leaning over the table. Now he settled back in his chair. 'Harry, I swear I'll do my best to get us out of this. But I wish I had a better grasp of what we're up against. It all comes from New Wave. But exactly what have they done, and how can it be stopped? And how can I hope to deal with it when I don't even *understand* it?'

To that point Chrissie had felt that the conversation had been way over her head, even though all of it had been fascinating and though some of it had stirred the learning feeling in her. But now she felt that she had to contribute: 'Are you really *sure* it's not aliens?'

'We're sure,' Tessa said, smiling at her, and Sam ruffled her hair.

'Well,' Chrissie said, 'what I mean is, maybe what went wrong at New Wave is that aliens landed *there* and used it as a base, and maybe they want to turn us all into machines, like the Coltranes, so we can serve them as slaves – which, when you think about it, is more sensible than wanting to eat us. They're aliens, after all, which means they have alien stomachs and alien digestive juices, and we'd probably be real hard to digest, give them heartburn, maybe even diarrhea.'

Sam, who was sitting in the chair beside Chrissie, took both her hands and held them gently in his, as aware of her abraded palm as he was aware of his own injured wrist. 'Chrissie, I don't know if you've been paying too much attention to what Harry's been saying—'

'Oh, yes,' she said at once. 'All of it.'

'Well, then you'll understand when I tell you that wanting to blame all these horrors on aliens is yet another way of shifting the responsibility from where it really belongs – on us, on people, on our very real and very great capacity to do harm to one another. It's hard to believe that anybody, even crazy men, would want to make the Coltranes into what they became, but somebody evidently did want just that. If we try to blame it on aliens – or the devil or God or trolls or whatever – we won't be likely to see the situation clearly enough to figure out how to save ourselves. You understand?'

'Sort of.'

He smiled at her. He had a very nice smile, though he didn't flash it much. 'I think you understand it more than sort of.'

'More than sort of,' Chrissie agreed. 'It'd sure be nice if it was aliens, because we'd just have to find their nest or their hive or whatever, burn them out real good, maybe blow up their spaceship, and it would be over and done with. But if it's not aliens, if it's us – people like us – who did all this, then maybe it's never quite over and done with.'

With increasing frustration, Loman Watkins cruised from one end of Moonlight Cove to the other, back and forth, around and around in the rain, seeking Shaddack. He had revisited the house on the north point to be sure Shaddack had not returned there, and also to check the garage to see which vehicle was missing. Now he was looking for Shaddack's charcoal-gray van with tinted windows, but he was unable to locate it.

Wherever he went, conversion teams and search parties were at work. Though the unconverted were not likely to notice anything too unusual about those men's passage through town, Loman was constantly aware of them.

At the north and south roadblocks on the county route and at the main blockade on the eastern end of Ocean Avenue, out toward the interstate, Loman's officers were continuing to deal with outsiders wanting to enter Moonlight Cove. Exhaust plumes rose from the idling patrol cars, mingling with the wisps of fog that had begun to slither through the rain. The red and blue emergency beacons were reflected in the wet macadam, so it seemed as if streams of blood, oxygenated and oxygen-depleted, flowed along the pavement.

There weren't many would-be visitors because the town was neither the county seat nor a primary shopping center for people in outlying communities. Furthermore, it was close to the end of the county road, and there were no destinations beyond it, so no one wanted to pass through on the way to somewhere else. Those who did want to come into town were turned away, if at all possible, with a story about a toxic spill at New Wave. Those who seemed at all skeptical were arrested, conveyed to the jail, and locked in cells until a decision could be made either to kill or convert them. Since the establishment of the quarantine in the early hours of the morning, only a score of people had been stopped at the blockades, and only six had been jailed.

Shaddack had chosen his proving ground well. Moonlight Cove was relatively isolated and therefore easier to control.

Loman was of a mind to order the roadblocks dismantled, and to drive over to Aberdeen Wells, where he could spill the whole story to the county sheriff. He wanted to blow the Moonhawk Project wide open.

He was no longer afraid of Shaddack's rage or of dying. Well . . . not true. He was afraid of Shaddack and of death, but they held less fear for him than the prospect of becoming something like Denny had become. He would have as soon entrusted himself to the mercies of the sheriff in Aberdeen and the federal authorities – even scientists who, cleaning up the mess in Moonlight Cove, might be sorely tempted to dissect him – than stay in town and inevitably surrender the last few fragments of his humanity either to regression or to some nightmare wedding of his body and mind with a computer.

But if he ordered his officers to stand down, they would be suspicious, and their loyalty lay more with Shaddack than with him, for they were bound to Shaddack by terror. They were still more frightened of their New Wave master than of anything else, for they had not seen what Denny had become and did not yet realize that their future might hold in store something even worse than regression to a savage state. Like Moreau's beastmen, they kept The Law as best they could, not daring – at least for now – to betray their maker. They would probably try to stop Loman from sabotaging the Moonhawk Project, and he might wind up dead or, worse, locked in a jail cell.

He couldn't risk revealing his counter revolutionary commitment, for then 'he might never have a chance to deal with Shaddack. In his mind's eye he saw himself caged at the jail, with Shaddack smiling coldly at him through the bars, as they wheeled in a computer with which they somehow intended to fuse him.

Molten silver eyes . . .

He kept on the move in the rain-hammered day, squinting through the streaked windshield. The wipers thumped steadily, as though ticking off time. He was acutely aware that midnight was drawing nearer.

He was the puma-man, on the prowl, and Moreau was out there in the island jungle that was Moonlight Cove.

• 31 •

Initially the protean creature was content to feed on the things it found when it extended thin tendrils of itself down the drain in the cellar floor or through fine cracks in the walls and into the moist surrounding earth. Beetles. Grubs. Earthworms. It no longer knew the names of those things, but it avidly consumed them.

Soon, however, it depleted the supply of insects and worms within ten yards of the house. It needed a more substantial meal.

It churned, seethed, perhaps striving to marshal its amorphous tissues into a shape in which it could leave the cellar and seek prey. But it had no memory of previous forms and no desire whatsoever to impose structural order on itself.

The consciousness which inhabited that jellid mass no longer had more than the dimmest sense of self-awareness, yet it was still able to remake itself to an extent that would satisfy its needs. Suddenly a score of lipless, toothless mouths opened in that fluid form. A blast of sound, mostly beyond the range of human hearing, erupted from it.

Throughout the moldering structure above the shapeless beast, dozens of mice were scurrying, nibbling at food, nest-building, and grooming themselves. They stopped, as one, when the call blared up from the cellar.

The creature could sense them above, in the crumbling walls, though it thought of them not as mice but as small warm masses of living flesh. Food. Fuel. It wanted them. It *needed* them.

It attempted to express that need in the form of a wordless but compelling summons.

In every corner of the house, mice twitched. They brushed at their faces with forepaws, as if they'd scurried through cobwebs and were trying to scrape those clingy, gossamer strands out of their fur.

A small colony of eight bats lived in the attic, and they also reacted to the urgent call. They dropped from the rafters on which they hung, and flew in frenzied, random patterns in the long upper room, repeatedly swooping within a fraction of an inch of the walls and one another.

But nothing came to the creature in the basement. Though the call had reached the small animals for which it had been intended, it did not have the desired effect.

The shapeless thing fell silent.

Its many mouths closed.

One by one the bats returned to their perches in the attic.

The mice sat as if in shock for a moment, then resumed their usual activities.

A couple of minutes later, the protean beast tried again with a different pattern of sounds, still pitched beyond human hearing but more alluring than before.

The bats flung themselves from their perches and roiled through the attic in such turmoil that an observer might have thought they numbered a hundred instead of only eight. The beating of their wings was louder than the rush of rain on the leaky roof.

Everywhere, mice rose on their hind feet, sitting at attention, ears pricked. Those in the lower reaches of the house, nearer the source of the summons, shivered violently, as though they saw before them a crouched and grinning cat.

Screeching, the bats swooped through a hole in the attic floor, into an empty room on the second story, where they circled and soared and dove ceaselessly.

Two mice on the ground floor began to creep toward the kitchen, where the door to the basement stood open. But both stopped on the threshold of that room, frightened and confused.

Below, the shapeless entity tripled the power of its call.

One of the mice in the kitchen suddenly bled from the ears and fell dead.

Upstairs, the bats began to bounce off walls, their radar shot.

The cellar dweller cut back somewhat on the force of its summons.

The bats immediately swooped out of the upstairs room, into the hallway, down the stairwell, and along the ground-floor hall. As they went, they flew over a double score of scurrying mice.

Below, the creature's many mouths had connected, forming one large orifice in the center of the pulsing mass.

In swift succession the bats flew straight into that gaping maw like black playing cards being tossed one at a time into a waste can. They embedded themselves in the oozing protoplasm and were swiftly dissolved by powerful digestive acids.

An army of mice and four rats – even two chipmunks that eagerly abandoned their nest inside the dining-room wall – swarmed down the steep cellar steps, falling over one another, squeaking excitedly. They fed themselves to the waiting entity.

After that flurry of movement, the house was still.

The creature stopped its siren song. For the moment.

• 32 •

Officer Neil Penniworth was assigned to patrol the northwest quadrant of Moonlight Cove. He was alone in the car because even with the hundred New Wave employees detailed to the police department during the night, their manpower was stretched thin.

Right now, he preferred to work without a partner. Since the episode at Peyser's house, when the smell of blood and the sight of Peyser's altered form had enticed Penniworth to regress, he had been afraid to be around other people. He had avoided total degeneration last night . . . but only by the thinnest of margins. If he witnessed someone else in the act of regression, the urge might stir within him, too, and this time he was not sure that he could successfully repress that dark yearning.

He was equally afraid to be alone. The struggle to hold fast to his remaining shreds of humanity, to resist chaos, to be responsible, was wearying, and he longed to escape this new, hard life. Alone, with no one to see him if he began to surrender the very form and substance of himself, with no one to talk him out of it or even to protest his degeneration, he would be lost.

The weight of his fear was as real as a slab of iron, crushing the life out of him. At times he had difficulty drawing breath, as though his lungs were banded by steel and restricted from full expansion.

The dimensions of the black-and-white seemed to shrink, until he felt almost as confined as he would have been in a straitjacket. The metronomic thump of the windshield wipers grew louder, at least to his ears, until the volume was as thunderous as an endless series of cannon volleys. Repeatedly during the morning and early afternoon, he pulled off the road, flung open the door, and scrambled out into the rain, drawing deep breaths of the cool air.

As the day progressed, however, even the world outside of the car began to seem smaller than it had been. He stopped on Holliwell Road, half a mile west of New Wave's headquarters, and got out of the cruiser, but he felt no better. The low roof of gray clouds denied him the sight of the limitless sky. Like semitransparent curtains of tinsel and thinnest silk, the rain and fog hung between him and the rest of the world. The humidity was cloying, stifling. Rain overflowed gutters, churned in muddy torrents through roadside ditches, dripped from every branch and leaf of every tree, pattered on the macadam pavement, tapped hollowly on the patrol car, sizzled, gurgled, chuckled, snapped against his face, beat upon him with such force that it seemed he was being driven to his knees by thousands of tiny hammers, each too small to be effective in itself but with brutal cumulative effect.

Neil clambered back into the car with as much eagerness as he had scrambled out of it.

He understood that it was neither the claustrophobic interior of the cruiser nor the enervating enwrapment of the rain that he was desperately trying to escape. The actual oppressor was his life as a New Person. Able to feel only fear, he was locked in an emotional closet of such unendurably narrow dimensions that he could not move at all. He was not suffocating because of external entanglements and constrictions; rather, he was bound from within, because of what Shaddack had made of him.

Which meant there was no escape.

Except, perhaps, by regression.

Neil could not bear life as he must now live it. On the other hand he was repelled and terrified by the thought of devolution into some subhuman form.

His dilemma appeared insoluble.

He was as distressed by his inability to stop thinking about his predicament as he was by the predicament itself. It pried constantly at his mind. He could find no surcease.

The closest he came to being able to put his worry – and some of his fear – out of mind was when he was working with the mobile VDT in the patrol car. When he checked the computer bulletin board to see if messages awaited him, when he accessed the Moonhawk schedule to learn how conversions were progressing, or undertook any other task with the computer, his attention became so focused on the interaction with the machine that briefly his anxiety subsided and his nagging claustrophobia faded.

From adolescence, Neil had been interested in computers, though he had never become a hacker. His interest was less obsessive than that. He'd started with computer games, of course, but later had been given an inexpensive PC. Later still he had bought a modem with some of the money earned at a summer job. Though he could not afford much long-distance telephone time and never spent leisurely hours using the modem to reach far from the backwaters of Moonlight Cove into the fascinating data nets available in the outside world, he found his forays into on-line systems engrossing and fun.

Now, as he sat in the parked car along Holliwell Road, using the VDT, he thought that the inner world of the computer was admirably clean, comparatively simple, predictable, and sane. So unlike human existence – whether that of New People or Old. In there, logic and reason ruled. Cause and effect and side-effect were always analyzed and made perfectly clear. In there, all was black and white – or, when gray, the gray was carefully measured, quantified and qualified. Cold facts were easier to deal with than feelings. A universe formed purely of data, abstracted from matter and event, seemed so much more desirable than the real universe of cold and heat, sharp and blunt, smooth and rough, blood and death, pain and fear.

Calling up menu after menu, Neil probed ever deeper into the Moonhawk research files within Sun. He needed none of the data that he summoned forth but found solace in the process of obtaining it.

He began to see the terminal screen not as a cathode-ray tube on which information was displayed, but as a window into another world. A world of facts. A world free of troubling contradictions . . . and responsibility. In there, nothing could be felt; there was only the known and the unknown, either an abundance of facts about a particular subject or a dearth of them, but not *feeling*; never feeling; feeling was the curse of those whose existence was dependent upon flesh and bone.

A window into another world.

Neil touched the screen.

He wished the window could be opened and that he could climb through it to that place of reason, order, peace.

With the fingertips of his right hand, he traced circles across the warm glass screen.

Strangely, he thought of Dorothy, swept up from the plains of Kansas with her dog Toto, spun high into the tornado, and dropped out of that depression-era grayness into a world far more intriguing. If only some electronic tornado could erupt from the VDT and carry him to a better place . . .

His fingers passed through the screen.

He snatched his hand back in astonishment.

The glass had not ruptured. Chains of words and numbers glowed on the tube, as before.

At first he tried to convince himself that what he had seen had been a hallucination. But he did not believe that.

He flexed his fingers. They appeared unhurt.

He looked out at the stormswept day. The windshield wipers were not switched on. Rain rippled down the glass, distorting the world beyond; everything out there looked twisted, mutated, strange. There could never be order, sanity, and peace in such a place as that.

Tentatively he touched the computer screen once more. It felt solid.

Again, he thought of how desirable the clean, predictable world of the computer would be – and as before his hand slipped through the glass, up to the wrist this time. The screen had opened around him and sealed tight to him, as if it were an organic membrane. The data continued to blaze on the tube, the words and numbers forming lines around his intruding hand.

His heart was racing. He was afraid but also excited.

He tried to wiggle his fingers in that mysterious, inner warmth. He could not feel them. He began to think they had dissolved or been cut off, and that when he withdrew his hand from the machine, the stump of his wrist would spout blood.

He withdrew it anyway.

His hand was whole.

But it was not quite a hand any more. The flesh on the upper side, from the tips of his fingernails to his wrist, appeared to be veined with copper and threads of glass. In those glass filaments beat a steady and luminous pulse.

He turned his hand over. The undersides of his fingers and his palm resembled the surface of a cathode-ray tube. Data burned there, green letters on a background glassy and dark. When he compared the words and numbers on his hand to those on the car's VDT, he saw they were identical. The information on the VDT changed; simultaneously, so did that on his hand.

Abruptly, he understood that regression into bestial form was not the only avenue of escape open to him, that he could enter into the world of electronic thought and magnetic memory, of knowledge without fleshly desire, of awareness without feeling. This was not an insight strictly – or even primarily – intellectual in nature. It wasn't just instinctive understanding, either. On some level more profound than either intellect or instinct, he knew that he could remake himself more thoroughly than even Shaddack had remade him.

He lowered his hand from the tilted computer screen to the data-processing unit in the console between the seats. As easily as he had penetrated the glass, he let his hand slide through the keyboard and cover plate, into the guts of the machine.

He was like a ghost, able to pass through walls, ectoplasmic.

A coldness crept up his arm.

The data on the screen was replaced by cryptic patterns of light.

He leaned back in his seat.

The coldness had reached his shoulder. It flowed into his neck.

He sighed.

He felt something happening to his eyes. He wasn't sure what. He could have looked at the rearview mirror. He didn't care. He decided to close his eyes and let them become whatever was necessary as part of this second and more complete conversion.

This altered state was infinitely more appealing than that of the regressive. Irresistible.

The coldness was in his face now. His mouth was numb.

Something also was happening inside his head. He was becoming as aware of the inner geography of his brain circuits and synapses as he was of the exterior world. His body was not as much a part of him as it had once been; he sensed less through it, as if his nerves had been mostly abraded away; he could not even tell if it was warm or chilly in the car unless he concentrated on accumulating that data. His body was just a machine casing, after all, and a rack for sensors, designed to protect and serve the inner him, the calculating mind.

The coldness was inside his skull.

It felt like scores, then hundreds, then thousands of ice-cold spiders scurrying over the surface of his brain, burrowing into it.

Suddenly he remembered that Dorothy had found Oz to be a living nightmare and ultimately had wanted desperately to find her way back to Kansas. Alice, too, had found madness and terror down the rabbit hole, beyond the looking glass . . .

A million cold spiders.

Inside his skull.

A billion.

Cold, cold.

Scurrying.

• 33 •

Still circling through Moonlight Cove, seeking Shaddack, Loman saw two regressives sprint across the street.

He was on Paddock Lane, at the southern end of town, where the properties were big enough for people to keep horses. Ranch houses lay on both sides, with small private stables beside or behind them. The homes set back from the street, behind split-rail or white ranch fencing, beyond deep and lushly landscaped lawns.

The pair of regressives erupted from a dense row of mature three-foot-high azaleas that were still bushy but flowerless this late in the season. They streaked on all fours across the roadway, leaped a ditch, and crashed through a hedgerow, vanishing behind it.

Although immense pines were lined up along both sides of Paddock Lane, adding their shadows to the already darkish day, Loman was sure of what he had seen. They had been modeled after dream creatures rather than any single animal of the real world: part wolf, perhaps, part cat, part reptile. They were swift and looked powerful. One of them had turned its head toward him, and in the shadows its eyes had glowed as pink-red as those of a rat.

He slowed but did not stop. He no longer cared about identifying and apprehending regressives. For one thing, he'd already identified them to his satisfaction: all of the converted. He knew that stopping them could be accomplished only by stopping Shaddack. He was after much bigger game.

However, he was unnerved to see them brazenly on the prowl in daylight, at two-thirty in the afternoon. Heretofore they had been secretive creatures of the night, hiding the shame of their regression by seeking their altered states only well after sunset. If they were prepared to venture forth before nightfall, the Moonhawk Project was disintegrating into chaos even faster than he had expected. Moonlight Cove was not merely teetering on the brink of hell but had already tipped over the edge and into the pit.

• 34 •

They were in Harry's third-floor bedroom again, where they had passed the last hour and a half, brainstorming and urgently discussing their options. No lamps were on. Watery afternoon light washed the room, contributing to the somber mood.

'So we're agreed there are two ways we might send a message out of town,' Sam said.

'But in either case,' Tessa said uneasily, 'you have to go out there and cover a lot of ground to get where you need to go.'

Sam shrugged.

Tessa and Chrissie had taken off their shoes and sat on the bed, their backs against the headboard. The girl clearly intended to stay close to Tessa; she seemed to have imprinted on her the way a baby chick, freshly hatched from the egg, imprints on the nearest adult bird, whether it's the mother or not.

Tessa said, 'It's not going to be as easy as slipping two doors south to the Coltrane house. Not in daylight.'

'You think I ought to wait until it gets dark?' Sam asked.

'Yes. The fog will come in more heavily, too, as the afternoon fades.'

She meant what she said, though she was worried about the delay. During the hours that they bided their time, more people would be converted. Moonlight Cove would become an increasingly alien, dangerous, and surprise-filled environment.

Turning to Harry, Sam said, 'What time's it get dark?'

Harry was in his wheelchair. Moose had returned to his master, thrusting his burly head under the arm of the chair and onto Harry's lap, content to sit for long stretches in that awkward posture in return for just a little petting and scratching and an occasional reassuring word.

Harry said, 'These days, twilight comes before six o'clock.'

Sam was sitting at the telescope, though at the moment he was not using it. A few minutes ago he had surveyed the streets and reported seeing more activity than earlier – plenty of car and foot patrols. As steadily fewer local residents remained unconverted, the conspirators behind Moonhawk were growing bolder in their policing actions, less concerned than they'd once been about calling attention to themselves.

Glancing at his watch, Sam said, 'I can't say I like the idea of wasting three hours or more. The sooner we get the word out, the more people we'll save from . . . from whatever's being done to them.'

'But if you get caught because you didn't wait for nightfall,' Tessa said, 'then the chances of saving *anyone* become a hell of a lot slimmer.'

'The lady has a point,' Harry said.

'A good one,' Chrissie said. 'Just because they're not aliens doesn't mean they're going to be any easier to deal with.'

Because even the working telephones would allow a caller to dial only approved numbers within town, they'd given up on that hope. But Sam had realized that any PC connected by modem with the supercomputer at New Wave – Harry said they called it Sun – might provide a way out of town, an electronic highway on which they could circumvent the current restrictions on the phone lines and the roadblocks.

As Sam had noted last night while using the VDT in the police car, Sun maintained direct contacts with scores of other computers – including several FBI data banks, both those approved for wide access and those supposedly sealed to all but Bureau agents. If he could sit at a VDT, link in to Sun, and through Sun link to a Bureau computer, then he could transmit a call for help that would appear on Bureau computer screens and spew out in hard copy from the laser printers in their offices.

They were assuming, of course, that the restrictions on outside contact that applied to all other phone lines in town did *not* apply to the lines by which Sun maintained its linkages with the broader world. If Sun's routes out of Moonlight Cove were clipped off, too, they were utterly without hope.

Understandably, Sam was reluctant to enter the houses of those who worked for New Wave, afraid that he would encounter more people like the Coltranes. That left only two ways to attain access to a PC that could be linked to Sun.

First, he could try to get into a black-and-white and use one of their mobile terminals, as he'd done last night. But they were alert to his presence now, making it harder to sneak into an unused patrol car. Furthermore, all of the cars were probably now in use, as the cops searched diligently for him and, no doubt, for Tessa as well. And even if a cruiser were parked behind the municipal building, that area was at the moment bound to be a lot busier than the last time he had been there.

Second, they could use the computers at the high school on Roshmore Way. New Wave had donated them not out of a noble concern for the educational quality of local schools but as one more means of tying the community to it. Sam believed, and Tessa agreed, that the school's terminals probably had the capacity to link with Sun.

But Moonlight Cove Central, as the combination junior-senior high was called, stood on the west side of Roshmore Way, two blocks west of Harry's house and a full block south. In ordinary times it was a pleasant five-minute walk. But with the streets under surveillance and every house potentially a watchtower occupied by enemies, reaching Central School now without being seen was about as easy as crossing a minefield.

'Besides,' Chrissie said, 'they're still in class at Central. You couldn't just walk in there and use a computer.'

'Especially,' Tessa said, 'since you can figure the teachers were among the first converted.'

'What time are classes over?' Sam asked.

'Well, at Thomas Jefferson we get out at three o'clock, but they go an extra half hour at Central.'

'Three-thirty,' Sam said.

Checking his watch, Harry said, 'Forty-seven minutes yet. But even then, there'll be after-school activities, won't there?'

'Sure,' Chrissie said. 'Band, probably football practice, a few other clubs that don't meet during regular activity period.'

'What time would all that be done with?'

'I know band practice is from a quarter to four till a quarter to five,' Chrissie said, 'because I'm friends with a kid one year older than me who's in the band. I play a clarinet. I want to be in the band, too, next year. If there is a band. If there is a next year.'

'So, say . . . by five o'clock the place is cleared out.'

'Football practice runs later than that.'

'Would they practice today, in pouring rain?'

'I guess not.'

'If you're going to wait until five or five-thirty,' Tessa said, 'then you might as well wait just a little while longer and head down there after dark.'

Sam nodded. 'I guess so.'

'Sam, you're forgetting,' Harry said.

'What?'

'Sometime shortly after you leave here, maybe as early as six o' clock sharp, they'll be coming to convert me.'

'Jesus, that's right!' Sam said.

Moose slipped his head off his master's lap and from beneath the arm of the wheelchair. He sat erect, black ears pricked, as if he understood what had been said and was already anticipating the doorbell or listening for a knock downstairs.

'I believe you *do* have to wait for nightfall before you go, to have a better chance,' Harry said, 'but then you'll have to take Tessa and Chrissie with you. It won't be safe to leave them here.'

'We'll have to take you too,' Chrissie said at once. 'You and Moose. I don't know if they convert dogs, but we have to take Moose just to be sure. We wouldn't want to have to worry about him being turned into a machine or something.'

Moose chuffed.

'Can he be trusted not to bark?' Chrissie asked. 'We wouldn't want him to yap at something at a crucial moment. I guess we could always wind a long strip of gauze bandage around his mouth, muzzle him, which is sort of cruel and would probably hurt his feelings, since muzzling him would mean we don't entirely trust him, but it wouldn't hurt him physically, of course, and I'm sure we could make it up to him later with a juicy steak or—'

Suddenly recognizing an unusual solemnity in the silence of her companions, the girl fell silent too. She blinked at Harry, at Sam, and frowned at Tessa, who still sat on the bed beside her.

Darker clouds had begun to plate the sky since they had come upstairs, and the room was receding deeper into shadows. But at the moment Tessa could see Harry Talbot's face almost too clearly in the gray dimness. She was aware of how he was striving to conceal his fear, succeeding for the most part, managing a genuine smile and an unruffled tone of voice, betrayed only by his expressive eyes.

To Chrissie, Harry said, 'I won't be going with you, honey.'

'Oh,' the girl said. She looked at him again, her gaze slipping down from Harry to the wheelchair on which he sat. 'But you came to our school that day to talk to us. You leave the house sometimes. You must have a way to get out.'

Harry smiled. 'The elevator goes down to the garage on the cellar level. I don't drive any more, so there's no car down there, and I can easily roll out into the driveway, to the sidewalk.'

'Well, then!' Chrissie said.

Harry looked at Sam and said, 'But I can't go anywhere on these streets, steep as they are in some places, without someone along. The chair has brakes, and the motor has quite a lot of pull, but half the time not enough for these slopes.'

'We'll be with you,' Chrissie said earnestly. 'We can help.'

'Dear girl, you can't sneak quickly through three blocks of occupied territory and drag me with you at the same time,' Harry said firmly. 'For one thing, you'll have to stay off the streets as much as possible, move from yard to yard and between houses as much as you can, while I can only roll on pavement, especially in this weather, with the ground so soggy.'

'We can carry you.'

'No,' Sam said. 'We can't. Not if we hope to get to the school and get a message out to the Bureau. It's a short distance but full of danger, and we've got to travel light. Sorry, Harry.'

'No need to apologize,' Harry said. 'I wouldn't have it any other way. You think I want to be dragged or shoulder-carried like a bag of cement across half the town?'

In obvious distress, Chrissie got off the bed and stood with her small hands fisted at her sides. She looked from Tessa to Sam to Tessa again, silently pleading with them to think of a way to save Harry.

Outside the gray sky was mottled now with ugly clouds that were nearly black.

The rain eased up, but Tessa sensed that they were entering a brief lull, after which the downpour would continue with greater force than ever.

Both the spiritual and the physical gloom deepened.

Moose whined softly.

Tears shimmered in Chrissie's eyes, and she seemed unable to bear looking at Harry. She went to a north window and stared down at the house next door and at the street beyond – staying just far enough back from the glass to avoid being spotted by anyone outside.

Tessa wanted to comfort her.

She wanted to comfort Harry too.

More than that . . . she wanted to make everything *right*.

As writer-producer-director, she was a mover and shaker, good at taking charge, making things happen. She always knew how to solve a problem, what to do in a crisis, how to keep the cameras rolling once a project had begun. But now she was at a loss. She could not always script reality with the assurance she brought to the writing of her films; sometimes the real world resisted conforming to her demands. Maybe that was why she had chosen a career over a family, even after having enjoyed a wonderful family atmosphere as a child. The real world of daily life and struggle was sloppy, unpredictable, full of loose ends; she couldn't count on being able to tie it all up the way she could when she took aspects of it and reduced them to a neatly structured film. Life was life, broad and rich . . . but film was only essences. Maybe she dealt better with essences than with life in all its gaudy detail.

Her genetically received Lockland optimism, previously as bright as a spotlight, had not deserted her, though it definitely had dimmed for the time being.

Harry said, 'It's going to be all right.'

'How?' Sam asked.

'I'm probably last on their list,' Harry said. 'They wouldn't be worried about cripples and blind people. Even if we learn something's up, we can't try to get out of town and get help. Mrs. Sagerian – she lives over on Pinecrest – she's blind, and I'll bet she and I are the last two on the schedule. They'll wait to do us until near midnight. You see if they don't. Bet on it. So what you've got to do is go to the high school and get through to the Bureau, bring help in here pronto, before midnight comes, and then I'll be all right.'

Chrissie turned away from the window, her cheeks wet with tears. 'You really think so, Mr. Talbot? You really, honestly think they won't come here until midnight?'

With his head tilted to one side in a perpetual twist that was, depending on how you looked at it, either jaunty or heart-wrenching, Harry winked at the girl, though she was farther away from him than Tessa and probably didn't see the wink. 'If I'm jiving you, honey, may God strike me with lightning this instant.'

Rain fell but no lightning struck.

'See?' Harry said, grinning.

Though the girl clearly wanted to believe the scenario that Harry had painted for her, Tessa knew that they could not count on his being the last or next to last on the final conversion schedule. What he'd said made a little sense, actually, but it was just too neat. Like a narrative development in a film script. Real life, as she had just reminded herself, was sloppy, unpredictable. She desperately wanted to believe that Harry would be safe until a few minutes till midnight, but the reality was that he would be at extreme risk as soon as the clock struck six and the final series of conversions was under way.

• 35 •

Shaddack remained in Paula Parkins's garage through most of the afternoon.

Twice he put up the big door, switched on the van's engine, and pulled into the driveway to better monitor Moonhawk's progress on the VDT. Both times, satisfied with the data, he rolled back into the garage and lowered the door again.

The mechanism was clicking away. He had designed it, built it, wound it up, and pushed the start button. Now it could go through its paces without him.

He passed the hours sitting behind the wheel, daydreaming about the time when the final stage of Moonhawk would be completed and all the world would be brought into the fold. When no Old People existed, he would have redefined the word 'power,' for no man before him in all of history would have known such total control. Having remade the species, he could then program its destiny to his own desires. All of humankind would be one great hive, buzzing industriously, serving his vision. As he daydreamed, his erection grew so hard that it began to ache dully.

Shaddack knew many scientists who genuinely seemed to believe that the purpose of technological progress was to improve the lot of humanity, lift the species up from the mud and carry it, eventually, to the stars. He saw things differently. To his way of thinking, the sole purpose of technology was to concentrate power in his hands. Previous would-be remakers of the world had relied on political power, which always ultimately meant the power of the legal gun. Hitler, Stalin, Mao, Pol Pot, and others had sought power through intimidation and mass murder, wading to the throne through lakes of blood, and all of them had ultimately failed to achieve what silicon circuitry was in the process of bestowing upon Shaddack. The pen was not mightier than the sword, but the microprocessor was mightier than vast enemies.

If they knew what he had undertaken and what dreams of conquest still preoccupied him, virtually all other men of science would say that he was bent, sick, deranged. He didn't care. They were wrong, of course. Because they didn't realize who he was. The child of the moonhawk. He had destroyed those who had posed as his parents, and he had not been discovered or punished, which was proof that the rules and laws governing other men were not meant to apply to him. His *true* mother and father were spirit forces, disembodied, powerful. They had protected him from punishment because the murders that he'd committed in Phoenix so long ago were a sacred offering to his real progenitors, a statement of his faith and trust in them. Other scientists would misunderstand him because they could not know that all of existence centered around him, that the universe itself existed only because *he* existed, and that if he ever died – which was unlikely – then the universe would simultaneously cease to exist. He was the center of creation. He was the only man who mattered. The great spirits had told him this. The great spirits had whispered these truths in his ear, waking and sleeping, for more than thirty years.

Child of the moonhawk . . .

As the afternoon waned, he became ever more excited about the approaching completion of the first stage of the project, and he could no longer endure temporary exile in the Parkins garage. Though it had seemed wise to absent himself from places in which Loman Watkins might find him, he was having increasing difficulty justifying the need to hide out. Events at Mike Peyser's house last night no longer seemed so catastrophic to him, merely a minor setback; he was confident that the problem of the regressives would eventually be solved. His genius resulted from the direct line between him and higher spiritual forces, and no difficulty was beyond resolution when the great spirits desired his success. The threat he'd felt from Watkins steadily diminished in his memory, too, until the police chief's promise to find him seemed empty, even pathetic.

He was the child of the moonhawk. He was surprised that he had forgotten such an important truth and had run scared. Of course, even Jesus had spent his time in the garden, briefly frightened, and had wrestled with his demons. The Parkins garage was, Shaddack saw, his own Gethsemane, where he had taken refuge to cast out those last doubts that plagued him.

He was the child of the moonhawk.

At four-thirty he put up the garage door.

He started the van and pulled down the driveway.

He was the child of the moonhawk.

He turned onto the county road and headed toward town.

He was the child of the moonhawk, heir to the crown of light, and at midnight he would ascend the throne.

Pack Martin – his name was actually Packard because his mother named him after a car that had been her father's pride – lived in a house trailer on the southeast edge of town. It was an old trailer, its enameled finish faded and crackled like the glaze on an ancient vase. It was rusted in a few spots, dented, and set on a concrete-block foundation in a lot that was mostly weeds. Pack knew that many people in Moonlight Cove thought his place was an eyesore, but he just plain did not give a damn.

The trailer had electrical hookup, an oil furnace, and plumbing, which was enough to meet his needs. He was warm, dry, and had a place to keep his beer. It was a veritible palace.

Best of all, the trailer had been paid for twenty-five years ago, with money he had inherited from his mother, so no mortgage hung over him. He had a little of the inheritance left, too, and rarely touched the principal. The interest amounted to nearly three hundred dollars a month, and he also had his disability check, earned by virtue of a fall he had taken three weeks after being inducted into the Army. The only real work in which Pack had ever engaged was all the reading and studying he had done to learn and memorize all of the subtlest and most complex symptoms of serious back injury, before reporting per the instructions on his draft notice.

He was born to be a man of leisure. He had known that much about himself from a young age. Work and him had nothing for each other. He figured he'd been scheduled to be born into a wealthy family, but something had gotten screwed up and he'd wound up as the son of a waitress who'd been just sufficiently industrious to provide him with a minimum inheritance.

But he envied no one. Every month he bought twelve or fourteen cases of cheap beer at the discount store out on the highway, and he had his TV, and with a bologna and mustard sandwich now and then, maybe some Fritos, he was happy enough.

By four o'clock that Tuesday afternoon, Pack was well into his second six-pack of the day, slumped in his tattered armchair, watching a game show on which the prize girl's prime hooters, always revealed in low-cut dresses, were a lot more interesting than the MC, the contestants, or the questions.

The MC said, 'So what's your choice? Do you want what's behind screen number one, screen number two, or screen number three?'

Talking back to the tube, Pack said, 'I'll take what's in that cutie's Maidenform, thank you very much,' and he swigged more beer.

Just then someone knocked on the door.

Pack did not get up or in any way acknowledge the knock. He had no friends, so visitors were of no interest to him. They were always either community do-gooders bringing him a box of food that he didn't want, or offering to cut down his weeds and clean up his property, which he didn't want, either, because he liked his weeds.

They knocked again.

Pack responded by turning up the volume on the TV.

They knocked harder.

'Go away,' Pack said.

They really *pounded* on the door, shaking the whole damn trailer.

'What the hell?' Pack said. He clicked off the TV and got up.

The pounding was not repeated, but Pack heard a strange scraping noise against the side of the trailer.

And the place creaked on its foundation, which it sometimes did when the wind was blowing hard. Today, there was no wind.

'Kids,' Pack decided.

The Aikhorn family, which lived on the other side of the county road and two hundred yards to the south, had kids so ornery they ought to have been put to sleep with injections, pickled in formaldehyde, and displayed in some museum of criminal behavior. Those brats got a kick out of pushing cherry bombs through chinks in the foundation blocks, under the trailer, waking him with a bang in the middle of the night.

The scraping at the side of the trailer stopped, but now a couple of kids were walking around on the roof.

That was too much. The metal roof didn't leak, but it had seen better days, and it was liable to bend or even separate at the seams under the weight of a couple of kids.

Pack opened the door and stepped out into the rain, shouting obscenities at them. But when he looked up he didn't see any kids on the roof. What he saw, instead, was something out of a '50s bug movie, big as a man, with clacking mandibles and multifaceted eyes, and a mouth framed by small pincers. The weird thing was that he also saw a few features of a human face in that monstrous countenance, just enough so he thought he recognized Daryl Aikhorn, father of the brats. '*Neeeeeeeeeeed,*' it said, in a voice half Aikhorn's and half an insectile keening. It leaped at him, and as it came, a wickedly sharp stinger telescoped from its replusive body. Even before that yard-long, serrated spear skewered his belly and thrust all the way through him, Pack knew that the days of beer and bologna sandwiches and Fritos and disability checks and game-show girls with perfect hooters were over.

Randy Hapgood, fourteen, sloshed through the dirty calf-deep water in an overflowing gutter and sneered contemptuously, as if to say that nature would have to come up with an obstacle a thousand times more formidable than that if she hoped to daunt him. He refused to wear a raincoat and galoshes because such gear was not fashionably cool. You didn't see rad blondes hanging on the arms of nerds who carried umbrellas, either. There were no rad girls hanging on Randy, as far as that went, but he figured they just hadn't yet noticed how cool he was, how indifferent to weather and everything else that humbled other guys.

He was soaked and miserable – but whistling jauntily to conceal it – when he got home from Central at twenty minutes till five, after band practice, which had been cut short because of the bad weather. He stripped out of his wet denim jacket and hung it on the back of the pantry door. He slipped out of his soggy tennis shoes, as well.

'I'm *heeeeerrreeeee,*' he shouted, parodying the little girl in *Poltergeist.*

No one answered him.

He knew his parents were home, because lights were on and the door was unlocked. Lately they'd been working at home more and more. They were in some sort of product research at New Wave, and they were able to put in a full day on their dual terminals upstairs, in the back room, without actually going in to the office.

Randy got a Coke out of the refrigerator, popped the tab, took a swig, and headed upstairs to dry out while he told Pete and Marsha about his day. He didn't call them mom and dad, and that was all right with them; they were cool. Sometimes he thought they were even too cool. They drove a Porsche, and their clothes were always six months ahead of what everyone else was wearing, and they'd talk about anything with him, *anything*, including sex, as frankly as if they were his pals. If he ever *did* find a rad blonde who wanted to hang on him, he'd be afraid to bring her home to meet his folks, for fear she'd think his dad was infinitely cooler than he was. Sometimes he wished Pete and Marsha were fat, frumpy, dressed out of date, and stuffily insisted on being called mom and dad. Competition in school for grades and popularity was fierce enough without having to feel that he was also in competition at home with his parents.

As he reached the top of the stairs, he called out again, 'In the immortal words of the modern American intellectual, John Rambo: "Yo!" '

They still didn't answer him.

Just as Randy reached the open door to the workroom at the back of the hall, a case of the creeps hit him. He shivered and frowned but didn't stop, however, because his self-image of ultimate cool did not allow him to be spooked.

He stepped across the threshold, ready with a wisecrack about their failure to respond to his calls. Too late, he was flash-frozen in place by fear.

Pete and Marsha were sitting on opposite sides of the large work table, where their computer terminals stood back to back. No, they were not exactly sitting there; they were wired into the chairs and the computers by scores of hideous, segmented cables that grew out of them – or out of the machine; it was hard to tell which – and not only anchored them to their computers but to their chairs and, finally, to the floor, into which the cables disappeared. Their faces were still vaguely recognizable, though wildly altered, half pale flesh and half metal, with a slightly melted look.

Randy could not breathe.

But abruptly he could move, and he scrambled backward.

The door slammed behind him.

He whirled.

Tentacles – half organic, half metallic – erupted from the wall. The entire room was weirdly, malevolently alive; the walls seemed to be filled with alien machinery. The tentacles were quick. They lashed around him, pinned his arms, thoroughly snared him, and turned him toward his parents.

They were still in their chairs but were no longer facing their computers. They stared at him with radiant green eyes that appeared to be boiling in their sockets, bubbling and churning.

Randy screamed. He thrashed, but the tentacles held him.

Pete opened his mouth, and half a dozen silvery spheres, like large ball bearings, shot from him and struck Randy in the chest.

Pain exploded through the boy. But it didn't last more than a couple of seconds. Instead, the hot pain became an icy-cold, crawling sensation that worked through his entire body and up into his face.

He tried to scream again. No sound escaped him.

The tentacles shrank back into the wall, pulling him with them, until his back was pinned tightly against the plaster.

The coldness was in his head now. Crawling, crawling.

Again, he tried to scream. This time a sound came from him. A thin, electronic oscillation.

Tuesday afternoon, wearing warm wool slacks and a sweatshirt and a cardigan over the sweatshirt because she found it hard to stay warm these days, Meg Henderson sat at the kitchen table by the window, with a glass of chenin blanc, a plate of onion crackers, a wedge of Gouda, and a Nero Wolfe novel by Rex Stout. She had read all of the Wolfe novels ages ago, but she was rereading them. Returning to old novels was comforting because the people in them never changed. Wolfe was still a genius and gourmet. Archie was still a man of action. Fritz still ran the best private kitchen in the world. None of them had aged since last she'd met them, either, which was a trick she wished she had learned.

Meg was eighty years old, and she looked eighty, every minute of it; she didn't kid herself. Occasionally, when she saw herself in a mirror, she stared in amazement, as if she had not lived with that face for the better part of a century and was looking at a stranger. Somehow she expected to see a reflection of her youth because inside she was still that girl. Fortunately she didn't *feel* eighty. Her bones were creaky, and her muscles had about as much tone as those of Jabba the Hut in the third *Star Wars* movie she'd watched on the VCR last week, but she was free of arthritis and other major complaints, thank God. She still lived in her bungalow on Concord Circle, an odd little half-moon street that began and ended from Serra Avenue on the east end of town. She and Frank had bought the place forty years ago, when they had both been teachers at Thomas Jefferson School, in the days when it had been a combined school for all grades. Moonlight Cove had been much smaller then. For fourteen years, since Frank died, she had lived in the bungalow alone. She could get around, clean, and cook for herself, for which she was grateful.

She was even more grateful for her mental acuity. More than physical infirmity, she dreaded senility or a stroke that, while leaving her physically functional, would steal her memory and alter her personality. She tried to keep her mind flexible by reading a lot of books of all different kinds, by renting a variety of videos for her VCR, and by avoiding at all costs the mind-numbing slop that passed for entertainment on television.

By four-thirty Tuesday afternoon, she was halfway through the novel, though she paused at the end of each chapter to look out at the rain. She liked rain. She liked whatever weather God chose to throw at the world – storms, hail, wind, cold, heat – because the variety and extremes of creation were what made it so beautiful.

While looking at the rain, which earlier had declined from a fierce downpour to a drizzle but was once more falling furiously, she saw three large, dark, and utterly fantastic creatures appear out of the stand of trees at the rear of her property, fifty feet from the window at which she sat. They halted for a moment as a thin mist eddied around their feet, as if they were dream monsters that had taken shape from those scraps of fog and might melt away as suddenly as they had arisen. But then they raced toward her back porch.

As they drew swiftly nearer, Meg's first impression of them was reinforced. They were like nothing on this earth . . . unless perhaps gargoyles could come alive and climb down from cathedral roofs.

She knew at once that she must be in the early stages of a truly massive stroke, because that was what she had always feared would at last claim her. But she was surprised that it would begin like this, with such a weird hallucination.

That was all it could be, of course – hallucination preceding the bursting of a cerebral blood vessel that must be already swelling and pressing on her brain. She waited for a painful exploding sensation inside her head, waited for her face and body to twist to the left or right as one side or the other was paralyzed.

Even when the first of the gargoyles crashed through the window, showering the table with glass, spilling the chenin blanc, knocking Meg off her chair, and falling to the floor atop her, all teeth and claws, she marveled that a stroke could produce such vivid, convincing illusions, though she was not surprised by the intensity of the pain. She'd always known that death would hurt.

Dora Hankins, the receptionist in the main lobby at New Wave, was accustomed to seeing people leave work as early as four-thirty. Though the official quitting time was five o'clock, a lot of workers put in hours at home, on their own PCs, so no one strictly enforced the eight-hour office day. Since they'd been converted, there had been no need for rules, anyway, because they were all working for the same goal, for the new world that was coming, and the only discipline they needed was their fear of Shaddack, of which they had plenty.

By 4:55, when no one at all had passed through the lobby, Dora was apprehensive. The building was oddly silent, though hundreds of people were working there in offices and labs farther back on the ground floor and in the two floors overhead. In fact the place seemed deserted.

At five o'clock no one had yet left for the day, and Dora had decided to see what was going on. She abandoned her post at the main reception desk, walked to the end of the large marble lobby, through a brass door, into a less grand corridor floored with vinyl tile. Offices lay on both sides. She went into the first room on the left, where eight women served as a secretarial pool for minor department heads who had no personal secretaries of their own.

The eight were at their VDTs. In the fluorescent light, Dora had no trouble seeing how intimately flesh and machine had joined.

Fear was the only emotion Dora had felt in weeks.She thought she had known it in all its shades and degrees. But now it fell over her with greater force, darker and more intense, than anything she had experienced before.

A glistening probe erupted from the wall to Dora's right. It was more metallic than not, yet it dripped what appeared to be yellowish mucus. The thing shot straight to one of the secretaries and bloodlessly pierced the back of her head. From the top of one of the other women's heads, another probe erupted, rose like a snake to the music of a charmer's flute, hesitated, then with tremendous speed snapped to the ceiling, piercing the acoustic tile without disturbing it, and vanished toward rooms above.

Dora sensed that all of the computers and people of New Wave had somehow linked into a single entity and that the building itself was swiftly being incorporated into it. She wanted to run but couldn't move – maybe because she knew any escape attempt would prove futile.

A moment later, they plugged her into the network.

———

Betsy Soldonna was carefully taping up a sign on the wall behind the front desk at the Moonlight Cove Town Library. It was part of Fascinating Fiction Week, a campaign to get kids to read more fiction.

She was the assistant librarian, but on Tuesdays, when her boss, Cora Danker, was off, Betsy worked alone. She liked Cora, but Betsy also liked being by herself. Cora was a talker, filling every free minute with gossip or her boring observations on the characters and plots of her favorite TV programs. Betsy, a lifelong bibliophile obsessed with books, would have been delighted to talk endlessly about what she'd read, but Cora, though head librarian, hardly read at all.

Betsy tore a fourth piece of Scotch tape off the dispenser and fixed the last corner of the poster to the wall. She stepped back to admire her work.

She had made the poster herself. She was proud of her modest artistic talent. In the drawing, a boy and a girl were holding books and staring bug-eyed at the open pages before them. Their hair was standing on end. The girl's eyebrows appeared to have jumped off her face, as had the boy's ears. Above them was the legend BOOKS ARE PORTABLE FUNHOUSES, FILLED WITH THRILLS AND SURPRISES.

From back in the stacks at the other end of the library came a curious sound – a grunt, a choking cough, and then what might have been a snarl. Next came the unmistakable clatter of a row of books falling from a shelf to the floor.

The only person in the library, other than Betsy, was Dale Foy, a retiree who'd been a cashier at Lucky's supermarket until three years ago when he'd turned sixty-five. He was always searching for thriller writers he had never read before and complaining that none of them was as good as the really old-time tale spinners, by which he meant John Buchan rather than Robert Louis Stevenson.

Betsy suddenly had the terrible feeling that Mr. Foy had suffered a heart attack in one of the aisles, that she had heard him gurgling for help, and that he had pulled the books to the floor when he'd grabbed at a shelf. In her mind she could see him writhing in agony, unable to breathe, his face turning blue and his eyes bulging, a bloody foam bubbling at his lips . . .

Years of heavy reading had stropped Betsy's imagination until it was as sharp as a straight razor made from fine German steel.

She hurried around the desk and along the head of the aisles, looking into each of the narrow corridors, which were flanked by nine-foot-high shelves. 'Mr. Foy? Mr. Foy, are you all right?'

In the last aisle she found the fallen books but no sign of Dale Foy. Puzzled, she turned to go back the way she had come, and *there* was Foy behind her. But changed. And even Betsy Soldonna's sharp imagination could not have conceived of the thing that Foy had become – or of the things that he was about to do to her. The next few minutes were as filled with surprises as any hundred books she had ever read, though there was not a happy ending.

———————

Because of the dark storm clouds that clotted the sky, an early twilight crept over Moonlight Cove, and the entire town seemed to be celebrating Fascinating Fiction Week at the library. The dying day was, for many, filled with thrills and surprises, just like a funhouse in the most macabre carnival that had ever pitched its tents.

• 37 •

Sam swept the beam of the flashlight around the attic. It had a rough board floor but no light fixture. Nothing was stored there except dust, spider webs, and a multitude of dead, dry bees that had built nests in the rafters during the summer and had died either due to the work of an exterminator or at the end of their span.

Satisfied, he returned to the trapdoor and went backward down the wooden rungs, into the closet of Harry's third-floor bedroom. They had removed many of the hanging clothes to be able to open the trap and draw down the collapsible ladder.

Tessa, Chrissie, Harry, and Moose were waiting for him just outside the closet door, in the steadily darkening bedroom.

Sam said, 'Yeah, it'll do.'

'I haven't been up there since before the war,' Harry said.

'A little dirty, a few spiders, but you'll be safe. If you're not at the end of their list, if they *do* come for you early, they'll find the house empty, and they'll never think of the attic. Because how could a man with two bad legs and one bad arm drag himself up there?'

Sam was not sure that he believed what he was saying. But for his own peace of mind as well as Harry's, he wanted to believe.

'Can I take Moose up there with me?'

'Take that handgun you mentioned,' Tessa said, 'but not Moose. Well-behaved as he is, he might bark at just the wrong moment.'

'Will Moose be safe down here . . . when *they* come?' Chrissie wondered.

'I'm sure he will be,' Sam said. 'They don't want dogs. Only people.'

'We better get you up there, Harry,' Tessa said. 'It's twenty past five. We've got to be out of here soon.'

The bedroom was filling with shadows almost as rapidly as a glass filling with blood-dark wine.

PART THREE

THE NIGHT BELONGS TO THEM

*Montgomery told me that the Law
. . . became oddly weakened about
nightfall; that then the animal was
at its strongest; a spirit of adventure sprang up in them at the dusk;
they would dare things they never
seemed to dream about by day.*

H.G. WELLS,
THE ISLAND OF DR. MOREAU

• 1 •

In the scrub-covered hills that surrounded the abandoned Icarus Colony, gophers and field mice and rabbits and a few foxes scrambled out of their burrows and shivered in the rain, listening. In the two nearest stands of pine, sweet gum, and autumn-stripped birch, one just to the south and one immediately east of the old colony, squirrels and raccoons stood to attention.

The birds were the first to respond. In spite of the rain, they flew from their sheltered nests in the trees, in the dilapidated old barn, and in the crumbling eaves of the main building itself. Cawing and screeching, they spiraled into the sky, darted and swooped, then streaked directly to the house. Starlings, wrens, crows, owls, and hawks all came in shrill and flapping profusion. Some flew against the walls, as if struck blind, battering insistently until they broke their necks, or until they snapped their wings and fell to the ground where they fluttered and squeaked until they were exhausted or had perished. Others, equally frenzied, found open doorways and windows through which they entered without damaging themselves.

Though wildlife within a two-hundred-yard radius had heard the call, only the nearer animals responded obediently. Rabbits leaped, squirrels scurried, coyotes loped, foxes dashed, and raccoons waddled in that curious way of theirs, through wet grass and rain-bent weeds and mud, toward the source of the siren song. Some were predators and some, by nature, were timid prey, but they moved side by side without conflict. It might have been a scene from an animated Disney film – the neighborly and harmonious folk of field and forest responding to the sweet guitar or harmonica music of some elderly black man who, when they gathered around him, would tell them stories of magic and great adventure. But there was no kindly, tale-spinning Negro where they were going, and the music that drew them was dark, cold, and without melody.

• 2 •

While Sam struggled to lift Harry up the ladder and into the attic, Tessa and Chrissie took the wheelchair to the basement garage. It was a heavy-duty motorized model, not a light collapsible chair, and would not fit through the trap. Tessa and Chrissie parked it just inside the big garage door, so it looked as if Harry had gotten this far in his chair and had left the house, perhaps in a friend's car.

'You think they'll fall for it?' Chrissie asked worriedly.

'There's a chance,' Tessa said.

'Maybe they'll even think Harry left town yesterday before the roadblocks went up.'

Tessa agreed, but she knew – and suspected Chrissie knew – that the chance of the ruse working was slim. If Sam and Harry really had been as confident in the attic trick as they pretended, they would have wanted Chrissie to be tucked up there, too, instead of sent out into the storm-lashed, nightmare world of Moonlight Cove.

They rode the elevator back to the third floor, where Sam was just folding the ladder and pushing the trapdoor into place. Moose watched him curiously.

'Five-forty-two,' Tessa said, checking her watch.

Sam snatched up the closet pole, which he'd had to remove to pull down the trap, and he reinserted it into its braces. 'Help me put the clothes back.'

Shirts and slacks, still on hangers, had been transferred to the bed. Working together, passing the garments like amateur firemen relaying pails of water, they quickly restored the closet to its former appearance.

Tessa noticed that traces of fresh blood were soaking through the thick gauze bandage on Sam's right wrist. His wounds were pulling open from the exertion. Although they weren't mortal injuries, they must hurt a lot, and anything that weakened or distracted him during the ordeal ahead decreased their chances of success.

Closing the door, Sam said, 'God, I hate to leave him there.'

'Five-forty-six,' Tessa reminded him.

While Tessa pulled on her leather jacket, and while Chrissie slipped into a too-large but waterproof blue nylon windbreaker that belonged to Harry, Sam reloaded his revolver. He had used up all the rounds in his pockets while at the Coltranes'. But Harry owned a .45 revolver and a .38 pistol, both of which he had taken with him into the attic, and he had a box of ammunition for each, so Sam had taken a score or so of the .38 cartridges.

Holstering the gun, he went to the telescope and studied the streets that lay west and south toward Central School. 'Still lots of activity,' he reported.

'Patrols?' Tessa asked.

'But also lots of rain. And fog's coming in faster, thicker.'

Thanks to the storm, an early twilight was upon them and already fading. Although some bleak light still burned above the churning clouds, night might as well have fallen, for cloaks of gloom lay over the wet and huddled town.

'Five-fifty,' Tessa said.

Chrissie said, 'If Mr. Talbot's at the top of their list, they could be here any minute.'

Turning from the telescope, Sam said, 'All right. Let's go.'

Tessa and Chrissie followed him out of the bedroom. They took the stairs down to the first floor.

Moose used the elevator.

• 3 •

Shaddack was a child tonight.

Circling repeatedly through Moonlight Cove, from the sea to the hills, from Holliwell Road on the north to Paddock Lane on the south, he could not remember ever having been in a better mood. He altered the patterns of his patrol, largely to be sure that eventually he would cover every block of every street in town; the sight of each house and every citizen on foot in the storm affected him in a way they never had previously, because soon they would be his to do with as he pleased.

He was filled with excitement and anticipation, the likes of which he had not felt since Christmas Eve when he was a young boy. Moonlight Cove was a huge toy, and in a few hours, when midnight struck, when this dark eve ticked over into the holiday, he would be able to have so much fun with his marvelous toy. He would indulge in games which he had long wanted to play but which he had denied himself. Henceforth, no urge or desire would be denied, for despite the bloodiness or outrageousness of whatever game he chose, there would be no referees, no authorities, to penalize him.

And like a child sneaking into a closet to filch coins from his father's coat to buy ice cream, he was so completely transported by contemplation of the rewards that he had virtually forgotten there was a potential for disaster. Minute by minute, the threat of the regressives faded from his awareness. He did not entirely forget about Loman Watkins, but he no longer was able to remember exactly why he had spent the day hiding from the police chief in the garage at the Parkins house.

More than thirty years of unrelenting self-control, strenuous and undeviating application of his mental and physical resources, beginning with the day he had murdered his parents and Runningdeer, thirty years of repressing his needs and desires and of sublimating them in his work, had at last led him to the brink of his dream's realization. *He could not doubt.* To doubt his mission or worry about its outcome would be to question his sacred destiny and insult the great spirits who had favored him. He was now incapable of even seeing a downside; he turned his mind away from any incipient thought of disaster.

He sensed the great spirits in the storm.

He sensed them moving secretly through his town.

They were there to witness and approve his ascension to the throne of destiny.

He had eaten no cactus candy since the day he had killed his mother, father, and the Indian, but over the years he had been subject to vivid flashbacks. They came upon him unexpectedly. One moment he would be in this world, and the next instant he would be in that other place, the eerie world parallel to this one, where the cactus candy had always conveyed him, a reality in which colours were simultaneously more vivid and more subtle, where every object seemed to have more angles and dimensions than in the ordinary world, where he seemed to be strangely weightless – buoyant as a helium-filled balloon – and where the voices of spirits spoke to him. The flashbacks had been frequent during the year following the murders, striking him about twice a week, then had gradually declined in number – though not in intensity – through his teenage years. Those dreamy, fuguelike spells, which usually lasted an hour or two but could occasionally last half a day, were responsible in part for his reputation, with family and teachers, of being a somewhat detached child. They all had sympathy for him, naturally, because they assumed that whatever detachment he displayed was a result of the shattering trauma that he had endured.

Now, cruising in his van, he was phasing slowly into that cactus-candy condition. This flashback was unexpected, too, but it didn't *snap* upon him as all the others had. He sort of . . . drifted into it, deeper, deeper. And the further he went, the more he suspected that this time he would not be pulled rudely back from that realm of higher consciousness. From now on he would be a resident of both worlds, which was how the great spirits themselves lived, with awareness of both the higher and the lower states of existence. He even began to think that what he was undergoing now, spiritually, was a conversion of his own, a thousand times more profound than that the citizens of Moonlight Cove had undergone.

In this exalted state, everything was special and wondrous to Shaddack. The twinkling lights of the rainswept town seemed like jewels sprinkled through the descending darkness. The molten, silvery beauty of the rain itself astonished him, as did the swiftly dimming, gorgeously turbulent gray sky.

As he braked at the intersection of Paddock Lane and Saddleback Drive, he touched his breast, feeling the telemetry device he wore from a chain around his neck, unable for a moment to remember what it was, and *that* seemed mysterious and wonderful, as well. Then he recalled that the device monitored and broadcast his heartbeat, which was received by a unit at New Wave. It was effective over a distance of five miles, and worked even when he was indoors. If the reception of his heartbeat was interrupted for more than one minute, Sun was programmed to feed a destruct order, via microwave, to the microsphere computers in all of the New People.

A few minutes later, on Bastenchurry Road, when he touched the device, the memory of its purpose again proved elusive. He sensed that it was a powerful object, that whoever wore it held the lives of others in his hands, and the fantasy-tripping child in him decided that it must be an amulet, bestowed upon him by the great spirits, one more sign that he stood astride the two worlds, one foot in the ordinary plane of ordinary men and one foot in the higher realm of the great spirits, the gods of the cactus candy.

His slowly phased-in flashback, like time-released medication, had carried him back into the condition of his youth, at least to those seven years when he'd been in the thrall of Runningdeer. He was a child. And he was a demigod. He was the favored child of the moonhawk, so he could do anything he wanted to anyone, *anyone*, and as he continued to drive, he fantasized about just what he might want to do . . . and to whom.

Now and then he laughed softly and slightly shrilly, and his eyes gleamed like those of a cruel and twisted boy studying the effects of fire on captive ants.

• 4 •

As Moose padded around them and wagged his tail so hard it seemed in danger of flying off, Chrissie waited in the kitchen with Tessa and Sam until more light bled out of the dying day.

At last Sam said, 'All right. Stay close. Do what I say every step of the way.'

He looked at Chrissie and Tessa for a long moment before actually opening the door; without any of them speaking a word, they hugged one another. Tessa kissed Chrissie on the cheek, then Sam kissed her, and Chrissie returned their kisses. She didn't have to be told why they all suddenly felt so affectionate. They were people, *real* people, and expressing their feelings was important, because before the night was out they might not be real people any more. Maybe they wouldn't ever again feel the kinds of things real people felt, so those feelings were more precious by the second.

Who knew what those weird shape-changers felt? Who would *want* to know?

Besides, if they didn't reach Central, it would be because one of the search parties or a couple of the Boogeymen nailed them along the way. In that case this might be their last chance to say goodbye to one another.

Finally Sam led them onto the porch.

Carefully, Chrissie closed the door behind them. Moose didn't try to get out. He was too good and noble a dog for such cheap stunts. But he did stick his snout in the narrowing crack, sniffing at her and trying to lick her hand, so she was afraid she was going to pinch his nose. He pulled back at the last moment, and the door clicked shut.

Sam led them down the steps and across the yard toward the house to the south of Harry's. No lights were on there. Chrissie hoped no one was home, but she figured some monstrous creature was at one of the dark windows right now, peering out at them and licking its chops.

The rain seemed colder than when she'd been on the run last night, but that might have been because she had just come out of the warm, dry house. Only the palest gray glow still illuminated the sky to the west. The icy, slashing droplets seemed to be tearing the last of that light out of the clouds and driving it into the earth, pulling down a deep, damp darkness. Before they had even reached the fence separating Harry's property from the next, Chrissie was grateful for the hooded nylon windbreaker, even though it was so big on her that it made her feel as if she was a little kid playing dress-up in her parents' clothes.

It was a picket fence, easy to clamber over. They followed Sam across the neighbor's backyard to another fence. Chrissie was over that one, too, and into yet another yard, with Tessa close behind her, before she realized they had reached the Coltranes' place.

She looked at the blank windows. No lights on here, either, which was a good thing, because if there *had* been lights, that would mean someone had found what was left of the Coltranes after their battle with Sam.

Crossing the yard toward the next fence, Chrissie was overcome by the fear that the Coltranes had somehow reanimated themselves after Sam had fired all of those bullets into them, that they were standing in the kitchen and looking out the windows right this minute, that they had seen their nemesis and his two companions, and that they were even now opening the back door. She expected two robot-things to come clanking out of the house and across the porch, radar eyes aglow, reaching out with metal arms and working massive metal hands, sort of like tin versions of the walking dead in old zombie movies, miniature radar-dish antennae whirling around and around on their heads, steam hissing from body vents.

Her fear must have slowed her, because Tessa almost stumbled into her from behind and gave her a gentle push to urge her along. Chrissie crouched and hurried to the south side of the yard.

Sam helped her over a wrought-iron fence with spearlike points on the staves. She would probably have gored herself if she'd had to scale it alone. Chrissie shishkebab.

People were home at the next house, and Sam took refuge behind some shrubbery to study the lay of things before continuing. Chrissie and Tessa quickly joined him there.

While clambering over the last fence, she'd rubbed the abraded palm of her left hand, even though it was bandaged. It hurt, but she gritted her teeth and made no complaint.

Parting the branches of what appeared to be a mulberry bush, Chrissie peered at the house, which was only twenty feet away. She saw four people through the kitchen windows. They were preparing dinner together. A middle-aged couple, a gray haired man, and a teenage girl.

She wondered if they had been converted yet. She suspected not, but there was no way to be sure. And since the robots and Boogeymen sometimes hid in clever human disguises, you couldn't trust anyone, not even your best friend . . . or your parents. Pretty much the same as when aliens were taking over.

'Even if they look out, they won't see us,' Sam said. 'Come on.'

Chrissie followed him from the cover of the mulberry bush and across the open lawn toward the next property line, thanking God for the fog, which was getting denser by the minute.

Eventually they reached the house at the end of the block. The south side of that lawn fronted the cross street, Bergenwood Way, which led down to Conquistador.

When they were two thirds of the way across the lawn, less than twenty feet from the street, a car turned the corner a block and a half uphill and started down. Following Sam's lead, Chrissie threw herself flat on the soggy lawn because there was no nearby shrubbery behind which to take refuge. If they tried to scramble too far, the driver of the approaching car might get close enough to spot them while they were still scuttling for cover.

No streetlamps flanked Bergenwood, which was in their favor. The last of the ashen light was gone from the western sky – another boon.

As the car drew nearer, moving slowly either because of the bad weather or because its occupants were part of a patrol, its headlights were diffused by the fog, which seemed not to be reflecting that light but glowing with a radiance of its own. Objects in the night for yards on both sides of the car were half revealed and weirdly distorted by those slowly churning, ground-hugging, luminous clouds.

When the car was less than a block away, someone riding in the back seat switched on a handheld spotlight. He directed it out his side window, playing it over the front lawns of the houses that faced on Bergenwood and the side lawns of houses facing the cross streets. At the moment the beam was pointed in the opposite direction, south, toward the other side of Bergenwood. But by the time they had driven this far, they might decide to spotlight the properties to the north of Bergenwood.

'Backtrack,' Sam said fiercely. 'But stay down and crawl, *crawl*.'

The car reached the intersection, half a block uphill.

Chrissie crawled after Sam, not straight back the way they had come but toward the nearby house. She didn't see anywhere he could hide, because the back-porch railing was pretty open and there were no large shrubs. Maybe he figured to slip around the side of the house until the patrol passed, but she didn't think she and Tessa would make it to the corner in time.

When she glanced over her shoulder, she saw that the spotlight was still sweeping the front lawns and between the houses on the south flank of the street. However, there was also the side-glow effect of the headlights to worry about, and that was going to wash across *this* lawn in a few seconds.

She was half crawling and half slithering on her belly, moving fast, though no doubt squashing lots of snails and earthworms that had come out to bask on the wet grass, which didn't bear thinking about. She came to a concrete walkway close to the house – and realized that Sam had disappeared.

She halted on her hands and knees, looking left and right.

Tessa appeared at her side. 'Cellar steps, honey. Hurry!'

Scrambling forward, she discovered a set of exterior concrete steps leading down to a cellar entrance. Sam was crouched at the bottom, where collected rainwater gurgled softly as it trickled into a drain in front of the closed cellar door. Chrissie joined him in that haven, slipping below ground level, and Tessa followed. About four seconds later a spotlight swept across the wall of the house and even played for a moment inches above their heads, on the concrete lip of the stairwell.

They huddled in silence, unmoving, for a minute or so after the spotlight swung away from them and the car passed. Chrissie was sure that something inside the house had heard them, that the door at Sam's back would fly open at any second, that something would leap at them, a creature part werewolf and part computer, snarling and beeping, its mouth bristling with both teeth and programming keys, saying something like, 'To be killed, please press ENTER and proceed.'

She was relieved when at last Sam whispered, 'Go.'

They recrossed the lawn toward Bergenwood Way. This time the street remained conveniently deserted.

As Harry promised, a stone-lined drainage channel ran alongside Bergenwood. According to Harry, who had played in it when he was a kid, the channel was about three feet wide and maybe five feet deep. Judging by those dimensions, a foot or more of runoff surged through it at the moment. Those currents were swift, almost black, revealed at the bottom of the shadow-pooled trench only by an occasional dark glint and chuckle of roiling water.

The channel offered a considerably less conspicuous route than the open street. They moved uphill a few yards until they found the mortared, iron handholds that Harry had promised they'd find every hundred feet along the open sections of the channel. Sam climbed down first, Chrissie went second, and Tessa brought up the rear.

Sam hunched over to keep his head below street level, and Tessa hunched a bit less than he did. But Chrissie didn't have to hunch at all. Being eleven had its advantages, especially when you were on the run from werewolves or ravenous aliens or robots or Nazis, and at one time or another during the past twenty-four hours, she had been on the run from the first three, but not from Nazis, too, thank God, though who knew what might happen next.

The churning water was cold around her feet and calves. She was surprised to discover that although it only reached her knees it had considerable force. It pushed and tugged relentlessly, as if it were a living thing with a mean desire to topple her. She was not in any danger of falling as long as she stood in one place with feet widely planted, but she was not sure how long she could maintain her balance while walking. The watercourse sloped steeply downhill. The old stone floor, after several decades of rainy seasons, was well polished by runoff.

Because of that combination of factors, the channel was the next best thing to an amusement-park flume ride.

If she fell, she'd be swept all the way downhill, to within half a block of the bluff, where the channel widened and dropped straight down into the earth. Harry had said something about safety bars dividing the passage into narrow slots just before the downspout, but she figured that if she were swept down there and had to rely on those bars, they would prove to be missing or rusted out, leaving a straight shot to the bottom. The system came out again at the base of the cliffs, then led part of the way across the beach, discharging the run-off onto the sand or, at high tide, into the sea.

She had no difficulty picturing herself tumbling and twisting helplessly, choking on filthy water, desperately but unsuccessfully grabbing at the stone channel for purchase, suddenly plummeting a couple of hundred feet straight down, banging against the walls of the shaft when it went vertical, breaking bones, smashing her head to bits, hitting the bottom with . . .

Well, yes, she *could* easily picture it, but suddenly she didn't see any wisdom in doing so.

Fortunately Harry had warned them of this problem, so Sam had come prepared. From under his jacket and around his waist, he unwound a length of rope that he had removed from a long-unused pulley system in Harry's garage. Though the rope was old, Sam said it was still strong, and Chrissie hoped he was right. He had tied one end around his waist before leaving the house. Now he looped the other end through Chrissie's belt and finally tied it around Tessa's waist, leaving approximately eight feet of play between each of them. If one of them fell – well, face it, Chrissie was far and away the one most likely to fall and most likely to be swept to a wet and bloody death – the others could stand fast until she had time to regain her footing.

That was the plan, anyway.

Securely linked, they started down the channel. Sam and Tessa hunched over so no one in a passing car would see their heads bobbing above the stone rim of the watercourse, and Chrissie hunched over a bit, too, keeping her feet wide apart, sort of troll-walking as she had done last night in the tunnel under the meadow.

Per Sam's instructions, she held on to the line in front of her with both hands, taking up the slack when she drew close to him, to avoid tripping on it, then paying it out again when she fell back a couple of feet. Behind her, Tessa was doing the same thing; Chrissie felt the subtle tug of the rope on her belt.

They were heading toward a culvert half a block downhill. The channel went underground at Conquistador and stayed subterranean not just through the intersection but for two entire blocks, surfacing again at Roshmore.

Chrissie kept glancing up, past Sam at the mouth of the pipe, not liking what she saw. It was round, concrete rather than stone. It was wider than the rectangular channel, about five feet in diameter, no doubt so workmen could get into it easily and clean it out if it became choked with debris. However, neither the shape nor the size of the culvert made her uneasy; it was the absolute blackness of it that prickled the nape of her neck, for it was darker even than the essence of night at the bottom of the drainage channel itself – absolutely, absolutely black – and it seemed as if they were marching into the gaping mouth of some prehistoric behemoth.

A car cruised by slowly on Bergenwood, another on Conquistador. Their headlights were refracted by the incoming bank of fog, so the night itself seemed to glow, but little of that queer luminosity reached down into the watercourse, and none of it penetrated the mouth of the culvert.

When Sam crossed the threshold of that tunnel and, within two steps, disappeared entirely from sight, Chrissie followed without hesitation, although not without trepidation. They proceeded at a slower pace, for the floor of the culvert was not merely steeply sloped but curved, as well, and even more treacherous than the stone drainage channel.

Sam had a flashlight, but Chrissie knew he didn't want to use it near either end of the tunnel. The backsplash of the beam might be visible from outside and draw the attention of one of the patrols.

The culvert was as utterly lightless as the inside of a whale's belly. Not that she knew what a whale's belly was like, inside, but she doubted it was equipped with a lamp or even a Donald Duck night light, like the one she'd had when she was years younger. The whale's belly image seemed fitting because she had the creepy feeling that the pipe was really a stomach and that the rushing water was digestive juice, and that already her tennis shoes and the legs of her jeans were dissolving in that corrosive flood.

Then she fell. Her feet slipped on something, perhaps a fungus that was growing on the floor and attached so tightly to the concrete that the runoff had not torn it away. She let go of the line and windmilled her arms, trying to keep her balance, but she went down with a tremendous splash, and instantly found herself borne away by the water.

She had enough presence of mind not to scream. A scream would draw one of the search teams – or worse.

Gasping for breath, spluttering as water slopped into her mouth, she collided with Sam's legs, knocking him off balance. She felt him falling. She wondered how long they'd all lie, dead and decomposing, at the bottom of the long vertical drain, out at the foot of the bluff, before their bloated, purple remains were found.

• 5 •

In the tomb-perfect darkness, Tessa heard the girl fall, and she immediately halted, planting her legs as wide and firm as she could on that sloped and curved floor, keeping both hands on the security line. Within a second that rope pulled taut as Chrissie was swept away by the water.

Sam grunted, and Tessa realized that the girl had been carried into him. Slack developed on the line for an instant, but then it went taut again, pulling her forward, which she took to mean that Sam was staggering ahead, trying to stay on his feet, with the girl pressing against his lower legs and threatening to knock them out from under him. If Sam had been brought down, too, and seized by tumultuous currents, the line would not have been merely taut; the drag would have been great enough to wrench Tessa off her feet.

She heard a lot of splashing ahead. A soft curse from Sam.

The water was creeping higher. At first she thought she was imagining it, but then she realized the torrent had risen to above her knees.

The damned darkness was the worst of it, not being able to see anything, virtually blind, unable to be sure what was happening.

Abruptly she was jerked forward again. Two, three – oh, God – half a dozen steps.

Sam, don't fall!

Stumbling, almost losing her balance, realizing that they were on the edge of disaster, Tessa leaned backward on the line, using its tautness to steady herself instead of rushing forward with the hope of developing slack again. She hoped to God she didn't resist too much and get yanked off her feet.

She swayed. The line pulled hard at her waist. Without slack to loop through her hands, she was unable to take most of the strain with her arms.

The pressure of water against the back of her legs was growing.

Her feet skidded.

Like videotape fast-forwarded through an editing machine, strange thoughts flew through her mind, scores of them in a few seconds, all unbidden, and some of them surprised her. She thought about living, surviving, about not wanting to die, and that wasn't so surprising, but then she thought about Chrissie, about not wanting to fail the girl, and in her mind she saw a detailed image of her and Chrissie together, in a cozy house somewhere, living as mother and daughter, and she was surprised at how much she *wanted* that, which seemed wrong because Chrissie's parents were not dead, as far as anyone knew, and might not even be hopelessly changed, because the conversion – whatever it was – just might be reversible. Chrissie's family might be put back together again. Tessa couldn't see a picture of that in her mind. It didn't seem as much a possibility as she and Chrissie together. But it might happen. Then she thought of Sam, of never having a chance to make love to him, and *that* startled her, because although he was sort of attractive, she truly hadn't realized she was drawn to him in any romantic way. Of course his grit in the face of spiritual despair was appealing, and his perfectly serious four-reasons-for-living shtick made him an intriguing challenge. Could she give him a fifth? Or supplant Goldie Hawn as the fourth? But until she found herself tottering on the brink of a watery death, she didn't realize how very much he had attracted her in such a short time.

Her feet skidded again. Beneath the surging water, the floor was much more slippery than it had been in the stone channel, as if moss grew on the concrete. Tessa tried to dig in her heels.

Sam cursed under his breath. Chrissie made a coughing-choking sound.

The depth of water in the center of the tunnel had risen to about eighteen or twenty inches.

A moment later the line jerked hard, then went completely slack.

The rope had snapped. Sam and Chrissie had been swept down into the tunnel.

The gurgle-slosh-slap of gushing water echoed off the walls, and echoes of the echoes overlaid previous echoes, and Tessa's heart was pounding so loud she could hear it, but still she should have heard their cries, too, as they were carried away. Yet for one awful moment they were silent.

Then Chrissie coughed again. Only a few feet away.

A flashlight snapped on. Sam was hooding most of the lens with his hand.

Chrissie was sideways in the passage, pressed up out of the worst of the flow, her back and the palms of both hands braced against the side of the tunnel.

Sam stood with his feet planted wide apart. Water churned and foamed around his legs. He had gotten turned around. He was facing uphill now.

The rope hadn't snapped, after all; the tension had been released because both Sam and Chrissie had regained their equilibrium.

'You all right?' Sam whispered to the girl.

She nodded, still gagging on the dirty water she had swallowed. She wrinkled her face in distaste, spat once, twice, and said, 'Yuch.'

Looking at Tessa, Sam said, 'Okay?'

She couldn't speak. A rock-hard lump had formed in her throat. She swallowed a few times, blinked. A delayed wave of relief passed through her, reducing the almost unbearable pressure in her chest, and at last she said, 'Okay. Yeah. Okay.'

• 6 •

Sam was relieved when they got to the end of the culvert without another fall. He stood for a moment, just outside the lower mouth of the drain, happily looking up at the sky. Because of the thick fog, he couldn't actually see the sky, but that was a technicality; he felt relieved to be out in the open air again, if still knee-deep in muddy water.

They were virtually in a river now. Either the rain was falling harder in the hills, at the far east end of town, or some breakwater in the system had collapsed. The level had swiftly risen well past midthigh on Sam and nearly to Chrissie's waist, and the deluge poured from the conduit at their back with impressive power. Keeping their footing in those cataracts was getting more difficult by the second.

He turned, reached for the girl, drew her close, and said, 'I'm going to hold tight to your arm from here on.'

She nodded.

The night was grave-deep, and even inches from her face, he could see only a shadowy impression of her features. When he looked up at Tessa, who stood a few feet behind the girl, she was little more than a black shape and might not have been Tessa at all.

Holding fast to the girl, he turned and looked again at the way ahead.

The tunnel had extended for two blocks before pouring the flood forth into another one-block length of open drainage channel, just as Harry had remembered from the days when he had been a kid and, against every admonition of his parents, had played in the drainage system. Thank God for disobedient children.

One block ahead of them, this new section of stone watercourse fed into another concrete culvert. *That* pipe, according to Harry, terminated at the mouth of the long vertical drain at the west end of town. Supposedly, in the last ten feet of the main sloping line, a row of sturdy, vertical iron bars was set twelve inches apart and extended floor to ceiling, creating a barrier through which only water and smaller objects could pass. There was virtually no chance of being carried all the way into that two-hundred-foot drop.

But Sam didn't want to risk it. There must be no more falls. After being washed to the end and crashing against the safety barrier, if they were not suffering from myriad broken bones, if they were able to get to their feet and move, climbing back up that long culvert, on a steep slope, against the onrushing force of the water, was not an ordeal he was willing to contemplate, let alone endure.

All of his life he had felt he'd failed people. Though he had been only seven when his mother had died in the accident, he'd always been eaten by guilt related to her death, as if he ought to have been able to save her in spite of his tender age and in spite of having been pinned in the wreckage of the car with her. Later, Sam had never been able to please his drunken, mean, sorry son-of-a-bitch of a father – and had suffered grievously for that failure. Like Harry, he felt that he had failed the people of Vietnam, though the decision to abandon them had been made by authorities who far outranked him and with whom he could have had no influence. Neither of the Bureau agents who had died with him had died *because* of him, yet he felt he had failed them too. He had failed Karen, somehow, though people told him he was mad to think that he had any responsibility for her cancer; it was just that he couldn't help thinking that if he had loved her more, loved her harder, she would have found the strength and the will to pull through. God knew, he had failed his own son, Scott.

Chrissie squeezed his hand.

He returned the squeeze.

She seemed so small.

Earlier in the day, gathered in Harry's kitchen, they'd had a conversation about responsibility. Now, suddenly, he realized that his sense of responsibility was so highly developed that it bordered on obsession, but he still agreed with what Harry had said: A man's commitment to others, especially to friends and family, could never be excessive. He had never imagined that one of the key insights of his life would come to him while he was standing nearly waist-deep in muddy water in a drainage canal, on the run from enemies both human and inhuman, but that was where he received it. He realized that his problem was not the alacrity with which he shouldered responsibility or the unusual weight of it that he was willing to carry. No, hell no, his problem was that he had allowed his sense of responsibility to obstruct his ability to cope with failure. All men failed from time to time, and often the fault lay not in the man himself but in the role of fate. When he failed, he had to learn not only to go on but to *enjoy* going on. Failure could not be allowed to bleed him of the very pleasure of life. Such a turning away from life was blasphemous, if you believed in God – and just plain stupid if you didn't. It was like saying, 'Men fail, but *I* shouldn't fail, because I'm more than just a man, I'm somewhere up there between the angels and God.' He saw why he had lost Scott: because he had lost his own love of life, his sense of fun, and had ceased to be able to share anything meaningful with the boy – or to halt Scott's own descent into nihilism when it had begun.

At the moment, if he had tried to count his reasons for living, the list would have had more than four items. It would have had hundreds. *Thousands.*

All of this understanding came to him in an instant, while he was holding Chrissie's hand, as if the flow of time had been stretched by some quirk of relativity. He realized that if he failed to save the girl or Tessa, but got out of this mess himself, he would nevertheless have to rejoice at his own salvation and get on with life. Although their situation was dark and their hope slim, his spirits soared, and he almost laughed aloud. The living nightmare they were enduring in Moonlight Cove had profoundly shaken him, rattling important truths into him, truths which were simple and should have been easy to see during his long years of torment, but which he received gratefully in spite of their simplicity and his own previous thickheadedness. Maybe the truth was always simple when you found it.

Yeah, okay, maybe he could go on now even if he failed in his responsibilities to others, even if he lost Chrissie and Tessa – but, shit, he wasn't *going* to lose them. Damned if he was.

Damned if he was.

He held Chrissie's hand and cautiously edged along the stone channel, grateful for the comparative unevenness of that pavement and the moss-free traction it provided. The water was just deep enough to give him a slight buoyant feeling, which made it harder to put each foot down after he lifted it, so instead of walking, he dragged his feet along the bottom.

In less than a minute they reached a set of iron rungs mortared into the masonry of the channel wall. Tessa moved in, and for a while they all just hung there, gripping iron, grateful for the solid feel of it and the anchor it provided.

A couple of minutes later, when the rain abruptly slacked off, Sam was ready to move again. Being careful not to step on Tessa's and Chrissie's hands, he climbed a couple of rungs and looked out at the street.

Nothing moved but the fog.

This section of open watercourse flanked Moonlight Cove Central School. The athletic field was just a few feet from him, and, sitting beyond that open space, barely visible in the darkness and mist, was the school itself, illuminated only by a couple of dim security lamps.

The property was encircled by a nine-foot-high chain-link fence. But Sam wasn't daunted by that. Fences always had gates.

• 7 •

Harry waited in the attic, hoping for the best, expecting the worst.

He was propped against the outer wall of the long, unlit chamber, tucked in the corner at the extreme far end from the trapdoor through which he had been lifted. There was nothing in that upper room behind which he could hide.

But if someone went so far as to empty out the master-bedroom closet, pull down the trap, open the folding stairs, and poke his head up to look around, maybe he wouldn't be diligent about probing every corner of the place. When he saw bare boards and a flurry of spiders on his first sweep of the flash, maybe he would click off the beam and retreat.

Absurd, of course. Anyone who went to the trouble to look into the attic at all would look into it properly, exploring every corner. But whether that hope was absurd or not, Harry clung to it; he was good at nurturing hope, making hearty stew from the thinnest broth of it, because for half his life, hope was mostly what had sustained him.

He was not uncomfortable. As preparation for the unheated attic, with Sam's help to speed the dressing process, he had put on wool socks, warmer pants than what he had been wearing, and two sweaters.

Funny, how a lot of people seemed to think that a paralyzed man could feel nothing in his unresponsive extremities. In some cases, that was true; all nerves were blunted, all feeling lost. But spinal injuries came in myriad types; short of a total severing of the cord, the range of sensations left to the victim varied widely.

In Harry's case, though he had lost all use of one arm and one leg and nearly all use of the other leg, he could still feel heat and cold. When something pricked him he was aware – if not of pain – at least of a blunt pressure.

Physically, he felt much less than when he'd been a whole man; no argument about that. But all feelings were not physical. Though he was sure that few people would believe him, his handicap actually had enriched his emotional life. Though by necessity something of a recluse, he had learned to compensate for a dearth of human contact. Books had helped. Books opened the world to him. And the telescope. But mostly his unwavering will to lead as full a life as possible was what had kept him whole in mind and heart.

If these were his final hours, he would blow out the candle with no bitterness when the time came to extinguish it. He regretted what he had lost, but more important, he treasured what he had kept. In the last analysis, he felt that he had lived a life that was in the balance good, worthwhile, precious.

He had two guns with him. A .45 revolver. A .38 pistol. If they came into the attic after him, he would use the pistol on them until it was empty. Then he would make them eat all but one of the rounds in the revolver. That last cartridge would be for himself.

He had brought no extra bullets. In a crisis, a man with one good hand could not reload fast enough to make the effort more than a comic finale.

The drumming of rain on the roof had subsided. He wondered if this was just another lull in the storm or if it was finally ending.

It would be nice to see the sun again.

He worried more about Moose than about himself. The poor damn dog was down there alone. When the Boogeymen or their makers came at last, he hoped they wouldn't harm old Moose. And if they came into the attic and forced him to kill himself, he hoped that Moose would not be long without a good home.

· 8 ·

To Loman, as he cruised, Moonlight Cove seemed both dead and teeming with life.

Judged by the usual signs of life in a small town, the burg was an empty husk, as defunct as any sun-dried ghost town in the heart of the Mohave. The shops, bars, and restaurants were closed. Even the usually crowded Perez Family Restaurant was shuttered, dark; no one had showed up to open for business. The only pedestrians out walking in the aftermath of the storm were foot patrols or conversion teams. Likewise, the police units and two-man patrols in private cars had the streets to themselves.

However, the town seethed with perverse life. Several times he saw strange, swift figures moving through the darkness and fog, still secretive but far bolder than they had been on other nights. When he stopped or slowed to study those marauders, some of them paused in deep shadows to gaze at him with baleful yellow or green or smoldering red eyes, as if they were contemplating their chances of attacking his black-and-white and pulling him out of it before he could take his foot off the brake pedal and get out of there. Watching them, he was filled with a longing to abandon his car, his clothes, and the rigidity of his human form, to join them in their simpler world of hunting, feeding, and rutting. Each time he quickly turned away from them and drove on before they – or he – could act upon such impulses. Here and there he passed houses in which eerie lights glowed, and against the windows of which moved shadows so grotesque and unearthly that his heart quickened and his palms went damp, though he was well removed from them and probably beyond their reach. He did not stop to investigate what creatures might inhabit those places or what tasks they were engaged upon, for he sensed that they were kin to the thing Denny had become and that they were more dangerous, in many ways, than the prowling regressives.

He now lived in a Lovecraftian world of primal and cosmic forces, of monstrous entities stalking the night, where human beings were reduced to little more than cattle, where the Judeo-Christian universe of a love-motivated God had been replaced by the creation of the old gods who were driven by dark lusts, a taste for cruelty, and a never-satisfied thirst for power. In the air, in the eddying fog, in the shadowed and dripping trees, in the unlit streets, and even in the sodium-yellow glare of the lamps on the main streets, there was the pervasive sense that nothing good could happen that night ... but that any-thing *else* could happen, no matter how fantastical or bizarre.

Having read uncounted paperbacks over the years, he was familiar with Lovecraft. He had not liked him a hundredth as much as Louis L'Amour, largely because L'Amour had dealt with reality, while H.P. Lovecraft had traded in the impossible. Or so it had seemed to Loman at the time. Now he knew that men could create, in the real world, hells equal to any that the most imaginative writer could dream up.

Lovecraftian despair and terror flooded through Moonlight Cove in greater quantities than those in which the recent rain had fallen. As he drove through those transmuted streets, Loman kept his service revolver on the car seat beside him, within easy reach.

Shaddack.

He must find Shaddack.

Going south on Juniper, he stopped at the intersection with Ocean Avenue. At the same time another black-and-white braked at the stop sign directly opposite Loman, headed north.

No traffic was moving on Ocean. Rolling his window down, Loman pulled slowly across the intersection and braked beside the other cruiser, with no more than a foot separating them.

From the number on the door, above the police-department shield, Loman knew it was Neil Penniworth's patrol car. But when he looked through the side window, he did not see the young officer. He saw something that might once have been Penniworth, still vaguely human, illuminated by the gauge and speedometer lights but more directly by the glow of the mobile VDT in there. Twin cables, like the one that had erupted from Denny's forehead to join him more intimately with his PC, had sprouted from Penniworth's skull; and although the light was poor, it appeared as if one of those extrusions snaked through the steering wheel and into the dashboard, while the other looped down toward the console-mounted computer. The shape of Penniworth's skull had changed dramatically, too, drawing forward, bristling with spiky features that must have been sensors of some kind and that gleamed softly like burnished metal in the light of the VDT; his shoulders were larger, queerly scalloped and pointed; he appeared earnestly to have sought the form of a baroque robot. His hands were not on the steering wheel, but perhaps he did not even have hands any more; Loman suspected that Penniworth had not just become one with his mobile computer terminal but with the patrol car itself.

Penniworth slowly turned his head to face Loman.

In his eyeless sockets, crackling white fingers of electricity wiggled and jittered ceaselessly.

Shaddack had said that the New People's freedom from emotion had given them the ability to make far greater use of their innate brain power, even to the extent of exerting mental control over the form and function of matter. Their consciousness now dictated their form; to escape a world in which they were not permitted emotion, they could become whatever they chose – though they could not return to the Old People they had been. Evidently life as a cyborg was free of angst, for Penniworth had sought release from fear and longing – perhaps some kind of obliteration, as well – in this monstrous incarnation.

But what did he feel now? What purpose did he have? And did he remain in that altered state because he truly preferred it? Or was he like Peyser – trapped either for physical reasons or because an aberrant aspect of his own psychology would not permit him to reassume the human form to which, otherwise, he desired to return?

Loman reached for the revolver on the seat beside him.

A segmented cable burst from the driver's door of Penniworth's car, without shredding metal, extruding as if a part of the door had melted and re-formed to produce it – except that it looked at least semiorganic. The probe struck Loman's side window with a snap.

The revolver eluded Loman's sweaty hand, for he could not take his eyes off the probe to look for the gun.

The glass did not crack, but a quarter-size patch bubbled and melted in an instant, and the probe weaved into the car, straight at Loman's face. It had a fleshy sucker mouth, like an eel, but the tiny, sharply pointed teeth within it looked like steel.

He ducked his head, forgot about the revolver, and tramped the accelerator to the floor. The Chevy almost seemed to rear back for a fraction of a second; then with a surge of power that pressed Loman into the seat, it shot forward, south on Juniper.

For a moment the probe between the cars stretched to maintain contact, brushed the bridge of Loman's nose – and abruptly was gone, reeled back into the vehicle from which it had come.

He drove fast all the way to the end of Juniper before slowing down to make a turn. The wind of his passage whistled at the hole that the probe had melted in his window.

Loman's worst fear seemed to be unfolding. Those New People who didn't choose regression were going to transform themselves – or be transformed at the demand of Shaddack – into hellish hybrids of man and machine.

Find Shaddack. Murder the maker and release the anguished monsters he had made.

9

Preceded by Sam and followed by Tessa, Chrissie squelched through the mushy turf of the athletic field. In places the soggy grass gave way to gluey mud, which pulled noisily at her shoes, and she thought she sounded like a sort of goofy alien herself, plodding along on big, sucker-equipped feet. Then it occurred to her that in a way she *was* an alien in Moonlight Cove tonight, a different sort of creature from what the majority of the citizens had become.

They were two thirds of the way across the field when they were halted by a shrill cry that split the night as cleanly as a sharp ax would split a dry cord of wood. That unhuman voice rose and fell and rose again, savage and uncanny but familiar, the call of one of those beasts that she'd thought were invading aliens. Though the rain had stopped, the air was laden with moisture, and in that humidity, the unearthly shriek carried well, like the bell-clear notes of a distant trumpet.

Worse, the call at once was answered by the beast's excited kin. At least half a dozen equally chilling shrieks arose from perhaps as far south as Paddock Lane and as far north as Holliwell Road, from the high hills in the east end of town and from the beach-facing bluffs only a couple of blocks to the west.

All of a sudden Chrissie longed for the cold, lightless culvert churning with waist-deep water so filthy that it might have come from the devil's own bathtub. This open ground seemed wildly dangerous by comparison.

A new cry arose as the others faded, and it was closer than any that had come before it. Too close.

'Let's get inside,' Sam said urgently.

Chrissie was beginning to admit to herself that she might not make a good Andre Norton heroine, after all. She was scared, cold, grainy-eyed with exhaustion, starting to feel sorry for herself, and hungry again. She was sick and tired of adventure. She yearned for warm rooms and lazy days with good books and trips to movie theaters and wedges of double-fudge cake. By this time a true adventure-story heroine would have worked out a series of brilliant stratagems that would have brought the beasts in Moonlight Cove to ruin, would have found a way to turn the robot-people into harmless car-washing machines, and would be well on her way to being crowned princess of the kingdom by acclamation of the respectful and grateful citizenry.

They hurried to the end of the field, rounded the bleachers, and crossed the deserted parking lot to the back of the school.

Nothing attacked them.

Thank you, God. Your friend, Chrissie.

Something howled again.

Sometimes even God seemed to have a perverse streak.

There were six doors at different places along the back of the school. They moved from one to another, as Sam tried them all and examined the locks in the hand-hooded beam of his flashlight. He apparently couldn't pick any of them, which disappointed her, because she'd imagined FBI men were so well trained that in an emergency they could open a bank vault with spit and a hairpin.

He also tried a few windows and spent what seemed a long time peering through the panes with his flashlight. He was examining not the rooms beyond but the inner sills and frames of the windows.

At the last door – which was the only one that had glass in the top of it, the others being blank rectangles of metal – Sam clicked off the flashlight, looked solemnly at Tessa, and spoke to her in a low voice. 'I don't think there's an alarm system here. Could be wrong. But there's no alarm tape on the glass and as far as I can see no hard-wired contacts along the frames or at the window latches.'

'Are those the only two kinds of alarms they might have?' Tessa whispered.

'Well, there're motion-detection systems, either employing sonic transmitters or electric eyes. But they'd be too elaborate for just a school, and probably too sensitive for a building like this.'

'So now what?'

'Now I break a window.'

Chrissie expected him to withdraw a roll of masking tape from a pocket of his coat and tape one of the panes to soften the sound of shattering glass and to prevent the shards from falling noisily to the floor inside. That was how they usually did it in books. But he just turned sideways to the door, drew his arm forward, then rammed it back and drove his elbow through the eight-inch-square pane in the lower-right corner of the window grid. Glass broke and clattered to the floor with an awful racket. Maybe he had forgotten to bring his tape.

He reached through the empty pane, felt for the locks, disengaged them, and went inside first. Chrissie followed him, trying not to step on the broken glass.

Sam switched on the flashlight. He didn't hood it quite so much as he had done outside, though he was obviously trying to keep the backwash of the beam off the windows.

They were in a long hallway. It was full of the cedar-pine smell that came from the crumbly green disinfectant and dust-attractor that for years the janitors had sprinkled on the floors and then swept up, until the tiles and walls had become impregnated with the scent. The aroma was familiar to her from Thomas Jefferson Elementary, and she was disappointed to find it here. She had thought of high school as a special, mysterious place, but how special or mysterious could it be if they used the same disinfectant as at the grade school?

Tessa quietly closed the outside door behind them.

They stood listening for a moment.

The school was silent.

They moved down the hall, looking into classrooms and lavatories and supply closets on both sides, searching for the computer lab. In a hundred and fifty feet they reached a junction with another hall. They stood in the intersection for a moment, heads cocked, listening again.

The school was still silent.

And dark. The only light in any direction was the flashlight, which Sam still held in his left hand but which he no longer hooded with his right. He had withdrawn his revolver from his holster and needed his right hand for that.

After a long wait, Sam said, 'Nobody's here.'

Which did seem to be the case.

Briefly Chrissie felt better, safer.

On the other hand, if he really believed they were the only people in the school, why didn't he put his gun away?

10

As he drove through his domain, impatient for midnight, which was still five hours away, Thomas Shaddack had largely regressed to a childlike condition. Now that his triumph was at hand, he could cast off the masquerade of a grown man, which he had so long sustained, and he was relieved to do so. He had never been an adult, really, but a boy whose emotional development had been forever arrested at the age of twelve, when the message of the moonhawk had not only come to him but been *imbedded* in him; he had thereafter faked emotional ascension into adulthood to match his physical growth.

But it was no longer necessary to pretend.

On one level, he had always known this about himself, and had considered it to be his great strength, an advantage over those who had put childhood behind them. A boy of twelve could harbor and nurture a dream with more determination than could an adult, for adults were constantly distracted by conflicting needs and desires. A boy on the edge of puberty, however, had the single-mindedness to focus on and dedicate himself unswervingly to a single Big Dream. Properly bent, a twelve-year-old boy was the perfect monomaniac.

The Moonhawk Project, his Big Dream of godlike power, would not have reached fruition if he had matured in the usual way. He owed his impending triumph to arrested development.

He was a boy again, not secretly any more but openly, eager to satisfy his every whim, to take whatever he wanted, to do anything that broke the rules. Twelve-year-old boys reveled in breaking the rules, challenging authority. At their worst, twelve-year-old boys were naturally lawless, on the verge of hormonal-induced rebellion.

But he was more than lawless. He was a boy flying on cactus candy that had been eaten long ago but that had left a psychic if not a physical residue. He was a boy who knew that he was a god. *Any* boy's potential for cruelty paled in comparison to the cruelty of gods.

To pass the time until midnight, he imagined what he would do with his power when the last of Moonlight Cove had fallen under his command. Some of his ideas made him shiver with a strange mixture of excitement and disgust.

He was on Iceberry Way when he realized the Indian was with him. He was surprised when he turned his head and saw Runningdeer sitting in the passenger seat. Indeed he stopped the van in the middle of the street and stared in disbelief, shocked and afraid.

But Runningdeer did not menace him. In fact the Indian didn't even speak to him or look at him, but stared straight ahead, through the windshield.

Slowly understanding came to Shaddack. The Indian's spirit was his now, his possession as surely as was the van. The great spirits had given him the Indian as an advisor, as a reward for having made a success of Moonhawk. But *he*, not Runningdeer, was in control this time, and the Indian would speak only when spoken to.

'Hello, Runningdeer,' he said.

The Indian looked at him. 'Hello, Little Chief.'

'You're mine now.'

'Yes, Little Chief.'

For just a brief flicker of time, it occurred to Shaddack that he was mad and that Runningdeer was an illusion coughed up by a sick mind. But monomaniacal boys do not have the capacity for an extended examination of their mental condition, and the thought passed out of his mind as quickly as it had entered.

To Runningdeer, he said, 'You'll do what I say.'

'Always.'

Immensely pleased, Shaddack let up on the brake pedal and drove on. The headlights revealed an amber-eyed thing of fantastic shape, drinking from a puddle on the pavement. He refused to regard it as a thing of consequence, and when it loped away, he let it vanish from his memory as swiftly as it disappeared from the night-mantled street.

Casting a sly glance at the Indian, he said, 'You know one thing I'm going to do some day?'

'What's that, Little Chief?'

'When I've converted everyone, not just the people in Moonlight Cove but everyone in the world, when no one stands against me, then I'll spend some time tracking down your family, all of your remaining brothers, sisters, even your cousins, and I'll find all of *their* children, and all their wives and husbands, and all their *children's* wives and husbands . . . and I'll make them pay for your crimes, I'll really, really make them pay.' A whining petulance had entered his voice. He disapproved of the tone he heard himself using, but he could not lose it. 'I'll kill all the men, hack them to bloody bits and pieces, do it myself. I'll let them know that it's because of their relation to you that they've got to suffer, and they'll despise you and curse your name, they'll be sorry you ever existed. And I'll rape all the women and hurt them, hurt them all, really bad, and then I'll kill them too. What do you think of that? Huh?'

'If it's what you want, Little Chief.'

'Damn right it's what I want.'

'Then you may have it.'

'Damn right I may have it.'

Shaddack was surprised when tears came to his eyes. He stopped at an intersection and didn't move on. 'It wasn't right what you did to me.'

The Indian said nothing.

'Say it wasn't right!'

'It wasn't right, Little Chief.'

'It wasn't right at all.'

'It wasn't right.'

Shaddack pulled a handkerchief from his pocket and blew his nose. He blotted his eyes. Soon his tears dried up.

He smiled at the nightscape revealed through the windshield. He sighed. He glanced at Runningdeer.

The Indian was staring forward, silent.

Shaddack said, 'Of course, without you, I might never have been the child of the moonhawk.'

11

The computer lab was on the ground floor, in the center of the building, near a confluence of corridors. Windows looked out on a courtyard but could not be seen from any street, which allowed Sam to switch on the overhead lights.

It was a large chamber, laid out like a language lab, with each VDT in its own three-sided cubicle. Thirty computers – upper end, hard-disk systems – were lined up along three walls and in a back-to-back row down the middle of the room.

Looking around at the wealth of hardware, Tessa said, 'New Wave sure was generous, huh.'

'Maybe "thorough" is a better word,' Sam said.

He walked along a row of VDTs, looking for telephone lines and modems, but he found none.

Tessa and Chrissie stayed back by the open lab door, peering out at the dark hallway.

Sam sat down at one of the machines and switched it on. The New Wave logo appeared in the center of the screen.

With no telephones, no modems, maybe the computers really had been given to the school for student training, without the additional intention of tying the kids to New Wave during some stage of the Moonhawk Project.

The logo blinked off, and a menu appeared on the screen. Because they were hard-disk machines with tremendous capacity, their programs were already loaded and ready to go as soon as the system was powered up. The menu offered him five choices:

    A. TRAINING 1
    B. TRAINING 2
    C. WORD PROCESSING
    D. ACCOUNTING
    E. OTHER

He hesitated, not because he couldn't decide what letter to push but because he was suddenly afraid of using the machine. He vividly remembered the Coltranes. Though it had seemed to him that they had elected to meld with their computers, that their transformation began within them, he had no way of knowing for sure that it had not been the other way around. Maybe the computers had somehow reached out and *seized* them. That seemed impossible. Besides, thanks to Harry's observations, they knew that people in Moonlight Cove were being converted by an injection, not by some insidious force that passed semimagically through computer keys into the pads of their fingers. He was hesitant nevertheless.

Finally he pressed E and got a list of school subjects:

    A. ALL LANGUAGES
    B. MATH
    C. ALL SCIENCES
    D. HISTORY
    E. ENGLISH
    F. OTHER

He pressed F. A third menu appeared, and the process continued until he finally got a menu on which the final selection was NEW WAVE. When he keyed in that choice, words began to march across the screen.

> HELLO, STUDENT.
> YOU ARE NOW IN CONTACT WITH THE SUPER-COMPUTER
> AT NEW WAVE MICROTECHNOLOGY.
> MY NAME IS SUN.
> I AM HERE TO SERVE YOU.

The school machines were wired directly to New Wave. Modems were unnecessary.

> WOULD YOU LIKE TO SEE MENUS?
> OR WILL YOU SPECIFY INTEREST?

Considering the wealth of menus in the police department's system alone, which he had reviewed last night in the patrol car, he figured he could sit here all evening just looking at menu after menu after submenu before he found what he wanted. He typed in: MOONLIGHT COVE POLICE DEPARTMENT.

> THIS FILE RESTRICTED.
> PLEASE DO NOT ATTEMPT TO PROCEED WITHOUT THE
> ASSISTANCE OF YOUR TEACHER.

He supposed that the teachers had individual code numbers that, depending on whether or not they were converted, would allow them to access otherwise restricted data. The only way to hit on one of their codes was to begin trying random combinations of digits, but since he didn't even know how many numbers were in a code, there were millions if not billions of possibilities. He could sit there until his hair turned white and his teeth fell out, and not luck into a good number.

Last night he had used Officer Reese Dorn's personal computer-access code, and he wondered whether it worked only on a designated police-department VDT or whether any computer tied to Sun would accept it. Nothing lost for trying. He typed in 262699.

The screen cleared. Then: HELLO, OFFICER DORN.

Again he requested the police department data system.

This time it was given to him.

> CHOOSE ONE
> A. DISPATCHER
> B. CENTRAL FILES
> C. BULLETIN BOARD
> D. OUT-SYSTEM MODEM

He pressed D.

He was shown a list of computers nationwide with which he could link through the police-department's modem.

His hands were suddenly damp with sweat. He was sure something was going to go wrong, if only because nothing had been easy thus far, not from the minute he had driven into town.

He glanced at Tessa. 'Everything okay?'

She squinted at the dark hallway, then blinked at him. 'Seems to be. Any luck?'

'Yeah ... maybe.' He turned to the computer again and said softly, 'Please ...'

He scanned the long roster of possible outsystem links. He found FBI KEY, which was the name of the latest and most sophisticated of the Bureau's computer networks – a highly secure, interoffice data-storage, -retrieval, and -transmission system housed at headquarters in Washington, which had been installed only within the past year. Supposedly no one but approved agents at the home office and in the Bureau's field offices, accessing with their own special codes, were able to use FBI KEY.

So much for high security.

Still expecting trouble, Sam selected FBI KEY. The menu disappeared. The screen remained blank for a moment. Then on the display, which proved to be a full-color monitor, the FBI shield appeared in blue and gold. The word KEY appeared below it.

Next, a series of questions was flashed on the screen – WHAT IS YOUR BUREAU ID NUMBER? NAME? DATE OF BIRTH? DATE OF BUREAU INDUCTION? MOTHER'S MAIDEN NAME? – and when he answered those, he was rewarded with access.

'Bingo!' he said, daring to be optimistic.

Tessa said, 'What's happened?'

'I'm in the Bureau's main system in D.C.'

'You're a hacker,' Chrissie said.

'I'm a fumbler. But I'm in.'

'Now what?' Tessa asked.

'I'll ask for the current operator in a minute. But first I want to send greetings to every damned office in the country, make them all sit up and take notice.'

'Greetings?'

From the extensive FBI KEY menu, Sam called up item G – IMMEDIATE INTEROFFICE TRANSMISSION. He intended to send a message to every Bureau field office in the country, not just to San Francisco, which was the closest and the one from which he hoped to obtain help. There was one chance in a million that the night operator in San Francisco would overlook the message among reams of other transmissions, in spite of the ACTION ALERT heading he would tag on to it. If that happened, if someone was asleep at the wheel at this most inopportune of moments, they wouldn't be asleep for long, because every office in the country would be asking HQ for more details about the Moonlight Cove bulletin and requesting an explanation of why they had been fed an alert about a situation outside their regions.

He did not understand half of what was happening in this town. He could not have explained, in the shorthand of a Bureau bulletin, even as much as he *did* understand. But he quickly crafted a summary which he believed was as accurate as it had to be – and which he hoped would get them off their duffs and running.

ACTION ALERT
MOONLIGHT COVE, CALIFORNIA.
* SCORES DEAD. CONDITION DETERIORATING. HUN-
DREDS MORE COULD DIE WITHIN HOURS.
* NEW WAVE MICROTECHNOLOGY ENGAGED IN ILLICIT
EXPERIMENTS ON HUMAN SUBJECTS, WITHOUT THEIR
KNOWLEDGE. CONSPIRACY OF WIDEST SCOPE.
* THOUSANDS OF PEOPLE CONTAMINATED.
* REPEAT, ENTIRE POPULATION OF TOWN CONTAMI-
NATED.
* SITUATION EXTREMELY DANGEROUS.
*CONTAMINATED CITIZENS SUFFER LOSS OF FACULTIES,
EXHIBIT TENDENCY TO EXTREME VIOLENCE.
* REPEAT, EXTREME VIOLENCE.
* REQUEST IMMEDIATE QUARANTINE BY ARMY SPECIAL
FORCES. ALSO REQUEST IMMEDIATE, MASSIVE, ARMED
BACKUP BY BUREAU PERSONNEL.

He gave his position at the high school on Roshmore so incoming support
would have a place to start looking for him, though he was not certain that he,
Tessa, and Chrissie could safely continue to take refuge there until reinforcements arrived. He signed off with his name and Bureau ID number.

That message was not going to prepare them for the shock of what they
would find in Moonlight Cove, but at least it would get them on the move and
encourage them to come prepared for anything.

He typed TRANSMIT, but then had a thought and wiped the word from the
screen. He typed REPEAT TRANSMISSION.

The computer asked NUMBER OF REPEATS?

He typed 99.

The computer acknowledged the order.

Then he typed TRANSMIT again and pressed the ENTER button.

WHAT OFFICES?

He typed ALL.

The screen went blank. Then: TRANSMITTING.

At that moment every KEY laser printer in every Bureau field office in the
country was printing out the first of ninety-nine repeats of his message. Night
staffers everywhere soon would be climbing the walls.

He almost whooped with delight.

But there was more to be done. They were not out of this mess yet.

Sam quickly returned to the KEY menu and tapped selection A – NIGHT
OPERATOR. Five seconds later he was in touch with the agent manning the
KEY post at the Bureau's central communications room in Washington. A
number flashed on the screen – the operator's ID – followed by a name,
ANNE DENTON. Taking immense satisfaction in using high technology to
bring the downfall of Thomas Shaddack, New Wave, and the Moonhawk
Project, Sam entered into a long-distance, unspoken, electronic conversation
with Anne Denton, intending to spell out the horrors of Moonlight Cove in
more detail.

Though Loman no longer was interested in the activities of the police department, he switched on the VDT in his car every ten minutes or so to see if anything was happening. He expected Shaddack to be in touch with members of the department from time to time. If he was lucky enough to catch a VDT dialogue between Shaddack and other cops, he might be able to pinpoint the bastard's location from something that was said.

He didn't leave the computer on all the time because he was afraid of it. He didn't think it would jump at him and suck out his brains or anything, but he did recognize that working with it too long might induce in him a temptation to become what Neil Penniworth and Denny had become – in the same way that being around the regressives had given rise to a powerful urge to devolve.

He had just pulled to the side of Holliwell Road, where his restless cruising had taken him, had switched on the machine, and was about to call up the dialogue channel to see if anyone was engaged in conversation, when the word ALERT appeared in large letters on the screen. He pulled his hand back from the keyboard as if something had nipped at him.

The computer said, SUN REQUESTS DIALOGUE.

Sun? The supercomputer at New Wave? Why would it be accessing the police department's system?

Before another officer at headquarters or in another car could query the machine, Loman took charge and typed DIALOGUE APPROVED.

REQUEST CLARIFICATION, Sun said.

Loman typed YES, which could mean GO AHEAD.

Structuring its questions from its own self-assessment program, which allowed it to monitor its own workings as if it were an outside observer, Sun said, ARE TELEPHONE CALLS TO AND FROM UNAPPROVED NUMBERS IN MOONLIGHT COVE AND ALL NUMBERS OUTSIDE STILL RESTRICTED?

YES.

ARE SUN'S RESERVED TELEPHONE LINES INCLUDED IN AFOREMENTIONED PROHIBITION? the New Wave computer asked, speaking of itself in third person.

Confused, Loman typed UNCLEAR.

Patiently leading him through it step by step, Sun explained that it had its own dedicated phone lines, outside the main directory, by which its users could call other computers all over the country and access them.

He already knew this, so he typed YES.

ARE SUN'S RESERVED TELEPHONE LINES INCLUDED IN AFOREMENTIONED PROHIBITION? it repeated.

If he'd had Denny's interest in computers, he might have tumbled immediately to what was happening, but he was still confused. So he typed WHY? – meaning WHY DO YOU ASK?

OUT-SYSTEM MODEM NOW IN USE.

BY WHOM?

SAMUEL BOOKER.

Loman would have laughed if he had been capable of glee. The agent had found a way out of Moonlight Cove, and now the shit was going to hit the fan at last.

Before he could query Sun as to Booker's activities and whereabouts, another name appeared on the upper left corner of the screen – SHADDACK – indicating that New Wave's own Moreau was watching the dialogue on his VDT and was cutting in. Loman was content to let his maker and Sun converse uninterrupted.

Shaddack asked for more details.

Sun responded: FBI KEY SYSTEM ACCESSED.

Loman could imagine Shaddack's shock. The beast master's demand appeared on the screen: OPTIONS. Which meant he desperately wanted a menu of options from Sun to deal with the situation.

Sun presented him with five choices, the fifth of which was SHUT DOWN, and Shaddack chose that one.

A moment later Sun reported: FBI KEY SYSTEM LINK SHUT DOWN.

Loman hoped that Booker had gotten enough of a message out to blow Shaddack and Moonhawk out of the water.

On the screen, from Shaddack to Sun: BOOKER'S TERMINAL?

YOU REQUIRE LOCATION?

YES.

MOONLIGHT COVE CENTRAL SCHOOL, COMPUTER LAB.

Loman was three minutes from Central.

He wondered how close Shaddack was to the school. It didn't matter. Near or far, Shaddack would bust his ass to get there and prevent Booker from compromising the Moonhawk Project – or to take vengeance if it had already been compromised.

At last Loman knew where he could find his maker.

· 13 ·

When Sam was only six exchanges into his dialogue with Anne Denton in Washington, the link was cut off. The screen went blank.

He wanted to believe he had been disconnected by ordinary line problems somewhere along the way. But he knew that wasn't the case.

He got up from his chair so fast that he knocked it over.

Chrissie jumped in surprise, and Tessa said, 'What is it? What's wrong?'

'They know we're here,' Sam said. 'They're coming.'

· 14 ·

Harry heard the doorbell ring down in the house below him.

His stomach twisted. He felt as if he were in a roller-coaster, just pulling away from the boarding ramp.

The bell rang again.

A long silence followed. They knew he was crippled. They would give him time to answer.

Finally it rang again.

He looked at his watch. Only 7:24. He took no comfort in the fact that they had not put him at the end of their schedule.

The bell rang again. Then again. Then insistently.

In the distance, muffled by the two intervening floors, Moose began barking.

· 15 ·

Tessa grabbed Chrissie's hand. With Sam, they hurried out of the computer lab. The batteries in the flashlight must not have been fresh, for the beam was growing dimmer. She hoped it would last long enough for them to find their way out. Suddenly the school's layout – which had been uncomplicated when they had not been in a life-or-death rush to negotiate its byways – seemed like a maze.

They crossed a junction of four halls, entered another corridor, and went about twenty yards before Tessa realized they were going the wrong direction. 'This isn't how we came in.'

'Doesn't matter,' Sam said. 'Any door out will do.'

They had to go another ten yards before the failing flashlight beam was able to reach all the way to the end of the hall, revealing that it was a dead end.

'This way,' Chrissie said, pulling loose of Tessa and turning back into the darkness from which they'd come, forcing them either to follow or abandon her.

· 16 ·

Shaddack figured they wouldn't have tried to break into Central on any side that faced a street, where they might be seen – and the Indian agreed – so he drove around to the back. He passed metal doors that would have provided too formidable a barrier, and studied the windows, trying to spot a broken pane.

The last rear door, the only one with glass in the top, was in an angled extension of the building. He was driving toward it for a moment, just before the service road swung to the left to go around that wing, and from a distance of only a few yards, with all the other panes reflecting the glare of his headlights, his attention was caught by the missing glass at the bottom right.

'There,' he told Runningdeer.

'Yes, Little Chief.'

He parked near the door and grabbed the loaded Remington 12-gauge semi-automatic pistol-grip shotgun from the van's floor behind him. The box of extra shells was on the passenger seat. He opened it, grabbed four or five, stuffed them in a coat pocket, grabbed four or five more, then got out of the van and headed toward the door with the broken window.

· 17 ·

Four soft thuds reverberated through the house, even into the attic, and Harry thought he heard glass breaking far away.

Moose barked furiously. He sounded like the most vicious attack dog ever bred, not a sweet black lab. Maybe he would prove willing to defend home and master in spite of his naturally good temperament.

Don't do it, boy, Harry thought. Don't try to be a hero. Just crawl away in a corner somewhere and let them pass, lick their hands if they offer them, and don't—

The dog squealed and fell silent.

No, Harry thought, and a pang of grief tore through him. He had lost not just a dog but his best friend.

Moose, too, had a sense of duty.

Silence settled over the house. They would be searching the ground floor now.

Harry's grief and fear receded as his anger grew. Moose. Dammit, poor harmless Moose. He could feel the flush of rage in his face. He wanted to kill them all.

He picked up the .38 in his one good hand and held it on his lap. They wouldn't find him for a while, but he felt better with the gun in his hand.

In the service he had won competition medals for both rifle sharpshooting and performance with a handgun. That had been a long time ago. He had not fired a gun, even in practice, for more than twenty years, since that faraway and beautiful Asian land, where on a morning of exceptionally lovely blue skies, he had been crippled for life. He kept the .38 and the .45 cleaned and oiled, mostly out of habit; a soldier's lessons and routines were learned for life – and now he was glad of that.

A clank.

A rumble-purr of machinery.

The elevator.

· 18 ·

Halfway down the correct hallway, holding the dimming flashlight in his left hand and the revolver in his other, just as he caught up with Chrissie, Sam heard a siren approaching outside. It was not on top of them, but it was too close. He couldn't tell if the patrol car was actually closing in on the back of the school, toward which they were headed, or coming to the front entrance.

Apparently Chrissie was uncertain too. She stopped running and said, 'Where, Sam? Where?'

From behind them Tessa said, 'Sam, the doorway!'

For an instant he didn't understand what she meant. Then he saw the door swinging open at the end of the hall, about thirty yards away, the same door by which they had entered. A man stepped inside. The siren was still wailing, drawing nearer, so there were more of them on the way, a whole platoon of them. The guy who'd come through the door was just the first – tall, six feet five if he was one inch, but otherwise only a shadow, minimally backlighted by the security lamp outside and to the right of the door.

Sam squeezed off a shot with his .38, not bothering to determine if this man was an enemy, because they were all enemies, every last one of them – their name was legion – and he knew the shot was wide. His marksmanship was lousy because of his injured wrist, which hurt like hell after their misadventures in the culvert. With the recoil, pain burst out of that joint and all the way to his shoulder, then back again, Jesus, pain sloshing around like acid inside him, from shoulder to fingertips. Half the strength went out of his hand. He almost dropped the gun.

As the roar of Sam's shot slammed back to him from the walls of the corridor, the guy at the far end opened fire with a weapon of his own, but he had heavy artillery. A shotgun. Fortunately he was not good with it. He was aiming too high, not aware of how the kick would throw the muzzle up. Consequently the first blast went into the ceiling only ten yards ahead of him, tearing out one of the unlit fluorescent fixtures and a bunch of acoustic tiles. His reaction confirmed his lack of experience with guns; he overcompensated for the kick, swinging the muzzle too far down as he pulled the trigger a second time, so the follow-up round struck the floor far short of target.

Sam did not remain an idle observer of the misdirected gunfire. He seized Chrissie and pushed her to the left, across the corridor and through a door into a dark room, even as the second flock of buckshot gouged chunks out of the vinyl flooring. Tessa was right behind them. She threw the door shut and leaned against it, as if she thought that she was Superwoman and that any pellets penetrating the door would bounce harmlessly from her back.

Sam shoved the woefully dim flashlight at her. 'With my wrist, I'm going to need both hands to manage the gun.'

Tessa swept the weak yellow beam around the chamber. They were in the band room. To the right of the door, tiered platforms – full of chairs and music stands – rose up to the back wall. To the left was a large open area, the band director's podium, a blond-wood and metal desk. And two doors. Both standing open, leading to adjoining rooms.

Chrissie needed no urging to follow Tessa toward the nearer of those doors, and Sam brought up the rear, moving backward, covering the hall door through which they had come.

Outside, the siren had died. Now there would be more than one man with a shotgun.

• 19 •

They had searched the first two floors. They were in the third-floor bedroom.

Harry could hear them talking. Their voices rose to him through their ceiling, his floor. But he couldn't quite make out what they were saying.

He almost hoped they would spot the attic trap in the closet and would decide to come up. He wanted a chance to blow a couple of them away. For Moose. After twenty long years of being a victim, he was sick to death of it; he wanted a chance to let them know that Harry Talbot was still a man to be reckoned with – and that although Moose was only a dog, his was nevertheless a life taken only with serious consequences.

20

In the eddying fog, Loman saw the single patrol car parked beside Shaddack's van. He braked next to it just as Paul Amberlay got out from behind the wheel. Amberlay was lean and sinewy and very bright, one of Loman's best young officers, but he looked like a high-school boy now, too small to be a cop – and scared.

When Loman got out of his car, Amberlay came to him, gun in hand, visibly shaking. 'Only you and me? Where the hell's everybody else? This is a major alert.'

'Where's everybody else?' Loman asked. 'Just listen, Paul. Just listen.'

From every part of town, scores of wild voices were lifted in eerie song, either calling to one another or challenging the unseen moon that floated above the wrung-out clouds.

Loman hurried to the back of the patrol car and opened the trunk. His unit, like every other, carried a 20-gauge riot gun for which he'd never had a use in peaceable Moonlight Cove. But New Wave, which had generously equipped the force, did not stint on equipment even if it was perceived as unnecessary. He pulled the shotgun from its clip mounting on the back wall of the trunk.

Joining him, Amberlay said, 'You telling me they've regressed, all of them, everyone on the force, except you and me?'

'Just listen,' Loman repeated as he leaned the 20-gauge against the bumper.

'But that's crazy!' Amberlay insisted. 'Jesus, God, you mean this whole thing is coming down on us, the whole damn thing?'

Loman grabbed a box of shells that was in the right wheel-well of the trunk, tore off the lid. 'Don't *you* feel the yearning, Paul?'

'No!' Amberlay said too quickly. 'No, I don't feel it, I don't feel anything.'

'I feel it,' Loman said, putting five rounds in the 20-gauge – one in the chamber, four in the magazine. 'Oh, Paul, I sure as hell feel it. I want to tear off my clothes and change, *change*, and just run, be free, go with them, hunt and kill and run with them.'

'Not me, no, never,' Amberlay said.

'Liar,' Loman said. He brought up the loaded gun and fired at Amberlay pointblank, blowing his head off.

He couldn't have trusted the young officer, couldn't have turned his back on him, not with the urge to regress so strong in him, and those voices in the night singing their siren songs.

As he stuffed more shells into his pockets, he heard a shotgun blast from inside the school.

He wondered if that gun was in the hands of Booker or Shaddack. Struggling to control his raging terror, fighting off the hideous and powerful urge to shed his human form, Loman went inside to find out.

21

Tommy Shaddack heard another shotgun, but he didn't think much about that because, after all, they were in a war now. You could hear what a war it was by just stepping out in the night and listening to the shrieks of the combatants echoing down through the hills to the sea. He was more focused on getting

Booker, the woman, and the girl he'd seen in the hall, because he knew the woman must be the Lockland bitch and the girl must be Chrissie Foster, though he couldn't figure how they had joined up.

War. So he handled it the way soldiers did in the good movies, kicking the door open, firing a round into the room before entering. No one screamed. He guessed he hadn't hit anyone, so he fired again, and still no one screamed, so he figured they were already gone from there. He crossed the threshold, fumbled for the light switch, found it, and discovered he was in the deserted band room.

Evidently they had left by one of the two other doors, and when he saw that, he was angry, really angry. The only time in his life that he had fired a gun was in Phoenix, when he had shot the Indian with his father's revolver, and that had been close-up, where he could not miss. But still he had expected that he would be *good* with a gun. After all, Jeez, he had watched a lot of war movies, cowboy movies, cop shows on television, and it didn't look hard, not hard at all, you just pointed the muzzle and pulled the trigger. But it hadn't been that easy, after all, and Tommy was angry, furious, because they shouldn't make it look so easy in the movies and on the boob tube when, in fact, the gun jumped in your hands as if it was alive.

He knew better now, and he was going to brace himself when he fired, spread his legs and brace himself, so his shots wouldn't be blowing holes in the ceiling or bouncing off the floor any more. He would nail them cold the next time he got a whack at them, and they'd be sorry for making him chase them, for not just lying down and being dead when he *wanted* them to be dead.

• 22 •

The door out of the band room had led into a hall that served ten soundproofed practice rooms, where student musicians could mutilate fine music for hours at a time without disturbing anyone. At the end of that narrow corridor, Tessa pushed through another door and coaxed just enough out of the flashlight to see that they were in a chamber as large as the band room. It also featured tiered platforms rising to the back. A student-drawn sign on one wall, complete with winged angels singing, proclaimed, 'This the home of THE WORLD'S BEST CHORUS.'

As Chrissie and Sam followed her into the room, a shotgun roared in the distance. It sounded as if it was outside. But even as the door to the corridor of practice rooms swung shut behind them, another shotgun discharged, closer than the first, probably back at the door to the band room. Then a second blast from the same location.

Just like in the band room, two more doors led out of the choral chamber, but the first one she tried was a dead end; it went into the chorus director's office.

They dashed to the other exit, beyond which they found a corridor illuminated only by a red, twenty-four-hour-a-day emergency sign – STAIRS – immediately to their right. Not EXIT, just STAIRS, which meant this was an interior well with no access to the outside. 'Take her up,' Sam urged Tessa.

'But—'

'Up! They're probably coming in the ground floor by every entrance, anyway.'

'What're you—'

'Gonna make a little stand here,' he said.

A door crashed open and a shotgun exploded back in the chorus room.

'Go!' Sam whispered.

• 23 •

Harry heard the closet door open in the bedroom below.

The attic was cold, but he was streaming sweat as if in a sauna. Maybe he hadn't needed the second sweater.

Go away, he thought. Go away.

Then he thought, Hell, no, come on, come and get it. You think I want to live forever?

• 24 •

Sam went down on one knee in the hall outside the chorus room, taking a stable position to compensate somewhat for his weak right wrist. He held the swinging door open six inches, both arms thrust through the gap, the .38 gripped in his right hand, his left hand clamped around his right wrist.

He could see the guy across the room, silhouetted in the lights of the band-room corridor behind him. Tall. Couldn't see his face. But something about him struck a chord of familiarity.

The gunman didn't see Sam. He was only being cautious, laying down a spray of pellets before he entered. He pulled the trigger. The click was loud in the silent room. He pumped the shotgun. *Clackety-clack*. No ammo.

That meant a change in Sam's plans. He surged to his feet and through the swinging door, back into the chorus room, no longer able to wait for the guy to switch on the overhead lights or step farther across the threshold, because now was the time to take him, before he reloaded. Firing as he went, Sam squeezed off the four remaining rounds in the .38, trying his damnedest to make every slug count. On the second or third shot, the guy in the doorway squealed, God, he squealed like a kid, his voice high-pitched and quavering, as he threw himself back into the practice-room corridor, out of sight.

Sam kept moving, fumbling in his jacket pocket with his left hand, grabbing at the spare cartridges, while with his right hand he snapped open the revolver's cylinder and shook out the expended brass casings. When he reached the closed door to the narrow hall that connected chorus room to band room, the door through which the tall man had vanished, he pressed his back to the wall and jammed fresh rounds into the Smith & Wesson, snapped the cylinder shut.

He kicked the door open and looked into the hall, where the overhead fluorescents were lit.

It was deserted.

No blood on the floor.

Damn. His right hand was half numb. He could feel his wrist swelling tight under the bandage, which was now soaked with fresh blood. At the rate his shooting was deteriorating, he was going to have to walk right up to the bastard and ask him to bite on the muzzle in order to make the shot count.

The doors to the ten practice rooms, five on each side, were closed. The door at the far end, where the hall led into the band room, was open, and the lights were on there. The tall guy could be there or in any of the ten practice rooms. But wherever he was, he had probably slipped at least a couple of shells into that shotgun, so the moment to pursue him had passed.

Sam backed up, letting the door between the hall and the chorus room slip shut. Even as he let go of it, as it was swinging back into place, he glimpsed the tall man stepping through the open door of the band room about forty feet away.

It was Shaddack himself.

The shotgun boomed.

The soundproofed door, gliding shut at the crucial moment, was thick enough to stop the pellets.

Sam turned and ran across the chorus room, into the hall, and up the stairs, where he had sent Tessa and Chrissie.

When he reached the top flight, he found them waiting for him in the upper hall, in the soft red glow of another STAIRS sign.

Below, Shaddack entered the stairwell.

Sam turned, stepped back onto the landing and descended the first step. He leaned over the railing, looked down, glimpsed part of his pursuer, and squeezed off two shots.

Shaddack squealed like a boy again. He ducked back against the wall, away from the open center of the well, where he could not be seen.

Sam didn't know whether he'd scored a hit or not. Maybe. What he *did* know was that Shaddack wasn't mortally wounded; he was still coming, easing up step by step, staying against the outer wall. And when that geek reached the lower landing, he would take the turn suddenly, firing the shotgun repeatedly at whoever waited above.

Silently Sam retreated from the upper landing, into the hall once more. The scarlet light of the STAIRS sign fell on Chrissie's and Tessa's faces . . . an illusion of blood.

• 25 •

A clink. A scraping sound.

Clink-scrape. Clink-scrape.

Harry knew what he was hearing. Clothes hangers sliding on a metal rod.

How could they have known? Hell, maybe they had smelled him up here. He was sweating like a horse, after all. Maybe the conversion improved their senses.

The clinking and scraping stopped.

A moment later he heard them lifting the closet rod out of its braces so they could lower the trap.

• 26 •

The fading flashlight kept winking out, and Tessa had to shake it, jarring the batteries together, to get a few more seconds of weak and fluttery light from it.

They had stepped out of the hall, into what proved to be a chemistry lab with black marble lab tables and steel sinks and high wooden stools. Nowhere to hide.

They checked the windows, hoping there might be a roof just under them. No. A two-story drop to a concrete walk.

At the end of the chemistry lab was a door, through which they passed into a ten-foot-square storage room full of chemicals in sealed tins and bottles, some labeled with skulls and crossbones, some with DANGER in bright red letters. She supposed there were ways to use the contents of that closet as a weapon, but they didn't have time to inventory the supplies, looking for interesting substances to mix together. Besides, she'd never been a great science student, recalled nothing whatsoever of her chemistry classes, and would probably blow herself up with the first bottle she opened. From the expression on Sam's face, she knew that he saw no more hope there than she did.

A rear door in the storage closet opened onto a second lab that seemed to double as a biology classroom. Anatomy charts hung on one wall. The room offered no better place to hide than had the previous lab.

Holding Chrissie close against her side, Tessa looked at Sam and whispered, 'Now what? Wait here and hope he can't find us . . . or keep moving?'

'I think it's safer to keep moving,' Sam said. 'Easier to be cornered if we sit still.'

She nodded agreement.

He eased past her and Chrissie, leading the way between the lab benches, toward the door to the hall.

From behind them, either in the dark chemical-storage room or in the unlit chemistry lab beyond it, came a soft but distinct *clink*.

Sam halted, motioned Tessa and Chrissie ahead of him, and turned to cover the exit from the storage room.

With Chrissie at her side, Tessa stepped to the hall door, turned the knob slowly, quietly, and eased the door outward.

Shaddack came from the darkness in the corridor, into the pale and inconstant pulse of light from her flash, and rammed the barrel of his shotgun into her stomach. 'You're gonna be sorry now,' he said excitedly.

• 27 •

They pulled the trapdoor down. A shaft of light from the closet shot up to the rafters, but it didn't illuminate the far corner in which Harry sat with his useless legs splayed out in front of him.

His bad hand was curled in his lap, while his good hand fiercely clasped the pistol.

His heart was hammering harder and faster than it had in twenty years, since the battlefields of Southeast Asia. His stomach was churning. His throat was so tight he could barely breathe. He was dizzy with fear. But, God in heaven, he sure felt *alive*.

With a squeak and clatter, they unfolded the ladder.

· 28 ·

Tommy Shaddack shoved the muzzle into her belly and almost blew her guts out, almost wasted her, before he realized how *pretty* she was, and then he didn't want to kill her any more, at least not right away, not until he'd made her do some things with him, do some things *to* him. She'd have to do whatever he wanted, anything, whatever he told her to do, or he could just smear her across the wall, yeah, she was his, and she better realize that, or she'd be sorry, he'd make her sorry.

Then he saw the girl beside her, a pretty little girl, only ten or twelve, and she excited him even more. He could have her first, and then the older one, have them any which way he wanted them, make them *do* things, all sorts of things, and then hurt them, that was his right, they couldn't deny him, not him, because all the power was in his hands now, he had seen the moonhawk *three* times.

He pushed through the open door, into the room, keeping the gun in the woman's belly, and she backed up to accommodate him, pulling the girl with her. Booker was behind them, a startled expression on his face. Tommy Shaddack said, 'Drop your gun and back away from it, or I'll make raspberry jelly out of this bitch, I swear I will, you can't move fast enough to stop me.'

Booker hesitated.

'Drop it!' Tommy Shaddack insisted.

The agent let go of the revolver and sidestepped away from it.

Keeping the muzzle of the Remington hard against the woman's belly, he made her edge around until she could reach the light switch and click on the fluorescents. The room leaped out of shadows.

'Okay, now, all of you,' Tommy Shaddack said, 'sit down on those three stools, by that lab bench, yeah, there, and don't do anything funny.'

He stepped back from the woman and covered them all with the shotgun. They looked scared, and that made him laugh.

Tommy was getting excited now, really excited, because he had decided he would kill Booker in front of the woman and the girl, not swift and clean but slowly, the first shot in the legs, let him lie on the floor and wriggle a while, the second shot in the gut but not from such a close range that it finished him instantly, make him hurt, make the woman and the girl watch, show them what a customer they had in Tommy Shaddack, what a damned tough customer, make them grateful for being spared, so grateful they'd get on their knees and let him *do* things to them, do all the things he had wanted to do for thirty years but which he had denied himself, let off thirty years of steam right here, right now, tonight . . .

· 29 ·

Beyond the house, filtering into the attic through vents in the eaves, came eerie howling, point and counterpoint, first solo and then chorus. It sounded as if the gates of hell had been thrown open, letting denizens of the pit pour forth into Moonlight Cove.

Harry worried about Sam, Tessa, and Chrissie.

Below him, the unseen conversion team locked the collapsible ladder in place. One of them began to climb into the attic.

Harry wondered what they would look like. Would they be just ordinary men – old Doc Fitz with a syringe and a couple of deputies to assist him? Or would they be Boogeymen? Or some of the machine-men Sam had talked about?

The first one ascended through the open trap. It was Dr. Worthy, the town's youngest physician.

Harry considered shooting him while he was still on the ladder. But he hadn't fired a gun in twenty years, and he didn't want to waste his limited ammunition. Better to wait for a closer shot.

Worthy didn't have a flashlight. Didn't seem to need one. He looked straight toward the darkest corner, where Harry was propped, and said, 'How did you know we were coming, Harry?'

'Cripple's intuition,' Harry said sarcastically.

Along the center of the attic, there was plenty of headroom to allow Worthy to walk upright. He rose from a crouch as he came out from under the sloping rafters near the trap, and when he had taken four steps forward, Harry fired twice at him.

The first shot missed, but the second hit low in the chest.

Worthy was flung backward, went down hard on the bare boards of the attic floor. He lay there for a moment, twitching, then sat up, coughed once, and got to his feet.

Blood glistened all over the front of his torn white shirt. He had been hit hard, yet he had recovered in seconds.

Harry remembered what Sam had said about how the Coltranes had refused to stay dead. *Go for the data processor.*

He aimed for Worthy's head and fired twice again, but at that distance – about twenty-five feet – and at that angle, shooting up from the floor, he couldn't hit anything. He hesitated with only four rounds left in the pistol's clip.

Another man was climbing through the trap.

Harry shot at him, trying to drive him back down.

He came on, unperturbed.

Three rounds in the pistol.

Keeping his distance, Dr. Worthy said, 'Harry, we're not here to harm you. I don't know what you've heard or *how* you've heard about the project, but it isn't a bad thing . . .'

His voice trailed off, and he cocked his head as if to listen to the inhuman cries that filled the night outside. A peculiar look of longing, visible even in the dim wash of light from the open trap, crossed Worthy's face.

He shook himself, blinked, and remembered that he had been trying to sell his elixir to a reluctant customer. 'Not a bad thing at all, Harry. Especially for you. You'll walk again, Harry, walk as well as anyone. You'll be whole again. Because after the Change, you'll be able to heal yourself. You'll be free of paralysis.'

'No, thanks. Not at that price.'

'What price, Harry?' Worthy asked, spreading his arms, palms up. 'Look at me. What price have I paid?'

'Your soul?' Harry said.

A third man was coming up the ladder.

The second man was listening to the ululant cries that came in through the attic vents. He gritted his teeth, ground them together forcefully, and blinked very fast. He raised his hands and covered his face with them, as if he were suddenly anguished.

Worthy noticed his companion's situation. 'Vanner, are you all right?'

Vanner's hands . . . *changed.* His wrists swelled and grew gnarly with bone, and his fingers lengthened, all in a couple of seconds. When he took his hands from his face, his jaw was thrusting forward like that of a werewolf in mid-transformation. His shirt tore at the seams as his body reconfigured itself. He snarled, and teeth flashed.

'. . . *need,*' Vanner said, '. . . *need, need, want, need* . . .'

'No!' Worthy shouted.

The third man, who had just come out of the trap, rolled onto the floor, changing as he did so, flowing into a vaguely insectile but thoroughly repulsive form.

Before he quite knew what he was doing, Harry emptied the .38 at the insect-thing, pitched it away, snatched the .45 revolver off the board floor beside him, also fired three rounds from that, evidently striking the thing's brain at least once. It kicked, twitched, fell back down through the trap, and did not clamber upward again.

Vanner had undergone a complete lupine metamorphosis and seemed to have patterned himself after something that he had seen in a movie, because he looked familiar to Harry, as if Harry had seen that same movie, though he could not quite remember it. Vanner shrieked in answer to the creatures whose cries pealed through the night outside.

Tearing frantically at his clothes, as if the pressure of them against his skin was driving him mad, Worthy was changing into a beast quite different from either Vanner or the third man. Some grotesque physical incarnation of his own mad desires.

Harry had only three rounds left, and he had to save the last one for himself.

• 30 •

Earlier, after surviving the ordeal in the culvert, Sam had promised himself that he would learn to accept failure, which had been all well and good until now, when failure was again at hand.

He could *not* fail, not with both Chrissie and Tessa depending on him. If no other opportunity presented itself, he would at least leap at Shaddack the moment before he believed the man was ready to pull the trigger.

Judging that moment might be difficult. Shaddack looked and sounded insane. The way his mind was short-circuiting, he might pull the trigger in the middle of one of those high, quick, nervous, boyish laughs, without any indication that the moment had come.

'Get off your stool,' he said to Sam.

'What?'

'You heard me, dammit, get off your stool. Lay on the floor, over there, or I'll make you sorry, I sure will, I'll make you very sorry.' He gestured with the muzzle of the shotgun. 'Get off your stool and lay on the floor *now*.'

Sam didn't want to do it because he knew Shaddack was separating him from Chrissie and Tessa only to shoot him.

He hesitated, then slid off the stool because there was nothing else he could do. He moved between two lab benches, to the open area that Shaddack had indicated.

'Down,' Shaddack said. 'I want to see you down there on the floor, groveling.'

Dropping to one knee, Sam slipped a hand into an inner pocket of his leather jacket, fished out the metal loid that he had used to pop the lock at the Coltranes' house, and flicked it away from himself, with the same snap of his wrist that he would have used to toss a playing card at a hat.

The loid sailed low across the floor, toward the windows, until it clattered through the rungs of a stool and clinked off the base of a marble lab bench.

The madman swung the Remington toward the sound.

With a shout of rage and determination, Sam came up fast and threw himself at Shaddack.

· 31 ·

Tessa grabbed Chrissie and hustled her away from the struggling men, to the wall beside the hall door. They crouched there, where she hoped they would be out of the line of fire.

Sam had come up under the shotgun before Shaddack could swing back from the distraction. He grabbed the barrel with his left hand and Shaddack's wrist with his weakened right hand, and pressed him backward, pushing him off balance, slamming him against another lab bench.

When Shaddack cried out, Sam snarled with satisfaction, as if *he* might turn into something that howled in the night.

Tessa saw him ram a knee up between Shaddack's legs, hard into his crotch. The tall man screamed.

'All *right*, Sam!' Chrissie said approvingly.

As Shaddack gagged and spluttered and tried to double over in an involuntary reaction to the pain in his damaged privates, Sam tore the shotgun out of his hands and stepped back—

—and a man in a police uniform came into the room from the chemistry storage closet, carrying a shotgun of his own. 'No! Drop your weapon. Shaddack is *mine*.'

· 32 ·

The thing that had been Vanner moved toward Harry, growling low in its throat, drooling yellowish saliva. Harry fired twice, struck it both times, but failed to kill it. The gaping wounds seemed to close up before his eyes.

One round left.

'. . . *need, need* . . .'

Harry put the barrel of the .45 in his mouth, pressed the muzzle against his palate, gagging on the hot steel.

The hideous, wolfish thing loomed over him. The swollen head was three times as big as it ought to have been, out of proportion to its body. Most of the head was mouth, and most of the mouth was teeth, not even the teeth of a wolf but the inward-curving teeth of a shark. Vanner had not been satisfied to model himself entirely after just one of nature's predators, but wanted to make of himself something more murderous and efficiently destructive than anything nature had contemplated.

When Vanner was only three feet from him, leaning in to bite, Harry pulled the gun out of his own mouth, said, 'Hell, no,' and shot the damn thing in the head. It toppled back, landed with a crash, and stayed down.

Go for the data-processor.

Elation swept through Harry, but it was short-lived. Worthy had completed his transformation and seemed to have been thrown into a frenzy by the carnage in the room and the escalating shrieks that came through the attic vents from the world beyond. He turned his lantern eyes on Harry, and in them was a look of unhuman hunger.

No more bullets.

• 33 •

Sam was squarely under the cop's gun, with no room to maneuver. He had to drop the Remington that he'd taken off Shaddack.

'I'm on your side,' the cop repeated.

'No one's on our side,' Sam said.

Shaddack was gasping for breath and trying to stand up straight. He regarded the officer with abject terror.

With the coldest premeditation Sam had ever seen, with no hint of emotion whatsoever, not even anger, the cop turned his 20-gauge shotgun on Shaddack, who was no longer a threat to anyone, and fired four rounds. As if punched by a giant, Shaddack flew backward over two stools and into the wall.

The cop threw the gun aside and moved quickly to the dead man. He tore open the sweat-suit jacket that Shaddack wore under his coat and ripped loose a strange object, a largish rectangular medallion, that had hung from a gold chain around the man's neck.

Holding up that curious artifact, he said, 'Shaddack's dead. His heartbeat isn't being broadcast any more, so Sun is even now putting the final program into effect. In half a minute or so we'll all know peace. Peace at last.'

At first Sam thought the cop was saying they were all going to die, that the thing in his hand was going to kill them, that it was a bomb or something. He backed quickly toward the door and saw that Tessa evidently had the same expectation. She had pulled Chrissie up from where they'd been crouching, and had opened the door.

But if there was a bomb, it was a silent one, and the radius of its small explosion remained within the police officer. Suddenly his face contorted. Between clenched teeth, he said, 'God.' It was not an exclamation but a plea or perhaps an inadequate description of something he had just seen, for in that moment he fell down dead from no cause that Sam could see.

When they stepped out through the back door by which they had entered, the first thing Sam noticed was that the night had fallen silent. The shrill cries of the shape-changers no longer echoed across the fogbound town.

The keys were in the van's ignition.

'You drive,' he told Tessa.

His wrist was swollen worse than ever. It was throbbing so hard that each pulse of pain reverberated through every fiber of him.

He settled in the passenger seat.

Chrissie curled in his lap, and he wrapped his arms around her. She was uncharacteristically silent. She was exhausted, on the verge of collapse, but Sam knew the cause of her silence was more profound than weariness.

Tessa slammed her door and started the engine. She didn't have to be told where to go.

On the drive to Harry's place, they discovered that the streets were littered with the dead, not the corpses of ordinary men and women but – as their headlights revealed beyond a doubt – of creatures out of a painting by Hieronymus Bosch, twisted and phantasmagorical forms. She drove slowly, maneuvering around them, and a couple of times she had to pull up on the sidewalk to get past a pack of them that had gone down together, apparently felled by the same unseen force that had dropped the policeman back at Central.

Shaddack's dead. His heartbeat isn't being broadcast any more, so Sun is even now putting the final program into effect . . .

After a while Chrissie lowered her head against Sam's chest and would not look out the windshield.

Sam kept telling himself that the fallen creatures were phantoms, that no such things could have actually come into existence, either by the application of the highest of high technology or by sorcery. He expected them to vanish every time a shroud of fog briefly obscured them, but when the fog moved off again, they were still huddled on the pavement, sidewalks, and lawns.

Immersed in all that horror and ugliness, he could not believe that he had been so foolish as to pass years of precious life in gloom, unwilling to see the beauty of the world. He'd been a singular fool. When the dawn came he would never thereafter fail to look upon a flower and appreciate the wonder of it, the beauty that was beyond man's abilities of creation.

'Tell me now?' Tessa asked as they pulled within a block of Harry's redwood house.

'Tell you what?'

'What you saw. Your near-death experience. What did you see on the Other Side that scared you so?'

He laughed shakily. 'I was an idiot.'

'Probably,' she said. 'Tell me and let me judge.'

'Well, I can't tell you exactly. It was more an *understanding* than a seeing, a spiritual rather than visual perception.'

'So what did you understand?'

'That we go on from this world,' he said. 'That there's either life for us on another plane, one life after another on an endless series of planes . . . or that we live again on this plane, reincarnate. I'm not sure which, but I felt it deeply, *knew* it when I reached the end of that tunnel and saw the light, that brilliant light.'

She glanced at him. 'And *that's* what terrified you?'

'Yes.'

'That we live again?'

'Yes. Because I found life so bleak, you see, just a series of tragedies, just pain. I'd lost the ability to appreciate the beauty of life, the joy, so I didn't want to die and have to start in all over again, not any sooner than absolutely necessary. At least in *this* life I'd become hardened, inured to the pain, which gave me an advantage over starting out as a child again in some new incarnation.'

'So your fourth reason for living wasn't technically a fear of death,' she said.

'I guess not.'

'It was a fear of having to live again.'

'Yes.'

'And now?'

He thought a moment. Chrissie stirred in his lap. He stroked her damp hair. At last he said, 'Now, I'm *eager* to live again.'

• 35 •

Harry heard noises downstairs – the elevator, then someone in the third-floor bedroom. He tensed, figuring two miracles were one too many to hope for, but then he heard Sam calling to him from the bottom of the ladder.

'Here, Sam! Safe! I'm okay.'

A moment later Sam climbed into the attic.

'Tessa? Chrissie?' Harry asked anxiously.

'They're downstairs. They're both all right.'

'Thank God.' Harry let out a long breath, as if it had been pent up in him for hours. 'Look at these brutes, Sam.'

'Rather not.'

'Maybe Chrissie was right about alien invaders after all.'

'Something stranger,' Sam said.

'What?' Harry said as Sam knelt beside him and gingerly pushed Worthy's mutated body off his legs.

'Damned if I know,' Sam said. 'Not even sure I want to know.'

'We're entering an age when we make our own reality, aren't we? Science is giving us that ability, bit by bit. Used to be only madmen could do that.'

Sam said nothing.

Harry said, 'Maybe making our own reality isn't wise. Maybe the natural order is the best one.'

'Maybe. On the other hand, the natural order could do with some perfecting here and there. I guess we've got to try. We just have to hope to God that the men who do the tinkering aren't like Shaddack. You okay, Harry?'

'Pretty good, thanks.' He smiled. 'Except, of course, I'm still a cripple. See this hulking thing that was Worthy? He was leaning in to rip my throat out, I had no more bullets, he had his claws at my neck, and then he just fell dead, bang. Is that a miracle or what?'

'Been a miracle all over town,' Sam said. 'They all seemed to have died when Shaddack died . . . linked somehow. Come on, let's get you down from here, out of this mess.'

'They killed Moose, Sam.'

'The hell they did. Who do you think Chrissie and Tessa are fussing over downstairs?'

Harry was stunned. 'But I heard—'

'Looks like maybe somebody kicked him in the head. He's got this bloody, skinned-up spot along one side of his skull. Might've been knocked unconscious, but he doesn't seem to've suffered a concussion.'

• 36 •

Chrissie rode in the back of the van with Harry and Moose, with Harry's good arm around her and Moose's head in her lap. Slowly she began to feel better. She was not herself, no, and maybe she never would feel like her old self again, but she was better.

They went to the park at the head of Ocean Avenue, at the east end of town. Tessa drove right up over the curb, bouncing them around, and parked on the grass.

Sam opened the rear doors of the van so Chrissie and Harry could sit side by side in their blankets and watch him and Tessa at work.

Braver than Chrissie would have been, Sam went into the nearby residential areas, stepping over and around the dead things, and jump-started cars that were parked along the streets. One by one, he and Tessa drove them into the park and arranged them in a huge ring, with the engines running and the headlights pointing in toward the middle of the circle.

Sam said that people would be coming in helicopters, even in the fog, and that the circle of light would mark a proper landing pad for them. With twenty cars, their headlights all blazing on high beam, the inside of that ring was as bright as noon.

Chrissie liked the brightness.

Even before the landing pad was fully outlined, a few people began to appear in the streets, live people, and not weird looking at all, without fangs and stingers and claws, standing fully erect – altogether normal, judging by appearances. Of course, Chrissie had learned that you could never confidently judge anyone by appearances because they could be anything inside; they could be something inside that would astonish even the editors of the *National Enquirer*. You couldn't even be sure of your own parents.

But she couldn't think about that.

She didn't *dare* think about what had happened to her folks. She knew that what little hope she still held for their salvation was probably false hope, but she wanted to hold on to it for just a while longer, anyway.

The few people who appeared in the streets began to gravitate toward the park while Tessa and Sam finished pulling the last few cars into the ring. They all looked dazed. The closer they approached, the more uneasy Chrissie became.

'They're all right,' Harry assured her, cuddling her with his one good arm.

'How can you be sure?'

'You can see they're scared shitless. Oops. Maybe I shouldn't say "shitless," teach you bad language.'

' "Shitless" is okay,' she said.

Moose made a mewling sound and shifted in her lap. He probably had the kind of headache that only karate experts usually got from smashing bricks with their heads.

'Well,' Harry said, 'look at them – they're scared plenty bad, which probably tags them as our kind. You never saw one of those others acting scared, did you?'

She thought about it a moment. 'Yeah. I did. That cop who shot Mr. Shaddack at the school. He was scared. He had more fear in his eyes, a lot more, than I've ever seen in anybody else's.'

'Well, these people are all right, anyway,' Harry told her as the dazed stragglers approached the van. 'They're some of the ones who were scheduled to be converted before midnight, but nobody got around to them. Must be others in their houses, barricaded in there, afraid to come out, think the whole world's gone crazy, probably think aliens are on the loose, like you thought. Besides, if these people were more of those shape-changers, they wouldn't be staggering up to us so hesitantly. They'd have loped right up the hill, leaped in here, and eaten our noses, plus whatever other parts of us they consider to be delicacies.'

That explanation appealed to her, even made her smile thinly, and she relaxed a little.

But just a second later, Moose jerked his burly head off her lap, yipped, and scrambled to his feet.

Outside, the people approaching the van cried out in surprise and fear, and Chrissie heard Sam say, 'What the blazing *hell?*'

She threw aside her warm blankets and scrambled out of the back of the van to see what was happening.

Behind her, alarmed in spite of the reassurances that he had just given her, Harry said, 'What is it? What's wrong?'

For a moment she wasn't sure what had startled everyone, but then she saw the animals. They swarmed through the park – scores of mice, a few hungry rats, cats of all descriptions, half a dozen dogs, and maybe a couple of dozen squirrels that had scampered down from the trees. More mice and rats and cats were racing out of the mouths of the streets that intersected Ocean Avenue, pouring up that main drag, running pell-mell, frenzied, cutting through the park and angling over to the county road. They reminded her of something she'd read about once, and she only had to stand there for a few seconds, watching them pour by her, before she remembered: lemmings. Periodically, when the lemming population became too great in a particular area, the little creatures ran and ran, straight toward the sea, into the surf, and drowned themselves. All these animals were acting like lemmings, tearing off in the same direction, letting nothing stand in their way, drawn by nothing apparent and therefore evidently following an inner compulsion.

Moose jumped out of the van and joined the fleeing multitudes.

'Moose, no!' she shouted.

He stumbled, as if he had tripped over the cry that she had flung after him.

He looked back, then snapped his head toward the county road again, as if he had been jerked by an invisible chain. He took off at top speed.

'Moose!'

He stumbled once more and actually fell this time, rolled, and scrambled onto his feet.

Somehow Chrissie knew that the image of lemmings was apt, that these animals were rushing to their graves, though away from the sea, toward some other and more hideous death that was a part of all the rest that had happened in Moonlight Cove. If she did not stop Moose, they would never see him again.

The dog ran.

She sprinted after him.

She was bone weary, burnt out, aching in every muscle and joint, and afraid, but she found the strength and will to pursue the Labrador because no one else seemed to understand that he and the other animals were running toward death. Tessa and Sam, smart as they were, didn't get it. They were just standing, gaping at the spectacle. So Chrissie tucked her arms against her sides, pumped her legs, and ran for all she was worth, picturing herself as Chrissie Foster, World's Youngest Olympic Marathon Champion, pounding around the course, with thousands cheering her from the sidelines. *'Chrissie, Chrissie, Chrissie, Chrissie . . .'* And as she ran, she screamed at Moose to stop, because every time he heard his name, he faltered, hesitated, and she gained a little ground on him. Then they were through the park, and she nearly fell in the deep ditch alongside the county road, leaped it at the last instant, not because she saw it in time but because she had her eye on Moose and saw *him* leap something. She landed perfectly, not losing a stride. The next time Moose faltered in response to his name, she was on him, grabbing at him, seizing his collar. He growled and nipped at her, and she said, 'Moose,' in such a way as to shame him. That was the only time he tried to bite her but, Lord, he strained mightily to pull loose. Hanging on to him took everything she had, and he even dragged her, big as she was, about fifty or sixty feet along the road. His big paws scrabbled at the blacktop as he struggled to follow the wave of small animals that was receding into the night and fog.

By the time the dog calmed down enough to be willing to go back toward the park, Tessa and Sam joined Chrissie. 'What's happening?' Sam asked.

'They're all running to their deaths,' Chrissie said. 'I just couldn't let Moose go with them.'

'To their deaths? How do you know?'

'I don't know. But . . . what else?'

They stood on the dark and foggy road for a moment, looking after the animals, which had vanished into the blackness.

Tessa said, 'What else indeed?'

• 37 •

The fog was thinning, but visibility was still no more than about a quarter of a mile.

Standing with Tessa in the middle of the circle of cars, Sam heard the choppers shortly after ten o'clock, before he saw their lights. Because the mist distorted sound, he actually could not tell from which direction they were approaching, but he figured they were coming in from the south, along the coast, staying a couple of hundred yards out to sea, where there were no hills to worry about in the fog. Packed with the most sophisticated instruments, they could virtually fly blind. The pilots would be wearing night-vision goggles, coming in under five hundred feet in respect of the poor weather.

Because the FBI maintained tight relationships with the armed services, especially the Marines, Sam pretty much knew what to expect. This would be a Marine Reconnaissance force composed of the standard elements required by such a situation: one CH-46 helicopter carrying the recon team itself – probably twelve men detached from a Marine Assault Unit – accompanied by two Cobra gunships.

Turning around, looking in every direction, Tessa said, 'I don't see them.'

'You won't,' Sam said. 'Not until they're almost on top of us.'

'They fly without lights?'

'No. They're equipped with blue lights, which can't be seen well from the ground, but which give them a damned good view through their night-vision goggles.'

Ordinarily, when responding to a terrorist threat, the CH-46 – called the 'Sea Knight,' officially, but referred to as 'The Frog' by grunts – would have gone, with its Cobra escorts, to the north end of town. Three fire teams, composed of four men each, would have disembarked and swept through Moonlight Cove from north to south, checking out the situation, rendez-vousing at the other end for evacuation as necessary.

But because of the message Sam had sent to the Bureau before Sun's links to the outside world had been cut off, and because the situation did not involve terrorists and was, in fact, singularly strange, SOP was discarded for a bolder approach. The choppers overflew the town repeatedly, descending to within twenty or thirty feet of the treetops. At times their strange bluish-green lights were visible, but nothing whatsoever could be seen of their shape or size; because of their Fiberglas blades, which were much quieter than the old metal blades that once had been used, the choppers at times seemed to glide silently in the distance and might have been alien craft from a far world even stranger than this one.

At last they hovered near the circle of light in the park.

They did not put down at once. With the powerful rotors flinging the fog away, they played a searchlight over the people in the park who stood outside the illuminated landing pad, and they spent minutes examining the grotesque bodies in the street.

Finally, while the Cobras remained aloft, the CH-46 gentled down almost reluctantly in the ring of cars. The men who poured from the chopper were toting automatic weapons, but otherwise they didn't look like soldiers because, thanks to Sam's message, they were dressed in biologically secure white suits, carrying their own air-supply tanks on their backs. They might have been astronauts instead of Marines.

Lieutenant Ross Dalgood, who looked baby-faced behind the faceplate of his helmet, came straight to Sam and Tessa, gave his name and rank, and greeted Sam by name, evidently because he'd been shown a photograph before his mission had gotten off the ground. 'Biological hazard, Agent Booker?'

'I don't think so,' Sam said, as the chopper blades cycled down from a hard rhythmic cracking to a softer, wheezing chug.

'But you don't know?'

'I don't know,' he admitted.

'We're the advance,' Dalgood said. 'Lots more on the way – regular Army and your Bureau people are coming in by highway. Be here soon.'

The three of them – Dalgood, Sam, and Tessa – moved between two of the encircling cars, to one of the dead things that lay on a sidewalk bordering the park.

'I didn't believe what I saw from the air,' Dalgood said.

'Believe it,' Tessa said.

'What the hell?' Dalgood said.

Sam said, 'Boogeymen.'

• 38 •

Tessa worried about Sam. She and Chrissie and Harry returned to Harry's house at one in the morning, after being debriefed three times by men in decontamination suits. Although they had terrible nightmares, they managed to get a few hours' sleep. But Sam was gone all night. He had not returned by the time they finished breakfast at eleven o'clock Wednesday morning.

'He may think he's indestructible,' she said, 'but he's not.'

'You care about him,' Harry said.

'Of course I care about him.'

'I mean *care* about him.'

'Well . . . I don't know.'

'I know.'

'I know too,' Chrissie said.

Sam returned at one o'clock, grimy and gray-faced. She'd made up the spare bed with fresh sheets, and he tumbled into it still half dressed.

She sat in a chair by the bed, watching him sleep. Occasionally he groaned and thrashed. He called her name and Chrissie's – and sometimes Scott's – as if he had lost them and was wandering in search of them through a dangerous and desolate place.

Bureau men in decontamination suits came for him at six o'clock, Wednesday evening, after he'd slept less than five hours. He went away for the rest of that night.

By then all the bodies, in their multitudinous biologies, had been collected from where they had fallen, tagged, sealed in plastic bags, and put into cold storage for the attention of the pathologists.

That night Tessa and Chrissie shared the same bed. Lying in the half-dark room, where a towel had been thrown over a lamp to make a night light, the girl said, 'They're gone.'

'Who?'

'My mom and dad.'

'I think they are.'

'Dead.'

'I'm sorry, Chrissie.'

'Oh, I know. I know you are. You're very nice.' Then for a while she cried in Tessa's arms.

Much later, nearer sleep, she said, 'You talked to Sam a little. Did he say if they figured out . . . about those animals last night . . . where they were all running to?'

'No,' Tessa said. 'They haven't got a clue yet.'

'That spooks me.'

'Me too.'

'I mean, that they haven't got a clue.'

'I know,' Tessa said. 'That's what I mean too.'

<h2 style="text-align:center">• 39 •</h2>

By Thursday morning, teams of Bureau technicians and outside consultants from the private sector had pored through enough of the Moonhawk data in Sun to determine that the project had dealt strictly with the implantation of a nonbiological control mechanism that had resulted in profound physiological changes in the victims. No one yet had the glimmer of an idea as to how it worked, as to how the microspheres could have resulted in such radical metamorphoses, but they were certain no bacterium, virus, or other engineered organism had been involved. It was purely a matter of machines.

The Army troops, enforcing the quarantine against news-media interlopers and civilian curiosity-seekers, still had their work to do, but they were grateful to be able to strip out of their hot and clumsy decon suits. So were the hundreds of scientists and Bureau agents who were bivouacked throughout town.

Although Sam would surely be returning in the days ahead, he and Tessa and Chrissie were cleared for evacuation early Friday morning. A sympathetic court, with the counsel of a host of federal and state officials, had already granted Tessa temporary custody of the girl. They said see-you-soon to Harry, not goodbye, and were lifted out by one of the Bureau's Bell JetRanger executive helicopters.

To keep on-site researchers from having their views colored by sensationalistic and inaccurate news accounts, a media blackout was in force in Moonlight Cove, and Sam did not fully realize the impact of the Moonhawk story until they flew over the Army roadblock near the interstate. Hundreds of press vehicles were strewn along the road and parked in fields. The pilot flew low enough for Sam to see all the cameras turned upward to shoot them as they passed over the mob.

'It's almost as bad on the county route, north of Holliwell Road,' the chopper pilot said, 'where they set up the other block. Reporters from all over the world, sleeping on the ground 'cause they don't want to go away to some motel and wake up to find that Moonlight Cove was opened to the press while they were snoozing.'

'They don't have to worry,' Sam said. 'It's not going to be opened to the press – or to anyone but researchers – for weeks.'

The JetRanger transported them to San Francisco International Airport, where they had reservations for three seats on a PSA flight south to Los Angeles. In the terminal, scanning the news racks, Sam read a couple of headlines:

ARTIFICIAL INTELLIGENCE BEHIND COVE TRAGEDY
SUPERCOMPUTER RUNS AMOK

That was nonsense, of course. New Wave's supercomputer, Sun, was not an artificial intelligence. No such thing had yet been built anywhere on earth, though legions of scientists were racing to be the first to father a true, thinking, electronic mind. Sun had not run amok; it had only served, as all computers do.

Paraphrasing Shakespeare, Sam thought: The fault lies not in our technology but in ourselves.

These days, however, people blamed screwups in the system on computers – just as, centuries ago, members of less sophisticated cultures had blamed the alignment of celestial bodies.

Tessa quietly pointed out another headline:

SECRET PENTAGON EXPERIMENT BEHIND
MYSTERIOUS DISASTER

The Pentagon was a favorite Boogeyman in some circles, almost beloved for its real and imagined evils because believing it was the root of all malevolence made life simpler and easier to understand. To those who felt that way, the Pentagon was almost the bumbling old Frankenstein monster in his clodhopper shoes and too-small black suit, scary but understandable, perverse and to be shunned yet comfortably predictable and preferable to consideration of worse and more complex villains.

Chrissie pulled from the rack a rare special edition of a major national tabloid, filled with stories about Moonlight Cove. She showed them the main headline:

ALIENS LAND ON CALIFORNIA COAST
RAVENOUS FLESH-EATERS SACK TOWN

They looked at one another solemnly for a moment, then smiled. For the first time in a couple of days, Chrissie laughed. It was not a hearty laugh, just a chuckle, and there might have been a touch of irony in it that was too sharp for an eleven-year-old girl, not to mention a trace of melancholy, but it *was* a laugh. Hearing her laugh, Sam felt better.

• 40 •

Joel Ganowicz, of United Press International, had been on the perimeter of Moonlight Cove, at one roadblock or another, since early Wednesday morning. He bunked in a sleeping bag on the ground, used the woods as a toilet, and paid an unemployed carpenter from Aberdeen Wells to bring meals to him. Never in his career had he been so committed to a story, willing to rough it to this extent. And he was not sure why. Yes, certainly, it was the biggest story of the decade, maybe bigger than that. But why did he feel this need to hang in there, to learn every scrap of the truth? Why was he obsessed? His behavior was a puzzle to him.

He wasn't the only one obsessed.

Though the story of Moonlight Cove had been leaked to the media in piecemeal fashion over three days and had been explored in detail during a four-hour press conference on Thursday evening, and though reporters had exhaustively interviewed many of the two hundred survivors, no one had had enough. The singular horror of the deaths of the victims – and the number, nearly three thousand, many times the number at Jonestown – stunned newspaper and TV audiences no matter how often they heard the specifics. By Friday morning the story was hotter than ever.

Yet Joel sensed that it wasn't even the grizliness of the facts or the spectacular statistics that gripped the public interest. It was something deeper than that.

At ten o'clock Friday morning, Joel was sitting on his bedroll in a field alongside the county route, just ten yards away from the police checkpoint north of Holliwell, basking in a surprisingly warm October morning and thinking about that very thing. He was starting to believe that maybe this news hit home hard because it was about not just the relatively modern conflict of man and machine but about the eternal human conflict, since time immemorial, between responsibility and irresponsibility, between civilization and savagery, between contradictory human impulses toward faith and nihilism.

Joel was still thinking about that when he got up and started to walk. Somewhere along the way he stopped thinking about much of anything, but he started walking more briskly.

He was not alone. Others at the roadblock, fully half the two hundred who had been waiting there, turned almost as one and walked east into the fields with sudden deliberation, neither hesitating along the way nor wandering in parabolic paths, but cutting straight up across a sloped meadow, over scrub-covered hills, and through a stand of trees.

The walkers startled those who had not felt the abrupt call to go for a stroll, and some reporters tagged along for a while, asking questions, then shouting questions. None of the walkers answered.

Joel was possessed by a feeling that there was a place he must go to, a special place, where he would never again have to worry about anything, a place where all would be provided, where he would have no need to worry about the future. He didn't know what that magic place looked like, but he knew he'd recognize it when he saw it. He hurried forward excitedly, compelled, *drawn*.

Need.

The protean thing in the basement of the Icarus Colony was in the grip of need. It had not died when the other children of Moonhawk had perished, for the microsphere computer within it had dissolved when it had first sought the freedom of utter shapelessness; it had not been able to receive the microwave-transmitted death order from Sun. Even if the command had been received, it would not have been acted upon, for the cellar-dwelling creature had no heart to stop.

Need.

Its need was so intense that it pulsed and writhed. This need was more profound than mere desire, more terrible than any pain.

Need.

Mouths had opened all over its surface. The thing called out to the world around it in a voice that seemed silent but was not, a voice that spoke not to the ears of its prey but to their minds.

And they were coming.

Its needs would soon be fulfilled.

———

Colonel Lewis Tarker, commanding officer at the Army field headquarters in the park at the eastern end of Ocean Avenue, received an urgent call from Sergeant Sperlmont, who was in charge of the county-route roadblock. Sperlmont reported losing six of his twelve men when they just walked off like zombies, with maybe a hundred reporters who were in the same strange condition.

'Something's up,' he told Tarker. 'This isn't over yet, sir.'

———

Tarker immediately got hold of Oren Westrom, the Bureau man who was heading the investigation into Moonhawk and with whom all of the military aspects of the operation had to be coordinated.

'It isn't over,' Tarker told Westrom. 'I think those walkers are even weirder than Sperlmont described them, weird in some way he can't quite convey. I know him, and he's more spooked than he thinks he is.'

———

Westrom, in turn, ordered the Bureau's JetRanger into the air. He explained the situation to the pilot, Jim Lobbow, and said, 'Sperlmont's going to have some of his men track them on the ground, see where the hell they're going – and why. But in case that gets difficult, I want you spotting from the air.'

'On my way,' Lobbow said.

'You filled up on fuel recently?'

'Tanks are brimming.'

'Good.'

———

Nothing worked for Jim Lobbow but flying a chopper.

He had been married three times, and every marriage had ended in divorce. He'd lived with more women than he could count; even without the pressure of marriage weighing him down, he could not sustain a relationship. He had one child, a son, by his second marriage, but he saw the boy no more than three times a year, never for longer than a day at a time. Though he'd been brought up in the Catholic Church, and though all his brothers and sisters were regulars at Mass, that did not work for Jim. Sunday always seemed to be the only morning he could sleep in, and when he considered going to a weekday service it seemed like too much trouble. Though he dreamed of being an entrepreneur, every small business he started seemed doomed to failure; he was repeatedly startled to find how much work went into a business, even one that seemed designed for absentee management, and sooner or later it always became too much trouble.

But nobody was a better chopper pilot than Jim Lobbow. He could take one up in weather that grounded everyone else, and he could set down or pick up in any terrain, any conditions.

He took the JetRanger up at Westrom's orders and swung out over the county-route roadblock, getting there in no time because the day was blue and clear, and the roadblock was just a mile and a quarter from the park where he kept the chopper. On the ground, a handful of regular Army troops, still at the barricade, were waving him due east, up into the hills.

Lobbow went where they told him, and in less than a minute he found the walkers toiling busily up scrub-covered hills, scuffing their shoes, tearing their clothes, but scrambling forward in a frenzy. It was definitely weird.

A funny buzzing filled his head. He thought something was wrong with his radio headphones, and he pulled them off for a moment, but that wasn't it. The buzzing didn't stop. Actually it wasn't a buzzing at all, not a sound, but a *feeling*.

And what do I mean by that? he wondered.

He tried to shrug it off.

The walkers were circling east-southeast as they went, and he flew ahead of them, looking for some landmark, anything unusual toward which they might be headed. He came almost at once to the decaying Victorian house, the tumbledown barn, and the collapsed outbuildings.

Something about the place drew him.

He circled it once, twice.

Though it was a complete dump, he suddenly had the crazy idea that he would be happy there, free, with no worries any more, no ex-wives nagging at him, no child-support to pay.

Over the hills to the northwest, the walkers were coming, all hundred or more of them, not walking any more but running. They stumbled and fell but got up and ran again.

And Jim knew why they were coming. He circled over the house again, and it was the most appealing place he had ever seen, a source of surcease. He wanted that freedom, that release, more than he had ever wanted anything in his life. He took the JetRanger up in a steep climb, leveled out, swooped south, then west, then north, then east, coming all the way around again, back toward the house, the wonderful house, he had to be there, had to go there, had to go, and he took the chopper straight in through the front porch, directly at the door that hung open and half off its hinges, through the wall, plowing straight into the heart of the house, burying the chopper in the heart—

———

Need.

The creature's many mouths sang of its need, and it knew that momentarily its needs would be met. It throbbed with excitement.

Then vibrations. Hard vibrations. Then heat.

It did not recoil from the heat, for it had surrendered all the nerves and complex biological structures required to register pain.

The heat had no meaning for the beast – except that heat was not food and therefore did not fulfill its needs.

Burning, dwindling, it tried to sing the song that would draw what it required, but the roaring flames filled its mouths and soon silenced it.

═══════

Joel Ganowicz found himself standing two hundred feet from a ramshackle house that had exploded in flames. It was a tremendous blaze, fire shooting a hundred feet into the clear sky, black smoke beginning to billow up, the old walls of the place collapsing in upon themselves with alacrity, as if eager to give up the pretense of usefulness. The heat washed over him, forcing him to squint and back away, even though he was not particularly close to it. He couldn't understand how a little dry wood could burn that intensely.

He realized that he could not remember how the fire had started. He was just suddenly *there*, in front of it.

He looked at his hands. They were abraded and filthy.

The right knee was torn out of his corduroys, and his Rockports were badly scuffed.

He looked around and was startled to see scores of people in his same condition, tattered and dirty and dazed. He couldn't remember how he had gotten there, and he definitely didn't recall setting out on a group hike.

The house sure was burning, though. Wouldn't be a stick of it left, just a cellarful of ashes and hot coals.

He frowned and rubbed his forehead.

Something had happened to him. Something . . . He was a reporter, and his curiosity was gradually reasserting itself. Something had happened, and he ought to find out what. Something disturbing. *Very* disturbing. But at least it was over now.

He shivered.

• 41 •

When they entered the house in Sherman Oaks, the music on Scott's stereo, upstairs, was turned so loud that the windows were vibrating.

Sam climbed the steps to the second floor, motioning for Tessa and Chrissie to follow. They were reluctant, probably embarrassed, feeling out of place, but he was not certain he could do what had to be done if he went up there alone.

The door to Scott's room was open.

The boy was lying on his bed, wearing black jeans and a black denim shirt. His feet were toward the headboard, his head at the foot of the mattress, propped up on pillows, so he could stare at all of the posters on the wall behind the bed: black-metal rockers wearing leather and chains, some of them with bloody hands, some with bloody lips as if they were vampires who had just fed, others holding skulls, one of them french-kissing a skull, another holding out cupped hands filled with glistening maggots.

Scott didn't hear Sam enter. With the music at that volume, he wouldn't have heard a thermonuclear blast in the adjacent bathroom.

At the stereo Sam hesitated, wondering if he was doing the right thing. Then he listened to the bellowed words of the number on the machine, backed up by iron slabs of guitar chords. It was a song about killing your parents, about drinking their blood, then 'taking the gaspipe escape.' Nice. Oh, very nice stuff. That decided him. He punched a button and cut off the CD in midplay.

Startled, Scott sat straight up in bed. 'Hey!'

Sam took the CD out of the player, dropped it on the floor, and ground it under his heel.

'Hey, Christ, what the hell are you doing?'

Forty or fifty CDs, mostly black-metal albums, were stored in open-front cases on a shelf above the stereo. Sam swept them to the floor.

'Hey, come on,' Scott said, 'what're you, nuts?'

'Something I should've done long ago.'

Noticing Tessa and Chrissie, who stood just outside the door, Scott said, 'Who the hell are they?'

Sam said, 'They the hell are friends.'

Really working himself into a rage, all lathered up, the boy said, 'What the fuck are they doing here, man?'

Sam laughed. He was feeling almost giddy. He wasn't sure why. Maybe because he was finally doing something about this situation, assuming responsibility for it. He said, 'They the fuck are with me.' And he laughed again.

He felt sorry that he had exposed Chrissie to this, but then he looked at her and saw that she was not only unshaken but giggling. He realized that all the angry and bad words in the world couldn't hurt her, not after what she had endured. In fact, after what they'd all seen in Moonlight Cove, Scott's teenage nihilism *was* funny and even sort of innocent, altogether ridiculous.

Sam stood on the bed and began to tear the posters off the wall, and Scott started screaming at him, opening up full volume, a real tantrum this time. Sam finished with those posters he could reach only from the bed, got down, and turned toward those on another wall.

Scott grabbed him.

Gently, Sam pushed the boy aside and clawed at the other posters.

Scott struck him.

Sam took the blow, then looked at him.

Scott's face was brilliant red, his nostrils dilated, his eyes bulging with hatred.

Smiling, Sam embraced him in a bear hug.

At first Scott clearly didn't understand what was happening. He thought his father was just making a grab for him, going to punish him, so he tried to pull away. But suddenly it dawned on him – Sam could *see* it dawn on him – he was being hugged, his old man was for God's sake embracing him, and in front of people – strangers. When that realization hit him, the boy *really* began to struggle, twisting and thrashing, pushing hard against Sam, desperate to escape, because this didn't fit into his belief in a loveless world, especially if he started to respond.

That was it, yes, damn, Sam understood now. That was the reason behind Scott's alienation. A fear that he'd respond to love, respond and be spurned . . . or find the responsibility of commitment too much to bear.

In fact, for a moment, the boy met his father's love with love of his own, hugged him tight. It was as if the real Scott, the kid hidden under the layers of hipness and cynicism, had peeked through and smiled. Something good remained in him, good and pure, something that could be salvaged.

But then the boy began to curse Sam in more explicit and colorful terms than he had used previously. Sam only hugged him harder, closer, and now Sam began to tell him that he loved him, desperately loved him, told him not the way that he had told him he loved him on the telephone when he had called him from Moonlight Cove on Monday night, not with any degree of reservation occasioned by his own sense of hopelessness, because he *had* no sense of hopelessness any more. This time, when he told Scott that he loved him, he spoke in a voice cracking with emotion, told him again and again, demanded that his love be heard.

Scott was crying now, and Sam was not surprised to find that he was crying, too, but he didn't think they were crying for the same reason yet, because the boy was still struggling to get away, his energy depleted, but still struggling. So Sam held on to him and talked to him: 'Listen, kid, you're going to care about me, one way or the other, sooner or later. Oh, yes. You're going to know that I care about you, and then you're going to care about me, and not just me, no, you're going to care about yourself, too, and it's not going to stop there, either, hell, no, you're going to find out you can care about a lot of people, that it feels good to care. You're going to care about that woman standing there in the doorway, and you're going to care about that little girl, you're going to care about her like you'd care about a sister, you're going to *learn*, you're going to get the damn machine out of you and learn to be loved and to love. There's a guy going to come visit us, a guy who's got one good hand and no good legs, and *he* believes life is worth living. Maybe he's going to stay a while, see how he likes it, see how he feels about it, 'cause maybe he can show you what I was too slow to show you – that it's good, life's good. And this guy's got a dog, what a dog, you're going to love that dog, probably the dog first.' Sam laughed and held fast to Scott. 'You can't say "Get outta my face" to a dog and expect him to listen or care, he won't get out of your face, so you'll have to love him first. But then you'll get around to loving me, because that's what I'm going to be – a dog, just a smiling old dog, padding around the place, hanging on, impervious to insult, an old dog.'

Scott had stopped struggling. He was probably just exhausted. Sam was sure that he had not really gotten through the boy's rage. Hadn't more than scratched the surface. Sam had let an evil into their lives, the evil of self-indulgent despair, which he transmitted to the boy, and now rooting it out would be a hard job. They had a long way to go, months of struggle, maybe even years, lots of hugging, lots of holding on tight and not letting go.

Looking over Scott's shoulder, he saw that Tessa and Chrissie had stepped into the room. They were crying too. In their eyes he saw an awareness that matched his, a recognition that the battle for Scott had only begun.

But it *had* begun. That was the wonderful thing. It *had* begun.

THE BAD PLACE

Teachers often affect our lives more than they realize. From high school days to the present, I have had teachers to whom I will remain forever indebted, not merely because of what they taught me, but because they provided the invaluable examples of dedication, kindness, and generosity of spirit that have given me an unshakable faith in the basic goodness of the human species. This book is dedicated to:

David O'Brien
Thomas Doyle
Richard Forsythe
John Bodnar
Carl Campbell
Steve and Jean Hernishin

Every eye sees its own special vision;
every ear hears a most different song.
In each man's troubled heart, an incision
would reveal a unique, shameful wrong.

Stranger fiends hide here in human guise
than reside in the valleys of Hell.
But goodness, kindness and love arise
in the heart of the poor beast, as well.

The Book of Counted Sorrows

• 1 •

The night was becalmed and curiously silent, as if the alley were an abandoned and windless beach in the eye of a hurricane, between the tempest past and the tempest coming. A faint scent of smoke hung on the motionless air, although no smoke was visible.

Sprawled facedown on the cold pavement, Frank Pollard did not move when he regained consciousness; he waited in the hope that his confusion would dissipate. He blinked, trying to focus. Veils seemed to flutter within his eyes. He sucked deep breaths of the cool air, tasting the invisible smoke, grimacing at the acrid tang of it.

Shadows loomed like a convocation of robed figures, crowding around him. Gradually his vision cleared, but in the weak yellowish light that came from far behind him, little was revealed. A large trash dumpster, six or eight feet from him, was so dimly outlined that for a moment it seemed ineffably strange, as though it were an artifact of an alien civilization. Frank stared at it for a while before he realized what it was.

He did not know where he was or how he had gotten there. He could not have been unconscious longer than a few seconds, for his heart was pounding as if he had been running for his life only moments ago.

Fireflies in a windstorm . . .

That phrase took flight through his mind, but he had no idea what it meant. When he tried to concentrate on it and make sense of it, a dull headache developed above his right eye.

Fireflies in a windstorm . . .

He groaned softly.

Between him and the dumpster, a shadow among shadows moved, quick and sinuous. Small but radiant green eyes regarded him with icy interest.

Frightened, Frank pushed up onto his knees. A thin, involuntary cry issued from him, almost less like a human sound than like the muted wail of a reed instrument.

The green-eyed observer scampered away. A cat. Just an ordinary black cat.

Frank got to his feet, swayed dizzily, and nearly fell over an object that had been on the blacktop beside him. Gingerly he bent down and picked it up: a flight bag made of supple leather, packed full, surprisingly heavy. He supposed it was his. He could not remember. Carrying the bag, he tottered to the dumpster and leaned against its rusted flank.

Looking back, he saw that he was between rows of what seemed to be two-story stucco apartment buildings. All of the windows were black. On both sides, the tenants' cars were pulled nose-first into covered parking stalls. The queer yellow glow, sour and sulfurous, almost more like the product of a gas flame than the luminescence of an incandescent electric bulb, came from a streetlamp at the end of the block, too far away to reveal the details of the alleyway in which he stood.

As his rapid breathing slowed and as his heartbeat decelerated, he abruptly realized that he did not know who he was. He knew his name – Frank Pollard – but that was all. He did not know how old he was, what he did for a living, where he had come from, where he was going, or why. He was so startled by his predicament that for a moment his breath caught in his throat; then his heartbeat soared again, and he let his breath out in a rush.

Fireflies in a windstorm . . .

What the hell did that mean?

The headache above his right eye corkscrewed across his forehead.

He looked frantically left and right, searching for an object or an aspect of the scene that he might recognize, anything, an anchor in a world that was suddenly too strange. When the night offered nothing to reassure him, he turned his quest inward, desperately seeking something familiar in himself, but his own memory was even darker than the passageway around him.

Gradually he became aware that the scent of smoke had faded, replaced by a vague but nauseating smell of rotting garbage in the dumpster. The stench of decomposition filled him with thoughts of death, which seemed to trigger a vague recollection that he was on the run from someone – or something – that wanted to kill him. When he tried to recall why he was fleeing, and from whom, he could not further illuminate that scrap of memory; in fact, it seemed more an awareness based on instinct than a genuine recollection.

A puff of wind swirled around him. Then calm returned, as if the dead night was trying to come back to life but had managed just one shuddering breath. A single piece of wadded paper, swept up by that insufflation, clicked along the pavement and scraped to a stop against his right shoe.

Then another puff.

The paper whirled away.

Again the night was dead calm.

Something was happening. Frank sensed that these short-lived whiffs of wind had some malevolent source, ominous meaning.

Irrationally, he was sure that he was about to be crushed by a great weight. He looked up into the clear sky, at the bleak and empty blackness of space and at the malignant brilliance of the distant stars. If something was descending toward him, Frank could not see it.

The night exhaled once more. Harder this time. Its breath was sharp and dank.

He was wearing running shoes, white athletic socks, jeans, and a long-sleeved blue-plaid shirt. He had no jacket, and he could have used one. The air was not frigid, just mildly bracing. But a coldness was in him, too, a gelid fear, and he shivered uncontrollably between the cool caress of the night air and that inner chill.

The gust of wind died.

Stillness reclaimed the night.

Convinced that he had to get out of there – and fast – he pushed away from the dumpster. He staggered along the alley, retreating from the end of the block where the streetlamp glowed, into darker realms, with no destination in mind, driven only by the sense that this place was dangerous and that safety, if indeed safety could be found, lay elsewhere.

The wind rose again, and with it, this time, came an eerie whistling, barely audible, like the distant music of a flute made of some strange bone.

Within a few steps, as Frank became surefooted and as his eyes adapted to the murky night, he arrived at a confluence of passageways. Wrought-iron gates in pale stucco arches lay to his left and right.

He tried the gate on the left. It was unlocked, secured only by a simple gravity latch. The hinges squeaked, eliciting a wince from Frank, who hoped the sound had not been heard by his pursuer.

By now, although no adversary was in sight, Frank had no doubt that he was the object of a chase. He knew it as surely as a hare knew when a fox was in the field.

The wind huffed again at his back, and the flutelike music, though barely audible and lacking a discernible melody, was haunting. It pierced him. It sharpened his fear.

Beyond the black iron gate, flanked by feathery ferns and bushes, a walkway led between a pair of two-story apartment buildings. Frank followed it into a rectangular courtyard somewhat revealed by low-wattage security lamps at each end. First-floor apartments opened onto a covered promenade; the doors of the second-floor units were under the tile roof of an iron-railed balcony. Lightless windows faced a swath of grass, beds of azaleas and succulents, and a few palms.

A frieze of spiky palm-frond shadows lay across one palely illuminated wall, as motionless as if they were carved on a stone entablature. Then the mysterious flute warbled softly again, the reborn wind huffed harder than before, and the shadows danced, danced. Frank's own distorted, dark reflection whirled briefly over the stucco, among the terpsichorean silhouettes, as he hurried across the courtyard. He found another walkway, another gate, and ultimately the street on which the apartment complex faced.

It was a side street without lampposts. There, the reign of the night was undisputed.

The blustery wind lasted longer than before, churned harder. When the gust ended abruptly, with an equally abrupt cessation of the unmelodic flute, the night seemed to have been left in a vacuum, as though the departing turbulence had taken with it every wisp of breathable air. Then Frank's ears popped as if from a sudden altitude change; as he rushed across the deserted street toward the cars parked along the far curb, air poured in around him again.

He tried four cars before finding one unlocked, a Ford. Slipping behind the wheel, he left the door open to provide some light.

He looked back the way he had come.

The apartment complex was dead-of-the-night still. Wrapped in darkness. An ordinary building yet inexplicably sinister.

No one was in sight.

Nevertheless, Frank knew someone was closing in on him.

He reached under the dashboard, pulled out a tangle of wires, and hastily hot-wired the engine before realizing that such a larcenous skill suggested a life outside of the law. Yet he didn't feel like a thief. He had no sense of guilt and no antipathy for – or fear of – the police. In fact, at the moment, he would have welcomed a cop to help him deal with whoever or whatever was on his tail. He felt not like a criminal, but like a man who had been on the run for an exhaustingly long time, from an implacable and relentless enemy.

As he reached for the handle of the open door, a brief pulse of pale blue light washed over him, and the driver's-side windows of the Ford exploded. Tempered glass showered into the rear seat, gummy and minutely fragmented. Since the front door was not closed, that window didn't spray over him; instead, most of it fell out of the frame, onto the pavement.

Yanking the door shut, he glanced through the gap where the glass had been, toward the gloom-enfolded apartments, saw no one.

Frank threw the Ford in gear, popped the brake, and tramped hard on the accelerator. Swinging away from the curb, he clipped the rear bumper of the car parked in front of him. A brief peal of tortured metal rang sharply across the night.

But he was still under attack: A scintillant blue light, at most one second in duration, lit up the car; over its entire breadth the windshield crazed with thousands of jagged lines, though it had been struck by nothing he could see. Frank averted his face and squeezed his eyes shut just in time to avoid being blinded by flying fragments. For a moment he could not see where he was going, but he didn't let up on the accelerator, preferring the danger of collision to the greater risk of braking and giving his unseen enemy time to reach him. Glass rained over him, spattered across the top of his bent head; luckily, it was safety glass, and none of the fragments cut him.

He opened his eyes, squinting into the gale that rushed through the now empty windshield frame. He saw that he'd gone half a block and had reached the intersection. He whipped the wheel to the right, tapping the brake pedal only lightly, and turned onto a more brightly lighted thoroughfare.

Like Saint Elmo's fire, sapphire-blue light glimmered on the chrome, and when the Ford was halfway around the corner, one of the rear tires blew. He had heard no gunfire. A fraction of a second later, the other rear tire blew.

The car rocked, slewed to the left, began to fishtail.

Frank fought the steering wheel.

Both front tires ruptured simultaneously.

The car rocked again, even as it glided sideways, and the sudden collapse of the front tires compensated for the leftward slide of the rear end, giving Frank a chance to grapple the spinning steering wheel into submission.

Again, he had heard no gunfire. He didn't know why all of this was happening – yet he did.

That was the truly frightening part: On some deep subconscious level he *did* know what was happening, what strange force was swiftly destroying the car around him, and he also knew that his chances of escaping were poor.

A flicker of twilight blue . . .

The rear window imploded. Gummy yet prickly wads of safety glass flew past him. Some smacked the back of his head, stuck in his hair.

Frank made the corner and kept going on four flats. The sound of flapping rubber, already shredded, and the grinding of metal wheel rims could be heard even above the roar of the wind that buffeted his face.

He glanced at the rearview mirror. The night was a great black ocean behind him, relieved only by widely spaced streetlamps that dwindled into the gloom like the lights of a double convoy of ships.

According to the speedometer, he was doing thirty miles an hour just after coming out of the turn. He tried to push it up to forty in spite of the ruined tires, but something clanged and clinked under the hood, rattled and whined, and the engine coughed, and he could not coax any more speed out of it.

When he was halfway to the next intersection, the headlights either burst or winked out. Frank couldn't tell which. Even though the streetlamps were widely spaced, he could see well enough to drive.

The engine coughed, then again, and the Ford began to lose speed. He didn't brake for the stop sign at the next intersection. Instead he pumped the accelerator but to no avail.

Finally the steering failed too. The wheel spun uselessly in his sweaty hands.

Evidently the tires had been completely torn apart. The contact of the steel wheel rims with the pavement flung up gold and turquoise sparks.

Fireflies in a windstorm . . .

He still didn't know what that meant.

Now moving about twenty miles an hour, the car headed straight toward the righthand curb. Frank tramped the brakes, but they no longer functioned.

The car hit the curb, jumped it, grazed a lamppost with a sound of sheet metal kissing steel, and thudded against the bole of an immense date palm in front of a white bungalow. Lights came on in the house even as the final crash was echoing on the cool night air.

Frank threw the door open, grabbed the leather flight bag from the seat beside him, and got out, shedding fragments of splintery safety glass.

Though only mildly cool, the air chilled his face because sweat trickled down from his forehead. He could taste salt when he licked his lips.

A man had opened the front door of the bungalow and stepped onto the porch. Lights flicked on at the house next door.

Frank looked back the way he had come. A thin cloud of luminous sapphire dust seemed to blow through the street. As if shattered by a tremendous surge of current, the bulbs in the streetlamps exploded along the two blocks behind him, and shards of glass, glinting like ice, rained on the blacktop. In the resultant gloom, he thought he saw a tall, shadowy figure, more than a block away, coming after him, but he could not be sure.

To Frank's left, the guy from the bungalow was hurrying down the walk toward the palm tree where the Ford had come to rest. He was talking, but Frank wasn't listening to him.

Clutching the leather satchel, Frank turned and ran. He was not sure what he was running from, or why he was so afraid, or where he might hope to find a haven, but he ran nonetheless because he knew that if he stood there only a few seconds longer, he would be killed.

· **2** ·

The windowless rear compartment of the Dodge van was illuminated by tiny red, blue, green, white, and amber indicator bulbs on banks of electronic surveillance equipment but primarily by the soft green glow from the two computer screens, which made that claustrophobic space seem like a chamber in a deep-sea submersible.

Dressed in a pair of Rockport walking shoes, beige cords, and a maroon sweater, Robert Dakota sat on a swivel chair in front of the twin video display terminals. He tapped his feet against the floor-boards, keeping time, and with his right hand he happily conducted an unseen orchestra.

Bobby was wearing a headset with stereo earphones and with a small microphone suspended an inch or so in front of his lips. At the moment he was listening to Benny Goodman's 'One O'Clock Jump,' the primo version of Count Basie's classic swing composition, six and a half minutes of heaven. As Jess Stacy took up another piano chorus and as Harry James launched into the brilliant trumpet stint that led to the most famous rideout in swing history, Bobby was deep into the music.

But he was also acutely aware of the activity on the display terminals. The one on the right was linked, via microwave, with the computer system at the Decodyne Corporation, in front of which his van was parked. It revealed what Tom Rasmussen was up to in those offices at 1:10 Thursday morning: no good.

One by one, Rasmussen was accessing and copying the files of the software-design team that had recently completed Decodyne's new and revolutionary wordprocessing program, 'Whizard'. The Whizard files carried well-constructed lockout instructions – electronic drawbridges, moats, and ramparts. Tom Rasmussen was an expert in computer security, however, and there was no fortress that he could not penetrate, given enough time. Indeed, if Whizard had not been developed on a secure in-house computer system with no links to the outside world, Rasmussen would have slipped into the files from beyond the walls of Decodyne, via a modem and telephone line.

Ironically, he had been working as the night security guard at Decodyne for five weeks, having been hired on the basis of elaborate – and nearly convincing – false papers. Tonight he had breached Whizard's final defenses. In a while he would walk out of Decodyne with a packet of floppy diskettes worth a fortune to the company's competitors.

'One O'Clock Jump' ended.

Into the microphone Bobby said, 'Music stop.'

That vocal command cued his computerized compact-disk system to switch off, opening the headset for communication with Julie, his wife and business partner.

'You there, babe?'

From her surveillance position in a car at the farthest end of the parking lot behind Decodyne, she had been listening to the same music through her own headset. She sighed. 'Did Vernon Brown ever play better trombone than the night of the Carnegie concert?'

'What about Krupa on the drums?'

'Auditory ambrosia. And an aphrodisiac. The music makes me want to go to bed with you.'

'Can't. Not sleepy. Besides, we're being private detectives, remember?'

'I like being lovers better.'

'We don't earn our daily bread by making love.'

'I'd pay you,' she said.

'Yeah? How much?'

'Oh, in daily-bread terms . . . half a loaf.'

'I'm worth a whole loaf.'

Julie said, 'Actually, you're worth a whole loaf, two croissants, and a bran muffin.'

She had a pleasing, throaty, and altogether sexy voice that he loved to listen to, especially through headphones, when she sounded like an angel whispering in his ears. She would have been a marvelous big-band singer if she had been around in the 1930s and '40s – and if she had been able to carry a tune. She was a great swing dancer, but she couldn't croon worth a damn; when she was in the mood to sing along with old recordings by Margaret Whiting or the Andrews Sisters or Rosemary Clooney or Marion Hutton, Bobby had to leave the room out of respect for the music.

She said, 'What's Rasmussen doing?'

Bobby checked the second video display, to his left, which was linked to Decodyne's interior security cameras. Rasmussen thought he had overridden the cameras and was unobserved; but they had been watching him for the last few weeks, night after night, and recording his every treachery on videotape.

'Old Tom's still in George Ackroyd's office, at the VDT there.' Ackroyd was project director for Whizard. Bobby glanced at the other display, which duplicated what Rasmussen was seeing on Ackroyd's computer screen. 'He just copied the last Whizard file onto diskette.'

Rasmussen switched off the computer in Ackroyd's office.

Simultaneously the linked VDT in front of Bobby went blank.

Bobby said, 'He's finished. He's got it all now.'

Julie said, 'The worm. He must be feeling smug.'

Bobby turned to the display on his left, leaned forward, and watched the black-and-white image of Rasmussen at Ackroyd's terminal. 'I think he's grinning.'

'We'll wipe that grin off his face.'

'Let's see what he does next. Want to make a bet? Will he stay in there, finish his shift, and waltz out in the morning – or leave right now?'

'Now,' Julie said. 'Or soon. He won't risk getting caught with the floppies. He'll leave while no one else is there.'

'No bet. I think you're right.'

The transmitted image on the monitor flickered, rolled, but Rasmussen did not get out of Ackroyd's chair. In fact, he slumped back, as if exhausted. He yawned and rubbed his eyes with the heels of his hands.

'He seems to be resting, gathering his energy,' Bobby said.

'Let's have another tune while we wait for him to move.'

'Good idea.' He gave the CD player the start-up cue – 'Begin music' – and was rewarded with Glenn Miller's 'In the Mood.'

On the monitor, Tom Rasmussen rose from the chair in Ackroyd's dimly lighted office. He yawned again, stretched, and crossed the room to the big windows that looked down on Michaelson Drive, the street on which Bobby was parked.

If Bobby had slipped forward, out of the rear of the van and into the driver's compartment, he probably would have been able to see Rasmussen standing up there at the second-floor window, silhouetted by the glow of Ackroyd's desk lamp, staring out at the night. He stayed where he was, however, satisfied with the view on the screen.

Miller's band was playing the famous 'In the Mood' riff, again and again, gradually fading away, almost disappearing entirely but . . . *now* blasting back at full power to repeat the entire cycle.

In Ackroyd's office, Rasmussen finally turned from the window and looked up at the security camera that was mounted on the wall near the ceiling. He seemed to be staring straight at Bobby, as if aware of being watched. He moved a few steps closer to the camera, smiling.

Bobby said, 'Music stop,' and the Miller band instantly fell silent. To Julie, he said, 'Something strange here . . .'

'Trouble?'

Rasmussen stopped just under the security camera, still grinning up at it. From the pocket of his uniform shirt, he withdrew a folded sheet of typing paper, which he opened and held toward the lens. A message had been printed in bold black letters: GOODBYE, ASSHOLE.

'Trouble for sure,' Bobby said.

'How bad?'

'I don't know.'

An instant later he did know: Automatic weapon fire shattered the night – he could hear the clatter even with his earphones on – and armor-piercing slugs tore through the walls of the van.

Julie evidently picked up the gunfire through her headset. 'Bobby, no!'

'Get the hell out of there, babe! Run!'

Even as he spoke, Bobby tore free of the headset and dived off his chair, lying as flat against the floorboards as he could.

• 3 •

Frank Pollard sprinted from street to street, from alley to alley, sometimes cutting across the lawns of the dark houses. In one backyard a large black dog with yellow eyes barked and snapped at him all the way to the board fence, briefly snaring one leg of his pants as he clambered over that barrier. His heart was pounding painfully, and his throat was hot and raw because he was sucking in great draughts of the cool, dry air through his open mouth. His legs ached. As if made of iron, the flight bag pulled on his right arm, and with each lunging step that he took, pain throbbed in his wrist and shoulder socket. But he did not pause and did not glance back, because he felt as if something monstrous was at his heels, a creature that never required rest and that would turn him to stone with its gaze if he dared set eyes upon it.

In time he crossed an avenue, devoid of traffic at that late hour, and hurried along the entrance walk to another apartment complex. He went through a gate into another courtyard, this one centered by an empty swimming pool with a cracked and canted apron.

The place was lightless, but Frank's vision had adapted to the night, and he could see well enough to avoid falling into the drained pool. He was searching for shelter. Perhaps there was a communal laundry room where he could force the lock and hide.

He had discovered something else about himself as he fled his unknown pursuer: He was thirty or forty pounds overweight and out of shape. He desperately needed to catch his breath – and think.

As he was hurrying past the doors of the ground-floor units, he realized that a couple of them were standing open, sagging on ruined hinges. Then he saw that cracks webbed some windows, holes pocked a few, and other panes were missing altogether. The grass was dead, too, as crisp as ancient paper, and the shrubbery was withered; a seared palm tree leaned at a precarious angle. The apartment complex was abandoned, awaiting a wrecking crew.

He came to a set of crumbling concrete stairs at the north end of the courtyard, glanced back. Whoever . . . whatever was following him was still not in sight. Gasping, he climbed to the second-floor balcony and moved from one apartment to another until he found a door ajar. It was warped; the hinges were stiff, but they worked without much noise. He slipped inside, pushing the door shut behind him.

The apartment was a well of shadows, oil-black and pooled deep. Faint ash-gray light outlined the windows but provided no illumination to the room.

He listened intently.

The silence and darkness were equal in depth.

Cautiously, Frank inched toward the nearest window, which faced the balcony and courtyard. Only a few shards of glass remained in the frame, but lots of fragments crunched and clinked under his feet. He trod carefully, both to avoid cutting a foot and to make as little noise as possible.

At the window he halted, listened again.

Stillness.

As if it was the gelid ectoplasm of a slothful ghost, a sluggish current of cold air slid inward across the few jagged points of the glass that had not already fallen from the frame.

Frank's breath steamed in front of his face, pale ribbons of vapor in the gloom.

The silence remained unbroken for ten seconds, twenty, thirty, a full minute. Perhaps he had escaped.

He was just about to turn away from the window when he heard footsteps outside. At the far end of the courtyard. On the walkway that led in from the street. Hard-soled shoes rang against the concrete, and each footfall echoed hollowly off the stucco walls of the surrounding buildings.

Frank stood motionless and breathed through his mouth, as if the stalker could be counted on to have the hearing of a jungle cat.

When he entered the courtyard from the entrance walkway, the stranger halted. After a long pause he began to move again; though the overlapping echoes made sounds deceptive, he seemed to be heading slowly north along the apron of the pool, toward the same stairs by which Frank, himself, had climbed to the second floor of the apartment complex.

Each deliberate, metronomic footfall was like the heavy tick of a headsman's clock mounted on a guillotine railing, counting off the seconds until the appointed hour of the blade's descent.

• 4 •

As if alive, the Dodge van shrieked with every bullet that tore through its sheet-metal walls, and the wounds were inflicted not one at a time but by the score, with such relentless fury the assault had to involve at least two machine guns. While Bobby Dakota lay flat on the floor, trying to catch God's attention with fervent heaven-directed prayers, fragments of metal rained down on him.

One of the computer screens imploded, then the other terminal, too, and all the indicator lights went out, but the interior of the van was not entirely dark; showers of amber and green and crimson and silver sparks erupted from the damaged electronic units as one steel-jacketed round after another pierced equipment housings and shattered circuit boards. Glass fell on him, too, and splinters of plastic, bits of wood, scraps of paper; the air was filled with a virtual blizzard of debris. But the noise was the worst of it; in his mind he saw himself sealed inside a great iron drum, while half a dozen big bikers, stoned on PCP, pounded on the outside of his prison with tire irons, really huge bikers with massive muscles and thick necks and coarse peltlike beards and wildly colorful Death's-head tattoos on their arms – hell, tattoos on their *faces* – guys as big as Thor, the Viking god, but with blazing, psychotic eyes.

Bobby had a vivid imagination. He had always thought that was one of his best qualities, one of his strengths. But he could not simply imagine his way out of this mess.

With every passing second, as slugs continued to crash into the van, he grew more astonished that he had not been hit. He was pressed to the floor, as tight as a carpet, and he tried to imagine that his body was only a quarter of an inch thick, a target with an incredibly low profile, but he still expected to get his ass shot off.

He had not anticipated the need for a gun; it wasn't that kind of case. At least it hadn't *seemed* to be that kind of case. A .38 revolver was in the van glovebox, well beyond his reach, which did not cause him a lot of frustration, actually, because a single handgun against a pair of automatic weapons was not much use.

The gunfire stopped.

After that cacophony of destruction, the silence was so profound, Bobby felt as if he had gone deaf.

The air reeked of hot metal, overheated electronic components, scorched insulation – and gasoline. Evidently the van's tank had been punctured. The engine was still chugging, and a few sparks spat out of the shattered equipment surrounding Bobby, and his chances of escaping a flash fire were a whole lot worse than his chances of winning fifty million bucks in the state lottery.

He wanted to get the hell out of there, but if he burst out of the van, they might be waiting with machine guns to cut him down. On the other hand, if he continued to hug the floor in the darkness, counting on them to give him up for dead without checking on him, the Dodge might flare like a campfire primed with starter fluid, toasting him as crisp as a marshmallow.

He had no difficulty imagining himself stepping out of the van and being hit immediately by a score of bullets, jerking and twitching in a spasmodic death dance across the blacktop street, like a broken marionette jerked around on tangled strings. But he found it even easier to imagine his skin peeling off in the fire, flesh bubbling and smoking, hair *whooshing* up like a torch, eyes melting, teeth turning coal-black as flames seared his tongue and followed his breath down his throat to his lungs.

Sometimes a vivid imagination was definitely a curse.

Suddenly the gasoline fumes became so heavy that he had trouble drawing breath, so he started to get up.

Outside, a car horn began to blare. He heard a racing engine drawing rapidly nearer.

Someone shouted, and a machine gun opened fire again.

Bobby hit the floor, wondering what the hell was going on, but as the car with the blaring horn drew nearer, he realized what must be happening: Julie. Julie was happening. Sometimes she was like a natural force; she happened the way a storm happened, the way lightning happened, abruptly crackling down a dark sky. He had told her to get out of there, to save herself, but she had not listened to him; he wanted to kick her butt for being so bullheaded, but he loved her for it too.

· 5 ·

Sidling away from the broken window, Frank tried to time his steps to those of the man in the courtyard below, with the hope that any noise he made, treading on glass, would be covered by his unseen enemy's advance. He figured that he was in the living room of the apartment, that it was pretty much empty except for whatever detritus had been left behind by the last tenants or had blown through the missing windows, and indeed he made it across that chamber and into a hallway in relative silence, without colliding with anything.

He hurriedly felt his way along the hall, which was as black as a predator's lair. It smelled of mold and mildew and urine. He passed the entrance to a room, kept going, turned right through the next doorway, and shuffled to another broken window. This one had no splinters of glass left in the frame, and it did not face the courtyard but looked onto a lamplit and deserted street.

Something rustled behind him.

He turned, blinking blindly at the gloom, and almost cried out.

But the sound must have been made by a rat scurrying along the floor, close to the wall, across dry leaves or bits of paper. Just a rat.

Frank listened for footsteps, but if the stalker was still homing in on him, the hollow heel clicks of his approach were completely muffled by the walls that now intervened.

He looked out the window again. The dead lawn lay below, as dry as sand and twice as brown, offering little cushion. He dropped the leather flight bag, which landed with a thud. Wincing at the prospect of the leap, he climbed onto the sill, crouching in the broken-out window, hands braced against the frame, where for a moment he hesitated.

A gust of wind ruffled his hair and coolly caressed his face. But it was a normal draught, nothing like the preternatural whiffs of wind that, earlier, had been accompanied by the unearthly and unmelodic music of a distant flute.

Suddenly, behind Frank, a blue flash pulsed out of the living room, down the hall, and through the doorway. The strange tide of light was trailed closely by an explosion and a concussion wave that shook the walls and seemed to churn the air into a more solid substance. The front door had been blasted to pieces; he heard chunks of it raining down on the floor of the apartment a couple of rooms away.

He jumped out of the window, landed on his feet. But his knees gave way, and he fell flat on the dead lawn.

At that same moment a large truck turned the corner. Its cargo bed had slat sides and a wooden tailgate. The driver smoothly shifted gears and drove past the apartment house, apparently unaware of Frank.

He scrambled to his feet, plucked the satchel off the barren lawn, and ran into the street. Having just rounded the corner, the truck was not moving fast, and Frank managed to grab the tailgate and pull himself up, one-handed, until he was standing on the rear bumper.

As the truck accelerated, Frank looked back at the decaying apartment complex. No mysterious blue light glimmered at any of the windows; they were all as black and empty as the sockets of a skull.

The truck turned right at the next corner, moving away into the sleepy night.

Exhausted, Frank clung to the tailgate. He would have been able to hold on better if he had dropped the leather flight bag, but he held fast to it because he suspected that its contents might help him to learn who he was and from where he had come and from what he was running.

<h2 style="text-align:center">• 6 •</h2>

Cut and run! Bobby actually thought she would cut and run when trouble struck – *'Get the hell out of there, babe! Run!'* – would cut and run just because he told her to, as if she was an obedient little wifey, not a full-fledged partner in the agency, not a damned good investigator in her own right, just a token backup who couldn't take the heat when the furnace kicked on. Well, to hell with that.

In her mind she could see his lovable face – merry blue eyes, pug nose, smattering of freckles, generous mouth – framed by thick honey-gold hair that was mussed (as was most often the case) like that of a small boy who had just gotten up from a nap. She wanted to bop his pug nose just hard enough to make his blue eyes water, so he'd have no doubt how the cut-and-run suggestion annoyed her.

She had been on surveillance behind Decodyne, at the far end of the corporate parking lot, in the deep shadows under a massive Indian laurel. The moment Bobby signaled trouble, she started the Toyota's engine. By the time she heard gunfire over the earphones, she had shifted gears, popped the emergency brake, switched on the headlights, and jammed the accelerator toward the floor.

At first she kept the headset on, calling Bobby's name, trying to get an answer from him, hearing only the most godawful ruckus from his end. Then the set went dead; she couldn't hear anything at all, so she pulled it off and threw it into the backseat.

Cut and run! Damn him!

When she reached the end of the last row in the parking lot, she let up on the accelerator with her right foot, simultaneously tapping the brake pedal with her left foot, finessing the small car into a slide, which carried it onto the access road that led around the big building. She turned the steering wheel into the slide, then gave the heap some gas again even before the back end had stopped skidding and shuddering. The tires barked, and the engine shrieked, and with a rattle-squeak-twang of tortured metal, the car leaped forward.

They were shooting at Bobby, and Bobby probably wasn't even able to shoot back, because he was lax about carrying a gun on every job; he went armed only when it seemed that the current business was likely to involve violence. The Decodyne assignment had looked peaceable enough; sometimes industrial espionage could turn nasty, but the bad guy in this case was Tom Rasmussen, a computer nerd and a greedy son of a bitch, clever as a dog reading Shakespeare on a high wire, with a record of theft via computer but with no blood on his hands. He was the high-tech equivalent of a meek, embezzling bank clerk – or so he had seemed.

But Julie was armed on *every* job. Bobby was the optimist; she was the pessimist. Bobby expected people to act in their own best interests and be reasonable, but Julie half expected every apparently normal person to be, in secret, a crazed psychotic. A Smith & Wesson .357 Magnum was held by a clip to the back of the glovebox lid, and an Uzi – with two spare, thirty-round magazines – lay on the other front seat. From what she had heard on the earphones before they'd gone dead, she was going to need that Uzi.

The Toyota virtually *flew* past the side of Decodyne, and she wheeled hard left, onto Michaelson Drive, almost rising onto two wheels, almost losing control, but not quite. Ahead, Bobby's Dodge was parked at the curb in front of the building, and another van – a dark blue Ford – was stopped in the street, doors open wide.

Two men, who had evidently been in the Ford, were standing four or five yards from the Dodge, chopping the hell out of it with automatic weapons, blasting away with such ferocity that they seemed not to be after the man inside but to have some bizarre personal grudge against the Dodge itself. They stopped firing, turned toward her as she came out of the driveway onto Michaelson, and hurriedly jammed fresh magazines into their weapons.

Ideally, she would close the hundred-yard gap between herself and the men, pull the Toyota sideways in the street, slip out, and use the car as cover to blow out the tires on their Ford and pin them down until police arrived. But she didn't have time for all of that. They were already raising the muzzles of their weapons.

She was unnerved at how lonely the night streets looked at this hour in the heart of metropolitan Orange County, barren of traffic, washed by the urine-yellow light of the sodium-vapor streetlamps. They were in an area of banks and office buildings, no residences, no restaurants or bars within a couple of blocks. It might as well have been a city on the moon, or a vision of the world after it had been swept by an Apocalyptic disease that had left only a handful of survivors.

She didn't have time to handle the two gunmen by the book, and she could not count on help from any quarter, so she would have to do what they least expected: play kamikaze, use her *car* as a weapon.

The instant she had the Toyota fully under control, she pressed the accelerator tight to the floorboards and rocketed straight at the two bastards. They opened fire, but she was already slipping down in the seat and leaning sideways a little, trying to keep her head below the dashboard and still hold the wheel relatively steady. Bullets snapped and whined off the car. The windshield burst. A second later Julie hit one of the gunmen so hard that the impact snapped her head forward, against the wheel, cutting her forehead, snapping her teeth together forcefully enough to make her jaw ache; even as pain needled through her face, she heard the body bounce off the front bumper and slam onto the hood.

With blood trickling down her forehead and dripping from her right eye-brow, Julie jabbed at the brakes and sat up at the same time. She was confronted by a man's wide-eyed corpse jammed in the frame of the empty windshield. His face was in front of the steering wheel – teeth chipped, lips torn, chin slashed, cheek battered, left eye missing – and one of his broken legs was inside the car, hooked down over the dashboard.

Julie found the brake pedal and pumped it. With the sudden drop in speed, the dead man was dislodged. His limp body rolled across the hood, and when the car slid to a shaky halt, he vanished over the front end.

Heart racing, blinking to keep the stinging blood from blurring the vision in her right eye, Julie snatched the Uzi from the seat beside her, shoved open the door, and rolled out, moving fast and staying low.

The other gunman was already in the blue Ford van. He gave it gas before remembering to shift out of park, so the tires screamed and smoked.

Julie squeezed off two short bursts from the Uzi, blowing out both tires on her side of the van.

But the gunman didn't stop. He shifted gears at last and tried to drive past her on two ruined tires.

The guy might have killed Bobby; now he was getting away. He would prob-ably never be found if Julie didn't stop him. Reluctantly she swung the Uzi higher and emptied the magazine into the side window of the van. The Ford accelerated, then suddenly slowed and swung to the right, at steadily diminish-ing speed, in a long arc that carried it to the far curb, where it came to a halt with a jolt.

No one got out.

Keeping an eye on the Ford, Julie leaned into her car, plucked a spare magazine from the seat, and reloaded the Uzi. She approached the idling van cautiously and pulled open the door, but caution was not required because the man behind the wheel was dead. Feeling a little sick, she reached in and switched off the engine.

Briefly, as she turned from the Ford and hurried toward the bullet-riddled Dodge, the only sounds she could hear were the soughing of a faint breeze in the lush corporate landscaping that flanked the street, punctuated by the gentle hiss and rattle of palm fronds. Then she also heard the idling engine of the Dodge, simultaneously smelled gasoline, and shouted, 'Bobby!'

Before she reached the white van, the back doors creaked open, and Bobby came out, shedding twists of metal, chunks of plastic, bits of glass, wood chips, and scraps of paper. He was gasping, no doubt because the gasoline fumes had driven most of the breathable air out of the Dodge's rear quarters.

Sirens rose in the distance.

Together they quickly walked away from the van. They had gone only a few steps when orange light flared and flames rose in a *wooooosh* from the gasoline pooled on the pavement, enveloping the vehicle in bright shrouds. They hur-ried beyond the corona of intense heat that surrounded the Dodge and stood for a moment, blinking at the wreckage, then at each other.

The sirens were drawing nearer.

He said, 'You're bleeding.'

'Just skinned my forehead a little.'

'You sure?'

'It's nothing. What about you?'

He sucked in a deep breath. 'I'm okay.'

'Really?'

'Yeah.'

'You weren't hit?'

'Unmarked. It's a miracle.'

'Bobby?'

'What?'

'I couldn't handle it if you'd turned up dead in there.'

'I'm not dead. I'm fine.'

'Thank God,' she said.

Then she kicked his right shin.

'Ow! What the hell?'

She kicked his left shin.

'Julie, dammit!'

'Don't you ever tell me to cut and run.'

'What?'

'I'm a full half of this partnership in *every* way.'

'But—'

'I'm as smart as you, as fast as you—'

He glanced at the dead man on the street, the other one in the Ford van, half visible through the open door, and he said, 'That's for sure, babe.'

'—as tough as you—'

'I know, I know. Don't kick me again.'

She said, 'What about Rasmussen?'

Bobby looked up at the Decodyne building. 'You think he's still in there?'

'The only exits from the parking lot are onto Michaelson, and he hasn't come out this way, so unless he fled on foot, he's in there, all right. We've got to nail him before he slides out of the trap with those diskettes.'

'Nothing worthwhile on the diskettes anyway,' Bobby said.

Decodyne had been on to Rasmussen from the time he applied for the job, because Dakota & Dakota Investigations – which was contracted to handle the company's security checks – had penetrated the hacker's highly sophisticated false ID. Decodyne's management wanted to play along with Rasmussen long enough to discover to whom he would pass the Whizard files when he got them; they intended to prosecute the money man who had hired Rasmussen, for no doubt the hacker's employer was one of Decodyne's primary competitors. They had allowed Tom Rasmussen to think he had compromised the security cameras, when in fact he had been under constant observation. They also had allowed him to break down the file codes and access the information he wanted, but unknown to him they had inserted secret instructions in the files, which insured that any diskettes he acquired would be full of trash data of no use to anyone.

Flames roared and crackled, consuming the van. Julie watched chimeras of reflected flames slither and caper up the glass walls and across the blank, black windows of Decodyne, as if they were striving to reach the roof and coalesce there in the form of gargoyles.

Raising her voice slightly to compete with the fire and with the shriek of approaching sirens, she said, 'Well, we thought he believed he'd circumvented the videotape records of the security cameras, but apparently he knew we were on to him.'

'Sure did.'

'So he also might've been smart enough to search for an anti-copying directive in the files – and find a way around it.'

Bobby frowned. 'You're right.'

'So he's probably got Whizard, unscrambled, on those diskettes.'

'Damn, I don't want to go in there. I've been shot at enough tonight.'

A police cruiser turned the corner two blocks away and sped toward them, siren screaming, emergency lights casting off alternating waves of blue and red light.

'Here come the professionals,' Julie said. 'Why don't we let them take over now?'

'We were hired to do the job. We have an obligation. PI honor is a sacred thing, you know. What would Sam Spade think of us?'

She said, 'Sam Spade can go spit up a rope.'

'What would Philip Marlowe think?'

'Philip Marlowe can go spit up a rope.'

'What will our client think?'

'Our *client* can go spit up a rope.'

'Dear, "spit" isn't the popular expression.'

'I know, but I'm a lady.'

'You certainly are.'

As the black-and-white braked in front of them, another police car turned the corner behind it, siren wailing, and a third entered Michaelson Drive from the other direction.

Julie put her Uzi on the pavement and raised her hands to avoid unfortunate misunderstandings. 'I'm *really* glad you're alive, Bobby.'

'You going to kick me again?'

'Not for a while.'

• 7 •

Frank Pollard hung on to the tailgate and rode the truck nine or ten blocks, without drawing the attention of the driver. Along the way he saw a sign welcoming him to the city of Anaheim, so he figured he was in southern California, although he still didn't know if this was where he lived or whether he was from out of town. Judging by the chill in the air, it was winter – not truly cold but as frigid as it got in these climes. He was unnerved to realize that he did not know the date or even the month. Shivering, he dropped off the truck when it slowed and turned onto a serviceway that led through a warehouse district. Huge, corrugated-metal buildings – some newly painted and some streaked with rust, some dimly lit by security lamps and some not – loomed against the star-spattered sky.

Carrying the flight bag, he walked away from the warehouses. The streets in that area were lined with shabby bungalows. The shrubs and trees were overgrown in many places: untrimmed palms with full skirts of dead fronds; bushy hibiscuses with half-closed pale blooms glimmering softly in the gloom; jade hedges and plumthorn hedges so old they were more woody than leafy; bougainvillea draped over roofs and fences, bristling with thousands of untamed, questing trailers. His soft-soled shoes made no sound on the sidewalk, and his shadow alternately stretched ahead of him and then behind, as he approached and then passed one lamppost after another.

Cars, mostly older models, some rusted and battered, were parked at curbs and in driveways; keys might have dangled from the ignitions of some of them, and he could have jump-started any he chose. However, he noted that the cinderblock walls between the properties – as well as the walls of a decrepit and abandoned house – shimmered with the spray-painted, ghostly, semi-phosphorescent graffiti of Latino gangs, and he didn't want to tinker with a set of wheels that might belong to one of their members. Those guys didn't bother rushing to a phone to call the police if they caught you trying to steal one of their cars; they just blew your head off or put a knife in your neck. Frank had enough trouble already, even with his head intact and his throat unpunctured, so he kept walking.

Twelve blocks later, in a neighborhood of well-kept houses and better cars, he began searching for a set of wheels that would be easy to boost. The tenth vehicle he tried was a one-year-old green Chevy, parked near a streetlamp, the doors unlocked, the keys tucked under the driver's seat.

Intent on putting a lot of distance between himself and the deserted apartment complex where he had last encountered his unknown pursuer, Frank switched on the Chevy's heater, drove from Anaheim to Santa Ana, then south on Bristol Avenue toward Costa Mesa, surprised by his familiarity with the streets. He seemed to know the area well. He recognized buildings, shopping centers, parks, and neighborhoods past which he drove, though the sight of them did nothing to rekindle his burnt-out memory. He still could not recall who he was, where he lived, what he did for a living, what he was running from, or how he had come to wake up in an alleyway in the middle of the night.

Even at that dead hour – the car clock indicated it was 2:48 – he figured his chances of encountering a traffic cop were greater on a freeway, so he stayed on the surface streets through Costa Mesa and the eastern and southern fringes of Newport Beach. At Corona Del Mar he picked up the Pacific Coast Highway and followed it all the way to Laguna Beach, encountering a thin fog that gradually thickened as he progressed southward.

Laguna, a picturesque resort town and artists' colony, shelved down a series of steep hillsides and canyon walls to the sea, most of it cloaked now in the thick fog. Only an occasional car passed him, and the mist rolling in from the Pacific became sufficiently dense to force him to reduce his speed to fifteen miles an hour.

Yawning and gritty-eyed, he turned onto a side street east of the highway and parked at the curb in front of a dark, two-story, gabled, Cape Cod house that looked out of place on these Western slopes. He wanted to get a motel room, but before he tried to check in somewhere, he needed to know if he had any money or credit cards. For the first time all night, he had a chance to look for ID, as well. He searched the pockets of his jeans, but to no avail.

He switched on the overhead light, pulled the leather flight bag onto his lap and opened it. The satchel was filled with tightly banded stacks of twenty- and hundred-dollar bills.

The thin soup of gray mist was gradually stirring itself into a thicker stew. A couple of miles closer to the ocean, the night probably was clotted with fog so dense that it would almost have lumps.

Coatless, protected from the night only by a sweater, but warmed by the fact that he had narrowly avoided almost certain death, Bobby leaned against one of the patrol cars in front of Decodyne and watched Julie as she paced back and forth with her hands in the pockets of her brown leather jacket. He never got tired of looking at her. They had been married seven years, and during that time they had lived and worked and played together virtually twenty-four hours a day, seven days a week. Bobby had never been the kind who liked to hang out with a bunch of guys at a bar or ball game – partly because it was difficult to find other guys in their middle thirties who were interested in the things that he cared about: big band music, the arts and pop culture of the '30s and '40s, and classic Disney comic books. Julie wasn't a lunch-with-the-girls type, either, because not many thirty-year-old women were into the Big Band Era, Warner Brothers Cartoons, martial arts, or advanced weapons training. In spite of spending so much time together, they remained fresh to each other, and she was still the most interesting and appealing woman he had ever known.

'What's taking them so long?' she asked, glancing up at the now-lighted windows of Decodyne, bright but fuzzy rectangles in the mist.

'Be patient with them, dear,' Bobby said. 'They don't have the dynamism of Dakota and Dakota. They're just a humble SWAT team.'

Michaelson Drive was blocked off. Eight police vehicles – cars and vans – were scattered along the street. The chilly night crackled with the static and metallic voices sputtering out of police-band radios. An officer was behind the wheel of one of the cars, and other uniformed men were positioned at both ends of the block, and two more were visible at the front doors of Decodyne; the rest were inside, looking for Rasmussen. Meanwhile, men from the police lab and coroner's office were photographing, measuring, and removing the bodies of the two gunmen.

'What if he gets away with the diskettes?' Julie asked.

'He won't.'

She nodded. 'Sure, I know what you're thinking – Whizard was developed on a closed-system computer with no links beyond Decodyne. But there's another system in the company, with modems and everything, isn't there? What if he takes the diskettes to one of *those* terminals and sends them out by phone?'

'Can't. The second system, the outlinked system, is totally different from the one on which Whizard was developed. Incompatible.'

'Rasmussen is clever.'

'There's also a night lockout that keeps the outlinked system shut down.'

'Rasmussen is clever,' she repeated.

She continued to pace in front of him.

The skinned spot on her forehead, where she had met the steering wheel when she'd jammed on the brakes, was no longer bleeding, though it looked raw and wet. She had wiped her face with tissues, but smears of dried blood, which looked almost like bruises, had remained under her right eye and along her jawline. Each time Bobby focused on those stains or on the shallow wound, a pang of anxiety quivered through him at the realization of what might have happened to her, to both of them.

Not surprisingly, her injury and the blood on her face only accentuated her beauty, making her appear more fragile and therefore more precious. Julie *was* beautiful, although Bobby realized that she appeared more so to his eyes than to others, which was all right because, after all, his eyes were the only ones through which he could look at her. Though it was kinking up a bit now in the moist night air, her chestnut-brown hair was usually thick and lustrous. She had wide-set eyes as dark as semi-sweet chocolate, skin as smooth and naturally tan as toffee ice cream, and a generous mouth that always tasted sweet to him. Whenever he watched her without her being fully aware of the intensity of his attention, or when he was apart from her and tried to conjure an image of her in his mind, he always thought of her in terms of food: chestnuts, chocolate, toffee, cream, sugar, butter. He found this amusing, but he also understood the profundity of his choice of similes: She reminded him of food because she, *more* than food, sustained him.

Activity at the entrance to Decodyne, about sixty feet away, at the end of a palm-flanked walkway, drew Julie's attention and then Bobby's. Someone from the SWAT team had come to the doors to report to the guards stationed there. A moment later one of the officers motioned for Julie and Bobby to come forward.

When they joined him, he said, 'They found this Rasmussen. You want to see him, make sure he has the right diskettes?'

'Yeah,' Bobby said.

'Definitely,' Julie said, and her throaty voice didn't sound at all sexy now, just tough.

• 9 •

Keeping a lookout for any Laguna Beach police who might be running graveyard-shift patrols, Frank Pollard removed the bundles of cash from the flight bag and piled them on the car seat beside him. He counted fifteen packets of twenty-dollar bills and eleven bundles of hundreds. He judged the thickness of each wad to be approximately one hundred bills, and when he did the mathematics in his head he came up with $140,000. He had no idea where the money had come from or whether it belonged to him.

The first of two small, zippered side compartments in the bag yielded another surprise – a wallet that contained no cash and no credit cards but two important pieces of identification: a Social Security card and a California driver's license. With the wallet was a United States passport. The photographs on the passport and license were of the same man: thirtyish, brown hair, a round face, prominent ears, brown eyes, an easy smile, and dimples. Realizing he had also forgotten what he looked like, he tilted the rearview mirror and was able to see enough of his face to match it with the one on the ID. The problem was . . . the license and passport bore the name James Roman, not Frank Pollard.

He unzipped the second of the two smaller compartments, and found another Social Security card, passport, and California driver's license. These were all in the name of George Farris, but the photos were of Frank.

James Roman meant nothing to him.

George Farris was also meaningless.

And Frank Pollard, whom he believed himself to be, was only a cipher, a man without any past that he could recall.

'What the hell am I tangled up in?' he said aloud. He needed to hear his own voice to convince himself that he was, in fact, not just a ghost reluctant to leave this world for the one to which death had entitled him.

As the fog closed around his parked car, blotting out most of the night beyond, a terrible loneliness overcame him. He could think of no one to whom he could turn, nowhere to which he could retreat and be assured of safety. A man without a past was also a man without a future.

• 10 •

When Bobby and Julie stepped out of the elevator onto the third floor, in the company of a police officer named McGrath, Julie saw Tom Rasmussen sitting on the polished gray vinyl tiles, his back against the wall of the corridor, his hands cuffed in front of him and linked by a length of chain to shackles that bound his ankles together. He was pouting. He had tried to steal software worth tens of millions of dollars, if not hundreds of millions, and from the window of Ackroyd's office he had cold-bloodedly given the signal to have Bobby killed, yet here he was pouting like a child because he had been caught. His weasel face was puckered, and his lower lip was thrust out, and his yellow-brown eyes looked watery, as though he might break into tears if anyone dared to say a cross word. The mere sight of him infuriated Julie. She wanted to kick his teeth down his throat, all the way into his stomach, so he could re-chew whatever he had last eaten.

The cops had found him in a supply closet, behind boxes that he had rearranged to make a pitifully obvious hiding place. Evidently, standing at Ackroyd's window to watch the fireworks, he had been surprised when Julie had appeared in the Toyota. She had driven the Toyota into the Decodyne parking lot early in the day and had stayed far back from the building, in the shadows beneath the boughs of the laurel, where no one had spotted her. Instead of fleeing the moment he saw the first gunman run down, Rasmussen had hesitated, no doubt wondering who *else* was out there. Then he heard the sirens, and his only option was to hide out in the hope they would only search the building casually and conclude that he had escaped. With a computer, he was a genius, but when it came to making cool decisions under fire, Rasmussen was not half as bright as he thought he was.

Two heavily armed cops were watching over him. But because he was huddled and shivering and on the verge of tears, they were a bit ludicrous in their bulletproof vests, cradling automatic weapons, squinting in the fluorescent glare, and looking grim.

Julie knew one of the officers, Sampson Garfeuss, from her own days with the sheriff's department, where Sampson also served before joining the City of Irvine force. Either his parents had been prescient or he had striven mightily to live up to his name, for he was both tall and broad and rocklike. He held a lidless box that contained four small floppy diskettes. He showed it to Julie and said, 'Is this what he was after?'

'Could be,' she said, accepting the box.

Taking the diskettes from her, Bobby said, 'I'll have to go down one floor to Ackroyd's office, switch on the computer, pop these in, and see what's on them.'

'Go ahead,' Sampson said.

'You'll have to accompany me,' Bobby said to McGrath, the officer who had brought them up on the elevator. 'Keep a watch on me, make sure I don't tamper with these things.' He indicated Tom Rasmussen. 'We don't want this piece of slime claiming they were blank disks, saying I framed him by copying the real stuff onto them myself.'

As Bobby and McGrath went into one of the elevators and descended to the second floor, Julie hunkered down in front of Rasmussen. 'You know who I am?'

Rasmussen looked at her but said nothing.

'I'm Bobby Dakota's wife. Bobby was in that van your goons shot up. It was my Bobby you tried to kill.'

He looked away from her, at his cuffed wrists.

She said, 'Know what I'd like to do to you?' She held one of her hands down in front of his face, and wiggled her manicured nails. 'For starters, I'd like to grab you by the throat, hold your head against the wall, and ram two of these nice, sharp fingernails straight through your eyes, all the way in, deep, real deep in your fevered little brain, and twist them around, see if maybe I can unscramble whatever's messed up in there.'

'Jesus, lady,' Sampson's partner said. His name was Burdock. Beside anyone but Sampson, he would have been a big man.

'Well,' she said, 'he's too screwed up to get any help from a prison psychiatrist.'

Sampson said, 'Don't do anything foolish, Julie.'

Rasmussen glanced at her, meeting her eyes for only a second, but that was long enough for him to understand the depth of her anger and to be frightened by it. A flush of childish embarrassment and temper had accompanied his pout, but now his face went pale. To Sampson, in a voice that was too shrill and quaverous to be as tough as he intended, Rasmussen said, 'Keep this crazy bitch away from me.'

'She's not actually crazy,' Sampson said. 'Not clinically speaking, at least. Pretty hard to have anyone declared crazy these days, I'm afraid. Lots of concern about their civil rights, you know. No, I wouldn't say she's crazy.'

Without looking away from Rasmussen, Julie said, 'Thank you so much, Sam.'

'You'll notice I didn't say anything about the other half of his accusation,' Sampson said good-naturedly.

'Yeah, I got your point.'

While she talked to Sampson, she kept her attention on Rasmussen.

Everyone harbored a special fear, a private boogeyman built to his own specifications and crouched in a dark corner of his mind, and Julie knew what Tom Rasmussen feared more than anything in the world. Not heights. Not confining spaces. Not crowds, cats, flying, insects, dogs, or darkness. Dakota & Dakota had developed a thick file on him in recent weeks, and had turned up the fact that he suffered from a phobia of blindness. In prison, every month with the regularity of a true obsessive, he had demanded an eye exam, claiming his vision was deteriorating, and he'd petitioned to be tested periodically for syphilis, diabetes, and other diseases that, untreated, could result in blindness. When not in prison – and he had been there twice – he had a standing, monthly appointment with an ophthalmologist in Costa Mesa.

Still squatting in front of Rasmussen, Julie took hold of his chin. He flinched. She twisted his head toward her. She thrust two fingers of her other hand at him, raked them down his cheek, making red welts on his wan skin, but not hard enough to draw blood.

He squealed and tried to strike her with his cuffed hands, but he was inhibited by both his fear and the chain that tethered his wrists to his ankles. 'What the hell you think you're doing?'

She spread the same two fingers with which she'd scratched him, and now she poked them at him, stopping just two inches short of his eyes. He winced, made a mewling sound, and tried to pull loose of her, but she held him fast by the chin, forcing a confrontation.

'Me and Bobby have been together eight years, married more than seven, and they've been the best years of my life, but you come along and think you can just squash him the way you'd squash a bug.'

She slowly brought her fingertips closer to his eyes. An inch and a half. One inch.

Rasmussen tried to pull back. His head was against the wall. He had nowhere to go.

The sharp tips of her manicured fingernails were less than half an inch from his eyes.

'This is police brutality,' Rasmussen said.

'I'm not a cop,' Julie said.

'*They* are,' he said, rolling his eyes at Sampson and Burdock. 'Better get this bitch away from me, I'll sue your asses off.'

With her fingernails she flicked his eyelashes.

His attention snapped back to her. He was breathing fast, and suddenly he was sweating too.

She flicked his lashes again, and smiled.

The dark pupils in his yellow-brown eyes were open wide.

'You bastards better hear me, I swear, I'll sue, they'll kick you off the force—'

She flicked his lashes again.

He closed his eyes tight. '– they'll take away your Goddamned uniforms and badges, they'll throw *you* in prison, and you know what happens to ex-cops in prison, they get the shit kicked out of them, broken, killed, *raped*!' His voice spiraled up, cracked on the last word, like the voice of an adolescent boy.

Glancing at Sampson to be sure she had his tacit if not active approval to carry this just a little further, glancing also at Burdock and seeing that he was not as placid as Sampson but would probably stay out of it for a while yet, Julie pressed her fingernails against Rasmussen's eyelids.

He attempted to squeeze his eyes even more tightly shut.

She pressed harder. 'You tried to take Bobby away from me, so I'll take your eyes away from you.'

'You're *nuts*!'

She pressed still harder.

'Make her stop,' Rasmussen demanded of the two cops.

'If you didn't want me to have my Bobby to look at, why should I let you look at anything ever again?'

'What do you want?' Perspiration poured down Rasmussen's face; he looked like a candle in a bonfire, melting fast.

'Who gave you permission to kill Bobby?'

'Permission? What do you mean? Nobody. I don't need—'

'You wouldn't have tried to touch him if your employer hadn't told you to do it.'

'I knew he was on to me,' Rasmussen said frantically, and because she had not let up the pressure with her nails, thin tears flowed from under his eyelids. 'I knew he was out there, tumbled to him five or six days ago, even though he used different vans, trucks, even that orange van with the county seal on it. So I had to do something, didn't I? I couldn't walk away from the job, too much money at stake. I couldn't just let him nail me when I finally got Whizard, so I had to do something. Listen, Jesus, it was as simple as that.'

'You're just a computer freak, a hired hacker – morally bent, sleazy, but you're no tough guy. You're soft, squishy-soft. You wouldn't plan a hit on your own. Your boss told you to do it.'

'I don't have a boss. I'm freelance.'

'Somebody still pays you.'

She risked more pressure, not with the points of her nails but with the flat surfaces, although Rasmussen was so swept away by a rapture of fear that he might still imagine he could feel those filed edges gradually carving through the delicate shields of his eyelids. He must be seeing interior starfields now, bursts and whorls of color, and maybe he was feeling some pain. He was shaking; his shackles clinked and rattled. More tears squeezed from beneath his lids.

'Delafield.' The word erupted from him, as if he had been trying simultaneously to hold it back and to expel it with all his might. 'Kevin Delafield.'

'Who's he?' Julie asked, still holding Rasmussen's chin with one hand, her fingernails against his eyes, unrelenting.

'Microcrest Corporation.'

'That's who hired you for this?'

He was rigid, afraid to move a fraction of an inch, convinced that the slightest shift in his position would force her fingernails into his eyes. 'Yeah. Delafield. A nutcase. A renegade. They don't understand about him at Microcrest. They just know he gets results for them. When this hits the fan they'll be surprised by it, blown away. So let go of me. What more do you want?'

She let go of him.

Immediately he opened his eyes, blinked, testing his vision, then broke down and sobbed with relief.

As Julie stood, the nearby elevator doors opened, and Bobby returned with the officer who had accompanied him downstairs to Ackroyd's office. Bobby looked at Rasmussen, cocked his head at Julie, clucked his tongue, and said, 'You've been naughty, haven't you, dear? Can't I take you anywhere?'

'I just had a conversation with Mr Rasmussen. That's all.'

'He seems to have found it stimulating,' Bobby said.

Rasmussen sat slumped forward with his hands over his eyes, weeping uncontrollably.

'We disagreed about something,' Julie said.

'Movies, books?'

'Music.'

'Ah.'

Sampson Garfeuss said softly, 'You're a wild woman, Julie.'

'He tried to have Bobby killed,' was all she said.

Sampson nodded. 'I'm not saying I don't admire wildness sometimes . . . a little. But you sure as hell owe me one.'

'I do,' she agreed.

'You owe me more than one,' Burdock said. 'This guy's going to file a complaint. You can bet your ass on it.'

'Complaint about what?' Julie asked. 'He's not even marked.'

Already the faint welts on Rasmussen's cheek were fading. Sweat, tears, and a case of the shakes were the only evidence of his ordeal.

'Listen,' Julie told Burdock, 'he cracked because I just happened to know exactly the right weak point where I could give him a little tap, like cutting a diamond. It worked because scum like him thinks everyone else is scum, too, thinks *we're* capable of doing what he'd do in the same situation. I'd never put out his eyes, but he might've put mine out if our roles were reversed, so he thought for sure I'd do him like he would've done me. All I did was use his own screwed up attitudes against him. Psychology. Nobody can file a complaint about the application of a little psychology.' She turned to Bobby and said, 'What was on those diskettes?'

'Whizard. Not trash data. The whole thing. These have to be the files he duplicated. He only made one set while I was watching, and after the shooting started he didn't have time to make backup copies.'

The elevator bell rang, and their floor number lit on the board. When the doors opened, a plainclothes detective they knew, Gil Dainer, stepped into the hallway.

Julie took the package of diskettes from Bobby, handed them to Dainer.

She said, 'This is evidence. The whole case might rest on it. You think you can keep track of it?'

Dainer grinned. 'Gosh, ma'am, I'll try.'

• 11 •

Frank Pollard – alias James Roman, alias George Farris – looked in the trunk of the stolen Chevy and found a small bundle of tools wrapped in a felt pouch and tucked in the wheel well. He used a screwdriver to take the plates off the car.

Half an hour later, after cruising some of the higher and even quieter neighborhoods in fogbound Laguna, he parked on a dark side street and exchanged the Chevy's plates for those on an Oldsmobile. With luck, the owner of the Olds would not notice the new plates for a couple of days, maybe even a week or longer; until he reported the switch, the Chevy would not match anything on a police hot sheet and would, therefore, be relatively safe to drive. In any case, Frank intended to get rid of the car by tomorrow night and either boost a new one or use some of the cash in the flight bag to buy legal wheels.

Though he was exhausted, he didn't think it wise to check into a motel. Four-thirty in the morning was a damned odd hour for anyone to be wanting a room. Furthermore, he was unshaven, and his thick hair was matted and oily, and both his jeans and checkered blue flannel shirt were dirty and rumpled from his recent adventures. The last thing he wanted to do was call attention to himself, so he decided to catch a few hours of sleep in the car.

He drove farther south, into Laguna Niguel, where he parked on a quiet residential street, under the immense boughs of a date palm. He stretched out on the backseat, as comfortably as possible without benefit of sufficient legroom or pillows, and closed his eyes.

For the moment he was not afraid of his unknown pursuer, because he felt that the man was no longer nearby. Temporarily, at least, he had given his enemy the shake, and had no need to lie awake in fear of a hostile face suddenly appearing at the window. He was also able to put out of his mind all questions about his identity and the money in the flight bag; he was so tired – and his thought processes were so fuzzy – that any attempt to puzzle out solutions to those mysteries would be fruitless.

He was kept awake, however, by the memory of how *strange* the events in Anaheim had been, a few hours ago. The foreboding gusts of wind. The eerie flutelike music. Imploding windows, exploding tires, failed brakes, failed steering . . .

Who had come into that apartment behind the blue light? Was 'who' the right word . . . or would it be more accurate to ask *what* had been searching for him?

During his urgent flight from Anaheim to Laguna, he'd not had the leisure to reflect upon those bizarre incidents, but now he could not turn his mind from them. He sensed that he had survived an encounter with something unnatural. Worse, he sensed that he knew what it was – and that his amnesia was self-induced by a deep desire to forget.

After a while, even the memory of those preternatural events weren't enough to keep him awake. The last thing that crossed his waking mind, as he slipped off on a tide of sleep, was that four-word phrase that had come to him when he had first awakened in the deserted alleyway: *Fireflies in a windstorm* . . .

• 12 •

By the time they had cooperated with the police at the scene, made arrangements for their disabled vehicles, and talked with the three corporate officers who showed up at Decodyne, Bobby and Julie did not get home until shortly before dawn. They were dropped at their door by a police cruiser, and Bobby was glad to see the place.

They lived on the east side of Orange, in a three-bedroom, sort-of-ersatz-Spanish tract house, which they had bought new two years ago, largely for its investment potential. Even at night the relative youth of the neighborhood was apparent in the landscaping: None of the shrubbery had reached full size; the trees were still too immature to loom higher than the rain gutters on the houses.

Bobby unlocked the door. Julie went in, and he followed. The sound of their footsteps on the parquet floor of the foyer, echoing hollowly off the bare walls of the adjacent and utterly empty living room, was proof that they were not committed to the house for the long term. To save money toward the fulfillment of The Dream, they had left the living room, dining room, and two bedrooms unfurnished. They installed cheap carpet and cheaper draperies. Not a penny had been spent on other improvements. This was merely a way station en route to The Dream, so they saw no point in lavishing funds on the decor.

The Dream. That was how they thought of it – with a capital T and a capital D. They kept their expenses as low as possible, in order to fund The Dream. They didn't spend much on clothes or vacations, and they didn't buy fancy cars. With hard work and iron determination, they were building Dakota & Dakota Investigations into a major firm that could be sold for a large capital gain, so they plowed a lot of earnings back into the business to make it grow. For The Dream.

At the back of the house, the kitchen and family room – and the small breakfast area that separated them – were furnished. This – and the master bedroom upstairs – was where they lived when at home.

The kitchen had a Spanish-tile floor, beige counters, and dark oak cabinets. No money had been spent on decorative accessories, but the room had a cozy feeling because some necessities of a functioning kitchen were on display: a net bag filled with half a dozen onions, copper pots dangling from a ceiling rack, cooking utensils, bottles of spices. Three green tomatoes were ripening on the windowsill.

Julie leaned against the counter, as if she could not stand another moment without support, and Bobby said, 'You want a drink?'

'Booze at dawn?'

'I was thinking more of milk or juice.'

'No thanks.'

'Hungry?'

She shook her head. 'I just want to fall into bed. I'm beat.'

He took her in his arms, held her close, cheek to cheek, with his face buried in her hair. Her arms tightened around him.

They stood that way for a while, saying nothing, letting the residual fear evaporate in the gentle heat they generated between them. Fear and love were indivisible. If you allowed yourself to care, to love, you made yourself vulnerable, and vulnerability led to fear. He found meaning in life through his relationship with her, and if she died, meaning and purpose would die too.

With Julie still in his arms, Bobby leaned back and studied her face. The smudges of dried blood had been wiped away. The skinned spot on her forehead was beginning to scab over with a thin yellow membrane. However, the imprint of their recent ordeal consisted of more than the abrasion on her forehead. With her tan complexion, she could never be said to look pale, even in moments of the most profound anxiety; a detectable grayness seeped into her face, however, at times like this, and at the moment her cinnamon-and-cream skin was underlaid with a shade of gray that made him think of headstone marble.

'It's over,' he assured her, 'and we're okay.'

'It's not over in my dreams. Won't be for weeks.'

'A thing like tonight adds to the legend of Dakota and Dakota.'

'I don't want to be a legend. Legends are all dead.'

'We'll be *living* legends, and that'll bring in business. The more business we build, the sooner we can sell out, grab The Dream.' He kissed her gently on each corner of her mouth. 'I have to call in, leave a long message on the agency machine, so Clint will know how to handle everything when he goes to work.'

'Yeah. I don't want the phone to start ringing only a couple of hours after I hit the sheets.'

He kissed her again and went to the wall phone beside the refrigerator. As he was dialing the office number, he heard Julie walk to the bathroom off the short hall that connected the kitchen to the laundryroom. She closed the bathroom door just as the answering machine picked up: *'Thank you for calling Dakota and Dakota. No one—'*

Clint Karaghiosis – whose Greek-American family had been fans of Clint Eastwood from the earliest days of his first television show, 'Rawhide' – was Bobby's and Julie's right-hand man at the office. He could be trusted to handle any problem. Bobby left a long message for him, summarizing the events at Decodyne and noting specific tasks that had to be done to wrap up the case.

When he hung up, he stepped down into the adjoining family room, switched on the CD player, and put on a Benny Goodman disk. The first notes of 'King Porter Stomp' brought the dead room to life.

In the kitchen again, he got a quart can of eggnog from the refrigerator. They had bought it two weeks ago for their quiet, at-home, New Year's Eve celebration, but had not opened it, after all, on the holiday. He opened it now and half-filled two waterglasses.

From the bathroom he heard Julie make a tortured sound; she was finally throwing up. It was mostly just dry heaves because they had not eaten in eight or ten hours, but the spasms sounded violent. Throughout the night, Bobby had expected her to succumb to nausea, and he was surprised that she had retained control of herself this long.

He retrieved a bottle of white rum from the bar cabinet in the family room and spiked each serving of eggnog with a double shot. He was gently stirring the drinks with a spoon to blend in the rum, when Julie returned, looking even grayer than before.

When she saw what he was doing, she said, 'I don't need that.'

'I know what you need. I'm psychic. I knew you'd toss your cookies after what happened tonight. Now I know you need *this*.' He stepped to the sink and rinsed off the spoon.

'No, Bobby, really, I can't drink that.' The Goodman music didn't seem to be energizing her.

'It'll settle your stomach. And if you don't drink it, you're not going to sleep.' Taking her by the arm, crossing the breakfast area, and stepping down into the family room, he said, 'You'll lie awake worrying about me, about Thomas,' – Thomas was her brother – 'about the world and everyone in it.'

They sat on the sofa, and he did not turn on any lamps. The only light was what reached them from the kitchen.

She drew her legs under her and turned slightly to face him. Her eyes shone with a soft, reflected light. She sipped the eggnog.

The room was now filled with the strains of 'One Sweet Letter From You,' one of Goodman's most beautiful thematic statements, with a vocal by Louise Tobin.

They sat and listened for a while.

Then Julie said, 'I'm tough, Bobby, I really am.'

'I know you are.'

'I don't want you thinking I'm lame.'

'Never.'

'It wasn't the shooting that made me sick, or using the Toyota to run that guy down, or even the thought of almost losing you—'

'I know. It was what you had to do to Rasmussen.'

'He's a slimy little weasel-faced bastard, but even he doesn't deserve to be broken like that. What I did to him stank.'

'It was the only way to crack the case, because it wasn't near cracked till we'd found out who hired him.'

She drank more eggnog. She frowned down at the milky contents of her glass, as if the answer to some mystery could be found there.

Following Tobin's vocal, Ziggy Elman came in with a lusty trumpet solo, followed by Goodman's clarinet. The sweet sounds made that boxy, tract-house room seem like the most romantic place in the world.

'What I did . . . I did for The Dream. Giving Decodyne Rasmussen's employer will please them. But breaking him was somehow . . . worse than wasting a man in a fair gunfight.'

Bobby put one hand on her knee. It was a nice knee. After all these years, he was still sometimes surprised by her slenderness and the delicacy of her bone structure, for he always thought of her as being strong for her size, solid, indomitable. 'If you hadn't put Rasmussen in that vise and squeezed him, I would've done it.'

'No, you wouldn't have. You're scrappy, Bobby, and you're smart and you're tough, but there're certain things you can never do. This was one of them. Don't jive me just to make me feel good.'

'You're right,' he said. 'I couldn't have done it. But I'm glad you did. Decodyne's *very* big time, and this could've set us back years if we'd flubbed it.'

'Is there anything we won't do for The Dream?'

Bobby said, 'Sure. We wouldn't torture small children with red-hot knives, and we wouldn't shove innocent old ladies down long flights of stairs, and we wouldn't club a basketful of newborn puppies to death with an iron bar – at least not without good reason.'

Her laughter lacked a full measure of humor.

'Listen,' he said, 'you're a good person. You've got a good heart, and nothing you did to Rasmussen blackens it at all.'

'I hope you're right. It's a hard world sometimes.'

'Another drink will soften it a little.'

'You know the calories in these? I'll be fat as a hippo.'

'Hippos are cute,' he said, taking her glass and heading back toward the kitchen to pour another drink. 'I love hippos.'

'You won't want to *make* love to one.'

'Sure. More to hold, more to love.'

'You'll be crushed.'

'Well, of course, I'll always insist on taking the top.'

Candy was going to kill. He stood in the dark living room of a stranger's house, shaking with need. Blood. He needed blood.

Candy was going to kill, and there was nothing he could do to stop himself. Not even thinking of his mother could shame him into controlling his hunger.

His given name was James, but his mother – an unselfish soul, exceedingly kind, brimming with love, a saint – always said he was her little candy boy. Never James. Never Jim or Jimmy. She'd said he was sweeter than anything on earth, and 'little candy boy' eventually had become 'candy boy,' and by the time he was six the sobriquet had been shortened and capitalized, and he had become Candy for good. Now, at twenty-nine, that was the only name to which he would answer.

Many people thought murder was a sin. He knew otherwise. Some were born with a taste for blood. God had made them what they were and expected them to kill chosen victims. It was all part of His mysterious plan.

The only sin was to kill when God and your mother did not approve of the victim, which was exactly what he was about to do. He was ashamed. But he was also in need.

He listened to the house. Silence.

Like unearthly and dusky beasts, the shadowy forms of the living-room furniture huddled around him.

Breathing hard, trembling, Candy moved into the dining room, kitchen, family room, then slowly along the hallway that led to the front of the house. He made no sound that would have alerted anyone asleep upstairs. He seemed to glide rather than walk, as if he were a specter instead of a real man.

He paused at the foot of the stairs and made one last feeble attempt to overcome his murderous compulsion. Failing, he shuddered and let out his pent-up breath. He began to climb toward the second floor, where the family was probably sleeping.

His mother would understand and forgive him.

She had taught him that killing was good and moral – but only when necessary, only when it benefited the family. She had been terribly angry with him on those occasions when he had killed out of sheer compulsion, with no good reason. She'd had no need to punish him physically for his errant ways, because her displeasure gave him more agony than any punishment she could have devised. For days at a time she refused to speak to him, and that silent treatment caused his chest to swell with pain, so it seemed as if his heart would spasm and cease to beat. She looked straight through him, too, as if he no longer existed. When the other children spoke of him, she said, 'Oh, you mean your late brother, Candy, your poor dead brother. Well, remember him if you want, but only among yourselves, not to me, never to me, because I don't want to remember him, not that bad seed. He was no good, that one, no good at all, wouldn't listen to his mother, not him, always thought he knew better. Just the sound of his name makes me sick, *revolts* me, so don't mention him in my hearing.' Each time that Candy had been temporarily banished to the land of the dead for having misbehaved, no place was set for him at the table, and he had to stand in a corner, watching the others eat, as if he was a visiting spirit. She would not favor him with either a frown or a smile, and she would not stroke his hair or touch his face with her warm soft hands, and she would not let him cuddle against her or put his weary head upon her breast, and at night he had to find his way into a troubled sleep without being guided there by either her bedtime stories or sweet lullabies. In that total banishment he learned more of Hell than he ever hoped to know.

But she would understand why Candy could not control himself tonight, and she'd forgive him. Sooner or later she always forgave him because her love for him was like the love of God for all His children: perfect, rich with forbearance and mercy. When she deemed that Candy had suffered enough, she always had looked *at* him again, smiled for him, opened her arms wide. In her new acceptance of him, he had experienced as much of Heaven as he needed to know.

She was in Heaven now, herself. Seven long years! God, how he missed her. But she was watching him even now. She would know he had lost control tonight, and she would be disappointed in him.

He climbed the stairs, rushing up two risers at a time, staying close to the wall, where the steps were less likely to squeak. He was a big man but graceful and light on his feet, and if some of the stair treads were loose or tired with age, they did not creak under him.

In the upstairs hall he paused, listening. Nothing.

A dim night light was part of the overhead smoke alarm. The glow was just bright enough for Candy to see two doors on the right of the hall, two on the left, and one at the far end.

He crept to the first door on the right, eased it open, and slipped into the room beyond. He closed the door again and stood with his back to it.

Although his need was great, he forced himself to wait for his eyes to adjust to the gloom. Ashen light, from a streetlamp at least half a block away, glimmered faintly at the two windows. He noticed the mirror, first, a frosty rectangle in which the meager radiance was murkily reflected; then he began to make out the shape of the dresser beneath it. A moment later he was also able to see the bed and, dimly, the huddled form of someone lying under a light-colored blanket that was vaguely phosphorescent.

Candy stepped cautiously to the bed, took hold of the blanket and sheets and hesitated, listening to the soft rhythmic breathing of the sleeper. He detected a trace of perfume mingled with a pleasant scent of warm skin and recently shampooed hair. A girl. He could always tell girl-smell from boy-smell. He also sensed that this one was young, perhaps a teenager. If his need had not been so intense, he would have hesitated much longer than he did, for the moments preceding a kill were exciting, almost better than the act itself.

With a dramatic flick of his arm, as if he were a magician throwing back the cloth that had covered an empty cage to reveal a captive dove of sorcerous origins, he uncovered the sleeper. He fell upon her, crushing her into the mattress with his body.

She woke instantly and tried to scream, even though he had surely knocked the wind out of her. Fortunately, he had unusually large and powerful hands, and he had found her face even as she began to raise her voice, so he was able to thrust his palm under her chin and hook his fingers in her cheeks and clamp her mouth shut.

'Be quiet, or I'll kill you,' he whispered, his lips brushing against her delicate ear.

Making a muffled, panicky sound, she squirmed under him, though to no avail. Judging by the feel of her, she was a girl, not a woman, perhaps no younger than twelve, certainly no older than fifteen. She was no match for him.

'I don't want to hurt you. I just *want* you, and when I'm done with you, I'll leave.'

That was a lie, for he had no desire to rape her. Sex was of no interest to him. Indeed, sex disgusted him; involving unmentionable fluids, depending upon the shameless use of the same organs associated with urination, sex was an unspeakably repulsive act. Other people's fascination with it only proved to Candy that men and women were members of a fallen species and that the world was a cesspool of sin and madness.

Either because she believed his pledge not to kill her or because she was now half-paralyzed with fear, she stopped resisting. Maybe she just needed all of her energy to breathe. Candy's full weight – two hundred and twenty pounds – was pressing on her chest, restricting her lungs. Against his hand, with which he clamped her mouth shut, he could feel her cool inhalations as her nostrils flared, followed by short, hot exhalations.

His vision had continued to adapt to the poor light. Although he still could not make out the details of her face, he could see her eyes shining darkly in the gloom, glistening with terror. He could also see that she was a blonde; her pale hair caught even the dull gray glow from the windows and shone with burnished-silver highlights.

With his free hand, he gently pushed her hair back from the right side of her neck. He shifted his position slightly, moving down on her in order to bring his lips to her throat. He kissed the tender flesh, felt the strong throb of her pulse against his lips, then bit deep and found the blood.

She bucked and thrashed beneath him, but he held her down and held her fast, and she could not dislodge his greedy mouth from the wound he had made. He swallowed rapidly but could not consume the thick, sweet fluid as fast as it was offered. Soon, however, the flow diminished. The girl's convulsions became less violent, as well, then faded altogether, until she was as still beneath him as if she had been nothing more than a tangled mound of bedclothes.

He rose from her and switched on the bedside lamp just long enough to see her face. He always wanted to see their faces, after their sacrifices if not before. He also liked to look into their eyes, which seemed not sightless but gifted with a vision of the far place to which their souls had gone. He did not entirely understand his curiosity. After all, when he ate a steak, he did not wonder what the cow had looked like. This girl – and each of the others on whom he'd fed – should have been nothing more than one of the cattle to him. Once, in a dream, when he had finished drinking from a ravaged throat, his victim, although dead, had spoken to him, asking him why he wanted to look upon her in death. When he had said that he didn't know the answer to her question, she had suggested that perhaps, on those occasions when he had killed in the dark, he later needed to see his victims' faces because, in some unlit corner of his heart, he half expected to find his own face looking up at him, ice-white and dead-eyed. 'Deep down,' the dream-victim had said, 'you know that you're already dead yourself, burnt out inside. You realize that you have far more in common with your victims after you've killed them than before.' Those words, though spoken only in a dream, and though amounting to the purest nonsense, had nevertheless brought him awake with a sharp cry. He was alive, not dead, powerful and vital, a man with appetites as strong as they were unusual. The dream-victim's words stayed with him over the years, and when they echoed through his memory at times like this, they made him anxious. Now, as always, he refused to dwell on them. He turned his attention, instead, to the girl on the bed.

She appeared to be about fourteen, quite pretty. Captivated by her flawless complexion, he wondered if her skin would feel as perfect as it looked, as smooth as porcelain, if he dared to stroke it with his fingertips. Her lips were slightly parted, as if they had been gently prised open by her spirit as it departed her. Her wonderfully blue, clear eyes seemed enormous, too big for her face – and as wide as a winter sky.

He would have liked to gaze upon her for hours.

Letting a sigh of regret escape him, he switched off the lamp.

He stood for a while in the darkness, enveloped by the pungent aroma of blood.

When his eyes had readjusted to the gloom, he returned to the hall, not bothering to close the girl's door behind him. He entered the room across from hers and found it untenanted.

But in the room next to that one, Candy smelled a trace of stale sweat, and heard snoring. This one was a boy, seventeen or eighteen, not a big kid but not small either, and he put up more of a struggle than his sister. However, he was sleeping on his stomach, and when Candy threw back the covers and fell upon him, the boy's face was jammed hard into the pillow and mattress, smothering him and making it difficult for him to shout a warning. The fight was violent but brief. The boy passed out from lack of oxygen, and Candy flopped him over. When he went for the exposed throat, Candy let out a low and eager cry that was louder than any sound the boy had made.

Later, when he opened the door to the fourth bedroom, the first pewter light of dawn had pierced the windows. Shadows still huddled in the corners, but the deeper darkness had been chased off. The early light was too thin to elicit color from objects, and everything in the room seemed to be one shade of gray or another.

An attractive blonde in her late thirties was asleep on one side of a king-size bed. The sheets and blanket on the other half of the bed were hardly disturbed, so he figured the woman's husband had either moved out or was away on business. He noted a half-full glass of water and a plastic bottle of prescription drugs on the nightstand. He picked up the pharmacy bottle and saw that it was two-thirds full of small pills: a sedative, according to the label. From the label, he also learned her name: Roseanne Lofton.

Candy stood for a while, staring down at her face, and an old longing for maternal solace stirred in him. Need continued to drive him, but he did not want to take her violently, did not want to rip her open and drain her in a few minutes. He wanted this one to last.

He had the urge to suckle on this woman as he had suckled on his mother's blood when she would permit him that grace. Occasionally, when he was in her favor, his mother would make a shallow cut in the palm of her hand or puncture one of her fingers, then allow him to curl up against her and be nursed on her blood for an hour or longer. During that time a great peace stole over him, a bliss so profound that the world and all its pain ceased to be real to him, because his mother's blood was like no other, untainted, pure as the tears of a saint. Through such small wounds, of course, he was able to drink no more than an ounce or two of her, but that meager dribble was more precious and more nourishing to him than the gallons he might have drained from a score of other people. The woman before him would not have such ambrosia within her veins, but if he closed his eyes while he suckled on her, and if he let his mind reel backward to memories of the days before his mother's death, he might recapture at least some of the exquisite serenity he had known then . . . and experience a faint echo of that old thrill.

At last, without casting the covers aside, Candy gently lowered himself to the bed and stretched out beside the woman, watching as her heavy-lidded eyes fluttered and then opened. She blinked at him as he cuddled next to her, and for a moment she seemed to think that she was still dreaming, for no expression tightened the muscles of her slack face.

'All I want is your blood,' he said softly.

Abruptly she cast off the lingering effects of the sedative, and her eyes filled with alarm.

Before she could spoil the beauty of the moment by screaming or resisting, thereby shattering the illusion that she was his mother and was giving voluntarily of herself, he struck the side of her neck with his heavy fist. Then he struck her again. Then he hammered the side of her face twice. She slumped unconscious against the pillow.

He squirmed under the covers to be close against her, withdrew her hand, and nipped her palm with his teeth. He put his head on the pillow, lying face to face with her, holding her hand between them, drinking the slow trickle from her palm. He closed his eyes after a while and tried to imagine that she was his mother, and eventually a gratifying peace stole over him. However, though he was happier at that moment than he had been in a long time, it was not a deep happiness, merely a veneer of joy that brightened the surface of his heart but left the inner chambers dark and cold.

· 14 ·

After only a few hours of sleep, Frank Pollard woke in the backseat of the stolen Chevy. The morning sun, streaming through the windows, was bright enough to make him wince.

He was stiff, achy, and unrested. His throat was dry, and his eyes burned as if he had not slept for days.

Groaning, Frank swung his legs off the seat, sat up, and cleared his throat. He realized that both of his hands were numb; they felt cold and dead, and he saw that he had curled them into fists. He had evidently been sleeping that way for some time, because at first he could not unclench. With considerable effort, he opened his right fist – and a handful of something black and grainy poured through his tingling fingers.

He stared, perplexed, at the fine grains that had spilled down the leg of his jeans and onto his right shoe. He raised his hand to take a closer look at the residue that had stuck to his palm. It looked and smelled like sand.

Black sand? Where had he gotten it?

When he opened his left hand, more sand spilled out.

Confused, he looked through the car windows at the residential neighborhood around him. He saw green lawns, dark topsoil showing through where the grass was sparse, mulch-filled planting beds, redwood chips mounded around some shrubs, but nothing like what he had held in his tightly clenched fists.

He was in Laguna Niquel, so the Pacific Ocean was nearby, rimmed by broad beaches. But those beaches were white, not black.

As full circulation returned to his cramped fingers, he leaned back in the seat, raised his hands in front of his face, and stared at the black grains that speckled his sweat-damp skin. Sand, even black sand, was a humble and innocent substance, but the residue on his hands troubled him as deeply as if it had been fresh blood.

'Who the hell am I, what's happening to me?' he wondered aloud.

He knew that he needed help. But he didn't know to whom he could turn.

• 15 •

Bobby was awakened by a Santa Ana wind soughing in the trees outside. It whistled under the eaves, and forced a chorus of ticks and creaks from the cedar-shingle roof and the attic rafters.

He blinked sleep-matted eyes and squinted at the numbers on the bedroom ceiling. 12:07. Because they sometimes worked odd hours and slept during the day, they had installed exterior Rolladen security shutters, leaving the room coal-mine dark except for the projection clock's pale green numerals, which floated on the ceiling like some portentous spirit message from Beyond.

Because he had gone to bed near dawn, and instantly to sleep, he knew the numbers on the ceiling meant that it was shortly past noon, not midnight. He had slept perhaps six hours. He lay unmoving for a moment, wondering if Julie was awake.

She said, 'I am.'

'You're spooky,' he said. 'You knew what I was thinking.'

'That's not spooky,' she said. 'That's married.'

He reached for her, and she came into his arms.

For a while they just held each other, satisfied to be close. But by mutual and unspoken desire, they began to make love.

The projection clock's glowing green numerals were too pale to relieve the absolute darkness, so Bobby could see nothing of Julie as they clung together. However, he 'saw' her through his hands. As he reveled in the smoothness and warmth of her skin, the elegant curves of her breasts, the discovery of angularity precisely where angularity was desirable, the tautness of muscle, and the fluid movement of muscle and bone, he might have been a blind man using his hands to describe an inner vision of ideal beauty.

The wind shook the world outside, in sympathy with the climaxes that shook Julie. And when Bobby could withhold himself no longer, when he cried out and emptied himself into her, the skirling wind cried, too, and a bird that had taken shelter in a nearby eave was blown from its perch with a rustle of wings and a spiraling shriek.

For a while they lay side by side in the blackness, their breath mingling, touching each other almost reverently. They did not want or need to speak; talk would have diminished the moment.

The aluminum-slat shutters vibrated softly on the huffing wind.

Gradually the afterglow of lovemaking gave way to a curious uneasiness, the source of which Bobby could not identify. The enveloping blackness began to seem oppressive, as if a continued absence of light was somehow contributing to a thickening of the air, until it would become as viscid and unbreathable as syrup.

Though he had just made love to her, he was stricken by the crazy notion that Julie was not actually there with him, that what he had coupled with was a dream, or the congealing darkness itself, and that she had been stolen from him in the night, whisked away by some power he could not fathom, and that she was forever beyond his reach.

His childish fear made him feel foolish, but he rose onto one elbow and turned on one of the wall-mounted bedside lamps.

When he saw Julie lying beside him, smiling, her head raised on a pillow, the level of his inexplicable anxiety abruptly dropped. He let out a rush of breath, surprised to discover that he'd pent it up in the first place. But a peculiar tension remained in him, and the sight of Julie, safe and undamaged but for the scabbing spot on her forehead, was insufficient to completely relax him.

'What's wrong?' she asked, as perceptive as ever.

'Nothing,' he lied.

'Bit of a headache from all that rum in the eggnog?'

What troubled him was not a hangover, but the queer, unshakable feeling that he was going to lose Julie, that something out there in a hostile world was coming to take her away. As the optimist in the family, he wasn't usually given to grim forebodings of doom; accordingly, this strange augural chill frightened him more than it would have if he had been regularly subject to such disturbances.

'Bobby?' she said, frowning.

'Headache,' he assured her.

He leaned down and gently kissed her eyes, then again, forcing her to close them so she could not see his face and read the anxiety that he was unable to conceal.

Later, after showering and dressing, they ate a hasty breakfast while standing at the kitchen counter: English muffins and raspberry jam, half a banana each, and black coffee. By mutual agreement, they were not going to the office. A brief call to Clint Karaghiosis confirmed that the wrap-up on the Decodyne case was nearly completed, and that no other business needed their urgent personal attention.

Their Suzuki Samurai waited in the garage, and Bobby's spirits rose at the sight of it. The Samurai was a small sports truck with four-wheel drive. He had justified its purchase by pitching its dual nature – utilitarian and recreational – to Julie, especially noting its comparatively reasonable price tag, but in fact he had wanted it because it was fun to drive. She had not been deceived, and she had gone for it because she, too, thought it was fun to drive. This time, she was willing to let him have the wheel when he suggested she drive.

'I did enough driving last night,' she said as she buckled herself into her shoulder harness.

Dead leaves, twigs, a few scraps of paper, and less identifiable detritus whirled and tumbled along the windswept streets. Dust devils spun out of the east, as the Santa Anas – named for the mountains out of which they arose – poured down through the canyons and across the arid, scrub-stubbled hills that Orange County's industrious developers had not yet graded and covered with thousands of nearly identical wood-and-stucco pieces of the California dream. Trees bent to the surging oceans of air that moved in powerful and erratic tides toward the real sea in the west. The previous night's fog was gone, and the day was so clear that, from the hills, Catalina Island could be seen twenty-six miles off the Pacific's distant coast.

Julie popped an Artie Shaw CD into the player, and the smooth melody and softly bouncing rhythms of 'Begin the Beguine' filled the car. The mellow saxophones of Les Robinson, Hank Freeman, Tony Pastor, and Ronnie Perry provided strange counterpoint to the chaos and dissonance of the Santa Ana winds.

From Orange, Bobby drove south and west toward the beach cities – Newport, Corona Del Mar, Laguna, Dana Point. He traveled as much as possible on those few of the urbanized county's blacktop byways that could still be called back roads. They even passed a couple of orange groves, with which the county had once been carpeted, but which had mostly fallen to the relentless advance of the tracts and malls.

Julie became more talkative and bubbly as the miles rolled up on the odometer, but Bobby knew that her spritely mood was not genuine. Each time they set out to visit her brother Thomas, she worked hard to inflate her spirits. Although she loved Thomas, every time that she was with him, her heart broke anew, so she had to fortify herself in advance with manufactured good humor.

'Not a cloud in the sky,' she said, as they passed the old Irvine Ranch fruit-packing plant. 'Isn't it a beautiful day, Bobby?'

'A wonderful day,' he agreed.

'The wind must've pushed the clouds all the way to Japan, piled them up miles high over Tokyo.'

'Yeah. Right now California litter is falling on the Ginza.'

Hundreds of red bougainvillea blossoms, stripped from their vines by the wind, blew across the road, and for a moment the Samurai seemed to be caught in a crimson snowstorm. Maybe it was because they had just spoken of Japan, but there was something oriental about the whirl of petals. He would not have been surprised to glimpse a kimono-clad woman at the side of the road, dappled in sunshine and shadow.

'Even a windstorm is beautiful here,' Julie said. 'Aren't we lucky, Bobby? Aren't we lucky to be living in this special place?'

Shaw's 'Frenesi' struck up, string-rich swing. Every time he heard the song, Bobby was almost able to imagine that he was in a movie from the 1930s or '40s, that he would turn a corner and encounter his old friend Jimmy Stewart or maybe Bing Crosby, and they'd go off to have lunch with Cary Grant and Jean Arthur and Katharine Hepburn, and screwball things would happen.

'What movie are you in?' Julie asked. She knew him too well.

'Haven't figured it yet. Maybe *The Philadelphia Story*.'

By the time they pulled into the parking lot of Cielo Vista Care Home, Julie had whipped herself into a state of high good humor. She got out of the Samurai, faced west, and grinned at the horizon, which was delineated by the marriage of sea and sky, as if she had never before encountered a sight to match it. In truth it was a stunning panorama, because Cielo Vista stood on a bluff half a mile from the Pacific, overlooking a long stretch of southern California's Gold Coast. Bobby admired it, too, shoulders hunched slightly and head tucked down in deference to the cool and blustery wind.

When Julie was ready, she took Bobby's hand and squeezed it hard, and they went inside.

Cielo Vista Care Home was a private facility, operated without government funds, and its architecture eschewed all of the standard institutional looks. Its two-story Spanish facade of pale peach stucco was accented by white marble cornerpieces, doorframes, and window lintels; white-painted French windows and doors were recessed in graceful arches, with deep sills. The sidewalks were shaded by lattice arbors draped with a mix of purple- and yellow-blooming bougainvillea, from which the wind drew a chorus of urgent whispers. Inside, the floors were gray vinyl tile, speckled with peach and turquoise, and the walls were peach with white base and crown molding, which lent the place a warm and airy ambience.

They paused in the foyer, just inside the front door, while Julie withdrew a comb from her purse and pulled the wind tangles from her hair. After stopping at the front desk in the cozy visitors' lobby, they followed the north hall to Thomas's first-floor room.

His was the second of the two beds, nearest the windows, but he was neither there nor in his armchair. When they stopped in his open doorway, he was sitting at the worktable that belonged to both him and his roommate, Derek. Bent over the table, using a pair of scissors to clip a photograph from a magazine, Thomas appeared curiously both hulking and fragile, thickset yet delicate; physically, he was solid but mentally and emotionally he was frail, and that inner weakness shone through to belie the outer image of strength. With his thick neck, heavy rounded shoulders, broad back, proportionally short arms, and stocky legs, Thomas had a gnomish look, but when he became aware of them and turned his head to see who was there, his face was not graced by the cute and beguiling features of a fairytale creature; it was instead a face of cruel genetic destiny and biological tragedy.

'Jules!' he said, dropping the scissors and magazine, nearly knocking over his chair in his haste to get up. He was wearing baggy jeans and a green-plaid flannel shirt. He seemed ten years younger than his true age. 'Jules, Jules!'

Julie let go of Bobby's hand and stepped into the room, opening her arms to her brother. 'Hi, honey.'

Thomas hurried to her in that shuffling walk of his, as if his shoes were heeled and soled with enough iron to preclude his lifting them. Although he was twenty years old, ten years younger than Julie, he was four inches shorter than she, barely five feet. He had been born with Down's syndrome, a diagnosis that even a layman could read in his face: His brow was sloped and heavy; inner epicanthic folds gave his eyes an oriental cast; the bridge of his nose was flat; his ears were low-set on a head that was slightly too small to be in proportion to his body; the rest of his features had those soft, heavy contours often associated with mental retardation. Though it was a countenance shaped more for expressions of sadness and loneliness, it now defied its naturally downcast lines and formed itself into a wondrous smile, a warm grin of pure delight.

Julie always had that effect on Thomas.

Hell, she has that effect on *me*, Bobby thought.

Stooping only slightly, Julie threw her arms around her brother when he came to her, and for a while they hugged each other.

'How're you doing?' she asked.

'Good,' Thomas said. 'I'm good.' His speech was thick but not at all difficult to understand, for his tongue was not as deformed as those of some victims of DS; it was a little larger than it should have been but not fissured or protruding. 'I'm real good.'

'Where's Derek?'

'Visiting. Down the hall. He'll be back. I'm real good. Are you good?'

'I'm fine, honey. Just great.'

'I'm just great too. I love you, Jules,' Thomas said happily, for with Julie he was always free of the shyness that colored his relations with everyone else. 'I love you so much.'

'I love you, too, Thomas.'

'I was afraid . . . maybe you wouldn't come.'

'Don't I always come?'

'Always,' he said. At last he relaxed his grip on his sister and peeked around her. 'Hi, Bobby.'

'Hi, Thomas. You're lookin' good.'

'Am I?'

'If I'm lyin', I'm dyin'.'

Thomas laughed. To Julie, he said, 'He's funny.'

'Do I get a hug too?' Bobby asked. 'Or do I have to stand here with my arms out until someone mistakes me for a hatrack?'

Hesitantly, Thomas let go of his sister. He and Bobby embraced. After all these years, Thomas was still not entirely comfortable with Bobby, not because they had bad chemistry between them or any bad feelings, but because Thomas didn't like change very much and adapted to it slowly. Even after more than seven years, his sister being married was a change, something that still felt new to him.

But he likes me, Bobby thought, maybe even as much as I like him.

Liking DS victims was not difficult, once you got past the pity that initially distanced you from them, because most of them had an innocence and guilelessness that was charming and refreshing. Except when inhibited by shyness or embarrassment about their differences, they were usually forthright, more truthful than other people, and incapable of the petty social games and scheming that marred so many relationships among 'ordinary' people. The previous summer, at Cielo Vista's Fourth of July picnic, a mother of one of the other patients had said to Bobby, 'Sometimes, watching them, I think there's something in them – a gentleness, a special kindness – that's closer to God than anything in us.' Bobby felt the truth of that observation now, as he hugged Thomas and looked down into his sweet, lumpish face.

'Did we interrupt a poem?' Julie asked.

Thomas let go of Bobby and hurried to the worktable, where Julie was looking at the magazine from which he had been clipping a picture when they'd arrived. He opened his current scrapbook – fourteen others were filled with his creations and shelved in a corner bookcase near his bed – and pointed to a two-page spread of pasted-in clippings that were arranged in lines and quatrains, like poetry.

'This was yesterday. Finished yesterday,' Thomas said. 'Took me a looooong time, and it was hard, but now it was . . . *is* . . . right.'

Four or five years ago, Thomas had decided that he wanted to be a poet like someone he had seen and admired on television. The degree of mental retardation among victims of Down's syndrome varied widely, from mild to severe; Thomas was somewhere just above the middle of the spectrum, but he did not possess the intellectual capacity to learn to write more than his name. That didn't stop him. He had asked for paper, glue, a scrapbook, and piles of old magazines. Since he rarely asked for anything, and since Julie would have moved a mountain on her back to get him whatever he wanted, the items on his list were soon in his possession. 'All kinds of magazines,' he'd said, 'with different pretty pictures . . . but ugly too . . . all kinds.' From *Time*, *Newsweek*, *Life*, *Hot Rod*, *Omni*, *Seventeen*, and dozens of other publications, he snipped whole pictures and parts of pictures, arranging them as if they were words, in a series of images that made a statement that was important to him. Some of his 'poems' were only five images long, and some involved hundreds of clippings arranged in orderly stanzas or, more often, in loosely structured lines that resembled free verse.

Julie took the scrapbook from him and went to the armchair by the window, where she could concentrate on his newest composition. Thomas remained at the worktable, watching her anxiously.

His picture poems did not tell stories or have recognizable thematic narratives, but neither were they merely random jumbles of images. A church spire, a mouse, a beautiful woman in an emerald-green ball gown, a field of daisies, a can of Dole pineapple rings, a crescent moon, pancakes in a stack with syrup drizzling down, rubies gleaming on a black-velvet display cloth, a fish with mouth agape, a child laughing, a nun praying, a woman crying over the blasted body of a loved one in some Godforsaken war zone, a pack of Lifesavers, a puppy with floppy ears, black-clad nuns with starched white wimples – from those and thousands of other pictures in his treasured boxes of clippings, Thomas selected the elements of his compositions. From the beginning Bobby recognized an uncanny *rightness* to many of the poems, a symmetry too fundamental to be defined, juxtapositions that were both naive and profound, rhythms as real as they were elusive, a personal vision plain to see but too mysterious to comprehend to any significant degree. Over the years, Bobby had seen the poems become better, more satisfying, though he understood them so little that he could not explain how he could discern the improvement; he just knew that it was there.

Julie looked up from the two-page spread in the scrapbook and said, 'This is wonderful, Thomas. It makes me want to . . . run outside in the grass . . . and stand under the sky and maybe even dance, just throw my head back and laugh. It makes me glad to be alive.'

'Yes!' Thomas said, slurring the word, clapping his hands.

She passed the book to Bobby, and he sat on the edge of the bed to read it.

The most intriguing thing about Thomas's poems was the emotional response they invariably evoked. None left a reader untouched, as an array of randomly assembled images might have done. Sometimes, when looking at Thomas's work, Bobby laughed out loud, and sometimes he was so moved that he had to blink back tears, and sometimes he felt fear or sadness or regret or wonder. He did not know why he responded to any particular piece as he did; the effect always defied analysis. Thomas's compositions functioned on some primal level, eliciting reaction from a region of the mind far deeper than the subconscious.

The latest poem was no exception. Bobby felt what Julie had felt: that life was good; that the world was beautiful; elation in the very fact of existence.

He looked up from the scrapbook and saw that Thomas was awaiting his reaction as eagerly as he had awaited Julie's, perhaps a sign that Bobby's opinion was cherished as much as hers, even if he still didn't rate as long or as ardent a hug as Julie did. 'Wow,' he said softly. 'Thomas, this one gives me such a warm, tingly feeling that . . . I think my toes are curling.'

Thomas grinned.

Sometimes Bobby looked at his brother-in-law and felt that two Thomases shared that sadly deformed skull. Thomas number one was the moron, sweet but feebleminded. Thomas number two was just as smart as anyone, but he occupied only a small part of the damaged brain that he shared with Thomas number one, a chamber in the center, from which he had no direct communication with the outside world. All of Thomas number two's thoughts had to be filtered through Thomas number one's part of the brain, so they ended up sounding no different from Thomas number one's thoughts; therefore the world could not know that number two was in there, thinking and feeling and fully *alive* – except through the evidence of the picture poems, the essence of which survived even after filtered through Thomas number one.

'You've got such a talent,' Bobby said, and he meant it – almost envied it.

Thomas blushed and lowered his eyes. He rose and quickly shuffled to the softly humming refrigerator that stood beside the door to the bathroom. Meals were served in the communal dining room, where snacks and drinks were provided on request, but patients with sufficient mental capacity to keep their rooms neat were allowed to have their own refrigerators stocked with their favorite snacks and drinks, to encourage as much independence as possible. He withdrew three cans of Coke. He gave one to Bobby, one to Julie. With the third he returned to the chair at the worktable, sat down, and said, 'You been catchin' bad guys?'

'Yeah, we're keeping the jails full,' Bobby said.

'Tell me.'

Julie leaned forward in the armchair, and Thomas scooted his straight-backed chair closer to her, until their knees touched, and she recounted the highlights of the events at Decodyne last night. She made Bobby more heroic than he'd really been, and she played down her own involvement a little, not only out of modesty but in order not to frighten Thomas with too clear a picture of the danger in which she had put herself. Thomas was tough in his own way; if he hadn't been, he would have curled up on his bed long ago, facing into the corner, and never gotten up again. But he was not tough enough to endure the loss of Julie. He would be devastated even to imagine that she was vulnerable. So she made her daredevil driving and the shoot-out sound funny, exciting but not really dangerous. Her revised version of events entertained Bobby nearly as much as it did Thomas.

After a while, as usual, Thomas became overwhelmed by what Julie was telling him, and the tale grew more confusing than entertaining. 'I'm full up,' he said, which meant he was still trying to process everything he had been told, and didn't have room for any more just now. He was fascinated by the world outside Cielo Vista, and he often longed to be a part of it, but at the same time he found it too loud and bright and colorful to be handled in more than small doses.

Bobby got one of the older scrapbooks from the shelves and sat on the bed, reading picture poems.

Thomas and Julie sat in their chairs, Cokes put aside, knees to knees, leaning forward and holding hands, sometimes looking at each other, sometimes not, just being together, close. Julie needed that as much as Thomas did.

Julie's mother had been killed when Julie was twelve. Her father had died eight years later, two years before Bobby and Julie had been married. She'd been only twenty at the time, working as a waitress to put herself through college and to pay her half of the rent on a studio apartment she shared with another student. Her parents had never been rich, and though they had kept Thomas at home, the expense of looking after him had depleted what little savings they'd ever had. When her dad died, Julie had been unable to afford an apartment for her and Thomas, to say nothing of the time required to help him cope in a civilian environment, so she'd been forced to commit him to a state institution for mentally disabled children. Though Thomas never held it against her, she viewed the commitment as a betrayal of him.

She had intended to get a degree in criminology, but she dropped out of school in her third year and applied to the sheriff's academy. She had worked as a deputy for fourteen months by the time Bobby met and married her; she had been living on peanuts, her life style hardly better than that of a bag lady, saving most of her salary in hope of putting together a nest egg that would allow her to buy a small house someday and take Thomas in with her. Shortly after they were married, when Dakota Investigations became Dakota & Dakota, they brought Thomas to live with them. But they worked irregular hours, and although some victims of Down's syndrome were capable of living to a degree on their own, Thomas needed someone nearby at all times. The cost of three daily shifts of qualified companions was even more than the cost of high-level care at a private institution like Cielo Vista; but they would have borne it if they

could have found enough reliable help. When it became impossible to conduct their business, have a life of their own, and take care of Thomas, too,
they brought him to Cielo Vista. It was as comfortable a care institution as
existed, but Julie viewed it as her second betrayal of her brother. That he
was happy at Cielo Vista, even thrived there, did not lighten her burden of
guilt.

One part of The Dream, an important part, was to have the time and financial resources to bring Thomas home again.

Bobby looked up from the scrapbook just as Julie said, 'Thomas, think you'd
like to go out with us for a while?'

Thomas and Julie were still holding hands, and Bobby saw his brother-in-
law's grip tighten at the suggestion of an excursion.

'We could just go for a drive,' Julie said. 'Down to the sea. Walk on the shore.
Get an ice cream cone. What do you say?'

Thomas looked nervously at the nearest window, which framed a portion of
clear blue sky, where white sea gulls periodically swooped and capered. 'It's bad
out.'

'Just a little windy, honey.'

'Don't mean the wind.'

'We'll have fun.'

'It's bad out,' he repeated. He chewed on his lower lip.

At times he was eager to venture out into the world, but at other times he
withdrew from the prospect as if the air beyond Cielo Vista was purest poison.
Thomas could never be argued or cajoled out of that agoraphobic mood, and
Julie knew not to push the issue.

'Maybe next time,' she said.

'Maybe,' Thomas said, looking at the floor. 'But today's *really* bad. I . . . sort
of feel it . . . the badness . . . cold all over my skin.'

For a while Bobby and Julie tried various subjects, but Thomas was talked
out. He said nothing, did not make eye contact, and gave no indication that he
even heard them.

They sat together in silence, then, until after a few minutes Thomas said,
'Don't go yet.'

'We're not going,' Bobby assured him.

'Just 'cause I can't talk . . . don't mean I want you gone.'

'We know that, kiddo,' Julie said.

'I . . . need you.'

'I need you too,' Julie said. She lifted one of her brother's thick-fingered
hands and kissed his knuckles.

• 16 •

After buying an electric razor at a drugstore, Frank Pollard shaved and washed
as best he could in a service-station restroom. He stopped at a shopping mall
and bought a suitcase, underwear, socks, a couple of shirts, another pair of
jeans, and incidentals. In the mall parking lot, with the stolen Chevy rocking
slightly in the gusting wind, he packed the other purchases in the suitcase.
Then he drove to a motel in Irvine, where he checked in under the name of

George Farris, using one of the sets of ID he possessed, making a cash deposit because he lacked a credit card. He had cash in abundance.

He could have stayed in the Laguna area; but he sensed that he should not remain in one place too long. Maybe his wariness was based on hard experience. Or maybe he had been on the run for so long that he had become a creature of motion who could never again be truly comfortable at rest.

The motel room was large, clean, and tastefully decorated. The designer had been swept up in the southwest craze: whitewashed wood, rattan side chairs with cushions upholstered in peach and pale-blue patterns, seafoam-green drapes. Only the mottled-brown carpet, evidently chosen for its ability to conceal stains and wear, spoiled the effect; by contrast, the light-hued furnishings seemed not merely to stand on the dark carpet but to float above it, creating spatial illusions that were disconcerting, even slightly eerie.

For most of the afternoon Frank sat on the bed, using a pile of pillows as a backrest. The television was on, but he did not watch it. Instead, he probed at the black hole of his past. Hard as he tried, he could still not recall anything of his life prior to waking in the alleyway the previous night. Some strange and exceedingly malevolent shape loomed at the edge of recollection, however, and he wondered uneasily if forgetfulness actually might be a blessing.

He needed help. Given the cash in the flight bag and his two sets of ID, he suspected that he would be unwise to seek assistance from the authorities. He withdrew the Yellow Pages from one of the nightstands and studied the listings for private investigators. But a PI called to mind old Humphrey Bogart movies and seemed like an anachronism in this modern age. How could a guy in a trenchcoat and a snap-brimmed fedora help him recover his memory?

Eventually, with the wind singing threnodies at the window, Frank stretched out to get some of the sleep he had missed last night.

A few hours later, just an hour before dusk, he woke suddenly, whimpering, gasping for breath. His heart pounded furiously.

When he sat up and swung his legs over the side of the bed, he saw that his hands were wet and scarlet. His shirt and jeans were smeared with blood. Some, though surely not all of it, was his own blood, for both of his hands bore deep, oozing scratches. His face stung, and in the bathroom, the mirror revealed two long scratches on his right cheek, one on his left cheek, and a fourth on his chin.

He could not understand how this could have happened in his sleep. If he had torn at himself in some bizarre dream frenzy – and he could recall no dream – or if someone else had clawed him while he slept, he would have awakened at once. Which meant that he had been awake when it had happened, then had stretched out on the bed again and gone back to sleep – and had forgotten the incident, just as he had forgotten his life prior to that alleyway last night.

He returned in panic to the bedroom and looked on the other side of the bed, then in the closet. He was not sure what he was looking for. Maybe a dead body. He found nothing.

The very thought of killing anyone made him sick. He knew he did not have the capacity to kill, except perhaps in self-defense. So who had scratched his face and hands? Whose blood was on him?

In the bathroom again, he stripped out of his stained clothes and rolled them into a tight bundle. He washed his face and hands. He had bought a styptic

pencil along with other shaving gear; he used that to stop the scratches from
bleeding.

When he met his own eyes in the mirror, they were so haunted that he had to
look away.

Frank dressed in fresh clothes and snatched the car keys off the dresser. He
was afraid of what he might find in the Chevy.

At the door, as he disengaged the dead bolt, he realized that neither the frame
nor the door itself was smeared with blood. If he had left during the afternoon
and returned, bleeding from his hands, he would not have had the presence
of mind to wipe the door clean before climbing into bed. Anyway, he had
seen no bloody washcloth or tissues with which a cleanup might have been
accomplished.

Outside, the sky was clear; the westering sun was bright. The motel's palm
trees shivered in a cool wind, and a constant susurration rose from them,
punctuated by an occasional series of hard clacks as the thick spines of the
fronds met like snapping, wooden teeth.

The concrete walkway outside his room was not spotted with blood. The
interior of the car was free of blood. No blood marked the dirty rubber mat in
the trunk, either.

He stood by the open trunk, blinking at the sun-washed motel and parking
lot around him. Three doors down, a man and woman in their twenties were
unloading luggage from their black Pontiac. Another couple and their grade-
school-age daughter were hurrying along the covered walkway, apparently
heading toward the motel restaurant. Frank realized that he could not have gone
out and committed murder and returned, blood-soaked and in broad daylight,
without being seen.

In his room again, he went to the bed and studied the rumpled sheets. They
were crimson-spotted, but not a fraction as saturated as they would have been if
the attack – whatever its nature – had happened there. Of course, if all the
blood was his, it might have spilled mostly on the front of his shirt and jeans.
But he still could not believe that he had clawed himself in his sleep – one hand
ripping at the other, both hands tearing at his face – without waking.

Besides, he had been scratched by someone with sharp fingernails. His own
nails were blunt, bitten down to the quick.

• 17 •

South of Cielo Vista Home, between Corona Del Mar and Laguna, Bobby
tucked the Samurai into a corner of a parking lot at a public beach. He and Julie
walked down to the shore.

The sea was marbled blue and green, with thin veins of gray. The water was
dark in the troughs, lighter and more colorful where the waves rose and were
half pierced by the rays of the fat, low sun. In serried ranks the breakers moved
toward the strand, big but not huge, wearing caps of foam that the wind
snatched from them.

Surfers in black wetsuits paddled their boards out toward where the swell
rose, seeking a last ride before twilight. Others, also in wetsuits, sat around a
couple of big coolers, drinking hot beverages from thermos bottles or Coors

from the can. The day was too cool for sunbathing, and except for the surfers, the beach was deserted.

Bobby and Julie walked south until they found a low knoll, far enough back from the water to escape the spray. They sat on the stiff grass that flourished in patches in the sandy, salt-tinged soil.

When at last she spoke, Julie said, 'A place like this, with a view like this. Not a big place.'

'Doesn't have to be. A living room, one bedroom for us and one for Thomas, maybe a cozy little den lined with books.'

'We don't even need a dining room, but I'd like a big kitchen.'

'Yeah. A kitchen you can really live in.'

She sighed. 'Music, books, real home-cooked meals instead of junk food grabbed on the fly, lots of time to sit on the porch and enjoy the view – and the three of us together.'

That was the rest of The Dream: a place by the sea and – by otherwise living simply – enough financial security to retire twenty years early.

One of the things that had drawn Bobby to Julie – and Julie to him – was their shared awareness of the shortness of life. Everyone knew that life was too short, of course, but most people pushed that thought out of mind, living as if there were endless tomorrows. If most people weren't able to deceive themselves about death, they could not have cared so passionately about the outcome of a ball game, the plot of a soap opera, the blatherings of politicians, or a thousand other things that actually meant nothing when considered against the inevitable fall of the endless night that finally came to everyone. They could not have endured to waste a minute standing in a supermarket line and would not have suffered hours in the company of bores or fools. Maybe a world lay beyond this one, maybe even Heaven, but you couldn't count on it; you could count only on darkness. Self-deception in this case was a blessing. Neither Bobby nor Julie was a gloom-monger. She knew how to enjoy life as well as anyone, and so did he, even if neither of them could buy the fragile illusion of immortality that served most people as a defense against the unthinkable. Their awareness expressed itself not in anxiety or depression, but in a strong resolve not to spend their lives in a hurly-burly of meaningless activity, to find a way to finance long stretches of time together in their own serene little tide pool.

As her chestnut hair streamed in the wind, Julie squinted at the far horizon, which was filling up with honey-gold light as the sinking sun drizzled toward it. 'What frightens Thomas about being out in the world is people, too many people. But he'd be happy in a little house by the sea, a quiet stretch of coast, few people. I'm sure he would.'

'It'll happen,' Bobby assured her.

'By the time we build the agency big enough to sell, the southern coast will be too expensive. But north of Santa Barbara is pretty.'

'It's a long coast,' Bobby said, putting an arm around her. 'We'll still be able to find a place in the south. And we'll have time to enjoy it. We're not going to live forever, but we're young. Our numbers aren't going to come up for years and years yet.'

But he remembered the premonition that had shivered through him in bed that morning, after they had made love, the feeling that something malevolent was out there in the windswept world, coming to take Julie away from him.

The sun had touched the horizon and begun to melt into it. The golden light deepened swiftly to orange and then to bloody red. The grass and tall weeds behind them rustled in the wind, and Bobby looked over his shoulder at the spirals of airborne sand that swirled across the slope between the beach and the parking lot, like pale spirits that had fled a graveyard with the coming of twilight. From the east a wall of night was toppling over the world. The air had grown downright cold.

• **18** •

Candy slept all day in the front bedroom that had once been his mother's, breathing her special scent. Two or three times a week, he carefully shook a few drops of her favorite perfume – Chanel No. 5 – onto a white, lace-trimmed handkerchief, which he kept on the dresser beside her silver comb-and-brush set, so each breath he took in the room reminded him of her. Occasionally he half woke from slumber to readjust the pillows or pull the covers more tightly around him, and the trace of perfume always lulled him as if it were a tranquilizer; each time he happily drifted back into his dreams.

He slept in sweatpants and a T-shirt, because he had a hard time finding pajamas large enough and because he was too modest to sleep in the nude or even in his underwear. Being unclothed embarrassed Candy, even when no one was around to see him.

All of that long Thursday afternoon, hard winter sun filled the world outside, but little got past the flower-patterned shades and rose-colored drapes that guarded the two windows. The few times he woke and blinked at the shadows, Candy saw only the pearl-gray glimmer of the dresser mirror and glints from the silver-framed photographs on the nightstand. Drugged by sleep and by the freshly applied perfume on the handkerchief, he could easily imagine that his beloved mother was in her rocking chair, watching over him, and he felt safe.

He came fully awake shortly before sunset and lay for a while with his hands folded behind his head, staring up at the underside of the canopy that arched over the four-poster; he could not see it, but he knew it was there, and in his mind he could conjure up a vivid image of the fabric's rosebud pattern. For a while he thought about his mother, about the best times of his life, now all gone, and then he thought about the girl, the boy, and the woman he had killed last night. He tried to recall the taste of their blood, but that memory was not as intense as those involving his mother.

After a while he switched on a bedside lamp and looked around at the comfortably familiar room: rosebud wallpaper; rosebud bedspread; rosebud blinds; rose-colored drapes and carpets; dark mahogany bed, dresser, and highboy. Two afghans – one green like the leaves of a rose, one the shade of the petals – were draped over the arms of the rocking chair.

He went into the adjoining bathroom, locked and tested the door. The only light came from the fluorescent panels in the soffit, over the sink, for he had long ago lathered black paint on the small, high window.

He studied his face in the mirror for a moment because he liked the way he looked. He could see his mother in his face. He had her blond hair, so pale it was almost white, and her sea-blue eyes. His face was all hard planes and strong features, with none of her beauty or gentleness, though his full mouth was as generous as hers.

As he undressed, he avoided looking down at himself. He was proud of his powerful shoulders and arms, his broad chest, and his muscular legs, but even catching a glimpse of the sex thing made him feel dirty and mildly ill. He sat on the toilet to make water, so he wouldn't have to touch himself. During his shower, when he soaped his crotch, he first pulled on a mitten that he had sewn from a pair of washcloths, so the flesh of his hand would not have to touch the wicked flesh below.

When he had dried off and dressed – athletic socks, running shoes, dark gray cords, black shirt – he hesitantly left the reliable shelter of his mother's old room. Night had fallen, and the upstairs hall was poorly lit by two low-wattage bulbs in a ceiling fixture that was coated with gray dust and missing half its pendant crystals. To his left was the head of the staircase. To his right were his sisters' room, his old room, and the other bath, the doors to which stood open; no lights were on back there. The oak floor creaked, and the threadbare runner did little to soften his footsteps. He sometimes thought he should give the rest of the house a thorough cleaning, maybe even spring for some new carpeting and fresh paint; however, though he kept his mother's room spotless and in good repair, he was not motivated to spend time or money on the rest of the house, and his sisters had little interest in – or talent for – homemaking.

A flurry of soft footfalls alerted him to the approach of the cats, and he stopped short of the stairs, afraid of treading on one of their paws or tails as they poured into the upstairs hall. A moment later they streamed over the top step and swarmed around him: twenty-six of them, if his most recent count was not out of date. Eleven were black, several more were chocolate-brown or tobacco-brown or charcoal-gray, two were deep gold, and only one was white. Violet and Verbina, his sisters, preferred dark cats, the darker the better.

The animals milled around him, walking over his shoes, rubbing against his legs, curling their tails around his calves. Among them were two Angoras, an Abyssinian, a tailless Manx, a Maltese and a tortoise-shell, but most were mongrel cats of no easily distinguished lineage. Some had green eyes, some yellow, some silver-gray, some blue, and they all regarded him with great interest. Not one of them purred or meowed; their inspection was conducted in absolute silence.

Candy did not particularly like cats, but he tolerated these not only because they belonged to his sisters but because, in a way, they were virtually an extension of Violet and Verbina. To have hurt them, to have spoken harshly to them, would have been the same as striking out at his sisters, which he could never do because his mother, on her deathbed, had admonished him to provide for the girls and protect them.

In less than a minute the cats had fulfilled their mission and, almost as one, turned from him. With much swishing of tails and flexing of feline muscles and rippling of fur, they flowed like a single beast to the head of the stairs and down.

By the time he reached the first step, they were at the landing, turning, slipping out of sight. He descended to the lower hall, and the cats were gone. He passed the lightless and musty smelling parlor. The odor of mildew drifted out of the study, where shelves were filled with the moldering romance novels that his mother had liked so much, and when he passed through the dimly lit dining room, litter crunched under his shoes.

Violet and Verbina were in the kitchen. They were identical twins. They were equally blond, with the same fair and faultless skin, with the same china-blue eyes, smooth brows, high cheekbones, straight noses with delicately carved nostrils, lips that were naturally red without lipstick, and small even teeth as bone-white as those of their cats.

Candy tried to like his sisters, and failed. For his mother's sake he could not *dis*like them, so he remained neutral, sharing the house with them but not as a real family might share it. They were too thin, he thought, fragile looking, almost frail, and too pale, like creatures that infrequently saw the sun – which in fact seldom warmed them, since they rarely went outside. Their slim hands were well manicured, for they groomed themselves as constantly as if they, too, were cats; but, to Candy, their fingers seemed excessively long, unnaturally flexible and nimble. Their mother had been robust, with strong features and good color, and Candy often wondered how such a vital woman could have spawned this pallid pair.

The twins had piled up cotton blankets, six thick, in one corner of the big kitchen, to make a large area where the cats could lie comfortably, though the padding was actually for Violet and Verbina, so they could sit on the floor among the cats for hours at a time. When Candy entered the room, they were on the blankets, with cats all around them and in their laps. Violet was filing Verbina's fingernails with an emery board. Neither of them looked up, though of course they had already greeted him through the cats. Verbina had never spoken a word within Candy's hearing, not in her entire twenty-five years – the twins were four years younger than he was – but he was not sure whether she was unable to talk, merely unwilling to talk, or shy of talking only when around him. Violet was nearly as silent as her sister, but she did speak when necessary; apparently, at the moment, she had nothing that needed to be said.

He stood by the refrigerator, watching them as they huddled over Verbina's pale right hand, grooming it, and he supposed that he was unfair in his judgment of them. Other men might find them attractive in a strange way. Though, to him, their limbs seemed too thin, other men might see them as supple and erotic, like the legs of dancers and the arms of acrobats. Their skin was clear as milk, and their breasts were full. Because he was blessedly free of any interest in sex, he was not qualified to judge their appeal.

They habitually wore as little as possible, as little as he would tolerate before ordering them to put on more clothes. They kept the house excessively warm in winter, and most often dressed – as now – in T-shirts and short shorts or panties, barefoot and bare-limbed. Only his mother's room, which was now his, was kept cooler, because he had closed the vents up there. Without his presence to demand a degree of modesty, they would have roamed the house in the nude.

Lazily, lazily, Violet filed Verbina's thumbnail, and they both stared at it as intently as if the meaning of life was to be read in the curve of the half-moon or the arc of the nail itself.

Candy raided the refrigerator, removing a chunk of canned ham, a package of Swiss cheese, mustard, pickles, and a quart of milk. He got bread from one of the cupboards and sat in a railback chair at the age-yellowed table.

The table, chairs, cabinets, and woodwork had once been glossy white, but they had not been painted since before his mother died. They were yellow-white now, gray-white in the seams and corners, crackle-finished by time. The daisy-patterned wallpaper was soiled and, in a couple of places, peeling along the seams, and the chintz curtains hung limp with grease and dust.

Candy made and consumed two thick ham-and-cheese sandwiches. He gulped the milk straight from the carton.

Suddenly all twenty-six cats, which had been sprawling languidly around the twins, sprang up simultaneously, proceeded to the pet door in the bottom of the larger kitchen door, and went outside in orderly fashion. Time to make their toilet, evidently. Violet and Verbina didn't want the house smelling of litter boxes.

Candy closed his eyes and took a long swallow of milk. He would have preferred it at room temperature or even slightly warm. It tasted vaguely like blood, though not as pleasantly pungent; it would have been more like blood if it had not been chilled.

Within a couple of minutes the cats returned. Now Verbina was lying on her back, with her head propped on a pillow, eyes closed, lips moving as if talking to herself, though no sound issued from her. She extended her other slender hand so her sister could meticulously file those nails too. Her long legs were spread, and Candy could see between her smooth thighs. She was wearing only a T-shirt and flimsy peach-colored panties that defined rather than concealed the cleft of her womanhood. The silent cats swarmed to her, draped themselves over her, more concerned about propriety than she was, and they regarded Candy accusatorily, as if they knew that he'd been staring.

He lowered his eyes and studied the crumbs on the table.

Violet said, 'Frankie was here.'

At first he was more surprised by the fact that she had spoken than by what she had said. Then the meaning of those three words reverberated through him as if he were a brass gong struck by a mallet. He stood up so abruptly that he knocked over his chair. 'He was here? In the house?'

Neither the cats nor Verbina twitched at the crash of the chair or the sharpness of his voice. They lay somnolent, indifferent.

'Outside,' Violet said, still sitting on the floor beside her reclining sister, working on the other twin's nails. She had a low, almost whispery voice. 'Watching the house from the Eugenia hedge.'

Candy glanced at the night beyond the windows. 'When?'

'Around four o'clock.'

'Why didn't you wake me?'

'He wasn't here long. He's never here long. A minute or two, then he goes. He's afraid.'

'You saw him?'

'I knew he was there.'

'You didn't try to stop him from leaving?'

'How could I?' She sounded irritable now, but her voice was no less seductive than it had been. 'The cats went after him, though.'

'Did they hurt him?'

'A little. Not bad. But he killed Samantha.'

'Who?'

'Our poor little puss. Samantha.'

Candy did not know the cats' names. They had always seemed to be not just a pack of cats but a single creature, most often moving as one, apparently thinking as one.

'He killed Samantha. Smashed her head against one of the stone pilasters at the end of the walk.' At last Violet looked up from her sister's hand. Her eyes seemed to be a paler blue than before, icy. 'I want you to hurt him, Candy. I want you to hurt him real bad, the way he hurt our cat. I don't care if he is our brother—'

'He isn't our brother any more, not after what he did,' Candy said furiously.

'I want you to do to him what he did to our poor Samantha. I want you to smash him, Candy, I want you to crush his head, crack his skull open until his brains ooze out.' She continued to speak softly, but he was riveted by her words. Sometimes, like now, when her voice was even more sensuous than usual, it seemed not merely to play upon his ears but to slither into his head, where it lay gently on his brain, like a mist, a fog. 'I want you to pound him, hit him and tear him until he's just splintered bones and ruptured guts, and I want you to rip out his eyes. I want him to be sorry he hurt Samantha.'

Candy shook himself. 'If I get my hands on him, I'll kill him, all right, but not because of what he did to your cat. Because of what he did to our *mother*. Don't you remember what he did to *her*? How can you worry about getting revenge for a cat when we still haven't made him pay for our mother, after seven long years?'

She looked stricken, turned her face from him, and fell silent.

The cats flowed off Verbina's recumbent form.

Violet stretched out half atop her sister, half beside her. She put her head on Verbina's breasts. Their bare legs were entwined.

Rising part of the way out of her trancelike state, Verbina stroked her sister's silken hair.

The cats returned and cuddled against both twins wherever there was a warm hollow to welcome them.

'Frank was here,' Candy said aloud but largely to himself, and his hands curled into tight fists.

A fury grew in him, like a small turning wheel of wind far out on the sea but soon to whirl itself into a hurricane. However, rage was an emotion he dared not indulge; he must control himself. A storm of rage would water the seeds of his dark need. His mother would approve of killing Frank, for Frank had betrayed the family; his death would benefit the family. But if Candy let his anger at his brother swell into a rage, then was unable to find Frank, he would have to kill someone else, because the need would be too great to deny. His mother, in Heaven, would be ashamed of him, and for a while she would turn her face from him and deny that she had ever given birth to him.

Looking up at the ceiling, toward the unseen sky and the place at God's court where his mother dwelled, Candy said, 'I'll be okay. I won't lose control. I won't.'

He turned from his sisters and the cats, and he went outside to see if any trace of Frank remained near the Eugenia hedge or at the pilaster where he'd killed Samantha.

Bobby and Julie ate dinner at Ozzie's in Orange, then shifted to the adjoining bar. The music was provided by Eddie Day, who had a smooth, supple voice; he played contemporary stuff but also tunes from the fifties and early sixties. It wasn't Big Band, but some early rock-and-roll had a swing beat. They could swing to numbers like 'Dream Lover,' rumba to 'La Bamba,' and cha-cha to any disco ditty that crept into Eddie's repertoire, so they had a good time.

Whenever possible, Julie liked to go dancing after she visited Thomas at Cielo Vista. In the thrall of the music, keeping time to the beat, focused on the patterns of the dance, she was able to put everything else out of her mind – even guilt, even grief. Nothing else freed her so completely. Bobby liked to dance, too, especially swing. Tuck in, throw out, change places, sugarpush, do a tight whip, tuck in again, throw out, trade places with both hands linked, back to basic position . . . Music soothed, but dance had the power to fill the heart with joy and to numb those parts of it that were bruised.

During the musicians' break, Bobby and Julie sipped beer at a table near the edge of the parquet dance floor. They talked about everything except Thomas, and eventually they got around to The Dream – specifically, how to furnish the seaside bungalow if they ever bought it. Though they would not spend a fortune on furniture, they agreed that they could indulge themselves with two pieces from the swing era: maybe a bronze and marble Art Deco cabinet by Emile-Jacques Ruhlmann, and *definitely* a Wurlitzer jukebox.

'The model 950,' Julie said. 'It was gorgeous. Bubble tubes. Leaping gazelles on the front panels.'

'Fewer than four thousand were made. Hitler's fault. Wurlitzer retooled for war production. The Model 500 is pretty too – or the 700.'

'Nice, but they're not the 950.'

'Not as *expensive* as the 950, either.'

'You're counting pennies when we're talking ultimate beauty?'

He said, 'Ultimate beauty is the Wurlitzer 950?'

'That's right. What else?'

'To me, you're the ultimate beauty.'

'Sweet,' she said. 'But I still want the 950.'

'To you, aren't *I* the ultimate beauty?' He batted his eyelashes.

'To me, you're just a difficult man who won't let me have my Wurlitzer 950,' she said, enjoying the game.

'What about a Seeburg? A Packard Pla-mor? Okay. A Rock-ola?'

'Rock-ola made some beautiful boxes,' she agreed. 'We'll buy one of those *and* the Wurlitzer 950.'

'You'll spend our money like a drunken sailor.'

'I was born to be rich. Stork got confused. Didn't deliver me to the Rockefellers.'

'Wouldn't you like to get your hands on that stork now?'

'Got him years ago. Cooked him, ate him for Christmas dinner. He was delicious, but I'd still rather be a Rockefeller.'

'Happy?' Bobby asked.

'Delirious. And it's not just the beer. I don't know why, but tonight I feel better than I've felt in ages. I think we're going to get where we want to go,

Bobby. I think we're going to retire early and live a long happy life by the sea.'

His smile faded as she talked. Now he was frowning.

She said, 'What's wrong with you, Sourpuss?'

'Nothing.'

'Don't kid me. You've been a little strange all day. You've tried to hide it, but something's on your mind.'

He sipped his beer. Then: 'Well, you've got this good feeling that everything's going to be fine, but I've got a bad feeling.'

'You? Mr Blue Skies?'

He was still frowning. 'Maybe you should confine yourself to office work for a while, stay off the firing line.'

'Why?'

'My bad feeling.'

'Which is?'

'That I'm going to lose you.'

'Just try.'

• 20 •

With its invisible baton, the wind conducted a chorus of whispery voices in the hedgerow. The dense Eugenias formed a seven-foot-high wall around three sides of the two-acre property, and they would have been higher than the house itself if Candy had not used power trimmers to chop off the tops of them a couple of times each year.

He opened the waist-high, wrought-iron gate between the two stone pilasters, and stepped out onto the graveled shoulder of the county road. To his left, the two-lane blacktop wound up into the hills for another couple of miles. To his right, it dropped down toward the distant coast, past houses on lots that were more parsimoniously proportioned the nearer they were to the shore, until in town they were only a tenth as big as the Pollard place. As the land descended westward, lights were clustered in ever greater concentration – then stopped abruptly, several miles away, as if crowding against a black wall; that wall was the night sky and the lightless expanse of the deep, cold sea.

Candy moved along the high hedge, until he sensed that he had reached the place where Frank had stood. He held up both big hands, letting the wind-fluttered leaves tremble against his palms, as if the foliage might impart to him some psychic residue of his brother's brief visit. Nothing.

Parting the branches, he peered through the gap at the house, which looked larger at night than it really was, as if it had eighteen or twenty rooms instead of ten. The front windows were dark; along the side, toward the back, where the light was filtered through greasy chintz curtains, a kitchen window was filled with a yellow glow. But for that one light, the house might have appeared abandoned. Some of the Victorian gingerbread had warped and broken away from the eaves. The porch roof was sagging, and a few railing balusters were broken, and the front steps were swaybacked. Even by the meager light of the low crescent moon, he could see the house needed painting; bare wood, like glimpses of dark bone, showed in many places, and the remaining paint was either peeling or as translucent as an albino's skin.

Candy tried to put himself in Frank's mind, to imagine why Frank kept returning. Frank was afraid of Candy, and he had reason to be. He was afraid of his sisters, too, and of all the memories that the house held for him, so he should have stayed away. But he crept back with frequency, in search of something – perhaps something that even he did not understand.

Frustrated, Candy let the branches fall together, retraced his steps along the hedge, and stopped at one gatepost, then the other, searching for the spot where Frank had fended off the cats and smashed Samantha's skull. Though far milder now than it had been earlier, the wind nevertheless had dried the blood that had stained the stones, and darkness hid the residue. Still, Candy was sure he could find the killing place. He gingerly touched the pilaster high and low, on all four faces, as if he expected a portion of it to be hot enough to sear his skin. But though he patiently traced the outlines of the rough stones and the mortar seams, too much time had passed; even his exceptional talents could not extract his brother's lingering aura.

He hurried along the cracked and canted walkway, out of the chilly night and into the stiflingly warm house again, into the kitchen, where his sisters were sitting on the blankets in the cats' corner. Verbina was behind Violet, a comb in one hand and a brush in the other, grooming her sister's flaxen hair.

Candy said, 'Where's Samantha?'

Tilting her head, looking up at him perplexedly, Violet said, 'I told you. Dead.'

'Where's the *body*?'

'Here,' Violet said, making a sweeping gesture with both hands to indicate the quiescent felines sprawled and curled around her.

'Which one?' Candy asked. Half of the creatures were so still that any of them might have been the dead one.

'All,' Violet said. 'They're all Samantha now.'

Candy had been afraid of that. Each time one of the cats died, the twins drew the rest of the pack into a circle, placed the corpse at the center, and without speaking commanded the living to partake of the dead.

'Damn,' Candy said.

'Samantha still lives, she's still a part of us,' Violet said. Her voice was as low and whispery as before, but dreamier than usual. 'None of our pusses ever really leaves us. Part of him . . . or her . . . stays in each of us . . . and we're all stronger because of that, stronger and purer, and always together, always and forever.'

Candy did not ask if his sisters had shared in the feast, for he already knew the answer. Violet licked the corner of her mouth, as if remembering the taste, and her moist lips glistened; a moment later Verbina's tongue slid across her lips too.

Sometimes Candy felt as if the twins were members of an entirely different species from him, for he could seldom fathom their attitudes and behavior. And when they looked at him – Verbina, in perpetual silence – their faces and eyes revealed nothing of their thoughts or feelings; they were as inscrutable as the cats.

He only dimly grasped the twins' bond with the cats. It was their blessed mother's gift to them just as his many talents were his mother's generous bequest to him, so he did not question the rightness or wholesomeness of it.

Still, he wanted to hit Violet because she hadn't saved the body for him. She had known Frank had touched it, that it could be of use to Candy, but she had not saved it until he'd awakened, had not come to wake him early. He wanted to smash her, but she was his sister, and he couldn't hurt his sisters; he had to provide for them, protect them. His mother was watching.

'The parts that couldn't be eaten?' he asked.

Violet gestured toward the kitchen door.

He switched on the outside light and stepped onto the back porch. Small knobs of bone and vertebrae were scattered like queerly shaped dice on the unpainted floorboards. Only two sides of the porch were open; the house angled around the other two flanks of it, and in the niche where the house walls met, Candy found a piece of Samantha's tail and scraps of fur, jammed there by the night wind. The half-crushed skull was on the top step. He snatched it up and moved down onto the unmown lawn.

The wind, which had been declining since late afternoon, suddenly stopped altogether. The cool air would have carried the faintest sound a great distance; but the night was hushed.

Usually Candy could touch an object and see who had recently handled it before him. Sometimes he could even see where some of those people had gone after putting the object down, and when he went looking for them, they were always to be found where his clairvoyance had led him. Frank had killed the cat, and Candy hoped that contact with the remains would spark an inner vision that would put him on his brother's trail again.

Every speck of flesh had been stripped from Samantha's broken pate, and its contents had been emptied as well. Picked clean, licked smooth, dried by the wind, it might have been a portion of a fossil from a distant age. Candy's mind was filled not with images of Frank but of the other cats and Verbina and Violet, and finally he threw down the damaged skull in disgust.

His frustration sharpened his anger. He felt the need rising in him. He dared not let the need bloom . . . but resisting it was infinitely harder than resisting the charms of women and other sins. He *hated* Frank. He hated him so much, so deeply, had hated him so constantly for seven years, that he could not bear the thought that he had slept through an opportunity to destroy him.

Need . . .

He dropped to his knees on the weedy lawn. He fisted his hands and hunched his shoulders and clenched his teeth, trying to make a rock of himself, an unmovable mass that would not be swayed one inch by the most urgent need, not one hair's width by even the most dire necessity, the most demanding hunger, the most passionate craving. He prayed to his mother to give him strength. The wind began to pick up again, and he believed it was a devil wind that would blow him toward temptation, so he fell forward on the ground and dug his fingers into the yielding earth, and he repeated his mother's sacred name – Roselle – whispered her name furiously into the grass and dirt, again and again, desperate to quell the germination of his dark need. Then he wept. Then he got up. And went hunting.

• 21 •

Frank went to a theater and sat through a movie but was unable to concentrate on the story. He ate dinner at El Torito, though he didn't really taste the food; he just pushed down the enchiladas and rice as if feeding fuel to a furnace. For a couple of hours he drove aimlessly back and forth across the middle and southern reaches of Orange County, staying on the move only because, for the time being, he felt safer when in motion. Finally he returned to the motel.

He kept probing at the dark wall in his mind, behind which his entire life was concealed. Diligently, he sought the tiniest chink through which he might glimpse a memory. If he could find one crack, he was sure that the entire facade of amnesia would come tumbling down. But the barrier was smooth and flawless.

When he switched off the lights, he could not sleep.

The Santa Anas had abated. He could not blame his insomnia on the noisy winds.

Although the amount of blood on the sheets had been minimal and though it had dried since he'd awakened from his nap earlier in the day, he decided that the thought of lying in bloodstained bedclothes was preventing him from nodding off. He snapped on a lamp, stripped the bed, turned up the heat, stretched out in the darkness again, and tried to sleep without covers. No good.

He told himself that his amnesia – and the resultant loneliness and sense of isolation – was keeping him awake. Although there was some truth in that, he knew that he was kidding himself.

The real reason he could not sleep was fear. Fear of where he might go while sleepwalking. Fear of what he might do. Fear of what he might find in his hands when he woke up.

• 22 •

Derek slept. In the other bed. Snoring softly.

Thomas couldn't sleep. He got up and stood by the window, looking out. The moon was gone. The dark was very big.

He didn't like the night. It scared him. He liked sunshine, and flowers all bright, and grass looking green, and blue sky all over so you felt like there was a lid on the world keeping everything down here on the ground and in place. At night all the colors were gone, and the world was empty, like somebody took the lid off and let in a lot of nothingness, and you looked up at all that nothingness and you felt you might just float away like the colors, float up and away and out of the world, and then in the morning when they put the lid back on, you wouldn't be here, you'd be out there somewhere, and you could never get back in again. Never.

He put his fingertips against the window. The glass was cool.

He wished he could sleep away the night. Usually he slept okay. Not tonight.

He was worried about Julie. He always worried about her a little. A brother was supposed to worry. But this wasn't a little worry. This was a lot.

It started just that morning. A funny feeling. Not funny ha-ha. Funny strange. Funny scary. Something real bad's going to happen to Julie, the feeling said. Thomas got so upset, he tried to warn her. He TVed a warning to her. They said the pictures and voices and music on the TV were sent through the air, which he first thought was a lie, that they were making fun of his being dumb, expecting him to believe *anything*, but then Julie said it was true, so sometimes he tried to TV his thoughts to her, because if you could send pictures and music and voices through the air, thoughts ought to be easy. *Be careful, Julie*, he TVed. *Look out, be careful, something bad's going to happen.*

Usually, when he felt things about someone, that someone was Julie. He knew when she was happy. Or sad. When she was sick, he sometimes curled up on his bed and put his hands on his own belly. He always knew when she was coming to visit.

He felt things about Bobby too. Not at first. When Julie first brought Bobby around, Thomas felt nothing. But slowly he felt more. Until now he felt almost as much about Bobby as about Julie.

He felt things about some other people too. Like Derek. Like Gina, another Down's kid at The Home. And like a couple of the aides, one of the visiting nurses. But he didn't feel half as much about them as he did about Bobby and Julie. He figured that maybe the more he loved somebody, the bigger he felt things – *knew* things – about them.

Sometimes when Julie was worried about him, Thomas wanted real bad to tell her that he knew how she felt, and that he was all right. Because just knowing he understood would make her happier. But he didn't have the words. He couldn't explain how or why he sometimes felt other people's feelings. And he didn't want to try to tell them about it because he was afraid of looking dumb.

He *was* dumb. He knew that. He wasn't as dumb as Derek, who was very nice, good to room with, but who was real slow. They sometimes said 'slow' instead of 'dumb' when they talked in front of you. Julie never did. Bobby never did. But some people said 'slow' and thought you didn't get it. He got it. They had bigger words, too, and he really didn't understand those, but he sure understood 'slow.' He didn't *want* to be dumb, nobody gave him a choice, and sometimes he TVed a message to God, asking God to make him not dumb any more, but either God wanted him to stay dumb always and forever – but why? – or God just didn't get the messages.

Julie didn't get the messages either. Thomas always knew when he got through to someone with a TVed thought. He never got to Julie.

But he could sometimes get through to Bobby, which was funny. Not ha-ha funny. Strange funny. Interesting funny. When Thomas TVed a thought to Julie, Bobby sometimes got it instead. Like this morning. When he'd TVed a warning to Julie—

—*Something bad's going to happen, Julie, something real bad is coming*—

—Bobby had picked it up. Maybe because Thomas and Bobby both loved Julie. Thomas didn't know. He couldn't figure. But it sure happened. Bobby tuned in.

Now Thomas stood at the window, in his pajamas, and looked out at the scary night, and he felt the Bad Thing out there, felt it like a ripple in his blood, like a tingle in his bones. The Bad Thing was far away, not anywhere near Julie, but coming.

Today, during Julie's visit, Thomas wanted to tell her about the Bad Thing coming. But he couldn't find a way to say it and make sense, and he was scared of sounding dumb. Julie and Bobby knew he was dumb, sure, but he hated to sound dumb in front of them, to *remind* them how dumb he was. Every time he almost started to tell her about the Bad Thing, he just forgot how to use words. He had the words in his head, all lined up in a row, ready to say, but then suddenly they were mixed up, and he couldn't make them get back in the right order, so he couldn't say the words because they'd be just words without meaning anything, and he'd look really, really dumb.

Besides, he didn't know what to tell her the Bad Thing was. He thought maybe it was a person, a real terrible person out there, going to do something to Julie, but it didn't exactly feel like a person. Partly a person, but something else. Something that made Thomas feel cold not just on his outside but on his inside, too, like standing in a winter wind and eating ice cream at the same time.

He shivered.

He didn't want to get these ugly feelings about whatever was out there, but he couldn't just go back to bed and tune out, either, because the more he felt about the far-away Bad Thing, the better he could warn Julie and Bobby when the thing wasn't so far away any more.

Behind him, Derek murmured in a dream.

The Home was real quiet. All the dumb people were deep asleep. Except Thomas. Sometimes he liked to be awake when everyone else wasn't. Sometimes that made him feel smarter than all of them put together, seeing things they couldn't see and knowing things they couldn't know because they were asleep and he wasn't.

He stared at the nothingness of night.

He put his forehead against the glass.

For Julie's sake, he reached. Into the nothingness. Toward the far-away.

He opened himself. To the feelings. To the ripple-tingle.

A big ugly-nasty hit him. Like a wave. It came out of the night and hit him, and he stumbled back from the window and fell on his butt beside the bed, and then he couldn't feel the Bad Thing at all, it was gone, but what he had felt was so big and so ugly that his heart was pounding and he could hardly breathe, and right away he TVed to Bobby:

Run, go, get away, save Julie, the Bad Thing's coming, the Bad Thing, run, run.

· 23 ·

The dream was filled with the music of Glenn Miller's '*Moonlight Serenade*,' though like everything in dreams, the song was indefinably different from the real tune. Bobby was in a house that was at once familiar yet totally strange, and somehow he knew it was the seaside bungalow to which he and Julie were going to retire young. He drifted into the living room, over a dark Persian carpet, past comfortable-looking upholstered chairs, a huge old chesterfield with rounded back and thick cushions, a Ruhlmann cabinet with bronze panels, an Art Deco lamp, and overflowing bookshelves. The music was coming from outside, so he went out there. He enjoyed the easy transitions of the dream, moving through a door without opening it, crossing a wide porch and descending wooden stairs without ever quite lifting a foot. The sea rumbled to one side, and the phosphorescent foam of the breakers glowed faintly in the night. Under a palm tree, in the sand, with a scattering of shells around it, stood a Wurlitzer 950, ablaze with gold and red light, bubble tubes percolating, gazelles perpetually leaping, figures of Pan perpetually piping, record-changing mechanism gleaming like real silver, and a large black platter spinning on the turntable. Bobby felt as if 'Moonlight Serenade' would go on forever, which would have been fine with him, because he had never been more mellow, more at peace, and he sensed that Julie had come out of the house behind him, that she was waiting on the damp sand near the water's edge, and that she wanted to dance with him, so he turned, and there she was, exotically illuminated by the Wurlitzer, and he took a step toward her—

Run, go, get away, save Julie, the Bad Thing's coming, the Bad Thing, run, run!

The indigo ocean suddenly leapt as if under the lash of a storm, and spume exploded into the night air.

Hurricane winds shook the palms.

The Bad Thing! Run! Run!

The world tilted. Bobby stumbled toward Julie. The sea surged up around her. It wanted her; it was going to seize her; it was water with a will, a thinking sea with a malevolent consciousness gleaming darkly in its depths.

The Bad Thing!

The Glenn Miller tune speeded up, whirling at doubletime.

The Bad Thing!

The soft, romantic light from the Wurlitzer flamed brighter, stung his eyes, yet did not drive back the night. It was radiating light as if the door to Hell had opened, but the darkness around them only intensified, yielding nothing to that supernatural blaze.

THE BAD THING! THE BAD THING!

The world tilted again. Heaved and rolled.

Bobby staggered across the carnival-ride beach, toward Julie, who seemed unable to move. She was being swallowed by the churning oil-black sea.

THE BAD THING THE BAD THING THE BAD THING!

With the hard crack of riven stone, the sky split above them, but no lightning stabbed out of that crumbling vault.

Geysers of sand erupted around Bobby. Inky water exploded out of sudden gaping holes in the beach.

He looked back. The bungalow was gone. The sea rose on all sides. The beach was dissolving under his feet.

Screaming, Julie disappeared under the water.

BADTHINGBADTHINGBADTHINGBADTHING!

A twenty-foot wave loomed over Bobby. It broke. He was swept away. He tried to swim. The flesh on his arms and hands bubbled and blistered and began to peel off, revealing glints of ice-white bone. The midnight seawater was an acid. His head went under. He gasped, broke the surface, but the corrosive sea had already kissed away his lips, and he felt his gums receding from his teeth, and his tongue turned to rancid mush in the salty rush of caustic brine that he had swallowed. Even the spray-filled air was erosive, eating away his lungs in an instant, so when he tried to breathe he could not. He went down, flailing at the waves with arms and hands that were only bone, caught in an undertow, sucked into everlasting darkness, dissolution, oblivion.

BADTHING!

Bobby sat straight up in bed.

He was screaming, but no cry issued from him. When he realized he had been dreaming, he stopped trying to scream, and finally a low and miserable sound escaped him.

He had thrown off the sheets. He sat on the edge of the bed, feet on the floor, both hands on the mattress, steadying himself as if he was still on that heaving beach or struggling to swim in those roiling tides.

The green numbers of the projection clock glowed faintly on the ceiling: 2:43.

For a while the drum-loud thud of his own heart filled him with sound from within, and he was deaf to the outer world. But after a few seconds he heard Julie breathing steadily, rhythmically, and he was surprised that he had not awakened her. Evidently he had not been thrashing in his sleep.

The panic that infused the dream had not entirely left him. His anxiety began to swell again, partly because the room was as lightless as that devouring sea. Afraid of waking Julie, he did not switch on the bedside lamp.

As soon as he was able to stand, he got up and circled the bed in the perfect blackness. The bathroom was on her side, but a clear path was provided, and he found his way as he had on countless other nights, without difficulty, guided both by experience and instinct.

He eased the door shut behind him and switched on the lights. For a moment the fluorescent brilliance prevented him from looking into the glary surface of the mirror above the double sinks. When at last he regarded his reflection, he saw that his flesh had not been eaten away. The dream had been frighteningly vivid, unlike anything he'd known before; in some strange way it had been even more real than waking life, with intense colors and sounds that pulsed through his slumbering mind with the fulgurate dazzle of light along the filament of an incandescent bulb. Though aware that it had been a dream, he had half feared that the nightmare ocean had left its corrosive mark on him even after he woke.

Shuddering, he leaned against the counter. He turned on the cold water, bent forward, and splashed his face. Dripping, he looked at his reflection again and met his eyes. He whispered to himself: 'What the hell was *that*?'

• 24 •

Candy prowled.

The eastern end of the Pollard family's two-acre property dropped into a canyon. The walls were steep, composed mostly of dry crumbling soil veined in places by pink and gray shale. Only the expansive root systems of the hardy, desert vegetation – chaparral, thick clumps of bunchgrass, pampas grass, scattered mesquite – kept the slopes from eroding extensively in every heavy rain. A few eucalyptuses, laurels, and melaleucas grew on the walls of the canyon, and where the floor was broad enough, melaleucas and California live oaks sank roots deep into the earth along the runoff channel. That channel was only a dry streambed now, but during a heavy rain it overflowed.

Fleet and silent in spite of his size, Candy followed the canyon eastward, moving upslope, until he came to a junction with another declivity that was too narrow to be called a canyon. There, he turned north. The land continued to climb, though not as steeply as before. Sheer walls soared on both sides of him, and in places the passage was nearly pinched off, narrowing to only a couple of feet. Brittle tumbleweeds, blown into the ravine by the wind, had collected in mounds at some of those choke points, and they scratched Candy as he pushed through them.

Without even a fragment moon, the night was unusually dark at the bottom of that fissure in the land, but he seldom stumbled and never hesitated. His gifts did not include superhuman vision; he was as blinded by lightlessness as anyone. However, even in the blackest night, he knew when obstacles lay before him, sensed the contours of the land so well that he could proceed with surefooted confidence. He did not know how this sixth sense served him, and he did nothing to engage it; he simply had an uncanny awareness of his relationship with his surroundings, knew his place at all times, much as the best high-wire walkers, though blindfolded, could proceed with self-assurance along a taut line above the upturned faces of a circus crowd.

This was another gift from his mother.

All of her children were gifted. But Candy's talents exceeded those of Violet, Verbina, and Frank.

The narrow passage opened into another canyon, and Candy turned east again, along a rocky runoff channel, hurrying now as his need grew. Though ever more widely separated, houses were still perched high above, on the canyon rim; their bright windows were too far away to illuminate the ground before him, but now and then he glanced up longingly because within those homes was the blood he needed.

God had given Candy a taste for blood, made him a predator, and therefore God was responsible for whatever Candy did; his mother had explained all of that long ago. God wanted him to be selective in his killing; but when Candy was unable to restrain himself, the ultimate blame was God's, for He had instilled the blood lust in Candy but had not provided him with the strength to control it.

Like all predators, Candy's mission was to thin the sick and the weak from the herd. In his case, morally degenerate members of the human herd were the intended prey: thieves, liars, cheats, adulterers. Unfortunately he did not always recognize sinners when he met them. Fulfilling his mission had been far easier when his mother had been alive, for she had no trouble spotting the blighted souls for him.

Tonight he would try as best he could to confine his killing to wild animals. Slaughtering people – especially close to home – was chancy; it might bring him under the eye of the police. He could risk killing locals only when they had crossed the family in some way and simply could not be allowed to live.

If he was unable to satisfy his need with animals, he would go somewhere, anywhere, and kill people. His mother, up there in Heaven, would be angry with him and disappointed by his lack of control, but God would not be able to blame him. After all, he was only what God had made him.

With the lights of the last house well behind him, he stopped in a grove of melaleucas. The day's strong winds had drained out of the high hills, down through the canyons, and out to sea; currently the air seemed utterly still.

Drooping trailers hung from the branches of the melaleucas, and every long, blade-sleek leaf was motionless.

His eyes had adapted to the darkness. The trees were silver in the dim starlight, and their cascading trailers contributed to an illusion that he was surrounded by a silent waterfall or frozen in a paperweight blizzard. He could even make out the ragged scrolls of bark that curled away from the trunks and limbs in the perpetual peeling process that lent a unique beauty to the species.

He could not see any prey.

He could hear no furtive movement of wildlife in the brush.

However, he knew that many small creatures, filled with warm blood, were huddled nearby in burrows, in secret nests, in drifts of old leaves, and in the sheltered niches of rocks. The very thought of them made him half mad with hunger.

He held his arms out in front of him, palms facing away from him, fingers spread. Blue light, the shade of pale topaz, faint as the glow of a quarter moon, perhaps a second in duration, pulsed from his hands. The leaves trembled, and the sparse bunchgrass stirred, then all was still as darkness reclaimed the canyon floor.

Again, blue light shone forth from his hands, as if they were hooded lanterns from which the shutters had been briefly lifted. This time the light was twice as bright as before, a deeper blue, and it lasted perhaps two seconds. The leaves rustled, and a few of the drooping trailers swayed, and the grass shivered for thirty or forty feet in front of him.

Disturbed by those queer vibrations, something scurried toward Candy, started past him. With that special sense of his surroundings that did not rely on sight or sound or smell, he reached to his left and snatched at the unseen darting creature. His reflexes were as uncanny as anything else about him, and he seized his prey. A field mouse. For an instant it froze in terror. Then it squirmed in his grasp, but he held fast to it.

His power had no effect on living things. He could not stun his prey with the telekinetic energy that radiated from his open palms. He could not draw them forth or call them to him, only frighten them out of hiding. He could have shattered one of the melaleucas or sent geysers of dirt and stones into the air, but no matter how hard he strained, he could not have stirred one hair on the mouse by using just his mind. He didn't know why he was hampered by that limitation. Violet and Verbina, whose gifts were not half as impressive as his, seemed to have power *only* over living things, smaller animals like the cats. Plants bent to Candy's will, of course, and sometimes insects, but nothing with a mind, not even something with a mind as weak as that of a mouse.

Kneeling under the silvery trees, he was swaddled in gloom so deep that he could see nothing of the mouse except its dimly gleaming eyes. He brought the fist-wrapped creature to his mouth.

It made a thin, terrified sound, more of a peep than a squeal.

He bit off its head, spat it out, and fastened his lips upon the torn neck. The blood was sweet, but there was too little of it.

He cast the dead rodent aside and raised his arms again, palms out, fingers spread. This time the splash of spectral light was an intense, electric, sapphire blue. Although it was of no longer duration than before, its effect was startlingly greater. A half dozen waves of vibrations, each a fraction of a second apart, slammed up the inclined floor of the canyon. The tall trees shook, and the hundreds of drooping trailers lashed the air, and the leaves thrashed with a sound like swarms of bees. Pebbles and smaller stones were flung up from the ground, and loose rocks rattled against one another. Every blade of bunchgrass stood up stiff and straight, like hair on a frightened man's nape, and a few clumps tore out of the soil and tumbled away into the night, along with showers of dead leaves, as if a wind had captured them. But no wind disturbed the night – only the brief burst of sapphire light and the powerful vibrations that accompanied it.

Wildlife erupted from concealment, and some of the animals streamed toward him, heading down the canyon. He had learned long ago that they never recognized his scent as that of a human being. They were as likely to flee toward him as away from him. Either he had no scent that they could detect . . . or they smelled something wild in him, something more like themselves than like a human being, and in their panic they did not realize that he was a predator.

They were visible, at best, as shapeless dark forms, streaking past him, like shadows flung off by a spinning lamp. But he also sensed them with his psychic gift. Coyotes loped by, and a panicked raccoon brushed against his leg; he did not reach out for those, because he wanted to avoid being badly clawed or bitten. At least a double score of mice streamed within reach, as well, but he wanted something more full of life, heavy with blood.

He snatched at what he thought was a squirrel, missed, but a moment later seized a rabbit by its hind legs. It shrieked. It thrashed with its less formidable forepaws, but he got hold of those, too, not only immobilizing the creature but paralyzing it with fear.

He held it up to his face.

Its fur had a dusty, musky smell.

Its red eyes glistened with terror.

He could hear its thunderous heart.

He bit into its throat. The fur, hide, and muscle resisted his teeth, but blood flowed.

The rabbit twitched, not in an attempt to escape but as if to express its resignation to its fate; they were slow spasms, strangely sensuous, as if the creature almost welcomed death. Over the years Candy had seen this behavior in countless small animals, especially in rabbits, and he always thrilled to it, for it gave him a heady sense of power, made him feel as one with the fox and the wolf.

The spasms ceased, and the rabbit went limp in his hands. Though it was still alive, it had acknowledged the imminence of death and had entered a trancelike state in which it evidently felt no pain. This seemed to be a grace that God bestowed on small prey.

Candy bit into its throat again, harder this time, deeper, then bit again, deeper still, and the life of the rabbit spurted and bubbled into his greedy mouth.

Far away in another canyon, a coyote howled. It was answered by others in its pack. A chorus of eerie voices rose and fell and rose again, as if the coyotes were aware that they were not the only hunters in the night, as if they smelled the fresh kill.

When he had supped, Candy cast the drained corpse aside.

His need was still great. He would have to break open the blood reservoirs within more rabbits or squirrels before his thirst was slaked.

He got to his feet and headed farther up into the canyon, where the wildlife had not been disturbed by his first use of the power, where creatures of many kinds waited in their burrows and hidey-holes to be harvested. The night was deep and bountiful.

• **25** •

Maybe it was just Monday morning blues. Maybe it was the bruised sky and the promise of rain that formed her mood. Or maybe she was tense and sour because the violent events at Decodyne were only four days in the past and therefore still too fresh. But for some reason, Julie did not want to take on this Frank Pollard's case. Or any other new case, for that matter. They had a few ongoing security contracts with firms they had served for years, and she wanted to stick to that comfortable, familiar business. Most of the work they did was about as risky as going to the supermarket for a quart of milk, but danger was a potential of the job, and the degree of danger in each new case was unknown. If a frail, elderly lady had come to them that Monday morning, seeking help in finding a lost cat, Julie probably would have regarded her as a menace on a par with an ax-wielding psychopath. She was edgy. After all, if luck had not been with them last week, Bobby would now be *four days dead*.

Sitting forward in her chair, leaning over her sturdy metal and Formica desk, arms crossed on the green felt blotter, Julie studied Pollard. He could not meet her eyes, and that evasion aroused her suspicion in spite of his harmless – even appealing – appearance.

He looked as if he ought to have a Vegas comedian's name – Shecky, Buddy, something like that. He was about thirty years old, five ten, maybe a hundred and eighty pounds, which on him was thirty pounds too much; however, it was his face that was most suited for a career in comedy. Except for a couple of curious scratches that were mostly healed, it was a pleasant mug: open, kind, round enough to be jolly, deeply dimpled. A permanent flush tinted his cheeks, as if he had been standing in an arctic wind for most of his life. His nose was reddish, too, apparently not from too great a fondness for booze, but from having been broken a few times; it was lumpish enough to be amusing, but not sufficiently squashed to make him look like a thug.

Shoulders slumped, he sat in one of the two leather and chrome chairs in front of Julie's desk. His voice was soft and pleasant, almost musical. 'I need help. I don't know where else to go for it.'

In spite of his comedic looks, his manner was bleak. Though it was mellifluous, his voice was heavy with despair and weariness. With one hand he periodically wiped his face, as if pulling off cobwebs, then peered at his hand with puzzlement each time it came away empty.

The backs of his hands were marked with scabbed-over scratches, too, a couple of which were slightly swollen and inflamed.

'But frankly,' he said, 'seeking help from private detectives seems ridiculous, as if this isn't real life but a TV show.'

'I've got heartburn, so it's real life, all right,' Bobby said. He was standing at one of the big sixth-floor windows that faced out toward the mist-obscured sea and down on the nearby buildings of Fashion Island, the Newport Beach shopping center adjacent to the office tower in which Dakota & Dakota leased a seven-room suite. He turned from the view, leaned against the sill, and extracted a roll of Rolaids from the pocket of his Ultrasuede jacket. 'TV detectives never suffer heartburn, dandruff, or the heartbreak of psoriasis.'

'Mr Pollard,' Julie said, 'I'm sure Mr Karaghiosis has explained to you that strictly speaking we aren't private detectives.'

'Yes.'

'We're security consultants. We primarily work with corporations and private institutions. We have eleven employees with sophisticated skills and years of security experience, which is a lot different from the one-man PI fantasies on TV. We don't shadow men's wives to see if they're being unfaithful, and we don't do divorce work or any of the other things that people usually come to private detectives for.'

'Mr Karaghiosis explained that to me,' Pollard said, looking down at his hands, which were clenched on his thighs.

From the sofa to the left of the desk, Clint Karaghiosis said, 'Frank told me his story, and I really think you ought to hear why he needs us.'

Julie noted that Clint had used the would-be client's first name, which he had never done before during six years with Dakota & Dakota. Clint was solidly built – five foot eight, a hundred and sixty pounds. He looked as though he had once been an inanimate assemblage of chunks of granite and slabs of marble, flint and fieldstone, slate and iron and lodestone, which some alchemist had transmuted into living flesh.

His broad countenance, though handsome enough, also looked as if it had been chiseled from rock. In a search for a sign of weakness in his face, one could say only that, though strong, some features were not as strong as others. He had a rocklike personality too: steady, reliable, imperturbable. Few people impressed Clint, and fewer still pierced his reserve and elicited more than a polite, businesslike response from him. His use of the client's first name seemed to be a subtle expression of sympathy for Pollard and a vote of confidence in the truthfulness of whatever tale the man had to tell.

'If Clint thinks this is something for us, that's good enough for me,' Bobby said. 'What's your problem, Frank?'

Julie was not impressed that Bobby had used the client's first name so immediately, casually. Bobby liked everyone he met, at least until they emphatically proved themselves unworthy of being liked. In fact, you had to stab him in the back repeatedly, virtually giggling with malice, before he would finally and regretfully consider the possibility that maybe he *shouldn't* like you. Sometimes she thought she had married a big puppy that was pretending to be human.

Before Pollard could begin, Julie said, 'One thing, first. If we decide to accept your case – and I stress the *if* – we aren't cheap.'

'That's no problem,' Pollard said. He lifted a leather flight bag from the floor at his feet. It was one of two he'd brought with him. He put it on his lap and unzipped it. He withdrew a couple of packs of currency and put them on the desk. Twenties and hundreds.

As Julie took the money to inspect it, Bobby pushed away from the windowsill and went to Pollard's side. He looked down into the flight bag and said, 'It's crammed full.'

'One hundred and forty thousand dollars,' Pollard said.

Upon quick inspection, the money on the desk did not appear to be counterfeit. Julie pushed it aside and said, 'Mr Pollard, are you in the habit of carrying so much cash?'

'I don't know,' Pollard said.

'You don't know?'

'I don't know,' he repeated miserably.

'He literally doesn't know,' Clint said. 'Hear him out.'

In a voice at once subdued yet heavy with emotion, Pollard said, 'You've got to help me find out where I go at night. What in God's name am I doing when I should be sleeping?'

'Hey, this sounds interesting,' Bobby said, sitting down on one corner of Julie's desk.

Bobby's boyish enthusiasm made Julie nervous. He might commit them to Pollard before they knew enough to be sure that it was wise to take the case. She also didn't like him sitting on her desk. It just didn't seem businesslike. She felt that it gave the prospective client an impression of amateurism.

From the sofa, Clint said, 'Should I start the tape?'

'Definitely,' Bobby said.

Clint was holding a compact, battery-powered tape recorder. He flicked the switch and set the recorder on the coffee table in front of the sofa, with the built-in microphone aimed at Pollard, Julie, and Bobby.

The slightly chubby, round-faced man looked up at them. The rings of bluish skin around his eyes, the watery redness of the eyes themselves, and the paleness of his lips belied any image of robust health to which his ruddy cheeks might have lent credence. A hesitant smile flickered across his mouth. He met Julie's eyes for no more than a second, looked down at his hands again. He seemed frightened, beaten, altogether pitiable. In spite of herself she felt a pang of sympathy for him.

As Pollard began to speak, Julie sighed and slumped back in her chair. Two minutes later, she was leaning forward again, listening intently to Pollard's soft voice. She did not want to be fascinated, but she was. Even phlegmatic Clint Karaghiosis, hearing the story for the second time, was obviously captivated by it.

If Pollard was not a liar or a raving lunatic – and most likely he was both – then he was caught up in events of an almost supernatural nature. Julie did not believe in the supernatural. She tried to remain skeptical, but Pollard's demeanor and evident conviction persuaded her against her will.

Bobby began making holy-jeez-gosh-wow sounds and slapping the desk in astonishment at the revelation of each new twist in the tale. When the client – no. Pollard. Not 'the client.' He wasn't their client yet. Pollard. When Pollard told them about waking in a motel room Thursday afternoon, with blood on his hands, Bobby blurted, 'We'll take the case!'

'Bobby, wait!' Julie said. 'We haven't heard everything Mr Pollard came here to tell us. We shouldn't—'

'Yeah, Frank,' Bobby said, 'what the hell happened *then*?'

Julie said, 'What I mean is, we have to hear his whole story before we can possibly know whether or not we can help him.'

'Oh, we can help him, all right,' Bobby said. 'We—'

'Bobby,' she said firmly, 'could I see you alone for a moment?' She got up, crossed the office, opened the door to the adjoining bathroom, and turned on the light in there.

Bobby said, 'Be right back, Frank.' He followed Julie into the bathroom, closing the door behind them.

She switched on the ceiling exhaust fan to help muffle their voices, and spoke in a whisper. 'What's wrong with you?'

'Well, I have flat feet, no arches at all, and I've got that ugly mole in the middle of my back.'

'You're impossible.'

'Flat feet and a mole are too many faults for you to handle? You're a hard woman.'

The room was small. They were standing between the sink and the toilet, almost nose to nose. He kissed her forehead.

'Bobby, for God's sake, you just told Pollard we'll take his case. Maybe we won't.'

'Why wouldn't we? It's *fascinating*.'

'For one thing, he sounds like a nut.'

'No, he doesn't.'

'He says some strange power caused that car to disintegrate, blew out street-lights. Strange flute music, mysterious blue lights . . . This guy's been reading the *National Inquirer* too long.'

'But that's just it. A true nut would already be able to explain what happened to him. He'd claim he'd met God or Martians. This guy is baffled, looking for answers. That strikes me as a sane response.'

'Besides, we're in business, Bobby. Business. Not for fun. For money. We're not a couple of damned hobbyists.'

'He's got money. You saw it.'

'What if it's hot money?'

'Frank's no thief.'

'You know him less than an hour and you're sure he's no thief? You're so trusting, Bobby.'

'Thank you.'

'It wasn't a compliment. How can you do the kind of work you do, and be so trusting?'

He grinned. 'I trusted you, and that turned out okay.'

She refused to be charmed. 'He says he doesn't know where he got the money, and just for the sake of the argument, let's say we buy that part of the story. And let's also say you're right about him not being a thief. So maybe he's a drug dealer. Or something else. There's a thousand ways it could be hot money without being stolen. And if we find out that it's hot, we can't keep what he pays us. We'll have to turn it over to the cops. We'll have wasted our time and energy. Besides . . . it's going to be messy.'

'Why do you say that?' he asked.

'Why do I say that? He just told you about waking up in a motel room with blood all over his hands!'

'Keep your voice down. You might hurt his feelings.'

'God forbid!'

'Remember, there was no body. It must've been his own blood.'

Frustrated, she said, 'How do we know there was no body? Because he says there wasn't? He might be such a nutcase that he wouldn't even notice the body if he stepped in its steaming bowels and stumbled over its decapitated head.'

'What a vivid image.'

'Bobby, he says maybe he clawed at himself, but that's not very damned likely. Probably some poor woman, some innocent girl, maybe even a child, a helpless schoolgirl, was attacked by that man, dragged into his car, raped and beaten and raped again, forced to perform every humiliating act a perverse mind could imagine, then driven to some lonely desert canyon, maybe tortured with needles and knives and God knows what, then clubbed to death, and pitched naked into a dry wash, where coyotes are even now chewing on the softer parts of her, with flies crawling in and out of her open mouth.'

'Julie, you're forgetting something.'

'What?'

'*I'm* the one with the overactive imagination.'

She laughed. She couldn't help it. She wanted to thump his skull hard enough to knock some sense into him, but she laughed instead and shook her head.

He kissed her cheek, then reached for the doorknob.

She put her hand on his. 'Promise we won't take the case until we've heard his whole story and have time to think about it.'

'All right.'

They returned to the office.

Beyond the windows, the sky resembled a sheet of steel that had been scorched black in places, with a few scattered incrustations of mustard-yellow corrosion. Rain had not begun to fall, but the air seemed tense in expectation of it.

The only lights in the room were two brass lamps on tables that flanked the sofa, and a silk-shaded brass floorlamp in one corner. The overhead fluorescents were not on, because Bobby hated the glare and believed that an office should be as cozily lighted as a den in a private home. Julie thought an office should look and feel like an office. But she humored Bobby and usually left the fluorescents off. Now as the oncoming storm darkened the day, she wanted to switch on the overheads and chase away the shadows that had begun to gather in those corners untouched by the amber glow of the lamps.

Frank Pollard was still in his chair, staring at the framed posters of Donald Duck, Mickey Mouse, and Uncle Scrooge that adorned the walls. They were another burden under which Julie labored. She was a fan of Warner Brothers' cartoons, because they had a harder edge than Disney's creations, and she owned videotape collections of them, plus a couple of animation cells of Daffy Duck, but she kept that stuff at home. Bobby brought the Disney cartoon characters into the office because (he said) they relaxed him, made him feel good, and helped him think. No clients ever questioned their professional abilities merely because of the unconventional artwork on their walls, but she still worried about what they might think.

She went behind her desk again, and again Bobby perched on it.

After winking at Julie, Bobby said, 'Frank, I was premature in accepting the case. We really can't make that decision until we've heard your whole story.'

'Sure,' Frank said, looking quickly at Bobby, at Julie, then down at his scratched hands, which were now clutching the open flight bag. 'That's perfectly understandable.'

'Of course it is,' Julie said.

Clint switched on the tape recorder again.

Exchanging the flight bag on his lap for the one on the floor, Pollard said, 'I should give you these.' He unzippered the second satchel and withdrew a plastic bag that contained a small portion of the handfuls of black sand he'd been clutching when he had awakened after his brief sleep Thursday morning. He also withdrew the bloody shirt he had been wearing when he had arisen from his even shorter nap later that same day. 'I saved them because . . . well, they seemed like evidence. Clues. Maybe they'll help you figure out what's going on, what I've done.'

Bobby accepted the shirt and the sand, examined them briefly, then put them on the desk beside him.

Julie noted that the shirt had been thoroughly saturated with blood, not merely spotted. Now the dry brownish stains made the material stiff.

'So you were in the motel Thursday afternoon,' Bobby prompted.

Pollard nodded. 'Nothing much happened that night. I went to a movie, couldn't get interested in it. Drove around a while. I was tired, real tired, in spite of the nap, but I couldn't sleep at all. I was afraid to sleep. Next morning I moved to another motel.'

'When did you finally sleep again?' Julie asked.

'The next evening.'

'Friday evening that was?'

'Yeah. I tried to stay awake with lots of coffee. Sat at the counter in the little restaurant attached to the motel, and drank coffee until I started to float off the stool. Stomach got so acidic, I had to stop. Went back to my room. Every time I started nodding off, I went out for a walk. But it was pointless. I couldn't stay awake forever. I was coming apart at the seams. Had to get some rest. So I went to bed shortly past eight that evening, fell asleep instantly, and didn't wake up until half past five in the morning.'

'Saturday morning.'

'Yeah.'

'And everything was okay?' Bobby asked.

'At least there was no blood. But there was something else.'

They waited.

Pollard licked his lips, nodded as if confirming to himself his willingness to continue. 'See, I'd gone to bed in my boxer shorts . . . but when I woke up I was fully clothed.'

'So you were sleepwalking, and you dressed in your sleep,' Julie said.

'But the clothes I was wearing weren't any I'd seen before.'

Julie blinked. 'Excuse me?'

'They weren't the clothes I was wearing when I came to in that alleyway two nights before, and they weren't the clothes I bought at the mall on Thursday morning.'

'Whose clothes were they?' Bobby asked.

'Oh, they must be mine,' Pollard said, 'because they fit me too well to belong to anyone else. They fit perfectly. Even the shoes fit perfectly. I couldn't have lifted that outfit from someone else and been lucky enough to have it all fit so well.'

Bobby slipped off the desk and began to pace. 'So what are you saying? That you left that motel in your underwear, went out to some store, bought clothes, and nobody objected to your immodesty or even questioned you about it?'

Shaking his head, Pollard said, 'I don't know.'

Clint Karaghiosis said, 'He could've dressed in his room, while sleep-walking, then went out, bought other clothes, changed into them.'

'But why would he do that?' Julie asked.

Clint shrugged. 'I'm just offering a possible explanation.'

'Mr Pollard,' Bobby said, 'why would you have done something like that?'

'I don't know.' Pollard had used those three words so often that he was wearing them out; each time he repeated them, his voice seemed softer and fuzzier than before. 'I don't think I did. It doesn't feel right – as an explanation, I mean. Besides, I didn't fall asleep in the motel until after eight o'clock. I probably couldn't have gotten up again, gone out, and bought the clothes before the stores closed.'

'Some places are open until ten o'clock,' Clint said.

'There was a narrow window of opportunity,' Bobby agreed.

'I don't think I would've broken into a store after hours,' Pollard said. 'Or stolen the clothes. I don't think I'm a thief.'

'We know you're not a thief,' Bobby said.

'We don't know any such thing,' Julie said sharply.

Bobby and Clint looked at her, but Pollard continued to stare at his hands, too shy or confused to defend himself.

She felt like a bully for having questioned his honesty. Which was nuts. They knew nothing about him. Hell, if he was telling the truth, he knew nothing about himself.

Julie said, 'Listen, whether he bought or stole the clothes is not the point here. I can't accept either. At least not with our current scenario. It's just too outrageous – the man going to a mall or K-Mart or someplace in his under-wear, outfitting himself, while he's sleepwalking. Could he do all that and not wake up – and appear to be awake to other people? I don't think so. I don't know anything about sleepwalking, but if we research it, I don't think we'll find such a thing is possible.'

'Of course, it wasn't just the clothes,' Clint said.

'No, not just the clothes,' Pollard said. 'When I woke up, there was a large paper bag on the bed beside me, like one of those you get at a supermarket if you don't want plastic. I looked inside, and it was full of . . . money. More cash.'

'How much?' Bobby asked.

'I don't know. A lot.'

'You didn't count it?'

'It's back at the motel where I'm staying now, the new place. I keep moving. I feel safer that way. Anyway, you can count it later if you want. I tried to count it, but I've lost my ability to do even simple arithmetic. Yeah, that sounds screwy, but it's what happened. Couldn't add the numbers. I keep trying but . . . numbers just don't mean much to me any more.' He lowered his head, put his face in his hands. 'First I lost my memory. Now I'm losing essential skills, like math. I feel as if . . . as if I'm coming apart . . . dissolving . . . until there's going to be none of me left, just a body, no mind at all . . . gone.'

'That won't happen, Frank,' Bobby said. 'We won't let it. We'll find out who you are and what all this means.'

'Bobby,' Julie said warningly.

'Hmmm?' He smiled obtusely.

She got up from her desk and went into the bathroom.

'Ah, Jeez.' Bobby followed her, closed the door, and turned on the fan, 'Julie, we *have* to help the poor guy.'

'The man is obviously experiencing psychotic fugues. He's doing these things in a blacked-out condition. He gets up in the middle of the night, yeah, but he's not sleepwalking. He's awake, alert, but in a fugue state. He could steal, kill – and not remember any of it.'

'Julie, I'll bet you that was his own blood on his hands. He may be having blackouts, fugues, whatever you want to call them, but he's not a killer. How much you want to bet?'

'And you still say he's not a thief? On a regular basis he wakes up with a bagful of money, doesn't know where he got it, but he's not a thief? You think maybe he counterfeits money during these amnesiac spells? No, I'm sure you think he's too nice to be a counterfeiter.'

'Listen,' he said, 'we've got to go with gut feelings sometimes, and my gut feeling is that Frank is a good guy. Even Clint thinks he's a good guy.'

'Greeks are notoriously gregarious. They like everybody.'

'You telling me Clint is your typical Greek social animal? Are we talking about the same Clint? Last name – Karaghiosis? Guy who looks as if he was cast from concrete, and smiles about as often as a cigar store Indian?'

The light in the bathroom was too bright. It bounced off the mirror, white sink, white walls, and white ceramic tiles. Thanks to the glare and Bobby's good-natured if iron-willed determination to help Pollard, Julie was getting a headache.

She closed her eyes. 'Pollard's pathetic,' she admitted.

'Want to go back in there and hear him out?'

'All right. But, dammit, don't tell him we'll help him until we've heard everything. All right?'

They returned to the office.

The sky no longer looked like cold, scorched metal. It was darker than before, and churning, molten. Though only the mildest breeze stirred at ground level, strong winds apparently were at work in higher altitudes, for dense black thunderheads were being harried inland from the sea.

Like metal filings drawn to magnets, shadows had piled up in some corners. Julie reached for the switch to snap on the overhead fluorescents. Then she saw Bobby looking around with obvious pleasure at the softly lustrous, burnished brass surfaces of the lamps, at the way the polished oak end tables and coffee table glimmered in the fall of warm buttery light, and she left the switch unflicked.

She sat behind her desk again. Bobby perched on the edge of it, legs dangling.

Clint clicked on the tape recorder, and Julie said, 'Frank . . . Mr Pollard, before you continue your story, I'd like you to answer a few important questions for me. In spite of the blood on your hands, and the scratches, you believe you're incapable of hurting anyone?'

'Yeah. Except maybe in self-defense.'

'And you don't think you're a thief?'

'No. I can't . . . I don't see myself as a thief, no.'

'Then why haven't you gone to the police for help?'

He was silent. He clutched the open flight bag on his lap and peered into it, as if Julie was speaking to him from its interior.

She said, 'Because if you *really* feel certain you're an innocent man in all regards, the police are best equipped to help you find out who you are and who's pursuing you. You know what I think? I think you're not as certain of your innocence as you pretend. You know how to hot-wire a car, and although any man with reasonable knowledge of automobiles could perform that trick, it's at least an indication of criminal experience. And then there's the money, all that money, bagfuls of it. You don't remember committing any crimes, but in your heart you're convinced you have, so you're afraid to go to the cops.'

'That's part of it,' he acknowledged.

She said, 'You do understand, I hope, that if we take your case, and if we turn up evidence that you've committed a criminal act, we'll have to convey that information to the police.'

'Of course. But I figure if I went to the cops first, they wouldn't even look for the truth. They'd make up their minds that I was guilty of something even before I finished telling my story.'

'And of course *we* wouldn't do that,' Bobby said, turning his head to favor Julie with a meaningful look.

Pollard said, 'Instead of helping me, they'd look around for some recent crimes to pin on me.'

'The police don't work that way,' Julie assured him.

'Of course they do,' Bobby said mischievously. He slid off the desk and began to pace back and forth from the Uncle Scrooge poster to one of Mickey Mouse. 'Haven't we seen 'em do that a thousand times on TV shows? Haven't we all read Hammett and Chandler?'

'Mr Pollard,' Julie said, 'I was a police officer once—'

'Proves my point,' Bobby said. 'Frank, if you'd gone to the cops, you'd no doubt already have been booked, tried, convicted, and sentenced to a thousand years.'

'There's a more important reason I can't go to the cops. That would be like going public. Maybe the press would hear about me, and be real eager to do a story about this poor guy with amnesia and bags of cash. Then he would know where to find me. I can't risk that.'

Bobby said, 'Who is "he", Frank?'

'The man who was chasing me the other night.'

'The way you said it, I thought you'd remembered his name, had a specific person in mind.'

'No. I don't know who he is. I'm not even entirely sure *what* he is. But I know he'll come for me again if he learns where I am. So I've got to keep my head down.'

From the sofa, Clint said, 'I better flip the tape over.'

They waited while he popped the cassette out of the recorder.

Although it was only three o'clock, the day was in the grip of a false twilight indistinguishable from the real one. The breeze at ground level was striving to match the wind that drove the clouds at higher altitudes; a thin fog poured in from the west, exhibiting none of the lazy motion with which fogs usually advanced, swirling and churning, a molten flux that seemed to be trying to solder the earth to the thunderheads above.

When Clint had the recorder going again, Julie said, 'Frank, is that the end of it? When you woke Saturday morning, wearing new clothes, with the paper bag full of money on the bed beside you?'

'No. Not the end.' He raised his head, but he didn't look at her. He stared past her at the dreary day beyond the windows, though he seemed to be gazing at something much farther away than Newport Beach. 'Maybe it's never going to end.'

From the second flight bag out of which he had earlier withdrawn the bloody shirt and the sample of black sand, he produced a one-pint mason jar of the type used to store home-canned fruits and vegetables, with a sturdy, hinged glass lid that clamped on a rubber gasket. The jar was filled with what appeared to be rough, uncut, dully gleaming gems. Some were more polished than others; they sparkled, flared.

Frank released the lid, tipped the jar, and poured some of the contents onto the imitation blond-wood Formica desktop.

Julie leaned forward.

Bobby stepped in for a closer look.

The less irregular gems were round, oval, teardrop, or lozenge-shaped; some aspects of each stone were smoothly curved, and some were naturally beveled with lots of sharp edges. Other gems were lumpy, jagged, pocked. Several were as large as fat grapes, others as small as peas. They were all red, though they varied in their degree of coloration. They vigorously refracted the light, a pool of scarlet glitter on the pale surface of the desk; the gems marshaled the diffuse glow of the lamps through their prisms, and cast shimmering spears of crimson toward the ceiling and one wall, where the acoustic tiles and Sheetrock appeared to be marked by luminous wounds.

'Rubies?' Bobby asked.

'They don't look quite like rubies,' Julie said. 'What are they, Frank?'

'I don't know. They might not even be valuable.'

'Where'd you get them?'

'Saturday night I couldn't sleep much at all. Just minutes at a time. I kept tossing and turning, popping awake again as soon as I dozed off. Afraid to sleep. And I didn't nap Sunday afternoon. But by yesterday evening, I was so exhausted, I couldn't keep my eyes open any more. I slept in my clothes, and when I got up this morning, my pants pockets were full of these things.'

Julie plucked one of the more polished stones from the pile and held it to her right eye, looking through it toward the nearest lamp. Even in its raw state, the gem's color and clarity were exceptional. They might, as Frank implied, be only semiprecious, but she suspected that they were, in fact, of considerable value.

Bobby said, 'Why're you keeping them in a mason jar?'

'Because I had to go buy one anyway to keep *this*,' Frank said.

From the flight bag he produced a larger, quart-size jar and placed it on the desk.

Julie turned to look at it and was so startled that she dropped the gem she had been examining. An insect, nearly as large as her hand, lay in that glass container. Though it had a dorsal shell like a beetle – midnight black with blood-red markings around the entire rim – the thing within that carapace more closely resembled a spider than a beetle. It had the eight, sturdy, hairy legs of a tarantula.

'What the hell?' Bobby grimaced. He was mildly entomophobic. When he encountered any insect more formidable than a housefly, he called upon Julie to capture or kill it, while he watched from a distance.

'Is it alive?' Julie asked.

'Not now,' Frank said.

Two forearms, like miniature lobster claws, extended from under the front of the thing's shell, one on each side of the head, though they differed from the appendages of a lobster in that the pincers were far more highly articulated than those of any common crustacean. They somewhat resembled hands, with four curved, chitinous segments, each jointed at the base; the edges were wickedly serrated.

'If that thing got hold of your finger,' Bobby said, 'I bet it could snip it off. You say it was alive, Frank?'

'When I woke up this morning, it was crawling on my chest.'

'Good God!' Bobby paled visibly.

'It was sluggish.'

'Yeah? Well, it sure looks quick as a damned cockroach.'

'I think it was dying already,' Frank said. 'I screamed, brushed it off. It just lay there on its back, on the floor, kicking kinda feebly for a few seconds, then it was still. I stripped the case off one of the bed pillows, scooped the thing into it, knotted the top so it wouldn't crawl away if it was still alive. Then I discovered the gems in my pockets, so I bought two mason jars, one for the bug, and it hasn't moved since I put it in there, so I figure it's dead. You ever see anything like it?'

'No,' Julie said.

'Thank God, no,' Bobby agreed. He was not leaning over the jar for a closer look, as Julie was. In fact he had taken a step back from the desk, as if he thought the creepy-crawler might be able, in a wink, to cut its way through the glass.

Julie picked up the jar and turned it so she could look at the bug face-on. Its satin-black head was almost as big as a plum and half hidden under the carapace. Multifaceted, muddy yellow eyes were set high on the sides of the face, and under each of them was what appeared to be another eye, a third smaller than the one above it and reddish-blue. Queer patterns of tiny holes, half a dozen thornlike extrusions, and three clusters of silky-looking hairs marked the otherwise smooth, shiny surface of that hideous countenance. Its small mouth, open now, was a circular orifice in which she saw what appeared to be rings of tiny but sharp teeth.

Staring at the occupant of the jar, Frank said, 'Whatever the hell I'm mixed up in, it's a bad thing. It's a real bad thing, and I'm afraid.'

Bobby twitched. In a thoughtful voice, speaking more to himself than to them, Bobby said, 'Bad thing . . .'

Putting the jar down, Julie said, 'Frank, we'll take the case.'

'All right!' Clint said, and switched off the recorder.

Turning away from the desk, heading toward the bathroom, Bobby said, 'Julie, I need to see you alone for a moment.'

For the third time they stepped into the bathroom together, closed the door behind them, and switched on the fan.

Bobby's face was grayish, like a highly detailed portrait done in pencil; even his freckles were colorless. His customarily merry blue eyes were not merry now.

He said, 'Are you crazy? You told him we'll take the case.'

Julie blinked in surprise. 'Isn't that what you wanted?'

'No.'

'Ah. Then I guess I heard you wrong. Must be too much wax in my ears. Solid as cement.'

'He's probably a lunatic, dangerous.'

'I'd better go to a doctor, have my ears professionally cleaned.'

'This wild story he's made up is just—'

She held up one hand, halting him in midsentence. 'Get real, Bobby. He didn't imagine that bug. What is that thing? I've never even seen pictures of anything like it.'

'What about the money? He must've stolen it.'

'Frank's no thief.'

'What – did God tell you that? Because there's no other way you could know. You only met Pollard little more than an hour ago.'

'You're right,' she said. 'God told me. And I always listen to God because if you don't listen to Him, then He's likely to visit a plague of teeming locusts on you or maybe set your hair on fire with a lightning bolt. Listen, Frank's so lost, adrift, I feel sorry for him. Okay?'

He stared at her, chewing on his pale lower lip for a moment, then finally said, 'We work good together because we complement each other. You're strong where I'm weak, and I'm strong where you're weak. In many ways we're not at all alike, but we belong together because we fit like pieces of a puzzle.'

'What's your point?'

'One way we're different but complementary is our motivation. This line of work suits me because I get a kick out of helping people who're in trouble through no fault of their own. I like to see good triumph. Sounds like a comic-book hero, but it's the way I feel. You, on the other hand, are primarily motivated by a desire to stomp the bad guys. Yeah, sure, I like to see the bad guys all crumpled and whimpering, too, but it's not as important to me as it is to you. And, of course, you're happy to help innocent people, but with you that's secondary to the stomping and crushing. Probably because you're still working out your rage over the murder of your mother.'

'Bobby, if I want psychoanalysis, I'll get it in a room where the primary piece of furniture is a couch – not a toilet.'

Her mother had been taken hostage in a bank holdup when Julie was twelve. The two perpetrators had been high on amphetamines and low on common sense and compassion. Before it was all over, five of the six hostages were dead, and Julie's mother was not the lucky one.

Turning to the mirror, Bobby looked at her reflection, as if he was uncomfortable meeting her eyes directly. 'My point is – suddenly you're acting like me, and that's no good, that destroys our balance, disrupts the harmony of this relationship, and it's the harmony that has always kept us alive, successful and alive. You want to take this case because you're fascinated, it excites your imagination, and because you'd like to help Frank, he's so pitiful. Where's your usual outrage? I'll tell you where it is. You don't have any because, at this moment anyway, there's no one to elicit it, no bad guy. Okay, there's the guy he says chased him that night, but we don't even know if he's real or just a figment of Frank's fantasy. Without an obvious bad guy to focus your anger, I should have to drag you into this every step of the way, and that's what I was doing, but now you're doing the dragging, and that worries me. It doesn't feel right.'

She let him ramble on, with their gazes locked in the mirror, and when at last he finished, she said, 'No, that's not your point.'

'What do you mean?'

'I mean, everything you just said is smoke. What's really bothering you, Robert?'

His reflection tried to stare down her reflection.

She smiled. 'Come on. Tell me. We never keep secrets.'

Bobby-in-the-mirror looked like some bad imitation of the real Bobby Dakota. The real Bobby, her Bobby, was full of fun and life and energy. Bobby-in-the-mirror was gray-faced, almost grim; his vitality had been sapped by worry.

'Robert?' she prodded.

'You remember last Thursday when we woke?' he said. 'The Santa Anas were blowing. We made love.'

'I remember.'

'And right after we'd made love . . . I had the strange, terrible feeling that I was going to lose you, that something out there in the wind was . . . coming to get you.'

'You told me about it later that night, at Ozzie's, when we were talking about jukeboxes. But the windstorm ended, and nothing got me. Here I am.'

'That same night, Thursday night, I had a nightmare, the most vivid damn dream you can imagine.' He told her about the little house on the beach, the jukebox standing in the sand, the thunderous inner voice – THE BAD THING IS COMING, THE BAD THING, BAD THING! – and about the corrosive sea that had swallowed both of them, dissolving their flesh and dragging their bones into lightless depths. 'It rocked me. You can't conceive of how *real* it seemed. Sounds crazy but . . . that dream was almost more real than real life. I woke up, scared as bad as I've ever been. You were sleeping, and I didn't wake you. Didn't tell you about it later because I didn't see the point of worrying you and because . . . well, it seems childish to put much stock in a dream. I haven't had the nightmare again. But since then – Friday, Saturday, yesterday – I've had moments when a strange anxiety sort of shivers through me, and I think maybe some bad thing is coming to get you. And now, out there in the office, Frank said he was mixed up in a bad thing, a real bad thing, that's how he put it, and right away I made the connection. Julie, maybe this case is the bad thing I dreamed about. Maybe we shouldn't take it.'

She stared at Bobby-in-the-mirror for a moment, wondering how to reassure him. Finally she decided that, because their roles had reversed, she should deal with him as Bobby would deal with her in a similar situation. Bobby would not resort to logic and reason – which were her tools – but would charm and humor her out of a funk.

Instead of responding directly to his concerns, she said, 'As long as we're getting things off our chests, you know what bothers me? The way you sit on my desk sometimes when we're talking to a prospective client. With some clients, it might make sense for *me* to sit on the desk, wearing a short skirt, showing some leg, 'cause I have good legs, even if I say so myself. But you never wear skirts, short or otherwise, and you don't have the gams for it, anyway.'

'Who's talking about desks?'

'I am,' she said, turning away from the mirror and looking at him directly. 'We leased a seven-room suite instead of eight, to save money, and by the time the rest of the staff was set up, we had only one office for ourselves, which seemed okay. There's plenty of room in there for two desks, but you say you don't want one. Desks are too formal for you. All you need is a couch to lie on while making calls, you say, yet when clients come in, you sit on my desk.'

'Julie—'

'Formica is a hard, nearly impervious surface, but sooner or later you'll have spent so much time sitting on my desk, it'll be marked by a permanent imprint of your ass.'

Because she wouldn't look at the mirror, he had to turn away from it, too, and face her. 'Didn't you hear what I said about the dream?'

'Now, don't get me wrong. You've got a cute ass, Bobby, but I don't want the imprint on my desktop. Pencils will keep rolling into the depression. Dust will collect in it.'

'What's going on here?'

'I want to warn you that I'm thinking of having the top of my desk wired, so I can electrify it with a flick of a switch. You sit on it then, and you'll know what a fly feels like when it settles on one of those electronic bug zappers.'

'You're being difficult, Julie. Why're you being difficult?'

'Frustration. I haven't gotten to stomp or crush any bad guys lately. Makes me irritable.'

He said, 'Hey, wait a minute. You're not being difficult.'

'Of course I'm not.'

'You're being *me!*'

'Exactly.' She kissed his right cheek and patted his left. 'Now, let's go back out there and take the case.'

She opened the door and stepped out of the bathroom.

With some amusement, Bobby said, 'I'll be damned,' and followed her into the office.

Frank Pollard was talking quietly with Clint, but he fell silent and looked up hopefully as they entered.

Shadows clung to the corners like monks to their cloisters, and for some reason the amber glow from the three lamps reminded her of the scintillant and mysterious light of serried votive candles in a church.

The puddle of scarlet gems still glimmered on the desk.

The bug was still in a death crouch in the mason jar.

'Did Clint explain our fee schedule?' she asked Pollard.

'Yes.'

'Okay. In addition, we'll need ten thousand dollars as an advance against expenses.'

Outside, lightning scarred the bellies of the clouds. The bruised sky ruptured, and cold rain spattered against the windows.

26

Violet had been awake for more than an hour, and during most of that time she had been a hawk, swooping high on the wind, darting down now and then to make a swift kill. The open sky was nearly as real to her as it was to the bird that she had invaded. She glided on thermal currents, the air offering little resistance to the sleek fore edges of her wings, with only the lowering gray clouds above, and the whole huddled world below.

She was also aware of the shadowy bedroom in which her body and a portion of her mind remained. Violet and Verbina usually slept during the day, for to sleep away the night was to waste the best of times. They shared a room on the second floor, one king-size bed, never more than an arm's reach from each other, though usually entwined. That Monday afternoon, Verbina was still asleep, naked, on her belly, with her head turned away from her sister, occasionally mumbling wordlessly into her pillow. Her warm flank pressed against Violet. Even while Violet was with the hawk, she was aware of her twin's body heat, smooth skin, slow rhythmic breathing, sleepy murmurings, and distinct scent. She smelled the dust in the room, too, and the stale odor of the long unwashed sheets – and the cats, of course.

She not only smelled the cats, which slept upon the bed and the surrounding floor or lay lazily licking themselves, but lived in each of them. While a part of her consciousness remained in her own pale flesh and a part soared with the feathered predator, other aspects of her held tenancy in each of the cats, twenty-five of them now that poor Samantha was gone. Simultaneously Violet experienced the world through her own senses, through those of the hawk, and through the fifty eyes and twenty-five noses and fifty ears and hundred paws and twenty-five tongues of the pack. She could smell her own body odor not merely through her own nose but through the noses of all the cats: the faint soapy residue of last night's bath; the pleasantly lingering tang of lemon-scented shampoo; the staleness that always followed sleep; halitosis ripe with the vapor ghosts of the raw eggs and onions and raw liver that she had eaten that morning before going to bed with the rising sun. Each member of the pack had a sharper olfactory sense than she did, and each perceived her scent differently from the way she did; they found her natural fragrance strange yet comforting, intriguing yet familiar.

She could smell, see, hear and feel herself through her sister's senses, as well, for she was always inextricably linked with Verbina. At will, she could swiftly enter or disengage from the minds of other lifeforms, but Verbina was the only other *person* with whom she could join in that way. It was a permanent link, which they had shared since birth, and though Violet could disengage from the hawk or the cats whenever she wished, she could never disengage from her twin. Likewise, she could control the minds of animals as well as inhabit them, but she was not able to control her sister. Their link was not that of puppetmaster and puppet, but special and sacred.

All of her life, Violet had lived at the confluence of many rivers of sensation, bathed in great churning currents of sound and scent and sight and taste and touch, experiencing the world not only through her own senses but those of countless surrogates. For part of her childhood, she had been autistic, so overwhelmed by sensory input that she could not cope; she had turned inward, to her secret world of rich, varied, and profound experience, until she had learned to control the incoming flood, harnessing it instead of being swept away. Only then had she chosen to relate to the people around her, abandoning autism, and she had not learned to talk until she was six years old. She had never risen out of those deep, fast currents of extraordinary sensation to stand on the comparatively dry bank of life on which other people existed, but at least she had learned to interact with her mother, Candy, and others to a limited degree.

Verbina had never coped half as well as Violet, and evidently never would. Having chosen a life almost exclusively defined by sensation, she exhibited little or no concern for the exercise and development of her intellect. She had never learned to talk, showed only the vaguest interest in anyone but her sister, and immersed herself with joyous abandonment in the ocean of sensory stimuli that surged around her. Running as a squirrel, flying as a hawk or gull, rutting as a cat, loping and killing as a coyote, drinking cool water from a stream through the mouth of a raccoon or field mouse, entering the mind of a bitch in heat as other dogs mounted her, simultaneously sharing the terror of the cornered rabbit and the savage excitement of the predatory fox, Verbina enjoyed a breadth of life that no one else but Violet could ever know. And she preferred the constant thrill of immersion in the wildness of the world to the comparatively mundane existence of other people.

Now, although Verbina still slept, a part of her was with Violet in the soaring hawk, for even sleep did not necessitate the complete disconnection of their links to other minds. The continuous sensory input of the lesser species was not only the primary fabric from which their lives were cut, but the stuff of which their dreams were formed, as well.

Under storm clouds that grew darker by the minute, the hawk glided high over the canyon behind the Pollard property. It was hunting.

Far below, among pieces of dried and broken tumbleweed, between spiny clumps of gorse, a fat mouse broke cover. It scurried along the canyon floor, alert for signs of enemies at ground level but oblivious to the feathered death that observed it from far above.

Instinctively aware that the mouse could hear the flapping of wings from a great distance and would scramble into the nearest haven at the first sound of them, the hawk silently tucked its wings back, half folding them against its body, and dived steeply, angling toward the rodent. Though she had shared this experience countless times before, Violet held her breath as they plummeted twelve hundred feet, dropping past ground level and farther down into the ravine; and though she actually was safely on her back in bed, her stomach seemed to turn within her, and a primal terror swelled within her breast even as she let out a thin squeal of pleasurable excitement.

On the bed beside Violet, her sister also softly cried out.

On the canyon floor the mouse froze, sensing onrushing doom but not certain from which quarter it was coming.

The hawk deployed its wings as foils at the last moment; abruptly the true substance of the air became apparent and provided a welcome braking resistance. Letting its hindquarters precede it, extending its legs, opening its claws, the hawk seized the mouse even as the creature reacted to the sudden spread of wings and tried to flee.

Though remaining with the hawk, Violet entered the mind of the mouse an instant before the predator had taken it. She felt the icy satisfaction of the hunter and the hot fear of the prey. From the perspective of the hawk, she felt the plump mouse's flesh puncture and split under the sharp and powerful assault of her talons, and from the perspective of the mouse, she was wracked by searing pain and was aware of a dreadful rupturing within. The bird peered down at the squealing rodent in its grasp, and shivered with a wild sense of dominance and power, with a realization that hunger would again be sated. It loosed a caw of triumph that echoed along the canyon. Feeling small and helpless in the grip of its winged assailant, in the thrall of excruciating fear so intense as to be strangely akin to the most exquisite of sensory pleasures, the mouse looked up into the steely, merciless eyes and ceased to struggle, went limp, resigned itself to death. It saw the fierce beak descending, was aware of being rent, but no longer felt pain, only numb resignation, then a brief moment of shattering bliss, then nothing, nothing. The hawk tipped back its head and let bloody ribbons and warm knots of flesh fall down its gullet.

On the bed Violet turned on her side to face her sister. Having been shaken from sleep by the power of the experience with the hawk, Verbina came into Violet's arms. Naked, pelvis to pelvis, belly to belly, breasts to breasts, the twins held each other and shuddered uncontrollably. Violet gasped against Verbina's tender throat, and through her link with Verbina's mind, she felt that hot flood of her own breath and the warmth it brought to her sister's skin. They made wordless sounds and clung to each other, and their frantic breathing did not begin to subside until the hawk tore the last red sliver of nourishing meat from the mouse's hide and, with a flurry of wings, threw itself into the sky again.

Below was the Pollard property: the Eugenia hedge; the gabled, slate-roofed, weathered-looking house; the twenty-year-old Buick that had belonged to their mother and that Candy sometimes drove; clusters of primroses burning with red and yellow and purple blooms in a narrow and untended flowerbed that extended the length of the decrepit back porch. Violet also saw Candy far below, at the northeast corner of the sprawling property.

Still holding fast to her sister, gracing Verbina's throat and cheek and temple with a lace of gentle kisses, Violet simultaneously directed the hawk to circle above her brother. Through the bird, she watched him as he stood, head bowed, at their mother's grave, mourning her as he had mourned her every day, without exception, since her death those many years ago.

Violet did not mourn. Her mother had been as much a stranger to her as anyone in the world, and she had felt nothing special at the woman's passing. Indeed, because Candy was gifted, too, Violet felt closer to him than she had to her mother, which was not saying much because she did not really know him or care a great deal about him. How could she be close to anyone if she could not enter his mind and live with him, through him? That incredible intimacy was what welded her to Verbina, and it marked the myriad relationships she enjoyed with all the fowl and fauna that populated nature's world. She simply did not know how to relate to anyone without that intense, innermost connection, and if she could not love, she could not mourn.

Far below the wheeling hawk, Candy dropped to his knees beside the grave.

27

Monday afternoon. Thomas sat at his worktable. Making a picture poem.

Derek helped. Or thought he did. He sorted through a box of magazine clippings. He chose pictures, gave them to Thomas. If the picture was right, Thomas trimmed it, pasted it on the page. Most of the time it wasn't right, so he put it aside and asked for another picture and another until Derek gave him something he could use.

He didn't tell Derek the awful truth. The awful truth was that he wanted to make the poem by himself. But he couldn't hurt Derek's feelings. Derek was hurt enough. Too much. Being dumb really hurt, and Derek was dumber than Thomas. Derek was dumber looking, too, which was more hurt. His forehead sloped more than Thomas's. His nose was flatter, and his head had a squashy shape. Awful truth.

Later, tired of making the picture poem, Thomas and Derek went to the wreck room, and that was where it happened. Derek got hurt. He got hurt so much he cried. A girl did it. Mary. In the wreck room.

Some people were playing a game of marbles in one corner. Some were watching TV. Thomas and Derek were sitting on a couch near some windows, Being Sociable when anyone came around. The aides always wanted people at The Home to Be Sociable. It was good for you to Be Sociable. When no one came around to Be Sociable with them, Thomas and Derek were watching hummingbirds at a feeder that hung outside the windows. Hummingbirds didn't really hum, but they zipped around and were a lot of fun to watch. Mary, who was new at The Home, didn't zip around and wasn't fun to watch, but she hummed a lot. No, she buzzed. Buzz, buzz, buzz, all the time.

Mary knew about eye cues. She said they really mattered, eye cues, and maybe they did, though Thomas had never heard of them and didn't understand what they were, but then a lot of things he didn't understand were important. He knew what eyes were, of course. He knew a cue was a stick you hit balls with because they had a pool table right there in the wreck room, near where he and Derek were sitting, though nobody used it much. He figured it would be a bad thing, real bad, if you stuck yourself in the eye with a cue, but this Mary said eye cues were good and she had a big one for a Down's kid.

'I'm a high-end moron,' she said, real happy with herself, you could tell.

Thomas didn't know what a moron was, but he couldn't see a high end to Mary anywhere, she was fat and mostly droopy all over.

'You're probably a moron, too, Thomas, but you ain't high-end like me. I'm almost normal, and you ain't as close normal as me.'

All this only confused Thomas.

It confused Derek even more, you could tell, and in his thick and sometimes hard to understand voice, Derek said, 'Me? No moron.' He shook his head. 'Cowboy.' He smiled. 'Cowboy.'

Mary laughed at him. 'You ain't no cowboy or ever going to be. What you are is you're an imbecile.'

They had to ask her to say it a few times before they got it, but even then they didn't really get it. They could say it but didn't know what it was any more than they knew what one of these eye cues looked like.

'You've got your normal people,' Mary said, 'then morons under them, then imbeciles, who're dumber than morons, and then you got idiots, who're dumber than even imbeciles. Me, I'm a high-end moron, and I ain't going to be here forever, I'm going to be good, behave, work hard to be normal, and someday go back to the halfway house.'

'Halfway where?' Derek asked, which was what Thomas wondered too.

Mary laughed at him. 'Halfway to being normal, which is more than you'll ever be, you poor damn imbecile.'

This time Derek realized she was looking down on him, making fun, and he tried not to cry, but he did. He got red in the face and cried, and Mary grinned sort of wild, she was all puffed up, excited, like she'd won some big prize. She'd used a bad word – damn – and should be ashamed, but she wasn't, you could tell. She said the other word again, which Thomas now saw was a bad word, too, 'imbecile,' and she kept saying it, until poor Derek got up and ran, and even then she shouted it after him.

Thomas went back to their room, looking for Derek, and Derek was in the closet with the door shut, bawling. Some of the aides came, and they talked to Derek real nice, but he didn't want to come out of the closet. They had to talk to him a long time to get him to come out of there, but even then he couldn't stop crying, and so after a while they had to Give Him Something. Once in a while when you were sick, like with the flew, the aides asked you to Take Something, which meant a pill of one shape or another, one color or another, big or little. But when they had to Give You Something, it always meant a needle, which was a bad thing. They never had to Give Something to Thomas because he was always good. But sometimes Derek, nice as he was, got to feeling so bad about himself that he couldn't stop crying, and sometimes he hit himself, just hit himself in the face, until he broke himself open and got blood on himself, and even then he wouldn't stop, so they had to Give Him Something For His Own Good. Derek never hit anyone else, he was nice, but For His Own Good he sometimes had to be made to relax or sometimes even made to sleep, which was what happened the day Mary the high-end moron called him an imbecile.

After Derek was made to sleep, one of the aides sat beside Thomas at the worktable. It was Cathy. Thomas liked Cathy. She was older than Julie but not as old as somebody's mother. She was pretty. Not as pretty as Julie but pretty, with a nice voice and eyes you weren't afraid to look into. She took one of Thomas's hands in both of hers, and she asked if he was okay. He said he was, but he really wasn't, and she knew it. They talked a while. That helped. Being Sociable.

She told him about Mary, so he'd understand, and that helped too. 'She's so frustrated, Thomas. She was out there in the world for a while, at a halfway house, and she even had a part-time job, making a little money of her own. She was trying so hard, but it didn't work, she had too many problems, so she had to be institutionalized again. I think she regrets what she did to Derek. She's just so disappointed that she needed to feel superior to someone.'

'I am . . . *was* . . . was out there in the world once,' Thomas said.

'I know you were, honey.'

'With my dad. Then with my sister. And Bobby.'

'Did you like it out there?'

'Some of it . . . scared me. But when I was with Julie and Bobby . . . I liked that part.'

On his bed, Derek was snoring now.

The afternoon was half gone. The sky was getting ugly-stormy. The room had shadows everywhere. Only the desk lamp was on. Cathy's face looked pretty in the lampglow. Her skin was like peach-colored satin. He knew what satin was like. Julie once had a dress of satin.

For a while he and Cathy were quiet.

Then he said, 'Sometimes it's hard.'

She put her hand on his head. Smoothed his hair. 'Yeah, I know, Thomas. I know.'

She was so nice. He didn't know why he started to cry when she was so nice, but he did. Maybe it was because she *was* so nice.

Cathy scooted her chair closer to his. He leaned against her. She put her arms around him. He cried and cried. Not hard terrible crying like Derek. Soft. But he couldn't stop. He tried not to cry because crying made him feel dumb, and he hated feeling dumb.

Through his tears, he said, 'I *hate* feeling dumb.'

'You're not dumb, honey.'

'Yeah, I am. Hate it. But I can't be nothing else. I try not to think about being dumb, but you can't not think about it when it's what you are, and when other people aren't, and they go out in the world every day and they live, but you don't go out in the world and don't even want to but, oh, you *want* to, even when you say you don't.' That was a lot for him to say, and he was surprised that he had said it all, surprised but also frustrated because he wanted so bad to tell her how it felt, being dumb, being afraid of going out in the world, and he'd failed, hadn't been able to find the right words, so the feeling was still all bottled up in him. 'Time. There's lots of time, see, when you're dumb and can't go out in the world, lots of time to fill up, but then there really ain't *enough* time, not enough for learning how to be not afraid of things, and I've got to learn how not to be afraid so I can go back and be with Julie and Bobby, which I want to do real bad, before all the time runs out. There's too big amounts of time and not enough, and that sounds dumb, don't it?'

'No, Thomas. It doesn't sound dumb.'

He didn't move out of her arms. He wanted to be hugged.

Cathy said, 'You know, sometimes life is hard for everyone. Even for smart people. Even for the smartest of them all.'

With one hand he wiped at his damp eyes. 'It is? Sometimes is it hard for you?'

'Sometimes. But I believe there's a God, Thomas, and that He put us here for a reason, and that every hardship we have to face is a test, and that we're better for enduring them.'

He raised his head to look at her. Such nice eyes. Good eyes. They were eyes that loved you. Like Julie's eyes or Bobby's.

Thomas said, 'God made me dumb to test me?'

'You're not dumb, Thomas. Not in some ways. I don't like to hear you call yourself dumb. You're not as smart as some, but that's not your fault. You're different, that's all. Being . . . different is your hardship, and you're coping with it well.'

'I am?'

'Beautifully. Look at you. You're not bitter. You're not sullen. You reach out to people.'

'Being Sociable.'

She smiled, pulled a tissue from the box of Kleenex on the worktable, and wiped the tears from his face. 'Of all the smart people in the world, Thomas, not a one of them handles hardship better than you do, and most not as well.'

He knew she meant what she said, and her words made him happy, even if he didn't quite believe life was ever hard for smart people.

She stayed a while. Made sure he was okay. Then she left.

Derek was still snoring.

Thomas sat at the worktable. Tried to make more poem.

After a while he went to the window. Rain was coming down now. It trickled on the glass. The afternoon was almost gone. Night was soon coming down on top of the rain.

He put his hands against the glass. He reached into the rain, into the gray day, into the nothingness of the night that was slowly sneaking up on them.

The Bad Thing was still out there. He could feel it. A man but not a man. Something more than a man. Very bad. Ugly-nasty. He'd felt it for days, but he hadn't TVed a warning to Bobby since last week because the Bad Thing wasn't coming any closer. It was far away, right now Julie was safe, and if he TVed too many warnings to Bobby, then Bobby would stop paying attention to them, and when the Bad Thing finally showed up, Bobby wouldn't believe in it any more, and then it would get to Julie because Bobby wouldn't be paying attention.

What Thomas most feared was that the Bad Thing would take Julie to the Bad Place. Their mother went to the Bad Place when Thomas was two years old, so he'd never known her. Then their dad went to the Bad Place later, leaving Thomas with just Julie.

He didn't mean Hell. He knew about Heaven and Hell. Heaven was God's. The devil owned Hell. If there was a Heaven, he was sure his mom and dad went there. You wanted to go up to Heaven if you could. Things were better there. In Hell, the aides weren't nice.

But, to Thomas, the Bad Place wasn't just Hell. It was Death. Hell was *a* bad place, but Death was *the* Bad Place. Death was a word you couldn't picture. Death meant everything stopped, went away, all your time ran out, over, done, kaput. How could you picture that? A thing wasn't real if you couldn't picture it. He couldn't *see* Death, couldn't get a picture of it in his head, not if he thought about it the way other people seemed to think about it. He was just too dumb, so he had to picture it in his head as a *place*. They said Death came to take you, and it had come to take his father one night, his heart had attacked him, but if it came to take you, then it had to take you to some *place*. And that was the Bad Place. It's where you were taken and never allowed to come back. Thomas didn't know what happened to a person there. Maybe nothing nasty. Except you weren't allowed to come back and see people you loved, which made it nasty enough, no matter if the food was good over there. Maybe some people went on to Heaven, some to Hell, but you couldn't come back from either one, so both were part of the Bad Place, just different rooms. And he wasn't sure Heaven and Hell were real, so maybe all there was in the Bad Place was darkness and cold and so much empty space that when you went over there you couldn't even find the people who'd gone ahead of you.

That scared him most of all. Not just losing Julie to the Bad Place, but not being able to find her when he went over there himself.

He was already afraid of the night. All that big empty. The lid off the world.

So if just the night itself was so scary, the Bad Place would be lots worse. It was sure to be bigger than the night, and daylight never came in the Bad Place.

Outside, the sky got darker.

Wind blew the palms.

Rain ran down the glass.

The Bad Thing was far away.

But it would come closer. Soon.

• 28 •

Candy was having one of those days when he could not accept that his mother was dead. Every time he crossed a threshold or turned a corner, he expected to see her. He thought he heard her rocking in the parlor, humming softly to herself as she knitted a new afghan, but when he went in there to look, the rocking chair was filmed with dust and draped with a shawl of cobwebs. Once, he hurried into the kitchen, expecting to find her in a brightly flowered housedress overlaid with a ruffle-trimmed white apron, dropping neat spoonfuls of cookie batter on baking sheets or perhaps mixing a cake, but, of course, she was not there. In a moment of acute emotional turmoil, Candy raced upstairs, certain that he would find his mother in bed, but when he burst into her room, he remembered that it was *his* room now, and that she was gone.

Eventually, to jar himself out of that strange and troubling mood, he went into the backyard and stood by her lonely grave in the northeast corner of the large property. He had buried her there, seven years ago, under a solemn winter sky similar to the one that currently hid the sun, with a hawk circling above just as one circled now. He had dug her grave, wrapped her in sheets scented with Chanel No. 5, and lowered her into the ground secretly, because interment on private property, not designated as a gravesite, was against the law. If he had allowed her to be buried elsewhere, he would have had to go live there with her, for he could not have endured being separated from her mortal remains for any great length of time.

Candy dropped to his knees.

Over the years the original mound of earth had settled, until her grave was marked by a shallow concavity. The grass was sparser there, the blades coarse, wiry, different from the rest of the lawn, though he did not know why; even in the months following her burial, the grass above her had not flourished. No headstone memorialized her passing; although the backyard was sheltered by the high hedge, he could not risk calling attention to her illegal resting place.

Staring at the ground before him, Candy wondered if a headstone would help him accept her death. If every day he saw her name and the date of her death deeply cut into a slab of marble, that sight should slowly but permanently engrave the loss upon his heart, sparing him days like this, when he was disturbed by a queer forgetfulness and by a hope that could never be fulfilled.

He stretched out on the grave, his head turned to one side with an ear against the earth, as if he half expected to hear her speaking to him from her subterranean bed. Pressing his body hard into the unyielding ground, he longed to feel the vitality that she had once radiated, the singular energy that had flowed from her like heat from the open door of a furnace, but he felt nothing. Though his mother had been a special woman, Candy knew it was absurd to expect her corpse, after seven years, to radiate even a ghost of the love that she had lavished upon him when she was alive; nevertheless, he was grievously disappointed when not even the faintest aura shimmered upward through the dirt from her sacred bones.

Hot tears burned in his eyes, and he tried to hold them back. But a faint rumble of thunder passed through the sky, and a few fat droplets of rain began to fall, and neither the storm nor his tears could be restrained.

She lay only five or six feet beneath him, and he was overcome by an urge to claw his way down to her. He knew her flesh would have deteriorated, that he would find only bones cradled in a vile muck of unthinkable origin, but he wanted to hold her and be held, even if he had to arrange her skeletal arms around himself in a staged embrace. He actually ripped at the grass and tore up a few handfuls of topsoil. Soon, however, he was wracked by powerful sobs that swiftly exhausted him and left him too weak to struggle with reality any longer.

She was dead.

Gone.

Forever.

As the cold rain fell in greater volume, pounding on Candy's back, it seemed to leech his hot grief from him and fill him, instead, with icy hatred. Frank had killed their mother; he *must* pay for that crime with his own life. Lying on a muddy grave and weeping like a child would not bring Candy one step closer to vengeance. Finally he got up and stood with his hands fisted at his sides, letting the storm sluice some of the mud and grief from him.

He promised his mother that he would be more relentless and diligent in his pursuit of her killer. The next time he got a lead on Frank, he would not lose him.

Looking up at the cloud-choked and streaming sky, addressing his mother in heaven, he said, 'I'll find Frankie, kill him, crush him, I will. I'll smash his skull open and cut his hateful brain into pieces and flush it down a toilet.'

The rain seemed to penetrate him, driving a chill deep into his marrow, and he shuddered.

'If I find anyone who lifted a hand to help him, I'll cut their hands off. I'll tear out the eyes of anyone who looked at Frankie with sympathy. I swear I will. And I'll cut out the tongues of any bastards who spoke kind words to him.'

Suddenly the rain fell with greater force than before, hammering the grass flat, crackling through the leaves of a nearby oak, stirring a chorus of whispers from the Eugenias. It snapped against his face, making him squint, but he did not lower his eyes from Heaven.

'If he's found anyone to care about, anyone at all, I'll take them away from him like he took you from me. I'll break them open, get the blood out of them, and throw them away like garbage.'

He had made these same promises many times during the past seven years, but he made them now with no less passion than he had before.

'Like garbage,' he repeated through clenched teeth.

His need for vengeance was no less fierce now than it had been on the day of her murder seven years ago. His hatred of Frank was, if anything, harder and sharper than ever.

'Like garbage.'

An ax of lightning cleaved the contusive sky. Briefly a long, jagged laceration gaped open in the dark clouds, which for a moment seemed to him not like clouds at all but like the infinitely strange and throbbing body of some godlike being, and through the lightning-rent flesh he thought he glimpsed the shining mystery beyond.

• 29 •

Clint dreaded the rainy season in southern California. Most of the year was dry, and in the on-again-off-again drought of the past decade, some winters were marked by only a few storms. When rain finally fell, the natives seemed to have forgotten how to drive in it. As gutters overflowed, the streets clogged with traffic. The freeways were worse; they looked like infinitely long car washes in which the conveyors had broken down.

While the gray light slowly faded out of that Monday afternoon, he drove first to Palomar Laboratories in Costa Mesa. It was a large, single-story concrete-block building one block west of Bristol Avenue. Their medical-lab division analyzed blood samples, pap smears, and biopsies, among other things, but they also performed industrial- and geological-sample analyses of all kinds.

He parked his Chevy in the adjoining lot. Carrying a plastic bag from Von's supermarket, he sloshed through the deep puddles, head bent against the driving rain, and went into the small reception lounge, dripping copiously.

An attractive young blonde sat on a stool behind the counter at the reception window. She was wearing a white uniform and a purple cardigan. She said, 'You should have an umbrella.'

Clint nodded, put the supermarket bag on the counter, and began to untie the knot in the straps, to open it.

'At least a raincoat,' she said.

From an inside jacket pocket, he withdrew a Dakota & Dakota card, passed it to her.

'Is this who you want billed?' she asked.

'Yeah.'

'Have you used our service before?'

'Yeah.'

'You have an account?'

'Yeah.'

'I haven't seen you in here before.'

'No.'

'My name's Lisa. I've only been here about a week. Never had a private eye come in before, least since I've started.'

From the large white sack he withdrew three smaller, clear, Ziploc bags and lined them up side by side.

'You got a name?' she asked, cocking her head, smiling at him.

'Clint.'

'You go around without an umbrella or raincoat in this weather, Clint, you'll catch your death, even as sturdy as you look.'

'First, the shirt,' Clint said, pushing that bag forward. 'We want the bloodstains analyzed. Not just typed. We want the whole nine yards. A complete genetic workup too. Take samples from four different parts of the shirt, because there might be more than one person's blood on it. If so, do a workup on both.'

Lisa frowned at Clint, then at the shirt in the bag. She began filling out an analysis order.

'Same program on this one,' he said, pushing forward the second bag. It contained a folded sheet of Dakota & Dakota stationery that was mottled with several spots of blood. Back at the office, Julie had sterilized a pin in a match flame, stuck Frank Pollard's thumb, and squeezed the crimson samples onto the paper. 'We want to know if any of the blood on the shirt matches what's on this stationery.'

The third bag contained the black sand.

'Is this a biological substance?' Lisa asked.

'I don't know. Looks like sand.'

'Because if it's a biological substance, it should go to our medical division, but if it's not biological it should go to the industrial lab.'

'Send a little to both. And put a rush on it.'

'Costs more.'

'Whatever.'

As she filled out the third form, she said, 'There's a few beaches in Hawaii with black sand, you ever been there?'

'No.'

'Kaimu. That's the name of one of the black beaches. Comes from a volcano, somehow. The sand, I mean. You like beaches?'

'Yeah.'

She looked up, her pen poised over the form, and gave him a big smile. Her lips were full. Her teeth were very white. 'I *love* the beach. Nothing I like better than putting on a bikini and soaking up some sun, really just *baking* in the sun, and I don't care what they say about a tan being bad for you. Life's short anyway, you know? Might as well look good while we're here. Besides, being in the sun makes me feel . . . oh, not lazy exactly, because I don't mean it saps my energy, just the opposite, it makes me feel full of energy, but a lazy energy, sort of the way a lioness walks – you know? – strong looking but easy. The sun makes me feel like a lioness.'

He said nothing.

She said, 'It's erotic, the sun. I guess that's what I'm trying to say. You lay out in the sun enough, on a nice beach, and all your inhibitions sort of melt away.'

He just stared at her.

After she finished filling out the analysis orders, gave him copies, and attached each order to the correct sample, Lisa said, 'Listen, Clint, we're living in a modern world, right?'

He didn't know what she meant.

She said, 'We're all liberated these days, am I right? So if a girl finds a guy attractive, she doesn't have to wait for him to make the move.'

Oh, Clint thought.

Leaning back on her stool, maybe to let him see how her full breasts filled out her white uniform blouse, she smiled and said, 'Would you be interested in a dinner, movie?'

'No.'

Her smile froze.

'Sorry,' he said.

He folded the copies of the work orders and put them in the same jacket pocket from which earlier he had withdrawn a business card.

She was glaring at him, and he realized he'd hurt her feelings.

Searching for something to say, all he could come up with was, 'I'm gay.'

She blinked and shook her head as if recovering from a stunning blow. Like sun piercing clouds, her smile broke through the gloom on her face. 'Had to be to resist this package, I guess.'

'Sorry.'

'Hey, it's not your fault. We are what we are, huh?'

He went into the rain again. It was getting colder. The sky looked like the ruins of a burned-out building at which the fire department had arrived too late: wet ashes, dripping cinders.

• 30 •

As night fell on that rainy Monday, Bobby Dakota stood at the hospital window and said, 'Not much of a view, Frank. Unless you're keen on parking lots.' He turned and surveyed the small, white room. Hospitals always gave him the creeps, but he did not express his true feelings to Frank. 'The decor sure won't be featured in *Architectural Digest* anytime soon, but it's comfy enough. You've got TV, magazines, and three meals a day in bed. I noticed some of the nurses are real lookers, too, but please try to keep your hands off the nuns, okay?'

Frank was paler than ever. The dark circles around his eyes had grown like spreading inkblots. He not only looked as if he belonged in a hospital but as if he had been there for weeks already. He used the power controls to tilt the bed up. 'Are these tests really necessary?'

'Your amnesia might have a physical cause,' Julie said. 'You heard Dr Freeborn. They'll look for cerebral abscesses, neoplasms, cysts, clots, all kinds of things.'

'I'm not sure about this Freeborn,' Frank said worriedly.

Sanford Freeborn was Bobby's and Julie's friend, as well as their physician. A few years ago they had helped him get his brother out of deep trouble.

'Why? What's wrong with Sandy?'

Frank said, 'I don't know him.'

'You don't know anybody,' Bobby said. 'That's your problem. Remember? You're an amnesiac.'

After accepting Frank as a client, they had taken him directly to Sandy Freeborn's office for a preliminary examination. All Sandy knew was that Frank could remember nothing but his name. They had not told him about the bags of money, the blood, black sand, red gems, weird insect, or any of the rest of it. Sandy didn't ask why Frank had come to them instead of the police or why they had accepted a case so far outside their usual purview; one of the things that made him a good friend was his reliable discretion.

Nervously adjusting the sheets, Frank said, 'You think a private room is really necessary?'

Julie nodded. 'You also want us to find out what you do at night, where you go, which means monitoring you, tight security.'

'A private room's expensive,' Frank said.

'You can afford the finest care,' Bobby said.

'The money in those bags might not be mine.'

Bobby shrugged. 'Then you'll have to work off your hospital bill – change a few hundred beds, empty a few thousand bedpans, perform some brain surgery free of charge. You might *be* a brain surgeon. Who knows? With amnesia, it's just as likely you've forgotten that you're a surgeon as that you're a used-car salesman. Worth a try. Get a bone saw, cut off the top of some guy's head, have a peek in there, see if anything looks familiar.'

Leaning against the bed rail, Julie said, 'When you're not in radiology or some other department, undergoing tests, we'll have a man with you, watching over you. Tonight it's Hal.'

Hal Yamataka had already taken his station in an uncomfortable-looking upholstered chair provided for visitors. He was to one side of the bed, between Frank and the door, in a position to watch both his charge and, if Frank was in the mood, the wall-mounted television. Hal resembled a Japanese version of Clint Karaghiosis: about five foot seven or eight, broad in the shoulders and chest, as solid looking as if he had been built by a mason who knew how to fit stones tight together and hide the mortar. In case nothing worth watching was on television and his charge proved to be a lousy conversationalist, he had brought a John D. MacDonald novel.

Looking at the rain-washed window, Frank said, 'I guess I'm just . . . scared.'

'No need to be scared,' Bobby said. 'Hal's not as dangerous as he looks. He's never killed anyone he liked.'

'Only once,' Hal said.

Bobby said, 'You once killed someone you liked? Over what?'

'He asked to borrow my comb.'

'There you go, Frank,' Bobby said. 'Just don't ask to borrow his comb, and you're safe.'

Frank was in no mood to be kidded. 'I can't stop thinking about waking up with blood on my hands. I'm afraid maybe I've already hurt someone. I don't want to hurt anyone else.'

'Oh, you can't hurt Hal,' Bobby said. 'He's an impenetrable oriental.'

'Inscrutable,' Hal said. 'I'm an *inscrutable* oriental.'

'I don't want to hear about your sex problems, Hal. Anyway, if you didn't eat so much sushi and didn't have raw-fish breath, you'd get scruted as often as anyone.'

Reaching over the bed railing, Julie took one of Frank's hands.

He smiled weakly. 'Your husband always like this, Mrs Dakota?'

'Call me Julie. Do you mean, does he always act like a wiseass or a child? Not always, but most of the time, I'm afraid.'

'You hear that, Hal?' Bobby said. 'Women and amnesiacs – they have no sense of humor.'

To Frank, Julie said, 'My husband believes everything in life should be fun, even car accidents, even funerals—'

'Even dental hygiene,' Bobby said.

'—and he'd probably be making jokes about fallout in the middle of a nuclear war. That's just the way he is. He can't be cured—'

'She's tried,' Bobby said. 'She sent me to a happiness detox center. They promised to knock some gloom into me. Couldn't.'

'You'll be safe here,' Julie said, squeezing Frank's hand before letting go of it. 'Hal will look after you.'

• 31 •

The entomologist's house was in the Turtle Rock development in Irvine, within easy driving distance of the university. Low, black, mushroom-shaped Malibu lamps threw circles of light on the rain-puddled walkway that led to the softly gleaming oak doors.

Carrying one of Frank Pollard's leather flight bags, Clint stepped onto the small covered porch and rang the bell.

A man spoke to him through an intercom set just below the bell push. 'Who is it, please?'

'Dr Dyson Manfred? I'm Clint Karaghiosis. From Dakota and Dakota.'

Half a minute later, Manfred opened the door. He was at least ten inches taller than Clint, six feet five or six, and thin. He was wearing black slacks, a white shirt, and a green necktie; the top button of the shirt was undone, and the tie hung loose.

'Good God, man, you're soaked.'

'Just damp.'

Manfred moved back, opening the door wide, and Clint stepped into the tile-floored foyer.

As he closed the door, Manfred said, 'Ought to have a raincoat or umbrella on a night like this.'

'It's invigorating.'

'What is?'

'Bad weather,' Clint said.

Manfred looked at him as if he was strange, but in Clint's view it was Manfred himself who was strange. The guy was too thin, all bones. He could not fill his clothes; his trousers hung shapelessly on his knobby hips, and his shoulders poked at the fabric of his shirt as if only bare, sharp bones lay under there. Angular and graceless, he looked as if he had been assembled from a pile of dry sticks by an apprentice god. His face was long and narrow, with a high brow and a lantern jaw, and his well-tanned, leathery skin seemed to be stretched so tight over his cheekbones that it might split. He had peculiar amber eyes that regarded Clint with an expression of cool curiosity no doubt familiar to the thousands of bugs he had pinned to specimen boards.

Manfred's gaze traveled down Clint to the floor, where water was puddling around his running shoes.

'Sorry,' Clint said.

'It'll dry. I was in my study. Come along.'

Glancing into the living room, to his right, Clint noted fleur-de-lis wallpaper, a thick Chinese rug, too many overstuffed chairs and sofas, antique English furniture, wine-red velour drapes, and tables cluttered with bibelots that glimmered in the lamplight. It was a very Victorian room, not in harmony with the California lines and layout of the house itself.

He followed the entomologist past the living room, along a short hall to the study. Manfred had a singular, stilting gait. Tall and sticklike as he was, with shoulders hunched and head thrust forward slightly, he seemed as unevolved and prehistoric as a praying mantis.

Clint had expected a university professor's study to be crammed full of books, but only forty or fifty volumes were shelved in one case to the left of the desk. There were cabinets with wide, shallow drawers that probably were filled with creepy-crawlies, and on the walls were insects in specimen boxes, framed under glass.

When he saw Clint staring at one collection in particular, Manfred said, 'Cockroaches. Beautiful creatures.'

Clint did not reply.

'The simplicity of their design and function, I mean. Few would find them beautiful in appearance, of course.'

Clint couldn't shake the feeling that the bugs were really alive.

Manfred said, 'What do you think of that big fellow in the corner of the collection?'

'He's big, sir.'

'Madagascar hissing roach. The scientific name's *Gromphadorrhina portentosa*. That one's over eight and a half centimeters long, about three and a half inches. Absolutely beautiful, isn't he?'

Clint said nothing.

Settling into the chair behind his desk, Manfred somehow folded his long bony arms and legs into that compact space, the way a large spider could scrunch itself into a tiny ball.

Clint did not sit down. Having put in a long day, he was eager to go home.

Manfred said, 'I received a call from the university chancellor. He asked me to cooperate with your Mr Dakota in any way I could.'

UCI – the University of California at Irvine – had long been striving to become one of the country's premier universities. The current chancellor and the one before him had sought to attain that status by offering enormous salaries and generous fringe benefits to world-class professors and researchers at other institutions. Before committing substantial resources in the form of a well-upholstered job offer, however, the university hired Dakota & Dakota to conduct a background investigation on the prospective faculty member. Even a brilliant physicist or biologist could have too great a thirst for whiskey, a nose for cocaine, or an unfortunate attraction to underage girls. UCI wanted to buy brainpower, respectability, and academic glory, not scandal; Dakota & Dakota served them well.

Manfred propped his elbows on the arms of his chair and steepled his fingers, which were so long that they looked as if they must have at least one extra knuckle each. 'What's the problem?' he asked.

Clint opened the leather flight bag and removed the quart-size, wide-mouth mason jar. He put it on the entomologist's desk.

The bug in the jar was at least twice as big as the Madagascar hissing roach on the wall.

For a moment Dr Dyson Manfred seemed to have been quick-frozen. He didn't move a finger; his eyes didn't blink. He stared intently at the creature in the jar. At last he said, 'What is this – a hoax?'

'It's real.'

Manfred leaned forward, hunching over the desk and lowering his head until his nose almost touched the thick glass behind which the insect crouched. 'Alive?'

'Dead.'

'Where did you find this – not here in southern California?'

'Yes.'

'Impossible.'

'What is it?' Clint asked.

Manfred looked up at him, scowling. 'I've never seen anything like it. And if *I* haven't seen anything like it, neither has anyone else. It's of the phylum *Arthropoda*, I'm sure, which includes such things as spiders and scorpions, but whether it can be classed an insect, I can't say, not until I've examined it. If it *is* an insect, it's of a new species. Where, exactly, did you find it, and why on earth would it be of interest to private detectives?'

'I'm sorry, sir, but I can't tell you anything about the case. I have to protect the client's privacy.'

Manfred carefully turned the jar around in his hands, studying the resident from every side. 'Just incredible. I must have it.' He looked up, and his amber eyes were no longer cool and appraising, but gleaming with excitement. 'I must have this specimen.'

'Well, I intended to leave it with you for examination,' Clint said. 'But as to whether you can have permanent possession—'

'Yes. Permanent.'

'That's up to my boss and the client. Meanwhile we want to know what it is, where it comes from, everything you can tell us about it.'

With exaggerated care, as if handling the finest crystal instead of ordinary glass, Manfred put the jar on the blotter. 'I'll make a complete photographic and video-tape record of the specimen from every angle and in extreme close-up. Then it'll be necessary to dissect it, though that'll be done with utmost dare, I assure you.'

'Whatever.'

'Mr Karaghiosis, you seem terribly blasé about this. Do you fully understand what I've said? This would appear to be an entirely new species, which would be extraordinary. Because how could any such species, producing individuals of this size, be overlooked for so long? This is going to be big news in the world of entomology, Mr Karaghiosis, very big news.'

Clint looked at the bug in the bottle.

He said, 'Yeah, I figured.'

• 32 •

From the hospital, Bobby and Julie drove a company Toyota into the county's western flatlands to Garden Grove, looking for 884 Serape Way, the address on the driver's license that Frank held in the name of George Farris.

Julie peered through the rain-dappled side windows and forward between the thumping windshield wipers, checking house numbers.

The street was lined with bright sodium-vapor lamps and thirty-year-old, single-story homes. They had been built in two basic, boxy models, but an illusion of individuality was provided by a variety of trim. This one was stucco with brick accents. That one was stucco with cedar-shingle panels – or Bouquet Canyon stone or desert bark or volcanic rock.

California was not all Beverly Hills, Bel Air, and Newport Beach, not all mansions and seaside villas, which was the television image. Economies of home design had made the California dream accessible to the waves of immigrants that for decades had flooded in from back east, and now from farther shores – as was evident from Vietnamese- and Korean-language bumper stickers on some cars parked along Serape.

'Next block,' Julie said. 'My side.'

Some people said such neighborhoods were a blot on the land, but to Bobby they were the essence of democracy. He had been raised on a street like Serape Way, north in Anaheim instead of Garden Grove, and it had never seemed ugly. He remembered playing with other kids on long summer evenings, when the sun set with orange and crimson flares, and the feathery silhouettes of the backlit palms were as black as ink drawings against the sky; at twilight the air sometimes smelled of star jasmine and echoed with the cry of a lingering sea gull far to the west. He remembered what it meant to be a kid with a bicycle in California – the vistas for exploration, the grand possibilities for adventure; every street of stucco homes, seen for the first time and from the seat of a Schwinn, had seemed exotic.

Two coral trees dominated the yard at 884 Serape. The white blooms of the azalea bushes were softly radiant in the bleak night.

Tinted by the sodium-vapor streetlamps, the falling rain looked like molten gold. But as Bobby hurried along the walkway behind Julie, the rain was almost as cold as sleet on his face and hands. He was wearing a warmly lined nylon jacket with a hood, but he shivered.

Julie rang the doorbell. The porch light came on, and Bobby sensed someone looking them over through the fisheye lens in the front door. He pushed back his hood and smiled.

The door opened on a security chain, and an Asian man peered out. He was in his forties, short, slender, with black hair fading to gray at the temples. 'Yes?'

Julie showed him her private investigator's license and explained that they were looking for someone named George Farris.

'Police?' The man frowned. 'Nothing wrong, no need for police.'

'No, see, we're private investigators,' Bobby explained.

The man's eyes narrowed. He looked as if he would close the door in their faces, but abruptly he brightened, smiled. 'Oh, you're PI! Like on TV.' He took the chain off the door and let them in.

Actually he didn't just let them in, he welcomed them as if they were honored guests. Within three minutes flat, they learned his name was Tuong Tran Phan (the order of his names having been rearranged to accommodate the Western custom of putting the surname last), that he and his wife, Chinh, were among the boat people who fled Vietnam two years after the fall of Saigon, that they had worked in laundries and dry cleaners, and eventually opened two dry-cleaning stores of their own. Tuong insisted on taking their coats. Chinh – a petite woman with delicate features, dressed in baggy black slacks and a yellow silk blouse – said she would provide refreshments, even though Bobby explained that only a few minutes of their time were required.

Bobby knew first-generation Vietnamese-Americans were sometimes suspicious of policemen, even to the extent of being reluctant to call for help when they were victims of crime. The South Vietnamese police often had been corrupt, and the North Vietnamese overlords, who seized the South after the U.S. withdrawal, had been murderous. Even after fifteen years or longer in the States, many Vietnamese remained at least somewhat distrustful of all authorities.

In the case of Tuong and Chinh Phan, however, that suspicion did not extend to private investigators. Evidently they had seen so many heroic television gumshoes, they believed all PIs were champions of the underdog, knights with blazing .38s instead of lances. In their roles as liberators of the oppressed, Bobby and Julie were conducted, with some ceremony, to the sofa, which was the newest and best piece of furniture in the living room.

The Phans marshaled their exceptionally good-looking children in the living room for introductions: thirteen-year-old Rocky, ten-year-old Sylvester, twelve-year-old Sissy, and six-year-old Meryl. They were obviously born-and-raised Americans, except that they were refreshingly more courteous and well mannered than many of their contemporaries. When introductions had been made, the kids returned to the kitchen, where they had been doing their schoolwork.

In spite of their polite protestations, Bobby and Julie were swiftly served coffee laced with condensed milk and exquisite little Vietnamese pastries. The Phans had coffee as well.

Tuong and Chinh sat in worn armchairs that were visibly less comfortable than the sofa. Most of their furniture was in simple contemporary styles and neutral colors. A small Buddhist shrine stood in one corner; fresh fruit lay on the red altar, and several sticks of incense bristled from ceramic holders. Only one stick was lit, and a pale-blue ribbon of fragrant smoke curled upward. The only other Asian elements were black-lacquered tables.

'We're looking for a man who might once have lived at this address,' Julie said, selecting one of the petits fours from the tray on which Mrs Phan had served them. 'His name's George Farris.'

'Yes. He lived here,' Tuong said, and his wife nodded.

Bobby was surprised. He had been certain that the Farris name and the address had been randomly matched by a document forger, that Frank had never lived here. Frank had been equally certain that Pollard, not Farris, was his real name.

'You bought this house from George Farris?' Julie asked.

Tuong said, 'No, he was dead.'

'Dead?' Bobby asked.

'Five or six years ago,' Tuong said. 'Terrible cancer.'

Then Frank Pollard *wasn't* Farris and hadn't lived here. The ID was entirely fake.

'We bought house just a few months ago from widow,' Tuong said. His English was good, though occasionally he dropped the article before the noun. 'No, what I mean to say – from widow's estate.'

Julie said, 'So Mrs Farris is dead too.'

Tuong turned to his wife, and a meaningful look passed between them. He said, 'It is very sad. Where does such a man come from?'

Julie said, 'What man are you speaking of, Mr Phan?'

'The one who killed Mrs Farris, her brother, two daughters.'

Something seemed to slither and coil in Bobby's stomach. He instinctively liked Frank Pollard and was certain of his innocence, but suddenly a worm of doubt bored into the fine, polished apple of his conviction. Could it be just a coincidence that Frank was carrying the ID of a man whose family had been slaughtered – or was Frank responsible? He was chewing a bite of cream-filled pastry, and though it was tasty, he had trouble swallowing it.

'It was late July,' Chinh said. 'During the heat wave, which you may remember.' She blew on her coffee to cool it. Bobby noticed that most of the time Chinh spoke perfect English, and he suspected that her occasional infelicities of language were conscious mistakes that she inserted in order not to seem more well spoken than her husband, a subtle and thoroughly Asian courtesy. 'We buy house last October.'

'They never catch the killer,' Tuong Phan said.

'Do they have a description of him?' Julie asked.

'I don't think so.'

Reluctantly Bobby glanced at Julie. She appeared to be as shaken as he was, but she did not give him an I-told-you-so look.

She said, 'How were they murdered? Shot? Strangled?'

'Knife, I think. Come. I show you where bodies were found.'

The house had three bedrooms and two bathrooms, but one bath was being remodeled. The tile had been torn off the walls, floor, and counter. The cabinets were being rebuilt with quality oak.

Julie followed Tuong into the bathroom, and Bobby stayed at the doorway with Mrs Phan.

The rattle-hiss of the rain echoed down through the ceiling vent.

Tuong said, 'Body of younger Farris daughter was here, on the floor. She was thirteen. Terrible thing. Much blood. The grout between tiles was permanently stained, all had to come out.'

He led them into the bedroom his daughters shared. Twin beds, nightstands, and two small desks left little room for anything else. But Sissy and Meryl had squeezed in a lot of books.

Tuong Phan said, 'Mrs Farris's brother, staying with her for a week, was killed here. In his bed. Blood was on walls, carpet.'

'We saw the house before it was listed with a real-estate agent, before the carpet was replaced and the walls repainted,' Chinh Phan said. 'This room was the worst. It gave me bad dreams for a while.'

They proceeded to the sparely furnished master bedroom: a queen-size bed, nightstands, two ginger-jar lamps, but no bureau or chest of drawers. The clothes that would not fit in the closet were arranged along one wall, in cardboard storage boxes with clear plastic lids.

Their frugality struck Bobby as similar to his and Julie's. Perhaps they, too, had a dream for which they were working and saving.

Tuong said, 'Mrs Farris was found in this room, in her bed. Terrible things were done to her. She was bitten, but they never wrote about that in newspapers.'

'Bitten?' Julie asked. 'By what?'

'Probably by killer. On the face, throat . . . other places.'

'If they didn't write about it in the papers,' Bobby said, 'how do you know about the bites?'

'Neighbor who found bodies still lives next door. She says that both older daughter and Mrs Farris were bitten.'

Mrs Phan said, 'She's not the kind to imagine such things.'

'Where was the second daughter found?' Julie asked.

'Please follow me.' Tuong led them back the way they had come, through the living room and dining room, into the kitchen.

The four Phan children were sitting around a breakfast table. Three of them were diligently reading textbooks and taking notes. No television or radio provided distraction, and they appeared to be enjoying their studies. Even Meryl, who was a first-grader and probably had no homework to speak of, was reading a children's book.

Bobby noticed two colorful charts posted on the wall near the refrigerator. The first displayed each kid's grades and major test results since the start of the school year in September. The other was a list of household chores for which each child was responsible.

Throughout the country, universities were in a bind, because an inordinately large percentage of the best applicants for admission were of Asian extraction. Blacks and Hispanics complained about being aced out by another minority, and whites shouted reverse racism when denied admission in favor of an Asian student. Some attributed Asian-Americans' success to a conspiracy, but Bobby saw the simple explanation for their achievements everywhere in the Phan house: They tried harder. They embraced the ideals upon which the country had been based – including hard work, honesty, goal-oriented self-denial, and the freedom to be whatever one wanted to be. Ironically, their great success was partly due to the fact that so many born Americans had become cynical about those same ideals.

The kitchen was open to a family room that was furnished as humbly as the rest of the house.

Tuong said, 'Older Farris girl found here on sofa. Seventeen.'

'Very pretty girl,' Chinh said sadly.

'She, like mother, was bitten. So our neighbor says.'

Julie said, 'What about the other victims, the younger daughter and Mrs Farris's brother – were they bitten too?'

'Don't know,' Tuong said.

'The neighbor didn't see their bodies,' Chinh said.

They were silent for a moment, looking at the place where the dead girl had been found, as if the enormity of this crime was such that the stain of it should somehow have reappeared on this brand new carpet. Rain droned on the roof.

Bobby said, 'Doesn't it sometimes bother you to live here? Not because murders took place in these rooms, but because the killer was never found. Don't you worry about him coming back some night?'

Chinh nodded.

Tuong said, 'Everywhere is danger. Life itself is danger. Less risky never being born.' A faint smile flickered across his face and was gone. 'Leaving Vietnam in tiny boat was more danger than this.'

Glancing at the table in the adjoining kitchen, Bobby saw the four kids still deeply involved with their studies. The prospect of a murderer returning to the scene of this crime did not faze them.

'In addition to dry-cleaning,' Chinh said, 'we remodel houses, sell them. This is fourth. We will live here maybe another year, remodeling room by room, then sell, take a profit.'

Tuong said, 'Because of murders, some people would not consider moving here after the Farrises. But danger is also opportunity.'

'When we finish with the house,' Chinh said, 'it won't just be remodeled. It will be clean, spiritually clean. Do you understand? The innocence of the house will be restored. We will have chased out the evil that the killer brought here, and we'll have left our own spiritual imprint on these rooms.'

Nodding, Tuong said, 'That is a satisfaction.'

Removing the forged driver's license from his pocket, Bobby held it so his fingers covered the name and address, leaving the photograph visible. 'Do you recognize this man?'

'No,' Tuong said, and Chinh agreed.

As Bobby put the license away, Julie said, 'Do you know what George Farris looked like?'

'No,' Tuong said. 'As I told you, he died of cancer, many years before his family was killed.'

'I thought maybe you'd seen a photo of him here in the house, before the Farris's belongings were removed.'

'No. Sorry.'

Bobby said, 'You mentioned earlier that you didn't buy the house through a realtor. You worked with the estate?'

'Yes. Mrs Farris's other brother inherited everything.'

'Do you happen to have his name and address?' Bobby asked. 'I think we'll need to talk to him.'

· **33** ·

Dinnertime came. Derek woke up. He was groggy but hungry too. He leaned on Thomas when they walked to the dining room. Food got eaten. Spaghetti. Meatballs. Salad. Good bread. Chocolate cake. Cold milk.

Back in their room, they watched TV. Derek fell asleep again. It was a bad night on TV. Thomas sighed with disgust. After an hour or so, he stopped the set. None of the shows was smart enough to care about. They were too stupid-silly even for a moron, which Mary said he was. Maybe imbeciles would like them. Probably not.

He used the bathroom. Brushed his teeth. Washed his face. He didn't look in the mirror. He didn't like mirrors because they showed him what he was.

After changing into pajamas, he got in bed and made the lamp go dark, even though it was only 8:30. He turned on his side, with his head propped on two pillows, and studied the night sky framed by the nearest window. No stars. Clouds. Rain. He liked rain. When a storm came down, it was like a lid on the night, and you didn't feel like you might float up in all that darkness and just disappear.

He listened to the rain. It whispered. It cried tears on the window.

Far away, the Bad Thing was loose. Ugly-nasty waves spread out from it the way ripples spread across a pond when you dropped a stone in the water. The Bad Thing was like a big stone dropped into the night, a thing that didn't belong in this world, and with a little effort Thomas could sense the waves from it breaking over him.

He reached out. Felt it. A throbbing thing. Cold and full of anger. Mean. He wanted to get closer. Learn what it was.

He tried TVing questions at it. What are you? Where are you? What do you want? Why are you going to hurt Julie?

Suddenly, like a big magnet, the Bad Thing began pulling him. He'd never felt anything like that before. When he tried to TV his thoughts to Bobby or Julie, they didn't grab him and pull at him the way this Bad Thing did.

A part of his mind seemed to unravel like a ball of string, and the loose end sailed through the window and way up into the night, through the darkness, until it found the Bad Thing. Suddenly Thomas was very close to the Bad Thing, too close. It was all around him, big ugly and so strange that Thomas felt like he'd dropped into a swimming pool full of ice and razor blades. He didn't know if it was a man, couldn't see its shape, only feel it; it might be pretty on the outside, but on the inside it was throbbing and dark and deep nasty. He sensed the Bad Thing was eating. The food was still alive and squirming. Thomas was scared big, and right away he tried to pull back, but for a moment the ugly mind held him tight, and he could get away only by picturing the mind-string rewinding itself onto the ball.

When the mind-string was all wound up again, Thomas turned away from the window, onto his stomach. He was breathing real fast. He listened to his heart boom.

He had a sick-making taste in his mouth. The same taste he got sometimes when he bit his tongue, not meaning to, and the same taste as when the dentist yanked one of his teeth, meaning to. Blood.

Sick and scared, he sat up in bed and made the lamp come on right away. He took a tissue from the box on the nightstand. He spit into it and looked to see if there was blood. There wasn't. Just spit.

He tried again. No blood.

He knew what that meant. He'd been too close to the Bad Thing. Maybe even *inside* the Bad Thing, just for a blink. The ugly taste in his mouth was the same taste the Bad Thing tasted, tearing with its teeth at some living, squirming food. Thomas didn't have blood in his mouth, he just had a memory of blood in his mouth. But that was bad enough; this time wasn't at all like biting his tongue or getting a tooth yanked, because this time what he tasted wasn't his own blood.

Though enough warmth was in the room, he started shivering and couldn't stop.

———

Candy prowled the canyons, in the grip of urgent need, rattling wild animals out of burrows and nests. He was kneeling in the mud beside a huge oak, pummeled by rain, sucking blood from the ravished throat of a rabbit, when he felt someone place a hand atop his head.

He threw down the rabbit and sprang to his feet, turning around as he did so. Nobody was there. Two of his sisters' blackest cats were twenty feet behind him, visible only because their eyes were luminous in the gloom; they had been following him since he'd left the house. Otherwise he was alone.

For a second or two, he still felt the hand on his head, though no hand was there. Then the queer sensation passed.

He studied the shadows on all sides and listened to the rain snapping through the oak leaves.

Finally, shrugging off the episode, driven by his fierce need, he proceeded farther east, moving upslope. A two-foot-wide stream had formed on the canyon floor, six or eight inches deep, not large enough to hamper his progress.

The drenched cats followed. He did not want them with him, but he knew from experience that he would not be able to chase them away. They did not always accompany him, but when they chose to follow in his tracks, they could not be dissuaded.

After he had gone about a hundred yards, he dropped to his knees again, held his hands in front of him, and allowed the power to erupt once more. Shimmering sapphire light swept through the night. Brush shook, trees stirred, and rocks clattered against one another. In the wake of the light, clouds of dust flew up, ghostly silver columns that rippled like wind-stirred shrouds, then vanished into the darkness.

A bevy of animals burst from cover, and some raced toward Candy. He snatched at a rabbit, missed, but seized a squirrel. It tried to bite him, but he swung it hard by one leg, bashing its head against the muddy ground, stunning it.

Violet was with Verbina in the kitchen. They were sitting on the layered blankets with twenty-three of their twenty-five cats.

Parts of her mind – and parts of her sister's – were in Cinders and Lamia, the black cats through which they were accompanying their brother. Watching Candy seize and destroy his prey, Cinders and Lamia were excited, and Violet was excited too. Electrified.

The wet January night was deep, illumined only by the ambient light from the communities to the west, which was reflected off the bellies of the low clouds. In that wilderness, Candy was the wildest creature of them all, a fierce and powerful and merciless predator who crept swiftly and silently through the rugged canyons, taking what he needed and wanted. He was so strong and limber that he appeared to flow up the canyon, over rocks and fallen timber, around prickly brush, as if he were not a man of flesh and blood, but the rippled moon-shadow of some flying creature soaring high above the earth.

When Candy seized the squirrel and bashed its head against the ground, Violet divided the part of her mind that was in Lamia and Cinders, and also entered the squirrel. It was stunned by the blow. It struggled feebly and looked at Candy with unalloyed terror.

Candy's big, strong hands were on the squirrel, but it seemed to Violet that they were on her, as well, moving over her bare legs, hips, belly, and breasts.

Candy snapped its spine against his bent knee.

Violet shuddered. Verbina whimpered and clung to her sister.

The squirrel no longer had any feeling in its extremities.

With a low growl, Candy bit the animal's throat. He tore at its hide, chewing open the blood-rich vessels.

Violet felt the hot blood spurting out of the squirrel, felt Candy's mouth fastened hungrily to the wound. It almost seemed as though no surrogate lay between them, as if his lips were pressed firmly to Violet's throat and as if her own blood was flooding into his mouth. She wished that she could enter Candy's mind and be on both the giving and receiving end of the blood, but she could only meld with animals.

She no longer had the strength to sit up. She settled back onto the blankets, only half aware that she was softly chanting a monotonous litany: '*Yes, yes, yes, yes, yes . . .*'

Verbina rolled atop her sister.

Around them the cats tumbled together in a roiling mass of fur and tails and whiskered faces.

Thomas tried again. For Julie's sake. He reached out toward the cold, glowing mind of the Bad Thing. Right away the Bad Thing drew him toward it. He let his mind unwind like a big ball of string. It pierced the window, zoomed into the night, made contact.

He TVed questions: What are you? Where are you? What do you want? Why are you going to hurt Julie?

Just as Candy threw aside the dead squirrel and got to his feet, he felt the hand on his head again. He twitched, turned, and flailed at the darkness with both fists.

No one was behind him. With radiant amber eyes, the two cats watched him from about twenty feet away, dark blots on the pale silt. All the wildlife in the immediate vicinity had fled. If someone was spying on him, the intruder was concealed in the brush farther back along the canyon or in a niche on one of the canyon walls, certainly not near enough to have touched him.

Besides, he still felt the hand. He rubbed at the top of his head, half expecting to find leaves stuck in his wet hair. Nothing.

But the pressure of a hand remained, even increased, and was so well defined that he could feel the outlines of four fingers, a thumb, and the curve of a palm against his skull.

What . . . where . . . what . . . why . . .?

Those words echoed inside his head. No voice had broken through the drizzling sounds of the rain.

What . . . where . . . what . . . why . . .?

Candy turned in a full circle, angry and confused.

A crawling sensation arose in his head, different from anything he had ever known before. As if something was burrowing in his brain.

'Who are you?' he said aloud.
What . . . where . . . what . . . why?
'Who are you?'

<hr>

The Bad Thing was a man. Thomas knew that now. An ugly-inside man and something else, too, but still at least partly a man.

The Bad Thing's mind was like a whirlpool, blacker than black, swirling real fast, sucking Thomas down, down, wanting to gobble him alive. He tried to break loose. Swim away. Wasn't easy. The Bad Thing was going to pull him into the Bad Place, and he'd never be able to come back. He thought he was a goner. But his fear of the Bad Place, of going where Julie and Bobby would never find him and where he'd be alone, was so big he finally tore free and rewound himself into his room at Cielo Vista.

He slid down on the mattress and drew the covers over his head, so he couldn't see the night beyond the window, and so nothing out there in the night could see him.

• 34 •

Walter Havalow, Mrs George Farris's surviving brother and heir to her modest estate, lived in a richer neighborhood than the Phans, but he was poorer in courtesy and good manners. His English tudor house in Villa Park had beveled-glass windows filled with a light that Julie found warm and beckoning, but Havalow stood in the doorway and did not invite them inside even after he had studied their PI license and returned it to her.

'What do you want?'

Havalow was tall, potbellied, with thinning blond hair and a thick mustache that was part blond and part red. His penetrating hazel eyes marked him as a man of intelligence, but they were cold, watchful, and calculating – the eyes of a Mafia accountant.

'As I explained,' Julie said, 'the Phans told us you could help. We need a photograph of your late brother-in-law, George Farris.'

'Why?'

'Well, as I said, there's a man going around pretending to be Mr Farris, and he's a player in a case we're working on.'

'Can't be my brother-in-law. He's dead.'

'Yes, we know. But this imposter's ID is very good, and it would help us to have a photo of the real George Farris. I'm sorry I can't tell you anything more. I'd be violating our client's privacy.'

Havalow turned away and closed the door in their faces.

Bobby looked at Julie and said, 'Mr Conviviality.'

Julie rang the bell again.

After a moment, Havalow opened the door. 'What?'

'I know we arrived unannounced,' Julie said, struggling to remain cordial, 'and I apologize for the intrusion, but a photo of your—'

'I was just going to get the picture,' he said impatiently. 'I'd have it in hand by now if you hadn't rung the bell again.' He turned away from them and closed the door a second time.

'Is it our body odor?' Bobby wondered.

'What a jerk.'

'You think he's really coming back?'

'He doesn't, I'll break the door down.'

Behind them, rain dripped off the overhang that sheltered the last ten feet of the walkway, and water gurgled hollowly through a downspout – cold sounds.

Havalow returned with a shoe box full of snapshots. 'My time is valuable. If you want my cooperation, you'll keep that in mind.'

Julie resisted her worst instincts. Rudeness irritated the hell out of her. She fantasized knocking the box out of his grasp, seizing one of his hands, and bending the index finger as far back as it would go, thus straining the digital nerve on the front of his hand while simultaneously pinching the radial and median nerves on the back, forcing him to kneel. Then a knee driven into the underside of his chin, a swift chop to the back of his neck, a well-placed kick to his soft, protruding belly . . .

Havalow rummaged through the box and extracted a Polaroid of a man and a woman sitting at a redwood picnic table on a sunny day. 'That's George and Irene.'

Even in the yellowish light of the porch lamp, Julie could see that George Farris had been a rangy man with a long narrow face, the exact physical opposite of Frank Pollard.

'Why would someone be claiming he's George?' Havalow asked.

'We're dealing with a possible criminal who uses multiple fake IDs,' Julie said. 'George Farris is just one of his identities. No doubt your brother-in-law's name was probably chosen at random by the document forger this guy used. Forgers sometimes use the names and addresses of the deceased.'

Havalow frowned. 'You think it's possible this man using George's name is the same guy who killed Irene, my brother, my two nieces?'

'No,' Julie said immediately. 'We're not dealing with a killer here. Just a confidence man, a swindler.'

'Besides,' Bobby said, 'no killer would link himself to murders he'd committed by getting an ID in the name of his victim's husband.'

Making eye contact with Julie, clearly trying to determine how much they were snowing him, Havalow said, 'This guy your client?'

'No,' Julie lied. 'He ripped off our client, and we've been hired to track him down, so he can be forced to make restitution.'

Bobby said, 'Can we borrow this photo, sir?'

Havalow hesitated. He was still making eye contact with Julie.

Bobby handed Havalow a Dakota & Dakota business card. 'We'll get the picture back to you. There's our address, phone number. I understand your reluctance to part with a family photo, especially since your sister and brother-in-law are no longer alive, but if—'

Apparently deciding that they were not lying, Havalow said, 'Hell, take it. I'm not sentimental about George. Never could stand him. Always thought my sister was a fool for marrying him.'

'Thank you,' Bobby said. 'We—'

Havalow stepped back and closed the door.

Julie rang the bell.

Bobby said, 'Please don't kill him.'

Scowling with impatience, Havalow opened the door.

Stepping between Julie and Havalow, Bobby held out the forged driver's license bearing George Farris's name and Frank's picture. 'One more thing, sir, and we'll get out of your hair.'

'I live to a very tight schedule,' Havalow said.

'Have you seen this man before?'

Irritated, Havalow took the driver's license and inspected it. 'Doughy face, bland features. There're a million like him within a hundred miles of here – wouldn't you say?'

'And you've never seen him?'

'Are you slow-witted? Do I have to put it in short, simple sentences? No. I have never seen him.'

Retrieving the license, Bobby said, 'Thanks for your time and—'

Havalow closed the door. Hard.

Julie reached for the bell.

Bobby stayed her hand. 'We've got everything we came for.'

'I want—'

'I know what you want,' Bobby said, 'but torturing a man to death is against the law in California.'

He hustled her away from the house, into the rain.

In the car again, she said, 'That rude, self-important bastard!'

Bobby started the engine and switched on the windshield wipers. 'We'll stop at the mall, buy you one of those giant teddy bears, paint Havalow's name on it, let you tear the guts out of it. Okay?'

'Who the hell does he think he is?'

While Julie glowered back at the house, Bobby drove away from it. 'He's Walter Havalow, babe, and he's got to be himself until he dies, which is a worse punishment than anything you could do to him.'

A few minutes later, when they were out of Villa Park, Bobby drove into the lot at a Ralph's supermarket and tucked the Toyota into a parking space. He doused the headlights, switched off the wipers, but left the engine running so they would have heat.

Only a few cars were in front of the market. Puddles as large as swimming pools reflected the store lights.

Bobby said, 'What've we learned?'

'That we *loathe* Walter Havalow.'

'Yes, but what have we learned that's germane to the case? Is it just a coincidence that Frank's been using George Farris's name and Farris's family was slaughtered?'

'I don't believe in coincidence.'

'Neither do I. But I still don't think Frank is a killer.'

'Neither do I, though anything's possible. But what you said to Havalow was true – surely Frank wouldn't kill Irene Farris and everyone else in the house, then carry around fake ID that links him to them.'

Rain began to fall harder than before, drumming noisily on the Toyota. The heavy curtain of water blurred the supermarket.

Bobby said, 'You want to know what I think? I think Frank was using Farris's name, and whoever's after him found out about it.'

'Mr Blue Light, you mean. The guy who supposedly can make a car fall apart around you and magically induce streetlights to blow out.'

'Yeah, him,' Bobby said.

'If he exists.'

'Mr Blue Light discovered Frank was using the Farris name, and went to that address, hoping to find him. But Frank had never been there. It was just a name and address his document forger picked at random. So when Mr Blue didn't find Frank, he killed everyone in the house, maybe because he thought they were lying to him and hiding Frank, or maybe just because he was in a rage.'

'*He'd* have known how to deal with Havalow.'

'So you think I'm right, I'm on to something?'

She thought about it. 'Could be.'

He grinned at her. 'Isn't it fun being a detective?'

'Fun?' she said incredulously.

'Well, I meant "interesting". '

'We're either representing a man who killed four people, or we're representing a man who's been targeted by a brutal murderer, and that strikes you as fun?'

'Not as much fun as sex, but more fun than bowling.'

'Bobby, sometimes you make me nuts. But I love you.'

He took her hand. 'If we're going to pursue the investigation, I'm damned well going to enjoy it as much as I can. But I'll drop the case in a minute if you want.'

'Why? Because of your dream? Because of the Bad Thing?' She shook her head. 'No. We start letting a weird dream spook us, pretty soon *anything* will spook us. We'll lose our confidence, and you can't do this kind of work without confidence.'

Even in the dim backsplash from the dashboard lights, she could see the anxiety in his eyes.

Finally he said, 'Yeah, that's what I knew you'd say. So let's get to the bottom of it as fast as we can. According to his other driver's license, he's James Roman, and he lives in El Toro.'

'It's almost eight-thirty.'

'We can be there, find the house . . . maybe forty-five minutes. That's not too late.'

'All right.'

Instead of putting the car in gear, he slid his seat back and stripped out of his down-lined nylon jacket. 'Unlock the glovebox and give me my gun. From now on I'm wearing it everywhere.'

Each of them had a license to carry a concealed weapon. Julie struggled out of her own jacket, then retrieved two shoulder holsters from under her seat. She took both revolvers out of the glovebox: two snubnosed Smith & Wesson .38 Chief's Specials, reliable and compact guns that could be carried inconspicuously beneath ordinary clothing with little or no help from a tailor.

―――

The house was gone. If anyone named James Roman had lived there, he had new lodgings now. A bare concrete slab lay in the middle of the lot, surrounded by grass, shrubbery, and several trees, as if the structure had been snared from above by intergalactic moving men and neatly spirited away.

Bobby parked in the driveway, and they got out of the Toyota to have a closer look at the property. Even in the slashing rain, a nearby streetlamp cast enough light to reveal that the lawn was trampled, gouged by tires, and bare in spots; it was also littered with splinters of wood, pale bits of Sheetrock, crumbled stucco, and a few fragments of glass that sparkled darkly.

The strongest clue to the fate of the house was to be found in the condition of the shrubbery and trees. Those bushes closest to the slab were all either dead or badly damaged, and on closer inspection appeared to be scorched. The nearest tree was leafless, and its stark black limbs lent an anachronistic feeling of Halloween to the drizzly January night.

'Fire,' Julie said. 'Then they tore down what was left.'

'Let's talk to a neighbor.'

The empty lot was flanked by houses. But lights glowed only at the house on the north side.

The man who answered the doorbell was about fifty-five, six feet two, solidly built, with gray hair and a neatly trimmed gray mustache. His name was Park Hampstead, and he had the air of a retired military man. He invited them in, with the proviso that they leave their sodden shoes on the front porch. In their socks, they followed him to a breakfast nook off the kitchen, where the yellow vinyl dinette upholstery was safe from their damp clothing; even so, Hampstead made them wait while he draped thick peach-colored beach towels over two of the chairs.

'Sorry,' he said, 'but I'm something of a fussbudget.'

The house had bleached-oak floors and modern furniture, and Bobby noticed that it was spotless in every corner.

'Thirty years in the Marine Corps left me with an abiding respect for routine, order, and neatness,' Hampstead explained. 'In fact, when Sharon died three years ago – she was my wife – I think maybe I got a little crazy about neatness. The first six or eight months after her funeral, I cleaned the place top to bottom at least twice a week, because as long as I was cleaning, my heart didn't hurt so bad. Spent a fortune on Windex, paper towels, Fantastik, and sweeper bags. Let me tell you, no military pension can support the End Dust habit I developed! I got over that stage. I'm still a fussbudget but not *obsessed* with neatness.'

He had just brewed a fresh pot of coffee, so he poured for them as well. The cups, saucers, and spoons were all spotless. Hampstead provided each of them with a crisply folded paper napkin, then sat across the table from them.

'Sure,' he said, after they raised the issue, 'I knew Jim Roman. Good neighbor. He was a chopper jockey out of the El Toro Air Base. That was my last station before retirement. Jim was a hell of a nice guy, the kind who'd give you the shirt off his back, then ask if you needed money to buy a matching tie.'

'Was?' Julie asked.

'He die in the fire?' Bobby asked, remembering the scorched shrubbery and soot-blackened concrete slab next door.

Hampstead frowned. 'No. He died about six months after Sharon. Make it . . . two and a half years ago. His chopper crashed on maneuvers. He was only forty-one, eleven years younger than me. Left a wife, Maralee. A fourteen-year-old daughter named Valerie. Twelve-year-old son, Mike. Real nice kids.

Terrible thing. They were a close family, and Jim's accident devastated them. They had some relatives back in Nebraska, but no one they could really turn to.' Hampstead stared past Bobby, at the softly humming refrigerator, and his eyes swam out of focus. 'So I tried to step in, help out, advise Maralee on finances, give a shoulder to lean on and an ear to listen when the kids needed that. Took 'em to Disneyland and Knott's from time to time, you know, that sort of thing. Maralee told me lots of times what a godsend I was, but it was really me who needed them more than the other way around, because doing things for them was what finally began to take my mind off losing Sharon.'

Julie said, 'So the fire happened more recently?'

Hampstead did not respond. He got up, went to the sink, opened the cupboard door below, returned with a spray bottle of Windex and a dish towel, and began to wipe the refrigerator door, which already appeared to be as clean as the antiseptic surfaces in a hospital surgery. 'Valerie and Mike were terrific kids. After a year or so it almost got to seem like they were *my* kids, the ones me and Sharon never had. Maralee grieved for Jim a long time, almost two years, before she began to remember she was a woman in her prime. Maybe what started to happen between her and me would've upset Jim, but I don't think so; I think he'd have been happy for us, even if I was eleven years older than her.'

When he finished wiping the refrigerator, Hampstead inspected the door from the side, at an angle to the light, apparently searching for a fingerprint or smudge. As if he had just heard the question that Julie had asked a minute ago, he suddenly said, 'The fire was two months ago. I woke up in the middle of the night, heard sirens, saw an orange glow at the window, got up, looked out . . .'

He turned away from the refrigerator, studied the kitchen for a moment, then went to the nearest tile-topped counter and began to spritz and wipe that gleaming surface.

Julie looked at Bobby. He shook his head. Neither of them said anything.

After a moment Hampstead continued: 'Got over to their house just ahead of the firemen. Went in through the front door. Made it into the foyer, then to the foot of the steps, but couldn't get up to the bedroom, the heat was too intense, and the smoke. I called their names, nobody answered. If I'd heard an answer maybe I would've found the strength to go up there somehow in spite of the flames. I guess I must've blacked out for a few seconds and been carried out by firemen, 'cause I woke up on the front lawn, coughing, choking, a paramedic bent over me, giving me oxygen.'

'All three of them died?' Bobby asked.

'Yeah,' Hampstead said.

'What caused the fire?'

'I'm not sure they ever figured that out. I might've heard something about a short in the wiring, but I'm not sure. I think they even suspected arson for a while, but that never led anywhere. Doesn't much matter, does it?'

'Why not?'

'Whatever caused it, they're all three dead.'

'I'm sorry,' Bobby said softly.

'Their lot's been sold. Construction starts on a new house sometime this spring. More coffee?'

'No, thank you,' Julie said.

Hampstead surveyed the kitchen, then moved to the stainless-steel range hood, which he began to clean in spite of the fact that it was spotless. 'I apologize for the mess. Don't know how the place gets like this when it's just me living here. Sometimes I think there must be gremlins sneaking behind my back, messing things up to torment me.'

'No need for gremlins,' Julie said. 'Life itself gives us all the torment we can handle.'

Hampstead turned away from the range hood. For the first time since he had gotten up from the table and begun his cleaning ritual, he made eye contact with them. 'No gremlins,' he agreed. 'Nothing as simple and easy to handle as gremlins.' He was a big man and obviously tough from years of military training and discipline, but the shimmering, watery evidence of grief brimmed in his eyes, and at the moment he seemed as lost and helpless as a child.

In the car again, staring through the rain-spattered windshield at the vacant lot where the Roman house had once stood, Bobby said, 'Frank finds out that Mr Blue Light knows about the Farris ID, so he gets new ID in the name of James Roman. But Mr Blue eventually learns about that, too, and he goes looking for Frank at the Roman address, where he discovers only the widow and the kids. He kills them, same way he killed the Farris family, but this time he sets fire to the house to cover the crime. Is that the way it looks to you?'

'Could be,' Julie said.

'He burns the bodies because he bites them, like the Phans told us, and the bite marks help the police tie his crimes together, so he wants to throw the cops off the trail.'

Julie said, 'Then why doesn't he burn them every time?'

'Because that would be just as much of a giveaway as the bite marks. Sometimes he burns the bodies, sometimes he doesn't, and maybe sometimes he disposes of them so they're never even found.'

They were both silent for a moment. Then she said, 'So we're dealing with a mass murderer, a serial killer, who's evidently a raving psychotic.'

'Or a vampire,' Bobby said.

'Why's he after Frank?'

'I don't know. Maybe Frank once tried to drive a wooden stake through his heart.'

'Not funny.'

'I agree,' Bobby said. 'Right now, nothing seems funny.'

· 35 ·

From Dyson Manfred's house full of insect specimens in Irvine, Clint Karaghiosis drove through the chilly rain to his own house in Placentia. It was a homey two-bedroom bungalow with a rolled-shingle roof, a deep front porch in the California Craftsman style, and French windows full of warm amber light. By the time he got there, the car heater had pretty much dried his rain-soaked clothes.

Felina was in the kitchen when Clint entered by way of the connecting door from the garage. She hugged him, kissed him, held fast to him for a moment, as if surprised to see him alive again.

She believed that his job was fraught with danger every day, though he had often explained that he did mostly boring legwork. He chased facts instead of culprits, pursued a trail of paper rather than blood.

He understood his wife's concern, however, because he worried unreasonably about her too. For one thing, she was an attractive woman with black hair, an olive complexion, and startlingly beautiful gray eyes; in this age of lenient judges, with a surfeit of merciless sociopaths on the streets, a good-looking woman was regarded by some as fair game. Furthermore, though the office where Felina worked as a data processor was only three blocks from their house, an easy walk even in bad weather, Clint nevertheless worried about the danger she faced at the busiest of the intersections that she had to cross; in an emergency, a warning cry or blaring horn would not alert her to onrushing death.

He could not let her know how much he worried, for she was justly proud that she was so independent in spite of her deafness. He did not want to diminish her self-respect by indicating in any way that he was not entirely confident of her ability to deal with every rotten tomato that fate threw at her. So he daily reminded himself that she had lived twenty-nine years without coming to serious harm, and he resisted the urge to be overly protective.

While Clint washed his hands at the sink, Felina set the kitchen table for a late dinner. An enormous pot of homemade vegetable soup was heating on the stove, and together they ladled out two large bowls of it. He got a shaker of Parmesan cheese from the refrigerator, and she unwrapped a loaf of crusty Italian bread.

He was hungry, and the soup was excellent – thick with vegetables and chunks of lean beef – but by the time Felina had finished her first bowlful, Clint had eaten less than half of his, because he repeatedly paused to talk to her. She could not read his lips well when he tried to converse and eat at the same time, and for the moment his hunger was less compelling than his need to tell her about his day. She refilled her bowl and refreshed his.

Beyond the walls of his own small home, he was only slightly more talkative than a stone, but in Felina's company he was as loquacious as a talkshow host. He didn't just prattle, either, but settled with surprising ease into the role of a polished raconteur. He had learned how to deliver an anecdote in such a way as to sharpen its impact and maximize Felina's response, for he loved to elicit a laugh from her or watch her eyes widen with surprise. In all of Clint's life, she was the first person whose opinion of him truly mattered, and he wanted her to think of him as smart, clever, witty, and fun.

Early in their relationship he had wondered if her deafness had anything to do with his ability to open up to her. Deaf since birth, she had never heard the spoken word and therefore had not learned to speak clearly. She responded to Clint – and would later tell him about her own day – by way of sign language, which he had studied in order to understand her nimble-fingered speech. Initially he had thought that the main encouragement to intimacy was her disability, which ensured that his innermost feelings and secrets, once revealed to her, would go no further; a conversation with Felina was nearly as private as a conversation with himself. In time, however, he finally understood that he opened up to her in spite of her deafness, not because of it, and that he wanted her to share his every thought and experience – and to share hers in return – simply because he loved her.

When he told Felina how Bobby and Julie had adjourned to the bathroom for three private chats during Frank Pollard's appointment, she laughed delightedly. He loved that sound; it was so warm and singularly melodious, as if the great joy in life that she could not express in spoken words was entirely channeled into her laughter.

'They're some pair, the Dakotas,' he said. 'When you first meet them, they seem so dissimilar in some ways, you figure they can't possibly work well together. But then you get to know them, you see how they fit like two pieces of a puzzle, and you realize they've got a nearly perfect relationship.'

Felina put down her soup spoon and signed: *So do we.*

'We sure do.'

We fit better than puzzle pieces. We fit like a plug and socket.

'We sure do,' he agreed, smiling. Then he picked up on the sly sexual connotation of what she'd said, and he laughed. 'You're a filthy-minded wench, aren't you?'

She grinned and nodded.

'Plug and socket, huh?'

Big plug, tight socket, good fit.

'Later on, I'll check your wiring.'

I am in desperate need of a first-rate electrician. But tell me more about this new client.

Thunder cracked and clattered across the night outside, and a sudden gust of wind rattled the rain against the window. The sounds of the storm made the warm and aromatic kitchen even more inviting by comparison. Clint sighed with contentment, then was touched by a brief sadness when he realized that the deeply satisfying sense of shelter, induced by the sounds of thunder and rain, was a specific pleasure that Felina could never experience or share with him.

From his pants pocket he withdrew one of the red gems that Frank Pollard had brought to the office. 'I borrowed this one 'cause I wanted you to see it. The guy had a jarful of them.'

She pinched the grape-sized stone between thumb and index finger and held it up to the light. *Beautiful,* she signed with her free hand. She put the gem beside her soup bowl, on the cream-white Formica surface of the kitchen table. *Is it very valuable?*

'We don't know yet,' he said. 'We'll get an opinion from a gemologist tomorrow.'

I think it's valuable. When you take it back to the office, make sure there's no hole in your pocket. I have a hunch you'd have to work a long time to pay for it if you lost it.

The stone took in the kitchen light, bounced it from prism to prism, and cast it back with a bright tint, painting Felina's face with luminous crimson spots and smears. She seemed to be spattered with blood.

A queer foreboding overtook Clint.

She signed, *What're you frowning about?*

He didn't know what to say. His uneasiness was out of proportion to the cause of it. A cold prickling swiftly progressed from the base of his spine all the way to the back of his neck, as if dominoes of ice were falling in a row. He reached out and moved the gem a few inches, so the blood-red reflections fell on the wall beside Felina instead of on her face.

• 36 •

By one-thirty in the morning, Hal Yamataka was thoroughly hooked by the John D. MacDonald novel, *The Last One Left*. The room's only chair wasn't the most comfortable seat he'd ever parked his butt in, and the antiseptic smell of the hospital always made him a bit queasy, and the chile rellenos he'd eaten for dinner were still coming back on him, but the book was so involving that eventually he forgot all of those minor discomforts.

He even forgot Frank Pollard for a while, until he heard a brief hiss, like air escaping under pressure, and felt a sudden draft. He looked away from the book, expecting to see Pollard sitting up in the bed or trying to get out of it, but Pollard was not there.

Startled, Hal sprang up, dropping the book.

The bed was empty. Pollard had been there all night, asleep for the last hour, but now he was gone. The place was not brightly lit because the fluorescents behind the bed were turned off, but the shadows beyond the reading lamp were too shallow to conceal a man. The sheets were not tossed aside but were draped neatly across the mattress, and both of the side railings were locked in place, as if Frank Pollard had evaporated like a figure carved from Dry Ice.

Hal was certain that he would have heard Pollard lower one of the railings, get out of bed, then lift the railing into place again. Surely he would have heard Pollard climbing *over* it too.

The window was closed. Rain washed down the glass, glimmering with silvery reflections of the room's light. They were on the sixth floor, and Pollard could not escape by the window, yet Hal checked it, noting that it was not merely closed but locked.

Stepping to the door of the adjoining bathroom, he said, 'Frank?' When no one answered, he entered. The bathroom was deserted.

Only the narrow closet remained as a viable hiding place. Hal opened it and found two hangers that held the clothes Pollard had been wearing when he'd checked into the hospital. The man's shoes were there, too, with his socks neatly rolled and tucked into them.

'He can't have gotten past me and into the hall,' Hal said, as if giving voice to that contention would magically make it true.

He pulled open the heavy door and rushed into the corridor. No one was in sight in either direction.

He turned to the left, hurried to the emergency exit at the end of the hall, and opened the door. Standing on the sixth-floor landing, he listened for footsteps rising or descending, heard none, peered over the iron railing, down into the well, then up. He was alone.

Retracing his steps, he returned to Pollard's room and glanced inside at the empty bed. Still disbelieving, he proceeded to the junction of corridors, where he turned right and went to the glass-walled nurses' station.

None of the five night-shift nurses had seen Pollard on the move. Since the elevators were directly opposite the nurses' station, where Pollard would have had to wait in full view of the people on duty, it seemed unlikely that he had left the hospital by that route.

'I thought you were watching over him,' said Grace Fulgham, the gray-haired supervisor of the sixth-floor night staff. Her solid build, indomitable manner, and life-worn but kind face would have made her perfect for the female lead if Hollywood ever started remaking the old Tugboat Annie or Ma and Pa Kettle movies. 'Wasn't that your job?'

'I never left the room, but—'

'Then how did he get past you?'

'I don't know,' Hal said, chagrined. 'But the important thing is . . . he's suffering from partial amnesia, somewhat confused. He might wander off any-where, out of the hospital, God knows where. I can't figure how he got past me, but we have to find him.'

Mrs Fulgham and a younger nurse named Janet Soto began a swift and quiet inspection of all the rooms along Pollard's corridor.

Hal accompanied Nurse Fulgham. As they were checking out 604, where two elderly men snored softly, he heard eerie music, barely audible. As he turned, seeking the source, the notes faded away.

If Nurse Fulgham heard the music, she did not remark on it. A moment later in the next room, 606, when those strains arose once more, marginally louder than before, she whispered, 'What *is* that?'

To Hal it sounded like a flute. The unseen flautist produced no discernible melody, but the flow of notes was haunting nonetheless.

They reentered the hall as the music stopped again, and just as a draft swept along the corridor.

'Someone's left a window open – or probably a stairway door,' the nurse said quietly but pointedly.

'Not me,' Hal assured her.

Janet Soto stepped out of the room across the hall just as the blustery draft abruptly died. She frowned at them, shrugged, then headed toward the next room on her side.

The flute warbled softly. The draft struck up again, stronger than before, and beneath the astringent odors of the hospital, Hal thought he detected a faint scent of smoke.

Leaving Grace Fulgham to her search, Hal hurried toward the far end of the corridor. He intended to check the door at the head of the emergency stairs, to make sure that he hadn't left it open.

From the corner of his eye, he saw the door to Pollard's room beginning to swing shut, and he realized that the draft must be coming from in there. He pushed through the door before it could close, and saw Frank sitting up in bed, looking confused and frightened.

The draft and flute had given way to stillness, silence.

'Where did you go?' Hal asked, approaching the bed.

'Fireflies,' Pollard said, apparently dazed. His hair was spiked and tangled, and his round face was pale.

'Fireflies?'

'Fireflies in a windstorm,' Pollard said.

Then he vanished. One second he was sitting in bed, as real and solid as anyone Hal had ever known, and the next second he was gone as inexplicably and neatly as a ghost abandoning a haunt. A brief hiss, like air escaping from a punctured tire, accompanied his departure.

Hal swayed as if he had been stricken. For a moment his heart seemed to seize up, and he was paralyzed by surprise.

Nurse Fulgham stepped into the doorway. 'No sign of him in any of the rooms off this corridor. He might've gone up or down another floor – don't you think?'

'Uh . . .'

'Before we check out the rest of this level, maybe I'd better call security and get them moving on a search of the entire hospital. Mr Yamataka?'

Hal glanced at her, then back at the empty bed. 'Uh . . . yeah. Yeah, that's a good idea. He might wander off to . . . God knows where.'

Nurse Fulgham hurried away.

Weak-kneed, Hal went to the door, closed it, put his back against it, and stared at the bed across the room. After a while he said, 'Are you there, Frank?'

He received no answer. He had not expected one. Frank Pollard had not turned invisible; he had *gone* somewhere, somehow.

Not sure why he was less wonderstruck than frightened by what he had seen, Hal hesitantly crossed the room to the bed. He gingerly touched the stainless-steel railing, as if he thought that Pollard's vanishing act had tapped some elemental force, leaving a deadly residual current in the bed. But no sparks crackled under his fingertips; the metal was cool and smooth.

He waited, wondering how soon Pollard would reappear, wondering if he ought to call Bobby now or wait until Pollard materialized, wondering if the man *would* materialize again or disappear forever. For the first time in memory, Hal Yamataka was gripped by indecision; he was ordinarily a quick thinker, and quick to act, but he had never come face to face with the supernatural before.

The only thing he knew for sure was that he must not let Fulgham or Soto or anyone else in the hospital know what had really happened. Pollard was caught up in a phenomenon so strange that word of it would spread quickly from the hospital staff to the press. Protecting a client's privacy was always one of Dakota & Dakota's prime objectives, but in this case it was even more important than usual. Bobby and Julie had said that someone was hunting for Pollard, evidently with violent intentions; therefore, keeping the press out of the case might be essential if the client was to survive.

The door opened, and Hal jumped as if he'd been stuck with a hatpin.

In the doorway stood Grace Fulgham, looking as if she had just either guided a tugboat through stormy seas or chopped and carried a couple of cords of firewood that Pa had been too lazy to deal with. 'Security's putting a man at every exit to stop him if he tries to leave, and we're mobilizing the nursing staff on each floor to look for him. Do you intend to join the search?'

'Uh, well, I've got to call the office, my boss . . .'

'If we find him, where will we find you?'

'Here. Right here. I'll be here, making some calls.'

She nodded and went away. The door eased shut after her.

A privacy curtain hung from a ceiling track that described an arc around three sides of the bed. It was bunched against the wall, but Hal Yamataka drew it to the foot of the bed, blocking the view from the doorway, in case Pollard materialized just as someone stepped in from the corridor.

His hands were shaking, so he jammed them in his pockets. Then he took his left hand out to look at his wristwatch: 1:48.

Pollard had been missing for perhaps eighteen minutes – except, of course, for the few seconds during which he had flickered into existence and talked about fireflies in a windstorm. Hal decided to wait until two o'clock to call Bobby and Julie.

He stood at the foot of the bed, clutching the railing with one hand, listening to the night wind crying at the window and the rain snapping against the glass. The minutes crawled past like snails on an incline, but at least the wait gave him time to calm down and think about how he would tell Bobby what had happened.

As the hands on his watch lined up at two o'clock, he went the rest of the way around the bed and was reaching for the phone on the nightstand when he heard the eerie ululation of a distant flute. The half-drawn bed curtain fluttered in a sudden draft.

He returned to the foot of the bed and looked past the end of the curtain to the hallway door. It was closed. That was not the source of the draft.

The flute died. The air in the room grew still, leaden.

Abruptly the curtain shivered and rippled, gently rattling the bearings in the overhead track, and a breath of cool air swept around the room, ruffling his hair. The atonal, ghostly music rose again.

With the door shut and the window closed tight, the only possible source of the draft was the ventilation grille in the wall above the nightstand. But when Hal stood on his toes and raised his right hand in front of that outlet, he felt nothing issuing from it. The chilly currents of air appeared to have sprung up within the room itself.

He turned in a circle, moved this way and that, trying to get a fix on the flute. Actually, it didn't sound like a flute when he listened closely; it was more like a fluctuant wind whistling through a lot of pipes at the same time, big ones and little ones, threading together many vague but separate sounds into a loosely woven keening that was simultaneously eerie and melancholy, mournful yet somehow . . . threatening. It faded, then returned a third time. To his surprise and bewilderment, the tuneless notes seemed to be issuing from the empty air above the bed.

Hal wondered if anyone else in the hospital could hear the flute this time. Probably not. Though the music was louder now than when it had begun, it remained faint; in fact, if he had been asleep, the mysterious serenade would not have been loud enough to wake him.

Before Hal's eyes, the air over the bed shimmered. For a moment he could not breathe, as if the room had become a temporary vacuum chamber. He felt his ears pop the way they did during a too-rapid altitude change.

The strange warbling and the draft died together, and Frank Pollard reappeared as abruptly as he had vanished. He was lying on his side, with his knees drawn up in the fetal position. For a few seconds he was disoriented; when he realized where he was, he clutched the bed railing and pulled himself into a sitting position. The skin around his eyes was puffy and dark, but otherwise he was dreadfully pale. His face had a greasy sheen to it, as if it wasn't perspiration pouring from him but clear beads of oil. His blue cotton pajamas were rumpled, darkly mottled with sweat, and caked with dirt in places.

He said, 'Stop me.'

'What the hell's going on here?' Hal asked, his voice cracking.

'Out of control.'

'Where did you go?'

'For God's sake, help me.' Pollard was still clutching the bed rail with his right hand, but he reached entreatingly toward Hal with his left. 'Please, please . . .'

Stepping closer to the bed, Hal reached out—

—and Pollard vanished, this time not only with a hissing sound, as before, but with a shriek and sharp crack of tortured metal. The stainless-steel railing, which he had been gripping so fiercely, had torn loose of the bed and vanished with him.

Hal Yamataka stared in astonishment at the hinges to which the adjustable railing had been fixed. They were twisted and torn, as if made of cardboard. A force of incredible power had pulled Pollard out of that room, snapping quarter-inch steel.

Staring at his own outstretched hand, Hal wondered what would have happened to him if he had been gripping Pollard. Would he have disappeared with the man? To where? Not someplace he would want to be: he was sure of that.

Or maybe only part of him would have gone with Pollard. Maybe he would have come apart at a joint, just as the bed railing had done. Maybe his arm would have ripped out of his shoulder socket with a crack almost as sharp as that with which the steel hinges had separated, and maybe he would have been left screaming in pain, with blood squirting from snapped vessels.

He snatched his hand back, as if afraid Pollard might suddenly reappear and seize it.

As he rounded the bed to the phone, he thought that his legs were going to fail him. His hands were shaking so badly, he almost dropped the receiver and had difficulty dialing the Dakotas' home number.

• 37 •

When Bobby and Julie left for the hospital the night looked deeper than usual; streetlamps and headlights did not fully penetrate the gloom. Shatters of rain fell with such force, they appeared to bounce off the blacktop streets, as if they were hard fragments of a disintegrating vault that arched through the night above.

Julie drove because Bobby was only three-quarters awake. His eyes were heavy, and he couldn't stop yawning, and his thoughts were fuzzy at the edges. They had gone to bed only three hours before Hal Yamataka had awakened them. If Julie had to get by on only that much sleep, she could do it, but Bobby needed at least six – preferably eight – hours in the sack in order to function well.

That was a minor difference between them, no big deal. But because of several such minor differences, Bobby suspected that Julie was tougher overall than he was, even if he could whip her ten times out of ten in an arm-wrestling competition.

He chuckled softly.

She said, 'What?'

She braked for a traffic light as it phased to red. Its bloody image was reflected in distorted patterns by the black, mirrorlike surface of the rain-slick street.

'I'm crazy to give you an advantage by admitting this, but I was thinking that in some ways you're tougher than me.'

She said, 'That's no revelation. I've always known I'm tougher.'

'Oh, yeah? If we arm wrestle, I'll whip you every time.'

'How sad.' She shook her head. 'Do you really think beating up someone smaller than you, and a woman to boot, makes you a macho man?'

'I could beat up a lot of women *bigger* than me,' Bobby assured her. 'And if they're old enough, I could take them on two or three or four at a time. In fact, you throw half a dozen big grandmothers at me, and I'll take them all on with one hand tied behind my back!'

The traffic light turned green, and she drove on.

'I'm talking *big* grandmothers,' he said. 'Not frail little old ladies. Big, fat, solid grandmothers, six at a time.'

'That is impressive.'

'Damn right. Though it'd help if I had a tire iron.'

She laughed, and he grinned. But they could not forget where they were going or why, and their smiles faded to a pair of matching frowns. They drove in silence. The thump of the windshield wipers, which ought to have lulled Bobby to sleep, kept him awake instead.

Finally Julie said, 'You think Frank actually vanished in front of Hal's eyes, the way he says?'

'I've never known Hal to lie or give in to hysteria.'

'Me neither.'

She turned left at the next corner. A few blocks ahead, beyond billowing curtains of rain, the lights of the hospital appeared to pulse and flicker and stream like an iridescent liquid, which made it look every bit as miragelike as a phantom oasis shimmering behind veils of heat rising from desert sands.

When they entered the room, Hal was standing at the foot of the bed, which was largely concealed by the privacy curtain. He looked like a guy who had not only seen a ghost, but had embraced it and kissed it on its cold, damp, putrescent lips.

'Thank God, you're here.' He looked past them, into the hall. 'The head nurse wants to call the cops, file a missing person—'

'We've dealt with that,' Bobby said. 'Dr Freeborn talked to her by phone, and we've signed a release absolving the hospital.'

'Good.' Gesturing toward the open door, Hal said, 'We'll want to keep this as private as we can.'

After closing the door, Julie joined them at the foot of the bed.

Bobby noted the missing railing and broken hinges. 'What's this?'

Hal swallowed hard. 'He was holding the railing when he vanished . . . and it went with him. I didn't mention it on the phone, 'cause I figured you already thought I was nuts, and this would confirm it.'

'Tell us now,' Julie said quietly. They were all talking softly, for otherwise Nurse Fulgham was certain to stop by and remind them that most of the patients on the floor were sleeping.

When Hal finished his story, Bobby said, 'The flute, the peculiar breeze . . . that's what Frank told us *he* heard shortly after he regained consciousness that night in the alleyway, and somehow he knew it meant someone was coming.'

Some of the dirt that Hal had observed on Frank's pajamas, after his second reappearance, was on the bed sheets. Julie plucked up a pinch of it. 'Not dirt exactly.'

Bobby examined the grains on her fingertips. 'Black sand.'

To Hal, Julie said, 'Frank hasn't reappeared since he vanished with the railing?'

'No.'

'And when was that?'

'A couple of minutes after two o'clock. Maybe two-oh-two, two-oh-three, something like that.'

'About an hour and twenty minutes ago,' Bobby said.

They stood in silence, staring at the mountings from which the bed railing had been torn. Outside, a squall of wind threw rain against the window with sufficient force to make it sound like out-of-season Halloween pranksters pitching handfuls of dried corn.

Finally Bobby looked at Julie. 'What do we do now?'

She blinked. 'Don't ask me. This is the first case I've ever worked on that involves witchcraft.'

'Witchcraft?' Hal said nervously.

'Just a figure of speech,' Julie assured him.

Maybe, Bobby thought. He said, 'We've got to assume he'll come back before morning, perhaps a couple of times, and sooner or later he'll stay put. This must be what happens every night when he sleeps; this is the traveling he doesn't remember when he wakes up.'

'Traveling,' Julie said. Under the circumstances, that ordinary word seemed as exotic and full of mystery as any in the language.

———

Careful not to wake the patients, they borrowed two additional chairs from other rooms along the corridor. Hal sat tensely just inside the closed door of room 638, in a position to prevent any of the hospital staff from walking in unimpeded. Julie sat at the foot of the bed, and Bobby stationed himself at the side of it nearest the window, where the railing was still in place.

They waited.

From her chair, Julie only had to turn her head slightly to look across the room at Hal. When she glanced the other way she could see Bobby. But because of the privacy curtain that was drawn along the side of the bed with the missing railing, Hal and Bobby were not in each other's line of sight.

She wondered if Hal would have been astonished to see how quickly Bobby went to sleep. Hal was still pumped up by what had happened, and Julie, only having heard about Frank's sorcerous disappearance second-hand, was nonetheless eagerly – and nervously – anticipating the chance to witness the same bit of magic herself. Bobby was a man of considerable imaginative powers, with a childlike sense of wonder, so he was probably more excited about these events than either she or Hal was; furthermore, because of his premonition of trouble, he suspected that the case was going to be full of surprises, some nasty, and these events no doubt alarmed him. Yet he could slump against the inadequately padded arm of his chair, let his chin drop against his chest, and doze off. He would never be felled by stress. At times his sense of proportion, his ability to put *anything* in a manageable perspective, seemed superhuman. When Bobby McFerrin's song 'Don't Worry, Be Happy' had been a hit a couple of years ago, she had not been surprised that her own Bobby had been enamoured of it; the tune was essentially his personal anthem. Apparently by an act of will, he could readily achieve serenity, and she admired that.

By 4:40, when Bobby had been slumbering contentedly for nearly an hour, she watched him doze with admiration that rapidly escalated to unhealthy envy. She had the urge to give his chair a kick, toppling him out of it. She restrained herself only because she suspected that he would merely yawn, curl up on his side, and sleep even more comfortably on the floor, at which point her envy would become so all-consuming that she would simply have to kill him where he lay. She imagined herself in court: *I know murder is wrong, Judge, but he was just too laid back to live.*

A cascade of soft, almost melancholy notes fell out of the air in front of her.

'The flute!' Hal said, leaving his chair with the suddenness of a popcorn kernel bursting off a heated pan.

Simultaneously, a breath of cool air stirred through the room, without apparent source.

Getting to her feet, Julie whispered, 'Bobby!'

She shook him by the shoulder, and he came awake just as the atonal music faded and the air turned crypt-still.

Bobby rubbed his eyes with his palms, and yawned. 'What's wrong?'

Even as he spoke, the haunting music swelled again, faint but louder than before. Not music, actually, just noise. And Hal was right: listening closely, you could also tell it was not a flute.

She stepped toward the bed.

Hal had left his station by the door. He put a hand on her shoulder, halting her. 'Be careful.'

Frank had reported three – maybe four – separate trillings of the faux flute, and as many agitations of the air, before Mr Blue Light had appeared on his trail that night in Anaheim, and Hal had noticed that three episodes had preceded each of Frank's own reappearances. However, those accompanying phenomena evidently could not be expected in an immutable pattern, for when the second rivulet of unharmonious notes finished spilling out of the ether, the air immediately above the bed shimmered, as if a double handful of pale tarnished sequins had been swept up and set aflutter in rising currents of heat, and suddenly Frank Pollard winked into existence atop the rumpled sheets.

Julie's ears popped.

'Holy cow!' Bobby said, which was just what Julie would have expected him to say.

She, on the other hand, was unable to speak.

Gasping, Frank Pollard sat up in bed. His face was bloodless. Around his rheumy eyes, the skin looked bruised. Sour perspiration glistened on his face and beaded in his beard stubble.

He was holding a pillowcase half filled with something. The end was twisted and held shut with a length of cord. He let go of it, and it fell off the side of the bed where the railing was missing, striking the floor with a soft *plop*.

When he spoke, his voice was hoarse and strange. 'Where am I?'

'You're in the hospital, Frank,' Bobby said. 'It's all right. You're where you belong now.'

'Hospital . . .' Frank said, savoring the word as if he had just heard it – and was now pronouncing it – for the first time. He looked around, obviously bewildered; he still didn't know where he was. 'Don't let me slip—'

He vanished mid-sentence. A brief hiss accompanied his abrupt departure, as if the air in the room was escaping through a puncture in the skin of reality.

'Damn!' Julie said.

'Where were his pajamas?' Hal said.

'What?'

'He was wearing shoes, khaki pants, a shirt and sweater,' Hal said, 'but the last time I saw him, a couple of hours ago, he still had on his pajamas.'

At the far end of the room, the door began to open but bumped against Hal's empty chair. Nurse Fulgham poked her head through the gap. She looked down at the chair, then across the room at Hal and Julie, then at Bobby, who stepped to the foot of the bed to peer past his two associates and the half-drawn privacy curtain.

Their astonishment at Frank's vanishing act must have been ill concealed, for the woman frowned and said, 'What's wrong?'

Julie quickly crossed the room as Grace Fulgham slid the chair aside and opened the door all the way. 'Everything's fine. We just spoke by phone with our man heading up the search, and he says they've found someone who saw Mr Pollard earlier tonight. We know which way he was heading, so now it's only a matter of time until we find him.'

'We didn't expect you'd be here so long,' Fulgham said, frowning past Julie at the curtained bed.

Even through the heavy door, maybe she had heard the faint warble of the flute that wasn't a flute.

'Well,' Julie said, 'this is the easiest place from which to coordinate the search.'

By standing just inside the door, with Hal's empty chair between them, Julie was trying to block the nurse's advance without appearing to do so. If Fulgham got past the curtain, she might notice the missing railing, the black sand in the bed, and the pillowcase that was filled with God-knew-what. Questions about any of those things might be difficult to answer convincingly, and if the nurse remained in the room too long, she might be there when Frank returned.

Julie said, 'I'm sure we haven't disturbed any of the other patients. We've been very quiet.'

'No, no,' Nurse Fulgham said, 'you haven't disturbed anyone. We just wondered if you might like some coffee to help keep you awake.'

'Oh.' Julie turned to look at Hal and Bobby. 'Coffee?'

'No,' the two men said simultaneously. Then, speaking over each other, Hal said, 'No, thank you,' and Bobby said, 'Very kind of you.'

'I'm wide awake,' Julie said, frantic to be rid of the woman, but trying to sound casual, 'and Hal doesn't drink coffee, and Bobby, my husband, can't handle caffeine because of prostate problems.' I'm babbling, she thought. 'Anyway, we'll be leaving soon now, I'm sure.'

'Well,' the nurse said, 'if you change your mind . . .'

After Fulgham left, letting the door close behind her, Bobby whispered, 'Prostate trouble?'

Julie said, 'Too much caffeine causes prostate trouble. Seemed like a convincing detail to explain why, with all your yawning, you didn't want coffee.'

'But I don't have a prostate problem. Makes me sound like an old fart.'

'I have it,' Hal said. 'And I'm not an old fart.'

'What is this?' Julie said. 'We're *all* babbling.'

She pushed the chair in front of the door and returned to the bed, where she picked up the pillowcase that Frank Pollard had brought from . . . from wherever he had been.

'Careful,' Bobby said. 'Last time Frank mentioned a pillowcase, it was the one he trapped that insect in.'

Julie gingerly set the bag on a chair and watched it closely. 'Doesn't seem to be anything squirming around in it.' She started to untie the knotted cord from the neck of the sack.

Grimacing, Bobby said, 'If you let out something big as a house cat, with a lot of legs and feelers, I'm going straight to a divorce lawyer.'

The cord slipped free. She pulled open the pillowcase, and looked inside. 'Oh, God.'

Bobby took a couple of steps backward.

'No, not that,' she assured him. 'No bugs. Just more cash.' She reached into the sack and withdrew a couple of bundles of hundred-dollar bills. 'If it's all hundreds, there could be as much as a quarter of a million in here.'

'What's Frank doing?' Bobby wondered. 'Laundering money for the mob in the Twilight Zone?'

Hollow, lonely, tuneless piping pierced the air again, and like a needle pulling thread, the sound brought with it a draft that rustled the curtain.

Shivering, Julie turned to look at the bed.

The flutelike notes faded with the draft, then soon rose again, faded, rose, and faded a fourth time as Frank Pollard reappeared. He was on his side, arms against his chest, hands fisted, grimacing, his eyes squeezed shut, as if he were preparing himself to receive the killing blow of an ax.

Julie stepped toward the bed, and again Hal stopped her.

Frank sucked in a deep breath, shuddered, made a low anguished mewling, opened his eyes – and vanished. Within two or three seconds, he appeared yet again, still shuddering. But immediately he vanished, reappeared, vanished, reappeared, vanished, as if he were an image flickering on a television set with poor signal reception. At last he stuck fast to the fabric of reality and lay on the bed, moaning.

After rolling off his side, onto his back, he gazed at the ceiling. He raised his fists from his chest, uncurled them, and stared at his hands, baffled, as if he had never seen fingers before.

'Frank?' Julie said.

He did not respond to her. With his fingertips he explored the contours of his face, as if a Braille reading of his features would recall to him the forgotten specifics of his appearance.

Julie's heart was racing, and every muscle in her body felt as if it had been twisted up as tight as an overwound clock spring. She was not afraid, really. It was not a tension engendered by fear but by the sheer *strangeness* of what had happened. 'Frank, are you okay?'

Blinking through the interstices of his fingers, he said, 'Oh. It's you, Mrs Dakota. Yeah . . . Dakota. What's happened? Where am I?'

'You're in the hospital now,' Bobby said. 'Listen, the important question isn't where you are, but where the hell have you *been*?'

'Been? Well . . . what do you mean?'

Frank tried to sit up in bed, but he seemed temporarily to lack the strength to get off his back.

Picking up the bed controls, Bobby elevated the upper half of the mattress. 'You weren't in this room during most of the last few hours. It's almost five in the morning, and you've been jumping in and out of here like . . . like . . . like a crew member of the Starship *Enterprise* who keeps beaming back up to the mothership!'

'*Enterprise*? Beaming up? What're you talking about?'

Bobby looked at Julie. 'Whoever this guy is, wherever he comes from, we now know for sure that he's been living out past the edge of modern culture, on the fringe. You ever known a modern American who hasn't at least *heard* of Star Trek?'

To Bobby, Julie said, 'Thanks for your analysis, Mr Spock.'

'Mr Spock?' Frank said.

'See!' Bobby said.

'We can question Frank later,' Julie said. 'He's confused right now, anyway. We've got to get him out of here. If that nurse comes back and sees him, how do we explain his reappearance? Is she really going to believe he wandered back *into* the hospital, past security and the nursing staff, up six floors, with nobody spotting him?'

'Yeah,' Hal said, 'and though he seems to be back for good, what if he pops away again, in front of her eyes?'

'Okay, so we'll get him out of bed and sneak him down those stairs at the end of the hall,' Julie said, 'out to the car.'

As they talked about him, Frank turned his head back and forth, following the conversation. He appeared to be watching a tennis match for the first time, unable to comprehend the rules of the game.

Bobby said, 'Once we've gotten him out of here, we can tell Fulgham he's been found just a few blocks away and that we're meeting with him to determine whether he wants – or even needs – to be returned to the hospital. He's our client, after all, not our ward, and we have to respect his wishes.'

Without having to wait for tests to be conducted, they now knew that Frank was not suffering strictly from physical ailments like cerebral abscesses, clots, aneurysms, cysts or neoplasms. His amnesia did not spring from brain tumors, but from something far stranger and more exotic than that. No malignancy, regardless of how singular its nature, would invest its victim with the power to step into the fourth dimension – or to wherever Frank was stepping when he vanished.

'Hal,' Julie said, 'get Frank's other clothes from the closet, bundle them up, and stuff them in the pillowcase with the money.'

'Will do.'

'Bobby, help me get Frank out of bed, see if he can stand on his own feet. He looks awful weak.'

The remaining bed railing stuck for a moment when Bobby tried to lower it, but he struggled with it because they could not take Frank out of bed on the other side without drawing back the privacy curtain and exposing him to anyone who might push open the door.

'You could've done me a big favor and packed this rail off to Oz with the other one,' Bobby told Frank, and Frank said, 'Oz?'

When the railing finally folded down, out of the way, Julie found that she was hesitant to touch Frank, for fear of what might happen to her – or parts of her – if he pulled another disappearing act. She had seen the shattered hinges of the bed railing; she was also keenly aware that Frank had not brought the railing back with him, but had abandoned it in the otherwhere or otherwhen to which he traveled.

Bobby hesitated, too, but overcame his apprehension, grabbing the man's legs and swinging them over the edge of the bed, taking hold of his arm and helping him into a sitting position. In some ways she might be tougher than Bobby, but when it came to encounters with the unknown, he was clearly more flexible and quick to adapt than she was.

Finally she quelled her fear, and together she and Bobby assisted Frank off the bed and onto his feet. His legs buckled under him, and they had to support him. He complained of weakness and dizziness.

Stuffing the other set of clothes in the pillowcase, Hal said, 'If we have to, Bobby and I can carry him.'

'I'm sorry to be so much trouble,' Frank said.

To Julie, he had never sounded or looked more pathetic, and she felt a flush of guilt about her reluctance to touch him.

Flanking Frank, their arms around him to provide support, Julie and Bobby walked him back and forth, past the rain-washed window, giving him a chance to recover the use of his legs. Gradually his strength and balance returned.

'But my pants keep trying to fall down,' Frank said.

They propped him against the bed, and he leaned on Julie while Bobby lifted the blue cotton sweater to see if the belt needed to be cinched in one notch. The tongue end of the belt was weakened by scores of small holes, as if industrious insects had been boring at it. But what insects ate leather? When Bobby touched the tarnished brass buckle, it crumbled as though made of flaky pastry dough.

Gaping at the glittering crumbs of metal on his fingers, Bobby said, 'Where do you shop for clothes, Frank? In a dumpster?'

In spite of Bobby's light tone, Julie knew he was unnerved. What substance or circumstances could so profoundly alter the composition of brass? When he brushed his fingers against the bed sheets to wipe off the curious residue, she flinched, half expecting his flesh to have been contaminated by the contact with the brass, and to crumble as the buckle had done.

After cinching Frank's pants with the belt that he had worn when he'd checked into the hospital, Hal helped Bobby slip their client out of the room. With Julie scouting the way, they went quickly and quietly along the hall and through the fire door at the head of the emergency stairs. Frank's skin remained cold to the touch, and he was still clammy with perspiration; but the effort brought a flush to his cheeks, which made him look less like a walking corpse.

Julie hurried to the bottom of the stairwell to see what lay beyond the lower door. With the thump and scrape of their footsteps echoing hollowly off the bare concrete walls, the three men went down four flights without much difficulty. At the fourth-floor landing, however, they had to pause to let Frank catch his breath.

'Are you always this weak when you wake up and don't remember where you've been?' Bobby asked.

Frank shook his head. His words issued in a thin wheeze: 'No. Always frightened . . . tired, but not as bad . . . as this. I feel like . . . whatever I'm doing . . . wherever I'm going . . . it's taking a bigger and bigger toll. I'm not . . . not going to survive . . . a lot more of this.'

As Frank was talking, Bobby noticed something peculiar about the man's blue cotton sweater. The pattern of the cable knit was wildly irregular in places, as if the knitting machine had briefly gone berserk. And on the back, near his right shoulderblade, a patch of fibers was missing; the hole was the size of a block of four postage stamps, though with irregular rather than straight edges. But it wasn't just a hole. A piece of what appeared to be khaki filled the gap, not merely sewn on but woven tightly into the surrounding cotton yarn, as if at the garment factory itself. Khaki of the same shade and hard finish as the pants that Frank was wearing.

A shiver of dread pierced Bobby, although he was not sure why. His subconscious mind seemed to understand how the patch had come to be and what it meant, and grasped some hideous consequence not yet fulfilled, while his conscious mind was baffled.

He saw that Hal, on the other side of Frank, had noticed the patch, too, and was frowning.

Julie ascended the stairs while Bobby was staring in puzzlement at the khaki swatch. 'We're in luck,' she said. 'There're two doors at the bottom. One leads into a hallway off the lobby, where we'd probably run into a security man, even though they aren't looking for Frank any more. But the other door leads into the parking garage, the same level our car's on. How you doing Frank? You going to be okay?'

'Getting my . . . second wind,' he said less wheezily than before.

'Look at this,' Bobby said, calling Julie's attention to the khaki woven into the blue cotton sweater.

While Julie studied the peculiar patch, Bobby let go of Frank and, on a hunch, stooped down to examine the legs of his client's pants. He found a corresponding irregularity: blue cotton yarn from the sweater was woven into the slacks. It was not one spot of the same size and shape as that in the sweater, but a series of three smaller holes near the cuff on the right leg; however, he was sure that more accurate measurements would confirm what he knew from a quick look – that the total amount of blue yarn in those three holes would just about fill the hole in the shoulder of the sweater.

'What's wrong?' Frank asked.

Bobby didn't respond but took hold of the somewhat baggy leg of the pants and pulled it taut, so he could get a better look at the three patches. Actually, 'patches' was an inaccurate word because these abnormalities in the fabric did not look like repairs; they were too well blended with the material around them to be handwork.

Julie squatted beside him and said, 'First, we've got to get Frank out of here, back to the office.'

'Yeah, but this is real strange,' Bobby said, indicating the irregularities in the pants. 'Strange and . . . important somehow.'

'What's wrong?' Frank repeated.

'Where'd you get these clothes?' Bobby asked him.

'Well . . . I don't know.'

Julie pointed to the white athletic sock on Frank's right foot, and Bobby saw at once what had caught her attention: several blue threads, precisely the color of the sweater. They were not loose, clinging to the sock. They were woven into the very fabric of it.

Then he noticed Frank's left shoe. It was a dark brown hiking shoe, but a few thin, squiggly white lines marred the leather on the toe. When he studied them closely, he saw that the lines appeared to be coarse threads like those in the athletic socks; scraping at them with one fingernail, he discovered they were not stuck to the shoe, but were an integral part of the surface of the leather.

The missing yarn of the sweater had somehow become a part of both the khaki pants and one of the socks; the displaced threads of the sock had become part of the shoe on the other foot.

'What's wrong?' Frank repeated, more fearfully than before.

Bobby hesitated to look up, expecting to see that the filaments of displaced shoe leather were embedded in Frank's face, and that the displaced flesh was magically entwined with the cable knit of the sweater. He stood and forced himself to confront his client.

Aside from the dark and puffy rings around his eyes, the sickly pallor relieved only by the flush on his upper cheeks, and the fear and confusion that gave him a tormented look, nothing was wrong with his face. No leather ornamentation. No khaki stitched into his lips. No filaments of blue yarn or plastic shoelace tips or button fragments bristling from his eyeballs.

Silently castigating himself for his overactive imagination, Bobby patted Frank's shoulder. 'It's okay. It's all right. We'll figure it out later. Come on, let's get you out of here.'

In the embrace of darkness, enwrapped by the scent of Chanel No. 5, under the very blankets and sheets that had once warmed his mother and that he had so carefully preserved, Candy dozed and awakened repeatedly with a start, though he could not remember any nightmares.

Between periods of fitful sleep, he dwelt on the incident in the canyon, earlier that night, when he had been hunting and had felt an unseen presence put a hand on his head. He'd never before experienced anything like that. He was disturbed by the encounter, unsure whether it was threatening or benign, and anxious to understand it.

He first wondered if it had been his mother's angelic presence, hovering above him. But he quickly dismissed that explanation. If his mother had stepped through the veil between this world and the next, he would have recognized her spirit, her singular aura of love, warmth, and compassion. He would have fallen to his knees under the weight of her ghostly hand and wept with joy at her visitation.

Briefly he had considered that one or both of his inscrutable sisters possessed a heretofore unrevealed talent for psychic contact and reached out to him for unknown reasons. After all, somehow they controlled their cats and appeared to have equal influence over other small animals. Maybe they could enter human minds as well. He didn't want that pale, cold-eyed pair invading his privacy. At times he looked at them and thought of snakes – sinuous albino snakes, silent and watchful – with desires as alien as any that motivated reptiles. The possibility that they could intrude into his mind was chilling, even if they could not control him.

But between bouts of sleep, he abandoned that idea. If Violet and Verbina possessed such abilities, they would have enslaved him long ago, as thoroughly as they had enslaved the cats. They would have forced him to do degrading, obscene things; they did not possess his self-control in matters of the flesh and would live, if they could, in constant violation of God's most fundamental commandments.

He could not understand why his mother had sworn him to keep and protect them, any more than he could understand how she could love them. Of course her compassion for those miscreant offspring was only one more example of her saintly nature. Forgiveness and understanding flowed from her like clear, cool water from an artesian well.

For a while he dozed. When he woke with a start again, he turned on his side and watched the faint light of dawn appear along the edges of the drawn blinds.

He considered the possibility that the presence in the canyon had been his brother Frank. But that was also unlikely. If Frank had possessed telepathic abilities, he would have found a way to employ them to destroy Candy a long, long time ago. Frank was less talented than his sisters and much less talented than his brother Candy.

Then who had approached him twice in the canyon, insistently pressing into his mind? Who sent the disconnected words that echoed in his head: *What . . . where . . . what . . . why . . . what . . . where . . . what . . . why . . .?*

Last night, he'd tried to get a mental grip on the presence. When it hastily withdrew from him, he had tried to let part of his consciousness soar up into the night with it, but he had been unable to sustain a pursuit on that psychic plane. He sensed, however, that he might be able to develop that ability.

If the unwelcome presence ever returned, he would try to knot a filament of his mind to it and trace it to its source. In his twenty-nine years, his own siblings were the only people he had encountered with what might be called psychic abilities. If someone out there in the world was also gifted, he must learn who it was. Such a person, not born of his sainted mother, was a rival, a threat, an enemy.

Though the sun beyond the blinded windows had not fully risen, he knew that he would not be able to doze again. He threw back the covers, crossed the dark and furniture-crowded room with the assurance of a blind man in a familiar place, and went into the adjoining bathroom. After locking the door, he undressed without glancing in the mirror. He peed forcefully without looking down at his hateful organ. When he showered, he soaped and rinsed the sex thing only with the washcloth mitten that he'd made and that protected his innocent hand from being corrupted by the monstrous, wicked flesh below.

<h2 style="text-align:center">• 39 •</h2>

From the hospital in Orange, they went directly to their offices in Newport Beach. They had a lot of work to do on Frank's behalf, and his worsening plight evoked in them a greater sense of urgency than ever. Frank rode with Hal, and Julie followed in order to be able to offer assistance if unforeseen developments occurred during the trip. The entire case seemed to be a *series* of unforeseen developments.

By the time they reached their deserted offices – the Dakota & Dakota staff would not arrive for a couple of hours yet – the sun was fully risen behind the clouds in the east. A thin strip of blue sky, like a crack under the door of the storm, was visible over the ocean to the west. As the four of them passed through the reception lounge into their inner sanctum, the rain halted abruptly, as if a godly hand had turned a celestial lever; the water on the big windows stopped flowing in shimmering sheets, and coalesced into hundreds of small beads that glimmered with a mercury-gray sheen in the cloud-dulled morning light.

Bobby indicated the bulging pillowcase that Hal was carrying. 'Take Frank into the bathroom, help him change into the clothes he was wearing when we checked him into the hospital. Then we'll have a real close look at the clothes he's wearing now.'

Frank had recovered his balance and most of his strength. He did not need Hal's assistance. But Julie knew Bobby wouldn't let Frank go anywhere unchaperoned from now on. They needed to keep an eye on him constantly, in order not to miss any clues that might lead to an explanation of his sudden vanishments and reappearances.

Before attending to Frank, Hal removed the rumpled clothes from the pillowcase. He left the rest of its contents on Julie's desk.

'Coffee?' Bobby asked.

'Desperately,' Julie said.

He went out to the pantry that opened off the lounge, to start up one of their two Mr Coffee machines.

Sitting at her desk, Julie emptied the pillowcase. It contained thirty bundles of hundred-dollar bills in packs bound by rubber bands. She fanned the edges of the bills in ten bundles to ascertain if lower denominations were included; they were all hundreds. She chose two packets at random and counted them. Each contained one hundred bills. Ten thousand in each. By the time Bobby returned with mugs, spoons, cream, sugar, and a pot of hot coffee, all on a tray, Julie had concluded that this was the largest of Frank's three hauls to date.

'Three hundred K,' she said, as Bobby put the tray on her desk.

He whistled softly. 'What's that bring the total to?'

'With this, we'll be holding six hundred thousand for him.'

'Soon have to get a bigger office safe.'

Hal Yamataka put Frank's other set of clothes on the coffee table. 'Something's wrong with the zipper in the pants. I don't mean just that it doesn't work, which it doesn't. I mean, something's very *wrong* with it.'

Hal, Frank, and Julie pulled up chairs around the low glass-topped table, and drank strong black coffee while Bobby sat on the couch and carefully inspected the garments. In addition to the oddities he had noticed at the hospital, he discovered that most of the teeth in the pants zipper were metal, as they should have been, while about forty others, interspersed at random, appeared to be hard black rubber; in fact, the slide was jammed on a couple of the rubber ones.

Bobby stared in puzzlement at the anomalous zipper, slowly moving a finger up and down one of the notched tracks, until he was suddenly struck by inspiration. He picked up one of the shoes Frank had been wearing and examined the heel. It looked perfectly normal, but in the heel of the second shoe, thirty or forty tiny, brass-bright bits of metal were embedded in the rubber, flush with the surface of it.

'Anybody have a penknife?' Bobby asked.

Hal withdrew one from his pocket. Bobby used it to pry loose a couple of the shiny rectangles, which appeared to have been set in the rubber when it was still molten. Zipper teeth. They fell onto the glass table: *tink . . . tink*. At a glance he estimated that the amount of rubber displaced by those teeth was equal to what he had found in the zipper.

Sitting in the Dakotas' Disney-embellished office, Frank Pollard was overwhelmed by a weariness that was cartoonish in its extremity, the degree of utter exhaustion sufficient to render Donald Duck so limp that he might slip off a chair and pour onto the floor in a puddle of mallard flesh and feathers. It had been seeping into him day by day, hour by hour, since he had awakened in that alleyway last week; but now it suddenly poured through him as if a dike had broken. This surging flood of weariness had a density not of water but of liquid lead, and he felt enormously heavy; he could lift a foot or move a limb only with effort, and even keeping his head up was a strain on his neck. Virtually every joint in his body ached dully, even his elbow and wrist and finger joints, but especially his knees, hips, and shoulders. He felt feverish, not acutely ill, but as if his strength had been steadily sapped by a low-grade viral infection from which he had been suffering his entire life. Weariness had not dulled his senses; on the contrary, it abraded his nerve endings as surely as a fine-grade sandpaper might have done. Loud sounds made him cringe, bright light made him squint in pain, and he was exquisitely sensitive to heat and cold and the textures of everything he touched.

His exhaustion seemed only in part a result of his inability to sleep more than a couple of hours a night. If Hal Yamataka and the Dakotas could be believed – and Frank saw no reason for them to lie to him – he performed an incredible vanishing act several times during the night, though upon returning to his bed and staying put there, he could recall nothing of what he had done. Whatever the cause of those disappearances, no matter where he had gone or how or why, the very act of vanishing seemed likely to require an expenditure of energy as surely as walking or running or lifting heavy weights or any other physical act; therefore, perhaps his weakness and profound weariness were largely the result of his mysterious night journeys.

Bobby Dakota had pried only a couple of the brass teeth from the heel of the shoe. After studying them for a moment, he put down the penknife, leaned back against the sofa, and looked thoughtfully at the gloomy but rainless sky beyond the office's big windows. They were all silent, waiting to hear what he deduced from the condition of those clothes and shoes.

Even exhausted, preoccupied with his own fears, and after only a one-day association with the Dakotas, Frank realized that Bobby was the more imaginative and mentally nimble of the two. Julie was probably smarter than her husband; but she was also a more methodical thinker than he was, far less likely than he was to make sudden leaps of logic to arrive at insightful deductions and imaginative solutions. Julie would more often be right than Bobby was, but on those occasions when the firm resolved a client's problems *quickly*, the resolution would usually be attributable to Bobby. They made a good pair, and Frank was relying on their complementary natures to save him.

Turning to Frank again, Bobby said, 'What if, somehow, you can teleport yourself, send yourself from here to there in a wink?'

'But that's . . . magic,' Frank said. 'I don't believe in magic.'

'Oh, I do,' Bobby said. 'Not witches and spells and genies in bottles, but I believe in the possibility of fantastic things. The very fact that the world exists, that we're alive, that we can laugh and sing and feel the sun on our skin . . . that seems like a kind of magic to me.'

'Teleport myself? If I can, I don't *know* I can. Evidently I have to fall asleep first. Which means teleportation must be a function of my subconscious mind, essentially involuntary.'

'You weren't asleep when you reappeared in the hospital room or any of the other times you vanished,' Hal said. 'Maybe the first time, but not later. Your eyes were open. You spoke to me.'

'But I don't remember it,' Frank said frustratedly. 'I only remember going to sleep, then suddenly I was lying awake in bed, in a lot of distress, confused, and you were all there.'

Julie sighed. 'Teleportation. How can that be possible?'

'You saw it.' Bobby shrugged. He picked up his coffee and took a sip, more relaxed than anyone in the room, as though having a client with an astonishing psychic power was, if not an ordinary occurrence, at least a situation that all of them should have realized was simply inevitable, given enough years in the private security business.

'I saw him disappear,' Julie agreed, 'but I'm not sure that proves he . . . teleported.'

'When he disappeared,' Bobby said, 'he went *somewhere*. Right?'

'Well . . . yes.'

'And going from one place to another, instantaneously, as an act of sheer willpower . . . as far as I'm concerned, that's teleportation.'

'But how?' Julie asked.

Bobby shrugged again. 'Right now, it doesn't matter how. Just accept the assumption of teleportation as a place to start.'

'As a theory,' Hal said.

'Okay,' Julie agreed. 'Theoretically, let's assume Frank can teleport himself.'

To Frank, who was sealed off from his own experience by amnesia, that was like assuming iron was lighter than air in order to allow an argument for the possibility of steel-plated blimps. But he was willing to go along with it.

Bobby said, 'Good, all right, then that assumption explains the condition of these clothes.'

'How?' Frank asked.

'It'll take a while to get to the clothes. Stay with me. First, consider that maybe teleporting yourself requires that the atoms of your body temporarily disassociate themselves from one another, then come together again an instant later at another place. Same thing goes for the clothes you're wearing and for anything on which you've got a firm grip, like the bed railing.'

'Like the teleportation pod in that movie,' Hal said. '*The Fly*.'

'Yeah,' Bobby said, clearly getting excited now. He put down his coffee and slid forward on the edge of the sofa, gesticulating as he spoke. 'Sort of like that. Except the power to do this is maybe all in Frank's mind, not in a futuristic machine. He just sort of *thinks* himself somewhere else, disassembles himself in a fraction of a second – *poof!* – and reassembles himself at his destination. Of course, I'm also assuming the mind remains intact even during the time the body is dispersed in disconnected atoms, because it would have to be the sheer power of the mind that transports those billions of particles and keeps them together like a shepherd collie herding sheep, then welds them to one another again in the right configurations at the far end.'

Though his weariness was sufficient to have resulted from an impossibly complex and strenuous task like the one Bobby had just described, Frank was unconvinced. 'Well, gee, I don't know . . . This isn't something you go to school to learn. UCLA doesn't have a course in teleportation. So it's . . . instinct? Even supposing I instinctively know how to break my body down into a stream of atomic particles and send it somewhere else, then put it together again . . . how can any human mind, even the greatest genius ever born, be powerful enough to keep track of those billions of particles and get them all back exactly as they belong? It'd take a hundred geniuses, a thousand, and I'm not even *one*. I'm no dummy, but I'm no brighter than the average guy.'

'You've answered your own question,' Bobby said. 'You don't need superhuman intelligence for this, 'cause teleportation isn't primarily a function of intelligence. It's not instinct, either. It's just . . . well, an ability programmed into your genes, like vision or hearing or the sense of smell. Think of it this way: any scene you look at is composed of billions of separate points of color and light and shade and texture, yet your eyes instantly order those billions of bits of input into a coherent scene. You don't have to *think* about seeing. You just see, it's automatic. You understand what I meant about magic? Vision is almost magical. With teleportation, there's probably a trigger mechanism you have to pull – like *wishing* yourself to be elsewhere – but thereafter the process is pretty much automatic; the mind makes it happen the way it makes instantaneous sense of all the data coming in through your eyes.'

Frank closed his eyes tight and concentrated on wishing himself into the reception lounge. When he opened his eyes and was still in the inner office, he said, 'It doesn't work. It's not that easy. I can't do it at will.'

Hal said, 'Bobby, are you saying all of us have this ability, and only Frank has figured out how to use it?'

'No, no. This is probably a scrap of genetic material unique to Frank, maybe even a talent that sprung from genetic *damage.*'

They were all silent, absorbing what Bobby had conjectured.

Outside, the layer of clouds was cracking, peeling, and the old blue paint of the sky was showing through in more places every minute. But the brightening day did not lift Frank's spirits.

Finally Hal Yamataka indicated the pile of garments on the coffee table. 'How does all this explain the condition of those clothes?'

Bobby picked up the blue cotton sweater and held it so they could see the khaki swatch on the back. 'Okay, let's suppose the mind can automatically shepherd all the molecules of its own body through the teleportation process without a single error. It can also deal with other things Frank wants to take with him, like his clothes—'

'And bags full of money,' Julie said.

'But why the bed railing?' Hal asked. 'No reason for him to want to take that with him.'

To Frank, Bobby said, 'You can't remember it now, but you clearly knew what was happening while you were caught up in that series of teleportations. You were trying to stop, you asked Hal to help you stop, and you seized the railing to stop yourself, to anchor yourself to the hospital room. You were *concentrating* on your grip on that railing, so when you went, you took it with you. As for the clothes getting scrambled the way they are . . . Maybe your mind concentrates first on getting your body back together in the proper order because error-free physical re-creation is crucial to your survival, but then sometimes you might not have the energy left to do as good a job on secondary things like clothes.'

'Well,' Frank said, 'I can't remember prior to last week, but this is the first time anything like this has happened since then, even though I've apparently been . . . traveling more nights than not. Then again, even if my clothes have come through okay, *I* seem to be getting more weary, weaker, and more confused day by day . . .'

He did not have to finish the thought, because the worry in their eyes and faces made clear their understanding. If he was teleporting, and if it was a strenuous act that bled him of strength that could not be restored by rest, he was gradually going to get less meticulous about the reconstitution of his clothes and whatever other items he tried to carry with him. But more important – he might begin to have difficulty reconstituting his body, as well. He might return from one of his late-night rambles and find fragments of his sweater woven into the back of his hand, and the skin replaced by that cotton might turn up as a pale patch in the dark leather of his shoe, and the displaced leather from the shoe might appear as an integral part of his tongue . . . or as strands of alien cells twisted through his brain tissue.

Fear, never far away and circling like a shark in the depths of Frank's mind, abruptly shot to the surface, called forth by the worry and pity that he saw in the faces of those on whom he was depending for salvation. He closed his eyes, but that was a rotten idea because he had a vision of his own face when he shut out theirs, his face as it might look after a disastrous reconstitution at the end of a future telekinetic journey: eight or ten misplaced teeth sprouting from his right eye socket; the evicted eye staring lidlessly from the middle of the cheek below; his nose smeared in hideous lumps of flesh and gristle across the side of his face. In the vision he opened his misshapen mouth, perhaps to scream, and within were two fingers and a portion of his hand, rooted where the tongue should have been.

He opened his eyes as a low cry of terror and misery escaped him.

He was shuddering. He couldn't stop.

Having freshened everyone's coffee and, at Bobby's suggestion, having laced Frank's mug with bourbon in spite of the early hour, Hal went to the nook off the reception lounge to brew another pot.

After Frank had been fortified with a few sips of the spiked coffee, Julie showed the photograph to him and watched his reaction carefully. 'You recognize either of the people in this?'

'No. They're strangers to me.'

'The man,' Bobby said, 'is George Farris. The *real* George Farris. We got the picture from his brother-in-law.'

Frank studied the photograph with renewed interest. 'Maybe I knew him, and that's why I borrowed his name – but I can't recall ever seeing him before.'

'He's dead,' Julie said, and thought that Frank's surprise was genuine. She explained how Farris had died, years ago . . . and then how his family had been slaughtered far more recently. She told him about James Roman, too, and how Roman's family died in a fire in November.

With what appeared to be sincere dismay and confusion, Frank said, 'Why all these deaths? Is it coincidence?'

Julie leaned forward. 'We think Mr Blue killed them.'

'Who?'

'Mr Blue Light. The man you said pursued you that night in Anaheim, the man you think is hunting you for some reason. We believe he discovered you were traveling under the names Farris and Roman, so he went to the addresses he got for them, and when he didn't find you there, he killed everyone, either while trying to squeeze information out of them or . . . just for the hell of it.'

Frank looked stricken. His pale face grew even paler, as if it were an image doing a slow fade on a movie screen. The bleak look in his eyes intensified. 'If I hadn't been using that fake ID, he never would've gone to those people. It's because of me they died.'

Feeling sorry for the guy, ashamed of the suspicion that had driven her to approach the issue in this manner, Julie said, 'Don't let it eat you, Frank. Most likely, the paper artist who forged your documents took the names at random from a list of recent deaths. If he'd used another approach, the Farris and Roman families would never have come to Mr Blue's attention. But it's not your fault the forger used the quick and lazy method.'

Frank shook his head, tried to speak, could not.

'You *can't* blame yourself,' Hal said from the doorway, where he had evidently been standing long enough to have gotten the gist of the photo's importance. He seemed genuinely distressed to see Frank so anguished. Like Clint, Hal had been won over by Frank's gentle voice, self-effacing manner, and cherubic demeanor.

Frank cleared his throat, and finally the words broke loose: 'No, no, it's on me, my God, all those people dead because of me.'

In Dakota & Dakota's computer center, Bobby and Frank sat in two spring-backed, typist chairs with rubber wheels, and Bobby switched on one of the three state-of-the-art IBM PCs, each of which was outlinked to the world through its own modem and phone line. Though bright enough to work by, the overhead lights were soft and diffuse to prevent glare on the terminal screens, and the room's one window was covered with blackout drapes for the same reason.

Like policemen in the silicon age, modern private detectives and security consultants relied on the computer to make their work easier and to compile a breadth and depth of information that could never be acquired by the old-fashioned gumshoe methods of Sam Spade and Philip Marlowe. Pounding the pavement, interviewing witnesses and potential suspects, and conducting surveillances were still aspects of their job, of course, but without the computer they would be as ineffective as a blacksmith trying to fix a flat tire with a hammer and anvil and other tools of his trade. As the twentieth century progressed through its last decade, private investigators who were ignorant of the microchip revolution existed only in television dramas and the curiously dated world of most PI novels.

Lee Chen, who had designed and now operated their electronic data-gathering system, would not arrive in the office until around nine o'clock. Bobby did not want to wait nearly an hour to start putting the computer to work on Frank's case. He was not a primo hacker, as Lee was, but he knew all the hardware, had the ability to learn new software quickly when he needed to, and was almost as comfortable tracking down information in cyberspace as he was poring through files of age-yellowed newspapers.

Using Lee's code book, which he removed from a locked desk drawer, Bobby first entered a Social Security Administration data network that contained files to which broad public access was legal. Other files in the same system were restricted and supposedly inaccessible behind walls of security codes required by various right-to-privacy laws.

From the open files, he inquired as to the number of men named Frank Pollard in the Administration's records, and within seconds the response appeared on the screen: counting variations of Frank, such as Franklin and Frankie and Franco – plus names like Francis, for which Frank might be a diminutive – there were six hundred and nine Frank Pollards in possession of Social Security numbers.

'Bobby,' Frank said anxiously, 'does that stuff on the screen make sense to you? Are those words, real words, or jumbled letters?'

'Huh? Of course they're words.'

'Not to me. They don't look like anything to me. Gibberish.'

Bobby picked up a copy of *Byte* magazine that was lying between two of the computers, opened it to an article, and said, 'Read that.'

Frank accepted the magazine, stared at it, flipped ahead a couple of pages, then a couple more. His hands began to shake. The magazine rattled in his grip. 'I can't. Jesus, I've lost that too. Yesterday, I lost the ability to do math, and now I can't read any more, and I get more confused, foggy in the head, and I ache in every joint, every muscle. This teleporting's wearing me down, killing me. I'm falling apart, Bobby, mentally and physically, faster all the time.'

'It's going to be all right,' Bobby said, though his confidence was largely feigned. He was pretty sure they would get to the bottom of this, would learn who Frank was and where he went at night and how and why; however, he could see that Frank was declining fast, and he would not have bet money that they'd find all the answers while Frank was still alive, sane, and able to benefit from their discoveries. Nevertheless, he put his hand on Frank's shoulder and gave it a gentle reassuring squeeze. 'Hang in there, buddy. Everything's going to be okay. I really think it is. I really do.'

Frank took a deep breath and nodded.

Turning to the display terminal again, feeling guilty about the lie he'd just told, Bobby said, 'You remember how old you are, Frank?'

'No.'

'You look about thirty-two, thirty-three.'

'I feel older.'

Softly whistling Duke Ellington's 'Satin Doll,' Bobby thought a moment, then asked the SSA computer to eliminate those Frank Pollards younger than twenty-eight and older than thirty-eight. That left seventy-two of them.

'Frank, do you think you've ever lived anywhere else, or are you a dyed-in-the-wool Californian?'

'I don't know.'

'Let's assume you're a son of the sunshine state.'

He asked the SSA computer to whittle down the remaining Frank Pollards to those who applied for their Social Security numbers while living in California (fifteen), then to those whose current addresses on file were in California (six).

The public-access portion of the Social Security Administration's data network was forbidden by law to reveal Social Security numbers to casual researchers. Bobby referred to the instructions in Lee Chen's code book and entered the restricted files through a complicated series of maneuvers that circumvented SSA security.

He was unhappy about breaking the law, but it was a fact of high-tech life that you never got the maximum benefit from your data-gathering system if you played strictly by the rules. Computers were instruments of freedom, and governments were to one degree or another instruments of repression; the two could not always exist in harmony.

He obtained the six numbers and addresses for the Frank Pollards living in California.

'Now what?' Frank wondered.

'Now,' Bobby said, 'I use these numbers and addresses to cross reference with the California Department of Motor Vehicles, all of the armed forces, state police, major city police, and other government agencies to get descriptions of these six Frank Pollards. As we learn their height, weight, hair color, color of their eyes, race . . . we'll gradually eliminate them one by one. Better yet, if one of them is you, and if you've ever served in the military or been arrested for a crime, we might even be able to turn up a picture of you in one of those files and confirm your identity with a photo match.'

Sitting at the desk, catercorner from each other, Julie and Hal removed the rubber bands from more than half of the packets of cash. They sorted through the hundred-dollar bills, trying to determine if some of them had consecutive serial numbers that might indicate they were stolen from a bank, savings and loan, or other institution.

Suddenly Hal looked up and said, 'Why do those flutelike sounds and drafts precede Frank when he teleports himself?'

'Who knows?' Julie said. 'Maybe it's displaced air following him down some tunnel in another dimension, from the place he left to the place he's going.'

'I was just thinking . . . If this Mr Blue is real, and if he's searching for Frank, and if Frank heard those flutes and felt those gusts in that alleyway . . . then Mr Blue is also able to teleport.'

'Yeah. So?'

'So Frank's not unique. Whatever he is, there's another one like him. Maybe even more than one.'

'Here's something else to think about,' Julie said. 'If Mr Blue can teleport himself, and if he finds out where Frank is, we won't be able to defend a hiding place from him. He'll be able to pop up among us. And what if he arrived with a submachine gun, spraying bullets as he materialized?'

After a moment of silence, Hal said, 'You know, gardening has always seemed like a pleasant profession. You need a lawnmower, a weed whacker, a few simple tools. There's not much overhead, and you hardly ever get shot at.'

Bobby followed Frank into the office, where Julie and Hal were examining the money. Putting a sheet of paper on the desk, he said, 'Move over, Sherlock Holmes. The world now has a greater detective.'

Julie angled the page so she and Hal could read it together. It was a laser-printed copy of the information that Frank had filed with the California Department of Motor Vehicles when he had last applied for an extension of his driver's license.

'The physical statistics match,' she said. 'Is your first name really Francis and your middle name Ezekiel?'

Frank nodded. 'I didn't remember until I saw it. But it's me, all right. Ezekiel.'

Tapping the printout, she said, 'This address in El Encanto Heights – does it ring a bell?'

'No. I can't even tell you where El Encanto is.'

'It's adjacent to Santa Barbara,' Julie said.

'So Bobby tells me. But I don't remember being there. Except . . .'

'What?'

Frank went to the window and looked out toward the distant sea, above which the sky was now entirely blue. A few early gulls swooped in arcs so huge and smoothly described that their exuberance was thrilling to watch. Clearly, Frank was neither thrilled by the birds nor charmed by the view.

Finally, still facing the window, he said, 'I don't recall being in El Encanto Heights . . . except that every time I hear the name, my stomach sort of sinks, you know, like I'm on a roller coaster that's just taken a plunge. And when I try to think about El Encanto, strain to remember it, my heart pounds, and my mouth goes dry, and it's a little harder to get my breath. So I think I must be repressing any memories I have of the place, maybe because something happened to me there, something bad . . . something I'm too scared to remember.'

Bobby said, 'His driver's license expired seven years ago, and according to the DMV's records, he never tried to renew it. In fact, sometime this year he'd have been weeded out of even their dead files, so we were lucky to find this before they expunged it.' He laid two more printouts on the desk. 'Move over Holmes *and* Sam Spade.'

'What're these?'

'Arrest reports. Frank was stopped for traffic violations, once in San Francisco a little more than six years ago. The second time was on Highway 101, north of Ventura, five years ago. He didn't have a valid driver's license either time and, because of odd behavior, was taken into custody.'

The photographs that were a part of both arrest records showed a slightly younger, even pudgier man who was without a doubt their current client.

Bobby pushed aside some of the money and sat on the edge of her desk. 'He escaped from jail both times, so they're looking for him even after all these years, though probably not too hard, since he wasn't arrested for a major crime.'

Frank said, 'I draw a blank on that too.'

'Neither report indicates *how* he escaped,' Bobby said, 'but I suspect he didn't saw his way through the bars or dig a tunnel or whittle a gun out of a bar of soap or use any of the long-accepted, traditional methods of jailbreak. Oh, no, not our Frank.'

'He teleported,' Hal guessed. 'Vanished when no one was looking.'

'I'd bet on it,' Bobby agreed. 'And after that he began to carry false ID good enough to satisfy any cop who pulled him over.'

Looking at the papers before her, Julie said, 'Well, Frank, at least we know this is your real name, and we've nailed down a real address for you up there in Santa

Barbara County, not just another motel room. We're beginning to make headway.'

Bobby said, 'Move over Holmes, Spade, *and* Miss Marple.'

Unable to embrace their optimism, Frank returned to the chair in which he'd been sitting earlier. 'Headway. But not enough. And not fast enough.' He leaned forward with his arms on his thighs, hands clasped between his spread knees, and stared morosely at the floor. 'Something unpleasant just occurred to me. What if I'm not only making mistakes with my clothes when I reconstitute myself? What if I've *already* begun to make mistakes with my own biology too? Nothing major. Nothing visible. Hundreds or thousands of tiny mistakes on a cellular level. That would explain why I feel so lousy, so tired and sore. And if my brain tissue isn't coming back together right . . . that would explain why I'm confused, fuzzy-headed, unable to read or do math.'

Julie looked at Hal, at Bobby, and knew that both men wanted to allay Frank's fear but were unable to do so because the scenario that he had outlined was not only possible but likely.

Frank said, 'The brass buckle looked perfectly normal until Bobby touched it . . . then it turned to dust.'

• 40 •

All night long, when sleep made Thomas's head empty, ugly dreams filled it up. Dreams of eating small live things. Dreams of drinking blood. Dreams of being the Bad Thing.

He finished sleeping all of a sudden, sitting up in bed, trying to scream but unable to find any sounds in himself. For a while he sat there, shaking, being afraid, breathing so hard and fast his chest ached.

The sun was back, and the night was gone away, and that made him feel better. Getting out of bed, he stepped into his slippers. His pajamas were cold with sweat. He shivered. He pulled on a robe. He went to the window, looked out and up, liking the blue sky very much. Leftover rain made the green lawn look soggy, the sidewalks darker than usual, and the dirt in the flowerbeds almost black, and in the puddles you could see the blue sky again like a face in a mirror. He liked all of that, too, because the whole world looked clean and new after all the rain emptied out of the sky.

He wondered if the Bad Thing was still far away, or closer, but he didn't reach out to it. Because last night it tried to hold him. Because it was so strong he almost couldn't get away from it. And because even when he *did* get away, it tried to follow him. He'd felt it hanging on, coming back across the night with him, and he'd shaken it off real quick like, but maybe next time he wouldn't be so lucky, and maybe it would come all the way, right into his room with him, not just its mind but the Bad Thing itself. He didn't understand how that could happen, but somehow he knew it might. And if the Bad Thing came to The Home, being awake would be like being asleep with a nightmare filling up your head. Terrible things would happen, and there would be no hope.

Turning away from the window, starting toward the closed door to the bathroom, Thomas glanced at Derek's bed and saw Derek dead. He was on his back. His face was bashed, bruised, swollen. His eyes were open big, you could see them shine in the light from the window and the low light from the lamp beside the bed. His mouth was open, too, like he was shouting, but all the sound was out of him like air out of a popped balloon, and he would not have any more sound in him ever again, you could tell. Blood was let out of him, too, lots of it, and a pair of scissors were stuck in his belly, deep in, with not much more than the handles showing, the same scissors Thomas used to clip pictures from magazines for his poems.

He felt a big twist of pain in his heart, like maybe somebody was sticking scissors in him too. But it wasn't hurt-pain so much as what he called 'feel-pain,' because it was losing Derek that he was feeling, not real hurt. It was as bad as real hurt, though, because Derek was his friend, he liked Derek. He was scared, too, because he somehow knew the Bad Thing had let the life out of Derek, the Bad Thing was here at The Home. Then he realized this could happen just the way things sometimes happened in TV stories, with the cops coming and believing that Thomas killed Derek, blaming Thomas, and everyone hating Thomas for what he'd done, but he hadn't done it, and all the while the Bad Thing was still loose to do more killing, maybe even doing to Julie what it'd done to Derek.

The hurt, the fear for himself, the fear for Julie – all of it was too much. Thomas gripped the footboard of his own bed and closed his eyes and tried to get air into himself. It wouldn't come. His chest was tight. Then the air came in, and so did an ugly-nasty smell, which in a while he realized was the stink of Derek's blood, so he gagged and almost puked.

He knew he had to Get Control of Himself. The aides didn't like it when you Lost Control of Yourself, so they Gave You Something For Your Own Good. He'd never Lost Control before and didn't want to lose it now.

He tried not to smell the blood. Took long deep breaths. Made himself open his eyes to look at the dead body. He figured looking at it the second time wouldn't be as bad as the first. He knew it was going to be there this time, so it wouldn't be such a big surprise.

The surprise was – the body was gone.

Thomas closed his eyes, put one hand to his face, looked again between spread fingers. The body still wasn't there.

He started shaking because what he thought, first, was that this was like some other TV stories he'd seen where nasty-dead bodies were walking around like live bodies, rotting and getting wormy, with bones showing in places, killing people for no reason and even sometimes eating them. He could never watch much of one of those stories. He sure didn't want to *be* in one.

He was so scared he almost TVed to Bobby – *Dead people, look out, look out, dead people hungry and mean and walking around* – but stopped himself when he saw there wasn't blood on Derek's blankets and sheets. The bed wasn't rumpled, either. Neatly made. No walking dead person was quick enough to get out of bed, change sheets and blankets, make everything right just in the few little seconds while Thomas's eyes were closed. Then he heard the shower pouring down on the floor of the stall in the bathroom, and he heard Derek singing soft the way he always did when he washed himself. For just a moment, in his head, Thomas had a picture of a dead person taking a shower, trying to be neat, but rotten chunks were falling off with the dirt, showing more bones, clogging the drain. Then he realized Derek was never really dead. Thomas hadn't really seen a body on the bed. What he'd seen was something else he'd learned from TV stories – he'd seen a vision. A sidekick vision. He was a sidekick.

Derek hadn't been killed. What Thomas saw, just for a moment, was Derek being dead tomorrow or some other day after tomorrow. It might be something that would happen no matter what Thomas did to stop it, or it might be something that would happen only if he let it happen, but at least it wasn't something that *already* happened.

He let go of the footboard and went to his worktable. His legs were shaky. He was glad to sit down. He opened the top drawer of the cabinet that stood beside the table. He saw his scissors in there, where they should be, with his colored pencils and pens and paper clips and Scotch tape and stapler – and a half-eaten Hershey's bar in an open wrapper, which *shouldn't* be in there because it would Draw Bugs. He took the candy out of the drawer and stuffed it in a pocket of his robe, reminding himself to put it in the refrigerator later.

For a while he stared at the scissors, listened to Derek sing in the shower, and thought how the scissors were jammed in Derek's belly, letting all the music and other sounds out of him forever, sending him to the Bad Place. Finally he touched the black plastic handles. They felt all right, so he touched the metal blades, but that was bad, real bad, as if leftover lightning from a storm was in the blades and jumped into him when he touched them. Sizzling, crackling white light flashed through him. He snatched his hand back. His fingers tingled. He closed the drawer and hurried back to bed and sat there with the covers pulled around his shoulders the way TV Indians wrapped themselves in blankets when they sat at TV campfires.

The shower stopped. So did the singing. After a while Derek came out of the bathroom, followed by a cloud of damp, soapy-smelling air. He was dressed for the day. His wet hair was combed back from his forehead.

He was not a rotting dead person. He was all alive, every part of him, at least every part you could see, and no bones poked out anywhere.

'Good morning,' Derek said, the words slurred and muffled by his crooked mouth and too-big tongue. He smiled.

'Good morning.'

'You sleep good?'

'Yeah,' Thomas said.

'Breakfast soon.'

'Yeah.'

'Maybe sticky buns.'

'Maybe.'

'I like sticky buns.'

'Derek?'

'Huh?'

'If I ever tell you . . .'

Derek waited, smiling.

Thomas thought out what he wanted to say, then continued: 'If I ever tell you the Bad Thing's coming, and I tell you to run, don't just stand around like a dumb person. You just *run*.'

Derek stared at him, thinking about it, still smiling, then after a while he said, 'Sure, okay.'

'Promise?'

'Promise. But what's a bad thing?'

'I don't know really, for sure, but I'll feel when it's coming, I think, and tell you, and you'll run.'

'Where?'

'Anywhere. Down the hall. Find some aides, stay with them.'

'Sure. You better wash. Breakfast soon. Maybe sticky buns.'

Thomas unwrapped himself from the blanket and got out of bed. He stepped into his slippers again and walked to the bathroom.

Just as Thomas was opening the bathroom door, Derek said, 'You mean at breakfast?'

Thomas turned. 'Huh?'

'You mean a bad thing might come at breakfast?'

'Might,' Thomas said.

'Could it be . . . poached eggs?'

'Huh?'

'The bad thing – could it be poached eggs? I don't like poached eggs, all slimy, yuck, that'd be real bad, not good at all like cereal and bananas and sticky buns.'

'No, no,' Thomas said. 'The bad thing isn't poached eggs. It's a person, some funny-weird person. I'll feel when it's coming, and tell you, and you'll run.'

'Oh. Yeah, sure. A person.'

Thomas went into the bathroom, closed the door. He didn't have much beard. He had an electric razor, but he only used it a couple-few times a month, and today he didn't need it. He brushed his teeth, though. And he peed. He made the water start in the shower. Only then did he let himself laugh, because enough time had passed so Derek wouldn't even wonder if Thomas was laughing at him.

Poached eggs!

Though Thomas usually didn't like seeing himself, seeing how lumpy and wrong and dumb his face was, he peeked at the steam-streaked mirror. One time long ago, past when he could remember, he'd been laughing when he'd happened to see himself in a mirror, and for once – surprise! – he hadn't felt so bad about how he looked. When he laughed he looked more like a normal person. Just pretending to laugh didn't make him look more normal, it had to be real laughing, and smiling didn't do it, either, because a smile wasn't enough of a laugh to change his face. In fact, a smile could sometimes look so sad, he couldn't stand seeing himself at all.

Poached eggs.

Thomas shook his head, and when his laughter finished he turned from the mirror.

To Derek the most worst bad thing he could think of was poached eggs and no sticky buns, which was very funny ha-ha. You try to tell Derek about walking dead people and scissors sticking out of bellies and something that eats little live animals, and old Derek would look at you and smile and nod and not get it at all.

For as long as he could remember, Thomas had wished he was a normal person, not dumb, and many times he thanked God for at least making him not as dumb as poor Derek. But now he half wished he was dumber, so he could get those ugly-nasty vision-pictures out of his mind, so he could forget about Derek going to die and the Bad Thing coming and Julie being in danger, so he'd have nothing to worry about except poached eggs, which wouldn't be much of a worry at all, since he sort of *liked* poached eggs.

When Clint Karaghiosis arrived at Dakota & Dakota shortly before nine o'clock, Bobby took him by the shoulder, turned him around, and went back to the elevators with him. 'You drive, and I'll fill you in on what's happened during the night. I know you've got other cases to tend to, but the Pollard thing is getting hotter by the minute.'

'Where're we going?'

'First, Palomar Labs. They called. Test results are ready.'

Only a few clouds remained in the sky, and they were all far off toward the mountains, moving away like the billowing sails of great galleons on an eastward journey. It was a quintessential southern California day: blue, pleasantly warm, everything green and fresh, and rush-hour traffic so hideously snarled that it could transform an ordinary citizen into a foaming-at-the-mouth sociopath with a yearning to pull the trigger of a semiautomatic weapon.

Clint avoided freeways, but even surface streets were clogged. By the time Bobby recounted everything that had transpired since they had seen each other yesterday afternoon, they were still ten minutes from Palomar in spite of the questions occasioned by Clint's amazement – subdued like all of his reactions, but amazement nonetheless – over the discovery that Frank was evidently able to teleport himself.

Finally Bobby changed the subject because talking too much about psychic phenomena to a phlegmatic guy like Clint made him feel like an airhead, as if he had lost his grip on reality. While they inched along Bristol Avenue, he said, 'I can remember when you could go anywhere in Orange County and *never* get caught in traffic.'

'Not so long ago.'

'I remember when you didn't have to sign a developer's waiting list to buy a house. Demand wasn't five times supply.'

'Yeah.'

'And I remember when orange groves were all over Orange County.'

'Me too.'

Bobby sighed. 'Hell, listen to me, like an old geezer, babbling about the good old days. Pretty soon, I'll be talking about how nice it was when there were still dinosaurs around.'

'Dreams,' Clint said. 'Everyone's got a dream, and the one more people have than any other is the California dream, so they never stop coming, even though so many have come now that the dream isn't really quite attainable any more, not the original dream that started it all. Of course, maybe a dream should be unattainable, or at least at the outer limits of your reach. If it's too easy, it's meaningless.'

Bobby was surprised by the long burst of words from Clint, but more surprised to hear the man talking about something as intangible as dreams. 'You're already a Californian, so what's your dream?'

After a brief hesitation, Clint said, 'That Felina will be able to hear someday. There're so many medical advancements these days, new discoveries and treatments and techniques all the time.'

As Clint turned left off Bristol, onto the side street where Palomar Laboratories stood, Bobby decided that was a good dream, a damned fine dream, maybe even better than his and Julie's dream about buying time and getting a chance to bring Thomas out of Cielo Vista and into a remade family.

They parked in the lot beside the huge concrete-block building in which Palomar Laboratories was housed. As they were walking toward the front door, Clint said, 'Oh, by the way, the receptionist here thinks I'm gay, which is fine with me.'

'What?'

Clint went inside without saying more, and Bobby followed him to the reception window. An attractive blonde sat at the counter.

'Hi, Lisa,' Clint said.

'Hi!' She punctuated her response by cracking her chewing gum.

'Dakota and Dakota.'

'I remember,' she said. 'Your stuff's ready. I'll get it.'

She glanced at Bobby and smiled, and he smiled, too, though her expression seemed a little peculiar to him.

When she returned with two large, sealed manila envelopes – one labeled SAMPLES, the other ANALYSES – Clint handed the second one to Bobby. They stepped to one side of the lounge, away from the counter.

Bobby tore open the envelope and skimmed the documents inside. 'Cat's blood.'

'You serious?'

'Yeah. When Frank woke up in that motel, he was covered with cat's blood.'

'I knew he was no killer.'

Bobby said, 'The cat may have an opinion about that.'

'The other stuff is?'

'Well . . . bunch of technical terms here . . . but what it comes down to is that it's what it looks like. Black sand.'

Stepping back to the reception counter, Clint said, 'Lisa, you remember we talked about a black-sand beach in Hawaii?'

'Kaimu,' she said. 'It's a dynamite place.'

'Yeah, Kaimu. Is it the only one?'

'Black-sand beach, you mean? No. There's Punaluu, which is a real sweet place too. Those are on the big island. I guess there must be more on the other islands, cause there's volcanoes all over the place, aren't there?'

Bobby joined them at the counter. 'What do volcanoes have to do with it?'

Lisa took her chewing gum out of her mouth and put it aside on a piece of paper. 'Well, the way I heard it, really hot lava flows into the sea, and when it meets the water, there're these huge explosions, which throw off zillions and zillions of these really teeny-tiny beads of black glass, and then over a long period of time the waves rub all the beads together until they're ground down into sand.'

'They have these beaches anywhere but Hawaii?' Bobby wondered.

She shrugged. 'Probably. Clint, is this fella your . . . friend?'

'Yeah,' Clint said.

'I mean, you know, your *good* friend?'

'Yeah,' Clint said, without looking at Bobby.

Lisa winked at Bobby. 'Listen, you make Clint take you to Kaimu, 'cause I'll tell you something – it's really terrific to go out on a black beach at night, make love under the stars, because it's soft, for one thing, but mainly because black sand doesn't reflect moonlight like regular sand. It seems like you're floating in space, darkness all around, it really sharpens your senses, if you know what I mean.'

'Sounds terrific,' Clint said. 'Take care, Lisa.' He headed for the door.

As Bobby turned to follow Clint, Lisa said, 'You make him take you to Kaimu, you hear? You'll have a good time.'

Outside, Bobby said, 'Clint, you've got some explaining to do.'

'Didn't you hear her? These little beads of black glass—'

'That's not what I'm talking about. Hey, look at you, you're grinning. I don't think I've ever seen you grinning. I don't think I *like* you grinning.'

• 42 •

By nine o'clock, Lee Chen had arrived at the offices, opened a bottle of orange-flavored seltzer, and settled in the computer room midst his beloved hardware, where Julie was waiting for him. He was five six, slender but wiry, with a warm brass complexion and jet-black hair that bristled in a modified punk style. He wore red tennis shoes and socks, baggy black cotton pants with a white belt, a black and charcoal-gray shirt with a subtle leaf pattern, and a black jacket with narrow lapels and big shoulder pads. He was the most stylishly dressed employee at DAKOTA & Dakota, even compared to Cassie Hanley, their receptionist, who was an unashamed clotheshorse.

While Lee sat in front of his computers, sipping seltzer, Julie filled him in on what had happened at the hospital and showed him the printouts of the information Bobby had acquired earlier that morning. Frank Pollard sat with them, in the third chair, where Julie could keep an eye on him. Throughout their conversation, Lee exhibited no surprise at what he was being told, as if his computers had bestowed on him such enormous wisdom and foresight that nothing – not even a man capable of teleportation – could surprise him. Julie knew that Lee, as well as everyone else in the Dakota & Dakota family, would never leak a word of any client's business to anyone; but she didn't know how much of his supercool demeanor was real and how much was a conscious image that he put on every morning with his ultra-vogueish clothes.

Though his unshakable nonchalance might be partly feigned, his talent for computers was unquestionably real. When Julie had finished her condensed version of recent events, Lee said, 'Okay, what do you need from me now?' There was no doubt on either his part or hers that eventually he could provide whatever she required.

She gave him a steno pad. Double rows of currency serial numbers filled the first ten pages. 'Those are random samplings of the bills in each of the bags of cash we're holding for Frank. Can you find out if it's hot money – stolen, maybe an extortion or ransom payment?'

Lee quickly paged through the lists. 'No consecutive numbers? That makes it harder. Usually cops don't have a record of the serial numbers of stolen money unless it was brand-new bills, which are still bound in packets, consecutively numbered, right off the press.'

'Most of this cash is fairly well circulated.'

'There's an outside chance it might still be from a ransom or extortion payoff, like you said. The cops would've taken down all the numbers before they let the victim make the drop, just in case the perp made a clean getaway. It looks bleak, but I'll try. What else?'

Julie said, 'An entire family in Garden Grove, last name Farris, was murdered last year.'

'Because of me,' Frank said.

Lee propped his elbows on the arms of his chair, leaned back, and steepled his fingers. He looked like a wise Zen master who had been forced to don the clothes of an avant-garde artist after getting the wrong suitcase at the airport. 'No one really dies, Mr Pollard. They just go on from here. Grief is good, but guilt is pointless.'

Though she knew too few computer fanatics to be certain, Julie suspected that not many found a way to combine the hard realities of science and technology with religion. But in fact, Lee had arrived at a belief in God through his work with computers and his interest in modern physics. He once explained to her why a profound understanding of the dimensionless space inside a computer network, combined with a modern physicist's view of the universe, led inevitably to faith in a Creator, but she hadn't followed a thing he'd said.

She gave Lee Chen the dates and details of the Farris and Roman murders. 'We think they were all killed by the same man. I haven't got a clue to his real name, so I call him Mr Blue. Considering the savagery of the murders, we suspect he's a serial killer with a long list of victims. If we're right, the murders have been so widely spread or Mr Blue has covered his tracks so well that the press has never made connections between the crimes.'

'Otherwise,' Frank said, 'they'd have sensationalized it on their front pages. Especially if this guy regularly bites his victims.'

'But since most police agencies are computer-linked these days,' Julie said, 'they might've made connections across jurisdictions, saw what the press didn't. There might be one or more quiet, ongoing investigations between local, state, and federal authorities. We need to know if any police in California – or the FBI nationally – are on to Mr Blue, and we need to know anything they've learned about him, no matter how trivial.'

Lee smiled. In the middle of his brass-hued face, his teeth were like pegs of highly polished ivory. 'That means going past the public-access files in their computers. I'll have to break their security, one agency after another, all the way into the FBI.'

'Difficult?'

'Very. But I'm not without experience.' He pushed his jacket sleeves farther up on his arms, flexed his fingers, and turned to the terminal keyboard as if he were a concert pianist about to interpret Mozart. He hesitated and glanced sideways at Julie. 'I'll work into their systems indirectly to discourage trace-backs. I won't damage any data or breach national security, so I probably won't even be noticed. But if someone spots me snooping and puts a tracer on me that I don't see or can't shake, they might pull your PI license for this.'

'I'll sacrifice myself, take the blame. Bobby's license won't be pulled, too, so the agency won't go down. How long will this take?'

'Four or five hours, maybe more, maybe a lot more. Can somebody bring me lunch at noon? I'd rather eat here and not take a break.'

'Sure. What would you like?'

'Big Mac, double order of fries, vanilla shake.'

Julie grimaced. 'How come a high-tech guy like you never heard of cholesterol?'

'Heard of it. Don't care. If we never really die, cholesterol can't kill me. It can only move me out of this life a little sooner.'

• 43 •

Archer van Corvaire cracked open the Levolor blind and peered through the thick bulletproof glass in the front door of his Newport Beach shop. He squinted suspiciously at Bobby and Clint, though he knew and expected them. At last he unlocked the door and let them in.

Van Corvaire was about fifty-five but invested a lot of time and money in the maintenance of a youthful appearance. To thwart time, he'd undergone dermabrasion, face-lifts, and liposuction; to improve on nature, he'd had a nose job, cheek implants, and chin restructuring. He wore a toupée of such exquisite craftsmanship, it would have passed for his own dyed-black hair – except that he sabotaged the illusion by insisting on not merely a replacement but a lush, unnatural pompadour. If he ever got into a swimming pool wearing that toupée, it would look like the conning tower of a submarine.

After reengaging both dead bolts, he turned to Bobby. 'I never do business in the morning. I take only afternoon appointments.'

'We appreciate the exception you've made for us,' Bobby said.

Van Corvaire sighed elaborately. 'Well, what is it?'

'I have a stone I'd like you to appraise for me.'

He squinted, which wasn't appealing, since his eyes were already as narrow as those of a ferret. Before his name change thirty years ago, he'd been Jim Bob Spleener, and a friend would have told him that when he squinted suspiciously he looked very much like a Spleener and not at all like a van Corvaire. 'An appraisal? That's all you want?'

He led them through the small but plush salesroom: hand-textured plaster ceiling; bleached suede walls; whitewashed oak floors; custom area carpet by Patterson, Flynn & Martin in shades of peach, pale blue and sandstone; a modern white sofa flanked by pickled-finish, burlwood tables by Bau; four elegant rattan chairs encircling a round table with a glass top thick enough to survive a blow from a sledgehammer.

One small merchandise display case stood off to the left. Van Corvaire's business was conducted entirely by appointment; his jewelry was custom designed for the very rich and tasteless, people who would find it necessary to buy hundred-thousand-dollar necklaces to wear to a thousand-dollar-a-plate charity dinner, and never grasp the irony.

The back wall was mirrored, and van Corvaire watched himself with obvious pleasure all the way across the room. He hardly took his eyes off his reflection until he passed through the door into the workroom.

Bobby wondered if the guy ever got so entranced by his image that he walked smack into it. He didn't like van Corvaire, but the narcissistic creep's knowledge of gems and jewelry was often useful.

Years ago, when Dakota & Dakota Investigations was just Dakota Investigations, without the ampersand and the redundancy (better never put it that way around Julie, who would appreciate the clever wordplay but would make him eat the 'redundancy' part), Bobby had helped van Corvaire recover a fortune in unmounted diamonds stolen by a lover. Old van Corvaire desperately wanted his gems but didn't want the woman sent to prison, so he went to Bobby instead of to the police. That was the only soft spot Bobby had ever seen in van Corvaire; in the intervening years the jeweler no doubt had grown a callous over it too.

Bobby fished one of the marble-size red stones from his pocket. He saw the jeweler's eyes widen.

With Clint standing to one side of him, with Bobby behind him and looking over his shoulder, van Corvaire sat on a high stool at a workbench and examined the rough-cut stone through a loupe. Then he put it on the lighted glass table of a microscope and studied it with that more powerful instrument.

'Well?' Bobby asked.

The jeweler did not respond. He rose, elbowing them out of the way, and went to another stool, farther along the workbench. There, he used one scale to weigh the stone and another to determine if its specific gravity matched that of any known gems.

Finally, he moved to a third stool that was positioned in front of a vise. From a drawer he withdrew a ring box in which three large, cut gems lay on a square of blue velvet.

'Junk diamonds,' he said.

'They look nice to me,' Bobby said.

'Too many flaws.'

He selected one of those stones and fixed it in the vise with a couple of turns of the crank. Gripping the red beauty in a small pair of pliers, he used one of its sharper edges to attempt to score the polished facet of the diamond in the vise, pressing with considerable effort. Then he put the pliers and red gem aside, picked up another jeweler's loupe, leaned forward, and studied the junk diamond.

'A faint scratch,' he said. 'Diamond cuts diamond.' He held the red stone between thumb and forefinger, staring at it with obvious fascination – and greed. 'Where did you get this?'

'Can't tell you,' Bobby said. 'So it's just a red diamond?'

'*Just*? The red diamond may be the rarest precious stone in the world! You must let me market it for you. I have clients who'd pay anything to have this as the centerstone of a necklace or pendant. It'll probably be too big for a ring even after final cut. It's huge!'

'What's it worth?' Clint asked.

'Impossible to say until it's finish-cut. Millions, certainly.'

'Millions?' Bobby said doubtfully. 'It's big but not *that* big.'

Van Corvaire finally tore his gaze from the stone and looked up at Bobby. 'You don't understand. Until now, there were only seven known red diamonds in the world. This is the eighth. And when it's cut and polished, it'll be one of the two largest. This comes as close to priceless as anything gets.'

Outside Archer van Corvaire's small shop, where heavy traffic roared past on

Pacific Coast Highway, with disco-frenetic flares of sunlight flashing off the chrome and glass, it was hard to believe that the tranquility of Newport Harbor and its burden of beautiful yachts were just beyond the buildings on the far side of the street. In a sudden moment of enlightenment, Bobby realized that his entire life (and perhaps nearly everyone else's) was like this street at this precise point in time: all bustle and noise, glare and movement, a desperate rush to break out of the herd, to achieve something and transcend the frantic whirl of commerce, thereby earning respite for reflection and a shot at serenity – when all the time serenity was only a few steps away, on the far side of the street, just out of sight.

That realization contributed to a heretofore subtle feeling that the Pollard case was somehow a trap – or, more accurately, a squirrel cage that spun faster and faster even as he scampered frantically to get a footing on its rotating floor. He stood for a few seconds by the open door of the car, feeling ensnared, caged. At that moment he was not sure why, in spite of the obvious dangers, he had been so eager to take on Frank's problems and put all that he cared about at risk. He knew now that the reasons he had quoted to Julie and to himself – sympathy for Frank, curiosity, the excitement of a wildly different kind of job – were merely justifications, not reasons, and that his true motivation was something he did not yet understand.

Unnerved, he got in the car and pulled the door shut as Clint started the engine.

'Bobby, how many red diamonds would you say are in the mason jar? A hundred?'

'More. A couple hundred.'

'Worth what – hundreds of millions?'

'Maybe a billion or more.'

They stared at each other, and for a while neither of them spoke. It wasn't that no words were adequate to the situation; instead, there was *too much* to say and no easy way to determine where to begin.

At last Bobby said, 'But you couldn't convert the stones to cash, not quickly anyway. You'd have to dribble them onto the market over a lot of years to prevent a sudden dilution of their rarity and value, but also to avoid causing a sensation, drawing unwanted attention, and maybe having to answer some unanswerable questions.'

'After they've mined diamonds for hundreds of years, all over the world, and only found seven red ones . . . where the hell did Frank come up with a jarful?'

Bobby shook his head and said nothing.

Clint reached into his pants pocket and withdrew one of the diamonds, smaller than the specimen that Bobby had brought for Archer van Corvaire's appraisal. 'I took this home to show it to Felina. I was going to return it to the jar when I got to the office, but you hustled me out before I had a chance. Now that I know what it is, I don't want it in my possession a minute longer.'

Bobby took the stone and put it in his pocket with the larger diamond. 'Thank you, Clint.'

Dr Dyson Manfred's study, in his house in Turtle Rock, was the most uncomfortable place Bobby had ever been. He had been happier last week, flattened on

the floor of his van, trying to avoid being chopped to bits by automatic weapon fire than he was among Manfred's collection of many-legged, cara-
paced, antenna-bristled, mandibled, and thoroughly repulsive exotic
bugs.

Repeatedly, in his peripheral vision, Bobby saw something move in one of
the many glass-covered boxes on the wall, but every time he turned to ascertain
which hideous creature was about to slip out from under the frame, his fear
proved unfounded. All of the nightmarish specimens were pinned and motionless, lined up neatly beside one another, none missing. He also would have
sworn that he heard things skittering and slithering inside the shallow drawers
of the many cases that he knew contained more insects, but he supposed that
those sounds were every bit as imaginary as the phantom movements glimpsed
from the corners of his eyes.

Though he knew Clint to be a born stoic, Bobby was impressed by the
apparent ease with which the guy endured the creepy-crawly decor. This was an
employee he must never lose. He decided on the spot to give Clint a significant
raise in salary before the day was out.

Bobby found Dr Manfred nearly as disquieting as his collection. The tall,
thin, long-limbed entomologist seemed to be the offspring of a professional
basketball player and one of those African stick insects that you saw in nature
films and hoped never to encounter in real life.

Manfred stood behind his desk, his chair pushed out of the way, and they
stood in front of it. Their attention was directed upon a two-foot-long, one-foot-
wide, white-enamel, inch-deep lab tray which occupied the center of the
desktop and over which was draped a small white towel.

'I have had no sleep since Mr Karaghiosis brought this to me last night,'
Manfred said, 'and I won't sleep much tonight, either, just turning over all the
remaining questions in my mind. This dissection was the most fascinating of
my career, and I doubt that I'll ever again experience anything in my life to
equal it.'

The intensity with which Manfred spoke – and the implication that neither
good food nor good sex, neither a beautiful sunset nor a fine wine, could be a
fraction as satisfying as insect dismemberment – gave Bobby a queasy stomach.

He glanced at the fourth man in the room, if only to divert his attention
briefly from their bugophile host. The guy was in his late forties, as round as
Manfred was angular, as pink as Manfred was pale, with red-gold hair, blue
eyes, and freckles. He sat on a chair in the corner, straining the seams of his gray
jogging suit, with his hands fisted on his heavy thighs, looking like a good
Boston Irish fellow who had been trying to eat his way into a career as a Sumo
wrestler. The entomologist hadn't introduced or even referred to the well-
padded observer. Bobby figured that introductions would be made when
Manfred was ready. He decided not to force the issue – if only because the
round man silently regarded them with a mixture of wonder, suspicion, fear,
and intense curiosity that encouraged Bobby to believe they would not be
pleased to hear what he had to tell them when, at last, he spoke.

With long-fingered, spidery hands – which Bobby might have sprayed with
Raid if he'd had any – Dyson Manfred removed the towel from the white-
enamel tray, revealing the remains of Frank's insect. The head, a couple of the
legs, one of the highly articulated pincers, and a few other unidentifiable parts

had been cut off and put aside. Each grisly piece rested on a soft pad of what appeared to be cotton cloth, almost as a jeweler might present a fine gem on velvet to a prospective buyer. Bobby stared at the plum-size head with its small reddish-blue eye, then at its two large muddy-yellow eyes that were too similar in color to Dyson Manfred's. He shivered. The main part of the bug was in the middle of the tray, on its back. The exposed underside had been slit open, the outer layers of tissue removed or folded back, and the inner workings revealed.

Using the gleaming point of a slender scalpel, which he handled with grace and precision, the entomologist began by showing them the respiratory, ingestive, digestive, and excretory systems of the bug. Manfred kept referring to the 'great art' of the biological design, but Bobby saw nothing that equaled a painting by Matisse; in fact, the guts of the thing were even more repellent than its exterior. One term – 'polishing chamber' – struck him as odd, but when he asked for a further explanation, Manfred only said, 'in time, in time,' and went on with his lecture.

When the entomologist finished, Bobby said, 'Okay, we know how the thing ticks, so what does that tell us about it that we might want to know? For instance, where does it come from?'

Manfred stared at him, unresponding.

Bobby said, 'The South American jungles?'

Manfred's peculiar amber eyes were hard to read, and his silence puzzling.

'Africa?' Bobby said. The entomologist's stare was beginning to make him twitchier than he already was.

'Mr Dakota,' Manfred said finally, 'you're asking the wrong question. Let me ask the interesting ones for you. What does this creature eat? Well, to put it in the simplest terms that any layman can understand – it eats a broad spectrum of minerals, rock, and soil. What does it ex—'

'It eats dirt?' Clint asked.

'That's an even simpler way to express it,' Manfred said. 'Not precise, mind you, but simpler. We don't yet understand how it breaks down those substances or how it obtains energy from them. There are aspects of its biology that we can see perfectly clearly but that still remain mysterious.'

'I thought insects ate plants or each other or . . . dead meat,' Bobby said.

'They do,' the entomologist confirmed. 'This thing is not an insect – or any other class of the phylum *Arthropoda*, for that matter.'

'Sure looks like an insect to me,' Bobby said, glancing down at the partly dismantled bug and grimacing involuntarily.

'No,' Manfred said, '*this* is a creature that evidently bores through soil and stone, capable of ingesting that material in chunks as large as fat grapes. And the next question is, "If that's what it eats, what does it excrete?" And the answer, Mr Dakota, is that it excretes diamonds.'

Bobby jerked as if the entomologist had hit him.

He glanced at Clint, who looked as surprised as Bobby felt. The Pollard case had induced several changes in the Greek, and now it had robbed him of his poker face.

In a tone of voice that suggested Manfred was playing them for fools, Clint said, 'You're telling us it turns dirt into diamonds?'

'No, no,' Manfred said. 'It methodically eats through veins of diamond-bearing carbon and other material, until it finds the gems. Then it swallows them in their encrusted jackets of minerals, *digests* those minerals, passes the rough diamond into the polishing chamber, where any remaining extraneous matter is worn away by vigorous contact with these hundreds of fine, wirelike bristles that line the chamber.' With the scalpel he pointed to the feature of the bug that he had just described. 'Then it squirts the raw diamond out the other end.'

The entomologist opened the center drawer of his desk, removed a white handkerchief, unfolded it, and revealed three red diamonds, all considerably smaller than the one Bobby had taken to van Corvaire, but probably worth hundreds of thousands, maybe millions, apiece.

'I found these at various points in the creature's system.'

The largest of the three was still partially encased in a mottled brown-black-gray mineral crust.

'They're diamonds?' Bobby said, playing ignorant. 'I've never seen red diamonds.'

'Neither had I. So I went to another professor, a geologist who happens to be a gemologist as well, got him out of bed at midnight to show these to him.'

Bobby glanced at the would-be Irish Sumo wrestler, but the man did not rise from his chair or speak, so he evidently was not the geologist.

Manfred explained what Bobby and Clint already knew – that these scarlet diamonds were among the rarest things on earth – while they pretended that it was all news to them. 'This discovery strengthened my suspicions about the creature, so I went straight to Dr Gavenall's house and woke *him* shortly before two o'clock this morning. He threw on sweats and sneakers, and we came right back here, and we've been here ever since, working this out together, unable to believe our own eyes.'

At last the round man rose and stepped to the side of the desk.

'Roger Gavenall,' Manfred said, by way of introduction. 'Roger is a geneticist, a specialist in recombinant DNA, and widely known for his creative projections of macroscale genetic engineering that might conceivably progress from current knowledge.'

'Sorry,' Bobby said, 'I lost you at "Roger is . . ." We'll need some more of that layman's language, I'm afraid.'

'I'm a geneticist and futurist,' Gavenell said. His voice was unexpectedly melodic, like that of a television gameshow host. 'Most genetic engineering, for the foreseeable future, will take place on a *micro*scopic scale – creating new and useful bacteria, repairing flawed genes in the cells of human beings to correct inherited weaknesses and prevent inherited disease. But eventually we'll be able to create whole new species of animals and insects, *macro*scale engineering – useful things like voracious mosquito eaters that will eliminate the need to spray Malathion in tropical regions like Florida. Cows that are maybe half the size of today's cows and a lot more metabolically efficient, so they require less food, yet produce twice as much milk.'

Bobby wanted to suggest that Gavenall consider combining the two biological inventions to produce a small cow that ate only enormous quantities of mosquitoes and produced *three* times as much milk. But he kept his mouth shut, certain that neither of the scientists would appreciate his humor. Anyway, he had to admit that his compulsion to make a joke of this was an attempt to deal with his own deep-seated fear of the ever-increasing weirdness of the Pollard case.

'This thing,' Gavenall said, indicating the deconstructed bug in the lab tray, 'isn't anything that nature created. It's clearly an engineered lifeform, so astonishingly task-specific in every aspect of its biology that it's essentially a biological machine. A diamond scavenger.'

Using a pair of forceps and the scalpel, Dyson Manfred gently turned over the insect that wasn't an insect, so they could see its midnight-black shell rimmed with red markings.

Bobby thought he heard whispery movement in many parts of the study, and he wished Manfred would let some sunlight into the room. The windows were covered with interior wood shutters, and the slats were tightly shut. Bugs liked darkness and shadows, and the lamps here seemed insufficiently bright to dissuade them from scurrying out of the shallow drawers, over Bobby's shoes, up his socks, and under the legs of his pants.

Hanging his pendulous belly over the desk, indicating the crimson edging on the carapace, Gavenall said, 'On a hunch Dyson and I shared, we showed a representation of this pattern to an associate in the mathematics department, and he confirmed that it's an obvious binary code.'

'Like the universal product code that's on everything you buy at the grocery store,' the entomologist explained.

Clint said, 'You mean the red marks are the bug's *number*?'

'Yes.'

'Like . . . well, like a license plate?'

'More or less,' Manfred said. 'We haven't taken a chip of the red material for analysis yet, but we suspect it'll prove to be a ceramic material, painted onto the shell or spray-bonded in some fashion.'

Gavenall said, 'Somewhere there are a lot of these things, industriously digging for diamonds, red diamonds, and each of them carries a coded serial number that identifies it to whomever created it and set it to work.'

Bobby grappled with that concept for a moment, trying to find a way to see it as a part of the world in which he lived, but it simply did not fit. 'Okay, Dr Gavenall, you're able to envision engineered creatures like this—'

'I couldn't have envisioned this,' Gavenall said adamantly. 'It never would've occurred to me. I could only recognize it for what it was, for what it must be.'

'All right, but nevertheless you recognized what it must be, which is something neither Clint nor I could've done. So now tell me – who could make something like this damned thing?'

Manfred and Gavenall exchanged a meaningful look and were both silent for a long moment, as if they knew the answer to his question but were reluctant to reveal it. Finally, lowering his gameshow-host voice to an even more mellifluous note, Gavenall said, 'The genetic knowledge and engineering skill required to produce this thing do not yet exist. We're not even close to being able to . . . to . . . not even *close*.'

Bobby said, 'How long until science advances far enough to make this thing possible?'

'No way of arriving at a precise answer,' Manfred said.

'Guess.'

'Decades?' Gavenall said. 'A century? Who knows?'

Clint said, 'Wait a minute. What're you telling us? That this thing comes from the future, that it came through some . . . some time warp from the next century?'

'Either that,' Gavenall said, 'or . . . it doesn't come from this world at all.'

Stunned, Bobby looked down at the bug with no less revulsion but with considerably more wonder and respect than he'd had a moment ago. 'You really think this might be a biological machine created by people from another world? An alien artifact?'

Manfred worked his mouth but produced no sound, as if rendered speechless by the prospect of what he was about to say.

'Yes,' Gavenall said, 'an alien artifact. Seems more likely to me than the possibility that it came tumbling back to us through some hole in time.'

Even as Gavenall spoke, Dyson Manfred continued to work his mouth in a frustrated attempt to break the silence that gripped him, and his lantern jaw gave him the look of a praying mantis masticating a grisly lunch. When words at last issued from him, they came in a rush: 'We want you to understand, we will not, flatly will not, return this specimen. We'd be derelict as scientists to allow this incredible thing to reside in the hands of laymen, we must preserve and protect it, and we will, even if we have to do so by force.'

A flush of defiance lent a glow of health to the entomologist's pale, angular face for the first time since Bobby had met him.

'Even if by force,' he repeated.

Bobby had no doubt that he and Clint could beat the crap out of the human stick bug and his rotund colleague, but there was no reason to do so. He didn't care if they kept the thing in the lab tray – as long as they agreed to some ground rules about how and when they would go public with it.

All he wanted right now was to get out of that bughouse, into warm sunlight and fresh air. The whispery sounds from the specimen drawers, though certainly imaginary, grew louder and more frenzied by the minute. His entomophobia would soon kick him off the ledge of reason and send him screaming from the room; he wondered if his anxiety was apparent or if he was sufficiently self-controlled to conceal it. He felt a bead of sweat slip down his left temple, and had the answer.

'Let's be absolutely frank,' Gavenall said. 'It's not only our obligation to science that requires us to maintain possession of this specimen. Revelation of this find will *make* us, academically and financially. Neither one of us is a slouch in his field, but this will catapult us to the top, the very top, and we're willing to do whatever is necessary to protect our interests here.' His blue eyes had narrowed, and his open Irish face had closed up into a hard mask of determination. 'I'm not saying I'd kill to keep that specimen . . . but I'm not saying I wouldn't, either.'

Bobby sighed. 'I've done a lot of research for UCI into the backgrounds of prospective faculty members, so I know the academic world can be as competitive and vicious and dirty – dirtier – than either politics or show business. I'm not going to fight you on this. But we've got to reach an agreement about when you can go public with it. I don't want you doing anything that would bring my client to the attention of the press until we've resolved his case and are sure he's . . . out of danger.'

'And when will that be?' Manfred asked.

Bobby shrugged. 'A day or two. Maybe a week. I doubt it'll drag on much longer than that.'

The entomologist and geneticist beamed at each other, obviously delighted. Manfred said, 'That's no problem at all. We'll need much longer than that to finish studying the specimen, prepare our first paper for publication, and devise a strategy to deal with both the scientific community and the media.'

Bobby imagined that he heard one of the shallow drawers sliding open in the case behind him, forced outward by the weight of a vile torrent of giant, squirming Madagascar roaches.

'But I'll take the three diamonds with me,' he said. 'They're quite valuable, and they belong to my client.'

Manfred and Gavenall hesitated, made a token protest, but quickly agreed. Clint took the stones and rewrapped them in the handkerchief. The scientists' capitulation convinced Bobby there had been more than three diamonds in the bug, probably at least five, leaving them with two stones to support their thesis regarding the bug's origins and purpose.

'We'll want to meet your client, interview him,' Gavenall said.

'That's up to him,' Bobby said.

'It's essential. We *must* interview him.'

'That's his decision,' Bobby said. 'You've gotten most of what you wanted. Eventually he may agree, and then you'll have everything you're after. But don't push it now.'

The round man nodded. 'Fair enough. But tell me . . . where *did* he find the thing?'

'He doesn't remember. He has amnesia.' The drawer behind him was open now. He could hear the shells of the huge roaches clicking and scraping together as they poured out of confinement and down the front of the cabinet, swarming toward him. 'We really have to go,' he said. 'We don't have another minute to spare.' He left the study quickly, trying not to look as if he was bolting for his life.

Clint followed him, as did the two scientists, and at the front door, Manfred said, 'I'm going to sound as if I ought to be writing stories for some sensational tabloid, but if this *is* an alien artifact that came into your client's hands, do you think he could have gotten it inside a . . . well, a spaceship? Those people who claim to have been abducted and forced to undergo examinations aboard spaceships . . . they always seem to go through a period of amnesia first, before learning the truth.'

'Those people are crackpots or frauds,' Gavenall said sharply. 'We can't let ourselves be associated with that sort of thing.' He frowned, and the frown deepened into a scowl, and he said, 'Unless in this case it's true.'

Looking back at them from the stoop, grateful to be outside, Bobby said, 'Maybe it is. I'm at a point where I'll believe anything till it's disproved. But I'll tell you this . . . my feeling is that whatever is happening to my client is something a lot stranger than alien abduction.'

'A lot,' Clint agreed.

Without further elaboration, they went down the front walkway to the car. Bobby opened his door and stood for a moment, reluctant to get into Clint's Chevy. The mild breeze washing down the Irvine hills felt so *clean* after the stale air in Manfred's study.

He put one hand in his pocket, felt the red diamonds, and said softly, 'Bug shit.'

When he finally got into the car and slammed the door, he barely resisted the urge to reach under his shirt to determine if the things he still felt crawling on him were real.

Manfred and Gavenall stood on the front stoop, watching Bobby and Clint, as if half expecting their car to tip back on its rear bumper and shoot straight into the sky to rendezvous with some great glowing craft out of a Spielberg movie.

Clint drove two blocks, turned at the corner, and pulled to the curb as soon as they were out of sight. 'Bobby, where in the hell *did* Frank get that thing?'

Bobby could only answer him with another question: 'How many different places does he go when he teleports? The money, the red diamonds and the bug, the black sand – and how far away are some of those places? Really *far* away?'

'And who is he?' Clint asked.

'Frank Pollard from El Encanto Heights.'

'But I mean, who is that?' Clint thumped one fist against the steering wheel. 'Who the hell *is* Frank Pollard from El Encanto?'

'I think what you really want to know is not who he is. More important . . . *what* is he?'

• 44 •

By surprise Bobby came to visit.

Lunch was eaten before Bobby came. Dessert was still in Thomas's mind. Not the taste of it. The memory. Vanilla ice cream, fresh strawberries. The way dessert made you feel.

He was alone in his room, sitting in his armchair, thinking about making a picture poem that would have the feeling of eating ice cream and strawberries, not the taste but the good feeling, so some day when you didn't have any ice cream or strawberries, you could just look at the poem and get that same good feeling even without eating anything. Of course, you couldn't use pictures of ice cream or strawberries in the poem, because that wouldn't be a poem, that would be only *saying* how good ice cream and strawberries made you feel. A poem didn't just say, it showed you and made you feel.

Then Bobby came through the door, and Thomas was so happy he forgot the poem, and they hugged. Somebody was with Bobby, but it wasn't Julie, so Thomas was disappointed. He was embarrassed, too, because it turned out he'd met the person with Bobby a couple of times before, over the years, but he didn't remember him right away, which made him feel dumb. It was Clint. Thomas said the name to himself, over and over, so maybe he'd remember next time: *Clint, Clint, Clint, Clint, Clint*.

'Julie couldn't come,' Bobby said, 'she's babysitting a client.'

Thomas wondered why a baby would ever need a private eye, but he didn't ask. In TV only grownups needed private eyes, which were called private *eyes* because they looked out for you, though he wasn't sure why they were called private. He also wondered how a baby could pay for a private eye, because he knew eyes like Bobby and Julie worked for money like everyone else, but babies didn't work, they were too little to do anything. So where'd this one get the money to pay Bobby and Julie? He hoped they didn't get cheated out of their money, they worked hard for it.

Bobby said, 'She told me to tell you she loves you even more than she did yesterday, and she'll love you even more tomorrow.'

They hugged again because this time Thomas was giving the hug to Bobby for Julie.

Clint asked if he could see the latest scrapbook of poems. He took it across the room and sat in Derek's armchair, which was okay because Derek wasn't in it, he was in the wreck room.

Bobby moved the chair from the worktable, putting it closer to the armchair that belonged to Thomas. He sat, and they talked about what a big blue day it was and how nice the flowers looked where they were all bright outside Thomas's window.

For a while they talked about lots of things, and Bobby was funny – except when they talked about Julie, he changed. He was worried for Julie, you could tell. When he talked about her, he was like a good picture poem – he didn't say his worry, but he showed it and made you feel it.

Thomas was already worried for Julie, so Bobby's worry made him feel even worse, made him scared for her.

'We've got our hands full with the current case,' Bobby said, 'so neither one of us might be able to visit again until this weekend or the first of the week.'

'Okay, sure,' Thomas said, and a big coldness rushed in from somewhere and filled him up. Each time Bobby mentioned the new case, the one with the baby, his picture poem of worry was even easier to read.

Thomas wondered if this was the case where they were going to meet up with the Bad Thing. He was pretty sure it was. He thought he should tell Bobby about the Bad Thing, but he couldn't find a way. No matter how he told it, he'd sound like the dumbest dumb person who ever lived at The Home. It was better to wait until the danger was coming a lot nearer, then TV to Bobby a real hard warning that'd scare him into looking out for the Bad Thing and shooting it when he saw it. Bobby would pay attention to a TVed warning because he wouldn't know where it came from, that it came from just a dumb person.

And Bobby could shoot, too, all private eyes could shoot because most days it was bad out there in the world, and you knew you were going to meet up with somebody who was going to shoot at you first or try to run you down with a car or stab you or strangle you or, once in a while, try to throw you off a building, or even Try To Make It Look Like Suicide, and since most good guys didn't carry guns around with them, private eyes who watched over them had to be good shooters.

After a while Bobby had to go. Not to the bathroom but back to work. So they hugged again. And then Bobby and Clint were gone, and Thomas was alone.

He went to the window. Looked out. The day was good, better than night. But even with the sun pushing most darkness out past the edge of the world, and even with the rest of the darkness hiding from the sun behind trees and buildings, there was badness in the day. The Bad Thing hadn't gone out past the edge of the world with the night. It was still there, somewhere in the day, you could tell.

Last night, when he got too close to the Bad Thing and it tried to grab him, he was so afraid, he pulled away quick like. He had a feeling the Bad Thing was trying to find out who he was and where he was, and then was going to come to

The Home and eat him like it ate the little animals. So he pretty much made up his mind not to get real close to it again, stay far away, but now he couldn't do that because of Julie and the baby. If Bobby, who never worried, was so worried for Julie, then Thomas needed to be even more worried for her than he was. And if Julie and Bobby thought the baby should be watched over, then Thomas had to worry about the baby, too, because what was important to Julie was important to him.

He reached out into the day.

It was there. Far away yet.

He didn't get close.

He was scared.

But for Julie, for Bobby, for the baby, he'd have to stop being scared, get closer, and be sure he knew all the time where the Bad Thing was and whether it was coming this way.

· 45 ·

Jackie Jaxx did not arrive at the offices of Dakota & Dakota until ten past four that Tuesday afternoon, a full hour after Bobby and Clint returned, and to Julie's annoyance he spent half an hour creating an atmosphere that he found conducive to his work. He felt the room was too bright, so he closed the blinds on the large windows, though the approaching winter twilight and an incoming bank of clouds over the Pacific had already robbed the day of much of its light. He tried different arrangements with the three brass lamps, each of which was equipped with a three-way bulb, giving him what seemed an infinite number of combinations; he finally left one of them at seventy watts, one at thirty, and one off completely. He asked Frank to move from the sofa to one of the chairs, decided that wasn't going to work, moved Julie's big chair out from behind the desk and put him in that, then arranged four other chairs in a semicircle in front of it.

Julie suspected that Jackie could have worked effectively with the blinds open and all of the lamps on. He was a performer, however, even when off the stage, and he could not resist being theatrical.

In recent years magicians had forsaken fake show-biz monikers like The Great Blackwell and Harry Houdini in favor of names that at least seemed like real ones, but Jackie was a throwback. Just as Houdini's real name was Ehrich Weiss, so Jackie had been baptized David Carver. Because he performed comic magic, he had avoided mysterious-sounding names. And because, since puberty, he had yearned to be part of the nightclub and Vegas scene, he had chosen a new identity that, to him and those in his social circle, sounded like Nevada royalty. While other kids thought about being teachers, doctors, real estate salesmen or auto mechanics, young Davey Carver had dreamed of being someone like Jackie Jaxx; now, God help him, he was living his dream.

Although he was currently between a one-week engagement in Reno and a stint as the opening act for Sammy Davis in Vegas, Jackie showed up not in blue jeans or an ordinary suit, but in an outfit he could have worn during performances: a black leisure suit with emerald-green piping on the lapels and cuffs of the jacket, a matching green shirt, and black patent-leather shoes. He was thirty-six years old, five feet eight, thin, cancerously tanned, with hair that he dyed ink-black and teeth that were unnaturally, *ferociously* white, thanks to the modern miracle of dental bonding.

Three years ago Dakota & Dakota had been hired by the Las Vegas hotel with which Jackie had a long-term contract, and charged with the sticky task of uncovering the identity of a blackmailer who was trying to extort most of the magician's income. The case had many unexpected twists and turns, but by the time they reached the end, the thing that most surprised Julie was that she had gotten over her initial distaste for the magician and had come to sort of like him. Sort of.

Finally Jackie settled on the chair directly in front of Frank. 'Julie, you and Clint sit to my right. Bobby, to my left, please.'

Julie saw no good reason why she couldn't sit in whichever of the three chairs she chose, but she played along.

Half of Jackie's Vegas act involved the hypnotizing and comic exploitation of audience members. His knowledge of hypnotic technique was so extensive, and his understanding of the functioning of the mind in a trance state was so profound, that he was frequently invited to participate in medical conferences with physicians, psychologists, and psychiatrists who were exploring practical uses of hypnosis. Perhaps they could have persuaded a psychiatrist to help them pierce Frank's amnesia with hypnotic regression therapy. But it was doubtful that any doctor was as qualified for the task as Jackie Jaxx.

Besides, no matter what fantastic things Jackie learned about Frank, he could be counted on to keep his mouth shut. He owed a lot to Bobby and Julie, and in spite of his faults, he was a man who paid his debts and had at least a vestigial sense of loyalty that was rare in the me-me-me culture of show business.

In the moody amber light of the two brass lamps, with the world darkening rapidly beyond the drawn blinds, Jackie's smooth and well-projected voice, full of low rounded tones and an occasional dramatic vibrato, commanded not just Frank's attention but everyone else's as well. He used a beveled teardrop crystal on a gold chain to focus Frank's attention, after suggesting that the others look at Frank's face rather than at the bauble, to avoid unwanted entrancement.

'Frank, please watch the light winking in the crystal, a very soft and lovely light fluttering from one facet to another, one facet to another, a very warm and appealing light, warm, fluttering . . .'

After a while, lulled somewhat herself by Jackie's calculated patter, Julie noticed Frank's eyes glaze over.

Beside her, Clint switched on the small tape recorder that he had used when Frank had told them his story yesterday afternoon.

Still twisting the chain back and forth between his thumb and forefinger to make the crystal spin on the end of it, Jackie said, 'All right, Frank, you are now slipping into a very relaxed state, a deeply relaxed state, where you will hear only my voice, no other, and will respond only to my voice, no other . . .'

When he had conveyed Frank into a deep trance and finished giving him instructions related to the interrogation ahead, Jackie told him to close his eyes. Frank obliged.

Jackie put the crystal down. He said, 'What is your name?'

'Frank Pollard.'

'Where do you live?'

'I don't know.'

Having been briefed on the phone by Julie earlier in the day, aware of the information they were seeking from their client, Jackie said, 'Have you ever lived in El Encanto?'

A hesitation. Then: 'Yes.'

Frank's voice was strangely flat. His face was so haggard and deathly pale that he seemed almost like an exhumed corpse that had been sorcerously revitalized for the purpose of serving as a bridge between the members of a séance and those to whom they wished to speak in the land of the dead.

'Do you recall your address in El Encanto?'

'No.'

'Was your address 1458 Pacific Hill Road?'

A frown flickered across Frank's face and was gone almost as soon as it came, 'Yes. That's what . . . Bobby found . . . with the computer.'

'But do you actually remember that place?'

'No.'

Jackie adjusted his Rolex watch, then used both hands to smooth back his thick, black hair. 'When did you live in El Encanto, Frank?'

'I don't know.'

'You must tell me the truth.'

'Yeah.'

'You cannot lie to me, Frank, or hide anything from me. That is impossible in your current state. When did you live there?'

'I don't know.'

'Did you live there alone?'

'I don't know.'

'Do you remember being in the hospital last night, Frank?'

'Yeah.'

'And you . . . disappeared?'

'They say I did.'

'Where did you disappear to, Frank?'

Silence.

'Frank, where did you disappear to?'

'I . . . I'm afraid.'

'Why?'

'I . . . don't know. I can't think.'

'Frank, do you remember waking up in your car last Thursday morning, parked along a street in Laguna Beach?'

'Yeah.'

'Your hands were full of black sand.'

'Yeah.' Frank wiped his hands on his thighs, as if he could feel the black grains clinging to his sweaty palms.

'Where did you get that sand, Frank?'

'I don't know.'

'Take your time. Think about it.'

'I don't know.'

'Do you remember checking into a motel later . . . napping . . . then waking up with blood all over yourself?'

'I remember,' Frank said, and he shuddered.

'Where did that blood come from, Frank?'

'I don't know,' he said miserably.

'It was cat blood, Frank. Did you know it was cat blood?'

'No.' His eyelids fluttered, but he did not open his eyes. 'Just cat blood? Really?'

'Do you remember encountering a cat that day?'

'No.'

Clearly, a more aggressive technique would be required to get the answers they needed. Jackie began to talk Frank backward in time, gradually regressing him to his admission to the hospital yesterday evening, then farther back toward the moment he had awakened in that Anaheim alleyway in the earliest hours of Thursday morning, knowing nothing but his name. Beyond that point might lie his memory, if he could be induced to step through the veil of amnesia and recover his past.

Julie leaned slightly forward in her chair and looked past Jackie Jaxx, wondering how Bobby was enjoying the show. She figured the spinning crystal and other hocus pocus would appeal to his boyish spirit of adventure, and that he would be smiling and bright-eyed.

Instead he was somber. His teeth must have been clenched, for his jaw muscles bulged. He had told her what they learned at Dyson Manfred's house, and she had been as astonished and shaken as he and Clint. But that didn't seem to explain his current mood. Maybe he was still unnerved by the memory of the bugs in the entomologist's study. Or maybe he continued to be troubled by that dream he'd had last week: *the bad thing is coming, the bad thing . . .*

She had dismissed his dream as unimportant. Now she wondered if it had been genuinely prophetic. After all the weirdness that Frank had brought into their lives, she was more willing to give credence to such things as omens, visions, and prescient dreams.

The bad thing is coming, the bad thing . . .

Maybe the bad thing was Mr Blue.

Jackie regressed Frank to the alleyway, to the very moment when he had first awakened in a strange place, disoriented and confused. 'Now go back further, Frank, just a little further, back just a few more seconds, and a few more, back, back, beyond the total darkness in your mind, beyond that black wall in your mind . . .'

Since the questioning had begun, Frank had appeared to dwindle in Julie's desk chair, as if made of wax and subjected to a flame. He had grown paler, too, if that was possible, as white as candle paraffin. But now, as he was forced backward through the darkness in his mind, toward the light of memory on the other side, he sat up straighter, put his hands on the arms of the chair and clutched the vinyl almost tightly enough to cause the upholstery to split. He seemed to be growing, returning to his former size, as if he had drunk one of the magic elixirs that Alice had consumed in her adventures at the far end of the rabbit hole.

'Where are you now?' Jackie asked.

Frank's eyes twitched beneath his closed lids. An inarticulate, strangled sound issued from him. 'Uh . . . uh . . .'

'Where are you now?' Jackie insisted gently but firmly.

'Fireflies,' Frank said shakily. 'Fireflies in a windstorm!' He began to breathe rapidly, raggedly, as if he were having trouble drawing air into his lungs.

'What do you mean by that, Frank?'

'Fireflies . . .'

'Where are you, Frank?'

'Everywhere. Nowhere.'

'We don't have fireflies in southern California, Frank, so you must be somewhere else. Think, Frank. Look around yourself now and tell me where you are.'

'Nowhere.'

Jackie made a few more attempts to get Frank to describe his surroundings and be more specific as to the nature of the fireflies, all to no avail.

'Move him on from there,' Bobby said. 'Farther back.'

Julie glanced at the recorder in Clint's hand and saw the spools turning behind the plastic window in the tapedeck.

With his melodic and vibrant voice, in seductively rhythmic cadences, Jackie ordered Frank to regress past the firefly-speckled darkness.

Suddenly Frank said, 'What am I doing here?' He was not referring to the offices of Dakota & Dakota, but to the place that Jackie Jaxx had drawn him to in his memory. 'Why here?'

'Where are you, Frank?'

'The house. What in the hell am I doing here, why did I come here? This is crazy, I shouldn't be here.'

'Whose house is it, Frank?' Bobby asked.

Because he had been instructed to hear only the hypnotist's voice, Frank did not respond until Jackie repeated the question. Then: 'Her house. It's *her* house. She's dead, of course, been dead seven years, but it's still her house, always will be, the bitch will haunt the place, you can't destroy that kind of evil, not entirely, part of it lingers in the rooms where she lived, in everything she touched.'

'Who was she, Frank?'

'Mother.'

'Your mother? What was her name?'

'Roselle. Roselle Pollard.'

'This is the house on Pacific Hill Road?'

'Yeah. Look at it, my God, what a place, what a dark place, what a bad place. Can't people see what a bad place it is? Can't they see that something terrible lives in there?' He was crying. Tears glimmered in his eyes, then streamed down his cheeks. Anguish twisted his voice. 'Can't they see what's in there, what lives there, what hides there and *breeds* in that bad place? Are people blind? Or do they just not *want* to see?'

Julie was riveted by Frank's tortured voice and by the agony that had wrenched his face into an approximation of the pained countenance of a lost and frightened child. But she turned away from him and peered past the hypnotist to see if Bobby had reacted to the words 'bad place.'

He was looking at her. The expression of distress that darkened his blue eyes was proof enough that the reference had not escaped him.

At the other end of the room, carrying a sheaf of printouts, Lee Chen entered from the reception lounge. He closed the door quietly. Julie put a finger to her lips, then motioned him to the sofa.

Jackie spoke soothingly to Frank, trying to allay the fear that had electrified him.

Suddenly Frank let out a sharp cry of fear. He sounded more like a frightened animal than like a man. He sat up even straighter. He was trembling. He opened his eyes, but obviously did not see anything in the room; he was still in a trance. 'Oh, my God, he's coming, he's coming now, the twins must've told him I'm here, he's coming!'

Frank's unalloyed terror was so pure and intense that some of it was communicated to Julie. Her heartbeat speeded up, and she began to breathe more rapidly, shallowly.

Trying to keep his subject relaxed enough to be cooperative, Jackie said, 'Calm down, Frank. Relax and be calm. Nobody can hurt you. Nothing unpleasant will happen. Be calm, relaxed, calm . . .'

Frank shook his head. 'No. No, he's coming, he's coming, he's going to get me this time. Dammit, why did I come back here? Why did I come back and give him a chance at me?'

'Relax now—'

'He's there!' Frank tried to rise to his feet, seemed unable to find the strength, and dug his fingers even deeper into the vinyl padding on the arms of the chair. 'He's right *there*, and he sees me, he sees me.'

Bobby said, 'Who is he, Frank?' and Jackie repeated the question.

'Candy. It's Candy!' When he was asked again for the name of this person he feared, he repeated: 'Candy.'

'His name is Candy?'

'He *sees* me!'

In a more forceful and commanding voice than before, Jackie said, 'You will relax, Frank. You *will* be calm and relaxed.'

But Frank only grew more agitated. He had broken into a sweat. Fixed on something in a far place and time, his eyes were wild. His terror seemed to be sweeping him into a heart-bursting panic.

'I don't have much control of him,' Jackie said worriedly. 'I'm going to have to bring him out of it.'

Bobby slid forward to the edge of his chair. 'No, not yet. In a minute but not yet. Ask him about this Candy. Who is the guy?'

Jackie repeated the question.

Frank said, 'He's death.'

Frowning, Jackie said, 'That's not a clear answer, Frank.'

'He's death walking, he's death living, he's my brother, *her* child, her favorite child, her *spawn*, and I hate him, he wants to kill me, here he comes!'

With a wretched bleat of terror, Frank started to push up from the chair.

Jackie ordered him to stay where he was.

Frank sat down reluctantly, but his terror only grew, because he could still see Candy coming toward him.

Jackie tried to bring him out of that place in the past, forward to the present, and out of his trance, but to no avail.

'Got to get away now, now, *now*,' Frank said desperately.

Julie was frightened for him. She'd never seen anyone look more pathetic or vulnerable. He was drenched in sweat, shaking violently. His hair had fallen over his forehead, into his eyes, but it did not interfere with the vision of terror that he had called up from his past. He clutched the arms of the chair so fiercely that a fingernail on his right hand finally punctured the vinyl upholstery.

'I've got to get out of here,' Frank repeated urgently.

Jackie told him to stay put.

'No, I've got to get away from him!'

To Bobby, Jackie Jaxx said, 'This has never happened to me, I've lost control of him. Jesus, look at him, I'm afraid the guy's going to have a heart attack.'

'Come on, Jackie, you've got to help him,' Bobby said sharply. He got off his chair, squatted beside Frank, putting his hand on Frank's in a gesture of comfort and reassurance.

'Bobby, don't,' Clint said, standing up so fast that he dropped the tape recorder he'd been balancing on his thigh.

Bobby didn't respond to Clint, for he was too focused on Frank, who seemed to be shaking himself to pieces in front of them. The guy was like a boiler with a jammed release valve, filled to the bursting point not with steam pressure but with manic terror. Bobby was trying to calm him, where Jackie had failed.

For an instant Julie didn't understand what had made Clint shoot to his feet. But she realized that Bobby had seen something the rest of them had missed: fresh blood on Frank's right hand. Bobby hadn't put his hand over Frank's merely to offer comfort; he was trying, as gently as possible, to loosen Frank's grip on the arm of the chair, because Frank had torn open the vinyl and cut himself, perhaps repeatedly, on an exposed staple or upholstery tack.

'He's coming, got to get away!' Frank let go of the chair, grabbed Bobby's hand, and got to his feet, pulling Bobby up with him.

Suddenly Julie understood what Clint feared, and she stood up so fast that she knocked her chair over. 'Bobby, no!'

Thrown into a panic by the vision of his murderous brother, Frank screamed. With a hiss like steam escaping from a locomotive engine, he vanished. And took Bobby with him.

• 46 •

Fireflies in a windstorm.

Bobby seemed to be floating in space, for he had no sense of his body's position, couldn't tell if he was lying or sitting or standing, right side up or upside down, as if weightless in an immense void. He had no sense of smell or taste. He could hear nothing. He could feel neither heat nor cold nor texture nor weight. The only thing he could see was limitless blackness that seemed to stretch to the ends of the universe – and millions upon millions of tiny fireflies, ephemeral as sparks, that swarmed around him. Actually, he was not sure he saw them at all, because he was not aware of having eyes with which to look at them; it was more as if he was . . . *aware* of them, not through any of the usual senses but through some inner sight, the mind's eye.

At first he panicked. The extreme sensory deprivation convinced him that he was paralyzed, without feeling in any limb or inch of skin, felled by a massive cerebral hemorrhage, deafened and blinded and trapped forever in a damaged brain that had severed all its connections to the outside world.

Then he became aware that he was in motion, not drifting in the blackness as he had first thought, but speeding through it, *rocketing* at a tremendous, frightening speed. He became aware of being drawn forward as if he were a bit of lint flying toward some vacuum cleaner of cosmic power, and all around him the fireflies swirled and tumbled. It was like being on an amusement park ride so huge and fast that only God could have designed it for His own pleasure, though there was no pleasure whatsoever in it for Bobby as he roller-coastered through pitch blackness, trying to scream.

He hit the forest floor on his feet, swayed, and almost fell against Frank, in front of whom he was standing. Frank still had a painfully tight grip on his hand.

Bobby was desperate for air. His chest ached; his lungs seemed to have shriveled up. He sucked in a deep breath, another, exhaling explosively.

He saw the blood, which was on both of their hands now. An image of torn upholstery flashed through his mind. Jackie Jaxx. Bobby remembered.

When Bobby tried to pull loose of his client, Frank held him fast and said, 'Not here. No, I can't risk this. Too dangerous. Why am I here?'

Steeped in the scent of pines, Bobby surveyed the surrounding primeval forest, which was thick with shadows as dusk introduced night to the world. The air was frigid, and the bristling boughs of the giant evergreens drooped under a weight of snow, but he saw nothing frightening in that scene.

Then he realized that Frank was staring past him. He turned to discover they were on the edge of the forest. A snow-covered meadow sloped up gently behind them. At the top was a long cabin, not a rustic shack but an elaborate structure that clearly showed the input of an architect, a vacation retreat for someone with plenty of disposable income. A mantle of snow was draped over the main roof, another over the porch roof, each decorated with a fringe of icicles that glittered in the last beams of cold sunlight. No lights glowed at the windows. No smoke curled up from any of the three chimneys. The place appeared to be deserted.

'He knows about this,' Frank said, still panicked. 'I bought it under another name, but he found out about it, and he came here, almost killed me here, and he's probably keeping tabs on it, checking in regularly, hoping to catch me again.'

Bobby was numbed less by the subzero cold than by the realization that he had teleported out of their office and onto this slope in the Sierras or some other mountains. He finally found his voice and said, 'Frank, what—'

Darkness.

Fireflies.

Velocity.

He hit the floor rolling, slammed into a coffee table, and felt Frank let go of his hand. The table crashed over, spilling a vase and other decorative – and breakable – items onto a hardwood floor.

He'd sustained a solid knock to the head. When he pushed onto his knees and tried to stand, he was too dizzy to get up.

Frank was already on his feet, looking around, breathing hard. 'San Diego. This was my apartment once. He found out about it. Had to get out fast.'

When Frank reached down to help Bobby get up, Bobby unthinkingly accepted his hand, the uninjured one.

'Someone else lives here now,' Frank said. 'Must be off at work, we're lucky.'

Darkness.

Fireflies.

Velocity.

Bobby found himself standing at a rusted iron gate between two stone pilasters, looking at a Victorian-style house with a sagging porch roof, broken balusters, and swaybacked steps. The sidewalk was cracked and canted, and weeds flourished in an unmown lawn. In the gloaming it looked like every kid's conception of a seriously haunted house, and he suspected it would look even worse in broad daylight.

Frank gasped. 'Jesus, no, not here!'

Darkness.

Fireflies.

Velocity.

Papers fluttered to the floor from a massive mahogany desk, as if a wind had swept through the room, though the air was still now. They were in a book-lined study with French windows. An old man had risen from a wing-backed leather chair. He was wearing gray flannel slacks, a white shirt, a blue cardigan, and a look of surprise.

Frank said, 'Doc,' and with his free hand reached toward the startled elder.

Darkness.

Bobby had figured out that all was lightless and featureless because, for the moment, he did not exist as a coherent physical entity; he had no eyes, no ears, no nerve endings with which to feel. But understanding brought no diminishment of his fear.

Fireflies.

The millions of tiny, whirling points of light were probably the atomic particles of which his flesh was constructed, being shepherded along sheerly by the power of Frank's mind.

Velocity.

They were teleporting, and the process was probably just about instantaneous, requiring only microseconds from physical dissolution to reconstitution, though subjectively it seemed longer.

The decrepit house again. It must be the place in the hills north of Santa Barbara. They were upslope from the gate, along the Eugenia hedge that encircled the property.

Frank let out a low cry of terror the instant that he saw where he was.

Bobby was afraid of running into Candy just as much as Frank was, but also afraid of Frank, and of teleporting—

Darkness.

Fireflies.

Velocity.

This time they didn't materialize with the balance and stability of their arrival in the old man's study or at the peeling house with the rusted gate, but with the clumsiness of their intrusion into that apartment in San Diego. Bobby stumbled a few steps up a slope, still in Frank's grip as firmly as if they had been handcuffed, and they both fell to their knees on the plush, well-cropped grass.

Frantically Bobby tried to wrench loose of Frank. But Frank held fast with superhuman strength and pointed to a gravestone only a few feet in front of them. Bobby looked around and saw that they were alone in a cemetery, where massive coral trees and palms loomed eerily in the purple-gray twilight.

'He was our neighbor,' Frank said.

Gasping for breath, unable to speak, still twisting his hand in an attempt to escape Frank's iron grip, Bobby saw the name NORBERT JAMES KOLREEN in the granite headstone.

'She had him killed,' Frank said, 'had her precious Candy kill him just because she felt he'd been rude to her. *Rude* to her! The crazy bitch.'

Darkness.

Fireflies.

Velocity.

The book-lined study. The old man in the doorway now, looking into the room at them.

Bobby felt as if he had been on a corkscrew roller coaster for hours, turning upside down at high speed, again and again, until he couldn't be sure any more if he was actually moving . . . or standing still while the rest of the world spun and looped around him.

'I shouldn't have come here, Dr Fogarty,' Frank said worriedly. Blood dripped off his injured hand, spotting a pale-green section of the Chinese carpet. 'Candy might've seen me at the house, might be trying to follow. Don't want to lead him to you.'

Fogarty said, 'Frank, wait—'

Darkness.

Fireflies.

Velocity.

They were in the backyard of the decaying house, thirty or forty feet from steps and a porch that were as spavined and dilapidated as those at the front of the place. Lights shone in the first floor windows.

'I want to go, I want to be out of here,' Frank said.

Bobby expected to teleport at once, and steeled himself for it, but nothing happened.

'I want *out* of here,' Frank said again. When they did not pop from that place to another, Frank cursed in frustration.

Suddenly the kitchen door opened, and a woman stepped into sight. She stopped on the threshold and stared at them. The fading, muddy purple twilight barely exposed her, and the light from the kitchen silhouetted her but did not reveal any details of her face. Whether it was a trick of the strange illumination or an accurate revelation of her form, Bobby could not know, but when starkly outlined, she presented a powerfully erotic picture: sylphlike, gracefully thin yet clearly and lushly feminine, a smoky phantom that seemed either thinly clad or nude, and that issued a call of desire without making a sound. There was a powerful lubriciousness in this mysterious woman that made her the equal of any siren that had ever induced sailors to run their ships onto hull-gouging rocks.

'My sister Violet,' Frank said with obvious dread and disgust.

Bobby noticed movement around her feet, a swarming of shadows. They poured down the steps, onto the lawn, and he saw they were cats. Their eyes were iridescent in the gloom.

He was gripping Frank every bit as hard as Frank was gripping him, for now he feared release as much as he had previously feared continued captivity. 'Frank, get us out of here.'

'I can't. I don't have control of this, of myself.'

There were a dozen cats, two dozen, still more. As they rushed off the porch and across the first few yards of unmown grass, they were silent. Then, simultaneously, they cried out, as if they were a single creature. Their wail of anger and hunger instantly cured Bobby of his nausea and made his stomach quiver, instead, with terror.

'Frank!'

He wished he hadn't taken off his shoulder holster back at the office. His gun was back there on Julie's desk, of no use to him, but as he glimpsed the bared teeth of the oncoming horde, he figured the revolver wouldn't stop them anyway, at least not enough of them.

The nearest of the cats leaped—

Julie was standing by her office chair, where it had been moved into the center of the room for the session of hypnotic therapy. She was unable to step away from it because she had last seen Bobby when he had been next to that chair, and it was where she felt closest to him. 'How long now?'

Clint was standing at her side. He looked at his watch. 'Less than six minutes.'

Jackie Jaxx was in the bathroom, splashing his face with cold water. Still on the sofa with a sheaf of printouts, Lee Chen was not as relaxed as he had been six and a half minutes ago. His Zen calm had been shattered. He was holding those papers in both hands, as if afraid they would vanish from his grasp, and his eyes were as wide now as they had been the moment that Bobby and Frank disappeared.

Julie was lightheaded with fear, but she was determined not to lose control of herself. Though there seemed to be nothing that she could do to help Bobby, an opportunity for action might arise when she least expected it, and she wanted to be calm and ready. 'Last night, Hal said that Frank returned the first time about eighteen minutes after he'd left.'

Clint nodded. 'Then we've twelve minutes to go.'

'After his second disappearance, he didn't return for hours.'

'Listen,' Clint said, 'if they don't show up here again in twelve minutes or an hour or three hours, that doesn't mean anything terrible has happened to Bobby. It's not going to be the same every time.'

'I know. What I'm more worried about is . . . the damn bed railing.'

Clint said nothing.

Unable to keep her voice even, she said, 'Frank never did bring it back. What happened to it?'

'He'll bring Bobby back,' Clint said. 'He won't leave Bobby out there . . . wherever he goes.'

She wished she felt confident about that.

Darkness.

Fireflies.

Velocity.

Rain poured straight down in warm torrents, as if Bobby and Frank had materialized under a waterfall. It pasted their clothes to them in an instant. There was no wind whatsoever, as if the tremendous weight and ferocity of the rainfall had drowned the wind as it would a fire; the air was steamy-humid. They had traveled far enough around the globe to have left twilight behind; the sun was up there somewhere behind the steely plating of gray clouds.

They were on their sides this time, facing each other like two inebriates who had been arm wrestling and had fallen drunkenly off their stools onto the floor of the barroom, where they still lay with their hands locked in competition. They were not in a bar, however, but in lush tropical foliage: ferns; dark green plants with rubbery deeply crenulated foliage; ground-hugging succulent vines with leaves as plump as gum candies and berries the same shade as the flesh of a Mandarin orange.

Bobby pulled away from Frank, and this time his client let him go without a struggle. He scrambled to his feet and pushed through the slick, spongy, clinging flora.

He didn't know where he was going and didn't care. He just had to put a little space between himself and Frank, distance himself from the danger that Frank now represented to him. He was overwhelmed by what had happened, over-loaded with new experiences that he needed to consider and to which he had to adapt before he could go on.

Within half a dozen steps he broke out of the tropical brush and onto a dark expanse of land, the nature of which at first eluded him. The rain came down not in droplets and not in sheets, but in roaring, silver-gray cascades that dramatically reduced visibility; it swept his hair over his eyes, too, which didn't help. He supposed some people, sitting by windows in dry rooms, might even have seen beauty in the storm, but there was just too damned much rain, a flood; it met the earth and the greenery with a cacophonous roar that threatened to deafen him. The rain not only exhausted him but made him wildly and irration-ally angry, as if he was being pelted not by rain but by spittle, great gobs of phlegmy spit, and as if the roar was actually the combined voices of thousands of onlookers showering him with insults and other abuse. He stumbled forward through the peculiarly mushy soil – not muddy, but mushy – looking for someone to blame for the rain, someone to shout at and shake and maybe even punch. In six or eight steps, however, he saw the breakers rolling ashore in a tumult of white foam, and he knew he was standing on a black-sand beach. That realization stopped him cold.

'Frank!' he shouted, and when he turned to look back the way he had come, he saw that Frank was following him, a few steps behind and round-backed, as if he were an old man unable to stand up to the force of the rain, or as if his spine had been warped by all the moisture. 'Frank, dammit, where are we?'

Frank stopped, unbent his back slightly, lifted his head, and blinked stu-pidly. 'What?'

Raising his voice even further, Bobby shouted above the tumult: 'Where are we?'

Pointing to Bobby's left, Frank indicated an enigmatic, rain-shrouded struc-ture that stood like the ancient shrine of a long-dead religion, perhaps a hundred feet farther down the black beach. 'Lifeguard station!' He pointed the other direction, up the beach, indicating a large wooden building considerably farther from them but less mysterious because its size made it easier to see. 'Restaurant. One of the most popular on the island.'

'What island?'

'The big island.'

'What big island?'

'Hawaii. We're standing on Punaluu Beach.'

'This was where *Clint* was supposed to take me,' Bobby said. He laughed, but it was a strange, wild laugh that spooked him, so he stopped.

Frank said, 'The house I bought and abandoned is back there.' He indicated the direction from which they had come. 'Overlooking a golf course. I loved the place. I was happy there for eight months. Then *he* found me. Bobby, we have to get out of here.'

Frank took a few steps toward Bobby, out of the mushy area and onto that section of the beach where the sand was better compacted.

'That's far enough,' Bobby ordered when Frank was six or eight feet from him. 'Don't come any closer.'

'Bobby, we have to go now, right away. I can't teleport exactly when I want. That'll happen when it happens, but at least we have to get away from this part of the island. He knows I lived here. He's familiar with this area. And he may be following us.'

The fiery anger in Bobby was not quenched by the rain; it grew hotter than ever. 'You lying bastard.'

'It's true, really,' Frank said, obviously surprised by Bobby's vehemence. They were close enough to converse without shouting now, but Frank still spoke louder than usual to be heard over the crackle-hiss-patter-rumble of the deluge. 'Candy came here after me, and he was worse than I'd ever seen him, more horrible, more evil. He came into my house with a baby, an infant he'd picked up somewhere, only months old, he'd probably killed its parents. He bit into that poor baby's throat, Bobby, then laughed and offered me its blood, taunted me with it. He drinks blood, you know, *she* taught him to drink blood, and he relishes it now, thrives on it. And when I wouldn't join him at the baby's throat, he threw it aside the way you'd discard an empty beer can, and he came for me, but I . . . traveled.'

'I didn't mean you were lying about him.' A wave broke closer to shore than the others, washing around Bobby's feet and leaving short-lived, lacelike traceries of foam on the black sand. 'I mean you lied to us about your amnesia. You remember everything. You know exactly who you are.'

'No, no.' Frank shook his head and made negating gestures with his hands. 'I didn't know. It *was* a blank. And maybe it'll be a blank again when I stop traveling and stay put someplace.'

'Lying shit!' Bobby said.

He stooped, scooped up handfuls of wet black sand and threw it at Frank in a blind fury, two more sopping handfuls, then two more. He began to realize that he was behaving like a child throwing a tantrum.

Frank flinched from the wet sand but waited patiently for Bobby to stop. 'This isn't like you,' he said, when at last Bobby relented.

'To hell with you.'

'Your rage is out of all proportion to anything you imagine I've done to you.'

Bobby knew that was true. As he wiped his wet sand-covered hands on his shirt and tried to catch his breath, he began to understand that he was not angry at Frank but at what Frank represented to him. Chaos. Teleportation was a funhouse ride in which the monsters and dangers were not illusory, in which the constant threat of death was to be taken seriously, in which there were no rules, no verities that could be relied upon, where up was down and in was out. Chaos. They had ridden the back of a bull named chaos, and Bobby had been flat-out terrified.

'You okay?' Frank asked.

Bobby nodded.

More than fear was involved. On a level deeper than intellect or even instinct, perhaps as deep as the soul itself, Bobby had been *offended* by that chaos. Until now he had not realized what a powerful need he had for stability and order. He'd always thought of himself as a free spirit who thrived on change and the unexpected. But now he saw that he had limits and that, in fact, beneath the devil-may-care attitude he sometimes struck, beat the steady heart of a stability-loving traditionalist. He suddenly understood that his passion for swing music had roots of which he'd never been aware: the elegant and complex rhythms and melodies of big-band jazz appealed to his bebop surface *and* to the secret seeker of order who dwelt in his heart. No wonder he liked Disney cartoons, in which Donald Duck might run wild and Mickey might get in a tangled mess with Pluto, but in which order triumphed in the end. Not for him the chaotic universe of Warner Brothers' Looney Tunes, in which reason and logic seldom won more than a temporary victory.

'Sorry, Frank,' he said at last. 'Give me a second. This sure isn't the place for it, but I'm having an epiphany.'

'Listen, Bobby, please, I'm telling the truth. Evidently I can remember everything when I travel. The very fact of traveling tears down the wall blocking my memory, but as soon as I stop traveling, the wall goes up again. It's part of the degeneration I'm undergoing, I guess. Or maybe it's just a desperate need to forget what's happened to me in the past, what's happening now, and what will sure as hell happen to me in the days to come.'

Though no wind had risen, some of the breakers were larger now, washing deep onto the beach. They battered the backs of Bobby's legs and, on retreating, buried his feet in coaly sand.

Struggling to explain himself, Frank said, 'See, traveling isn't easy for me, like it is for Candy. He can control where he wants to go, and when. He can travel just by deciding to do it, virtually by wishing himself someplace, like you suggested I might be able to do. But I can't. My talent for teleportation isn't really a talent, it's a curse.' His voice grew shaky. 'I didn't even know I could do it until seven years ago, the day that bitch died. All of us who came from her womb are cursed, we can't escape it. I thought I could escape somehow by killing her, but that didn't release me.'

After the events of the past hour, Bobby thought nothing could surprise him, but he was startled by the confession Frank had made. This pathetic, sad-eyed, dimpled, comic-faced, pudgy man seemed an unlikely perpetrator of matricide. 'You killed your own mother?'

'Never mind about her. We haven't time for her.' Frank looked back toward the brush out of which they had come, and both ways along the beach, but they were still alone in the downpour. 'If you'd known her, if you'd suffered under her hand,' Frank said, his voice shaking with anger, 'if you'd known the atrocities she was capable of, you'd have picked up an ax and chopped at her too.'

'You took an ax and gave your mother forty whacks?' That crazy sound burst from Bobby again, a laugh as wet as the rain but not as warm, and again he was spooked by himself.

'I discovered I could teleport when Candy had me backed into a corner, going to kill me for having killed her. And that's the only time I can travel – when it's a matter of survival.'

'Nobody was threatening you last night in the hospital.'

'Well, see, when I start traveling in my sleep, I think maybe I'm trying to escape from Candy in a dream, which triggers teleportation. Traveling always wakes me, but then I can't stop, I keep popping from place to place, sometimes staying a few seconds, sometimes an hour or more, and it's beyond my control, like I'm being bounced around inside a goddamn cosmic pinball machine. It exhausts me. It's killing me. You can *see* how it's killing me.'

Frank's earnest persistence and the numbing, relentless roar of the rain had washed away Bobby's rage. He was still somewhat afraid of Frank, of the potential for chaos that Frank represented, but he was no longer angry.

'Years ago,' Frank said, 'dreams started me traveling maybe one night a month, but gradually the frequency increased, until the last few weeks it happens almost every time I go to sleep. And when we finally wind up in your office or wherever this episode is going to come to an end, you'll remember everything that's happened to us, but I won't. And not only because I *want* to forget, but because what you suspected is true – I'm not always putting myself back together without mistakes.'

'Your mental confusion, loss of intellectual skills, amnesia – they're symptoms of those mistakes.'

'Yeah. I'm sure there's sloppy reconstruction and cell damage every time I travel, nothing dramatic in any one trip, but the effect is incremental . . . and accelerating. Sooner or later it's going to go criticial, and I'll either die or experience some weird biological meltdown. Coming to you for help was pointless, no matter how good you are at what you do, because nobody can help me. Nobody.'

Bobby had already reached that conclusion, but he was still curious. 'What is it with your family, Frank? Your brother has the power to make that car disintegrate around you, the power to blow out those streetlamps, and he can teleport. And what was that business with the cats?'

'My sisters, the twins, they have this thing with animals.'

'How come all of you possess these . . . abilities? Who *was* your mother, your father?'

'We don't have time for that now, Bobby. Later. I'll try to explain later.' He held out his cut hand, which had either stopped bleeding or was sluiced free of blood by the rain. 'I could pop out of here any moment, and you'd be stranded.'

'No thanks,' Bobby said, shunning his client's hand. 'Call me an old fuddy-duddy, but I'd prefer an airliner.' He patted his hip pocket. 'Got my wallet, credit cards. I can be back in Orange County tomorrow, and I don't have to take a chance that I'll arrive there with my left ear where my nose should be.'

'But Candy's probably going to follow us, Bobby. If you're here when he shows up, he'll kill you.'

Bobby turned to his right and started to walk toward the distant restaurant. 'I'm not afraid of anyone named Candy.'

'You better be,' Frank said, grabbing his arm and halting him.

Jerking away as if making contact with his client was tantamount to contracting the bubonic plague, Bobby said, 'How could he follow us anyway?'

When Frank worriedly surveyed the beach again, Bobby realized that because of the pounding rain and the underlying crash of the surf, they might not hear the telltale flutelike sounds that would warn them of Candy's imminent arrival.

Frank said, 'Sometimes, when he touches something you recently touched, he sees an image of you in his mind, and sometimes he can see where you went after you put the object down, and he can follow you.'

'But I didn't touch anything back there at the house.'

'You stood on the back lawn.'

'So?'

'If he can find the place where the grass is trampled, find where we stood, he might be able to put his fingers to the grass and see us, see this place, and come after us.'

'For God's sake, Frank, you make this guy sound supernatural.'

'He's the next thing to it.'

Bobby almost said he would take his chances with brother Candy, regardless of his godlike powers. Then he remembered what the Phans had told him about the savage murders of the Farris family. He also remembered the Roman family, their brutalized bodies torched to cover the ragged gashes that Candy's teeth had torn in their throats. He recalled what Frank had said about Candy offering him the fresh blood of a living baby, factored in the unmitigated terror in Frank's eyes at that very moment, and thought of the inexplicable prophetic dream he'd had about the 'bad thing.' At last he said, 'All right, okay, if he shows up, and if you're able to pop out of here before he kills us both, then I'd be better off with you. I'll take your hand, but only until we walk up to that restaurant, call a cab, and are on our way to the airport.' He gripped Frank's hand reluctantly. 'As soon as we're out of this area, I let go.'

'All right. Good enough,' Frank said.

Squinting as the rain battered their faces, they headed toward the restaurant. The structure, which stood perhaps a hundred and fifty yards away, appeared to be made of gray, weathered wood and lots of glass. Bobby thought he saw dim lights in the place, but he could not be sure; the large windows were no doubt tinted, which filtered out what fraction of the lampglow was not already hidden by the veils of rain.

Every third or fourth incoming wave was now much larger than the others, reached farther onto the beach, and sloshed around their legs with enough force to unbalance them. They moved toward the higher end of the strand, away from the breakers, but the sand was far softer there; it sucked at their shoes and made progress more laborious.

Bobby thought of Lisa, the blond receptionist at Palomar Labs. He pictured her coming along the beach right now, taking a crazy-romantic walk in the warm rain with some guy who'd brought her to the islands, pictured her face when she saw him strolling the black-sand beach hand-in-hand with another man, cheating on Clint.

This time his laughter didn't have a scary edge.

Frank said, 'What?'

Before Bobby could even start to explain, he saw that someone actually was heading in their general direction through the obscuring rain. It was a dark figure, not Lisa, a man, and he was only about thirty yards away.

He hadn't been there a moment ago.

'It's him,' Frank said.

Even at a distance the guy looked big. He spotted them and turned directly toward them.

Bobby said, 'Get us out of here, Frank.'

'I can't do it on demand. You know that.'

'Then let's run,' he urged, and he tried to pull Frank along the beach, toward the abandoned lifeguard tower and whatever lay beyond.

But after floundering a few steps through the sand, Frank stopped and said, 'No, I can't, I'm worn out. I'm going to have to pray that I pop out of here in time.'

He looked worse than worn out. He looked half dead.

Bobby turned toward Candy again, and saw the dark brother slogging through the soft, wet sand much faster than they had managed but still with some difficulty. 'Why doesn't he just teleport from there to here in a flash, overwhelm us?'

Frank's horror at the sight of his oncoming nemesis was so complete that he didn't appear capable of speech. Yet the words came with the shallow breaths that rasped out of him: 'Short hops, under a few hundred feet, aren't possible. Don't know why.'

Maybe if the trip was too short, the mind had a fraction of a second less than the minimum time required to deconstruct and fully reconstruct the body. It didn't matter what the reason was. Even if he couldn't teleport across the remaining stretch of sand, Candy was going to reach them in seconds.

He was only thirty feet away and closing, a massive juggernaut of a man, with a neck thick enough to support a car balanced on his head, and arms that would give him an advantage in a wrestling match with a four-ton industrial robot. His blond hair was almost white. His face was broad and sharp-featured and hard – and as cruel as the face of one of those pre-psychotic young boys who liked to set ants on fire with matches and test the effects of full-strength lye on neighborhood dogs. Charging through the storm, kicking up gouts of wet black sand with each step, he looked less like a man than like a demon with a fierce hunger for human souls.

Holding fast to his client's hand, Bobby said, 'Frank, for God's sake, let's get out of here.'

When Candy was close enough for Bobby to see blue eyes as wild and vicious as those of a rattlesnake on Benzedrine, he let out a wordless roar of triumph. He flung himself at them.

Darkness.

Fireflies.

Velocity.

Pale morning light filtered from a clear sky into the narrow pass-through between two rotting, ramshackle buildings so crusted in the filth of ages that it was impossible to determine what material had been used to construct their walls. Bobby and Frank were standing in knee-deep garbage that had been tossed out of the windows of the two-story structures and left to decompose into a reeking sludge that steamed like a compost pile. Their magical arrival had startled a colony of roaches that scuttled away from them, and caused swarms of fat black flies to leap up from their breakfast. Several sleek rats sat up on their haunches to see what had arrived among them, but they were too bold to be scared off.

The tenements on both sides had some windows completely open to the outside, some covered with what looked like oiled paper, none with glass. Though no people were in sight, from the rooms within the aged walls came voices: laughter here; an angry exchange there; chanting, as of a mantra, softly drifting down from the second floor of the building on the right. It was all in a foreign tongue with which Bobby was not familiar, though he suspected they might be in India, perhaps Bombay or Calcutta.

Because of the ineluctable stench, which by comparison made the stink of a slaughterhouse seem like a new perfume by Calvin Klein, and because of the insistently buzzing flies that exhibited great interest in an open mouth and nostrils, Bobby was unable to get his breath. He choked, put his free hand over his mouth, still could not breathe, and knew he was going to faint facefirst into the vile, steaming muck.

Darkness.

Fireflies.

Velocity.

In a place of stillness and silence, shafts of afternoon sunshine pierced mimosa branches and dappled the ground with golden light. They stood on a red oriental footbridge over a koi pond in a Japanese garden, where sculpted bonzai and other meticulously tended plants were positioned among carefully raked beds of pebbles.

'Oh, yes,' Frank said with a mixture of wonder and pleasure and relief. 'I lived here, too, for a while.'

They were alone in the garden. Bobby realized that Frank always materialized in sheltered places where he was unlikely to be seen in the act, or in circumstances – such as the middle of a cloudburst – that almost ensured even a public place like a beach would be conveniently deserted. Evidently, in addition to the unimaginably demanding task of deconstruction-travel-reconstruction, his mind was also capable of scouting the way ahead and choosing a discreet point of arrival.

Frank said, 'I was the longest-residing guest they'd ever had. It's a traditional Japanese inn on the outskirts of Kyoto.'

Bobby became aware that they were both totally dry. Their clothes were wrinkled, in need of an ironing, but when Frank had deconstructed them in Hawaii, he had not teleported the molecules of water that had saturated their clothes and hair.

'They were so kind here,' Frank said, 'respectful of my privacy, yet so attentive and kind.' He sounded wistful and terminally weary, as if he would have liked to have stopped his traveling right there, even if stopping meant dying at the hand of his brother.

Bobby was relieved to see that Frank also had not brought with them any of the slime from the narrow alley in Calcutta, or wherever. Their shoes and pants were clean.

Then he noticed something on the toe of his right shoe. He bent forward to look at it.

'I wish we could stay here,' Frank said. 'Forever.'

One of the roaches from that filth-choked alley was now a part of Bobby's footwear. One of the biggest advantages of being self-employed was freedom from neckties and uncomfortable shoes, so he was wearing, as usual, a pair of soft Rockport Supersports, and the roach was not merely stuck on the putty-colored leather but bristling from it and melded *with* it. The roach was not squirming, obviously dead, but it was there, or at least part of it was, some bits of it apparently having been left behind.

'But we've got to keep moving,' Frank said, oblivious of the roach. 'He's trying to follow us. We have to lose him if—'

Darkness.

Fireflies.

Velocity.

They were on a high place, a rocky trail, with an incredible panorama below them.

'Mount Fuji,' Frank said, not as if he had known where they were going but as if pleasantly surprised to be there. 'About halfway up.'

Bobby was not interested in the exotic view or concerned about the chill in the air. He was entirely preoccupied by the discovery that the roach was no longer a part of the toe of his shoe.

'The Japanese once thought Fuji was sacred. I guess they still do, or some of them do. And you can see why. It's magnificent.'

'Frank, what happened to the roach?'

'What roach?'

'There was a roach welded into the leather of this shoe. I saw it back there in the garden. You evidently brought it along from that disgusting alleyway. Where is it now?'

'I don't know.'

'Did you just drop its atoms along the way?'

'I don't know.'

'Or are its atoms still with me but somewhere else?'

'Bobby, I just don't know.'

In Bobby's mind was an image of his own heart, hidden within the dark cavity of his chest, beating with the mystery of all hearts but with a new secret all its own – the bristling legs and shiny carapace of a roach embedded in the muscle tissue that formed the walls of the atrium or a ventricle.

An insect might be *inside* of him, and even if the thing was dead, its presence within was intolerable. An attack of entomophobia hit him with the equivalent force of a hammer blow to the gut, knocking the wind out of him, sending undulate waves of nausea through him. He struggled to breathe, at the same time striving not to vomit on the sacred ground of Mount Fuji.

Darkness.

Fireflies.

Velocity.

They hit more violently this time, as if they had materialized in midair and had fallen a few feet onto the ground. They didn't manage to hold on to each other, and they didn't land on their feet, either. Separated from Frank, Bobby rolled down a gentle incline, over small objects that clattered and clicked under him and poked painfully into his flesh. When he tumbled to a halt, gasping and frightened, he was facedown on gray soil almost as powdery as ashes. Scattered around him, sparkling brightly against that ashen backdrop, were hundreds if not thousands of red diamonds in the rough.

Raising his head, he saw that the diamond miners were there in unnerving numbers: a score of huge insects just like the one they had taken to Dyson Manfred. Caught, as he was, in a whirlpool of panic, Bobby believed that every one of those bugs was fixated on him, all those multifaceted eyes turned toward him, all those tarantula legs churning through the powdery gray soil in his direction.

He felt something crawling on his back, knew what it must be, and rolled over, pinning the thing between him and the ground. He felt it squirming frantically beneath him. Propelled by revulsion, he was suddenly on his feet, without quite remembering how he had gotten up. The bug was still clinging to the back of his shirt; he could feel its weight, its quick-footed advance from the small of his back to his neck. He reached behind, tore it off himself, cried out in disgust as it kicked against his hand, and pitched it as far away as he could.

He heard himself breathing hard and making queer little sounds of fear and desperation. He didn't like what he heard, but he was unable to silence himself.

A foul taste filled his mouth. He figured he had ingested some of the powdery soil. He spat, but his spittle looked clean, and he realized that the air itself was what he tasted. The warm air was thick, not humid exactly but *thick*, like nothing he had experienced before. And in addition to the bitter taste, it had a distinctly different but equally unpleasant smell, like sour milk with a whiff of sulfur.

Turning around, surveying the terrain, he realized that he was standing in a shallow bowl in the land, about four feet deep at its lowest point, and about a hundred feet in diameter. The sloped walls were marked by evenly spaced holes, a double layer of them, and more of the biologically engineered insects were squirming into some of those bores, out of others, no doubt seeking – and returning with – diamonds.

Because it was only four feet deep, he could see above the rim of the bowl. Across the huge, barren, and slightly sloped plain in which this depression was set, he saw what appeared to be scores of similar features, like age-smoothed meteor craters, though they were so evenly spaced that they had to be unnatural. He was in the middle of a giant mining operation.

Kicking at an insect that had crept too close to him, Bobby turned to look at the last quarter of his surroundings. Frank was there, at the far side of the crater, on his hands and knees. Bobby was relieved by the sight of him, but he was definitely not relieved by what he saw in the sky beyond Frank.

The moon was visible in broad daylight, but it was not like the gossamer ghost moon that sometimes could be seen in a clear sky. It was a mottled gray-yellow sphere six times normal size, looming ominously over the land, as if about to collide with the larger world around which it should have been revolving at a respectable distance.

But that was not the worst. A huge and strangely shaped aircraft hung silently at perhaps an altitude of four or five hundred feet, so alien in every aspect that it brought home to Bobby the understanding that had thus far eluded him. He was not on his own world any longer.

'Julie,' he said, because suddenly he realized how terribly far from her he had traveled.

At the far side of the crater, as he was getting to his feet, Frank Pollard vanished.

• 47 •

As day dimmed and dark came, Thomas stood at the window or sat in his chair or stretched out on his bed, sometimes reaching toward the Bad Thing to be sure it wasn't coming closer. Bobby was worried when he visited, so Thomas was worried too. A lump of fear kept rising in his throat, but he kept swallowing it because he had to be brave and protect Julie.

He didn't get as close to the Bad Thing as last night. Not close enough to let it grab him with its mind. Not close enough to let it follow him when he quick-like reeled his own mind-string back to The Home. But close. A lot closer than Thomas liked.

Every time he pushed at the Bad Thing to make sure it was still there, up north someplace, where it belonged, he knew the Bad Thing felt him snooping. That spooked Thomas. The Bad Thing knew he was snooping around, but didn't do anything, and sometimes Thomas felt maybe the Bad Thing was waiting like a toad.

Once, in the garden behind The Home, Thomas watched a toad sit real still for a long time, while a bright yellow flutterby, pretty and quick, bounced from leaf to leaf, flower to flower, back and forth, round and round, close to the toad, then not so close, then closer than ever, then way out of reach, then closer again, like it was teasing the toad, but the toad didn't move, not an inch, like maybe it was a fake toad or just a stone that looked like a toad. So the flutterby felt safe, or maybe it just liked the game too much, and it came even closer. *Wham!* The toad's tongue shot out like one of those roll-up tooters they'd let the dumb people have one New Year's Eve, and it caught the flutterby, and the green toad ate the yellow flutterby, every bit, and that was the end of the game.

If the Bad Thing was playing a toad, Thomas was going to be real careful not to be a flutterby.

Then, just when Thomas figured he should start washing himself and changing clothes for supper, just when he was going to pull back from the Bad Thing, it went somewhere. He felt it go, bang, there one second and far away the next, slipping past where he could keep a watch on it, out across the world, going the same place where the sun was taking the last of the daylight. He couldn't figure how it could go so fast, unless maybe it was on a jetplane having good food and a fine whine, smiling at pretty girls in uniforms who put little pillows behind the Bad Thing's seat and gave it magazines and smiled back at it so nice and so much you expected them to kiss it like everybody was always kissing on daytime TV. Okay, yeah, probably a jetplane.

Thomas tried some more to find the Bad Thing. Then, by the time day was all gone and night all there, he gave up. He got off his bed and got ready for supper, hoping maybe the Bad Thing was gone away and never coming back, hoping Julie was safe forever now, and hoping there was chocolate cake for dessert.

———

Bobby charged across the floor of the diamond-strewn crater, kicking at the bugs in his way. As he ran he told himself that his eyes had deceived him and that his mind was playing nasty tricks, that Frank had not actually teleported out of there without him. But when he arrived at the spot where Frank had been, he found only a couple of footprints in the powdery soil.

A shadow fell across him, and he looked up as the alien craft drifted in blimplike silence over the crater, coming to a full stop directly above him, still about five hundred feet overhead. It was nothing like starships in the movies, neither organic looking nor a flying chandelier. It was lozenge shaped, at least five hundred feet long, and perhaps two hundred feet in diameter. Immense. On the ends, sides, and top, it bristled with hundreds if not thousands of pointed black metal spines, big as church spires, which made it look a little like a mechanical porcupine in a permanent defensive posture. The underside, which Bobby could see best of all, was smooth, black, and featureless, lacking not only the massive spines but markings, remote sensors, portholes, airlocks, and all the other apparatus one might expect.

Bobby did not know if the ship's repositioning was coincidental or whether he was under observation. If he was being watched, he didn't want to think about the nature of the creatures that might be peering down at him, and he sure as hell didn't want to consider what their intentions toward him might be. For every movie that featured an adorable alien with the power to turn kids' bicycles into airborne vehicles, there were ten others in which the aliens were ravenous flesh eaters with dispositions so vicious as to make any New York headwaiter think twice about being rude, and Bobby was certain that this was one thing Hollywood had gotten right. It was a hostile universe out there, and dealing with his fellow human beings was scary enough for him; he didn't need to make contact with a whole new race that had devised countless new cruelties of its own.

Besides, his capacity for terror was already filled to the brim, running over; he could contain no more. He was abandoned on a distant world, where the air – he began to suspect – might contain only enough oxygen and other required gases to keep him alive for a short while, insects the size of kittens were crawling all around him, and there was a possibility that a much smaller dead insect was actually fused with the tissue of one of his internal organs, and a psychotic blond giant with superhuman powers and a taste for blood was on his trail – and the odds were billions to one that he would ever see Julie again, or kiss her, or touch her, or see her smile.

A series of tremendous, throbbing vibrations issued from the ship and shook the ground around Bobby. His teeth chattered, and he nearly fell.

He looked for somewhere to hide. There was nothing in the crater to afford concealment, and nowhere to run on the flat plain beyond.

The vibrations stopped.

Even in the deep shadow thrown by the ship, Bobby saw a horde of identical insects begin to scuttle out of the boreholes in the crater walls, one after the other. They had been called forth.

Though no apparent openings appeared in the belly of the ship, a score or more of low-energy lasers – some yellow, some white, some blue, some red – began to play over the floor of the crater. Each beam was the diameter of a silver dollar, and each moved independently of the others. Like spotlights, they repeatedly swept the crater and everything in it, sometimes moving parallel to one another, sometimes crisscrossing one another, in a display that further disoriented Bobby and gave him the feeling that he was caught in the middle of a silent fireworks show.

He remembered what Manfred and Gavenall had told him about the crimson decorations along the rim of the bug's shell, and he saw that the white lasers were focusing only on the insects, busily scanning the markings around each carapace. Their owners were taking roll call. He saw a white beam fidget over the broken corpus of one of the bugs he had kicked, and after a moment a red beam joined it to study the carcass. Then the red beam jumped to Bobby, and a couple of other beams of different hue also found him, as if he was a can of peas being identified and added to someone's grocery bill at a supermarket checkout.

The floor of the crater was teeming with insects now, so many that Bobby could see neither the gray soil nor the litter of excreted diamonds over which they clambered. He told himself that they were not really bugs; they were just biological machines, engineered by the same race that had built the ship hanging over him. But that didn't help much because they still looked more like bugs than like machines. They had been designed to mine diamonds; they were not attracted to him whatsoever; but their disinterest did not make him feel better, because his phobia guaranteed that *he* was interested in *them*. His shadow-chilled skin prickled with gooseflesh. Short-circuiting nerve endings sputtered with false reports of things crawling on him, so he felt as if bugs swarmed over him from head to foot. They were actually creeping over his shoes, but none of them tried to scurry up his legs; he was grateful, because he was sure he would go mad if they began to climb him.

He used his hand as a visor over his eyes, to avoid being dazzled by the lasers that were playing on him. He saw something gleaming in the scanner beams only a few feet away: a curved section of what appeared to be hollow steel tubing. It was sticking out of the powdery soil, partly buried, further concealed by the bugs that scurried and jittered around it. Nevertheless, at first sight Bobby knew what it was, and he was overcome with a horrible sinking feeling. He shuffled forward, trying not to crush any of the insects because, for all he knew, the alien penalty for the additional destruction of property might be instant incineration. When he could reach the glinting curve of metal, he seized it and pulled it loose of the soft earth. It was the missing railing from the hospital bed.

'How long?' Julie demanded.

'Twenty-one minutes,' Clint said.

They still stood near the chair where Frank had been sitting and beside which Bobby had been stooping.

THE BAD PLACE 759

Lee Chen had gotten off the sofa, so Jackie Jaxx could lie down. The magician-hypnotist had draped a damp washcloth over his forehead. Every couple of minutes he protested that he could not really make people disappear, though no one had accused him of being responsible for what had happened to Frank and Bobby.

Having retrieved a bottle of Scotch, glasses, and ice from the office wet bar, Lee Chen was pouring six stiff drinks, one for each person in the room, as well as for Frank and Bobby. 'If you don't need a drink to steady your nerves now,' Lee had said, 'you'll need one to celebrate when they come back safe.' He had already downed one Scotch himself. The drink he poured now would be his second. This was the first time in his life he had drunk hard liquor – or needed it.

'How long?' Julie demanded.

'Twenty-two minutes,' Clint said.

And I'm still sane, she thought wonderingly. Bobby, damn you, come back to me. Don't you leave me alone forever. How am I going to dance alone? How am I going to live alone? How am I going to live?

Bobby dropped the bed railing, and the lasers winked off, leaving him in the shadow of the spiny ship, which seemed darker than before the beams appeared. As he looked up to see what would happen next, another light issued from the underside of the craft, too pale to make him squint. This one was precisely the diameter of the crater. In that queer, pearly glow, the insects began to rise off the ground, as if they were weightless. At first only ten or twenty floated upward, but then twenty more and a hundred after that, rising as lazily and effortlessly as so many bits of dandelion fluff, turning slowly, their tarantula legs motionless, the eerie light gone out of their eyes, as if they had been switched off. In a minute or two, the floor of the crater was depopulated of insects, and the horde was being drawn up effortlessly in that sepulchral silence that accompanied all of the craft's maneuvers except for the base vibrations that had called the insect miners from their bores.

Then the silence was broken by a flutelike warble.

'Frank!' Bobby cried in relief, and turned as a gust of vile-smelling wind washed over him.

As the cold, hollow piping echoed across the crater again, there was a subtle change in the hue of the light that issued from the ship above. Now the thousands of red diamonds rose from the ash-gray soil in which they lay and followed the insects upward, gleaming dully here and brightly there, so many of them that it seemed as if Bobby was standing in a rain of blood.

Another whirl of evil-scented wind cast up a cloud of the ashy soil, reducing visibility, and Bobby turned in eager expectation of Frank's arrival. Until he remembered that it might not be Frank but the brother.

The piping came a third time, and the subsequent puff of wind carried the dust away from him, so he saw Frank arrive less than ten feet from him.

'Thank God!'

As Bobby stepped forward, the pearly light underwent a second subtle change. Reaching for Frank's hand, he felt himself become weightless. When he looked down he saw his feet drift off the floor of the crater.

Frank grabbed at his outstretched hand and seized it.

Nothing had ever felt better to Bobby than Frank's firm grip, and for a moment he felt safe. Then he became aware that Frank had risen from the ground too. They were both being drawn upward in the wake of the insects and diamonds, toward the belly of the alien vessel, toward God-only-knew what nightmare inside.

Darkness.

Fireflies.

Velocity.

They were on Punaluu beach again, and the rain was coming down harder than before.

'Where the hell was that last place?' Bobby demanded, still holding fast to his client.

'I don't know,' Frank said. 'It scares the hell out of me, it's so weird, but sometimes I seem to be . . . drawn there.'

He hated Frank for having taken him there; he loved Frank for having returned for him. When he shouted above the rain, neither love nor hate was in his voice, just borderline hysteria: 'I thought you could only travel to places you've been?'

'Not necessarily. Anyway, I've been there before.'

'But how did you get there the first time, it's another world, it can't have been familiar to you – right, Frank?'

'I don't know. I just don't understand any of it, Bobby.'

Though face to face with Frank, Bobby took a while to notice how much the man's appearance had deteriorated since they had teleported from the Dakota & Dakota offices in Newport Beach. Although the storm once more had soaked him to the skin in seconds and left his clothes hanging on him shapelessly, it wasn't just the rain that made him look disheveled, beaten, and sickly. His eyes were more sunken than ever; the whites of them were yellow, as if he had contracted jaundice, and the flesh around them was so darkly bruised that he appeared to have painted a pair of fake shiners on himself with black shoe polish. His skin was paler than pale, a deathly gray, and his lips were bluish, as though his circulatory system was failing. Bobby felt guilty about having shouted at him, so he put his free hand on Frank's shoulder and told him he was sorry, that it was all right, that they were still fighting on the same side of this war, and that everything would turn out just fine – as long as Frank didn't take them back to that crater.

Frank said, 'Sometimes it's like I'm almost in touch with . . . with the minds of those people, creatures, whatever they are in that ship.' They were leaning on each other now, forehead to forehead, seeking mutual support in their exhaustion. 'Maybe I've got another gift I'm not aware of, like for most of my life I wasn't aware of being able to teleport until Candy backed me into a corner and tried to kill me. Maybe I'm mildly telepathic. Maybe the wavelength my telepathy functions on is the major wavelength of that race's brain activity. Maybe I feel them out there, even across billions of light-years of space. Maybe that's why I feel as if I'm being drawn to them, called to them.'

Pulling back a few inches from Frank, Bobby looked into his tortured eyes for a long moment. Then he smiled and pinched Frank's cheek, and said, 'You devil, you've really done a lot of thinking about this, haven't you, really put the old noodle to work on it, huh?'

Frank smiled.

Bobby laughed.

Then they were both laughing, holding each other up by leaning into each other, the way teepee poles held one another up, and a part of their laugh was healthy, a release of tension, but part of it was that mad laughter that had troubled Bobby earlier. Clinging to his client, he said, 'Frank, your life is chaos, you're *living* in chaos, and you can't go on like this. It's going to destroy you.'

'I know.'

'You've got to find a way to stop it.'

'There is no way.'

'You've got to try, buddy, you've got to try. Nobody can handle this. I couldn't live like this for one day, and you've done it for seven years!'

'No. It wasn't this bad most of that time. It's just lately, the last few months, it's accelerated.'

'A few months,' Bobby said wonderingly. 'Hell, if we don't give your brother the slip soon and get back to the office and step off this merry-go-round in the next few minutes, I swear to God I'm going to crack. Frank, I need order, order and stability, familiarity. I need to know that what I do today will determine where I am and who I am and what I have to show for it tomorrow. Nice orderly progression, Frank, cause and effect, logic and reason.'

Darkness.

Fireflies.

Velocity.

'How long?'

'Twenty-seven . . . almost twenty-eight minutes.'

'Where the hell *are* they?'

'Julie,' Clint said, 'I think you ought to sit down. You're shaking like a leaf, your color's not good.'

'I'm all right.'

Lee Chen handed her a glass of Scotch. 'Have a drink.'

'No.'

'It might help,' Clint said.

She grabbed the glass from Lee, drained it in a couple of long swallows, and shoved it back into his hand.

'I'll get you another,' he said.

'Thanks.'

From the sofa, Jackie Jaxx said, 'Listen, is anyone going to sue me over this?'

Julie no longer sort of liked the hypnotist. She loathed him as much as she had loathed him when they had first met him in Vegas and taken on his case. She wanted to go kick his head in. Though she knew the urge to kick him was irrational, that he really had not been the cause of Bobby's disappearance, she wanted to kick him anyway. That was the impulsive side of her, the quick-to-anger side of which she was not proud. But she couldn't always control it, because it was part of her genetic makeup or, as Bobby suspected, a predilection to violent response that had begun to form in her on the day, during her twelfth year, when a drug-crazed sociopath had brutally killed her mother. Either way, she knew Bobby was sometimes dismayed by that dark side of her, much as he loved everything else, so she made a bargain with both Bobby and God: *Listen, Bobby, wherever you are – and you listen, too, God – if this just ends well, if I can just have my Bobby back with me, I won't be this way any more, I won't want to kick in Jackie's head any more, or anyone else's head, either, I'll turn over a new leaf, I swear I will, just let Bobby come back to me safe and sound.*

They were on a beach again, but this one had white sand that was slightly phosphorescent in the early darkness. The strand disappeared into a medium-thick fog in both directions. No rain was falling, and the air was not as warm as it had been at Punaluu.

Bobby shivered in the chill, moist air. 'Where are we?'

'I'm not sure,' Frank said, 'but I think we're probably on the Monterey Peninsula somewhere.' A car passed on a highway a hundred yards behind them. 'That's probably Seventeen-Mile Drive. You know it? The road from Carmel through Pebble Beach—'

'I know it.'

'I love the peninsula, Big Sur to the south,' Frank said. 'It's another one of the places I was happy . . . for a while.'

Their voices were strangely muffled by the mist. Bobby liked the solid ground beneath his feet, and the thought that he was not only on his own planet but in his own country and in his own state; but he would have preferred a place with more concrete details, where fog did not obscure the landscape. The white blindness of fog was another form of chaos, and he had had more than enough disorder to last him for the rest of his life.

Frank said, 'Oh, and by the way, back there in Hawaii a minute ago, you were worried about giving Candy the slip, but you don't need to be concerned. We lost him several stops ago in Kyoto, or maybe on the slopes of Mount Fuji.'

'For God's sake, if we don't have to worry about leading him back to the office, let's go home.'

'Bobby, I don't have—'

'Any control. Yeah, I know, I heard, it's no big secret. But I'll tell you something – you've got control on some level, way down deep in the subconscious, more control than you think you have.'

'No. I—'

'Yes. Because you came back to that crater for me,' Bobby said. 'You told me you hate the place, that it's more frightening than anywhere you've ever been, but you came back and got me. You didn't leave me there with the bed railing.'

'Pure chance that I came back.'

'I don't think so.'

Darkness.

Fireflies.

Velocity.

They made the soft, pretty *bing-bong* signal come out of the wall, because that was how they told all the people in The Home it was just ten minutes before supper was going to be eaten.

Derek was already out the door by the time Thomas got up from his chair. Derek liked food. Everyone liked food, of course. But Derek liked food enough for three people.

Thomas got to the doorway, and Derek was already down the hall, walking fast in that funny way he did, almost to The Dining Room. Thomas looked back at the window.

Night was at the window.

He didn't like seeing night at the window, which was why he usually kept the drapes closed after the light went out of the world. But after he got himself ready for supper, he had tried to find the Bad Thing out there, and it helped a little to see the night when he was trying to send a mind-string into it.

The Bad Thing was still so far away it couldn't be felt. But he wanted to try once more before going to eat food and Be Sociable. He reached out through the window, up into the big dark, spinning the mind-string toward where the Bad Thing used to be – and it was back. He felt it right away, knew it felt him, too, and he remembered the green toad eating the bouncy yellow flutterby, and he pulled back into his room faster than a toad tongue could snap out and catch him.

He didn't know if he should be happy or scared that it was back. When it was gone away, Thomas was happy, because maybe it was going to be gone away a long time, but he was also a little scared because when it was gone away, he didn't know exactly where it was.

It was back.

He waited in the doorway a while.

Then he went to eat food. There was roast chicken. There was frenched fries. There was carrots and peas. There was coleslaw. There was Homemade bread, and people said there was going to be some chocolate cake and ice cream for dessert, though the people that said it was dumb people, so you couldn't be sure. It all looked good, and it smelled good, and it even tasted good. But Thomas kept thinking about how the flutterby might've tasted to the toad, and he couldn't eat much of anything.

Bouncing like two balls in tandem, they traveled to an empty lot in Las Vegas, where a cool desert wind spun a tumbleweed past them and where Frank said he had once lived in a house that was now demolished; to that cabin at the top of a snowy mountain meadow, where they had first teleported after leaving the office; to the graveyard in Santa Barbara; to the top of an Aztec ziggurat in the lush Mexican jungles, where the humid night air was full of buzzing mosquitoes and the cries of unknown beasts, and where Bobby almost fell down the terraced side of the pyramidal structure before he realized how high they were and how precariously perched; to the offices of Dakota & Dakota—

They were popping around so quickly, remaining in each place such a brief time – in fact, briefer with each stop – that for a moment he stood in a corner of his own office, blinking stupidly, before he realized where he was and what he had to do. He tore his hand away from Frank, and he said, 'Stop it now, stop here.' But Frank vanished even as Bobby spoke.

Julie was all over him an instant later, hugging him so tightly that she hurt his ribs. He hugged her, too, and kissed her a long time before coming up for air. Her hair smelled clean, and her skin smelled sweeter than he remembered. Her eyes were brighter than memory allowed, and more beautiful.

Though by nature he was not much of a toucher, Clint put a hand on Bobby's shoulder. 'God, it's good to see you, good to have you back.' There was even a catch in his voice. 'Had us worried there for a while.'

Lee Chen handed him a glass of Scotch on the rocks. 'Don't do that again, okay?'

'Don't plan to,' Bobby said.

No longer the smooth and self-assured performer, Jackie Jaxx had had enough for one night. 'Listen, Bobby, I'm sure that whatever you have to tell us is fascinating, and you're bound to've come back with a lot of boffo anecdotes, wherever you went, but I for one don't want to hear about it.'

'Boffo anecdotes?' Bobby said.

Jackie shook his head. 'Don't want to hear 'em. Sorry. It's my fault, not yours. I like show biz 'cause it's a narrow life, you know? A thin little slice of the real world, but exciting 'cause it's all bright colors and loud music. You don't have to *think* in show biz, you can just be. I just want to *be*, you know? Perform, hang out, have fun. I got opinions, sure, colorful and loud opinions about everything, show biz opinions, but I don't know a damn thing, and I don't *want* to know a damn thing, and I sure as hell don't want to know about what happened here tonight, 'cause it's the kind of thing that turns your world upside down, makes you curious, makes you think, and then pretty soon you're no longer happy with all the things that made you happy before.' He raised both hands, as if to forestall argument, and said, 'I'm outta here,' and a moment later he was.

At first, as he told the others what had happened to him, Bobby walked slowly around the room, marveling at ordinary items, finding wonder in the mundane, relishing the solidity of things. He put his hand on Julie's desk, and it seemed to him that nothing in the world was more wondrous than humble Formica – all those molecules of man-made chemicals lined up in perfect, stable order. The framed prints of Disney characters, the inexpensive furniture, the half-empty bottle of Scotch, the flourishing pothos plant on a stand by the windows – all of those things were suddenly precious to him.

He had been traveling only thirty-nine minutes. He took almost as long to tell them a condensed version. He had popped out of the office at 4:47 and returned at 5:26, but he'd done enough traveling – via teleportation or otherwise – to last the rest of his life.

On the sofa, with Julie and Clint and Lee gathered around, Bobby said, 'I want to stay right here in California. I don't need to see Paris. Don't need London. Not any more. I want to stay where I have my favorite chair, sleep every night in a bed that's familiar—'

'Damn right you will,' Julie interjected.

'—drive my little yellow Samurai, open a medicine cabinet where the Anacin and toothpaste and mouthwash and steptic pencil and Bactine and Band-Aids are exactly where they ought to be.'

By 6:15 Frank had not reappeared. During Bobby's account of his adventures, no one mentioned Frank's second disappearance or wondered aloud when he would return. But all of them kept glancing at the chair from which he had vanished initially and at the corner of the room from which he had dematerialized the second time.

'How long do we wait here for him?' Julie finally asked.

'I don't know,' Bobby said. 'But I have a feeling . . . a real bad feeling . . . that maybe Frank's not going to regain control of himself this time, that he's just going to keep popping from one place to another, faster and faster, until sooner or later he's unable to put himself back together again.'

• 48 •

When he came straight from Japan into the kitchen of his mother's house, Candy was seething with anger, and when he saw the cats on the table, where he ate his meals, his anger grew into a full-blown rage. Violet was sitting in a chair at the table; her ever-silent sister was in another chair beside her, hanging on her. Cats lay under their chairs and around their feet, and five of the biggest were on the table, eating bits of ham that Violet fed them.

'What're you doing?' he demanded.

Violet did not acknowledge him either with a word or a glance. Her gaze was locked with that of a dark gray mongrel that was sitting as erect as a statue of an Egyptian temple cat, patiently nibbling at a few small bits of meat offered on her pale palm.

'I'm talking to you,' he said sharply, but she did not respond.

He was sick of her silences, weary to death of her infinite strangeness. If not for the promise that he had made to his mother, he would have torn Violet open right there and fed on her. Too many years had passed since he had tasted the ambrosia in his sainted mother's veins, and he had often thought that the blood in Violet and Verbina was, in a way, the same blood that had flowed in Roselle. He wondered – and sometimes dreamed – of how his sisters' blood might feel upon the tongue, how it might taste.

Looming over her, staring down as she continued to commune with the gray cat, he said, 'This is where I *eat*, damn you!'

Violet still said nothing, and Candy struck her hand, knocking the remaining bits of ham helter-skelter. He swept the plate of ham off the table, as well, and took tremendous satisfaction in the sound of it shattering on the floor.

The five cats on the table were not the least startled by his fury, and the greater number on the floor remained unfazed by the ping and clatter of china fragments.

At last Violet turned her head, tilted it back, and looked up at Candy.

Simultaneously with their mistress, the cats on the table turned their heads to look haughtily at him, too, as if they wished him to understand what a singular honor they were bestowing upon him simply by granting him their attention.

That same attitude was apparent in the disdain in Violet's eyes and in the faint smirk that curled the edges of her ripe mouth. More than once he had found her direct gaze withering, and he had turned away from her, rattled and confused. Certain that he was her superior in every way, he was perplexed by her unfailing ability to defeat him or force him into a hasty retreat with just a look.

But this time would be different. He had never been as furious as he was at that moment, not even seven years ago when he had found his mother's bloody, sundered body and had learned the ax had been wielded by Frank. He was angrier now because that old rage had never subsided; it had fed on itself all these years, and on the humiliation of repeatedly failing to get his hands on Frank when the opportunities to do so arose. Now it was a midnight-black bile that coursed in his veins and bathed the muscles of his heart and nourished the cells of his brain where visions of vengeance were spawned in profusion.

Refusing to be cowed by her stare, he seized her thin arm and jerked her violently to her feet.

Verbina made a soft, woeful sound upon her separation from her sister, as if they were Siamese twins, for God's sake, as if tissue had been torn, bones split.

Shoving his face close to Violet's, he sprayed her with spittle as he spoke: 'Our mother had *one* cat, just one, she liked things clean and neat, she wouldn't approve of this mess, this stinking brood of yours.'

'Who cares,' Violet said in a tone of voice that was at once disinterested and mocking. 'She's dead.'

Grabbing her by both arms, he lifted her off her feet. The chair behind her fell over as he swung her away from it. He slammed her up against the pantry door so hard that the sound was like an explosion, rattling the loose kitchen windows and some dirty silverware on a nearby counter. He had the satisfaction of seeing her face contort with pain and her eyes roll back in her head as she nearly passed out from the blow. If he had smashed her against the door any harder, her spine might have cracked. He dug his fingers cruelly into the pale flesh of her upper arms, pulled her away from the door, and slammed her into it again, though not as hard as before, just making the point that it *might* have been as hard, that it could be as hard the next time if she displeased him.

Her head had fallen forward, for she was teetering on the edge of consciousness. Effortlessly, he held her against the door, with her feet eight inches off the floor, as if she weighed nothing at all, thereby forcing her to consider his incredible strength. He waited for her to come around.

She was having difficulty getting her breath, and when at last she stopped gasping and raised her head to face him, he expected to see a different Violet. He had never struck her before. A fateful line had been crossed, one over which he never expected to trespass. With his promise to his mother in mind, he had kept his sisters safe from the often dangerous world outside, provided them with food, kept them warm in cold weather and cool in the heat, dry when it rained, but year after year he had performed his brotherly duties with growing frustration, appalled by their increasingly shameless and mysterious behavior. Now he realized that disciplining them was a natural part of protecting them; up in Heaven, his mother had probably despaired of his ever realizing the need for discipline. Thanks to his rage, he had stumbled upon enlightenment. It felt good to hurt Violet a little, just enough to bring her to her senses and to prevent her from spiraling further into the decadence and animal sensuality to which she had surrendered herself. He knew he was right to punish her. He waited eagerly for her to lift her head and face him, for he knew that they had entered a new relationship and that the awareness of these profound changes would be evident in her eyes.

At last, breathing somewhat normally, she raised her head and met Candy's gaze. To his surprise, none of his own enlightenment had been visited upon his sister. Her white-blond hair had fallen across her face, and she stared through it, like a jungle animal peering through its wind-tossed mane. In her icy blue eyes, he perceived something stranger and more primitive than anything he had seen there before. A gleeful wildness. Indefinable hungers. Need. Though she had been hurt when he had thrown her against the pantry door, a smile played on her full lips again. She opened her mouth, and he felt her hot breath against his face as she said, 'You're strong. Even the cats like the feel of your strong hands on me . . . and so does Verbina.'

He became aware of her long bare legs. The flimsiness of her panties. The way her red T-shirt had pulled up to expose her flat belly. The swell of her full breasts, which seemed even fuller than they were because of the leanness of the rest of her. The sharp outlines of her nipples against the material of the shirt. The smoothness of her skin. Her smell.

Revulsion burst through him like pus from a secret inner abscess, and he let go of her. Turning, he saw that the cats were looking at him. Worse, they were still lying where they had been when he had pulled Violet from her chair, as if they had not been frightened by his outrage even briefly. He knew their equanimity meant that Violet had not been frightened, either, and that her erotic response to his fury – and her mocking smile – was not in the least feigned.

Verbina was slumped in her chair, her head bowed, for she was no more able to look at him directly now than she had ever been. But she was grinning, and her left hand was between her legs, her long fingers tracing lazy circles on the thin material of her panties, under which lay the dark cleft of her sex. He needed no more proof that some of Violet's sick desire had communicated itself to Verbina, and he turned away from her too.

He tried to leave the room quickly, but without looking as if he was fleeing from them.

In his scented bedroom, safely among his mother's belongings, Candy locked the door. He was not sure why he felt safer with the lock engaged, though he was certain it was not because he feared his sisters. There was nothing about them to fear. They were to be pitied.

For a while he sat in Roselle's rocker, remembering the times, as a child, when he'd curled in her lap and contentedly sucked blood from a self-inflicted wound in her thumb or in the meaty part of her palm. Once, but unfortunately only once, she had made a half-inch incision in one of her breasts and held him to her bosom while he drank her blood from the same flesh where other mothers gave, and other children received, the milk of maternity.

He had been five years old that night when, in this very room and in this chair, he tasted the blood of her breast. Frank, seven years old then, had been asleep in the room at the end of the hall, and the twins, who'd only recently reached their first birthday, were asleep in a crib in the room across from their mother's. Being alone with her when all the others slept – oh, how unique and treasured that made him feel, especially since she was sharing with him the rich liquid of her arteries and veins, which she never offered to his siblings; it was a sacred communion, dispensed and received, that remained their secret.

He recalled being in something of a swoon that night, not merely because of the heavy taste of her rich blood and the unbounded love that was represented by the gift of it, but because of the metronomic rocking of the chair and the lulling rhythms of her voice. As he sucked, she smoothed his hair away from his brow and spoke to him of God's intricate plan for the world. She explained, as she had done many times before, that God condoned the use of violence when it was committed in the defense of those who were good and righteous. She told him how God had created men who thrived on blood, so they might be used as the earthly instruments of God's vengeance on behalf of the righteous. Theirs was a righteous family, she said, and God had sent Candy to them to be their protector. None of this was new. But though his mother had spoken of these things many times during their secret communions, Candy never grew tired of hearing them again. Children often relish the retelling of a favorite story. And as with certain particularly magical tales, this story somehow did not become more familiar with retelling but curiously more mysterious and appealing.

That night in his fifth year, however, the story took a new turn. The time had come, his mother said, for him to apply the truly amazing talents he had been given, and embark upon the mission for which God had created him. He had begun to exhibit his phenomenal talents when he was three, the same age at which Frank's far more meager gifts had become evident. His telekinetic abilities – primarily his talent for telekinetic transportation of his own body – particularly enchanted Roselle, and she quickly saw the potential. They would never want for money as long as he could teleport at night into places where cash and valuables were locked away: bank vaults; the jewelry-rich, walk-in safes in Beverly Hills mansions. And if he could materialize within the homes of the Pollard family's enemies, while they slept, vengeance could be taken without fear of discovery or reprisal.

'There's a man named Salfont,' his mother cooed to him as he took his nourishment from her wounded breast. 'He's a lawyer, one of those jackals who prey on upstanding folks, nothing good about him at all, not that one. He handled my father's estate – that's your dear grandpa, little Candy – probated the will, charged too much, way too much, he was greedy. They're all greedy, those lawyers.'

The quiet, gentle tone in which she spoke was at odds with the anger she was expressing, but that contradiction added to the sweet, hypnotic quality of her message.

'I've tried for years to get part of the fee returned to me, like I deserve. I've gone to other lawyers, but they all say his fee was reasonable, they all stick up for each other, they're alike, peas in a pod, rotten little peas in rotten little pods. Took him to court, but judges are nothing except lawyers in black robes, they make me sick, the greedy lot of them. I've worried at this for years, little Candy, can't get it out of my mind. That Donald Salfont, living in his big house in Montecito, overcharging people, overcharging *me*, he ought to have to pay for that. Don't you think so, little Candy? Don't you think he ought to pay?'

He was five years old and not yet big for his age, as he would be from the time he was nine or ten. Even if he could teleport into Salfont's bedroom, the advantage of surprise might not be sufficient to ensure success. If either Salfont or his wife happened to be awake when Candy arrived, or if the first slash of the knife failed to kill the lawyer and brought him awake in a defensive panic, Candy would not be able to overpower him. He wouldn't be in danger of getting caught or harmed, for he could teleport home in a wink; but he would risk being recognized. Police would believe a man like Salfont, even as regards such a fantastic accusation as murder lodged against a five-year-old boy. They would visit the Pollard place, asking questions, poking around, and God knew what they might find or come to suspect.

'So you can't kill him, though he deserves it,' Roselle whispered as she rocked her favorite child. She stared down intently into his eyes as he looked up from her exposed breast. 'Instead, what you have to do is take something from him as vengeance for the money he took from me, something precious to him. There's a new baby in the Salfont house. I read about it in the paper a few months ago, a little girl baby they called Rebekah Elizabeth. What kind of name is that for a girl, I ask you? Sounds high-falutin' to me, the kind of name a fancy lawyer and his wife give a baby 'cause they think them and theirs is better than other people. Elizabeth is a queen's name, you see, and you just look up what Rebekah is in the Bible, see if they don't think way too much of themselves and their little brat. Rebekah . . . she's almost six months now, they've had her long enough to miss her when she's gone, miss her bad. I'll drive you past their house tomorrow, my precious little Candy boy, let you see where it is, and tomorrow night you'll go there and visit the Lord's vengeance on them, my vengeance. They'll say a rat got into the room, or something of the sort, and they'll blame themselves until the day they're dead too.'

The throat of Rebekah Salfont had been tender, her blood salty. Candy enjoyed the adventure of it, the thrill of entering the house of strangers without their permission or knowledge. Killing the girl while grownups slept in the adjoining room, unaware, filled him with a sense of power. He was just a boy, yet he slipped past their defenses and struck a blow for his mother, which in a way made him the man of the Pollard house. That heady feeling added an element of glory to the excitement of the kill.

His mother's requests for vengeance were thereafter irresistible.

For the first few years of his mission, infants and very young children were his only prey. Sometimes, in order not to present a pattern to the police, he did not bite them but disposed of them in other ways, and occasionally he took hold of them and teleported out of the house with them, so no body was ever found.

Even so, if Roselle's enemies had all been from in and around Santa Barbara, the pattern could not have been hidden. But often she required vengeance against people in far places, about whom she read in newspapers and magazines.

He remembered, in particular, a family in New York State, who won millions of dollars in the lottery. His mother had felt that their good fortune had been at the expense of the Pollard family, and that they were too greedy to be permitted to live. Candy had been fourteen at the time, and he had not understood his mother's reasoning – but he had not questioned it, either. She was the only source of truth to him, and the thought of disobedience never crossed his mind. He had killed all five members of that family in New York, then burned their house to the ground with their bodies in it.

His mother's thirst for vengeance followed a predictable cycle. Immediately after Candy killed someone for her, she was happy, filled with plans for the future; she would bake special treats for him and sing melodically while she worked in the kitchen, and she would begin a new quilt or an elaborate needle-point project. But over the next four weeks her happiness would dim like a light bulb on a rheostat, and almost one month to the day after the killing, having lost interest in baking and crafts, she would begin to talk about other people who had wronged her and, by extension, the Pollard family. Within two to four more weeks, she would have settled on a target, and Candy would be dispatched to fulfill his mission. Consequently, he killed on only six or seven occasions each year.

That frequency satisfied Roselle, but the older Candy got, the less it satisfied him. He had not merely acquired a thirst for blood but a craving that occasion-ally overwhelmed him. The thrill of the hunt also intoxicated him, and he longed for it as an alcoholic longed for the bottle. Not least of all, the mindless hostility of the world toward his blessed mother motivated him to kill more often. Sometimes it seemed that virtually everyone was against her, scheming to harm her physically or to take money that was rightfully hers. She had no dearth of enemies. He remembered days when fear oppressed her; then at her direction all the blinds and drapes were drawn, the doors locked and sometimes even barricaded with chairs and other furniture, against the onslaught of adver-saries who never came but who *might* have. On those bad days she became despondent and told him that so many people were out to get her that even he could not protect her forever. When he begged her to turn him loose, she refused and only said, 'It's hopeless.'

Then, as now, he tried to supplement the approved murders with his forays into the canyons in search of small animals. But those blood feasts, rich as they sometimes were, never quenched his thirst as thoroughly as when the vessel was human.

Saddened by too many memories, Candy rose from the rocking chair and nervously paced the room. The blind was up, and he glanced with increasing interest at the night beyond the window.

After failing to catch Frank and the stranger who had teleported into the backyard with him, after the confrontation with Violet had taken that unexpec-ted turn and left him with undissipated rage, he was smoldering, hot to kill, but in need of a target. With no enemy of the family in sight, he would have to slaughter either innocent people or the small creatures that lived in the canyons. The problem was – he dreaded evoking his sainted mother's disappointment, up there in Heaven, yet he had no appetite for the thin blood of timid beasts.

His frustration and need built by the minute. He knew he was going to do something he would later regret, something that would make Roselle turn her face from him for a time.

Then, just when he felt he might explode, he was saved by the intrusion of a genuine enemy.

A hand touched the back of his head.

He whirled around, feeling the hand withdraw as he turned.

It had been a phantom hand. No one was there.

But he knew it was the same presence that he had sensed in the canyon last night. Someone out there, not of the Pollard family, had psychic ability of his own, and the very fact that Roselle was not his mother made him an enemy to be found and eliminated. The same person had visited Candy several times earlier in the afternoon, reaching out tentatively, probing at him but not making full contact.

Candy returned to the rocking chair. If a real enemy was going to put in an appearance, it would be worth waiting for him.

A few minutes later, he felt the touch again. Light, hesitant, quickly withdrawn.

He smiled. He started rocking. He even hummed softly – one of his mother's favorite songs.

Banking the coals of rage eventually made them burn brighter. By the time the shy visitor grew bolder, the fire would be white hot, and the flames would consume him.

• 49 •

At ten minutes to seven, the doorbell rang. Felina Karaghiosis did not hear it, of course. But each room of the house had a small red signal lamp in one corner or another, and she could not miss the flashing light that was activated by the bell.

She went into the foyer and looked through the sidelight next to the front door. When she saw Alice Kasper, a neighbor from three doors down the street, she switched off the dead bolt, removed the security chain from its slot, and let her in.

'Hi, kid. How ya doin'?'

I like your hair, Felina signed.

'Do ya really? Just got it cut, and the girl said did I want the same old one, or did I want to catch up with the times, and I thought what the hell. I'm not too old to be sexy, do ya think?'

Alice was only thirty-three, five years older than Felina. She had exchanged her trademark blond curls for a more modern cut that would require a new source of income just to pay for all the mousse she was going to use, but she looked great.

Come in. Want a drink?

'I'd love a drink, kid, and right now I could use six of 'em, but I gotta say no. My in-laws came over, and we're about to either play cards with 'em or shoot 'em – it depends on their attitude.'

Of all the people Felina knew in her day-to-day life, Alice was the only one, other than Clint, who understood sign language. Given the fact that most people harbored a prejudice against the deaf, to which they could not admit but on which they acted, Alice was her only girlfriend. But Felina happily would have given up their friendship if Mark Kasper – Alice's son, for whom she had learned sign language – had not been born deaf.

'Why I came over, we got a call from Clint, asking me to tell ya he's not on his way home yet, but he expects to get here maybe by eight. Since when does he work so late?'

They've got a big case. That always means some overtime.

'He's going to take ya out to dinner, and says to tell ya it's been an incredible day. I guess that's about the case, huh? Must be fascinating, married to a detective. And he's sweet, too. You're lucky, kid.'

Yes. But so is he.

Alice laughed. 'Right on! And if he comes home this late another night, don't settle for dinner. Make him buy ya a diamond.'

Felina thought of the red diamond he had brought home yesterday, and she wished she could tell Alice about it. But Dakota & Dakota business, especially concerning an ongoing case in which the client was in jeopardy, was as sacred in their house as the privacies of the marriage bed.

'Saturday, our place, six-thirty? Jack'll cook up a mess of his chili, and we'll play pinochle and eat chili and drink beer and fart till we pass out. Okay?'

Yes.

'And tell Clint, it's okay – we won't expect him to talk.'

Felina laughed, then signed: *He's getting better.*

'That's 'cause you're civilizing him, kid.'

They hugged again, and Alice left.

Felina closed the door, looked at her wristwatch, and saw that it was seven o'clock. She had only an hour to get ready for dinner, and she wanted to look especially good for Clint, not because this was a special occasion, but because she *always* wanted to look good for him. She headed for the bedroom, then realized that only the automatic lock was engaged on the front door. She returned to the foyer, twisted the thumbscrew that slid the dead bolt home, and slipped the security chain in place.

Clint worried about her too much. If he came home and found that she hadn't remembered the dead bolt, he'd age a year in a minute, right before her eyes.

· 50 ·

After being off duty all day, Hal Yamataka responded to a call from Clint and came to the offices at 6:35 Tuesday night, to stand a watch in case Frank returned after the rest of them had left. Clint met him in the reception lounge and briefed him there over a cup of coffee. He had to be brought up to date on what had happened during his absence, and after he heard what had gone down, he again wistfully considered a career in gardening.

Nearly everyone in his family either had a gardening business or owned a little nursery, and all of them did well, most of them better than what Hal made working for Dakota & Dakota, some of them a great deal better. His folks, his three brothers, and various well-meaning uncles tried repeatedly to persuade him that he should work for them or come into business with them, but he resisted. It was not that he had anything against running a nursery, selling gardening supplies, landscape planning, tree pruning, or even gardening itself. But in southern California the term 'Japanese gardener' was a cliché, not a career, and he couldn't abide the thought of being any kind of stereotype.

He had been a heavy reader of adventure and suspense novels all his life, and he yearned to be a character like one of those he read about, especially a character worthy of being a lead in a John D. MacDonald novel, because John D's lead characters were as rich in insight as they were in courage, every bit as sensitive as they were tough. In his heart Hal knew that his work at Dakota & Dakota was usually as mundane as the daily grind of a gardener, and that the opportunities for heroism in the security industry were far fewer than they appeared to be to outsiders. But selling a bag of mulch or a can of Spectricide or a flat of marigolds, you couldn't kid yourself that you were a romantic figure or had any chance of being one. And, after all, self-image was often the better part of reality.

'If Frank shows up here,' Hal said, 'what do I do with him?'

'Pack him in a car and take him to Bobby and Julie.'

'You mean their house?'

'No. Santa Barbara. They're driving up there tonight, staying at the Red Lion Inn, so tomorrow they can start digging into the Pollard family's background.'

Frowning, Hal leaned forward on the reception-lounge sofa. 'Thought you said they don't figure ever to see Frank again.'

'Bobby says he thinks Frank is coming apart, won't last through this latest series of travels. That's just his feeling.'

'So then who's their client?'

'Until he fires them, Frank is.'

'Sounds iffy to me. Be straight with me, Clint. What's really got them so committed to this one, especially considering how crazy-dangerous it seems to get, hour by hour?'

'They like Frank. *I* like Frank.'

'I said be straight.'

Clint sighed. 'Damned if I know. Bobby came back here spooked out of his mind. But he won't let go of it. You'd think they'd pull in their horns, at least until Frank shows up again, if he does. This brother of his, this Candy, he sounds like the devil himself, too much for anyone to handle. Bobby and Julie are stubborn sometimes, but they're not stupid, and I'd expect them to let go of this, now that they've seen it's a job big enough for God, not a private detective. But here we are.'

<hr/>

Bobby and Julie huddled with Lee Chen at the desk, while he shared with them the information he had thus far obtained.

'The money might be stolen, but it's spendable,' Lee said. 'I can't find those serial numbers on any currency hot sheets – federal, state, or local.'

Bobby had already thought of several sources from which Frank might have obtained the six hundred thousand now in the office safe. 'Find a business with a high cash flow, where they don't always get to a bank with the receipts at the end of the day, and you've got a potential target. Say it's a supermarket, stays open till midnight, and it's not a good idea for a manager to tote a lot of cash to a bank for automatic deposit, so there's a safe in the market. After the place closes, you teleport inside, if you're Frank, and use whatever other powers you have to open that safe, put the day's receipts in a grocery bag, and vanish. You're not going to find big chunks of cash, a couple hundred thousand at a time, but you hit three or four markets in an hour, and you've got your haul.'

Evidently Julie had been pondering the same question, for she said, 'Casinos. They all have accounting rooms you can find on the blueprints, the ones the IRS gets into with a little effort. But they've got hidden rooms, too, where the skim goes. Like big walk-in safes. Fort Knox would envy them. You use whatever minor psychic abilities you have to figure the location of one of those hidden rooms, teleport in when it's deserted, and just take what you want.'

'Frank lived in Vegas for a while,' Bobby said. 'Remember, I told you about the vacant lot he took me to, where he'd had a house.'

'He wouldn't be limited to Vegas,' Julie said. 'Reno, Tahoe, Atlantic City, the Caribbean, Macao, France, England, Monte Carlo – anywhere there's big-time gambling.'

This talk of easy access to unlimited amounts of cash excited Bobby, though he was not sure why. After all, it was Frank who could teleport, not him, and he was ninety-five percent sure they were never going to see Frank again.

Spreading a sheaf of printouts across the desktop, Lee Chen said, 'The money's the least interesting thing. You remember, you wanted me to find out if the cops are on to Mr Blue?'

'Candy,' Bobby said. 'We have a name for him now.'

Lee scowled. 'I liked Mr Blue better. It had more style.'

Entering the room, Hal Yamataka said, 'I don't think I trust the style judgment of a guy who wears red sneakers and socks.'

Lee shook his head. 'We Chinese spend thousands of years working up an intimidating image for all Asians, so we can keep these hapless Westerners off balance, and you Japanese blow it all by making those Godzilla movies. You can't be inscrutable and make Godzilla movies.'

'Yeah? You show me *anybody* who understands a Godzilla movie after the first one.'

They made an interesting pair, these two: one slender, modish, with delicate features, an enthusiastic child of the silicon age; the other squat, broad, with a face as blunt as a hammer, a guy who was about as high-tech as a rock.

But to Bobby the most interesting thing was that, until this moment, he had never thought about the fact that a disproportionately large percentage of Dakota & Dakota's small staff was Asian-American. There were two more – Nguyen Tuan Phu and Jamie Quang, both Vietnamese. Four out of eleven people. Though he and Hal once in a while made East-West jokes, Bobby never thought of Lee and Hal and Nguyen and Jamie as composing any subset of employees; they were just themselves, as different from one another as apples are different from pears and oranges and peaches. But Bobby realized that this predilection for Asian-American co-workers revealed something about himself, something more than just an obvious and admirable racial blindness, but he could not figure out what it was.

Hal said, 'And *nothing* gets more inscrutable than the whole concept of Mothra. By the way, Bobby, Clint's gone home to Felina. We should all be so lucky.'

'Lee was telling us about Mr Blue,' Julie said.

'Candy,' Bobby said.

Indicating the data he had extracted from various police records nationwide, Lee said, 'Most police agencies began to be computerized and interlinked only about nine years ago – in any sophisticated way, that is. So that's all the further back a lot of electronically accessible files go. But during that time, there have been seventy-eight brutal murders, in nine states, that have enough similarities to raise the possibility of a single perp. Just the possibility, mind you. But FBI got interested enough last year to put a three-man team on it, one in the office and two in the field, to coordinate local and state investigations.'

'Three men?' Hal said. 'Doesn't sound like high priority.'

'The Bureau's always been overextended,' Julie said. 'And over the last thirty years, since it's been unfashionable for judges to hand out long criminal sentences, the bad guys outnumber them worse than ever. Three men, full time – that's a serious commitment at this stage.'

Extracting a printout from the pile on the desk, Lee summarized the essential data on it. 'All of the killings have these points in common. First – the victims were all bitten, most on the throat, but virtually no part of the body is sacred to this guy. Second – many of them were beaten, suffered head injuries. But loss of blood, from the bites – usually the jugular vein and carotid artery in the throat – was a substantial contributing factor to the death in virtually every instance, regardless of other injuries.'

'On top of everything else, the guy's a vampire?' Hal asked.

Taking the question seriously – as, indeed, they had to consider every possibility in this bizarre case, regardless of how outlandish it seemed – Julie said, 'Not a vampire in the supernatural sense. From what we've learned, the Pollard family is for some reason generously gifted. You know that magician on TV, the Amazing Randi, who offers to pay a hundred thousand bucks to anyone who proves they have psychic power? This Pollard clan would bankrupt his ass. But that doesn't mean there's anything supernatural about them. They're not demons, or possessed, or the children of the devil – nothing like that.'

'It's just some extra bit of genetic material,' Bobby said.

'Exactly. If Candy acts like a vampire, biting people in the throat, that's just a manifestation of psychological illness,' Julie said. 'It doesn't mean he's one of the living dead.'

Bobby vividly remembered the blond giant charging him and Frank on the rainswept black beach at Punaluu. The guy was as formidable as a locomotive. If Bobby had a choice of going up against either Candy Pollard or Dracula, he might choose the undead Count. Nothing as simple as a clove of garlic, a crucifix, or a well-placed wooden stake would effectively deter Frank's brother.

Lee said, 'Another similarity. In those instances where victims didn't leave doors or windows unlocked, there was no indication of how the killer gained entrance. And in many instances police found doors dead bolted from the inside, windows locked from the inside, as if the murderer had gone up the chimney when he was done.'

'Seventy-eight,' Julie said, and shivered.

Lee dropped the paper onto the desk. 'They figure there're more, maybe a lot more, because sometimes this guy has attempted to cover his trail – the bite marks – by further mutilating or even burning the bodies. Though the cops weren't fooled in *these* cases, you can figure they were fooled in others. So the count's higher than seventy-eight, and that's just the last nine years.'

'Good job, Lee,' Julie said, and Bobby seconded that.

'I'm not done yet,' Lee said. 'I'm going to order in a pizza, do some more digging.'

'You've been here more than ten hours today,' Bobby said. 'That's already above and beyond the call. Got to have downtime, Lee.'

'If you believe, as I do, that time is subjective, then you've got an infinite supply. Later, at home, I'll stretch a few hours into a couple of weeks and return tomorrow quite rested.'

Hal Yamataka shook his head and sighed. 'Hate to admit it, Lee, but you're damned good at this mysterious oriental crap.'

Lee smiled enigmatically. 'Thank you.'

⸻

After Bobby and Julie went home to pack an overnight bag for the trip to Santa Barbara, and after Lee returned to the computer room, Hal settled on the sofa in the bosses' office, slipped off his shoes, and put his feet up on the coffee table. He still had the paperback of *The Last One Left*, which he'd read twice before, and which he had started to reread last night in the hospital. If Bobby was right when he said they might never see Frank again, Hal was in for an uneventful evening and would probably get half the book read.

Maybe his happiness at Dakota & Dakota had nothing to do with the prospect of excitement, avoiding a stereotypical job as a gardener, and having the admittedly slim chance to be a hero. Maybe the thing that most affected his career decision was the realization that he simply could not mow a lawn or trim a hedge or plant fifty flats of flowers and read a book at the same time.

⸻

Derek sat in his chair. Pointed the raygun at the TV and made it be on. He said, 'You don't want to watch news?'

'No,' Thomas said. He was on his bed, propped up with pillows, looking at the night being dark outside the window.

'Good. Me neither.' Derek pushed buttons on the raygun. A new picture came on the screen. 'You don't want to watch a game show?'

'No.' All Thomas wanted to do was snoop on the Bad Thing.

'Good.' Derek pushed buttons, and the invisible rays made the screen show a new picture. 'You don't want to watch the Three Stooges pretending to be funny?'

'No.'

'What you want to watch?'

'Don't matter. Whatever you want to watch.'

'Really?'

'Whatever you want to watch,' Thomas repeated.

'Gee, that's nice.' He made lots of pictures on the screen until he found a space movie where spacemen in spacesuits were poking around in some spooky place. Derek made a happy sigh and said, 'This is good. I like their hats.'

'Helmets,' Thomas said. 'Space helmets.'

'I wish I had a hat like that.'

When he reached out into the big dark again, Thomas decided not to picture a mind-string unraveling toward the Bad Thing. Instead he pictured a raygun, shooting some invisible rays. Boy, did that work better! *Wham*, he was right there with the Bad Thing in a flash, and he felt it stronger, too, so strong he got scared and clicked off the raygun and got all of himself back into his room with the rest of himself right away.

'They got telephones in their hats,' Derek said. 'See, they're talking through their hats.'

On the TV, the spacemen were in an even spookier place, poking around, which was one of the things spacemen did the most, even though something ugly-nasty was usually in those spooky places just waiting for them. Spacemen never learned.

Thomas looked away from the screen.

At the window.

The dark.

Bobby was scared for Julie. Bobby knew stuff Thomas didn't know. If Bobby was scared for Julie, Thomas had to be brave and do What Was Right.

The raygun idea worked such a lot better it scared him, but he figured it was really good because he could easier snoop on the Bad Thing. He could get to the Bad Thing faster and get away from it faster, too, so he could snoop on it more often and not be scared about it maybe grabbing the mind-string and coming back to The Home with him. Grabbing an invisible raygun ray was harder, even for a thing as fast and smart and mean as the Bad Thing.

So he pictured pushing buttons on a raygun again, and a part of him went through the dark – *wham!* – and to the Bad Thing right away. He felt how mad the Bad Thing was, madder than ever, and thinking lots of thoughts about blood that made Thomas half sick. Thomas wanted to come right back to The Home. The Bad Thing felt him, you could tell. He didn't like the Bad Thing feeling him, knowing he was there with it, but he stayed just a couple clock ticks longer, trying to see any thoughts about Julie in all those thoughts about blood. If the Bad Thing had thoughts about Julie, Thomas would TV a warning right away to Bobby. He was happy he couldn't find Julie in the Bad Thing's mind, and he quick raygunned back to The Home.

'Where you think I could get a hat like that?' Derek asked.

'Helmet.'

'Even has a light on it, see?'

Rising up a little from this pillows, Thomas said, 'You know what kind of a story this is?'

Derek shook his head. 'What kind of story?'

'It's the kind where any second something ugly-nasty jumps up and sucks off a spacemen's face or maybe crawls in his mouth and down his belly and makes a nest in there.'

Derek made a disgusted face. 'Yuck. I don't like that kind of stories.'

'I know,' Thomas said. 'That's why I warned you.'

While Derek made a lot of different pictures come on the screen, one quick after the other, to get far away from the spaceman who was going to get his face sucked off, Thomas tried to think how long he should wait before he snooped on the Bad Thing again. Bobby was real worried, you could tell, even if he tried to hide it, and Bobby was not a Dumb Person, so it was a good idea to check on the Bad Thing pretty regular, in case maybe it all of a sudden thought about Julie and got up and went after her.

'You want to watch this?' Derek asked.

On the screen was a picture of this guy in a hockey mask with a big knife in his hand, going quiet-like across a room where a girl was asleep in a bed.

'Better raygun up another picture,' Thomas said.

Because the rush hour was past, because Julie knew all the best shortcuts, but mainly because she was not in a mood to be cautious or respect the traffic laws, they made great time from the office to their home on the east end of Orange.

On the way Bobby told her about the Calcutta roach that had been part of his shoe when he and Frank had arrived on that red bridge in the garden in Kyoto. 'But when we popped to Mount Fuji, my shoe was okay, the roach was gone.'

She slowed at an intersection, but she was the only traffic in sight, so she didn't obey the four-way stop. 'Why didn't you tell me about this at the office?'

'Wasn't time for every detail.'

'What do you think happened to the roach?'

'I don't know. That's what bothers me.'

They were on Newport Avenue, just past Crawford Canyon. Sodium-vapor streetlamps cast a queer light on the roadway.

Atop the steep hills to the left, several huge English Tudor and French houses, blazing like giant luxury liners, looked wildly out of place, partly because the insanely high value of such upscale real estate ensured the construction of immense houses out of proportion to the tiny lots they stood on, but also partly because Tudor and French architectural styles clashed with the semitropical landscape. It was all part of the California circus, some of which he hated, most of which he loved. Those houses never bothered him before, and given the serious problems he and Julie faced, he couldn't figure why they bothered him now. Maybe he was so jumpy that even these minor disharmonies reminded him of the chaos that had almost engulfed him during his travels with Frank.

He said, 'Do you have to drive so fast?'

'Yes,' she said curtly. 'I want to get home, get packed, get to Santa Barbara, learn what we can about the Pollard family, get finished with this whole damn creepy case.'

'If you feel that way, why don't we just drop it here? Frank comes back, we give him his money, his jar of red diamonds, tell him we're sorry, we think he's a prince of a guy, but we're out of it.'

'We can't,' she said.

He chewed on his lower lip, then said, 'I know. But I can't figure why we're compelled to hang in there with this one.'

They crested the hill and speeded north, past the entrance to Rocking Horse Ridge. Their own development was only a couple of streets ahead, on the left. As she finally began to brake for the turn, she glanced at him and said, 'You really don't know why we can't bug out of it?'

'No. You saying you do?'

'I know.'

'Tell me.'

'You'll figure it out eventually.'

'Don't be mysterious. That's not like you.'

She swung the company Toyota into their development, then onto their street. 'I tell you what I think, it'll upset you. You'll deny it, we'll argue, and I don't want to argue with you.'

'Why will we argue?'

She pulled into their driveway, put the car in park, switched off the lights and engine, and turned to him. Her eyes shone in the dark. 'When you understand why we can't let go, you won't like what it says about us, and you'll argue that I'm wrong, that we're just a couple of sweet kids, really. You like to see us as a couple of sweet kids, savvy but basically innocent at the same time, like a young Jimmy Stewart and Donna Reed. I really love you for that, for being such a dreamer about the world and us, and it'll hurt me when you want to argue.'

He almost started to argue with her about whether he would argue with her. Then he stared at her for a moment and finally said, 'I've had this feeling that I'm not facing up to something, that when this is all over and I realize why I was so determined to see this through to the end, my motivations won't be as noble as I think they are now. It's a damn weird feeling. As if I don't really know myself.'

'Maybe we spend all our lives learning to know ourselves. And maybe we never really do – completely.'

She kissed him lightly, quickly, and got out of the car.

As he followed her up the sidewalk to the front door, he glanced at the sky. The clarity of the day had been short-lived. A pall of clouds concealed the moon and stars. The sky was very dark, and he was gripped by the curious certainty that a great and terrible weight was falling toward them, black against the black heavens and therefore invisible, but falling fast, faster . . .

• 51 •

Candy kept a chokehold on his fury, which strained like an attack dog trying to break its leash.

He rocked and rocked, and gradually the shy visitor grew bolder. Repeatedly he felt the invisible hand on his head. Initially it lay upon him as lightly as an empty silk glove, and it stayed only briefly before flitting away. But as he pretended to be disinterested in both the hand and the person to whom it belonged, the visitor grew more daring, the hand heavier and less nervous.

Though Candy made no effort to probe at the mind of the intruder, for fear of scaring him away, some of the stranger's thoughts came to him nonetheless. He did not think the visitor was aware that images and words from his own mind were slipping into Candy's; they were just leaking out of him as if they were trickles of water seeping from pinsize holes in a rusty bucket.

The name 'Julie' came several times. And once an image floated along with the name – an attractive woman with brown hair and dark eyes. Candy wasn't sure if it was the visitor's face or the face of someone the visitor knew – or even if it was the face of anyone who really existed. There were aspects that made it seem unreal: a pale light radiated from it, and the features were so kind and serene that it looked like the holy countenance of a saint in an illustrated Bible.

The word 'flutterby' leaked out of the visitor's mind more than once, sometimes with other words, like 'remember the flutterby' or 'don't be a flutterby.' And each time that word flitted through his mind, the visitor quickly withdrew.

But he kept coming back. Because Candy did nothing to make him feel unwelcome.

Candy rocked and rocked. The chair made a soft sound: *creak . . . creak . . . creak . . . creak.*

He waited.

He kept an open mind.

   . . . *creak* . . . *creak* . . . *creak* . . .

Twice the name 'Bobby' seeped from the visitor's mind, and the second time a fuzzy image of a face was linked to it, another very kind face. It was idealized, like Julie's face. Recognition stirred in Candy, but Bobby's visage was not as clear or detailed as Julie's, and Candy did not want to concentrate on it because the visitor might notice his interest and be frightened off.

During his long and patient courtship of the shy intruder, many other words and images came to Candy, but he didn't know what to make of them:

—men in spacesuits—

—'Bad Thing'—

—a guy in a hockey mask—

—'The Home'—

—'Dumb People'—

—a bathrobe, a half-eaten Hershey's bar, and a sudden frantic thought: *Draw Bugs, no good, Draw Bugs, got to Be Neat*—

More than ten minutes passed without contact, and Candy started to worry that the intruder had gone away for good. But suddenly he was back. This time the contact was strong, more intimate than ever.

When Candy sensed that the visitor was more confident, he knew the time had come to act. He pictured his mind as a steel trap, the visitor as an inquisitive mouse, and he pictured the trap springing, the bar pinning the visitor to the killplate.

Shocked, the visitor tried to pull away. Candy held him and pushed across the telepathic bridge between them, trying to storm his adversary's mind to find out who he was, where he was, and what he wanted.

Candy had no telepathic power of his own, nothing to equal even the weak telepathic gifts of the intruder; he had never read anyone's mind before, and he did not know how to go about it. As it turned out, he did not need to do anything except open himself and receive what the visitor gave him. Thomas was his name, and he was terrified of Candy, of having Done Something Really Dumb, and of putting Julie in danger; that trinity of terrors shattered his mental defenses and caused him to disgorge a flood of information.

In fact, there was too much information for Candy to make sense of it, a babble of words and images. He tried desperately to sort through it for clues to Thomas's identity and location.

Dumb People, Cielo Vista, The Home, everybody here has bad eye cues, Care Home, good food, TV, The Best Place For Us, Cielo Vista, the aides are nice, we watch the hummingbirds, the world is bad out there, too bad for us out there, Cielo Vista Care Home . . .

With some astonishment, Candy realized that the visitor was someone with a subnormal intellect – he even picked up the term 'Down's syndrome' – and he was afraid that he was not going to be able to sort enough meaningful thoughts from the babble to get a fix on Thomas's location. Depending on the size of his IQ, Thomas might not know where Cielo Vista Care Home was, even though he apparently lived there.

Then a series of images spun out of Thomas's mind, a well-linked chain of serial memories that still caused him some emotional pain: the trip to Cielo Vista in a car with Julie and Bobby, on the day they first checked him into the place.

This was different from most of Thomas's other thoughts and memories, in that it was richly detailed and so clearly retained that it unreeled like a length of motion-picture film, giving Candy all he needed to know. He saw the highways over which they had driven that day, saw the route markers flashing past the car window, saw every landmark at every turn, all of which Thomas had struggled mightily to memorize because all through the trip he kept thinking, *If I don't like it there, if people are mean there, if it's too scary there, if it's too much being alone there, I got to know how I find the way back to Bobby and Julie anytime I want, remember this, remember all of this, turn there at the 7-11, right there at the 7-11, don't forget that 7-11, and now go past those three palm trees. What if they don't come visit me? No, that's a bad thing to think, they love me, they'll come. But what if they don't? Look there, remember that house, you go past that house, remember that house with the blue roof—*

Candy got it all, as precise a fix as he could have obtained from a geographer who would have spoken precisely in degrees and minutes of longitude and latitude. It was more than he needed to know to make use of his gift. He opened the trap and let Thomas go.

He got up from the rocker.

He pictured Cielo Vista Care Home as it appeared so exquisitely detailed in Thomas's memory.

He pictured Thomas's room on the first floor of the north wing, at the northwest corner.

Darkness, billions of hot sparks spinning in the void, velocity.

———

Because Julie was in a let's-move-and-get-it-done mood, they had stopped at the house only fifteen minutes, long enough to throw toiletries and a change of clothes in an overnight bag. At McDonald's, on Chapman Avenue in Orange, she swung by the drive-through window and got dinner to eat on the way: Big Macs, fries, diet colas. Before they reached the Costa Mesa Freeway, while Bobby was still divvying up the extra packets of mustard and opening the containers that held the Big Macs, Julie had clipped the radar detector to the rearview mirror, plugged it in the Toyota's cigarette lighter, and switched it on. Bobby had never before eaten fast food at high speed, but he figured they averaged eighty-five miles an hour north on the Costa Mesa to the Riverside Freeway west to the Orange Freeway north, and he was still finishing his french fries when they were only a couple of exits away from the Foothill Freeway east of Los Angeles. Though the rush hour was well past and the traffic unusually light, maintaining that pace required a lot of lane changing and nerve.

He said, 'We keep this up, I'll never have a chance to die from the cholesterol in this Big Mac.'

'Lee says cholesterol doesn't kill us.'

'Is that what he says?'

'He says we live forever, and all cholesterol can do is move us out of this life a little sooner. Same thing must be true if I slip up and roll this sucker a few times.'

'I don't think that'll happen,' he said. 'You're the best driver I've ever seen.'

'Thank you, Bobby. You're the best passenger.'

'The only thing I wonder . . .'

'Yeah?'

'If we don't really die, just move on, and I don't have to worry about anything – why the hell did I bother to get *diet* colas?'

━━━━

Thomas rolled off the bed, onto his feet. 'Derek, go, get out, he's coming!'

Derek was watching a horse talking on TV, and he didn't hear Thomas.

The TV was in the room's middle, between the beds, and by the time Thomas got there and grabbed Derek to make him listen, a funny sound was all around them, not funny ha-ha but funny weird, like somebody whistling but not whistling. There was wind, too, a couple of puffs, not warm or cold either, but it made Thomas shiver when it blew on him.

Pulling Derek off his chair, Thomas said, 'Bad Thing's coming, you get out, you go, like I said before, *now!*'

Derek just made a dumb face at him, then smiled, like he figured Thomas was pretending to be funny the way the Three Stooges pretended. He'd forgot all about the promise he made Thomas. He'd thought the Bad Thing was going to be poached eggs for breakfast, and when poached eggs never showed up on his plate, he figured he was safe, but now he wasn't safe and didn't know it.

More funny-weird whistling. More wind.

Giving Derek a shove, making him get started for the door, Thomas shouted, 'Run!'

The whistling stopped, the wind stopped, and all of a sudden from nowhere the Bad Thing was there. Between them and the open door.

It was a man, like Thomas already knew it was, but it was more than just a man. It was darkness poured in the shape of a man, like a piece of the night itself that came in through the window, and not just because it wore a black T-shirt and black pants but because it was all deep dark inside, you could tell.

Right away Derek was afraid. Nobody needed to tell him this was a Bad Thing, not now when he could see it with his own eyes. But he didn't see it was too late to run, and he went straight at the Bad Thing, like maybe he could push past it, which must have been what he was figuring because even Derek wasn't dumb enough to figure he could knock it down, it was so big.

The Bad Thing grabbed him and lifted him before he had any chance to get around it, lifted him right up off the floor, like he didn't weigh any more than a pillow. Derek screamed, and the Bad Thing slammed him against the wall so hard his scream stopped, and pictures of Derek's mom and dad and brother fell off the wall, not the one where Derek got slammed but another wall all the way around the room from him and over his bed.

The Bad Thing was so fast. That was the worst thing about it, how awful fast it was. It slammed Derek against the wall, Derek's mouth fell open but no more sound came from him, the Bad Thing slammed him again, right away, harder, though the first time was hard enough for anybody, and Derek's eyes went funny. The Bad Thing took him away from the wall and slammed him down on the worktable. The table kind of shivered like it would fall apart, but it didn't. Derek's head was over the table edge, hanging down, so Thomas was looking at his face, upside-down eyes blinking fast, upside-down mouth open real wide but no sound coming out. He looked up from Derek's face, looked right across Derek's body at the Bad Thing, which was looking at him and grinning, like all this was a joke, funny ha-ha, which it wasn't, no way. Then it picked up the scissors on the edge of the worktable, the ones Thomas used to make his picture poems, the ones that almost fell on the floor when it slammed Derek on the table. It made the scissors go into Derek and bring the blood out of him, into poor Derek who wouldn't hurt no one himself, except himself, who wouldn't know *how* to hurt anyone. And the Bad Thing made the scissors go in again and bring more blood out of another place in Derek, and in again, and again. Then blood wasn't coming out of just four places on Derek's chest and belly where the scissors had been made to go in, but out of his mouth and nose too. The Bad Thing lifted Derek off the table, the scissors still sticking out of his front, and threw him like he was just a pillow. No, like he was a garbage bag, threw him the way the Santa Nation Men threw the garbage bags onto their Santa Nation Truck. Derek landed on his bed, on his back on his bed, with the scissors still in him, and didn't move and was gone to the Bad Place, you could tell. And the worst thing was it all happened so fast, faster than Thomas could think what to do to stop it.

Footsteps in the hall, people running.

Thomas yelled for help.

Pete, one of the aides, showed up in the doorway. Pete saw Derek on the bed, scissors in him, blood coming out everywhere, and he got afraid, you could see him get it. He turned to the Bad Thing and said, 'Who—'

The Bad Thing grabbed him by the neck, and Pete made a sound like something was stuck in his throat. He put both his hands on the Bad Thing's arm, which seemed bigger than Pete's two arms together, but he couldn't make the Bad Thing let go. The Bad Thing lifted him by his neck, making his chin turn up and his head bend back, and then took hold of him by the belt, too, and pitched him back out the door, into the hall. Pete hit a nurse who came running up just then, and they both went down on the floor out there in the hall, all tangled up, her screaming.

All of this in a few clock ticks. So *fast*.

The Bad Thing made the door shut with a bang, saw you couldn't lock it, then did the funniest thing of all, funny-weird, funny-scary. He held both his hands out at the door, and this blue light came from his hands the way not-blue came from a flashlight. Sparks flew from hinges and around the knob and all around the door edges. Everything metal smoked and turned all soft, like butter when you put it on mashed potatoes. It was a Fire Door. They said you had to keep your door closed if you ever saw fire in the hall, not try to run in the hall, but keep your door closed and stay put. They called it a Fire Door because fire couldn't get through it, they said, and Thomas always wondered why they didn't call it a Fire Can't Get Through It Door, but he never asked. The thing was, a Fire Door was all metal, so it couldn't burn, but now it melted around the edges, and so did the metal frame, they melted together, it didn't look like you could ever get through that door again.

People started pounding on the door from out there in the hall, tried to make it open, couldn't, and shouted for Thomas and Derek. Thomas knew some voices and who they belonged to, and he wanted to yell for them to help quick because he was in trouble, but he couldn't make a sound any better than poor Derek.

The Bad Thing made the blue light stop. Then it turned and looked at

Thomas. It smiled at him. It didn't have a nice smile. It said, 'Thomas?'

Thomas was surprised he could stand up, he was so scared. He was against the wall by the window, and he thought of maybe making the lock open on the window and push it up and get out, which he knew how to do because of Emergency Drills. But he knew he wasn't fast enough, no way, because the Bad Thing was the fastest he ever saw.

It took a step toward him, and another step. 'Are you Thomas?'

For a while he still couldn't find the way to make sounds. He could just move his mouth and sort of pretend to make sounds. Then while he was doing that, he figured maybe if he told a lie and said he wasn't Thomas, the Bad Thing would believe him and just go away. So when all of a sudden he could make sounds, and then words, he said, 'No. I . . . no . . . not Thomas. He's gone out in the world now, he's got a big eye cue, he's a high-end moron, so they moved him out in the world.'

The Bad Thing laughed. It was a laugh that had no funny in it, the worst Thomas ever heard. The Bad Thing said, 'Who the hell are you, Thomas? Where do you come from? How come a dummy like you can do something *I* can't?'

Thomas didn't answer. He didn't know what to say. He wished the people in the hall would stop pounding on the door and find some other way to get in, because pounding wasn't working. Maybe they could call the cops and tell them to bring the Jaws of Life, yeah, the Jaws of Life, like you saw them use on the TV news when a person was in a wrecked car and couldn't get out. They could use the Jaws of Life to pull open the door the way they pulled at smashed-up cars to get people out of them. He hoped the cops wouldn't say, we're sorry but we can only open car doors with the Jaws of Life, we can't open Care Home doors, because then he was finished for sure.

'You going to answer me, Thomas?' the Bad Thing asked.

Derek's TV chair got turned around in the fight, and now it was between Thomas and the Bad Thing. The Bad Thing held one hand out at the chair, just one, and the blue light went *whoosh*! and the chair blew up in splinters, like all the toothpicks in the world. Thomas threw his hands over his face just fast enough so no splinters went in his eyes. Some went in the backs of his hands and even in his cheeks and chin, and he could feel some of them in his shirt, poking his belly, but he didn't feel any hurt because he was so busy feeling scared.

He took his hands from his eyes right away, because he had to see where the Bad Thing was. Where it was was right on top of him, with soft bits of the chair's insides floating in the air in front of its face.

'Thomas?' it said, and it put one of its big hands on the front of Thomas's neck the way it did Pete a while ago.

Thomas heard words coming from himself, and he couldn't believe he was making them, but he was. Then when he heard what he said to the Bad Thing, he couldn't believe he said it, but he did: 'You're not Being Sociable.'

The Bad Thing grabbed him by the belt and kept hold of him by the neck and lifted him off the floor and pulled him away from the wall, then slammed him into the wall, the same way it did Derek, and, oh, it hurt worse than Thomas ever before hurt in his life.

———

The interior garage door had a dead bolt but no security chain. Pocketing his keys,

Clint entered the kitchen at ten minutes past eight and saw Felina sitting at the table, reading a magazine while she waited for him.

She looked up and smiled, and his heart thumped faster at the sight of her, just like in every sappy love story ever written. He wondered how this could have happened to him. He had been so self-contained before Felina. He had been proud of the fact that he needed no one for intellectual stimulation or emotional support, and that he was therefore not vulnerable to the pains and disappointments of human relationships. Then he had met her. When he caught his breath, he had been as vulnerable as anyone – and glad of it.

She looked terrific in a simple blue dress with a red belt and matching red shoes. She was so strong yet so gentle, so tough yet so fragile.

He went to her, and for a while they stood by the refrigerator, next to the sink, holding each other and kissing, neither of them speaking in either of the ways they could. Clint thought they would have been happy, just then, even if both of them had been deaf and mute, capable of neither lip reading nor sign language, because at that moment what made them happy was the very fact of being together, which no words could adequately express anyway.

Finally he said, 'What a day! Can't wait to tell you all about it. Let me clean up real quick, change clothes. We'll be out of here by eight-thirty, go over to Caprabello's, get a corner booth, some wine, some pasta, some garlic bread—'

Some heartburn.

He laughed because it was true. They both loved Caprabello's, but the food was spicy. They always suffered for the indulgence.

He kissed her again, and she sat down with her magazine, and he went through the dining room and down the hall to the bathroom. While he let the water run in the sink to get it hot, he plugged in his electric razor and began to shave, grinning at himself in the mirror because he was such a damned lucky guy.

The Bad Thing was right in his face, snarling at him, lots of questions, too many for Thomas to think about and answer even if he was sitting in a chair quiet and happy, instead of lifted off the floor and held against the wall with his whole back hurting so bad he had to cry. He kept saying, 'I'm full up, I'm full up.' Always when he said that, people stopped asking him things or telling him things, they let him take time to make his head clear. But the Bad Thing was not like other people. It didn't care if his head was clear, it just wanted answers. Who was Thomas? Who was his mother? Who was his father? Where did he come from? Who was Julie? Who was Bobby? Where was Julie? Where was Bobby?

Then the Bad Thing said, 'Hell, you're just a dummy. You don't *know* the answers, do you? You're just as stupid as you are stupid-looking.'

It pulled Thomas away from the wall, held him off the floor with one hand on his neck, so Thomas couldn't breathe good. It slapped Thomas in the face, hard, and Thomas didn't want to keep crying, but he couldn't stop, he hurt and was scared.

'Why do they let people like you live?' the Bad Thing asked.

It let go of Thomas, and Thomas dropped on the floor. The Bad Thing looked down at him in a mean way that made Thomas angry almost as much as it made him scared. Which was funny-weird, because he almost never was angry. And this was the first time he was ever angry and scared both at the same time. But the Bad Thing was looking at him like he was just a bug or some dirt on the floor that had to be made clean.

'Why don't they kill you people at birth? What're you good for? Why don't they kill you at birth and chop you up and make dog food out of you?'

Thomas had memories of how people, out there in the world, looked at him that way or said mean things, and how Julie always Told Them Off. She said Thomas didn't have to be nice to people like that, said he could tell them they were Being Rude. Now Thomas was angry like he had Every Right To Be, and even if Julie never told him he could be angry about these things, he probably would be angry anyway, because some things you just *knew* were right or wrong.

The Bad Thing kicked him in the leg, and was going to kick him again, you could tell, but a noise was made at the window. Some of the aides were at the window. They broke a little square of glass and reached through, wanting to find the lock.

When the glass made a breaking sound, the Bad Thing turned from Thomas and held its hands up at the window, like it was asking the aides to stop wanting in. But Thomas knew what it was going to do was make the blue light.

Thomas wanted to warn the aides, but he figured nobody would hear him or listen to him until it was too late. So while the Bad Thing's back was turned, he crawled across the floor, away from the Bad Thing, even if crawling hurt, even if he had to go through spots of Derek's blood, all wet, and it made him sick on top of being angry and scared.

Blue light. Very bright.

Something exploded.

He heard glass falling and worse, like maybe not just the whole window blew out on the aides but part of the wall too.

People screamed. Most of the screams cut off quick-like, but one of them went on, it was real bad, like somebody out in the dark past the blown-up window was made to hurt even worse than Thomas.

Thomas didn't look back because he was all the way around the side of Derek's bed now, where he couldn't see the window anyway from where he was on the floor. And, besides, he knew what he wanted now, where he wanted to go, and he had to get there before the Bad Thing got interested in him again.

Quick-like, he crawled to the top end of the bed and looked up and saw Derek's arm hanging over the side, blood running down under his shirtsleeve and across his hand and drip-drip-dripping off his fingers. He didn't want to touch a dead person, not even a dead person he liked. But this was what he had to do, and he was used to having to do all sorts of things he wished he didn't – that was what life was like. So he grabbed the edge of the bed and pulled himself up as fast as he could, trying not to feel the bad hurt in his back and in his kicked leg, because feeling it would make him stiff and slow. Derek was right there, eyes open, mouth open, blood-wet, so sad, so scary, on top of the pictures of his folks that fell off the wall, still dead, off for always and ever to the Bad Place. Thomas grabbed the scissors sticking out of Derek, pulled them loose, telling himself it was okay because Derek couldn't feel anything now, or ever.

'You!' the Bad Thing said.

Thomas turned to see where the Bad Thing was, and where it was was right behind him, all the way around the bed, coming at him. So he shoved the scissors at it, hard as he could, and the Bad Thing's face made a surprised look. The scissors went in the front of the Bad Thing's shoulder. The Bad Thing looked even more surprised. The blood came.

Letting go of the scissors, Thomas said, 'For Derek,' then said, 'for me.'

He wasn't sure what would happen, but he figured that making the blood come would hurt the Bad Thing and maybe make it dead, like it made Derek dead. Across the room he saw where the window wasn't any more and where part of the wall wasn't any more, some smoke coming from the broken ends of things. He figured he was going to run over there and go through the hole, even if the night was out there on the other side.

But he never figured on what *did* happen, because the Bad Thing acted like the scissors weren't even in it, like blood wasn't being let loose from it, and it grabbed him and lifted him up again. It slammed him into Derek's dresser, which was a lot more hurt than the wall because the dresser was made with knobs and edges the wall didn't have.

He heard something crack in him, heard something tear. But the funny thing was, he wasn't crying any more and didn't *want* to cry any more, like he'd used up all the tears in himself.

The Bad Thing put its face close to Thomas's face, so their eyes were only a couple inches apart. He didn't like looking in the Bad Thing's eyes. They were scary. They were blue, but it was like they were really dark, like under the blue was a lot of stuff as black as the night out past the gone window.

But the other funny thing was, he wasn't as scared as he was a while ago, like he'd used up all his being scared just like he'd used up his tears. He looked in the Bad Thing's eyes, and he saw all that big dark, bigger than the dark that came over the world each day when the sun went away, and he knew it was wanting to make him dead, *going* to make him dead, and that was okay. He was not so afraid of being made dead as he always thought he would be. It was still a Bad Place, death, and he wished he didn't have to go there, but he had a funny-nice feeling about the Bad Place all of a sudden, a feeling that maybe it wouldn't be so lonely over there as he always figured it was, not even as lonely as it was on this side. He felt maybe someone was over there who loved him, someone who loved him more than even Julie loved him, even more than their dad used to love him, someone who was all bright, no dark at all, so bright you could only look at Him sideways.

The Bad Thing held Thomas against the dresser with one hand, and with its other hand it pulled the scissors out of itself.

Then it put the scissors in Thomas.

This light started to fill up Thomas, this light that loved him, and he knew he was going away. He hoped when he was all gone, Julie would know how brave he was right at the end, how he stopped crying and stopped being scared and fought back. And then all of a sudden he remembered he hadn't TVed a warning to Bobby that the Bad Thing might be coming for them, too, and he started to do that.

—the scissors went in again—

Then he all of a sudden knew something even more important he had to do. He had to let Julie know that the Bad Place was not so bad, after all, there was a light over there that loved you, you could tell. She needed to know about it because deep down she really didn't believe it. She figured it was all dark and lonely the way Thomas once figured it was, so she counted each clock tick and worried about all she had to do before her time ran out, all she had to learn and see and feel and get, all she had to do for Thomas and for Bobby so they'd be okay if Something Happened To Her.

—and the scissors went in again—

And she was happy with Bobby, but she was never going to be *real* happy until she knew she didn't have to be so angry about everything ending in a big dark. She was so nice it was hard to figure she was angry inside, but she was. Thomas only figured it out now, as the light was filling him up, figured out how terrible angry Julie was. She was angry that all the hard work and all the hope and all the dreams and all the trying and doing and loving didn't matter in the end because you were sooner or later made dead forever.

—the scissors—

If she knew about the light, she could stop being angry deep down. So Thomas TVed that, too, along with a warning, and with three last words to her and to Bobby, words of his own, all three things at once, hoping they wouldn't get mixed up:

The Bad Thing's coming, look out, the Bad Thing, there's a light that loves you, the Bad Thing, I love you too, and there's a light, there's a light, THE BAD THING'S COMING—

At 8:15 they were on the Foothill Freeway, rocketing toward the junction with the Ventura Freeway, which they would follow across the San Fernando Valley almost to the ocean before turning north toward Oxnard, Ventura, and eventually Santa Barbara. Julie knew she should slow down, but she couldn't. Speed relieved her tension a little; if she stayed even close to the fifty-five-mile-an-hour limit, she was pretty sure that she would start to scream before they were past Burbank.

A Benny Goodman tape was on the stereo. The exuberant melodies and syncopated rhythms seemed in time and sympathy with the headlong rush of the car; and if they had been in a movie, Goodman's sounds would have been perfect background music to the tenebrous panorama of light-speckled night hills through which they passed from city to city, suburb to suburb.

She knew why she was so tense. In a way she could never have anticipated, The Dream was within their grasp – but they could lose everything as they reached for it. Everything. Hope. Each other. Their lives.

Sitting in the seat beside her, Bobby trusted her so implicitly that he could doze at more than eighty miles an hour, even though he knew that she, too, had slept only three hours last night. From time to time she glanced at him, just because it felt good to have him there.

He did not yet understand why they were going north to check out the Pollard family, stretching their obligation to the client beyond reason, but his bafflement sprang from the fact that he was nearly as good a man as he appeared to be. He sometimes bent the rules and broke the laws on behalf of their clients, but he was more scrupulous in his personal life than anyone Julie had ever known. She had been with him once when a newspaper-vending machine gave him a copy of the Sunday *Los Angeles Times*, then malfunctioned and returned three of his four quarters to him, whereupon he had repaid all three into the coin slot, even though that same machine had malfunctioned to his disadvantage on other occasions over the years and was into him for a couple of bucks. 'Yeah, well,' he'd said, blushing when she had laughed at his goody-goody deed, 'maybe the machine can be crooked and still live with itself, but I can't.'

Julie could have told him that they were hanging with the Pollard case because they saw a once-in-a-lifetime shot at really big bucks, the Main Chance for which every hustler in the world was looking and which most of them would never find. From the moment Frank had shown them all that cash in the flight bag and told them about the second cache back at the motel, they were locked in like rats in a maze, drawn forward by the smell of cheese, even though each of them had taken a turn at protesting any interest in the game. When Frank came back to that hospital room from God-knew-where, with another three hundred thousand, neither she nor Bobby even raised the issue of illegality, though it was by that time no longer possible to pretend that Frank was entirely an innocent. By then the smell of cheese was too strong to be resisted at all. They were plunging ahead because they saw the chance to use Frank to cash out of the rat race and buy into The Dream sooner than they had expected. They were willing to use dirty money and questionable means to get to their desired end, more willing than they could admit to each other, though Julie supposed it could be said in their favor that they were not yet so greedy that they could simply steal the money and the diamonds from Frank and abandon him to the mercies of his psychotic brother; or maybe even their sense of duty to their client was a lie now, a virtue they could point to later when they tried to justify, to themselves, their other less-than-noble acts and impulses.

She *could* have told him all that, but she didn't, because she did not want to argue with him. She had to let him figure it out at his own pace, accept it in his own way. If she tried to tell him before he was able to understand it, he'd deny what she said. Even if he admitted to a fraction of the truth, he'd trot out an argument about the rightness of The Dream, the basic morality of it, and use that to justify the means to the end. But she didn't think a noble end could remain purely noble if arrived at by immoral means. And though she could not turn away from this Main Chance, she worried that when they achieved The Dream it would be sullied, not what it might have been.

Yet she drove on. Fast. Because speed relieved some of her fear and tension. It numbed caution too. And without caution she was less likely to retreat from the dangerous confrontation with the Pollard family that seemed inevitable if they were to seize the opportunity to obtain immense and liberating wealth.

They were in a clearing in traffic, with nothing close behind them and trailing the nearest forward car by about a quarter of a mile, when Bobby cried out and sat up in his seat as if warning her of an imminent collision. He jerked forward, pulling the shoulder harness taut, and put his hands on his head, as though stricken by a sudden migraine.

Frightened, she let up on the accelerator, lightly tapped the brake pedal, and said, 'Bobby, what is it?'

In a voice coarsened by fear and sharpened by urgency, speaking above the music of Benny Goodman, he said, 'Bad Thing, the Bad thing, look out, there's a light, there's a light that loves you—'

Candy looked down at the bloody body at his feet and knew that he should not have killed Thomas. Instead, he should have taken him away to a private place and tortured the answers out of him even if it took hours for the dummy to remember everything Candy needed to know. It could even have been fun.

But he was in a rage greater than any he had ever known, and he was less in control of himself than at any time in his life since the day he had found his mother's dead body. He wanted vengeance not only for his mother but for himself and for everyone in the world who ever deserved revenge and never got it. God had made him an instrument of revenge, and now Candy longed desperately to fulfill his purpose as he had never fulfilled it before. He yearned not merely to tear open the throat and drink the blood of one sinner, but of a great multitude of sinners. If ever his rage was to be dissipated, he needed not only to drink blood but to become drunk on it, bathe in it, wade through rivers of it, stand on land saturated with it. He wanted his mother to free him from all the rules that had restricted his rage before, wanted God to turn him *loose*.

He heard sirens in the distance, and knew that he must go soon.

Hot pain throbbed in his shoulder, where the scissors had parted muscle and scraped bone, but he would deal with that when he traveled. In reconstituting himself, he could easily remake his flesh whole and healthy.

Stalking through the debris that littered the floor, he looked for something that might give him a clue to the whereabouts of either the Julie or the Bobby of whom Thomas had spoken. They might know who Thomas had been and why he had possessed a gift that not even Candy's blessed mother had been able to impart.

He touched various objects and pieces of furniture, but all he could extract from them were images of Thomas and Derek and some of the aides and nurses who took care of them. Then he saw a scrapbook lying open on the floor, beside the table on which he had butchered Derek. The open pages were full of all kinds of pictures that had been pasted in lines and peculiar patterns. He picked the book up and leafed through it, wondering what it was, and when he tried to see the face of the last person who had handled it, he was rewarded with someone other than a dummy or a nurse.

A hard-looking man. Not as tall as Candy but almost as solid.

The sirens were less than a mile away now, louder by the second.

Candy let his right hand glide over the cover of the scrapbook, seeking . . . seeking . . .

Sometimes he could sense only a little, sometimes a lot. This time he *had* to be successful, or this room was going to be a dead end in his search for the meaning of the dummy's power.

Seeking . . .

He received a name. Clint.

Clint had sat in Derek's chair sometime during the afternoon, paging through this odd collection of pictures.

When he tried to see where Clint had gone, after leaving this room, he saw a

Chevy that Clint was driving on the freeway, then a place called Dakota & Dakota. Then the Chevy again, on a freeway at night, and then a small house in a place called Placentia.

The approaching sirens were very close now, probably coming up the driveway into the Cielo Vista parking lot.

Candy threw the book down. He was ready to go.

He had only one more thing to do before he teleported. When he had discovered that Thomas was a dummy, and when he had realized that Cielo Vista was a place full of them, he had been angered and offended by the home's existence.

He held his hands two feet apart, palm facing palm. Sky-blue light glowed between them.

He remembered how neighbors and other people had talked about his sisters – and also about him when, as a boy, he had been kept out of school because of his problems. Violet and Verbina looked and acted mentally deficient, and they probably did not care if people called them retards. Ignorant people labeled him retarded, too, because they thought he was excused from school for being as learning disabled and strange as his sisters. (Only Frank attended classes like a normal child.)

The light began to coalesce into a ball. As more power poured out of his hands and into the ball, it acquired a deeper shade of blue and seemed to take on substance, as if it were a solid object floating in the air.

Candy had been bright, with no learning disabilities at all. His mother taught him to read, write, and do math; so he got angry when he overheard people say he was a deadhead. He had been excused from school for other reasons, of course, mainly because of the sex thing. When he got older and bigger, nobody called him retarded or made jokes about him, at least not within his hearing.

The sapphire-blue sphere looked almost as solid as a genuine sapphire, but as big as a basketball. It was nearly ready.

Having been unjustly tagged with the retarded label, Candy had not grown up with sympathy for the genuinely disabled, but with an intense loathing for them that he hoped would make it clear to even ignorant people that he definitely was not – and never had been – one of *them*. To think such a thing of him – or of his sisters, for that matter – was an insult to his sainted mother, who was incapable of bringing a moron into the world.

He cut off the flow of power and took his hands away from the sphere. For a moment he stared at it, smiling, thinking about what it would do to this offensive place.

Through the missing window and the partially shattered walls, the wail of the sirens became deafening, then suddenly subsided from a high-pitched shriek to a low growl that spiraled toward silence.

'Help's here, Thomas,' he said, and laughed.

He put one hand against the sapphire sphere and gave it a shove. It shot across the room as if it were a ballistic missile fired from its silo. It smashed through the wall behind Derek's bed, leaving a ragged hole as big as anything a cannonball could have made, through the wall beyond that, and through every additional wall that stood before it, spewing flames as it went, setting fire to everything along its path.

Candy heard people screaming and a hard explosion, as he did a fadeout on his way to the house in Placentia.

Bobby stood at the side of the freeway, holding on to the open car door, gasping for breath. He had been sure he was going to throw up, but the urge had passed.

'Are you all right?' Julie asked anxiously.

'I . . . think so.'

Traffic shot past. Each vehicle was trailed by a wake of wind and a roar that gave Bobby the peculiar feeling that he and Julie and the Toyota were still moving, doing eighty-five with him holding on to the open door and her with a hand on his shoulder, magically keeping their balance and avoiding roadburn as they dragged their feet along the pavement, with nobody driving.

The dream had seriously unsettled and disoriented him.

'Not a dream, really,' he told her. He continued to keep his head down, peering at bits of loose gravel on the paved shoulder of the highway, half expecting a return of the cramping nausea. 'Not like the dream I had before, about us and the jukebox and the ocean of acid.'

'But about "the bad thing" again.'

'Yeah. You couldn't call it a dream, though, because it was just this . . . this burst of words, inside my head.'

'From where?'

'I don't know.'

He dared to lift his head, and though a whirl of dizziness swept through him, the nausea did not return.

He said, ' "Bad thing . . . look out . . . there's a light that loves you . . ." I can't remember it all. It was so strong, so hard, like somebody shouting at me through a bullhorn that was pressed against my ear. Except that's not right, either, because I didn't really hear the words, they were just there, in my head. But they *felt* loud, if that makes any sense. And there weren't images, like in a dream. Instead there were these feelings, as strong as they were confused. Fear and joy, anger and forgiveness . . . and right at the end of it, this strange sense of peace that I . . . can't describe.'

A Peterbilt thundered toward them, towing the biggest trailer the law allowed. Sweeping out of the night behind its blazing headlights, it looked like a leviathan swimming up from a deep marine trench, all raw power and cold rage, with a hunger that could never be satisfied. For some reason, as it boomed past them, Bobby thought of the man he had seen on the beach at Punaluu, and he shuddered.

Julie said, 'Are you okay?'

'Yeah.'

'Are you sure?'

He nodded. 'A little dizzy. That's all.'

'What now?'

He looked at her. 'What else? We go on to Santa Barbara, El Encanto Heights, bring this thing to an end . . . somehow.'

———

Candy arrived in the archway between a living room and dining room. No one was in either place.

He heard a buzzing sound farther back in the house, and after a moment he identified it as an electric razor. It stopped. Then he heard water running in a sink, and the drone of a bathroom exhaust fan.

He intended to head straight for the hall and the bath, take the man by surprise. But he heard a rustle of paper from the opposite direction.

He crossed the dining room and stepped into the kitchen doorway. It was smaller than the kitchen in his mother's house, but it was as spotlessly clean and orderly as his mother's kitchen had not been since her death.

A woman in a blue dress was sitting at the table, her back to him. She was leaning over a magazine, turning the pages one after the other, as if looking for something of interest to read.

Candy possessed a far greater control of his telekinetic talents than Frank enjoyed, and in particular could teleport more efficiently and swiftly than Frank, creating less air displacement and less noise from molecular resistance. Nevertheless, he was surprised that she had not gotten up to investigate, for the sounds he had made during arrival had been only one small room away from her and, surely, odd enough to prick her curiosity.

She turned a few more pages, then leaned forward to read.

He could not see much of her from behind. Her hair was thick, lustrous, and so black it seemed to have been spun on the same loom as the night. Her shoulders and back were slender. Her legs, which were both to one side of the chair and crossed at the ankles, were shapely. If he had been a man with any interest in sex, he supposed he would have been excited by the curve of her calves.

Wondering what she looked like – and suddenly overwhelmed by a need to know how her blood would taste – he stepped out of the open doorway and took three steps to her. He made no effort to be silent, but she did not look up. The first she became aware of him was when he seized a handful of her hair and dragged her, kicking and flailing, out of her chair.

He turned her around and was instantly excited by her. He was indifferent to her shapely legs, the flare of her hips, the trimness of her waist, the fullness of her breasts. Though beautiful, it was not even her face that electrified him. Something else. A quality in her gray eyes. Call it vitality. She was more alive than most people, vibrant.

She did not scream but let out a low grunt of fear or anger, then struck him furiously with both fists. She pounded his chest, battered his face.

Vitality! Yes, this one was full of life, bursting with life, and her vitality thrilled him far more than any bounty of sexual charms.

He could still hear the distant splash of water, the rattle-hum of the bathroom exhaust fan, and he was confident that he could take her without drawing the attention of the man – as long as he could prevent her from screaming. He struck her on the side of the head with his fist, hammered her before she could scream. She slumped against him, not unconscious but dazed.

Shaking with the anticipation of pleasure, Candy placed her on her back, on the table, with her legs trailing over the edge. He spread her legs and leaned between them, but not to commit rape, nothing as disgusting as that. As he lowered his face toward hers, she first blinked at him in confusion, still rattle-brained from the blows she had taken. Then her eyes began to clear. He saw horrified comprehension return to her, and he went quickly for her throat, bit deep, and found the blood, which was clean and sweet, intoxicating.

She thrashed beneath him.

She was so alive. So wonderfully alive. For a while.

When the deliveryman brought the pizza, Lee Chen took it into Bobby and Julie's office and offered some to Hal.

Putting his book aside but not taking his stockinged feet off the coffee table, Hal said, 'You know what that stuff does to your arteries?'

'Why's everyone so concerned about my arteries today?'

'You're such a nice young man. We'd hate to see you dead before you're thirty. Besides, we'd always wonder what clothes you might've worn next, if you'd lived.'

'Not anything like what you're wearing, I assure you.'

Hal leaned over and looked in the box that Lee held down to him. 'Looks pretty good. Rule of thumb – any pizza they'll bring to you, they're selling service instead of good food. But this doesn't look bad at all, you can actually tell where the pizza ends and the cardboard begins.'

Lee tore the lid off the box, put it on the coffee table, and put two slices of pizza on that makeshift plate. 'There.'

'You're not going to give me half?'

'What about the cholesterol?'

'Hell, cholesterol's just a little animal fat, it isn't arsenic.'

When the woman's strong heart stopped beating, Candy pulled back from her. Though blood still seeped from her ravaged throat, he did not touch another drop of it. The thought of drinking from a corpse sickened him. He remembered his sisters' cats, eating their own each time one of the pack died, and he grimaced.

Even as he raised his wet lips from her throat, he heard a door open farther back in the house. Footsteps approached.

Candy quickly circled the table, putting it and the dead woman between himself and the doorway to the dining room. From the vision induced by the dummy's scrapbook of pictures, Candy knew that Clint would not be as easy to handle as most people were. He preferred to put a little distance between them, give himself time to size up his opponent rather than take the guy by surprise.

Clint appeared in the doorway. Except for his outfit – gray slacks, navy-blue blazer, maroon V-neck, white shirt – he looked the same as the psychic impression he had left on the book. He had pumped a lot of iron in his time. His hair was thick, black, and combed straight back from his forehead. He had a face like carved granite, and a hard look in his eyes.

Excited by the recent kill, by the taste of blood still in his mouth, Candy watched the man with interest, wondering what would happen next. There were all sorts of ways it could go, and not one of them would be dull.

Clint did not react as Candy expected. He did not show surprise when he saw the woman sprawled dead upon the table; he did not seem horrified, shattered by the loss of her, or outraged. Something major changed in his stony face, though below the surface, like tectonic plates shifting under the mantle of the earth's crust.

Finally he met Candy's gaze, and said, 'You.'

The note of recognition in that single word was unsettling. For a moment Candy could think of no way this man could know him – then he remembered Thomas.

The possibility that Thomas had told this man – and perhaps others – about Candy was the most frightening turn in Candy's life since his mother's death. His service in God's army of avengers was a deeply private matter, a secret that should not have been spread beyond the Pollard family. His mother had warned him that it was all right to be proud of doing God's work, but that his pride would lead him to a fall if he boasted of his divine favor to others. 'Satan,' she had told him, 'constantly seeks the names of lieutenants in God's army – which is what you are – and when he finds them, he destroys them with worms that eat them alive from within, worms fat as snakes, and he rains fire on them too. If you can't keep the secret, you'll die and go to Hell for your big mouth.'

'Candy,' Clint said.

The use of his name erased whatever doubt remained that the secret had been passed outside the family and that Candy was in deep trouble, though he had not broken the code of silence himself.

He imagined that even now Satan, in some dark and steaming place, had tilted his head and said, 'Who? Who did you say? What was his name? Candy? Candy who?'

As furious as he was frightened, Candy started around the kitchen table, wondering if Clint had learned about him from Thomas. He was determined to break the man, make him talk before killing him.

In a move as unexpected as his rock-calm acceptance of the woman's murder, Clint reached inside his jacket, withdrew a revolver, and fired two shots.

He might have fired more than two, but those were the only ones Candy heard. The first round hit him in the stomach, the second in the chest, pitching him backward. Fortunately he sustained no damage to head or heart. If his brain tissue had been scrambled, disturbing the mysterious and fragile connection between brain and mind, leaving his mind trapped within his ruined brain before he had a chance to separate the two, he would not have possessed the mental ability to teleport, leaving him vulnerable to a coup de grace. And if his heart had been stopped instantaneously by a well-placed bullet, before he could dematerialize, he would have fallen down dead where he'd stood. Those were the only wounds that might finish him. He was many things, but he was not immortal; so he was grateful to God for letting him get out of that kitchen and back to his mother's house alive.

The Ventura Freeway. Julie drove fast, though not as fast as she had earlier. On the tapedeck: Artie Shaw's 'Nightmare.'

Bobby brooded, staring through the side window at the nightscape. He could not stop thinking about the blare of words that had seared through him, loud as a bomb blast and bright as a blast-furnace fire. He had come to terms with the dream that had frightened him last week; everyone had bad dreams. Though exceptionally vivid, almost more real than real life, there had been nothing uncanny about it – or so he had convinced himself. But this was different. He could not believe that these urgent, lava-hot words had erupted from his own subconscious. A dream, with complex Freudian messages couched in elaborate scenes and symbols – yes, that was understandable; after all, the subconscious dealt in euphemisms and metaphors. But this wordburst had been blunt, direct, like a telegraph delivered on a wire plugged directly into his cerebral cortex.

When he wasn't brooding, Bobby was fidgeting. Because of Thomas.

For some reason, the longer he dwelt on the blaze of words, the more Thomas slipped into his thoughts. He could see no connection between the two, so he tried to put Thomas out of mind and concentrate on turning up an explanation for the experience. But Thomas gently, insistently returned, again and again. After a while Bobby got the uneasy feeling there *was* a link between the wordburst and Thomas, though he had no ghost of an idea what it might be.

Worse, as the miles rolled up on the odometer and they reached the western end of the valley, Bobby began to sense that Thomas was in danger. And because of me and Julie, Bobby thought.

Danger from whom, from what?

The biggest danger that Bobby and Julie faced, right now, was Candy Pollard. But even that jeopardy lay in the future, for Candy didn't know about them yet; he was not aware that they were working on Frank's behalf, and he might never become aware of it, depending on how things went in Santa Barbara and El Encanto Heights. Yes, he had seen Bobby on the beach at Punaluu, with Frank, but he had no way of knowing who Bobby was. Ultimately, even if Candy became aware of Dakota & Dakota's association with Frank, there was no way that Thomas could be drawn into the affair; Thomas was another, separate part of their lives. Right?

'Something wrong?' Julie said as she pulled the Toyota one lane to the left, to pass a big rig hauling Coors.

He could see nothing to be gained by telling her that Thomas might be in danger. She would be upset, worried. And for what? He was just letting his vivid imagination run away with him. Thomas was perfectly safe down there in Cielo Vista.

'Bobby, what's wrong?'

'Nothing.'

'Why're you fidgeting?'

'Prostate trouble.'

═══

Chanel No. 5, a softly glowing lamp, cozy rose-patterned fabrics and wallpaper . . .

He laughed with relief when he materialized in the bedroom, the bullets left behind in that kitchen in Placentia, over a hundred miles away. His wounds had knit up as if they had never existed. He had lost perhaps an ounce of blood and a few flecks of tissue, because one of the bullets had passed through him and out his back, carrying that material with it before he'd transported himself beyond the revolver's range. Everything else was as it should be, however, and his flesh did not harbor even the memory of pain.

He stood in front of the dresser for half a minute, breathing deeply of the perfume that wafted up from the saturated handkerchief. The scent gave him courage and reminded him of the abiding need to make them pay for his mother's murder, all of them, not just Frank but the whole world, which had conspired against her.

He looked at his face in the mirror. The gray-eyed woman's blood was no longer on his chin and lips; he had left it behind him, as he might leave water behind when teleporting out of a rainstorm. But the taste of it was still in his mouth. And his reflection was without a doubt that of vengeance personified.

Depending on the element of surprise and his ability to target his point of arrival precisely now that he was familiar with the kitchen, he returned to Clint's house. He intended to enter at the dining room doorway, immediately behind the man, directly opposite the point from which he had dematerialized.

Either the experience of being shot had shaken him more than he realized, or the rage jittering through him had passed the critical point at which it interfered with his concentration. Whatever the reason, he did not arrive where he intended, but by the door to the garage, one quarter instead of halfway around the room from his last position, to the right of Clint and not near enough to rush him and seize the gun before it could be fired.

Except Clint was not present. And the woman's body had been removed from the table. Only the blood remained as proof that she perished there.

Candy could not have been gone more than a minute – the time he had spent in his mother's room, plus a couple of seconds in transit each way. He expected to return to find Clint bent over the corpse, either grieving or checking desperately for a pulse. But as soon as he realized Candy was gone, the man must have taken the body in his arms and . . . And what? He must have fled the house, of course, hoping against hope that a faint thread of life remained unbroken in the woman, getting her out of the way in case Candy returned.

Cursing softly – then immediately begging his mother's and God's forgiveness for his foul language – Candy tried the door into the garage. It was locked. If he had left by that exit, Clint wouldn't have paused to lock up behind himself.

He hurried out of the kitchen, through the dining room, toward the foyer off the living room, to check out the front lawn and the street. But he heard a noise from deeper in the house, and halted before he reached the front door. He changed direction, cautiously following the hallway back to the bedrooms.

A light was on in one of those rooms. He eased to the door and risked a glance inside.

Clint had just put the woman on the queen-size bed. As Candy watched, the man pulled her skirt down over her knees. He still had the revolver in one hand.

For the second time in less than an hour, Candy heard faraway sirens swelling in the night. The neighbors probably had heard the gunfire and called the police.

Clint saw him in the doorway but did not bring up the gun. He did not say anything, either, and the expression on his stoic face remained unchanged. He seemed like a deaf mute. The strangeness of the man's demeanor made Candy nervous and uncertain.

He thought there was a pretty good chance that Clint had emptied the gun at him in the kitchen, even though he had teleported out of there with the impact of the second slug. Most likely, he had fired every round reflexively, his trigger finger ruled by rage or fear or whatever he was feeling. He could not have carried the woman into the bedroom and reloaded the gun, too, in the minute or so that Candy had been gone, which meant Candy might be in no danger if he just walked up to the guy and took the weapon away from him.

But he stayed in the doorway. Either of those two shots *could* have been dead-center in his heart. The power within him was great, but he could not exercise it quickly enough to vaporize an oncoming bullet.

Instead of dealing with Candy in any fashion, the man turned away from him, walked around the foot of the bed to the other side, and stretched out beside the woman.

'What the hell?' Candy said aloud.

Clint took hold of her dead hand. His other hand held the .38 revolver. He turned his head on the pillow to look toward her, and his eyes glistened with what might have been unshed tears. He put the muzzle of the gun under his chin, and annihilated himself.

Candy was so stunned that he was unable to move for a moment or think what to do next. He was jolted out of his paralysis by the ululant sirens, and realized that the trail from Thomas to Bobby and Julie, whoever they were, might end here if he did not discover what link the dead man on the bed shared with them. If he ever hoped to learn who Thomas had been, how Clint had known his name, or how many others knew of him, if he wanted to learn how much danger he was in and how he might slide out of it, he couldn't waste this opportunity.

He hurried to the bed, rolled the dead man onto his side, and withdrew the wallet from his pants pocket. He flipped it open and saw the private investigator's license. Opposite it, in another plastic window, was a business card for Dakota & Dakota.

Candy remembered a vague image of the Dakota & Dakota offices, which had come to him in Thomas's room when he had obtained a vision of Clint from the scrapbook. There was an address on the card. And below the name Clint Karaghiosis, in smaller type, were the names Robert and Julia Dakota.

Outside, the sirens had died. Someone was pounding on the front door. Two voices shouted, 'Police!'

Candy threw the wallet aside and took the gun out of the dead man's hand. He broke open the cylinder. It was a five-shot weapon, and all of the chambers were filled with expended cartridges. Clint had fired four rounds in the kitchen, but even in his moment of vengeful fury, he had possessed enough control to save the last bullet for himself.

'Just because of a woman?' Candy said uncomprehendingly, as if the dead man might answer him. 'Because you couldn't get sex from her any more now? Why does sex matter so much? Couldn't you get sex from another woman? Why was sex with this one so important, you didn't want to live without it?'

They were still pounding on the door. Someone spoke through a bullhorn, but Candy didn't pay attention to what was being said.

He dropped the gun and wiped his hand on his pants, because he suddenly felt unclean. The dead man had handled the gun, and the dead man seemed to have been obsessed with sex. Without question, the world was a cesspool of lust and debauchery, and Candy was glad that God and his mother had spared him from the sick desires that seemed to infect nearly everyone else.

He left that house of sinners.

<h1 style="text-align:center">• 53 •</h1>

Slumped on the sofa, Hal Yamataka had a slice of pizza in one hand and the MacDonald novel in the other, when he heard the hollow flutelike warble. He dropped both the book and the food, and shot to his feet.

'Frank?'

The half-open door swung slowly inward, not because it was being pushed open by anyone but because a sudden draft, sweeping in from the reception lounge, was strong enough to move it.

'Frank?' Hal repeated.

As he crossed the room, the sound faded and the draft died. But by the time he reached the doorway, the unmelodic notes returned, and a burst of wind ruffled his hair.

To the left stood the receptionist's desk, untended at this hour. Directly opposite the desk was the door to the public corridor that served the other companies on this level, and it was closed. The only other door, at the far end of the rectangular lounge, was also closed; it led to a hallway that was interior to the Dakota & Dakota suite, off which were six other offices – including the computer room where Lee was still at work – and a bathroom. The piping and the wind could not have reached him through those closed doors; therefore, the point of origin was clearly the reception lounge.

Stepping to the center of the room, he looked around expectantly.

The flute sounds and turbulence rose a third time.

Hal said, 'Frank,' as he became aware, out of the corner of his eye, that a man had arrived near the door to the public hall, to Hal's right and almost behind him.

But when he turned, he saw that it was not Frank. The traveler was a stranger, but Hal knew him at once. Candy. It could be no one else, for this was the man Bobby had described from the beach at Punaluu, and whose description Hal had received from Clint.

Hal was built low and wide, he kept in good shape, and he could remember no instance in his life when he'd been physically intimidated by another man. Candy was eight inches taller than he, but Hal had handled men taller than that. Candy was clearly an endomorph, one of those guys destined from birth to have a strong-boned body layered with slabs of muscle, even if he exercised lightly or not at all; and he was clearly no stranger to the discipline and painful rituals of barbells, dumbbells, and slantboards. But Hal had an endomorphic body type as well, and was as hard as frozen beef. He was not intimidated by Candy's height or muscles. What frightened him was the aura of insanity, rage, and violence the man radiated as powerfully as a week-old corpse would radiate the stink of death.

The instant that Frank's brother hit the room, Hal smelled his mad ferocity as surely as a healthy dog would detect the rabid odor of a sick one, and he acted accordingly. He wasn't wearing shoes, wasn't carrying a gun, and wasn't aware of anything near at hand that might be used as a weapon, so he spun around and ran back toward the bosses' office, where he knew a loaded Browning 9mm semiautomatic pistol was kept in a spring clip on the underside of Julie's desk as insurance against the unexpected. Until now the gun had never been needed.

Hal was not the martial-arts whiz that his formidable appearance and ethnicity led everyone to believe he was, but he did know some Tai Kwan Do. The problem was, only a fool would resort to *any* form of martial arts as a first defense against a charging bull with a bumblebee up its butt.

He made the doorway before Candy grabbed him by his shirt and tried to pull him off his feet. The shirt tore along the seams, leaving the madman with a handful of cloth.

But Hal was wrenched off balance. He stumbled into the office and collided with Julie's big chair, which was still standing in the middle of the room with four other chairs arranged in a semicircle in front of it, as Jackie Jaxx had required for Frank's session of hypnosis. He grabbed at Julie's chair for support. It was on wheels, which rolled grudgingly on the carpet, though well enough to send it skidding treacherously out from under him.

The psycho crashed into him, ramming him against the chair and the chair against the desk. Leaning into Hal, with massive fists that felt like the iron heads of sledgehammers, Candy delivered a flurry of punches to his midsection.

Hal's hands were down, leaving him briefly defenseless, but he clasped them, with his thumbs aligned, and rammed them upward, between Candy's piledriving arms, catching him in the adam's apple. The blow was hard enough to make Candy gag on his own cry of pain, and Hal's thumbnails gouged the madman's flesh, skidding all the way up under his chin, tearing the skin as they went.

Choking, unable to draw breath through his bruised and spasming esophagus, Candy staggered backward, both hands to his throat.

Hal pushed away from the chair, against which he had been pinned, but he didn't go after Candy. Even the blow he'd delivered was the equivalent of a tap with a flyswatter to the snout of that bull with the bee up its butt. An overconfident charge would no doubt end in a swift goring. Instead, hurting from the punches to his gut, with the sour taste of pizza sauce in the back of his throat, he hurried around the desk, hot to get his hands on that 9mm Browning.

The desk was large, and the dimensions of the kneehole were correspondingly spacious. He wasn't sure where the pistol was clipped, and he didn't want to bend down to look under because he would have to take his eyes off Candy. He slid his hand from left to right along the underside of the desktop, then reached deeper and slid it back the other way.

Just as he touched the butt of the pistol, he saw Candy thrust out both hands, palms forward, as if the guy knew Hal had found a gun and was saying, *Don't shoot, I surrender, stop.* But as Hal tugged the Browning free of the metal spring clamp, he discovered that Candy didn't have surrender in mind: blue light flashed out of the madman's palms.

The heavy desk abruptly behaved like a wire-rigged, balsawood prop in a movie about poltergeists. Even as Hal was raising the gun, the desk slammed into him and carried him backward, into the huge window behind him. The desk was wider than the window, and the ends of it met the wall, which prevented it from sailing straight through the glass.

But Hal was in the center of the window, and the low sill hit him behind the knees, so nothing inhibited his plunge. For an instant the jangling Levolor blinds seemed as if they might restrain him, but that was wishful thinking; he carried them with him, through the glass, and into the night, dropping the Browning without ever having fired it.

He was surprised how long it took to fall six stories, which was not such a terribly great distance, though a deadly one. He had time to marvel at how slowly the lighted office window receded from him, time to think about people he had loved and dreams never fulfilled, time even to notice that the clouds, which had returned at twilight, were shedding light sprinkles of rain. His last thought was about the garden behind his small house in Costa Mesa, where he tended an array of flowers year around and secretly enjoyed every moment of it: the exquisitely soft texture of a coral-red impatiens petal, and on its edge a single tiny drop of morning dew, glistening—

Candy shoved the heavy desk aside and leaned out of the sixth-floor window. A cool updraft rose along the side of the building and buffeted his face.

The shoeless man lay on his back on a broad concrete walk below, illuminated by the amber backsplash of a landscape spotlight. He was surrounded by broken glass, tangled metal blinds, and a swiftly spreading blot of his own blood.

Coughing, still having a little difficulty drawing deep enough breaths, with one hand pressed to the stinging flesh of his battered throat, Candy was upset by the man's death. Actually, not by the fact of it but by the timing of it. First, he'd wanted to interrogate him to learn who Bobby and Julie were, and what association they had with the psychic Thomas.

And when Candy had teleported into the reception lounge, the guy had thought he was Frank; he had spoken Frank's name. The people at Dakota & Dakota were somehow associated with Frank – knew all about his ability to teleport! – and therefore would know where to find the mother-murdering wretch.

Candy supposed the office would hold answers to at least some of his questions, but he was concerned that police, responding to the dead man's plunge, would necessitate a departure before he turned up all the information he needed. Sirens were the background music to this night's adventures.

No sirens had arisen yet, however. Maybe he had gotten lucky; maybe no one had seen the man fall. It was unlikely that anyone was at work at any of the other companies in the office building; it was, after all, ten minutes till nine. Perhaps janitors were polishing floors somewhere, or emptying wastebaskets, but they might not have heard enough to warrant investigation.

The man had plummeted to his death with surprisingly little protest. He had not screamed. An instant before impact, the start of a shout had flown from him, but it had been too short to attract notice. The explosion of the glass and the tinny clanging of the blinds had been loud enough, but the action had been over before anyone could have located the source of the sound.

A four-lane street encircled the Fashion Island shopping center and also served the office towers that, like this one, stood on the outer rim. Apparently, however, no cars had been on it when the man had fallen.

Now two appeared to the left, one behind the other. Both passed without slowing. A row of shrubberies, between the sidewalk and the street, prevented motorists from seeing the corpse where it lay. The office-tower ring of the sprawling complex was clearly not an area that attracted pedestrians at night, so the dead man might remain undiscovered until morning.

He looked across the street, at the restaurants and stores that were on this flank of the mall, five or six hundred yards away. A few people on foot, shrunken by distance, moved between the parked cars and the entrances to the businesses. No one appeared to have seen anything – and in fact it would not have been that easy to spot a darkly dressed man plunging past a mostly dark building, aloft and visible for only seconds before gravity finished him.

Candy cleared his throat, wincing in pain, and spat toward the dead man below.

He tasted blood. This time it was his own.

Turning away from the window, he surveyed the office, wondering where he would find the answers he sought. If he could locate Bobby and Julie Dakota, they might be able to explain Thomas's telepathy and more important, they might be able to deliver Frank into his hands.

After twice responding to an alarm from the radar detector and avoiding two speed traps in the west valley, Julie cranked the Toyota back up to eighty-five, and they dusted LA off their heels.

A few raindrops spattered the windshield, but the sprinkles did not last. She switched the wipers off moments after turning them on.

'Santa Barbara in maybe an hour,' she said, 'as long as a cop with a sense of duty doesn't come along.'

The back of her neck ached, and she was deeply weary, but she didn't want to trade places with Bobby; she didn't have the patience to be a passenger tonight. Her eyes were sore but not heavy; she could not possibly have slept. The events of the day had murdered sleep, and alertness was assured by concern about what might lie ahead, not just on the highway before them but in El Encanto Heights.

Ever since he'd been awakened by what he called the 'wordburst,' Bobby had been moody. She could tell he was worried about something, but he didn't seem to want to talk about it yet.

After a while, in an obvious attempt to take his mind off the wordburst and whatever gloomy ruminations it had inspired, he tried to strike up a conversation about something utterly different. He lowered the volume on the stereo, thereby frustrating the intended effect of Glenn Miller's 'American Patrol,' and said, 'You ever stop to think, four out of our eleven employees are Asian-Americans?'

She didn't glance away from the road. 'So?'

'So why is that, do you think?'

'Because we hire only first-rate people, and it so happened that four of the first-rate people who wanted to work for us were Chinese, Japanese, and Vietnamese.'

'That's part of it.'

'Just part?' she said. 'So what's the other part? You think maybe the wicked Fu Manchu turned a mind-control ray on us from his secret fortress in the Tibetan mountains and *made* us hire 'em?'

'That's part of it too,' he said. 'But another part of it is – I'm attracted to the Asian personality. Or to what people think of when they think of the Asian personality: intelligence, a high degree of self-discipline, neatness, a strong sense of tradition and order.'

'Those are pretty much traits of everyone who works for us, not just Jamie, Nguyen, Hal, and Lee.'

'I know. But what makes me so comfortable with Asian-Americans is that I buy into the stereotype of them, I feel everything will go along in an orderly, stable fashion when I'm working with them, and I *need* to buy into the stereotype because . . . well, I'm not the kind of guy I've always thought I was. You ready to hear something shocking?'

'Always,' Julie said.

Often, when Lee Chen was laboring in the computer room, he popped a CD in his Sony Walkman and listened to music through earphones. He always kept the door closed to avoid distraction, and no doubt some of his fellow employees thought he was somewhat antisocial; however, when he was engaged in the penetration of a complex and well-protected data network, like the array of police systems he was still plundering, he needed to concentrate. Occasionally music distracted him as much as anything, depending on his mood, but most of the time it was conducive to his work. The minimalist New Age piano solos of George Winston were sometimes just the thing, but more often he needed rock-'n'-roll. Tonight it was Huey Lewis and The News: 'Hip to Be Square' and 'The Power of Love,' 'The Heart of Rock & Roll' and 'You Crack Me Up.' Focused intently on the terminal screen (his window on the mesmerizing world of cyberspace), with 'Bad Is Bad' pouring into his ears through the headset, he might not have heard a thing if, in the world outside, God had peeled back the sky and announced the imminent destruction of the human race.

A cool draft circulated through the room from the broken window, but growing frustration generated a compensatory heat in Candy. He moved slowly around the spacious office, handling various objects, touching the furniture, trying to finesse a vision that would reveal the whereabouts of the Dakotas and Frank. Thus far he'd had no luck.

He could have pored through the contents of the desk drawers and filing cabinets, but that would have taken hours, since he didn't know where they might have filed the information he was seeking. He also realized he might not recognize the right stuff when he found it, for it might be in a folder or envelope bearing a case name or code that was meaningless to him. And though his mother had taught him to read and write, and though he had been a voracious reader just like her – until he lost interest in books upon her death – teaching himself many subjects as well as any university could have done, he nevertheless trusted what his special gifts could reveal to him more than anything he might find on paper.

Besides, he had already stepped into the lounge, obtained the Dakotas' home address and phone number, and called to see if they were there. An answering machine had picked up on the third ring, and he had left no message. He didn't just want to know where the Dakotas lived, where they might turn up in time; he needed to know where they were *now*, this minute, because he was in a fever to get at them and wring answers from them.

He picked up a third Scotch-and-soda glass. They were all over the room. The psychic residue on the tumbler gave him an instant, vivid image of a man named Jackie Jaxx, and he pitched it aside in anger. It bounced off the sofa, onto the carpet, without shattering.

This Jaxx person left a colorful and noisy psychic impression everywhere in his wake, the way a dog with poor bladder control would mark each step on his route with a dribble of stinking urine. Candy sensed that Jaxx was currently with a large number of people, at a party in Newport Beach, and he also sensed that trying to find Frank or the Dakotas through Jaxx would be wasted effort. Even so, if Jaxx had been alone now, easily taken, Candy would have gone straight to him and slaughtered him, just because the guy's lingering aura was so brassy and annoying.

Either he had not yet found an object that one of the Dakotas had touched long enough to leave an imprint, or neither of them was the type who left a rich, lingering psychic residue in his wake. For reasons Candy could not fathom, some people were harder to trace than others.

He had always found tracing Frank to be of medium difficulty, but tonight catching that scent was harder than usual. Repeatedly he sensed that Frank had been in the room, but at first he could locate nothing in which the aura of his brother was coagulated.

Next he turned to the four chairs, beginning with the largest. When he skimmed his sensitive fingertips lightly over the upholstery, he quivered with excitement, for he knew at once that Frank had sat there recently. A small tear marred the vinyl on one arm, and when Candy put his thumb upon the rent, particularly vivid visions of Frank assaulted him.

Too many visions. He was rewarded with a whole series of place images, where Frank had traveled after rising from the chair: the High Sierras; the apartment in San Diego in which he had lived briefly four years ago; the rusted front gate of their mother's house on Pacific Hill road; a graveyard; a book-lined study in which he'd stayed such a short time that Candy could get only the vaguest impression of it; Punaluu Beach, where Candy had nearly caught him . . . There were so many images, from so many travels, layered one atop another, that he could not clearly see the later stops.

Disgusted, he pushed the chair out of his way and turned to the coffee table, where two more tumblers stood. Both contained melted ice and Scotch. He picked one up and had a vision of Julie Dakota.

While Julie drove toward Santa Barbara as if they were competing in time trials for the Indianapolis 500, Bobby told her the shocking thing: that he was not, at heart, the laid-back guy he appeared to be on the surface; that during his hectic travels with Frank – especially during the moments when he had been reduced to a disembodied mind and a frantic whirl of disconnected atoms – he'd discovered within himself a rich vein of love for stability and order that ran deeper than he could ever have imagined, a motherlode of stick-in-the-mudness; that his delight in swing music arose more from an appreciation for the meticulosity of its structures than from the dizzying musical freedom embodied in jazz; that he was not half the free-spirited man he'd thought he was . . . and far more of a conservative embracer of tradition that he would have hoped.

'In short,' he said, 'all this time when you thought you were married to an easy-going young-James-Garner type, you've actually been wed to an any-age-Charles-Bronson type.'

'I can live with you anyway, Charlie.'

'This is serious. Sort of. I've tipped into my late thirties, I'm no child. I should've known this about myself a long time ago.'

'You did.'

'Huh?'

'You love order, reason, logic – that's why you got into a line of work where you could right wrongs, help the innocent, punish the bad. That's why you share The Dream with me – so we can get our little family in order, step out of the chaos of the world as it is these days and buy into some peace and quiet. That's why you won't let me have the Wurlitzer 950 – those bubble tubes and leaping gazelles are just a little too chaotic for you.'

He was silent a moment, surprised by her answer.

The lightless vastness of the sea lay to the west.

He said, 'Maybe you're right. Maybe I've always known what I am, deep down. But then isn't it unnerving that I've fooled myself with my own act for so long?'

'You haven't. You're easy-going *and* a bit of Charles Bronson, which is a good thing. Otherwise we probably couldn't communicate at all, since I've got more Bronson in me than anyone but Bronson.'

'God, that's true!' he said, and they both laughed.

The Toyota's speed had declined to under seventy. She put it up to eighty and said, 'Bobby . . . what's really on your mind?'

'Thomas.'

She glanced at him. 'What about Thomas?'

'Since that wordburst, I can't shake the feeling he's in danger.'

'What did that have to do with him?'

'I don't know. But I'd feel better if we could find a phone and put in a call to Cielo Vista. Just to be . . . sure.'

She let their speed fall dramatically. Within three miles they exited the freeway and pulled into a service station. There was a full-service lane. While the attendant washed their windows, checked the oil, and filled the tank with premium unleaded, they went inside and used the pay phone.

It was a modern electronic version allowing everything from coin to credit calls, on the wall next to a rack of snack crackers, candy bars, and packages of beer nuts. A condom machine was there, too, right out in the open, thanks to the social chaos wrought by AIDS. Using their AT&T credit card, Bobby called Cielo Vista Care Home in Newport.

It didn't ring or give a busy signal. He heard an odd series of electronic sounds, then a recording informed him that the number he had dialed was temporarily out of service as a result of unspecified line problems. The droning voice suggested that he try later.

He dialed the operator, who tried the same number, with the same results. She said, 'I'm sorry, sir. Please call your party later.'

'What line problems could they be having?'

'I wouldn't know, sir, but I'm sure service'll be restored soon.'

He had tilted the phone away from his ear, so Julie could lean in and hear both sides of the exchange. When he hung up, he looked at her. 'Let's go back. I got this hunch Thomas needs us.'

'Go back? We're little more than half an hour from Santa Barbara now. Much further to go home.'

'He may need us. It's not a strong hunch, I admit, but it's persistent and . . . weird.'

'If he needs help urgently,' she said, 'then we'd never get to him in time, anyway. And if it's not so urgent, it'll be okay if we go on to Santa Barbara, call again from the motel. If he's sick or been hurt or something, the extra driving from here to Santa Barbara and back will only add about an hour.'

'Well . . .'

'He's my brother, Bobby. I care about him as much as you do, and I say it'll be all right. I love you, but you've never shown enough talent as a psychic to make me hysterical about this.'

He nodded. 'You're right. I'm just . . . jumpy. My nerves haven't settled down since all that traveling with Frank.'

Back on the highway, a few thin tendrils of fog were creeping in from the sea. Sprinkles of rain fell again, then stopped after less than a minute. The heaviness of the air, and an indefinable but undeniable quality of oppressiveness in the utterly black night sky, portended a major storm.

When they had gone a couple of miles, Bobby said, 'I should've called Hal at the office. While he's sitting around there waiting for Frank, he could use some of our contacts with the phone company, the cops, make sure everything's jake at Cielo Vista.'

'If the lines are still out when you make the call from the motel,' Julie said, 'then you can bother Hal about it.'

From the weak psychic residue on the drinking glass, Candy received an image of Julie Dakota that was recognizably the same face that had seeped from Thomas's mind earlier in the evening – except that it was not as idealized as it had been in Thomas's memory. With his sixth sense he saw that she had gone home from the office, to the address he had obtained earlier from the secretary's Rolodex. She had been there a short time, then had gone somewhere in a car with another person, most likely the man named Bobby. He could see no more, and he wished that the traces she left behind had been as strong as those of Jaxx.

He put down the tumbler and decided to go to her house. Though she and

Bobby were not there now, he might be able to find an object that would, like the liquor glass, lead him another step or two along their trail. If he found nothing, he could return here and continue his search, assuming the police had not arrived in response to the discovery of the dead man outside.

Lee switched off the computer, then cut off the CD player too – Huey Lewis and The News were in the middle of 'Walking On a Thin Line' – and removed the earphones.

Happy after a long and productive session in the land of silicon and gallium arsenide, he stood, stretched, yawned, and checked his watch. A little after nine. He'd been at work for twelve hours.

He should have wanted nothing more than to flop in bed and sleep half a day. But he figured he'd zip back to his condo, which was ten minutes from the office, freshen up, and catch some nightlife. Last week he'd found a new club, Nuclear Grin, where the music was loud and hard-edged, the drinks unwatered, the crowd's politics unconsciously libertarian, and the women hot. He wanted to dance a little, drink a little, and find someone who wanted to screw her brains out.

In this age of new diseases, sex was risky; it sometimes seemed that drinking from the same glass as someone else was suicidal. But after a day in the painstakingly logical microchip universe, you had to get a little wild, take some risks, dance on the edge of chaos, to get some balance in your life.

Then he remembered how Frank and Bobby had vanished in front of his eyes. He wondered if maybe he hadn't already had enough wildness for one day.

He picked up the latest printouts. It was more stuff that he had gleaned from police records, regarding the decidedly weird behavior of Mr Blue, who would never need to get a little wild for balance, since he was *already* chaos walking around in shoes. Lee opened the door, switched off the lights, went down the hall and through another door into the lounge, intending to leave the printouts on Julie's desk and say goodnight to Hal before splitting.

When he walked into Bobby and Julie's office, it looked like the National Wrestling Federation had sanctioned a match there between tag teams of three-hundred-pound hulks. Furniture was overturned, and Scotch glasses, some of them broken, were scattered over the floor. Julie's desk was aslant and askew: tilting on one shattered leg; the top no longer properly aligned with the base, as if someone had gone at it with prybars and hammers.

'Hal?'

No answer.

He gingerly pushed open the door to the adjoining bathroom.

'Hal?'

The bathroom was deserted.

He went to the broken window. A few small shards of glass still clung to the frame. Caught the light. Jagged.

With one hand against the wall, Lee Chen carefully leaned out. He looked down. In a much different tone of voice, he said, 'Hal?'

Candy materialized in the foyer of the Dakotas' house, which was dark and silent. He stood quietly for a moment, head cocked, until he was confident that he was alone.

His throat was healed. He was whole again, and excited by the prospects of the night.

He began the search from there, putting his hand on the doorknob in hope of finding some of the residue that, while lacking physical substance, nevertheless provided the nourishment for his visions. He felt nothing, no doubt partly because the Dakotas had touched it only briefly upon entering and departing the house.

Of course, a person could handle a hundred items, leaving psychic images of himself on only one of them, then touch the same hundred an hour later and contaminate every one with his aura. The reason for that was as mysterious, to Candy, as was so many people's interest in sex. He remained as grateful to his mother for this talent as he was for all the others, but tracking his prey with psychometry was not always an easy or infallible process.

The Dakotas' living room and dining room were unfurnished, which gave him little to work with, although for some reason the emptiness made him feel comfortable and at home. That response puzzled him. The rooms in his mother's house were all furnished – as much with mold and fungus and dust these days as with chairs, sofas, tables, and lamps; but he suddenly realized that, like the Dakotas, he lived in such a small percentage of the house that most of its chambers might as well have been bare, carpetless, and sealed off.

The Dakotas' kitchen and family room were furnished and obviously lived in. Though it was unlikely that they had used the family room during their brief stop between the office and wherever they had gone from here, he hoped they might have lingered in the kitchen for a bite of food or a drink. But the handles of the cabinets, microwave, oven, and refrigerator provided him with no images whatsoever.

On his way to the second floor, Candy climbed the steps slowly, letting his left hand slide searchingly along the oak balustrade. At several points along the way, he was rewarded by psychic images that, while brief and not clear, encouraged him, and led him to believe that he would find what he needed in their bedroom or bathroom.

• 54 •

Instead of immediately dialing 911 to report the murder of Hal Yamataka, Lee ran first to the reception desk and, as he had been trained, removed a small brown notebook from the back of the bottom drawer on the right side. For the benefit of employees, like Lee, who did not often get into the field and seldom interfaced directly with the county's many police agencies but might one day need to deal with them in an emergency, Bobby had composed a list of some of the officers, detectives, and administrators who were most professional, reasonable, and reliable in every major jurisdiction. The brown notebook contained a second list of cops to avoid: those who had an instinctive dislike for anyone in the private investigation and security business; those who were just pains in the ass in general; and those who were always on the lookout for a little green grease to lubricate the wheels of justice. It was a testament to the high quality of the county's law enforcement that the first list was much longer than the second.

According to Bobby and Julie, it was preferable to try to *manage* the introduction of the police into a situation that required them, even going so far as to try to select one of the detectives who would show up at the scene – if it was a scene that needed detectives. Relying on the luck of the draw or a dispatcher's whim was considered unwise.

Lee wondered if he should even call the cops. He had no doubt who had killed Hal. Mr Blue. Candy. But also he knew that Bobby would not want to reveal more about Frank and the case than was truly necessary; the agency-client privilege was not as legally airtight as that of lawyer-client or doctor-patient, but it was important too. Since Julie and Bobby were on the road and temporarily unreachable, Lee could get no guidance on what and how much to say to the police.

But he couldn't let a dead body lie in front of the building, hoping nobody would notice! Especially not when the victim was a man he had known and liked.

Call the cops, then. But play dumb.

Consulting the notebook, Lee dialed the Newport Beach Police and asked for Detective Harry Ladsbroke, but Ladsbroke was off duty. So was Detective Janet Heisinger. Detective Kyle Ostov was available, however, and when he came on the line he sounded reassuringly big and competent; his voice was a mellow baritone, and he spoke crisply.

Lee identified himself, aware that his own voice was higher than usual, almost squeaky, and that he was speaking too fast. 'There's been a . . . well, a murder.'

Before Lee could go on, Ostov said, 'Jesus, you mean Bobby and Julie know already? I just found out myself. It was pushed on to me to tell them, and I was just sitting here, trying to figure how best to break the news. I had my hand on the phone, going to call them, when you rang through. How're they taking it?'

Confused, Lee said, 'I don't think they know. I mean, it must have happened just a few minutes ago.'

'A little longer than that,' Ostov said.

'When did you guys find out? I just looked, and there weren't any patrol cars, nothing.' Finally the shakes hit him. 'God, I was talking to him not that long ago, took him some pizza, and now he's splattered all over the concrete six floors down.'

Ostov was silent. Then: 'What murder are you talking about, Lee?'

'Hal Yamataka. There must've been a fight here, and then—' He stopped, blinked, and said, 'What murder are *you* talking about?'

'Thomas,' Ostov said.

Lee felt sick. He had only met Thomas once, but he knew that Julie and Bobby were devoted to him.

Ostov said, 'Thomas *and* his roommate. And maybe more in the fire if they didn't get them all out of the building in time.'

The computer that Lee had been born with was not functioning as smoothly as the ones made by IBM in his office, and he needed a moment to grasp the implications of the information that he and Ostov had exchanged. 'They've got to be connected, don't they?'

THE BAD PLACE

'I'd bet on it. You know of anybody who has a grudge against Julie and Bobby?'

Lee looked around the reception lounge, thought about the other deserted rooms at Dakota & Dakota, the lonely offices on the rest of the sixth floor, and the unpeopled levels below the sixth. He thought of Candy, too, all those people bitten and torn, the giant Bobby had seen on Punaluu Beach, the way the guy could zap himself from place to place. He began to feel very much alone. 'Detective Ostov, could you get some people here really fast?'

'I've entered the call on the computer while I've been talking to you,' Ostov said. 'A couple of units are on the way now.'

With his fingertips, Candy traced lazy circles on the surface of the dresser, then explored the contours of each brass handle on the drawers. He touched the light switch on the wall and the switches on both bedside lamps. He let his hands glide over doorframes on the off-chance that one of his intended prey might have paused and leaned there while in conversation, examined the handles on the mirrored closet doors, and caressed each number and switchpad on the remote-control device for the TV, hoping that they had clicked on the set even during the short time they had been home.

Nothing.

Because he needed to be calm and methodical in his search if he were to succeed, Candy had to repress his rage and frustration. But his anger grew even as he struggled to contain it, and in him the thirst of anger was always a thirst for blood, that wine of vengeance. Only blood would slake his thirst, quench his fury, and allow him an interlude of relative peace.

By the time he moved from the Dakotas' bedroom into the adjoining bath, Candy was possessed of a *need* for blood almost as undeniable and critical as his need for air. Looking at the mirror, he did not see himself for a moment, as if he cast no reflection; he saw only red blood, as if the mirror were a porthole on one of the lower decks of a ship in Hell, on a cruise through a sea of gore. When that illusion faded and he saw his own face, he quickly looked away.

He clenched his jaws, struggled even harder to control himself, and touched the hot-water faucet, searching, seeking . . .

The motel room in Santa Barbara was spacious, quiet, clean, and furnished without the jarring clash of colors and patterns that seemed de rigueur in most American motels – but it was not a place in which Julie would have chosen to receive the terrible news that came to her there. The blow seemed greater, the ache in the heart more piercing, for having to be borne in a strange and impersonal place.

She really had thought that Bobby was letting his imagination run away with him again, that Thomas was perfectly fine. Because the phone was on the nightstand, he sat on the edge of the bed to make the call, and Julie watched him and listened from a chair only a few feet away. When he got that recording again, explaining that the Cielo Vista number was temporarily out of service due to line problems, she was vaguely uneasy but still sure that all was well with her brother.

However, when he called the office in Newport to talk with Hal, got Lee Chen instead, and spent the first minute or so listening in shocked silence, responding with a cryptic word or two, she knew this was to be a night that cleaved her life, and that the years to come inevitably would be darker than the years she had lived on the other side of that cleft. As he began to ask questions of Lee, Bobby avoided looking at Julie, which confirmed her intuition and made her heart pound faster. When at last he glanced at her, she had to look away from the sadness in his eyes. His questions to Lee were clipped, and she couldn't ascertain much from them. Maybe she didn't want to.

Finally the call seemed to be drawing to an end. 'No, you've done well, Lee. Keep handling it just the way you have been. What? Thank you, Lee. No, we'll be all right. We'll be okay, Lee. One way or another, we'll be okay.'

When Bobby hung up, he sat for a moment, staring at his hands, which he clasped between his knees.

Julie did not ask him what had happened, as if what Lee had told him was not yet fact, as if her question was a dark magic and as if the unrevealed tragedy would not become real until she asked about it.

Bobby got off the bed and knelt on the floor in front of her chair. He took both of her hands in his and gently kissed them.

She knew then that the news was as bad as it could get.

Softly he said, 'Thomas is dead.'

She had steeled herself for that news, but the words cut deep.

'I'm sorry, Julie. God, I'm so sorry. And it doesn't end there.' He told her about Hal. 'And just a couple minutes before he talked to me, Lee received a call about Clint and Felina. Both dead.'

The horror was too much to assimilate. Julie had liked and respected Hal, Clint, and Felina enormously, and her admiration for the deaf woman's courage and self-sufficiency was unbounded. It was unfair that she could not mourn each of them individually; they deserved that much. She also felt that she was somehow betraying them because her sorrow at their deaths was only a pale reflection of the grief she felt at the loss of Thomas, though that was, of course, the only way it could be.

Her breath caught in her throat, and when it flew free, it was not just an exhalation but a sob. That was no good. She could not allow herself to break down. At no point in her life had she needed to be as strong as she needed to be now; the murders committed in Orange County tonight were the first in a domino-fall of death that would take down her and Bobby, too, if misery dulled their edge.

While Bobby continued to kneel before her and reveal more details – Derek was dead, too, and perhaps others at Cielo Vista – she gripped his hands tightly, inexpressibly grateful to have him for an anchor in this turbulence. Her vision was blurry, but she held back the tears with a sheer effort of will – though she dared not make eye contact with Bobby just yet; that would be the end of her self-control.

When he finished, she said, 'It was Frank's brother, of course,' and was dismayed by the way her voice quavered.

'Almost certainly,' Bobby said.

'But how did he find out Frank was our client?'

'I don't know. He saw me on the beach at Punaluu—'

'Yeah, but didn't follow you. He had no way of knowing who you were. And for God's sake, how did he find out about Thomas?'

'There's some crucial bit of information missing, so we can't understand the pattern.'

'What's the bastard after?' she said. Now her voice was marked by nearly as much anger as grief, and that was good.

'He's hunting Frank,' Bobby said. 'For seven years Frank was a loner, and that made him harder to find. Now Frank has friends, and that gives Candy more ways to search for him.'

'I as good as killed Thomas when I took the case,' she said.

'You didn't want to take it. I had to talk you into it.'

'I talked *you* into it, you wanted to back out.'

'If there's guilt, we share it, but there isn't any. We took on a new client, that's all, and everything . . . just happened.'

Julie nodded and finally met his eyes. Although his voice had remained steady, tears slid down his cheeks. Preoccupied with her own grief, she had forgotten that the friends lost were his as well as hers, and that he had come to love Thomas nearly as much as she did. She had to look away from him again.

'Are you okay?' he asked.

'For now, I have to be. Later, I want to talk about Thomas, how brave he was about being different, how he never complained, how sweet he was. I want to talk about all of it, you and me, and I don't want us to forget. Nobody's ever going to build a monument to Thomas, he wasn't famous, he was just a little guy who never did anything great except be the best person he knew how, and the only monument he's ever going to have is our memories. So we'll keep him alive, won't we?'

'Yes.'

'We'll keep him alive . . . until we're gone. But that's for later, when there's time. Now we have to keep ourselves alive, because that son of a bitch will be coming for us, won't he?'

'I think he will,' Bobby said.

He rose from his knees and pulled her up from the chair.

He was wearing his dark-brown Ultrasuede jacket with the shoulder holster under it. She'd taken off her corduroy blazer and her holster; she put both of them on again. The weight of the revolver, against her left side, felt good. She hoped she'd have a chance to use it.

Her vision had cleared; her eyes were dry. She said, 'One thing for sure – no more dreams for me. What good is it, having dreams, when they never come true?'

'Sometimes they do.'

'No. They never came true for my mom or dad. Never came true for Thomas, did they? Ask Clint and Felina if their dreams came true, see what they say. You ask George Farris's family if they think being slaughtered by a maniac was the fulfillment of their dreams.'

'Ask the Phans,' Bobby said quietly. 'They were boat people on the South China Sea, with hardly any food and less money, and now they own dry-cleaning shops and remodel two-hundred-thousand-dollar houses for resale, and they have those terrific kids.'

'Sooner or later, they'll get it in the neck too,' she said, unsettled by the bitterness in her voice and the black despair that churned like a whirlpool within her, threatening to swallow her up. But she could not stop the churning. 'Ask Park Hampstead, down there in El Toro, whether he and his wife were thrilled when she developed terminal cancer, and ask him how his dream about him and Maralee Roman worked after he finally got over the death of his wife. Nasty bugger named Candy got in the way of that one. Ask all the poor suckers lying in the hospital with cerebral hemorrhages, cancer. Ask those who get Alzheimer's in their fifties, just when their golden years are supposed to start. Ask the little kids in wheelchairs from muscular dystrophy, and ask all the parents of those other kids down there in Cielo Vista how Down's Syndrome fits in with *their* dreams. Ask—'

She cut herself off. She was losing control, and she could not afford to do so tonight.

She said, 'Come on, let's go.'

'Where?'

'First, we find the house where that bitch raised him. Cruise by, get the lay of it. Maybe just seeing it will give us ideas.'

'I've seen it.'

'I haven't.'

'All right.' From a nightstand drawer he removed a telephone directory for Santa Barbara, Montecito, Goleta, Hope Ranch, El Encanto Heights, and other surrounding communities. He brought it with him to the door.

She said, 'What do you want that for?'

'We'll need it later. I'll explain in the car.'

Sprinkles of rain were falling again. The Toyota's engine was still so hot from the drive north that in spite of the cool night air, steam rose from its hood as the beads of rainwater evaporated. Far away a brief, low peal of thunder rolled across the sky. Thomas was dead.

———

He received images as faint and distorted as reflections on the wind-rippled surface of a pond. They came repeatedly as he touched the faucets, the rim of the sink, the mirror, the medicine cabinet and its contents, the light switch, the controls for the shower. But none of his visions was detailed, and none provided a clue as to where the Dakotas had gone.

Twice he was jolted by vivid images, but they were related to disgusting sexual episodes between the Dakotas. A tube of vaginal lubricant and a box of Kleenex were contaminated with older psychic residue that had inexplicably lingered beyond its time, making him privy to sinful practices that he had no desire to witness. He quickly snatched his hands away from those surfaces and waited for his nausea to pass. He was incensed that the need to track Frank through these decadent people had forced him into a situation where his senses had been so brutally affronted.

Infuriated by his lack of success and by the unclean contact with images of their sin (which he seemed unable to expel from his mind), he decided that he must burn the evil out of this house in the name of God. Burn it out. Incinerate it. So that maybe his mind would be cleansed again as well.

He stepped out of the bathroom, raised his hands, and sent an immensely destructive wave of power across the bedroom. The wooden headboard of the big bed disintegrated, flames leaped from the quilted spread and blankets, the nightstands flew apart, and every drawer in the dresser shot out and dumped its contents on the floor, where they instantly caught fire. The drapes were consumed as if made from magicians' flashpaper, and the two windows in the far wall burst, letting in a draft that fanned the blaze.

Candy often wished the mysterious light that came from him could affect people and animals, rather than just inanimate things, plants, and a few insects. There were times when he would have gone into a city and melted the flesh from the bones of ten thousand sinners in a single night, a hundred thousand. It didn't matter which city, they were all festering sewers of iniquity, populated by depraved masses who worshiped evil and practiced every repulsive degeneracy. He had never seen anyone in any of them, not a single person, who seemed to him to live in God's grace. He would have made them run screaming in terror, would have tracked them down in their secret places, would have splintered their bones with his power, hammered their flesh to pulp, made their heads explode, and torn off the offensive sex things that preoccupied them. If he had been that gifted, he would not have shown them any of the mercy with which their Creator always treated them, so they would have realized, then, how grateful and obedient they should have been to their God, who always so patiently tolerated even their worst transgressions.

Only God and Candy's mother had such unlimited compassion. He did not share it.

The smoke alarm went off in the hall. He walked out there, pointed a finger at it, and blew it to bits.

This part of his gift seemed more powerful tonight than ever. He was a great engine of destruction.

The Lord must be rewarding his purity by increasing his power.

He thanked God that his own saintly mother had never descended into the pits of depravity in which so much of humanity swam. No man had ever touched her *that* way, so her children were born without the stain of original sin. He knew this to be true, for she had told him – and had shown him that it was.

He descended to the first floor and set the living room carpet on fire with a bolt from his left hand.

Frank and the twins had never appreciated the immaculate aspect of their conceptions, and in fact had thrown away that incomparable state of grace to embrace sin and do the devil's work. Candy would never make that mistake.

Overhead he heard the roar of flames, the crash of a partition. In the morning, when the sun revealed a smoldering pile of blackened rubble, the remains of this nest of corruption would be a testament to the ultimate perdition of all sinners.

Candy felt cleansed. The psychic images of the Dakotas' fevered degeneracy had been expunged from his mind.

He returned to the offices of Dakota & Dakota to continue his search for them.

Bobby drove, for he didn't think Julie ought to be behind the wheel any more tonight. She had been awake for more than nineteen hours, not a marathon all-nighter yet, but she was exhausted; and her bottled-up grief over Thomas's death could not help but cloud her judgment and dull her reflexes. At least he had napped a couple of times since Hal's call from the hospital had awakened them last night.

He crossed most of Santa Barbara and entered Goleta before bothering to look for a service station where they could ask for directions to Pacific Hill Road.

At his request, Julie opened the telephone directory on her lap, and with the assistance of a small flashlight taken from the glove compartment, she looked under the Fs for Fogarty. He didn't know the first name, but he was only interested in a male Fogarty who carried the title of doctor.

'He might not live in this area,' Bobby said, 'but I have a hunch he does.'

'Who is he?'

'When Frank and I were traveling, we stopped in this guy's study, twice.' He told her about both brief visits.

'How come you didn't mention him before?'

'At the office, when I told you what happened to me, where Frank and I had gone, I had to condense some of it, and this Fogarty seemed comparatively uninteresting, so I left him out. But the longer I've had time to think about it, the more it seems to me that he might be a key player in this. See, Frank popped us out of there so fast because he seemed especially reluctant to endanger Fogarty by leading Candy to him. If Frank's especially concerned about the man, then we ought to have a talk with him.'

She hunched over the directory, studying it closely. 'Fogarty, James. Fogarty, Jennifer. Fogarty, Kevin . . .'

'If he's not a medical doctor and doesn't use the title daily, or if "Doc" is a nickname, we're in trouble. Even if he is a medical doctor, don't bother looking in the Yellow Pages under "physicians," because this guy is up in years, got to be retired.'

'Here!' she said. 'Fogarty, Dr Lawrence J.'

'There's an address?'

'Yes.' She tore the page out of the book.

'Great. As soon as you've seen the infamous Pollard place, we'll pay Fogarty a visit.'

Though Bobby had visited the house three times, he had traveled there with Frank, and he had not known the precise location of 1458 Pacific Hill Road any more than he had known exactly what flank of Mount Fuji that trail had ascended. They found it easily, however, by following the directions they received from a long-haired guy with a handlebar mustache at a Union 76 station.

Though the houses along Pacific Hill Road enjoyed an El Encanto Heights address, they were actually neither in that suburb nor in Goleta – which separated El Encanto from Santa Barbara – but in a narrow band of county land that lay between the two and that led east into a wilderness preserve of mesquite, chapparral, desert brush, and pockets of California live oaks and other hardy trees.

The Pollard house was near the end of Pacific Hill, on the edge of developed land, with few neighbors. Oriented west-southwest, it overlooked the charmed

Pacific-facing communities so beautifully sited on the terraced hills below. At night the view was spectacular – a sea of lights leading to a real sea cloaked in darkness – and no doubt the immediate neighborhood remained rural and free of expensive new houses only because of development restrictions related to the proximity of the preserve.

Bobby recognized the Pollard place at once. The headlights revealed little more than the Eugenia hedge and the rusted iron gate between two tall stone pilasters. He slowed as they went by it. The ground floor was dark. In one upstairs room a light was on; a pale glow leaked around the edges of a drawn blind.

Leaning over to look past Bobby, Julie said, 'Can't see much.'

'There isn't much to see. It's a crumbling pile.'

They drove over a quarter of a mile to the end of the road, turned, and went back. Coming downhill, the house was on Julie's side, and she insisted he slow to a crawl, to allow her more time to study it.

As they eased past the gate, Bobby saw a light on at the back of the house, too, on the first floor. He couldn't actually see a lighted window, just the glow that fell through it and painted a pale, frosty rectangle on the side yard.

'It's all hidden in shadows,' Julie said at last, turning to look back at the property as it fell behind them. 'But I can see enough to know that it's a bad place.'

'Very,' Bobby said.

———

Violet lay on her back on the bed in her dark room with her sister, warmed by the cats, which were draped over them and huddled around them. Verbina lay on her right side, cuddled against Violet, one hand on Violet's breasts, her lips against Violet's bare shoulder, her warm breath spilling across Violet's smooth skin.

They were not settling down to sleep. Neither of them cared to sleep at night, for that was the wild time, when a greater number and variety of nature's hunters were on the prowl and life was more exciting.

At that moment they were not merely in each other and in all of the cats that shared the bed with them, but in a hungry owl that soared the night, scanning the earth for mice that weren't wise enough to fear the gloom and remain in burrows. No creature had night vision as sharp as the owl, and its claws and beak were even sharper.

Violet shivered in anticipation of the moment when a mouse or other small creature would be seen below, slipping through tall grass that it believed offered concealment. From past experience she knew the terror and pain of the prey, the savage glee of the hunter, and she yearned now to experience both again, simultaneously.

At her side Verbina murmured dreamily.

Swooping high, gliding, spiraling down, swooping up again, the owl had not yet seen its dinner when the car came up the hill and slowed almost to a stop in front of the Pollard house. It drew Violet's attention, of course, and through her the attention of the owl, but she lost interest when the car speeded up again and drove on. Seconds later, however, her interest was renewed when it returned and coasted almost to a stop, once more, at the front gate.

She directed the owl to circle the vehicle at a height of about sixty feet. Then she sent it out ahead of the car and brought it even lower, to about twenty feet, before guiding it around again to approach the curious motorist head-on.

From an altitude of only twenty feet, the vision of the owl was more than acute enough to see the driver and the passenger in the front seat. There was a woman Violet had never seen before – but the driver was familiar. A moment later she realized that he was the man who had appeared with Frank in the backyard, at twilight that very same day!

Frank had killed their precious Samantha, for which Frank must die, and now here was a man who knew Frank, who might lead them to Frank, and on the bed around Violet, the other cats stirred and made low growling sounds as her passion for vengeance was transitted to them. A tailless Manx and a black mongrel leaped from the bed, raced through the open bedroom door, down the steps, into the kitchen, out the pet door, around the house, and into the street. The car was moving away, gaining speed, heading downhill, and Violet wanted to pursue it not only by air but on foot, to ensure that she would not lose track of it.

Candy arrived in the reception lounge at Dakota & Dakota. Cool cross-drafts circulated from the broken window in the next room and two open doors in this one, setting up opposing currents. The faint sounds announcing his arrival had evidently been masked by the bursts of static and harsh voices coming from the portable police radios that the cops had clipped to their belts. One policeman stood in the entrance to Julie and Bobby's private office, and the other was at the open door to the sixth-floor corridor. Each of them was talking to someone out of sight, and both had their backs turned to Candy, which Candy knew was a sign that God was still looking out for him.

Though he was angered by this obstacle to his search for the Dakotas, he got out of there at once, materializing in his bedroom, nearly a hundred and fifty miles to the north. He needed time to think if there was some way that he could pick up their trail again, a place where they had been tonight – besides their office and their house – at which he could seek more visions of them.

When they backtracked to the Union 76 station, the long-haired, mustachioed man who had given them directions to Pacific Hill Road was able to tell them how to find the street on which Fogarty lived. He even knew the man. 'Nice old guy. Stops by here for gas now and then.'

'Is he a medical doctor?' Bobby asked.

'Used to be. Been retired quite a while.'

Shortly after ten o'clock, Bobby parked at the curb in front of Lawrence Fogarty's house. It was a quaint Spanish two-story with the style of French windows that had been featured in the study to which Bobby and Frank had twice traveled, and lights were on throughout the first floor. The glass in the many panes was beveled, at least on the front of the house, and the lamplight inside was warmly refracted by those cut edges. When Bobby and Julie got out of the car, he smelled woodsmoke, and saw a homey white curl rising from a chimney into the still, cool, humid pre-storm air. In the odd and vaguely purple, crepuscular glow of a nearby streetlamp, a few pink flowers were visible on the azaleas, but the bushes were not as laden with early blooms as those farther south in Orange County. An ancient tree with a multiple trunk and enormous branches looked over more than half the house, so it seemed like a wonderfully cozy and sheltered haven in some Spanish version of a Hobbity fantasy world.

As they followed the front walkway, something dashed between two low Malibu lights, crossed their path, and startled Julie. It stopped on the lawn after passing them, and studied them with radiant green eyes.

'Just a cat,' Bobby said.

Usually he liked cats, but when he saw this one, he shivered.

It moved again, vanishing into shadows and shrubs at the side of the house.

What spooked him was not this particular creature, but the memory of the feline horde at the Pollard house, which had raced to attack him and Frank, in eerie silence initially but then with the shrill single-voiced squeal of a banshee regiment, and with a most uncatlike unanimity of purpose. On the prowl alone, swift and curious, this cat was quite ordinary, possessed only of the mystery and haughtiness common to every member of his species.

At the end of the walk, three front steps led up to an archway, through which they entered a small veranda.

Julie rang the bell, which was soft and musical, and when no one answered after half a minute, she rang it again.

As the second set of chimes faded, the stillness was disturbed by the rustle of feathered wings, as some night bird settled onto the veranda roof above them.

When Julie was about to reach for the bell push again, the porch light came on, and Bobby sensed they were being scrutinized through the security lens. After a moment the door opened, and Dr Fogarty stood before them in an outfall of light from the hall behind him.

He looked the same as Bobby remembered him, and he recognized Bobby as well. 'Come in,' he said, stepping aside to admit them. 'I half expected you. Come in – not that any of you is welcome.'

• 55 •

'In the library,' Fogarty said, leading them back through the hall to a room on the left.

The library, where Frank had taken him during their travels, was the place Bobby had referred to as the study when he had described it to Julie. As the exterior of the house had a Hobbity-fantasy coziness in spite of its Spanish style, so this room seemed exactly the sort of place where one imagined that Tolkien, on many a long Oxford evening, had taken pen to paper to create the adventures of Frodo. That warm and welcoming space was gently illuminated by a brass floorlamp and a stained-glass table lamp that was either a genuine Tiffany or an excellent imitation. Books lined the walls under a deeply coffered ceiling, and a thick Chinese carpet – dark green and beige around the border, mostly pale green in the middle – graced a dark tongue-and-groove oak floor. The water-clear finish on the large mahogany desk had a deep luster; on the green felt blotter, the elements of a gold-plated, bone-handled desk set – including a letter opener, magnifying glass, and scissors – were lined up neatly behind a gold fountain pen in a square marble holder. The Queen Anne sofa was upholstered in a tapestry that perfectly complemented the carpet, and when Bobby turned to look at the wing-backed chair where he'd first seen Fogarty earlier in the day – he twitched with astonishment at the sight of Frank.

'Something's happened to him,' Fogarty said, pointing to Frank. He was unaware of Bobby's and Julie's surprise, apparently operating under the assumption that they had come to his house specifically because they had known they would find Frank there.

Frank's physical appearance had deteriorated since Bobby had last seen him at 5:26 that afternoon, in the office in Newport Beach. If his eyes had been sunken then, they were as deep as pits now; the dark rings around them had widened, too, and some of the blackness seemed to have leeched out of those bruises to impart a deathly gray tint to the rest of his face. His previous pallor had looked healthy by comparison.

The worst thing about him, however, was the blank expression with which he regarded them. No recognition lit his eyes; he seemed to be staring through them. His facial muscles were slack. His mouth hung open about an inch, as if he had started to speak a long time ago but had not yet managed to remember the first word of what he had wanted to say. At Cielo Vista Care Home, Bobby had seen only a few patients with faces as empty as this, but they had been among the most severely retarded, several steps down the ladder from Thomas.

'How long has he been here?' Bobby asked, moving toward Frank.

Julie seized his arm and held him back. 'Don't!'

'He arrived shortly before seven o'clock,' Fogarty said.

So Frank had traveled for nearly another hour and a half after he had returned Bobby to the office.

Fogarty said, 'He's been here over three hours, and I don't know what the blazing hell I'm supposed to do with him. Now and then he comes around a little bit, looks at you when you talk to him, even responds more or less to what you say. Then sometimes he's positively garrulous, runs on and on, won't answer your questions but sure wants to talk *at* a person, you couldn't shut him up with a two-by-four. He's told me a lot about you, for instance, more than I care to know.' He frowned and shook his head. 'You two may be crazy enough to get involved in this nightmare, but I'm not, and I resent being *dragged* into it.'

At first glance, the impression that Dr Lawrence Fogarty made was that of a kindly grandfather who, in his day, had been the type of devoted and selfless physician who became revered by his community, known and beloved by one and all. He was still wearing the slippers, gray slacks, white shirt, and blue cardigan in which Bobby had first seen him earlier, and the image was completed by a pair of half-lens reading glasses, over which he regarded them. With his thick white hair, blue eyes, and gentle rounded features, he would have made a perfect Santa Claus if he had been fifty or sixty pounds heavier.

But on a second and closer look, his blue eyes were steely, not warm. His rounded features were *too* soft, and revealed not gentility so much as lack of character, as though they had been acquired through a lifetime of self-indulgence. His wide mouth would have given kindly old Doc Fogarty a winning smile, but its generous dimension served equally well to lend the look of a predator to the real Doc Fogarty.

'So Frank's told you about us,' Bobby said. 'But we don't know anything about you, and I think we need to.'

Fogarty scowled. 'Better that you don't know about me. Better by far for *me*. Just get him out of here, take him away.'

'You want us to take Frank off your hands,' Julie said coldly, 'then you've got to tell us who you are, how you fit into this, what you know about it.'

Meeting Julie's gaze, then Bobby's, the old man said, 'He's not been here in five years. Today, when he came with you, Dakota, I was shocked, I'd thought I was finished with him forever. And when he came back tonight . . .'

Frank's eyes had not focused, but he had cocked his head to one side. His mouth was still ajar like the door to a room from which the resident had fled in haste.

Regarding Frank sourly, Fogarty said, 'I've never seen him like this, either. I wouldn't want him on my hands if he was his old self, let alone when he's half a vegetable. All right, all right, we'll talk. But once we've talked, he's *your* responsibility.'

Fogarty went behind the mahogany desk and sat in a chair that was upholstered in the same dark maroon leather as was the wingback in which Frank slumped.

Although their host had not offered them a seat, Bobby went to the sofa. Julie followed and slipped past him at the last moment, sitting on the end of the sofa closest to Frank. She favored Bobby with a look that essentially said, *You're too impulsive, if he groans or sighs or blows a spit bubble, you'll put a hand on him to comfort him, and then you'll be gone in a wink to Hoboken or Hell, so keep your distance.*

Removing his tortoiseshell reading glasses and putting them on the blotter, Fogarty squeezed his eyes shut and pinched the bridge of his nose between thumb and forefinger, as if to banish a headache with an effort of will or collect his thoughts or both. Then he opened his eyes, blinked at them across the desk, and said, 'I'm the doctor who delivered Roselle Pollard when she was born forty-six years ago, February of 1946. I'm also the doctor who delivered each of her kids – Frank, the twins, and James . . . or Candy as he now prefers. Over the years I treated Frank for the usual childhood-adolescent illnesses, and I guess that's why he thinks he can come to me now, when he's in trouble. Well, he's wrong. I'm no goddamned TV doctor who wants to be everybody's confidant and Dutch uncle. I treated them, they paid me, and that should be the end of it. Fact is . . . I only ever really treated Frank and his mother, because the girls and James never got sick, unless we're talking mental illness, in which case they were sick at birth and never got well.'

Because Frank's head was tilted, a thin, silver stream of drool slipped out of the right corner of his mouth and along his chin.

Julie said, 'You evidently know about the powers her children have—'

'I didn't know, really, until seven years ago, the day that Frank killed her. I was retired by then, but he came to me, told me more than I ever wanted to know, dragged me into this nightmare, wanted me to help. How could I help?

How can anyone help? It's none of my business anyway.'

'But why do they have these powers?' Julie said. 'Do you have any clue, any theories?'

Fogarty laughed. It was a hard, sour laugh that would have dispelled any illusions Bobby had about him if those illusions had not already been dispelled two minutes after he'd met the man. 'Oh, yes, I have theories, lots of information to support the theories too, some of it stuff you'll wish you never heard. I'm not going to get myself involved in the mess, not me, but I can't help now and then thinking about it. Who could? It's a sick and twisted and *fascinating* mess. My theory is that it starts with Roselle's father. Supposedly her father was some itinerant who knocked up her mother, but I always knew that was a lie. Her father was Yarnell Pollard, her mother's brother. Roselle was a child of rape and incest.'

A look of distress must have crossed Bobby's face or Julie's, for Fogarty let out another bark of cold laughter, clearly amused by their sympathetic response.

The old physician said, 'Oh, that's nothing. That's the least of it.'

The tailless Manx – Zitha by name – took up sentry duty in the concealment of an azalea shrub near the front door.

The old Spanish house had exterior window ledges, and the second cat – as black as midnight, and named Darkle – sprang to another one in search of the room to which the old man had taken the younger man and woman. Darkle put his nose to the glass. A set of interior shutters inhibited snooping, but the wide louvres were only half closed, and Darkle was able to see several cross-sections of the room by raising or lowering his head.

Hearing Frank's name spoken, the cat stiffened, because Violet had stiffened in her bed high on Pacific Hill.

The old man was there, among the books, and the couple as well. When everyone sat down, Darkle had to lower his head to peer between another pair of tilted louvres. Then he saw that Frank was not only one of the subjects of their conversation but actually present in a high-backed chair that stood at just enough of an angle to the window to reveal part of his face, and one hand lying limply on the wide, maroon-leather arm.

Leaning over his desk and smiling humorlessly as he talked, Doc Fogarty resembled a troll that had crawled out from its lair beneath a bridge, not content to wait for unsuspecting children to pass by, prepared to forage for his grisly dinner.

Bobby reminded himself not to let his imagination run away with him. He needed to keep an unbiased perspective on Fogarty, in order to determine the truthfulness and value of what the old man had to tell them. Their lives might depend on it.

'The house was built in the thirties by Deeter and Elizabeth Pollard. He'd made some money in Hollywood, producing a bunch of cheap Westerns, other junk. Not a fortune, but enough that he was fairly sure he could give up films and Los Angeles, which he hated, move up here, get into some small businesses, and do all right for the rest of his life. They had two children. Yarnell was fifteen when they came here in 1938, and Cynthia was only six years old. In '45, when Deeter and Elizabeth were killed in a car crash – hit head-on by a drunk driving a truck full of cabbages down from the Santa Ynez valley, if you can believe it – Yarnell became the man of the house at the age of twenty-two, and the legal guardian of his thirteen-year-old sister.'

Julie said, 'And . . . forced himself on her, you said?'

Fogarty nodded. 'I'm sure of it. Because over the next year, Cynthia became withdrawn, weepy. People attributed it to the death of her folks, but it was Yarnell using her, I think. Not just because he wanted the sex – though she was a pretty little thing, and you could hardly fault his taste – but because being man of the house appealed to him, he liked authority. And he was the type who wasn't happy until his authority was absolute, his dominance complete.'

Bobby was horrified by the words 'you could hardly fault his taste' and what they implied about the depth of the moral abyss in which Fogarty lived.

Oblivious of the disgust with which his visitors were regarding him, Fogarty continued: 'Yarnell was strong-willed, reckless, caused his folks a lot of heart-ache before they died, all kinds of heartache but mostly related to drugs. He was an acidhead before they had a name for it, before they even had LSD. Peyote, mescaline . . . all of the natural hallucinogens you can distill from certain cactuses, mushrooms and other fungi. Wasn't the drug culture back then that we have now, but crap was around. He got into hallucinogens through a relationship he had with a character actor who appeared in a lot of his father's movies, got started when he was fifteen, and I tell you all this because my theory is it's the key to everything you want to know.'

'The fact that Yarnell was an acidhead,' Julie said. 'That's the key?'

'That and the fact he impregnated his own sister. The chemicals probably did genetic damage, and a lot of it, by the time he was twenty-two. They usually do. In his case some very *strange* genetic damage. Then, when you add in the fact that the gene pool was very limited, being as Cynthia was his sister, you might expect there's a high chance the offspring will be a freak of some kind.'

Frank made a low sound, then sighed.

They all looked at him, but he was still detached. Though his eyes blinked rapidly for a moment, they did not come back into focus. Saliva still drooled from the right corner of his mouth; a string of it hung from his chin.

Though Bobby felt that he should get some Kleenex and blot Frank's face, he restrained himself, largely because he was afraid of Julie's reaction.

'So about a year after their parents died, Yarnell and Cynthia came to me, and she was pregnant,' Fogarty said. 'They had this story about some itinerant farmworker raping her, but it didn't ring true, and I pretty much figured out the real story just watching how they were with each other. She'd tried to conceal the pregnancy by wearing loose clothes and by staying in the house entirely during her last few months, and I never could understand that behavior; it was as if they thought the problem would just go away one day. By the time they came to me, abortion was out of the question. Hell, she was in the early stages of labor.'

The longer he listened to Fogarty, the more it seemed to Bobby that the air in the library was foul and growing fouler, thick with a humidity as sour as sweat.

'Claiming that he wanted to protect Cynthia as much as possible from public scorn, Yarnell offered me a pretty fat fee if I'd keep her out of the hospital and deliver the baby right in my office, which was a little risky, in case there were complications. But I needed the money, and if anything went really wrong, there were ways to cover it. I had this nurse at the time who could assist me – Norma, she was pretty flexible about things.'

Just great, Bobby thought. The sociopathic physician had found himself a sociopathic nurse, a couple who would be right in the social swim of things among the medical staff at Dachau or Auschwitz.

Julie put a hand on Bobby's knee and squeezed, as if the contact reassured her that she was not listening to a mad doctor in a dream.

'You should have seen what came out of that girl's oven,' Fogarty said. 'A freak it was, just as you'd expect.'

'Wait a minute,' Julie said. 'I thought you said the baby was Roselle. Frank's mother.'

'It was,' Fogarty said. 'And she was such a spectacular little freak that she'd have been worth a fortune to any carnival sideshow willing to risk the anger of the law to exhibit her.' He paused, enjoying their anticipation. 'She was an hermaphrodite.'

For a moment the word meant nothing to Bobby, and then he said, 'You don't mean – she had both sexes, male and female?'

'Oh, but that's exactly what I mean.' Fogarty bounced up from his chair and began to pace, suddenly energized by the conversation. 'Hermaphroditism is an extremely rare birth defect in humans, it's an amazing thing to have the opportunity to deliver one. You have *traverse* hermaphroditism, where you have the external organs of one sex and the internal of the other, lateral hermaphroditism . . . several other types. But the thing is . . . Roselle was the rarest of all, she possessed the complete internal and external organs of both sexes.' He plucked a thick medical reference book from one of the shelves and handed it to Julie. 'Check page one forty-six for photos of the kind of thing I'm talking about.'

Julie handed the volume to Bobby so fast it seemed as if she thought it was a snake.

Bobby, in turn, put it beside himself on the sofa, unopened. The last thing he needed, with his imagination, was the assistance of clinical photographs.

His hands and feet had gone cold, as though the blood had rushed from his extremities to his head, to nourish his brain, which was spinning furiously. He wished that he could *stop* thinking about what Fogarty was telling them. It was gross. But the worst thing about it was, judging by the physician's strange smile, Bobby sensed that what they had heard thus far was all just the bread on this horror sandwich; the meat was yet to come.

Pacing again, Fogarty said, 'Her vagina was about where you'd expect, the male equipment somewhat displaced. Urination was through the male part, but the female appeared reproductively complete.'

'I think we get the picture,' Julie said. 'We don't need all the technical details.'

Fogarty came to them, stood looking down at them, and his eyes were as bright and lively as if he were recounting a charming medical anecdote that had bewitched legions of delighted companions at dinner parties over the years.

'No, no, you must understand what she was, if you're going to understand all that happened next.'

───────

Though her own mind was split into many parts – sharing the bodies of Verbina, all the cats, and the owl on Fogarty's porch roof – Violet was most acutely aware of what she was receiving through the senses of Darkle, as he perched upon the windowsill outside the study. With the cat's sharp hearing, Violet missed not a word of the conversation, in spite of the intervening pane of glass. She was enthralled.

She seldom paused to think about her mother, although Roselle was still in this old house in so many ways. She seldom thought about *any* human being, for that matter, except herself and her twin sister – less often Candy and Frank – because she had so little in common with other people. Her life was with the wild things. In them emotions were so much more primitive and intense, pleasure so much more easily found and enjoyed without guilt. She hadn't really known her mother or been close to her; and Violet would not have been close, even if her mother had been willing to share affection with anyone but Candy.

But now Violet was riveted by what Fogarty was telling them, not because it was news to her (which it was), but because anything that had affected Roselle's life this completely also had profound effects on Violet's life. And of the countless attitudes and perceptions that Violet had absorbed from the myriad wild creatures whose minds and bodies she shared, a fascination with self was perhaps paramount. She had an animal's narcissistic preoccupation with grooming, with her own wants and needs. From her point of view, nothing in the world was of interest unless it served her, satisfied her, or affected the possibility of her future happiness.

Dimly she realized that she should find her brother and tell him that Frank was less than two miles away from them. Not long ago she had heard the wind-music of Candy's return.

───────

Fogarty turned away from Bobby and Julie and circled behind his desk again, where he walked along the bookshelves, snapping his finger against the spines of the volumes to punctuate his story.

As the physician spoke of this family that had seemingly *sought* genetic catastrophe, Julie could not help but think of how Thomas's affliction had been visited upon him even though his parents had lived healthy and normal lives. Fate played as cruelly with the innocent as with the guilty.

'When he saw the baby's abnormality, I think Yarnell would have killed it and thrown it out with the garbage – or at least put it in the hands of an institution. But Cynthia wouldn't part with it, she said it was her child, deformed or not, and she named it Roselle, after her dead grandmother. I suspect she wanted to keep it largely because she saw how it repulsed him, and she wanted to have Roselle around as a permanent reminder to him of the consequences of what he had forced her to do.'

'Couldn't surgery have been used to make her one sex or another?' Bobby asked.

'Easier today. Iffier then.'

Fogarty had stopped at the desk, where he had removed a bottle of Wild Turkey and a glass from one of the side drawers. He poured a few ounces of bourbon for himself and recapped the bottle without offering them a drink. That was fine with Julie. Though Fogarty's house was spotless, she wouldn't have felt clean after drinking or eating anything in it.

After taking a swallow of the warm bourbon, neat, Fogarty said, 'Besides, wouldn't want to remove one set of organs only to discover that, as the child grew older, it proved to look and act more like the sex you denied it than like the one it was permitted. Secondary sex characteristics are visible in infants, of course, but not as easily read – certainly not in 1946. Anyway, Cynthia wouldn't have authorized surgery. Remember what I said – she probably welcomed the child's deformity as a weapon against her brother.'

'You could have stepped between them and the baby,' Bobby said. 'You could've brought the child's plight to the attention of public health authorities.'

'Why on earth would I want to do that? For the psychological wellbeing of the child, you mean? Don't be naive.' He drank some more bourbon. 'I was paid well to make the delivery and keep my mouth shut about it, and that was fine by me. They took her home, stuck to their story about the itinerant rapist.'

Julie said, 'The baby . . . Roselle . . . she had no serious medical problems?'

'None,' Fogarty said. 'Other than this abnormality, she was as healthy as a horse. Her mental skills and her body developed right on schedule, like any child, and before long it became obvious that, to all outward appearances, she was going to look like a woman. As she grew even older, you could see she'd never be an attractive filly, mind you, more on the sturdy side than a fashion model, thick legs and all that, but quite feminine enough.'

Frank remained vacant-eyed and detached, but a muscle in his left cheek twitched twice.

The bourbon apparently relaxed the physician, for he sat behind his desk again, leaned forward, and clasped his hands around the glass. 'In 1959, when Roselle was thirteen, Cynthia died. Killed herself, actually. Blew her brains out. The following year, about seven months after his sister's suicide, Yarnell came to the office with his daughter – that is, with Roselle. He never called her his daughter, maintaining the fiction that she was only his bastard niece. Anyway, Roselle was pregnant at fourteen, same age at which Cynthia had given birth to her.'

'Good God!' Bobby said.

The shocks kept piling one atop another with such speed that Julie was almost ready to grab the whiskey bottle off the desk, drink straight from it, and never mind that it was Fogarty's booze.

Enjoying their reactions, Fogarty sipped the bourbon and gave them time to absorb the shock.

Julie said, 'Yarnell raped the daughter he had fathered by his own sister?'

Fogarty waited a little longer, savoring the moment. Then: 'No, no. He found the girl repellent, and I'm confident he wouldn't have touched her. I'm sure what Roselle told me was the truth.' He sipped more bourbon. 'Cynthia had developed quite a religious streak between the time she gave birth to Roselle and the day she killed herself, and she had passed on that passion for God to Roselle. The girl knew the Bible backward and forward. So Roselle came in here, pregnant. Said she'd decided she should have a child. Said God had made her special – that's what she called hermaphroditism, *special!* – because she was to be a pure vessel by which blessed children could be brought into the world. Therefore she had collected the semen from her male half and mechanically inserted it into her female half.'

Bobby shot up from the sofa as if one of its springs had broken under him, and he grabbed the bottle of Wild Turkey from the desk. 'You have another glass?'

Fogarty pointed to a bar cabinet in the corner, which Julie had not noticed before. Bobby opened the double doors, revealing not only more glasses but additional fifths of Wild Turkey. Evidently the physician kept a bottle in his desk drawer only so he would not have to walk across the room for it. Bobby poured two glasses full, with no ice, and brought one back to Julie.

To Fogarty, she said, 'Of course, I never thought Roselle was barren. She did bear children, we know that. But I assumed you meant the male part of her was sterile.'

'Fertile as a male *and* as a female. She couldn't actually join herself to herself, so to speak. So she resorted to artificial insemination, as I said.'

Late that afternoon, in the office in Newport, when Bobby had tried to explain how traveling with Frank was like a bobsled ride off the edge of the world, Julie had not really understood why he was so unnerved by the experience. Now she thought she had an inkling of what he had meant, for the chaos of the Pollard family's relationships and sexual identities made her skin crawl and filled her with a dark suspicion that nature was even stranger and more hospitable to anarchy than she had feared.

'Yarnell wanted me to abort the fetus, and abortion was a fairly lucrative sideline in those days, though illegal and hush-hush. But the girl had hidden her pregnancy from him for seven months, as he and Cynthia had tried to hide a pregnancy fourteen years earlier. It was much too late for an abortion then. The girl would've died, hemorrhaging. Besides, I would no more have aborted that fetus than I'd have shot myself in the foot. Imagine the degree of inbreeding involved here: the hermaphroditic child of brother-sister incest impregnates herself! Her child's mother is also its father. Its grandmother is also its great-aunt, and its grandfather is its great-uncle! One tight genetic line – and genes damaged by Yarnell's use of hallucinogenics, remember. Virtually a guarantee of a freak of one kind or another, and I wouldn't have missed it for the world.'

Julie took a long swallow of the bourbon. It tasted sour and stung her throat. She didn't care. She needed it.

'I'd become a doctor because the pay was good,' Fogarty said. 'Later, when I gravitated toward illegal abortions, the pay was better, and it became my main business. Not much danger, either, because I knew what I was doing, and I could buy off an authority now and then if I had to. When you're getting those fat fees, you don't have to schedule many office visits, you can have a lot of free time, money and leisure, the best of both worlds. But having settled for a career like that, what I *never* figured was that I'd encounter anything as medically interesting, as fascinating, as *entertaining* as this Pollard mess.'

The only consideration that caused Julie to refrain from going across the room and kicking the crap out of the old man was not his age but the fact that he would leave the story unfinished and some vital piece of information unrevealed.

'But the birth of Roselle's first child wasn't the event I'd thought it would be,' Fogarty said. 'In spite of the odds, the baby she produced was healthy and, from all indications, perfectly normal. That was 1960, and the baby was Frank.'

In the wingback chair, Frank whimpered softly but remained in his semicomatose condition.

Still listening to Doc Fogarty through Darkle, Violet sat up and swung her bare legs over the edge of the bed, dispossessing some of the cats from their resting places, and eliciting a murmur of protest from Verbina, who was seldom content to share just a mental link with her sister and needed the reassurance of physical contact. With cats swarming at her feet, seeing through their eyes as well as her own and therefore not blinded by the darkness, Violet started toward the open door to the lightless upstairs hall.

Then she remembered that she was nude, and she turned back for panties and T-shirt.

She wasn't afraid of Candy's disapproval – or of Candy himself. In fact, she would welcome his violent attentions, for that would be the ultimate game of hunter and prey, hawk and mouse, brother and sister. Candy was the only wild creature into whose mind she couldn't intrude; though wild, he was also human and beyond the reach of her powers. If he tore out her throat, however, then her blood would get into him, and she would become a part of him in the only manner she ever could. Likewise, that was the only way he could get into her: by biting his way in, by chewing into her, the only way.

On any other night, she would have called to him and let him see her nude, with the hope that her shamelessness would at last provoke him to violence. But she could not pursue her fondest desire right now, not when Frank was nearby and still unpunished for what he had done to their poor puss, Samantha.

When she had dressed, she returned to the hall, moved along it in the gloom – still in complete touch with Darkle and Zitha and the wild world – and stopped before the door to their mother's room, into which Candy had moved upon her death. A thin line of light showed along the sill.

'Candy,' she said. 'Candy, are you there?'

Like a memory from wars past or a presentiment of an ultimate war to come, a searing flash of lightning and a sky-shattering crash of thunder shook the night. The windows of the study vibrated. It was the first thunder Bobby had heard since the faint and distant peal when they had come out of the motel, nearly an hour and a half ago. In spite of the fireworks in the sky, rain was not yet falling. But though the tempest was slow moving, it was almost upon them. The pyrotechnics of a storm was an ideal backdrop to Fogarty's tale.

'I was disappointed in Frank,' Fogarty said, taking a second bottle of bourbon from his capacious desk drawer and refilling his glass. 'No fun at all. So normal. But two years later, she was pregnant again! This time the delivery was every bit as entertaining as I'd expected Frank's to be. A baby boy again, and she called him James. Her second virgin birth, she said, and she didn't mind at all that he was as much of a mess as she was. She said that was just proof that he, too, was favored by God and brought into the world without a need to wallow in the depravity of sex. I knew then that she was as mad as a hatter.'

Bobby knew he had to remain sober, and he was aware of the danger of too much bourbon after a night of too little sleep. But he had a hunch that he was burning it off as fast as he drank it, at least for now. He took another sip before he said, 'You're not telling us that beefy hulk is hermaphroditic too?'

'Oh, no.' Fogarty said. 'Worse than that.'

Candy opened the door. 'What do you want?'

'He's here, in town, right now,' she said.

His eyes widened. 'You mean Frank?'

'Yes.'

'Worse,' Bobby said numbly.

He got up from the sofa long enough to put his glass on the desk. It was still three-quarters full, but he suddenly decided that even bourbon would not be an effective tranquilizer in this case.

Julie seemed to reach the same conclusion, and put her glass aside too.

'James – or Candy, if you wish – was born with four testes instead of two, but with no male organ. Now, at birth, male infants all carry their testes safely in their abdominal cavity, and the testes descend later, during infant maturation. But Candy's never descended and never could, because there was no scrotum for them to descend into. And for another thing, there's a strange excrescence of bone that would prevent their descent. So they've remained within his abdominal cavity. But I would guess they've functioned well, busily producing quite large amounts of testosterone, which is related to development of musculature and partly explains his formidable size.'

'So he's incapable of having sex,' Bobby said.

'With his testicles undescended and no organ for copulation, I'd say he's got a shot at being the most chaste man who ever lived.'

Bobby had come to loathe the old man's laugh. 'But with four gonads, he's producing a flood of testosterone, and that does more than help build muscles – doesn't it?'

Fogarty nodded. 'To put it in the language of a medical journal: excess testosterone, over an extended period of time, alters normal brain function, sometimes radically, and is a causative factor of socially unacceptable levels of aggression. To put it in layman's language: this guy is seriously stoked with sexual tension he can't possibly release, he's rechanneled that energy into other outlets, mainly acts of incredible violence, and he's as dangerous as any monster any moviemaker ever dreamed up.'

Although she had released the owl as the storm drew near, Violet still inhabited Darkle and Zitha, taking their fear away from them when the lightning flared and the thunder boomed. Even as she stood before Candy, at the door to his room, she was listening to Fogarty tell the Dakotas about her brother's deformity. She knew about it already, of course, for within the family their mother had referred to it as God's sign that Candy was the most special of all of them. Likewise, in some way Violet had been aware that this deformity was related to the great wildness in Candy, the thing that made him so powerfully attractive.

Now she stood before him, wanting to touch his huge arms, feel the sculpted muscles, but she restrained herself. 'He's at Fogarty's house.'

That surprised him. 'Mother said Fogarty was an instrument of God. He brought us into the world, four virgin births. Why would he harbor Frank? Frank's on the dark side now.'

'That's where he is,' Violet said. 'And a couple. His name's Bobby. Hers is Julie.'

'Dakota,' he whispered.

'At Fogarty's. Make him pay for Samantha, Candy. Bring him back here after you've killed him, and let us feed him to the cats. He hated the cats, and he'll hate being part of them forever.'

Julie's temper, not always easily controlled, was dangerously near the flash-point. As lightning shocked the night outside and thunder again protested, she counseled herself about the necessity for diplomacy.

Nevertheless, she said, 'You've known all these years that Candy is a vicious killer, and you've done nothing to alert anyone to the danger?'

'Why should I?' Fogarty asked.

'Haven't you ever heard of social responsibility?'

'It's a nice phrase, but meaningless.'

'People have been brutally murdered because you let that man—'

'People will always and forever be brutally murdered. History is full of brutal murder. Hitler murdered millions. Stalin, many millions more. Mao Tse-tung, more millions than anyone. They're all considered monsters now, but they had their admirers in their time, didn't they? And there're people even now who'll tell you Hitler and Stalin only did what they had to do, that Mao was just keeping the public order, disposing of ruffians. So many people *admire* those murderers who are bold about it and who cloak their bloodlust in noble causes like brotherhood and political reform and justice – and social responsibility. We're all meat, just meat, and in our hearts we know it, so we secretly applaud the men bold enough to treat us as we are. Meat.'

By now she knew that he was a sociopath, with no conscience, no capacity for love, and no ability to empathize with other people. Not all of them were street hoodlums – or even high-class, high-tech thieves like Tom Rasmussen, who had tried to kill Bobby last week. Some got to be doctors – or lawyers, TV ministers, politicians. None of them could be reasoned with, for they had no normal human feelings.

He said, 'Why should I tell anyone about Candy Pollard? I'm safe from him because his mother always called me God's instrument, told her wretched spawn I was to be respected. It's none of my business. He's covered his mother's murder to avoid having the police tramping through the house, told people she moved to a nice oceanside condo near San Diego. I don't think anybody believes that crazy bitch would suddenly lighten up and become a beach bunny, but nobody questions it because nobody wants to get involved. Everybody feels it's *none of their business.* Same with me. Whatever outrages Candy adds to the world's pain are negligible. At least, given his peculiar psychology and physiology, his outrages will be more imaginative than most.

'Besides, when Candy was about eight, Roselle came to thank me for bringing her four into the world, and for keeping my own counsel, so that Satan was unaware of their blessed presence on earth. That's exactly how she put it! And as a token of her appreciation, she gave me a suitcase full of money, enough to make early retirement possible. I couldn't figure where she'd gotten it. The money that Deeter and Elizabeth piled up in the thirties had long ago dwindled away. So she told me a little bit about Candy's ability, not much, but enough to explain that she'd never want for cash. That was the first time I realized there was a genetic boon tied to the genetic disaster.'

Fogarty raised his glass of bourbon in a toast that they did not return. 'To God's mysterious ways.'

Like the archangel come to declare the end of the world in the Book of The Apocalypse, Candy arrived just as the heavens sundered and the rain began to fall in earnest, although this was not black rain as would be the deluge of Armageddon, nor was it a storm of fire. Not yet. Not yet.

He materialized in the darkness between two widely spaced streetlamps, almost a block from the doctor's house, to be sure that the soft trumpets that unfailingly announced his arrival would not be audible to anyone in Fogarty's library. As he walked toward the house through the hammering rain, he believed that his power, provided by God, had now grown so enormous that nothing could prevent him from taking or achieving anything he desired.

'In sixty-six, the twins were born, and physically they were as normal as Frank,' Fogarty said as rain suddenly splattered noisily against the window. 'No fun in that. I couldn't believe it, really. Three out of four of the kids, perfectly healthy. I'd been expecting all sorts of cute twists – harelips at the very least, misshapen skulls, cleft faces, withered limbs or extra heads!'

Bobby took Julie's hand. He needed the contact.

He wanted to get out of there. He felt burnt out. Hadn't they heard enough?

But that was the problem: he didn't know what was left to hear, or how much of it might be crucial to finding a way of dealing with the Pollards.

'Of course, when Roselle brought me that suitcase full of money, I began to learn that the children *were* all freaks, mentally if not physically. And seven years ago, when Frank killed her, he came to me, as if I owed him something

– understanding, shelter. He told me more about them than I wanted to know, too much. For the next two years, he'd periodically return here, just appear like a ghost that wanted to haunt *me* instead of a place. But he finally understood there was nothing for him here, and for five years he stayed out of my life. Until today, tonight.'

In his wingback chair, Frank moved. He shifted his body and tipped his head from the right to the left. Otherwise, he was no more alert than he had been since they had entered the room. The old man had said that Frank had come around a few times and had been talkative, but it couldn't be proved by his behavior during the past hour or so.

Julie, who was the closest to Frank, frowned and leaned toward him, peering at the right side of his head.

'Oh, my God.'

She spoke those three words in a bleak tone of voice that was as effective a refrigerant as anything used in an air conditioner.

With a chill skittering up his spine, Bobby slid along the sofa, crowding her against the other end, and looked past her at the side of Frank's head. Wished he had not. Tried to look away. Couldn't.

When Frank's head had been tilted to his right, almost lying against his shoulder, they had not been able to see that temple. After leaving Bobby at the office, still out of control, traveling against his will, Frank evidently had returned to one of those craters where the engineered insects shat out their diamonds. His flesh was lumpy all the way along his temple to his jaw, and in some places the rough gemstones that were the cause of the lumpiness poked through, gleaming, intimately melded with his tissue. For whatever reason, he had scooped up a handful to bring with him, but when reconstituting himself he had made a mistake.

Bobby wondered what treasures might be buried in the soft gray matter within Frank's skull.

'I saw that too,' Fogarty said. 'And look at the palm of his right hand.'

Although Julie protested, Bobby pinched the sleeve of Frank's jacket and pulled until he twisted the man's arm off the chair and revealed his palm. He had found the partial roach that had once been welded into his own shoe. At least it appeared to be the same one. It was sprouting from the meaty part of Frank's hand, carapace gleaming, dead eyes staring up toward Frank's index finger.

———

Candy circled the house in the rain, passing a black cat on a windowsill. It turned its head to glance at him, then put its face to the windowpane again.

At the rear of the house, he stepped quietly onto the porch and tried the back door. It was locked.

Vague blue light pulsed from his hand as he gripped the knob. The lock slipped, the door opened, and he stepped inside.

———

Julie had heard and seen enough, too much.

Eager to get away from Frank, she rose from the sofa and walked to the desk, where she considered her unfinished bourbon. But that was no answer. She was dreadfully tired, struggling to repress her grief for Thomas, striving even harder to make some sense out of the grotesque family history that Fogarty had revealed to them. She did not need the complication of any more bourbon, appealing as it might look there in the glass.

She said to the old man, 'So what hope do we have of dealing with Candy?'

'None.'

'There must be a way.'

'No.'

'There must be.'

'Why?'

'Because he can't be allowed to win.'

Fogarty smiled. 'Why not?'

'Because he's the bad guy, dammit! And we're the good guys. Not perfect, maybe, not without flaws, but we're the good guys, all right. And that's why we have to win, because if we don't, then the whole game is meaningless.'

Fogarty leaned back in his chair. 'My point exactly. It *is* all meaningless. We're not good, and we're not bad, we're just meat. We don't have souls, there's no hope of transcendence for a slab of meat, you wouldn't expect a hamburger to go to heaven after someone ate it.'

She had never hated anyone as much as she hated Fogarty at that moment, partly because he was so smug and hateful, but partly because she recognized, in his arguments, something perilously close to the things she had said to Bobby in the motel, after she had learned about Thomas's death. She had said there was no point in having dreams, that they never came true, that death was always there watching even if you *were* lucky enough to grasp your personal brass ring. And loathing life, just because it led sooner or later to death . . . well, that was the same as saying people were nothing but meat.

'We have just pleasure and pain,' the old physician said, 'so it doesn't matter who's right or who's wrong, who wins or loses.'

'What's his weakness?' she demanded angrily.

'None I can see.' Fogarty seemed pleased by the hopelessness of their position. If he had been practicing medicine in the early 1940s, he had to be nearing eighty, though he looked younger. He was acutely aware of how little time remained to him, and was no doubt resentful of anyone younger; and given his cold perspective on life, their deaths at Candy Pollard's hands would entertain him. 'No weaknesses at all.'

Bobby disagreed, or tried to. 'Some might say that his weakness is his mind, his screwed-up psychology.'

Fogarty shook his head. 'And I'd argue that he's made a strength of his screwed-up psychology. He's used this business about being the instrument of God's vengeance to armor himself very effectively from depression and self-doubt and anything else that might trip him up.'

In the wingback chair, Frank abruptly sat up straighter, shook himself as if to cast off his mental confusion the way a dog might shake water from its sodden coat after coming in from the rain. He said, 'Where . . . Why do I . . . Is it . . . is it . . . is it . . .?'

'Is it what, Frank?' Bobby asked.

'Is it happening?' Frank said. His eyes seemed slowly to be clearing. 'Is it finally happening?'

'Is what finally happening, Frank?'

His voice was hoarse. 'Death. Is it finally happening? Is it?'

Candy had crept quietly through the house, into the hallway that led to the library. As he moved toward the open door on the left, he heard voices. When he recognized one of them as Frank's, he could barely contain himself.

According to Violet, Frank was crippled. His control of his telekinetic talent had always been erratic, which is why Candy had enjoyed some hope of one day catching him and finishing him before he could travel to a place of safety. Perhaps the moment of triumph had arrived.

When he reached the door, he found himself looking at the woman's back. He could not see her face, but he was sure that it would be the same one that had been suffused in a beatific glow in Thomas's mind.

Beyond her he glimpsed Frank, and saw Frank's eyes widen at the sight of him. If the mother-killer had been too mentally confused to teleport out of Candy's reach, as Violet had claimed, he was now casting off that confusion. He looked as if he might pop out of there long before Candy could lay a hand on him.

Candy had intended to throw the library into a turmoil by sending a wave of energy through the doorway ahead of him, setting the books on fire and shattering the lamps, with the purpose of panicking and distracting the Dakotas and Doc Fogarty, giving him a chance to go straight for Frank. But now he was forced to change his plans by the sight of his brother trembling on the edge of dematerialization.

He entered the room in a rush and seized the woman from behind, curling his right arm around her neck and jerking her head back, so she – and the two men – would understand at once that he could snap her neck in an instant, whenever he chose. Even so, she slashed backward with one foot, scraping the heel of her shoe down his shin, stomping on his foot, all of which hurt like hell; it was some martial-art move, and he could tell by the way she tried to counterbalance his grip and stance that she had a lot of training in such things. So he jerked her head back again, even harder, and flexed his biceps, which pinched her windpipe, hurting her enough to make her realize that resistance was suicidal.

Fogarty watched from his chair, alarmed but not sufficiently to rise to his feet, and the husband came off the sofa with a gun in his hand, Mr Quick-Draw Artist, but Candy was not concerned about either of them. His attention was on Frank, who had risen from his chair and appeared about to blink out of there, off to Punaluu and Kyoto and a score of other places.

'Don't do it, Frank!' he said sharply. 'Don't run away. It's time we settled, time you paid for what you did to our mother. You come to the house, accept God's punishment, and end it now, tonight. I'm going there with this bitch. She tried to help you, I guess, so maybe you won't want to see her suffer.'

The husband was going to do something crazy; seeing Julie in Candy's grip had clearly unhinged him. He was searching for a shot, a way to get Candy without getting her, and he might even risk firing at Candy's head, though Candy was half crouching behind the woman. Time to get out of there.

'Come to the house,' he told Frank. 'You come into the kitchen, let me end it for you, and I'll let her go. I swear on our mother's name, I'll let her go. But if you don't come in fifteen minutes, I'll put this bitch on the table, and I'll have my dinner, Frank. You want me to feed on her after she tried to help you, Frank?'

Candy thought he heard a gunshot just as he got out of there. In any event, it had been too late. He rematerialized in the kitchen of the house on Pacific Hill Road, with Julie Dakota still locked in the crook of his arm.

• 56 •

No longer concerned about the danger of touching Frank, Bobby grabbed handfuls of his jacket and shoved him backward against the wide-louvred shutters on the library window. 'You heard him, Frank. Don't run. Don't run this time, or I'll hang on to you and never let go, no matter where you take me, I swear to God, you'll wish you'd put your neck on Candy's platter instead of mine.' He slammed Frank against the shutters to make his point, and behind him he heard Lawrence Fogarty's soft, knowing laughter.

Registering the terror and confusion in his client's eyes, Bobby realized that his threats would not achieve the effect he desired. In fact, threats would almost certainly frighten Frank into flight, even if he wanted to help Julie. Worse, by stooping to violence as a first resort, he was treating Frank not as a person but as meat, confirming the depraved code by which the corrupt old physician had led his entire life, and that was almost as intolerable as losing Julie.

He let go of Frank.

'I'm sorry. Listen, I'm sorry, I just got a little crazy.'

He studied the man's eyes, searching for some indication that sufficient intelligence remained in the damaged brain for the two of them to reach an understanding. He saw fear, stark and terrible, and he saw a loneliness that made him want to cry. He saw a lost look, too, not unlike what he had sometimes seen in Thomas's eyes when they had taken him on an excursion from Cielo Vista, 'out in the world,' as he had said.

Aware that perhaps two minutes of Candy's fifteen-minute deadline had passed, trying to remain calm nonetheless, Bobby took Frank's right hand, turned it palm up, and forced himself to touch the dead roach that was now integrated with the man's soft white flesh. The insect felt crisp and bristly against his fingers, but he did not permit his disgust to show.

'Does this hurt, Frank? This bug mixed up with your own cells here, does it hurt you?'

Frank stared at him, finally shook his head. No.

Heartened by the establishment of even this much dialogue, Bobby gently put his fingertips to Frank's right temple, feeling the lumps of precious gems like unburst boils or cancerous tumors.

'Do you hurt here, Frank? Are you in pain?'

'No,' Frank said, and Bobby's heart pounded with excitement at the escalation to a spoken response.

From a pocket of his jeans, Bobby removed a folded Kleenex and gently blotted away the spittle that still glistened on Frank's chin.

The man blinked, and his eyes seemed to focus better.

From behind Bobby, still in the leather chair at the desk, perhaps with a glass of bourbon in his hand, almost certainly with that infuriatingly smug smile plastered on his face, Fogarty said, 'Twelve minutes left.'

Bobby ignored the physician. Maintaining eye contact with his client, his fingertips still on Frank's temple, he said quietly, 'It's been a hard life for you, hasn't it? You were the normal one, the most normal one, and when you were a kid you always wanted to fit in at school, didn't you, the way your sisters and brother never could. And it took you a long time to realize your dream wasn't going to happen, you weren't going to fit in, because no matter how normal you were compared to the rest of your family, you'd still come from that goddamned house, out of that *cesspool*, which made you forever an outsider to other people. They might not see the stain on your heart, might not know the dark memories in you, but *you* saw, and *you* remembered, and you felt yourself unworthy because of the horror that was your family. Yet you were also an outsider at home, much too sane to fit in there, too sensitive to the nightmare of it. So all your life, you've been alone.'

'All my life,' Frank said. 'And always will be.'

He wasn't going to travel now. Bobby would have bet on it.

'Frank, I can't help you. No one can. That's a hard truth, but I won't lie to you. I'm not going to con you or threaten you.'

Frank said nothing, but maintained eye contact.

'Ten minutes,' Fogarty said.

'The only thing I can do for you, Frank, is show you a way to give your life meaning at last, a way to end it with purpose and dignity, and maybe find peace in death. I have an idea, a way that you might be able to kill Candy and save Julie, and if you can do that, you'll have gone out a hero. Will you come with me, Frank, listen to me, and not let Julie die?'

Frank didn't say yes, but he didn't say no, either. Bobby decided to take heart from the lack of a negative response.

'We've got to get moving, Frank. But don't try teleporting to the house, because then you'll just lose control again, pop off to hell and back a hundred times. We'll go in my car. We can be there in five minutes.'

Bobby took his client's hand. He made a point of taking the one with the roach embedded in it, hoping Frank would remember that he had a fear of bugs and perceive that his willingness to overrule the phobia was a testament to his sincerity.

They crossed the room to the door.

Rising from his chair, Fogarty said, 'You're going to your death, you know.'

Without glancing back at the physician, Bobby said, 'Well, seems to me, you went to yours decades ago.'

He and Frank walked out into the rain and were drenched by the time they got into the car.

Behind the wheel, Bobby glanced at his watch. Less than eight minutes to go.

He wondered why he accepted Candy's word that the fifteen-minute deadline would be observed, why he was so sure that the madman had not already torn out her throat. Then he remembered something she had said to him once:

Sweetcakes, as long as you're breathing, Tinkerbell will live.

Gutters overflowed, and a sudden wind wound skeins of rain, like silver yarn, through his headlights.

As he drove the storm-swept streets and turned east on Pacific Hill Road, he explained how Frank, through his sacrifice of himself, could rid the world of Candy and undo his mother's evil the way he had wanted to undo it – but had failed – when he had taken the ax to her. It was a simple concept. He was able to go over it several times even in the few minutes they had before pulling to a stop at the rusted iron gate.

Frank did not respond to anything that Bobby said. There was no way to be sure he understood what he must do – or if he had even heard a word of it. He stared straight ahead, his mouth open an inch or so, and sometimes his head ticked back and forth, back and forth, in time with the windshield wipers, as if he were watching Jackie Jaxx's crystal pendant swinging on its gold chain.

By the time they got out of the car, went through the gate, and approached the decrepit house, with less than two minutes of the deadline left, Bobby was reduced to proceeding entirely on faith.

When Candy brought her into the filthy kitchen, pushed her into one of the chairs at the table, and let go of her, Julie reached at once for the revolver in the shoulder holster under her corduroy jacket. He was too fast for her, however, and tore it from her hand, breaking two of her fingers in the process.

The pain was excruciating, and that was on top of the soreness in her neck and throat from the ruthless treatment he had dealt out at Fogarty's, but she refused to cry or complain. Instead, when he turned away from her to toss the gun into a drawer beyond her reach, she leapt up from the chair and sprinted for the door.

He caught her, lifted her off her feet, swung her around, and body-slammed her onto the kitchen table so hard she nearly passed out. He brought his face close to hers and said, 'You're going to taste good, like Clint's woman, all that vitality in your veins, all that energy, I want to feel you spurting in my mouth.'

Her attempts at resistance and escape had not arisen from courage as much as from terror, some of which sprang from the experience of deconstruction and reconstitution, which she hoped never to have to endure again. Now her fear doubled as his lips lowered to within an inch of hers and as his charnal-house breath washed over her face. Unable to look away from his blue eyes, she thought these were what Satan's eyes would be like, not dark as sin, not red as the fires of Hell, not crawling with maggots, but gloriously and beautifully blue – and utterly devoid of all mercy and compassion.

If all the worst of human savagery from time immemorial could be condensed into one individual, if all of the species' hunger for blood and violence and raw power could be embodied in one monstrous figure, it would have looked like Candy Pollard at that moment. When he finally pulled back from her, like a coiled serpent grudgingly reconsidering its decision to strike, and when he dragged her off the table and shoved her back into the chair, she was cowed, perhaps for the first time in her life. She knew that if she exhibited any further resistance, he would kill her on the spot and feed on her.

Then he said an astonishing thing: 'Later, when I'm done with Frank, you'll tell me where Thomas got his power.'

She was so intimidated by him that she had difficulty finding her voice. 'Power? What do you mean?'

'He's the only one I've ever encountered, outside our family. The Bad Thing, he called me. And he kept trying to keep tabs on me telepathically because he knew sooner or later you and I would cross paths. How can he have had any gifts when he wasn't born of my virgin mother? Later, you'll explain that to me.'

As she sat, actually too terrified either to cry or shake, in a storm's-eye calm, cradling her injured hand in the other, she had to find room in her for a sense of wonder too. Thomas? Psychically gifted? Could it be true that all the time she worried about taking care of him, he was to some extent taking care of her?

She heard a strange sound approaching from the front of the house. A moment later, at least twenty cats poured into the kitchen through the hall doorway, tails sweeping over one another.

Among the pack came the Pollard twins, long-legged and barefoot, one in panties and a red T-shirt, the other in panties and a white T-shirt, as sinuous as their cats. They were as pale as spirits, but there was nothing soft or ineffectual about them. They were lean and vital, filled with that tightly coiled energy that you always knew was in a cat even when it appeared to be lazing in the sun. They were ethereal in some ways, yet at the same time earthy and strong, powerfully sensual. Their presence in the house must have cranked up the unnatural tensions in their brother, who was doubly male in the matter of testes but lacking the crucial valve that would have allowed release.

They approached the table. One of them stared at Julie, while the other hung on her sister and averted her eyes. The bold one said, 'Are you Candy's girl-friend?' There was unmistakable mockery of her brother in the question.

'You shut up,' Candy said.

'If you're not his girlfriend,' the bold one said, in a voice as soft as rustling silk, 'you could come upstairs with us, we have a bed, the cats wouldn't mind, and I think I'd like you.'

'Don't you talk like that in your mother's house,' Candy said fiercely.

His anger was real, but Julie could see that he was also more than a little unnerved by his sister.

Both women, even the shy one, virtually radiated wildness, as if they might do anything that occurred to them, regardless of how outrageous, without compunction or inhibitions.

Julie was nearly as scared of them as she was of Candy.

From the front of the moldering house, echoing above the roar of the rain on the roof, came a knocking.

As one, the cats dashed from the kitchen, down the hall to the front door, and less than a minute later they returned as escort to Bobby and Frank.

Entering the kitchen, Bobby was overcome with gratitude – to God, even to Candy – at the sight of Julie alive. She was haggard, gaunt with fear and pain, but she had never looked more beautiful to him.

She had never been so subdued, either, or so unsure of herself, and in spite of the banshee chorus of emotions that roared and shrieked in him, he found capacity to contain a separate sadness and anger about that.

Though he was still hoping that Frank would come through for him, Bobby had been prepared to use his revolver if worse came to worst or if an unexpected advantage presented itself. But as soon as he walked in the room, the madman said, 'Remove your gun from your holster and empty the cartridges out of it.'

As Bobby had entered, Candy had moved behind the chair in which Julie sat, and had put one hand on her throat, his fingers hooked like talons. Inhumanly strong as he was, he could no doubt tear her throat out in a second or two, even though he lacked real talons.

Bobby withdrew the Smith & Wesson from his shoulder holster, handling it in such a way as to demonstrate that he had no intention of using it. He broke out the cylinder, shook the five cartridges onto the floor, and put the revolver down on a nearby counter.

Candy Pollard's excitement grew visibly second by second, from the moment Bobby and Frank appeared. Now he removed his hand from Julie's throat, stepped away from her, and glared triumphantly at Frank.

As far as Bobby could tell, it was a wasted glare. Frank was there in the kitchen with them – but not there. If he was aware of everything that was happening and understood the meaning of it, he was doing a good job of pretending otherwise.

Pointing to the floor at his feet, Candy said, 'Come here and kneel, you mother-killer.'

The cats fled from the section of the cracked linoleum which the madman had indicated.

The twins stood hipshot but alert. Bobby had seen cats feign indifference in the same way but reveal their actual involvement by the prick of their ears. With Violet and Verbina, their true interest was betrayed by the throbbing of their pulses in their temples and, almost obscenely, by the erection of their nipples against the fabric of their T-shirts.

'I said come here and kneel,' Candy repeated. 'Or will you really betray the only people who ever lifted a hand to help you in these last seven years? Kneel, or I'll kill the Dakotas, both of them, I'll kill them *now*.'

Candy projected the awesome presence not of a psychotic but of a genuinely supernatural being, as if his name were Legion and forces beyond human ken worked through him.

Frank moved forward one step, away from Bobby's side.

Another step.

Then he stopped and looked around at the cats, as if something about them puzzled him.

Bobby could never know if Frank had intended to evoke the bloody consequences that ensued from his next act, whether his words were calculated, or whether he was speaking out of befuddlement and was as surprised as anyone by the turmoil that followed. Whatever the case, he frowned at the cats, looked up at the bolder of the twins, and said, 'Ah, is mother still here, then? Is she still here in the house with us?'

The shy twin stiffened, but the bold one actually appeared to relax, as if Frank's question had spared her the trouble of deciding on the right time and place to make the revelation herself. She turned to Candy and favored him with the most subtly textured smile Bobby had ever seen: it was mocking, but it was a would-be lover's invitation, as well; it was tentative with fear, but simultaneously challenging; hot with lust, cool with dread; and above all, it was wild, as uncivilized and ferocious as any expression on the face of any creature that roamed any field or forest in the world.

Her smile was met by Candy with an expression of stark horror and disbelief that made him appear, briefly and for the first time, almost human. 'You didn't,' he said.

The bold twin's smile broadened. 'After you buried her, we dug her up. She's part of us now, and always will be, part of us, part of the pack.'

The cats swished their tails and stared at Candy.

The cry that erupted from him was less than human, and the speed with which he reached the bold twin was uncanny. He drove her against the refrigerator with his body, crushed her against it, grabbed her by the face with his right hand and slammed her head against the yellowed enamel surface, then again. Lifting her bodily, his hands around her narrow waist, he tried to throw her as a furious child might cast away a doll, but cat-quick she wrapped her limber legs around his waist and locked her ankles behind him, so she was riding him with her breasts before his face. He pounded at her with his fists, but she would not let go. She held on until the blows stopped raining on her, then loosened her lock on him so she slid down far enough to bring her pale throat near his mouth. He seized the opportunity that she thrust upon him and tore the life out of her with his teeth.

The cats squealed hideously, though not as one creature this time, and fled the kitchen by several routes.

To the sound of his anguished screams and her eerily erotic cries, Candy extinguished his sister's life in less than a minute. Neither Bobby nor Julie attempted to intervene, for it was clear that to do so would be like stepping into the funnel of a tornado, ensuring their death but leaving the storm undiminished. Frank only stood in that curious detachment that was now his only attitude.

Candy turned immediately to the shy twin and destroyed her even more quickly, as she offered no resistance.

As the psychotic giant dropped the brutalized corpse, Frank at last obeyed the order he had been given, closed the distance between them, and surprised his brother by taking his hand. Then, as Bobby had hoped, Frank traveled and Candy went with him, not under his own power but as a sidecar rider, the way Bobby had gone.

After the tumult, the silence was shocking.

Sweating, clearly ill from what she had witnessed, Julie pushed back her chair. The wooden legs stuttered on the linoleum.

'No,' Bobby said, and quickly came to her, stooped beside her, encouraging her to sit down. He took her uninjured hand. 'Wait, not yet, stay out of the way . . .'

The hollow piping.

A blustery whirl of wind.

'Bobby,' she said, panicking, 'they're coming back, let's go, let's get out of here while we have the chance.'

He held her in the chair. 'Don't look. I have to look, be sure, make certain Frank understood, but you don't need to see.'

The atonal music trilled again, and the wind stirred up the scent of the dead women's blood.

'What are you talking about?' she demanded.

'Close your eyes.'

She did not close her eyes, of course, because she had never been one to look away or run away from anything.

The Pollards reappeared, back from the brief visit they had made in tandem to someplace as far away as Mount Fuji or as close as Doc Fogarty's house, more likely to several places. Recklessly rapid and repeated travel was the key to the success of the trick, just as Bobby had outlined it to Frank in the car. The brothers were no longer two distinct human beings, for Frank's had been the guiding consciousness on their journeys, and his ability to shepherd them through error-free reconstitution was declining rapidly, worse with each jaunt. They were fused, more biologically tangled than any Siamese twins. Frank's left arm disappeared into Candy's right side, as if he had reached in there to fish among his brother's internal organs. Candy's right leg melted into Frank's left, giving them only three to stand on.

There were more strangenesses, but that was all Bobby could comprehend before they vanished again. Frank needed to keep moving, stay in control, give Candy no chance to exert his own power, until the scramble was so complete that proper reconstitution of either of them would be impossible.

Realizing what was happening, Julie sat perfectly still, her broken hand curled in her lap, holding fast to Bobby with her good hand. He knew she understood, without being told, that Frank was sacrificing himself for them, and that the least they could do for him was bear witness to his courage, just as they would keep Thomas and Hal and Clint and Felina alive in memory.

That was one of the most fundamental and sacred duties good friends and family performed for one another: they tended the flame of memory, so no one's death meant an immediate vanishment from the world; in some sense the deceased would live on after their passing, at least as long as those who loved them lived. Such memories were an essential weapon against the chaos of life and death, a way to ensure some continuity from generation to generation, an endorsement of order and of meaning.

Piping, wind: the brothers returned from another series of rapid deconstructions and reconstitutions, and now they were essentially one creature of cataclysmic biology. The body was large, well over seven feet tall, broad and hulking, for it incorporated the mass of both of them. The single head had a nightmare face: Frank's brown eyes were badly misaligned; a slanted mouth gaped between them where a nose should have been; and a second mouth pocked the left cheek. Two tortured, screaming voices filled the kitchen. Another face was set in the chest, mouthless but with two eye sockets, in one of which lay an unblinking eye as blue as Candy's; the other socket was filled with bristling teeth.

The slouching beast vanished, then returned once more, after less than a minute. This time it was an undifferentiated mass of tissue, dark in some places and hideously pink in others, prickled with bone fragments, tufted with sparse clumps of hair, marbled with veins that pulsed to different beats. Along the way, Frank had no doubt visited that alleyway in Calcutta or some place like it, for he had conveyed with him dozens of roaches, not just one, and rats as well; they were incorporated into the tissue everywhere that Bobby looked, further ensuring that Candy's flesh was too diffused and polluted ever to be properly reconstituted. The monstrous and obviously dysfunctional assemblage fell to the floor, flopped and shuddered, and finally lay still. Some of the rodents and insects continued to quiver and writhe, trying to get free; inextricably bonded to the dead mass, they also would soon perish.

• 57 •

The house was simple, on a section of the coast that was not yet fashionable. The back porch faced the sea, and wooden steps led down to a scrubby yard that ended at the beach. There were twelve palm trees.

The living room was furnished with a couple of chairs, a love seat, a coffee table, and a Wurlitzer 950 stocked with records from the Big-Band era. The floor was bleached oak, tightly made, and sometimes they pushed the furniture to the walls, rolled up the area rug, punched up some numbers on the juke, and danced together, just the two of them.

That was mostly in the evenings.

In the mornings, if they didn't make love, they pored through recipe books in the kitchen and whipped up baked goods together, or just sat with coffee by the window, watched the sea, and talked.

They had books, two decks of cards, an interest in the birds and animals that lived along the shore, memories both good and bad, and each other. Always, each other.

Sometimes they talked about Thomas and wondered at the gift he'd possessed and had kept secret all his life. She said it made you humble to think of it, made you realize everyone and everything was more complex and mysterious than you could know.

To get the police off their backs, they had admitted working on a case for one Frank Pollard from El Encanto Heights, who believed his brother James was trying to kill him over a misunderstanding. They said they felt James may have been a complete psychotic who had killed their employees and Thomas, merely because they had dared to try to settle the matter between the brothers. Subsequently, when the Pollard house up north was found torched with gasoline, with a confusing array of skeletal remains in the aftermath, police pressure was slowly lifted from Dakota & Dakota. It was believed that Mr James Pollard had killed his twin sisters and his brother, as well, and was currently on the run, armed and dangerous.

The agency had been sold. They didn't miss it. She no longer felt she could save the world, and he no longer needed to help her save herself.

Money, a few more red diamonds, and negotiations had convinced Dyson Manfred and Roger Gavenall to invent another source for the biologically engineered bug when, eventually, they published their work on it. Without the cooperation of Dakota & Dakota, they would never know the actual source, anyway.

In the finished attic of the beach house they kept the boxes and bags of cash they had brought back from Pacific Hill Road. Candy and his mother had tried to compensate for the chaos of their lives by storing up millions in a second-floor bedroom, just as Bobby and Julie had suspected before they had ever gotten to El Encanto Heights. Only a small portion of the Pollards' treasure was now in the beach-house attic, but it was more than two people could spend; the rest had been burned, along with everything else, when they'd torched the house on Pacific Hill Road.

In time he came to accept the fact that he could be a good man and still sometimes have dark thoughts or selfish motives. She said this was maturity, and that it wasn't such a bad thing to live outside of Disneyland by the time you reached middle age.

She said she'd like a dog.

He said fine, if they could agree on a breed.

She said you clean up its poop.

He said you clean up its poop, I'll take care of the petting and Frisbee throwing.

She said she had been wrong that night in Santa Barbara when, in her despair, she had claimed no dreams ever came true. They came true all the time. The problem was, you sometimes had your sights set on a particular dream and missed all the others that turned out your way: like finding him, she said, and being loved.

One day she told him she was going to have a baby. He held her close for a long time before he could find the words to express his happiness. They dressed to go out for champagne and dinner at the Ritz, then decided they would rather celebrate at home, on the porch, overlooking the sea, listening to old Tommy Dorsey recordings.

They built sandcastles. Huge ones. They sat on the back porch and watched the incoming tide wreck their constructions.

Sometimes they talked about the wordburst he had received in the car on the freeway, from Thomas at the moment of his death. They wondered about the words 'there is a light that loves you,' and dared to consider dreaming the biggest dream of all – that people never really die.

They got a black Labrador.

They named him Sookie, just because it sounded silly.

Some nights she was afraid. Occasionally, so was he.

They had each other. And time.